THE WORLD'S CLASSICS

THE PORTRAIT OF A LADY

HENRY JAMES was born in New York in 1843 of ancestry both Irish and Scottish. He received a remarkably cosmopolitan education in New York, London, Paris, and Geneva, and entered law school at Harvard in 1862. After 1866, he lived mostly in Europe, at first writing critical articles, reviews, and short stories for American periodicals. He lived in London for more than twenty years, and in 1898 moved to Rye, where his later novels were written. Under the influence of an ardent sympathy for the British cause in the First World War, Henry James was in 1915 naturalized a British subject. He died in 1916.

In his early novels, which include *Roderick Hudson* (1875) and *The Portrait of a Lady* (1881), he was chiefly concerned with the impact of the older civilization of Europe upon American life. He analysed English character with extreme subtlety in such novels as *What Maisie Knew* (1897) and *The Awkward Age* (1899). In his last three great novels, *The Wings of the Dove* (1902), *The Ambassadors* (1903), and *The Golden Bowl* (1904), he returned to the 'international' theme of the contrast of American and European character.

NICOLA BRADBURY is a Lecturer in English at Reading University, and the author of *Henry James: The Later Novels* (Oxford University Press, 1979).

THE WORLD'S CLASSICS

HENRY JAMES

The Portrait of a Lady

Edited with an introduction by

NICOLA BRADBURY

Oxford New York
OXFORD UNIVERSITY PRESS
1995

Oxford University Press, Walton Street, Oxford OX2 6DP
Oxford New York
Athens Auckland Bangkok Bombay
Calcutta Cape Town Dar es Salaam Delhi
Florence Hong Kong Istanbul Karachi
Kuala Lumpur Madras Madrid Melbourne
Mexico City Nairobi Paris Singapore
Taipei Tokyo Toronto

and associated companies in
Berlin Ibadan

Oxford is a trade mark of Oxford University Press

The Portrait of a Lady *first published in book form 1881*
The New York Edition first published 1907
First published as a World's Classics paperback 1981
Reissued with Introduction and Notes 1995

British Library Cataloguing in Publication Data
Data available

Library of Congress Cataloging in Publication Data
James, Henry, 1843–1916.
The portrait of a lady / edited with an introduction by Nicola Bradbury.
p. cm.—(The world's classics)
"Revised with introduction and notes"—T.p. verso.
Includes bibliographical references (p.).
1. Europe—Social life and customs—19th century—Fiction.
2. Young women—Europe—Fiction.
3. Americans—Europe—Fiction.
I. Bradbury, Nicola. II. Title. III. Series.
PS2116.P6 1995b 813'.4—dc20 94–39396
ISBN 0–19–282362–0

1 3 5 7 9 10 8 6 4 2

Typeset by Pure Tech Corporation, Pondicherry, India
Printed in Great Britain by
BPC Paperbacks Ltd.
Aylesbury, Bucks

CONTENTS

INTRODUCTION

The Portrait of a Lady announces itself as a work of art. The title suggests something inward, perhaps mannered, even complicit with a classbound society. A portrait depicts someone—perhaps just the face, or head and shoulders—sitting, posed, both for the painter and his audience: perhaps the patron, or those with privileged access to the view. So the phrase creates a sense of stasis, of surface, and elaborate framing. The personal is transformed into something else: a commodity. Beauty co-operates with art at the behest of wealth: aesthetic and financial values corroborating a rigid hierarchy which is endorsed by the artist for the public gaze. And, indeed, the values of art, the lures of both aestheticism and collecting, and their connections with the social construction of femininity, the shaping of a girl into a lady, are amongst the strongest and darkest themes of *The Portrait of a Lady*. The novel does not just depict but explores the central figure of Isabel Archer, showing, not telling, how she comes to a full sense of her own being, amidst forces which threaten to distort, exploit, or constrain her.

For this work of art is more than ornament. Behind its surfaces, within the frame, caught up in its lines of perspective, the picture proposes a dramatic scene, where spectators are enticed into perception of the unseen—motives and restraints—while the figures portrayed move into vortices of desire, projection, and interpretation. This 'portrait' is not a mere memorial, but work in progress, coming into being as we read. Art here is at work, hard work, for James found it exciting 'to see deep difficulty braved'(12). Accordingly, he creates in this great novel, the climax of his early career, anticipating his later and most demanding fiction, a situation which is full of dangers yet meets difficulties as a challenge.

James harks back to the simplicities of Romance as he adopts the Cinderella story for his basic fable, and echoes the Pygmalion legend. The neglected child rescued by the love of a Prince; the sculptor who makes a statue so beautiful that he loses his heart to her and she must come alive. These two myths sketch possibilities of creation and transformation through marriage or art. Through them James addresses ancient themes: the strength of desire in achieving identity, its hidden costs and dangers. But in recasting his waif as a bright and vigorous American girl, he takes account of her historical moment and of his own experience both in life and literature. James Buzard points out: 'James thought that the Civil War had marked a new era for "the American mind"; the War also appeared to mark a new era in American travel to Europe—much as the Napoleonic Wars had done for British travellers to the Continent.'[1] James himself had made this 'reverse pilgrimage', and he takes his heroine from New England to the old country, and from there to the Continent, not to escape, but to discover her self. True, most of those she meets are also Americans, living in Europe. James's 'international theme' opens up cultural comparitivism.

Three great moments of civilization inform and invigorate Isabel's journey. Late nineteenth-century America, Victorian England, and Renaissance Italy give contours to experience. Their possibilities and dangers are evoked through details of place and setting, from continent to country, cities, houses, gardens, furniture; above all through pictures and artistic possessions. This 'background' not only gives James's *Portrait* depth and lustre: it locates his subject in a wider context, evoking ancient struggles in the drama of the imagination. The novel's cultural traces constitute a resonantly historical, rich, and far from innocent heritage, one which conditions the present, for a heroine who may be naïve but who is greedy for experience, and ironically eager to be granted a vision of the ghosts of the old world.

First, there is the Italian Renaissance, with its own ambivalent classical heritage of display and suffering, princes, poets, gladiators, in the Florence and Rome of the novel—extended to the East by Lord Warburton's and then Isabel's travels, and rippling through the later glories of Paris, with its Empire and its Revolution. Art here is a political product as well as an

[1] *The Beaten Track: European Tourism, Literature and the Ways to Culture, 1800-1918* (Oxford University Press, 1993), 217.

aesthetic pursuit. It acts as a display of power, commemorates patronage, but hints at corruption. Browning's poem 'My Last Duchess' (1842), where the tyrant's absolute command is rifted with the self-torment of suspicion, as the speaker betrays his own jealousy in displaying the portrait of his wife like a trophy, makes an intriguing companion piece to *The Portrait of a Lady*.

A different temper derives from the eighteenth-century Enlightenment, which, together with contemporary Liberal politics, forms one of the traces of 'Englishness' in the novel, mediated by the strong English novel tradition. Ian Watt[2] linked the philosophy of John Locke with the rise of the novel: for Locke saw that abstraction and generalization must be preceded by the 'principle of individuation', which locates the special and particular. Isabel, whose imagination is informed by novel-reading, has a self-conscious protagonist's interest in what sets her apart from others; but one distinction lies in her strong sense of ethical responsibility, her tendency towards abstraction and general principles. This moral energy is recognizably American: a complex inheritance from the Pilgrim Fathers transformed by Emersonian transcendentalism, with its stress on self-reliance, and inflected by a post-Civil War pragmatism.

James's anchoring of conventional romance in cultural space raises many critical questions: biographical and psychological, historical and contextual issues, intimate and disturbing in a way which belies the impersonal formality of his chosen title. F. R. Leavis[3] contrasted James's treatment of his heroine with George Eliot's fiery Gwendolen Harleth in *Daniel Deronda* (1876), and James himself mentions her in his Preface; but the idealistic Dorothea Brooke from *Middlemarch* (1871) is also there: the two defining perhaps the stretches of marital despair and a range of response to such misery. From further back (though a similar date) arises from James's own life the ghost of his cousin Minny Temple, who faced her vital crisis alone. She might, like James himself, and like Daisy Miller, and so many of his protagonists, have ventured from America to find her future in Europe. Instead, on 8 March 1870, ten years

[2] *The Rise of the Novel* (1957). [3] *The Great Tradition* (1948).

before *The Portrait of a Lady*, and aged only 24, Minny died. She haunts James's novels to the last, where Milly Theale in *The Wings of the Dove* (1902) is removed in full career, only to make her absence felt through her generosity beyond the grave. One of the key scenes in that novel confronts the heroine with her uncanny likeness in the shape of a Bronzino portrait of a lady long since dead, when 'Milly recognized her exactly in words that had nothing to do with her'(Ch. 10). Milly Theale was fresh in James's mind when he came to revise *The Portrait of a Lady* for his own artistic monument: the collected New York edition of his works. Amongst textual critics, Philip Horne[4] gives an exemplary investigation of how the persistence of themes and techniques through James's procedures of revision re-enacts the processes of conception and expression engaged in individual texts.

We can see from the author's 1907 Preface to *The Portrait of a Lady* how conscious he was of all these issues. Turning from the anecdotal history of composition to the abstract 'architectural' construction of the novel, then moving on to consider the entire 'house of fiction', which he imagines with countless windows, each pierced or yet pierceable 'by the need of the individual vision and the pressure of the individual will'(8), James subtly interlinks through his figurative logic the motives and the means of art, the textual drama and those of creation and reading. Despite his firm rejection in his essay on 'The Art of Fiction' (1886) of demands for morality in novels, James here declares unequivocally 'the perfect dependence of the "moral" sense of a work of art on the amount of felt life concerned in producing it'(7).

That life centres in James's protagonist, Isabel Archer, because she herself is 'concerned in producing' her own being. What appears mere self-indulgence at the opening of James's Preface, as he talks about the difficulties of writing in Venice, or the hindrance of romantic and historic cues 'too rich in their own life and too charged with their own meanings'(3), gradually shifts its focus and function as he considers what may emerge from 'a wasted effort of attention'(4). This line

[4] *Henry James and Revision: The New York Edition* (1990).

of discussion is neither authorial nostalgia nor a dilatory gathering of forces: it announces an investigation into the mysteries of the imagination and whether its powers may be accessible to authorial will. That query engages James the author and master in writing and revision—creatively and critically—and he addresses it experimentally through his heroine. He makes Isabel Archer, 'the mere slim shade of an intelligent but presumptuous girl'(10), both a proponent and also a victim of 'the need of the individual vision and the pressure of the individual will'. She becomes 'a certain young woman affronting her destiny'(10).

'Certain', indeed: both select and sure. For Isabel's distinction lies in her self consciousness. James exploits this technically to direct our interest: 'Stick to *that*—for the centre; put the heaviest weight into that scale, which will be so largely the scale of her relation to herself'(12). He uses it rhetorically, to enhance her adventures: 'Without her sense of them, her sense *for* them . . . they are next to nothing at all; but isn't the beauty and the difficulty just in showing their mystic conversion by that sense, conversion into the stuff of drama, or, even more delightful word still, of "story"?'(16) He also values it in terms of figurative potential, within the novel, where 'Her nature had, in her conceit, a certain garden-like quality, a suggestion of perfume and murmuring boughs, of shady bowers and lengthening vistas, which made her feel that introspection was, after all, an exercise in the open air, and that a visit to the recesses of one's spirit was harmless when one returned from it with a lapful of roses'(71).

A vignette—the girl as a garden—grows within the space of a sentence from mere cliché into picture, scene, and story: one full of clues about Isabel, the novel, and how to read it. We see the drama of Isabel's imagination at work, but her fanciful self-portrait is framed by the narrator's irony in a way which brings both into question. Is this small pastoral comical or poignant? The double force of 'nature', as personality and the living world, is both ironized and celebrated in the equally ambivalent 'conceit': which could be self-deluding or creative imagination. 'Nature' here is not wild, but a garden; it is both the garden of Eden, a space for the spirit, and the confection of artists and poets, a bower of roses. Everything is alive, with scent, sound, touch, as well as sight. It is a scene to be entered, not merely gazed upon: 'an exercise in the open air'. There is, however, 'after all', another quality lurking here: the shading of ambiguity; the closure of 'a lapful of roses'; the sense of 'recesses'; even the denial of harm.

The Portrait of a Lady opens in a garden, on an English summer afternoon, just in time for tea. It is the picture of peace. But the shadows are already growing; and the people themselves are shades: an old man and his son who will greet Isabel's sudden arrival warmly, but will not survive the progress which they help under way. James presents this 'little eternity' pictorially, through light, mass, colour and line: there is an air of abstraction and desultory talk, almost of half-life, until the entrance of 'a tall girl in a black dress'(30) initiates the drama. Isabel's journey, from the 'dusky corners' of New England through those of the old world, takes her into several gardens—in England, at Gardencourt, Lockleigh, and even in London; outside Florence at Gilbert Osmond's villa, and at Palazzo Crescentini where Ralph challenges her engagement; in Rome, where public parks are formal, but the Campagna and the ruins of the Coliseum provide wild flowers of memory and imagination. Their spaces are defined by encroaching shadows. Like Milton's protagonists in *Paradise Lost*, whose closing words[5] echo through James's text, Isabel finds, 'The world lay all before her—she could do whatever she chose'(348). The power 'to do some of the things she wants'(204), to be 'as good as her best opportunities'(207) is a gift which enriches but exposes her to experience beyond the garden in a fallen world. Her last movement will be again in this first garden, but away from darkness on the straight path towards the light.

Foreshortening the story in this way underlines the shapeliness and design of the work; but it is worth remembering the confession in James's Preface: 'It is a long novel, and I was long in writing it'(3), and what he recognized in his Notebooks: 'The *whole* of anything is never told; you can only take

[5] As Adam and Eve leave Eden in *Paradise Lost* (Book 12), 'The world was all before them, where to choose | Their place of rest.'

what groups together' (*Notebooks*, p. 15). *The Portrait of a Lady* moves, at first confidently, then more questioningly, with Isabel, through experience, towards knowledge, but not closure. It is surprising, on rereading, to note the proportions of narrative space allowed to different phases of her life, and find how much of the novel passes before Madame Merle makes her entry, and how much more before Isabel's engagement: then how rapid is the final denouement. The story actually breaks off for three years two-thirds of the way through, on the marriage of Isabel to Osmond: a speaking narrative silence or structural fissure. The picture is neither static nor complete. Through the jolts of experience it becomes a dramatic scene, infused with the power of what can never fully be revealed. Long as it is, *The Portrait of a Lady* bears the traces of stories untold, perhaps impossible to imagine unfolding—those of Pansy in the future, Mrs Touchett, Madame Merle, in the past, for example. Their darkness and silence throws into relief the urgency of Isabel's determination to define herself.

After his memorable opening, James gives a brief flashback to Isabel's origins. In principle, the narrative follows her movements, from place to place, and from person to person; but that first retrograde step is more than a hiccup: it signals the need to notice both gaps and hesitancies in her progress. One of three daughters, long motherless, now orphaned, Isabel is 'rescued' from Albany by her Aunt Touchett, who seems to be a cross between a fairy godmother and Dickens's Betsey Trotwood from *David Copperfield*. Through her Isabel meets Mr Touchett and her cousin Ralph; each in his own way promotes her progress. Isabel rejects an American and an English offer of marriage, from Caspar Goodwood and Lord Warburton; but, having inherited her uncle's fortune, she attracts a third proposal, from the expatriate Gilbert Osmond, who lives in retirement outside Florence. Three sisters, three Touchetts, three suitors; the pattern grows menacing as Isabel finds herself involved in yet further triangles. One is with her husband and his daughter Pansy, herself almost ready to be married. Another involves Lord Warburton, formerly Isabel's suitor, now a potential fiancé for her stepdaughter. The last links both

Isabel and Pansy with Madame Merle, an old friend of the family who introduced her to Osmond. It is untangling the mystery of this relationship which breaks the spell of Isabel's marriage, and allows her to return to Gardencourt and speak to Ralph about the inheritance he made over to her, and what followed from the dangerous gift.

Ralph's covert generosity and Madame Merle's clandestine arrangements propose competing fictions to shape Isabel's fortunes. One is benign, the other ruthless, but both might be seen as using her. Ralph tells his father, with the conscious self-mockery of cliché, 'I should like to put a little wind in her sails'(204). In a different idiom of self-assessment, Madame Merle, holding a cracked coffee-cup as Osmond departs, 'looked at it rather abstractedly. "Have I been so vile all for nothing?" she vaguely wailed'(559). Isabel is surrounded by persons of powerful purpose. Patronage and intrigue offer two modes of exploitation.

Isabel is vulnerable. We are told, 'With all her love of knowledge she had a natural shrinking from raising curtains and looking into unlighted corners. The love of knowledge coexisted in her mind with the finest capacity for ignorance'(220). But this warning comes just before an important debate between Isabel and Madame Merle about what constitutes identity. Madame Merle, the woman of the world, knows: 'There's no such thing as an isolated man or woman; we're each of us made up of some cluster of appurtenances. What shall we call our "self"? Where does it begin? where does it end? It overflows into everything that belongs to us—and then it flows back again. . . . One's self—for other people—is one's expression of self; and one's house, one's furniture, one's garments, the books one reads, the company one keeps—these things are all expressive'(223). Yet Isabel retorts, 'I don't agree with you. I think just the other way. . . . Nothing that belongs to me is any measure of me; everything's on the contrary a limit, a barrier, and a perfectly arbitrary one'(223). The exchange is characterized, both teasingly and accurately, as 'very metaphysical'. It is central to the novel, for it questions the codes and values of expression, asking exactly what this portrait shows and is, and whether the two can ever be identified. What is the force of fiction, the truth of appearances, the weight of Isabel's story?

Feminist criticism has found James's work fascinating and *The Portrait of a Lady* a test case. Long celebrated for his quasi-feminine sensibility, particularly to the undercurrents of pathos in those human situations where good manners prevented plain speaking, James has recently been accused of complicity with the dominant patriarchy, perhaps motivated by his own repressed homosexuality, and Isabel's fate has been cited as evidence. She longs to assert her independence, but is brought down. Given the wherewithal by her benevolent uncle, she is betrayed by femininity on two fronts: the treachery of a female friend, and her own romantic fantasies, which lead her into a doomed marriage. So argues Alfred Habegger,[6] who suggests that James was determined to outwrite the female authors of popular romance whose fiction outsold his.

Responding to this charge requires careful discrimination in *The Portrait of a Lady*. The elements of romance are present, yet its formulas are questioned by experience. The familiar plot is recast by James's chosen character: and this throws the narrative process itself into a new light. Given Isabel, what becomes of her? Given that, what does James make of it? His narrator, initially patronizing, presents a young woman whose 'imagination was by habit ridiculously active; when the door was not open it jumped out of the window'(48). She is wilfully prone to fancy, naughtily declaring to her practical friend Henrietta, 'A swift carriage, of a dark night, rattling with four horses over roads that one can't see—that's my idea of happiness'(187). The contours of romance shape the heroine's fortunes—whether by her wish or authorial decree, or both. This strain is underlined throughout the narrative by references to mythology, poetry, and painting which are not simply decorative but functional. There are echoes (not all relating to Isabel, who is also defined through the reflection and refraction of surrounding characters) of Eve, of Juno, Niobe, Proserpine, and figures of the Madonna, indicating the

[6] *Henry James and the 'Woman Business'* (Cambridge University Press, 1989).

antiquity and complexity of a woman's predicament and pain in progressing from innocence to knowledge, and suggesting how sexuality and maternity may both empower and imprison her. When Madame Merle calls upon the newly enriched Isabel, she asks Mrs Touchett, 'Am I not to see your happy niece?' and is told, 'You may see her; but you'll not be struck with her being happy. She has looked as solemn, these three days, as a Cimabue Madonna!'(231) This analogy invites us to appreciate the culture of women who produce and register such terms; but exposes a certain coolness in their capacity to do so in this situation. Yet the reference is richly suggestive. Mention of the Florentine artist leads (surreptitiously) towards the crucial next phase of Isabel's story, when Madame Merle will take the heiress there to meet Osmond. Cimabue's work is elaborately beautiful: an aesthetic bridge between the Florentine Renaissance and Byzantine tradition: two cultures equally noted for political cunning. It is rather pale, frozen into stillness. The Madonna is, like Isabel, virginal: afigure of potential and of grace; but one who has been given a great responsibility, carrying predestined pain.

Intertextuality constructs a kind of force field around Isabel: a predisposition of the arts to recognize her case. This perhaps corroborates her imaginative conception of herself as her own creation. Or perhaps it works ironically for the narrator, framing her 'conceit' as one amongst many such fabrications. There is a third possibility: that the whole novel's aesthetic self-consciousness reflects on both the protagonist and the author, aligning their creative and critical purposes in a way which makes irony itself a poignant celebration of the lost cause which is desire deflected by experience: imagination realized. Isabel's idea of herself and James's ambition for his novel are doomed as all longings must be, but equally graced by their daring, and the insistence of artistic references acts as a sympathetic resonance to this. Awareness enhances the beauty of their courage.

These aspects of the *Portrait* create complex currents through the work. Consider one of James's artistic resources: allusions to other writers. Shakespeare, Milton, Byron,

Browning, could be grouped as poets, but their temper is quite different. References to eighteenth-century English essayists (146) cast a quizzical light on the nineteenth-century novelists (146); Vittoria Colonna implicitly questions Machiavelli (283); 'the American Corinne'(305)[7] is an epithet for Osmond's mother which preposterously juxtaposes poetic pretensions in New English and French society. Isabel, 'poor girl', we are told, 'liked to be thought clever, but she hated to be thought bookish'(51). The narrator, however, is at least equally inclined to literariness. His own linguistic virtuosity is satirically magnified into the suspicious fluency which his sophisticated characters display in French: Madame Merle holds expression, like music, 'just *du bout des doigts*'(193) (with her fingertips), and with such expertise that Isabel supposes, 'She's a Frenchwoman . . . she says that as if she were French'(193).

On the textual front, there is a certain self-mockery in the narrator's humour (sometimes ventriloquized through Ralph) at the expense of Henrietta Stackpole, the female journalist, whose broadsheet candour contrasts refreshingly with the more oblique enquiries and communications of all those Americans in the novel who have been more deeply touched or contaminated by European culture. Henrietta is no Greek myth, but a thoroughly modern phenomenon. At the outset, 'Henrietta, for Isabel, was chiefly a proof that a woman might suffice to herself and be happy'(70). There will be a different lesson before the close. James's Preface reveals some compunction over his use of Henrietta. She is a convenience to the novelist, an easy target, more naïve and brash than the heroine, who sees that she 'doesn't sufficiently recognize the existence of knockers'(112) Yet Henrietta has virtues. She appreciates 'that free play of intelligence which, to her sense, rendered Isabel's character a sister-spirit'(114): a tribute to the credit of both friends. Her good faith eventually wins even the irreverent Ralph to accept her escort on his journey home to die. To the last, however, Henrietta is used as a contrasting measure of Isabel's stature, in the controversial closing scenes. When Caspar Goodwood presses his passionate declaration

[7] Corinne, a poet, is the eponymous heroine of a novel (1807) by Mme de Staël: See note to p. 305.

and Isabel turns away, the narrative slyly signals ironically where its approval lies, by showing Henrietta on his side.

Counterpointing intertextuality with old-fashioned characterization by exploiting Henrietta's profession as her nature too permits the narrative both subtlety and economy. Even broad satire works self-reflexively, and becomes exploratory. Similarly, the pictorial 'packing' of James's text is haunting and diverse in its effects. Visual riches beautify Isabel's world. Gardencourt has a picture gallery whose 'vague squares of rich colour'(63) she asks Ralph to show her immediately, even in the failing light (Isabel likes to linger in semi-darkness). He prefers to gaze at her. Henrietta prefers to walk in the garden. The paintings become a touchstone. Architecture may do the same: moving between solid realism and symbolism. The very façade of Osmond's Tuscan villa emblazons visual significance as 'the mask, not the face, of the house. It had heavy lids but no eyes; the house in reality looked another way—looked off behind'(249). He scarcely needs further introduction; but he is fully characterized in this 'seat of ease, indeed of luxury, telling of arrangements subtly studied and refinements frankly proclaimed'(250) by his collection. Amidst his things are 'a few small, odd, elaborate pictures, chiefly in watercolour'(250): his 'own productions'. These surroundings grimly foreshadow the furnishings of married life in the aptly named cold, dark, hard Palazzo Roccanera, Rome. As night falls there in the 'meditative vigil'(Ch. 42) which James singles out in his Preface(17), Isabel's 'dwelling' becomes the outward and visible sign of an inner prison. She has chosen Osmond's devotion: has taken up residence in his conception of her. His mind has become the confines of her existence. To Isabel's perception the actual and metaphorical merge with a syntactical claustrophobia which re-enacts her dramatic plight:

> She could live it over again, the incredulous terror with which she had taken the measure of her dwelling. Between those four walls she had lived ever since; they were to surround her for the rest of her life. It was the house of darkness, the house of dumbness, the house of suffocation. Osmond's beautiful mind gave it neither light nor air; Osmond's beautiful mind indeed seemed to peep down from a small high window and mock at her. (461)

Osmond is seated by the window in his study when Isabel finally comes to leave him to attend to her dying cousin. She walks in, without knocking, and finds him copying the print of a drawing of an antique coin: the devalued image of his third-hand aestheticism. When she challenges him, 'I suppose that if I go you'll not expect me to come back', what he asks is, 'Are you out of your mind?'(572) Her mind, at last, is its own place.

The constraints of courtesy, stretched here but not ignored, constitute an expressive vocabulary of forms for the novelist. Action in *The Portrait of a Lady* is essentially 'very metaphysical', like the debate between Isabel and Madame Merle: it is a matter of the mind, of Isabel's responses and perceptions. But this conceptual development is realized in textual terms through a more obvious kind of drama: encounters, meetings, conversations, partings, which chart Isabel's 'adventures'. Comportment here gives clues to inner values: it is the sight of Osmond sitting while Madame Merle stands that first alerts Isabel to something askance in the relation between them: 'the thing made an image'(438). In this novel every deflection from decorum is significant. Scrupulous manners give away as much as lapses; and Pansy's obedience to her father, Madame Merle's conduct as a house guest, Mrs Touchett's rigid adherence to propriety reveal as much about them as Henrietta's blithe disappearance to the Continent with an ex-Lancer, or the Countess Gemini's excesses. From the first Isabel has some understanding of this. Weighing up the merits of Henrietta and Madame Merle, early on at Gardencourt, she perceives that 'Madame Merle was not superficial—not she. She was deep, and her nature spoke none the less in her behaviour because it spoke a conventional tongue'(213). Although she recognizes the operation of this semiotic code, however—'What's language at all but a convention?'(214)—Isabel cannot yet see the full implications of this gap between behaviour and what it expresses.

To an innocent, 'deep' is not the signal of danger; darkness is seductive; suffering sounds glamorous. The heroine's naïvety may be held up to narrative irony; yet her sense of a space behind the superficial is also vital to the workings of the text. That space is where the imagination operates, for narrator and reader as well as the protagonist. In plot, but even more in tone, Isabel's story relies both on speech and on silence; on secrecy, and on the inferences that can only be drawn from what remains unsaid. Besides stories untold, this novel finds its shape through scenes off-stage, encounters unwitnessed, histories suppressed. Philip Horne charts James 'revising his intentions in the process of thinking out the action'(210) in his Notebooks, and recognizes 'potent indirections' and 'inferential excitement'(212) in 'a complex play of silences and understandings'(214) which supplant the extravagance of melodrama implicit in the storyline of inheritance, exploitation, and betrayal. Clearly the machinations of Merle and Osmond require concealment; their history must be hidden for the plot to succeed. But equally we need actually to see Isabel confronting all her lovers in the impressive sequence of proposal scenes, if we are to appreciate the courage as well as the deceptiveness of the choices which determine her destiny. Some aspects of the story must be veiled, others even embarrassingly naked, to achieve the textual drama of discovery. Yet James's use of silence goes further than this. He does not merely manipulate the sympathies or excitement of the reader, but explores the potential of the story. Seclusion, omission, hesitancy, challenge overt statement, hinting at an intensity of experience which only imagination can apprehend. Unlike the irony of the early chapters, or the melodrama of revelation, this oblique expression through what is withheld has the effect of dissolving narrative boundaries between omniscience and discovery, and brings author, character, and reader closer together. The hierarchy of representation from superior authorial knowledge dissolves in mutual attempts at perception and recognition. Gazing at the portrait creates the sense of its eyes following you.

When we meet Isabel she is already orphaned, and decency shrouds the dying of Mr Touchett and of Ralph—though we are allowed to see Isabel's parting from her cousin, and apprehend the wordless summons which calls her to his deathbed(516). The loss of her own child is never spoken of but by Madame Merle(390): a poignantly ironic exception.

Extinction is the deepest darkness in *The Portrait of a Lady*: a bleakness so absolute that it must be understood, not represented. Isabel's imaginative potency is exhibited against this ground. Her freedom comes at that cost; her fortune is inherited; and yet her orientation is towards life, not morbid hoarding. From the first she hopes to see the ghost of Gardencourt, and is 'not afraid, you know'(65). Ironically, she rapidly intuits a history of suffering in Madame Merle, but she fancies this 'aristocratic'(212), and congratulates her new friend on the capacity to feel. When an older and a wiser Isabel eventually returns to attend the dying Ralph and see his familiar ghost, she has already dealt with worse horrors: with betrayal, and despair; and she has seen Pansy entombed in her father's displeasure, and Madame Merle banished to America. Now it is Mrs Touchett's 'inexpressiveness, her want of regret, of disappointment'(606) which touch her niece's pity. With a marvellous expressive economy, the imagination of one emerges in defining the lack of the other, so that we see by example the value of experience. Seated 'at an abbreviated table in the melancholy dining room' (the first adjective predicating the second) Isabel creates a poignant still life out of her aunt's emotional starvation. She recasts the literal as a symbolic scene: the imagined aftermath of a banquet untasted. It is nearly, but not quite, a last supper. Everything bespeaks lost opportunities. Blankness, not pain, is most wretched. This perception is attributed not to Mrs Touchett but to Isabel, and expressed with remarkable delicacy in conditional and negative terms, as she imagines her aunt's desolation: 'Unmistakeably she would have found it a blessing to-day to be able to feel a defeat, a mistake, even a shame or two'(606).

During the earlier vigil (Chapter 42) in Rome we are told, 'Suffering, with Isabel, was an active condition; it was not a chill, a stupor, a despair; it was a passion of thought, of speculation, of response to every pressure'(456). Unlike the instincts of the 'collectors', Osmond, and by proxy Madame Merle, this important capacity is not acquisitive but reciprocal. Rosier rises towards it when he sells his lovingly selected 'bibelots' for a very small fortune because he values Pansy more, although his gesture gets him nowhere with her father.

The triumph comes in defeat, and it is one of recognition. There is an element of appraisal, but not appropriation. Beyond longing, this stands clear of the rebounding force of desire, and does not possess but liberates both subject and object.

This is truly metaphysical, and it is Isabel's distinction to display it. As she returns to Gardencourt (Chapter 53), Isabel takes on the status of watcher rather than watched. Carried along in the suspended animation of travel, shock, and grief, she becomes herself a vehicle of thought: 'She had plenty to think about; but it was neither reflexion nor conscious purpose that filled her mind. Disconnected visions passed through it, and sudden dull gleams of memory, of expectation'(595). Active and passive impulses, though connected, are not identified with the crisis, but meet in Isabel's imagination. The whole story comes together for her, even the future opening out: 'She saw herself, in the distant years, still in the attitude of a woman who had her life to live, and these intimations contradicted the spirit of the present hour'(596). Pain, after all, is contingent, not material to her being.

The concluding scenes of parting from Ralph (Chapter 54) and then from Goodwood (Chapter 55), preceded by the vigil with her aunt, amount to an exploration of what Isabel's mature vision means in terms of the narrative, by contrasting her imagination with her aunt's failure, Ralph's original project, and Goodwood's determination. Enjoying, perhaps greedily, her potential for life, so different from his own, Ralph made his cousin rich: '—that was not happy'(612). It was a generous, but yet a directive gesture: the act of an author, setting the conditions of her story. Goodwood would take her now, give her a future: 'Ah, be mine as I'm yours!'(627). Isabel's response recognizes, without bitterness or denial, what each implies for her. With Ralph, exonerated from selfishness, a shared vision is at last possible: 'nothing mattered now but the only knowledge that was not pure anguish—the knowledge that they were looking at the truth together'(612). With Goodwood, acknowledgement of the other is a liberation: 'she felt each thing in his hard manhood that had least pleased her, each aggressive fact of his face, his figure, his presence, justified of its intense identity and made one with this act of possession. So had she heard of those wrecked and under water following a train of images before they sink. But when darkness returned she was free'(627). The power to know, to feel, to recognize, and then to be free, marks Isabel's independence of all fictions which might enclose her, whether from other characters or the author. The 'very straight path' she finds eventually is that of her own integrity.

NOTE ON THE TEXT

The Portrait of a Lady was first published in twelve parts in *Macmillan's Magazine* and the *Atlantic Monthly* from October 1880. Book publication in England and America came in 1881. Between magazine and book James made his first textual revisions, mostly to individual words. But for the selective New York Edition of his works twenty-six years later he returned to this greatest of his early novels with a 'late James' eye, ear, and sixth sense for what lies behind appearances. Thousands of changes were made: none lengthy, but together significant.

Four critics have examined James's revisions. Anthony Mazzella shows James's attentiveness by picking up changes to the first *volume* of the 1907 text foreshadowing the controversial end of the novel. Sydney Krause, comparing early and late revisions, argues that both show similar tendencies in style and thought, consistently refining and strengthening the original conception. This is what F. O. Matthiessen concludes, as he relates the revised *Portrait* to James's 'Major Phase'. Nina Baym, however, finds the New York text damaged by a late James enhancement of the aesthetic and intellectual at the expense of impulsive feeling: for her the purpose of the novel is baffled as its imaginative focus shifts.

Are the New York revisions an improvement? What do they reveal about James's concerns, stylistic or thematic: about the workings of his imagination? Can awareness of them help us to understand the novel, resolve or clarify its critical problems?

Some changes are straightforward: colloquialisms and contractions in speech make the text flow faster and less formally. But pace may point up a disingenuous ease. When Madame Merle tells Mrs Touchett, 'You make me feel an idiot' for failing to notice Osmond's approach to courtship, her veiled contempt is nearer the surface than in the original 'You make me feel like a fool' (p. 300). James refines her duplicities: 'Again Madame Merle was silent, while her thoughtful smile drew up her mouth *even more charmingly than usual* toward the left corner.' Against this, Mrs Touchett's increasingly abrasive speech becomes poignantly clumsy: 'You must know this: whether that *curious creature's really* making love to my niece . . . Don't tell me about his *probably quite cold-blooded* love-affairs; they're nothing to me.' (My italics indicate revisions.) James's irony is racier, Madame Merle's manipulation more reprehensible.

Editing out two pages analysing Osmond's motives for marrying Isabel, and altering the images that remain, again James heightens the chiaroscuro of manipulation and betrayal. Instead of an Isabel 'as bright and soft as an April cloud', we find: 'she would have been as smooth to his general need of her as handled ivory to the palm.' Osmond's ambition 'to succeed greatly' becomes, in a crass colloquialism, 'the desire to have something or other to show for his parts'. A blunted sensibility, despite his refined aestheticism, accounts for the degeneration from 'When at last the best did present itself Osmond recognised it like a gentleman' to vulgar self-interest: 'His "style" was what the girl had discovered with a little help; and now, beside herself enjoying it, she should publish it to the world without his having any of the trouble. She should do the thing *for* him, and he would not have waited in vain' (p. 331).

If Isabel's dangers grow more blatant, her support appears increasingly inadequate. Henrietta Stackpole, originally a delightful mixture of girlish enthusiasm and American feminist, is given over to Ralph's wry relish as something nearer a caricature. 'She was very well dressed, in fresh, dove-coloured draperies' becomes 'She rustled, she shimmered . . .' From 'scrupulously, fastidiously neat', he develops a preposterous typographical characterization: 'she was as crisp and new and comprehensive as a first issue before the folding. From top to toe she had probably no misprint. . . . she struck him as not at all in the large type, the type of horrid "headings", that he had expected.' Her New World qualities are grossly exaggerated: the 'odour of the prairies' which Isabel enjoys, and which Ralph at first calls 'decidedly fragrant', becomes overpowering: ' "Henrietta . . . does smell of the Future—it almost knocks one down!" ' Her 'fine' courage grows positively resplendent: 'as Isabel had said, she was brave: she went into cages, she flourished lashes, like a spangled lion-tamer.' No wonder this Henrietta 'prompted mirth' in Ralph, who 'had long since decided that the *crescendo* of mirth should be the flower of his declining days'.

The New York Ralph is distinguished by laughter and flowers: a 'luxury of laughter', and, accepting his illness, 'His serenity was but the array of wild flowers niched in his ruin.' Such slender adjustments change Ralph little; but they maintain an imaginative correspondence between him and the more 'conscious' Isabel. Their vital sympathy, perfected at Ralph's death, helps clarify the issues of feeling and understanding which are then confirmed in the final chapter when Isabel turns from Goodwood's passion to her duty in Rome.

The deathbed scene with Ralph shows that Isabel's consciousness does not exclude emotion. James's increased colloquialism and added images, more concrete and precise, create a new strength of feeling. Not 'nervous and even frightened', but 'nervous and scared—as scared as if the objects about her had begun to show for conscious things, watching her trouble with grotesque grimaces', Isabel's reflection 'that things change but little, while people change so much' acquires particularized elegiac intensity: 'She envied the security of valuable "pieces" which change by no hair's breadth, only grow in value, while their owners lose inch by inch youth, happiness, beauty . . .' (p. 604). On Isabel's 'hot cheek' Mrs Touchett's lips feel 'very thin indeed': the physical touch substantiates her aunt's emotional deprivation. But her own awareness is vigorous, far from arid. Her speculation on Mrs Touchett's 'regret', the 'desire for the recreation of grief', is generously, even extravagantly, extended: 'Unmistakeably she would have found it a blessing to-day to be able to feel a defeat, a mistake, even a shame or two. She wondered if she were not even missing those enrichments of consciousness and privately trying—reaching out for some aftertaste of life, dregs of the banquet; the testimony of pain or the cold recreation of remorse.' This is the Isabel whom Ralph could assure not only ' "that if you have been hated, you have also been loved" ', but ' "loved. Ah but, Isabel—*adored!*" '

Goodwood's adoration is of another kind. The late James

accentuates both attraction and repulsion—not hesitation—in Isabel's response. 'Pressingly close' to her, the American's presence embodies a complex sexual force. James's rewording reveals a respect for 'something really formidable in his resolution' (1881: 'something awful in his persistency'). But Goodwood's melodramatic diction betrays him: ' "It will have cost you your life? Say it will"—and he flared almost into anger: "give me one word of truth! When I know such a horror as that, how can I keep myself from wishing to save you?" ' Isabel's sense of his emotion is conveyed with metaphorical extravagance: 'this was the hot wind of the desert, at the approach of which the others dropped dead, like mere sweet airs of the garden. It wrapped her about; it lifted her off her feet; while the very taste of it, as of something potent, acrid and strange, forced open her set teeth.' The stylistic crescendo, 'harsh and terrible', of Goodwood's passion prepares for his notoriously extended kiss,

> like white lightning, a flash that spread, and spread again, and stayed; and it was extraordinarily as if, while she took it, she felt each thing in his hard manhood that had least pleased her, each aggressive fact of his face, his figure, his presence, justified of its intense identity and made one with this act of possession. So had she heard of those wrecked and under water following a train of images before they sink.

The whole weight of James's revisions argues against any failure on his part to recognize the potent sexuality here. And his recognition, surely, becomes Isabel's. It is neither insensibility nor cowardice, but experience, that emerges from this kiss, 'But when darkness returned she was free.'

(1981)

SELECT BIBLIOGRAPHY

Anesko, Michael, *'Friction with the Market': Henry James and the Profession of Authorship* (Oxford University Press, 1986).

Baym, Nina, 'Revision and Thematic Change in *The Portrait of a Lady*', *Modern Fiction Studies*, 22 (Summer 1976), 183–200.

Bazzanella, Dominic J., 'The Conclusion to *The Portrait of a Lady* Re-Examined', *American Literature*, 41 (Mar. 1969), 55–63.

Bell, Ian F. A., *Henry James and the Past* (London: Macmillan, 1993).

Booth, Wayne C., *The Rhetoric of Fiction* (Chicago University Press, 1961).

Buitenhuis, Peter (ed.), *Twentieth Century Interpretations of The Portrait of a Lady: A Collection of Critical Essays* (Englewood Cliffs, NJ: Prentice-Hall, 1968).

Buzard, James, *The Beaten Track, European Tourism, Literature, and the Ways to 'Culture' 1900–1918* (Oxford: Clarendon Press, 1993).

Cross, Mary, *Henry James: The Contingencies of Style* (London: Macmillan, 1993).

Dupee, F. W. (ed.), *The Question of Henry James: A Collection of Critical Essays* (New York: Holt & Co., 1945).

Edel, Leon, *Henry James: A Life*, (London, 1987).

Freedman, Jonathan, *Professions of Taste: Henry James, British Aestheticism, and Commodity Culture* (Stanford, Calif.: Stanford University Press, 1990).

Fowler, Virginia C., *Henry James's American Girl: The Embroidery on the Canvas* (Madison, Wis.: University of Wisconsin Press, 1984).

Gale, Robert L., *The Caught Image: Figurative Language in the Fiction of Henry James* (Chapel Hill, NC: University of North Carolina Press, 1964).

Gard, Roger (comp.), *Henry James: The Critical Heritage* (London: Routledge & Kegan Paul, 1968).

Graham, Kenneth, *Henry James: The Drama of Fulfilment: An Approach to the Novels* (Oxford: Clarendon Press, 1975).

Habegger, Alfred, *Henry James and the 'Woman Business'* (Cambridge University Press, 1989).

Hocks, Richard A., *Henry James and Pragmatistic Thought: A Study in the Relationship between the Philosophy of William and the Literary Art of Henry James* (Chapel Hill, NC: University of North Carolina Press, 1974).

Horne, Philip, *Henry James and Revision: The New York Edition* (Oxford: Clarendon Press, 1990).

James, Henry, *The Art of the Novel: Critical Prefaces*, with introduction by R. P. Blackmur, 1934; repr. New York: Scribner, 1962).

—— *Autobiography: A Small Boy and Others, Notes of a Son and Brother, The Middle Years*, ed. Frederick W. Dupee (New York, 1956).

—— *Henry James Letters*, ed. Leon Edel, 4 vols. (Cambridge, Mass., 1974–84).

—— *The Complete Notebooks of Henry James: The Authoritative and Definitive Edition*, ed. Leon Edel and Lyall H. Powers, (New York and Oxford, 1987).

Jolly, Roslyn, *Henry James: History, Narrative, Fiction* (Oxford: Clarendon Press, 1993).

Krause, Sidney J., 'James's Revisions of Style of *The Portrait of a Lady*', *American Literature*, 30 (Mar. 1958), 67–88.

Leavis, F. R., *The Great Tradition: George Eliot, Henry James, Joseph Conrad* (1948; new edn. London: Chatto & Windus, 1960).

Long, Robert Emmet, *The Great Succession: Henry James and the Legacy of Hawthorne* (University of Pittsburgh Press, 1979).

Matthiessen, F. O., *Henry James: The Major Phase* (Oxford: Clarendon Press, 1944; repr. with appendix, 1963).

Mazzella, Anthony J., 'James's *The Portrait of a Lady*', *Explicator*, 30 (Jan. 1972), Item 37.

Poirier, Richard, *The Comic Sense of Henry James: A Study of the Early Novels* (London: Chatto & Windus, 1960).

Porte, Joel (ed.), *New Essays on James's The Portrait of a Lady* (Cambridge University Press, 1990).

Segal, Ora, *The Lucid Reflector: The Observer in Henry James's Fiction* (New Haven, Conn.: Yale University Press, 1969).
Seltzer, Mark, *Henry James and the Art of Power* (Ithaca, NY: Cornell University Press, 1984).
Tanner, Tony (ed.), *Henry James: Modern Judgments* (London: Macmillan, 1968).
—— *Henry James: The Writer and his Work* (Amherst, Mass.: University of Massachusetts Press, 1985).
Tintner, Adeline, *The Museum World of Henry James* (Ann Arbor, Mich.: UMI Research Press, 1986).
Torgovnick, Marianna, *The Visual Arts, Pictorialism and the Novel, James, Conrad, and Woolf* (Princeton, NJ: Princeton University Press, 1985).
Veeder, William, *Henry James: The Lessons of the Master: Popular Fiction and Personal Style in the Nineteenth Century*, (University of Chicago Press, 1975).
Winner, Viola Hopkins, *Henry James and the Visual Arts*, (Charlottesville, Va.: University Press of Virginia, 1970).

CHRONOLOGY OF HENRY JAMES

1843	Born 15 April at No. 21 Washington Place, New York City.
1843–4	Taken abroad by parents to Paris and London: period of residence at Windsor.
1845–55	Childhood in Albany and New York.
1855–8	Attends schools in Geneva, London, Paris, and Boulogne-sur-mer and is privately tutored.
1858	James family settles in Newport, Rhode Island.
1859	At scientific school in Geneva. Studies German in Bonn.
1860	At school in Newport. Receives back injury on eve of Civil War while serving as volunteer fireman. Studies art briefly. Friendship with John La Farge.
1862–3	Spends term in Harvard Law School.
1864	Family settles in Boston and then in Cambridge. Early anonymous story and unsigned reviews published.
1865	First signed story published in *Atlantic Monthly*.
1869–70	Travels in England, France, and Italy. Death of his beloved cousin Minny Temple.
1870	Back in Cambridge, publishes first novel in *Atlantic*, *Watch and Ward*.
1872–4	Travels with sister Alice and aunt in Europe; writes impressionistic travel sketches for the *Nation*. Spends autumn in Paris and goes to Italy to write first large novel.
1874–5	On completion of *Roderick Hudson* tests New York City as residence; writes much literary journalism for *Nation*. First three books published: *Transatlantic Sketches*, *A Passionate Pilgrim* (tales), and *Roderick Hudson*.
1875–6	Goes to live in Paris. Meets Ivan Turgenev and through him Flaubert, Zola, Daudet, Maupassant, and Edmond de Goncourt. Writes *The American*.
1876–7	Moves to London and settles in 3 Bolton Street, Piccadilly. Revisits Paris, Florence, Rome.
1878	'Daisy Miller' published in London establishes fame on both sides of the Atlantic. Publishes first volume of essays, *French Poets and Novelists*.
1879–82	*The Europeans*, *Washington Square*, Confidence, *The Portrait of a Lady*.

1882–3	Revisits Boston: first visit to Washington. Death of parents.
1884–6	Returns to London. Sister Alice comes to live near him. Fourteen-volume collection of novels and tales published. Writes *The Bostonians* and *The Princess Casamassima*, published in the following year.
1886	Moves to flat at 34 De Vere Gardens West.
1887	Sojourn in Italy, mainly Florence and Venice. 'The Aspern Papers', *The Reverberator*, 'A London Life'. Friendship with grand-niece of Fenimore Cooper—Constance Fenimore Woolson.
1888	*Partial Portraits* and several collections of tales.
1889–90	*The Tragic Muse*.
1890–1	Dramatizes *The American*, which has a short run. Writes four comedies, rejected by producers.
1892	Alice James dies in London.
1894	Miss Woolson commits suicide in Venice. James journeys to Italy and visits her grave in Rome.
1895	He is booed at first night of his play *Guy Domville*. Deeply depressed, he abandons the theatre.
1896–7	*The Spoils of Poynton, What Maisie Knew*.
1898	Takes long lease of Lamb House, in Rye, Sussex. 'The Turn of the Screw' published.
1899–1900	*The Awkward Age, The Sacred Fount*. Friendship with Conrad and Wells.
1902–4	*The Ambassadors, The Wings of the Dove*, and *The Golden Bowl*. Friendships with H. C. Andersen and Jocelyn Persse.
1905	Revisits USA after 20-year absence, lectures on Balzac and the speech of Americans.
1906–10	*The American Scene*. Edits selective and revised 'New York Edition' of his works in 24 volumes. Friendship with Hugh Walpole.
1910	Death of brother, William James.
1913	Sargent paints his portrait as 70th birthday gift from some 300 friends and admirers. Writes autobiographies, *A Small Boy and Others*, and *Notes of a Son and Brother*.
1914	*Notes on Novelists*. Visits wounded in hospitals.
1915	Becomes a British subject.
1916	Given Order of Merit. Dies 28 February in Chelsea, aged 72. Funeral in Chelsea Old Church. Ashes buried in Cambridge, Mass., family plot.

1976 Commemorative tablet unveiled in Poets' Corner of Westminster Abbey, 17 June.

THE PORTRAIT OF A LADY

PREFACE

'THE PORTRAIT OF A LADY' was, like 'Roderick Hudson,' begun in Florence, during three months spent there in the spring of 1879. Like 'Roderick' and like 'The American,' it had been designed for publication in 'The Atlantic Monthly,' where it began to appear in 1880. It differed from its two predecessors, however, in finding a course also open to it, from month to month, in 'Macmillan's Magazine'; which was to be for me one of the last occasions of simultaneous 'serialisation' in the two countries that the changing conditions of literary intercourse between England and the United States had up to then left unaltered. It is a long novel, and I was long in writing it; I remember being again much occupied with it, the following year, during a stay of several weeks made in Venice. I had rooms on Riva Schiavoni, at the top of a house near the passage leading off to San Zaccaria; the waterside life, the wondrous lagoon spread before me, and the ceaseless human chatter of Venice came in at my windows, to which I seem to myself to have been constantly driven, in the fruitless fidget of composition, as if to see whether, out in the blue channel, the ship of some right suggestion, of some better phrase, of the next happy twist of my subject, the next true touch for my canvas, mightn't come into sight. But I recall vividly enough that the response most elicited, in general, to these restless appeals was the rather grim admonition that romantic and historic sites, such as the land of Italy abounds in, offer the artist a questionable aid to concentration when they themselves are not to be the subject of it. They are too rich in their own life and too charged with their own meanings merely to help him out with a lame phrase; they draw him away from his small question to their own greater ones; so that, after a little, he feels, while thus yearning toward them in his difficulty, as if he were asking an army of glorious veterans to help him to arrest a peddler who has given him the wrong change.

There are pages of the book which, in the reading over, have seemed to make me see again the bristling curve of the wide

Riva, the large colour-spots of the balconied houses and the repeated undulation of the little hunchbacked bridges, marked by the rise and drop again, with the wave, of foreshortened clicking pedestrains. The Venetian footfall and the Venetian cry—all talk there, wherever uttered, having the pitch of a call across the water—come in once more at the window, renewing one's old impression of the delighted senses and the divided, frustrated mind. How can places that speak *in general* so to the imagination not give it, at the moment, the particular thing it wants? I recollect again and again, in beautiful places, dropping into that wonderment. The real truth is, I think, that they express, under this appeal, only too much—more than, in the given case, one has use for; so that one finds one's self working less congruously, after all, so far as the surrounding picture is concerned, than in presence of the moderate and the neutral, to which we may lend something of the light of our vision. Such a place as Venice is too proud for such charities; Venice doesn't borrow, she but all magnificently gives. We profit by that enormously, but to do so we must either be quite off duty or be on it in her service alone. Such, and so rueful, are these reminiscences; though on the whole, no doubt, one's book, and one's 'literary effort' at large, were to be the better for them. Strangely fertilising, in the long run, does a wasted effort of attention often prove. It all depends on *how* the attention has been cheated, has been squandered. There are high-handed insolent frauds, and there are insidious sneaking ones. And there is, I fear, even on the most designing artist's part, always witless enough good faith, always anxious enough desire, to fail to guard him against their deceits.

Trying to recover here, for recognition, the germ of my idea, I see that it must have consisted not at all in any conceit of a 'plot,' nefarious name, in any flash, upon the fancy, of a set of relations, or in any one of those situations that, by a logic of their own, immediately fall, for the fabulist, into movement, into a march or a rush, a patter of quick steps; but altogether in the sense of a single character, the character and aspect of a particular engaging young woman, to which all the usual elements of a 'subject,' certainly of a setting, were to need to be super-added. Quite as interesting as the young woman herself, at her best, do I find, I must again repeat, this projection of memory upon the whole matter of the growth, in one's imagination, of some such apology for a motive. These are the fascinations of the fabulist's art, these lurking forces of expansion, these necessities of upspringing in the seed, these beautiful determinations, on the part of the idea entertained, to grow as tall as possible, to push into the light and the air and thickly flower there; and, quite as much, these fine possibilities of recovering, from some good standpoint on the ground gained, the intimate history of the business—of retracing and reconstructing its steps and stages. I have always fondly remembered a remark that I heard fall years ago from the lips of Ivan Turgenieff in regard to his own experience of the usual origin of the fictive picture. It began for him almost always with the vision of some person or persons, who hovered before him, soliciting him, as the active or passive figure, interesting him and appealing to him just as they were and by what they were. He saw them, in that fashion, as *disponibles*,* saw them subject to the chances, the complications of existence, and saw them vividly, but then had to find for them the right relations, those that would most bring them out; to imagine, to invent and select and piece together the situations most useful and favourable to the sense of the creatures themselves, the complications they would be most likely to produce and to feel.

'To arrive at these things is to arrive at my "story," ' he said, 'and that's the way I look for it. The result is that I'm often accused of not having "story" enough. I seem to myself to have as much as I need—to show my people, to exhibit their relations with each other; for that is all my measure. If I watch them long enough I see them come together, I see them *placed*, I see them engaged in this or that act and in this or that difficulty. How they look and move and speak and behave, always in the setting I have found for them, is my account of them—of which I dare say, alas, *que cela manque souvent d'architecture*.* But I would rather, I think, have too little architecture than too much—when there's danger of its interfering with my measure of the truth. The French of course like more of it than I give—having by their own genius such a hand for it; and indeed one must give all one can. As for the origin of one's wind-blown germs themselves, who shall say, as you ask, where *they* come from? We have to go too far back, too far behind, to say. Isn't it all we can say that they come from every quarter of heaven, that they are *there* at almost any turn of the road? They accumulate, and we are always picking them over, selecting among them. They are the breath of life—by which I mean that life, in its own way, breathes them upon us. They are so, in a manner prescribed and imposed—floated into our minds by the current of life. That reduces to imbecility the vain critic's quarrel, so often, with one's subject, when he hasn't the wit to accept it. Will he point out then which other it should properly have been?—his office being, essentially *to* point out. *Il en serait bien embarrassé.** Ah, when he points out what I've done or failed to do with it, that's another matter: there he's on his ground. I give him up my "architecture," ' my distinguished friend concluded, 'as much as he will.'

So this beautiful genius, and I recall with comfort the gratitude I drew from his reference to the intensity of suggestion that may reside in the stray figure, the unattached character, the image *en disponibilité.** It gave me higher warrant than I seemed then to have met for just that blest habit of one's own imagination, the trick of investing some conceived or encountered individual, some brace or group of individuals, with the germinal property and authority. I was myself so much more antecedently conscious of my figures than of their setting—a too preliminary, a preferential interest in which struck me as in general such a putting of the cart before the horse. I might envy, though I couldn't emulate, the imaginative writer so constituted as to see his fable first and to make out its agents afterwards: I could think so little of any fable that didn't need its agents positively to launch it; I could think so little of any situation that didn't depend for its interest on the nature of the persons situated, and thereby on their way of taking it. There are methods of so-called presentation, I believe—among novelists who have appeared to flourish—that offer the situation as indifferent to that support; but I have not lost the sense of the value for me, at the time, of the admirable Russian's testimony to my not needing, all superstitiously, to try and perform any such gymnastic. Other echoes from the same source linger with me, I confess, as unfadingly—if it be not all indeed one much-embracing echo. It was impossible after that not to read, for one's uses, high lucidity into the tormented and disfigured and bemuddled question of the objective value, and even quite into that of the critical appreciation, of 'subject' in the novel.

One had had from an early time, for that matter, the instinct of the right estimate of such values and of its reducing to the inane the dull dispute over the 'immoral' subject and the moral. Recognising so promptly the one measure of the worth of a given subject, the question about it that, rightly answered, disposes of all others—is it valid, in a word, is it genuine, is it sincere, the result of some direct impression or perception of life?—I had found small edification, mostly, in a critical pretension that had neglected from the first all delimitation of ground and all definition of terms. The air of my earlier time shows, to memory, as darkened, all round, with that vanity—unless the difference to-day be just in one's own final impatience, the lapse of one's attention. There is, I think, no more nutritive or suggestive truth in this connexion than that of the perfect dependence of the 'moral' sense of a work of art on the amount of felt life concerned in producing it. The question comes back thus, obviously, to the kind and the degree of the artist's prime sensibility, which is the soil out of which his subject springs. The quality and capacity of that soil, its ability to 'grow' with due freshness and straightness any vision of life, represents, strongly or weakly, the projected morality. That element is but another name for the more or less close connexion of the subject with some mark made on the intelligence, with some sincere experience. By which, at the same time, of course, one is far from contending that this enveloping air of the artist's humanity—which gives the last touch to the worth of the work—is not a widely and wondrously varying element; being on one occasion a rich and magnificent medium and on another a comparatively poor and ungenerous one. Here we get exactly the high price of the novel as a literary form—its power not only, while preserving that form with closeness, to range through all the differences of the individual relation to its general subject-matter, all the varieties of outlook on life, of disposition to reflect and project, created by conditions that are never the same from man to man (or, so far as that goes, from man to woman), but positively to appear more true to its character in proportion as it strains, or tends to burst, with a latent extravagance, its mould.

The house of fiction has in short not one window, but a million—a number of possible windows not to be reckoned, rather; every one of which has been pierced, or is still pierceable, in its vast front, by the need of the individual vision and by the pressure of the individual will. These apertures, of dissimilar shape and size, hang so, all together, over the human scene that we might have expected of them a greater sameness of report than we find. They are but windows at the best, mere holes in a dead wall, disconnected, perched aloft; they are not hinged doors opening straight upon life. But they have this mark of their own that at each of them stands a figure with a pair of eyes, or at least with a field-glass, which forms, again and again, for observation, a unique instrument, insuring to the person making use of it an impression distinct from every other. He and his neighbours are watching the same show, but one seeing more where the other sees less, one seeing black where the other sees white, one seeing big where the other sees small, one seeing coarse where the other sees fine. And so on, and so on; there is fortunately no saying on what, for the particular pair of eyes, the window may *not* open; 'fortunately' by reason, precisely, of this incalculability of range. The spreading field, the human scene, is the 'choice of subject'; the pierced aperture, either broad or balconied or slit-like and low-browed, is the 'literary form'; but they are, singly or together, as nothing without the posted presence of the watcher—without, in other words, the consciousness of the artist. Tell me what the artist is, and I will tell you of what he has *been* conscious. Thereby I shall express to you at once his boundless freedom and his 'moral' reference.

All this is a long way round, however, for my word about my dim first move toward 'The Portrait,' which was exactly my grasp of a single character—an acquisition I had made, moreover, after a fashion not here to be retraced. Enough that I was, as seemed to me, in complete possession of it, that I had been so for a long time, that this had made it familiar and yet had not blurred its charm, and that, all urgently, all tormentingly, I saw it in motion and, so to speak, in transit. This amounts to saying that I saw it as bent upon its fate—some fate or other; *which*, among the possibilities, being precisely the question. Thus I had my vivid individual—vivid, so strangely, in spite of being still at large, not confined by the conditions, not engaged in the tangle, to which we look for much of the impress that constitutes an identity. If the apparition was still all to be placed how came it to be vivid?—since we puzzle such quantities out, mostly, just by the business of placing them. One could answer such a question beautifully, doubtless, if one could do so subtle, if not so monstrous, a thing as to write the history of the growth of one's imagination. One would describe then what, at a given time, had extraordinarily happened to it, and one would so, for instance, be in a position to tell, with an approach to clearness, how, under favour of occasion, it had been able to take over (take over straight from life) such and such a constituted, animated figure or form. The figure has to that extent, as you see, *been* placed—placed in the imagination that detains it, preserves, protects, enjoys it, conscious of its presence in the dusky, crowded, heterogeneous back-shop of the mind very much as a wary dealer in precious odds and ends, competent to make an 'advance' on rare objects confided to him, is conscious of the rare little 'piece' left in deposit by the reduced, mysterious lady of title or the speculative amateur, and which is already there to disclose its merit afresh as soon as a key shall have clicked in a cupboard-door.

That may be, I recognise, a somewhat superfine analogy for the particular 'value' I here speak of, the image of the young feminine nature that I had had for so considerable a time all curiously at my disposal; but it appears to fond memory quite to fit the fact—with the recall, in addition, of my pious desire but to place my treasure right. I quite remind myself thus of the dealer resigned not to 'realise,' resigned to keeping the precious object locked up indefinitely rather than commit it, at no matter what price, to vulgar hands. For there *are* dealers in these forms and figures and treasures capable of that refinement. The point is, however, that this single small corner-stone, the conception of a certain young woman affronting her destiny, had begun with being all my outfit for the large building of 'The Portrait of a Lady.' It came to be a square and spacious house—or has at least seemed so to me in this going over it again; but, such as it is, it had to be put up round my young woman while she stood there in perfect isolation. That is to me, artistically speaking, the circumstance of interest; for I have lost myself once more, I confess, in the curiosity of analysing the structure. By what process of logical accretion was this slight 'personality,' the mere slim shade of an intelligent but presumptuous girl, to find itself endowed with the high attributes of a Subject?—and indeed by what thinness, at the best, would such a subject not be vitiated? Millions of presumptuous girls, intelligent or not intelligent, daily affront their destiny, and what is it open to their destiny to *be*, at the most, that we should make an ado about it? The novel is of its very nature an 'ado,' an ado about something, and the larger the form it takes the greater of course the ado. Therefore, consciously, that was what one was in for—for positively organising an ado about Isabel Archer.

One looked it well in the face, I seem to remember, this extravagance; and with the effect precisely of recognising the charm of the problem. Challenge any such problem with any intelligence, and you immediately see how full it is of substance; the wonder being, all the while, as we look at the world, how absolutely, how inordinately, the Isabel Archers, and even much smaller female fry, insist on mattering. George Eliot has admirably noted it—'In these frail vessels is borne onward through the ages the treasure of human affection.' In 'Romeo and Juliet' Juliet has to be important, just as, in 'Adam Bede' and 'The Mill on the Floss' and 'Middlemarch' and 'Daniel Deronda,' Hetty Sorrel and Maggie Tulliver and Rosamond Vincy and Gwendolen Harleth have to be; with that much of firm ground, that much of bracing air, at the disposal all the while of their feet and their lungs. They are typical, none the less, of a class difficult, in the individual case, to make a centre of interest; so difficult in fact that many an expert painter, as for instance Dickens and Walter Scott, as for instance even, in the main, so subtle a hand as that of R. L. Stevenson, has preferred to leave the task unattempted. There are in fact writers as to whom we make out that their refuge from this is to assume it to be not worth their attempting; by which pusillanimity in truth their honour is scantly saved. It is never an attestation of a value, or even of our imperfect sense of one, it is never a tribute to any truth at all, that we shall represent that value badly. It never makes up, artistically, for an artist's dim feeling about a thing that he shall 'do' the thing as ill as possible. There are better ways than that, the best of all of which is to begin with less stupidity.

It may be answered meanwhile, in regard to Shakespeare's and to George Eliot's testimony, that their concession to the 'importance' of their Juliets and Cleopatras and Portias (even with Portia as the very type and model of the young person intelligent and presumptuous) and to that of their Hettys and Maggies and Rosamonds and Gwendolens, suffers the abatement that these slimnesses are, when figuring as the main props of the theme, never suffered to be sole ministers of its appeal, but have their inadequacy eked out with comic relief and underplots, as the playwrights say, when not with murders and battles and the great mutations of the world. If they are shown as 'mattering' as much as they could possibly pretend to, the proof of it is in a hundred other persons, made of much stouter stuff, and each involved moreover in a hundred relations which matter to *them* concomitantly with that one. Cleopatra matters, beyond bounds, to Antony, but his colleagues, his antagonists, the state of Rome and the impending battle also prodigiously matter; Portia matters to Antonio, and to Shylock, and to the Prince of Morocco, to the fifty aspiring princes, but for these gentry there are other lively concerns; for Antonio, notably, there are Shylock and Bassanio and his lost ventures and the extremity of his predicament. This extremity indeed, by the same token, matters to Portia—though its doing so becomes of interest all by the fact that Portia matters to *us*. That she does so, at any rate, and that almost everything comes round to it again, supports my contention as to this fine example of the value recognised in the mere young thing. (I say 'mere' young thing because I guess that even Shakespeare, preoccupied mainly though he may have been with the passions of princes, would scarce have pretended to found the best of his appeal for her on her high social position.) It is an example exactly of the deep difficulty braved—the difficulty of making George Eliot's 'frail vessel,' if not the all-in-all for our attention, at least the clearest of the call.

Now to see deep difficulty braved is at any time, for the really addicted artist, to feel almost even as a pang the beautiful incentive, and to feel it verily in such sort as to wish the danger intensified. The difficulty most worth tackling can only be for him, in these conditions, the greatest the case permits of. So I remember feeling here (in presence, always, that is, of the particular uncertainty of my ground), that there would be one way better than another—oh, ever so much better than any other!—of making it fight out its battle. The frail vessel, that charged with George Eliot's 'treasure,' and thereby of such importance to those who curiously approach it, has likewise possibilities of importance to itself, possibilities which permit of treatment and in fact peculiarly require it from the moment they are considered at all. There is always the escape from any close account of the weak agent of such spells by using as a bridge for evasion, for retreat and flight, the view of her relation to those surrounding her. Make it predominantly a view of *their* relation and the trick is played: you give the general sense of her effect, and you give it, so far as the raising on it of a superstructure goes, with the maximum of ease. Well, I recall perfectly how little, in my now quite established connexion, the maximum of ease appealed to me, and how I seemed to get rid of it by an honest transposition of the weights in the two scales. 'Place the centre of the subject in the young woman's own consciousness,' I said to myself, 'and you get as interesting and as beautiful a difficulty as you could wish. Stick to *that*—for the centre; put the heaviest weight into *that* scale, which will be so largely the scale of her relation to herself. Make her only interested enough, at the same time, in the things that are not herself, and this relation needn't fear to be too limited. Place meanwhile in the other scale the lighter weight (which is usually the one that tips the balance of interest): press least hard, in short, on the consciousness of your heroine's satellites, especially the male; make it an interest contributive only to the greater one. See, at all events, what can be done in this way. What better field could there be for a due ingenuity? The girl hovers, inextinguishable, as a charming creature, and the job will be to translate her into the highest terms of that formula, and as nearly as possible moreover into *all* of them. To depend upon her and her little concerns wholly to see you through will necessitate, remember, your really "doing" her.'

So far I reasoned, and it took nothing less than that technical rigour, I now easily see, to inspire me with the right confidence for erecting on such a plot of ground the neat and careful and proportioned pile of bricks that arches over it and that was thus to form, constructionally speaking, a literary monument. Such is the aspect that to-day 'The Portrait' wears for me: a structure reared with an 'architectural' competence, as Turgenieff would have said, that makes it, to the author's own sense, the most proportioned of his productions after 'The Ambassadors'—which was to follow it so many years later and which has, no doubt, a superior roundness. On one thing I was determined; that, though I should clearly have to pile brick upon brick for the creation of an interest, I would leave no pretext for saying that anything is out of line, scale or perspective. I would build large—in fine embossed vaults and painted arches, as who should say, and yet never let it appear that the chequered pavement, the ground under the reader's feet, fails to stretch at every point to the base of the walls. That precautionary spirit, on re-persual of the book, is the old note that most touches me: it testifies so, for my own ear, to the anxiety of my provision for the reader's amusement. I felt, in view of the possible limitations of my subject, that no such provision could be excessive, and the development of the latter was simply the general form of that earnest quest. And I find indeed that this is the only account I can give myself of the evolution of the fable: it is all under the head thus named that I conceive the needful accretion as having taken place, the right complications as having started. It was naturally of the essence that the young woman should be herself complex; that was rudimentary—or was at any rate the light in which Isabel

Archer had originally dawned. It went, however, but a certain way, and other lights, contending, conflicting lights, and of as many different colours, if possible, as the rockets, the Roman candles and Catherine-wheels of a 'pyrotechnic display,' would be employable to attest that she was. I had, no doubt, a groping instinct for the right complications, since I am quite unable to track the footsteps of those that constitute, as the case stands, the general situation exhibited. They are there, for what they are worth, and as numerous as might be; but my memory, I confess, is a blank as to how and whence they came.

I seem to myself to have waked up one morning in possession of them—of Ralph Touchett and his parents, of Madame Merle, of Gilbert Osmond and his daughter and his sister, of Lord Warburton, Caspar Goodwood and Miss Stackpole, the definite array of contributions to Isabel Archer's history. I recognised them, I knew them, they were the numbered pieces of my puzzle, the concrete terms of my 'plot.' It was as if they had simply, by an impulse of their own, floated into my ken, and all in response to my primary question: 'Well, what will she *do*?' Their answer seemed to be that if I would trust them they would show me; on which, with an urgent appeal to them to make it at least as interesting as they could, I trusted them. They were like the group of attendants and entertainers who come down by train when people in the country give a party; they represented the contract for carrying the party on. That was an excellent relation with them—a possible one even with so broken a reed (from her slightness of cohesion) as Henrietta Stackpole. It is a familiar truth to the novelist, at the strenuous hour, that, as certain elements in any work are of the essence, so others are only of the form; that as this or that character, this or that disposition of the material, belongs to the subject directly, so to speak, so this or that other belongs to it but indirectly—belongs intimately to the treatment. This is a truth, however, of which he rarely gets the benefit—since it could be assured to him, really, but by criticism based upon perception, criticism which is too little of this world. He must not think of benefits, moreover, I freely recognise, for that way dishonour lies: he has, that is, but one to think of—the benefit, whatever it may be, involved in his having cast a spell upon the simpler, the very simplest, forms of attention. This is all he is entitled to; he is entitled to nothing, he is bound to admit, that can come to him, from the reader, as a result on the latter's part of any act of reflection or discrimination. He may *enjoy* this finer tribute—that is another affair, but on condition only of taking it as a gratuity 'thrown in,' a mere miraculous windfall, the fruit of a tree he may not pretend to have shaken. Against reflection, against discrimination, in his interest, all earth and air conspire; wherefore it is that, as I say, he must in many a case have schooled himself, from the first, to work but for a 'living wage.' The living wage is the reader's grant of the least possible quantity of attention required for consciousness of a 'spell.' The occasional charming 'tip' is an act of his intelligence over and beyond this, a golden apple, for the writer's lap, straight from the wind-stirred tree. The artist may of course, in wanton moods, dream of some Paradise (for art) where the direct appeal to the intelligence might be legalised; for to such extravagances as these his yearning mind can scarce hope ever completely to close itself. The most he can do is to remember they *are* extravagances.

All of which is perhaps but a gracefully devious way of saying that Henrietta Stackpole was a good example, in 'The Portrait,' of the truth to which I just adverted—as good an example as I could name were it not that Maria Gostrey, in 'The Ambassadors,' then in the bosom of time, may be mentioned as a better. Each of these persons is but wheels to the coach; neither belongs to the body of that vehicle, or is for a moment accommodated with a seat inside. There the subject alone is ensconced, in the form of its 'hero and heroine,' and of the privileged high officials, say, who ride with the king and queen. There are reasons why one would have liked this to be felt, as in general one would like almost anything to be felt, in one's work, that one has one's self contributively felt. We have seen, however, how idle is that pretension, which I should be sorry to make too much of. Maria Gostrey and Miss Stackpole then are cases, each, of the light *ficelle*,* not of the true agent; they may run beside the coach 'for all they are worth,' they may cling to it till they are out of breath (as poor Miss Stackpole all so visibly does), but neither, all the while, so much as gets her foot on the step, neither ceases for a moment to tread the dusty road. Put it even that they are like the fishwives who helped to bring back to Paris from Versailles, on that most ominous day of the first half of the French Revolution, the carriage of the royal family. The only thing is that I may well be asked, I acknowledge, why then, in the present fiction, I have suffered Henrietta (of whom we have indubitably too much) so officiously, so strangely, so almost inexplicably, to pervade. I will presently say what I can for that anomaly and in the most conciliatory fashion.

A point I wish still more to make is that if my relation of confidence with the actors in my drama who *were*, unlike Miss Stackpole, true agents, was an excellent one to have arrived at, there still remained my relation with the reader, which was another affair altogether and as to which I felt no one to be trusted but myself. That solicitude was to be accordingly expressed in the artful patience with which, as I have said, I piled brick upon brick. The bricks, for the whole counting-over—putting for bricks little touches and inventions and enhancements by the way—affect me in truth as wellnigh innumerable and as ever so scrupulously fitted together and packed in. It is an effect of detail, of the minutest; though, if one were in this connection to say all, one would express the hope that the general, the ampler air of the modest monument still survives. I do at least seem to catch the key to a part of this abundance of small anxious, ingenious illustration as I recollect putting my finger, in my young woman's interest, on the most obvious of her predicates. 'What will she "do"? Why, the first thing she'll do will be to come to Europe; which in fact will form, and all inevitably, no small part of her principal adventure. Coming to Europe is even for the "frail vessels," in this wonderful age, a mild adventure; but what is truer than that on one side—the side of their independence of flood and field, of the moving accident, of battle and murder and sudden death—her adventures are to be mild? Without her sense of them, her sense *for* them, as one may say, they are next to nothing at all; but isn't the beauty and the difficulty just in showing their mystic conversion by that sense, conversion into the stuff of drama or, even more delightful word still, of "story"?' It was all as clear, my contention, as a silver bell. Two very good instances, I think, of this effect of conversion, two cases of the rare chemistry, are the pages in which Isabel, coming into the drawing-room at Gardencourt, coming in from a wet walk or whatever, that rainy afternoon, finds Madame Merle in possession of the place, Madame Merle seated, all absorbed but all serene, at the piano, and deeply recognises, in the striking of such an hour, in the presence there, among the gathering shades, of this personage, of whom a moment before she had never so much as heard, a turning-point in her life. It is dreadful to have too much, for any artistic demonstration, to dot one's i's and insist on one's intentions, and I am not eager to do it now; but the question here was that of producing the maximum of intensity with the minimum of strain.

The interest was to be raised to its pitch and yet the elements to be kept in their key; so that, should the whole thing duly impress, I might show what an 'exciting' inward life may do for the person leading it even while it remains perfectly normal. And I cannot think of a more consistent application of that ideal unless it be in the long statement, just beyond the middle of the book, of my young woman's extraordinary meditative vigil on the occasion that was to become for her such a landmark. Reduced to its essence, it is but the vigil of searching criticism; but it throws the action further forward than twenty 'incidents' might have done. It was designed to have all the vivacity of incident and all the economy of picture. She sits up, by her dying fire, far into the night, under the spell of recognitions on which she finds the last sharpness suddenly wait. It is a representation simply of her motionlessly *seeing*, and an attempt withal to make the mere still lucidity of her act as 'interesting' as the surprise of a caravan or the identification of a pirate. It represents, for that matter, one of the identifications dear to the novelist, and even indispensable to him; but it all goes on without her being approached by another person and without her leaving her chair. It is obviously the best thing in the book, but it is only a supreme illustration of the general plan. As to Henrietta, my apology for whom I just left incomplete, she exemplifies, I fear, in her superabundance, not an element of my plan, but only an excess of my zeal. So early was to begin my tendency to *overtreat*, rather than undertreat (when there was choice or danger) my subject. (Many members of my craft, I gather, are far from agreeing with me, but I have always held overtreating the minor disservice.) 'Treating' that of 'The Portrait' amounted to never forgetting, by any lapse, that the thing was under a special obligation to be amusing. There was the danger of the noted 'thinness'—which was to be averted, tooth and nail, by cultivation of the lively. That is at least how I see it to-day. Henrietta must have been at that time a part of my wonderful notion of the lively. And then there was another matter. I had, within the few preceding years, come to live in London, and the 'international' light lay, in those days, to my sense, thick and rich upon the scene. It was the light in which so much of the picture hung. But that *is* another matter. There is really too much to say.

HENRY JAMES

I

UNDER certain circumstances there are few hours in life more agreeable than the hour dedicated to the ceremony known as afternoon tea. There are circumstances in which, whether you partake of the tea or not—some people of course never do,—the situation is in itself delightful. Those that I have in mind in beginning to unfold this simple history offered an admirable setting to an innocent pastime. The implements of the little feast had been disposed upon the lawn of an old English country-house, in what I should call the perfect middle of a splendid summer afternoon. Part of the afternoon had waned, but much of it was left, and what was left was of the finest and rarest quality. Real dusk would not arrive for many hours; but the flood of summer light had begun to ebb, the air had grown mellow, the shadows were long upon the smooth, dense turf. They lengthened slowly, however, and the scene expressed that sense of leisure still to come which is perhaps the chief source of one's enjoyment of such a scene at such an hour. From five o'clock to eight is on certain occasions a little eternity; but on such an occasion as this the interval could be only an eternity of pleasure. The persons concerned in it were taking their pleasure quietly, and they were not of the sex which is supposed to furnish the regular votaries of the ceremony I have mentioned. The shadows on the perfect lawn were straight and angular; they were the shadows of an old man sitting in a deep wicker-chair near the low table on which the tea had been served, and of two younger men strolling to and fro, in desultory talk, in front of him. The old man had his cup in his hand; it was an unusually large cup, of a different pattern from the rest of the set and painted in brilliant colours. He disposed of its contents with much circumspection, holding it for a long time close to his chin, with his face turned to the house. His companions had either finished their tea or were indifferent to their privilege; they smoked cigarettes as they continued to stroll. One of them, from time to time, as he passed, looked with a certain attention at the elder man, who, unconscious of observation, rested his eyes upon the rich red front of his dwelling. The house that rose beyond the lawn was a structure to repay such consideration and was the most characteristic object in the peculiarly English picture I have attempted to sketch.

It stood upon a low hill, above the river—the river being the Thames at some forty miles from London. A long gabled front of red brick, with the complexion of which time and the weather had played all sorts of pictorial tricks, only, however, to improve and refine it, presented to the lawn its patches of ivy, its clustered chimneys, its windows smothered in creepers. The house had a name and a history; the old gentleman taking his tea would have been delighted to tell you these things: how it had been built under Edward the Sixth, had offered a night's hospitality to the great Elizabeth (whose august person had extended itself upon a huge, magnificent and terribly angular bed which still formed the principal honour of the sleeping apartments), had been a good deal bruised and defaced in Cromwell's wars, and then, under the Restoration, repaired and much enlarged; and how, finally, after having been remodelled and disfigured in the eighteenth century, it had passed into the careful keeping of a shrewd American banker, who had bought it originally because (owing to circumstances too complicated to set forth) it was offered at a great bargain: bought it with much grumbling at its ugliness, its antiquity, its incommodity, and who now, at the end of twenty years, had become conscious of a real aesthetic passion for it, so that he knew all its points and would tell you just where to stand to see them in combination and just the hour when the shadows of its various protuberances—which fell so softly upon the warm, weary brickwork—were of the right measure. Besides this, as I have said, he could have counted off most of the successive owners and occupants, several of whom were known to general fame; doing so, however, with an undemonstrative conviction that the latest phase of its destiny was not the least honourable. The front of the house overlooking that portion of the lawn with which we are concerned was not the entrance-front; this was in quite another quarter. Privacy here reigned supreme, and the wide carpet of turf that covered the level hill-top seemed but the extension of a luxurious interior. The great still oaks and beeches flung down a shade as dense as that of velvet curtains; and the place was furnished, like a room, with cushioned seats, with rich-coloured rugs, with the books and papers that lay upon the grass. The river was at some distance; where the ground began to slope the lawn, properly speaking, ceased. But it was none the less a charming walk down to the water.

The old gentleman at the tea-table, who had come from America thirty years before, had brought with him, at the top of his baggage, his American physiognomy; and he had not only brought it with him, but he had kept it in the best order, so that, if necessary, he might have taken it back to his own country with perfect confidence. At present, obviously, nevertheless, he was not likely to displace himself; his journeys were over and he was taking the rest that precedes the great rest. He had a narrow, clean-shaven face, with features evenly distributed and an expression of placid acuteness. It was evidently a face in which the range of representation was not large, so that the air of contented shrewdness was all the more of a merit. It seemed to tell that he had been successful in life, yet it seemed to tell also that his success had not been exclusive and invidious, but had had much of the inoffensiveness of failure. He had certainly had a great experience of men, but there was an almost rustic simplicity in the faint smile that played upon his lean, spacious cheek and lighted up his humorous eye as he at last slowly and carefully deposited his big tea-cup upon the table. He was neatly dressed, in well-brushed black; but a shawl was folded upon his knees, and his feet were encased in thick, embroidered slippers. A beautiful collie dog lay upon the grass near his chair, watching the master's face almost as tenderly as the master took in the still more magisterial physiognomy of the house; and a little bristling, bustling terrier bestowed a desultory attendance upon the other gentlemen.

One of these was a remarkably well-made man of five-and-thirty, with a face as English as that of the old gentleman I have just sketched was something else; a noticeably handsome face, fresh-coloured, fair and frank, with firm, straight features, a lively grey eye and the rich adornment of a chestnut beard. This person had a certain fortunate, brilliant exceptional look—the air of a happy temperament fertilised by a high civilisation—which would have made almost any observer envy him at a venture. He was booted and spurred, as if he had dismounted from a long ride; he wore a white hat, which looked too large for him; he held his two hands behind him, and in one of them—a large, white, well-shaped fist—was crumpled a pair of a soiled dog-skin gloves.

His companion, measuring the length of the lawn beside him, was a person of quite a different pattern, who, although he might have excited grave curiosity, would not, like the other, have provoked you to wish yourself, almost blindly, in his place. Tall, lean, loosely and feebly put together, he had an ugly, sickly, witty, charming face, furnished, but by no means decorated, with a straggling moustache and whisker. He looked clever and ill—a combination by no means felicitous; and he wore a brown velvet jacket. He carried his hands in his pockets, and there was something in the way he did it that showed the habit was inveterate. His gait had a shambling, wandering quality; he was not very firm on his legs. As I have said, whenever he passed the old man in the chair he rested his eyes upon him; and at this moment, with their faces brought into relation, you would easily have seen they were father and son. The father caught his son's eye at last and gave him a mild, responsive smile.

'I'm getting on very well,' he said.

'Have you drunk your tea?' asked the son.

'Yes, and enjoyed it.'

'Shall I give you some more?'

The old man considered, placidly. 'Well, I guess I'll wait and see.' He had, in speaking, the American tone.

'Are you cold?' the son enquired.

The father slowly rubbed his legs. 'Well, I don't know. I can't tell till I feel.'

'Perhaps some one might feel for you,' said the younger man, laughing.

'Oh, I hope some one will always feel for me! Don't you feel for me, Lord Warburton?'

'Oh yes, immensely,' said the gentleman addressed as Lord Warburton, promptly. 'I'm bound to say you look wonderfully comfortable.'

'Well, I suppose I am, in most respects.' And the old man looked down at his green shawl and smoothed it over his knees. 'The fact is I've been comfortable so many years that I suppose I've got so used to it I don't know it.'

'Yes, that's the bore of comfort,' said Lord Warburton. 'We only know when we're uncomfortable.'

'It strikes me we're rather particular,' his companion remarked.

'Oh yes, there's no doubt we're particular,' Lord Warburton murmured. And then the three men remained silent a while; the two younger ones standing looking down at the other, who presently asked for more tea. 'I should think you would be very unhappy with that shawl,' Lord Warburton resumed while his companion filled the old man's cup again.

'Oh no, he must have the shawl!' cried the gentleman in the velvet coat. 'Don't put such ideas as that into his head.'

'It belongs to my wife,' said the old man simply.

'Oh, if it's for sentimental reasons——' And Lord Warburton made a gesture of apology.

'I suppose I must give it to her when she comes,' the old man went on.

'You'll please to do nothing of the kind. You'll keep it to cover your poor old legs.'

'Well, you mustn't abuse my legs,' said the old man. 'I guess they are as good as yours.'

'Oh, you're perfectly free to abuse mine,' his son replied, giving him his tea.

'Well, we're two lame ducks; I don't think there's much difference.'

'I'm much obliged to you for calling me a duck. How's your tea?'

'Well, it's rather hot.'

'That's intended to be a merit.'

'Ah, there's a great deal of merit,' murmured the old man, kindly. 'He's a very good nurse, Lord Warburton.'

'Isn't he a bit clumsy?' asked his lordship.

'Oh no, he's not clumsy—considering that he's an invalid himself. He's a very good nurse—for a sick-nurse. I call him my sick-nurse because he's sick himself.'

'Oh, come, daddy!' the ugly young man exclaimed.

'Well, you are; I wish you weren't. But I suppose you can't help it.'

'I might try: that's an idea,' said the young man.

'Were you ever sick, Lord Warburton?' his father asked.

Lord Warburton considered a moment. 'Yes, sir, once, in the Persian Gulf.'

'He's making light of you, daddy,' said the other young man. 'That's a sort of joke.'

'Well, there seem to be so many sorts now,' daddy replied, serenely. 'You don't look as if you had been sick, any way, Lord Warburton.'

'He's sick of life; he was just telling me so; going on fearfully about it,' said Lord Warburton's friend.

'Is that true, sir?' asked the old man gravely.

'If it is, your son gave me no consolation. He's a wretched fellow to talk to—a regular cynic. He doesn't seem to believe in anything.'

'That's another sort of joke,' said the person accused of cynicism.

'It's because his health is so poor,' his father explained to Lord Warburton. 'It affects his mind and colours his way of looking at things; he seems to feel as if he had never had a chance. But it's almost entirely theoretical, you know; it doesn't seem to affect his spirits. I've hardly ever seen him when he wasn't cheerful—about as he is at present. He often cheers me up.'

The young man so described looked at Lord Warburton and laughed. 'Is it a glowing eulogy or an accusation of levity? Should you like me to carry out my theories, daddy?'

'By Jove, we should see some queer things!' cried Lord Warburton.

'I hope you haven't taken up that sort of tone,' said the old man.

'Warburton's tone is worse than mine; he pretends to be bored. I'm not in the least bored; I find life only too interesting.'

'Ah, *too* interesting; you shouldn't allow it to be that, you know!'

'I'm never bored when I come here,' said Lord Warburton. 'One gets such uncommonly good talk.'

'Is that another sort of joke?' asked the old man. 'You've no excuse for being bored anywhere. When I was your age I had never heard of such a thing.'

'You must have developed very late.'

'No, I developed very quick; that was just the reason. When I was twenty years old I was very highly developed indeed. I was working tooth and nail. You wouldn't be bored if you had something to do; but all you young men are too idle. You think too much of your pleasure. You're too fastidious, and too indolent, and too rich.'

'Oh, I say,' cried Lord Warburton, 'you're hardly the person to accuse a fellow-creature of being too rich!'

'Do you mean because I'm a banker?' asked the old man.

'Because of that, if you like; and because you have—haven't you?—such unlimited means.'

'He isn't very rich,' the other young man mercifully pleaded. 'He has given away an immense deal of money.'

'Well, I suppose it was his own,' said Lord Warburton; 'and in that case could there be a better proof of wealth? Let not a public benefactor talk of one's being too fond of pleasure.'

'Daddy's very fond of pleasure—of other people's.'

The old man shook his head. 'I don't pretend to have contributed anything to the amusement of my contemporaries.'

'My dear father, you're too modest!'

'That's a kind of joke, sir,' said Lord Warburton.

'You young men have too many jokes. When there are no jokes you've nothing left.'

'Fortunately there are always more jokes,' the ugly young man remarked.

'I don't believe it—I believe things are getting more serious. You young men will find that out.'

'The increasing seriousness of things, then—that's the great opportunity of jokes.'

'They'll have to be grim jokes,' said the old man. 'I'm

convinced there will be great changes; and not all for the better.'

'I quite agree with you, sir,' Lord Warburton declared. 'I'm very sure there will be great changes, and that all sorts of queer things will happen. That's why I find so much difficulty in applying your advice; you know you told me the other day that I ought to "take hold" of something. One hesitates to take hold of a thing that may the next moment be knocked sky-high.'

'You ought to take hold of a pretty woman,' said his companion. 'He's trying hard to fall in love,' he added, by way of explanation, to his father.

'The pretty women themselves may be sent flying!' Lord Warburton exclaimed.

'No, no, they'll be firm,' the old man rejoined; 'they'll not be affected by the social and political changes I just referred to.'

'You mean they won't be abolished? Very well, then, I'll lay hands on one as soon as possible and tie her round my neck as a life-preserver.'

'The ladies will save us,' said the old man; 'that is the best of them will—for I make a difference between them. Make up to a good one and marry her, and your life will become much more interesting.'

A momentary silence marked perhaps on the part of his auditors a sense of the magnanimity of this speech, for it was a secret neither for his son nor for his visitor that his own experiment in matrimony had not been a happy one. As he said, however, he made a difference; and these words may have been intended as a confession of personal error; though of course it was not in place for either of his companions to remark that apparently the lady of his choice had not been one of the best.

'If I marry an interesting woman I shall be interested: is that what you say?' Lord Warburton asked. 'I'm not at all keen about marrying—your son misrepresented me; but there's no knowing what an interesting woman might do with me.'

'I should like to see your idea of an interesting woman,' said his friend.

'My dear fellow, you can't see ideas—especially such highly

ethereal ones as mine. If I could only see it myself—that would be a great step in advance.'

'Well, you may fall in love with whomsoever you please; but you mustn't fall in love with my niece,' said the old man.

His son broke into a laugh. 'He'll think you mean that as a provocation! My dear father, you've lived with the English for thirty years, and you've picked up a good many of the things they say. But you've never learned the things they don't say!'

'I say what I please,' the old man returned with all his serenity.

'I haven't the honour of knowing your niece,' Lord Warburton said. 'I think it's the first time I've heard of her.'

'She's a niece of my wife's; Mrs Touchett brings her to England.'

Then young Mr Touchett explained. 'My mother, you know, has been spending the winter in America, and we're expecting her back. She writes that she has discovered a niece and that she has invited her to come out with her.'

'I see—very kind of her,' said Lord Warburton. 'Is the young lady interesting?'

'We hardly know more about her than you; my mother has not gone into details. She chiefly communicates with us by means of telegrams, and her telegrams are rather inscrutable. They say women don't know how to write them, but my mother has thoroughly mastered the art of condensation. "Tired America, hot weather awful, return England with niece, first steamer decent cabin." That's the sort of message we get from her—that was the last that came. But there had been another before, which I think contained the first mention of the niece. "Changed hotel, very bad, impudent clerk, address here. Taken sister's girl, died last year, go to Europe, two sisters, quite independent." Over that my father and I have scarcely stopped puzzling; it seems to admit of so many interpretations.'

'There's one thing very clear in it,' said the old man; 'she has given the hotel-clerk a dressing.'

'I'm not sure even of that, since he has driven her from the field. We thought at first that the sister mentioned might be the sister of the clerk; but the subsequent mention of a niece seems to prove that the allusion is to one of my aunts. Then there was a question as to whose the two other sisters were; they are probably two of my late aunt's daughters. But who's "quite independent," and in what sense is the term used?—that point's not yet settled. Does the expression apply more particularly to the young lady my mother has adopted, or does it characterise her sisters equally?—and is it used in a moral or in a financial sense? Does it mean that they've been left well off, or that they wish to be under no obligations? or does it simply mean that they're fond of their own way?'

'Whatever else it means, it's pretty sure to mean that,' Mr Touchett remarked.

'You'll see for yourself,' said Lord Warburton. 'When does Mrs Touchett arrive?'

'We're quite in the dark; as soon as she can find a decent cabin. She may be waiting for it yet; on the other hand she may already have disembarked in England.'

'In that case she would probably have telegraphed to you.'

'She never telegraphs when you would expect it—only when you don't,' said the old man. 'She likes to drop on me suddenly; she thinks she'll find me doing something wrong. She has never done so yet, but she's not discouraged.'

'It's her share in the family trait, the independence she speaks of.' Her son's appreciation of the matter was more favourable. 'Whatever the high spirit of those young ladies may be, her own is a match for it. She likes to do everything for herself and has no belief in any one's power to help her. She thinks me of no more use than a postage-stamp without gum, and she would never forgive me if I should presume to go to Liverpool to meet her.'

'Will you at least let me know when your cousin arrives?' Lord Warburton asked.

'Only on the condition I've mentioned—that you don't fall in love with her!' Mr Touchett replied.

'That strikes me as hard. Don't you think me good enough?'

'I think you too good—because I shouldn't like her to marry you. She hasn't come here to look for a husband, I hope; so many young ladies are doing that, as if there were no good ones at home. Then she's probably engaged; American girls are usually engaged, I believe. Moreover I'm not sure, after all, that you'd be a remarkable husband.'

'Very likely she's engaged; I've known a good many American girls, and they always were; but I could never see that it made any difference, upon my word! As for my being a good husband,' Mr Touchett's visitor pursued, 'I'm not sure of that either. One can but try!'

'Try as much as you please, but don't try on my niece,' smiled the old man, whose opposition to the idea was broadly humorous.

'Ah, well,' said Lord Warburton with a humour broader still, 'perhaps, after all, she's not worth trying on!'

II

WHILE this exchange of pleasantries took place between the two Ralph Touchett wandered away a little, with his usual slouching gait, his hands in his pockets and his little rowdyish terrier at his heels. His face was turned toward the house, but his eyes were bent musingly on the lawn; so that he had been an object of observation to a person who had just made her appearance in the ample doorway for some moments before he perceived her. His attention was called to her by the conduct of his dog, who had suddenly darted forward with a little volley of shrill barks, in which the note of welcome, however, was more sensible than that of defiance. The person in question was a young lady, who seemed immediately to interpret the greeting of the small beast. He advanced with great rapidity and stood at her feet, looking up and barking hard; whereupon, without hesitation, she stooped and caught him in her hands, holding him face to face while he continued his quick chatter. His master now had had time to follow and to see that Bunchie's new friend was a tall girl in a black dress, who at first sight looked pretty. She was bare-headed, as if she were staying in the house—a fact which conveyed perplexity to the son of its master, conscious of that immunity from visitors which had for some time been rendered necessary by the latter's ill-health. Meantime the two other gentlemen had also taken note of the new-comer.

'Dear me, who's that strange woman?' Mr Touchett had asked.

'Perhaps it's Mrs Touchett's niece—the independent young lady,' Lord Warburton suggested. 'I think she must be, from the way she handles the dog.'

The collie, too, had now allowed his attention to be diverted, and he trotted toward the young lady in the doorway, slowly setting his tail in motion as he went.

'But where's my wife then?' murmured the old man.

'I suppose the young lady has left her somewhere: that's a part of the independence.'

The girl spoke to Ralph, smiling, while she still held up the terrier. 'Is this your little dog, sir?'

'He was mine a moment ago; but you've suddenly acquired a remarkable air of property in him.'

'Couldn't we share him?' asked the girl. 'He's such a perfect little darling.'

Ralph looked at her a moment; she was unexpectedly pretty. 'You may have him altogether,' he then replied.

The young lady seemed to have a great deal of confidence, both in herself and in others; but this abrupt generosity made her blush. 'I ought to tell you that I'm probably your cousin,' she brought out, putting down the dog. 'And here's another!' she added quickly, as the collie came up.

'Probably?' the young man exclaimed, laughing. 'I supposed it was quite settled! Have you arrived with my mother?'

'Yes, half an hour ago.'

'And has she deposited you and departed again?'

'No, she went straight to her room, and she told me that, if I should see you, I was to say to you that you must come to her there at a quarter to seven.'

The young man looked at his watch. 'Thank you very much; I shall be punctual.' And then he looked at his cousin. 'You're very welcome here. I'm delighted to see you.'

She was looking at everything, with an eye that denoted clear perception—at her companion, at the two dogs, at the two gentlemen under the trees, at the beautiful scene that surrounded her. 'I've never seen anything so lovely as this place. I've been all over the house; it's too enchanting.'

'I'm sorry you should have been here so long without our knowing it.'

'Your mother told me that in England people arrived very quietly; so I thought it was all right. Is one of those gentlemen your father?'

'Yes, the elder one—the one sitting down,' said Ralph.

The girl gave a laugh. 'I don't suppose it's the other. Who's the other?'

'He's a friend of ours—Lord Warburton.'

'Oh, I hoped there would be a lord; it's just like a novel!'

And then, 'Oh you adorable creature!' she suddenly cried, stooping down and picking up the small dog again.

She remained standing where they had met, making no offer to advance or to speak to Mr Touchett, and while she lingered so near the threshold, slim and charming, her interlocutor wondered if she expected the old man to come and pay her his respects. American girls were used to a great deal of deference, and it had been intimated that this one had a high spirit. Indeed Ralph could see that in her face.

'Won't you come and make acquaintance with my father?' he nevertheless ventured to ask. 'He's old and infirm—he doesn't leave his chair.'

'Ah, poor man, I'm very sorry!' the girl exclaimed, immediately moving forward. 'I got the impression from your mother that he was rather—rather intensely active.'

Ralph Touchett was silent a moment. 'She hasn't seen him for a year.'

'Well, he has a lovely place to sit. Come along, little hound.'

'It's a dear old place,' said the young man, looking sidewise at his neighbour.

'What's his name?' she asked, her attention having again reverted to the terrier.

'My father's name?'

'Yes,' said the young lady with amusement; 'but don't tell him I asked you.'

They had come by this time to where old Mr Touchett was sitting, and he slowly got up from his chair to introduce himself.

'My mother has arrived,' said Ralph, 'and this is Miss Archer.'

The old man placed his two hands on her shoulders, looked at her a moment with extreme benevolence and then gallantly kissed her. 'It's a great pleasure to me to see you here; but I wish you had given us a chance to receive you.'

'Oh, we were received,' said the girl. 'There were about a dozen servants in the hall. And there was an old woman curtseying at the gate.'

'We can do better than that—if we have notice!' And the old

man stood there smiling, rubbing his hands and slowly shaking his head at her. 'But Mrs Touchett doesn't like receptions.'

'She went straight to her room.' 'Yes—and locked herself in. She always does that. Well, I suppose I shall see her next week.' And Mrs Touchett's husband slowly resumed his former posture.

'Before that,' said Miss Archer. 'She's coming down to dinner—at eight o'clock. Don't you forget a quarter to seven,' she added, turning with a smile to Ralph.

'What's to happen at a quarter to seven?'

'I'm to see my mother,' said Ralph.

'Ah, happy boy!' the old man commented. 'You must sit down—you must have some tea,' he observed to his wife's niece.

'They gave me some tea in my room the moment I got there,' this young lady answered. 'I'm sorry you're out of health,' she added, resting her eyes upon her venerable host.

'Oh, I'm an old man, my dear; it's time for me to be old. But I shall be the better for having you here.'

She had been looking all round her again—at the lawn, the great trees, the reedy, silvery Thames, the beautiful old house; and while engaged in this survey she had made room in it for her companions; a comprehensiveness of observation easily conceivable on the part of a young woman who was evidently both intelligent and excited. She had seated herself and had put away the little dog; her white hands, in her lap, were folded upon her black dress; her head was erect, her eye lighted, her flexible figure turned itself easily this way and that, in sympathy with the alertness with which she evidently caught impressions. Her impressions were numerous, and they were all reflected in a clear, still smile. 'I've never seen anything so beautiful as this.'

'It's looking very well,' said Mr Touchett. 'I know the way it strikes you. I've been through all that. But you're very beautiful yourself,' he added with a politeness by no means crudely jocular and with the happy consciousness that his advanced age gave him the privilege of saying such things—even to young persons who might possibly take alarm at them.

What degree of alarm this young person took need not be exactly measured; she instantly rose, however, with a blush which was not a refutation. 'Oh yes, of course I'm lovely!' she returned with a quick laugh. 'How old is your house? Is it Elizabethan?'

'It's early Tudor,' said Ralph Touchett.

She turned toward him, watching his face. 'Early Tudor? How very delightful! And I suppose there are a great many others.'

'There are many much better ones.'

'Don't say that, my son!' the old man protested. 'There's nothing better than this.'

'I've got a very good one; I think in some respect it's rather better,' said Lord Warburton, who as yet had not spoken, but who had kept an attentive eye upon Miss Archer. He slightly inclined himself, smiling; he had an excellent manner with women. The girl appreciated it in an instant; she had not forgotten that this was Lord Warburton. 'I should like very much to show it to you,' he added.

'Don't believe him,' cried the old man; 'don't look at it! It's a wretched old barrack—not to be compared with this.'

'I don't know—I can't judge,' said the girl, smiling at Lord Warburton.

In this discussion Ralph Touchett took no interest whatever; he stood with his hands in his pockets, looking greatly as if he should like to renew his conversation with his new-found cousin. 'Are you very fond of dogs?' he enquired by way of beginning. He seemed to recognise that it was an awkward beginning for a clever man.

'Very fond of them indeed.'

'You must keep the terrier, you know,' he went on, still awkwardly.

'I'll keep him while I'm here, with pleasure.'

'That will be for a long time, I hope.'

'You're very kind. I hardly know. My aunt must settle that.'

'I'll settle it with her—at a quarter to seven.' And Ralph looked at his watch again.

'I'm glad to be here at all,' said the girl.

'I don't believe you allow things to be settled for you.'

'Oh yes; if they're settled as I like them.'

'I shall settle this as I like it,' said Ralph. 'It's most unaccountable that we should never have known you.'

'I was there—you had only to come and see me.'

'There? Where do you mean?'

'In the United States: in New York and Albany and other American places.'

'I've been there—all over, but I never saw you. I can't make it out.'

Miss Archer just hesitated. 'It was because there had been some disagreement between your mother and my father, after my mother's death, which took place when I was a child. In consequence of it we never expected to see you.'

'Ah, but I don't embrace all my mother's quarrels—heaven forbid!' the young man cried. 'You've lately lost your father?' he went on more gravely.

'Yes; more than a year ago. After that my aunt was very kind to me; she came to see me and proposed that I should come with her to Europe.'

'I see,' said Ralph. 'She has adopted you.'

'Adopted me?' The girl stared, and her blush came back to her, together with a momentary look of pain which gave her interlocutor some alarm. He had underestimated the effect of his words. Lord Warburton, who appeared constantly desirous of a nearer view of Miss Archer, strolled toward the two cousins at the moment, and as he did so she rested her wider eyes on him. 'Oh no; she has not adopted me. I'm not a candidate for adoption.'

'I beg a thousand pardons,' Ralph murmured. 'I meant—I meant—' He hardly knew what he meant.

'You meant she has taken me up. Yes; she likes to take people up. She has been very kind to me; but,' she added with a certain visible eagerness of desire to be explicit, 'I'm very fond of my liberty.'

'Are you talking about Mrs Touchett?' the old man called out from his chair. 'Come here, my dear, and tell me about her. I'm always thankful for information.'

The girl hesitated again, smiling. 'She's really very benevolent,' she answered; after which she went over to her uncle, whose mirth was excited by her words.

Lord Warburton was left standing with Ralph Touchett, to whom in a moment he said: 'You wished a while ago to see my idea of an interesting woman. There it is!'

III

Mrs Touchett was certainly a person of many oddities, of which her behaviour on returning to her husband's house after many months was a noticeable specimen. She had her own way of doing all that she did, and this is the simplest description of a character which, although by no means without liberal motions, rarely succeeded in giving an impression of suavity. Mrs Touchett might do a great deal of good, but she never pleased. This way of her own, of which she was so fond, was not intrinsically offensive—it was just unmistakeably distinguished from the ways of others. The edges of her conduct were so very clear-cut that for susceptible persons it sometimes had a knife-like effect. That hard fineness came out in her deportment during the first hours of her return from America, under circumstances in which it might have seemed that her first act would have been to exchange greetings with her husband and son. Mrs Touchett, for reasons which she deemed excellent, always retired on such occasions into impenetrable seclusion, postponing the more sentimental ceremony until she had repaired the disorder of dress with a completeness which had the less reason to be of high importance as neither beauty nor vanity were concerned in it. She was a plain-faced old woman, without graces and without any great elegance, but with an extreme respect for her own motives. She was usually prepared to explain these—when the explanation was asked as a favour; and in such a case they proved totally different from those that had been attributed to her. She was virtually separated from her husband, but she appeared to perceive nothing irregular in the situation. It had become clear, at an early stage of their community, that they should never desire the same thing at the same moment, and this appearance had prompted her to rescue disagreement from the vulgar realm of accident. She did what she could to erect it into a law—a much more edifying aspect of it—by going to live in Florence, where she bought a house and established herself; and by leaving her husband to take care of the English branch of his bank. This arrangement greatly pleased her; it was so felicitously definite. It struck her husband in the same light, in a foggy square in London, where it was at times the most definite fact he discerned; but he would have preferred that such unnatural things should have a greater vagueness. To agree to disagree had cost him an effort; he was ready to agree to almost anything but that, and saw no reason why either assent or dissent should be so terribly consistent. Mrs Touchett indulged in no regrets nor speculations, and usually came once a year to spend a month with her husband, a period during which she apparently took pains to convince him that she had adopted the right system. She was not fond of the English style of life, and had three or four reasons for it to which she currently alluded; they bore upon minor points of that ancient order, but for Mrs Touchett they amply justified non-residence. She detested bread-sauce, which, as she said, looked like a poultice and tasted like soap; she objected to the consumption of beer by her maid-servants; and she affirmed that the British laundress (Mrs Touchett was very particular about the appearance of her linen) was not a mistress of her art. At fixed intervals she paid a visit to her own country; but this last had been longer than any of its predecessors.

She had taken up her niece—there was little doubt of that. One wet afternoon, some four months earlier than the occurrence lately narrated, this young lady had been seated alone with a book. To say she was so occupied is to say that her solitude did not press upon her; for her love of knowledge had a fertilising quality and her imagination was strong. There was at this time, however, a want of fresh taste in her situation which the arrival of an unexpected visitor did much to correct. The visitor had not been announced; the girl heard her at last walking about the adjoining room. It was in an old house at Albany, a large, square, double house, with a notice of sale in the windows of one of the lower apartments. There were two entrances, one of which had long been out of use but had never been removed. They were exactly alike—large white doors, with an arched frame and wide side-lights, perched upon little 'stoops' of red stone, which descended sidewise to the brick pavement of the street. The two houses together formed a single dwelling, the party-wall having been removed and the rooms placed in communication. These rooms, above-stairs, were extremely numerous, and were painted all over exactly alike, in a yellowish white which had grown sallow with time. On the third floor there was a sort of arched passage, connecting the two sides of the house, which Isabel and her sisters used in their childhood to call the tunnel and which, though it was short and well-lighted, always seemed to the girl to be strange and lonely, especially on winter afternoons. She had been in the house, at different periods, as a child; in those days her grandmother lived there. Then there had been an absence of ten years, followed by a return to Albany before her father's death. Her grandmother, old Mrs Archer, had exercised, chiefly within the limits of the family, a large hospitality in the early period, and the little girls often spent weeks under her roof—weeks of which Isabel had the happiest memory. The manner of life was different from that of her own home—larger, more plentiful, practically more festal; the discipline of the nursery was delightfully vague and the opportunity of listening to the conversation of one's elders (which with Isabel was a highly-valued pleasure) almost unbounded. There was a constant coming and going; her grandmother's sons and daughters and their children appeared to be in the enjoyment of standing invitations to arrive and remain, so that the house offered to a certain extent the appearance of a bustling provincial inn kept by a gentle old landlady who sighed a great deal and never presented a bill. Isabel of course knew nothing about bills; but even as a child she thought her grandmother's home romantic. There was a covered piazza behind it, furnished with a swing which was a source of tremulous interest; and beyond this was a long garden, sloping down to the stable and containing peach-trees of barely credible familiarity. Isabel had stayed with her grandmother at various seasons, but somehow all her visits had a flavour of peaches. On the other side, across the street, was an old house that was called the Dutch House—a peculiar structure dating from the earliest colonial time, composed of bricks that had been painted yellow, crowned with a gable that was pointed out to strangers, defended by a rickety wooden paling and standing sidewise to the street. It was occupied by a primary school for children of both sexes, kept or rather let go, by a demonstrative lady of whom Isabel's chief recollection was that her hair was fastened with strange bedroomy combs at the temples and that she was the widow of some one of consequence. The little girl had been offered the opportunity of laying a foundation of knowledge in this establishment; but having spent a single day in it, she had protested against its laws and had been allowed to stay at home, where, in the September days, when the windows of the Dutch House were open, she used to hear the hum of childish voices repeating the multiplication-table—an incident in which the elation of liberty and the pain of exclusion were indistinguishably mingled. The foundation of her knowledge was really laid in the idleness of her grandmother's house, where, as most of the other inmates were not reading people, she had uncontrolled use of a library full of books with frontispieces, which she used to climb upon a chair to take down. When she had found one to her taste—she was guided in the selection chiefly by the frontispiece—she carried it into a mysterious apartment which lay beyond the library and which was called, traditionally, no one knew why, the office. Whose office it had been and at what period it had flourished, she never learned; it was enough for her that it contained an echo and a pleasant musty smell and that it was a chamber of disgrace for old pieces of furniture whose infirmities were not always apparent (so that the disgrace seemed unmerited and rendered them victims of injustice) and with which, in the manner of children, she had established relations almost human, certainly dramatic. There was an old haircloth sofa in especial, to which she had confided a hundred childish sorrows. The place owed much of its mysterious melancholy to the fact that it was properly entered from the second door of the house, the door that had been condemned, and that it was secured by bolts which a particularly slender little girl found it impossible to slide. She knew that this silent, motionless portal opened into the street; if the side-lights had not been filled with green paper she might have looked out upon the little brown stoop and the well-worn brick pavement. But she had no wish to look out, for this would have interfered with her theory that there was a strange, unseen place on the other side—a place which became to the child's imagination, according to its different moods, a region of delight or of terror.

It was in the 'office' still that Isabel was sitting on that melancholy afternoon of early spring which I have just mentioned. At this time she might have had the whole house to choose from, and the room she had selected was the most depressed of its scenes. She had never opened the bolted door nor removed the green paper (renewed by other hands) from its side-lights; she had never assured herself that the vulgar street lay beyond. A crude, cold rain fell heavily; the springtime was indeed an appeal—and it seemed a cynical, insincere appeal—to patience. Isabel, however, gave as little heed as possible to cosmic treacheries; she kept her eyes on her book and tried to fix her mind. It had lately occurred to her that her mind was a good deal of a vagabond, and she had spent much ingenuity in training it to a military step and teaching it to advance, to halt, to retreat, to perform even more complicated manœuvres, at the word of command. Just now she had given it marching orders and it had been trudging over the sandy plains of a history of German Thought. Suddenly she became aware of a step very different from her own intellectual pace; she listened a little and perceived that some one was moving in the library, which communicated with the office. It struck her first as the step of a person from whom she was looking for a visit, then almost immediately announced itself as the tread of a woman and a stranger—her possible visitor being neither. It had an inquisitive, experimental quality which suggested that it would not stop short of the threshold of the office; and in fact the doorway of this apartment was presently occupied by a lady who paused there and looked very hard at our heroine. She was a plain, elderly woman, dressed in a comprehensive waterproof mantle; she had a face with a good deal of rather violent point.

'Oh,' she began, 'is that where you usually sit?' She looked about at the heterogeneous chairs and tables.

'Not when I have visitors,' said Isabel, getting up to receive the intruder.

She directed their course back to the library while the visitor continued to look about her. 'You seem to have plenty of other rooms; they're in rather better condition. But everything's immensely worn.'

'Have you come to look at the house?' Isabel asked. 'The servant will show it to you.'

'Send her away; I don't want to buy it. She has probably gone to look for you and is wandering about upstairs; she didn't seem at all intelligent. You had better tell her it's no matter.' And then, since the girl stood there hesitating and wondering, this unexpected critic said to her abruptly: 'I suppose you're one of the daughters?'

Isabel thought she had very strange manners. 'It depends upon whose daughters you mean.'

'The late Mr Archer's—and my poor sister's.'

'Ah,' said Isabel slowly, 'you must be our crazy Aunt Lydia!'

'Is that what your father told you to call me? I'm your Aunt Lydia, but I'm not at all crazy: I haven't a delusion! And which of the daughters are you?'

'I'm the youngest of the three, and my name's Isabel.'

'Yes; the others are Lilian and Edith. And are you the prettiest?'

'I haven't the least idea,' said the girl.

'I think you must be.' And in this way the aunt and the niece made friends. The aunt had quarrelled years before with her brother-in-law, after the death of her sister, taking him to task for the manner in which he brought up his three girls. Being a high-tempered man he had requested her to mind her own business, and she had taken him at his word. For many years she held no communication with him and after his death had addressed not a word to his daughters, who had been bred in that disrespectful view to her which we have just seen Isabel betray. Mrs Touchett's behaviour was, as usual, perfectly deliberate. She intended to go to America to look after her investments (with which her husband, in spite of his great financial position, had nothing to do) and would take advantage of this opportunity to enquire into the condition of her nieces. There was no need of writing, for she should attach no importance to any account of them she should elicit by letter; she believed, always, in seeing for one's self. Isabel found, however, that she knew a good deal about them, and knew about the marriage of the two elder girls; knew that their poor father had left very little money, but that the house in Albany, which had passed into his hands, was to be sold for their benefit; knew, finally, that Edmund Ludlow, Lilian's husband, had taken upon himself to attend to this matter, in consideration of which the young couple, who had come to Albany during Mr Archer's illness, were remaining there for the present and, as well as Isabel herself, occupying the old place.

'How much money do you expect for it?' Mrs Touchett asked of her companion, who had brought her to sit in the front parlour, which she had inspected without enthusiasm.

'I haven't the least idea,' said the girl.

'That's the second time you have said that to me,' her aunt rejoined. 'And yet you don't look at all stupid.'

'I'm not stupid; but I don't know anything about money.'

'Yes, that's the way you were brought up—as if you were to inherit a million. What have you in point of fact inherited?'

'I really can't tell you. You must ask Edmund and Lilian; they'll be back in half an hour.'

'In Florence we should call it a very bad house,' said Mrs Touchett; 'but here, I dare say, it will bring a high price. It ought to make a considerable sum for each of you. In addition to that you *must* have something else; it's most extraordinary your not knowing. The position's of value, and they'll probably pull it down and make a row of shops. I wonder you don't do that yourself; you might let the shops to great advantage.'

Isabel stared; the idea of letting shops was new to her. 'I hope they won't pull it down,' she said; 'I'm extremely fond of it.'

'I don't see what makes you fond of it; your father died here.'

'Yes; but I don't dislike it for that,' the girl rather strangely returned. 'I like places in which things have happened—even if they're sad things. A great many people have died here; the place has been full of life.'

'Is that what you call being full of life?'

'I mean full of experience—of people's feelings and sorrows. And not of their sorrows only, for I've been very happy here as a child.'

'You should go to Florence if you like houses in which things have happened—especially deaths. I live in an old palace in which three people have been murdered; three that were known and I don't know how many more besides.'

'In an old palace?' Isabel repeated.

'Yes, my dear; a very different affair from this. This is very bourgeois.'

Isabel felt some emotion, for she had always thought highly of her grandmother's house. But the emotion was of a kind which led her to say: 'I should like very much to go to Florence.'

'Well, if you'll be very good, and do everything I tell you I'll take you there,' Mrs Touchett declared.

Our young woman's emotion deepened; she flushed a little and smiled at her aunt in silence. 'Do everything you tell me? I don't think I can promise that.'

'No, you don't look like a person of that sort. You're fond of your own way; but it's not for me to blame you.'

'And yet, to go to Florence,' the girl exclaimed in a moment, 'I'd promise almost anything!'

Edmund and Lilian were slow to return, and Mrs Touchett had an hour's uninterrupted talk with her niece, who found her a strange and interesting figure: a figure essentially—almost the first she had ever met. She was as eccentric as Isabel had always supposed; and hitherto, whenever the girl had heard people described as eccentric, she had thought of them as offensive or alarming. The term had always suggested to her something grotesque and even sinister. But her aunt made it a matter of high but easy irony, or comedy, and led her to ask herself if the common tone, which was all she had known, had ever been as interesting. No one certainly had on any occasion so held her as this little thin-lipped, bright-eyed, foreign-looking woman, who retrieved an insignificant appearance by a distinguished manner and, sitting there in a well-worn water-proof, talked with striking familiarity of the courts of Europe.

There was nothing flighty about Mrs Touchett, but she recognised no social superiors, and, judging the great ones of the earth in a way that spoke of this, enjoyed the consciousness of making an impression on a candid and susceptible mind. Isabel at first had answered a good many questions, and it was from her answers apparently that Mrs Touchett derived a high opinion of her intelligence. But after this she had asked a good many, and her aunt's answers, whatever turn they took, struck her as food for deep reflexion. Mrs Touchett waited for the return of her other niece as long as she thought reasonable, but as at six o'clock Mrs Ludlow had not come in she prepared to take her departure.

'Your sister must be a great gossip. Is she accustomed to staying out so many hours?'

'You've been out almost as long as she,' Isabel replied; 'she can have left the house but a short time before you came in.'

Mrs Touchett looked at the girl without resentment; she appeared to enjoy a bold retort and to be disposed to be gracious. 'Perhaps she hasn't had so good an excuse as I. Tell her at any rate that she must come and see me this evening at that horrid hotel. She may bring her husband if she likes, but she needn't bring you. I shall see plenty of you later.'

IV

MRS LUDLOW was the eldest of the three sisters, and was usually thought the most sensible; the classification being in general that Lilian was the practical one, Edith the beauty and Isabel the 'intellectual' superior. Mrs Keyes, the second of the group, was the wife of an officer of the United States Engineers, and as our history is not further concerned with her it will suffice that she was indeed very pretty and that she formed the ornament of those various military stations, chiefly in the unfashionable West, to which, to her deep chagrin, her husband was successively relegated. Lilian had married a New York lawyer, a young man with a loud voice and an enthusiasm for his profession; the match was not brilliant, any more than Edith's, but Lilian had occasionally been spoken of as a young woman who might be thankful to marry at all—she was so much plainer than her sisters. She was, however, very happy, and now, as the mother of two peremptory little boys and the mistress of a wedge of brown stone violently driven into Fifty-third Street, seemed to exult in her condition as in a bold escape. She was short and solid, and her claim to figure was questioned, but she was conceded presence, though not majesty; she had moreover, as people said, improved since her marriage, and the two things in life of which she was most distinctly conscious were her husband's force in argument and her sister Isabel's originality. 'I've never kept up with Isabel—it would have taken *all* my time,' she had often remarked; in spite of which, however, she held her rather wistfully in sight; watching her as a motherly spaniel might watch a free greyhound. 'I want to see her safely married—that's what I want to see,' she frequently noted to her husband.

'Well, I must say I should have no particular desire to marry her,' Edmund Ludlow was accustomed to answer in an extremely audible tone.

'I know you say that for argument; you always take the opposite ground. I don't see what you've against her except that she's so original.'

'Well, I don't like originals; I like translations,' Mr Ludlow had more than once replied. 'Isabel's written in a foreign tongue. I can't make her out. She ought to marry an Armenian or a Portuguese.'

'That's just what I'm afraid she'll do!' cried Lilian, who thought Isabel capable of anything.

She listened with great interest to the girl's account of Mrs Touchett's appearance and in the evening prepared to comply with their aunt's commands. Of what Isabel then said no report has remained, but her sister's words had doubtless prompted a word spoken to her husband as the two were making ready for their visit. 'I do hope immensely she'll do something handsome for Isabel; she has evidently taken a great fancy to her.'

'What is it you wish her to do?' Edmund Ludlow asked. 'Make her a big present?'

'No indeed; nothing of the sort. But take an interest in her—sympathise with her. She's evidently just the sort of person to appreciate her. She has lived so much in foreign society; she told Isabel all about it. You know you've always thought Isabel rather foreign.'

'You want her to give her a little foreign sympathy, eh? Don't you think she gets enough at home?'

'Well, she ought to go abroad,' said Mrs Ludlow. 'She's just the person to go abroad.'

'And you want the old lady to take her, is that it?'

'She has offered to take her—she's dying to have Isabel go. But what I want her to do when she gets her there is to give her all the advantages. I'm sure all we've got to do,' said Mrs Ludlow, 'is to give her a chance.'

'A chance for what?'

'A chance to develop.'

'Oh Moses!' Edmund Ludlow exclaimed. 'I hope she isn't going to develop any more!'

'If I were not sure you only said that for argument I should feel very badly,' his wife replied. 'But you know you love her.'

'*Do* you know I love you?' the young man said, jocosely, to Isabel a little later, while he brushed his hat.

'I'm sure I don't care whether you do or not!' exclaimed the girl; whose voice and smile, however, were less haughty than her words.

'Oh, she feels so grand since Mrs Touchett's visit,' said her sister.

But Isabel challenged this assertion with a good deal of seriousness. 'You must not say that, Lily. I don't feel grand at all.'

'I'm sure there's no harm,' said the conciliatory Lily.

'Ah, but there's nothing in Mrs Touchett's visit to make one feel grand.'

'Oh,' exclaimed Ludlow, 'she's grander than ever!'

'Whenever I feel grand,' said the girl, 'it will be for a better reason.'

Whether she felt grand or no, she at any rate felt different, felt as if something had happened to her. Left to herself for the evening she sat a while under the lamp, her hands empty, her usual avocations unheeded. Then she rose and moved about the room, and from one room to another, preferring the places where the vague lamplight expired. She was restless and even agitated; at moments she trembled a little. The importance of what had happened was out of proportion to its appearance; there had really been a change in her life. What it would bring with it was as yet extremely indefinite; but Isabel was in a situation that gave a value to any change. She had a desire to leave the past behind her and, as she said to herself, to begin afresh. This desire indeed was not a birth of the present occasion; it was as familiar as the sound of the rain upon the window and it had led to her beginning afresh a great many times. She closed her eyes as she sat in one of the dusky corners of the quiet parlour; but it was not with a desire for dozing forgetfulness. It was on the contrary because she felt too wide-eyed and wished to check the sense of seeing too many things at once. Her imagination was by habit ridiculously active; when the door was not open it jumped out of the window. She was not accustomed indeed to keep it behind bolts; and at important moments, when she would have been thankful to make use of her judgement alone, she paid the penalty of having given undue encouragement to the faculty of seeing without judging. At present, with her sense that the note of change had been struck, came gradually a host of images of the things she was leaving behind her. The years and hours of her life came back to her, and for a long time, in a stillness broken only by the ticking of the big bronze clock, she passed them in review. It had been a very happy life and she had been a very fortunate person—this was the truth that seemed to emerge most vividly. She had had the best of everything, and in a world in which the circumstances of so many people made them unenviable it was an advantage never to have known anything particularly unpleasant. It appeared to Isabel that the unpleasant had been even too absent from her knowledge, for she had gathered from her acquaintance with literature that it was often a source of interest and even of instruction. Her father had kept it away from her—her handsome, much-loved father, who always had such an aversion to it. It was a great felicity to have been his daughter; Isabel rose even to pride in her parentage. Since his death she had seemed to see him as turning his braver side to his children and as not having managed to ignore the ugly quite so much in practice as in aspiration. But this only made her tenderness for him greater; it was scarcely even painful to have to suppose him too generous, too good-natured, too indifferent to sordid considerations. Many persons had held that he carried this indifference too far, especially the large number of those to whom he owed money. Of their opinions Isabel was never very definitely informed; but it may interest the reader to know that, while they had recognised in the late Mr Archer a remarkably handsome head and a very taking manner (indeed, as one of them had said, he was always taking something), they had declared that he was making a very poor use of his life. He had squandered a substantial fortune, he had been deplorably convivial, he was known to have gambled freely. A few very harsh critics went so far as to say that he had not even brought up his daughters. They had had no regular education and no permanent home; they had been at once spoiled and neglected; they had lived with nursemaids and governesses (usually very bad ones) or had been sent to superficial schools, kept by the French, from which, at the end of a month, they had been removed in tears. The view of the matter would have excited Isabel's indignation, for to her own sense her opportunities had been large. Even when her father had left his daughters for three months at Neufchatel with a French *bonne** who had eloped with a Russian nobleman staying at the same hotel—even in this irregular situation (an incident of the girl's eleventh year) she had been neither frightened nor ashamed, but had thought it a romantic episode in a liberal education. Her father had a large way of looking at life, of which his restlessness and even his occasional incoherency of conduct had been only a proof. He wished his daughters, even as children, to see as much of the world as possible; and it was for this purpose that, before Isabel was fourteen, he had transported them three times across the Atlantic, giving them on each occasion, however, but a few months' view of the subject proposed: a course which had whetted our heroine's curiosity without enabling her to satisfy it. She ought to have been a partisan of her father, for she was the member of his trio who most 'made up' to him for the disagreeables he didn't mention. In his last days his general willingness to take leave of a world in which the difficulty of doing as one liked appeared to increase as one grew older had been sensibly modified by the pain of separation from his clever, his superior, his remarkable girl. Later, when the journeys to Europe ceased, he still had shown his children all sorts of indulgence, and if he had been troubled about money-matters nothing ever disturbed their irreflective consciousness of many possessions. Isabel, though she danced very well, had not the recollection of having been in New York a successful member of the choreographic circle; her sister Edith was, as every one said, so very much more fetching. Edith was so striking an example of success that Isabel could have no illusions as to what constituted this advantage, or as to the limits of her own power to frisk and jump and shriek—above all with rightness of effect. Nineteen persons out of twenty (including the younger sister herself) pronounced Edith infinitely the prettier of the two; but the twentieth, besides reversing this judgement, had the entertainment of thinking all the others æsthetic vulgarians. Isabel had in the depths of her nature an even more unquenchable desire to please than Edith; but the depths of this young lady's nature were a very out-of-the-way place, between which and the surface communication was interrupted by a dozen capricious forces. She saw the young men who came in large numbers to see her sister; but as a general thing they were afraid of her; they had a belief that some special preparation was required for talking with her. Her reputation of reading a great deal hung about her like the cloudy envelope of a goddess in an epic; it was supposed to engender difficult questions and to keep the conversation at a low temperature. The poor girl liked to be thought clever, but she hated to be thought bookish; she used to read in secret and, though her memory was excellent, to abstain from showy reference. She had a great desire for knowledge, but she really preferred almost any source of information to the printed page; she had an immense curiosity about life and was constantly staring and wondering. She carried within herself a great fund of life, and her deepest enjoyment was to feel the continuity between the movements of her own soul and the agitations of the world. For this reason she was fond of seeing great crowds and large stretches of country, of reading about revolutions and wars, of looking at historical pictures—a class of efforts as to which she had often committed the conscious solecism of forgiving them much bad painting for the sake of the subject. While the Civil War went on she was still a very young girl; but she passed months of this long period in a state of almost passionate excitement, in which she felt herself at times (to her extreme confusion) stirred almost indiscriminately by the valour of either army. Of course the circumspection of suspicious swains had never gone the length of making her a social proscript; for the number of those whose hearts, as they approached her, beat only just fast enough to remind them they had heads as well, had kept her unacquainted with the supreme disciplines of her sex and age. She had had everything a girl could have: kindness, admiration, bonbons, bouquets, the sense of exclusion from none of the privileges of the world she lived in, abundant opportunity for dancing, plenty of new dresses, the London *Spectator*, the latest publications, the music of Gounod, the poetry of Browning, the prose of George Eliot.

These things now, as memory played over them, resolved themselves into a multitude of scenes and figures. Forgotten things came back to her; many others, which she had lately thought of great moment, dropped out of sight. The result was kaleidoscopic, but the movement of the instrument was checked at last by the servant's coming in with the name of a gentleman. The name of the gentleman was Caspar Goodwood; he was a straight young man from Boston, who had known Miss Archer for the last twelve-month and who, thinking her the most beautiful young woman of her time, had pronounced the time, according to the rule I have hinted at, a foolish period of history. He sometimes wrote to her and had within a week or two written from New York. She had thought it very possible he would come in—had indeed all the rainy day been vaguely expecting him. Now that she learned he was there, nevertheless, she felt no eagerness to receive him. He was the finest young man she had ever seen, was indeed quite a splendid young man; he inspired her with a sentiment of high, of rare respect. She had never felt equally moved to it by any other person. He was supposed by the world in general to wish to marry her, but this of course was between themselves. It at least may be affirmed that he had travelled from New York to Albany expressly to see her; having learned in the former city, where he was spending a few days and where he had hoped to find her, that she was still at the State capital. Isabel delayed for some minutes to go to him; she moved about the room with a new sense of complications. But at last she presented herself and found him standing near the lamp. He was tall, strong and somewhat stiff; he was also lean and brown. He was not romantically, he was much rather obscurely, handsome; but his physiognomy had an air of requesting your attention, which it rewarded according to the charm you found in blue eyes of remarkable fixedness, the eyes of a complexion other than his own, and a jaw of the somewhat angular mould which is supposed to bespeak resolution. Isabel said to herself that it bespoke resolution to-night; in spite of which, in half an hour, Casper Goodwood, who had arrived hopeful as well as resolute, took his way back to his lodging with the feeling of a man defeated. He was not, it may be added, a man weakly to accept defeat.

V

RALPH TOUCHETT was a philosopher, but nevertheless he knocked at his mother's door (at a quarter to seven) with a good deal of eagerness. Even philosophers have their preferences, and it must be admitted that of his progenitors his father ministered most to his sense of the sweetness of filial dependence. His father, as he had often said to himself, was the more motherly; his mother, on the other hand, was paternal, and even, according to the slang of the day, gubernatorial. She was nevertheless very fond of her only child and had always insisted on his spending three months of the year with her. Ralph rendered perfect justice to her affection and knew that in her thoughts and her thoroughly arranged and servanted life his turn always came after the other nearest subjects of her solicitude, the various punctualities of performance of the workers of her will. He found her completely dressed for dinner, but she embraced her boy with her gloved hands and made him sit on the sofa beside her. She enquired scrupulously about her husband's health and about the young man's own, and, receiving no very brilliant account of either, remarked that she was more than ever convinced of her wisdom in not exposing herself to the English climate. In this case she also might have given way. Ralph smiled at the idea of his mother's giving way, but made no point of reminding her that his own infirmity was not the result of the English climate, from which he absented himself for a considerable part of each year.

He had been a very small boy when his father, Daniel Tracy Touchett, a native of Rutland, in the State of Vermont, came to England as subordinate partner in a banking-house where some ten years later he gained preponderant control. Daniel Touchett saw before him a life-long residence in his adopted country, of which, from the first, he took a simple, sane and accommodating view. But, as he said to himself, he had no intention of disamericanising, nor had he a desire to teach his only son any such subtle art. It had been for himself so very soluble a problem to live in England assimilated yet unconverted that it seemed to him equally simple his lawful heir should after his death carry on the grey old bank in the white American light. He was at pains to intensify this light, however, by sending the boy home for his education. Ralph spent several terms at an American school and took a degree at an American university, after which, as he struck his father on his return as even redundantly native, he was placed for some three years in residence at Oxford. Oxford swallowed up Harvard, and Ralph became at last English enough. His outward conformity to the manners that surrounded him was none the less the mask of a mind that greatly enjoyed its independence, on which nothing long imposed itself, and which, naturally inclined to adventure and irony, indulged in a boundless liberty of appreciation. He began with being a young man of promise; at Oxford he distinguished himself, to his father's ineffable satisfaction, and the people about him said it was a thousand pities so clever a fellow should be shut out from a career. He might have had a career by returning to his own country (though this point is shrouded in uncertainty) and even if Mr Touchett had been willing to part with him (which was not the case) it would have gone hard with him to put a watery waste permanently between himself and the old man whom he regarded as his best friend. Ralph was not only fond of his father, he admired him—he enjoyed the opportunity of observing him. Daniel Touchett, to his perception, was a man of genius, and though he himself had no aptitude for the banking mystery he made a point of learning enough of it to measure the great figure his father had played. It was not this, however, he mainly relished; it was the fine ivory surface, polished as by the English air, that the old man had opposed to possibilities of penetration. Daniel Touchett had been neither at Harvard nor at Oxford, and it was his own fault if he had placed in his son's hands the key to modern criticism. Ralph, whose head was full of ideas which his father had never guessed, had a high esteem for the latter's originality. Americans, rightly or wrongly, are commended for the ease with which they adapt themselves to foreign conditions; but Mr Touchett had made of the very limits of his pliancy half the ground of his general success. He had retained in their freshness most of his marks of primary pressure; his tone, as his son always noted with pleasure, was that of the more luxuriant parts of New England. At the end of his life he had become, on his own ground, as mellow as he was rich; he combined consummate shrewdness with the disposition superficially to fraternise, and his 'social position,' on which he had never wasted a care, had the firm perfection of an unthumbed fruit. It was perhaps his want of imagination and of what is called the historic consciousness; but to many of the impressions usually made by English life upon the cultivated stranger his sense was completely closed. There were certain differences he had never perceived, certain habits he had never formed, certain obscurities he had never sounded. As regards these latter, on the day he *had* sounded them his son would have thought less well of him.

Ralph, on leaving Oxford, had spent a couple of years in travelling; after which he had found himself perched on a high stool in his father's bank. The responsibility and honour of such positions is not, I believe, measured by the height of the stool, which depends upon other considerations: Ralph, indeed, who had very long legs, was fond of standing, and even of walking about, at his work. To this exercise, however, he was obliged to devote but a limited period, for at the end of some eighteen months he had become aware of his being seriously out of health. He had caught a violent cold, which fixed itself on his lungs and threw them into dire confusion. He had to give up work and apply, to the letter, the sorry injunction to take care of himself. At first he slighted the task; it appeared to him it was not himself in the least he was taking care of, but an uninteresting and uninterested person with whom he had nothing in common. This person, however, improved on acquaintance, and Ralph grew at last to have a certain grudging tolerance, even an undemonstrative respect, for him. Misfortune makes strange bedfellows, and our young man, feeling that he had something at stake in the matter—it usually struck him as his reputation for ordinary wit—devoted to his graceless charge an amount of attention of which note was duly taken and which had at least the effect of keeping the poor fellow alive. One of his lungs began to heal, the other promised to follow its example, and he was assured he might outweather a dozen winters if he would betake himself to those climates in which consumptives chiefly congregate. As he had grown extremely fond of London, he cursed the flatness of exile: but at the same time that he cursed he conformed, and gradually, when he found his sensitive organ grateful even for grim favours, he conferred them with a lighter hand. He wintered abroad, as the phrase is; basked in the sun, stopped at home when the wind blew, went to bed when it rained, and once or twice, when it had snowed overnight, almost never got up again.

A secret hoard of indifference—like a thick cake a fond old nurse might have slipped into his first school outfit—came to his aid and helped to reconcile him to sacrifice; since at the best he was too ill for aught but that arduous game. As he said to himself, there was really nothing he had wanted very much to do, so that he had at least not renounced the field of valour. At present, however, the fragrance of forbidden fruit seemed occasionally to float past him and remind him that the finest of pleasures is the rush of action. Living as he now lived was like reading a good book in a poor translation—a meagre entertainment for a young man who felt that he might have been an excellent linguist. He had good winters and poor winters, and while the former lasted he was sometimes the sport of a vision of virtual recovery. But this vision was dispelled some three years before the occurrence of the incidents with which this history opens: he had on that occasion remained later than usual in England and had been overtaken by bad weather before reaching Algiers. He arrived more dead than alive and lay there for several weeks between life and death. His convalescence was a miracle, but the first use he made of it was to assure himself that such miracles happen but once. He said to himself that his hour was in sight and that it behoved him to keep his eyes upon it, yet that it was also open to him to spend the interval as agreeably as might be consistent with such a preoccupation. With the prospect of losing them the simple use of his faculties became an exquisite pleasure; it seemed to him the joys of contemplation had never been sounded. He was far from the time when he had found it hard that he should be obliged to give up the idea of distinguishing himself; an idea none the less importunate for being vague and none the less delightful for having had to struggle in the same breast with bursts of inspiring self-criticism. His friends at present judged him more cheerful, and attributed it to a theory, over which they shook their heads knowingly, that he would recover his health. His serenity was but the array of wild flowers niched in his ruin.

It was very probably this sweet-tasting property of the observed thing in itself that was mainly concerned in Ralph's quickly-stirred interest in the advent of a young lady who was evidently not insipid. If he was consideringly disposed, something told him, here was occupation enough for a succession of days. It may be added, in summary fashion, that the imagination of loving—as distinguished from that of being loved—had still a place in his reduced sketch. He had only forbidden himself the riot of expression. However, he shouldn't inspire his cousin with a passion, nor would she be able, even should she try, to help him to one. 'And now tell me about the young lady,' he said to his mother. 'What do you mean to do with her?'

Mrs Touchett was prompt. 'I mean to ask your father to invite her to stay three or four weeks at Gardencourt.'

'You needn't stand on any such ceremony as that,' said Ralph. 'My father will ask her as a matter of course.'

'I don't know about that. She's my niece; she's not his.'

'Good Lord, dear mother; what a sense of property! That's all the more reason for his asking her. But after that—I mean after three months (for it's absurd asking the poor girl to remain but for three or four paltry weeks)—what do you mean to do with her?'

'I mean to take her to Paris. I mean to get her clothing.'

'Ah yes, that's of course. But independently of that?'

'I shall invite her to spend the autumn with me in Florence.'

'You don't rise above detail, dear mother,' said Ralph. 'I should like to know what you mean to do with her in a general way.'

'My duty!' Mrs Touchett declared. 'I suppose you pity her very much,' she added.

'No, I don't think I pity her. She doesn't strike me as inviting compassion. I think I envy her. Before being sure, however, give me a hint of where you see your duty.'

'In showing her four European countries—I shall leave her the choice of two of them—and in giving her the opportunity of perfecting herself in French, which she already knows very well.'

Ralph frowned a little. 'That sounds rather dry—even allowing her the choice of two of the countries.'

'If it's dry,' said his mother with a laugh, 'you can leave Isabel alone to water it! She is as good as a summer rain, any day.'

'Do you mean she's a gifted being?'

'I don't know whether she's a gifted being, but she's a clever girl—with a strong will and a high temper. She has no idea of being bored.'

'I can imagine that,' said Ralph; and then he added abruptly: 'How do you two get on?'

'Do you mean by that that I'm a bore? I don't think she finds me one. Some girls might, I know; but Isabel's too clever for that. I think I greatly amuse her. We get on because I understand her; I know the sort of girl she is. She's very frank, and I'm very frank: we know just what to expect of each other.'

'Ah, dear mother,' Ralph exclaimed, 'one always knows what to expect of *you*! You've never surprised me but once, and that's to-day—in presenting me with a pretty cousin whose existence I had never suspected.'

'Do you think her so very pretty?'

'Very pretty indeed; but I don't insist upon that. It's her general air of being some one in particular that strikes me. Who is this rare creature, and what is she? Where did you find her, and how did you make her acquaintance?'

'I found her in an old house at Albany, sitting in a dreary room on a rainy day, reading a heavy book and boring herself to death. She didn't know she was bored, but when I left her no doubt of it she seemed very grateful for the service. You may say I shouldn't have enlightened her—I should have let her alone. There's a good deal in that, but I acted conscientiously; I thought she was meant for something better. It occurred to me that it would be a kindness to take her about and introduce her to the world. She thinks she knows a great deal of it—like most American girls; but like most American girls she's ridiculously mistaken. If you want to know, I thought she would do me credit. I like to be well thought of, and for a woman of my age there's no greater convenience, in some ways, than an attractive niece. You know I had seen nothing of my sister's children for years; I disapproved entirely of the father. But I always meant to do something for them when he should have gone to his reward. I ascertained where they were to be found and, without any preliminaries, went and introduced myself. There are two others of them, both of whom are married; but I saw only the elder, who has, by the way, a very uncivil husband. The wife, whose name is Lily, jumped at the idea of my taking an interest in Isabel; she said it was just what her sister needed—that some one should take an interest in her. She spoke of her as you might speak of some young person of genius—in want of encouragement and patronage. It may be that Isabel's a genius; but in that case I've not yet learned her special line. Mrs Ludlow was especially keen about my taking her to Europe; they all regard Europe over there as a land of emigration, of rescue, a refuge for their superfluous population. Isabel herself seemed very glad to come, and the thing was easily arranged. There was a little difficulty about the money-question, as she seemed averse to being under pecuniary obligations. But she has a small income and she supposes herself to be travelling at her own expense.'

Ralph had listened attentively to this judicious report, by which his interest in the subject of it was not impaired. 'Ah, if she's a genius,' he said, 'we must find out her special line. Is it by chance for flirting?'

'I don't think so. You may suspect that at first, but you'll be wrong. You won't, I think, in any way, be easily right about her.'

'Warburton's wrong then!' Ralph rejoicingly exclaimed. 'He flatters himself he has made that discovery.'

His mother shook her head. 'Lord Warburton won't understand her. He needn't try.'

'He's very intelligent,' said Ralph; 'but it's right he should be puzzled once in a while.'

'Isabel will enjoy puzzling a lord,' Mrs Touchett remarked.

Her son frowned a little. 'What does she know about lords?'

'Nothing at all: that will puzzle him all the more.'

Ralph greeted these words with a laugh and looked out of the window. Then, 'Are you not going down to see my father?' he asked.

'At a quarter to eight,' said Mrs Touchett.

Her son looked at his watch. 'You've another quarter of an hour then. Tell me some more about Isabel.' After which, as Mrs Touchett declined his invitation, declaring that he must find out for himself, 'Well,' he pursued, 'she'll certainly do you credit. But won't she also give you trouble?'

'I hope not; but if she does I shall not shrink from it. I never do that.'

'She strikes me as very natural,' said Ralph.

'Natural people are not the most trouble.'

'No,' said Ralph; 'you yourself are a proof of that. You're extremely natural, and I'm sure you have never troubled any one. It *takes* trouble to do that. But tell me this; it just occurs to me. Is Isabel capable of making herself disagreeable?'

'Ah,' cried his mother, 'you ask too many questions! Find that out for yourself.'

His questions, however, were not exhausted. 'All this time,' he said, 'you've not told me what you intend to do with her.'

'Do with her? You talk as if she were a yard of calico. I shall do absolutely nothing with her, and she herself will do everything she chooses. She gave me notice of that.'

'What you meant then, in your telegram, was that her character's independent.'

'I never know what I mean in my telegrams—especially those I send from America. Clearness is too expensive. Come down to your father.'

'It's not yet a quarter to eight,' said Ralph.

'I must allow for his impatience,' Mrs Touchett answered.

Ralph knew what to think of his father's impatience; but, making no rejoinder, he offered his mother his arm. This put it in his power, as they descended together, to stop her a moment on the middle landing of the staircase—the broad, low, wide-armed staircase of time-blackened oak which was one of the most striking features of Gardencourt. 'You've no plan of marrying her?' he smiled.

'Marrying her? I should be sorry to play her such a trick! But apart from that, she's perfectly able to marry herself. She has every facility.'

'Do you mean to say she has a husband picked out?'

'I don't know about a husband, but there's a young man in Boston—!'

Ralph went on; he had no desire to hear about the young man in Boston. 'As my father says, they're always engaged!'

His mother had told him that he must satisfy his curiosity at the source, and it soon became evident he should not want for occasion. He had a good deal of talk with his young kinswoman when the two had been left together in the drawing-room. Lord Warburton, who had ridden over from his own house, some ten miles distant, remounted and took his departure before dinner; and an hour after this meal was ended Mr and Mrs Touchett, who appeared to have quite emptied the measure of their forms, withdrew, under the valid pretext of fatigue, to their respective apartments. The young man spent an hour with his cousin; though she had been travelling half the day she appeared in no degree spent. She was really tired; she knew it, and knew she should pay for it on the morrow; but it was her habit at this period to carry exhaustion to the furthest point and confess to it only when dissimulation broke down. A fine hypocrisy was for the present possible; she was interested; she was, as she said to herself, floated. She asked Ralph to show her the pictures; there were a great many in the house, most of them of his own choosing. The best were arranged in an oaken gallery, of charming proportions, which had a sitting-room at either end of it and which in the evening was usually lighted. The light was insufficient to show the pictures to advantage, and the visit might have stood over to the morrow. This suggestion Ralph had ventured to make; but Isabel looked disappointed—smiling still, however—and said: 'If you please I should like to see them just a little.' She was eager, she knew she was eager and now seemed so; she couldn't help it. 'She doesn't take suggestions,' Ralph said to himself; but he said it without irritation; her pressure amused and even pleased him. The lamps were on brackets, at intervals, and if the light was imperfect it was genial. It fell upon the vague squares of rich colour and on the faded gilding of heavy frames; it made a sheen on the polished floor of the gallery. Ralph took a candlestick and moved about, pointing out the things he liked; Isabel, inclining to one picture after another, indulged in little exclamations and murmurs. She was evidently a judge; she had a natural taste; he was struck with that. She took a candlestick herself and held it slowly here and there; she lifted it high, and as she did so he found himself pausing in the middle of the place and bending his eyes much less upon the pictures than on her presence. He lost nothing, in truth, by these wandering glances, for she was better worth looking at than most works of art. She was undeniably spare, and ponderably light, and proveably tall; when people had wished to distinguish her from the other two Miss Archers they had always called her the willowy one. Her hair, which was dark even to blackness, had been an object of envy to many women; her light grey eyes, a little too firm perhaps in her graver moments, had an enchanting range of concession. They walked slowly up one side of the gallery and down the other, and then she said: 'Well, now I know more than I did when I began!'

'You apparently have a great passion for knowledge,' her cousin returned.

'I think I have; most girls are horridly ignorant.'

'You strike me as different from most girls.'

'Ah, some of them *would*—but the way they're talked to!' murmured Isabel, who preferred not to dilate just yet on herself. Then in a moment, to change the subject, 'Please tell me—isn't there a ghost?' she went on.

'A ghost?'

'A castle-spectre, a thing that appears. We call them ghosts in America.'

'So we do here, when we see them.'

'You do see them then? You ought to, in this romantic old house.'

'It's not a romantic old house,' said Ralph. 'You'll be disappointed if you count on that. It's a dismally prosaic one; there's no romance here but what you may have brought with you.'

'I've brought a great deal; but it seems to me I've brought it to the right place.'

'To keep it out of harm, certainly; nothing will ever happen to it here, between my father and me.'

Isabel looked at him a moment. 'Is there never any one here but your father and you?'

'My mother, of course.'

'Oh, I know your mother; she's not romantic. Haven't you other people?'

'Very few.'

'I'm sorry for that; I like so much to see people.'

'Oh, we'll invite all the county to amuse you,' said Ralph.

'Now you're making fun of me,' the girl answered rather gravely. 'Who was the gentleman on the lawn when I arrived?'

'A county neighbour; he doesn't come very often.'

'I'm sorry for that; I liked him,' said Isabel.

'Why, it seemed to me that you barely spoke to him,' Ralph objected.

'Never mind, I like him all the same. I like your father too, immensely.'

'You can't do better than that. He's the dearest of the dear.'

'I'm so sorry he is ill,' said Isabel.

'You must help me to nurse him; you ought to be a good nurse.'

'I don't think I am; I've been told I'm not; I'm said to have too many theories. But you haven't told me about the ghost,' she added.

Ralph, however, gave no heed to this observation. 'You like my father and you like Lord Warburton. I infer also that you like my mother.'

'I like your mother very much, because—because——' And Isabel found herself attempting to assign a reason for her affection for Mrs Touchett.

'Ah, we never know why!' said her companion, laughing.

'I always know why,' the girl answered. 'It's because she

doesn't expect one to like her. She doesn't care whether one does or not.'

'So you adore her—out of perversity? Well, I take greatly after my mother,' said Ralph.

'I don't believe you do at all. You wish people to like you, and you try to make them do it.'

'Good heavens, how you see through one!' he cried with a dismay that was not altogether jocular.

'But I like you all the same,' his cousin went on. 'The way to clinch the matter will be to show me the ghost.'

Ralph shook his head sadly. 'I might show it to you, but you'd never see it. The privilege isn't given to every one; it's not enviable. It has never been seen by a young, happy, innocent person like you. You must have suffered first, have suffered greatly, have gained some miserable knowledge. In that way your eyes are opened to it. I saw it long ago,' said Ralph.

'I told you just now I'm very fond of knowledge,' Isabel answered.

'Yes, of happy knowledge—of pleasant knowledge. But you haven't suffered, and you're not made to suffer. I hope you'll never see the ghost!'

She had listened to him attentively, with a smile on her lips, but with a certain gravity in her eyes. Charming as he found her, she had struck him as rather presumptuous—indeed it was a part of her charm; and he wondered what she would say. 'I'm not afraid, you know,' she said: which seemed quite presumptuous enough.

'You're not afraid of suffering?'

'Yes, I'm afraid of suffering. But I'm not afraid of ghosts. And I think people suffer too easily,' she added.

'I don't believe *you* do,' said Ralph, looking at her with his hands in his pockets.

'I don't think that's a fault,' she answered. 'It's not absolutely necessary to suffer; we were not made for that.'

'You were not, certainly.'

'I'm not speaking of myself.' And she wandered off a little.

'No, it isn't a fault,' said her cousin. 'It's a merit to be strong.'

'Only, if you don't suffer they call you hard,' Isabel remarked.

They passed out of the smaller drawing-room, into which they had returned from the gallery, and paused in the hall, at the foot of the staircase. Here Ralph presented his companion with her bedroom candle, which he had taken from a niche. 'Never mind what they call you. When you do suffer they call you an idiot. The great point's to be as happy as possible.'

She looked at him a little; she had taken her candle and placed her foot on the oaken stair. 'Well,' she said, 'that's what I came to Europe for, to be as happy as possible. Good-night.'

'Good-night! I wish you all success, and shall be very glad to contribute to it!'

She turned away, and he watched her as she slowly ascended. Then, with his hands always in his pockets, he went back to the empty drawing-room.

VI

Isabel Archer was a young person of many theories; her imagination was remarkably active. It had been her fortune to possess a finer mind than most of the persons among whom her lot was cast; to have a larger perception of surrounding facts and to care for knowledge that was tinged with the unfamiliar. It is true that among her contemporaries she passed for a young woman of extraordinary profundity; for these excellent people never withheld their admiration from a reach of intellect of which they themselves were not conscious, and spoke of Isabel as a prodigy of learning, a creature reported to have read the classic authors—in translations. Her paternal aunt, Mrs Varian, once spread the rumour that Isabel was writing a book—Mrs Varian having a reverence for books, and averred that the girl would distinguish herself in print. Mrs Varian thought highly of literature, for which she entertained that esteem that is connected with a sense of privation. Her own large house, remarkable for its assortment of mosaic tables and decorated ceilings, was unfurnished with a library, and in the way of printed volumes contained nothing but half a dozen novels in paper on a shelf in the apartment of one of the Miss Varians. Practically, Mrs Varian's acquaintance with literature was confined to *The New York Interviewer*; as she very justly said, after you had read the *Interviewer* you had lost all faith in culture. Her tendency, with this, was rather to keep the *Interviewer* out of the way of her daughters; she was determined to bring them up properly, and they read nothing at all. Her impression with regard to Isabel's labours was quite illusory; the girl had never attempted to write a book and had no desire for the laurels of authorship. She had no talent for expression and too little of the consciousness of genius; she only had a general idea that people were right when they treated her as if she were rather superior. Whether or no she were superior, people were right in admiring her if they thought her so; for it seemed to her often that her mind moved more quickly than theirs, and this encouraged an impatience that might easily be confounded with superiority. It may be affirmed without delay that Isabel was probably very liable to the sin of self-esteem; she often surveyed with complacency the field of her own nature; she was in the habit of taking for granted, on scanty evidence, that she was right; she treated herself to occasions of homage. Meanwhile her errors and delusions were frequently such as a biographer interested in preserving the dignity of his subject must shrink from specifying. Her thoughts were a tangle of vague outlines which had never been corrected by the judgement of people speaking with authority. In matters of opinion she had had her own way, and it had led her into a thousand ridiculous zigzags. At moments she discovered she was grotesquely wrong, and then she treated herself to a week of passionate humility. After this she held her head higher than ever again; for it was of no use, she had an unquenchable desire to think well of herself. She had a theory that it was only under this provision life was worth living; that one should be one of the best, should be conscious of a fine organisation (she couldn't help knowing her organisation was fine), should move in a realm of light, of natural wisdom, of happy impulse, of inspiration gracefully chronic. It was almost as unnecessary to cultivate doubt of one's self as to cultivate doubt of one's best friend: one should try to be one's own best friend and to give one's self, in this manner, distinguished company. The girl had a certain nobleness of imagination which rendered her a good many services and played her a great many tricks. She spent half her time in thinking of beauty and bravery and magnanimity; she had a fixed determination to regard the world as a place of brightness, of free expansion, of irresistible action: she held it must be detestable to be afraid or ashamed. She had an infinite hope that she should never do anything wrong. She had resented so strongly, after discovering them, her mere errors of feeling (the discovery always made her tremble as if she had escaped from a trap which might have caught her and smothered her) that the chance of inflicting a sensible injury upon another person, presented only as a contingency, caused her at moments to hold her breath. That always struck her as the worst thing that could happen to her. On the whole, reflectively, she was in no uncertainty about the things that were wrong. She had no love of their look, but when she fixed them hard she recognised them. It was wrong to be mean, to be jealous, to be false, to be cruel; she had seen very little of the evil of the world, but she had seen women who lied and who tried to hurt each other. Seeing such things had quickened her high spirit; it seemed indecent not to scorn them. Of course the danger of a high spirit was the danger of inconsistency—the danger of keeping up the flag after the place has surrendered; a sort of behaviour so crooked as to be almost a dishonour to the flag. But Isabel, who knew little of the sorts of artillery to which young women are exposed, flattered herself that such contradictions would never be noted in her own conduct. Her life should always be in harmony with the most pleasing impression she should produce; she would be what she appeared, and she would appear what she was. Sometimes she went so far as to wish that she might find herself some day in a difficult position, so that she should have the pleasure of being as heroic as the occasion demanded. Altogether, with her meagre knowledge, her inflated ideals, her confidence at once innocent and dogmatic, her temper at once exacting and indulgent, her mixture of curiosity and fastidiousness, of vivacity and indifference, her desire to look very well and to be if possible even better, her determination to see, to try, to know, her combination of the delicate, desultory, flame-like spirit and the eager and personal creature of conditions: she would be an easy victim of scientific criticism if she were not intended to awaken on the reader's part an impulse more tender and more purely expectant.

It was one of her theories that Isabel Archer was very fortunate in being independent, and that she ought to make some very enlightened use of that state. She never called it the state of solitude, much less of singleness; she thought such descriptions weak, and, besides, her sister Lily constantly urged her to come and abide. She had a friend whose acquaintance she had made shortly before her father's death, who offered so high an example of useful activity that Isabel always thought of her as a model. Henrietta Stackpole had the advantage of an admired ability; she was thoroughly launched in journalism, and her letters to the *Interviewer*, from Washington, Newport, the White Mountains and other places, were universally quoted. Isabel pronounced them with confidence 'ephemeral,' but she esteemed the courage, energy and good-humour of the writer, who, without parents and without property, had adopted three of the children of an infirm and widowed sister and was paying their school-bills out of the proceeds of her literary labour. Henrietta was in the van of progress and had clear-cut views on most subjects; her cherished desire had long been to come to Europe and write a series of letters to the *Interviewer* from the radical point of view—an enterprise the less difficult as she knew perfectly in advance what her opinions would be and to how many objections most European institutions lay open. When she heard that Isabel was coming she wished to start at once; thinking, naturally, that it would be delightful the two should travel together. She had been obliged, however, to postpone this enterprise. She thought Isabel a glorious creature, and had spoken of her covertly in some of her letters, though she never mentioned the fact to her friend, who would not have taken pleasure in it and was not a regular student of the *Interviewer*. Henrietta, for Isabel, was chiefly a proof that a woman might suffice to herself and be happy. Her resources were of the obvious kind; but even if one had not the journalistic talent and a genius for guessing, as Henrietta said, what the public was going to want, one was not therefore to conclude that one had no vocation, no beneficent aptitude of any sort, and resign one's self to being frivolous and hollow. Isabel was stoutly determined not to be hollow. If one should wait with the right patience one would find some happy work to one's hand. Of course, among her theories, this young lady was not without a collection of views on the subject of marriage. The first on the list was a conviction of the vulgarity of thinking too much of it. From lapsing into eagerness on this point she earnestly prayed she might be delivered; she held that a woman ought to be able to live to herself, in the absence of exceptional flimsiness, and that it was perfectly possible to be happy without the society of a more or less coarse-minded person of another sex. The girl's prayer was very sufficiently answered; something pure and proud that there was in her—something cold and dry an unappreciated suitor with a taste for analysis might have called it—had hitherto kept her from any great vanity of conjecture on the article of possible husbands. Few of the men she saw seemed worth a ruinous expenditure, and it made her smile to think that one of them should present himself as an incentive to hope and a reward of patience. Deep in her soul—it was the deepest thing there—lay a belief that if a certain light should dawn she could give herself completely; but this image, on the whole, was too formidable to be attractive. Isabel's thoughts hovered about it, but they seldom rested on it long; after a little it ended in alarms. It often seemed to her that she thought too much about herself; you could have made her colour, any day in the year, by calling her a rank egoist. She was always planning out her development, desiring her perfection, observing her progress. Her nature had, in her conceit, a certain garden-like quality, a suggestion of perfume and murmuring boughs, of shady bowers and lengthening vistas, which made her feel that introspection was, after all, an exercise in the open air, and that a visit to the recesses of one's spirit was harmless when one returned from it with a lapful of roses. But she was often reminded that there were other gardens in the world than those of her remarkable soul, and that there were moreover a great many places which were not gardens at all—only dusky pestiferous tracts, planted thick with ugliness and misery. In the current of that repaid curiosity on which she had lately been floating, which had conveyed her to this beautiful old England and might carry her much further still, she often checked herself with the thought of the thousands of people who were less happy than herself—a thought which for the moment made her fine, full consciousness appear a kind of immodesty. What should one do with the misery of the world in a scheme of the agreeable for one's self? It must be confessed that this question never held her long. She was too young, too impatient to live, too unacquainted with pain. She always returned to her theory that a young woman whom after all every one thought clever should begin by getting a general impression of life. This impression was necessary to prevent mistakes, and after it should be secured she might make the unfortunate condition of others a subject of special attention.

England was a revelation to her, and she found herself as diverted as a child at a pantomime. In her infantine excursions to Europe she had seen only the Continent, and seen it from the nursery window; Paris, not London, was her father's Mecca, and into many of his interests there his children had naturally not entered. The images of that time moreover had grown faint and remote, and the old-world quality in everything that she now saw had all the charm of strangeness. Her uncle's house seemed a picture made real; no refinement of the agreeable was lost upon Isabel; the rich perfection of Gardencourt at once revealed a world and gratified a need. The large, low rooms, with brown ceilings and dusky corners, the deep embrasures and curious casements, the quiet light on dark, polished panels, the deep greenness outside that seemed always peeping in, the sense of well-ordered privacy in the centre of a 'property'—a place where sounds were felicitously accidental, where the tread was muffled by the earth itself and in the thick mild air all friction dropped out of contact and all shrillness out of talk—these things were much to the taste of our young lady, whose taste played a considerable part in her emotions. She formed a fast friendship with her uncle, and often sat by his chair when he had had it moved out to the lawn. He passed hours in the open air, sitting with folded hands like a placid, homely household god, a god of service, who had done his work and received his wages and was trying to grow used to weeks and months made up only of off-days. Isabel amused him more than she suspected—the effect she produced upon people was often different from what she supposed—and he frequently gave himself the pleasure of making her chatter. It was by this term that he qualified her conversation, which had much of the 'point' observable in that of the young ladies of her country, to whom the ear of the world is more directly presented than to their sisters in other lands. Like the mass of American girls Isabel had been encouraged to express herself; her remarks had been attended to; she had been expected to have emotions and opinions. Many of her opinions had doubtless but a slender value, many of her emotions passed away in the utterance; but they had left a trace in giving her the habit of seeming at least to feel and think, and in imparting moreover to her words when she was really moved that prompt vividness which so many people had regarded as a sign of superiority. Mr Touchett used to think that she reminded him of his wife when his wife was in her teens. It was because she was fresh and natural and quick to understand, to speak—so many characteristics of her niece—that he had fallen in love with Mrs Touchett. He never expressed this analogy to the girl herself, however; for if Mrs Touchett had once been like Isabel, Isabel was not at all like Mrs Touchett. The old man was full of kindness for her; it was a long time, as he said, since they had had any young life in the house; and our rustling, quickly-moving, clear-voiced heroine was as agreeable to his sense as the sound of flowing water. He wanted to do something for her and wished she would ask it of him. She would ask nothing but questions; it is true that of these she asked a quantity. Her uncle had a great fund of answers, though her pressure sometimes came in forms that puzzled him. She questioned him immensely about England, about the British constitution, the English character, the state of politics, the manners and customs of the royal family, the peculiarities of the aristocracy, the way of living and thinking of his neighbours; and in begging to be enlightened on these points she usually enquired whether they corresponded with the descriptions in the books. The old man always looked at her a little with his fine dry smile while he smoothed down the shawl spread across his legs.

'The books?' he once said; 'well, I don't know much about the books. You must ask Ralph about that. I've always ascertained for myself—got my information in the natural form. I never asked many questions even; I just kept quiet and took notice. Of course I've had very good opportunities—better than what a young lady would naturally have. I'm of an inquisitive disposition, though you mightn't think it if you were to watch me: however much you might watch me I should be watching you more. I've been watching these people for upwards of thirty-five years, and I don't hesitate to say that I've acquired considerable information. It's a very fine country on the whole—finer perhaps than what we give it credit for on the other side. There are several improvements I should like to see introduced; but the necessity of them doesn't seem to be generally felt as yet. When the necessity of a thing is generally felt they usually manage to accomplish it; but they seem to feel pretty comfortable about waiting till then. I certainly feel more at home among them than I expected to when I first came over; I suppose it's because I've had a considerable degree of success. When you're successful you naturally feel more at home.'

'Do you suppose that if I'm successful I shall feel at home?' Isabel asked.

'I should think it very probable, and you certainly will be successful. They like American young ladies very much over here; they show them a great deal of kindness. But you mustn't feel too much at home, you know.'

'Oh, I'm by no means sure it will *satisfy* me,' Isabel judicially emphasised. 'I like the place very much, but I'm not sure I shall like the people.'

'The people are very good people; especially if you like them.'

'I've no doubt they're good,' Isabel rejoined; 'but are they pleasant in society? They won't rob me nor beat me; but will they make themselves agreeable to me? That's what I like people to do. I don't hesitate to say so, because I always appreciate it. I don't believe they're very nice to girls; they're not nice to them in the novels.'

'I don't know about the novels,' said Mr Touchett. 'I believe the novels have a great deal of ability, but I don't suppose they're very accurate. We once had a lady who wrote novels staying here; she was a friend of Ralph's and he asked her down. She was very positive, quite up to everything; but she was not the sort of person you could depend on for evidence. Too free a fancy—I suppose that was it. She afterwards published a work of fiction in which she was understood to have given a representation—something in the nature of a caricature, as you might say—of my unworthy self. I didn't read it, but Ralph just handed me the book with the principal passages marked. It was understood to be a description of my conversation; American peculiarities, nasal twang, Yankee notions, stars and stripes. Well, it was not at all accurate; she couldn't have listened very attentively. I had no objection to her giving a report of my conversation, if she liked; but I didn't like the idea that she hadn't taken the trouble to listen to it. Of course I talk like an American—I can't talk like a Hottentot. However I talk, I've made them understand me pretty well over here. But I don't talk like the old gentleman in that lady's novel. He wasn't an American; we wouldn't have him over there at any price. I just mention that fact to show you that they're not always accurate. Of course, as I've no daughters, and as Mrs Touchett resides in Florence, I haven't had much chance to notice about the young ladies. It sometimes appears as if the young women in the lower class were not very well treated; but I guess their position is better in the upper and even to some extent in the middle.'

'Gracious,' Isabel exclaimed; 'how many classes have they? About fifty, I suppose.'

'Well, I don't know that I ever counted them. I never took much notice of the classes. That's the advantage of being an American here; you don't belong to any class.'

'I hope so,' said Isabel. 'Imagine one's belonging to an English class!'

'Well, I guess some of them are pretty comfortable—especially towards the top. But for me there are only two classes: the people I trust and the people I don't. Of those two, my dear Isabel, you belong to the first.'

'I'm much obliged to you,' said the girl quickly. Her way of taking compliments seemed sometimes rather dry; she got rid of them as rapidly as possible. But as regards this she was sometimes misjudged; she was thought insensible to them, whereas in fact she was simply unwilling to show how infinitely they pleased her. To show that was to show too much. 'I'm sure the English are very conventional,' she added.

'They've got everything pretty well fixed,' Mr Touchett admitted. 'It's all settled beforehand—they don't leave it to the last moment.'

'I don't like to have everything settled beforehand,' said the girl. 'I like more unexpectedness.'

Her uncle seemed amused at her distinctness of preference. 'Well, it's settled beforehand that you'll have great success,' he rejoined. 'I suppose you'll like that.'

'I shall not have success if they're too stupidly conventional. I'm not in the least stupidly conventional. I'm just the contrary. That's what they won't like.'

'No, no, you're all wrong,' said the old man. 'You can't tell what they'll like. They're very inconsistent; that's their principal interest.'

'Ah well,' said Isabel, standing before her uncle with her hands clasped about the belt of her black dress and looking up and down the lawn—'that will suit me perfectly!'

VII

The two amused themselves, time and again, with talking of the attitude of the British public as if the young lady had been in a position to appeal to it; but in fact the British public remained for the present profoundly indifferent to Miss Isabel Archer, whose fortune had dropped her, as her cousin said, into the dullest house in England. Her gouty uncle received very little company, and Mrs Touchett, not having cultivated relations with her husband's neighbours, was not warranted in expecting visits from them. She had, however, a peculiar taste; she liked to receive cards. For what is usually called social intercourse she had very little relish; but nothing pleased her more than to find her hall-table whitened with oblong morsels of symbolic pasteboard. She flattered herself that she was a very just woman, and had mastered the sovereign truth that nothing in this world is got for nothing. She had played no social part as mistress of Gardencourt, and it was not to be supposed that, in the surrounding country, a minute account should be kept of her comings and goings. But it is by no means certain that she did not feel it to be wrong that so little notice was taken of them and that her failure (really very gratuitous) to make herself important in the neighbourhood had not much to do with the acrimony of her allusions to her husband's adopted country. Isabel presently found herself in the singular situation of defending the British constitution against her aunt; Mrs Touchett having formed the habit of sticking pins into this venerable instrument. Isabel always felt an impulse to pull out the pins; not that she imagined they inflicted any damage on the tough old parchment, but because it seemed to her her aunt might make better use of her sharpness. She was very critical herself—it was incidental to her age, her sex and her nationality; but she was very sentimental as well, and there was something in Mrs Touchett's dryness that set her own moral fountains flowing.

'Now what's your point of view?' she asked of her aunt. 'When you criticise everything here you should have a point of view. Yours doesn't seem to be American—you thought everything over there so disagreeable. When I criticise I have mine; it's thoroughly American!'

'My dear young lady,' said Mrs Touchett, 'there are as many points of view in the world as there are people of sense to take them. You may say that doesn't make them very numerous! American? Never in the world; that's shockingly narrow. My point of view, thank God, is personal!'

Isabel thought this a better answer than she admitted; it was a tolerable description of her own manner of judging, but it would not have sounded well for her to say so. On the lips of a person less advanced in life and less enlightened by experience than Mrs Touchett such a declaration would savour of immodesty, even of arrogance. She risked it nevertheless in talking with Ralph, with whom she talked a great deal and with whom her conversation was of a sort that gave a large licence to extravagance. Her cousin used, as the phrase is, to chaff her; he very soon established with her a reputation for treating everything as a joke, and he was not a man to neglect the privileges such a reputation conferred. She accused him of an odious want of seriousness, of laughing at all things, beginning with himself. Such slender faculty of reverence as he possessed centred wholly upon his father; for the rest, he exercised his wit indifferently upon his father's son, this gentleman's weak lungs, his useless life, his fantastic mother, his friends (Lord Warburton in especial), his adopted, and his native country, his charming new-found cousin. 'I keep a band of music in my ante-room,' he said once to her. 'It has orders to play without stopping; it renders me two excellent services. It keeps the sounds of the world from reaching the private apartments, and it makes the world think that dancing's going on within.' It was dance-music indeed that you usually heard when you came within ear-shot of Ralph's band; the liveliest waltzes seemed to float upon the air. Isabel often found herself irritated by this perpetual fiddling; she would have liked to pass through the ante-room, as her cousin called it, and enter the private apartments. It mattered little that he had assured her they were a very dismal place; she would have been glad to undertake to sweep them and set them in order. It was but half-hospitality to let her remain outside; to punish him for which Isabel administered innumerable taps with the ferule of her straight young wit. It must be said that her wit was exercised to a large extent in self-defence, for her cousin amused himself with calling her 'Columbia' and accusing her of a patriotism so heated that it scorched. He drew a caricature of her in which she was represented as a very pretty young woman dressed, on the lines of the prevailing fashion, in the folds of the national banner. Isabel's chief dread in life at this period of her development was that she should appear narrow-minded; what she feared next afterwards was that she should really be so. But she nevertheless made no scruple of abounding in her cousin's sense and pretending to sigh for the charms of her native land. She would be as American as it pleased him to regard her, and if he chose to laugh at her she would give him plenty of occupation. She defended England against his mother, but when Ralph sang its praises on purpose, as she said, to work her up, she found herself able to differ from him on a variety of points. In fact, the quality of this small ripe country seemed as sweet to her as the taste of an October pear; and her satisfaction was at the root of the good spirits which enabled her to take her cousin's chaff and return it in kind. If her good-humour flagged at moments it was not because she thought herself ill-used, but because she suddenly felt sorry for Ralph. It seemed to her he was talking as a blind and had little heart in what he said.

'I don't know what's the matter with you,' she observed to him once; 'but I suspect you're a great humbug.'

'That's your privilege,' Ralph answered, who had not been used to being so crudely addressed.

'I don't know what you care for; I don't think you care for anything. You don't really care for England when you praise it; you don't care for America even when you pretend to abuse it.'

'I care for nothing but you, dear cousin,' said Ralph.

'If I could believe even that, I should be very glad.'

'Ah well, I should hope so!' the young man exclaimed.

Isabel might have believed it and not have been far from the truth. He thought a great deal about her; she was constantly present to his mind. At a time when his thoughts had been a good deal of a burden to him her sudden arrival, which promised nothing and was an openhanded gift of fate, had refreshed and quickened them, given them wings and something to fly for. Poor Ralph had been for many weeks steeped in melancholy; his outlook, habitually sombre, lay under the shadow of a deeper cloud. He had grown anxious about his father, whose gout, hitherto confined to his legs, had begun to ascend into regions more vital. The old man had been gravely ill in the spring, and the doctors had whispered to Ralph that another attack would be less easy to deal with. Just now he appeared disburdened of pain, but Ralph could not rid himself of a suspicion that this was a subterfuge of the enemy, who was waiting to take him off his guard. If the manœuvre should succeed there would be little hope of any great resistance. Ralph had always taken for granted that his father would survive him—that his own name would be the first grimly called. The father and son had been close companions, and the idea of being left alone with the remnant of a tasteless life on his hands was not gratifying to the young man, who had always and tacitly counted upon his elder's help in making the best of a poor business. At the prospect of losing his great motive Ralph lost indeed his one inspiration. If they might die at the same time it would be all very well; but without the encouragement of his father's society he should barely have patience to await his own turn. He had not the incentive of feeling that he was indispensable to his mother; it was a rule with his mother to have no regrets. He bethought himself of course that it had been a small kindness to his father to wish that, of the two, the active rather than the passive party should know the felt wound; he remembered that the old man had always treated his own forecast of an early end as a clever fallacy, which he should be delighted to discredit so far as he might by dying first. But of the two triumphs, that of refuting a sophistical son and that of holding on a while longer to a state of being which, with all abatements, he enjoyed, Ralph deemed it no sin to hope the latter might be vouchasfed to Mr Touchett.

These were nice questions, but Isabel's arrival put a stop to his puzzling over them. It even suggested there might be a compensation for the intolerable ennui of surviving his genial sire. He wondered whether he were harbouring 'love' for this spontaneous young woman from Albany; but he judged that on the whole he was not. After he had known her for a week he quite made up his mind to this, and every day he felt a little more sure. Lord Warburton had been right about her; she was a really interesting little figure. Ralph wondered how their neighbour had found it out so soon; and then he said it was only another proof of his friend's high abilities, which he had always greatly admired. If his cousin were to be nothing more than an entertainment to him, Ralph was conscious she was an entertainment of a high order. 'A character like that,' he said to himself—'a real little passionate force to see at play is the finest thing in nature. It's finer than the finest work of art—than a Greek bas-relief, than a great Titian, than a Gothic cathedral. It's very pleasant to be so well treated where one had least looked for it. I had never been more blue, more bored, than for a week before she came; I had never expected less that anything pleasant would happen. Suddenly I receive a Titian, by the post, to hang on my wall—a Greek bas-relief to stick over my chimney-piece. The key of a beautiful edifice is thrust into my hand, and I'm told to walk in and admire. My poor boy, you've been sadly ungrateful, and now you had better keep very quiet and never grumble again.' The sentiment of these reflexions was very just; but it was not exactly true that Ralph Touchett had had a key put into his hand. His cousin was a very brilliant girl, who would take, as he said, a good deal of knowing; but she needed the knowing, and his attitude with regard to her, though it was contemplative and critical, was not judicial. He surveyed the edifice from the outside and admired it greatly; he looked in at the windows and received an impression of proportions equally fair. But he felt that he saw it only by glimpses and that he had not yet stood under the roof. The door was fastened, and though he had keys in his pocket he had a conviction that none of them would fit. She was intelligent and generous; it was a fine free nature; but what was she going to do with herself? This question was irregular, for with most women one had no occasion to ask it. Most women did with themselves nothing at all; they waited, in attitudes more or less gracefully passive, for a man to come that way and furnish them with a destiny. Isabel's originality was that she gave one an impression of having intentions of her own. 'Whenever she executes them,' said Ralph, 'may I be there to see!'

It devolved upon him of course to do the honours of the place. Mr Touchett was confined to his chair, and his wife's position was that of rather a grim visitor; so that in the line of conduct that opened itself to Ralph duty and inclination were harmoniously mixed. He was not a great walker, but he strolled about the grounds with his cousin—a pastime for which the weather remained favourable with a persistency not allowed for in Isabel's somewhat lugubrious prevision of the climate; and in the long afternoons, of which the length was but the measure of her gratified eagerness, they took a boat on the river, the dear little river, as Isabel called it, where the opposite shore seemed still a part of the foreground of the landscape; or drove over the country in a phaeton—a low, capacious, thick-wheeled phaeton formerly much used by Mr Touchett, but which he had now ceased to enjoy. Isabel enjoyed it largely and, handling the reins in a manner which approved itself to the groom as 'knowing,' was never weary of driving her uncle's capital horses through winding lanes and byways full of the rural incidents she had confidently expected to find; past cottages thatched and timbered, past ale-houses latticed and sanded, past patches of ancient common and glimpses of empty parks, between hedgerows made thick by midsummer. When they reached home they usually found tea had been served on the lawn and that Mrs Touchett had not shrunk from the extremity of handing her husband his cup. But the two for the most part sat silent; the old man with his head back and his eyes closed, his wife occupied with her knitting and wearing that appearance of rare profundity with which some ladies consider the movement of their needles.

One day, however, a visitor had arrived. The two young persons, after spending an hour on the river, strolled back to the house and perceived Lord Warburton sitting under the trees and engaged in conversation, of which even at a distance the desultory character was appreciable, with Mrs Touchett. He had driven over from his own place with a portmanteau and had asked, as the father and son often invited him to do, for a dinner and a lodging. Isabel, seeing him for half an hour on the day of her arrival, had discovered in this brief space that she liked him; he had indeed rather sharply registered himself on her fine sense and she had thought of him several times. She had hoped she should see him again—hoped too that she should see a few others. Gardencourt was not dull; the place itself was sovereign, her uncle was more and more a sort of golden grandfather, and Ralph was unlike any cousin she had ever encountered—her idea of cousins having tended to gloom. Then her impressions were still so fresh and so quickly renewed that there was as yet hardly a hint of vacancy in the view. But Isabel had need to remind herself that she was interested in human nature and that her foremost hope in coming abroad had been that she should see a great many people. When Ralph said to her, as he had done several times, 'I wonder you find this endurable; you ought to see some of the neighbours and some of our friends, because we have really got a few, though you would never suppose it'—when he offered to invite what he called a 'lot of people' and make her acquainted with English society, she encouraged the hospitable impulse and promised in advance to hurl herself into the fray. Little, however, for the present, had come of his offers, and it may be confided to the reader that if the young man delayed to carry them out it was because he found the labour of providing for his companion by no means so severe as to require extraneous help. Isabel had spoken to him very often about 'specimens;' it was a word that played a considerable part in her vocabulary; she had given him to understand that she wished to see English society illustrated by eminent cases.

'Well now, there's a specimen,' he said to her as they walked up from the riverside and he recognised Lord Warburton.

'A specimen of what?' asked the girl.

'A specimen of an English gentleman.'

'Do you mean they're all like him?'

'Oh no; they're not all like him.'

'He's a favourable specimen then,' said Isabel; 'because I'm sure he's nice.'

'Yes, he's very nice. And he's very fortunate.'

The fortunate Lord Warburton exchanged a hand-shake with our heroine and hoped she was very well. 'But I needn't ask that,' he said, 'since you've been handling the oars.'

'I've been rowing a little,' Isabel answered; 'but how should you know it?'

'Oh, I know *he* doesn't row; he's too lazy,' said his lordship, indicating Ralph Touchett with a laugh.

'He has a good excuse for his laziness,' Isabel rejoined, lowering her voice a little.

'Ah, he has a good excuse for everything!' cried Lord Warburton, still with his sonorous mirth.

'My excuse for not rowing is that my cousin rows so well,' said Ralph. 'She does everything well. She touches nothing that she doesn't adorn!'

'It makes one want to be touched, Miss Archer,' Lord Warburton declared.

'Be touched in the right sense and you'll never look the worse for it,' said Isabel, who, if it pleased her to hear it said that her accomplishments were numerous, was happily able to reflect that such complacency was not the indication of a feeble mind, inasmuch as there were several things in which she excelled. Her desire to think well of herself had at least the element of humility that it always needed to be supported by proof.

Lord Warburton not only spent the night at Gardencourt, but he was persuaded to remain over the second day; and when the second day was ended he determined to postpone his departure till the morrow. During this period he addressed many of his remarks to Isabel, who accepted this evidence of his esteem with a very good grace. She found herself liking him extremely; the first impression he had made on her had had weight, but at the end of an evening spent in his society she scarce fell short of seeing him—though quite without luridity—as a hero of romance. She retired to rest with a sense of good fortune, with a quickened consciousness of possible felicities. 'It's very nice to know two such charming people as those,' she said, meaning by 'those' her cousin and her cousin's friend. It must be added moreover that an incident had occurred which might have seemed to put her good-humour to the test. Mr Touchett went to bed at half-past nine o'clock, but his wife remained in the drawing-room with the other members of the party. She prolonged her vigil for something less than an hour, and then, rising, observed to Isabel that it was time they should bid the gentlemen good-night. Isabel had as yet no desire to go to bed; the occasion wore, to her sense, a festive character, and feasts were not in the habit of terminating so early. So, without further thought, she replied, very simply—

'Need I go, dear aunt? I'll come up in half an hour.'

'It's impossible I should wait for you,' Mrs Touchett answered.

'Ah, you needn't wait! Ralph will light my candle,' Isabel gaily engaged.

'I'll light your candle; do let me light your candle, Miss Archer!' Lord Warburton exclaimed. 'Only I beg it shall not be before midnight.'

Mrs Touchett fixed her bright little eyes upon him a moment and transferred them coldly to her niece. 'You can't stay alone with the gentlemen. You're not—you're not at your blest Albany, my dear.'

Isabel rose, blushing. 'I wish I were,' she said.

'Oh, I say, mother!' Ralph broke out.

'My dear Mrs Touchett!' Lord Warburton murmured.

'I didn't make your country, my lord,' Mrs Touchett said majestically. 'I must take it as I find it.'

'Can't I stay with my own cousin?' Isabel enquired.

'I'm not aware that Lord Warburton is your cousin.'

'Perhaps *I* had better go to bed!' the visitor suggested. 'That will arrange it.'

Mrs Touchett gave a little look of despair and sat down again. 'Oh, if it's necessary I'll stay up till midnight.'

Ralph meanwhile handed Isabel her candlestick. He had been watching her; it had seemed to him her temper was involved—an accident that might be interesting. But if he had expected anything of a flare he was disappointed, for the girl simply laughed a little, nodded good-night and withdrew accompanied by her aunt. For himself he was annoyed at his mother, though he thought she was right. Above-stairs the two ladies separated at Mrs Touchett's door. Isabel had said nothing on her way up.

'Of course you're vexed at my interfering with you,' said Mrs Touchett.

Isabel considered. 'I'm not vexed, but I'm surprised—and a good deal mystified. Wasn't it proper I should remain in the drawing-room?'

'Not in the least. Young girls here—in decent houses—don't sit alone with the gentlemen late at night.'

'You were very right to tell me then,' said Isabel. 'I don't understand it, but I'm very glad to know it.'

'I shall always tell you,' her aunt answered, 'whenever I see you taking what seems to me too much liberty.'

'Pray do; but I don't say I shall always think your remonstrance just.'

'Very likely not. You're too fond of your own ways.'

'Yes, I think I'm very fond of them. But I always want to know the things one shouldn't do.'

'So as to do them?' asked her aunt.

'So as to choose,' said Isabel.

VIII

As she was devoted to romantic effects Lord Warburton ventured to express a hope that she would come some day and see his house, a very curious old place. He extracted from Mrs Touchett a promise that she would bring her niece to Lockleigh, and Ralph signified his willingness to attend the ladies if his father should be able to spare him. Lord Warburton assured our heroine that in the mean time his sisters would come and see her. She knew something about his sisters, having sounded him, during the hours they spent together while he was at Gardencourt, on many points connected with his family. When Isabel was interested she asked a great many questions, and as her companion was a copious talker she urged him on this occasion by no means in vain. He told her he had four sisters and two brothers and had lost both his parents. The brothers and sisters were very good people—'not particularly clever, you know,' he said, 'but very decent and pleasant;' and he was so good as to hope Miss Archer might know them well. One of the brothers was in the Church, settled in the family living, that of Lockleigh, which was a heavy, sprawling parish, and was an excellent fellow in spite of his thinking differently from himself on every conceivable topic. And then Lord Warburton mentioned some of the opinions held by his brother, which were opinions Isabel had often heard expressed and that she supposed to be entertained by a considerable portion of the human family. Many of them indeed she supposed she had held herself, till he assured her she was quite mistaken, that it was really impossible, that she had doubtless imagined she entertained them, but that she might depend that, if she thought them over a little, she would find there was nothing in them. When she answered that she had already thought several of the questions involved over very attentively he declared that she was only another example of what he had often been struck with—the fact that, of all the people in the world, the Americans were the most grossly superstitious. They were rank Tories and bigots, every one of them; there were no conservatives like American conservatives. Her uncle and her cousin were there to prove it; nothing could be more mediæval than many of their views; they had ideas that people in England nowadays were ashamed to confess to; and they had the impudence moreover, said his lordship, laughing, to pretend they knew more about the needs and dangers of this poor dear stupid old England than he who was born in it and owned a considerable slice of it—the more shame to him! From all of which Isabel gathered that Lord Warburton was a nobleman of the newest pattern, a reformer, a radical, a contemner of ancient ways. His other brother, who was in the army in India, was rather wild and pig-headed and had not been of much use as yet but to make debts for Warburton to pay—one of the most precious privileges of an elder brother. 'I don't think I shall pay any more,' said her friend; 'he lives a monstrous deal better than I do, enjoys unheard-of luxuries and thinks himself a much finer gentleman than I. As I'm a consistent radical I go in only for equality; I don't go in for the superiority of the younger brothers.' Two of his four sisters, the second and fourth, were married, one of them having done very well, as they said, the other only so-so. The husband of the elder, Lord Haycock, was a very good fellow, but unfortunately a horrid Tory; and his wife, like all good English wives, was worse than her husband. The other had espoused a smallish squire in Norfolk and, though married but the other day, had already five children. This information and much more Lord Warburton imparted to his young American listener, taking pains to make many things clear and to lay bare to her apprehension the peculiarities of English life. Isabel was often amused at his explicitness and at the small allowance he seemed to make either for her own experience or for her imagination. 'He thinks I'm a barbarian,' she said, 'and that I've never seen forks and spoons;' and she used to ask him artless questions for the pleasure of hearing him answer seriously. Then when he had fallen into the trap, 'It's a pity you can't see me in my war-paint and feathers,' she remarked; 'if I had known how kind you are to the poor savages I would have brought over my native costume!' Lord Warburton had travelled through the United States and knew much more about them than Isabel; he was so good as to say that America was the most charming country in the world, but his recollections of it appeared to encourage the idea that Americans in England would need to have a great many things explained to them. 'If I had only had you to explain things to me in America!' he said. 'I was rather puzzled in your country; in fact I was quite bewildered, and the trouble was that the explanations only puzzled me more. You know I think they often gave me the wrong ones on purpose; they're rather clever about that over there. But when I explain you can trust me; about what I tell you there's no mistake.' There was no mistake at least about his being very intelligent and cultivated and knowing almost everything in the world. Although he gave the most interesting and thrilling glimpses Isabel felt he never did it to exhibit himself, and though he had had rare chances and had tumbled in, as she put it, for high prizes, he was as far as possible from making a merit of it. He had enjoyed the best things of life, but they had not spoiled his sense of proportion. His quality was a mixture of the effect of rich experience—oh, so easily come by!—with a modesty at times almost boyish; the sweet and wholesome savour of which—it was as agreeable as something tasted—lost nothing from the addition of a tone of responsible kindness.

'I like your specimen English gentleman very much,' Isabel said to Ralph after Lord Warburton had gone.

'I like him too—I love him well,' Ralph returned. 'But I pity him more.'

Isabel looked at him askance. 'Why, that seems to me his only fault—that one can't pity him a little. He appears to have everything, to know everything, to *be* everything.'

'Oh, he's in a bad way!' Ralph insisted.

'I suppose you don't mean in health?'

'No, as to that he's detestably sound. What I mean is that he's a man with a great position who's playing all sorts of tricks with it. He doesn't take himself seriously.'

'Does he regard himself as a joke?'

'Much worse; he regards himself as an imposition—as an abuse.'

'Well, perhaps he is,' said Isabel.

'Perhaps he is—though on the whole I don't think so. But in that case what's more pitiable than a sentient, self-conscious abuse planted by other hands, deeply rooted but aching with a sense of its injustice? For me, in his place, I could be as solemn as a statue of Buddha. He occupies a position that appeals to my imagination. Great responsibilities, great opportunities, great consideration, great wealth, great power, a natural share in the public affairs of a great country. But he's all in a muddle about himself, his position, his power, and indeed about everything in the world. He's the victim of a critical age; he has ceased to believe in himself and he doesn't know what to believe in. When I attempt to tell him (because if I were he I know very well what I should believe in) he calls me a pampered bigot. I believe he seriously thinks me an awful Philistine; he says I don't understand my time. I understand it certainly better than he, who can neither abolish himself as a nuisance nor maintain himself as an institution.'

'He doesn't look very wretched,' Isabel observed.

'Possibly not; though, being a man of a good deal of charming taste, I think he often has uncomfortable hours. But what is it to say of a being of his opportunities that he's not miserable? Besides, I believe he is.'

'I don't,' said Isabel.

'Well,' her cousin rejoined, 'if he isn't he ought to be!'

In the afternoon she spent an hour with her uncle on the lawn, where the old man sat, as usual, with his shawl over his legs and his large cup of diluted tea in his hands. In the course of conversation he asked her what she thought of their late visitor.

Isabel was prompt. 'I think he's charming.'

'He's a nice person,' said Mr Touchett, 'but I don't recommend you to fall in love with him.'

'I shall not do it then; I shall never fall in love but on your recommendation. Moreover,' Isabel added, 'my cousin gives me rather a sad account of Lord Warburton.'

'Oh, indeed? I don't know what there may be to say, but you must remember that Ralph *must* talk.'

'He thinks your friend's too subversive—or not subversive enough! I don't quite understand which,' said Isabel.

The old man shook his head slowly, smiled and put down his cup. 'I don't know which either. He goes very far, but it's quite possible he doesn't go far enough. He seems to want to do away with a good many things, but he seems to want to remain himself. I suppose that's natural, but it's rather inconsistent.'

'Oh, I hope he'll remain himself,' said Isabel. 'If he were to be done away with his friends would miss him sadly.'

'Well,' said the old man, 'I guess he'll stay and amuse his friends. I should certainly miss him very much here at Gardencourt. He always amuses me when he comes over, and I think he amuses himself as well. There's a considerable number like him, round in society; they're very fashionable just now. I don't know what they're trying to do—whether they're trying to get up a revolution. I hope at any rate they'll put it off till after I'm gone. You see they want to disestablish everything; but I'm a pretty big landowner here, and I don't want to be disestablished. I wouldn't have come over if I had thought they were going to behave like that,' Mr Touchett went on with expanding hilarity. 'I came over because I thought England was a safe country. I call it a regular fraud if they are going to introduce any considerable changes; there'll be a large number disappointed in that case.'

'Oh, I do hope they'll make a revolution!' Isabel exclaimed. 'I should delight in seeing a revolution.'

'Let me see,' said her uncle, with a humorous intention; 'I forget whether you're on the side of the old or on the side of the new. I've heard you take such opposite views.'

'I'm on the side of both. I guess I'm a little on the side of everything. In a revolution—after it was well begun—I think I should be a high, proud loyalist. One sympathises more with them, and they've a chance to behave so exquisitely. I mean so picturesquely.'

'I don't know that I understand what you mean by behaving picturesquely, but it seems to me that you do that always, my dear.'

'Oh, you lovely man, if I could believe that!' the girl interrupted.

'I'm afraid, after all, you won't have the pleasure of going gracefully to the guillotine here just now,' Mr Touchett went on. 'If you want to see a big outbreak you must pay us a long visit. You see, when you come to the point it wouldn't suit them to be taken at their word.'

'Of whom are you speaking?'

'Well, I mean Lord Warburton and his friends—the radicals of the upper class. Of course I only know the way it strikes me. They talk about the changes, but I don't think they quite realise. You and I, you know, we know what it is to have lived under democratic institutions: I always thought them very comfortable, but I was used to them from the first. And then I ain't a lord; you're a lady, my dear, but I ain't a lord. Now over here I don't think it quite comes home to them. It's a matter of every day and every hour, and I don't think many of them would find it as pleasant as what they've got. Of course if they want to try, it's their own business; but I expect they won't try very hard.'

'Don't you think they're sincere?' Isabel asked.

'Well, they want to *feel* earnest,' Mr Touchett allowed; 'but it seems as if they took it out in theories mostly. Their radical views are a kind of amusement; they've got to have some amusement, and they might have coarser tastes than that. You see they're very luxurious, and these progressive ideas are about their biggest luxury. They make them feel moral and yet don't damage their position. They think a great deal of their position; don't let one of them ever persuade you he doesn't, for if you were to proceed on that basis you'd be pulled up very short.'

Isabel followed her uncle's argument, which he unfolded with his quaint distinctness, most attentively, and though she was unacquainted with the British aristocracy she found it in harmony with her general impressions of human nature. But she felt moved to put in a protest on Lord Warburton's behalf. 'I don't believe Lord Warburton's a humbug; I don't care what the others are. I should like to see Lord Warburton put to the test.'

'Heaven deliver me from my friends!' Mr Touchett answered. 'Lord Warburton's a very amiable young man—a very fine young man. He has a hundred thousand a year. He owns fifty thousand acres of the soil of this little island and ever so many other things besides. He has half a dozen houses to live in. He has a seat in Parliament as I have one at my own dinner-table. He has elegant tastes—cares for literature, for art, for science, for charming young ladies. The most elegant is his taste for the new views. It affords him a great deal of pleasure—more perhaps than anything else, except the young ladies. His old house over there—what does he call it, Lockleigh?—is very attractive; but I don't think it's as pleasant as this. That doesn't matter, however—he has so many others. His views don't hurt any one as far as I can see; they certainly don't hurt himself. And if there were to be a revolution he would come off very easily. They wouldn't touch him, they'd leave him as he is: he's too much liked.'

'Ah, he couldn't be a martyr even if he wished!' Isabel sighed. 'That's a very poor position.'

'He'll never be a martyr unless you make him one,' said the old man.

Isabel shook her head; there might have been something laughable in the fact that she did it with a touch of melancholy. 'I shall never make any one a martyr.'

'You'll never be one, I hope.'

'I hope not. But you don't pity Lord Warburton then as Ralph does?'

Her uncle looked at her a while with genial acuteness. 'Yes, I do, after all!'

IX

THE two Misses Molyneux, this nobleman's sisters, came presently to call upon her, and Isabel took a fancy to the young ladies, who appeared to her to show a most original stamp. It is true that when she described them to her cousin by that term he declared that no epithet could be less applicable than this to the two Misses Molyneux, since there were fifty thousand young women in England who exactly resembled them. Deprived of this advantage, however, Isabel's visitors retained that of an extreme sweetness and shyness of demeanour, and of having, as she thought, eyes like the balanced basins, the circles of 'ornamental water,' set, in parterres, among the geraniums.

'They're not morbid, at any rate, whatever they are,' our heroine said to herself; and she deemed this a great charm, for two or three of the friends of her girlhood had been regrettably open to the charge (they would have been so nice without it), to say nothing of Isabel's having occasionally suspected it as a tendency of her own. The Misses Molyneux were not in their first youth, but they had bright, fresh complexions and something of the smile of childhood. Yes, their eyes, which Isabel admired, were round, quiet and contented, and their figures, also of a generous roundness, were encased in sealskin jackets. Their friendliness was great, so great that they were almost embarrassed to show it; they seemed somewhat afraid of the young lady from the other side of the world and rather looked than spoke their good wishes. But they made it clear to her that they hoped she would come to luncheon at Lockleigh, where they lived with their brother, and then they might see her very, very often. They wondered if she wouldn't come over some day and sleep: they were expecting some people on the twenty-ninth, so perhaps she would come while the people were there.

'I'm afraid it isn't any one very remarkable,' said the elder sister; 'but I dare say you'll take us as you find us.'

'I shall find you delightful; I think you're enchanting just as you are,' replied Isabel, who often praised profusely.

Her visitors flushed, and her cousin told her, after they were gone, that if she said such things to those poor girls they would think she was in some wild, free manner practising on them: he was sure it was the first time they had been called enchanting.

'I can't help it,' Isabel answered. 'I think it's lovely to be so quiet and reasonable and satisfied. I should like to be like that.'

'Heaven forbid!' cried Ralph with ardour.

'I mean to try and imitate them,' said Isabel. 'I want very much to see them at home.'

She had this pleasure a few days later, when, with Ralph and his mother, she drove over to Lockleigh. She found the Misses Molyneux sitting in a vast drawing-room (she perceived afterwards it was one of several) in a wilderness of faded chintz; they were dressed on this occasion in black velveteen. Isabel liked them even better at home than she had done at Gardencourt, and was more than ever struck with the fact that they were not morbid. It had seemed to her before that if they had a fault it was a want of play of mind; but she presently saw they were capable of deep emotion. Before luncheon she was alone with them for some time, on one side of the room, while Lord Warburton, at a distance, talked to Mrs Touchett.

'Is it true your brother's such a great radical?' Isabel asked. She knew it was true, but we have seen that her interest in human nature was keen, and she had a desire to draw the Misses Molyneux out.

'Oh dear, yes; he's immensely advanced,' said Mildred, the younger sister.

'At the same time Warburton's very reasonable,' Miss Molyneux observed.

Isabel watched him a moment at the other side of the room; he was clearly trying hard to make himself agreeable to Mrs Touchett. Ralph had met the frank advances of one of the dogs before the fire that the temperature of an English August, in the ancient expanses, had not made an impertinence. 'Do you suppose your brother's sincere?' Isabel enquired with a smile.

'Oh, he must be, you know!' Mildred exclaimed quickly, while the elder sister gazed at our heroine in silence.

'Do you think he would stand the test?'

'The test?'

'I mean for instance having to give up all this.'

'Having to give up Lockleigh?' said Miss Molyneux, finding her voice.

'Yes, and the other places; what are they called?'

The two sisters exchanged an almost frightened glance. 'Do you mean—do you mean on account of the expense?' the younger one asked.

'I dare say he might let one or two of his houses,' said the other.

'Let them for nothing?' Isabel demanded.

'I can't fancy his giving up his property,' said Miss Molyneux.

'Ah, I'm afraid he is an imposter!' Isabel returned. 'Don't you think it's a false position?'

Her companions, evidently, had lost themselves. 'My brother's position?' Miss Molyneux enquired.

'It's thought a very good position,' said the younger sister. 'It's the first position in this part of the county.'

'I dare say you think me very irreverent,' Isabel took occasion to remark. 'I suppose you revere your brother and are rather afraid of him.'

'Of course one looks up to one's brother,' said Miss Molyneux simply.

'If you do that he must be very good—because you, evidently, are beautifully good.'

'He's most kind. It will never be known, the good he does.'

'His ability is known,' Mildred added; 'every one thinks it's immense.'

'Oh, I can see that,' said Isabel. 'But if I were he I should wish to fight to the death: I mean for the heritage of the past. I should hold it tight.'

'I think one ought to be liberal,' Mildred argued gently. 'We've always been so, even from the earliest times.'

'Ah well,' said Isabel, 'you've made a great success of it; I don't wonder you like it. I see you're very fond of crewels.'

When Lord Warburton showed her the house, after luncheon, it seemed to her a matter of course that it should be a noble picture. Within, it had been a good deal modernised—

some of its best points had lost their purity; but as they saw it from the gardens, a stout grey pile, of the softest, deepest, most weather-fretted hue, rising from a broad, still moat, it affected the young visitor as a castle in a legend. The day was cool and rather lustreless; the first note of autumn had been struck, and the watery sunshine rested on the walls in blurred and desultory gleams, washing them, as it were, in places tenderly chosen, where the ache of antiquity was keenest. Her host's brother, the Vicar, had come to luncheon, and Isabel had had five minutes' talk with him—time enough to institute a search for a rich ecclesiasticism and give it up as vain. The marks of the Vicar of Lockleigh were a big, athletic figure, a candid, natural countenance, a capacious appetite and a tendency to indiscriminate laughter. Isabel learned afterwards from her cousin that before taking orders he had been a mighty wrestler and that he was still, on occasion—in the privacy of the family circle as it were—quite capable of flooring his man. Isabel liked him—she was in the mood for liking everything; but her imagination was a good deal taxed to think of him as a source of spiritual aid. The whole party, on leaving lunch, went to walk in the grounds; but Lord Warburton exercised some ingenuity in engaging his least familiar guest in a stroll apart from the others.

'I wish you to see the place properly, seriously,' he said. 'You can't do so if your attention is distracted by irrelevant gossip.' His own conversation (though he told Isabel a good deal about the house, which had a very curious history) was not purely archæological; he reverted at intervals to matters more personal—matters personal to the young lady as well as to himself. But at last, after a pause of some duration, returning for a moment to their ostensible theme, 'Ah, well,' he said, 'I'm very glad indeed you like the old barrack. I wish you could see more of it—that you could stay here a while. My sisters have taken an immense fancy to you—if that would be any inducement.'

'There's no want of inducements,' Isabel answered; 'but I'm afraid I can't make engagements. I'm quite in my aunt's hands.'

'Ah, pardon me if I say I don't exactly believe that. I'm pretty sure you can do whatever you want.'

'I'm sorry if I make that impression on you; I don't think it's a nice impression to make.'

'It has the merit of permitting me to hope.' And Lord Warburton paused a moment.

'To hope what?'

'That in future I may see you often.'

'Ah,' said Isabel, 'to enjoy that pleasure I needn't be so terribly emancipated.'

'Doubtless not; and yet, at the same time, I don't think your uncle likes me.'

'You're very much mistaken. I've heard him speak very highly of you.'

'I'm glad you have talked about me,' said Lord Warburton. 'But, I nevertheless don't think he'd like me to keep coming to Gardencourt.'

'I can't answer for my uncle's tastes,' the girl rejoined, 'though I ought as far as possible to take them into account. But for myself I shall be very glad to see you.'

'Now that's what I like to hear you say. I'm charmed when you say that.'

'You're easily charmed, my lord,' said Isabel.

'No, I'm not easily charmed!' And then he stopped a moment. 'But you've charmed me, Miss Archer.'

These words were uttered with an indefinable sound which startled the girl; it struck her as the prelude to something grave: she had heard the sound before and she recognised it. She had no wish, however, that for the moment such a prelude should have a sequel, and she said as gaily as possible and as quickly as an appreciable degree of agitation would allow her: 'I'm afraid there's no prospect of my being able to come here again.'

'Never?' said Lord Warburton.

'I won't say "never"; I should feel very melodramatic.'

'May I come and see you then some day next week?'

'Most assuredly. What is there to prevent it?'

'Nothing tangible. But with you I never feel safe. I've a sort of sense that you're always summing people up.'

'You don't of necessity lose by that.'

'It's very kind of you to say so; but, even if I gain, stern justice is not what I most love. Is Mrs Touchett going to take you abroad?'

'I hope so.'

'Is England not good enough for you?'

'That's a very Machiavellian speech; it doesn't deserve an answer. I want to see as many countries as I can.'

'Then you'll go on judging, I suppose.'

'Enjoying, I hope, too.'

'Yes, that's what you enjoy most; I can't make out what you're up to,' said Lord Warburton. 'You strike me as having mysterious purposes—vast designs.'

'You're so good as to have a theory about me which I don't at all fill out. Is there anything mysterious in a purpose entertained and executed every year, in the most public manner, by fifty thousand of my fellow-countrymen—the purpose of improving one's mind by foreign travel?'

'You can't improve your mind, Miss Archer,' her companion declared. 'It's already a most formidable instrument. It looks down on us all; it despises us.'

'Despises you? You're making fun of me,' said Isabel seriously.

'Well, you think us "quaint"—that's the same thing. I won't be thought "quaint," to begin with; I'm not so in the least. I protest.'

'That protest is one of the quaintest things I've ever heard,' Isabel answered with a smile.

Lord Warburton was briefly silent. 'You judge only from the outside—you don't care,' he said presently. 'You only care to amuse yourself.' The note she had heard in his voice a moment before reappeared, and mixed with it now was an audible strain of bitterness—a bitterness so abrupt and inconsequent that the girl was afraid she had hurt him. She had often heard that the English are a highly eccentric people, and she had even read in some ingenious author that they are at bottom the most romantic of races. Was Lord Warburton suddenly turning romantic—was he going to make her a scene, in his own house, only the third time they had met? She was reassured quickly enough by her sense of his great good manners, which was not impaired by the fact that he had already touched the furthest limit of good taste in expressing his admiration of a young lady who had confided in his hospitality. She was right in trusting to his good manners, for he presently went on, laughing a little and without a trace of the accent that had discomposed her: 'I don't mean of course that you amuse yourself with trifles. You select great materials; the foibles, the afflictions of human nature, the peculiarities of nations!'

'As regards that,' said Isabel, 'I should find in my own nation entertainment for a lifetime. But we've a long drive, and my aunt will soon wish to start.' She turned back toward the others and Lord Warburton walked beside her in silence. But before they reached the others, 'I shall come and see you next week,' he said.

She had received an appreciable shock, but as it died away she felt that she couldn't pretend to herself that it was altogether a painful one. Nevertheless she made answer to his declaration, coldly enough, 'Just as you please.' And her coldness was not the calculation of her effect—a game she played in a much smaller degree than would have seemed probable to many critics. It came from a certain fear.

X

THE day after her visit to Lockleigh she received a note from her friend Miss Stackpole—a note of which the envelope, exhibiting in conjunction the postmark of Liverpool and the neat calligraphy of the quick-fingered Henrietta, caused her some liveliness of emotion. 'Here I am, my lovely friend,' Miss Stackpole wrote; 'I managed to get off at last. I decided only the night before I left New York—the *Interviewer* having come round to my figure. I put a few things into a bag, like a veteran journalist, and came down to the steamer in a street-car. Where are you and where can we meet? I suppose you're visiting at some castle or other and have already acquired the correct accent. Perhaps even you have married a lord; I almost hope you have, for I want some introductions to the first people and shall count on you for a few. The *Interviewer* wants some light on the nobility. My first impressions (of the people at large) are not rose-coloured; but I wish to talk them over with you, and you know that, whatever I am, at least I'm not superficial. I've also something very particular to tell you. Do appoint a meeting as quickly as you can; come to London (I should like so much to visit the sights with you) or else let me come to you, *wherever you are*. I will do so with pleasure; for you know everything interests me and I wish to see as much as possible of the inner life.'

Isabel judged best not to show this letter to her uncle; but she acquainted him with its purport, and, as she expected, he begged her instantly to assure Miss Stackpole, in his name, that he should be delighted to receive her at Gardencourt. 'Though she's a literary lady,' he said, 'I suppose that, being an American, she won't show me up, as that other one did. She has seen others like me.'

'She has seen no other so delightful!' Isabel answered; but she was not altogether at ease about Henrietta's reproductive instincts, which belonged to that side of her friend's character which she regarded with least complacency. She wrote to Miss Stackpole, however, that she would be very welcome under

Mr Touchett's roof; and this alert young woman lost no time in announcing her prompt approach. She had gone up to London, and it was from that centre that she took the train for the station nearest to Gardencourt, where Isabel and Ralph were in waiting to receive her.

'Shall I love her or shall I hate her?' Ralph asked while they moved along the platform.

'Whichever you do will matter very little to her,' said Isabel. 'She doesn't care a straw what men think of her.'

'As a man I'm bound to dislike her then. She must be a kind of monster. Is she very ugly?'

'No, she's decidedly pretty.'

'A female interviewer—a reporter in petticoats? I'm very curious to see her,' Ralph conceded. 'It's very easy to laugh at her but it is not easy to be as brave as she.'

'I should think not; crimes of violence and attacks on the person require more or less pluck. Do you suppose she'll interview *me*?'

'Never in the world. She'll not think you of enough importance.'

'You'll see,' said Ralph. 'She'll send a description of us all, including Bunchie, to her newspaper.'

'I shall ask her not to,' Isabel answered.

'You think she's capable of it then?'

'Perfectly.'

'And yet you've made her your bosom-friend?'

'I've not made her my bosom-friend; but I like her in spite of her faults.'

'Ah well,' said Ralph, 'I'm afraid I shall dislike her in spite of her merits.'

'You'll probably fall in love with her at the end of three days.'

'And have my love-letters published in the *Interviewer*? Never!' cried the young man.

The train presently arrived, and Miss Stackpole, promptly descending, proved, as Isabel had promised, quite delicately, even though rather provincially, fair. She was a neat, plump person, of medium stature, with a round face, a small mouth, a delicate complexion, a bunch of light brown ringlets at the back of her head and a peculiarly open, surprised-looking eye. The most striking point in her appearance was the remarkable fixedness of this organ, which rested without impudence or defiance, but as if in conscientious exercise of a natural right, upon every object it happened to encounter. It rested in this manner upon Ralph himself, a little arrested by Miss Stackpole's gracious and comfortable aspect, which hinted that it wouldn't be so easy as he had assumed to disapprove of her. She rustled, she shimmered, in fresh, dove-coloured draperies, and Ralph saw at a glance that she was as crisp and new and comprehensive as a first issue before the folding. From top to toe she had probably no misprint. She spoke in a clear, high voice—a voice not rich but loud; yet after she had taken her place with her companions in Mr Touchett's carriage she struck him as not all in the large type, the type of horrid 'headings,' that he had expected. She answered the enquiries made of her by Isabel, however, and in which the young man ventured to join, with copious lucidity; and later, in the library at Gardencourt, when she had made the acquaintance of Mr Touchett (his wife not having thought it necessary to appear) did more to give the measure of her confidence in her powers. 'Well, I should like to know whether you consider yourselves American or English,' she broke out. 'If once I knew I could talk to you accordingly.'

'Talk to us anyhow and we shall be thankful,' Ralph liberally answered.

She fixed her eyes on him, and there was something in their character that reminded him of large polished buttons—buttons that might have fixed the elastic loops of some tense receptacle: he seemed to see the reflection of surrounding objects on the pupil. The expression of a button is not usually deemed human, but there was something in Miss Stackpole's gaze that made him, as a very modest man, feel vaguely embarrassed—less inviolate, more dishonoured, than he liked. This sensation, it must be added, after he had spent a day or two in her company, sensibly diminished, though it never wholly lapsed. 'I don't suppose that you're going to undertake to persuade me that *you're* an American,' she said.

'To please you I'll be an Englishman, I'll be a Turk!'

'Well, if you can change about that way you're very welcome,' Miss Stackpole returned.

'I'm sure you understand everything and that differences of nationality are no barrier to you,' Ralph went on.

Miss Stackpole gazed at him still. 'Do you mean the foreign languages?'

'The languages are nothing. I mean the spirit—the genius.'

'I'm not sure that I understand you,' said the correspondent of the *Interviewer*, 'but I expect I shall before I leave.'

'He's what's called a cosmopolite,' Isabel suggested.

'That means he's a little of everything and not much of any. I must say I think patriotism is like charity—it begins at home.'

'Ah, but where does home begin, Miss Stackpole?' Ralph enquired.

'I don't know where it begins, but I know where it ends. It ended a long time before I got here.'

'Don't you like it over here?' asked Mr Touchett with his aged, innocent voice.

'Well, sir, I haven't quite made up my mind what ground I shall take. I feel a good deal cramped. I felt it on the journey from Liverpool to London.'

'Perhaps you were in a crowded carriage,' Ralph suggested.

'Yes, but it was crowded with friends—a party of Americans whose acquaintance I had made upon the steamer; a lovely group from Little Rock, Arkansas. In spite of that I felt cramped—I felt something pressing upon me; I couldn't tell what it was. I felt at the very commencement as if I were not going to accord with the atmosphere. But I suppose I shall make my own atmosphere. That's the true way—then you can breathe. Your surroundings seem very attractive.'

'Ah, we too are a lovely group!' said Ralph. 'Wait a little and you'll see.'

Miss Stackpole showed every disposition to wait and evidently was prepared to make a considerable stay at Gardencourt. She occupied herself in the mornings with literary labour; but in spite of this Isabel spent many hours with her friend, who, once her daily task performed, deprecated, in fact defied, isolation. Isabel speedily found occasion to desire her to desist from celebrating the charms of their common sojourn in print, having discovered, on the second morning of Miss Stackpole's visit, that she was engaged on a letter to the *Interviewer*, of which the title, in her exquisitely neat and legible hand (exactly that of the copybooks which our heroine remembered at school) was 'Americans and Tudors—Glimpses of Gardencourt.' Miss Stackpole, with the best conscience in the world, offered to read her letter to Isabel, who immediately put in her protest.

'I don't think you ought to do that. I don't think you ought to describe the place.'

Henrietta gazed at her as usual. 'Why, it's just what the people want, and it's a lovely place.'

'It's too lovely to be put in the newspapers, and it's not what my uncle wants.'

'Don't you believe that!' cried Henrietta. 'They're always delighted afterwards.'

'My uncle won't be delighted—nor my cousin either. They'll consider it a breach of hospitality.'

Miss Stackpole showed no sense of confusion; she simply wiped her pen, very neatly, upon an elegant little implement which she kept for the purpose, and put away her manuscript. 'Of course if you don't approve I won't do it; but I sacrifice a beautiful subject.'

'There are plenty of other subjects, there are subjects all round you. We'll take some drives; I'll show you some charming scenery.'

'Scenery's not my department; I always need a human interest. You know I'm deeply human, Isabel; I always was,' Miss Stackpole rejoined. 'I was going to bring in your cousin—the alienated American. There's a great demand just now for the alienated American, and your cousin's a beautiful specimen. I should have handled him severly.'

'He would have died of it!' Isabel exclaimed. 'Not of the severity, but of the publicity.'

'Well, I should have liked to kill him a little. And I should have delighted to do your uncle, who seems to me a much nobler type—the American faithful still. He's a grand old man; I don't see how he can object to my paying him honour.'

Isabel looked at her companion in much wonderment; it struck her as strange that a nature in which she found so much to esteem should break down so in spots. 'My poor Henrietta,' she said, 'you've no sense of privacy.'

Henrietta coloured deeply, and for a moment her brilliant eyes were suffused, while Isabel found her more than ever inconsequent. 'You do me great injustice,' said Miss Stackpole with dignity. 'I've never written a word about myself!'

'I'm very sure of that; but it seems to me one should be modest for others also!'

'Ah, that's very good!' cried Henrietta, seizing her pen again. 'Just let me make a note of it and I'll put it in somewhere.' She was a thoroughly good-natured woman, and half an hour later she was in as cheerful a mood as should have been looked for in a newspaper-lady in want of matter. 'I've promised to do the social side,' she said to Isabel; 'and how can I do it unless I get ideas? If I can't describe this place don't you know some place I *can* describe?' Isabel promised she would bethink herself, and the next day, in conversation with her friend, she happened to mention her visit to Lord Warburton's ancient house. 'Ah, you must take me there—that's just the place for me!' Miss Stackpole cried. 'I must get a glimpse of the nobility.'

'I can't take you,' said Isabel; 'but Lord Warburton's coming here, and you'll have a chance to see him and observe him. Only if you intend to repeat his conversation I shall certainly give him warning.'

'Don't do that,' her companion pleaded; 'I want him to be natural.'

'An Englishman's never so natural as when he's holding his tongue,' Isabel declared.

It was not apparent, at the end of three days, that her cousin had, according to her prophecy, lost his heart to their visitor, though he had spent a good deal of time in her society. They strolled about the park together and sat under the trees, and in the afternoon, when it was delightful to float along the Thames, Miss Stackpole occupied a place in the boat in which hitherto Ralph had had but a single companion. Her presence proved somehow less irreducible to soft particles than Ralph had expected in the natural perturbation of his sense of the perfect solubility of that of his cousin; for the correspondent of the *Interviewer* prompted mirth in him, and he had long since decided that the *crescendo* of mirth should be the flower of his declining days. Henrietta, on her side, failed a little to justify Isabel's declaration with regard to her indifference to masculine opinion; for poor Ralph appeared to have presented himself to her as an irritating problem, which it would be almost immoral not to work out.

'What does he do for a living?' she asked of Isabel the evening of her arrival. 'Does he go round all day with his hands in his pockets?'

'He does nothing,' smiled Isabel; 'he's a gentleman of large leisure.'

'Well, I call that a shame—when I have to work like a car-conductor,'* Miss Stackpole replied. 'I should like to show him up.'

'He's in wretched health; he's quite unfit for work,' Isabel urged.

'Pshaw! don't you believe it. I work when I'm sick,' cried her friend. Later, when she stepped into the boat on joining the water-party, she remarked to Ralph that she supposed he hated her and would like to drown her.

'Ah no,' said Ralph, 'I keep my victims for a slower torture. And you'd be such an interesting one!'

'Well, you do torture me; I may say that. But I shock all your prejudices; that's one comfort.'

'My prejudices? I haven't a prejudice to bless myself with. There's intellectual poverty for you.'

'The more shame to you; I've some delicious ones. Of course I spoil your flirtation, or whatever it is you call it, with your cousin; but I don't care for that, as I render her the service of drawing you out. She'll see how thin you are.'

'Ah, do draw me out!' Ralph exclaimed. 'So few people will take the trouble.'

Miss Stackpole, in this undertaking, appeared to shrink from no effort; resorting largely, whenever the opportunity offered, to the natural expedient of interrogation. On the following day the weather was bad, and in the afternoon the young man, by way of providing indoor amusement, offered to show her the pictures. Henrietta strolled through the long gallery in his society, while he pointed out its principal ornaments and mentioned the painters and subjects. Miss Stackpole looked at the pictures in perfect silence, committing herself to no opinion, and Ralph was gratified by the fact that she delivered herself of none of the little ready-made ejaculations of delight of which the visitors to Gardencourt were so frequently lavish. This young lady indeed, to do her justice, was but little addicted to the use of conventional terms; there was something earnest and inventive in her tone, which at times, in its strained deliberation, suggested a person of high culture speaking a foreign language. Ralph Touchett subsequently learned that she had at one time officiated as art-critic to a journal of the other world; but she appeared, in spite of this fact, to carry in her pocket none of the small change of admiration. Suddenly, just after he had called her attention to a charming Constable,* she turned and looked at him as if he himself had been a picture.

'Do you always spend your time like this?' she demanded.

'I seldom spend it so agreeably.'

'Well, you know what I mean—without any regular occupation.'

'Ah,' said Ralph, 'I'm the idlest man living.'

Miss Stackpole directed her gaze to the Constable again, and Ralph bespoke her attention for a small Lancret hanging near it, which represented a gentleman in a pink doublet and hose and a ruff, leaning against the pedestal of the statue of a nymph in a garden and playing the guitar to two ladies seated on the grass. 'That's my ideal of a regular occupation,' he said.

Miss Stackpole turned to him again, and, though her eyes had rested upon the picture, he saw she had missed the subject. She was thinking of something much more serious. 'I don't see how you can reconcile it to your conscience.'

'My dear lady, I *have* no conscience!'

'Well, I advise you to cultivate one. You'll need it the next time you go to America.'

'I shall probably never go again.'

'Are you ashamed to show yourself?'

Ralph meditated with a mild smile. 'I suppose that if one has no conscience one has no shame.'

'Well, you've got plenty of assurance,' Henrietta declared. 'Do you consider it right to give up your country?'

'Ah, one doesn't give up one's country any more than one gives up one's grandmother. They're both antecedent to choice—elements of one's composition that are not to be eliminated.'

'I suppose that means that you've tried and been worsted. What do they think of you over here?'

'They delight in me.'

'That's because you truckle to them.'

'Ah, set it down a little to my natural charm!' Ralph sighed.

'I don't know anything about your natural charm. If you've got any charm it's quite unnatural. It's wholly acquired—or at least you've tried hard to acquire it, living over here. I don't say you've succeeded. It's a charm that I don't appreciate, anyway. Make yourself useful in some way, and then we'll talk about it.'

'Well, now, tell me what I shall do,' said Ralph.

'Go right home, to begin with.'

'Yes, I see. And then?'

'Take right hold of something.'

'Well, now, what sort of thing?'

'Anything you please, so long as you take hold. Some new idea, some big work.'

'Is it very difficult to take hold?' Ralph enquired.

'Not if you put your heart into it.'

'Ah, my heart,' said Ralph. 'If it depends upon my heart—!'

'Haven't you got a heart?'

'I had one a few days ago, but I've lost it since.'

'You're not serious,' Miss Stackpole remarked; 'that's what's the matter with you.' But for all this, in a day or two, she again permitted him to fix her attention and on the later occasion assigned a different cause to her mysterious perversity. 'I know what's the matter with you, Mr Touchett,' she said. 'You think you're too good to get married.'

'I thought so till I knew you, Miss Stackpole,' Ralph answered; 'and then I suddenly changed my mind.'

'Oh pshaw!' Henrietta groaned.

'Then it seemed to me,' said Ralph, 'that I was not good enough.'

'It would improve you. Besides, it's your duty.'

'Ah,' cried the young man, 'one has so many duties! Is that a duty too?'

'Of course it is—did you never know that before? It's every one's duty to get married.'

Ralph meditated a moment; he was disappointed. There was something in Miss Stackpole he had begun to like; it seemed to him that if she was not a charming woman she was at least a very good 'sort.' She was wanting in distinction, but, as Isabel had said, she was brave: she went into cages, she flourished lashes, like a spangled lion-tamer. He had not supposed her to be capable of vulgar arts, but these last words struck him as a false note. When a marriageable young woman urges matrimony on an unencumbered young man the most obvious explanation of her conduct is not the altruistic impulse.

'Ah, well now, there's a good deal to be said about that,' Ralph rejoined.

'There may be, but that's the principal thing. I must say I think it looks very exclusive, going round all alone, as if you thought no woman was good enough for you. Do you think you're better than any one else in the world? In America it's usual for people to marry.'

'If it's my duty,' Ralph asked, 'is it not, by analogy, yours as well?'

Miss Stackpole's ocular surfaces unwinkingly caught the sun. 'Have you the fond hope of finding a flaw in my reasoning? Of course I've as good a right to marry as any one else.'

'Well then,' said Ralph, 'I won't say it vexes me to see you single. It delights me rather.'

'You're not serious yet. You never will be.'

'Shall you not believe me to be so on the day I tell you I desire to give up the practice of going round alone?'

Miss Stackpole looked at him for a moment in a manner which seemed to announce a reply that might technically be called encouraging. But to his great surprise this expression suddenly resolved itself into an appearance of alarm and even of resentment. 'No, not even then,' she answered dryly. After which she walked away.

'I've not conceived a passion for your friend,' Ralph said that evening to Isabel, 'though we talked some time this morning about it.'

'And you said something she didn't like,' the girl replied.

Ralph stared. 'Has she complained of me?'

'She told me she thinks there's something very low in the tone of Europeans towards women.'

'Does she call me a European?'

'One of the worst. She told me you had said to her something that an American never would have said. But she didn't repeat it.'

Ralph treated himself to a luxury of laughter. 'She's an extraordinary combination. Did she think I was making love to her?'

'No; I believe even Americans do that. But she apparently thought you mistook the intention of something she had said, and put an unkind construction on it.'

'I thought she was proposing marriage to me and I accepted her. Was that unkind?'

Isabel smiled. 'It was unkind to *me*. I don't want you to marry.'

'My dear cousin, what's one to do among you all?' Ralph demanded. 'Miss Stackpole tells me it's my bounden duty, and that it's hers, in general, to see I do mine!'

'She has a great sense of duty,' said Isabel gravely. 'She has indeed, and it's the motive of everything she says. That's what I like her for. She thinks it's unworthy of you to keep so many things to yourself. That's what she wanted to express. If you thought she was trying to—to attract you, you were very wrong.'

'It's true it was an odd way, but I did think she was trying to attract me. Forgive my depravity.'

'You're very conceited. She had no interested views, and never supposed you would think she had.'

'One must be very modest then to talk with such women,' Ralph said humbly. 'But it's a very strange type. She's too personal—considering that she expects other people not to be. She walks in without knocking at the door.'

'Yes,' Isabel admitted, 'she doesn't sufficiently recognize the existence of knockers; and indeed I'm not sure that she doesn't think them rather a pretentious ornament. She thinks one's door should stand ajar. But I persist in liking her.'

'I persist in thinking her too familiar,' Ralph rejoined, naturally somewhat uncomfortable under the sense of having been doubly deceived in Miss Stackpole.

'Well,' said Isabel, smiling, 'I'm afraid it's because she's rather vulgar that I like her.'

'She would be flattered by your reason!'

'If I should tell her I wouldn't express it in that way. I should say it's because there's something of the "people" in her.'

'What do you know about the people? and what does she, for that matter?'

'She knows a great deal, and I know enough to feel that she's a kind of emanation of the great democracy—of the continent, the country, the nation. I don't say that she sums it all up, that would be too much to ask of her. But she suggests it; she vividly figures it.'

'You like her then for patriotic reasons. I'm afraid it is on those very grounds I object to her.'

'Ah,' said Isabel with a kind of joyous sigh, 'I like so many things! If a thing strikes me with a certain intensity I accept it. I don't want to swagger, but I suppose I'm rather versatile. I like people to be totally different from Henrietta—in the style of Lord Warburton's sisters for instance. So long as I look at the Misses Molyneux they seem to me to answer a kind of ideal. Then Henrietta presents herself, and I'm straightway convinced by *her*; not so much in respect to herself as in respect to what masses behind her.'

'Ah, you mean the back view of her,' Ralph suggested.

'What she says is true,' his cousin answered; 'you'll never be serious. I like the great country stretching away beyond the rivers and across the prairies, blooming and smiling and spreading till it stops at the green Pacific! A strong, sweet, fresh odour seems to rise from it, and Henrietta—pardon my simile—has something of that odour in her garments.'

Isabel blushed a little as she concluded this speech, and the blush, together with the momentary ardour she had thrown into it, was so becoming to her that Ralph stood smiling at her for a moment after she had ceased speaking. 'I'm not sure the Pacific's so green as that,' he said; 'but you're a young woman of imagination. Henrietta, however, does smell of the Future—it almost knocks one down!'

XI

He took a resolve after this not to misinterpret her words even when Miss Stackpole appeared to strike the personal note most strongly. He bethought himself that persons, in her view, were simple and homogeneous organisms, and that he, for his own part, was too perverted a representative of the nature of man to have a right to deal with her in strict reciprocity. He carried out his resolve with a great deal of tact, and the young lady found in renewed contact with him no obstacle to the exercise of her genius for unshrinking enquiry, the general application of her confidence. Her situation at Gardencourt therefore, appreciated as we have seen her to be by Isabel and full of appreciation herself of that free play of intelligence which, to her sense, rendered Isabel's character a sister-spirit, and of the easy venerableness of Mr Touchett, whose noble tone, as she said, met with her full approval—her situation at Gardencourt would have been perfectly comfortable had she not conceived an irresistible mistrust of the little lady for whom she had at first supposed herself obliged to 'allow' as mistress of the house. She presently discovered, in truth, that this obligation was of the lightest and that Mrs Touchett cared very little how Miss Stackpole behaved. Mrs Touchett had defined her to Isabel as both an adventuress and a bore—adventuresses usually giving one more of a thrill; she had expressed some surprise at her niece's having selected such a friend, yet had immediately added that she knew Isabel's friends were her own affair and that she had never undertaken to like them all or to restrict the girl to those she liked.

'If you could see none but the people I like, my dear, you'd have a very small society,' Mrs Touchett frankly admitted; 'and I don't think I like any man or woman well enough to recommend them to you. When it comes to recommending it's a serious affair. I don't like Miss Stackpole—everything about her displeases me; she talks so much too loud and looks at one as if one wanted to look at *her*—which one doesn't. I'm sure she has lived all her life in a boarding-house, and I detest the manners and the liberties of such places. If you ask me if I prefer my own manners, which you doubtless think very bad, I'll tell you that I prefer them immensely. Miss Stackpole knows I detest boarding-house civilisation, and she detests me for detesting it, because she thinks it the highest in the world. She'd like Gardencourt a great deal better if it were a boarding-house. For me, I find it almost too much of one! We shall never get on together therefore, and there's no use trying.'

Mrs Touchett was right in guessing that Henrietta disapproved of her, but she had not quite put her finger on the reason. A day or two after Miss Stackpole's arrival she had made some invidious reflexions on American hotels, which excited a vein of counter-argument on the part of the correspondent of the *Interviewer*, who in the exercise of her profession had acquainted herself, in the western world, with every form of caravansary. Henrietta expressed the opinion that American hotels were the best in the world, and Mrs Touchett, fresh from a renewed struggle with them, recorded a conviction that they were the worst. Ralph, with his experimental geniality, suggested, by way of healing the breach, that the truth lay between the two extremes and that the establishments in question ought to be described as fair middling. This contribution to the discussion, however, Miss Stackpole rejected with scorn. Middling indeed! If they were not the best in the world they were the worst, but there was nothing middling about an American hotel.

'We judge from different points of view, evidently,' said Mrs Touchett. 'I like to be treated as an individual; you like to be treated as a "party".'

'I don't know what you mean,' Henrietta replied. 'I like to be treated as an American lady.'

'Poor American ladies!' cried Mrs Touchett with a laugh. 'They're the slaves of slaves.'

'They're the companions of feeemen,' Henrietta retorted.

'They're the companions of their servants—the Irish chambermaid and the negro waiter. They share their work.'

'Do you call the domestics in an American household

"slaves"?' Miss Stackpole enquired. 'If that's the way you desire to treat them, no wonder you don't like America.'

'If you've not good servants you're miserable,' Mrs Touchett serenely said. 'They're very bad in America, but I've five perfect ones in Florence.'

'I don't see what you want with five,' Henrietta couldn't help observing. 'I don't think I should like to see five persons surrounding me in that menial position.'

'I like them in that position better than in some others,' proclaimed Mrs Touchett with much meaning.

'Should you like me better if I were your butler, dear?' her husband asked.

'I don't think I should: you wouldn't at all have the *tenue*.'*

'The companions of freemen—I like that, Miss Stackpole,' said Ralph. 'It's a beautiful description.'

'When I said freemen I didn't mean you, sir!'

And this was the only reward that Ralph got for his compliment. Miss Stackpole was baffled; she evidently thought there was something treasonable in Mrs Touchett's appreciation of a class which she privately judged to be a mysterious survival of feudalism. It was perhaps because her mind was oppressed with this image that she suffered some days to elapse before she took occasion to say to Isabel: 'My dear friend, I wonder if you're growing faithless.'

'Faithless? Faithless to you, Henrietta?'

'No, that would be a great pain; but it's not that.'

'Faithless to my country then?'

'Ah, that I hope will never be. When I wrote to you from Liverpool I said I had something particular to tell you. You've never asked me what it is. Is it because you've suspected?'

'Suspected what? As a rule I don't think I suspect,' said Isabel. 'I remember now that phrase in your letter, but I confess I had forgotten it. What have you to tell me?'

Henrietta looked disappointed, and her steady gaze betrayed it. 'You don't ask that right—as if you thought it important. You're changed—you're thinking of other things.'

'Tell me what you mean, and I'll think of that.'

'Will you really think of it? That's what I wish to be sure of.'

'I've not much control of my thoughts, but I'll do my best,' said Isabel. Henrietta gazed at her, in silence, for a period which tried Isabel's patience, so that our heroine added at last: 'Do you mean that you're going to be married?'

'Not till I've seen Europe!' said Miss Stackpole. 'What are you laughing at?' she went on. 'What I mean is that Mr Goodwood came out in the steamer with me.'

'Ah!' Isabel responded.

'You say *that* right. I had a good deal of talk with him; he has come after you.'

'Did he tell you so?'

'No, he told me nothing; that's how I knew it,' said Henrietta cleverly. 'He said very little about you, but I spoke of you a good deal.'

Isabel waited. At the mention of Mr Goodwood's name she had turned a little pale. 'I'm very sorry you did that,' she observed at last.

'It was a pleasure to me, and I liked the way he listened. I could have talked a long time to such a listener; he was so quiet, so intense; he drank it all in.'

'What did you say about me?' Isabel asked.

'I said you were on the whole the finest creature I know.'

'I'm very sorry for that. He thinks too well of me already; he oughtn't to be encouraged.'

'He's dying for a little encouragement. I see his face now, and his earnest absorbed look while I talked. I never saw an ugly man look so handsome.'

'He's very simple-minded,' said Isabel. 'And he's not so ugly.'

'There's nothing so simplifying as a grand passion.'

'It's not a grand passion; I'm very sure it's not that.'

'You don't say that as if you were sure.'

Isabel gave rather a cold smile. 'I shall say it better to Mr Goodwood himself.'

'He'll soon give you a chance,' said Henrietta. Isabel offered no answer to this assertion, which her companion made with an air of great confidence. 'He'll find you changed,' the latter pursued. 'You've been affected by your new surroundings.'

'Very likely. I'm affected by everything.'

'By everything but Mr Goodwood!' Miss Stackpole exclaimed with a slightly harsh hilarity.

Isabel failed even to smile back and in a moment she said: 'Did he ask you to speak to me?'

'Not in so many words. But his eyes asked it—and his handshake, when he bade me good-bye.'

'Thank you for doing so.' And Isabel turned away.

'Yes, you're changed; you've got new ideas over here,' her friend continued. 'I hope so,' said Isabel; 'one should get as many new ideas as possible.'

'Yes; but they shouldn't interfere with the old ones when the old ones have been the right ones.'

Isabel turned about again. 'If you mean that I had any idea with regard to Mr Goodwood—!' But she faltered before her friend's implacable glitter.

'My dear child, you certainly encouraged him.'

Isabel made for the moment as if to deny this charge; instead of which, however, she presently answered: 'It's very true. I did encourage him.' And then she asked if her companion had learned from Mr Goodwood what he intended to do. It was a concession to her curiosity, for she disliked discussing the subject and found Henrietta wanting in delicacy.

'I asked him, and he said he meant to do nothing,' Miss Stackpole answered. 'But I don't believe that; he's not a man to do nothing. He is a man of high, bold action. Whatever happens to him he'll always do something, and whatever he does will always be right.'

'I quite believe that.' Henrietta might be wanting in delicacy, but it touched the girl, all the same, to hear this declaration.

'Ah, you *do* care for him!' her visitor rang out.

'Whatever he does will always be right,' Isabel repeated. 'When a man's of that infallible mould what does it matter to him what one feels?'

'It may not matter to him, but it matters to one's self.'

'Ah, what it matters to me—that's not what we're discussing,' said Isabel with a cold smile.

This time her companion was grave. 'Well, I don't care; you *have* changed. You're not the girl you were a few short weeks ago, and Mr Goodwood will see it. I expect him here any day.'

'I hope he'll hate me then,' said Isabel.

'I believe you hope it about as much as I believe him capable of it.'

To this observation our heroine made no return; she was absorbed in the alarm given her by Henrietta's intimation that Caspar Goodwood would present himself at Gardencourt. She pretended to herself, however, that she thought the event impossible, and, later, she communicated her disbelief to her friend. For the next forty-eight hours, nevertheless, she stood prepared to hear the young man's name announced. The feeling pressed upon her; it made the air sultry, as if there were to be a change of weather; and the weather, socially speaking, had been so agreeable during Isabel's stay at Gardencourt that any change would be for the worse. Her suspense indeed was dissipated the second day. She had walked into the park in company with the sociable Bunchie, and after strolling about for some time, in a manner at once listless and restless, had seated herself on a garden-bench, within sight of the house, beneath a spreading beech, where, in a white dress ornamented with black ribbons, she formed among the flickering shadows a graceful and harmonious image. She entertained herself for some moments with talking to the little terrier, as to whom the proposal of an ownership divided with her cousin had been applied as impartially as possible—as impartially as Bunchie's own somewhat fickle and inconstant sympathies would allow. But she was notified for the first time, on this occasion, of the finite character of Bunchie's intellect; hitherto she had been mainly struck with its extent. It seemed to her at last that she would do well to take a book; formerly, when heavy-hearted, she had been able, with the help of some well-chosen volume, to transfer the seat of consciousness to the organ of pure reason. Of late, it was not to be denied, literature had seemed a fading light, and even after she had reminded herself that her uncle's library was provided with a complete set of those authors which no gentleman's collection should be without, she sat motionless and empty-handed, her eyes bent on the cool green turf of the lawn. Her meditations were presently interrupted by the arrival of a servant who handed her a letter. The letter bore the London postmark and was addressed in a hand she knew—that came into her vision, already so held by him, with the vividness of the writer's voice or his face. This document proved short and may be given entire.

MY DEAR MISS ARCHER—I don't know whether you will have heard of my coming to England, but even if you have not it will scarcely be a surprise to you. You will remember that when you gave me my dismissal at Albany, three months ago, I did not accept it. I protested against it. You in fact appeared to accept my protest and to admit that I had the right on my side. I had come to see you with the hope that you would let me bring you over to my conviction; my reasons for entertaining this hope had been of the best. But you disappointed it; I found you changed, and you were able to give me no reason for the change. You admitted that you were unreasonable, and it was the only concession you would make; but it was a very cheap one, because that's not your character. No, you are not, and you never will be, arbitrary or capricious. Therefore it is that I believe you will let me see you again. You told me that I'm not disagreeable to you, and I believe it; for I don't see why that should be. I shall always think of you; I shall never think of any one else. I came to England simply because you are here; I couldn't stay at home after you had gone: I hated the country because you were not in it. If I like this country at present it is only because it holds you. I have been to England before, but have never enjoyed it much. May I not come and see you for half an hour? This at present is the dearest wish of yours faithfully

CASPAR GOODWOOD.

Isabel read this missive with such deep attention that she had not perceived an approaching tread on the soft grass. Looking up, however, as she mechanically folded it she saw Lord Warburton standing before her.

XII

SHE put the letter into her pocket and offered her visitor a smile of welcome, exhibiting no trace of discomposure and half surprised at her coolness.

'They told me you were out here,' said Lord Warburton; 'and as there was no one in the drawing-room and it's really you that I wish to see, I came out with no more ado.'

Isabel had got up; she felt a wish, for the moment, that he should not sit down beside her. 'I was just going indoors.'

'Please don't do that; it's much jollier here; I've ridden over from Lockleigh; it's a lovely day.' His smile was peculiarly friendly and pleasing, and his whole person seemed to emit that radiance of good-feeling and good fare which had formed the charm of the girl's first impression of him. It surrounded him like a zone of fine June weather.

'We'll walk about a little then,' said Isabel, who could not divest herself of the sense of an intention on the part of her visitor and who wished both to elude the intention and to satisfy her curiosity about it. It had flashed upon her vision once before, and it had given her on that occasion, as we know, a certain alarm. This alarm was composed of several elements, not all of which were disagreeable; she had indeed spent some days in analysing them and had succeeded in separating the pleasant part of the idea of Lord Warburton's 'making up' to her from the painful. It may appear to some readers that the young lady was both precipitate and unduly fastidious; but the latter of these facts, if the charge be true, may serve to exonerate her from the discredit of the former. She was not eager to convince herself that a territorial magnate, as she had heard Lord Warburton called, was smitten with her charms; the fact of a declaration from such a source carrying with it really more questions than it would answer. She had received a strong impression of his being a 'personage,' and she had occupied herself in examining the image so conveyed. At the risk of adding to the evidence of her self-sufficiency it must be said that there had been moments when this possibility of admiration by a personage represented to her an aggression almost to the degree of an affront, quite to the degree of an inconvenience. She had never yet known a personage; there had been no personages, in this sense, in her life; there were probably none such at all in her native land. When she had thought of individual eminence she had thought of it on the basis of character and wit—of what one might like in a gentleman's mind and in his talk. She herself was a character—she couldn't help being aware of that; and hitherto her visions of a completed consciousness had concerned themselves largely with moral images—things as to which the question would be whether they pleased her sublime soul. Lord Warburton loomed up before her, largely and brightly, as a collection of attributes and powers which were not to be measured by this simple rule, but which demanded a different sort of appreciation—an appreciation that the girl, with her habit of judging quickly and freely, felt she lacked patience to bestow. He appeared to demand of her something that no one else, as it were, had presumed to do. What she felt was that a territorial, a political, a social magnate had conceived the design of drawing her into the system in which he rather invidiously lived and moved. A certain instinct, not imperious, but persuasive, told her to resist—murmured to her that virtually she had a system and an orbit of her own. It told her other things besides—things which both contradicted and confirmed each other; that a girl might do much worse than trust herself to such a man and that it would be very interesting to see something of his system from his own point of view; that on the other hand, however, there was evidently a great deal of it which she should regard only as a complication of every hour, and that even in the whole there was something stiff and stupid which would make it a burden. Furthermore there was a young man lately come from America who had no system at all, but who had a character of which it was useless for her to try to persuade herself that the impression on her mind had been light. The letter she carried in her pocket all sufficiently reminded her of the contrary. Smile not, however, I venture to repeat, at this simple young woman from Albany who debated whether she should accept an English peer before he had offered himself and who was disposed to believe that on the whole she could do better. She was a person of great good faith, and if there was a great deal of folly in her wisdom those who judge her severely may have the satisfaction of finding that, later, she became consistently wise only at the cost of an amount of folly which will constitute almost a direct appeal to charity.

Lord Warburton seemed quite ready to walk, to sit or to do anything that Isabel should propose, and he gave her this assurance with his usual air of being particularly pleased to exercise a social virtue. But he was, nevertheless, not in command of his emotions, and as he strolled beside her for a moment, in silence, looking at her without letting her know it, there was something embarrassed in his glance and his misdirected laughter. Yes, assuredly—as we have touched on the point, we may return to it for a moment again—the English are the most romantic people in the world and Lord Warburton was about to give an example of it. He was about to take a step which would astonish all his friends and displease a great many of them, and which had superficially nothing to recommend it. The young lady who trod the turf beside him had come from a queer country across the sea which he knew a good deal about; her antecedents, her associations were very vague to his mind except in so far as they were generic, and in this sense they showed as distinct and unimportant. Miss Archer had neither a fortune nor the sort of beauty that justifies a man to the multitude, and he calculated that he had spent about twenty-six hours in her company. He had summed up all this—the perversity of the impulse, which had declined to avail itself of the most liberal opportunities to subside, and the judgement of mankind, as exemplified particularly in the more quickly-judging half of it: he had looked these things well in the face and then had dismissed them from his thoughts. He cared no more for them than for the rosebud in his buttonhole. It is the good fortune of a man who for the greater part of a lifetime has abstained without effort from making himself disagreeable to his friends, that when the need comes for such a course it is not discredited by irritating associations.

'I hope you had a pleasant ride,' said Isabel, who observed her companion's hesitancy.

'It would have been pleasant if for nothing else than that it brought me here.'

'Are you so fond of Gardencourt?' the girl asked, more and more sure that he meant to make some appeal to her; wishing not to challenge him if he hesitated, and yet to keep all the quietness of her reason if he proceeded. It suddenly came upon her that her situation was one which a few weeks ago she would have deemed deeply romantic: the park of an old English country-house, with the foreground embellished by a 'great' (as she supposed) nobleman in the act of making love to a young lady who, on careful inspection, should be found to present remarkable analogies with herself. But if she was now the heroine of the situation she succeeded scarcely the less in looking at it from the outside.

'I care nothing for Gardencourt,' said her companion. 'I care only for you.'

'You've known me too short a time to have a right to say that, and I can't believe you're serious.'

These words of Isabel's were not perfectly sincere, for she had no doubt whatever that he himself was. They were simply a tribute to the fact, of which she was perfectly aware, that those he had just uttered would have excited surprise on the part of a vulgar world. And, moreover, if anything beside the sense she had already acquired that Lord Warburton was not a loose thinker had been needed to convince her, the tone in which he replied would quite have served the purpose.

'One's right in such a matter is not measured by the time, Miss Archer; it's measured by the feeling itself. If I were to wait three months it would make no difference; I shall not be more sure of what I mean than I am to-day. Of course I've seen you very little, but my impression dates from the very first hour we met. I lost no time, I fell in love with you then. It was at first sight, as the novels say; I know now that's not a fancy-phrase, and I shall think better of novels for evermore. Those two days I spent here settled it; I don't know whether you suspected I was doing so, but I paid—mentally speaking I mean—the greatest possible attention to you. Nothing you said, nothing you did, was lost upon me. When you came to Lockleigh the other day—or rather when you went away—I was perfectly sure. Nevertheless I made up my mind to think it over and to question myself narrowly. I've done so; all these days I've done nothing else. I don't make mistakes about such things; I'm a very judicious animal. I don't go off easily, but when I'm touched, it's for life. It's for life, Miss Archer, it's for life,' Lord Warburton repeated in the kindest, tenderest, pleasantest voice Isabel had ever heard, and looking at her with eyes charged with the light of a passion that had sifted itself clear of the baser parts of emotion—the heat, the violence, the unreason—and that burned as steadily as a lamp in a windless place. By tacit consent, as he talked, they had walked more and more slowly, and at last they stopped and he took her hand. 'Ah, Lord Warburton, how little you know me!' Isabel said very gently. Gently too she drew her hand away.

'Don't taunt me with that; that I don't know you better makes me unhappy enough already; it's all my loss. But that's what I want, and it seems to me I'm taking the best way. If you'll be my wife, then I shall know you, and when I tell you all the good I think of you you'll not be able to say it's from ignorance.'

'If you know me little I know you even less,' said Isabel.

'You mean that, unlike yourself, I may not improve on acquaintance? Ah, of course that's very possible. But think, to speak to you as I do, how determined I must be to try and give satisfaction! You do like me rather, don't you?'

'I like you very much, Lord Warburton,' she answered; and at this moment she liked him immensely.

'I thank you for saying that; it shows you don't regard me as a stranger. I really believe I've filled all the other relations of life very creditably, and I don't see why I shouldn't fill this one—in which I offer myself to you—seeing that I care so much more about it. Ask the people who know me well; I've friends who'll speak for me.'

'I don't need the recommendation of your friends,' said Isabel.

'Ah now, that's delightful of you. You believe in me yourself.'

'Completely,' Isabel declared. She quite glowed there, inwardly, with the pleasure of feeling she did.

The light in her companion's eyes turned into a smile, and he gave a long exhalation of joy. 'If you're mistaken, Miss Archer, let me lose all I possess!'

She wondered whether he meant this for a reminder that he was rich, and, on the instant, felt sure that he didn't. He was sinking that, as he would have said himself; and indeed he might safely leave it to the memory of any interlocutor, especially of one to whom he was offering his hand. Isabel had prayed that she might not be agitated, and her mind was tranquil enough, even while she listened and asked herself what it was best she should say, to indulge in this incidental criticism. What she should say, had she asked herself? Her foremost wish was to say something if possible not less kind than what he had said to her. His words had carried perfect conviction with them; she felt she did, all so mysteriously, matter to him. 'I thank you more than I can say for your offer,' she returned at last. 'It does me great honour.'

'Ah, don't say that!' he broke out. 'I was afraid you'd say something like that. I don't see what you've to do with that sort of thing. I don't see why you should thank me—it's I who ought to thank you for listening to me: a man you know so little coming down on you with such a thumper! Of course it's a great question; I must tell you that I'd rather ask it than have it to answer myself. But the way you've listened—or at least your having listened at all—gives me some hope.'

'Don't hope too much,' Isabel said.

'Oh Miss Archer!' her companion murmured, smiling again, in his seriousness, as if such a warning might perhaps be taken but as the play of high spirits, the exuberance of elation.

'Should you be greatly surprised if I were to beg you not to hope at all?' Isabel asked.

'Surprised? I don't know what you mean by surprise. It wouldn't be that; it would be a feeling very much worse.'

Isabel walked on again; she was silent for some minutes. 'I'm very sure that, highly as I already think of you, my opinion of you, if I should know you well, would only rise. But I'm by no means sure that you wouldn't be disappointed. And I say that not in the least out of conventional modesty; it's perfectly sincere.'

'I'm willing to risk it, Miss Archer,' her companion replied.

'It's a great question, as you say. It's a very difficult question.'

'I don't expect you of course to answer it outright. Think it over as long as may be necessary. If I can gain by waiting I'll gladly wait a long time. Only remember that in the end my dearest happiness depends on your answer.'

'I should be very sorry to keep you in suspense,' said Isabel.

'Oh, don't mind. I'd much rather have a good answer six months hence than a bad one to-day.'

'But it's very probable that even six months hence I shouldn't be able to give you one that you'd think good.'

'Why not, since you really like me?'

'Ah, you must never doubt that,' said Isabel.

'Well then, I don't see what more you ask!'

'It's not what I ask; it's what I can give. I don't think I should suit you; I really don't think I should.'

'You needn't worry about that. That's my affair. You needn't be a better royalist than the king.'

'It's not only that,' said Isabel; 'but I'm not sure I wish to marry any one.'

'Very likely you don't. I've no doubt a great many women begin that way,' said his lordship, who, be it averred, did not in the least believe in the axiom he thus beguiled his anxiety by uttering. 'But they're frequently persuaded.'

'Ah, that's because they want to be!' And Isabel lightly laughed.

Her suitor's countenance fell, and he looked at her for a while in silence. 'I'm afraid it's my being an Englishman that makes you hesitate,' he said presently. 'I know your uncle thinks you ought to marry in your own country.'

Isabel listened to this assertion with some interest; it had never occurred to her that Mr Touchett was likely to discuss her matrimonial prospects with Lord Warburton. 'Has he told you that?'

'I remember his making the remark. He spoke perhaps of Americans generally.'

'He appears himself to have found it very pleasant to live in England.' Isabel spoke in a manner that might have seemed a little perverse, but which expressed both her constant perception of her uncle's outward felicity and her general disposition to elude any obligation to take a restricted view.

It gave her companion hope, and he immediately cried with warmth: 'Ah, my dear Miss Archer, old England's a very good sort of country, you know! And it will be still better when we've furbished it up a little.'

'Oh, don't furbish it, Lord Warburton; leave it alone. I like it this way.'

'Well then, if you like it, I'm more and more unable to see your objection to what I propose.'

'I'm afraid I can't make you understand.'

'You ought at least to try. I've a fair intelligence. Are you afraid—afraid of the climate? We can easily live elsewhere, you know. You can pick out your climate, the whole world over.'

These words were uttered with a breadth of candour that was like the embrace of strong arms—that was like the fragrance straight in her face, and by his clean, breathing lips, of she knew not what strange gardens, what charged airs. She would have given her little finger at that moment to feel strongly and simply the impulse to answer: 'Lord Warburton, it's impossible for me to do better in this wonderful world, I think, than commit myself, very gratefully, to your loyalty.' But though she was lost in admiration of her opportunity she managed to move back into the deepest shade of it, even as some wild, caught creature in a vast cage. The 'splendid' security so offered her was *not* the greatest she could conceive. What she finally bethought herself of saying was something very different—something that deferred the need of really facing her crisis. 'Don't think me unkind if I ask you to say no more about this to-day.'

'Certainly, certainly!' her companion cried. 'I wouldn't bore you for the world.'

'You've given me a great deal to think about, and I promise you to do it justice.'

'That's all I ask of you, of course—and that you'll remember how absolutely my happiness is in your hands.'

Isabel listened with extreme respect to this admonition, but she said after a minute: 'I must tell you that what I shall think about is some way of letting you know that what you ask is impossible—letting you know it without making you miserable.'

'There's no way to do that, Miss Archer. I won't say that if you refuse me you'll kill me; I shall not die of it. But I shall do worse; I shall live to no purpose.'

'You'll live to marry a better woman than I.'

'Don't say that, please,' said Lord Warburton very gravely. 'That's fair to neither of us.'

'To marry a worse one then.'

'If there are better women than you I prefer the bad ones. That's all I can say,' he went on with the same earnestness. 'There's no accounting for tastes.'

His gravity made her feel equally grave, and she showed it by again requesting him to drop the subject for the present. 'I'll speak to you myself—very soon. Perhaps I shall write to you.'

'At your convenience, yes,' he replied. 'Whatever time you take, it must seem to me long, and I suppose I must make the best of that.'

'I shall not keep you in suspense; I only want to collect my mind a little.'

He gave a melancholy sigh and stood looking at her a moment, with his hands behind him, giving short nervous shakes to his hunting-crop. 'Do you know I'm very much afraid of it—of that remarkable mind of yours?'

Our heroine's biographer can scarcely tell why, but the question made her start and brought a conscious blush to her cheek. She returned his look a moment, and then with a note in her voice that might almost have appealed to his compassion, 'So am I, my lord!' she oddly exclaimed.

His compassion was not stirred, however; all he possessed of the faculty of pity was needed at home. 'Ah! be merciful, be merciful,' he murmured.

'I think you had better go,' said Isabel. 'I'll write to you.'

'Very good; but whatever you write I'll come and see you, you know.' And then he stood reflecting, his eyes fixed on the observant countenance of Bunchie, who had the air of having understood all that had been said and of pretending to carry off the indiscretion by a simulated fit of curiosity as to the roots of an ancient oak. 'There's one thing more,' he went on. 'You know, if you don't like Lockleigh—if you think it's damp or anything of that sort—you need never go within fifty miles of it. It's not damp, by the way; I've had the house thoroughly examined; it's perfectly safe and right. But if you shouldn't fancy it you needn't dream of living in it. There's no difficulty whatever about that; there are plenty of houses. I thought I'd just mention it; some people don't like a moat, you know. Good-bye.'

'I adore a moat,' said Isabel. 'Good-bye.'

He held out his hand, and she gave him hers a moment—a moment long enough for him to bend his handsome bared head and kiss it. Then, still agitating, in his mastered emotion, his implement of the chase, he walked rapidly away. He was evidently much upset.

Isabel herself was upset, but she had not been affected as she would have imagined. What she felt was not a great responsibility, a great difficulty of choice; it appeared to her there had been no choice in the question. She couldn't marry Lord Warburton; the idea failed to support any enlightened prejudice in favour of the free exploration of life that she had hitherto entertained or was now capable of entertaining. She must write this to him, she must convince him, and that duty was comparatively simple. But what disturbed her, in the sense that it struck her with wonderment, was this very fact that it cost her so little to refuse a magnificent 'chance.' With whatever qualifications one would, Lord Warburton had offered her a great opportunity; the situation might have discomforts, might contain oppressive, might contain narrowing elements, might prove really but a stupefying anodyne; but she did her sex no injustice in believing that nineteen women out of twenty would have accommodated themselves to it without a pang. Why then upon her also should it not irresistibly impose itself? Who was she, what was she, that she should hold herself superior? What view of life, what design upon fate, what conception of happiness, had she that pretended to be larger than these large, these fabulous occasions? If she wouldn't do such a thing as that then she must do great things, she must do something greater. Poor Isabel found ground to remind herself from time to time that she must not be too proud, and nothing could be more sincere than her prayer to be delivered from such a danger: the isolation and loneliness of pride had for her mind the horror of a desert place. If it had been pride that interfered with her accepting Lord Warburton such a *bêtise** was singularly misplaced; and she was so conscious of liking him that she ventured to assure herself it was the very softness, and the fine intelligence, of sympathy. She liked him too much to marry him, that was the truth; something assured her there was a fallacy somewhere in the glowing logic of the proposition—as *he* saw it—even though she mightn't put her very finest finger-point on it; and to inflict upon a man who offered so much a wife with a tendency to criticise would be a peculiarly discreditable act. She had promised him she would consider his question, and when, after he had left her, she wandered back to the bench where he had found her and lost herself in meditation, it might have seemed that she was keeping her vow. But this was not the case; she was wondering if she were not a cold, hard, priggish person, and, on her at last getting up and going rather quickly back to the house, felt, as she had said to her friend, really frightened at herself.

XIII

It was this feeling and not the wish to ask advice—she had no desire whatever for that—that led her to speak to her uncle of what had taken place. She wished to speak to some one; she should feel more natural, more human, and her uncle, for this purpose, presented himself in a more attractive light than either her aunt or her friend Henrietta. Her cousin of course was a possible confidant; but she would have had to do herself violence to air this special secret to Ralph. So the next day, after breakfast, she sought her occasion. Her uncle never left his apartment till the afternoon, but he received his cronies, as he said, in his dressing-room. Isabel had quite taken her place in the class so designated, which, for the rest, included the old man's son, his physician, his personal servant, and even Miss Stackpole. Mrs Touchett did not figure in the list, and this was an obstacle the less to Isabel's finding her host alone. He sat in a complicated mechanical chair, at the open window of his room, looking westward over the park and the river, with his newspapers and letters piled up beside him, his toilet freshly and minutely made, and his smooth, speculative face composed to benevolent expectation.

She approached her point directly. 'I think I ought to let you know that Lord Warburton has asked me to marry him. I suppose I ought to tell my aunt; but it seems best to tell you first.'

The old man expressed no surprise, but thanked her for the confidence she showed him. 'Do you mind telling me whether you accepted him?' he then enquired.

'I've not answered him definitely yet; I've taken a little time to think of it, because that seems more respectful. But I shall not accept him.'

Mr Touchett made no comment upon this; he had the air of thinking that, whatever interest he might take in the matter from the point of view of sociability, he had no active voice in it. 'Well, I told you you'd be a success over here. Americans are highly appreciated.'

'Very highly indeed,' said Isabel. 'But at the cost of seeming both tasteless and ungrateful, I don't think I can marry Lord Warburton.'

'Well,' her uncle went on, 'of course an old man can't judge for a young lady. I'm glad you didn't ask me before you made up your mind. I suppose I ought to tell you,' he added slowly, but as if it were not of much consequence, 'that I've known all about it these three days.'

'About Lord Warburton's state of mind?'

'About his intentions, as they say here. He wrote me a very pleasant letter, telling me all about them. Should you like to see his letter?' the old man obligingly asked.

'Thank you; I don't think I care about that. But I'm glad he wrote to you; it was right that he should, and he would be certain to do what was right.'

'Ah well, I guess you do like him!' Mr Touchett declared. 'You needn't pretend you don't.'

'I like him extremely; I'm very free to admit that. But I don't wish to marry any one just now.'

'You think some one may come along whom you may like better. Well, that's very likely,' said Mr Touchett, who appeared to wish to show his kindness to the girl by easing off her decision, as it were, and finding cheerful reasons for it.

'I don't care if I don't meet any one else. I like Lord Warburton quite well enough.' She fell into that appearance of a sudden change of point of view with which she sometimes startled and even displeased her interlocutors.

Her uncle, however, seemed proof against either of these impressions. 'He's a very fine man,' he resumed in a tone which might have passed for that of encouragement. 'His letter was one of the pleasantest I've received for some weeks. I suppose one of the reasons I liked it was that it was all about you; that is all except the part that was about himself. I suppose he told you all that.'

'He would have told me everything I wished to ask him,' Isabel said.

'But you didn't feel curious?'

'My curiosity would have been idle—once I had determined to decline his offer.'

'You didn't find it sufficiently attractive?' Mr Touchett enquired.

She was silent a little. 'I suppose it was that,' she presently admitted. 'But I don't know why.'

'Fortunately ladies are not obliged to give reasons,' said her uncle. 'There's a great deal that's attractive about such an idea; but I don't see why the English should want to entice us away from our native land. I know that we try to attract them over there, but that's because our population is insufficient. Here, you know, they're rather crowded. However, I presume there's room for charming young ladies everywhere.'

'There seems to have been room here for you,' said Isabel, whose eyes had been wandering over the large pleasure-spaces of the park.

Mr Touchett gave a shrewd, conscious smile. 'There's room everywhere, my dear, if you'll pay for it. I sometimes think I've paid too much for this. Perhaps you also might have to pay too much.'

'Perhaps I might,' the girl replied.

That suggestion gave her something more definite to rest on than she had found in her own thoughts, and the fact of this association of her uncle's mild acuteness with her dilemma seemed to prove that she was concerned with the natural and reasonable emotions of life and not altogether a victim to intellectual eagerness and vague ambitions—ambitions reaching beyond Lord Warburton's beautiful appeal, reaching to something indefinable and possibly not commendable. In so far as the indefinable had an influence upon Isabel's behaviour at this juncture, it was not the conception, even unformulated, of a union with Caspar Goodwood; for however she might have resisted conquest at her English suitor's large quiet hands she was at least as far removed from the disposition to let the young man from Boston take positive possession of her. The sentiment in which she sought refuge after reading his letter was a critical view of his having come abroad; for it was part of the influence he had upon her that he seemed to deprive her of the sense of freedom. There was a disagreeably strong push, a kind of hardness of presence, in his way of rising before her. She had been haunted at moments by the image, by the danger, of his disapproval and had wondered—a consideration she had never paid in equal degree to any one else—whether he would like what she did. The difficulty was that more than any man she had ever known, more than poor Lord Warburton (she had begun now to give his lordship the benefit of this epithet), Caspar Goodwood expressed for her an energy—and she had already felt it as a power—that was of his very nature. It was in no degree a matter of his 'advantages'—it was a matter of the spirit that sat in his clear-burning eyes like some tireless watcher at a window. She might like it or not, but he insisted, ever, with his whole weight and force: even in one's usual contact with him one had to reckon with that. The idea of a diminished liberty was particularly disagreeable to her at present, since she had just given a sort of personal accent to her independence by looking so straight at Lord Warburton's big bribe and yet turning away from it. Sometimes Caspar Goodwood had seemed to range himself on the side of her destiny, to be the stubbornest fact she knew; she said to herself at such moments that she might evade him for a time, but that she must make terms with him at last—terms which would be certain to be favourable to himself. Her impulse had been to avail herself of the things that helped her to resist such an obligation; and this impulse had been much concerned in her eager acceptance of her aunt's invitation, which had come to her at an hour when she expected from day to day to see Mr Goodwood and when she was glad to have an answer ready for something she was sure he would say to her. When she had told him at Albany, on the evening of Mrs Touchett's visit, that she couldn't then discuss difficult questions, dazzled as she was by the great immediate opening of her aunt's offer of 'Europe,' he declared that this was no answer at all; and it was now to obtain a better one that he was following her across the sea. To say to herself that he was a kind of grim fate was well enough for a fanciful young woman who was able to take much for granted in him; but the reader has a right to a nearer and a clearer view.

He was the son of a proprietor of well-known cotton-mills in Massachusetts—a gentleman who had accumulated a considerable fortune in the exercise of this industry. Caspar at present managed the works, and with a judgement and a temper which, in spite of keen competition and languid years, had kept their prosperity from dwindling. He had received the better part of his education at Harvard College, where, however, he had gained renown rather as a gymnast and an oarsman than as a gleaner of more dispersed knowledge. Later on he had learned that the finer intelligence too could vault and pull and strain—might even, breaking the record, treat itself to rare exploits. He had thus discovered in himself a sharp eye for the mystery of mechanics, and had invented an improvement in the cotton-spinning process which was now largely used and was known by his name. You might have seen it in the newspapers in connection with this fruitful contrivance; assurance of which he had given to Isabel by showing her in the columns of the New York *Interviewer* an exhaustive article on the Goodwood patent—an article not prepared by Miss Stackpole, friendly as she had proved herself to his more sentimental interests. There were intricate, bristling things he rejoiced in; he liked to organise, to contend, to administer; he could make people work his will, believe in him, march before him and justify him. This was the art, as they said, of managing men—which rested, in him, further, on a bold though brooding ambition. It struck those who knew him well that he might do greater things than carry on a cotton-factory; there was nothing cottony about Caspar Goodwood, and his friends took for granted that he would somehow and somewhere write himself in bigger letters. But it was as if something large and confused, something dark and ugly, would have to call upon him: he was not after all in harmony with mere smug peace and greed and gain, an order of things of which the vital breath was ubiquitous advertisement. It pleased Isabel to believe that he might have ridden, on a plunging steed, the whirlwind of a great war—a war like the Civil strife* that had overdarkened her conscious childhood and his ripening youth.

She liked at any rate this idea of his being by character and in fact a mover of men—liked it much better than some other points in his nature and aspect. She cared nothing for his cotton-mill—the Goodwood patent left her imagination absolutely cold. She wished him no ounce less of his manhood, but she sometimes thought he would be rather nicer if he looked, for instance, a little differently. His jaw was too square and set and his figure too straight and stiff: these things suggested a want of easy consonance with the deeper rhythms of life. Then she viewed with reserve a habit he had of dressing always in the same manner; it was not apparently that he wore the same clothes continually, for, on the contrary, his garments had a way of looking rather too new. But they all seemed of the same piece; the figure, the stuff, was so drearily usual. She had reminded herself more than once that this was a frivolous objection to a person of his importance; and then she had amended the rebuke by saying that it would be a frivolous objection only if she were in love with him. She was not in love with him and therefore might criticise his small defects as well as his great—which latter consisted in the collective reproach of his being too serious, or, rather, not of his being so, since one could never be, but certainly of his seeming so. He showed his appetites and designs too simply and artlessly; when one was alone with him he talked too much about the same subject, and when other people were present he talked too little about anything. And yet he was of supremely strong, clean make—which was so much: she saw the different fitted parts of him as she had seen, in museums and portraits, the different fitted parts of armoured warriors—in plates of steel handsomely inlaid with gold. It was very strange: where, ever, was any tangible link between her impression and her act? Caspar Goodwood had never corresponded to her idea of a delightful person, and she supposed that this was why he left her so harshly critical. When, however, Lord Warburton, who not only did correspond with it, but gave an extension to the term, appealed to her approval, she found herself still unsatisfied. It was certainly strange.

The sense of her incoherence was not a help to answering Mr Goodwood's letter, and Isabel determined to leave it a while unhonoured. If he had determined to persecute her he must take the consequences; foremost among which was his being left to perceive how little it charmed her that he should come down to Gardencourt. She was already liable to the incursions of one suitor at this place, and though it might be pleasant to be appreciated in opposite quarters there was a kind of grossness in entertaining two such passionate pleaders at once, even in a case where the entertainment should consist of dismissing them. She made no reply to Mr Goodwood; but at the end of three days she wrote to Lord Warburton, and the letter belongs to our history.

DEAR LORD WARBURTON—A great deal of earnest thought has not led me to change my mind about the suggestion you were so kind as to make me the other day. I am not, I am really and truly not, able to regard you in the light of a companion for life; or to think of your home—your various homes—as the settled seat of my existence. These things cannot be reasoned about, and I very earnestly entreat you not to return to the subject we discussed so exhaustively. We see our lives from our own point of view; that is the privilege of the weakest and humblest of us; and I shall never be able to see mine in the manner you proposed. Kindly let this suffice you, and do me the justice to believe that I have given your proposal the deeply respectful consideration it deserves. It is with this very great regard that I remain sincerely yours,

ISABEL ARCHER.

While the author of this missive was making up her mind to despatch it Henrietta Stackpole formed a resolve which was accompanied by no demur. She invited Ralph Touchett to take a walk with her in the garden, and when he had assented with that alacrity which seemed constantly to testify to his high expectations, she informed him that she had a favour to ask of him. It may be admitted that at this information the young man flinched; for we know that Miss Stackpole had struck him as apt to push an advantage. The alarm was unreasoned, however; for he was clear about the area of her indiscretion as little as advised of its vertical depth, and he made a very civil profession of the desire to serve her. He was afraid of her and presently told her so. 'When you look at me in a certain way my knees knock together, my faculties desert me; I'm filled with trepidation and I ask only for strength to execute your commands. You've an address that I've never encountered in any woman.'

'Well,' Henrietta replied good-humouredly, 'if I had not known before that you were trying somehow to abash me I should know it now. Of course I'm easy game—I was brought up with such different customs and ideas. I'm not used to your arbitrary standards, and I've never been spoken to in America as you have spoken to me. If a gentleman conversing with me over there were to speak to me like that I shouldn't know what to make of it. We take everything more naturally over there, and, after all, we're a great deal more simple. I admit that; I'm very simple myself. Of course if you choose to laugh at me for it you're very welcome; but I think on the whole I would rather be myself than you. I'm quite content to be myself; I don't want to change. There are plenty of people that appreciate me just as I am. It's true they're nice fresh free-born Americans!' Henrietta had lately taken up the tone of helpless innocence and large concession. 'I want you to assist me a little,' she went on. 'I don't care in the least whether I amuse you while you do so; or, rather, I'm perfectly willing your amusement should be your reward. I want you to help me about Isabel.'

'Has she injured you?' Ralph asked.

'If she had I shouldn't mind, and I should never tell you. What I'm afraid of is that she'll injure herself.'

'I think that's very possible,' said Ralph.

His companion stopped in the garden-walk, fixing on him perhaps the very gaze that unnerved him. 'That too would amuse you, I suppose. The way you do say things! I never heard any one so indifferent.'

'To Isabel? Ah, not that!'

'Well, you're not in love with her, I hope.'

'How can that be, when I'm in love with Another?'

'You're in love with yourself, that's the Other!' Miss Stackpole declared. 'Much good may it do you! But if you wish to be serious once in your life here's a chance; and if you really care for your cousin here's an opportunity to prove it. I don't expect you to understand her; that's too much to ask. But you needn't do that to grant my favour. I'll supply the necessary intelligence.'

'I shall enjoy that immensely!' Ralph exclaimed. 'I'll be Caliban and you shall be Ariel.'*

'You're not at all like Caliban, because you're sophisticated, and Caliban was not. But I'm not talking about imaginary characters; I'm talking about Isabel. Isabel's intensely real. What I wish to tell you is that I find her fearfully changed.'

'Since you came, do you mean?'

'Since I came and before I came. She's not the same as she once so beautifully was.'

'As she was in America?'

'Yes, in America. I suppose you know she comes from there. She can't help it, but she does.'

'Do you want to change her back again?'

'Of course I do, and I want you to help me.'

'Ah,' said Ralph, 'I'm only Caliban; I'm not Prospero.'

'You were Prospero enough to make her what she has become. You've acted on Isabel Archer since she came here, Mr Touchett.'

'I, my dear Miss Stackpole? Never in the world. Isabel Archer has acted on me—yes; she acts on every one. But I've been absolutely passive.'

'You're too passive then. You had better stir yourself and be careful. Isabel's changing every day; she's drifting away—right out to sea. I've watched her and I can see it. She's not the bright American girl she was. She's taking different views, a different colour, and turning away from her old ideals. I want to save those ideals, Mr Touchett, and that's where you come in.'

'Not surely as an ideal?'

'Well, I hope not,' Henrietta replied promptly. 'I've got a fear in my heart that she's going to marry one of these fell Europeans, and I want to prevent it.'

'Ah, I see,' cried Ralph; 'and to prevent it you want me to step in and marry her?'

'Not quite; that remedy would be as bad as the disease, for you're the typical, the fell European from whom I wish to rescue her. No; I wish you to take an interest in another person—a young man to whom she once gave great encouragement and whom she now doesn't seem to think good enough. He's a thoroughly grand man and a very dear friend of mine, and I wish very much you would invite him to pay a visit here.'

Ralph was much puzzled by this appeal, and it is perhaps not to the credit of his purity of mind that he failed to look at it at first in the simplest light. It wore, to his eyes, a tortuous air, and his fault was that he was not quite sure that anything in the world could really be as candid as this request of Miss Stackpole's appeared. That a young woman should demand that a gentleman whom she described as her very dear friend should be furnished with an opportunity to make himelf agreeable to another young woman, a young woman whose attention had wandered and whose charms were greater—this was an anomaly which for the moment challenged all his ingenuity of interpretation. To read between the lines was easier than to follow the text, and to suppose that Miss Stackpole wished the gentleman invited to Gardencourt on her own account was the sign not so much of a vulgar as of an embarrassed mind. Even from this venial act of vulgarity, however, Ralph was saved, and saved by a force that I can only speak of as inspiration. With no more outward light on the subject than he already possessed he suddenly acquired the conviction that it would be a sovereign injustice to the correspondent of the *Interviewer* to assign a dishonourable motive to any act of hers. This conviction passed into his mind with extreme rapidity; it was perhaps kindled by the pure radiance of the young lady's imperturbable gaze. He returned this challenge a moment, consciously, resisting an inclination to frown as one frowns in the presence of larger luminaries. 'Who's the gentleman you speak of?'

'Mr Caspar Goodwood—of Boston. He has been extremely attentive to Isabel—just as devoted to her as he can live. He has followed her out her and he's at present in London. I don't know his address, but I guess I can obtain it.'

'I've never heard of him,' said Ralph.

'Well, I suppose you haven't heard of every one. I don't believe he has ever heard of you; but that's no reason why Isabel shouldn't marry him.'

Ralph gave a mild ambiguous laugh. 'What a rage you have for marrying people! Do you remember how you wanted to marry *me* the other day?'

'I've got over that. You don't know how to take such ideas. Mr Goodwood does, however; and that's what I like about him. He's a splendid man and a perfect gentleman, and Isabel knows it.'

'Is she very fond of him?'

'If she isn't she ought to be. He's simply wrapped up in her.'

'And you wish me to ask him here,' said Ralph reflectively.

'It would be an act of true hospitality.'

'Caspar Goodwood,' Ralph continued—'it's rather a striking name.'

'I don't care anything about his name. It might be Ezekiel Jenkins, and I should say the same. He's the only man I have ever seen whom I think worthy of Isabel.'

'You're a very devoted friend,' said Ralph.

'Of course I am. If you say that to pour scorn on me I don't care.'

'I don't say it to pour scorn on you; I'm very much struck with it.'

'You're more satiric than ever, but I advise you not to laugh at Mr Goodwood.'

'I assure you I'm very serious; you ought to understand that,' said Ralph.

In a moment his companion understood it. 'I believe you are; now you're too serious.'

'You're difficult to please.'

'Oh, you're very serious indeed. You won't invite Mr Goodwood.'

'I don't know,' said Ralph. 'I'm capable of strange things. Tell me a little about Mr Goodwood. What's he like?'

'He's just the opposite of you. He's at the head of a cotton-factory; a very fine one.'

'Has he pleasant manners?' asked Ralph.

'Splendid manners—in the American style.'

'Would he be an agreeable member of our little circle?'

'I don't think he'd care much about our little circle. He'd concentrate on Isabel.'

'And how would my cousin like that?'

'Very possibly not at all. But it will be good for her. It will call back her thoughts.'

'Call them back—from where?'

'From foreign parts and other unnatural places. Three

months ago she gave Mr Goodwood every reason to suppose he was acceptable to her, and it's not worthy of Isabel to go back on a real friend simply because she has changed the scene. I've changed the scene too, and the effect of it has been to make me care more for my old associations than ever. It's my belief that the sooner Isabel changes it back again the better. I know her well enough to know that she would never be truly happy over here, and I wish her to form some strong American tie that will act as a preservative.'

'Aren't you perhaps a little too much in a hurry?' Ralph enquired. 'Don't you think you ought to give her more of a chance in poor old England?' 'A chance to ruin her bright young life? One's never too much in a hurry to save a precious human creature from drowning.'

'As I understand it then,' said Ralph, 'you wish me to push Mr Goodwood overboard after her. Do you know,' he added, 'that I've never heard her mention his name?'

Henrietta gave a brilliant smile. 'I'm delighted to hear that; it proves how much she thinks of him.'

Ralph appeared to allow that there was a good deal in this, and he surrendered to thought while his companion watched him askance. 'If I should invite Mr Goodwood,' he finally said, 'it would be to quarrel with him.'

'Don't do that; he'd prove the better man.'

'You certainly are doing your best to make me hate him! I really don't think I can ask him. I should be afraid of being rude to him.'

'It's just as you please,' Henrietta returned. 'I had no idea you were in love with her yourself.'

'Do you really believe that?' the young man asked with lifted eyebrows.

'That's the most natural speech I've ever heard you make! Of course I believe it,' Miss Stackpole ingeniously said.

'Well,' Ralph concluded, 'to prove to you that you're wrong I'll invite him. It must be of course as a friend of yours.'

'It will not be as a friend of mine that he'll come; and it will not be to prove to me that I'm wrong that you'll ask him—but to prove it to yourself!'

These last words of Miss Stackpole's (on which the two

presently separated) contained an amount of truth which Ralph Touchett was obliged to recognise; but it so far took the edge from too sharp a recognition that, in spite of his suspecting it would be rather more indiscreet to keep than to break his promise, he wrote Mr Goodwood a note of six lines, expressing the pleasure it would give Mr Touchett the elder that he should join a little party at Gardencourt, of which Miss Stackpole was a valued member. Having sent his letter (to the care of a banker whom Henrietta suggested) he waited in some suspense. He had heard this fresh formidable figure named for the first time; for when his mother had mentioned on her arrival that there was a story about the girl's having an 'admirer' at home, the idea had seemed deficient in reality and he had taken no pains to ask questions the answers to which would involve only the vague or the disagreeable. Now, however, the native admiration of which his cousin was the object had become more concrete; it took the form of a young man who had followed her to London, who was interested in a cotton-mill and had manners in the most splendid of the American styles. Ralph had two theories about this intervener. Either his passion was a sentimental fiction of Miss Stackpole's (there was always a sort of tacit understanding among women, born of the solidarity of the sex, that they should discover or invent lovers for each other), in which case he was not to be feared and would probably not accept the invitation; or else he would accept the invitation and in this event prove himself a creature too irrational to demand further consideration. The latter clause of Ralph's argument might have seemed incoherent; but it embodied his conviction that if Mr Goodwood were interested in Isabel in the serious manner described by Miss Stackpole he would not care to present himself at Gardencourt on a summons from the latter lady. 'On this supposition,' said Ralph, 'he must regard her as a thorn on the stem of his rose; as an intercessor he must find her wanting in tact.'

Two days after he had sent his invitation he received a very short note from Caspar Goodwood, thanking him for it, regretting that other engagements made a visit to Gardencourt impossible and presenting many compliments to Miss Stackpole. Ralph handed the note to Henrietta, who, when she had read it, exclaimed: 'Well, I never have heard of anything so stiff!'

'I'm afraid he doesn't care so much about my cousin as you suppose,' Ralph observed.

'No, it's not that; it's some subtler motive. His nature's very deep. But I'm determined to fathom it, and I shall write to him to know what he means.'

His refusal of Ralph's overtures was vaguely disconcerting; from the moment he declined to come to Gardencourt our friend began to think him of importance. He asked himself what it signified to him whether Isabel's admirers should be desperadoes or laggards; they were not rivals of his and were perfectly welcome to act out their genius. Nevertheless he felt much curiosity as to the result of Miss Stackpole's promised enquiry into the causes of Mr Goodwood's stiffness—a curiosity for the present ungratified, inasmuch as when he asked her three days later if she had written to London she was obliged to confess she had written in vain. Mr Goodwood had not replied.

'I suppose he's thinking it over,' she said; 'he thinks everything over; he's not *really* at all impetuous. But I'm accustomed to having my letters answered the same day.' She presently proposed to Isabel, at all events, that they should make an excursion to London together. 'If I must tell the truth,' she observed, 'I'm not seeing much at this place, and I shouldn't think you were either. I've not even seen that aristocrat—what's his name?—Lord Washburton. He seems to let you severely alone.'

'Lord Warburton's coming to-morrow, I happen to know,' replied her friend, who had received a note from the master of Lockleigh in answer to her own letter. 'You'll have every opportunity of turning him inside out.'

'Well, he may do for one letter, but what's one letter when you want to write fifty? I've described all the scenery in this vicinity and raved about all the old women and donkeys. You may say what you please, scenery doesn't make a vital letter. I must go back to London and get some impressions of real life. I was there but three days before I came away, and that's hardly time to get in touch.'

As Isabel, on her journey from New York to Gardencourt, had seen even less of the British capital than this, it appeared a happy suggestion of Henrietta's that the two should go thither on a visit of pleasure. The idea struck Isabel as charming; she was curious of the thick detail of London, which had always loomed large and rich to her. They turned over their schemes together and indulged in visions of romantic hours. They would stay at some picturesque old inn—one of the inns described by Dickens*—and drive over the town in those delightful hansoms. Henrietta was a literary woman, and the great advantage of being a literary woman was that you could go everywhere and do everything. They would dine at a coffee-house and go afterwards to the play; they would frequent the Abbey* and the British Museum and find out where Doctor Johnson had lived, and Goldsmith and Addison.* Isabel grew eager and presently unveiled the bright vision to Ralph, who burst into a fit of laughter which scarce expressed the sympathy she had desired.

'It's a delightful plan,' he said. 'I advise you to go to the Duke's Head in Covent Garden,* an easy, informal, old-fashioned place, and I'll have you put down at my club.'*

'Do you mean it's improper?' Isabel asked. 'Dear me, isn't anything proper here? With Henrietta surely I may go anywhere; she isn't hampered in that way. She has travelled over the whole American continent and can at least find her way about this minute island.'

'Ah then,' said Ralph, 'let me take advantage of her protection to go up to town as well. I may never have a chance to travel so safely!'

XIV

MISS STACKPOLE would have prepared to start immediately; but Isabel, as we have seen, had been notified that Lord Warburton would come again to Gardencourt, and she believed it her duty to remain there and see him. For four or five days he had made no response to her letter; then he had written, very briefly, to say he would come to luncheon two days later. There was something in these delays and postponements that touched the girl and renewed her sense of his desire to be considerate and patient, not to appear to urge her too grossly; a consideration the more studied that she was so sure he 'really liked' her. Isabel told her uncle she had written to him, mentioning also his intention of coming; and the old man, in consequence, left his room earlier than usual and made his appearance at the two o'clock repast. This was by no means an act of vigilance on his part, but the fruit of a benevolent belief that his being of the company might help to cover any conjoined straying away in case Isabel should give their noble visitor another hearing. That personage drove over from Lockleigh and brought the elder of his sisters with him, a measure presumably dictated by reflexions of the same order as Mr Touchett's. The two visitors were introduced to Miss Stackpole, who, at luncheon, occupied a seat adjoining Lord Warburton's. Isabel, who was nervous and had no relish for the prospect of again arguing the question he had so prematurely opened, could not help admiring his good-humoured self-possession, which quite disguised the symptoms of that preoccupation with her presence it was natural she should suppose him to feel. He neither looked at her nor spoke to her, and the only sign of his emotion was that he avoided meeting her eyes. He had plenty of talk for the others, however, and he appeared to eat his luncheon with discrimination and appetite. Miss Molyneux, who had a smooth, nunlike forehead and wore a large silver cross suspended from her neck, was evidently preoccupied with Henrietta Stackpole, upon whom her eyes constantly rested in a manner suggesting a conflict between deep alienation and yearning wonder. Of the two ladies from Lockleigh she was the one Isabel had liked best; there was such a world of hereditary quiet in her. Isabel was sure moreover that her mild forehead and silver cross referred to some weird Anglican mystery—some delightful reinstitution perhaps of the quaint office of the canoness. She wondered what Miss Molyneux would think of her if she knew Miss Archer had refused her brother; and then she felt sure that Miss Molyneux would never know—that Lord Warburton never told her such things. He was fond of her and kind to her, but on the whole he told her little. Such, at least, was Isabel's theory; when, at table, she was not occupied in conversation she was usually occupied in forming theories about her neighbours. According to Isabel, if Miss Molyneux should ever learn what had passed between Miss Archer and Lord Warburton she would probably be shocked at such a girl's failure to rise; or no, rather (this was our heroine's last position) she would impute to the young American but a due consciousness of inequality.

Whatever Isabel might have made of her opportunities, at all events, Henrietta Stackpole was by no means disposed to neglect those in which she now found herself immersed. 'Do you know you're the first lord I've ever seen?' she said very promptly to her neighbour. 'I suppose you think I'm awfully benighted.'

'You've escaped seeing some very ugly men,' Lord Warburton answered, looking a trifle absently about the table.

'Are they very ugly? They try to make us believe in America that they're all handsome and magnificent and that they wear wonderful robes and crowns.'

'Ah, the robes and crowns are gone out of fashion,' said Lord Warburton, 'like your tomahawks and revolvers.'

'I'm sorry for that; I think an aristocracy ought to be splendid,' Henrietta declared. 'If it's not that, what is it?'

'Oh, you know, it isn't much, at the best,' her neighbour allowed. 'Won't you have a potato?'

'I don't care much for these European potatoes. I shouldn't know you from an ordinary American gentleman.'

'Do talk to me as if I *were* one,' said Lord Warburton. 'I

don't see how you manage to get on without potatoes; you must find so few things to eat over here.'

Henrietta was silent a little; there was a chance he was not sincere. 'I've had hardly any appetite since I've been here,' she went on at last; 'so it doesn't much matter. I don't approve of *you*, you know; I feel as if I ought to tell you that.'

'Don't approve of me?'

'Yes; I don't suppose any one ever said such a thing to you before, did they? I don't approve of lords as an institution. I think the world has got beyond them—far beyond.'

'Oh, so do I. I don't approve of myself in the least. Sometimes it comes over me—how I should object to myself if I were not myself, don't you know? But that's rather good, by the way—not to be vain-glorious.'

'Why don't you give it up then?' Miss Stackpole enquired.

'Give up—a—?' asked Lord Warburton, meeting her harsh inflexion with a very mellow one.

'Give up being a lord.'

'Oh, I'm so little of one! One would really forget all about it if you wretched Americans were not constantly reminding one. However, I do think of giving it up, the little there is left of it, one of these days.'

'I should like to see you do it!' Henrietta exclaimed rather grimly.

'I'll invite you to the ceremony; we'll have a supper and a dance.'

'Well,' said Miss Stackpole, 'I like to see all sides. I don't approve of a privileged class, but I like to hear what they have to say for themselves.'

'Mighty little, as you see!'

'I should like to draw you out a little more,' Henrietta continued. 'But you're always looking away. You're afraid of meeting my eye. I see you want to escape me.'

'No, I'm only looking for those despised potatoes.'

'Please explain about that young lady—your sister—then. I don't understand about her. Is she a Lady?'

'She's a capital good girl.'

'I don't like the way you say that—as if you wanted to change the subject. Is her position inferior to yours?'

'We neither of us have any position to speak of; but she's better off than I, because she has none of the bother.'

'Yes, she doesn't look as if she had much bother. I wish I had as little bother as that. You do produce quiet people over here, whatever else you may do.'

'Ah, you see one takes life easily, on the whole,' said Lord Warburton. 'And then you know we're very dull. Ah, we can be dull when we try!'

'I should advise you to try something else. I shouldn't know what to talk to your sister about; she looks so different. Is that silver cross a badge?'

'A badge?'

'A sign of rank.'

Lord Warburton's glance had wandered a good deal, but at this it met the gaze of his neighbour. 'Oh yes,' he answered in a moment; 'the women go in for those things. The silver cross is worn by the eldest daughters of Viscounts.' Which was his harmless revenge for having occasionally had his credulity too easily engaged in America. After luncheon he proposed to Isabel to come into the gallery and look at the pictures; and though she knew he had seen the pictures twenty times she complied without criticising this pretext. Her conscience now was very easy; ever since she sent him her letter she had felt particularly light of spirit. He walked slowly to the end of the gallery, staring at its contents and saying nothing; and then he suddenly broke out: 'I hoped you wouldn't write to me that way.'

'It was the only way, Lord Warburton,' said the girl. 'Do try and believe that.'

'If I could believe it of course I should let you alone. But we can't believe by willing it; and I confess I don't understand. I could understand your disliking me; that I could understand well. But that you should admit you do—'

'What have I admitted?' Isabel interrupted, turning slightly pale.

'That you think me a good fellow; isn't that it?' She said nothing, and he went on: 'You don't seem to have any reason, and that gives me a sense of injustice.'

'I have a reason, Lord Warburton.' She said it in a tone that made his heart contract.

'I should like very much to know it.'

'I'll tell you some day when there's more to show for it.'

'Excuse my saying that in the mean time I must doubt of it.'

'You make me very unhappy,' said Isabel.

'I'm not sorry for that; it may help you to know how I feel. Will you kindly answer me a question?' Isabel made no audible assent, but he apparently saw in her eyes something that gave him courage to go on. 'Do you prefer some one else?'

'That's a question I'd rather not answer.'

'Ah, you *do* then!' her suitor murmured with bitterness.

The bitterness touched her, and she cried out: 'You're mistaken! I don't.'

He sat down on a bench, unceremoniously, doggedly, like a man in trouble; leaning his elbows on his knees and staring at the floor. 'I can't even be glad of that,' he said at last, throwing himself back against the wall; 'for that would be an excuse.'

She raised her eyebrows in surprise. 'An excuse? Must I excuse myself?'

He paid, however, no answer to the question. Another idea had come into his head. 'Is it my political opinions? Do you think I go too far?'

'I can't object to your political opinions, because I don't understand them.'

'You don't care what I think!' he cried, getting up. 'It's all the same to you.'

Isabel walked to the other side of the gallery and stood there showing him her charming back, her light slim figure, the length of her white neck as she bent her head, and the density of her dark braids. She stopped in front of a small picture as if for the purpose of examining it; and there was something so young and free in her movement that her very pliancy seemed to mock at him. Her eyes, however, saw nothing; they had suddenly been suffused with tears. In a moment he followed her, and by this time she had brushed her tears away; but when she turned round her face was pale and the expression of her eyes strange. 'That reason that I wouldn't tell you—I'll tell it you after all. It's that I can't escape my fate.'

'Your fate?'

'I should try to escape it if I were to marry you.'

'I don't understand. Why should not *that* be your fate as well as anything else?'

'Because it's not,' said Isabel femininely. 'I know it's not. It's not my fate to give up—I know it can't be.'

Poor Lord Warburton stared, an interrogative point in either eye. 'Do you call marrying *me* giving up?'

'Not in the usual sense. It's getting—getting—getting a great deal. But it's giving up other chances.'

'Other chances for what?'

'I don't mean chances to marry,' said Isabel, her colour quickly coming back to her. And then she stopped, looking down with a deep frown, as if it were hopeless to attempt to make her meaning clear.

'I don't think it presumptuous in me to suggest that you'll gain more than you'll lose,' her companion observed.

'I can't escape unhappiness,' said Isabel. 'In marrying you I shall be trying to.'

'I don't know whether you'd try to, but you certainly would: that I must in candour admit!' he exclaimed with an anxious laugh.

'I mustn't—I can't!' cried the girl.

'Well, if you're bent on being miserable I don't see why you should make *me* so. Whatever charms a life of misery may have for you, it has none for me.'

'I'm not bent on a life of misery,' said Isabel. 'I've always been intensely determined to be happy, and I've often believed I should be. I've told people that; you can ask them. But it comes over me every now and then that I can never be happy in any extraordinary way; not by turning away, by separating myself.'

'By separating yourself from what?'

'From life. From the usual chances and dangers, from what most people know and suffer.'

Lord Warburton broke into a smile that almost denoted hope. 'Why, my dear Miss Archer,' he began to explain with the most considerate eagerness, 'I don't offer you any exoneration from life or from any chances or dangers whatever. I wish I could; depend upon it I would! For what do you take me, pray? Heaven help me, I'm not the Emperor of China! All I offer you is the chance of taking the common lot in a comfortable sort of way. The common lot? Why, I'm devoted to the common lot! Strike an alliance with me, and I promise you that you shall have plenty of it. You shall separate from nothing whatever—not even from your friend Miss Stackpole.'

'She'd never approve of it,' said Isabel, trying to smile and take advantage of this side-issue; despising herself too, not a little, for doing so.

'Are we speaking of Miss Stackpole?' his lordship asked impatiently. 'I never saw a person judge things on such theoretic grounds.'

'Now I suppose you're speaking of me,' said Isabel with humility; and she turned away again, for she saw Miss Molyneux enter the gallery, accompanied by Henrietta and by Ralph.

Lord Warburton's sister addressed him with a certain timidity and reminded him she ought to return home in time for tea, as she was expecting company to partake of it. He made no answer—apparently not having heard her; he was preoccupied, and with good reason. Miss Molyneux—as if he had been Royalty—stood like a lady-in-waiting.

'Well, I never, Miss Molyneux!' said Henrietta Stackpole. 'If I wanted to go he'd have to go. If I wanted my brother to do a thing he'd have to do it.'

'Oh, Warburton does everything one wants,' Miss Molyneux answered with a quick, shy laugh. 'How very many pictures you have!' she went on, turning to Ralph.

'They look a good many, because they're all put together,' said Ralph. 'But it's really a bad way.'

'Oh, I think it's so nice. I wish we had a gallery at Lockleigh. I'm so very fond of pictures,' Miss Molyneux went on, persistently, to Ralph, as if she were afraid Miss Stackpole would address her again. Henrietta appeared at once to fascinate and to frighten her.

'Ah yes, pictures are very convenient,' said Ralph, who appeared to know better what style of reflexion was acceptable to her.

'They're so very pleasant when it rains,' the young lady continued. 'It has rained of late so very often.'

'I'm sorry you're going away, Lord Warburton,' said Henrietta. 'I wanted to get a great deal more out of you.'

'I'm not going away,' Lord Warburton answered.

'Your sister says you must. In America the gentlemen obey the ladies.'

'I'm afraid we have some people to tea,' said Miss Molyneux, looking at her brother.

'Very good, my dear. We'll go.'

'I hoped you would resist!' Henrietta exclaimed. 'I wanted to see what Miss Molyneux would do.'

'I never do anything,' said this young lady.

'I suppose in your position it's sufficient for you to exist!' Miss Stackpole returned. 'I should like very much to see you at home.'

'You must come to Lockleigh again,' said Miss Molyneux, very sweetly, to Isabel, ignoring this remark of Isabel's friend.

Isabel looked into her quiet eyes a moment, and for that moment seemed to see in their grey depths the reflexion of everything she had rejected in rejecting Lord Warburton—the peace, the kindness, the honour, the possessions, a deep security and a great exclusion. She kissed Miss Molyneux and then she said: 'I'm afraid I can never come again.'

'Never again?'

'I'm afraid I'm going away.'

'Oh, I'm so very sorry,' said Miss Molyneux. 'I think that's so very wrong of you.'

Lord Warburton watched this little passage; then he turned away and stared at a picture. Ralph, leaning against the rail before the picture with his hands in his pockets, had for the moment been watching him.

'I should like to see you at home,' said Henrietta, whom Lord Warburton found beside him. 'I should like an hour's talk with you; there are a great many questions I wish to ask you.'

'I shall be delighted to see you,' the proprietor of Lockleigh answered; 'but I'm certain not to be able to answer many of your questions. When will you come?'

'Whenever Miss Archer will take me. We're thinking of

going to London, but we'll go and see you first. I'm determined to get some satisfaction out of you.'

'If it depends upon Miss Archer I'm afraid you won't get much. She won't come to Lockleigh; she doesn't like the place.'

'She told me it was lovely!' said Henrietta.

Lord Warburton hesitated. 'She won't come, all the same. You had better come alone,' he added.

Henrietta straightened herself, and her large eyes expanded. 'Would you make that remark to an English lady?' she enquired with soft asperity.

Lord Warburton stared. 'Yes, if I liked her enough.'

'You'd be careful not to like her enough. If Miss Archer won't visit your place again it's because she doesn't want to take me. I know what she thinks of me, and I suppose you think the same—that I oughtn't to bring in individuals.' Lord Warburton was at a loss; he had not been made acquainted with Miss Stackpole's professional character and failed to catch her allusion. 'Miss Archer has been warning you!' she therefore went on.

'Warning me?'

'Isn't that why she came off alone with you here—to put you on your guard?'

'Oh dear, no,' said Lord Warburton brazenly; 'our talk had no such solemn character as that.'

'Well, you've been on your guard—intensely. I suppose it's natural to you; that's just what I wanted to observe. And so, too, Miss Molyneux—she wouldn't commit herself. *You* have been warned, anyway,' Henrietta continued, addressing this young lady; 'but for you it wasn't necessary.'

'I hope not,' said Miss Molyneux vaguely.

'Miss Stackpole takes notes,' Ralph soothingly explained. 'She's a great satirist; she sees through us all and she works us up.'

'Well, I must say I never have had such a collection of bad material!' Henrietta declared, looking from Isabel to Lord Warburton and from this nobleman to his sister and to Ralph. 'There's something the matter with you all; you're as dismal as if you had got a bad cable.'

'You do see through us, Miss Stackpole,' said Ralph in a low tone, giving her a little intelligent nod as he led the party out of the gallery. 'There's something the matter with us all.'

Isabel came behind these two; Miss Molyneux, who decidedly liked her immensely, had taken her arm, to walk beside her over the polished floor. Lord Warburton strolled on the other side with his hands behind him and his eyes lowered. For some moments he said nothing; and then, 'Is it true you're going to London?' he asked.

'I believe it has been arranged.'

'And when shall you come back?'

'In a few days; but probably for a very short time. I'm going to Paris with my aunt.'

'When, then, shall I see you again?'

'Not for a good while,' said Isabel. 'But some day or other, I hope.'

'Do you really hope it?'

'Very much.'

He went a few steps in silence; then he stopped and put out his hand. 'Good-bye.'

'Good-bye,' said Isabel.

Miss Molyneux kissed her again, and she let the two depart. After it, without rejoining Henrietta and Ralph, she retreated to her own room; in which apartment, before dinner, she was found by Mrs Touchett, who had stopped on her way to the saloon. 'I may as well tell you,' said that lady, 'that your uncle has informed me of your relations with Lord Warburton.'

Isabel considered. 'Relations? They're hardly relations. That's the strange part of it: he has seen me but three or four times.'

'Why did you tell your uncle rather than me?' Mrs Touchett dispassionately asked.

Again the girl hesitated. 'Because he knows Lord Warburton better.'

'Yes, but I know you better.'

'I'm not sure of that,' said Isabel, smiling.

'Neither am I, after all; especially when you give me that rather conceited look. One would think you were awfully pleased with yourself and had carried off a prize! I suppose that when you refuse an offer like Lord Warburton's it's because you expect to do something better.'

'Ah, my uncle didn't say that!' cried Isabel, smiling still.

XV

It had been arranged that the two young ladies should proceed to London under Ralph's escort, though Mrs Touchett looked with little favour on the plan. It was just the sort of plan, she said, that Miss Stackpole would be sure to suggest, and she enquired if the correspondent of the *Interviewer* was to take the party to stay at her favourite boarding-house.

'I don't care where she takes us to stay, so long as there's local colour,' said Isabel. 'That's what we're going to London for.'

'I suppose that after a girl has refused an English lord she may do anything,' her aunt rejoined. 'After that one needn't stand on trifles.'

'Should you have liked me to marry Lord Warburton?' Isabel enquired.

'Of course I should.'

'I thought you disliked the English so much.'

'So I do; but it's all the greater reason for making use of them.'

'Is that your idea of marriage?' And Isabel ventured to add that her aunt appeared to her to have made very little use of Mr Touchett.

'Your uncle's not an English nobleman,' said Mrs Touchett, 'though even if he had been I should still probably have taken up my residence in Florence.'

'Do you think Lord Warburton could make me any better than I am?' the girl asked with some animation. 'I don't mean I'm too good to improve. I mean—I mean that I don't love Lord Warburton enough to marry him.'

'You did right to refuse him then,' said Mrs Touchett in her smallest, sparest voice. 'Only, the next great offer you get, I hope you'll manage to come up to your standard.'

'We had better wait till the offer comes before we talk about it. I hope very much I may have no more offers for the present. They upset me completely.'

'You probably won't be troubled with them if you adopt

permanently the Bohemian manner of life. However, I've promised Ralph not to criticise.'

'I'll do whatever Ralph says is right,' Isabel returned. 'I've unbounded confidence in Ralph.'

'His mother's much obliged to you!' this lady dryly laughed.

'It seems to me indeed she ought to feel it!' Isabel irrepressibly answered.

Ralph had assured her that there would be no violation of decency in their paying a visit—the little party of three—to the sights of the metropolis; but Mrs Touchett took a different view. Like many ladies of her country who had lived a long time in Europe, she had completely lost her native tact on such points, and in her reaction, not in itself deplorable, against the liberty allowed to young persons beyond the seas, had fallen into gratuitous and exaggerated scruples. Ralph accompanied their visitors to town and established them at a quiet inn in a street that ran at right angles to Piccadilly.* His first idea had been to take them to his father's house in Winchester Square, a large, dull mansion which at this period of the year was shrouded in silence and brown holland; but he bethought himself that, the cook being at Gardencourt, there was no one in the house to get them their meals, and Pratt's Hotel accordingly became their resting-place. Ralph, on his side, found quarters in Winchester Square, having a 'den' there of which he was very fond and being familiar with deeper fears than that of a cold kitchen. He availed himself largely indeed of the resources of Pratt's Hotel, beginning his day with an early visit to his fellow travellers, who had Mr Pratt in person, in a large bulging white waistcoat, to remove their dish-covers. Ralph turned up, as he said, after breakfast, and the little party made out a scheme of entertainment for the day. As London wears in the month of September* a face blank but for its smears of prior service, the young man, who occasionally took an apologetic tone, was obliged to remind his companion, to Miss Stackpole's high derision, that there wasn't a creature in town.

'I suppose you mean the aristocracy are absent,' Henrietta answered; 'but I don't think you could have a better proof that if they were absent altogether they wouldn't be missed. It seems to me the place is about as full as it can be. There's no one here, of course, but three or four millions of people. What is it you call them—the lower-middle class? They're only the population of London, and that's of no consequence.'

Ralph declared that for him the aristocracy left no void that Miss Stackpole herself didn't fill, and that a more contented man was nowhere at that moment to be found. In this he spoke the truth, for the stale September days, in the huge half-empty town, had a charm wrapped in them as a coloured gem might be wrapped in a dusty cloth. When he went home at night to the empty house in Winchester Square, after a chain of hours with his comparatively ardent friends, he wandered into the big dusky dining-room, where the candle he took from the hall-table, after letting himself in, constituted the only illumination. The square was still, the house was still; when he raised one of the windows of the dining-room to let in the air he heard the slow creak of the boots of a lone constable. His own step, in the empty place, seemed loud and sonorous; some of the carpets had been raised, and whenever he moved he roused a melancholy echo. He sat down in one of the armchairs; the big dark dining table twinkled here and there in the small candle-light; the pictures on the wall, all of them very brown, looked vague and incoherent. There was a ghostly presence as of dinners long since digested, of table-talk that had lost its actuality. This hint of the supernatural perhaps had something to do with the fact that his imagination took a flight and that he remained in his chair a long time beyond the hour at which he should have been in bed; doing nothing, not even reading the evening paper. I say he did nothing, and I maintain the phrase in the face of the fact that he thought at these moments of Isabel. To think of Isabel could only be for him an idle pursuit, leading to nothing and profiting little to any one. His cousin had not yet seemed to him so charming as during these days spent in sounding, tourist-fashion, the deeps and shallows of the metropolitan element. Isabel was full of premises, conclusions, emotions; if she had come in search of local colour she found it everywhere. She asked more questions than he could answer, and launched brave theories, as to historic cause and social effect, that he was equally unable to accept or to refute. The party went more than once to the

British Museum and to that brighter palace of art* which reclaims for antique variety so large an area of a monotonous suburb; they spent a morning in the Abbey and went on a penny-steamer to the Tower; they looked at pictures both in public and private collections and sat on various occasions beneath the great trees in Kensington Gardens. Henrietta proved an indestructible sight-seer and a more lenient judge than Ralph had ventured to hope. She had indeed many disappointments, and London at large suffered from her vivid remembrance of the strong points of the American civic idea; but she made the best of its dingy dignities and only heaved an occasional sigh and uttered a desultory 'Well!' which led no further and lost itself in retrospect. The truth was that, as she said herself, she was not in her element. 'I've not a sympathy with inanimate objects,' she remarked to Isabel at the National Gallery; and she continued to suffer from the meagreness of the glimpse that had as yet been vouchsafed to her of the inner life. Landscapes by Turner and Assyrian bulls were a poor substitute for the literary dinner-parties at which she had hoped to meet the genius and renown of Great Britain.

'Where are your public men, where are your men and women of intellect?' she enquired of Ralph, standing in the middle of Trafalgar Square as if she had supposed this to be a place where she would naturally meet a few. 'That's one of them on the top of the column, you say—Lord Nelson? Was he a lord too? Wasn't he high enough, that they had to stick him a hundred feet in the air? That's the past—I don't care about the past; I want to see some of the leading minds of the present. I won't say of the future, because I don't believe much in your future.' Poor Ralph had few leading minds among his acquaintance and rarely enjoyed the pleasure of buttonholing a celebrity; a state of things which appeared to Miss Stackpole to indicate a deplorable want of enterprise. 'If I were on the other side I should call,' she said, 'and tell the gentleman, whoever he might be, that I had heard a great deal about him and had come to see for myself. But I gather from what you say that this is not the custom here. You seem to have plenty of meaningless customs, but none of those that would help along. We *are* in advance, certainly. I suppose I shall have to give up the social side altogether;' and Henrietta, though she went about with her guidebook and pencil and wrote a letter to the *Interviewer* about the Tower (in which she described the execution of Lady Jane Grey*), had a sad sense of falling below her mission.

The incident that had preceded Isabel's departure from Gardencourt left a painful trace in our young woman's mind: when she felt again in her face, as from a recurrent wave, the cold breath of her last suitor's surprise, she could only muffle her head till the air cleared. She could not have done less than what she did; this was certainly true. But her necessity, all the same, had been as graceless as some physical act in a strained attitude, and she felt no desire to take credit for her conduct. Mixed with this imperfect pride, nevertheless, was a feeling of freedom which in itself was sweet and which, as she wandered through the great city with her ill-matched companions, occasionally throbbed into odd demonstrations. When she walked in Kensington Gardens she stopped the children (mainly of the poorer sort) whom she saw playing on the grass; she asked them their names and gave them sixpence and, when they were pretty, kissed them. Ralph noticed these quaint charities; he noticed everything she did. One afternoon, that his companions might pass the time, he invited them to tea in Winchester Square, and he had the house set in order as much as possible for their visit. There was another guest to meet them, an amiable bachelor, an old friend of Ralph's who happened to be in town and for whom prompt commerce with Miss Stackpole appeared to have neither difficulty nor dread. Mr Bantling, a stout, sleek, smiling man of forty, wonderfully dressed, universally informed and incoherently amused, laughed immoderately at everything Henrietta said, gave her several cups of tea, examined in her society the *bric-à-brac*, of which Ralph had a considerable collection, and afterwards, when the host proposed they should go out into the square and pretend it was a *fête-champêtre*,* walked round the limited enclosure several times with her and, at a dozen turns of their talk, bounded responsive—as with a positive passion for argument—to her remarks upon the inner life.

'Oh, I see; I dare say you found it very quiet at Gardencourt. Naturally there's not much going on there when there's such a lot of illness about. Touchett's very bad, you know; the doctors have forbidden his being in England at all, and he has only come back to take care of his father. The old man, I believe, has half a dozen things the matter with him. They call it gout, but to my certain knowledge he has organic disease so developed that you may depend upon it he'll go, some day soon, quite quickly. Of course that sort of thing makes a dreadfully dull house; I wonder they have people when they can do so little for them. Then I believe Mr Touchett's always squabbling with his wife; she lives away from her husband, you know, in that extraordinary American way of yours. If you want a house where there's always something going on, I recommend you to go down and stay with my sister, Lady Pensil, in Bedfordshire. I'll write to her to-morrow and I'm sure she'll be delighted to ask you. I know just what you want—you want a house where they go in for theatricals and picnics and that sort of thing. My sister's just that sort of woman; she's always getting up something or other and she's always glad to have the sort of people who help her. I'm sure she'll ask you down by return of post: she's tremendously fond of distinguished people and writers. She writes herself, you know; but I haven't read everything she has written. It's usually poetry, and I don't go in much for poetry—unless it's Byron.* I suppose you think a great deal of Byron in America,' Mr Bantling continued, expanding in the stimulating air of Miss Stackpole's attention, bringing up his sequences promptly and changing his topic with an easy turn of hand. Yet he none the less gracefully kept in sight of the idea, dazzling to Henrietta, of her going to stay with Lady Pensil in Bedfordshire. 'I understand what you want; you want to see some genuine English sport. The Touchetts aren't English at all, you know; they have their own habits, their own language, their own food—some odd religion even, I believe, of their own. The old man thinks it's wicked to hunt, I'm told. You must get down to my sister's in time for the theatricals, and I'm sure she'll be glad to give you a part. I'm sure you act well; I know you're very clever. My sister's forty years old and has seven children, but she's going to play the principal part. Plain as she is she makes up awfully well—I *will* say for her. Of course you needn't act if you don't want to.'

In this manner Mr Bantling delivered himself while they strolled over the grass in Winchester Square, which, although it had been peppered by the London soot, invited the tread to linger. Henrietta thought her blooming, easy-voiced bachelor, with his impressibility to feminine merit and his splendid range of suggestion, a very agreeable man, and she valued the opportunity he offered her. 'I don't know but I *would* go, if your sister should ask me. I think it would be my duty. What do you call her name?'

'Pensil. It's an odd name, but it isn't a bad one.'

'I think one name's as good as another. But what's her rank?'

'Oh, she's a baron's wife; a convenient sort of rank. You're fine enough and you're not too fine.'

'I don't know but what she'd be too fine for me. What do you call the place she lives in—Bedfordshire?'

'She lives away in the northern corner of it. It's a tiresome country, but I dare say you won't mind it. I'll try and run down while you're there.'

All this was very pleasant to Miss Stackpole, and she was sorry to be obliged to separate from Lady Pensil's obliging brother. But it happened that she had met the day before, in Piccadilly, some friends whom she had not seen for a year: the Miss Climbers, two ladies from Wilmington, Delaware, who had been travelling on the Continent and were now preparing to re-embark. Henrietta had had a long interview with them on the Piccadilly pavement, and though the three ladies all talked at once they had not exhausted their store. It had been agreed therefore that Henrietta should come and dine with them in their lodgings in Jermyn Street* at six o'clock on the morrow, and she now bethought herself of this engagement. She prepared to start for Jermyn Street, taking leave first of Ralph Touchett and Isabel, who, seated on garden chairs in another part of the enclosure, were occupied—if the term may be used—with an exchange of amenities less pointed than the practical colloquy of Miss Stackpole and Mr Bantling. When it had been settled between Isabel and her friend that they should be reunited at some reputable hour at Pratt's Hotel, Ralph remarked that the latter must have a cab. She couldn't walk all the way to Jermyn Street.

'I suppose you mean it's improper for me to walk alone!' Henrietta exclaimed. 'Merciful powers, have I come to this?'

'There's not the slightest need of your walking alone,' Mr Bantling gaily interposed. 'I should be greatly pleased to go with you.'

'I simply meant that you'd be late for dinner,' Ralph returned. 'Those poor ladies may easily believe that we refuse, at the last, to spare you.'

'You had better have a hansom, Henrietta,' said Isabel.

'I'll get you a hansom if you'll trust me,' Mr Bantling went on. 'We might walk a little till we meet one.'

'I don't see why I shouldn't trust him, do *you*?' Henrietta enquired of Isabel.

'I don't see what Mr Bantling could do to you,' Isabel obligingly answered; 'but, if you like, we'll walk with you till you find your cab.'

'Never mind; we'll go alone. Come on, Mr Bantling, and take care you get me a good one.'

Mr Bantling promised to do his best, and the two took their departure, leaving the girl and her cousin together in the square, over which a clear September twilight had now begun to gather. It was perfectly still; the wide quadrangle of dusky houses showed lights in none of the windows, where the shutters and blinds were closed; the pavements were a vacant expanse, and, putting aside two small children from a neighbouring slum, who, attracted by symptoms of abnormal animation in the interior, poked their faces between the rusty rails of the enclosure, the most vivid object within sight was the big red pillar-post on the southeast corner.

'Henrietta will ask him to get into the cab and go with her to Jermyn Street,' Ralph observed. He always spoke of Miss Stackpole as Henrietta.

'Very possibly,' said his companion.

'Or rather, no, she won't,' he went on. 'But Bantling will ask leave to get in.'

'Very likely again. I'm very glad they're such good friends.'

'She has made a conquest. He thinks her a brilliant woman. It may go far,' said Ralph.

Isabel was briefly silent. 'I call Henrietta a very brilliant woman, but I don't think it will go far. They would never really know each other. He has not the least idea what she really is, and she has no just comprehension of Mr Bantling.'

'There's no more usual basis of union than a mutual misunderstanding. But it ought not to be so difficult to understand Bob Bantling,' Ralph added. 'He is a very simple organism.'

'Yes, but Henrietta's a simpler one still. And, pray, what am I to do?' Isabel asked, looking about her through the fading light, in which the limited landscape-gardening of the square took on a large and effective appearance. 'I don't imagine that you'll propose that you and I, for our amusement, shall drive about London in a hansom.'

'There's no reason we shouldn't stay here—if you don't dislike it. It's very warm; there will be half an hour yet before dark; and if you permit it I'll light a cigarette.'

'You may do what you please,' said Isabel, 'if you'll amuse me till seven o'clock. I propose at that hour to go back and partake of a simple and solitary repast—two poached eggs and a muffin—at Pratt's Hotel.'

'Mayn't I dine with you?' Ralph asked.

'No, you'll dine at your club.'

They had wandered back to their chairs in the centre of the square again, and Ralph had lighted his cigarette. It would have given him extreme pleasure to be present in person at the modest little feast she had sketched; but in default of this he liked even being forbidden. For the moment, however, he liked immensely being alone with her, in the thickening dusk, in the centre of the multitudinous town; it made her seem to depend upon him and to be in his power. This power he could exert but vaguely; the best exercise of it was to accept her decisions submissively—which indeed there was already an emotion in doing. 'Why won't you let me dine with you?' he demanded after a pause.

'Because I don't care for it.'

'I suppose you're tired of me.'

'I shall be an hour hence. You see I have the gift of foreknowledge.'

'Oh, I shall be delightful meanwhile,' said Ralph. But he said nothing more, and as she made no rejoinder they sat some time in a stillness which seemed to contradict his promise of entertainment. It seemed to him she was preoccupied, and he wondered what she was thinking about; there were two or three very possible subjects. At last he spoke again. 'Is your objection to my society this evening caused by your expectation of another visitor?'

She turned her head with a glance of her clear, fair eyes. 'Another visitor? What visitor should I have?'

He had none to suggest; which made his question seem to himself silly as well as brutal. 'You've a great many friends that I don't know. You've a whole past from which I was perversely excluded.'

'You were reserved for my future. You must remember that my past is over there across the water. There's none of it here in London.'

'Very good, then, since your future is seated beside you. Capital thing to have your future so handy.' And Ralph lighted another cigarette and reflected that Isabel probably meant she had received news that Mr Caspar Goodwood had crossed to Paris. After he had lighted his cigarette he puffed it a while, and then he resumed. 'I promised just now to be very amusing; but you see I don't come up to the mark, and the fact is there's a good deal of temerity in one's undertaking to amuse a person like you. What do you care for my feeble attempts? You've grand ideas—you've a high standard in such matters. I ought at least to bring in a band of music or a company of mountebanks.'

'One mountebank's enough, and you do very well. Pray go on, and in another ten minutes I shall begin to laugh.'

'I assure you I'm very serious,' said Ralph. 'You do really ask a great deal.'

'I don't know what you mean. I ask nothing!'

'You accept nothing,' said Ralph. She coloured, and now suddenly it seemed to her that she guessed his meaning. But why should he speak to her of such things? He hesitated a little and then he continued: 'There's something I should like very much to say to you. It's a question I wish to ask. It seems to me I've a right to ask it, because I've a kind of interest in the answer.'

'Ask what you will,' Isabel replied gently, 'and I'll try to satisfy you.'

'Well then, I hope you won't mind my saying that Warburton has told me of something that has passed between you.'

Isabel suppressed a start; she sat looking at her open fan. 'Very good; I suppose it was natural he should tell you.'

'I have his leave to let you know he has done so. He has some hope still,' said Ralph.

'Still?'

'He had it a few days ago.'

'I don't believe he has any now,' said the girl.

'I'm very sorry for him then; he's such an honest man.'

'Pray, did he ask you to talk to me?'

'No, not that. But he told me because he couldn't help it. We're old friends, and he was greatly disappointed. He sent me a line asking me to come and see him, and I drove over to Lockleigh the day before he and his sister lunched with us. He was very heavy-hearted; he had just got a letter from you.'

'Did he show you the letter?' asked Isabel with momentary loftiness.

'By no means. But he told me it was a neat refusal. I was very sorry for him,' Ralph repeated.

For some moments Isabel said nothing; then at last, 'Do you know how often he had seen me?' she enquired. 'Five or six times.'

'That's to your glory.'

'It's not for that I say it.'

'What then do you say it for? Not to prove that poor Warburton's state of mind's superficial, because I'm pretty sure you don't think that.'

Isabel certainly was unable to say she thought it; but presently she said something else. 'If you've not been requested by Lord Warburton to argue with me, then you're doing it disinterestedly—or for the love of argument.'

'I've no wish to argue with you at all. I only wish to leave you alone. I'm simply greatly interested in your own sentiments.'

'I'm greatly obliged to you!' cried Isabel with a slightly nervous laugh.

'Of course you mean that I'm meddling in what doesn't concern me. But why shouldn't I speak to you of this matter without annoying you or embarrassing myself? What's the use of being your cousin if I can't have a few privileges? What's the use of adoring you without hope of a reward if I can't have a few compensations? What's the use of being ill and disabled and restricted to mere spectatorship at the game of life if I really can't see the show when I've paid so much for my ticket? Tell me this,' Ralph went on while she listened to him with quickened attention. 'What had you in mind when you refused Lord Warburton?'

'What had I in mind?'

'What was the logic—the view of your situation—that dictated so remarkable an act?'

'I didn't wish to marry him—if that's logic.'

'No, that's not logic—and I knew that before. It's really nothing, you know. What was it you *said* to yourself? You certainly said more than that.'

Isabel reflected a moment, then answered with a question of her own. 'Why do you call it a remarkable act? That's what your mother thinks too.'

'Warburton's such a thorough good sort; as a man, I consider he has hardly a fault. And then he's what they call here no end of a swell. He has immense possessions, and his wife would be thought a superior being. He unites the intrinsic and the extrinsic advantages.'

Isabel watched her cousin as to see how far he would go. 'I refused him because he was too perfect then. I'm not perfect myself, and he's too good for me. Besides, his perfection would irritate me.'

'That's ingenious rather than candid,' said Ralph. 'As a fact you think nothing in the world too perfect for you.'

'Do you think I'm so good?'

'No, but you're exacting, all the same, without the excuse of thinking yourself good. Nineteen women out of twenty, however, even of the most exacting sort, would have managed to do with Warburton. Perhaps you don't know how he has been stalked.'

'I don't wish to know. But it seems to me,' said Isabel, 'that one day when we talked of him you mentioned odd things in him.'

Ralph smokingly considered. 'I hope that what I said then had no weight with you; for they were not faults, the things I spoke of: they were simply peculiarities of his position. If I had known he wished to marry you I'd never have alluded to them. I think I said that as regards that position he was rather a sceptic. It would have been in your power to make him a believer.'

'I think not. I don't understand the matter, and I'm not conscious of any mission of that sort. You're evidently disappointed,' Isabel added, looking at her cousin with rueful gentleness. 'You'd have liked me to make such a marriage.'

'Not in the least. I'm absolutely without a wish on the subject. I don't pretend to advise you, and I content myself with watching you—with the deepest interest.'

She gave rather a conscious sigh. 'I wish I could be as interesting to myself as I am to you!'

'There you're not candid again; you're extremely interesting to yourself. Do you know, however,' said Ralph, 'that if you've really given Warburton his final answer I'm rather glad it has been what it was. I don't mean I'm glad for you, and still less of course for him. I'm glad for myself.'

'Are *you* thinking of proposing to me?'

'By no means. From the point of view I speak of that would be fatal; I should kill the goose that supplies me with the material of my inimitable omelettes.* I use that animal as the symbol of my insane illusions. What I mean is that I shall have the thrill of seeing what a young lady does who won't marry Lord Warburton.'

'That's what your mother counts upon too,' said Isabel.

'Ah, there will be plenty of spectators! We shall hang on the rest of your career. I shall not see all of it, but I shall probably see the most interesting years. Of course if you were to marry our friend you'd still have a career—a very decent, in fact a very brilliant one. But relatively speaking it would be a little prosaic. It would be definitely marked out in advance; it would be wanting in the unexpected. You know I'm extremely fond of the unexpected, and now that you've kept the game in your hands I depend on your giving us some grand example of it.'

'I don't understand you very well,' said Isabel, 'but I do so well enough to be able to say that if you look for grand examples of anything from me I shall disappoint you.'

'You'll do so only by disappointing yourself—and that will go hard with you!'

To this she made no direct reply; there was an amount of truth in it that would bear consideration. At last she said abruptly: 'I don't see what harm there is in my wishing not to tie myself. I don't want to begin life by marrying. There are other things a woman can do.'

'There's nothing she can do so well. But you're of course so many-sided.'

'If one's two-sided it's enough,' said Isabel.

'You're the most charming of polygons!' her companion broke out. At a glance from his companion, however, he became grave, and to prove it went on: 'You want to see life—you'll be hanged if you don't, as the young men say.'

'I don't think I want to see it as the young men want to see it. But I do want to look about me.'

'You want to drain the cup of experience.'

'No, I don't wish to touch the cup of experience. It's a poisoned drink! I only want to see for myself.'

'You want to see, but not to feel,' Ralph remarked.

'I don't think that if one's a sentient being one can make the distinction. I'm a good deal like Henrietta. The other day when I asked her if she wished to marry she said: "Not till I've seen Europe!" I too don't wish to marry till I've seen Europe.'

'You evidently expect a crowned head will be struck with you.'

'No, that would be worse than marrying Lord Warburton. But it's getting very dark,' Isabel continued, 'and I must go home.' She rose from her place, but Ralph only sat still and looked at her. As he remained there she stopped, and they exchanged a gaze that was full on either side, but especially on Ralph's, of utterances too vague for words.

'You've answered my question,' he said at last. 'You've told me what I wanted. I'm greatly obliged to you.'

'It seems to me I've told you very little.'

'You've told me the great thing: that the world interests you and that you want to throw yourself into it.'

Her silvery eyes shone a moment in the dusk. 'I never said that.'

'I think you meant it. Don't repudiate it. It's so fine!'

'I don't know what you're trying to fasten upon me, for I'm not in the least an adventurous spirit. Women are not like men.'

Ralph slowly rose from his seat and they walked together to the gate of the square. 'No,' he said; 'women rarely boast of their courage. Men do so with a certain frequency.'

'Men have it to boast of!'

'Women have it too. You've a great deal.'

'Enough to go home in a cab to Pratt's Hotel, but not more.'

Ralph unlocked the gate, and after they had passed out he fastened it. 'We'll find your cab,' he said; and as they turned toward a neighbouring street in which this quest might avail he asked her again if he mightn't see her safely to the inn.

'By no means,' she answered; 'you're very tired; you must go home and go to bed.'

The cab was found, and he helped her into it, standing a moment at the door. 'When people forget I'm a poor creature I'm often incommoded,' he said. 'But it's worse when they remember it!'

XVI

SHE had had no hidden motive in wishing him not to take her home; it simply struck her that for some days past she had consumed an inordinate quantity of his time, and the independent spirit of the American girl whom extravagance of aid places in an attitude that she ends by finding 'affected' had made her decide that for these few hours she must suffice to herself. She had moreover a great fondness for intervals of solitude, which since her arrival in England had been but meagrely met. It was a luxury she could always command at home and she had wittingly missed it. That evening, however, an incident occurred which—had there been a critic to note it—would have taken all colour from the theory that the wish to be quite by herself had caused her to dispense with her cousin's attendance. Seated toward nine o'clock in the dim illumination of Pratt's Hotel and trying with the aid of two tall candles to lose herself in a volume she had brought from Gardencourt, she succeeded only to the extent of reading other words than those printed on the page—words that Ralph had spoken to her that afternoon. Suddenly the well-muffled knuckle of the waiter was applied to the door, which presently gave way to his exhibition, even as a glorious trophy, of the card of a visitor. When this memento had offered to her fixed sight the name of Mr Caspar Goodwood she let the man stand before her without signifying her wishes.

'Shall I show the gentleman up, ma'am?' he asked with a slightly encouraging inflexion.

Isabel hesitated still and while she hesitated glanced at the mirror. 'He may come in,' she said at last; and waited for him not so much smoothing her hair as girding her spirit.

Caspar Goodwood was accordingly the next moment shaking hands with her, but saying nothing till the servant had left the room. 'Why didn't you answer my letter?' he then asked in a quick, full, slightly peremptory tone—the tone of a man whose questions were habitually pointed and who was capable of much insistence.

She answered by a ready question, 'How did you know I was here?'

'Miss Stackpole let me know,' said Caspar Goodwood. 'She told me you would probably be at home alone this evening and would be willing to see me.'

'Where did she see you—to tell you that?'

'She didn't see me; she wrote to me.'

Isabel was silent; neither had sat down; they stood there with an air of defiance, or at least of contention. 'Henrietta never told me she was writing to you,' she said at last. 'This is not kind of her.'

'Is it so disagreeable to you to see me?' asked the young man.

'I didn't expect it. I don't like such surprises.'

'But you knew I was in town; it was natural we should meet.'

'Do you call this meeting? I hoped I shouldn't see you. In so big a place as London it seemed very possible.'

'It was apparently repugnant to you even to write to me,' her visitor went on.

Isabel made no reply; the sense of Henrietta Stackpole's treachery, as she momentarily qualified it, was strong within her. 'Henrietta's certainly not a model of all the delicacies!' she exclaimed with bitterness. 'It was a great liberty to take.'

'I suppose I'm not a model either—of those virtues or of any others. The fault's mine as much as hers.'

As Isabel looked at him it seemed to her that his jaw had never been more square. This might have displeased her, but she took a different turn. 'No, it's not your fault so much as hers. What you've done was inevitable, I suppose, for *you*.'

'It was indeed!' cried Caspar Goodwood with a voluntary laugh. 'And now that I've come, at any rate, mayn't I stay?'

'You may sit down, certainly.'

She went back to her chair again, while her visitor took the first place that offered, in the manner of a man accustomed to pay little thought to that sort of furtherance. 'I've been hoping every day for an answer to my letter. You might have written me a few lines.'

'It wasn't the trouble of writing that prevented me; I could as easily have written you four pages as one. But my silence was an intention,' Isabel said. 'I thought it the best thing.'

He sat with his eyes fixed on hers while she spoke; then he lowered them and attached them to a spot in the carpet as if he were making a strong effort to say nothing but what he ought. He was a strong man in the wrong, and he was acute enough to see that an uncompromising exhibition of his strength would only throw the falsity of his position into relief. Isabel was not incapable of taking any advantage of position over a person of this quality, and though little desirous to flaunt it in his face she could enjoy being able to say 'You know you oughtn't to have written to me yourself!' and to say it with an air of triumph.

Caspar Goodwood raised his eyes to her own again; they seemed to shine through the vizard of a helmet. He had a strong sense of justice and was ready any day in the year—over and above this—to argue the question of his rights. 'You said you hoped never to hear from me again; I know that. But I never accepted any such rule as my own. I warned you that you should hear very soon.'

'I didn't say I hoped *never* to hear from you,' said Isabel.

'Not for five years then; for ten years; twenty years. It's the same thing.'

'Do you find it so? It seems to me there's a great difference. I can imagine that at the end of ten years we might have a very pleasant correspondence. I shall have matured my epistolary style.'

She looked away while she spoke these words, knowing them of so much less earnest a cast than the countenance of her listener. Her eyes, however, at last came back to him, just as he said very irrelevantly: 'Are you enjoying your visit to your uncle?'

'Very much indeed.' She stopped, but then she broke out. 'What good do you expect to get by insisting?'

'The good of not losing you.'

'You've no right to talk of losing what's not yours. And even from your own point of view,' Isabel added, 'you ought to know when to let one alone.'

'I disgust you very much,' said Caspar Goodwood gloomily; not as if to provoke her to compassion for a man conscious of this blighting fact, but as if to set it well before himself, so that he might endeavour to act with his eyes on it.

'Yes, you don't at all delight me, you don't fit in, not in any way, just now, and the worst is that your putting it to the proof in this manner is quite unnecessary.' It wasn't certainly as if his nature had been soft, so that pin-pricks would draw blood from it; and from the first of her acquaintance with him, and of her having to defend herself against a certain air that he had of knowing better what was good for her than she knew herself, she had recognised the fact that perfect frankness was her best weapon. To attempt to spare his sensibility or to escape from him edgewise, as one might do from a man who had barred the way less sturdily—this, in dealing with Caspar Goodwood, who would grasp at everything of every sort that one might give him, was wasted agility. It was not that he had not susceptibilities, but his passive surface, as well as his active, was large and hard, and he might always be trusted to dress his wounds, so far as they required it, himself. She came back, even for her measure of possible pangs and aches in him, to her old sense that he was naturally plated and steeled, armed essentially for aggression.

'I can't reconcile myself to that,' he simply said. There was a dangerous liberality about it; for she felt how open it was to him to make the point that he had not always disgusted her.

'I can't reconcile myself to it either, and it's not the state of things that ought to exist between us. If you'd only try to banish me from your mind for a few months we should be on good terms again.'

'I see. If I should cease to think of you at all for a prescribed time, I should find I could keep it up indefinitely.'

'Indefinitely is more than I ask. It's more even than I should like.'

'You know that what you ask is impossible,' said the young man, taking his adjective for granted in a manner she found irritating.

'Aren't you capable of making a calculated effort?' she demanded. 'You're strong for everything else; why shouldn't you be strong for that?'

'An effort calculated for what?' And then as she hung fire, 'I'm capable of nothing with regard to you,' he went on, 'but just of being infernally in love with you. If one's strong one loves only the more strongly.'

'There's a good deal in that;' and indeed our young lady felt the force of it—felt it thrown off, into the vast of truth and poetry, as practically a bait to her imagination. But she promptly came round. 'Think of me or not, as you find most possible; only leave me alone.'

'Until when?'

'Well, for a year or two.'

'Which do you mean? Between one year and two there's all the difference in the world.'

'Call it two then,' said Isabel with a studied effect of eagerness.

'And what shall I gain by that?' her friend asked with no sign of wincing.

'You'll have obliged me greatly.'

'And what will be my reward?'

'Do you need a reward for an act of generosity?'

'Yes, when it involves a great sacrifice.'

'There's no generosity without some sacrifice. Men don't understand such things. If you make the sacrifice you'll have all my admiration.'

'I don't care a cent for your admiration—not one straw, with nothing to show for it. When will you marry me? That's the only question.'

'Never—if you go on making me feel only as I feel at present.'

'What do I gain then by not trying to make you feel otherwise?'

'You'll gain quite as much as by worrying me to death!' Caspar Goodwood bent his eyes again and gazed a while into the crown of his hat. A deep flush overspread his face; she could see her sharpness had at last penetrated. This immediately had a value—classic, romantic, redeeming, what did she know?—for her; 'the strong man in pain' was one of the categories of the human appeal, little charm as he might exert in the given case. 'Why do you make me say such things to you?' she cried in a trembling voice. 'I only want to be gentle—to be thoroughly kind. It's not delightful to me to feel people care for me and yet to have to try and reason them out of it. I think others also ought to be considerate; we have each to judge for ourselves. I know you're considerate, as much as you can be; you've good reasons for what you do. But I really don't want to marry, or to talk about it at all now. I shall probably never do it—no, never. I've a perfect right to feel that way, and it's no kindness to a woman to press her so hard, to urge her against her will. If I give you pain I can only say I'm very sorry. It's not my fault; I can't marry you simply to please you. I won't say that I shall always remain your friend, because when women say that, in these situations, it passes, I believe, for a sort of mockery. But try me some day.'

Caspar Goodwood, during this speech, had kept his eyes fixed upon the name of his hatter, and it was not until some time after she had ceased speaking that he raised them. When he did so the sight of a rosy, lovely eagerness in Isabel's face threw some confusion into his attempt to analyse her words. 'I'll go home—I'll go to-morrow—I'll leave you alone,' he brought out at last. 'Only,' he heavily said, 'I hate to lose sight of you!'

'Never fear. I shall do no harm.'

'You'll marry some one else, as sure as I sit here,' Caspar Goodwood declared.

'Do you think that a generous charge?'

'Why not? Plenty of men will try to make you.'

'I told you just now that I don't wish to marry and that I almost certainly never shall.'

'I know you did, and I like your "almost certainly"! I put no faith in what you say.'

'Thank you very much. Do you accuse me of lying to shake you off? You say very delicate things.'

'Why should I not say that? You've given me no pledge of anything at all.'

'No, that's all that would be wanting!'

'You may perhaps even believe you're safe—from wishing to be. But you're not,' the young man went on as if preparing himself for the worst.

'Very well then. We'll put it that I'm not safe. Have it as you please.'

'I don't know, however,' said Caspar Goodwood, 'that my keeping you in sight would prevent it.'

'Don't you indeed? I'm after all very much afraid of you. Do you think I'm so very easily pleased?' she asked suddenly, changing her tone.

'No—I don't; I shall try to console myself with that. But there are a certain number of very dazzling men in the world, no doubt; and if there were only one it would be enough. The most dazzling of all will make straight for you. You'll be sure to take no one who isn't dazzling.'

'If you mean by dazzling brilliantly clever,' Isabel said—'and I can't imagine what else you mean—I don't need the aid of a clever man to teach me how to live. I can find it out for myself.'

'Find out how to live alone? I wish that, when you have, you'd teach *me*!'

She looked at him a moment; then with a quick smile, 'Oh, *you* ought to marry!' she said.

He might be pardoned if for an instant this exclamation seemed to him to sound the infernal note, and it is not on record that her motive for discharging such a shaft had been of the clearest. He oughtn't to stride about lean and hungry, however—she certainly felt *that* for him. 'God forgive you!' he murmured between his teeth as he turned away.

Her accent had put her slightly in the wrong, and after a moment she felt the need to right herself. The easiest way to do it was to place him where she had been. 'You do me great injustice—you say what you don't know!' she broke out. 'I shouldn't be an easy victim—I've proved it.'

'Oh, to me, perfectly.'

'I've proved it to others as well.' And she paused a moment. 'I refused a proposal of marriage last week; what they call—no doubt—a dazzling one.'

'I'm very glad to hear it,' said the young man gravely.

'It was a proposal many girls would have accepted; it had everything to recommend it.' Isabel had not proposed to herself to tell this story, but, now she had begun, the satisfaction of speaking it out and doing herself justice took possession of her. 'I was offered a great position and a great fortune—by a person whom I like extremely.'

Caspar watched her with intense interest. 'Is he an Englishman?'

'He's an English nobleman,' said Isabel.

Her visitor received this announcement at first in silence, but at last said: 'I'm glad he's disappointed.'

'Well then, as you have companions in misfortune, make the best of it.'

'I don't call him a companion,' said Caspar grimly.

'Why not—since I declined his offer absolutely?'

'That doesn't make him my companion. Besides, he's an Englishman.'

'And pray isn't an Englishman a human being?' Isabel asked.

'Oh, those people? They're not of *my* humanity, and I don't care what becomes of them.'

'You're very angry,' said the girl. 'We've discussed this matter quite enough.'

'Oh yes, I'm very angry. I plead guilty to that!'

She turned away from him, walked to the open window and stood a moment looking into the dusky void of the street, where a turbid gaslight alone represented social animation. For some time neither of these young persons spoke; Caspar lingered near the chimney-piece with eyes gloomily attached. She had virtually requested him to go—he knew that; but at the risk of making himself odious he kept his ground. She was too nursed a need to be easily renounced, and he had crossed the sea all to wring from her some scrap of a vow. Presently she left the window and stood again before him. 'You do me very little justice—after my telling you what I told you just now. I'm sorry I told you—since it matters so little to you.'

'Ah,' cried the young man, 'if you were thinking of *me* when you did it!' And then he paused with the fear that she might contradict so happy a thought.

'I was thinking of you a little,' said Isabel.

'A little? I don't understand. If the knowledge of what I feel for you had any weight with you at all, calling it a "little" is a poor account of it.'

Isabel shook her head as if to carry off a blunder. 'I've refused a most kind, noble gentleman. Make the most of that.'

'I thank you then,' said Caspar Goodwood gravely. 'I thank you immensely.'

'And now you had better go home.'

'May I not see you again?' he asked.

'I think it's better not. You'll be sure to talk of this, and you see it leads to nothing.'

'I promise you not to say a word that will annoy you.'

Isabel reflected and then answered: 'I return in a day or two to my uncle's, and I can't propose to you to come there. It would be too inconsistent.'

Caspar Goodwood, on his side, considered. 'You must do me justice too. I received an invitation to your uncle's more than a week ago, and I declined it.'

She betrayed surprise. 'From whom was your invitation?'

'From Mr Ralph Touchett, whom I suppose to be your cousin. I declined it because I had not your authorisation to accept it. The suggestion that Mr Touchett should invite me appeared to have come from Miss Stackpole.'

'It certainly never did from me. Henrietta really goes very far,' Isabel added.

'Don't be too hard on her—that touches *me*.'

'No; if you declined you did quite right, and I thank you for it.' And she gave a little shudder of dismay at the thought that Lord Warburton and Mr Goodwood might have met at Gardencourt: it would have been so awkward for Lord Warburton.

'When you leave your uncle where do you go?' her companion asked.

'I go abroad with my aunt—to Florence and other places.'

The serenity of this announcement struck a chill to the young man's heart; he seemed to see her whirled away into circles from which he was inexorably excluded. Nevertheless he went on quickly with his questions. 'And when shall you come back to America?'

'Perhaps not for a long time. I'm very happy here.'

'Do you mean to give up your country?'

'Don't be an infant!'

'Well, you'll be out of my sight indeed!' said Caspar Goodwood.

'I don't know,' she answered rather grandly. 'The world—with all these places so arranged and so touching each other—comes to strike one as rather small.'

'It's a sight too big for *me*!' Caspar exclaimed with a simplicity our young lady might have found touching if her face had not been set against concessions.

This attitude was part of a system, a theory, that she had lately embraced, and to be thorough she said after a moment: 'Don't think me unkind if I say it's just *that*—being out of your sight—that I like. If you were in the same place I should feel you were watching me, and I don't like that—I like my liberty too much. If there's a thing in the world I'm fond of,' she went on with a slight recurrence of grandeur, 'it's my personal independence.'

But whatever there might be of the too superior in this speech moved Caspar Goodwood's admiration; there was nothing he winced at in the large air of it. He had never supposed she hadn't wings and the need of beautiful free movements—he wasn't, with his own long arms and strides, afraid of any force in her. Isabel's words, if they had been meant to shock him, failed of the mark and only made him smile with the sense that here was common ground. 'Who would wish less to curtail your liberty than I? What can give me greater pleasure than to see you perfectly independent—doing whatever you like? It's to make you independent that I want to marry you.'

'That's a beautiful sophism,' said the girl with a smile more beautiful still.

'An unmarried woman—a girl of your age—isn't independent. There are all sorts of things she can't do. She's hampered at every step.'

'That's as she looks at the question,' Isabel answered with much spirit. 'I'm not in my first youth—I can do what I choose—I belong quite to the independent class. I've neither father nor mother; I'm poor and of a serious disposition; I'm not pretty. I therefore am not bound to be timid and conventional; indeed I can't afford such luxuries. Besides, I try to judge things for myself; to judge wrong, I think, is more honourable than not to judge at all. I don't wish to be a mere sheep in the flock; I wish to choose my fate and know something of human affairs beyond what other people think it compatible with propriety to tell me.' She paused a moment, but not long enough for her companion to reply. He was apparently on the point of doing so when she went on: 'Let me say this to you, Mr Goodwood. You're so kind as to speak of being afraid of my marrying. If you should hear a rumour that I'm on the point of doing so—girls are liable to have such things said about them—remember what I have told you about my love of liberty and venture to doubt it.'

There was something passionately positive in the tone in which she gave him this advice, and he saw a shining candour in her eyes that helped him to believe her. On the whole he felt reassured, and you might have perceived it by the manner in which he said, quite eagerly: 'You want simply to travel for two years? I'm quite willing to wait two years, and you may do what you like in the interval. If that's all you want, pray say so. I don't want you to be conventional; do I strike you as conventional myself? Do you want to improve your mind? Your mind's quite good enough for me; but if it interests you to wander about a while and see different countries I shall be delighted to help you in any way in my power.'

'You're very generous; that's nothing new to me. The best way to help me will be to put as many hundred miles of sea between us as possible.'

'One would think you were going to commit some atrocity!' said Caspar Goodwood.

'Perhaps I am. I wish to be free even to do that if the fancy takes me.'

'Well then,' he said slowly, 'I'll go home.' And he put out his hand, trying to look contented and confident.

Isabel's confidence in him, however, was greater than any he could feel in her. Not that he thought her capable of committing an atrocity; but, turn it over as he would, there was something ominous in the way she reserved her option. As she took his hand she felt a great respect for him; she knew how much he cared for her and she thought him magnanimous. They stood so for a moment, looking at each other, united by a hand-clasp which was not merely passive on her side. 'That's right,' she said very kindly, almost tenderly. 'You'll lose nothing by being a reasonable man.'

'But I'll come back, wherever you are, two years hence,' he returned with characteristic grimness.

We have seen that our young lady was inconsequent, and at this she suddenly changed her note. 'Ah, remember, I promise nothing—absolutely nothing!' Then more softly, as if to help him to leave her: 'And remember too that I shall not be an easy victim!'

'You'll get very sick of your independence.'

'Perhaps I shall; it's even very probable. When that day comes I shall be very glad to see you.'

She had laid her hand on the knob of the door that led into her room, and she waited a moment to see whether her visitor would not take his departure. But he appeared unable to move; there was still an immense unwillingness in his attitude and a sore remonstrance in his eyes. 'I must leave you now,' said Isabel; and she opened the door and passed into the other room.

This apartment was dark, but the darkness was tempered by a vague radiance sent up through the window from the court of the hotel, and Isabel could make out the masses of the furniture, the dim shining of the mirror and the looming of the big four-posted bed. She stood still a moment, listening, and at last she heard Caspar Goodwood walk out of the sitting-room and close the door behind him. She stood still a little longer, and then, by an irresistible impulse, dropped on her knees before her bed and hid her face in her arms.

XVII

SHE was not praying; she was trembling—trembling all over. Vibration was easy to her, was in fact too constant with her, and she found herself now humming like a smitten harp. She only asked, however, to put on the cover, to case herself again in brown holland,* but she wished to resist her excitement, and the attitude of devotion, which she kept for some time, seemed to help her to be still. She intensely rejoiced that Caspar Goodwood was gone; there was something in having thus got rid of him that was like the payment, for a stamped receipt, of some debt too long on her mind. As she felt the glad relief she bowed her head a little lower; the sense was there, throbbing in her heart; it was part of her emotion, but it was a thing to be ashamed of—it was profane and out of place. It was not for some ten minutes that she rose from her knees, and even when she came back to the sitting-room her tremor had not quite subsided. It had had, verily, two causes: part of it was to be accounted for by her long discussion with Mr Goodwood, but it might be feared that the rest was simply the enjoyment she found in the exercise of her power. She sat down in the same chair again and took up her book, but without going through the form of opening the volume. She leaned back, with that low, soft, aspiring murmur with which she often uttered her response to accidents of which the brighter side was not superficially obvious, and yielded to the satisfaction of having refused two ardent suitors in a fortnight. That love of liberty of which she had given Caspar Goodwood so bold a sketch was as yet almost exclusively theoretic; she had not been able to indulge it on a large scale. But it appeared to her she had done something; she had tasted of the delight, if not of battle, at least of victory; she had done what was truest to her plan. In the glow of this consciousness the image of Mr Goodwood taking his sad walk homeward through the dingy town presented itself with a certain reproachful force; so that, as at the same moment the door of the room was opened, she rose with an apprehension that he had come back. But it was only Henrietta Stackpole returning from her dinner.

Miss Stackpole immediately saw that our young lady had been 'through' something, and indeed the discovery demanded no great penetration. She went straight up to her friend, who received her without a greeting. Isabel's elation in having sent Caspar Goodwood back to America presupposed her being in a manner glad he had come to see her; but at the same time she perfectly remembered Henrietta had had no right to set a trap for her. 'Has he been here, dear?' the latter yearningly asked.

Isabel turned away and for some moments answered nothing. 'You acted very wrongly,' she declared at last.

'I acted for the best. I only hope you acted as well.'

'You're not the judge. I can't trust you,' said Isabel.

This declaration was unflattering, but Henrietta was much too unselfish to heed the charge it conveyed; she cared only for what it intimated with regard to her friend. 'Isabel Archer,' she observed with equal abruptness and solemnity, 'if you marry one of these people I'll never speak to you again!'

'Before making so terrible a threat you had better wait till I'm asked,' Isabel replied. Never having said a word to Miss Stackpole about Lord Warburton's overtures, she had now no impulse whatever to justify herself to Henrietta by telling her that she had refused that nobleman.

'Oh, you'll be asked quick enough, once you get off on the Continent. Annie Climber was asked three times in Italy—poor plain little Annie.'

'Well, if Annie Climber wasn't captured why should I be?'

'I don't believe Annie was pressed; but you'll be.'

'That's a flattering conviction,' said Isabel without alarm.

'I don't flatter you, Isabel, I tell you the truth!' cried her friend. 'I hope you don't mean to tell me that you didn't give Mr Goodwood some hope.'

'I don't see why I should tell you anything; as I said to you just now, I can't trust you. But since you're so much interested in Mr Goodwood I won't conceal from you that he returns immediately to America.'

'You don't mean to say you've sent him off?' Henrietta almost shrieked.

'I asked him to leave me alone; and I ask you the same, Henrietta.' Miss Stackpole glittered for an instant with dismay, and then passed to the mirror over the chimney-piece and took off her bonnet. 'I hope you've enjoyed your dinner,' Isabel went on.

But her companion was not to be diverted by frivolous propositions. 'Do you know where you're going, Isabel Archer?'

'Just now I'm going to bed,' said Isabel with persistent frivolity.

'Do you know where you're drifting?' Henrietta pursued, holding out her bonnet delicately.

'No, I haven't the least idea, and I find it very pleasant not to know. A swift carriage, of a dark night, rattling with four horses over roads that one can't see—that's my idea of happiness.'

'Mr Goodwood certainly didn't teach you to say such things as that—like the heroine of an immoral novel,' said Miss Stackpole. 'You're drifting to some great mistake.'

Isabel was irritated by her friend's interference, yet she still tried to think what truth this declaration could represent. She could think of nothing that diverted her from saying: 'You must be very fond of me, Henrietta, to be willing to be so aggressive.'

'I love you intensely, Isabel,' said Miss Stackpole with feeling.

'Well, if you love me intensely let me as intensely alone. I asked that of Mr Goodwood, and I must also ask it of you.'

'Take care you're not let alone too much.'

'That's what Mr Goodwood said to me. I told him I must take the risks.'

'You're a creature of risks—you make me shudder!' cried Henrietta. 'When does Mr Goodwood return to America?'

'I don't know—he didn't tell me.'

'Perhaps you didn't enquire,' said Henrietta with the note of righteous irony.

'I gave him too little satisfaction to have the right to ask questions of him.'

This assertion seemed to Miss Stackpole for a moment to bid defiance to comment; but at last she exclaimed: 'Well, Isabel, if I didn't know you I might think you were heartless!'

'Take care,' said Isabel; 'you're spoiling me.'

'I'm afraid I've done that already. I hope, at least,' Miss Stackpole added, 'that he may cross with Annie Climber!'

Isabel learned from her the next morning that she had determined not to return to Gardencourt (where old Mr Touchett had promised her a renewed welcome), but to await in London the arrival of the invitation that Mr Bantling had promised her from his sister Lady Pensil. Miss Stackpole related very freely her conversation with Ralph Touchett's sociable friend and declared to Isabel that she really believed she had now got hold of something that would lead to something. On the receipt of Lady Pensil's letter—Mr Bantling had virtually guaranteed the arrival of this document—she would immediately depart for Bedfordshire, and if Isabel cared to look out for her impressions in the *Interviewer* she would certainly find them. Henrietta was evidently going to see something of the inner life this time.

'Do you know where you're drifting, Henrietta Stackpole?' Isabel asked, imitating the tone in which her friend had spoken the night before.

'I'm drifting to a big position—that of the Queen of American Journalism. If my next letter isn't copied all over the West I'll swallow my pen-wiper!'

She had arranged with her friend Miss Annie Climber, the young lady of the continental offers, that they should go together to make those purchases which were to constitute Miss Climber's farewell to a hemisphere in which she at least had been appreciated; and she presently repaired to Jermyn Street to pick up her companion. Shortly after her departure Ralph Touchett was announced, and as soon as he came in Isabel saw he had something on his mind. He very soon took his cousin into his confidence. He had received from his mother a telegram to the effect that his father had had a sharp attack of his old malady, that she was much alarmed and that she begged he would instantly return to Gardencourt. On this occasion at least Mrs Touchett's devotion to the electric wire was not open to criticism.

'I've judged it best to see the great doctor, Sir Matthew Hope, first,' Ralph said; 'by great good luck he's in town. He's to see me at half-past twelve, and I shall make sure of his coming down to Gardencourt—which he will do the more readily as he has already seen my father several times, both there and in London. There's an express at two-forty-five, which I shall take; and you'll come back with me or remain here a few days longer, exactly as you prefer.'

'I shall certainly go with you,' Isabel returned. 'I don't suppose I can be of any use to my uncle, but if he's ill I shall like to be near him.'

'I think you're fond of him,' said Ralph with a certain shy pleasure in his face. 'You appreciate him, which all the world hasn't done. The quality's too fine.'

'I quite adore him,' Isabel after a moment said.

'That's very well. After his son he's your greatest admirer.'

She welcomed this assurance, but she gave secretly a small sigh of relief at the thought that Mr Touchett was one of those admirers who couldn't propose to marry her. This, however, was not what she spoke; she went on to inform Ralph that there were other reasons for her not remaining in London. She was tired of it and wished to leave it; and then Henrietta was going away—going to stay in Bedfordshire.

'In Bedfordshire?'

'With Lady Pensil, the sister of Mr Bantling, who has answered for an invitation.'

Ralph was feeling anxious, but at this he broke into a laugh. Suddenly, none the less, his gravity returned. 'Bantling's a man of courage. But if the invitation should get lost on the way?'

'I thought the British post-office was impeccable.'

'The good Homer sometimes nods,' said Ralph. 'However,' he went on more brightly, 'the good Bantling never does, and, whatever happens, he'll take care of Henrietta.'

Ralph went to keep his appointment with Sir Matthew Hope, and Isabel made her arrangements for quitting Pratt's Hotel. Her uncle's danger touched her nearly, and while she stood before her open trunk, looking about her vaguely for what she should put into it, the tears suddenly rose to her eyes. It was perhaps for this reason that when Ralph came back at two o'clock to take her to the station she was not yet ready. He found Miss Stackpole, however, in the sitting-room, where she had just risen from her luncheon, and this lady immediately expressed her regret at his father's illness.

'He's a grand old man,' she said; 'he's faithful to the last. If it's really to be the last—pardon my alluding to it, but you must often have thought of the possibility—I'm sorry that I shall not be at Gardencourt.'

'You'll amuse yourself much more in Bedfordshire.'

'I shall be sorry to amuse myself at such a time,' said Henrietta with much propriety. But she immediately added: 'I should like so to commemorate the closing scene.'

'My father may live a long time,' said Ralph simply. Then, adverting to topics more cheerful, he interrogated Miss Stackpole as to her own future.

Now that Ralph was in trouble she addressed him in a tone of larger allowance and told him that she was much indebted to him for having made her acquainted with Mr Bantling. 'He has told me just the things I want to know,' she said; 'all the society-items and all about the royal family. I can't make out that what he tells me about the royal family is much to their credit; but he says that's only my peculiar way of looking at it. Well, all I want is that he should give me the facts; I can put them together quick enough, once I've got them.' And she added that Mr Bantling had been so good as to promise to come and take her out that afternoon.

'To take you where?' Ralph ventured to enquire.

'To Buckingham Palace. He's going to show me over it, so that I may get some idea how they live.'

'Ah,' said Ralph, 'we leave you in good hands. The first thing we shall hear is that you're invited to Windsor Castle.'

'If they ask me, I shall certainly go. Once I get started I'm not afraid. But for all that,' Henrietta added in a moment, 'I'm not satisfied; I'm not at peace about Isabel.'

'What is her last misdemeanour?'

'Well, I've told you before, and I suppose there's no harm in my going on. I always finish a subject that I take up. Mr Goodwood was here last night.'

Ralph opened his eyes; he even blushed a little—his blush being the sign of an emotion somewhat acute. He remembered that Isabel, in separating from him in Winchester Square, had repudiated his suggestion that her motive in doing so was the expectation of a visitor at Pratt's Hotel, and it was a new pang to him to have to suspect her of duplicity. On the other hand, he quickly said to himself, what concern was it of his that she should have made an appointment with a lover? Had it not been thought graceful in every age that young ladies should make a mystery of such appointments? Ralph gave Miss Stackpole a diplomatic answer. 'I should have thought that, with the views you expressed to me the other day, this would satisfy you perfectly.'

'That he should come to see her? That was very well, as far as it went. It was a little plot of mine; I let him know that we were in London, and when it had been arranged that I should spend the evening out I sent him a word—the word we just utter to the "wise". I hoped he would find her alone; I won't pretend I didn't hope that you'd be out of the way. He came to see her, but he might as well have stayed away.'

'Isabel was cruel?'—and Ralph's face lighted with the relief of his cousin's not having shown duplicity.

'I don't exactly know what passed between them. But she gave him no satisfaction—she sent him back to America.'

'Poor Mr. Goodwood!' Ralph sighed.

'Her only idea seems to be to get rid of him,' Henrietta went on.

'Poor Mr. Goodwood!' Ralph repeated. The exclamation, it must be confessed, was automatic; it failed exactly to express his thoughts, which were taking another line.

'You don't say that as if you felt it. I don't believe you care.'

'Ah,' said Ralph, 'you must remember that I don't know this interesting young man—that I've never seen him.'

'Well, I shall see him, and I shall tell him not to give up. If I didn't believe Isabel would come round,' Miss Stackpole added—'well, I'd give up myself. I mean I'd give *her* up!'

XVIII

It had occurred to Ralph that, in the conditions, Isabel's parting with her friend might be of a slightly embarrassed nature, and he went down to the door of the hotel in advance of his cousin, who, after a slight delay, followed with the traces of an unaccepted remonstrance, as he thought, in her eyes. The two made the journey to Gardencourt in almost unbroken silence, and the servant who met them at the station had no better news to give them of Mr Touchett—a fact which caused Ralph to congratulate himself afresh on Sir Matthew Hope's having promised to come down in the five o'clock train and spend the night. Mrs Touchett, he learned, on reaching home, had been constantly with the old man and was with him at that moment; and this fact made Ralph say to himself that, after all, what his mother wanted was just easy occasion. The finer natures were those that shone at the larger times. Isabel went to her own room, noting throughout the house that perceptible hush which precedes a crisis. At the end of an hour, however, she came downstairs in search of her aunt, whom she wished to ask about Mr Touchett. She went into the library, but Mrs Touchett was not there, and as the weather, which had been damp and chill, was now altogether spoiled, it was not probable she had gone for her usual walk in the grounds. Isabel was on the point of ringing to send a question to her room, when this purpose quickly yielded to an unexpected sound—the sound of low music proceeding apparently from the saloon. She knew her aunt never touched the piano, and the musician was therefore probably Ralph, who played for his own amusement. That he should have resorted to this recreation at the present time indicated apparently that his anxiety about his father had been relieved; so that the girl took her way, almost with restored cheer, toward the source of the harmony. The drawing-room at Gardencourt was an apartment of great distances, and, as the piano was placed at the end of it furthest removed from the door at which she entered, her arrival was not noticed by the person seated before the instrument. This person was neither Ralph nor his mother; it was a lady whom Isabel immediately saw to be a stranger to herself, though her back was presented to the door. This back—an ample and well-dressed one—Isabel viewed for some moments with surprise. The lady was of course a visitor who had arrived during her absence and who had not been mentioned by either of the servants—one of them her aunt's maid—of whom she had had speech since her return. Isabel had already learned, however, with what treasures of reserve the function of receiving orders may be accompanied, and she was particularly conscious of having been treated with dryness by her aunt's maid, through whose hands she had slipped perhaps a little too mistrustfully and with an effect of plumage but the more lustrous. The advent of a guest was in itself far from disconcerting; she had not yet divested herself of a young faith that each new acquaintance would exert some momentous influence on her life. By the time she had made these reflexions she became aware that the lady at the piano played remarkably well. She was playing something of Schubert's—Isabel knew not what, but recognised Schubert—and she touched the piano with a discretion of her own. It showed skill, it showed feeling; Isabel sat down noiselessly on the nearest chair and waited till the end of the piece. When it was finished she felt a strong desire to thank the player, and rose from her seat to do so, while at the same time the stranger turned quickly round, as if but just aware of her presence.

'That's very beautiful, and your playing makes it more beautiful still,' said Isabel with all the young radiance with which she usually uttered a truthful rapture.

'You don't think I disturbed Mr Touchett then?' the musician answered as sweetly as this compliment deserved. 'The house is so large and his room so far away that I thought I might venture, especially as I played just—just *du bout des doigts*.'*

'She's a Frenchwoman,' Isabel said to herself; 'she says that as if she were French.' And this supposition made the visitor more interesting to our speculative heroine. 'I hope my uncle's doing well,' Isabel added. 'I should think that to hear such lovely music as that would really make him feel better.'

The lady smiled and discriminated. 'I'm afraid there are moments in life when even Schubert has nothing to say to us. We must admit, however, that they are our worst.'

'I'm not in that state now then,' said Isabel. 'On the contrary I should be so glad if you would play something more.'

'If it will give you pleasure—delighted.' And this obliging person took her place again and struck a few chords, while Isabel sat down nearer the instrument. Suddenly the new-comer stopped with her hands on the keys, half-turning and looking over her shoulder. She was forty years old and not pretty, though her expression charmed. 'Pardon me,' she said; 'but are you the niece—the young American?'

'I'm my aunt's niece,' Isabel replied with simplicity.

The lady at the piano sat still a moment longer, casting her air of interest over her shoulder. 'That's very well; we're compatriots.' And then she began to play.

'Ah then she's not French,' Isabel murmured; and as the opposite supposition had made her romantic it might have seemed that this revelation would have marked a drop. But such was not the fact; rarer even than to be French seemed it to be American on such interesting terms.

The lady played in the same manner as before, softly and solemnly, and while she played the shadows deepened in the room. The autumn twilight gathered in, and from her place Isabel could see the rain, which had now begun in earnest, washing the cold-looking lawn and the wind shaking the great trees. At last, when the music had ceased, her companion got up and, coming nearer with a smile, before Isabel had time to thank her again, said: 'I'm very glad you've come back; I've heard a great deal about you.'

Isabel thought her a very attractive person, but nevertheless spoke with a certain abruptness in reply to this speech. 'From whom have you heard about me?'

The stranger hesitated a single moment and then, 'From your uncle,' she answered. 'I've been here three days, and the first day he let me come and pay him a visit in his room. Then he talked constantly of you.'

'As you didn't know me that must rather have bored you.'

'It made me want to know you. All the more that since

then—your aunt being so much with Mr Touchett—I've been quite alone and have got rather tired of my own society. I've not chosen a good moment for my visit.'

A servant had come in with lamps and was presently followed by another bearing the tea-tray. On the appearance of this repast Mrs Touchett had apparently been notified, for she now arrived and addressed herself to the tea-pot. Her greeting to her niece did not differ materially from her manner of raising the lid of this receptacle in order to glance at the contents: in neither act was it becoming to make a show of avidity. Questioned about her husband she was unable to say he was better; but the local doctor was with him, and much light was expected from this gentleman's consultation with Sir Matthew Hope.

'I suppose you two ladies have made acquaintance,' she pursued. 'If you haven't I recommend you to do so; for so long as we continue—Ralph and I—to cluster about Mr Touchett's bed you're not likely to have much society but each other.'

'I know nothing about you but that you're a great musician,' Isabel said to the visitor.

'There's a good deal more than that to know,' Mrs Touchett affirmed in her little dry tone.

'A very little of it, I am sure, will content Miss Archer!' the lady exclaimed with a light laugh. 'I'm an old friend of your aunt's. I've lived much in Florence. I'm Madame Merle.' She made this last announcement as if she were referring to a person of tolerably distinct identity. For Isabel, however, it represented little; she could only continue to feel that Madame Merle had as charming a manner as any she had ever encountered.

'She's not a foreigner in spite of her name,' said Mrs Touchett. 'She was born—I always forget where you were born.'

'It's hardly worth while then I should tell you.'

'On the contrary,' said Mrs Touchett, who rarely missed a logical point; 'if I remembered your telling me would be quite superfluous.'

Madame Merle glanced at Isabel with a sort of world-wide

smile, a thing that over-reached frontiers. 'I was born under the shadow of the national banner.'

'She's too fond of mystery,' said Mrs Touchett; 'that's her great fault.'

'Ah,' exclaimed Madame Merle, 'I've great faults, but I don't think that's one of them; it certainly isn't the greatest. I came into the world in the Brooklyn navy-yard.* My father was a high officer in the United States Navy, and had a post—a post of responsibility—in that establishment at the time. I suppose I ought to love the sea, but I hate it. That's why I don't return to America. I love the land; the great thing is to love something.'

Isabel, as a dispassionate witness, had not been struck with the force of Mrs Touchett's characterisation of her visitor, who had an expressive, communicative, responsive face, by no means of the sort which, to Isabel's mind, suggested a secretive disposition. It was a face that told of an amplitude of nature and of quick and free motions and, though it had no regular beauty, was in the highest degree engaging and attaching. Madame Merle was a tall, fair, smooth woman; everything in her person was round and replete, though without those accumulations which suggest heaviness. Her features were thick but in perfect proportion and harmony, and her complexion had a healthy clearness. Her grey eyes were small but full of light and incapable of stupidity—incapable, according to some people, even of tears; she had a liberal, full-rimmed mouth which when she smiled drew itself upward to the left side in a manner that most people thought very odd, some very affected and a few very graceful. Isabel inclined to range herself in the last category. Madame Merle had thick, fair hair, arranged somehow 'classically' and as if she were a Bust, Isabel judged—a Juno or a Niobe;* and large white hands, of a perfect shape, a shape so perfect that their possessor, preferring to leave them unadorned, wore no jewelled rings. Isabel had taken her at first, as we have seen, for a Frenchwoman; but extended observation might have ranked her as a German—a German of high degree, perhaps an Austrian, a baroness, a countess, a princess. It would never have been supposed she had come into the world in Brooklyn—though one could doubtless not have carried through any argument that the air of distinction marking her in so eminent a degree was inconsistent with such a birth. It was true that the national banner had floated immediately over her cradle, and the breezy freedom of the stars and stripes might have shed an influence upon the attitude she there took towards life. And yet she had evidently nothing of the fluttered, flapping quality of a morsel of bunting in the wind; her manner expressed the repose and confidence which come from a large experience. Experience, however, had not quenched her youth; it had simply made her sympathetic and supple. She was in a word a woman of strong impulses kept in admirable order. This commended itself to Isabel as an ideal combination.

The girl made these reflexions while the three ladies sat at their tea, but that ceremony was interrupted before long by the arrival of the great doctor from London, who had been immediately ushered into the drawing-room. Mrs Touchett took him off to the library for a private talk; and then Madame Merle and Isabel parted, to meet again at dinner. The idea of seeing more of this interesting woman did much to mitigate Isabel's sense of the sadness now setting on Gardencourt.

When she came into the drawing-room before dinner she found the place empty; but in the course of a moment Ralph arrived. His anxiety about his father had been lightened; Sir Matthew Hope's view of his condition was less depressed than his own had been. The doctor recommended that the nurse alone should remain with the old man for the next three or four hours; so that Ralph, his mother and the great physician himself were free to dine at table. Mrs Touchett and Sir Matthew appeared; Madame Merle was the last.

Before she came Isabel spoke of her to Ralph, who was standing before the fireplace. 'Pray who is this Madame Merle?'

'The cleverest woman I know, not excepting yourself,' said Ralph.

'I thought she seemed very pleasant.'

'I was sure you'd think her very pleasant.'

'Is that why you invited her?'

'I didn't invite her, and when we came back from London I

didn't know she was here. No one invited her. She's a friend of my mother's, and just after you and I went to town my mother got a note from her. She had arrived in England (she usually lives abroad, though she has first and last spent a good deal of time here), and asked leave to come down for a few days. She's a woman who can make such proposals with perfect confidence; she's so welcome wherever she goes. And with my mother there could be no question of hesitating; she's the one person in the world whom my mother very much admires. If she were not herself (which she after all much prefers), she would like to be Madame Merle. It would indeed be a great change.'

'Well, she's very charming,' said Isabel. 'And she plays beautifully.'

'She does everything beautifully. She's complete.'

Isabel looked at her cousin a moment. 'You don't like her.'

'On the contrary, I was once in love with her.'

'And she didn't care for you, and that's why you don't like her.'

'How can we have discussed such things? Monsieur Merle was then living.'

'Is he dead now?'

'So she says.'

'Don't you believe her?'

'Yes, because the statement agrees with the probabilities. The husband of Madame Merle would be likely to pass away.'

Isabel gazed at her cousin again. 'I don't know what you mean. You mean something—that you don't mean. What was Monsieur Merle?'

'The husband of Madame.'

'You're very odious. Has she any children?'

'Not the least little child—fortunately.'

'Fortunately?'

'I mean fortunately for the child. She'd be sure to spoil it.'

Isabel was apparently on the point of assuring her cousin for the third time that he was odious; but the discussion was interrupted by the arrival of the lady who was the topic of it. She came rustling in quickly, apologising for being late, fastening a bracelet, dressed in dark blue satin, which exposed a white bosom that was ineffectually covered by a curious silver necklace. Ralph offered her his arm with the exaggerated alertness of a man who was no longer a lover.

Even if this had still been his condition, however, Ralph had other things to think about. The great doctor spent the night at Gardencourt and, returning to London on the morrow, after another consultation with Mr Touchett's own medical adviser, concurred in Ralph's desire that he should see the patient again on the day following. On the day following Sir Matthew Hope reappeared at Gardencourt, and now took a less encouraging view of the old man, who had grown worse in the twenty-four hours. His feebleness was extreme, and to his son, who constantly sat by his bedside, it often seemed that his end must be at hand. The local doctor, a very sagacious man, in whom Ralph had secretly more confidence than in his distinguished colleague, was constantly in attendance, and Sir Matthew Hope came back several times. Mr Touchett was much of the time unconscious; he slept a great deal; he rarely spoke. Isabel had a great desire to be useful to him and was allowed to watch with him at hours when his other attendants (of whom Mrs Touchett was not the least regular) went to take rest. He never seemed to know her, and she always said to herself 'Suppose he should die while I'm sitting here;' an idea which excited her and kept her awake. Once he opened his eyes for a while and fixed them upon her intelligently, but when she went to him, hoping he would recognise her, he closed them and relapsed into stupor. The day after this, however, he revived for a longer time; but on this occasion Ralph only was with him. The old man began to talk, much to his son's satisfaction, who assured him that they should presently have him sitting up.

'No, my boy,' said Mr Touchett, 'not unless you bury me in a sitting posture, as some of the ancients—was it the ancients?—used to do.'

'Ah, daddy, don't talk about that,' Ralph murmured. 'You mustn't deny that you're getting better.'

'There will be no need of my denying it if you don't say it,' the old man answered. 'Why should we prevaricate just at the last? We never prevaricated before. I've got to die some time, and it's better to die when one's sick than when one's well. I'm very sick—as sick as I shall ever be. I hope you don't want to prove that I shall ever be worse than this? That would be too bad. You don't? Well then.'

Having made this excellent point he became quiet; but the next time that Ralph was with him he again addressed himself to conversation. The nurse had gone to her supper and Ralph was alone in charge, having just relieved Mrs Touchett, who had been on guard since dinner. The room was lighted only by the flickering fire, which of late had become necessary, and Ralph's tall shadow was projected over wall and ceiling with an outline constantly varying but always grotesque.

'Who's that with me—is it my son?' the old man asked.

'Yes, it's your son, daddy.'

'And is there no one else?'

'No one else.'

Mr Touchett said nothing for a while; and then, 'I want to talk a little,' he went on.

'Won't it tire you?' Ralph demurred.

'It won't matter if it does. I shall have a long rest. I want to talk about *you*.'

Ralph had drawn nearer to the bed; he sat leaning forward with his hand on his father's. 'You had better select a brighter topic.'

'You were always bright; I used to be proud of your brightness. I should like so much to think you'd do something.'

'If you leave us,' said Ralph, 'I shall do nothing but miss you.'

'That's just what I don't want; it's what I want to talk about. You must get a new interest.

'I don't want a new interest, daddy. I have more old ones than I know what to do with.'

The old man lay there looking at his son; his face was the face of the dying, but his eyes were the eyes of Daniel Touchett. He seemed to be reckoning over Ralph's interests. 'Of course you have your mother,' he said at last. 'You'll take care of her.'

'My mother will always take care of herself,' Ralph returned.

'Well,' said his father, 'perhaps as she grows older she'll need a little help.'

'I shall not see that. She'll outlive me.'

'Very likely she will; but that's no reason—!' Mr Touchett let his phrase die away in a helpless but not quite querulous sigh and remained silent again.

'Don't trouble yourself about us,' said his son. 'My mother and I get on very well together, you know.'

'You get on by always being apart; that's not natural.'

'If you leave us we shall probably see more of each other.'

'Well,' the old man observed with wandering irrelevance, 'it can't be said that my death will make much difference in your mother's life.'

'It will probably make more than you think.'

'Well, she'll have more money,' said Mr Touchett. 'I've left her a good wife's portion, just as if she had been a good wife.'

'She has been one, daddy, according to her own theory. She has never troubled you.'

'Ah, some troubles are pleasant,' Mr Touchett murmured. 'Those you've given me for instance. But your mother has been less—less—what shall I call it? less out of the way since I've been ill. I presume she knows I've noticed it.'

'I shall certainly tell her so; I'm so glad you mention it.'

'It won't make any difference to her; she doesn't do it to please me. She does it to please—to please—' And he lay a while trying to think why she did it. 'She does it because it suits her. But that's not what I want to talk about,' he added. 'It's about *you*. You'll be very well off.'

'Yes,' said Ralph, 'I know that. But I hope you've not forgotten the talk we had a year ago—when I told you exactly what money I should need and begged you to make some good use of the rest.'

'Yes, yes, I remember. I made a new will—in a few days. I suppose it was the first time such a thing had happened—a young man trying to get a will made against him.'

'It is not against me,' said Ralph. 'It would be against me to have a large property to take care of. It's impossible for a man in my state of health to spend much money, and enough is as good as a feast.'

'Well, you'll have enough—and something over. There will be more than enough for one—there will be enough for two.'

'That's too much,' said Ralph.

'Ah, don't say that. The best thing you can do, when I'm gone, will be to marry.'

Ralph had foreseen what his father was coming to, and this suggestion was by no means fresh. It had long been Mr Touchett's most ingenious way of taking the cheerful view of his son's possible duration. Ralph had usually treated it facetiously; but present circumstances proscribed the facetious. He simply fell back in his chair and returned his father's appealing gaze.

'If I, with a wife who hasn't been very fond of me, have had a very happy life,' said the old man, carrying his ingenuity further still, 'what a life mightn't you have if you should marry a person different from Mrs Touchett. There are more different from her than there are like her.' Ralph still said nothing; and after a pause his father resumed softly: 'What do you think of your cousin?'

At this Ralph started, meeting the question with a strained smile. 'Do I understand you to propose that I should marry Isabel?'

'Well, that's what it comes to in the end. Don't you like Isabel?'

'Yes, very much.' And Ralph got up from his chair and wandered over to the fire. He stood before it an instant and then he stooped and stirred it mechanically. 'I like Isabel very much,' he repeated.

'Well,' said his father, 'I know she likes you. She has told me how much she likes you.'

'Did she remark that she would like to marry me?'

'No, but she can't have anything against you. And she's the most charming young lady I've ever seen. And she would be good to you. I have thought a great deal about it.'

'So have I,' said Ralph, coming back to the bedside again. 'I don't mind telling you that.'

'You *are* in love with her then? I should think you would be. It's as if she came over on purpose.'

'No, I'm not in love with her; but I should be if—if certain things were different.'

'Ah, things are always different from what they might be,' said the old man. 'If you wait for them to change you'll never do anything. I don't know whether you know,' he went on; 'but I suppose there's no harm in my alluding to it at such an hour as this: there was some one wanted to marry Isabel the other day, and she wouldn't have him.'

'I know she refused Warburton: he told me himself.'

'Well, that proves there's a chance for somebody else.'

'Somebody else took his chance the other day in London—and got nothing by it.'

'Was it you?' Mr Touchett eagerly asked.

'No, it was an older friend; a poor gentleman who came over from America to see about it.'

'Well, I'm sorry for him, whoever he was. But it only proves what I say—that the way's open to you.'

'If it is, dear father, it's all the greater pity that I'm unable to tread it. I haven't many convictions; but I have three or four that I hold strongly. One is that people, on the whole, had better not marry their cousins. Another is that people in an advanced stage of pulmonary disorder had better not marry at all.'

The old man raised his weak hand and moved it to and fro before his face. 'What do you mean by that? You look at things in a way that would make everything wrong. What sort of a cousin is a cousin that you had never seen for more than twenty years of her life? We're all each other's cousins, and if we stopped at that the human race would die out. It's just the same with your bad lung. You're a great deal better than you used to be. All you want is to lead a natural life. It is a great deal more natural to marry a pretty young lady that you're in love with than it is to remain single on false principles.'

'I'm not in love with Isabel,' said Ralph.

'You said just now that you would be if you didn't think it wrong. I want to prove to you that it isn't wrong.'

'It will only tire you, dear daddy,' said Ralph, who marvelled at his father's tenacity and at his finding strength to insist. 'Then where shall we all be?'

'Where shall you be if I don't provide for you? You won't have anything to do with the bank, and you won't have me to take care of. You say you've so many interests; but I can't make them out.'

Ralph leaned back in his chair with folded arms; his eyes were fixed for some time in meditation. At last, with the air of a man fairly mustering courage, 'I take a great interest in my cousin,' he said, 'but not the sort of interest you desire. I shall not live many years; but I hope I shall live long enough to see what she does with herself. She's entirely independent of me; I can exercise very little influence upon her life. But I should like to do something for her.'

'What should you like to do?'

'I should like to put a little wind in her sails.'

'What do you mean by that?'

'I should like to put it into her power to do some of the things she wants. She wants to see the world for instance. I should like to put money in her purse.'

'Ah, I'm glad you've thought of that,' said the old man. 'But I've thought of it too. I've left her a legacy—five thousand pounds.'

'That's capital; it's very kind of you. But I should like to do a little more.'

Something of that veiled acuteness with which it had been on Daniel Touchett's part the habit of a lifetime to listen to a financial proposition still lingered in the face in which the invalid had not obliterated the man of business. 'I shall be happy to consider it,' he said softly.

'Isabel's poor then. My mother tells me that she has but a few hundred dollars a year. I should like to make her rich.'

'What do you mean by rich?'

'I call people rich when they're able to meet the requirements of their imagination. Isabel has a great deal of imagination.'

'So have you, my son,' said Mr Touchett, listening very attentively but a little confusedly.

'You tell me I shall have money enough for two. What I want is that you should kindly relieve me of my superfluity and make it over to Isabel. Divide my inheritance into two equal halves and give her the second.'

'To do what she likes with?'

'Absolutely what she likes.'

'And without an equivalent?'

'What equivalent could there be?'

'The one I've already mentioned.'

'Her marrying—some one or other? It's just to do away with anything of that sort that I make my suggestion. If she has an easy income she'll never have to marry for a support. That's what I want cannily to prevent. She wishes to be free, and your bequest will make her free.'

'Well, you seem to have thought it out,' said Mr Touchett. 'But I don't see why you appeal to me. The money will be yours, and you can easily give it to her yourself.'

Ralph openly stared. 'Ah, dear father, *I* can't offer Isabel money!'

The old man gave a groan. 'Don't tell me you're not in love with her! Do you want *me* to have the credit of it?'

'Entirely. I should like it simply to be a clause in your will, without the slightest reference to me.'

'Do you want me to make a new will then?'

'A few words will do it; you can attend to it the next time you feel a little lively.'

'You must telegraph to Mr Hilary then. I'll do nothing without my solicitor.'

'You shall see Mr Hilary to-morrow.'

'He'll think we've quarrelled, you and I,' said the old man.

'Very probably; I shall like him to think it,' said Ralph, smiling; 'and, to carry out the idea, I give you notice that I shall be very sharp, quite horrid and strange, with you.'

The humour of this appeared to touch his father, who lay a little while taking it in. 'I'll do anything you like,' Mr Touchett said at last; 'but I'm not sure it's right. You say you want to put wind in her sails; but aren't you afraid of putting too much?'

'I should like to see her going before the breeze!' Ralph answered.

'You speak as if it were for your mere amusement.'

'So it is, a good deal.'

'Well, I don't think I understand,' said Mr Touchett with a sigh. 'Young men are very different from what I was. When I cared for a girl—when I was young—I wanted to do more than look at her. You've scruples that I shouldn't have had, and you've ideas that I shouldn't have had either. You say Isabel wants to be free, and that her being rich will keep her from marrying for money. Do you think that she's a girl to do that?'

'By no means. But she has less money than she has ever had before. Her father then gave her everything, because he used to spend his capital. She has nothing but the crumbs of that feast to live on, and she doesn't really know how meagre they are—she has yet to learn it. My mother has told me all about it. Isabel will learn it when she's really thrown upon the world, and it would be very painful to me to think of her coming to the consciousness of a lot of wants she should be unable to satisfy.'

'I've left her five thousand pounds. She can satisfy a good many wants with that.'

'She can indeed. But she would probably spend it in two or three years.'

'You think she'd be extravagant then?'

'Most certainly,' said Ralph, smiling serenely.

Poor Mr Touchett's acuteness was rapidly giving place to pure confusion. 'It would merely be a question of time then, her spending the larger sum?'

'No—though at first I think she'd plunge into that pretty freely: she'd probably make over a part of it to each of her sisters. But after that she'd come to her senses, remember she has still a lifetime before her, and live within her means.'

'Well, you *have* worked it out,' said the old man helplessly. 'You do take an interest in her, certainly.'

'You can't consistently say I go too far. You wished me to go further.'

'Well, I don't know,' Mr Touchett answered. 'I don't think I enter into your spirit. It seems to me immoral.'

'Immoral, dear daddy?'

'Well, I don't know that it's right to make everything so easy for a person.'

'It surely depends upon the person. When the person's good, your making things easy is all to the credit of virtue. To facilitate the execution of good impulses, what can be a nobler act?'

This was a little difficult to follow, and Mr Touchett considered it for a while. At last he said: 'Isabel's a sweet young thing; but do you think she's so good as that?'

'She's as good as her best opportunities,' Ralph returned.

'Well,' Mr Touchett declared, 'she ought to get a great many opportunities for sixty thousand pounds.'

'I've no doubt she will.'

'Of course I'll do what you want,' said the old man. 'I only want to understand it a little.'

'Well, dear daddy, don't you understand it now?' his son caressingly asked. 'If you don't we won't take any more trouble about it. We'll leave it alone.'

Mr Touchett lay a long time still. Ralph supposed he had given up the attempt to follow. But at last, quite lucidly, he began again. 'Tell me this first. Doesn't it occur to you that a young lady with sixty thousand pounds may fall a victim to the fortune-hunters?'

'She'll hardly fall a victim to more than one.'

'Well, one's too many.'

'Decidedly. That's a risk, and it has entered into my calculation. I think it's appreciable, but I think it's small, and I'm prepared to take it.'

Poor Mr Touchett's acuteness had passed into perplexity, and his perplexity now passed into admiration. 'Well, you *have* gone into it!' he repeated. 'But I don't see what good you're to get of it.'

Ralph leaned over his father's pillows and gently smoothed them; he was aware their talk had been unduly prolonged. 'I shall get just the good I said a few moments ago I wished to put into Isabel's reach—that of having met the requirements of my imagination. But it's scandalous, the way I've taken advantage of you!'

XIX

As Mrs Touchett had foretold, Isabel and Madame Merle were thrown much together during the illness of their host, so that if they had not become intimate it would have been almost a breach of good manners. Their manners were of the best, but in addition to this they happened to please each other. It is perhaps too much to say that they swore an eternal friendship, but tacitly at least they called the future to witness. Isabel did so with a perfectly good conscience, though she would have hesitated to admit she was intimate with her new friend in the high sense she privately attached to this term. She often wondered indeed if she ever had been, or ever could be, intimate with any one. She had an ideal of friendship as well as of several other sentiments, which it failed to seem to her in this case—it had not seemed to her in other cases—that the actual completely expressed. But she often reminded herself that there were essential reasons why one's ideal could never become concrete. It was a thing to believe in, not to see—a matter of faith, not of experience. Experience, however, might supply us with very creditable imitations of it, and the part of wisdom was to make the best of these. Certainly, on the whole, Isabel had never encountered a more agreeable and interesting figure than Madame Merle; she had never met a person having less of that fault which is the principal obstacle to friendship—the air of reproducing the more tiresome, the stale, the too-familiar parts of one's own character. The gates of the girl's confidence were opened wider than they had ever been; she said things to this amiable auditress that she had not yet said to any one. Sometimes she took alarm at her candour: it was as if she had given to a comparative stranger the key to her cabinet of jewels. These spiritual gems were the only ones of any magnitude that Isabel possessed, but there was all the greater reason for their being carefully guarded. Afterwards, however, she always remembered that one should never regret a generous error and that if Madame Merle had not the merits she attributed to her, so much the worse for Madame Merle.

There was no doubt she had great merits—she was charming, sympathetic, intelligent, cultivated. More than this (for it had not been Isabel's ill-fortune to go through life without meeting in her own sex several persons of whom no less could fairly be said), she was rare, superior and pre-eminent. There are many amiable people in the world, and Madame Merle was far from being vulgarly good-natured and restlessly witty. She knew how to think—an accomplishment rare in women; and she had thought to very good purpose. Of course, too, she knew how to feel; Isabel couldn't have spent a week with her without being sure of that. This was indeed Madame Merle's great talent, her most perfect gift. Life had told upon her; she had felt it strongly, and it was part of the satisfaction to be taken in her society that when the girl talked of what she was pleased to call serious matters this lady understood her so easily and quickly. Emotion, it is true, had become with her rather historic; she made no secret of the fact that the fount of passion, thanks to having been rather violently tapped at one period, didn't flow quite so freely as of yore. She proposed moreover, as well as expected, to cease feeling; she freely admitted that of old she had been a little mad, and now she pretended to be perfectly sane.

'I judge more than I used to,' she said to Isabel, 'but it seems to me one has earned the right. One can't judge till one's forty; before that we're too eager, too hard, too cruel, and in addition much too ignorant. I'm sorry for you; it will be a long time before you're forty. But every gain's a loss of some kind; I often think that after forty one *can't* really feel. The freshness, the quickness have certainly gone. You'll keep them longer than most people; it will be a great satisfaction to me to see you some years hence. I want to see what life makes of you. One thing's certain—it can't spoil you. It may pull you about horribly, but I defy it to break you up.'

Isabel received this assurance as a young soldier, still panting from a slight skirmish in which he has come off with honour, might receive a pat on the shoulder from his colonel. Like such a recognition of merit it seemed to come with authority. How could the lightest word do less on the part of a person who was prepared to say, of almost everything Isabel told her, 'Oh, I've been in that, my dear; it passes, like everything else.' On many of her interlocutors Madame Merle might have produced an irritating effect; it was disconcertingly difficult to surprise her. But Isabel, though by no means incapable of desiring to be effective, had not at present this impulse. She was too sincere, too interested in her judicious companion. And then moreover Madame Merle never said such things in the tone of triumph or of boastfulness; they dropped from her like cold confessions.

A period of bad weather had settled upon Gardencourt; the days grew shorter and there was an end to the pretty tea-parties on the lawn. But our young woman had long indoor conversations with her fellow visitor, and in spite of the rain the two ladies often sallied forth for a walk, equipped with the defensive apparatus which the English climate and the English genius have between them brought to such perfection. Madame Merle liked almost everything, including the English rain. 'There's always a little of it and never too much at once,' she said; 'and it never wets you and it always smells good.' She declared that in England the pleasures of smell were great—that in this inimitable island there was a certain mixture of fog and beer and soot which, however odd it might sound, was the national aroma, and was most agreeable to the nostril; and she used to lift the sleeve of her British overcoat and bury her nose in it, inhaling the clear, fine scent of the wool. Poor Ralph Touchett, as soon as the autumn had begun to define itself, became almost a prisoner; in bad weather he was unable to step out of the house, and he used sometimes to stand at one of the windows with his hands in his pockets and, from a countenance half-rueful, half-critical, watch Isabel and Madame Merle as they walked down the avenue under a pair of umbrellas. The roads about Gardencourt were so firm, even in the worst weather, that the two ladies always came back with a healthy glow in their cheeks, looking at the soles of their neat, stout boots and declaring that their walk had done them inexpressible good. Before luncheon, always, Madame Merle was engaged; Isabel admired and envied her rigid possession of her morning. Our heroine had always passed for a person of resources and had taken a certain pride in being one; but she wandered, as by the wrong side of the wall of a private garden, round the enclosed talents, accomplishments, aptitudes of Madame Merle. She found herself desiring to emulate them, and in twenty such ways this lady presented herself as a model. 'I should like awfully to be *so*!' Isabel secretly exclaimed, more than once, as one after another of her friend's fine aspects caught the light, and before long she knew that she had learned a lesson from a high authority. It took no great time indeed for her to feel herself, as the phrase is, under an influence. 'What's the harm,' she wondered, 'so long as it's a good one? The more one's under a good influence the better. The only thing is to see our steps as we take them—to understand them as we go. That, no doubt, I shall always do. I needn't be afraid of becoming too pliable; isn't it my fault that I'm not pliable enough?' It is said that imitation is the sincerest flattery; and if Isabel was sometimes moved to gape at her friend aspiringly and despairingly it was not so much because she desired herself to shine as because she wished to hold up the lamp for Madame Merle. She liked her extremely, but was even more dazzled than attracted. She sometimes asked herself what Henrietta Stackpole would say to her thinking so much of this perverted product of their common soil, and had a conviction that it would be severely judged. Henrietta would not at all subscribe to Madame Merle; for reasons she could not have defined this truth came home to the girl. On the other hand she was equally sure that, should the occasion offer, her new friend would strike off some happy view of her old: Madame Merle was too humorous, too observant, not to do justice to Henrietta, and on becoming acquainted with her would probably give the measure of a tact which Miss Stackpole couldn't hope to emulate. She appeared to have in her experience a touchstone for everything, and somewhere in the capacious pocket of her genial memory she would find the key to Henrietta's value. 'That's the great thing,' Isabel solemnly pondered; 'that's the supreme good fortune: to be in a better position for appreciating people than they are for appreciating you.' And she added that such, when one considered it, was simply the essence of the aristocratic situation. In this light, if in none other, one should aim at the aristocratic situation.

I may not count over all the links in the chain which led Isabel to think of Madame Merle's situation as aristocratic—a view of it never expressed in any reference made to it by that lady herself. She had known great things and great people, but she had never played a great part. She was one of the small ones of the earth; she had not been born to honours; she knew the world too well to nourish fatuous illusions on the article of her own place in it. She had encountered many of the fortunate few and was perfectly aware of those points at which their fortune differed from hers. But if by her informed measure she was no figure for a high scene, she had yet to Isabel's imagination a sort of greatness. To be so cultivated and civilised, so wise and so easy, and still make so light of it—that was really to be a great lady, especially when one so carried and presented one's self. It was as if somehow she had all society under contribution, and all the arts and graces it practised—or was the effect rather that of charming uses found *for* her, even from a distance, subtle service rendered by her to a clamorous world wherever she might be? After breakfast she wrote a succession of letters, as those arriving for her appeared innumerable: her correspondence was a source of surprise to Isabel when they sometimes walked together to the village post-office to deposit Madame Merle's offering to the mail. She knew more people, as she told Isabel, than she knew what to do with, and something was always turning up to be written about. Of painting she was devotedly fond, and made no more of brushing in a sketch than of pulling off her gloves. At Gardencourt she was perpetually taking advantage of an hour's sunshine to go out with a camp-stool and a box of water-colours. That she was a brave musician we have already perceived, and it was evidence of the fact that when she seated herself at the piano, as she always did in the evening, her listeners resigned themselves without a murmur to losing the grace of her talk. Isabel, since she had known her, felt ashamed of her own facility, which she now looked upon as basely inferior; and indeed, though she had been thought rather a prodigy at home, the loss to society when, in taking her place upon the music-stool, she turned her back to the room, was usually deemed greater than the gain. When Madame Merle was neither writing, nor painting, nor touching the piano, she was usually employed upon wonderful tasks of rich embroidery, cushions, curtains, decorations for the chimney-piece; an art in which her bold, free invention was as noted as the agility of her needle. She was never idle, for when engaged in none of the ways I have mentioned she was either reading (she appeared to Isabel to read 'everything important'), or walking out, or playing patience with the cards, or talking with her fellow inmates. And with all this she had always the social quality, was never rudely absent and yet never too seated. She laid down her pastimes as easily as she took them up; she worked and talked at the same time, and appeared to impute scant worth to anything she did. She gave away her sketches and tapestries; she rose from the piano or remained there, according to the convenience of her auditors, which she always unerringly divined. She was in short the most comfortable, profitable, amenable person to live with. If for Isabel she had a fault it was that she was not natural; by which the girl meant, not that she was either affected or pretentious, since from these vulgar vices no woman could have been more exempt, but that her nature had been too much overlaid by custom and her angles too much rubbed away. She had become too flexible, too useful, was too ripe and too final. She was in a word too perfectly the social animal that man and woman are supposed to have been intended to be; and she had rid herself of every remnant of that tonic wildness which we may assume to have belonged even to the most amiable persons in the ages before country-house life was the fashion. Isabel found it difficult to think of her in any detachment or privacy, she existed only in her relations, direct or indirect, with her fellow mortals. One might wonder what commerce she could possibly hold with her own spirit. One always ended, however, by feeling that a charming surface doesn't necessarily prove one superficial; this was an illusion in which, in one's youth, one had but just escaped being nourished. Madame Merle was not superficial—not she. She was deep, and her nature spoke none the less in her behaviour because it spoke a conventional tongue.

'What's language at all but a convention?' said Isabel. 'She has the good taste not to pretend, like some people I've met, to express herself by original signs.'

'I'm afraid you've suffered much,' she once found occasion to say to her friend in response to some allusion that had appeared to reach far.

'What makes you think that?' Madame Merle asked with the amused smile of a person seated at a game of guesses. 'I hope I haven't too much the droop of the misunderstood.'

'No; but you sometimes say things that I think people who have always been happy wouldn't have found out.'

'I haven't always been happy,' said Madame Merle, smiling still, but with a mock gravity, as if she were telling a child a secret. 'Such a wonderful thing!'

But Isabel rose to the irony. 'A great many people give me the impression of never having for a moment felt anything.'

'It's very true; there are many more iron pots certainly than porcelain. But you may depend on it that every one bears some mark; even the hardest iron pots have a little bruise, a little hole somewhere. I flatter myself that I'm rather stout, but if I must tell you the truth I've been shockingly chipped and cracked. I do very well for service yet, because I've been cleverly mended; and I try to remain in the cupboard—the quiet, dusky cupboard where there's an odour of stale spices—as much as I can. But when I've to come out and into a strong light—then, my dear, I'm a horror!'

I know not whether it was on this occasion or on some other that when the conversation had taken the turn I have just indicated she said to Isabel that she would some day a tale unfold.* Isabel assured her she should delight to listen to one, and reminded her more than once of this engagement. Madame Merle, however, begged repeatedly for a respite, and at last frankly told her young companion that they must wait till they knew each other better. This would be sure to happen; a long friendship so visibly lay before them. Isabel assented, but at the same time enquired if she mightn't be trusted—if she appeared capable of a betrayal of confidence.

'It's not that I'm afraid of your repeating what I say,' her fellow visitor answered; 'I'm afraid, on the contrary, of your taking it too much to yourself. You'd judge me too harshly; you're of the cruel age.' She preferred for the present to talk to Isabel of Isabel, and exhibited the greatest interest in our heroine's history, sentiments, opinions, prospects. She made her chatter and listened to her chatter with infinite good nature. This flattered and quickened the girl, who was struck with all the distinguished people her friend had known and with her having lived, as Mrs Touchett said, in the best company in Europe. Isabel thought the better of herself for enjoying the favour of a person who had so large a field of comparison; and it was perhaps partly to gratify the sense of profiting by comparison that she often appealed to these stores of reminiscence. Madame Merle had been a dweller in many lands and had social ties in a dozen different countries. 'I don't pretend to be educated,' she would say, 'but I think I know my Europe;' and she spoke one day of going to Sweden to stay with an old friend, and another of proceeding to Malta to follow up a new acquaintance. With England, where she had often dwelt, she was thoroughly familiar, and for Isabel's benefit threw a great deal of light upon the customs of the country and the character of the people, who 'after all,' as she was fond of saying, were the most convenient in the world to live with.

'You mustn't think it strange her remaining here at such a time as this, when Mr Touchett's passing away,' that gentleman's wife remarked to her niece. 'She is incapable of a mistake; she's the most tactful woman I know. It's a favour to me that she stays; she's putting off a lot of visits at great houses,' said Mrs Touchett, who never forgot that when she herself was in England her social value sank two or three degrees in the scale. 'She has her pick of places; she's not in want of a shelter. But I've asked her to put in this time because I wish you to know her. I think it will be a good thing for you. Serena Merle hasn't a fault.'

'If I didn't already like her very much that description might alarm me,' Isabel returned.

'She's never the least little bit "off." I've brought you out here and I wish to do the best for you. Your sister Lily told me she hoped I would give you plenty of opportunities. I give you one in putting you in relation with Madame Merle. She's one of the most brilliant women in Europe.'

'I like her better than I like your description of her,' Isabel persisted in saying.

'Do you flatter yourself that you'll ever feel her open to criticism? I hope you'll let me know when you do.'

'That will be cruel—to you,' said Isabel.

'You needn't mind me. You won't discover a fault in her.'

'Perhaps not. But I dare say I shan't miss it.'

'She knows absolutely everything on earth there is to know,' said Mrs Touchett.

Isabel after this observed to their companion that she hoped she knew Mrs Touchett considered she hadn't a speck on her perfection. On which 'I'm obliged to you,' Madame Merle replied, 'but I'm afraid your aunt imagines, or at least alludes to, no aberrations that the clock-face doesn't register.'

'So that you mean you've a wild side that's unknown to her?'

'Ah no, I fear my darkest sides are my tamest. I mean that having no faults, for your aunt, means that one's never late for dinner—that is for *her* dinner. I was not late, by the way, the other day, when you came back from London; the clock was just at eight when I came into the drawing-room: it was the rest of you that were before the time. It means that one answers a letter the day one gets it and that when one comes to stay with her one doesn't bring too much luggage and is careful not to be taken ill. For Mrs Touchett those things constitute virtue; it's a blessing to be able to reduce it to its elements.'

Madame Merle's own conversation, it will be perceived, was enriched with bold, free touches of criticism, which, even when they had a restrictive effect, never struck Isabel as ill-natured. It couldn't occur to the girl for instance that Mrs Touchett's accomplished guest was abusing her; and this for very good reasons. In the first place Isabel rose eagerly to the sense of her shades; in the second Madame Merle implied that there was a great deal more to say; and it was clear in the third that for a person to speak to one without ceremony of one's near relations was an agreeable sign of that person's intimacy with one's self. These signs of deep communion multiplied as the days elapsed, and there was none of which Isabel was more sensible than of her companion's preference for making Miss Archer herself a topic. Though she referred frequently to the incidents of her own career she never lingered upon them; she was as little of a gross egotist as she was of a flat gossip.

'I'm old and stale and faded,' she said more than once; 'I'm of no more interest than last week's newspaper. You're young and fresh and of to-day; you've the great thing—you've actuality. I once had it—we all have it for an hour. You, however, will have it for longer. Let us talk about you then; you can say nothing I shall not care to hear. It's a sign that I'm growing old—that I like to talk with younger people. I think it's a very pretty compensation. If we can't have youth within us we can have it outside, and I really think we see it and feel it better that way. Of course we must be in sympathy with it—that I shall always be. I don't know that I shall ever be ill-natured with old people—I hope not; there are certainly some old people I adore. But I shall never be anything but abject with the young; they touch me and appeal to me too much. I give you *carte blanche** then; you can even be impertinent if you like; I shall let it pass and horribly spoil you. I speak as if I were a hundred years old, you say? Well, I am, if you please; I was born before the French Revolution. Ah, my dear, *je viens de loin*;* I belong to the old, old world. But it's not of that I want to talk; I want to talk about the new. You must tell me more about America; you never tell me enough. Here I've been since I was brought here as a helpless child, and it's ridiculous, or rather it's scandalous, how little I know about that splendid, dreadful, funny country—surely the greatest and drollest of them all. There are a great many of us like that in these parts, and I must say I think we're a wretched set of people. You should live in your own land; whatever it may be you have your natural place there. If we're not good Americans we're certainly poor Europeans; we've no natural place here. We're mere parasites, crawling over the surface; we haven't our feet in the soil. At least one can know it and not have illusions. A woman perhaps can get on; a woman, it seems to me, has no natural place anywhere; wherever she finds herself she has to remain on the surface and, more or less, to crawl. You protest, my dear? you're horrified? you declare you'll never crawl? It's very true that I don't see you crawling; you stand more upright than a good many poor creatures. Very good; on the whole, I don't think you'll crawl. But the men, the Americans; *je vous demande un peu*,* what do they make of it over here? I don't envy them trying to arrange themselves. Look at poor Ralph Touchett: what sort of a figure do you call that? Fortunately he has a consumption; I say fortunately, because it gives him something to do. His consumption's his *carrière*;* it's a kind of position. You can say: "Oh, Mr Touchett, he takes care of his lungs, he knows a great deal about climates." But without that who would he be, what would he represent? "Mr Ralph Touchett: an American who lives in Europe." That signifies absolutely nothing—it's impossible anything should signify less. "He's very cultivated," they say: "he has a very pretty collection of old snuff-boxes." The collection is all that's wanted to make it pitiful. I'm tired of the sound of the word; I think it's grotesque. With the poor old father it's different; he has his identity, and it's rather a massive one. He represents a great financial house, and that, in our day, is as good as anything else. For an American, at any rate, that will do very well. But I persist in thinking your cousin very lucky to have a chronic malady so long as he doesn't die of it. It's much better than the snuff-boxes. If he weren't ill, you say, he'd do something?—he'd take his father's place in the house. My poor child, I doubt it; I don't think he's at all fond of the house. However, you know him better than I, though I used to know him rather well, and he may have the benefit of the doubt. The worst case, I think, is a friend of mine, a countryman of ours, who lives in Italy (where he also was brought before he knew better), and who is one of the most delightful men I know. Some day you must know him. I'll bring you together and then you'll see what I mean. He's Gilbert Osmond—he lives in Italy; that's all one can say about him or make of him. He's exceedingly clever, a man made to be distinguished; but, as I tell you, you exhaust the description when you say he's Mr Osmond who lives *tout bêtement** in Italy. No career, no name, no position, no fortune, no past, no future, no anything. Oh yes, he paints, if you please—paints in water-colours; like me, only better than I. His painting's pretty bad; on the whole I'm rather glad of that. Fortunately he's very indolent, so indolent that it amounts to a sort of position. He can say, "Oh, I do nothing; I'm too deadly lazy. You can do nothing to-day unless you get up at five o'clock in the morning." In that way he becomes a sort of exception; you feel he might do something if he'd only rise early. He never speaks of his painting—to people at large; he's too clever for that. But he has a little girl—a dear little girl; he does speak of *her*. He's devoted to her, and if it were a career to be an excellent father he'd be very distinguished. But I'm afraid that's no better than the snuff-boxes; perhaps not even so good. Tell me what they do in America,' pursued Madame Merle, who, it must be observed parenthetically, did not deliver herself all at once of these reflexions, which are presented in a cluster for the convenience of the reader. She talked of Florence, where Mr Osmond lived and where Mrs Touchett occupied a mediæval palace; she talked of Rome, where she herself had a little *pied-à-terre* with some rather good old damask. She talked of places, of people and even, as the phrase is, of 'subjects'; and from time to time she talked of their kind old host and of the prospect of his recovery. From the first she had thought this prospect small, and Isabel had been struck with the positive, discriminating, competent way in which she took the measure of his remainder of life. One evening she announced definitely that he wouldn't live.

'Sir Matthew Hope told me so as plainly as was proper,' she said; 'standing there, near the fire, before dinner. He makes himself very agreeable, the great doctor. I don't mean his saying that has anything to do with it. But he says such things with great tact. I had told him I felt ill at my ease, staying here at such a time; it seemed to me so indiscreet—it wasn't as if I could nurse. "You must remain, you must remain," he answered; "your office will come later." Wasn't that a very delicate way of saying both that poor Mr Touchett would go and that I might be of some use as a consoler? In fact, however, I shall not be of the slightest use. Your aunt will console herself; she, and she alone, knows just how much consolation she'll require. It would be a very delicate matter for another person to undertake to administer the dose. With your cousin it will be different; he'll miss his father immensely. But I should never presume to condole with Mr Ralph; we're not on those terms.' Madame Merle had alluded more than once to some undefined incongruity in her relations with Ralph Touchett; so Isabel took this occasion of asking her if they were not good friends.

'Perfectly, but he doesn't like me.'

'What have you done to him?'

'Nothing whatever. But one has no need of a reason for that.'

'For not liking you? I think one has need of a very good reason.'

'You're very kind. Be sure you have one ready for the day you begin.'

'Begin to dislike you? I shall never begin.'

'I hope not; because if you do you'll never end. That's the way with your cousin; he doesn't get over it. It's an antipathy of nature—if I can call it that when it's all on his side. I've nothing whatever against him and don't bear him the least little grudge for not doing me justice. Justice is all I want. However, one feels that he's a gentleman and would never say anything underhand about one. *Cartes sur table*,'* Madame Merle subjoined in a moment, 'I'm not afraid of him.'

'I hope not indeed,' said Isabel, who added something about his being the kindest creature living. She remembered, however, that on her first asking him about Madame Merle he had answered her in a manner which this lady might have thought injurious without being explicit. There was something between them, Isabel said to herself, but she said nothing more than this. If it were something of importance it should inspire respect; if it were not it was not worth her curiosity. With all her love of knowledge she had a natural shrinking from raising curtains and looking into unlighted corners. The love of knowledge coexisted in her mind with the finest capacity for ignorance.

But Madame Merle sometimes said things that startled her, made her raise her clear eyebrows at the time and think of the words afterwards. 'I'd give a great deal to be your age again,' she broke out once with a bitterness which, though diluted in her customary amplitude of ease, was imperfectly disguised by it. 'If I could only begin again—if I could have my life before me!'

'Your life's before you yet,' Isabel answered gently, for she was vaguely awe-struck.

'No; the best part's gone, and gone for nothing.'

'Surely not for nothing,' said Isabel.

'Why not—what have I got? Neither husband, nor child, nor fortune, nor position, nor the traces of a beauty that I never had.'

'You have many friends, dear lady.'

'I'm not so sure!' cried Madame Merle.

'Ah, you're wrong. You have memories, graces, talents——'

But Madame Merle interrupted her. 'What have my talents brought me? Nothing but the need of using them still, to get through the hours, the years, to cheat myself with some pretence of movement, of unconsciousness. As for my graces and memories the less said about them the better. You'll be my friend till you find a better use for your friendship.'

'It will be for you to see that I don't then,' said Isabel.

'Yes; I would make an effort to keep you.' And her companion looked at her gravely. 'When I say I should like to be your age I mean with your qualities—frank, generous, sincere like you. In that case I should have made something better of my life.'

'What should you have liked to do that you've not done?'

Madame Merle took a sheet of music—she was seated at the piano and had abruptly wheeled about on the stool when she first spoke—and mechanically turned the leaves. 'I'm very ambitious!' she at last replied.

'And your ambitions have not been satisfied? They must have been great.'

'They *were* great. I should make myself ridiculous by talking of them.'

Isabel wondered what they could have been—whether Madame Merle had aspired to wear a crown. 'I don't know what your idea of success may be, but you seem to me to have been successful. To me indeed you're a vivid image of success.'

Madame Merle tossed away the music with a smile. 'What's *your* idea of success?'

'You evidently think it must be a very tame one. It's to see some dream of one's youth come true.'

'Ah,' Madame Merle exclaimed, 'that I've never seen! But my dreams were so great—so preposterous. Heaven forgive me, I'm dreaming now!' And she turned back to the piano and began grandly to play. On the morrow she said to Isabel that her definition of success had been very pretty, yet frightfully sad. Measured in that way, who had ever succeeded? The dreams of one's youth, why they were enchanting, they were divine! Who had ever seen such things come to pass?

'I myself—a few of them,' Isabel ventured to answer.

'Already? They must have been dreams of yesterday.'

'I began to dream very young,' Isabel smiled.

'Ah, if you mean the aspirations of your childhood—that of having a pink sash and a doll that could close her eyes.'

'No, I don't mean that.'

'Or a young man with a fine moustache going down on his knees to you.'

'No, nor that either,' Isabel declared with still more emphasis.

Madame Merle appeared to note this eagerness. 'I suspect that's what you do mean. We've all had the young man with the moustache. He's the inevitable young man; he doesn't count.'

Isabel was silent a little but then spoke with extreme and characteristic inconsequence. 'Why shouldn't he count? There are young men and young men.'

'And yours was a paragon—is that what you mean?' asked her friend with a laugh. 'If you've had the identical young man you dreamed of, then that was success, and I congratulate you with all my heart. Only in that case why didn't you fly with him to his castle in the Apennines?'

'He has no castle in the Apennines.'

'What has he? An ugly brick house in Fortieth Street? Don't tell me that; I refuse to recognise that as an ideal.'

'I don't care anything about his house,' said Isabel.

'That's very crude of you. When you've lived as long as I you'll see that every human being has his shell and that you must take the shell into account. By the shell I mean the whole envelope of circumstances. There's no such thing as an isolated man or woman; we're each of us made up of some cluster of appurtenances. What shall we call our "self"? Where does it begin? where does it end? It overflows into everything that belongs to us—and then it flows back again. I know a large part of myself is in the clothes I choose to wear. I've a great respect for *things*! One's self—for other people—is one's expression of one's self; and one's house, one's furniture, one's garments, the books one reads, the company one keeps—these things are all expressive.'

This was very metaphysical; not more so, however, than several observations Madame Merle had already made. Isabel was fond of metaphysics, but was unable to accompany her friend into this bold analysis of the human personality. 'I don't agree with you. I think just the other way. I don't know whether I succeed in expressing myself, but I know that nothing else expresses me. Nothing that belongs to me is any measure of me; everything's on the contrary a limit, a barrier, and a perfectly arbitrary one. Certainly the clothes which, as you say, I choose to wear, don't express me; and heaven forbid they should!'

'You dress very well,' Madame Merle lightly interposed.

'Possibly; but I don't care to be judged by that. My clothes may express the dressmaker, but they don't express me. To begin with it's not my own choice that I wear them; they're imposed upon me by society.'

'Should you prefer to go without them?' Madame Merle enquired in a tone which virtually terminated the discussion.

I am bound to confess, though it may cast some discredit on the sketch I have given of the youthful loyalty practised by our heroine toward this accomplished woman, that Isabel had said nothing whatever to her about Lord Warburton and had been equally reticent on the subject of Caspar Goodwood. She had not, however, concealed the fact that she had had opportunities of marrying and had even let her friend know of how advantageous a kind they had been. Lord Warburton had left Lockleigh and was gone to Scotland, taking his sisters with him; and though he had written to Ralph more than once to ask about Mr Touchett's health the girl was not liable to the embarrassment of such enquiries as, had he still been in the neighbourhood, he would probably have felt bound to make in person. He had excellent ways, but she felt sure that if he had come to Gardencourt he would have seen Madame Merle, and that if he had seen her he would have liked her and betrayed to her that he was in love with her young friend. It so happened that during this lady's previous visits to Gardencourt—each of them much shorter than the present—he had either not been at Lockleigh or had not called at Mr Touchett's. Therefore, though she knew him by name as the great man of that county, she had no cause to suspect him as a suitor of Mrs Touchett's freshly-imported niece.

'You've plenty of time,' she had said to Isabel in return for the mutilated confidences which our young woman made her and which didn't pretend to be perfect, though we have seen that at moments the girl had compunctions at having said so much. 'I'm glad you've done nothing yet—that you have it still to do. It's a very good thing for a girl to have refused a few good offers—so long of course as they are not the best she's likely to have. Pardon me if my tone seems horribly corrupt; one must take the worldly view sometimes. Only don't keep on refusing for the sake of refusing. It's a pleasant exercise of power; but accepting's after all an exercise of power as well. There's always the danger of refusing once too often. It was not the one I fell into—I didn't refuse often enough. You're an exquisite creature, and I should like to see you married to a prime minister. But speaking strictly, you know, you're not what is technically called a *parti.** You're extremely good-looking and extremely clever; in yourself you're quite exceptional. You appear to have the vaguest ideas about your earthly possessions; but from what I can make out you're not embarrassed with an income. I wish you had a little money.'

'I wish I had!' said Isabel, simply, apparently forgetting for the moment that her poverty had been a venial fault for two gallant gentlemen.

In spite of Sir Matthew Hope's benevolent recommendation Madame Merle did not remain to the end, as the issue of poor Mr Touchett's malady had now come frankly to be designated. She was under pledges to other people which had at last to be redeemed, and she left Gardencourt with the understanding that she should in any event see Mrs Touchett there again, or else in town, before quitting England. Her parting with Isabel was even more like the beginning of a friendship than their meeting had been. 'I'm going to six places in succession, but I shall see no one I like so well as you. They'll all be old friends, however; one doesn't make new friends at my age. I've made a great exception for you. You must remember that and must think as well of me as possible. You must reward me by believing in me.'

By way of answer Isabel kissed her, and, though some women kiss with facility, there are kisses and kisses, and this embrace was satisfactory to Madame Merle. Our young lady, after this, was much alone; she saw her aunt and cousin only at meals, and discovered that of the hours during which Mrs Touchett was invisible only a minor portion was now devoted to nursing her husband. She spent the rest in her own apartments, to which access was not allowed even to her niece, apparently occupied there with mysterious and inscrutable exercises. At table she was grave and silent; but her solemnity was not an attitude—Isabel could see it was a conviction. She wondered if her aunt repented of having taken her own way so much; but there was no visible evidence of this—no tears, no sighs, no exaggeration of a zeal always to its own sense adequate. Mrs Touchett seemed simply to feel the need of thinking things over and summing them up; she had a little moral account-book—with columns unerringly ruled and a sharp steel clasp—which she kept with exemplary neatness. Uttered reflexion had with her ever, at any rate, a practical ring. 'If I had foreseen this I'd not have proposed your coming abroad now,' she said to Isabel after Madame Merle had left the house. 'I'd have waited and sent for you next year.'

'So that perhaps I should never have known my uncle? It's a great happiness to me to have come now.'

'That's very well. But it was not that you might know your uncle that I brought you to Europe.' A perfectly veracious speech; but, as Isabel thought, not as perfectly timed. She had leisure to think of this and other matters. She took a solitary walk every day and spent vague hours in turning over books in the library. Among the subjects that engaged her attention were the adventures of her friend Miss Stackpole, with whom she was in regular correspondence. Isabel liked her friend's private epistolary style better than her public; that is she felt her public letters would have been excellent if they had not been printed. Henrietta's career, however, was not so successful as might have been wished even in the interest of her private felicity; that view of the inner life of Great Britain which she was so eager to take appeared to dance before her like an *ignis fatuus*.* The invitation from Lady Pensil, for mysterious reasons, had never arrived; and poor Mr Bantling himself, with all his friendly ingenuity, had been unable to explain so grave a dereliction on the part of a missive that had obviously been sent. He had evidently taken Henrietta's affairs much to heart, and believed that he owed her a set-off to this illusory visit to Bedfordshire. 'He says he should think I would go to the Continent,' Henrietta wrote; 'and as he thinks of going there himself I suppose his advice is sincere. He wants to know why I don't take a view of French life; and it's a fact that I want very much to see the new Republic.* Mr Bantling doesn't care much about the Republic, but he thinks of going over to Paris anyway. I must say he's quite as attentive as I could wish, and at least I shall have seen one polite Englishman. I keep telling Mr Bantling that he ought to have been an American, and you should see how that pleases him. Whenever I say so he always breaks out with the same exclamation—"Ah, but really, come now!" ' A few days later she wrote that she had decided to go to Paris at the end of the week and that Mr Bantling had promised to see her off—perhaps even would go as far as Dover with her. She would wait in Paris till Isabel should arrive, Henrietta added; speaking quite as if Isabel were to start on her continental journey alone and making no allusion to Mrs Touchett. Bearing in mind his interest in their late companion, our heroine communicated several passages from this correspondence to Ralph, who followed with an emotion akin to suspense the career of the representative of the *Interviewer*.

'It seems to me she's doing very well,' he said, 'going over to Paris with an ex-Lancer!* If she wants something to write about she has only to describe that episode.'

'It's not conventional, certainly,' Isabel answered; 'but if you mean that—as far as Henrietta is concerned—it's not perfectly innocent, you're very much mistaken. You'll never understand Henrietta.'

'Pardon me, I understand her perfectly. I didn't at all at first, but now I've the point of view. I'm afraid, however, that Bantling hasn't; he may have some surprises. Oh, I understand Henrietta as well as if I had made her!'

Isabel was by no means sure of this, but she abstained from expressing further doubt, for she was disposed in these days to extend a great charity to her cousin. One afternoon less than a week after Madame Merle's departure she was seated in the library with a volume to which her attention was not fastened. She had placed herself in a deep window-bench, from which she looked out into the dull, damp park; and as the library stood at right angles to the entrance-front of the house she could see the doctor's brougham, which had been waiting for the last two hours before the door. She was struck with his remaining so long, but at last she saw him appear in the portico, stand a moment slowly drawing on his gloves and looking at the knees of his horse, and then get into the vehicle and roll away. Isabel kept her place for half an hour; there was a great stillness in the house. It was so great that when she at last heard a soft, slow step on the deep carpet of the room she was almost startled by the sound. She turned quickly away from the window and saw Ralph Touchett standing there with his hands still in his pockets, but with a face absolutely void of its usual latent smile. She got up and her movement and glance were a question.

'It's all over,' said Ralph.

'Do you mean that my uncle——?' And Isabel stopped.

'My dear father died an hour ago.'

'Ah, my poor Ralph!' she gently wailed, putting out her two hands to him.

XX

SOME fortnight after this Madame Merle drove up in a hansom cab to the house in Winchester Square. As she descended from her vehicle she observed, suspended between the dining-room windows, a large, neat, wooden tablet, on whose fresh black ground were inscribed in white paint the words—'This noble freehold mansion to be sold'; with the name of the agent to whom application should be made. 'They certainly lose no time,' said the visitor as, after sounding the big brass knocker, she waited to be admitted; 'it's a practical country!' And within the house, as she ascended to the drawing-room, she perceived numerous signs of abdication; pictures removed from the walls and placed upon sofas, windows undraped and floors laid bare. Mrs Touchett presently received her and intimated in a few words that condolences might be taken for granted.

'I know what you're going to say—he was a very good man. But I know it better than any one, because I gave him more chance to show it. In that I think I was a good wife.' Mrs Touchett added that at the end her husband apparently recognised this fact. 'He has treated me most liberally,' she said; 'I won't say more liberally than I expected, because I didn't expect. You know that as a general thing I don't expect. But he chose, I presume, to recognise the fact that though I lived much abroad and mingled—you may say freely—in foreign life, I never exhibited the smallest preference for any one else.'

'For any one but yourself,' Madame Merle mentally observed; but the reflexion was perfectly inaudible.

'I never sacrificed my husband to another,' Mrs Touchett continued with her stout curtness.

'Oh no,' thought Madame Merle; 'you never did anything for another!'

There was a certain cynicism in these mute comments which demands an explanation; the more so as they are not in accord either with the view—somewhat superficial perhaps—that we have hitherto enjoyed of Madame Merle's character or with the literal facts of Mrs Touchett's history; the more so, too, as Madame Merle had a well-founded conviction that her friend's last remark was not in the least to be construed as a side-thrust at herself. The truth is that the moment she had crossed the threshold she received an impression that Mr Touchett's death had had subtle consequences and that these consequences had been profitable to a little circle of persons among whom she was not numbered. Of course it was an event which would naturally have consequences; her imagination had more than once rested upon this fact during her stay at Gardencourt. But it had been one thing to foresee such a matter mentally and another to stand among its massive records. The idea of a distribution of property—she would almost have said of spoils—just now pressed upon her senses and irritated her with a sense of exclusion. I am far from wishing to picture her as one of the hungry mouths or envious hearts of the general herd, but we have already learned of her having desires that had never been satisfied. If she had been questioned, she would of course have admitted—with a fine proud smile—that she had not the faintest claim to a share in Mr Touchett's relics. 'There was never anything in the world between us,' she would have said. 'There was never that, poor man!'—with a fillip of her thumb and her third finger. I hasten to add, moreover, that if she couldn't at the present moment keep from quite perversely yearning she was careful not to betray herself. She had after all as much sympathy for Mrs Touchett's gains as for her losses.

'He has left me this house,' the newly-made widow said; 'but of course I shall not live in it; I've a much better one in Florence. The will was opened only three days since, but I've already offered the house for sale. I've also a share in the bank; but I don't yet understand if I'm obliged to leave it there. If not I shall certainly take it out. Ralph, of course, has Gardencourt; but I'm not sure that he'll have means to keep up the place. He's naturally left very well off, but his father has given away an immense deal of money; there are bequests to a string of third cousins in Vermont. Ralph, however, is very fond of Gardencourt and would be quite capable of living there—in summer—with a maid-of-all-work and a gardener's boy. There's one remarkable clause in my husband's will,' Mrs Touchett added. 'He has left my niece a fortune.'

'A fortune!' Madame Merle softly repeated.

'Isabel steps into something like seventy thousand pounds.'

Madame Merle's hands were clasped in her lap; at this she raised them, still clasped, and held them a moment against her bosom while her eyes, a little dilated, fixed themselves on those of her friend. 'Ah,' she cried, 'the clever creature!'

Mrs Touchett gave her a quick look. 'What do you mean by that?'

For an instant Madame Merle's colour rose and she dropped her eyes. 'It certainly is clever to achieve such results—without an effort!'

'There assuredly was no effort. Don't call it an achievement.'

Madame Merle was seldom guilty of the awkwardness of retracting what she had said; her wisdom was shown rather in maintaining it and placing it in a favourable light. 'My dear friend, Isabel would certainly not have had seventy thousand pounds left her if she had not been the most charming girl in the world. Her charm includes great cleverness.'

'She never dreamed, I'm sure, of my husband's doing anything for her; and I never dreamed of it either, for he never spoke to me of his intention,' Mrs Touchett said. 'She had no claim upon him whatever; it was no great recommendation to him that she was my niece. Whatever she achieved she achieved unconsciously.'

'Ah,' rejoined Madame Merle, 'those are the greatest strokes!'

Mrs Touchett reserved her opinion. 'The girl's fortunate; I don't deny that. But for the present she's simply stupefied.'

'Do you mean that she doesn't know what to do with the money?'

'That, I think, she has hardly considered. She doesn't know what to think about the matter at all. It has been as if a big gun were suddenly fired off behind her; she's feeling herself to see if she be hurt. It's but three days since she received a visit from the principal executor, who came in person, very gallantly, to notify her. He told me afterwards that when he had made his little speech she suddenly burst into tears. The money's to remain in the affairs of the bank, and she's to draw the interest.'

Madame Merle shook her head with a wise and now quite benignant smile. 'How very delicious! After she has done that two or three times she'll get used to it.' Then after a silence, 'What does your son think of it?' she abruptly asked.

'He left England before the will was read—used up by his fatigue and anxiety and hurrying off to the south. He's on his way to the Riviera and I've not yet heard from him. But it's not likely he'll ever object to anything done by his father.'

'Didn't you say his own share had been cut down?'

'Only at his wish. I know that he urged his father to do something for the people in America. He's not in the least addicted to looking after number one.'

'It depends upon whom he regards as number one!' said Madame Merle. And she remained thoughtful a moment, her eyes bent on the floor. 'Am I not to see your happy niece?' she asked at last as she raised them.

'You may see her; but you'll not be struck with her being happy. She has looked as solemn, these three days, as a Cimabue Madonna!'* And Mrs Touchett rang for a servant.

Isabel came in shortly after the footman had been sent to call her; and Madame Merle thought, as she appeared, that Mrs Touchett's comparison had its force. The girl was pale and grave—an effect not mitigated by her deeper mourning; but the smile of her brightest moments came into her face as she saw Madame Merle, who went forward, laid her hand on our heroine's shoulder and, after looking at her a moment, kissed her as if she were returning the kiss she had received from her at Gardencourt. This was the only allusion the visitor, in her great good taste, made for the present to her young friend's inheritance.

Mrs Touchett had no purpose of awaiting in London the sale of her house. After selecting from among its furniture the objects she wished to transport to her other abode, she left the rest of its contents to be disposed of by the auctioneer and took her departure for the Continent. She was of course accompanied on this journey by her niece, who now had plenty of leisure to measure and weigh and otherwise handle the windfall on which Madame Merle had covertly congratulated her. Isabel thought very often of the fact of her accession of means, looking at it in a dozen different lights; but we shall not now attempt to follow her train of thought or to explain exactly why her new consciousness was at first oppressive. This failure to rise to immediate joy was indeed but brief; the girl presently made up her mind that to be rich was a virtue because it was to be able to *do*, and that to do could only be sweet. It was the graceful contrary of the stupid side of weakness—especially the feminine variety. To be weak was, for a delicate young person, rather graceful, but, after all, as Isabel said to herself, there was a larger grace than that. Just now, it is true, there was not much to do—once she had sent off a cheque to Lily and another to poor Edith; but she was thankful for the quiet months which her mourning robes and her aunt's fresh widowhood compelled them to spend together. The acquisition of power made her serious; she scrutinised her power with a kind of tender ferocity, but was not eager to exercise it. She began to do so during a stay of some weeks which she eventually made with her aunt in Paris, though in ways that will inevitably present themselves as trivial. They were the ways most naturally imposed in a city in which the shops are the admiration of the world, and that were prescribed unreservedly by the guidance of Mrs Touchett, who took a rigidly practical view of the transformation of her niece from a poor girl to a rich one. 'Now that you're a young woman of fortune you must know how to play the part—I mean to play it well,' she said to Isabel once for all; and she added that the girl's first duty was to have everything handsome. 'You don't know how to take care of your things, but you must learn,' she went on; this was Isabel's second duty. Isabel submitted, but for the present her imagination was not kindled; she longed for opportunities, but these were not the opportunities she meant.

Mrs Touchett rarely changed her plans, and, having intended before her husband's death to spend a part of the winter in Paris, saw no reason to deprive herself—still less to deprive her companion—of this advantage. Though they would live in great retirement she might still present her niece, informally, to the little circle of her fellow countrymen dwelling upon the skirts of the Champs Elysées. With many of these amiable colonists Mrs Touchett was intimate; she shared their expatriation, their convictions, their pastimes, their ennui. Isabel saw them arrive with a good deal of assiduity at her aunt's hotel, and pronounced on them with a trenchancy doubtless to be accounted for by the temporary exaltation of her sense of human duty. She made up her mind that their lives were, though luxurious, inane, and incurred some disfavour by expressing this view on bright Sunday afternoons, when the American absentees were engaged in calling on each other. Though her listeners passed for people kept exemplarily genial by their cooks and dressmakers, two or three of them thought her cleverness, which was generally admitted, inferior to that of the new theatrical pieces. 'You all live here this way, but what does it lead to?' she was pleased to ask. 'It doesn't seem to lead to anything, and I should think you'd get very tired of it.'

Mrs Touchett thought the question worthy of Henrietta Stackpole. The two ladies had found Henrietta in Paris, and Isabel constantly saw her; so that Mrs Touchett had some reason for saying to herself that if her niece were not clever enough to originate almost anything, she might be suspected of having borrowed that style of remark from her journalistic friend. The first occasion on which Isabel had spoken was that of a visit paid by the two ladies to Mrs Luce, an old friend of Mrs Touchett's and the only person in Paris she now went to see. Mrs Luce had been living in Paris since the days of Louis Philippe;* she used to say jocosely that she was one of the generation of 1830—a joke of which the point was not always taken. When it failed Mrs Luce used to explain—'Oh yes, I'm one of the romantics;' her French had never become quite perfect. She was always at home on Sunday afternoons and surrounded by sympathetic compatriots, usually the same. In fact she was at home at all times, and reproduced with wondrous truth in her well-cushioned little corner of the brilliant city, the domestic tone of her native Baltimore. This reduced Mr Luce, her worthy husband, a tall, lean, grizzled, well-brushed gentleman who wore a gold eyeglass and carried his hat a little too much on the back of his head, to mere platonic praise of the 'distractions' of Paris—they were his great word—since you would never have guessed from what cares he escaped to them. One of them was that he went every day to the American banker's, where he found a post-office that was almost as sociable and colloquial an institution as in an American country town. He passed an hour (in fine weather) in a chair in the Champs Elysées, and he dined uncommonly well at his own table, seated above a waxed floor which it was Mrs Luce's happiness to believe had a finer polish than any other in the French capital. Occasionally he dined with a friend or two at the Café Anglais, where his talent for ordering a dinner was a source of felicity to his companions and an object of admiration even to the head-waiter of the establishment. These were his only known pastimes, but they had beguiled his hours for upwards of half a century, and they doubtless justified his frequent declaration that there was no place like Paris. In no other place, on these terms, could Mr Luce flatter himself that he was enjoying life. There was nothing like Paris, but it must be confessed that Mr Luce thought less highly of this scene of his dissipations than in earlier days. In the list of his resources his political reflections should not be omitted, for they were doubtless the animating principle of many hours that superficially seemed vacant. Like many of his fellow colonists Mr Luce was a high—or rather a deep—conservative, and gave no countenance to the government lately established in France. He had no faith in its duration and would assure you from year to year that its end was close at hand. 'They want to be kept down, sir, to be kept down; nothing but the strong hand—the iron heel—will do for them,' he would frequently say of the French people; and his ideal of a fine showy clever rule was that of the superseded Empire.* 'Paris is much less attractive than in the days of the Emperor; *he* knew how to make a city pleasant,' Mr Luce had often remarked to Mrs Touchett, who was quite of his own way of thinking and wished to know what one had crossed that odious Atlantic for but to get away from republics.

'Why, madam, sitting in the Champs Elysées, opposite to the Palace of Industry, I've seen the court-carriages from the Tuileries pass up and down as many as seven times a day. I remember one occasion when they went as high as nine. What do you see now? It's no use talking, the style's all gone. Napoleon knew what the French people want, and there'll be a dark cloud over Paris, *our* Paris, till they get the Empire back again.'

Among Mrs Luce's visitors on Sunday afternoons was a young man with whom Isabel had had a good deal of conversation and whom she found full of valuable knowledge. Mr Edward Rosier—Ned Rosier as he was called—was native to New York and had been brought up in Paris, living there under the eye of his father who, as it happened, had been an early and intimate friend of the late Mr Archer. Edward Rosier remembered Isabel as a little girl; it had been his father who came to the rescue of the small Archers at the inn at Neufchâtel (he was travelling that way with the boy and had stopped at the hotel by chance), after their *bonne* had gone off with the Russian prince and when Mr Archer's whereabouts remained for some days a mystery. Isabel remembered perfectly the neat little male child whose hair smelt of a delicious cosmetic and who had a *bonne* all his own, warranted to lose sight of him under no provocation. Isabel took a walk with the pair beside the lake and thought little Edward as pretty as an angel—a comparison by no means conventional in her mind, for she had a very definite conception of a type of features which she supposed to be angelic and which her new friend perfectly illustrated. A small pink face surmounted by a blue velvet bonnet and set off by a stiff embroidered collar had become the countenance of her childish dreams; and she had firmly believed for some time afterwards that the heavenly hosts conversed among themselves in a queer little dialect of French-English, expressing the properest sentiments, as when Edward told her that he was 'defended'* by his *bonne* to go near the edge of the lake, and that one must always obey to one's *bonne*. Ned Rosier's English had improved; at least it exhibited in a less degree the French variation. His father was dead and his *bonne* dismissed, but the young man still conformed to the spirit of their teaching—he never went to the edge of the lake. There was still something agreeable to the nostrils about him and something not offensive to nobler organs. He was a very gentle and gracious youth, with what are called cultivated tastes—an acquaintance with old china, with good wine, with the bindings of books, with the *Almanach de Gotha*,* with the best shops, the best hotels, the hours of railway-trains. He could order a dinner almost as well as Mr Luce, and it was probable that as his experience accumulated he would be a worthy successor to that gentleman, whose rather grim politics he also advocated in a soft and innocent voice. He had some charming rooms in Paris, decorated with old Spanish altar-lace, the envy of his female friends, who declared that his chimney-piece was better draped than the high shoulders of many a duchess. He usually, however, spent a part of every winter at Pau, and had once passed a couple of months in the United States.

He took a great interest in Isabel and remembered perfectly the walk at Neufchâtel, when she would persist in going so near the edge. He seemed to recognise this same tendency in the subversive enquiry that I quoted a moment ago, and set himself to answer our heroine's question with greater urbanity than it perhaps deserved. 'What does it lead to, Miss Archer? Why Paris leads everywhere. You can't go anywhere unless you come here first. Every one that comes to Europe has got to pass through. You don't mean it in that sense so much? You mean what good it does you? Well, how can you penetrate futurity? How can you tell what lies ahead? If it's a pleasant road I don't care where it leads. I like the road, Miss Archer; I like the dear old asphalte. You can't get tired of it—you can't if you try. You think you would, but you wouldn't; there's always something new and fresh. Take the Hôtel Drouot, now; they sometimes have three and four sales a week. Where can you get such things as you can here? In spite of all they say I maintain they're cheaper too, if you know the right places. I know plenty of places, but I keep them to myself. I'll tell you, if you like, as a particular favour; only you mustn't tell any one else. Don't you go anywhere without asking me first; I want you to promise me that. As a general thing avoid the

Boulevards; there's very little to be done on the Boulevards. Speaking conscientiously—*sans blague**—I don't believe any one knows Paris better than I. You and Mrs Touchett must come and breakfast with me some day, and I'll show you my things; *je ne vous dis que ça*!* There has been a great deal of talk about London of late; it's the fashion to cry up London. But there's nothing in it—you can't do anything in London. No Louis Quinze—nothing of the First Empire; nothing but their eternal Queen Anne.* It's good for one's bed-room, Queen Anne—for one's washing-room; but it isn't proper for a *salon*.* Do I spend my life at the auctioneer's?' Mr Rosier pursued in answer to another question of Isabel's. 'Oh no; I haven't the means. I wish I had. You think I'm a mere trifler; I can tell by the expression of your face—you've got a wonderfully expressive face. I hope you don't mind my saying that; I mean it as a kind of warning. You think I ought to do something, and so do I, so long as you leave it vague. But when you come to the point you see you have to stop. I can't go home and be a shopkeeper. You think I'm very well fitted? Ah, Miss Archer, you overrate me. I can buy very well, but I can't sell; you should see when I sometimes try to get rid of my things. It takes much more ability to make other people buy than to buy yourself. When I think how clever they must be, the people who make *me* buy! Ah no; I couldn't be a shopkeeper. I can't be a doctor; it's a repulsive business. I can't be a clergyman; I haven't got convictions. And then I can't pronounce the names right in the Bible. They're very difficult, in the Old Testament particularly. I can't be a lawyer; I don't understand—how do you call it?—the American *procédure*.* Is there anything else? There's nothing for a gentleman in America. I should like to be a diplomatist; but American diplomacy—that's not for gentlemen either. I'm sure if you had seen the last min——'

Henrietta Stackpole, who was often with her friend when Mr Rosier, coming to pay his compliments late in the afternoon, expressed himself after the fashion I have sketched, usually interrupted the young man at this point and read him a lecture on the duties of the American citizen. She thought him most unnatural; he was worse than poor Ralph Touchett.

Henrietta, however, was at this time more than ever addicted to fine criticism, for her conscience had been freshly alarmed as regards Isabel. She had not congratulated this young lady on her augmentations and begged to be excused from doing so.

'If Mr Touchett had consulted me about leaving you the money,' she frankly asserted, 'I'd have said to him "Never!" '

'I see,' Isabel had answered. 'You think it will prove a curse in disguise. Perhaps it will.'

'Leave it to some one you care less for—that's what I should have said.'

'To yourself for instance?' Isabel suggested jocosely. And then, 'Do you really believe it will ruin me?' she asked in quite another tone.

'I hope it won't ruin you; but it will certainly confirm your dangerous tendencies.'

'Do you mean the love of luxury—of extravagance?'

'No, no,' said Henrietta; 'I mean your exposure on the moral side. I approve of luxury; I think we ought to be as elegant as possible. Look at the luxury of our western cities; I've seen nothing over here to compare with it. I hope you'll never become grossly sensual; but I'm not afraid of that. The peril for you is that you live too much in the world of your own dreams. You're not enough in contact with reality—with the toiling, striving, suffering, I may even say sinning, world that surrounds you. You're too fastidious; you've too many graceful illusions. Your newly-acquired thousands will shut you up more and more to the society of a few selfish and heartless people who will be interested in keeping them up.'

Isabel's eyes expanded as she gazed at this lurid scene. 'What are my illusions?' she asked. 'I try so hard not to have any.'

'Well,' said Henrietta, 'you think you can lead a romantic life, that you can live by pleasing yourself and pleasing others. You'll find you're mistaken. Whatever life you lead you must put your soul in it—to make any sort of success of it; and from the moment you do that it ceases to be romance, I assure you: it becomes grim reality! And you can't always please yourself; you must sometimes please other people. That, I admit, you're very ready to do; but there's another thing that's still more important—you must often *dis*please others. You must always be ready for that—you must never shrink from it. That doesn't suit you at all—you're too fond of admiration, you like to be thought well of. You think we can escape disagreeable duties by taking romantic views—that's your great illusion, my dear. But we can't. You must be prepared on many occasions in life to please no one at all—not even yourself.'

Isabel shook her head sadly; she looked troubled and frightened. 'This, for you, Henrietta,' she said, 'must be one of those occasions!'

It was certainly true that Miss Stackpole, during her visit to Paris, which had been professionally more remunerative than her English sojourn, had not been living in the world of dreams. Mr Bantling, who had now returned to England, was her companion for the first four weeks of her stay; and about Mr Bantling there was nothing dreamy. Isabel learned from her friend that the two had led a life of great personal intimacy and that this had been a peculiar advantage to Henrietta, owing to the gentleman's remarkable knowledge of Paris. He had explained everything, shown her everything, been her constant guide and interpreter. They had breakfasted together, dined together, gone to the theatre together, supped together, really in a manner quite lived together. He was a true friend, Henrietta more than once assured our heroine; and she had never supposed that she could like any Englishman so well. Isabel could not have told you why, but she found something that ministered to mirth in the alliance the correspondent of the *Interviewer* had struck with Lady Pensil's brother; her amusement moreover subsisted in face of the fact that she thought it a credit to each of them. Isabel couldn't rid herself of a suspicion that they were playing somehow at cross-purposes—that the simplicity of each had been entrapped. But this simplicity was on either side none the less honourable. It was as graceful on Henrietta's part to believe that Mr Bantling took an interest in the diffusion of lively journalism and in consolidating the position of lady-correspondents as it was on the part of his companion to suppose that the cause of the *Interviewer*—a periodical of which he never formed a very definite conception—was, if subtly analysed (a task to which Mr Bantling felt himself quite equal), but the cause of Miss Stackpole's need of demonstrative affection. Each of these groping celibates supplied at any rate a want of which the other was impatiently conscious. Mr Bantling, who was of rather a slow and a discursive habit, relished a prompt, keen, positive woman, who charmed him by the influence of a shining, challenging eye and a kind of bandbox freshness, and who kindled a perception of raciness in a mind to which the usual fare of life seemed unsalted. Henrietta, on the other hand, enjoyed the society of a gentleman who appeared somehow, in his way, made, by expensive, roundabout, almost 'quaint' processes, for her use, and whose leisured state, though generally indefensible, was a decided boon to a breathless mate, and who was furnished with an easy, traditional, though by no means exhaustive, answer to almost any social or practical question that could come up. She often found Mr Bantling's answers very convenient, and in the press of catching the American post would largely and showily address them to publicity. It was to be feared that she was indeed drifting toward those abysses of sophistication as to which Isabel, wishing for a good-humoured retort, had warned her. There might be danger in store for Isabel; but it was scarcely to be hoped that Miss Stackpole, on her side, would find permanent rest in any adoption of the views of a class pledged to all the old abuses. Isabel continued to warn her good-humouredly; Lady Pensil's obliging brother was sometimes, on our heroine's lips, an object of irreverent and facetious allusion. Nothing, however, could exceed Henrietta's amiability on this point; she used to abound in the sense of Isabel's irony and to enumerate with elation the hours she had spent with this perfect man of the world—a term that had ceased to make with her, as previously, for opprobrium. Then, a few moments later, she would forget that they had been talking jocosely and would mention with impulsive earnestness some expedition she had enjoyed in his company. She would say: 'Oh, I know all about Versailles; I went there with Mr Bantling. I was bound to see it thoroughly—I warned him when we went out there that I was thorough: so we spent three days at the hotel and wandered all over the place. It was lovely weather—a kind of Indian summer, only not so good. We just lived in that park. Oh yes; you can't tell me anything about Versailles.' Henrietta appeared to have made arrangements to meet her gallant friend during the spring in Italy.

XXI

MRS TOUCHETT, before arriving in Paris, had fixed the day for her departure and by the middle of February had begun to travel southward. She interrupted her journey to pay a visit to her son, who at San Remo, on the Italian shore of the Mediterranean, had been spending a dull, bright winter beneath a slow-moving white umbrella. Isabel went with her aunt as a matter of course, though Mrs Touchett, with homely, customary logic, had laid before her a pair of alternatives.

'Now, of course, you're completely your own mistress and are as free as the bird on the bough. I don't mean you were not so before, but you're at present on a different footing—property erects a kind of barrier. You can do a great many things if you're rich which would be severely criticised if you were poor. You can go and come, you can travel alone, you can have your own establishment: I mean of course if you'll take a companion—some decayed gentlewoman, with a darned cashmere and dyed hair, who paints on velvet. You don't think you'd like that? Of course you can do as you please; I only want you to understand how much you're at liberty. You might take Miss Stackpole as your *dame de compagnie*;* she'd keep people off very well. I think, however, that it's a great deal better you should remain with me, in spite of there being no obligation. It's better for several reasons, quite apart from your liking it. I shouldn't think you'd like it, but I recommend you to make the sacrifice. Of course whatever novelty there may have been at first in my society has quite passed away, and you see me as I am—a dull, obstinate, narrow-minded old woman.'

'I don't think you're at all dull,' Isabel had replied to this.

'But you do think I'm obstinate and narrow-minded? I told you so!' said Mrs Touchett with much elation at being justified.

Isabel remained for the present with her aunt, because, in spite of eccentric impulses, she had a great regard for what was usually deemed decent, and a young gentlewoman without visible relations had always struck her as a flower without foliage. It was true that Mrs Touchett's conversation had never again appeared so brilliant as that first afternoon in Albany, when she sat in her damp waterproof and sketched the opportunities that Europe would offer to a young person of taste. This, however, was in a great measure the girl's own fault; she had got a glimpse of her aunt's experience, and her imagination constantly anticipated the judgements and emotions of a woman who had very little of the same faculty. Apart from this, Mrs Touchett had a great merit; she was as honest as a pair of compasses. There was a comfort in her stiffness and firmness; you knew exactly where to find her and were never liable to chance encounters and concussions. On her own ground she was perfectly present, but was never over-inquisitive as regards the territory of her neighbour. Isabel came at last to have a kind of undemonstrable pity for her; there seemed something so dreary in the condition of a person whose nature had, as it were, so little surface—offered so limited a face to the accretions of human contact. Nothing tender, nothing sympathetic, had ever had a chance to fasten upon it—no wind-sown blossom, no familiar softening moss. Her offered, her passive extent, in other words, was about that of a knife-edge. Isabel had reason to believe none the less that as she advanced in life she made more of those concessions to the sense of something obscurely distinct from convenience—more of them than she independently exacted. She was learning to sacrifice consistency to considerations of that inferior order for which the excuse must be found in the particular case. It was not to the credit of her absolute rectitude that she should have gone the longest way round to Florence in order to spend a few weeks with her invalid son; since in former years it had been one of her most definite convictions that when Ralph wished to see her he was at liberty to remember that Palazzo Crescentini contained a large apartment known as the quarter of the signorino.*

'I want to ask you something,' Isabel said to this young man the day after her arrival at San Remo—'something I've thought more than once of asking you by letter, but that I've hesitated on the whole to write about. Face to face, nevertheless, my question seems easy enough. Did you know your father intended to leave me so much money?'

Ralph stretched his legs a little further than usual and gazed a little more fixedly at the Mediterranean. 'What does it matter, my dear Isabel, whether I knew? My father was very obstinate.'

'So,' said the girl, 'you did know.'

'Yes; he told me. We even talked it over a little.'

'What did he do it for?' asked Isabel abruptly.

'Why, as a kind of compliment.'

'A compliment on what?'

'On your so beautifully existing.'

'He liked me too much,' she presently declared.

'That's a way we all have.'

'If I believed that I should be very unhappy. Fortunately I don't believe it. I want to be treated with justice; I want nothing but that.'

'Very good. But you must remember that justice to a lovely being is after all a florid sort of sentiment.'

'I'm not a lovely being. How can you say that, at the very moment when I'm asking such odious questions? I must seem to you delicate!'

'You seem to me troubled,' said Ralph.

'I am troubled.'

'About what?'

For a moment she answered nothing; then she broke out: 'Do you think it good for me suddenly to be made so rich? Henrietta doesn't.'

'Oh, hang Henrietta!' said Ralph coarsely. 'If you ask *me* I'm delighted at it.'

'Is that why your father did it—for your amusement?'

'I differ with Miss Stackpole,' Ralph went on more gravely. 'I think it very good for you to have means.'

Isabel looked at him with serious eyes. 'I wonder whether you know what's good for me—or whether you care.'

'If I know depend upon it I care. Shall I tell you what it is? Not to torment yourself.'

'Not to torment you, I suppose you mean.'

'You can't do that; I'm proof. Take things more easily. Don't ask yourself so much whether this or that is good for you. Don't question your conscience so much—it will get out of tune like a strummed piano. Keep it for great occasions. Don't try so much to form your character—it's like trying to pull open a tight, tender young rose. Live as you like best, and your character will take care of itself. Most things are good for you; the exceptions are very rare, and a comfortable income's not one of them.' Ralph paused, smiling; Isabel had listened quickly. 'You've too much power of thought—above all too much conscience,' Ralph added. 'It's out of all reason, the number of things you think wrong. Put back your watch. Diet your fever. Spread your wings; rise above the ground. It's never wrong to do that.'

She had listened eagerly, as I say; and it was her nature to understand quickly. 'I wonder if you appreciate what you say. If you do, you take a great responsibility.'

'You frighten me a little, but I think I'm right,' said Ralph, persisting in cheer.

'All the same what you say is very true,' Isabel pursued. 'You could say nothing more true. I'm absorbed in myself—I look at life too much as a doctor's prescription. Why indeed should we perpetually be thinking whether things are good for us, as if we were patients lying in a hospital? Why should I be so afraid of not doing right? As if it mattered to the world whether I do right or wrong!'

'You're a capital person to advise,' said Ralph; 'you take the wind out of *my* sails!'

She looked at him as if she had not heard him—though she was following out the train of reflexion which he himself had kindled. 'I try to care more about the world than about myself—but I always come back to myself. It's because I'm afraid.' She stopped; her voice had trembled a little. 'Yes, I'm afraid; I can't tell you. A large fortune means freedom, and I'm afraid of that. It's such a fine thing, and one should make such a good use of it. If one shouldn't one would be ashamed. And one must keep thinking; it's a constant effort. I'm not sure it's not a greater happiness to be powerless.'

'For weak people I've no doubt it's a greater happiness. For weak people the effort not to be contemptible must be great.'

'And how do you know I'm not weak?' Isabel asked.

'Ah,' Ralph answered with a flush that the girl noticed, 'if you are I'm awfully sold!'

The charm of the Mediterranean coast only deepened for our heroine on acquaintance, for it was the threshold of Italy, the gate of admirations. Italy, as yet imperfectly seen and felt, stretched before her as a land of promise, a land in which a love of the beautiful might be comforted by endless knowledge. Whenever she strolled upon the shore with her cousin—and she was the companion of his daily walk—she looked across the sea, with longing eyes, to where she knew that Genoa lay. She was glad to pause, however, on the edge of this larger adventure; there was such a thrill even in the preliminary hovering. It affected her moreover as a peaceful interlude, as a hush of the drum and fife in a career which she had little warrant as yet for regarding as agitated, but which nevertheless she was constantly picturing to herself by the light of her hopes, her fears, her fancies, her ambitions, her predilections, and which reflected these subjective accidents in a manner sufficiently dramatic. Madame Merle had predicted to Mrs Touchett that after their young friend had put her hand into her pocket half a dozen times she would be reconciled to the idea that it had been filled by a munificent uncle; and the event justified, as it had so often justified before, that lady's perspicacity. Ralph Touchett had praised his cousin for being morally inflammable, that is for being quick to take a hint that was meant as good advice. His advice had perhaps helped the matter; she had at any rate before leaving San Remo grown used to feeling rich. The consciousness in question found a proper place in rather a dense little group of ideas that she had about herself, and often it was by no means the least agreeable. It took perpetually for granted a thousand good intentions. She lost herself in a maze of visions; the fine things to be done by a rich, independent, generous girl who took a large human view of occasions and obligations were sublime in the mass. Her fortune therefore became to her mind a part of her better self; it gave her importance, gave her even, to her own imagination, a certain ideal beauty. What it did for her in the imagination of others is another affair, and on this point we must also touch in time. The visions I have just spoken of were mixed with other debates. Isabel liked better to think of the future than of the past; but at times, as she listened to the murmur of the Mediterranean waves, her glance took a backward flight. It rested upon two figures which, in spite of increasing distance, were still sufficiently salient; they were recognisable without difficulty as those of Caspar Goodwood and Lord Warburton. It was strange how quickly these images of energy had fallen into the background of our young lady's life. It was in her disposition at all times to lose faith in the reality of absent things; she could summon back her faith, in case of need, with an effort, but the effort was often painful even when the reality had been pleasant. The past was apt to look dead and its revival rather to show the livid light of a judgement-day. The girl moreover was not prone to take for granted that she herself lived in the mind of others—she had not the fatuity to believe she left indelible traces. She was capable of being wounded by the discovery that she had been forgotten; but of all liberties the one she herself found sweetest was the liberty to forget. She had not given her last shilling, sentimentally speaking, either to Caspar Goodwood or to Lord Warburton, and yet couldn't but feel them appreciably in debt to her. She had of course reminded herself that she was to hear from Mr Goodwood again; but this was not to be for another year and a half, and in that time a great many things might happen. She had indeed failed to say to herself that her American suitor might find some other girl more comfortable to woo; because, though it was certain many other girls would prove so, she had not the smallest belief that this merit would attract him. But she reflected that she herself might know the humiliation of change, might really, for that matter, come to the end of the things that were not Caspar (even though there appeared so many of them), and find rest in those very elements of his presence which struck her now as impediments to the finer respiration. It was conceivable that these impediments should some day prove a sort of blessing in disguise—a clear and quiet harbour enclosed by a brave granite breakwater. But that day could only come in its order, and she couldn't wait for it with folded hands. That Lord Warburton should continue to cherish her image seemed to her more than a noble humility or an enlightened pride ought to wish to reckon with. She had so definitely undertaken to preserve no record of what had passed between them that a corresponding effort on his own part would be eminently just. This was not, as it may seem, merely a theory tinged with sarcasm. Isabel candidly believed that his lordship would, in the usual phrase, get over his disappointment. He had been deeply affected—this she believed, and she was still capable of deriving pleasure from the belief; but it was absurd that a man both so intelligent and so honourably dealt with should cultivate a scar out of proportion to any wound. Englishmen liked moreover to be comfortable, said Isabel, and there could be little comfort for Lord Warburton, in the long run, in brooding over a self-sufficient American girl who had been but a casual acquaintance. She flattered herself that, should she hear from one day to another that he had married some young woman of his own country who had done more to deserve him, she should receive the news without a pang even of surprise. It would have proved that he believed she was firm—which was what she wished to seem to him. That alone was grateful to her pride.

XXII

On one of the first days of May, some six months after old Mr Touchett's death, a small group that might have been described by a painter as composing well was gathered in one of the many rooms of an ancient villa crowning an olive-muffled hill outside of the Roman gate of Florence. The villa was a long, rather blank-looking structure, with the far-projecting roof which Tuscany loves and which, on the hills that encircle Florence, when considered from a distance, makes so harmonious a rectangle with the straight, dark, definite cypresses that usually rise in groups of three or four beside it. The house had a front upon a little grassy, empty, rural piazza which occupied a part of the hill-top; and this front, pierced with a few windows in irregular relations and furnished with a stone bench lengthily adjusted to the base of the structure and useful as a lounging-place to one or two persons wearing more or less of that air of undervalued merit which in Italy, for some reason or other, always gracefully invests any one who confidently assumes a perfectly passive attitude—this antique, solid, weather-worn, yet imposing front had a somewhat incommunicative character. It was the mask, not the face of the house. It had heavy lids, but no eyes; the house in reality looked another way—looked off behind, into splendid openness and the range of the afternoon light. In that quarter the villa overhung the slope of its hill and the long valley of the Arno, hazy with Italian colour. It had a narrow garden, in the manner of a terrace, productive chiefly of tangles of wild roses and other old stone benches, mossy and sun-warmed. The parapet of the terrace was just the height to lean upon, and beneath it the ground declined into the vagueness of olive-crops and vineyards. It is not, however, with the outside of the place that we are concerned; on this bright morning of ripened spring its tenants had reason to prefer the shady side of the wall. The windows of the ground-floor, as you saw them from the piazza, were, in their noble proportions, extremely architectural; but their function seemed less to offer communication with the world than to defy the world to look in. They were massively cross-barred, and placed at such a height that curiosity, even on tiptoe, expired before it reached them. In an apartment lighted by a row of three of these jealous apertures—one of the several distinct apartments into which the villa was divided and which were mainly occupied by foreigners of random race long resident in Florence—a gentleman was seated in company with a young girl and two good sisters from a religious house. The room was, however, less sombre than our indications may have represented, for it had a wide, high door, which now stood open into the tangled garden behind; and the tall iron lattices admitted on occasion more than enough of the Italian sunshine. It was moreover a seat of ease, indeed of luxury, telling of arrangements subtly studied and refinements frankly proclaimed, and containing a variety of those faded hangings of damask and tapestry, those chests and cabinets of carved and time-polished oak, those angular specimens of pictorial art in frames as pedantically primitive, those perverse-looking relics of mediæval brass and pottery, of which Italy has long been the not quite exhausted storehouse. These things kept terms with articles of modern furniture in which large allowance had been made for a lounging generation; it was to be noticed that all the chairs were deep and well padded and that much space was occupied by a writing-table of which the ingenious perfection bore the stamp of London and the nineteenth century. There were books in profusion and magazines and newspapers, and a few small, odd, elaborate pictures, chiefly in water-colour. One of these productions stood on a drawing-room easel before which, at the moment we begin to be concerned with her, the young girl I have mentioned had placed herself. She was looking at the picture in silence.

Silence—absolute silence—had not fallen upon her companions; but their talk had an appearance of embarrassed continuity. The two good sisters had not settled themselves in their respective chairs; their attitude expressed a final reserve and their faces showed the glaze of prudence. They were plain, ample, mild-featured women, with a kind of business-like modesty to which the impersonal aspect of their stiffened linen and of the serge that draped them as if nailed on frames gave an advantage. One of them, a person of a certain age, in spectacles, with a fresh complexion and a full cheek, had a more discriminating manner than her colleague, as well as the responsibility of their errand, which apparently related to the young girl. This object of interest wore her hat—an ornament of extreme simplicity and not at variance with her plain muslin gown, too short for her years, though it must already have been 'let out'. The gentleman who might have been supposed to be entertaining the two nuns was perhaps conscious of the difficulties of his function, it being in its way as arduous to converse with the very meek as with the very mighty. At the same time he was clearly much occupied with their quiet charge, and while she turned her back to him his eyes rested gravely on her slim, small figure. He was a man of forty, with a high but well-shaped head, on which the hair, still dense, but prematurely grizzled, had been cropped close. He had a fine, narrow, extremely modelled and composed face, of which the only fault was just this effect of its running a trifle too much to points; an appearance to which the shape of the beard contributed not a little. This beard, cut in the manner of the portraits of the sixteenth century and surmounted by a fair moustache, of which the ends had a romantic upward flourish, gave its wearer a foreign, traditionary look and suggested that he was a gentleman who studied style. His conscious, curious eyes, however, eyes at once vague and penetrating, intelligent and hard, expressive of the observer as well as of the dreamer, would have assured you that he studied it only within well-chosen limits, and that in so far as he sought it he found it. You would have been much at a loss to determine his original clime and country; he had none of the superficial signs that usually render the answer to this question an insipidly easy one. If he had English blood in his veins it had probably received some French or Italian commixture; but he suggested, fine gold coin as he was, no stamp nor emblem of the common mintage that provides for general circulation; he was the elegant complicated medal struck off for a special occasion. He had a light, lean, rather languid-looking figure, and was apparently neither tall nor short. He was dressed as a man dresses who takes little other trouble about it than to have no vulgar things.

'Well, my dear, what do you think of it?' he asked of the young girl. He used the Italian tongue, and used it with perfect ease; but this would not have convinced you he was Italian.

The child turned her head earnestly to one side and the other. 'It's very pretty, papa. Did you make it yourself?'

'Certainly I made it. Don't you think I'm clever?'

'Yes, papa, very clever; I also have learned to make pictures.' And she turned round and showed a small, fair face painted with a fixed and intensely sweet smile.

'You should have brought me a specimen of your powers.'

'I've brought a great many; they're in my trunk.'

'She draws very—very carefully,' the elder of the nuns remarked, speaking in French.

'I'm glad to hear it. Is it you who have instructed her?'

'Happily no,' said the good sister, blushing a little. '*Ce n'est pas ma partie.** I teach nothing; I leave that to those who are wiser. We've an excellent drawing-master, Mr—Mr—what is his name?' she asked of her companion.

Her companion looked about at the carpet. 'It's a German name,' she said in Italian, as if it needed to be translated.

'Yes,' the other went on, 'he's a German, and we've had him many years.'

The young girl, who was not heeding the conversation, had wandered away to the open door of the large room and stood looking into the garden. 'And you, my sister, are French,' said the gentleman.

'Yes, sir,' the visitor gently replied. 'I speak to the pupils in my own tongue. I know no other. But we have sisters of other countries—English, German, Irish. They all speak their proper language.'

The gentleman gave a smile. 'Has my daughter been under the care of one of the Irish ladies?' And then, as he saw that his visitors suspected a joke, though failing to understand it, 'You're very complete,' he instantly added.

'Oh, yes, we're complete. We've everything, and everything's of the best.'

'We have gymnastics,' the Italian sister ventured to remark. 'But not dangerous.'

'I hope not. Is that *your* branch?' A question which provoked much candid hilarity on the part of the two ladies; on the subsidence of which their entertainer, glancing at his daughter, remarked that she had grown.

'Yes, but I think she has finished. She'll remain—not big,' said the French sister.

'I'm not sorry. I prefer women like books—very good and not too long. But I know,' the gentleman said, 'no particular reason why my child should be short.'

The nun gave a temperate shrug, as if to intimate that such things might be beyond our knowledge. 'She's in very good health; that's the best thing.'

'Yes, she looks sound.' And the young girl's father watched her a moment. 'What do you see in the garden?' he asked in French.

'I see many flowers,' she replied in a sweet, small voice and with an accent as good as his own.

'Yes, but not many good ones. However, such as they are, go out and gather some for *ces dames*.'*

The child turned to him with her smile heightened by pleasure. 'May I, truly?'

'Ah, when I tell you,' said her father.

The girl glanced at the elder of the nuns. 'May I, truly, *ma mère*?'*

'Obey monsieur your father, my child,' said the sister, blushing again.

The child, satisfied with this authorisation, descended from the threshold and was presently lost to sight. 'You don't spoil them,' said her father gaily.

'For everything they must ask leave. That's our system. Leave is freely granted, but they must ask it.'

'Oh, I don't quarrel with your system; I've no doubt it's excellent. I sent you my daughter to see what you'd make of her. I had faith.'

'One must have faith,' the sister blandly rejoined, gazing through her spectacles.

'Well, has my faith been rewarded? What have you made of her?'

The sister dropped her eyes a moment. 'A good Christian, monsieur.'

Her host dropped his eyes as well; but it was probable that the movement had in each case a different spring. 'Yes, and what else?'

He watched the lady from the convent, probably thinking she would say that a good Christian was everything; but for all her simplicity she was not so crude as that. 'A charming young lady—a real little woman—a daughter in whom you will have nothing but contentment.'

'She seems to me very *gentille*,'* said the father. 'She's really pretty.'

'She's perfect. She has no faults.'

'She never had any as a child, and I'm glad you have given her none.'

'We love her too much,' said the spectacled sister with dignity. 'And as for faults, how can we give what we have not? *Le couvent n'est pas comme le monde, monsieur.** She's our daughter, as you may say. We've had her since she was so small.'

'Of all those we shall lose this year she's the one we shall miss most,' the younger woman murmured deferentially.

'Ah, yes, we shall talk long of her,' said the other. 'We shall hold her up to the new ones.' And at this the good sister appeared to find her spectacles dim; while her companion, after fumbling a moment, presently drew forth a pocket-handkerchief of durable texture.

'It's not certain you'll lose her; nothing's settled yet,' their host rejoined quickly; not as if to anticipate their tears, but in the tone of a man saying what was most agreeable to himself.

'We should be very happy to believe that. Fifteen is very young to leave us.'

'Oh,' exclaimed the gentleman with more vivacity than he had yet used, 'it is not I who wish to take her away. I wish you could keep her always!'

'Ah, monsieur,' said the elder sister, smiling and getting up, 'good as she is, she's made for the world. *Le monde y gagnera.*'*

'If all the good people were hidden away in convents how would the world get on?' her companion softly enquired, rising also.

This was a question of a wider bearing than the good woman apparently supposed; and the lady in spectacles took a harmonising view by saying comfortably: 'Fortunately there are good people everywhere.'

'If you're going there will be two less here,' her host remarked gallantly.

For this extravagant sally his simple visitors had no answer, and they simply looked at each other in decent deprecation; but their confusion was speedily covered by the return of the young girl with two large bunches of roses—one of them all white, the other red.

'I give you your choice, mamman Catherine,' said the child. 'It's only the colour that's different, mamman Justine; there are just as many roses in one bunch as in the other.'

The two sisters turned to each other, smiling and hesitating, with 'Which will you take?' and 'No, it's for you to choose.'

'I'll take the red, thank you,' said mother Catherine in the spectacles. 'I'm so red myself. They'll comfort us on our way back to Rome.'

'Ah, they won't last,' cried the young girl. 'I wish I could give you something that would last!'

'You've given us a good memory of yourself, my daughter. That will last!'

'I wish nuns could wear pretty things. I would give you my blue beads,' the child went on.

'And do you go back to Rome to-night?' her father enquired.

'Yes, we take the train again. We've so much to do *là-bas*.'*

'Are you not tired?'

'We are never tired.'

'Ah, my sister, sometimes,' murmured the junior votaress.

'Not to-day, at any rate. We have rested too well here. *Que Dieu vous garde, ma fille*.'*

Their host, while they exchanged kisses with his daughter, went forward to open the door through which they were to pass; but as he did so he gave a slight exclamation, and stood looking beyond. The door opened into a vaulted ante-chamber, as high as a chapel and paved with red tiles; and into this ante-chamber a lady had just been admitted by a servant, a lad in shabby livery, who was now ushering her toward the apartment in which our friends were grouped. The gentleman at the door, after dropping his exclamation, remained silent; in silence too the lady advanced. He gave her no further audible greeting and offered her no hand, but stood aside to let her pass into the saloon. At the threshold she hesitated. 'Is there any one?' she asked.

'Some one you may see.'

She went in and found herself confronted with the two nuns and their pupil, who was coming forward, between them, with a hand in the arm of each. At the sight of the new visitor they all paused, and the lady, who had also stopped, stood looking at them. The young girl gave a little soft cry: 'Ah, Madame Merle!'

The visitor had been slightly startled, but her manner the next instant was none the less gracious. 'Yes, it's Madame Merle, come to welcome you home.' And she held out two hands to the girl, who immediately came up to her, presenting her forehead to be kissed. Madame Merle saluted this portion of her charming little person and then stood smiling at the two nuns. They acknowledged her smile with a decent obeisance, but permitted themselves no direct scrutiny of this imposing, brilliant woman, who seemed to bring in with her something of the radiance of the outer world.

'These ladies have brought my daughter home, and now they return to the convent,' the gentleman explained.

'Ah, you go back to Rome? I've lately come from there. It's very lovely now,' said Madame Merle.

The good sisters, standing with their hands folded into their sleeves, accepted this statement uncritically; and the master of the house asked his new visitor how long it was since she had left Rome. 'She came to see me at the convent,' said the young girl before the lady addressed had time to reply.

'I've been more than once, Pansy,' Madame Merle declared. 'Am I not your great friend in Rome?'

'I remember the last time best,' said Pansy, 'because you told me I should come away.'

'Did you tell her that?' the child's father asked.

'I hardly remember. I told her what I thought would please her. I've been in Florence a week. I hoped you would come to see me.'

'I should have done so if I had known you were there. One doesn't know such things by inspiration—though I suppose one ought. You had better sit down.'

These two speeches were made in a particular tone of voice—a tone half-lowered and carefully quiet, but as from habit rather than from any definite need. Madame Merle looked about her, choosing her seat. 'You're going to the door with these women? Let me of course not interrupt the ceremony. *Je vous salue, mesdames*,'* she added, in French, to the nuns, as if to dismiss them.

'This lady's a great friend of ours; you will have seen her at the convent,' said their entertainer. 'We've much faith in her judgement, and she'll help me to decide whether my daughter shall return to you at the end of the holidays.'

'I hope you'll decide in our favour, madame,' the sister in spectacles ventured to remark.

'That's Mr Osmond's pleasantry; I decide nothing,' said Madame Merle, but also as in pleasantry. 'I believe you've a very good school, but Miss Osmond's friends must remember that she's very naturally meant for the world.'

'That's what I've told monsieur,' sister Catherine answered. 'It's precisely to fit her for the world,' she murmured, glancing at Pansy, who stood, at a little distance, attentive to Madame Merle's elegant apparel.

'Do you hear that, Pansy? You're very naturally meant for the world,' said Pansy's father.

The child fixed him an instant with her pure young eyes. 'Am I not meant for you, papa?'

Papa gave a quick, light laugh. 'That doesn't prevent it! I'm of the world, Pansy.'

'Kindly permit us to retire,' said sister Catherine. 'Be good and wise and happy in any case, my daughter.'

'I shall certainly come back and see you,' Pansy returned, recommencing her embraces, which were presently interrupted by Madame Merle.

'Stay with me, dear child,' she said, 'while your father takes the good ladies to the door.'

Pansy stared, disappointed, yet not protesting. She was evidently impregnated with the idea of submission, which was due to any one who took the tone of authority; and she was a passive spectator of the operation of her fate. 'May I not see mamman Catherine get into the carriage?' she nevertheless asked very gently.

'It would please me better if you'd remain with me,' said Madame Merle, while Mr Osmond and his companions, who had bowed low again to the other visitor, passed into the ante-chamber.

'Oh yes, I'll stay,' Pansy answered; and she stood near Madame Merle, surrendering her little hand, which this lady took. She stared out of the window; her eyes had filled with tears.

'I'm glad they've taught you to obey,' said Madame Merle. 'That's what good little girls should do.'

'Oh yes, I obey very well,' cried Pansy with soft eagerness, almost with boastfulness, as if she had been speaking of her piano-playing. And then she gave a faint, just audible sigh.

Madame Merle, holding her hand, drew it across her own fine palm and looked at it. The gaze was critical, but it found nothing to deprecate; the child's small hand was delicate and fair. 'I hope they always see that you wear gloves,' she said in a moment. 'Little girls usually dislike them.'

'I used to dislike them, but I like them now,' the child made answer.

'Very good, I'll make you a present of a dozen.'

'I thank you very much. What colours will they be?' Pansy demanded with interest.

Madame Merle meditated. 'Useful colours.'

'But very pretty?'

'Are you very fond of pretty things?'

'Yes; but—but not too fond,' said Pansy with a trace of asceticism.

'Well, they won't be too pretty,' Madame Merle returned with a laugh. She took the child's other hand and drew her nearer; after which, looking at her a moment, 'Shall you miss mother Catherine?' she went on.

'Yes—when I think of her.'

'Try then not to think of her. Perhaps some day,' added Madame Merle, 'you'll have another mother.'

'I don't think that's necessary,' Pansy said, repeating her little soft conciliatory sigh. 'I had more than thirty mothers at the convent.'

Her father's step sounded again in the ante-chamber, and Madame Merle got up, releasing the child. Mr Osmond came in and closed the door; then, without looking at Madame Merle, he pushed one or two chairs back into their places. His visitor waited a moment for him to speak, watching him as he moved about. Then at last she said: 'I hoped you'd have come to Rome. I thought it possible you'd have wished yourself to fetch Pansy away.'

'That was a natural supposition; but I'm afraid it's not the first time I've acted in defiance of your calculations.'

'Yes,' said Madame Merle, 'I think you very perverse.'

Mr Osmond busied himself for a moment in the room—there was plenty of space in it to move about—in the fashion of a man mechanically seeking pretexts for not giving an attention which may be embarrassing. Presently, however, he had exhausted his pretexts; there was nothing left for him—unless he took up a book—but to stand with his hands behind him looking at Pansy. 'Why didn't you come and see the last of mamman Catherine?' he asked of her abruptly in French.

Pansy hesitated a moment, glancing at Madame Merle. 'I asked her to stay with me,' said this lady, who had seated herself again in another place.

'Ah, that was better,' Osmond conceded. With which he dropped into a chair and sat looking at Madame Merle; bent forward a little, his elbows on the edge of the arms and his hands interlocked.

'She's going to give me some gloves,' said Pansy.

'You needn't tell that to every one, my dear,' Madame Merle observed.

'You're very kind to her,' said Osmond. 'She's supposed to have everything she needs.'

'I should think she had had enough of the nuns.'

'If we're going to discuss that matter she had better go out of the room.'

'Let her stay,' said Madame Merle. 'We'll talk of something else.'

'If you like I won't listen,' Pansy suggested with an appearance of candour which imposed conviction.

'You may listen, charming child, because you won't understand,' her father replied. The child sat down, deferentially, near the open door, within sight of the garden, into which she directed her innocent, wistful eyes; and Mr Osmond went on irrelevantly, addressing himself to his other companion. 'You're looking particularly well.'

'I think I always look the same,' said Madame Merle.

'You always *are* the same. You don't vary. You're a wonderful woman.'

'Yes, I think I am.'

'You sometimes change your mind, however. You told me on your return from England that you wouldn't leave Rome again for the present.'

'I'm pleased that you remember so well what I say. That was my intention. But I've come to Florence to meet some friends who have lately arrived and as to whose movements I was at that time uncertain.'

'That reason's characteristic. You're always doing something for your friends.'

Madame Merle smiled straight at her host. 'It's less characteristic than your comment upon it—which is perfectly insincere. I don't, however, make a crime of that,' she added, 'because if you don't believe what you say there's no reason *why* you should. I don't ruin myself for my friends; I don't deserve your praise. I care greatly for myself.'

'Exactly; but yourself includes so many other selves—so much of every one else and of everything. I never knew a person whose life touched so many other lives.'

'What do you call one's life?' asked Madame Merle. 'One's appearance, one's movements, one's engagements, one's society?'

'I call *your* life your ambitions,' said Osmond.

Madame Merle looked a moment at Pansy. 'I wonder if she understands that,' she murmured.

'You see she can't stay with us!' And Pansy's father gave rather a joyless smile. 'Go into the garden, *mignonne*,* and pluck a flower or two for Madame Merle,' he went on in French.

'That's just what I wanted to do,' Pansy exclaimed, rising with promptness and noiselessly departing. Her father followed her to the open door, stood a moment watching her, and then came back, but remained standing, or rather strolling to and fro, as if to cultivate a sense of freedom which in another attitude might be wanting.

'My ambitions are principally for you,' said Madame Merle, looking up at him with a certain courage.

'That comes back to what I say. I'm part of your life—I and a thousand others. You're not selfish—I can't admit that. If you were selfish, what should I be? What epithet would properly describe me?'

'You're indolent. For me that's your worst fault.'

'I'm afraid it's really my best.'

'You don't care,' said Madame Merle gravely.

'No; I don't think I care much. What sort of a fault do you call that? My indolence, at any rate, was one of the reasons I didn't go to Rome. But it was only one of them.'

'It's not of importance—to me at least—that you didn't go; though I should have been glad to see you. I'm glad you're not in Rome now—which you might be, would probably be, if you had gone there a month ago. There's something I should like you to do at present in Florence.'

'Please remember my indolence,' said Osmond.

'I do remember it; but I beg you to forget it. In that way you'll have both the virtue and the reward. This is not a great labour, and it may prove a real interest. How long is it since you made a new acquaintance?'

'I don't think I've made any since I made yours.'

'It's time then you should make another. There's a friend of mine I want you to know.'

Mr Osmond, in his walk, had gone back to the open door again and was looking at his daughter as she moved about in the intense sunshine. 'What good will it do me?' he asked with a sort of genial crudity.

Madame Merle waited. 'It will amuse you.' There was nothing crude in this rejoinder; it had been thoroughly well considered.

'If you say that, you know, I believe it,' said Osmond, coming toward her. 'There are some points in which my confidence in you is complete. I'm perfectly aware, for instance, that you know good society from bad.'

'Society is all bad.'

'Pardon me. That isn't—the knowledge I impute to you—a common sort of wisdom. You've gained it in the right way—experimentally; you've compared an immense number of more or less impossible people with each other.'

'Well, I invite you to profit by my knowledge.'

'To profit? Are you very sure that I shall?'

'It's what I hope. It will depend on yourself. If I could only induce you to make an effort!'

'Ah, there you are! I knew something tiresome was coming. What in the world—that's likely to turn up here—is worth an effort?'

Madame Merle flushed as with a wounded intention. 'Don't be foolish, Osmond. No one knows better than you what *is* worth an effort. Haven't *I* seen you in old days?'

'I recognise some things. But they're none of them probable in this poor life.'

'It's the effort that makes them probable,' said Madame Merle.

'There's something in that. Who then is your friend?'

'The person I came to Florence to see. She's a niece of Mrs Touchett, whom you'll not have forgotten.'

'A niece? The word niece suggests youth and ignorance. I see what you're coming to.'

'Yes, she's young—twenty-three years old. She's a great friend of mine. I met her for the first time in England, several months ago, and we struck up a grand alliance. I like her immensely, and I do what I don't do every day—I admire her. You'll do the same.'

'Not if I can help it.'

'Precisely. But you won't be able to help it.'

'Is she beautiful, clever, rich, splendid, universally intelligent and unprecedentedly virtuous? It's only on those conditions that I care to make her acquaintance. You know I asked you some time ago never to speak to me of a creature who shouldn't correspond to that description. I know plenty of dingy people; I don't want to know any more.'

'Miss Archer isn't dingy; she's as bright as the morning. She corresponds to your description; it's for that I wish you to know her. She fills all your requirements.'

'More or less, of course.'

'No; quite literally. She's beautiful, accomplished, generous and, for an American, well-born. She's also very clever and very amiable, and she has a handsome fortune.'

Mr Osmond listened to this in silence, appearing to turn it over in his mind with his eyes on his informant. 'What do you want to do with her?' he asked at last.

'What you see. Put her in your way.'

'Isn't she meant for something better than that?'

'I don't pretend to know what people are meant for,' said Madame Merle. 'I only know what I can do with them.'

'I'm sorry for Miss Archer!' Osmond declared.

Madame Merle got up. 'If that's a beginning of interest in her I take note of it.'

The two stood there face to face; she settled her mantilla, looking down at it as she did so. 'You're looking very well,' Osmond repeated still less relevantly than before. 'You have some idea. You're never so well as when you've got an idea; they're always becoming to you.'

In the manner and tone of these two persons, on first meeting at any juncture, and especially when they met in the presence of others, was something indirect and circumspect, as if they had approached each other obliquely and addressed each other by implication. The effect of each appeared to be to intensify to an appreciable degree the self-consciousness of the other. Madame Merle of course carried off any embarrassment better than her friend; but even Madame Merle had not on this occasion the form she would have liked to have—the perfect self-possession she would have wished to wear for her host. The point to be made is, however, that at a certain moment the element between them, whatever it was, always levelled itself and left them more closely face to face than either ever was with any one else. This was what had happened now. They stood there knowing each other well and each on the whole willing to accept the satisfaction of knowing as a compensation for the inconvenience—whatever it might be—of being known. 'I wish very much you were not so heartless,' Madame Merle quietly said. 'It has always been against you, and it will be against you now.'

'I'm not so heartless as you think. Every now and then something touches me—as for instance your saying just now that your ambitions are for me. I don't understand it; I don't see how or why they should be. But it touches me, all the same.'

'You'll probably understand it even less as time goes on. There are some things you'll never understand. There's no particular need you should.'

'You, after all, are the most remarkable of women,' said Osmond. 'You have more in you than almost any one. I don't see why you think Mrs Touchett's niece should matter very much to me, when—when——' But he paused a moment.

'When I myself have mattered so little?'

'That of course is not what I meant to say. When I've known and appreciated such a woman as you.'

'Isabel Archer's better than I,' said Madame Merle.

Her companion gave a laugh. 'How little you must think of her to say that!'

'Do you suppose I'm capable of jealousy? Please answer me that.'

'With regard to me? No; on the whole I don't.'

'Come and see me then, two days hence. I'm staying at Mrs Touchett's—Palazzo Crescentini—and the girl will be there.'

'Why didn't you ask me that at first simply, without speaking of the girl?' said Osmond. 'You could have had her there at any rate.'

Madame Merle looked at him in the manner of a woman whom no question he could ever put would find unprepared. 'Do you wish to know why? Because I've spoken of you to her.'

Osmond frowned and turned away. 'I'd rather not know that.' Then in a moment he pointed out the easel supporting the little water-colour drawing.

'Have you seen what's there—my last?'

Madame Merle drew near and considered. 'Is it the Venetian Alps—one of your last year's sketches?'

'Yes—but how you guess everything!'

She looked a moment longer, then turned away. 'You know I don't care for your drawings.'

'I know it, yet I'm always surprised at it. They're really so much better than most people's.'

'That may very well be. But as the only thing you do—well, it's so little. I should have liked you to do so many other things: those were my ambitions.'

'Yes; you've told me many times—things that were impossible.'

'Things that were impossible,' said Madame Merle. And then in quite a different tone: 'In itself your little picture's very good.' She looked about the room—at the old cabinets, pictures, tapestries, surfaces of faded silk. 'Your rooms at least are perfect. I'm struck with that afresh whenever I come back; I know none better anywhere. You understand this sort of thing as nobody anywhere does. You've such adorable taste.'

'I'm sick of my adorable taste,' said Gilbert Osmond.

'You must nevertheless let Miss Archer come and see it. I've told her about it.'

'I don't object to showing my things—when people are not idiots.'

'You do it delightfully. As cicerone of your museum you appear to particular advantage.'

Mr Osmond, in return for this compliment, simply looked at once colder and more attentive. 'Did you say she was rich?'

'She has seventy thousand pounds.'

'*En écus bien comptés?*'*

'There's no doubt whatever about her fortune. I've seen it, as I may say.'

'Satisfactory woman!—I mean *you*. And if I go to see her shall I see the mother?'

'The mother? She has none—nor father either.'

'The aunt then—whom did you say?—Mrs Touchett.'

'I can easily keep her out of the way.'

'I don't object to her,' said Osmond; 'I rather like Mrs Touchett. She has a sort of old-fashioned character that's passing away—a vivid identity. But that long jackanapes the son—is he about the place?'

'He's there, but he won't trouble you.'

'He's a good deal of a donkey.'

'I think you're mistaken. He's a very clever man. But he's not fond of being about when I'm there, because he doesn't like me.'

'What could be more asinine than that? Did you say she has looks?' Osmond went on.

'Yes; but I won't say it again, lest you should be disappointed in them. Come and make a beginning; that's all I ask of you.'

'A beginning of what?'

Madame Merle was silent a little. 'I want you of course to marry her.'

'The beginning of the end? Well, I'll see for myself. Have you told her that?'

'For what do you take me? She's not so coarse a piece of machinery—nor am I.'

'Really,' said Osmond after some meditation, 'I don't understand your ambitions.'

'I think you'll understand this one after you've seen Miss Archer. Suspend your judgement.' Madame Merle, as she spoke, had drawn near the open door of the garden, where she stood a moment looking out. 'Pansy has really grown pretty,' she presently added.

'So it seemed to me.'

'But she has had enough of the convent.'

'I don't know,' said Osmond. 'I like what they've made of her. It's very charming.'

'That's not the convent. It's the child's nature.'

'It's the combination, I think. She's as pure as a pearl.'

'Why doesn't she come back with my flowers then?' Madame Merle asked. 'She's not in a hurry.'

'We'll go and get them.'

'She doesn't like me,' the visitor murmured as she raised her parasol and they passed into the garden.

XXIII

Madame Merle, who had come to Florence on Mrs Touchett's arrival at the invitation of this lady—Mrs Touchett offering her for a month the hospitality of Palazzo Crescentini—the judicious Madame Merle spoke to Isabel afresh about Gilbert Osmond and expressed the hope she might know him; making, however, no such point of the matter as we have seen her do in recommending the girl herself to Mr Osmond's attention. The reason of this was perhaps that Isabel offered no resistance whatever to Madame Merle's proposal. In Italy, as in England, the lady had a multitude of friends, both among the natives of the country and its heterogeneous visitors. She had mentioned to Isabel most of the people the girl would find it well to 'meet'—of course, she said, Isabel could know whomever in the wide world she would—and had placed Mr Osmond near the top of the list. He was an old friend of her own; she had known him these dozen years; he was one of the cleverest and most agreeable men—well, in Europe simply. He was altogether above the respectable average; quite another affair. He wasn't a professional charmer—far from it, and the effect he produced depended a good deal on the state of his nerves and his spirits. When not in the right mood he could fall as low as any one, saved only by his looking at such hours rather like a demoralised prince in exile. But if he cared or was interested or rightly challenged—just exactly rightly it had to be—then one felt his cleverness and his distinction. Those qualities didn't depend, in him, as in so many people, on his not committing or exposing himself. He had his perversities—which indeed Isabel would find to be the case with all the men really worth knowing—and didn't cause his light to shine equally for all persons. Madame Merle, however, thought she could undertake that for Isabel he would be brilliant. He was easily bored, too easily, and dull people always put him out; but a quick and cultivated girl like Isabel would give him a stimulus which was too absent from his life. At any rate he was a person not to miss. One shouldn't attempt to live in Italy without making a friend of Gilbert Osmond, who knew more about the country than any one except two or three German professors. And if they had more knowledge than he it was he who had most perception and taste—being artistic through and through. Isabel remembered that her friend had spoken of him during their plunge, at Gardencourt, into the deeps of talk, and wondered a little what was the nature of the tie binding these superior spirits. She felt that Madame Merle's ties always somehow had histories, and such an impression was part of the interest created by this inordinate woman. As regards her relations with Mr Osmond, however, she hinted at nothing but a long-established calm friendship. Isabel said she should be happy to know a person who had enjoyed so high a confidence for so many years. 'You ought to see a great many men,' Madame Merle remarked; 'you ought to see as many as possible, so as to get used to them.'

'Used to them?' Isabel repeated with that solemn stare which sometimes seemed to proclaim her deficient in the sense of comedy. 'Why, I'm not afraid of them—I'm as used to them as the cook to the butcher-boys.'

'Used to them, I mean, so as to despise them. That's what one comes to with most of them. You'll pick out, for your society, the few whom you don't despise.'

This was a note of cynicism that Madame Merle didn't often allow herself to sound; but Isabel was not alarmed, for she had never supposed that as one saw more of the world the sentiment of respect became the most active of one's emotions. It was excited, none the less, by the beautiful city of Florence, which pleased her not less than Madame Merle had promised; and if her unassisted perception had not been able to gauge its charms she had clever companions as priests to the mystery. She was in no want indeed of æsthetic illumination, for Ralph found it a joy that renewed his own early passion to act as cicerone to his eager young kinswoman. Madame Merle remained at home; she had seen the treasures of Florence again and again and had always something else to do. But she talked of all things with remarkable vividness of memory—she recalled the right-hand corner of the large Perugino and the position of the hands of the Saint Elizabeth in the picture next to it. She had her opinions as to the character of many famous works of art, differing often from Ralph with great sharpness and defending her interpretations with as much ingenuity as good-humour. Isabel listened to the discussions taking place between the two with a sense that she might derive much benefit from them and that they were among the advantages she couldn't have enjoyed for instance in Albany. In the clear May mornings before the formal breakfast—this repast at Mrs Touchett's was served at twelve o'clock—she wandered with her cousin through the narrow and sombre Florentine streets, resting a while in the thicker dusk of some historic church or the vaulted chambers of some dispeopled convent. She went to the galleries and palaces; she looked at the pictures and statues that had hitherto been great names to her, and exchanged for a knowledge which was sometimes a limitation a presentiment which proved usually to have been a blank. She performed all those acts of mental prostration in which, on a first visit to Italy, youth and enthusiasm so freely indulge; she felt her heart beat in the presence of immortal genius and knew the sweetness of rising tears in eyes to which faded fresco and darkened marble grew dim. But the return, every day, was even pleasanter than the going forth; the return into the wide, monumental court of the great house in which Mrs Touchett, many years before, had established herself, and into the high, cool rooms where the carven rafters and pompous frescoes of the sixteenth century looked down on the familiar commodities of the age of advertisement. Mrs Touchett inhabited an historic building in a narrow street whose very name recalled the strife of mediæval factions; and found compensation for the darkness of her frontage in the modicity of her rent and the brightness of a garden where nature itself looked as archaic as the rugged architecture of the palace and which cleared and scented the rooms in regular use. To live in such a place was, for Isabel, to hold to her ear all day a shell of the sea of the past. This vague eternal rumour kept her imagination awake.

Gilbert Osmond came to see Madame Merle, who presented him to the young lady lurking at the other side of the room. Isabel took on this occasion little part in the talk; she scarcely even smiled when the others turned to her invitingly; she sat there as if she had been at the play and had paid even a large sum for her place. Mrs Touchett was not present, and these two had it, for the effect of brilliancy, all their own way. They talked of the Florentine, the Roman, the cosmopolite world, and might have been distinguished performers figuring for a charity. It all had the rich readiness that would have come from rehearsal. Madame Merle appealed to her as if she had been on the stage, but she could ignore any learnt cue without spoiling the scene—though of course she thus put dreadfully in the wrong the friend who had told Mr Osmond she could be depended on. This was no matter for once; even if more had been involved she could have made no attempt to shine. There was something in the visitor that checked her and held her in suspense—made it more important she should get an impression of him than that she should produce one herself. Besides, she had little skill in producing an impression which she knew to be expected: nothing could be happier, in general, than to seem dazzling, but she had a perverse unwillingness to glitter by arrangement. Mr Osmond, to do him justice, had a well-bred air of expecting nothing, a quiet ease that covered everything, even the first show of his own wit. This was the more grateful as his face, his head, was sensitive; he was not handsome, but he was fine, as fine as one of the drawings in the long gallery above the bridge of the Uffizi. And his very voice was fine—the more strangely that, with its clearness, it yet somehow wasn't sweet. This had had really to do with making her abstain from interference. His utterance was the vibration of glass, and if she had put out her finger she might have changed the pitch and spoiled the concert. Yet before he went she had to speak.

'Madame Merle,' he said, 'consents to come up to my hill-top some day next week and drink tea in my garden. It would give me much pleasure if you would come with her. It's thought rather pretty—there's what they call a general view. My daughter too would be so glad—or rather, for she's too young to have strong emotions, *I* should be so glad—so very glad.' And Mr Osmond paused with a slight air of embarrassment, leaving his sentence unfinished. 'I should be so happy if you could know my daughter,' he went on a moment afterwards.

Isabel replied that she should be delighted to see Miss Osmond and that if Madame Merle would show her the way to the hill-top she should be very grateful. Upon this assurance the visitor took his leave; after which Isabel fully expected her friend would scold her for having been so stupid. But to her surprise that lady, who indeed never fell into the mere matter-of-course, said to her in a few moments: 'You were charming, my dear; you were just as one would have wished you. You're never disappointing.'

A rebuke might possibly have been irritating, though it is much more probable that Isabel would have taken it in good part; but, strange to say, the words that Madame Merle actually used caused her the first feeling of displeasure she had known this ally to excite. 'That's more than I intended,' she answered coldly. 'I'm under no obligation that I know of to charm Mr Osmond.'

Madame Merle perceptibly flushed, but we know it was not her habit to retract. 'My dear child, I didn't speak for him, poor man; I spoke for yourself. It's not of course a question as to his liking you; it matters little whether he likes you or not! But I thought you liked *him*.'

'I did,' said Isabel honestly. 'But I don't see what that matters either.'

'Everything that concerns you matters to me,' Madame Merle returned with her weary nobleness; 'especially when at the same time another old friend's concerned.'

Whatever Isabel's obligations may have been to Mr Osmond, it must be admitted that she found them sufficient to lead her to put to Ralph sundry questions about him. She thought Ralph's judgements distorted by his trials, but she flattered herself she had learned to make allowance for that.

'Do I know him?' said her cousin. 'Oh, yes, I "know" him; not well, but on the whole enough. I've never cultivated his society, and he apparently has never found mine indispensable to his happiness. Who is he, what is he? He's a vague, unexplained American who has been living these thirty years, or less, in Italy. Why do I call him unexplained? Only as a cover for my ignorance; I don't know his antecedents, his family, his origin. For all I do know he may be a prince in disguise; he rather looks like one, by the way—like a prince who has abdicated in a fit of fastidiousness and has been in a state of disgust ever since. He used to live in Rome; but of late years he has taken up his abode here; I remember hearing him say that Rome has grown vulgar. He has a great dread of vulgarity; that's his special line; he hasn't any other that I know of. He lives on his income, which I suspect of not being vulgarly large. He's a poor but honest gentleman—that's what he calls himself. He married young and lost his wife, and I believe he has a daughter. He also has a sister, who's married to some small Count or other, of these parts; I remember meeting her of old. She's nicer than he, I should think, but rather impossible. I remember there used to be some stories about her. I don't think I recommend you to know her. But why don't you ask Madame Merle about these people? She knows them all much better than I.'

'I ask you because I want your opinion as well as hers,' said Isabel.

'A fig for my opinion! If you fall in love with Mr Osmond what will you care for that?'

'Not much, probably. But meanwhile it has a certain importance. The more information one has about one's dangers the better.'

'I don't agree to that—it may make them dangers. We know too much about people in these days; we hear too much. Our ears, our minds, our mouths, are stuffed with personalities. Don't mind anything any one tells you about any one else. Judge every one and everything for yourself.'

'That's what I try to do,' said Isabel; 'but when you do that people call you conceited.'

'You're not to mind them—that's precisely my argument; not to mind what they say about yourself any more than what they say about your friend or your enemy.'

Isabel considered. 'I think you're right; but there are some things I can't help minding: for instance when my friend's attacked or when I myself am praised.'

'Of course you're always at liberty to judge the critic. Judge people as critics, however,' Ralph added, 'and you'll condemn them all!'

'I shall see Mr Osmond for myself,' said Isabel. 'I've promised to pay him a visit.'

'To pay him a visit?'

'To go and see his view, his pictures, his daughter—I don't know exactly what. Madame Merle's to take me; she tells me a great many ladies call on him.'

'Ah, with Madame Merle you may go anywhere, *de confiance*,'* said Ralph. 'She knows none but the best people.'

Isabel said no more about Mr Osmond, but she presently remarked to her cousin that she was not satisfied with his tone about Madame Merle. 'It seems to me you insinuate things about her. I don't know what you mean, but if you've any grounds for disliking her I think you should either mention them frankly or else say nothing at all.'

Ralph, however, resented this charge with more apparent earnestness than he commonly used. 'I speak of Madame Merle exactly as I speak *to* her: with an even exaggerated respect.'

'Exaggerated, precisely. That's what I complain of.'

'I do so because Madame Merle's merits are exaggerated.'

'By whom, pray? By me? If so I do her a poor service.'

'No, no; by herself.'

'Ah, I protest!' Isabel earnestly cried. 'If ever there was a woman who made small claims——!'

'You put your finger on it,' Ralph interrupted. 'Her modesty's exaggerated. She has no business with small claims—she has a perfect right to make large ones.'

'Her merits are large then. You contradict yourself.'

'Her merits are immense,' said Ralph. 'She's indescribably blameless; a pathless desert of virtue; the only woman I know who never gives one a chance.'

'A chance for what?'

'Well, say to call her a fool! She's the only woman I know who has but that one little fault.'

Isabel turned away with impatience. 'I don't understand you; you're too paradoxical for my plain mind.'

'Let me explain. When I say she exaggerates I don't mean it in the vulgar sense—that she boasts, overstates, gives too fine an account of herself. I mean literally that she pushes the search for perfection too far—that her merits are in themselves overstrained. She's too good, too kind, too clever, too learned, too accomplished, too everything. She's too complete, in a word. I confess to you that she acts on my nerves and that I feel about her a good deal as that intensely human Athenian felt about Aristides the Just.'*

Isabel looked hard at her cousin; but the mocking spirit, if it lurked in his words, failed on this occasion to peep from his face. 'Do you wish Madame Merle to be banished?'

'By no means. She's much too good company. I delight in Madame Merle,' said Ralph Touchett simply.

'You're very odious, sir!' Isabel exclaimed. And then she asked him if he knew anything that was not to the honour of her brilliant friend.

'Nothing whatever. Don't you see that's just what I mean? On the character of every one else you may find some little black speck; if I were to take half an hour to it, some day, I've no doubt I should be able to find one on yours. For my own, of course, I'm spotted like a leopard. But on Madame Merle's nothing, nothing, nothing!'

'That's just what I think!' said Isabel with a toss of her head. 'That is why I like her so much.'

'She's a capital person for you to know. Since you wish to see the world you couldn't have a better guide.'

'I suppose you mean by that that she's worldly?'

'Worldly? No,' said Ralph, 'she's the great round world itself!'

It had certainly not, as Isabel for the moment took it into her head to believe, been a refinement of malice in him to say that he delighted in Madame Merle. Ralph Touchett took his refreshment wherever he could find it, and he would not have forgiven himself if he had been left wholly unbeguiled by such a mistress of the social art. There are deep-lying sympathies and antipathies, and it may have been that, in spite of the administered justice she enjoyed at his hands, her absence from his mother's house would not have made life barren to him. But Ralph Touchett had learned more or less inscrutably to attend, and there could have been nothing so 'sustained' to attend to as the general performance of Madame Merle. He tasted her in sips, he let her stand, with an opportuneness she herself could not have surpassed. There were moments when he felt almost sorry for her; and these, oddly enough, were the moments when his kindness was least demonstrative. He was sure she had been yearningly ambitious and that what she had visibly accomplished was far below her secret measure. She had got herself into perfect training, but had won none of the prizes. She was always plain Madame Merle, the widow of a Swiss *négociant*,* with a small income and a large acquaintance, who stayed with people a great deal and was almost as universally 'liked' as some new volume of smooth twaddle. The contrast between this position and any one of some half-dozen others that he supposed to have at various moments engaged her hope had an element of the tragical. His mother thought he got on beautifully with their genial guest; to Mrs Touchett's sense two persons who dealt so largely in too-ingenious theories of conduct—that is of their own—would have much in common. He had given due consideration to Isabel's intimacy with her eminent friend, having long since made up his mind that he could not, without opposition, keep his cousin to himself; and he made the best of it, as he had done of worse things. He believed it would take care of itself; it wouldn't last forever. Neither of these two superior persons knew the other as well as she supposed, and when each had made an important discovery or two there would be, if not a rupture, at least a relaxation. Meanwhile he was quite willing to admit that the conversation of the elder lady was an advantage to the younger, who had a great deal to learn and would doubtless learn it better from Madame Merle than from some other instructors of the young. It was not probable that Isabel would be injured.

XXIV

It would certainly have been hard to see what injury could arise to her from the visit she presently paid to Mr Osmond's hill-top. Nothing could have been more charming than this occasion—a soft afternoon in the full maturity of the Tuscan spring. The companions drove out of the Roman Gate, beneath the enormous blank superstructure which crowns the fine clear arch of that portal and makes it nakedly impressive, and wound between high-walled lanes into which the wealth of blossoming orchards overdrooped and flung a fragrance, until they reached the small superurban piazza, of crooked shape, where the long brown wall of the villa occupied in part by Mr Osmond formed a principal, or at least a very imposing, object. Isabel went with her friend through a wide, high court, where a clear shadow rested below and a pair of light-arched galleries, facing each other above, caught the upper sunshine upon their slim columns and the flowering plants in which they were dressed. There was something grave and strong in the place; it looked somehow as if, once you were in, you would need an act of energy to get out. For Isabel, however, there was of course as yet no thought of getting out, but only of advancing. Mr Osmond met her in the cold ante-chamber—it was cold even in the month of May—and ushered her, with her conductress, into the apartment to which we have already been introduced. Madame Merle was in front, and while Isabel lingered a little, talking with him, she went forward familiarly and greeted two persons who were seated in the saloon. One of these was little Pansy, on whom she bestowed a kiss; the other was a lady whom Mr Osmond indicated to Isabel as his sister, the Countess Gemini. 'And that's my little girl,' he said, 'who has just come out of her convent.'

Pansy had on a scant white dress, and her fair hair was neatly arranged in a net; she wore her small shoes tied sandal-fashion about her ankles. She made Isabel a little conventual curtsey and then came to be kissed. The Countess Gemini simply nodded without getting up: Isabel could see she was a woman of high fashion. She was thin and dark and not at all pretty, having features that suggested some tropical bird—a long beak-like nose, small, quickly-moving eyes and a mouth and chin that receded extremely. Her expression, however, thanks to various intensities of emphasis and wonder, of horror and joy, was not inhuman, and, as regards her appearance, it was plain she understood herself and made the most of her points. Her attire, voluminous and delicate, bristling with elegance, had the look of shimmering plumage, and her attitudes were as light and sudden as those of a creature who perched upon twigs. She had a great deal of manner; Isabel, who had never known any one with so much manner, immediately classed her as the most affected of women. She remembered that Ralph had not recommended her as an acquaintance; but she was ready to acknowledge that to a casual view the Countess Gemini revealed no depths. Her demonstrations suggested the violent waving of some flag of general truce—white silk with fluttering streamers.

'You'll believe I'm glad to see you when I tell you it's only because I knew you were to be here that I came myself. I don't come and see my brother—I make him come and see me. This hill of his is impossible—I don't see what possesses him. Really, Osmond, you'll be the ruin of my horses some day, and if it hurts them you'll have to give me another pair. I heard them wheezing to-day; I assure you I did. It's very disagreeable to hear one's horses wheezing when one's sitting in the carriage; it sounds too as if they weren't what they should be. But I've always had good horses; whatever else I may have lacked I've always managed that. My husband doesn't know much, but I think he knows a horse. In general Italians don't, but my husband goes in, according to his poor light, for everything English. My horses are English—so it's all the greater pity they should be ruined. I must tell you,' she went on, directly addressing Isabel, 'that Osmond doesn't often invite me; I don't think he likes to have me. It was quite my own idea, coming to-day. I like to see new people, and I'm sure you're very new. But don't sit there; that chair's not what it looks. There are some very good seats here, but there are also some horrors.'

These remarks were delivered with a series of little jerks and pecks, of roulades of shrillness, and in an accent that was as some fond recall of good English, or rather of good American, in adversity.

'I don't like to have you, my dear?' said her brother. 'I'm sure you're invaluable.'

'I don't see any horrors anywhere,' Isabel returned, looking about her. 'Everything seems to me beautiful and precious.'

'I've a few good things,' Mr Osmond allowed; 'indeed I've nothing very bad. But I've not what I should have liked.'

He stood there a little awkwardly, smiling and glancing about; his manner was an odd mixture of the detached and the involved. He seemed to hint that nothing but the right 'values' was of any consequence. Isabel made a rapid induction: perfect simplicity was not the badge of his family. Even the little girl from the convent, who, in her prim white dress, with her small submissive face and her hands locked before her, stood there as if she were about to partake of her first communion, even Mr Osmond's diminutive daughter had a kind of finish that was not entirely artless.

'You'd have liked a few things from the Uffizi and the Pitti*—that's what you'd have liked,' said Madame Merle.

'Poor Osmond, with his old curtains and crucifixes!' the Countess Gemini exclaimed: she appeared to call her brother only by his family-name. Her ejaculation had no particular object; she smiled at Isabel as she made it and looked at her from head to foot.

Her brother had not heard her; he seemed to be thinking what he could say to Isabel. 'Won't you have some tea?—you must be very tired,' he at last bethought himself of remarking.

'No indeed, I'm not tired; what have I done to tire me?' Isabel felt a certain need of being very direct, of pretending to nothing; there was something in the air, in her general impression of things—she could hardly have said what it was—that deprived her of all disposition to put herself forward. The place, the occasion, the combination of people, signified more than lay on the surface; she would try to understand—she would not simply utter graceful platitudes. Poor Isabel was doubtless not aware that many women would have uttered graceful platitudes to cover the working of their observation. It must be confessed that her pride was a trifle alarmed. A man she had heard spoken of in terms that excited interest and who was evidently capable of distinguishing himself, had invited her, a young lady not lavish of her favours, to come to his house. Now that she had done so the burden of the entertainment rested naturally on his wit. Isabel was not rendered less observant, and for the moment, we judge, she was not rendered more indulgent, by perceiving that Mr Osmond carried his burden less complacently than might have been expected. 'What a fool I was to have let myself so needlessly in—!' she could fancy his exclaiming to himself.

'You'll be tired when you go home, if he shows you all his bibelots and gives you a lecture on each,' said the Countess Gemini.

'I'm not afraid of that; but if I'm tired I shall at least have learned something.'

'Very little, I suspect. But my sister's dreadfully afraid of learning anything,' said Mr Osmond.

'Oh, I confess to that; I don't want to know anything more—I know too much already. The more you know the more unhappy you are.'

'You should not undervalue knowledge before Pansy, who has not finished her education,' Madame Merle interposed with a smile.

'Pansy will never know any harm,' said the child's father. 'Pansy's a little convent-flower.'

'Oh, the convents, the convents!' cried the Countess with a flutter of her ruffles. 'Speak to me of the convents! You may learn anything there; I'm a convent-flower myself. I don't pretend to be good, but the nuns do. Don't you see what I mean?' she went on, appealing to Isabel.

Isabel was not sure she saw, and she answered that she was very bad at following arguments. The Countess then declared that she herself detested arguments, but that this was her brother's taste—he would always discuss. 'For me,' she said, 'one should like a thing or one shouldn't; one can't like everything, of course. But one shouldn't attempt to reason it out—you never know where it may lead you. There are some very good feelings that may have bad reasons, don't you know? And then there are very bad feelings, sometimes, that have good reasons. Don't you see what I mean? I don't care anything about reasons, but I know what I like.'

'Ah, that's the great thing,' said Isabel, smiling and suspecting that her acquaintance with this lightly-flitting personage would not lead to intellectual repose. If the Countess objected to argument Isabel at this moment had as little taste for it, and she put out her hand to Pansy with a pleasant sense that such a gesture committed her to nothing that would admit of a divergence of views. Gilbert Osmond apparently took a rather hopeless view of his sister's tone; he turned the conversation to another topic. He presently sat down on the other side of his daughter, who had shyly brushed Isabel's fingers with her own; but he ended by drawing her out of her chair and making her stand between his knees, leaning against him while he passed his arm round her slimness. The child fixed her eyes on Isabel with a still, disinterested gaze which seemed void of an intention, yet conscious of an attraction. Mr Osmond talked of many things; Madame Merle had said he could be agreeable when he chose, and to-day, after a little, he appeared not only to have chosen but to have determined. Madame Merle and the Countess Gemini sat a little apart, conversing in the effortless manner of persons who knew each other well enough to take their ease; but every now and then Isabel heard the Countess, at something said by her companion, plunge into the latter's lucidity as a poodle splashes after a thrown stick. It was as if Madame Merle were seeing how far she would go. Mr Osmond talked of Florence, of Italy, of the pleasure of living in that country and of the abatements to the pleasure. There were both satisfactions and drawbacks; the drawbacks were numerous; strangers were too apt to see such a world as all romantic. It met the case soothingly for the human, for the social failure—by which he meant the people who couldn't 'realise,' as they said, on their sensibility: they could keep it about them there, in their poverty, without ridicule, as you might keep an heirloom or an inconvenient entailed place that brought you in nothing. Thus there were advantages in living in the country which contained the greatest sum of beauty. Certain impressions you could get only there. Others, favourable to life, you never got, and you got some that were very bad. But from time to time you got one of a quality that made up for everything. Italy, all the same, had spoiled a great many people; he was even fatuous enough to believe at times that he himself might have been a better man if he had spent less of his life there. It made one idle and dilettantish and second-rate; it had no discipline for the character, didn't cultivate in you, otherwise expressed, the successful social and other 'cheek' that flourished in Paris and London. 'We're sweetly provincial,' said Mr Osmond, 'and I'm perfectly aware that I myself am as rusty as a key that has no lock to fit it. It polishes me up a little to talk with you—not that I venture to pretend I can turn that very complicated lock I suspect your intellect of being! But you'll be going away before I've seen you three times, and I shall perhaps never see you after that. That's what it is to live in a country that people come to. When they're disagreeable here it's bad enough; when they're agreeable it's still worse. As soon as you like them they're off again! I've been deceived too often; I've ceased to form attachments, to permit myself to feel attractions. You mean to stay—to settle? That would be really comfortable. Ah yes, your aunt's a sort of guarantee; I believe she may be depended on. Oh, she's an old Florentine; I mean literally an old one; not a modern outsider. She's a contemporary of the Medici;* she must have been present at the burning of Savonarola,* and I'm not sure she didn't throw a handful of chips into the flame. Her face is very much like some faces in the early pictures; little, dry, definite faces that must have had a good deal of expression, but almost always the same one. Indeed I can show you her portrait in a fresco of Ghirlandaio's.* I hope you don't object to my speaking that way of your aunt, eh? I've an idea you don't. Perhaps you think that's even worse. I assure you there's no want of respect in it, to either of you. You know I'm a particular admirer of Mrs Touchett.'

While Isabel's host exerted himself to entertain her in this somewhat confidential fashion she looked occasionally at Madame Merle, who met her eyes with an inattentive smile in which, on this occasion, there was no infelicitous intimation that our heroine appeared to advantage. Madame Merle eventually proposed to the Countess Gemini that they should go into the garden, and the Countess, rising and shaking out her feathers, began to rustle toward the door. 'Poor Miss Archer!' she exclaimed, surveying the other group with expressive compassion. 'She has been brought quite into the family.'

'Miss Archer can certainly have nothing but sympathy for a family to which you belong,' Mr Osmond answered, with a laugh which, though it had something of a mocking ring, had also a finer patience.

'I don't know what you mean by that! I'm sure she'll see no harm in me but what you tell her. I'm better than he says, Miss Archer,' the Countess went on. 'I'm only rather an idiot and a bore. Is that all he has said? Ah then, you keep him in good-humour. Has he opened on one of his favourite subjects? I give you notice that there are two or three that he treats *à fond.** In that case you had better take off your bonnet.'

'I don't think I know what Mr Osmond's favourite subjects are,' said Isabel, who had risen to her feet.

The Countess assumed for an instant an attitude of intense meditation, pressing one of her hands, with the finger-tips gathered together, to her forehead. 'I'll tell you in a moment. One's Machiavelli;* the other's Vittoria Colonna;* the next is Metastasio.'*

'Ah, with me,' said Madame Merle, passing her arm into the Countess Gemini's as if to guide her course to the garden, 'Mr Osmond's never so historical.'

'Oh you,' the Countess answered as they moved away, 'you yourself are Machiavelli—you yourself are Vittoria Colonna!'

'We shall hear next that poor Madame Merle is Metastasio!' Gilbert Osmond resignedly sighed.

Isabel had got up on the assumption that they too were to go into the garden; but her host stood there with no apparent inclination to leave the room, his hands in the pockets of his jacket and his daughter, who had now locked her arm into one of his own, clinging to him and looking up while her eyes moved from his own face to Isabel's. Isabel waited, with a certain unuttered contentedness, to have her movements directed; she liked Mr Osmond's talk, his company: she had what always gave her a very private thrill, the consciousness of a new relation. Through the open doors of the great room she saw Madame Merle and the Countess stroll across the fine grass of the garden; then she turned, and her eyes wandered over the things scattered about her. The understanding had been that Mr Osmond should show her his treasures; his pictures and cabinets all looked like treasures. Isabel after a moment went toward one of the pictures to see it better; but just as she had done so he said to her abruptly: 'Miss Archer, what do you think of my sister?'

She faced him with some surprise. 'Ah, don't ask me that—I've seen your sister too little.'

'Yes, you've seen her very little; but you must have observed that there is not a great deal of her to see. What do you think of our family tone?' he went on with his cool smile. 'I should like to know how it strikes a fresh, unprejudiced mind. I know what you're going to say—you've had almost no observation of it. Of course this is only a glimpse. But just take notice, in future, if you have a chance. I sometimes think we've got into a rather bad way, living off here among things and people not our own, without responsibilities or attachments, with nothing to hold us together or keep us up; marrying foreigners, forming artificial tastes, playing tricks with our natural mission. Let me add, though, that I say that much more for myself than for my sister. She's a very honest lady—more so than she seems. She's rather unhappy, and as she's not of a serious turn she doesn't tend to show it tragically: she shows it comically instead. She has got a horrid husband, though I'm not sure she makes the best of him. Of course, however, a horrid husband's an awkward thing. Madame Merle gives her excellent advice, but it's a good deal like giving a child a dictionary to learn a language with. He can look out the words, but he can't put them together. My sister needs a grammar, but unfortunately she's not grammatical. Pardon my troubling you with these details; my sister was very right in saying you've been taken into the family. Let me take down that picture; you want more light.'

He took down the picture, carried it toward the window,

related some curious facts about it. She looked at the other works of art, and he gave her such further information as might appear most acceptable to a young lady making a call on a summer afternoon. His pictures, his medallions and tapestries were interesting; but after a while Isabel felt the owner much more so, and independently of them, thickly as they seemed to overhang him. He resembled no one she had ever seen; most of the people she knew might be divided into groups of half a dozen specimens. There were one or two exceptions to this; she could think for instance of no group that would contain her aunt Lydia. There were other people who were, relatively speaking, original—original, as one might say, by courtesy—such as Mr Goodwood, as her cousin Ralph, as Henrietta Stackpole, as Lord Warburton, as Madame Merle. But in essentials, when one came to look at them, these individuals belonged to types already present to her mind. Her mind contained no class offering a natural place to Mr Osmond—he was a specimen apart. It was not that she recognised all these truths at the hour, but they were falling into order before her. For the moment she only said to herself that this 'new relation' would perhaps prove her very most distinguished. Madame Merle had had that note of rarity, but what quite other power it immediately gained when sounded by a man! It was not so much what he said and did, but rather what he withheld, that marked him for her as by one of those signs of the highly curious that he was showing her on the underside of old plates and in the corner of sixteenth-century drawings: he indulged in no striking deflections from common usage, he was an original without being an eccentric. She had never met a person of so fine a grain. The peculiarity was physical, to begin with, and it extended to impalpabilities. His dense, delicate hair, his overdrawn, retouched features, his clear complexion, ripe without being coarse, the very evenness of the growth of his beard, and that light, smooth slenderness of structure which made the movement of a single one of his fingers produce the effect of an expressive gesture—these personal points struck our sensitive young woman as signs of quality, of intensity, somehow as promises of interest. He was certainly fastidious and critical; he was probably irritable. His sensibility had governed him—possibly governed him too much; it had made him impatient of vulgar troubles and had led him to live by himself, in a sorted, sifted, arranged world, thinking about art and beauty and history. He had consulted his taste in everything—his taste alone perhaps, as a sick man consciously incurable consults at last only his lawyer: that was what made him so different from every one else. Ralph had something of this same quality, this appearance of thinking that life was a matter of connoisseurship; but in Ralph it was an anomaly, a kind of humorous excrescence, whereas in Mr Osmond it was the keynote, and everything was in harmony with it. She was certainly far from understanding him completely; his meaning was not at all times obvious. It was hard to see what he meant for instance by speaking of his provincial side—which was exactly the side she would have taken him most to lack. Was it a harmless paradox, intended to puzzle her? or was it the last refinement of high culture? She trusted she should learn in time; it would be very interesting to learn. If it was provincial to have that harmony, what then was the finish of the capital? And she could put this question in spite of so feeling her host a shy personage; since such shyness as his—the shyness of ticklish nerves and fine perceptions—was perfectly consistent with the best breeding. Indeed it was almost a proof of standards and touchstones other than the vulgar: he must be so sure the vulgar would be first on the ground. He wasn't a man of easy assurance, who chatted and gossiped with the fluency of a superficial nature; he was critical of himself as well as of others, and, exacting a good deal of others, to think them agreeable, probably took a rather ironical view of what he himself offered: a proof into the bargain that he was not grossly conceited. If he had not been shy he wouldn't have effected that gradual, subtle, successful conversion of it to which she owed both what pleased her in him and what mystified her. If he had suddenly asked her what she thought of the Countess Gemini, that was doubtless a proof that he was interested in her; it could scarcely be as a help to knowledge of his own sister. That he should be so interested showed an enquiring mind; but it was a little singular he should sacrifice his fraternal feeling to his curiosity. This was the most eccentric thing he had done.

There were two other rooms, beyond the one in which she had been received, equally full of romantic objects, and in these apartments Isabel spent a quarter of an hour. Everything was in the last degree curious and precious, and Mr Osmond continued to be the kindest of ciceroni* as he led her from one fine piece to another and still held his little girl by the hand. His kindness almost surprised our young friend, who wondered why he should take so much trouble for her; and she was oppressed at last with the accumulation of beauty and knowledge to which she found herself introduced. There was enough for the present; she had ceased to attend to what he said; she listened to him with attentive eyes, but was not thinking of what he told her. He probably thought her quicker, cleverer in every way, more prepared, than she was. Madame Merle would have pleasantly exaggerated; which was a pity, because in the end he would be sure to find out, and then perhaps even her real intelligence wouldn't reconcile him to his mistake. A part of Isabel's fatigue came from the effort to appear as intelligent as she believed Madame Merle had described her, and from the fear (very unusual with her) of exposing—not her ignorance; for that she cared comparatively little—but her possible grossness of perception. It would have annoyed her to express a liking for something he, in his superior enlightenment, would think she oughtn't to like; or to pass by something at which the truly initiated mind would arrest itself. She had no wish to fall into that grotesqueness—in which she had seen women (and it was a warning) serenely, yet ignobly, flounder. She was very careful therefore as to what she said, as to what she noticed or failed to notice; more careful than she had ever been before.

They came back into the first of the rooms, where the tea had been served; but as the two other ladies were still on the terrace, and as Isabel had not yet been made acquainted with the view, the paramount distinction of the place, Mr Osmond directed her steps into the garden without more delay. Madame Merle and the Countess had had chairs brought out, and as the afternoon was lovely the Countess proposed they should take their tea in the open air. Pansy therefore was sent to bid the servant bring out the preparations. The sun had got low, the golden light took a deeper tone, and on the mountains and the plain that stretched beneath them the masses of purple shadow glowed as richly as the places that were still exposed. The scene had an extraordinary charm. The air was almost solemnly still, and the large expanse of the landscape, with its gardenlike culture and nobleness of outline, its teeming valley and delicately-fretted hills, its peculiarly human-looking touches of habitation, lay there in splendid harmony and classic grace. 'You seem so well pleased that I think you can be trusted to come back,' Osmond said as he led his companion to one of the angles of the terrace.

'I shall certainly come back,' she returned, 'in spite of what you say about its being bad to live in Italy. What was that you said about one's natural mission? I wonder if I should forsake my natural mission if I were to settle in Florence.'

'A woman's natural mission is to be where she's most appreciated.'

'The point's to find out where that is.'

'Very true—she often wastes a great deal of time in the enquiry. People ought to make it very plain to her.'

'Such a matter would have to be made very plain to me,' smiled Isabel.

'I'm glad, at any rate, to hear you talk of settling. Madame Merle had given me an idea that you were of a rather roving disposition. I thought she spoke of your having some plan of going round the world.'

'I'm rather ashamed of my plans; I make a new one every day.'

'I don't see why you should be ashamed; it's the greatest of pleasures.'

'It seems frivolous, I think,' said Isabel. 'One ought to choose something very deliberately, and be faithful to that.'

'By that rule then, I've not been frivolous.'

'Have you never made plans?'

'Yes, I made one years ago, and I'm acting on it to-day.'

'It must have been a very pleasant one,' Isabel permitted herself to observe.

'It was very simple. It was to be as quiet as possible.'

'As quiet?' the girl repeated.

'Not to worry—not to strive nor struggle. To resign myself. To be content with little.' He spoke these sentences slowly, with short pauses between, and his intelligent regard was fixed on his visitor's with the conscious air of a man who has brought himself to confess something.

'Do you call that simple?' she asked with mild irony.

'Yes, because it's negative.'

'Has your life been negative?'

'Call it affirmative if you like. Only it has affirmed my indifference. Mind you, not my natural indifference—I *had* none. But my studied, my wilful renunciation.'

She scarcely understood him; it seemed a question whether he were joking or not. Why should a man who struck her as having a great fund of reserve suddenly bring himself to be so confidential? This was his affair, however, and his confidences were interesting. 'I don't see why you should have renounced,' she said in a moment.

'Because I could do nothing. I had no prospects, I was poor, and I was not a man of genius. I had no talents even; I took my measure early in life. I was simply the most fastidious young gentleman living. There were two or three people in the world I envied—the Emperor of Russia, for instance, and the Sultan of Turkey! There were even moments when I envied the Pope of Rome—for the consideration he enjoys. I should have been delighted to be considered to that extent; but since that couldn't be I didn't care for anything less, and I made up my mind not to go in for honours. The leanest gentleman can always consider himself, and fortunately I *was*, though lean, a gentleman. I could do nothing in Italy—I couldn't even be an Italian patriot. To do that I should have had to get out of the country; and I was too fond of it to leave it, to say nothing of my being too well satisfied with it, on the whole, as it then was, to wish it altered. So I've passed a great many years here on that quiet plan I spoke of. I've not been at all unhappy. I don't mean to say I've cared for nothing; but the things I've cared for have been definite—limited. The events of my life have been absolutely unperceived by any one save myself; getting an old silver crucifix at a bargain (I've never bought anything dear, of course), or discovering, as I once did, a sketch by Correggio on a panel daubed over by some inspired idiot.'

This would have been rather a dry account of Mr Osmond's career if Isabel had fully believed it; but her imagination supplied the human element which she was sure had not been wanting. His life had been mingled with other lives more than he admitted; naturally she couldn't expect him to enter into this. For the present she abstained from provoking further revelations; to intimate that he had not told her everything would be more familiar and less considerate than she now desired to be—would in fact be uproariously vulgar. He had certainly told her quite enough. It was her present inclination, however, to express a measured sympathy for the success with which he had preserved his independence. 'That's a very pleasant life,' she said, 'to renounce everything but Correggio!'*

'Oh, I've made in my way a good thing of it. Don't imagine I'm whining about it. It's one's own fault if one isn't happy.'

This was large; she kept down to something smaller. 'Have you lived here always?'

'No, not always. I lived a long time at Naples, and many years in Rome. But I've been here a good while. Perhaps I shall have to change, however; to do something else. I've no longer myself to think of. My daughter's growing up and may very possibly not care so much for the Correggios and crucifixes as I. I shall have to do what's best for Pansy.'

'Yes, do that,' said Isabel. 'She's such a dear little girl.'

'Ah,' cried Gilbert Osmond beautifully, 'she's a little saint of heaven! She is my great happiness!'

XXV

WHILE this sufficiently intimate colloquy (prolonged for some time after we cease to follow it) went forward Madame Merle and her companion, breaking a silence of some duration, had begun to exchange remarks. They were sitting in an attitude of unexpressed expectancy; an attitude especially marked on the part of the Countess Gemini, who, being of a more nervous temperament than her friend, practised with less success the art of disguising impatience. What these ladies were waiting for would not have been apparent and was perhaps not very definite to their own minds. Madame Merle waited for Osmond to release their young friend from her *tête-à-tête*, and the Countess waited because Madame Merle did. The Countess, moreover, by waiting, found the time ripe for one of her pretty perversities. She might have desired for some minutes to place it. Her brother wandered with Isabel to the end of the garden, to which point her eyes followed them.

'My dear,' she then observed to her companion, 'you'll excuse me if I don't congratulate you!'

'Very willingly, for I don't in the least know why you should.'

'Haven't you a little plan that you think rather well of?' And the Countess nodded at the sequestered couple.

Madame Merle's eyes took the same direction; then she looked serenely at her neighbour. 'You know I never understand you very well,' she smiled.

'No one can understand better than you when you wish. I see that just now you *don't* wish.'

'You say things to me that no one else does,' said Madame Merle gravely, yet without bitterness.

'You mean things you don't like? Doesn't Osmond sometimes say such things?'

'What your brother says has a point.'

'Yes, a poisoned one sometimes. If you mean that I'm not so clever as he you mustn't think I shall suffer from your sense of our difference. But it will be much better that you should understand me.'

'Why so?' asked Madame Merle. 'To what will it conduce?'

'If I don't approve of your plan you ought to know it in order to appreciate the danger of my interfering with it.'

Madame Merle looked as if she were ready to admit that there might be something in this; but in a moment she said quietly: 'You think me more calculating than I am.'

'It's not your calculating I think ill of; it's your calculating wrong. You've done so in this case.'

'You must have made extensive calculations yourself to discover that.'

'No, I've not had time. I've seen the girl but this once,' said the Countess, 'and the conviction has suddenly come to me. I like her very much.'

'So do I,' Madame Merle mentioned.

'You've a strange way of showing it.'

'Surely I've given her the advantage of making your acquaintance.'

'That indeed,' piped the Countess, 'is perhaps the best thing that could happen to her!'

Madame Merle said nothing for some time. The Countess's manner was odious, was really low; but it was an old story, and with her eyes upon the violet slope of Monte Morello she gave herself up to reflection. 'My dear lady,' she finally resumed, 'I advise you not to agitate yourself. The matter you allude to concerns three persons much stronger of purpose than yourself.'

'Three persons? You and Osmond of course. But is Miss Archer also very strong of purpose?'

'Quite as much so as we.'

'Ah then,' said the Countess radiantly, 'if I convince her it's her interest to resist you she'll do so successfully!'

'Resist us? Why do you express yourself so coarsely? She's not exposed to compulsion or deception.'

'I'm not sure of that. You're capable of anything, you and Osmond. I don't mean Osmond by himself, and I don't mean you by yourself. But together you're dangerous—like some chemical combination.'

'You had better leave us alone then,' smiled Madame Merle.

'I don't mean to touch you—but I shall talk to that girl.'

'My poor Amy,' Madame Merle murmured, 'I don't see what has got into your head.'

'I take an interest in her—that's what has got into my head. I like her.'

Madame Merle hesitated a moment. 'I don't think she likes you.'

The Countess's bright little eyes expanded and her face was set in a grimace. 'Ah, you *are* dangerous—even by yourself!'

'If you want her to like you don't abuse your brother to her,' said Madame Merle.

'I don't suppose you pretend she has fallen in love with him in two interviews.'

Madame Merle looked a moment at Isabel and at the master of the house. He was leaning against the parapet, facing her, his arms folded; and she at present was evidently not lost in the mere impersonal view, persistently as she gazed at it. As Madame Merle watched her she lowered her eyes; she was listening, possibly with a certain embarrassment, while she pressed the point of her parasol into the path. Madame Merle rose from her chair. 'Yes, I think so!' she pronounced.

The shabby footboy, summoned by Pansy—he might, tarnished as to livery and quaint as to type, have issued from some stray sketch of old-time manners, been 'put in' by the brush of a Longhi* or a Goya*—had come out with a small table and placed it on the grass, and then had gone back and fetched the tea-tray; after which he had again disappeared, to return with a couple of chairs. Pansy had watched these proceedings with the deepest interest, standing with her small hands folded together upon the front of her scanty frock; but she had not presumed to offer assistance. When the tea-table had been arranged, however, she gently approached her aunt.

'Do you think papa would object to my making the tea?'

The Countess looked at her with a deliberately critical gaze and without answering her question. 'My poor niece,' she said, 'is that your best frock?'

'Ah no,' Pansy answered, 'it's just a little *toilette** for common occasions.'

'Do you call it a common occasion when I come to see

you?—to say nothing of Madame Merle and the pretty lady yonder.'

Pansy reflected a moment, turning gravely from one of the persons mentioned to the other. Then her face broke into its perfect smile. 'I have a pretty dress, but even that one's very simple. Why should I expose it beside your beautiful things?'

'Because it's the prettiest you have; for me you must always wear the prettiest. Please put it on the next time. It seems to me they don't dress you so well as they might.'

The child sparingly stroked down her antiquated skirt. 'It's a good little dress to make tea—don't you think? Don't you believe papa would allow me?'

'Impossible for me to say, my child,' said the Countess. 'For me, your father's ideas are unfathomable. Madame Merle understands them better. Ask *her*.'

Madame Merle smiled with her usual grace. 'It's a weighty question—let me think. It seems to me it would please your father to see a careful little daughter making his tea. It's the proper duty of the daughter of the house—when she grows up.'

'So it seems to me, Madame Merle!' Pansy cried. 'You shall see how well I'll make it. A spoonful for each.' And she began to busy herself at the table.

'Two spoonfuls for me,' said the Countess, who, with Madame Merle, remained for some moments watching her. 'Listen to me, Pansy,' the Countess resumed at last. 'I should like to know what you think of your visitor.'

'Ah, she's not mine—she's papa's,' Pansy objected.

'Miss Archer came to see you as well,' said Madame Merle.

'I'm very happy to hear that. She has been very polite to me.'

'Do you like her then?' the Countess asked.

'She's charming—charming,' Pansy repeated in her little neat conversational tone. 'She pleases me thoroughly.'

'And how do you think she pleases your father?'

'Ah really, Countess!' murmured Madame Merle dissuasively. 'Go and call them to tea,' she went on to the child.

'You'll see if they don't like it!' Pansy declared; and departed to summon the others, who had still lingered at the end of the terrace.

'If Miss Archer's to become her mother it's surely interesting to know if the child likes her,' said the Countess.

'If your brother marries again it won't be for Pansy's sake,' Madame Merle replied. 'She'll soon be sixteen, and after that she'll begin to need a husband rather than a stepmother.'

'And will you provide the husband as well?'

'I shall certainly take an interest in her marrying fortunately. I imagine you'll do the same.'

'Indeed I shan't!' cried the Countess. 'Why should I, of all women, set such a price on a husband?'

'You didn't marry fortunately; that's what I'm speaking of. When I say a husband I mean a good one.'

'There are no good ones. Osmond won't be a good one.'

Madame Merle closed her eyes a moment. 'You're irritated just now; I don't know why,' she presently said. 'I don't think you'll really object either to your brother's or to your niece's marrying, when the time comes for them to do so; and as regards Pansy I'm confident that we shall some day have the pleasure of looking for a husband for her together. Your large acquaintance will be a great help.'

'Yes, I'm irritated,' the Countess answered. 'You often irritate me. Your own coolness is fabulous. You're a strange woman.'

'It's much better that we should always act together,' Madame Merle went on.

'Do you mean that as a threat?' asked the Countess rising.

Madame Merle shook her head as for quiet amusement. 'No indeed, you've not my coolness!'

Isabel and Mr Osmond were now slowly coming toward them and Isabel had taken Pansy by the hand. 'Do you pretend to believe he'd make her happy?' the Countess demanded.

'If he should marry Miss Archer I suppose he'd behave like a gentleman.'

The Countess jerked herself into a succession of attitudes. 'Do you mean as most gentlemen behave? That would be much to be thankful for! Of course Osmond's a gentleman; his own sister needn't be reminded of that. But does he think he can marry any girl he happens to pick out? Osmond's a gentleman, of course; but I must say I've *never*, no, no, never, seen any one of Osmond's pretensions! What they're all founded on is more than I can say. I'm his own sister; I might be supposed to know. Who is he, if you please? What has he ever done? If there had been anything particularly grand in his origin—if he were made of some superior clay—I presume I should have got some inkling of it. If there had been any great honours or splendours in the family I should certainly have made the most of them: they would have been quite in my line. But there's nothing, nothing, nothing. One's parents were charming people of course; but so were yours, I've no doubt. Every one's a charming person now-a-days. Even I'm a charming person; don't laugh, it has literally been said. As for Osmond, he has always appeared to believe that he's descended from the gods.'

'You may say what you please,' said Madame Merle, who had listened to this quick outbreak none the less attentively, we may believe, because her eye wandered away from the speaker and her hands busied themselves with adjusting the knots of ribbon on her dress. 'You Osmonds are a fine race—your blood must flow from some very pure source. Your brother, like an intelligent man, has had the conviction of it if he has not had the proofs. You're modest about it, but you yourself are extremely distinguished. What do you say about your niece? The child's a little princess. Nevertheless,' Madame Merle added, 'it won't be an easy matter for Osmond to marry Miss Archer. Yet he can try.'

'I hope she'll refuse him. It will take him down a little.'

'We mustn't forget that he is one of the cleverest of men.'

'I've heard you say that before, but I haven't yet discovered what he has done.'

'What he has done? He has done nothing that has had to be undone. And he has known how to wait.'

'To wait for Miss Archer's money? How much of it is there?'

'That's not what I mean,' said Madame Merle. 'Miss Archer has seventy thousand pounds.'

'Well, it's a pity she's so charming,' the Countess declared. 'To be sacrificed, any girl would do. She needn't be superior.'

'If she weren't superior your brother would never look at her. He must have the best.'

'Yes,' returned the Countess as they went forward a little to meet the others, 'he's very hard to satisfy. That makes me tremble for her happiness!'

XXVI

GILBERT OSMOND came to see Isabel again; that is he came to Palazzo Crescentini. He had other friends there as well, and to Mrs Touchett and Madame Merle he was always impartially civil; but the former of these ladies noted the fact that in the course of a fortnight he called five times, and compared it with another fact that she found no difficulty in remembering. Two visits a year had hitherto constituted his regular tribute to Mrs Touchett's worth, and she had never observed him select for such visits those moments, of almost periodical recurrence, when Madame Merle was under her roof. It was not for Madame Merle that he came; these two were old friends and he never put himself out for her. He was not fond of Ralph—Ralph had told her so—and it was not supposable that Mr Osmond had suddenly taken a fancy to her son. Ralph was imperturbable—Ralph had a kind of loose-fitting urbanity that wrapped him about like an ill-made overcoat, but of which he never divested himself; he thought Mr Osmond very good company and was willing at any time to look at him in the light of hospitality. But he didn't flatter himself that the desire to repair a past injustice was the motive of their visitor's calls; he read the situation more clearly. Isabel was the attraction, and in all conscience a sufficient one. Osmond was a critic, a student of the exquisite, and it was natural he should be curious of so rare an apparition. So when his mother observed to him that it was plain what Mr Osmond was thinking of, Ralph replied that he was quite of her opinion. Mrs Touchett had from far back found a place on her scant list for this gentleman, though wondering dimly by what art and what process—so negative and so wise as they were—he had everywhere effectively imposed himself. As he had never been an importunate visitor he had had no chance to be offensive, and he was recommended to her by his appearance of being as well able to do without her as she was to do without him—a quality that always, oddly enough, affected her as providing ground for a relation with her. It gave her no satisfaction, however, to think that he had taken it into his head to marry her niece. Such an alliance, on Isabel's part, would have an air of almost morbid perversity. Mrs Touchett easily remembered that the girl had refused an English peer; and that a young lady with whom Lord Warburton had not successfully wrestled should content herself with an obscure American dilettante, a middle-aged widower with an uncanny child and an ambiguous income, this answered to nothing in Mrs Touchett's conception of success. She took, it will be observed, not the sentimental, but the political, view of matrimony—a view which has always had much to recommend it. 'I trust she won't have the folly to listen to him,' she said to her son; to which Ralph replied that Isabel's listening was one thing and Isabel's answering quite another. He knew she had listened to several parties, as his father would have said, but had made them listen in return; and he found much entertainment in the idea that in these few months of his knowing her he should observe a fresh suitor at her gate. She had wanted to see life, and fortune was serving her to her taste; a succession of fine gentlemen going down on their knees to her would do as well as anything else. Ralph looked forward to a fourth, a fifth, a tenth besieger; he had no conviction she would stop at a third. She would keep the gate ajar and open a parley; she would certainly not allow number three to come in. He expressed this view, somewhat after this fashion, to his mother, who looked at him as if he had been dancing a jig. He had such a fanciful, pictorial way of saying things that he might as well address her in the deaf-mute's alphabet.

'I don't think I know what you mean,' she said; 'you use too many figures of speech; I could never understand allegories. The two words in the language I most respect are Yes and No. If Isabel wants to marry Mr Osmond she'll do so in spite of all your comparisons. Let her alone to find a fine one herself for anything she undertakes. I know very little about the young man in America; I don't think she spends much of her time in thinking of him, and I suspect he has got tired of waiting for her. There's nothing in life to prevent her marrying Mr Osmond if she only looks at him in a certain way. That's all very well; no one approves more than I of one's pleasing one's self. But she takes her pleasure in such odd things; she's capable of marrying Mr Osmond for the beauty of his opinions or for his autograph of Michael Angelo. She wants to be disinterested: as if she were the only person who's in danger of not being so! Will *he* be so disinterested when he has the spending of her money? That was her idea before your father's death, and it has acquired new charms for her since. She ought to marry some one of whose disinterestedness she shall herself be sure; and there would be no such proof of that as his having a fortune of his own.'

'My dear mother, I'm not afraid,' Ralph answered. 'She's making fools of us all. She'll please herself, of course; but she'll do so by studying human nature at close quarters and yet retaining her liberty. She has started on an exploring expedition, and I don't think she'll change her course, at the outset, at a signal from Gilbert Osmond. She may have slackened speed for an hour, but before we know it she'll be steaming away again. Excuse another metaphor.'

Mrs Touchett excused it perhaps, but was not so much reassured as to withhold from Madame Merle the expression of her fears. 'You who know everything,' she said, 'you must know this: whether that curious creature's really making love to my niece.'

'Gilbert Osmond?' Madame Merle widened her clear eyes and, with a full intelligence, 'Heaven help us,' she exclaimed, 'that's an idea!'

'Hadn't it occurred to you?'

'You make me feel an idiot, but I confess it hadn't. I wonder,' she added, 'if it has occurred to Isabel.'

'Oh, I shall now ask her,' said Mrs Touchett.

Madame Merle reflected. 'Don't put it into her head. The thing would be to ask Mr Osmond.'

'I can't do that,' said Mrs Touchett. 'I won't have him enquire of me—as he perfectly may with that air of his, given Isabel's situation—what business it is of mine.'

'I'll ask him myself,' Madame Merle bravely declared.

'But what business—for *him*—is it of yours?'

'It's being none whatever is just why I can afford to speak. It's so much less my business than any one's else that he can put me off with anything he chooses. But it will be by the way he does this that I shall know.'

'Pray let me hear then,' said Mrs Touchett, 'of the fruits of your penetration. If I can't speak to him, however, at least I can speak to Isabel.'

Her companion sounded at this the note of warning. 'Don't be too quick with her. Don't inflame her imagination.'

'I never did anything in life to any one's imagination. But I'm always sure of her doing something—well, not of *my* kind.'

'No, you wouldn't like this,' Madame Merle observed without the point of interrogation.

'Why in the world should I, pray? Mr Osmond has nothing the least solid to offer.'

Again Madame Merle was silent while her thoughtful smile drew up her mouth even more charmingly than usual toward the left corner. 'Let us distinguish. Gilbert Osmond's certainly not the first comer. He's a man who in favourable conditions might very well make a great impression. He has made a great impression, to my knowledge, more than once.'

'Don't tell me about his probably quite cold-blooded love-affairs; they're nothing to me!' Mrs Touchett cried. 'What you say's precisely why I wish he would cease his visits. He has nothing in the world that I know of but a dozen or two of early masters and a more or less pert little daughter.'

'The early masters are now worth a good deal of money,' said Madame Merle, 'and the daughter's a very young and very innocent and very harmless person.'

'In other words she's an insipid little chit. Is that what you mean? Having no fortune she can't hope to marry as they marry here; so that Isabel will have to furnish her either with a maintenance or with a dowry.'

'Isabel probably wouldn't object to being kind to her. I think she likes the poor child.'

'Another reason then for Mr Osmond's stopping at home! Otherwise, a week hence, we shall have my niece arriving at the conviction that her mission in life's to prove that a step-mother may sacrifice herself—and that, to prove it, she must first become one.'

'She would make a charming stepmother,' smiled Madame Merle; 'but I quite agree with you that she had better not decide upon her mission too hastily. Changing the form of one's mission's almost as difficult as changing the shape of one's nose: there they are, each, in the middle of one's face and one's character—one has to begin too far back. But I'll investigate and report to you.'

All this went on quite over Isabel's head; she had no suspicions that her relations with Mr Osmond were being discussed. Madame Merle had said nothing to put her on her guard; she alluded no more pointedly to him than to the other gentlemen of Florence, native and foreign, who now arrived in considerable numbers to pay their respects to Miss Archer's aunt. Isabel thought him interesting—she came back to that; she liked so to think of him. She had carried away an image from her visit to his hill-top which her subsequent knowledge of him did nothing to efface and which put on for her a particular harmony with other supposed and divined things, histories within histories: the image of a quiet, clever, sensitive, distinguished man, strolling on a moss-grown terrace above the sweet Val d'Arno and holding by the hand a little girl whose bell-like clearness gave a new grace to childhood. The picture had no flourishes, but she liked its lowness of tone and the atmosphere of summer twilight that pervaded it. It spoke of the kind of personal issue that touched her most nearly; of the choice between objects, subjects, contact—what might she call them?—of a thin and those of a rich association; of a lonely, studious life in a lovely land; of an old sorrow that sometimes ached to-day; of a feeling of pride that was perhaps exaggerated, but that had an element of nobleness; of a care for beauty and perfection so natural and so cultivated together that the career appeared to stretch beneath it in the disposed vistas and with the ranges of steps and terraces and fountains of a formal Italian garden—allowing only for arid places freshened by the natural dews of a quaint half-anxious, half-helpless fatherhood. At Palazzo Crescentini Mr Osmond's manner remained the same; diffident at first—oh self-conscious beyond doubt! and full of the effort (visible only to a sympathetic eye) to overcome this disadvantage; an effort which usually resulted in a great deal of easy, lively, very positive, rather aggressive, always suggestive talk. Mr Osmond's talk was not injured by the indication of an eagerness to shine; Isabel found no difficulty in believing that a person was sincere who had so many of the signs of strong conviction—as for instance an explicit and graceful appreciation of anything that might be said on his own side of the question, said perhaps by Miss Archer in especial. What continued to please this young woman was that while he talked so for amusement he didn't talk, as she had heard people, for 'effect.' He uttered his ideas as if, odd as they often appeared, he were used to them and had lived with them; old polished knobs and heads and handles, of precious substance, that could be fitted if necessary to new walking-sticks—not switches plucked in destitution from the common tree and then too elegantly waved about. One day he brought his small daughter with him, and she rejoiced to renew acquaintance with the child, who, as she presented her forehead to be kissed by every member of the circle, reminded her vividly of an *ingénue* in a French play. Isabel had never seen a little person of this pattern; American girls were very different—different too were the maidens of England. Pansy was so formed and finished for her tiny place in the world, and yet in imagination, as one could see, so innocent and infantine. She sat on the sofa by Isabel; she wore a small grenadine mantle and a pair of the useful gloves that Madame Merle had given her—little grey gloves with a single button. She was like a sheet of blank paper—the ideal *jeune fille** of foreign fiction. Isabel hoped that so fair and smooth a page would be covered with an edifying text.

The Countess Gemini also came to call upon her, but the Countess was quite another affair. She was by no means a blank sheet; she had been written over in a variety of hands, and Mrs Touchett, who felt by no means honoured by her visit, pronounced that a number of unmistakeable blots were to be seen upon her surface. The Countess gave rise indeed to some discussion between the mistress of the house and the visitor from Rome, in which Madame Merle (who was not such a fool as to irritate people by always agreeing with them) availed herself felicitously enough of that large licence of dissent which her hostess permitted as freely as she practised it. Mrs Touchett had declared it a piece of audacity that this highly compromised character should have presented herself at such a time of day at the door of a house in which she was esteemed so little as she must long have known herself to be at Palazzo Crescentini. Isabel had been made acquainted with the estimate prevailing under that roof: it represented Mr Osmond's sister as a lady who had so mismanaged her improprieties that they had ceased to hang together at all—which was at the least what one asked of such matters—and had become the mere floating fragments of a wrecked renown, incommoding social circulation. She had been married by her mother—a more administrative person, with an appreciation of foreign titles which the daughter, to do her justice, had probably by this time thrown off—to an Italian nobleman who had perhaps given her some excuse for attempting to quench the consciousness of outrage. The Countess, however, had consoled herself outrageously, and the list of her excuses had now lost itself in the labyrinth of her adventures. Mrs Touchett had never consented to receive her, though the Countess had made overtures of old. Florence was not an austere city; but, as Mrs Touchett said, she had to draw the line somewhere.

Madame Merle defended the luckless lady with a great deal of zeal and wit. She couldn't see why Mrs Touchett should make a scapegoat of a woman who had really done no harm, who had only done good in the wrong way. One must certainly draw the line, but while one was about it one should draw it straight: it was a very crooked chalk-mark that would exclude the Countess Gemini. In that case Mrs Touchett had better shut up her house; this perhaps would be the best course so long as she remained in Florence. One must be fair and not make arbitrary differences: the Countess had doubtless been imprudent, she had not been so clever as other women. She was a good creature, not clever at all; but since when had that been a ground of exclusion from the best society? For ever so long now one had heard nothing about her, and there could be no better proof of her having renounced the error of her ways than her desire to become a member of Mrs Touchett's circle.

Isabel could contribute nothing to this interesting dispute, not even a patient attention; she contented herself with having given a friendly welcome to the unfortunate lady, who, whatever her defects, had at least the merit of being Mr Osmond's sister. As she liked the brother Isabel thought it proper to try and like the sister: in spite of the growing complexity of things she was still capable of these primitive sequences. She had not received the happiest impression of the Countess on meeting her at the villa, but was thankful for an opportunity to repair the accident. Had not Mr Osmond remarked that she was a respectable person? To have proceeded from Gilbert Osmond this was a crude proposition, but Madame Merle bestowed upon it a certain improving polish. She told Isabel more about the poor Countess than Mr Osmond had done, and related the history of her marriage and its consequences. The Count was a member of an ancient Tuscan family, but of such small estate that he had been glad to accept Amy Osmond, in spite of the questionable beauty which had yet not hampered her career, with the modest dowry her mother was able to offer—a sum about equivalent to that which had already formed her brother's share of their patrimony. Count Gemini since then, however, had inherited money, and now they were well enough off, as Italians went, though Amy was horribly extravagant. The Count was a low-lived brute; he had given his wife every pretext. She had no children; she had lost three within a year of their birth. Her mother, who had bristled with pretensions to elegant learning and published descriptive poems and corresponded on Italian subjects with the English weekly journals, her mother had died three years after the Countess's marriage, the father, lost in the grey American dawn of the situation, but reputed originally rich and wild, having died much earlier. One could see this in Gilbert Osmond, Madame Merle held—see that he had been brought up by a woman; though, to do him justice, one would suppose it had been by a more sensible woman than the American Corinne,* as Mrs Osmond had liked to be called. She had brought her children to Italy after her husband's death, and Mrs Touchett remembered her during the year that followed her arrival. She thought her a horrible snob; but this was an irregularity of judgement on Mrs Touchett's part, for she, like Mrs Osmond, approved of political marriages. The Countess was very good company and not really the featherhead she seemed; all one had to do with her was to observe the simple condition of not believing a word she said. Madame Merle had always made the best of her for her brother's sake; he appreciated any kindness shown to Amy, because (if it had to be confessed for him) he rather felt she let down their common name. Naturally he couldn't like her style, her shrillness, her egotism, her violations of taste and above all of truth: she acted badly on his nerves, she was not *his* sort of woman. What was his sort of woman? Oh, the very opposite of the Countess, a woman to whom the truth should be habitually sacred. Isabel was unable to estimate the number of times her visitor had, in half an hour, profaned it: the Countess indeed had given her an impression of rather silly sincerity. She had talked almost exclusively about herself; how much she should like to know Miss Archer; how thankful she should be for a real friend; how base the people in Florence were; how tired she was of the place; how much she should like to live somewhere else—in Paris, in London, in Washington; how impossible it was to get anything nice to wear in Italy except a little old lace; how dear the world was growing everywhere; what a life of suffering and privation she had led. Madame Merle listened with interest to Isabel's account of this passage, but she had not needed it to feel exempt from anxiety. On the whole she was not afraid of the Countess, and she could afford to do what was altogether best—not to appear so.

Isabel had meanwhile another visitor, whom it was not, even behind her back, so easy a matter to patronise. Henrietta Stackpole, who had left Paris after Mrs Touchett's departure for San Remo and had worked her way down, as she said, through the cities of North Italy, reached the banks of the Arno about the middle of May. Madame Merle surveyed her with a single glance, took her in from head to foot, and after a pang of despair determined to endure her. She determined indeed to delight in her. She mightn't be inhaled as a rose, but she might be grasped as a nettle. Madame Merle genially squeezed her into insignificance, and Isabel felt that in foreseeing this liberality she had done justice to her friend's intelligence. Henrietta's arrival had been announced by Mr Bantling, who, coming down from Nice while she was at Venice, and expecting to find her in Florence, which she had not yet reached, called at Palazzo Crescentini to express his disappointment. Henrietta's own advent occurred two days later and produced in Mr Bantling an emotion amply accounted for by the fact that he had not seen her since the termination of the episode at Versailles. The humorous view of his situation was generally taken, but it was uttered only by Ralph Touchett, who, in the privacy of his own apartment, when Bantling smoked a cigar there, indulged in goodness knew what strong comedy on the subject of the all-judging one and her British backer. This gentleman took the joke in perfectly good part and candidly confessed that he regarded the affair as a positive intellectual adventure. He liked Miss Stackpole extremely; he thought she had a wonderful head on her shoulders, and found great comfort in the society of a woman who was not perpetually thinking about what would be said and how what she did, how what *they* did—and they had done things!—would look. Miss Stackpole never cared how anything looked, and, if she didn't care, pray why should he? But his curiosity had been roused; he wanted awfully to see if she ever *would* care. He was prepared to go as far as she—he didn't see why he should break down first.

Henrietta showed no signs of breaking down. Her prospects had brightened on her leaving England, and she was now in the full enjoyment of her copious resources. She had indeed been obliged to sacrifice her hopes with regard to the inner life; the social question, on the Continent, bristled with difficulties even more numerous than those she had encountered in England. But on the Continent there was the outer life, which was palpable and visible at every turn, and more easily convertible to literary uses than the customs of those opaque islanders. Out of doors in foreign lands, as she ingeniously remarked, one seemed to see the right side of the tapestry; out of doors in England one seemed to see the wrong side, which gave one no notion of the figure. The admission costs her historian a pang, but Henrietta, despairing of more occult things, was now paying much attention to the outer life. She had been studying it for two months at Venice, from which city she sent to the *Interviewer* a conscientious account of the gondolas, the Piazza, the Bridge of Sighs, the pigeons and the young boatman who chanted Tasso. The *Interviewer* was perhaps disappointed, but Henrietta was at least seeing Europe. Her present purpose was to get down to Rome before the malaria* should come on—she apparently supposed that it began on a fixed day; and with this design she was to spend at present but few days in Florence. Mr Bantling was to go with her to Rome, and she pointed out to Isabel that as he had been there before, as he was a military man and as he had a classical education—he had been bred at Eton, where they study nothing but Latin and Whyte-Melville,* said Miss Stackpole—he would be a most useful companion in the city of the Cæsars. At this juncture Ralph had the happy idea of proposing to Isabel that she also, under his own escort, should make a pilgrimage to Rome. She expected to pass a portion of the next winter there—that was very well; but meantime there was no harm in surveying the field. There were ten days left of the beautiful month of May—the most precious month of all to the true Rome-lover. Isabel would become a Rome-lover; that was a foregone conclusion. She was provided with a trusty companion of her own sex, whose society, thanks to the fact of other calls on this lady's attention, would probably not be oppressive. Madame Merle would remain with Mrs Touchett; she had left Rome for the summer and wouldn't care to return. She professed herself delighted to be left at peace in Florence; she had locked up her apartment and sent her cook home to Palestrina. She urged Isabel, however, to assent to Ralph's proposal, and assured her that a good introduction to Rome was not a thing to be despised. Isabel in truth needed no urging, and the party of four arranged its little journey. Mrs Touchett, on this occasion, had resigned herself to the absence of a duenna; we have seen that she now inclined to the belief that her niece should stand alone. One of Isabel's preparations consisted of her seeing Gilbert Osmond before she started and mentioning her intention to him.

'I should like to be in Rome with you,' he commented. 'I should like to see you on that wonderful ground.'

She scarcely faltered. 'You might come then.'

'But you'll have a lot of people with you.'

'Ah,' Isabel admitted, 'of course I shall not be alone.'

For a moment he said nothing more. 'You'll like it,' he went on at last. 'They've spoiled it, but you'll rave about it.'

'Ought I to dislike it because, poor old dear—the Niobe of Nations,* you know—it has been spoiled?' she asked.

'No, I think not. It has been spoiled so often,' he smiled. 'If I were to go, what should I do with my little girl?'

'Can't you leave her at the villa?'

'I don't know that I like that—though there's a very good old woman who looks after her. I can't afford a governess.'

'Bring her with you then,' said Isabel promptly.

Mr Osmond looked grave. 'She has been in Rome all winter, at her convent; and she's too young to make journeys of pleasure.'

'You don't like bringing her forward?' Isabel enquired.

'No, I think young girls should be kept out of the world.'

'I was brought up on a different system.'

'You? Oh, with you it succeeded, because you—you were exceptional.'

'I don't see why,' said Isabel, who, however, was not sure there was not some truth in the speech.

Mr Osmond didn't explain; he simply went on: 'If I thought it would make her resemble you to join a social group in Rome I'd take her there to-morrow.'

'Don't make her resemble me,' said Isabel. 'Keep her like herself.'

'I might send her to my sister,' Mr Osmond observed. He had almost the air of asking advice; he seemed to like to talk over his domestic matters with Miss Archer.

'Yes,' she concurred; 'I think that wouldn't do much towards making her resemble me!'

After she had left Florence Gilbert Osmond met Madame Merle at the Countess Gemini's. There were other people present; the Countess's drawing-room was usually well filled, and the talk had been general, but after a while Osmond left his place and came and sat on an ottoman half-behind, half-beside Madame Merle's chair. 'She wants me to go to Rome with her,' he remarked in a low voice.

'To go with her?'

'To be there while she's there. She proposed it.'

'I suppose you mean that you proposed it and she assented.'

'Of course I gave her a chance. But she's encouraging—she's very encouraging.'

'I rejoice to hear it—but don't cry victory too soon. Of course you'll go to Rome.'

'Ah,' said Osmond, 'it makes one work, this idea of yours!'

'Don't pretend you don't enjoy it—you're very ungrateful. You've not been so well occupied these many years.'

'The way you take it's beautiful,' said Osmond. 'I ought to be grateful for that.'

'Not too much so, however,' Madame Merle answered. She talked with her usual smile, leaning back in her chair and looking round the room. 'You've made a very good impression, and I've seen for myself that you've received one. You've not come to Mrs Touchett's seven times to oblige me.'

'The girl's not disagreeable,' Osmond quietly conceded.

Madame Merle dropped her eye on him a moment, during which her lips closed with a certain firmness. 'Is that all you can find to say about that fine creature?'

'All? Isn't it enough? Of how many people have you heard me say more?'

She made no answer to this, but still presented her talkative grace to the room. 'You're unfathomable,' she murmured at last. 'I'm frightened at the abyss into which I shall have cast her.'

He took it almost gaily. 'You can't draw back—you've gone too far.'

'Very good; but you must do the rest yourself.'

'I shall do it,' said Gilbert Osmond.

Madame Merle remained silent and he changed his place again; but when she rose to go he also took leave. Mrs Touchett's victoria was awaiting her guest in the court, and after he had helped his friend into it he stood there detaining her. 'You're very indiscreet,' she said rather wearily; 'you shouldn't have moved when I did.'

He had taken off his hat; he passed his hand over his forehead. 'I always forget; I'm out of the habit.'

'You're quite unfathomable,' she repeated, glancing up at the windows of the house, a modern structure in the new part of the town.

He paid no heed to this remark, but spoke in his own sense. 'She's really very charming. I've scarcely known any one more graceful.'

'It does me good to hear you say that. The better you like her the better for me.'

'I like her very much. She's all you described her, and into the bargain capable, I feel, of great devotion. She has only one fault.'

'What's that?'

'Too many ideas.'

'I warned you she was clever.'

'Fortunately they're very bad ones,' said Osmond.

'Why is that fortunate?'

'*Dame*,* if they must be sacrificed!'

Madame Merle leaned back, looking straight before her; then she spoke to the coachman. But her friend again detained her. 'If I go to Rome what shall I do with Pansy?'

'I'll go and see her,' said Madame Merle.

XXVII

I MAY not attempt to report in its fulness our young woman's response to the deep appeal of Rome, to analyse her feelings as she trod the pavement of the Forum or to number her pulsations as she crossed the threshold of Saint Peter's. It is enough to say that her impression was such as might have been expected of a person of her freshness and her eagerness. She had always been fond of history, and here was history in the stones of the street and the atoms of the sunshine. She had an imagination that kindled at the mention of great deeds, and wherever she turned some great deed had been acted. These things strongly moved her, but moved her all inwardly. It seemed to her companions that she talked less than usual, and Ralph Touchett, when he appeared to be looking listlessly and awkwardly over her head, was really dropping on her an intensity of observation. By her own measure she was very happy; she would even have been willing to take these hours for the happiest she was ever to know. The sense of the terrible human past was heavy to her, but that of something altogether contemporary would suddenly give it wings that it could wave in the blue. Her consciousness was so mixed that she scarcely knew where the different parts of it would lead her, and she went about in a repressed ecstasy of contemplation, seeing often in the things she looked at a great deal more than was there, and yet not seeing many of the items enumerated in her Murray.* Rome, as Ralph said, confessed to the psychological moment. The herd of reëchoing tourists had departed and most of the solemn places had relapsed into solemnity. The sky was a blaze of blue, and the plash of the fountains in their mossy niches had lost its chill and doubled its music. On the corners of the warm, bright streets one stumbled on bundles of flowers. Our friends had gone one afternoon—it was the third of their stay—to look at the latest excavations in the Forum, these labours having been for some time previous largely extended. They had descended from the modern street to the level of the Sacred Way, along which they wandered with a reverence of step which was not the same on the part of each. Henrietta Stackpole was struck with the fact that ancient Rome had been paved a good deal like New York, and even found an analogy between the deep chariot-ruts traceable in the antique street and the overjangled iron grooves which express the intensity of American life. The sun had begun to sink, the air was a golden haze, and the long shadows of broken column and vague pedestal leaned across the field of ruin. Henrietta wandered away with Mr Bantling, whom it was apparently delightful to her to hear speak of Julius Cæsar as a 'cheeky old boy,' and Ralph addressed such elucidations as he was prepared to offer to the attentive ear of our heroine. One of the humble archæologists who hover about the place had put himself at the disposal of the two, and repeated his lesson with a fluency which the decline of the season had done nothing to impair. A process of digging was on view in a remote corner of the Forum, and he presently remarked that if it should please the *signori* to go and watch it a little they might see something of interest. The proposal commended itself more to Ralph than to Isabel, weary with much wandering; so that she admonished her companion to satisfy his curiosity while she patiently awaited his return. The hour and the place were much to her taste—she should enjoy being briefly alone. Ralph accordingly went off with the cicerone while Isabel sat down on a prostrate column near the foundations of the Capitol. She wanted a short solitude, but she was not long to enjoy it. Keen as was her interest in the rugged relics of the Roman past that lay scattered about her and in which the corrosion of centuries had still left so much of individual life, her thoughts, after resting a while on these things, had wandered, by a concatenation of stages it might require some subtlety to trace, to regions and objects charged with a more active appeal. From the Roman past to Isabel Archer's future was a long stride, but her imagination had taken it in a single flight and now hovered in slow circles over the nearer and richer field. She was so absorbed in her thoughts, as she bent her eyes upon a row of cracked but not dislocated slabs covering the ground at her feet, that she had not heard the sound of approaching footsteps before a shadow was thrown across the line of her vision. She looked up and saw a gentleman—a gentleman who was not Ralph come back to say that the excavations were a bore. This personage was startled as she was startled; he stood there baring his head to her perceptibly pale surprise.

'Lord Warburton!' Isabel exclaimed as she rose.

'I had no idea it was you. I turned that corner and came upon you.'

She looked about her to explain. 'I'm alone, but my companions have just left me. My cousin's gone to look at the work over there.'

'Ah yes; I see.' And Lord Warburton's eyes wandered vaguely in the direction she had indicated. He stood firmly before her now; he had recovered his balance and seemed to wish to show it, though very kindly. 'Don't let me disturb you,' he went on, looking at her dejected pillar. 'I'm afraid you're tired.'

'Yes, I'm rather tired.' She hesitated a moment, but sat down again. 'Don't let me interrupt *you*,' she added.

'Oh dear, I'm quite alone, I've nothing on earth to do, I had no idea you were in Rome. I've just come from the East. I'm only passing through.'

'You've been making a long journey,'* said Isabel, who had learned from Ralph that Lord Warburton was absent from England.

'Yes, I came abroad for six months—soon after I saw you last. I've been in Turkey and Asia Minor; I came the other day from Athens.' He managed not to be awkward, but he wasn't easy, and after a longer look at the girl he came down to nature. 'Do you wish me to leave you, or will you let me stay a little?'

She took it all humanely. 'I don't wish you to leave me, Lord Warburton; I'm very glad to see you.'

'Thank you for saying that. May I sit down?'

The fluted shaft on which she had taken her seat would have afforded a resting-place to several persons, and there was plenty of room even for a highly-developed Englishman. This fine specimen of that great class seated himself near our young lady, and in the course of five minutes he had asked her several questions, taken rather at random and to which, as he put some of them twice over, he apparently somewhat missed catching the answer; had given her too some information about himself which was not wasted upon her calmer feminine sense. He repeated more than once that he had not expected to meet her, and it was evident that the encounter touched him in a way that would have made preparation advisable. He began abruptly to pass from the impunity of things to their solemnity, and from their being delightful to their being impossible. He was splendidly sunburnt; even his multitudinous beard had been burnished by the fire of Asia. He was dressed in the loose-fitting, heterogeneous garments in which the English traveller in foreign lands is wont to consult his comfort and affirm his nationality; and with his pleasant steady eyes, his bronzed complexion, fresh beneath its seasoning, his manly figure, his minimising manner and his general air of being a gentleman and an explorer, he was such a representative of the British race as need not in any clime have been disavowed by those who have a kindness for it. Isabel noted these things and was glad she had always liked him. He had kept, evidently in spite of shocks, every one of his merits—properties these partaking of the essence of great decent houses, as one might put it; resembling their innermost fixtures and ornaments, not subject to vulgar shifting and removable only by some whole break-up. They talked of the matters naturally in order; her uncle's death, Ralph's state of health, the way she had passed her winter, her visit to Rome, her return to Florence, her plans for the summer, the hotel she was staying at; and then of Lord Warburton's own adventures, movements, intentions, impressions and present domicile. At last there was a silence, and it said so much more than either had said that it scarce needed his final words. 'I've written to you several times.'

'Written to me? I've never had your letters.'

'I never sent them. I burned them up.'

'Ah,' laughed Isabel, 'it was better that you should do that than I!'

'I thought you wouldn't care for them,' he went on with a simplicity that touched her. 'It seemed to me that after all I had no right to trouble you with letters.'

'I should have been very glad to have news of you. You know how I hoped that—that—' But she stopped; there would be such a flatness in the utterance of her thought.

'I know what you're going to say. You hoped we should always remain good friends.' This formula, as Lord Warburton uttered it, was certainly flat enough; but then he was interested in making it appear so.

She found herself reduced simply to 'Please don't talk of all that'; a speech which hardly struck her as improvement on the other.

'It's a small consolation to allow me!' her companion exclaimed with force.

'I can't pretend to console you,' said the girl, who, all still as she sat there, threw herself back with a sort of inward triumph on the answer that had satisfied him so little six months before. He was pleasant, he was powerful, he was gallant; there was no better man than he. But her answer remained.

'It's very well you don't try to console me; it wouldn't be in your power,' she heard him say through the medium of her strange elation.

'I hoped we should meet again, because I had no fear you would attempt to make me feel I had wronged you. But when you do that—the pain's greater than the pleasure.' And she got up with a small conscious majesty, looking for her companions.

'I don't want to make you feel that; of course I can't say that. I only just want you to know one or two things—in fairness to myself, as it were. I won't return to the subject again. I felt very strongly what I expressed to you last year; I couldn't think of anything else. I tried to forget—energetically, systematically. I tried to take an interest in somebody else. I tell you this because I want you to know I did my duty. I didn't succeed. It was for the same purpose I went abroad—as far away as possible. They say travelling distracts the mind, but it didn't distract mine. I've thought of you perpetually, ever since I last saw you. I'm exactly the same. I love you just as much, and everything I said to you then is just as true. This instant at which I speak to you shows me again exactly how, to my great misfortune, you just insuperably *charm* me. There—I can't say less. I don't mean, however, to insist; it's only for a moment. I may add that when I came upon you a few minutes since, without the smallest idea of seeing you, I was, upon my honour, in the very act of wishing I knew where you were.' He had recovered his self-control, and while he spoke it became complete. He might have been addressing a small committee—making all quietly and clearly a statement of importance; aided by an occasional look at a paper of notes concealed in his hat, which he had not again put on. And the committee, assuredly, would have felt the point proved.

'I've often thought of you, Lord Warburton,' Isabel answered. 'You may be sure I shall always do that.' And she added in a tone of which she tried to keep up the kindness and keep down the meaning: 'There's no harm in that on either side.'

They walked along together, and she was prompt to ask about his sisters and request him to let them know she had done so. He made for the moment no further reference to their great question, but dipped again into shallower and safer waters. But he wished to know when she was to leave Rome, and on her mentioning the limit of her stay declared he was glad it was still so distant.

'Why do you say that if you yourself are only passing through?' she enquired with some anxiety.

'Ah, when I said I was passing through I didn't mean that one would treat Rome as if it were Clapham Junction.* To pass through Rome is to stop a week or two.'

'Say frankly that you mean to stay as long as I do!'

His flushed smile, for a little, seemed to sound her. 'You won't like that. You're afraid you'll see too much of me.'

'It doesn't matter what I like. I certainly can't expect you to leave this delightful place on my account. But I confess I'm afraid of you.'

'Afraid I'll begin again? I promise to be very careful.'

They had gradually stopped and they stood a moment face to face. 'Poor Lord Warburton!' she said with a compassion intended to be good for both of them.

'Poor Lord Warburton indeed! But I'll be careful.'

'You may be unhappy, but you shall not make *me* so. That I can't allow.'

'If I believed I could make you unhappy I think I should try it.' At this she walked in advance and he also proceeded. 'I'll never say a word to displease you.'

'Very good. If you do, our friendship's at an end.'

'Perhaps some day—after a while—you'll give me leave.'

'Give you leave to make me unhappy?'

He hesitated. 'To tell you again—' But he checked himself. 'I'll keep it down. I'll keep it down always.'

Ralph Touchett had been joined in his visit to the excavation by Miss Stackpole and her attendant, and these three now emerged from among the mounds of earth and stone collected round the aperture and came into sight of Isabel and her companion. Poor Ralph hailed his friend with joy qualified by wonder, and Henrietta exclaimed in a high voice 'Gracious, there's that lord!' Ralph and his English neighbour greeted with the austerity with which, after long separations, English neighbours greet, and Miss Stackpole rested her large intellectual gaze upon the sunburnt traveller. But she soon established her relation to the crisis. 'I don't suppose you remember me, sir.'

'Indeed I do remember you,' said Lord Warburton. 'I asked you to come and see me, and you never came.'

'I don't go everywhere I'm asked,' Miss Stackpole answered coldly.

'Ah well, I won't ask you again,' laughed the master of Lockleigh.

'If you do I'll go; so be sure!'

Lord Warburton, for all his hilarity, seemed sure enough. Mr Bantling had stood by without claiming a recognition, but he now took occasion to nod to his lordship, who answered him with a friendly 'Oh, you here, Bantling?' and a handshake.

'Well,' said Henrietta, 'I didn't know you knew him!'

'I guess you don't know every one I know,' Mr Bantling rejoined facetiously.

'I thought that when an Englishman knew a lord he always told you.'

'Ah, I'm afraid Bantling was ashamed of me,' Lord Warburton laughed again. Isabel took pleasure in that note; she gave a small sigh of relief as they kept their course homeward.

The next day was Sunday; she spent her morning over two long letters—one to her sister Lily, the other to Madame Merle; but in neither of these epistles did she mention the fact that a rejected suitor had threatened her with another appeal. Of a Sunday afternoon all good Romans (and the best Romans are often the northern barbarians) follow the custom of going to vespers at Saint Peter's; and it had been agreed among our friends that they would drive together to the great church. After lunch, an hour before the carriage came, Lord Warburton presented himself at the Hôtel de Paris and paid a visit to the two ladies, Ralph Touchett and Mr Bantling having gone out together. The visitor seemed to have wished to give Isabel a proof of his intention to keep the promise made her the evening before; he was both discreet and frank—not even dumbly importunate or remotely intense. He thus left her to judge what a mere good friend he could be. He talked about his travels, about Persia, about Turkey, and when Miss Stackpole asked him whether it would 'pay' for her to visit those countries assured her they offered a great field to female enterprise. Isabel did him justice, but she wondered what his purpose was and what he expected to gain even by proving the superior strain of his sincerity. If he expected to melt her by showing what a good fellow he was, he might spare himself the trouble. She knew the superior strain of everything about him, and nothing he could now do was required to light the view. Moreover his being in Rome at all affected her as a complication of the wrong sort—she liked so complications of the right. Nevertheless, when, on bringing his call to a close, he said he too should be at Saint Peter's and should look out for her and her friends, she was obliged to reply that he must follow his convenience.

In the church, as she strolled over its tesselated acres, he was the first person she encountered. She had not been one of the superior tourists who are 'disappointed' in Saint Peter's and find it smaller than its fame; the first time she passed beneath the huge leathern curtain that strains and bangs at the entrance, the first time she found herself beneath the far-arching dome and saw the light drizzle down through the air thickened with incense and with the reflections of marble and gilt, of mosaic and bronze, her conception of greatness rose and dizzily rose. After this it never lacked space to soar. She gazed and wondered like a child or a peasant, she paid her silent tribute to the seated sublime. Lord Warburton walked beside her and talked of Saint Sophia of Constantinople; she feared for instance that he would end by calling attention to his exemplary conduct. The service had not yet begun, but at Saint Peter's there is much to observe, and as there is something almost profane in the vastness of the place, which seems meant as much for physical as for spiritual exercise, the different figures and groups, the mingled worshippers and spectators, may follow their various intentions without conflict or scandal. In that splendid immensity individual indiscretion carries but a short distance. Isabel and her companions, however, were guilty of none; for though Henrietta was obliged in candour to declare that Michael Angelo's dome suffered by comparison with that of the Capitol at Washington, she addressed her protest chiefly to Mr Bantling's ear and reserved it in its more accentuated form for the columns of the *Interviewer*. Isabel made the circuit of the church with his lordship, and as they drew near the choir on the left of the entrance the voices of the Pope's singers were borne to them over the heads of the large number of persons clustered outside the doors. They paused a while on the skirts of this crowd, composed in equal measure of Roman cockneys and inquisitive strangers, and while they stood there the sacred concert went forward. Ralph, with Henrietta and Mr Bantling, was apparently within, where Isabel, looking beyond the dense group in front of her, saw the afternoon light, silvered by clouds of incense that seemed to mingle with the splendid chant, slope through the embossed recesses of high windows. After a while the singing stopped and then Lord Warburton seemed disposed to move off with her. Isabel could only accompany him; whereupon she found herself confronted with Gilbert Osmond, who appeared to have been standing at a short distance behind her. He now approached with all the forms—he appeared to have multiplied them on this occasion to suit the place.

'So you decided to come?' she said as she put out her hand.

'Yes, I came last night and called this afternoon at your hotel. They told me you had come here, and I looked about for you.'

'The others are inside,' she decided to say.

'I didn't come for the others,' he promptly returned.

She looked away; Lord Warburton was watching them; perhaps he had heard this. Suddenly she remembered it to be just what he had said to her the morning he came to Gardencourt to ask her to marry him. Mr Osmond's words had brought the colour to her cheek, and this reminiscence had not the effect of dispelling it. She repaired any betrayal by mentioning to each companion the name of the other, and fortunately at this moment Mr Bantling emerged from the choir, cleaving the crowd with British valour and followed by Miss Stackpole and Ralph Touchett. I say fortunately, but this is perhaps a superficial view of the matter; since on perceiving the gentleman from Florence Ralph Touchett appeared to take the case as not committing him to joy. He didn't hang back, however, from civility, and presently observed to Isabel, with due benevolence, that she would soon have all her friends about her. Miss Stackpole had met Mr Osmond in Florence, but she had already found occasion to say to Isabel that she liked him no better than her other admirers—than Mr Touchett and Lord Warburton, and even than little Mr Rosier in Paris. 'I don't know what it's in you,' she had been pleased to remark, 'but for a nice girl you do attract the most unnatural people. Mr Goodwood's the only one I've any respect for, and he's just the one you don't appreciate.'

'What's your opinion of Saint Peter's?' Mr Osmond was meanwhile enquiring of our young lady.

'It's very large and very bright,' she contented herself with replying.

'It's too large; it makes one feel like an atom.'

'Isn't that the right way to feel in the greatest of human temples?' she asked with rather a liking for her phrase.

'I suppose it's the right way to feel everywhere, when one *is* nobody. But I like it in a church as little as anywhere else.'

'You ought indeed to be a Pope!' Isabel exclaimed, remembering something he had referred to in Florence.

'Ah, I should have enjoyed that!' said Gilbert Osmond.

Lord Warburton meanwhile had joined Ralph Touchett, and the two strolled away together. 'Who's the fellow speaking to Miss Archer?' his lordship demanded.

'His name's Gilbert Osmond—he lives in Florence,' Ralph said.

'What is he besides?'

'Nothing at all. Oh yes, he's an American; but one forgets that—he's so little of one.'

'Has he known Miss Archer long?'

'Three or four weeks.'

'Does she like him?'

'She's trying to find out.'

'And will she?'

'Find out—?' Ralph asked.

'Will she like him?'

'Do you mean will she accept him?'

'Yes,' said Lord Warburton after an instant; 'I suppose that's what I horribly mean.'

'Perhaps not if one does nothing to prevent it,' Ralph replied.

His lordship stared a moment, but apprehended. 'Then we must be perfectly quiet?'

'As quiet as the grave. And only on the chance!' Ralph added.

'The chance she may?'

'The chance she may not?'

Lord Warburton took this at first in silence, but he spoke again. 'Is he awfully clever?'

'Awfully,' said Ralph.

His companion thought. 'And what else?'

'What more do you want?' Ralph groaned.

'Do you mean what more does *she?*'

Ralph took him by the arm to turn him: they had to rejoin the others. 'She wants nothing that *we* can give her.'

'Ah well, if she won't have You—!' said his lordship handsomely as they went.

XXVIII

On the morrow, in the evening, Lord Warburton went again to see his friends at their hotel, and at this establishment he learned that they had gone to the opera. He drove to the opera with the idea of paying them a visit in their box after the easy Italian fashion; and when he had obtained his admittance—it was one of the secondary theatres—looked about the large, bare, ill-lighted house. An act had just terminated and he was at liberty to pursue his quest. After scanning two or three tiers of boxes he perceived in one of the largest of these receptacles a lady whom he easily recognised. Miss Archer was seated facing the stage and partly screened by the curtain of the box; and beside her, leaning back in his chair, was Mr Gilbert Osmond. They appeared to have the place to themselves, and Warburton supposed their companions had taken advantage of the recess to enjoy the relative coolness of the lobby. He stood a while with his eyes on the interesting pair; he asked himself if he should go up and interrupt the harmony. At last he judged that Isabel had seen him, and this accident determined him. There should be no marked holding off. He took his way to the upper regions and on the staircase met Ralph Touchett slowly descending, his hat at the inclination of ennui and his hands where they usually were.

'I saw you below a moment since and was going down to you. I feel lonely and want company,' was Ralph's greeting.

'You've some that's very good which you've yet deserted.'

'Do you mean my cousin? Oh, she has a visitor and doesn't want me. Then Miss Stackpole and Bantling have gone out to a café to eat an ice—Miss Stackpole delights in an ice. I didn't think *they* wanted me either. The opera's very bad; the women look like laundresses and sing like peacocks. I feel very low.'

'You had better go home,' Lord Warburton said without affectation.

'And leave my young lady in this sad place? Ah no, I must watch over her.'

'She seems to have plenty of friends.'

'Yes, that's why I must watch,' said Ralph with the same large mock-melancholy.

'If she doesn't want you it's probable she doesn't want me.'

'No, you're different. Go to the box and stay there while I walk about.'

Lord Warburton went to the box, where Isabel's welcome was as to a friend so honourably old that he vaguely asked himself what queer temporal province she was annexing. He exchanged greetings with Mr Osmond, to whom he had been introduced the day before and who, after he came in, sat blandly apart and silent, as if repudiating competence in the subjects of allusion now probable. It struck her second visitor that Miss Archer had, in operatic conditions, a radiance, even a slight exaltation; as she was, however, at all times a keenly-glancing, quickly-moving, completely animated young woman, he may have been mistaken on this point. Her talk with him moreover pointed to presence of mind; it expressed a kindness so ingenious and deliberate as to indicate that she was in undisturbed possession of her faculties. Poor Lord Warburton had moments of bewilderment. She had discouraged him, formally, as much as a woman could; what business had she then with such arts and such felicities, above all with such tones of reparation—preparation? Her voice had tricks of sweetness, but why play them on *him?* The others came back; the bare, familiar, trivial opera began again. The box was large, and there was room for him to remain if he would sit a little behind and in the dark. He did so for half an hour, while Mr Osmond remained in front, leaning forward, his elbows on his knees, just behind Isabel. Lord Warburton heard nothing, and from his gloomy corner saw nothing but the clear profile of this young lady defined against the dim illumination of the house. When there was another interval no one moved. Mr Osmond talked to Isabel, and Lord Warburton kept his corner. He did so but for a short time, however; after which he got up and bade good-night to the ladies. Isabel said nothing to detain him, but it didn't prevent his being puzzled again. Why should she mark so one of his values—quite the wrong one—when she would have nothing to do with another, which was quite the right? He was angry with himself for being puzzled, and then angry for being angry. Verdi's music did little to comfort him, and he left the theatre and walked homeward, without knowing his way, through the tortuous, tragic streets of Rome, where heavier sorrows than his had been carried under the stars.

'What's the character of that gentleman?' Osmond asked of Isabel after he had retired.

'Irreproachable—don't you see it?'

'He owns about half England; that's his character,' Henrietta remarked. 'That's what they call a free country!'

'Ah, he's a great proprietor? Happy man!' said Gilbert Osmond.

'Do you call that happiness—the ownership of wretched human beings?' cried Miss Stackpole. 'He owns his tenants and has thousands of them. It's pleasant to own something, but inanimate objects are enough for me. I don't insist on flesh and blood and minds and consciences.'

'It seems to me you own a human being or two,' Mr Bantling suggested jocosely. 'I wonder if Warburton orders his tenants about as you do me.'

'Lord Warburton's a great radical,' Isabel said. 'He has very advanced opinions.'

'He has very advanced stone walls. His park's enclosed by a gigantic iron fence, some thirty miles round,' Henrietta announced for the information of Mr Osmond. 'I should like him to converse with a few of our Boston radicals.'

'Don't they approve of iron fences?' asked Mr Bantling.

'Only to shut up wicked conservatives. I always feel as if I were talking to *you* over something with a neat top-finish of broken glass.'

'Do you know him well, this unreformed reformer?' Osmond went on, questioning Isabel.

'Well enough for all the use I have for him.'

'And how much of a use is that?'

'Well, I like to like him.'

' "Liking to like"—why, it makes a passion!' said Osmond.

'No'—she considered—'keep that for liking to *dis*like.'

'Do you wish to provoke me then,' Osmond laughed, 'to a passion for *him?*'

She said nothing for a moment, but then met the light question with a disproportionate gravity. 'No, Mr Osmond; I don't think I should ever dare to provoke you. Lord Warburton, at any rate,' she more easily added, 'is a very nice man.'

'Of great ability?' her friend enquired.

'Of excellent ability, and as good as he looks.'

'As good as he's good-looking do you mean? He's very good-looking. How detestably fortunate!—to be a great English magnate, to be clever and handsome into the bargain, and, by way of finishing off, to enjoy your high favour! That's a man I could envy.'

Isabel considered him with interest. 'You seem to me to be always envying some one. Yesterday it was the Pope; to-day it's poor Lord Warburton.'

'My envy's not dangerous; it wouldn't hurt a mouse. I don't want to destroy the people—I only want to *be* them. You see it would destroy only myself.'

'You'd like to be the Pope?' said Isabel.

'I should love it—but I should have gone in for it earlier. But why'—Osmond reverted—'do you speak of your friend as poor?'

'Women—when they are very, very good—sometimes pity men after they've hurt them; that's their great way of showing kindness,' said Ralph, joining in the conversation for the first time and with a cynicism so transparently ingenious as to be virtually innocent.

'Pray, have I hurt Lord Warburton?' Isabel asked, raising her eyebrows as if the idea were perfectly fresh.

'It serves him right if you have,' said Henrietta while the curtain rose for the ballet.

Isabel saw no more of her attributive victim for the next twenty-four hours, but on the second day after the visit to the opera she encountered him in the gallery of the Capitol, where he stood before the lion of the collection, the statue of the Dying Gladiator.* She had come in with her companions, among whom, on this occasion again, Gilbert Osmond had his place, and the party, having ascended the staircase, entered the first and finest of the rooms. Lord Warburton addressed her alertly enough, but said in a moment that he was leaving the gallery. 'And I'm leaving Rome,' he added. 'I must bid you good-bye.' Isabel, inconsequently enough, was now sorry to hear it. This was perhaps because she had ceased to be afraid of his renewing his suit; she was thinking of something else. She was on the point of naming her regret, but she checked herself and simply wished him a happy journey; which made him look at her rather unlightedly. 'I'm afraid you'll think me very "volatile." I told you the other day I wanted so much to stop.'

'Oh no; you could easily change your mind.'

'That's what I have done.'

'*Bon voyage* then.'

'You're in a great hurry to get rid of me,' said his lordship quite dismally.

'Not in the least. But I hate partings.'

'You don't care what I do,' he went on pitifully.

Isabel looked at him a moment. 'Ah,' she said, 'you're not keeping your promise!'

He coloured like a boy of fifteen. 'If I'm not, then it's because I can't; and that's why I'm going.'

'Good-bye then.'

'Good-bye.' He lingered still, however. 'When shall I see you again?'

Isabel hesitated, but soon, as if she had had a happy inspiration: 'Some day after you're married.'

'That will never be. It will be after you are.'

'That will do as well,' she smiled.

'Yes, quite as well. Good-bye.'

They shook hands, and he left her alone in the glorious room, among the shining antique marbles. She sat down in the centre of the circle of these presences, regarding them vaguely, resting her eyes on their beautiful blank faces; listening, as it were, to their eternal silence. It is impossible, in Rome at least, to look long at a great company of Greek sculptures without feeling the effect of their noble quietude; which, as with a high door closed for the ceremony, slowly drops on the spirit the large white mantle of peace. I say in Rome especially, because the Roman air is an exquisite medium for such impressions. The golden sunshine mingles with them, the deep stillness of the past, so vivid yet, though it is nothing but a void full of names, seems to throw a solemn spell upon them. The blinds were partly closed in the windows of the Capitol, and a clear, warm shadow rested on the figures and made them more mildly human. Isabel sat there a long time, under the charm of their motionless grace, wondering to what, of their experience, their absent eyes were open, and how, to our ears, their alien lips would sound. The dark red walls of the room threw them into relief; the polished marble floor reflected their beauty. She had seen them all before, but her enjoyment repeated itself, and it was all the greater because she was glad again, for the time, to be alone. At last, however, her attention lapsed, drawn off by a deeper tide of life. An occasional tourist came in, stopped and stared a moment at the Dying Gladiator, and then passed out of the other door, creaking over the smooth pavement. At the end of half an hour Gilbert Osmond reappeared, apparently in advance of his companions. He strolled toward her slowly, with his hands behind him and his usual enquiring, yet not quite appealing smile. 'I'm surprised to find you alone, I thought you had company.'

'So I have—the best.' And she glanced at the Antinous and the Faun.*

'Do you call them better company than an English peer?'

'Ah, my English peer left me some time ago.' She got up, speaking with intention a little dryly.

Mr Osmond noted her dryness, which contributed for him to the interest of his question. 'I'm afraid that what I heard the other evening is true: you're rather cruel to that nobleman.'

Isabel looked a moment at the vanquished Gladiator. 'It's not true. I'm scrupulously kind.'

'That's exactly what I mean!' Gilbert Osmond returned, and with such happy hilarity that his joke needs to be explained. We know that he was fond of originals, of rarities, of the superior and the exquisite; and now that he had seen Lord Warburton, whom he thought a very fine example of his race and order, he perceived a new attraction in the idea of taking to himself a young lady who had qualified herself to figure in his collection of choice objects by declining so noble a hand. Gilbert Osmond had a high appreciation of this particular patriciate; not so much for its distinction, which he thought easily surpassable, as for its solid actuality. He had never forgiven his star for not appointing him to an English dukedom, and he could measure the unexpectedness of such conduct as Isabel's. It would be proper that the woman he might marry should have done something of that sort.

XXIX

RALPH TOUCHETT, in talk with his excellent friend, had rather markedly qualified, as we know, his recognition of Gilbert Osmond's personal merits; but he might really have felt himself illiberal in the light of that gentleman's conduct during the rest of the visit to Rome. Osmond spent a portion of each day with Isabel and her companions, and ended by affecting them as the easiest of men to live with. Who wouldn't have seen that he could command, as it were, both tact and gaiety?—which perhaps was exactly why Ralph had made his old-time look of superficial sociability a reproach to him. Even Isabel's invidious kinsman was obliged to admit that he was just now a delightful associate. His good-humour was imperturbable, his knowledge of the right fact, his production of the right word, as convenient as the friendly flicker of a match for your cigarette. Clearly he was amused—as amused as a man could be who was so little ever surprised, and that made him almost applausive. It was not that his spirits were visibly high—he would never, in the concert of pleasure, touch the big drum by so much as a knuckle: he had a mortal dislike to the high, ragged note, to what he called random ravings. He thought Miss Archer sometimes of too precipitate a readiness. It was pity she had that fault, because if she had not had it she would really have had none; she would have been as smooth to his general need of her as handled ivory to the palm. If he was not personally loud, however, he was deep, and during these closing days of the Roman May he knew a complacency that matched with slow irregular walks under the pines of the Villa Borghese, among the small sweet meadow-flowers and the mossy marbles. He was pleased with everything; he had never before been pleased with so many things at once. Old impressions, old enjoyments, renewed themselves; one evening, going home to his room at the inn, he wrote down a little sonnet to which he prefixed the title of 'Rome Revisited.' A day or two later he showed this piece of correct and ingenious verse to Isabel, explaining to her that it was an Italian fashion to commemorate the occasions of life by a tribute to the muse.

He took his pleasures in general singly: he was too often—he would have admitted that—too sorely aware of something wrong, something ugly; the fertilising dew of a conceivable felicity too seldom descended on his spirit. But at present he was happy—happier than he had perhaps ever been in his life, and the feeling had a large foundation. This was simply the sense of success—the most agreeable emotion of the human heart. Osmond had never had too much of it; in this respect he had the irritation of satiety, as he knew perfectly well and often reminded himself. 'Ah no, I've not been spoiled; certainly I've not been spoiled,' he used inwardly to repeat. 'If I do succeed before I die I shall thoroughly have earned it.' He was too apt to reason as if 'earning' this boon consisted above all of covertly aching for it and might be confined to that exercise. Absolutely void of it, also, his career had not been; he might indeed have suggested to a spectator here and there that he was resting on vague laurels. But his triumphs were, some of them, now too old; others had been too easy. The present one had been less arduous than might have been expected, but had been easy—that is had been rapid—only because he had made an altogether exceptional effort, a greater effort than he had believed it in him to make. The desire to have something or other to show for his 'parts'—to show somehow or other—had been the dream of his youth; but as the years went on the conditions attached to any marked proof of rarity had affected him more and more as gross and detestable; like the swallowing of mugs of beer to advertise what one could 'stand.' If an anonymous drawing on a museum wall had been conscious and watchful it might have known this peculiar pleasure of being at last and all of a sudden identified—as from the hand of a great master—by the so high and so unnoticed fact of style. His 'style' was what the girl had discovered with a little help; and now, beside herself enjoying it, she should publish it to the world without his having any of the trouble. She should do the thing *for* him, and he would not have waited in vain.

Shortly before the time fixed in advance for her departure this young lady received from Mrs Touchett a telegram running as follows: 'Leave Florence 4th June for Bellaggio, and take you if you have not other views. But can't wait if you dawdle in Rome.' The dawdling in Rome was very pleasant, but Isabel had different views, and she let her aunt know she would immediately join her. She told Gilbert Osmond that she had done so, and he replied that, spending many of his summers as well as his winters in Italy, he himself would loiter a little longer in the cool shadow of Saint Peter's. He would not return to Florence for ten days more, and in that time she would have started for Bellaggio. It might be months in this case before he should see her again. This exchange took place in the large decorated sitting-room occupied by our friends at the hotel; it was late in the evening, and Ralph Touchett was to take his cousin back to Florence on the morrow. Osmond had found the girl alone; Miss Stackpole had contracted a friendship with a delightful American family on the fourth floor and had mounted the interminable staircase to pay them a visit. Henrietta contracted friendships, in travelling, with great freedom, and had formed in railway-carriages several that were among her most valued ties. Ralph was making arrangements for the morrow's journey, and Isabel sat alone in a wilderness of yellow upholstery. The chairs and sofas were orange; the walls and windows were draped in purple and gilt. The mirrors, the pictures had great flamboyant frames; the ceiling was deeply vaulted and painted over with naked muses and cherubs. For Osmond the place was ugly to distress; the false colours, the sham splendour were like vulgar, bragging, lying talk. Isabel had taken in hand a volume of Ampère,* presented, on their arrival in Rome, by Ralph; but though she held it in her lap with her finger vaguely kept in the place she was not impatient to pursue her study. A lamp covered with a drooping veil of pink tissue-paper burned on the table beside her and diffused a strange pale rosiness over the scene.

'You say you'll come back; but who knows?' Gilbert Osmond said. 'I think you're much more likely to start on your voyage round the world. You're under no obligation to come back; you can do exactly what you choose; you can roam through space.'

'Well, Italy's a part of space,' Isabel answered. 'I can take it on the way.'

'On the way round the world? No, don't do that. Don't put us in a parenthesis—give us a chapter to ourselves. I don't want to see you on your travels. I'd rather see you when they're over. I should like to see you when you're tired and satiated,' Osmond added in a moment. 'I shall prefer you in that state.'

Isabel, with her eyes bent, fingered the pages of M. Ampère. 'You turn things into ridicule without seeming to do it, though not, I think, without intending it. You've no respect for my travels—you think them ridiculous.'

'Where do you find that?'

She went on in the same tone, fretting the edge of her book with the paper-knife. 'You see my ignorance, my blunders, the way I wander about as if the world belonged to me, simply because—because it has been put into my power to do so. You don't think a woman ought to do that. You think it bold and ungraceful.'

'I think it beautiful,' said Osmond. 'You know my opinions—I've treated you to enough of them. Don't you remember my telling you that one ought to make one's life a work of art? You looked rather shocked at first; but then I told you that it was exactly what you seemed to me to be trying to do with your own.'

She looked up from her book. 'What you despise most in the world is bad, is stupid art.'

'Possibly. But yours seem to me very clear and very good.'

'If I were to go to Japan next winter you would laugh at me,' she went on.

Osmond gave a smile—a keen one, but not a laugh, for the tone of their conversation was not jocose. Isabel had in fact her solemnity; he had seen it before. 'You have an imagination that startles one!'

'That's exactly what I say. You think such an idea absurd.'

'I would give my little finger to go to Japan; it's one of the countries I want most to see. Can't you believe that, with my taste for old lacquer?'

'I haven't a taste for old lacquer to excuse me,' said Isabel.

'You've a better excuse—the means of going. You're quite

wrong in your theory that I laugh at you. I don't know what has put it into your head.'

'It wouldn't be remarkable if you did think it ridiculous that I should have the means to travel when you've not; for you know everything, and I know nothing.'

'The more reason why you should travel and learn,' smiled Osmond. 'Besides,' he added as if it were a point to be made, 'I don't know everything.'

Isabel was not struck with the oddity of his saying this gravely; she was thinking that the pleasantest incident of her life—so it pleased her to qualify these too few days in Rome, which she might musingly have likened to the figure of some small princess of one of the ages of dress overmuffled in a mantle of state and dragging a train that it took pages or historians to hold up—that this felicity was coming to an end. That most of the interest of the time had been owing to Mr Osmond was a reflexion she was not just now at pains to make; she had already done the point abundant justice. But she said to herself that if there were a danger they should never meet again, perhaps after all it would be as well. Happy things don't repeat themselves, and her adventure wore already the changed, the seaward face of some romantic island from which, after feasting on purple grapes, she was putting off while the breeze rose. She might come back to Italy and find him different—this strange man who pleased her just as he was; and it would be better not to come than run the risk of that. But if she was not to come the greater the pity that the chapter was closed; she felt for a moment a pang that touched the source of tears. The sensation kept her silent, and Gilbert Osmond was silent too; he was looking at her. 'Go everywhere,' he said at last, in a low, kind voice; 'do everything; get everything out of life. Be happy—be triumphant.'

'What do you mean by being triumphant?'

'Well, doing what you like.'

'To triumph, then, it seems to me, is to fail! Doing all the vain things one likes is often very tiresome.'

'Exactly,' said Osmond with his quiet quickness. 'As I intimated just now, you'll be tired some day.' He paused a moment and then he went on: 'I don't know whether I had better not wait till then for something I want to say to you.'

'Ah, I can't advise you without knowing what it is. But I'm horrid when I'm tired,' Isabel added with due inconsequence.

'I don't believe that. You're angry, sometimes—that I can believe, though I've never seen it. But I'm sure you're never "cross." '

'Not even when I lose my temper?'

'You don't lose it—you find it, and that must be beautiful.' Osmond spoke with a noble earnestness. 'They must be great moments to see.'

'If I could only find it now!' Isabel nervously cried.

'I'm not afraid; I should fold my arms and admire you. I'm speaking very seriously.' He leaned forward, a hand on each knee; for some moments he bent his eyes on the floor. 'What I wish to say to you,' he went on at last, looking up, 'is that I find I'm in love with you.'

She instantly rose. 'Ah, keep that till I *am* tired!'

'Tired of hearing it from others?' He sat there raising his eyes to her. 'No, you may heed it now or never, as you please. But after all I must say it now.' She had turned away, but in the movement she had stopped herself and dropped her gaze upon him. The two remained a while in this situation, exchanging a long look—the large, conscious look of the critical hours of life. Then he got up and came near her, deeply respectful, as if he were afraid he had been too familiar. 'I'm absolutely in love with you.'

He had repeated the announcement in a tone of almost impersonal discretion, like a man who expected very little from it but who spoke for his own needed relief. The tears came into her eyes: this time they obeyed the sharpness of the pang that suggested to her somehow the slipping of a fine bolt—backward, forward, she couldn't have said which. The words he had uttered made him, as he stood there, beautiful and generous, invested him as with the golden air of early autumn; but, morally speaking, she retreated before them—facing him still—as she had retreated in the other cases before a like encounter. 'Oh don't say that, please,' she answered with an intensity that expressed the dread of having, in this case too, to choose and decide. What made her dread great was precisely the force which, as it would seem, ought to have banished all dread—the sense of something within herself, deep down, that she supposed to be inspired and trustful passion. It was there like a large sum stored in a bank—which there was a terror in having to begin to spend. If she touched it, it would all come out.

'I haven't the idea that it will matter much to you,' said Osmond. 'I've too little to offer you. What I have—it's enough for me; but it's not enough for you. I've neither fortune, nor fame, nor extrinsic advantages of any kind. So I offer nothing. I only tell you because I think it can't offend you, and some day or other it may give you pleasure. It gives me pleasure, I assure you,' he went on, standing there before her, considerately inclined to her, turning his hat, which he had taken up, slowly round with a movement which had all the decent tremor of awkwardness and none of its oddity, and presenting to her his firm, refined, slightly ravaged face. 'It gives me no pain, because it's perfectly simple. For me you'll always be the most important woman in the world.'

Isabel looked at herself in this character—looked intently, thinking she filled it with a certain grace. But what she said was not an expression of any such complacency. 'You don't offend me; but you ought to remember that, without being offended, one may be incommoded, troubled.' 'Incommoded': she heard herself saying that, and it struck her as a ridiculous word. But it was what stupidly came to her.

'I remember perfectly. Of course you're surprised and startled. But if it's nothing but that, it will pass away. And it will perhaps leave something that I may not be ashamed of.'

'I don't know what it may leave. You see at all events that I'm not overwhelmed,' said Isabel with rather a pale smile. 'I'm not too troubled to think. And I think that I'm glad we're separating—that I leave Rome to-morrow.'

'Of course I don't agree with you there.'

'I don't at all *know* you,' she added abruptly; and then she coloured as she heard herself saying what she had said almost a year before to Lord Warburton.

'If you were not going away you'd know me better.'

'I shall do that some other time.'

'I hope so. I'm very easy to know.'

'No, no,' she emphatically answered—'there you're not sincere. You're not easy to know; no one could be less so.'

'Well,' he laughed, 'I said that because I know myself. It may be a boast, but I do.'

'Very likely; but you're very wise.'

'So are you, Miss Archer!' Osmond exclaimed.

'I don't feel so just now. Still, I'm wise enough to think you had better go. Good-night.'

'God bless you!' said Gilbert Osmond, taking the hand which she failed to surrender. After which he added: 'If we meet again you'll find me as you leave me. If we don't I shall be so all the same.'

'Thank you very much. Good-bye.'

There was something quietly firm about Isabel's visitor; he might go of his own movement, but wouldn't be dismissed. 'There's one thing more. I haven't asked anything of you—not even a thought in the future; you must do me that justice. But there's a little service I should like to ask. I shall not return home for several days; Rome's delightful, and it's a good place for a man in my state of mind. Oh, I know you're sorry to leave it; but you're right to do what your aunt wishes.'

'She doesn't even wish it!' Isabel broke out strangely.

Osmond was apparently on the point of saying something that would match these words, but he changed his mind and rejoined simply: 'Ah well, it's proper you should go with her, very proper. Do everything that's proper; I go in for that. Excuse my being so patronising. You say you don't know me, but when you do you'll discover what a worship I have for propriety.'

'You're not conventional?' Isabel gravely asked.

'I like the way you utter that word! No, I'm not conventional: I'm convention itself. You don't understand that?' And he paused a moment, smiling. 'I should like to explain it.' Then with a sudden, quick, bright naturalness, 'Do come back again,' he pleaded. 'There are so many things we might talk about.'

She stood there with lowered eyes. 'What service did you speak of just now?'

'Go and see my little daughter before you leave Florence. She's alone at the villa; I decided not to send her to my sister, who hasn't at all my ideas. Tell her she must love her poor father very much,' said Gilbert Osmond gently.

'It will be a great pleasure to me to go,' Isabel answered. 'I'll tell her what you say. Once more good-bye.'

On this he took a rapid, respectful leave. When he had gone she stood a moment looking about her and seated herself slowly and with an air of deliberation. She sat there till her companions came back, with folded hands, gazing at the ugly carpet. Her agitation—for it had not diminished—was very still, very deep. What had happened was something that for a week past her imagination had been going forward to meet; but here, when it came, she stopped—that sublime principle somehow broke down. The working of this young lady's spirit was strange, and I can only give it to you as I see it, not hoping to make it seem altogether natural. Her imagination, as I say, now hung back: there was a last vague space it couldn't cross—a dusky, uncertain tract which looked ambiguous and even slightly treacherous, like a moorland seen in the winter twilight. But she was to cross it yet.

XXX

SHE returned on the morrow to Florence, under her cousin's escort, and Ralph Touchett, though usually restive under railway discipline, thought very well of the successive hours passed in the train that hurried his companion away from the city now distinguished by Gilbert Osmond's preference—hours that were to form the first stage in a larger scheme of travel. Miss Stackpole had remained behind; she was planning a little trip to Naples, to be carried out with Mr Bantling's aid. Isabel was to have three days in Florence before the 4th of June, the date of Mrs Touchett's departure, and she determined to devote the last of these to her promise to call on Pansy Osmond. Her plan, however, seemed for a moment likely to modify itself in deference to an idea of Madame Merle's. This lady was still at Casa Touchett; but she too was on the point of leaving Florence, her next station being an ancient castle in the mountains of Tuscany, the residence of a noble family of that country, whose acquaintance (she had known them, as she said, 'forever') seemed to Isabel, in the light of certain photographs of their immense crenellated dwelling which her friend was able to show her, a precious privilege. She mentioned to this fortunate woman that Mr Osmond had asked her to take a look at his daughter, but didn't mention that he had also made her a declaration of love.

'*Ah, comme cela se trouve!*'* Madame Merle exclaimed. 'I myself have been thinking it would be a kindness to pay the child a little visit before I go off.'

'We can go together then,' Isabel reasonably said: 'reasonably' because the proposal was not uttered in the spirit of enthusiasm. She had prefigured her small pilgrimage as made in solitude; she should like it better so. She was nevertheless prepared to sacrifice this mystic sentiment to her great consideration for her friend.

That personage finely meditated. 'After all, why should we both go; having, each of us, so much to do during these last hours?'

'Very good; I can easily go alone.'

'I don't know about your going alone—to the house of a handsome bachelor. He has been married—but so long ago!'

Isabel stared. 'When Mr Osmond's away what does it matter?'

'They don't know he's away, you see.'

'They? Whom do you mean?'

'Every one. But perhaps it doesn't signify.'

'If you were going why shouldn't I?' Isabel asked.

'Because I'm an old frump and you're a beautiful young woman.'

'Granting all that, you've not promised.'

'How much you think of your promises!' said the elder woman in mild mockery.

'I think a great deal of my promises. Does that surprise you?'

'You're right,' Madame Merle audibly reflected. 'I really think you wish to be kind to the child.'

'I wish very much to be kind to her.'

'Go and see her then; no one will be the wiser. And tell her I'd have come if you hadn't. Or rather,' Madame Merle added, '*don't* tell her. She won't care.'

As Isabel drove, in the publicity of an open vehicle, along the winding way which led to Mr Osmond's hill-top, she wondered what her friend had meant by no one's being the wiser. Once in a while, at large intervals, this lady, whose voyaging discretion, as a general thing, was rather of the open sea than of the risky channel, dropped a remark of ambiguous quality, struck a note that sounded false. What cared Isabel Archer for the vulgar judgements of obscure people? and did Madame Merle suppose that she was capable of doing a thing at all if it had to be sneakingly done? Of course not: she must have meant something else—something which in the press of the hours that preceded her departure she had not had time to explain. Isabel would return to this some day; there were sorts of things as to which she liked to be clear. She heard Pansy strumming at the piano in another place as she herself was ushered into Mr Osmond's drawing-room; the little girl was 'practising,' and Isabel was pleased to think she performed this duty with rigour. She immediately came in, smoothing down her frock, and did the honours of her father's house with a wide-eyed earnestness of courtesy. Isabel sat there half an hour, and Pansy rose to the occasion as the small, winged fairy in the pantomime soars by the aid of the dissimulated wire—not chattering, but conversing, and showing the same respectful interest in Isabel's affairs that Isabel was so good as to take in hers. Isabel wondered at her; she had never had so directly presented to her nose the white flower of cultivated sweetness. How well the child had been taught, said our admiring young woman; how prettily she had been directed and fashioned; and yet how simple, how natural, how innocent she had been kept! Isabel was fond, ever, of the question of character and quality, of sounding, as who should say, the deep personal mystery, and it had pleased her, up to this time, to be in doubt as to whether this tender slip were not really all-knowing. Was the extremity of her candour but the perfection of self-consciousness? Was it put on to please her father's visitor, or was it the direct expression of an unspotted nature? The hour that Isabel spent in Mr Osmond's beautiful empty, dusky rooms—the windows had been half-darkened, to keep out the heat, and here and there, through an easy crevice, the splendid summer day peeped in, lighting a gleam of faded colour or tarnished gilt in the rich gloom—her interview with the daughter of the house, I say, effectually settled this question. Pansy was really a blank page, a pure white surface, successfully kept so; she had neither art, nor guile, nor temper, nor talent—only two or three small exquisite instincts: for knowing a friend, for avoiding a mistake, for taking care of an old toy or a new frock. Yet to be so tender was to be touching withal, and she could be felt as an easy victim of fate. She would have no will, no power to resist, no sense of her own importance; she would easily be mystified, easily crushed: her force would be all in knowing when and where to cling. She moved about the place with her visitor, who had asked leave to walk through the other rooms again, where Pansy gave her judgement on several works of art. She spoke of her prospects, her occupations, her father's intentions; she was not egotistical, but felt the propriety of supplying the information so distinguished a guest would naturally expect.

'Please tell me,' she said, 'did papa, in Rome, go to see Madame Catherine? He told me he would if he had time. Perhaps he had not time. Papa likes a great deal of time. He wished to speak about my education; it isn't finished yet, you know. I don't know what they can do with me more; but it appears it's far from finished. Papa told me one day he thought he would finish it himself; for the last year or two, at the convent, the masters that teach the tall girls are so very dear. Papa's not rich, and I should be very sorry if he were to pay much money for me, because I don't think I'm worth it. I don't learn quickly enough, and I have no memory. For what I'm told, yes—especially when it's pleasant; but not for what I learn in a book. There was a young girl who was my best friend, and they took her away from the convent, when she was fourteen, to make—how do you say it in English?—to make a *dot.** You don't say it in English? I hope it isn't wrong; I only mean they wished to keep the money to marry her. I don't know whether it is for that that papa wishes to keep the money—to marry *me.* It costs so much to marry!' Pansy went on with a sigh; 'I think papa might make that economy. At any rate I'm too young to think about it yet, and I don't care for any gentleman; I mean for any but him. If he were not my papa I should like to marry him; I would rather be his daughter than the wife of—of some strange person. I miss him very much, but not so much as you might think, for I've been so much away from him. Papa has always been principally for holidays. I miss Madame Catherine almost more; but you must not tell him that. You shall not see him again? I'm very sorry, and he'll be sorry too. Of every one who comes here I like you the best. That's not a great compliment, for there are not many people. It was very kind of you to come to-day—so far from your house; for I'm really as yet only a child. Oh, yes, I've only the occupations of a child. When did *you* give them up, the occupations of a child? I should like to know how old you are, but I don't know whether it's right to ask. At the convent they told us that we must never ask the age. I don't like to do anything that's not expected; it looks as if one had not been properly taught. I myself—I should never like to be taken by surprise. Papa left directions for everything. I go to bed very early. When the sun goes off that side I go into the garden. Papa left strict orders that I was not to get scorched. I always enjoy the view; the mountains are so graceful. In Rome, from the convent, we saw nothing but roofs and bell-towers. I practise three hours. I don't play very well. You play yourself? I wish very much you'd play something for me; papa has the idea that I should hear good music. Madame Merle has played for me several times; that's what I like best about Madame Merle; she has great facility. I shall never have facility. And I've no voice—just a small sound like the squeak of a slate-pencil making flourishes.'

Isabel gratified this respectful wish, drew off her gloves and sat down to the piano, while Pansy, standing beside her, watched her white hands move quickly over the keys. When she stopped she kissed the child good-bye, held her close, looked at her long. 'Be very good,' she said; 'give pleasure to your father.'

'I think that's what I live for,' Pansy answered. 'He has not much pleasure; he's rather a sad man.'

Isabel listened to this assertion with an interest which she felt it almost a torment to be obliged to conceal. It was her pride that obliged her, and a certain sense of decency; there were still other things in her head which she felt a strong impulse, instantly checked, to say to Pansy about her father; there were things it would have given her pleasure to hear the child, to make the child, say. But she no sooner became conscious of these things than her imagination was hushed with horror at the idea of taking advantage of the little girl—it was of this she would have accused herself—and of exhaling into that air where he might still have a subtle sense for it any breath of her charmed state. She had come—she had come; but she had stayed only an hour. She rose quickly from the music-stool; even then, however, she lingered a moment, still holding her small companion, drawing the child's sweet slimness closer and looking down at her almost in envy. She was obliged to confess it to herself—she would have taken a passionate pleasure in talking of Gilbert Osmond to this innocent, diminutive creature who was so near him. But she said no other word; she only kissed Pansy once again. They went together through the vestibule, to the door that opened on the court; and there her young hostess stopped, looking rather wistfully beyond. 'I may go no further. I've promised papa not to pass this door.'

'You're right to obey him; he'll never ask you anything unreasonable.'

'I shall always obey him. But when will you come again?'

'Not for a long time, I'm afraid.'

'As soon as you can, I hope. I'm only a little girl,' said Pansy, 'but I shall always expect you.' And the small figure stood in the high, dark doorway, watching Isabel cross the clear, grey court and disappear into the brightness beyond the big *portone*,* which gave a wider dazzle as it opened.

XXXI

ISABEL came back to Florence, but only after several months; an interval sufficiently replete with incident. It is not, however, during this interval that we are closely concerned with her; our attention is engaged again on a certain day in the late springtime, shortly after her return to Palazzo Crescentini and a year from the date of the incidents just narrated. She was alone on this occasion, in one of the smaller of the numerous rooms devoted by Mrs Touchett to social uses, and there was that in her expression and attitude which would have suggested that she was expecting a visitor. The tall window was open, and though its green shutters were partly drawn the bright air of the garden had come in through a broad interstice and filled the room with warmth and perfume. Our young woman stood near it for some time, her hands clasped behind her; she gazed abroad with the vagueness of unrest. Too troubled for attention she moved in a vain circle. Yet it could not be in her thought to catch a glimpse of her visitor before he should pass into the house, since the entrance to the palace was not through the garden, in which stillness and privacy always reigned. She wished rather to forestall his arrival by a process of conjecture, and to judge by the expression of her face this attempt gave her plenty to do. Grave she found herself, and postively more weighted, as by the experience of the lapse of the year she had spent in seeing the world. She had ranged, she would have said, through space and surveyed much of mankind, and was therefore now, in her own eyes, a very different person from the frivolous young woman from Albany who had begun to take the measure of Europe on the lawn at Gardencourt a couple of years before. She flattered herself she had harvested wisdom and learned a great deal more of life than this light-minded creature had even suspected. If her thoughts just now had inclined themselves to retrospect, instead of fluttering their wings nervously about the present, they would have evoked a multitude of interesting pictures. These pictures would have been both landscapes and figure-pieces; the latter, however, would have been the more numerous. With several of the images that might have been projected on such a field we are already acquainted. There would be for instance the conciliatory Lily, our heroine's sister and Edmund Ludlow's wife, who had come out from New York to spend five months with her relative. She had left her husband behind her, but had brought her children, to whom Isabel now played with equal munificence and tenderness the part of maiden-aunt. Mr Ludlow, toward the last, had been able to snatch a few weeks from his forensic triumphs and, crossing the ocean with extreme rapidity, had spent a month with the two ladies in Paris before taking his wife home. The little Ludlows had not yet, even from the American point of view, reached the proper tourist-age; so that while her sister was with her Isabel had confined her movements to a narrow circle. Lily and the babies had joined her in Switzerland in the month of July, and they had spent a summer of fine weather in an Alpine valley where the flowers were thick in the meadows and the shade of great chestnuts made a resting-place for such upward wanderings as might be undertaken by ladies and children on warm afternoons. They had afterwards reached the French capital, which was worshipped, and with costly ceremonies, by Lily, but thought of as noisily vacant by Isabel, who in these days made use of her memory of Rome as she might have done, in a hot and crowded room, of a phial of something pungent hidden in her handkerchief.

Mrs Ludlow sacrificed, as I say, to Paris, yet had doubts and wonderments not allayed at that altar; and after her husband had joined her found further chagrin in his failure to throw himself into these speculations. They all had Isabel for subject; but Edmund Ludlow, as he had always done before, declined to be surprised, or distressed, or mystified, or elated, at anything his sister-in-law might have done or have failed to do. Mrs Ludlow's mental motions were sufficiently various. At one moment she thought it would be so natural for that young woman to come home and take a house in New York—the Rossiters', for instance, which had an elegant conservatory and was just round the corner from her own; at another she couldn't conceal her surprise at the girl's not marrying some member of one of the great aristocracies. On the whole, as I have said, she had fallen from high communion with the probabilities. She had taken more satisfaction in Isabel's accession of fortune than if the money had been left to herself; it had seemed to her to offer just the proper setting for her sister's slightly meagre, but scarce the less eminent figure. Isabel had developed less, however, than Lily had thought likely—development, to Lily's understanding, being somehow mysteriously connected with morning-calls and evening-parties. Intellectually, doubtless, she had made immense strides; but she appeared to have achieved few of those social conquests of which Mrs Ludlow had expected to admire the trophies. Lily's conception of such achievements was extremely vague; but this was exactly what she had expected of Isabel—to give it form and body. Isabel could have done as well as she had done in New York; and Mrs Ludlow appealed to her husband to know whether there was any privilege she enjoyed in Europe which the society of that city might not offer her. We know ourselves that Isabel had made conquests—whether inferior or not to those she might have effected in her native land it would be a delicate matter to decide; and it is not altogether with a feeling of complacency that I again mention that she had not rendered these honourable victories public. She had not told her sister the history of Lord Warburton, nor had she given her a hint of Mr Osmond's state of mind; and she had had no better reason for her silence than that she didn't wish to speak. It was more romantic to say nothing, and, drinking deep, in secret, of romance, she was as little disposed to ask poor Lily's advice as she would have been to close that rare volume forever. But Lily knew nothing of these discriminations, and could only pronounce her sister's career a strange anti-climax—an impression confirmed by the fact that Isabel's silence about Mr Osmond, for instance, was in direct proportion to the frequency with which he occupied her thoughts. As this happened very often it sometimes appeared to Mrs Ludlow that she had lost her courage. So uncanny a result of so exhilarating an incident as inheriting a fortune was of course perplexing to the cheerful Lily; it added to her general sense that Isabel was not at all like other people.

Our young lady's courage, however, might have been taken as reaching its height after her relations had gone home. She could imagine braver things than spending the winter in Paris—Paris had sides by which it so resembled New York, Paris was like smart, neat prose—and her close correspondence with Madame Merle did much to stimulate such flights. She had never had a keener sense of freedom, of the absolute boldness and wantonness of liberty, than when she turned away from the platform at the Euston Station on one of the last days of November, after the departure of the train that was to convey poor Lily, her husband and her children to their ship at Liverpool. It had been good for her to regale; she was very conscious of that; she was very observant, as we know, of what was good for her, and her effort was constantly to find something that was good enough. To profit by the present advantage till the latest moment she had made the journey from Paris with the unenvied travellers. She would have accompanied them to Liverpool as well, only Edmund Ludlow had asked her, as a favour, not to do so; it made Lily so fidgety and she asked such impossible questions. Isabel watched the train move away; she kissed her hand to the elder of her small nephews, a demonstrative child who leaned dangerously far out of the window of the carriage and made separation an occasion of violent hilarity, and then she walked back into the foggy London street. The world lay before her—she could do whatever she chose.* There was a deep thrill in it all, but for the present her choice was tolerably discreet; she chose simply to walk back from Euston Square to her hotel. The early dusk of a November afternoon had already closed in; the street-lamps, in the thick, brown air, looked weak and red; our heroine was unattended and Euston Square was a long way from Piccadilly. But Isabel performed the journey with a positive enjoyment of its dangers and lost her way almost on purpose, in order to get more sensations, so that she was disappointed when an obliging policeman easily set her right again. She was so fond of the spectacle of human life that she enjoyed even the aspect of gathering dusk in the London streets—the moving crowds, the hurrying cabs, the lighted shops, the flaring stalls, the dark, shining dampness of everything. That evening, at her hotel, she wrote to Madame Merle that she should start in a day or two for Rome. She made her way down to Rome without touching at Florence—having gone first to Venice and then proceeded southward by Ancona. She accomplished this journey without other assistance than that of her servant, for her natural protectors were not now on the ground. Ralph Touchett was spending the winter at Corfu, and Miss Stackpole, in the September previous, had been recalled to America by a telegram from the *Interviewer.* This journal offered its brilliant correspondent a fresher field for her genius than the mouldering cities of Europe, and Henrietta was cheered on her way by a promise from Mr Bantling that he would soon come over to see her. Isabel wrote to Mrs Touchett to apologise for not presenting herself just yet in Florence, and her aunt replied characteristically enough. Apologies, Mrs Touchett intimated, were of no more use to her than bubbles, and she herself never dealt in such articles. One either did the thing or one didn't, and what one 'would' have done belonged to the sphere of the irrelevant, like the idea of a future life or of the origin of things. Her letter was frank, but (a rare case with Mrs Touchett) not so frank as it pretended. She easily forgave her niece for not stopping at Florence, because she took it for a sign that Gilbert Osmond was less in question there than formerly. She watched of course to see if he would now find a pretext for going to Rome, and derived some comfort from learning that he had not been guilty of an absence.

Isabel, on her side, had not been a fortnight in Rome before she proposed to Madame Merle that they should make a little pilgrimage to the East. Madame Merle remarked that her friend was restless, but she added that she herself had always been consumed with the desire to visit Athens and Constantinople. The two ladies accordingly embarked on this expedition, and spent three months in Greece, in Turkey, in Egypt. Isabel found much to interest her in these countries, though Madame Merle continued to remark that even among the most classic sites, the scenes most calculated to suggest repose and reflexion, a certain incoherence prevailed in her. Isabel travelled rapidly and recklessly; she was like a thirsty person draining cup after cup. Madame Merle meanwhile, as lady-in-waiting to a princess circulating *incognita*, panted a little in her rear. It was on Isabel's invitation she had come, and she imparted all due dignity to the girl's uncountenanced state. She played her part with the tact that might have been expected of her, effacing herself and accepting the position of a companion whose expenses were profusely paid. The situation, however, had no hardships, and people who met this reserved though striking pair on their travels would not have been able to tell you which was patroness and which client. To say that Madame Merle improved on acquaintance states meagrely the impression she made on her friend, who had found her from the first so ample and so easy. At the end of an intimacy of three months Isabel felt she knew her better; her character had revealed itself, and the admirable woman had also at last redeemed her promise of relating her history from her own point of view—a consummation the more desirable as Isabel had already heard it related from the point of view of others. This history was so sad a one (in so far as it concerned the late M. Merle, a positive adventurer, she might say, though originally so plausible, who had taken advantage, years before, of her youth and of an inexperience in which doubtless those who knew her only now would find it difficult to believe); it abounded so in startling and lamentable incidents that her companion wondered a person so *éprouvée** could have kept so much of her freshness, her interest in life. Into this freshness of Madame Merle's she obtained a considerable insight; she seemed to see it as professional, as slightly mechanical, carried about in its case like the fiddle of the virtuoso, or blanketed and bridled like the 'favourite' of the jockey. She liked her as much as ever, but there was a corner of the curtain that never was lifted; it was as if she had remained after all something of a public performer, condemned to emerge only in character and in costume. She had once said that she came from a distance, that she belonged to the 'old, old' world, and Isabel never lost the impression that she was the product of a different moral or social clime from her own, that she had grown up under other stars.

She believed then that at bottom she had a different morality. Of course the morality of civilised persons has always much in common; but our young woman had a sense in her of values gone wrong or, as they said at the shops, marked down. She considered, with the presumption of youth, that a morality differing from her own must be inferior to it; and this conviction was an aid to detecting an occasional flash of cruelty, an occasional lapse from candour, in the conversation of a person who had raised delicate kindness to an art and whose pride was too high for the narrow ways of deception. Her conception of human motives might, in certain lights, have been acquired at the court of some kingdom in decadence, and there were several in her list of which our heroine had not even heard. She had not heard of everything, that was very plain; and there were evidently things in the world of which it was not advantageous to hear. She had once or twice had a positive scare; since it so affected her to have to exclaim, of her friend, 'Heaven forgive her, she doesn't understand me!' Absurd as it may seem this discovery operated as a shock, left her with a vague dismay in which there was even an element of foreboding. The dismay of course subsided, in the light of some sudden proof of Madame Merle's remarkable intelligence; but it stood for a high-water-mark in the ebb and flow of confidence. Madame Merle had once declared her belief that when a friendship ceases to grow it immediately begins to decline—there being no point of equilibrium between liking more and liking less. A stationary affection, in other words, was impossible—it must move one way or the other. However that might be, the girl had in these days a thousand uses for her sense of the romantic, which was more active than it had ever been. I do not allude to the impulse it received as she gazed at the Pyramids in the course of an excursion from Cairo, or as she stood among the broken columns of the Acropolis and fixed her eyes upon the point designated to her as the Strait of Salamis; deep and memorable as these emotions had remained. She came back by the last of March from Egypt and Greece and made another stay in Rome. A few days after her arrival Gilbert Osmond descended from Florence and remained three weeks, during which the fact of her being with his old friend Madame Merle, in whose house she had gone to lodge, made it virtually inevitable that he should see her every day. When the last of April came she wrote to Mrs Touchett that she should now rejoice to accept an invitation given long before, and went to pay a visit at Palazzo Crescentini, Madame Merle on this occasion remaining in Rome. She found her aunt alone; her cousin was still at Corfu. Ralph, however, was expected in Florence from day to day, and Isabel, who had not seen him for upwards of a year, was prepared to give him the most affectionate welcome.

XXXII

It was not of him, nevertheless, that she was thinking while she stood at the window near which we found her a while ago, and it was not of any of the matters I have rapidly sketched. She was not turned to the past, but to the immediate, impending hour. She had reason to expect a scene, and she was not fond of scenes. She was not asking herself what she should say to her visitor; this question had already been answered. What he would say to her—that was the interesting issue. It could be nothing in the least soothing—she had warrant for this, and the conviction doubtless showed in the cloud on her brow. For the rest, however, all clearness reigned in her; she had put away her mourning and she walked in no small shimmering splendour. She only felt older—ever so much, and as if she were 'worth more' for it, like some curious piece in an antiquary's collection. She was not at any rate left indefinitely to her apprehensions, for a servant at last stood before her with a card on his tray. 'Let the gentleman come in,' she said, and continued to gaze out of the window after the footman had retired. It was only when she had heard the door close behind the person who presently entered that she looked round.

Caspar Goodwood stood there—stood and received a moment, from head to foot, the bright, dry gaze with which she rather withheld than offered a greeting. Whether his sense of maturity had kept pace with Isabel's we shall perhaps presently ascertain; let me say meanwhile that to her critical glance he showed nothing of the injury of time. Straight, strong and hard, there was nothing in his appearance that spoke positively either of youth or of age; if he had neither innocence nor weakness, so he had no practical philosophy. His jaw showed the same voluntary cast as in earlier days; but a crisis like the present had in it of course something grim. He had the air of a man who had travelled hard; he said nothing at first, as if he had been out of breath. This gave Isabel time to make a reflexion: 'Poor fellow, what great things he's capable of, and what a pity he should waste so dreadfully his splendid force! What a pity too that one can't satisfy everybody!' It gave her time to do more—to say at the end of a minute: 'I can't tell you how I hoped you wouldn't come!'

'I've no doubt of that.' And he looked about him for a seat. Not only had he come, but he meant to settle.

'You must be very tired,' said Isabel, seating herself, and generously, as she thought, to give him his opportunity.

'No, I'm not at all tired. Did you ever know me to be tired?'

'Never; I wish I had! When did you arrive?'

'Last night, very late; in a kind of snail-train they call the express. These Italian trains go at about the rate of an American funeral.'

'That's in keeping—you must have felt as if you were coming to bury me!' And she forced a smile of encouragement to an easy view of their situation. She had reasoned the matter well out, making it perfectly clear that she broke no faith and falsified no contract; but for all this she was afraid of her visitor. She was ashamed of her fear; but she was devoutly thankful there was nothing else to be ashamed of. He looked at her with his stiff insistence, an insistence in which there was such a want of tact; especially when the dull dark beam in his eye rested on her as a physical weight.

'No, I didn't feel that; I couldn't think of you as dead. I wish I could!' he candidly declared.

'I thank you immensely.'

'I'd rather think of you as dead than as married to another man.'

'That's very selfish of you!' she returned with the ardour of a real conviction. 'If you're not happy yourself others have yet a right to be.'

'Very likely it's selfish; but I don't in the least mind your saying so. I don't mind anything you can say now—I don't feel it. The cruellest things you could think of would be mere pin-pricks. After what you've done I shall never feel anything—I mean anything but that. That I shall feel all my life.'

Mr Goodwood made these detached assertions with dry deliberateness, in his hard, slow American tone, which flung no atmospheric colour over propositions intrinsically crude.

The tone made Isabel angry rather than touched her; but her anger perhaps was fortunate, inasmuch as it gave her a further reason for controlling herself. It was under the pressure of this control that she became, after a little, irrelevant. 'When did you leave New York?'

He threw up his head as if calculating. 'Seventeen days ago.'

'You must have travelled fast in spite of your slow trains.'

'I came as fast as I could. I'd have come five days ago if I had been able.'

'It wouldn't have made any difference, Mr Goodwood,' she coldly smiled.

'Not to you—no. But to me.'

'You gain nothing that I see.'

'That's for me to judge!'

'Of course. To me it seems that you only torment yourself.' And then, to change the subject, she asked him if he had seen Henrietta Stackpole. He looked as if he had not come from Boston to Florence to talk of Henrietta Stackpole; but he answered, distinctly enough, that this young lady had been with him just before he left America. 'She came to see you?' Isabel then demanded.

'Yes, she was in Boston, and she called at my office. It was the day I had got your letter.'

'Did you tell her?' Isabel asked with a certain anxiety.

'Oh no,' said Caspar Goodwood simply; 'I didn't want to do that. She'll hear it quick enough; she hears everything.'

'I shall write to her, and then she'll write to me and scold me,' Isabel declared, trying to smile again.

Caspar, however, remained sternly grave. 'I guess she'll come right out,' he said.

'On purpose to scold me?'

'I don't know. She seemed to think she had not seen Europe thoroughly.'

'I'm glad you tell me that,' Isabel said. 'I must prepare for her.'

Mr Goodwood fixed his eyes for a moment on the floor; then at last, raising them, 'Does she know Mr Osmond?' he enquired.

'A little. And she doesn't like him. But of course I don't marry to please Henrietta,' she added. It would have been better for poor Caspar if she had tried a little more to gratify Miss Stackpole; but he didn't say so; he only asked, presently, when her marriage would take place. To which she made answer that she didn't know yet. 'I can only say it will be soon. I've told no one but yourself and one other person—an old friend of Mr Osmond's.'

'Is it a marriage your friends won't like?' he demanded.

'I really haven't an idea. As I say, I don't marry for my friends.'

He went on, making no exclamation, no comment, only asking questions, doing it quite without delicacy. 'Who and what then is Mr Gilbert Osmond?'

'Who and what? Nobody and nothing but a very good and very honourable man. He's not in business,' said Isabel. 'He's not rich; he's not known for anything in particular.'

She disliked Mr Goodwood's questions, but she said to herself that she owed it to him to satisfy him as far as possible. The satisfaction poor Caspar exhibited was, however, small; he sat very upright, gazing at her. 'Where does he come from? Where does he belong?'

She had never been so little pleased with the way he said 'belawng.' 'He comes from nowhere. He has spent most of his life in Italy.'

'You said in your letter he was American. Hasn't he a native place?'

'Yes, but he has forgotten it. He left it as a small boy.'

'Has he never gone back?'

'Why should he go back?' Isabel asked, flushing all defensively. 'He has no profession.'

'He might have gone back for his pleasure. Doesn't he like the United States?'

'He doesn't know them. Then he's very quiet and very simple—he contents himself with Italy.'

'With Italy and with you,' said Mr Goodwood with gloomy plainness and no appearance of trying to make an epigram. 'What has he ever done?' he added abruptly.

'That I should marry him? Nothing at all,' Isabel replied while her patience helped itself by turning a little to hardness.

'If he had done great things would you forgive me any better? Give me up, Mr Goodwood; I'm marrying a perfect nonentity. Don't try to take an interest in him. You can't.'

'I can't appreciate him; that's what you mean. And you don't mean in the least that he's a perfect nonentity. You think he's grand, you think he's great, though no one else thinks so.'

Isabel's colour deepened; she felt this really acute of her companion, and it was certainly a proof of the aid that passion might render perceptions she had never taken for fine. 'Why do you always come back to what others think? I can't discuss Mr Osmond with you.'

'Of course not,' said Caspar reasonably. And he sat there with his air of stiff helplessness, as if not only this were true, but there were nothing else that they might discuss.

'You see how little you gain,' she accordingly broke out—'how little comfort or satisfaction I can give you.'

'I didn't expect you to give me much.'

'I don't understand then why you came.'

'I came because I wanted to see you once more—even just as you are.'

'I appreciate that; but if you had waited a while, sooner or later we should have been sure to meet, and our meeting would have been pleasanter for each of us than this.'

'Waited till after you're married? That's just what I didn't want to do. You'll be different then.'

'Not very. I shall still be a great friend of yours. You'll see.'

'That will make it all the worse,' said Mr Goodwood grimly.

'Ah, you're unaccommodating! I can't promise to dislike you in order to help you to resign yourself.'

'I shouldn't care if you did!'

Isabel got up with a movement of repressed impatience and walked to the window, where she remained a moment looking out. When she turned round her visitor was still motionless in his place. She came toward him again and stopped, resting her hand on the back of the chair she had just quitted. 'Do you mean you came simply to look at me? That's better for you perhaps than for me.'

'I wished to hear the sound of your voice,' he said.

'You've heard it, and you see it says nothing very sweet.'

'It gives me pleasure, all the same.' And with this he got up.

She had felt pain and displeasure on receiving early that day the news he was in Florence and by her leave would come within an hour to see her. She had been vexed and distressed, though she had sent back word by his messenger that he might come when he would. She had not been better pleased when she saw him; his being there at all was so full of heavy implications. It implied things she could never assent to—rights, reproaches, remonstrance, rebuke, the expectation of making her change her purpose. These things, however, if implied, had not been expressed; and now our young lady, strangely enough, began to resent her visitor's remarkable self-control. There was a dumb misery about him that irritated her; there was a manly staying of his hand that made her heart beat faster. She felt her agitation rising, and she said to herself that she was angry in the way a woman is angry when she has been in the wrong. She was not in the wrong; she had fortunately not that bitterness to swallow; but, all the same, she wished he would denounce her a little. She had wished his visit would be short; it had no purpose, no propriety; yet now that he seemed to be turning away she felt a sudden horror of his leaving her without uttering a word that would give her an opportunity to defend herself more than she had done in writing to him a month before, in a few carefully chosen words, to announce her engagement. If she were not in the wrong, however, why should she desire to defend herself? It was an excess of generosity on Isabel's part to desire that Mr Goodwood should be angry. And if he had not meanwhile held himself hard it might have made him so to hear the tone in which she suddenly exclaimed, as if she were accusing him of having accused her: 'I've not deceived you! I was perfectly free!'

'Yes, I know that,' said Caspar.

'I gave you full warning that I'd do as I chose.'

'You said you'd probably never marry, and you said it with such a manner that I pretty well believed it.'

She considered this an instant. 'No one can be more surprised than myself at my present intention.'

'You told me that if I heard you were engaged I was not to believe it,' Caspar went on. 'I heard it twenty days ago from yourself, but I remembered what you had said. I thought there might be some mistake, and that's partly why I came.'

'If you wish me to repeat it by word of mouth, that's soon done. There's no mistake whatever.'

'I saw that as soon as I came into the room.'

'What good would it do you that I shouldn't marry?' she asked with a certain fierceness.

'I should like it better than this.'

'You're very selfish, as I said before.'

'I know that. I'm selfish as iron.'

'Even iron sometimes melts! If you'll be reasonable I'll see you again.'

'Don't you call me reasonable now?'

'I don't know what to say to you,' she answered with sudden humility.

'I shan't trouble you for a long time,' the young man went on. He made a step towards the door, but he stopped. 'Another reason why I came was that I wanted to hear what you would say in explanation of your having changed your mind.'

Her humbleness as suddenly deserted her. 'In explanation? Do you think I'm bound to explain?'

He gave her one of his long dumb looks. 'You were very positive. I did believe it.'

'So did I. Do you think I could explain if I would?'

'No, I suppose not. Well,' he added, 'I've done what I wished. I've seen you.'

'How little you make of these terrible journeys,' she felt the poverty of her presently replying.

'If you're afraid I'm knocked up—in any such way as that—you may be at your ease about it.' He turned away, this time in earnest, and no hand-shake, no sign of parting, was exchanged between them. At the door he stopped with his hand on the knob. 'I shall leave Florence to-morrow,' he said without a quaver.

'I'm delighted to hear it!' she answered passionately. Five minutes after he had gone out she burst into tears.

XXXIII

Her fit of weeping, however, was soon smothered, and the signs of it had vanished when, an hour later, she broke the news to her aunt. I use this expression because she had been sure Mrs Touchett would not be pleased; Isabel had only waited to tell her till she had seen Mr Goodwood. She had an odd impression that it would not be honourable to make the fact public before she should have heard what Mr Goodwood would say about it. He had said rather less than she expected, and she now had a somewhat angry sense of having lost time. But she would lose no more; she waited till Mrs Touchett came into the drawing-room before the mid-day breakfast, and then she began. 'Aunt Lydia, I've something to tell you.'

Mrs Touchett gave a little jump and looked at her almost fiercely. 'You needn't tell me; I know what it is.'

'I don't know how you know.'

'The same way that I know when the window's open—by feeling a draught. You're going to marry that man.'

'What man do you mean?' Isabel enquired with great dignity.

'Madame Merle's friend—Mr Osmond.'

'I don't know why you call him Madame Merle's friend. Is that the principal thing he's known by?'

'If he's not her friend he ought to be—after what she has done for him!' cried Mrs Touchett. 'I shouldn't have expected it of her; I'm disappointed.'

'If you mean that Madame Merle has had anything to do with my engagement you're greatly mistaken,' Isabel declared with a sort of ardent coldness.

'You mean that your attractions were sufficient, without the gentleman's having had to be lashed up? You're quite right. They're immense, your attractions, and he would never have presumed to think of you if she hadn't put him up to it. He has a very good opinion of himself, but he was not a man to take trouble. Madame Merle took the trouble *for* him.'

'He has taken a great deal for himself!' cried Isabel with a voluntary laugh.

Mrs Touchett gave a sharp nod. 'I think he must, after all, to have made you like him so much.'

'I thought he even pleased *you*.'

'He did, at one time; and that's why I'm angry with him.'

'Be angry with me, not with him,' said the girl.

'Oh, I'm always angry with you; that's no satisfaction! Was it for this that you refused Lord Warburton?'

'Please don't go back to that. Why shouldn't I like Mr Osmond, since others have done so?'

'Others, at their wildest moments, never wanted to marry him. There's nothing *of* him,' Mrs Touchett explained.

'Then he can't hurt me,' said Isabel.

'Do you think you're going to be happy? No one's happy, in such doings, you should know.'

'I shall set the fashion then. What does one marry for?'

'What *you* will marry for, heaven only knows. People usually marry as they go into partnership—to set up a house. But in your partnership you'll bring everything.'

'Is it that Mr Osmond isn't rich? Is that what you're talking about?' Isabel asked.

'He has no money; he has no name; he has no importance. I value such things and I have the courage to say it; I think they're very precious. Many other people think the same, and they show it. But they give some other reason.'

Isabel hesitated a little. 'I think I value everything that's valuable. I care very much for money, and that's why I wish Mr Osmond to have a little.'

'Give it to him then; but marry some one else.'

'His name's good enough for me,' the girl went on. 'It's a very pretty name. Have I such a fine one myself?'

'All the more reason you should improve on it. There are only a dozen American names. Do you marry him out of charity?'

'It was my duty to tell you, Aunt Lydia, but I don't think it's my duty to explain to you. Even if it were I shouldn't be able. So please don't remonstrate; in talking about it you have me at a disadvantage. I can't talk about it.'

'I don't remonstrate, I simply answer you: I must give some sign of intelligence. I saw it coming, and I said nothing. I never meddle.'

'You never do, and I'm greatly obliged to you. You've been very considerate.'

'It was not considerate—it was convenient,' said Mrs Touchett. 'But I shall talk to Madame Merle.'

'I don't see why you keep bringing her in. She has been a very good friend to me.'

'Possibly; but she has been a poor one to me.'

'What has she done to you?'

'She has deceived me. She had as good as promised me to prevent your engagement.'

'She couldn't have prevented it.'

'She can do anything; that's what I've always liked her for. I knew she could play any part; but I understood that she played them one by one. I didn't understand that she would play two at the same time.'

'I don't know what part she may have played to you,' Isabel said; 'that's between yourselves. To me she has been honest and kind and devoted.'

'Devoted, of course; she wished you to marry her candidate. She told me she was watching you only in order to interpose.'

'She said that to please you,' the girl answered; conscious, however, of the inadequacy of the explanation.

'To please me by deceiving me? She knows me better. Am I pleased to-day?'

'I don't think you're ever much pleased,' Isabel was obliged to reply. 'If Madame Merle knew you would learn the truth what had she to gain by insincerity?'

'She gained time, as you see. While I waited for her to interfere you were marching away, and she was really beating the drum.'

'That's very well. But by your own admission you saw I was marching, and even if she had given the alarm you wouldn't have tried to stop me.'

'No, but some one else would.'

'Whom do you mean?' Isabel asked, looking very hard at her aunt.

Mrs Touchett's little bright eyes, active as they usually were, sustained her gaze rather than returned it. 'Would you have listened to Ralph?'

'Not if he had abused Mr Osmond.'

'Ralph doesn't abuse people; you know that perfectly. He cares very much for you.'

'I know he does,' said Isabel; 'and I shall feel the value of it now, for he knows that whatever I do I do with reason.'

'He never believed you would do this. I told him you were capable of it, and he argued the other way.'

'He did it for the sake of argument,' the girl smiled. 'You don't accuse him of having deceived you; why should you accuse Madame Merle?'

'He never pretended he'd prevent it.'

'I'm glad of that!' cried Isabel gaily. 'I wish very much,' she presently added, 'that when he comes you'd tell him first of my engagement.'

'Of course I'll mention it,' said Mrs Touchett. 'I shall say nothing more to you about it, but I give you notice I shall talk to others.'

'That's as you please. I only meant that it's rather better the announcement should come from you than from me.'

'I quite agree with you; it's much more proper!' And on this the aunt and the niece went to breakfast, where Mrs Touchett, as good as her word, made no allusion to Gilbert Osmond. After an interval of silence, however, she asked her companion from whom she had received a visit an hour before.

'From an old friend—an American gentleman,' Isabel said with a colour in her cheek.

'An American gentleman of course. It's only an American gentleman who calls at ten o'clock in the morning.'

'It was half-past ten; he was in a great hurry; he goes away this evening.'

'Couldn't he have come yesterday, at the usual time?'

'He only arrived last night.'

'He spends but twenty-four hours in Florence?' Mrs Touchett cried. 'He's an American gentleman truly.'

'He is indeed,' said Isabel, thinking with perverse admiration of what Caspar Goodwood had done for her.

Two days afterward Ralph arrived; but though Isabel was sure that Mrs Touchett had lost no time in imparting to him the great fact, he showed at first no open knowledge of it. Their prompted talk was naturally of his health; Isabel had many questions to ask about Corfu. She had been shocked by his appearance when he came into the room; she had forgotten how ill he looked. In spite of Corfu he looked very ill to-day, and she wondered if he were really worse or if she were simply disaccustomed to living with an invalid. Poor Ralph made no nearer approach to conventional beauty as he advanced in life, and the now apparently complete loss of his health had done little to mitigate the natural oddity of his person. Blighted and battered, but still responsive and still ironic, his face was like a lighted lantern patched with paper and unsteadily held; his thin whisker languished upon a lean cheek; the exorbitant curve of his nose defined itself more sharply. Lean he was altogether, lean and long and loose-jointed; an accidental cohesion of relaxed angles. His brown velvet jacket had become perennial; his hands had fixed themselves in his pockets; he shambled and stumbled and shuffled in a manner that denoted great physical helplessness. It was perhaps this whimsical gait that helped to mark his character more than ever as that of the humorous invalid—the invalid for whom even his own disabilities are part of the general joke. They might well indeed with Ralph have been the chief cause of the want of seriousness marking his view of a world in which the reason for his own continued presence was past finding out. Isabel had grown fond of his ugliness; his awkwardness had become dear to her. They had been sweetened by association; they struck her as the very terms on which it had been given him to be charming. He was so charming that her sense of his being ill had hitherto had a sort of comfort in it; the state of his health had seemed not a limitation, but a kind of intellectual advantage; it absolved him from all professional and official emotions and left him the luxury of being exclusively personal. The personality so resulting was delightful; he had remained proof against the staleness of disease; he had had to consent to be deplorably ill, yet had somehow escaped being formally sick. Such had been the girl's impression of her cousin; and when she had pitied him it was only on reflection. As she reflected a good deal she had allowed him a certain amount of compassion; but she always had a dread of wasting that essence—a precious article, worth more to the giver than to any one else. Now, however, it took no great sensibility to feel that poor Ralph's tenure of life was less elastic than it should be. He was a bright, free, generous spirit, he had all the illumination of wisdom and none of its pedantry, and yet he was distressfully dying.

Isabel noted afresh that life was certainly hard for some people, and she felt a delicate glow of shame as she thought how easy it now promised to become for herself. She was prepared to learn that Ralph was not pleased with her engagement; but she was not prepared, in spite of her affection for him, to let this fact spoil the situation. She was not even prepared, or so she thought, to resent his want of sympathy; for it would be his privilege—it would be indeed his natural line—to find fault with any step she might take toward marriage. One's cousin always pretended to hate one's husband; that was traditional, classical; it was a part of one's cousin's always pretending to adore one. Ralph was nothing if not critical; and though she would certainly, other things being equal, have been as glad to marry to please him as to please any one, it would be absurd to regard as important that her choice should square with his views. What were his views after all? He had pretended to believe she had better have married Lord Warburton; but this was only because she had refused that excellent man. If she had accepted him Ralph would certainly have taken another tone; he always took the opposite. You could criticise any marriage; it was the essence of a marriage to be open to criticism. How well she herself, should she only give her mind to it, might criticise this union of her own! She had other employment, however, and Ralph was welcome to relieve her of the care. Isabel was prepared to be most patient and most indulgent. He must have seen that, and this made it the more odd he should say nothing. After three days had elapsed without his speaking our young woman wearied of waiting; dislike it as he would, he might at least go through the form. We, who know more about poor Ralph than his cousin, may easily believe that during the hours that followed his arrival at Palazzo Crescentini he had privately gone through many forms. His mother had literally greeted him with the great news, which had been even more sensibly chilling than Mrs Touchett's maternal kiss. Ralph was shocked and humiliated; his calculations had been false and the person in the world in whom he was most interested was lost. He drifted about the house like a rudderless vessel in a rock stream, or sat in the garden of the palace on a great cane chair, his long legs extended, his head thrown back and his hat pulled over his eyes. He felt cold about the heart; he had never liked anything less. What could he do, what could he say? If the girl were irreclaimable could he pretend to like it? To attempt to reclaim her was permissible only if the attempt should succeed. To try to persuade her of anything sordid or sinister in the man to whose deep art she had succumbed would be decently discreet only in the event of her being persuaded. Otherwise he should simply have damned himself. It cost him an equal effort to speak his thought and to dissemble; he could neither assent with sincerity nor protest with hope. Meanwhile he knew—or rather he supposed—that the affianced pair were daily renewing their mutual vows. Osmond at this moment showed himself little at Palazzo Crescentini; but Isabel met him every day elsewhere, as she was free to do after their engagement had been made public. She had taken a carriage by the month, so as not to be indebted to her aunt for the means of pursuing a course of which Mrs Touchett disapproved, and she drove in the morning to the Cascine. This suburban, wilderness, during the early hours, was void of all intruders, and our young lady, joined by her lover in its quietest part, strolled with him a while through the grey Italian shade and listened to the nightingales.

XXXIV

One morning, on her return from her drive, some half-hour before luncheon, she quitted her vehicle in the court of the palace and, instead of ascending the great staircase, crossed the court, passed beneath another archway and entered the garden. A sweeter spot at this moment could not have been imagined. The stillness of noontide hung over it, and the warm shade, enclosed and still, made bowers like spacious caves. Ralph was sitting there in the clear gloom, at the base of a statue of Terpsichore*—a dancing nymph with taper fingers and inflated draperies in the manner of Bernini;* the extreme relaxation of his attitude suggested at first to Isabel that he was asleep. Her light footstep on the grass had not roused him, and before turning away she stood for a moment looking at him. During this instant he opened his eyes; upon which she sat down on a rustic chair that matched with his own. Though in her irritation she had accused him of indifference she was not blind to the fact that he had visibly had something to brood over. But she had explained his air of absence partly by the languor of his increased weakness, partly by worries connected with the property inherited from his father—the fruit of eccentric arrangements of which Mrs Touchett disapproved and which, as she had told Isabel, now encountered opposition from the other partners in the bank. He ought to have gone to England, his mother said, instead of coming to Florence; he had not been there for months, and took no more interest in the bank than in the state of Patagonia.

'I'm sorry I waked you,' Isabel said; 'you look too tired.'

'I feel too tired. But I was not asleep. I was thinking of you.'

'Are you tired of that?'

'Very much so. It leads to nothing. The road's long and I never arrive.'

'What do you wish to arrive at?' she put to him, closing her parasol.

'At the point of expressing to myself properly what I think of your engagement.'

'Don't think too much of it,' she lightly returned.

'Do you mean that it's none of my business?'

'Beyond a certain point, yes.'

'That's the point I want to fix. I had an idea you may have found me wanting in good manners. I've never congratulated you.'

'Of course I've noticed that. I wondered why you were silent.'

'There have been a good many reasons. I'll tell you now,' Ralph said. He pulled off his hat and laid it on the ground; then he sat looking at her. He leaned back under the protection of Bernini, his head against his marble pedestal, his arms dropped on either side of him, his hands laid upon the rests of his wide chair. He looked awkward, uncomfortable; he hesitated long. Isabel said nothing; when people were embarrassed she was usually sorry for them, but she was determined not to help Ralph to utter a word that should not be to the honour of her high decision. 'I think I've hardly got over my surprise,' he went on at last. 'You were the last person I expected to see caught.'

'I don't know why you call it caught.'

'Because you're going to be put into a cage.'

'If I like my cage, that needn't trouble you,' she answered.

'That's what I wonder at; that's what I've been thinking of.'

'If you've been thinking you may imagine how I've thought! I'm satisfied that I'm doing well.'

'You must have changed immensely. A year ago you valued your liberty beyond everything. You wanted only to see life.'

'I've seen it,' said Isabel. 'It doesn't look to me now, I admit, such an inviting expanse.'

'I don't pretend it is; only I had an idea that you took a genial view of it and wanted to survey the whole field.'

'I've seen that one can't do anything so general. One must choose a corner and cultivate that.'

'That's what I think. And one must choose as good a corner as possible. I had no idea, all winter, while I read your delightful letters, that you were choosing. You said nothing about it, and your silence put me off my guard.'

'It was not a matter I was likely to write to you about. Besides, I knew nothing of the future. It has all come lately. If you had been on your guard, however,' Isabel asked, 'what would you have done?'

'I should have said "Wait a little longer." '

'Wait for what?'

'Well, for a little more light,' said Ralph with rather an absurd smile, while his hands found their way into his pockets.

'Where should my light have come from? From you?'

'I might have struck a spark or two.'

Isabel had drawn off her gloves; she smoothed them out as they lay upon her knee. The mildness of this movement was accidental, for her expression was not conciliatory. 'You're beating about the bush, Ralph. You wish to say you don't like Mr Osmond, and yet you're afraid.'

' "Willing to wound and yet afraid to strike"?* I'm willing to wound *him*, yes—but not to wound you. I'm afraid of you, not of him. If you marry him it won't be a fortunate way for me to have spoken.'

'*If* I marry him! Have you had any expectation of dissuading me?'

'Of course that seems to you too fatuous.'

'No,' said Isabel after a little; 'it seems to me too touching.'

'That's the same thing. It makes me so ridiculous that you pity me.'

She stroked out her long gloves again. 'I know you've a great affection for me. I can't get rid of that.'

'For heaven's sake don't try. Keep that well in sight. It will convince you how intensely I want you to do well.'

'And how little you trust me!'

There was a moment's silence; the warm noontide seemed to listen. 'I trust you, but I don't trust him,' said Ralph.

She raised her eyes and gave him a wide, deep look. 'You've said it now, and I'm glad you've made it so clear. But you'll suffer by it.'

'Not if you're just.'

'I'm very just,' said Isabel. 'What better proof of it can there be than that I'm not angry with you? I don't know what's the matter with me, but I'm not. I was when you began, but it has passed away. Perhaps I ought to be angry, but Mr Osmond wouldn't think so. He wants me to know everything; that's what I like him for. You've nothing to gain, I know that. I've never been so nice to you, as a girl, that you should have much reason for wishing me to remain one. You give very good advice; you've often done so. No, I'm very quiet; I've always believed in your wisdom,' she went on, boasting of her quietness, yet speaking with a kind of contained exaltation. It was her passionate desire to be just; it touched Ralph to the heart, affected him like a caress from a creature he had injured. He wished to interrupt, to reassure her; for a moment he was absurdly inconsistent; he would have retracted what he had said. But she gave him no chance; she went on, having caught a glimpse, as she thought, of the heroic line and desiring to advance in that direction. 'I see you've some special idea; I should like very much to hear it. I'm sure it's disinterested; I feel that. It seems a strange thing to argue about, and of course I ought to tell you definitely that if you expect to dissuade me you may give it up. You'll not move me an inch; it's too late. As you say, I'm caught. Certainly it won't be pleasant for you to remember this, but your pain will be in your own thoughts. I shall never reproach you.'

'I don't think you ever will,' said Ralph. 'It's not in the least the sort of marriage I thought you'd make.'

'What sort of marriage was that, pray?'

'Well, I can hardly say. I hadn't exactly a positive view of it, but I had a negative. I didn't think you'd decide for—well, for *that* type.'

'What's the matter with Mr Osmond's type, if it be one? His being so independent, so individual, is what *I* most see in him,' the girl declared. 'What do you know against him? You know him scarcely at all.'

'Yes,' Ralph said, 'I know him very little, and I confess I haven't facts and items to prove him a villain. But all the same I can't help feeling that you're running a grave risk.'

'Marriage is always a grave risk, and his risk's as grave as mine.'

'That's his affair! If he's afraid, let him back out. I wish to God he would.'

Isabel reclined in her chair, folding her arms and gazing a while at her cousin. 'I don't think I understand you,' she said at last coldly. 'I don't know what you're talking about.'

'I believed you'd marry a man of more importance.'

Cold, I say, her tone had been, but at this a colour like a flame leaped into her face. 'Of more importance to whom? It seems to me enough that one's husband should be of importance to one's self!'

Ralph blushed as well; his attitude embarrassed him. Physically speaking he proceeded to change it; he straightened himself, then leaned forward, resting a hand on each knee. He fixed his eyes on the ground; he had an air of the most respectful deliberation. 'I'll tell you in a moment what I mean,' he presently said. He felt agitated, intensely eager; now that he had opened the discussion he wished to discharge his mind. But he wished also to be superlatively gentle.

Isabel waited a little—then she went on with majesty. 'In everything that makes one care for people Mr Osmond is pre-eminent. There may be nobler natures, but I've never had the pleasure of meeting one. Mr Osmond's is the finest I know; he's good enough for me, and interesting enough, and clever enough. I'm far more struck with what he has and what he represents than with what he may lack.'

'I had treated myself to a charming vision of your future,' Ralph observed without answering this; 'I had amused myself with planning out a high destiny for you. There was to be nothing of this sort in it. You were not to come down so easily or so soon.'

'Come down, you say?'

'Well, that renders my sense of what has happened to you. You seemed to me to be soaring far up in the blue—to be, sailing in the bright light, over the heads of men. Suddenly some one tosses up a faded rosebud—a missile that should never have reached you—and straight you drop to the ground. It hurts me,' said Ralph audaciously, 'hurts me as if I had fallen myself!'

The look of pain and bewilderment deepened in his companion's face. 'I don't understand you in the least,' she repeated. 'You say you amused yourself with a project for my career—I don't understand that. Don't amuse yourself too much, or I shall think you're doing it at my expense.'

Ralph shook his head. 'I'm not afraid of your not believing that I've had great ideas for you.'

'What do you mean by my soaring and sailing?' she pursued. 'I've never moved on a higher plane than I'm moving on now. There's nothing higher for a girl than to marry a—a person she likes,' said poor Isabel, wandering into the didactic.

'It's your liking the person we speak of that I venture to criticise, my dear cousin. I should have said that the man for you would have been a more active, larger, freer sort of nature.' Ralph hesitated, then added: 'I can't get over the sense that Osmond is somehow—well, small.' He had uttered the last word with no great assurance; he was afraid she would flash out again. But to his surprise she was quiet; she had the air of considering.

'Small?' She made it sound immense.

'I think he's narrow, selfish. He takes himself so seriously!'

'He has a great respect for himself; I don't blame him for that,' said Isabel. 'It makes one more sure to respect others.'

Ralph for a moment felt almost reassured by her reasonable tone. 'Yes, but everything is relative; one ought to feel one's relation to things—to others. I don't think Mr Osmond does that.'

'I've chiefly to do with his relation to me. In that he's excellent.'

'He's the incarnation of taste,' Ralph went on, thinking hard how he could best express Gilbert Osmond's sinister attributes without putting himself in the wrong by seeming to describe him coarsely. He wished to describe him impersonally, scientifically. 'He judges and measures, approves and condemns, altogether by that.'

'It's a happy thing then that his taste should be exquisite.'

'It's exquisite, indeed, since it has led him to select you as his bride. But have you ever seen such a taste—a really exquisite one—ruffled?'

'I hope it may never be my fortune to fail to gratify my husband's.'

At these words a sudden passion leaped to Ralph's lips. 'Ah, that's wilful, that's unworthy of you! You were not meant to be measured in that way—you were meant for something better than to keep guard over the sensibilities of a sterile dilettante!'

Isabel rose quickly and he did the same, so that they stood for a moment looking at each other as if he had flung down a defiance or an insult. But 'You go too far,' she simply breathed.

'I've said what I had on my mind—and I've said it because I love you!'

Isabel turned pale: was he too on that tiresome list? She had a sudden wish to strike him off. 'Ah then, you're not disinterested!'

'I love you, but I love without hope,' said Ralph quickly, forcing a smile and feeling that in that last declaration he had expressed more than he intended.

Isabel moved away and stood looking into the sunny stillness of the garden; but after a little she turned back to him. 'I'm afraid your talk then is the wildness of despair! I don't understand it—but it doesn't matter. I'm not arguing with you; it's impossible I should; I've only tried to listen to you. I'm much obliged to you for attempting to explain,' she said gently, as if the anger with which she had just sprung up had already subsided. 'It's very good of you to try to warn me, if you're really alarmed; but I won't promise to think of what you've said: I shall forget it as soon as possible. Try and forget it yourself; you've done your duty, and no man can do more. I can't explain to you what I feel, what I believe, and I wouldn't if I could.' She paused a moment and then went on with an inconsequence that Ralph observed even in the midst of his eagerness to discover some symptom of concession. 'I can't enter into your idea of Mr Osmond; I can't do it justice, because I see him in quite another way. He's not important—no, he's not important; he's a man to whom importance is supremely indifferent. If that's what you mean when you call him "small," then he's as small as you please. I call that large—it's the largest thing I know. I won't pretend to argue with you about a person I'm going to marry,' Isabel repeated.

'I'm not in the least concerned to defend Mr Osmond; he's not so weak as to need my defence. I should think it would seem strange even to yourself that I should talk of him so quietly and coldly, as if he were any one else. I wouldn't talk of him at all to any one but you; and you, after what you've said—I may just answer you once for all. Pray, would you wish me to make a mercenary marriage—what they call a marriage of ambition? I've only one ambition—to be free to follow out a good feeling. I had others once, but they've passed away. Do you complain of Mr Osmond because he's not rich? That's just what I like him for. I've fortunately money enough; I've never felt so thankful for it as to-day. There have been moments when I should like to go and kneel down by your father's grave: he did perhaps a better thing than he knew when he put it into my power to marry a poor man—a man who has borne his poverty with such dignity, with such indifference. Mr Osmond has never scrambled nor struggled—he has cared for no worldly prize. If that's to be narrow, if that's to be selfish, then it's very well. I'm not frightened by such words, I'm not even displeased; I'm only sorry that you should make a mistake. Others might have done so, but I'm surprised that *you* should. You might know a gentleman when you see one—you might know a fine mind. Mr Osmond makes no mistakes! He knows everything, he understands everything, he has the kindest, gentlest, highest spirit. You've got hold of some false idea. It's a pity, but I can't help it; it regards you more than me.' Isabel paused a moment, looking at her cousin with an eye illumined by a sentiment which contradicted the careful calmness of her manner—a mingled sentiment, to which the angry pain excited by his words and the wounded pride of having needed to justify a choice of which she felt only the nobleness and purity, equally contributed. Though she paused Ralph said nothing; he saw she had more to say. She was grand, but she was highly solicitous; she was indifferent, but she was all in a passion. 'What sort of a person should you have liked me to marry?' she asked suddenly. 'You talk about one's soaring and sailing, but if one marries at all one touches the earth. One has human feelings and needs, one has a heart in one's bosom, and one must marry a particular individual. Your mother has never forgiven me for not having come to a better understanding with Lord Warburton, and she's horrified at my contenting myself with a person who has none of his great advantages—no property, no title, no honours, no houses, nor lands, nor position, nor reputation, nor brilliant belongings of any sort. It's the total absence of all these things that pleases me. Mr Osmond's simply a very lonely, a very cultivated and a very honest man—he's not a prodigious proprietor.'

Ralph had listened with great attention, as if everything she said merited deep consideration; but in truth he was only half thinking of the things she said, he was for the rest simply accommodating himself to the weight of his total impression—the impression of her ardent good faith. She was wrong, but she believed; she was deluded, but she was dismally consistent. It was wonderfully characteristic of her that, having invented a fine theory about Gilbert Osmond, she loved him not for what he really possessed, but for his very poverties dressed out as honours. Ralph remembered what he had said to his father about wishing to put it into her power to meet the requirements of her imagination. He had done so, and the girl had taken full advantage of the luxury. Poor Ralph felt sick; he felt ashamed. Isabel had uttered her last words with a low solemnity of conviction which virtually terminated the discussion, and she closed it formally by turning away and walking back to the house. Ralph walked beside her, and they passed into the court together and reached the big staircase. Here he stopped and Isabel paused, turning on him a face of elation—absolutely and perversely of gratitude. His opposition had made her own conception of her conduct clearer to her. 'Shall you not come up to breakfast?' she asked.

'No; I want no breakfast; I'm not hungry.'

'You ought to eat,' said the girl; 'you live on air.'

'I do, very much, and I shall go back into the garden and take another mouthful. I came thus far simply to say this. I told you last year that if you were to get into trouble I should feel terribly sold. That's how I feel to-day.'

'Do you think I'm in trouble?'

'One's in trouble when one's in error.'

'Very well,' said Isabel; 'I shall never complain of my trouble to you!' And she moved up the staircase.

Ralph, standing there with his hands in his pockets, followed her with his eyes; then the lurking chill of the high-walled court struck him and made him shiver, so that he returned to the garden to breakfast on the Florentine sunshine.

XXXV

ISABEL, when she strolled in the Cascine with her lover, felt no impulse to tell him how little he was approved at Palazzo Crescentini. The discreet opposition offered to her marriage by her aunt and her cousin made on the whole no great impression upon her; the moral of it was simply that they disliked Gilbert Osmond. This dislike was not alarming to Isabel; she scarcely even regretted it; for it served mainly to throw into higher relief the fact, in every way so honourable, that she married to please herself. One did other things to please other people; one did this for a more personal satisfaction; and Isabel's satisfaction was confirmed by her lover's admirable good conduct. Gilbert Osmond was in love, and he had never deserved less than during these still, bright days, each of them numbered, which preceded the fulfilment of his hopes, the harsh criticism passed upon him by Ralph Touchett. The chief impression produced on Isabel's spirit by this criticism was that the passion of love separated its victim terribly from every one but the loved object. She felt herself disjoined from every one she had ever known before—from her two sisters, who wrote to express a dutiful hope that she would be happy, and a surprise, somewhat more vague, at her not having chosen a consort who was the hero of a richer accumulation of anecdote; from Henrietta, who, she was sure, would come out, too late, on purpose to remonstrate; from Lord Warburton, who would certainly console himself, and from Caspar Goodwood, who perhaps would not; from her aunt, who had cold, shallow ideas about marriage, for which she was not sorry to display her contempt; and from Ralph, whose talk about having great views for her was surely but a whimsical cover for a personal disappointment. Ralph apparently wished her not to marry at all—that was what it really meant—because he was amused with the spectacle of her adventures as a single woman. His disappointment made him say angry things about the man she had preferred even to him: Isabel flattered herself that she believed Ralph had been angry.

It was the more easy for her to believe this because, as I say, she had now little free or unemployed emotion for minor needs, and accepted as an incident, in fact quite as an ornament, of her lot the idea that to prefer Gilbert Osmond as she preferred him was perforce to break all other ties. She tasted of the sweets of this preference, and they made her conscious, almost with awe, of the invidious and remorseless tide of the charmed and possessed condition, great as was the traditional honour and imputed virtue of being in love. It was the tragic part of happiness; one's right was always made of the wrong of some one else.

The elation of success, which surely now flamed high in Osmond, emitted meanwhile very little smoke for so brilliant a blaze. Contentment, on his part, took no vulgar form; excitement, in the most self-conscious of men, was a kind of ecstasy of self-control. This disposition, however, made him an admirable lover; it gave him a constant view of the smitten and dedicated state. He never forgot himself, as I say; and so he never forgot to be graceful and tender, to wear the appearance—which presented indeed no difficulty—of stirred senses and deep intentions. He was immensely pleased with his young lady; Madame Merle had made him a present of incalculable value. What could be a finer thing to live with than a high spirit attuned to softness? For would not the softness be all for one's self, and the strenuousness for society, which admired the air of superiority? What could be a happier gift in a companion than a quick, fanciful mind which saved one repetitions and reflected one's thought on a polished, elegant surface? Osmond hated to see his thought reproduced literally—that made it look stale and stupid; he preferred it to be freshened in the reproduction even as 'words' by music. His egotism had never taken the crude form of desiring a dull wife; this lady's intelligence was to be a silver plate, not an earthen one—a plate that he might heap up with ripe fruits, to which it would give a decorative value, so that talk might become for him a sort of served dessert. He found the silver quality in this perfection in Isabel; he could tap her imagination with his knuckle and make it ring. He knew perfectly, though he had not been told, that their union enjoyed little favour with the girl's relations; but he had always treated her so completely as an independent person that it hardly seemed necessary to express regret for the attitude of her family. Nevertheless, one morning, he made an abrupt allusion to it. 'It's the difference in our fortune they don't like,' he said. 'They think I'm in love with your money.'

'Are you speaking of my aunt—of my cousin?' Isabel asked. 'How do you know what they think?'

'You've not told me they're pleased, and when I wrote to Mrs Touchett the other day she never answered my note. If they had been delighted I should have had some sign of it, and the fact of my being poor and you rich is the most obvious explanation of their reserve. But of course when a poor man marries a rich girl he must be prepared for imputations. I don't mind them; I only care for one thing—for your not having the shadow of a doubt. I don't care what people of whom I ask nothing think—I'm not even capable perhaps of wanting to know. I've never so concerned myself, God forgive me, and why should I begin to-day, when I have taken to myself a compensation for everything? I won't pretend I'm sorry you're rich; I'm delighted. I delight in everything that's yours—whether it be money or virtue. Money's a horrid thing to follow, but a charming thing to meet. It seems to me, however, that I've sufficiently proved the limits of my itch for it: I never in my life tried to earn a penny, and I ought to be less subject to suspicion than most of the people one sees grubbing and grabbing. I suppose it's their business to suspect—that of your family; it's proper on the whole they should. They'll like me better some day; so will you, for that matter. Meanwhile my business is not to make myself bad blood, but simply to be thankful for life and love.' 'It has made me better, loving you,' he said on another occasion; 'it has made me wiser and easier and—I won't pretend to deny—brighter and nicer and even stronger. I used to want a great many things before and to be angry I didn't have them. Theoretically I was satisfied, as I once told you. I flattered myself I had limited my wants. But I was subject to irritation; I used to have morbid, sterile, hateful fits of hunger, of desire. Now I'm really satisfied, because I can't think of anything better. It's just as when one has been trying to spell out a book in the twilight and suddenly the lamp comes in. I had been putting out my eyes over the book of life and finding nothing to reward me for my pains; but now that I can read it properly I see it's a delightful story. My dear girl, I can't tell you how life seems to stretch there before us—what a long summer afternoon awaits us. It's the latter half of an Italian day—with a golden haze, and the shadows just lengthening, and that divine delicacy in the light, the air, the landscape, which I have loved all my life and which you love to-day. Upon my honour, I don't see why we shouldn't get on. We've got what we like—to say nothing of having each other. We've the faculty of admiration and several capital convictions. We're not stupid, we're not mean, we're not under bonds to any kind of ignorance or dreariness. You're remarkably fresh, and I'm remarkably well-seasoned. We've my poor child to amuse us; we'll try and make up some little life for her. It's all soft and mellow—it has the Italian colouring.'

They made a good many plans, but they left themselves also a good deal of latitude; it was a matter of course, however, that they should live for the present in Italy. It was in Italy that they had met, Italy had been a party to their first impressions of each other, and Italy should be a party to their happiness. Osmond had the attachment of old acquaintance and Isabel the stimulus of new, which seemed to assure her a future at a high level of consciousness of the beautiful. The desire for unlimited expansion had been succeeded in her soul by the sense that life was vacant without some private duty that might gather one's energies to a point. She had told Ralph she had 'seen life' in a year or two and that she was already tired, not of the act of living, but of that of observing. What had become of all her ardours, her aspirations, her theories, her high estimate of her independence and her incipient conviction that she should never marry? These things had been absorbed in a more primitive need—a need the answer to which brushed away numberless questions, yet gratified infinite desires. It simplified the situation at a stroke, it came down from above like the light of the stars, and it needed no explanation. There was explanation enough in the fact that he was her lover, her own, and that she should be able to be of use to him. She could surrender to him with a kind of humility, she could marry him with a kind of pride; she was not only taking, she was giving.

He brought Pansy with him two or three times to the Cascine—Pansy who was very little taller than a year before, and not much older. That she would always be a child was the conviction expressed by her father, who held her by the hand when she was in her sixteenth year and told her to go and play while he sat down a little with the pretty lady. Pansy wore a short dress and a long coat; her hat always seemed too big for her. She found pleasure in walking off, with quick, short steps, to the end of the alley, and then in walking back with a smile that seemed an appeal for approbation. Isabel approved in abundance, and the abundance had the personal touch that the child's affectionate nature craved. She watched her indications as if for herself also much depended on them—Pansy already so represented part of the service she could render, part of the responsibility she could face. Her father took so the childish view of her that he had not yet explained to her the new relation in which he stood to the elegant Miss Archer. 'She doesn't know,' he said to Isabel; 'she doesn't guess; she thinks it perfectly natural that you and I should come and walk here together simply as good friends. There seems to me something enchantingly innocent in that; it's the way I like her to be. No, I'm not a failure, as I used to think; I've succeeded in two things. I'm to marry the woman I adore, and I've brought up my child, as I wished, in the old way.'

He was very fond, in all things, of the 'old way'; that had struck Isabel as one of his fine, quiet, sincere notes. 'It occurs to me that you'll not know whether you've succeeded until you've told her,' she said. 'You must see how she takes your news. She may be horrified—she may be jealous.'

'I'm not afraid of that; she's too fond of you on her own account. I should like to leave her in the dark a little longer—to see if it will come into her head that if we're not engaged we ought to be.'

Isabel was impressed by Osmond's artistic, the plastic view, as it somehow appeared, of Pansy's innocence—her own appreciation of it being more anxiously moral. She was perhaps not the less pleased when he told her a few days later that he had communicated the fact to his daughter, who had made such a pretty little speech—'Oh, then I shall have a beautiful sister!' She was neither surprised nor alarmed; she had not cried, as he expected.

'Perhaps she had guessed it,' said Isabel.

'Don't say that; I should be disgusted if I believed that. I thought it would be just a little shock; but the way she took it proves that her good manners are paramount. That's also what I wished. You shall see for yourself; to-morrow she shall make you her congratulations in person.'

The meeting, on the morrow, took place at the Countess Gemini's, whither Pansy had been conducted by her father, who knew that Isabel was to come in the afternoon to return a visit made her by the Countess on learning that they were to become sisters-in-law. Calling at Casa Touchett the visitor had not found Isabel at home; but after our young woman had been ushered into the Countess's drawing-room Pansy arrived to say that her aunt would presently appear. Pansy was spending the day with that lady, who thought her of an age to begin to learn how to carry herself in company. It was Isabel's view that the little girl might have given lessons in deportment to her relative, and nothing could have justified this conviction more than the manner in which Pansy acquitted herself while they waited together for the Countess. Her father's decision, the year before, had finally been to send her back to the convent to receive the last graces, and Madame Catherine had evidently carried out her theory that Pansy was to be fitted for the great world.

'Papa has told me that you've kindly consented to marry him,' said this excellent woman's pupil. 'It's very delightful; I think you'll suit very well.'

'You think I shall suit *you?*'

'You'll suit me beautifully; but what I mean is that you and papa will suit each other. You're both so quiet and so serious. You're not so quiet as he—or even as Madame Merle; but you're more quiet than many others. He should not for instance have a wife like my aunt. She's always in motion, in agitation—to-day especially; you'll see when she comes in.

They told us at the convent it was wrong to judge our elders, but I suppose there's no harm if we judge them favourably. You'll be a delightful companion for papa.'

'For you too, I hope,' Isabel said.

'I speak first of him on purpose. I've told you already what I myself think of you; I liked you from the first. I admire you so much that I think it will be a good fortune to have you always before me. You'll be my model; I shall try to imitate you though I'm afraid it will be very feeble. I'm very glad for papa—he needed something more than me. Without you I don't see how he could have got it. You'll be my stepmother, but we mustn't use that word. They're always said to be cruel; but I don't think you'll ever so much as pinch or even push me. I'm not afraid at all.'

'My good little Pansy,' said Isabel gently, 'I shall be ever so kind to you.' A vague, inconsequent vision of her coming in some odd way to need it had intervened with the effect of a chill.

'Very well then, I've nothing to fear,' the child returned with her note of prepared promptitude. What teaching she had had, it seemed to suggest—or what penalties for non-performance she dreaded!

Her description of her aunt had not been incorrect; the Countess Gemini was further than ever from having folded her wings. She entered the room with a flutter through the air and kissed Isabel first on the forehead and then on each cheek as if according to some ancient prescribed rite. She drew the visitor to a sofa and, looking at her with a variety of turns of the head, began to talk very much as if, seated brush in hand before an easel, she were applying a series of considered touches to a composition of figures already sketched in. 'If you expect me to congratulate you I must beg you to excuse me. I don't suppose you care if I do or not; I believe you're supposed not to care—through being so clever—for all sorts of ordinary things. But I care myself if I tell fibs; I never tell them unless there's something rather good to be gained. I don't see what's to be gained with you—especially as you wouldn't believe me. I don't make professions any more than I make paper flowers or flouncey lampshades—I don't know how. My lampshades would be sure to take fire, my roses and my fibs to be larger than life. I'm very glad for my own sake that you're to marry Osmond; but I won't pretend I'm glad for yours. You're very brilliant—you know that's the way you're always spoken of; you're an heiress and very good-looking and original, not *banal;* so it's a good thing to have you in the family. Our family's very good, you know; Osmond will have told you that; and my mother was rather distinguished—she was called the American Corinne. But we're dreadfully fallen, I think, and perhaps you'll pick us up. I've great confidence in you; there are ever so many things I want to talk to you about. I never congratulate any girl on marrying; I think they ought to make it somehow not quite so awful a steel trap. I suppose Pansy oughtn't to hear all this; but that's what she has come to me for—to acquire the tone of society. There's no harm in her knowing what horrors she may be in for. When first I got an idea that my brother had designs on you I thought of writing to you, to recommend you, in the strongest terms, not to listen to him. Then I thought it would be disloyal, and I hate anything of that kind. Besides, as I say, I was enchanted for myself; and after all I'm very selfish. By the way, you won't respect me, not one little mite, and we shall never be intimate. I should like it, but you won't. Some day, all the same, we shall be better friends than you will believe at first. My husband will come and see you, though, as you probably know, he's on no sort of terms with Osmond. He's very fond of going to see pretty women, but I'm not afraid of you. In the first place I don't care what he does. In the second, you won't care a straw for him; he won't be a bit, at any time, your affair, and, stupid as he is, he'll see you're not his. Some day, if you can stand it, I'll tell you all about him. Do you think my niece ought to go out of the room? Pansy, go and practise a little in my boudoir.'

'Let her stay, please,' said Isabel. 'I would rather hear nothing that Pansy may not!'

XXXVI

One afternoon of the autumn of 1876, toward dusk, a young man of pleasing appearance rang at the door of a small apartment on the third floor of an old Roman house. On its being opened he enquired for Madame Merle; whereupon the servant, a neat, plain woman, with a French face and a lady's maid's manner, ushered him into a diminutive drawing-room and requested the favour of his name. 'Mr Edward Rosier,' said the young man, who sat down to wait till his hostess should appear.

The reader will perhaps not have forgotten that Mr Rosier was an ornament of the American circle in Paris, but it may also be remembered that he sometimes vanished from its horizon. He had spent a portion of several winters at Pau, and as he was a gentleman of constituted habits he might have continued for years to pay his annual visit to this charming resort. In the summer of 1876, however, an incident befell him which changed the current not only of his thoughts, but of his customary sequences. He passed a month in the Upper Engadine and encountered at Saint Moritz a charming young girl. To this little person he began to pay, on the spot, particular attention: she struck him as exactly the household angel he had long been looking for. He was never precipitate, he was nothing if not discreet, so he forbore for the present to declare his passion; but it seemed to him when they parted—the young lady to go down into Italy and her admirer to proceed to Geneva, where he was under bonds to join other friends—that he should be romantically wretched if he were not to see her again. The simplest way to do so was to go in the autumn to Rome, where Miss Osmond was domiciled with her family. Mr Rosier started on his pilgrimage to the Italian capital and reached it on the first of November. It was a pleasant thing to do, but for the young man there was a strain of the heroic in the enterprise. He might expose himself, unseasoned, to the poison of the Roman air, which in November lay, notoriously, much in wait. Fortune, however, favours the brave; and this adventurer, who took three grains of quinine a day, had at the end of a month no cause to deplore his temerity. He had made to a certain extent good use of his time; he had devoted it in vain to finding a flaw in Pansy Osmond's composition. She was admirably finished; she had had the last touch; she was really a consummate piece. He thought of her in amorous meditation a good deal as he might have thought of a Dresden-china shepherdess. Miss Osmond, indeed, in the bloom of her juvenility, had a hint of the rococo which Rosier, whose taste was predominantly for that manner, could not fail to appreciate. That he esteemed the productions of comparatively frivolous periods would have been apparent from the attention he bestowed upon Madame Merle's drawing-room, which, although furnished with specimens of every style, was especially rich in articles of the last two centuries. He had immediately put a glass into one eye and looked round; and then 'By Jove, she has some jolly good things!' he had yearningly murmured. The room was small and densely filled with furniture; it gave an impression of faded silk and little statuettes which might totter if one moved. Rosier got up and wandered about with his careful tread, bending over the tables charged with knick-knacks and the cushions embossed with princely arms. When Madame Merle came in she found him standing before the fireplace with his nose very close to the great lace flounce attached to the damask cover of the mantel. He had lifted it delicately, as if he were smelling it.

'It's old Venetian,' she said; 'it's rather good.'

'It's too good for this; you ought to wear it.'

'They tell me you have some better in Paris, in the same situation.'

'Ah, but I can't wear mine,' smiled the visitor.

'I don't see why you shouldn't! I've better lace than that to wear.'

His eyes wandered, lingeringly, round the room again. 'You've some very good things.'

'Yes, but I hate them.'

'Do you want to get rid of them?' the young man quickly asked.

'No, it's good to have something to hate: one works it off!'

'I love my things,' said Mr Rosier as he sat there flushed with all his recognitions. 'But it's not about them, nor about yours, that I came to talk to you.' He paused a moment and then, with greater softness: 'I care more for Miss Osmond than for all the *bibelots* in Europe!'

Madame Merle opened wide eyes. 'Did you come to tell me that?'

'I came to ask your advice.'

She looked at him with a friendly frown, stroking her chin with her large white hand. 'A man in love, you know, doesn't ask advice.'

'Why not, if he's in a difficult position? That's often the case with a man in love. I've been in love before, and I know. But never so much as this time—really never so much. I should like particularly to know what you think of my prospects. I'm afraid that for Mr Osmond I'm not—well, a real collector's piece.'

'Do you wish me to intercede?' Madame Merle asked with her fine arms folded and her handsome mouth drawn up to the left.

'If you could say a good word for me I should be greatly obliged. There will be no use in my troubling Miss Osmond unless I have good reason to believe her father will consent.'

'You're very considerate; that's in your favour. But you assume in rather an off-hand way that *I* think you a prize.'

'You've been very kind to me,' said the young man. 'That's why I came.'

'I'm always kind to people who have good Louis Quatorze.* It's very rare now, and there's no telling what one may get by it.' With which the left-hand corner of Madame Merle's mouth gave expression to the joke.

But he looked, in spite of it, literally apprehensive and consistently strenuous. 'Ah, I thought you liked me for myself!'

'I like you very much; but, if you please, we won't analyse. Pardon me if I seem patronising, but I think you a perfect little gentleman. I must tell you, however, that I've not the marrying of Pansy Osmond.'

'I didn't suppose that. But you've seemed to me intimate with her family, and I thought you might have influence.'

Madame Merle considered. 'Whom do you call her family?'

'Why, her father; and—how do you say it in English?—her *belle-mère*.'*

'Mr Osmond's her father, certainly; but his wife can scarcely be termed a member of her family. Mrs Osmond has nothing to do with marrying her.'

'I'm sorry for that,' said Rosier with an amiable sigh of good faith. 'I think Mrs Osmond would favour me.'

'Very likely—if her husband doesn't.'

He raised his eyebrows. 'Does she take the opposite line from him?'

'In everything. They think quite differently.'

'Well,' said Rosier, 'I'm sorry for that; but it's none of my business. She's very fond of Pansy.'

'Yes, she's very fond of Pansy.'

'And Pansy has a great affection for her. She has told me how she loves her as if she were her own mother.'

'You must, after all, have had some very intimate talk with the poor child,' said Madame Merle. 'Have you declared your sentiments?'

'Never!' cried Rosier, lifting his neartly-gloved hand. 'Never till I've assured myself of those of the parents.'

'You always wait for that? You've excellent principles; you observe the proprieties.'

'I think you're laughing at me,' the young man murmured, dropping back in his chair and feeling his small moustache. 'I didn't expect that of you, Madame Merle.'

She shook her head calmly, like a person who saw things as she saw them. 'You don't do me justice. I think your conduct in excellent taste and the best you could adopt. Yes, that's what I think.'

'I wouldn't agitate her—only to agitate her; I love her too much for that,' said Ned Rosier.

'I'm glad, after all, that you've told me,' Madame Merle went on. 'Leave it to me a little; I think I can help you.'

'I said you were the person to come to!' her visitor cried with prompt elation.

'You were very clever,' Madame Merle returned more dryly.

'When I say I can help you I mean once assuming your cause to be good. Let us think a little if it is.'

'I'm awfully decent, you know,' said Rosier earnestly. 'I won't say I've no faults, but I'll say I've no vices.'

'All that's negative, and it always depends, also, on what people call vices. What's the positive side? What's the virtuous? What have you got besides your Spanish lace and your Dresden teacups?'

'I've a comfortable little fortune—about forty thousand francs a year. With the talent I have for arranging, we can live beautifully on such an income.'

'Beautifully, no. Sufficiently, yes. Even that depends on where you live.'

'Well, in Paris. I would undertake it in Paris.'

Madame Merle's mouth rose to the left. 'It wouldn't be famous; you'd have to make use of the teacups, and they'd get broken.'

'We don't want to be famous. If Miss Osmond should have everything pretty it would be enough. When one's as pretty as she one can afford—well, quite cheap *faience.** She ought never to wear anything but muslin—without the sprig,' said Rosier reflectively.

'Wouldn't you even allow her the sprig? She'd be much obliged to you at any rate for that theory.'

'It's the correct one, I assure you; and I'm sure she'd enter into it. She understands all that; that's why I love her.'

'She's a very good little girl, and most tidy—also extremely graceful. But her father, to the best of my belief, can give her nothing.'

Rosier scarce demurred. 'I don't in the least desire that he should. But I may remark, all the same, that he lives like a rich man.'

'The money's his wife's; she brought him a large fortune.'

'Mrs Osmond then is very fond of her step-daughter; she may do something.'

'For a love-sick swain you have your eyes about you!' Madame Merle exclaimed with a laugh.

'I esteem a *dot* very much. I can do without it, but I esteem it.'

'Mrs Osmond,' Madame Merle went on, 'will probably prefer to keep her money for her own children.'

'Her own children? Surely she has none.'

'She may have yet. She had a poor little boy, who died two years ago, six months after his birth. Others therefore may come.'

'I hope they will, if it will make her happy. She's a splendid woman.'

Madame Merle failed to burst into speech. 'Ah, about her there's much to be said. Splendid as you like! We've not exactly made out that you're a *parti*. The absence of vices is hardly a source of income.'

'Pardon me, I think it may be,' said Rosier quite lucidly.

'You'll be a touching couple, living on your innocence!'

'I think you underrate me.'

'You're not so innocent as that? Seriously,' said Madame Merle, 'of course forty thousand francs a year and a nice character are a combination to be considered. I don't say it's to be jumped at, but there might be a worse offer. Mr Osmond, however, will probably incline to believe he can do better.'

'*He* can do so perhaps; but what can his daughter do? She can't do better than marry the man she loves. For she does, you know,' Rosier added eagerly.

'She does—I know it.'

'Ah,' cried the young man, 'I said you were the person to come to.'

'But I don't know how *you* know it, if you haven't asked her,' Madame Merle went on.

'In such a case there's no need of asking and telling; as you say, we're an innocent couple. How did *you* know it?'

'I who am not innocent? By being very crafty. Leave it to me; I'll find out for you.'

Rosier got up and stood smoothing his hat. 'You say that rather coldly. Don't simply find out how it is, but try to make it as it should be.'

'I'll do my best. I'll try to make the most of your advantages.'

'Thank you so very much. Meanwhile then I'll say a word to Mrs Osmond.'

'*Gardez-vous-en bien!*'* And Madame Merle was on her feet. 'Don't set her going, or you'll spoil everything.'

Rosier gazed into his hat; he wondered whether his hostess *had* been after all the right person to come to. 'I don't think I understand you. I'm an old friend of Mrs Osmond, and I think she would like me to succeed.'

'Be an old friend as much as you like; the more old friends she has the better, for she doesn't get on very well with some of her new. But don't for the present try to make her take up the cudgels for you. Her husband may have other views, and, as a person who wishes her well, I advise you not to multiply points of difference between them.'

Poor Rosier's face assumed an expression of alarm; a suit for the hand of Pansy Osmond was even a more complicated business than his taste for proper transitions had allowed. But the extreme good sense which he concealed under a surface suggesting that of a careful owner's 'best set' came to his assistance. 'I don't see that I'm bound to consider Mr Osmond so very much!' he exclaimed.

'No, but you should consider *her*. You say you're an old friend. Would you make her suffer?'

'Not for the world.'

'Then be very careful, and let the matter alone till I've taken a few soundings.'

'Let the matter alone, dear Madame Merle? Remember that I'm in love.'

'Oh, you won't burn up! Why did you come to me, if you're not to heed what I say?'

'You're very kind; I'll be very good,' the young man promised. 'But I'm afraid Mr Osmond's pretty hard,' he added in his mild voice as he went to the door.

Madame Merle gave a short laugh. 'It has been said before. But his wife isn't easy either.'

'Ah, she's a splendid woman!' Ned Rosier repeated, for departure.

He resolved that his conduct should be worthy of an aspirant who was already a model of discretion; but he saw nothing in any pledge he had given Madame Merle that made it improper he should keep himself in spirits by an occasional visit to Miss

Osmond's home. He reflected constantly on what his adviser had said to him, and turned over in his mind the impression of her rather circumspect tone. He had gone to her *de confiance*, as they put it in Paris; but it was possible he had been precipitate. He found difficulty in thinking of himself as rash—he had incurred this reproach so rarely; but it certainly was true that he had known Madame Merle only for the last month, and that his thinking her a delightful woman was not, when one came to look into it, a reason for assuming that she would be eager to push Pansy Osmond into his arms, gracefully arranged as these members might be to receive her. She had indeed shown him benevolence, and she was a person of consideration among the girl's people, where she had a rather striking appearance (Rosier had more than once wondered how she managed it) of being intimate without being familiar. But possibly he had exaggerated these advantages. There was no particular reason why she should take trouble for him; a charming woman was charming to every one, and Rosier felt rather a fool when he thought of his having appealed to her on the ground that she had distinguished him. Very likely—though she had appeared to say it in joke—she was really only thinking of his *bibelots*. Had it come into her head that he might offer her two or three of the gems of his collection? If she would only help him to marry Miss Osmond he would present her with his whole museum. He could hardly say so to her outright; it would seem too gross a bribe. But he should like her to believe it.

It was with these thoughts that he went again to Mrs Osmond's, Mrs Osmond having an 'evening'—she had taken the Thursday of each week—when his presence could be accounted for on general principles of civility. The object of Mr Rosier's well-regulated affection dwelt in a high house in the very heart of Rome; a dark and massive structure overlooking a sunny *piazzetta** in the neighbourhood of the Farnese Palace. In a palace, too, little Pansy lived—a palace by Roman measure, but a dungeon to poor Rosier's apprehensive mind. It seemed to him of evil omen that the young lady he wished to marry, and whose fastidious father he doubted of his ability to conciliate, should be immured in a kind of domestic fortress, a pile which bore a stern old Roman name, which smelt of historic deeds, of crime and craft and violence, which was mentioned in 'Murray' and visited by tourists who looked, on a vague survey, disappointed and depressed, and which had frescoes by Caravaggio* in the *piano nobile** and a row of mutilated statues and dusty urns in the wide, nobly-arched loggia overhanging the damp court where a fountain gushed out of a mossy niche. In a less preoccupied frame of mind he could have done justice to the Palazzo Roccanera; he could have entered into the sentiment of Mrs Osmond, who had once told him that on settling themselves in Rome she and her husband had chosen this habitation for the love of local colour. It had local colour enough, and though he knew less about architecture than about Limoges enamels he could see that the proportions of the windows and even the details of the cornice had quite the grand air. But Rosier was haunted by the conviction that at picturesque periods young girls had been shut up there to keep them from their true loves, and then, under the threat of being thrown into convents, had been forced into unholy marriages. There was one point, however, to which he always did justice when once he found himself in Mrs Osmond's warm, rich-looking reception-rooms, which were on the second floor. He acknowledged that these people were very strong in 'good things.' It was a taste of Osmond's own—not at all of hers; this she had told him the first time he came to the house, when, after asking himself for a quarter of an hour whether they had even better 'French' than he in Paris, he was obliged on the spot to admit that they had, very much, and vanquished his envy, as a gentleman should, to the point of expressing to his hostess his pure admiration of her treasures. He learned from Mrs Osmond that her husband had made a large collection before their marriage and that, though he had annexed a number of fine pieces within the last three years, he had achieved his greatest finds at a time when he had not the advantage of her advice. Rosier interpreted this information according to principles of his own. For 'advice' read 'cash,' he said to himself; and the fact that Gilbert Osmond had landed his highest prizes during his impecunious season confirmed his most cherished doctrine—the doctrine that a collector may freely be poor if he be only patient. In general, when Rosier presented himself on a Thursday evening, his first recognition was for the walls of the saloon; there were three or four objects his eyes really yearned for. But after his talk with Madame Merle he felt the extreme seriousness of his position; and now, when he came in, he looked about for the daughter of the house with such eagerness as might be permitted a gentleman whose smile, as he crossed a threshold, always took everything comfortable for granted.

XXXVII

PANSY was not in the first of the rooms, a large apartment with a concave ceiling and walls covered with old red damask; it was here Mrs Osmond usually sat—though she was not in her most customary place to-night—and that a circle of more especial intimates gathered about the fire. The room was flushed with subdued, diffused brightness; it contained the larger things and—almost always—an odour of flowers. Pansy on this occasion was presumably in the next of the series, the resort of younger visitors, where tea was served. Osmond stood before the chimney, leaning back with his hands behind him; he had one foot up and was warming the sole. Half a dozen persons, scattered near him, were talking together; but he was not in the conversation; his eyes had an expression, frequent with them, that seemed to represent them as engaged with objects more worth their while than the appearances actually thrust upon them. Rosier, coming in unannounced, failed to attract his attention; but the young man, who was very punctilious, though he was even exceptionally conscious that it was the wife, not the husband, he had come to see, went up to shake hands with him. Osmond put out his left hand,* without changing his attitude.

'How d'ye do? My wife's somewhere about.'

'Never fear; I shall find her,' said Rosier cheerfully.

Osmond, however, took him in; he had never in his life felt himself so efficiently looked at. 'Madame Merle has told him, and he doesn't like it,' he privately reasoned. He had hoped Madame Merle would be there, but she was not in sight; perhaps she was in one of the other rooms or would come later. He had never especially delighted in Gilbert Osmond, having a fancy he gave himself airs. But Rosier was not quickly resentful, and where politeness was concerned had ever a strong need of being quite in the right. He looked round him and smiled, all without help, and then in a moment, 'I saw a jolly good piece of Capo di Monte* to-day,' he said.

Osmond answered nothing at first; but presently, while he warmed his boot-sole, 'I don't care a fig for Capo di Monte!' he returned.

'I hope you're not losing your interest?'

'In old pots and plates? Yes, I'm losing my interest.'

Rosier for an instant forgot the delicacy of his position. 'You're not thinking of parting with a—a piece or two?'

'No, I'm not thinking of parting with anything at all, Mr Rosier,' said Osmond, with his eyes still on the eyes of his visitor.

'Ah, you want to keep, but not to add,' Rosier remarked brightly.

'Exactly. I've nothing I wish to match.'

Poor Rosier was aware he had blushed; he was distressed at his want of assurance. 'Ah, well, *I* have!' was all he could murmur; and he knew his murmur was partly lost as he turned away. He took his course to the adjoining room and met Mrs Osmond coming out of the deep doorway. She was dressed in black velvet; she looked high and splendid, as he had said, and yet oh so radiantly gentle! We know what Mr Rosier thought of her and the terms in which, to Madame Merle, he had expressed his admiration. Like his appreciation of her dear little stepdaughter it was based partly on his eye for decorative character, his instinct for authenticity; but also on a sense for uncatalogued values, for that secret of a 'lustre' beyond any recorded losing or rediscovering, which his devotion to brittle wares had still not disqualified him to recognise. Mrs Osmond, at present, might well have gratified such tastes. The years had touched her only to enrich her; the flower of her youth had not faded, it only hung more quietly on its stem. She had lost something of that quick eagerness to which her husband had privately taken exception—she had more the air of being able to wait. Now, at all events, framed in the gilded doorway, she struck our young man as the picture of a gracious lady. 'You see I'm very regular,' he said. 'But who should be if I'm not?'

'Yes, I've known you longer than any one here. But we mustn't indulge in tender reminiscences. I want to introduce you to a young lady.'

'Ah, please, what young lady?' Rosier was immensely obliging; but this was not what he had come for.

'She sits there by the fire in pink and has no one to speak to.'

Rosier hesitated a moment. 'Can't Mr Osmond speak to her? He's within six feet of her.'

Mrs Osmond also hesitated. 'She's not very lively, and he doesn't like dull people.'

'But she's good enough for me? Ah now, that's hard!'

'I only mean that you've ideas for two. And then you're so obliging.'

'So is your husband.'

'No, he's not—to me.' And Mrs Osmond vaguely smiled.

'That's a sign he should be doubly so to other women.'

'So I tell him,' she said, still smiling.

'You see I want some tea,' Rosier went on, looking wistfully beyond.

'That's perfect. Go and give some to my young lady.'

'Very good; but after that I'll abandon her to her fate. The simple truth is I'm dying to have a little talk with Miss Osmond.'

'Ah,' said Isabel, turning away, 'I can't help you there!'

Five minutes later, while he handed a tea-cup to the damsel in pink, whom he had conducted into the other room, he wondered whether, in making to Mrs Osmond the profession I have just quoted, he had broken the spirit of his promise to Madame Merle. Such a question was capable of occupying this young man's mind for a considerable time. At last, however, he became—comparatively speaking—reckless; he cared little what promises he might break. The fate to which he had threatened to abandon the damsel in pink proved to be none so terrible; for Pansy Osmond, who had given him the tea for his companion—Pansy was as fond as ever of making tea—presently came and talked to her. Into this mild colloquy Edward Rosier entered little; he sat by moodily, watching his small sweetheart. If we look at her now through his eyes we shall at first not see much to remind us of the obedient little girl who, at Florence, three years before, was sent to walk short distances in the Cascine while her father and Miss Archer talked together of matters sacred to elder people. But after a moment we shall perceive that if at nineteen Pansy has become a young lady she doesn't really fill out the part; that if she has grown very pretty she lacks in a deplorable degree the quality known and esteemed in the appearance of females as style; and that if she is dressed with great freshness she wears her smart attire with an undisguised appearance of saving it—very much as if it were lent her for the occasion. Edward Rosier, it would seem, would have been just the man to note these defects; and in point of fact there was not a quality of this young lady, of any sort, that he had not noted. Only he called her qualities by names of his own—some of which indeed were happy enough. 'No, she's unique—she's absolutely unique,' he used to say to himself; and you may be sure that not for an instant would he have admitted to you that she was wanting in style. Style? Why, she had the style of a little princess; if you couldn't see it you had no eye. It was not modern, it was not conscious, it would produce no impression in Broadway; the small, serious damsel, in her stiff little dress, only looked like an Infanta of Velasquez.* This was enough for Edward Rosier, who thought her delightfully old-fashioned. Her anxious eyes, her charming lips, her slip of a figure, were as touching as a childish prayer. He had now an acute desire to know just to what point she liked him—a desire which made him fidget as he sat in his chair. It made him feel hot, so that he had to pat his forehead with his handkerchief; he had never been so uncomfortable. She was such a perfect *jeune fille*,* and one couldn't make of a *jeune fille* the enquiry requisite for throwing light on such a point. A *jeune fille* was what Rosier had always dreamed of—a *jeune fille* who should yet not be French, for he had felt that this nationality would complicate the question. He was sure Pansy had never looked at a newspaper and that, in the way of novels, if she had read Sir Walter Scott* it was the very most. An American *jeune fille*—what could be better than that? She would be frank and gay, and yet would not have walked alone, nor have received letters from men, nor have been taken to the theatre to see the comedy of manners. Rosier could not deny that, as the matter stood, it would be a breach of hospitality to appeal directly to this unsophisticated creature; but he was now in imminent danger of asking himself if hospitality were the most sacred thing in the world. Was not the sentiment that he entertained for Miss Osmond of infinitely greater importance? Of greater importance to him—yes; but not probably to the master of the house. There was one comfort; even if this gentleman had been placed on his guard by Madame Merle he would not have extended the warning to Pansy; it would not have been part of his policy to let her know that a prepossessing young man was in love with her. But he *was* in love with her, the prepossessing young man; and all these restrictions of circumstance had ended by irritating him. What had Gilbert Osmond meant by giving him two fingers of his left hand? If Osmond was rude, surely he himself might be bold. He felt extremely bold after the dull girl in so vain a disguise of rose-colour had responded to the call of her mother, who came in to say, with a significant simper at Rosier, that she must carry her off to other triumphs. The mother and daughter departed together, and now it depended only upon him that he should be virtually alone with Pansy. He had never been alone with her before; he had never been alone with a *jeune fille*. It was a great moment; poor Rosier began to pat his forehead again. There was another room beyond the one in which they stood—a small room that had been thrown open and lighted, but that, the company not being numerous, had remained empty all the evening. It was empty yet; it was upholstered in pale yellow; there were several lamps; through the open door it looked the very temple of authorised love. Rosier gazed a moment through this aperture; he was afraid that Pansy would run away, and felt almost capable of stretching out a hand to detain her. But she lingered where the other maiden had left them, making no motion to join a knot of visitors on the far side of the room. For a little it occurred to him that she was frightened—too frightened perhaps to move; but a second glance assured him she was not, and he then reflected that she was too innocent indeed for that. After a supreme hesitation he asked her if he might go and look at the yellow room, which seemed so attractive yet so virginal. He had been there already with Osmond, to inspect the furniture, which was of the First French Empire, and especially to admire the clock (which he didn't really admire), an immense classic structure of that period. He therefore felt that he had now begun to manœuvre.

'Certainly, you may go,' said Pansy; 'and if you like I'll show you.' She was not in the least frightened.

'That's just what I hoped you'd say; you're so very kind,' Rosier murmured.

They went in together; Rosier really thought the room very ugly, and it seemed cold. The same idea appeared to have struck Pansy. 'It's not for winter evenings; it's more for summer,' she said. 'It's papa's taste; he has so much.'

He had a good deal, Rosier thought; but some of it was very bad. He looked about him; he hardly knew what to say in such a situation. 'Doesn't Mrs Osmond care how her rooms are done? Has she no taste?' he asked.

'Oh yes, a great deal; but it's more for literature,' said Pansy—'and for conversation. But papa cares also for those things. I think he knows everything.'

Rosier was silent a little. 'There's one thing I'm sure he knows!' he broke out presently. 'He knows that when I come here it's, with all respect to him, with all respect to Mrs Osmond, who's so charming—it's really,' said the young man, 'to see you!'

'To see me?' And Pansy raised her vaguely-troubled eyes.

'To see you; that's what I come for,' Rosier repeated, feeling the intoxication of a rupture with authority.

Pansy stood looking at him, simply, intently, openly; a blush was not needed to make her face more modest. 'I thought it was for that.'

'And it was not disagreeable to you?'

'I couldn't tell; I didn't know. You never told me,' said Pansy.

'I was afraid of offending you.'

'You don't offend me,' the young girl murmured, smiling as if an angel had kissed her.

'You like me then, Pansy?' Rosier asked very gently, feeling very happy.

'Yes—I like you.'

They had walked to the chimney-piece where the big cold Empire clock was perched; they were well within the room and beyond observation from without. The tone in which she had said these four words seemed to him the very breath of nature, and his only answer could be to take her hand and hold it a moment. Then he raised it to his lips. She submitted, still with her pure, trusting smile, in which there was something ineffably passive. She liked him—she had liked him all the while; now anything might happen! She was ready—she had been ready always, waiting for him to speak. If he had not spoken she would have waited for ever; but when the word came she dropped like the peach from the shaken tree. Rosier felt that if he should draw her toward him and hold her to his heart she would submit without a murmur, would rest there without a question. It was true that this would be a rash experiment in a yellow Empire *salottino*.* She had known it was for her he came, and yet like what a perfect little lady she had carried it off!

'You're very dear to me,' he murmured, trying to believe that there was after all such a thing as hospitality.

She looked a moment at her hand, where he had kissed it. 'Did you say papa knows?'

'You told me just now he knows everything.'

'I think you must make sure,' said Pansy.

'Ah, my dear, when once I'm sure of *you!*' Rosier murmured in her ear; whereupon she turned back to the other rooms with a little air of consistency which seemed to imply that their appeal should be immediate.

The other rooms meanwhile had become conscious of the arrival of Madame Merle, who, wherever she went, produced an impression when she entered. How she did it the most attentive spectator could not have told you, for she neither spoke loud, nor laughed profusely, nor moved rapidly, nor dressed with splendour, nor appealed in any appreciable manner to the audience. Large, fair, smiling, serene, there was something in her very tranquillity that diffused itself, and when people looked round it was because of a sudden quiet. On this occasion she had done the quietest thing she could do; after embracing Mrs Osmond, which was more striking, she had sat down on a small sofa to commune with the master of the house. There was a brief exchange of commonplaces between these two—they always paid, in public, a certain formal tribute to the commonplace—and then Madame Merle, whose eyes had been wandering, asked if little Mr Rosier had come this evening.

'He came nearly an hour ago—but he has disappeared,' Osmond said.

'And where's Pansy?'

'In the other room. There are several people there.'

'He's probably among them,' said Madame Merle.

'Do you wish to see him?' Osmond asked in a provokingly pointless tone.

Madame Merle looked at him a moment; she knew each of his tones to the eighth of a note. 'Yes, I should like to say to him that I've told you what he wants, and that it interests you but feebly.'

'Don't tell him that. He'll try to interest me more—which is exactly what I don't want. Tell him I hate his proposal.'

'But you don't hate it.'

'It doesn't signify; I don't love it. I let him see that, myself, this evening; I was rude to him on purpose. That sort of thing's a great bore. There's no hurry.'

'I'll tell him that you'll take time and think it over.'

'No, don't do that. He'll hang on.'

'If I discourage him he'll do the same.'

'Yes, but in the one case he'll try to talk and explain—which would be exceedingly tiresome. In the other he'll probably hold his tongue and go in for some deeper game. That will leave me quiet. I hate talking with a donkey.'

'Is that what you call poor Mr Rosier?'

'Oh, he's a nuisance—with his eternal majolica.'*

Madame Merle dropped her eyes; she had a faint smile. 'He's a gentleman, he has a charming temper; and, after all, an income of forty thousand francs!'

'It's misery—"genteel" misery,' Osmond broke in. 'It's not what I've dreamed of for Pansy.'

'Very good then. He has promised me not to speak to her.'

'Do you believe him?' Osmond asked absent-mindedly.

'Perfectly. Pansy has thought a great deal about him; but I don't suppose you consider that that matters.'

'I don't consider it matters at all; but neither do I believe she has thought of him.'

'That opinion's more convenient,' said Madame Merle quietly.

'Has she told you she's in love with him?'

'For what do you take her? And for what do you take me?' Madame Merle added in a moment.

Osmond had raised his foot and was resting his slim ankle on the other knee; he clasped his ankle in his hand familiarly—his long, fine forefinger and thumb could make a ring for it—and gazed a while before him. 'This kind of thing doesn't find me unprepared. It's what I educated her for. It was all for this—that when such a case should come up she should do what I prefer.'

'I'm not afraid that she'll not do it.'

'Well then, where's the hitch?'

'I don't see any. But, all the same, I recommend you not to get rid of Mr Rosier. Keep him on hand; he may be useful.'

'I can't keep him. Keep him yourself.'

'Very good; I'll put him into a corner and allow him so much a day.' Madame Merle had, for the most part, while they talked, been glancing about her; it was her habit in this situation, just as it was her habit to interpose a good many blank-looking pauses. A long drop followed the last words I have quoted; and before it had ended she saw Pansy come out of the adjoining room, followed by Edward Rosier. The girl advanced a few steps and then stopped and stood looking at Madame Merle and at her father.

'He has spoken to her,' Madame Merle went on to Osmond.

Her companion never turned his head. 'So much for your belief in his promises. He ought to be horsewhipped.'

'He intends to confess, poor little man!'

Osmond got up; he had now taken a sharp look at his daughter. 'It doesn't matter,' he murmured, turning away.

Pansy after a moment came up to Madame Merle with her little manner of unfamiliar politeness. This lady's reception of her was not more intimate; she simply, as she rose from the sofa, gave her a friendly smile.

'You're very late,' the young creature gently said.

'My dear child, I'm never later than I intend to be.'

Madame Merle had not got up to be gracious to Pansy; she moved toward Edward Rosier. He came to meet her and, very quickly, as if to get it off his mind, 'I've spoken to her!' he whispered.

'I know it, Mr Rosier.'

'Did she tell you?'

'Yes, she told me. Behave properly for the rest of the evening, and come and see me to-morrow at a quarter past five.' She was severe, and in the manner in which she turned her back to him there was a degree of contempt which caused him to mutter a decent imprecation.

He had no intention of speaking to Osmond; it was neither the time nor the place. But he instinctively wandered toward Isabel, who sat talking with an old lady. He sat down on the other side of her; the old lady was Italian, and Rosier took for granted she understood no English. 'You said just now you wouldn't help me,' he began to Mrs Osmond. 'Perhaps you'll feel differently when you know—when you know—!'

Isabel met his hesitation. 'When I know what?'

'That she's all right.'

'What do you mean by that?'

'Well, that we've come to an understanding.'

'She's all wrong,' said Isabel. 'It won't do.'

Poor Rosier gazed at her half-pleadingly, half-angrily; a sudden flush testified to his sense of injury. 'I've never been treated so,' he said. 'What is there against me, after all? That's not the way I'm usually considered. I could have married twenty times.'

'It's a pity you didn't. I don't mean twenty times, but once, comfortably,' Isabel added, smiling kindly. 'You're not rich enough for Pansy.'

'She doesn't care a straw for one's money.'

'No, but her father does.'

'Ah yes, he has proved that!' cried the young man.

Isabel got up, turning away from him, leaving her old lady without ceremony; and he occupied himself for the next ten minutes in pretending to look at Gilbert Osmond's collection of miniatures, which were neatly arranged on a series of small velvet screens. But he looked without seeing; his cheek burned; he was too full of his sense of injury. It was certain that he had never been treated that way before; he was not used to being thought not good enough. He knew how good he was, and if such a fallacy had not been so pernicious he could have laughed at it. He searched again for Pansy, but she had disappeared, and his main desire was now to get out of the house. Before doing so he spoke once more to Isabel; it was not agreeable to him to reflect that he had just said a rude thing to her—the only point that would now justify a low view of him.

'I referred to Mr Osmond as I shouldn't have done, a while ago,' he began. 'But you must remember my situation.'

'I don't remember what you said,' she answered coldly.

'Ah, you're offended, and now you'll never help me.'

She was silent an instant, and then with a change of tone: 'It's not that I won't; I simply can't!' Her manner was almost passionate.

'If you *could*, just a little, I'd never again speak of your husband save as an angel.'

'The inducement's great,' said Isabel gravely—inscrutably, as he afterwards, to himself, called it; and she gave him, straight in the eyes, a look which was also inscrutable. It made him remember somehow that he had known her as a child; and yet it was keener than he liked, and he took himself off.

XXXVIII

HE went to see Madame Merle on the morrow, and to his surprise she let him off rather easily. But she made him promise that he would stop there till something should have been decided. Mr Osmond had had higher expectations; it was very true that as he had no intention of giving his daughter a portion such expectations were open to criticism or even, if one would, to ridicule. But she would advise Mr Rosier not to take that tone; if he would possess his soul in patience he might arrive at his felicity. Mr Osmond was not favourable to his suit, but it wouldn't be a miracle if he should gradually come round. Pansy would never defy her father, he might depend on that; so nothing was to be gained by precipitation. Mr Osmond needed to accustom his mind to an offer of a sort that he had not hitherto entertained, and this result must come of itself—it was useless to try to force it. Rosier remarked that his own situation would be in the meanwhile the most uncomfortable in the world, and Madame Merle assured him that she felt for him. But, as she justly declared, one couldn't have everything one wanted; she had learned that lesson for herself. There would be no use in his writing to Gilbert Osmond, who had charged her to tell him as much. He wished the matter dropped for a few weeks and would himself write when he should have anything to communicate that it might please Mr Rosier to hear.

'He doesn't like your having spoken to Pansy. Ah, he doesn't like it at all,' said Madame Merle.

'I'm perfectly willing to give him a chance to tell me so!'

'If you do that he'll tell you more than you care to hear. Go to the house, for the next month, as little as possible, and leave the rest to me.'

'As little as possible? Who's to measure the possibility?'

'Let me measure it. Go on Thursday evenings with the rest of the world, but don't go at all at odd times, and don't fret about Pansy. I'll see that she understands everything. She's a calm little nature; she'll take it quietly.'

Edward Rosier fretted about Pansy a good deal, but he did as he was advised, and awaited another Thursday evening before returning to Palazzo Roccanera. There had been a party at dinner, so that though he went early the company was already tolerably numerous. Osmond, as usual, was in the first room, near the fire, staring straight at the door, so that, not to be distinctly uncivil, Rosier had to go and speak to him.

'I'm glad that you can take a hint,' Pansy's father said, slightly closing his keen, conscious eyes.

'I take no hints. But I took a message, as I supposed it to be.'

'You took it? Where did you take it?'

It seemed to poor Rosier he was being insulted, and he waited a moment, asking himself how much a true lover ought to submit to. 'Madame Merle gave me, as I understood it, a message from you—to the effect that you declined to give me the opportunity I desire, the opportunity to explain my wishes to you.' And he flattered himself he spoke rather sternly.

'I don't see what Madame Merle has to do with it. Why did you apply to Madame Merle?'

'I asked her for an opinion—for nothing more. I did so because she had seemed to me to know you very well.'

'She doesn't know me so well as she thinks,' said Osmond.

'I'm sorry for that, because she has given me some little ground for hope.'

Osmond stared into the fire a moment. 'I set a great price on my daughter.'

'You can't set a higher one than I do. Don't I prove it by wishing to marry her?'

'I wish to marry her very well,' Osmond went on with a dry impertinence which, in another mood, poor Rosier would have admired.

'Of course I pretend she'd marry well in marrying me. She couldn't marry a man who loves her more—or whom, I may venture to add, she loves more.'

'I'm not bound to accept your theories as to whom my daughter loves'—and Osmond looked up with a quick, cold smile.

'I'm not theorising. Your daughter has spoken.'

'Not to me,' Osmond continued, now bending forward a little and dropping his eyes to his boot-toes.

'I have her promise, sir!' cried Rosier with the sharpness of exasperation.

As their voices had been pitched very low before, such a note attracted some attention from the company. Osmond waited till this little movement had subsided; then he said, all undisturbed: 'I think she has no recollection of having given it.'

They had been standing with their faces to the fire, and after he had uttered these last words the master of the house turned round again to the room. Before Rosier had time to reply he perceived that a gentleman—a stranger—had just come in, unannounced, according to the Roman custom, and was about to present himself to his host. The latter smiled blandly, but somewhat blankly; the visitor had a handsome face and a large, fair beard, and was evidently an Englishman.

'You apparently don't recognise me,' he said with a smile that expressed more than Osmond's.

'Ah yes, now I do. I expected so little to see you.'

Rosier departed and went in direct pursuit of Pansy. He sought her, as usual, in the neighbouring room, but he again encountered Mrs Osmond in his path. He gave his hostess no greeting—he was too righteously indignant, but said to her crudely: 'Your husband's awfully cold-blooded.'

She gave the same mystical smile he had noticed before. 'You can't expect every one to be as hot as yourself.'

'I don't pretend to be cold, but I'm cool. What has he been doing to his daughter?'

'I've no idea.'

'Don't you take any interest?' Rosier demanded with his sense that she too was irritating.

For a moment she answered nothing; then, 'No!' she said abruptly and with a quickened light in her eyes which directly contradicted the word.

'Pardon me if I don't believe that. Where's Miss Osmond?'

'In the corner, making tea. Please leave her there.'

Rosier instantly discovered his friend, who had been hidden by intervening groups. He watched her, but her own attention was entirely given to her occupation. 'What on earth has he done to her?' he asked again imploringly. 'He declares to me she has given me up.'

'She has not given you up,' Isabel said in a low tone and without looking at him.

'Ah, thank you for that! Now I'll leave her alone as long as you think proper!'

He had hardly spoken when he saw her change colour, and became aware that Osmond was coming toward her accompanied by the gentleman who had just entered. He judged the latter, in spite of the advantage of good looks and evident social experience, a little embarrassed. 'Isabel,' said her husband, 'I bring you an old friend.'

Mrs Osmond's face, though it wore a smile, was, like her old friend's, not perfectly confident. 'I'm very happy to see Lord Warburton,' she said. Rosier turned away and, now that his talk with her had been interrupted, felt absolved from the little pledge he had just taken. He had a quick impression that Mrs Osmond wouldn't notice what he did.

Isabel in fact, to do him justice, for some time quite ceased to observe him. She had been startled; she hardly knew if she felt a pleasure or a pain. Lord Warburton, however, now that he was face to face with her, was plainly quite sure of his own sense of the matter; though his grey eyes had still their fine original property of keeping recognition and attestation strictly sincere. He was 'heavier' than of yore and looked older; he stood there very solidly and sensibly.

'I suppose you didn't expect to see me,' he said; 'I've but just arrived. Literally, I only got here this evening. You see I've lost no time in coming to pay you my respects. I knew you were at home on Thursdays.'

'You see the fame of your Thursdays has spread to England,' Osmond remarked to his wife.

'It's very kind of Lord Warburton to come so soon; we're greatly flattered,' Isabel said.

'Ah well, it's better than stopping in one of those horrible inns,' Osmond went on.

'The hotel seems very good; I think it's the same at which I saw you four years since. You know it was here in Rome that we first met; it's a long time ago. Do you remember where I bade you good-bye?' his lordship asked of his hostess. 'It was in the Capitol, in the first room.'

'I remember that myself,' said Osmond. 'I was there at the time.'

'Yes, I remember you there. I was very sorry to leave Rome—so sorry that, somehow or other, it became almost a dismal memory, and I've never cared to come back till to-day. But I knew you were living here,' her old friend went on to Isabel, 'and I assure you I've often thought of you. It must be a charming place to live in,' he added with a look, round him, at her established home, in which she might have caught the dim ghost of his old ruefulness.

'We should have been glad to see you at any time,' Osmond observed with propriety.

'Thank you very much. I haven't been out of England since then. Till a month ago I really supposed my travels over.'

'I've heard of you from time to time,' said Isabel, who had already, with her rare capacity for such inward feats, taken the measure of what meeting him again meant for her.

'I hope you've heard no harm. My life has been a remarkably complete blank.'

'Like the good reigns in history,' Osmond suggested. He appeared to think his duties as a host now terminated—he had performed them so conscientiously. Nothing could have been more adequate, more nicely measured, than his courtesy to his wife's old friend. It was punctilious, it was explicit, it was everything but natural—a deficiency which Lord Warburton, who, himself, had on the whole a good deal of nature, may be supposed to have perceived. 'I'll leave you and Mrs Osmond together,' he added. 'You have reminiscences into which I don't enter.'

'I'm afraid you lose a good deal!' Lord Warburton called after him, as he moved away, in a tone which perhaps betrayed overmuch an appreciation of his generosity. Then the visitor turned on Isabel the deeper, the deepest, consciousness of his look, which gradually became more serious. 'I'm really very glad to see you.'

'It's very pleasant. You're very kind.'

'Do you know that you're changed—a little?'

She just hesitated. 'Yes—a good deal.'

'I don't mean for the worse, of course; and yet how can I say for the better?'

'I think I shall have no scruple in saying that to *you*,' she bravely returned.

'Ah well, for me—it's a long time. It would be a pity there shouldn't be something to show for it.' They sat down and she asked him about his sisters, with other enquiries of a somewhat perfunctory kind. He answered her questions as if they interested him, and in a few moments she saw—or believed she saw—that he would press with less of his whole weight than of yore. Time had breathed upon his heart and, without chilling it, given it a relieved sense of having taken the air. Isabel felt her usual esteem for Time rise at a bound. Her friend's manner was certainly that of a contented man, one who would rather like people, or like her at least, to know him for such. 'There's something I must tell you without more delay,' he resumed. 'I've brought Ralph Touchett with me.'

'Brought him with you?' Isabel's surprise was great.

'He's at the hotel; he was too tired to come out and has gone to bed.'

'I'll go to see him,' she immediately said.

'That's exactly what I hoped you'd do. I had an idea you hadn't seen much of him since your marriage, that in fact your relations were a—a little more formal. That's why I hesitated—like an awkward Briton.'

'I'm as fond of Ralph as ever,' Isabel answered. 'But why has he come to Rome?' The declaration was very gentle, the question a little sharp.

'Because he's very far gone, Mrs Osmond.'

'Rome then is no place for him. I heard from him that he had determined to give up his custom of wintering abroad and to remain in England, indoors, in what he called an artificial climate.'

'Poor fellow, he doesn't succeed with the artificial! I went to see him three weeks ago, at Gardencourt, and found him thoroughly ill. He has been getting worse every year, and now he has no strength left. He smokes no more cigarettes! He had got up an artificial climate indeed; the house was as hot as

Calcutta. Nevertheless he had suddenly taken it into his head to start for Sicily. I didn't believe in it—neither did the doctors, nor any of his friends. His mother, as I suppose you know, is in America, so there was no one to prevent him. He stuck to his idea that it would be the saving of him to spend the winter at Catania. He said he could take servants and furniture, could make himself comfortable, but in point of fact he hasn't brought anything. I wanted him at least to go by sea, to save fatigue; but he said he hated the sea and wished to stop at Rome. After that, though I thought it all rubbish, I made up my mind to come with him. I'm acting as—what do you call it in America?—as a kind of moderator. Poor Ralph's very moderate now. We left England a fortnight ago, and he has been very bad on the way. He can't keep warm, and the further south we come the more he feels the cold. He has got rather a good man, but I'm afraid he's beyond human help. I wanted him to take with him some clever fellow—I mean some sharp young doctor; but he wouldn't hear of it. If you don't mind my saying so, I think it was a most extraordinary time for Mrs Touchett to decide on going to America.'

Isabel had listened eagerly; her face was full of pain and wonder. 'My aunt does that at fixed periods and lets nothing turn her aside. When the date comes round she starts; I think she'd have started if Ralph had been dying.'

'I sometimes think he *is* dying,' Lord Warburton said.

Isabel sprang up. 'I'll go to him then now.'

He checked her; he was a little disconcerted at the quick effect of his words. 'I don't mean I thought so to-night. On the contrary, to-day, in the train, he seemed particularly well; the idea of our reaching Rome—he's very fond of Rome, you know—gave him strength. An hour ago, when I bade him good-night, he told me he was very tired, but very happy. Go to him in the morning; that's all I mean. I didn't tell him I was coming here; I didn't decide to till after we had separated. Then I remembered he had told me you had an evening, and that it was this very Thursday. It occurred to me to come in and tell you he's here, and let you know you had perhaps better not wait for him to call. I think he said he hadn't written to you.' There was no need of Isabel's declaring that she would act upon Lord Warburton's information; she looked, as she sat there, like a winged creature held back. 'Let alone that I wanted to see you for myself,' her visitor gallantly added.

'I don't understand Ralph's plan; it seems to me very wild,' she said. 'I was glad to think of him between those thick walls at Gardencourt.'

'He was completely alone there; the thick walls were his only company.'

'You went to see him; you've been extremely kind.'

'Oh dear, I had nothing to do,' said Lord Warburton.

'We hear, on the contrary, that you're doing great things. Every one speaks of you as a great statesman, and I'm perpetually seeing your name in the *Times*, which, by the way, doesn't appear to hold it in reverence. You're apparently as wild a radical as ever.'

'I don't feel nearly so wild; you know the world has come round to me. Touchett and I have kept up a sort of parliamentary debate all the way from London. I tell him he's the last of the Tories, and he calls me the King of the Goths—says I have, down to the details of my personal appearance, every sign of the brute. So you see there's life in him yet.'

Isabel had many questions to ask about Ralph, but she abstained from asking them all. She would see for herself on the morrow. She perceived that after a little Lord Warburton would tire of that subject—he had a conception of other possible topics. She was more and more able to say to herself that he had recovered, and, what is more to the point, she was able to say it without bitterness. He had been for her, of old, such an image of urgency, of insistence, of something to be resisted and reasoned with, that his reappearance at first menaced her with a new trouble. But she was now reassured; she could see he only wished to live with her on good terms, that she was to understand he had forgiven her and was incapable of the bad taste of making pointed allusions. This was not a form of revenge, of course; she had no suspicion of his wishing to punish her by an exhibition of disillusionment; she did him the justice to believe it had simply occurred to him that she would now take a good-natured interest in knowing he was resigned. It was the resignation of a healthy, manly nature, in which sentimental wounds could never fester. British politics had cured him; she had known they would. She gave an envious thought to the happier lot of men, who are always free to plunge into the healing waters of action. Lord Warburton of course spoke of the past, but he spoke of it without implications; he even went so far as to allude to their former meeting in Rome as a very jolly time. And he told her he had been immensely interested in hearing of her marriage and that it was a great pleasure for him to make Mr Osmond's acquaintance—since he could hardly be said to have made it on the other occasion. He had not written to her at the time of that passage in her history, but he didn't apologise to her for this. The only thing he implied was that they were old friends, intimate friends. It was very much as an intimate friend that he said to her, suddenly, after a short pause which he had occupied in smiling, as he looked about him, like a person amused, at a provincial entertainment, by some innocent game of guesses—

'Well now, I suppose you're very happy and all that sort of thing?'

Isabel answered with a quick laugh; the tone of his remark struck her almost as the accent of comedy. 'Do you suppose if I were not I'd tell you?'

'Well, I don't know. I don't see why not.'

'I do then. Fortunately, however, I'm very happy.'

'You've got an awfully good house.'

'Yes, it's very pleasant. But that's not my merit—it's my husband's.'

'You mean he has arranged it?'

'Yes, it was nothing when we came.'

'He must be very clever.'

'He has a genius for upholstery,' said Isabel.

'There's a great rage for that sort of thing now. But you must have a taste of your own.'

'I enjoy things when they're done, but I've no ideas. I can never propose anything.'

'Do you mean you accept what others propose?'

'Very willingly, for the most part.'

'That's a good thing to know. I shall propose to you something.'

'It will be very kind. I must say, however, that I've in a few small ways a certain initiative. I should like for instance to introduce you to some of these people.'

'Oh, please don't; I prefer sitting here. Unless it be to that young lady in the blue dress. She has a charming face.'

'The one talking to the rosy young man? That's my husband's daughter.'

'Lucky man, your husband. What a dear little maid!'

'You must make her acquaintance.'

'In a moment—with pleasure. I like looking at her from here.' He ceased to look at her, however, very soon; his eyes constantly reverted to Mrs Osmond. 'Do you know I was wrong just now in saying you had changed?' he presently went on. 'You seem to me, after all, very much the same.'

'And yet I find it a great change to be married,' said Isabel with mild gaiety.

'It affects most people more than it has affected you. You see I haven't gone in for that.'

'It rather surprises me.'

'You ought to understand it, Mrs Osmond. But I do want to marry,' he added more simply.

'It ought to be very easy,' Isabel said, rising—after which she reflected, with a pang perhaps too visible, that she was hardly the person to say this. It was perhaps because Lord Warburton divined the pang that he generously forbore to call her attention to her not having contributed then to the facility.

Edward Rosier had meanwhile seated himself on an ottoman beside Pansy's tea-table. He pretended at first to talk to her about trifles, and she asked him who was the new gentleman conversing with her stepmother.

'He's an English lord,' said Rosier. 'I don't know more.'

'I wonder if he'll have some tea. The English are so fond of tea.'

'Never mind that; I've something particular to say to you.'

'Don't speak so loud—every one will hear,' said Pansy.

'They won't hear if you continue to look that way: as if your only thought in life was the wish the kettle would boil.'

'It has just been filled; the servants never know!'—and she sighed with the weight of her responsibility.

'Do you know what your father said to me just now? That you didn't mean what you said a week ago.'

'I don't mean everything I say. How can a young girl do that? But I mean what I say to *you*.'

'He told me you had forgotten me.'

'Ah no, I don't forget,' said Pansy, showing her pretty teeth in a fixed smile.

'Then everything's just the very same?'

'Ah no, not the very same. Papa has been terribly severe.'

'What has he done to you?'

'He asked me what *you* had done to me, and I told him everything. Then he forbade me to marry you.'

'You needn't mind that.'

'Oh yes, I must indeed. I can't disobey papa.'

'Not for one who loves you as I do, and whom you pretend to love?'

She raised the lid of the tea-pot, gazing into this vessel for a moment; then she dropped six words into its aromatic depths. 'I love you just as much.'

'What good will that do me?'

'Ah,' said Pansy, raising her sweet, vague eyes, 'I don't know that.'

'You disappoint me,' groaned poor Rosier.

She was silent a little; she handed a tea-cup to a servant. 'Please don't talk any more.'

'Is this to be all my satisfaction?'

'Papa said I was not to talk with you.'

'Do you sacrifice me like that? Ah, it's too much!'

'I wish you'd wait a little,' said the girl in a voice just distinct enough to betray a quaver.

'Of course I'll wait if you'll give me hope. But you take my life away.'

'I'll not give you up—oh no!' Pansy went on.

'He'll try and make you marry some one else.'

'I'll never do that.'

'What then are we to wait for?'

She hesitated again. 'I'll speak to Mrs Osmond and she'll help us.' It was in this manner that she for the most part designated her stepmother.

'She won't help us much. She's afraid.'

'Afraid of what?'

'Of your father, I suppose.'

Pansy shook her little head. 'She's not afraid of any one. We must have patience.'

'Ah, that's an awful word,' Rosier groaned; he was deeply disconcerted. Oblivious of the customs of good society, he dropped his head into his hands and, supporting it with a melancholy grace, sat staring at the carpet. Presently he became aware of a good deal of movement about him and, as he looked up, saw Pansy making a curtsey—it was still her little curtsey of the convent—to the English lord whom Mrs Osmond had introduced.

XXXIX

It will probably not surprise the reflective reader that Ralph Touchett should have seen less of his cousin since her marriage than he had done before that event—an event of which he took such a view as could hardly prove a confirmation of intimacy. He had uttered his thought, as we know, and after this had held his peace, Isabel not having invited him to resume a discussion which marked an era in their relations. That discussion had made a difference—the difference he feared rather than the one he hoped. It had not chilled the girl's zeal in carrying out her engagement, but it had come dangerously near to spoiling a friendship. No reference was ever again made between them to Ralph's opinion of Gilbert Osmond, and by surrounding this topic with a sacred silence they managed to preserve a semblance of reciprocal frankness. But there was a difference, as Ralph often said to himself—there was a difference. She had not forgiven him, she never would forgive him: that was all he had gained. She thought she had forgiven him; she believed she didn't care; and as she was both very generous and very proud these convictions represented a certain reality. But whether or no the event should justify him he would virtually have done her a wrong, and the wrong was of the sort that women remember best. As Osmond's wife she could never again be his friend. If in this character she should enjoy the felicity she expected, she would have nothing but contempt for the man who had attempted, in advance, to undermine a blessing so dear; and if on the other hand his warning should be justified the vow she had taken that he should never know it would lay upon her spirit such a burden as to make her hate him. So dismal had been, during the year that followed his cousin's marriage, Ralph's prevision of the future; and if his meditations appear morbid we must remember he was not in the bloom of health. He consoled himself as he might by behaving (as he deemed) beautifully, and was present at the ceremony by which Isabel was united to Mr Osmond, and which was performed in Florence in the month of June. He learned from his mother that Isabel at first had thought of celebrating her nuptials in her native land, but that as simplicity was what she chiefly desired to secure she had finally decided, in spite of Osmond's professed willingness to make a journey of any length, that this characteristic would be best embodied in their being married by the nearest clergyman in the shortest time. The thing was done therefore at the little American chapel, on a very hot day, in the presence only of Mrs Touchett and her son, of Pansy Osmond and the Countess Gemini. That severity in the proceedings of which I just spoke was in part the result of the absence of two persons who might have been looked for on the occasion and who would have lent it a certain richness. Madame Merle had been invited, but Madame Merle, who was unable to leave Rome, had written a gracious letter of excuses. Henrietta Stackpole had not been invited, as her departure from America, announced to Isabel by Mr Goodwood, was in fact frustrated by the duties of her profession; but she had sent a letter, less gracious than Madame Merle's, intimating that, had she been able to cross the Atlantic, she would have been present not only as a witness but as a critic. Her return to Europe had taken place somewhat later, and she had effected a meeting with Isabel in the autumn, in Paris, when she had indulged—perhaps a trifle too freely—her critical genius. Poor Osmond, who was chiefly the subject of it, had protested so sharply that Henrietta was obliged to declare to Isabel that she had taken a step which put a barrier between them. 'It isn't in the least that you've married—it is that you have married *him*,' she had deemed it her duty to remark; agreeing, it will be seen, much more with Ralph Touchett than she suspected, though she had few of his hesitations and compunctions. Henrietta's second visit to Europe, however, was not apparently to have been made in vain; for just at the moment when Osmond had declared to Isabel that he really must object to that newspaper-woman, and Isabel had answered that it seemed to her he took Henrietta too hard, the good Mr Bantling had appeared upon the scene and proposed that they should take a run down to Spain. Henrietta's letters from Spain had proved the most acceptable she had yet published, and there had been one in especial, dated from the Alhambra and entitled 'Moors and Moonlight,' which generally passed for her masterpiece. Isabel had been secretly disappointed at her husband's not seeing his way simply to take the poor girl for funny. She even wondered if his sense of fun, or of the funny—which would be his sense of humour, wouldn't it?—were by chance defective. Of course she herself looked at the matter as a person whose present happiness had nothing to grudge to Henrietta's violated conscience. Osmond had thought their alliance a kind of monstrosity; he couldn't imagine what they had in common. For him, Mr Bantling's fellow tourist was simply the most vulgar of women, and he had also pronounced her the most abandoned. Against this latter clause of the verdict Isabel had appealed with an ardour that had made him wonder afresh at the oddity of some of his wife's tastes. Isabel could explain it only by saying that she liked to know people who were as different as possible from herself. 'Why then don't you make the acquaintance of your washerwoman?' Osmond had enquired; to which Isabel had answered that she was afraid her washerwoman wouldn't care for her. Now Henrietta cared so much.

Ralph had seen nothing of her for the greater part of the two years that had followed her marriage; the winter that formed the beginning of her residence in Rome he had spent again at San Remo, where he had been joined in the spring by his mother, who afterwards had gone with him to England, to see what they were doing at the bank—an operation she couldn't induce him to perform. Ralph had taken a lease of his house at San Remo, a small villa which he had occupied still another winter; but late in the month of April of this second year he had come down to Rome. It was the first time since her marriage that he had stood face to face with Isabel; his desire to see her again was then of the keenest. She had written to him from time to time, but her letters told him nothing he wanted to know. He had asked his mother what she was making of her life, and his mother had simply answered that she supposed she was making the best of it. Mrs Touchett had not the imagination that communes with the unseen, and she now pretended to no intimacy with her niece, whom she rarely encountered. This young woman appeared to be living in a sufficiently honourable way, but Mrs Touchett still remained of the opinion that her marriage had been a shabby affair. It had given her no pleasure to think of Isabel's establishment, which she was sure was a very lame business. From time to time, in Florence, she rubbed against the Countess Gemini, doing her best always to minimise the contact; and the Countess reminded her of Osmond, who made her think of Isabel. The Countess was less talked of in these days; but Mrs Touchett augured no good of that: it only proved how she had been talked of before. There was a more direct suggestion of Isabel in the person of Madame Merle; but Madame Merle's relations with Mrs Touchett had undergone a perceptible change. Isabel's aunt had told her, without circumlocution, that she had played too ingenious a part; and Madame Merle, who never quarrelled with any one, who appeared to think no one worth it, and who had performed the miracle of living, more or less, for several years with Mrs Touchett and showing no symptom of irritation—Madame Merle now took a very high tone and declared that this was an accusation from which she couldn't stoop to defend herself. She added, however (without stooping), that her behaviour had been only too simple, that she had believed only what she saw, that she saw Isabel was not eager to marry and Osmond not eager to please (his repeated visits had been nothing; he was boring himself to death on his hill-top and he came merely for amusement). Isabel had kept her sentiments to herself, and her journey to Greece and Egypt had effectually thrown dust in her companion's eyes. Madame Merle accepted the event—she was unprepared to think of it as a scandal; but that she had played any part in it, double or single, was an imputation against which she proudly protested. It was doubtless in consequence of Mrs Touchett's attitude, and of the injury it offered to habits consecrated by many charming seasons, that Madame Merle had, after this, chosen to pass many months in England, where her credit was quite unimpaired. Mrs Touchett had done her a wrong; there are some things that can't be forgiven. But Madame Merle suffered in silence; there was always something exquisite in her dignity.

Ralph, as I say, had wished to see for himself; but while engaged in this pursuit he had yet felt afresh what a fool he had been to put the girl on her guard. He had played the wrong card, and now he had lost the game. He should see nothing, he should learn nothing; for him she would always wear a mask. His true line would have been to profess delight in her union, so that later, when, as Ralph phrased it, the bottom should fall out of it, she might have the pleasure of saying to him that he had been a goose. He would gladly have consented to pass for a goose in order to know Isabel's real situation. At present, however, she neither taunted him with his fallacies nor pretended that her own confidence was justified; if she wore a mask it completely covered her face. There was something fixed and mechanical in the serenity painted on it; this was not an expression, Ralph said—it was a representation, it was even an advertisement. She had lost her child; that was a sorrow, but it was a sorrow she scarcely spoke of; there was more to say about it than she could say to Ralph. It belonged to the past, moreover; it had occurred six months before and she had already laid aside the tokens of mourning. She appeared to be leading the life of the world; Ralph heard her spoken of as having a 'charming position.' He observed that she produced the impression of being peculiarly enviable, that it was supposed, among many people, to be a privilege even to know her. Her house was not open to every one, and she had an evening in the week to which people were not invited as a matter of course. She lived with a certain magnificence, but you needed to be a member of her circle to perceive it; for there was nothing to gape at, nothing to criticise, nothing even to admire, in the daily proceedings of Mr and Mrs Osmond. Ralph, in all this, recognised the hand of the master; for he knew that Isabel had no faculty for producing studied impressions. She struck him as having a great love of movement, of gaiety, of late hours, of long rides, of fatigue; an eagerness to be entertained, to be interested, even to be bored, to make acquaintances, to see people who were talked about, to explore the neighbourhood of Rome, to enter into relation with certain of the mustiest relics of its old society. In all this there was much less discrimination than in that desire for comprehensiveness of development on which he had been used to exercise his wit. There was a kind of violence in some of her impulses, of crudity in some of her experiments, which took him by surprise: it seemed to him that she even spoke faster, moved faster, breathed faster, than before her marriage. Certainly she had fallen into exaggerations—she who used to care so much for the pure truth; and whereas of old she had a great delight in good-humoured argument, in intellectual play (she never looked so charming as when in the genial heat of discussion she received a crushing blow full in the face and brushed it away as a feather), she appeared now to think there was nothing worth people's either differing about or agreeing upon. Of old she had been curious, and now she was indifferent, and yet in spite of her indifference her activity was greater than ever. Slender still, but lovelier than before, she had gained no great maturity of aspect; yet there was an amplitude and a brilliancy in her personal arrangements that gave a touch of insolence to her beauty. Poor human-hearted Isabel, what perversity had bitten her? Her light step drew a mass of drapery behind it; her intelligent head sustained a majesty of ornament. The free, keen girl had become quite another person; what he saw was the fine lady who was supposed to represent something. What did Isabel represent? Ralph asked himself; and he could only answer by saying that she represented Gilbert Osmond. 'Good heavens, what a function!' he then woefully exclaimed. He was lost in wonder at the mystery of things.

He recognised Osmond, as I say; he recognised him at every turn. He saw how he kept all things within limits; how he adjusted, regulated, animated their manner of life. Osmond was in his element; at last he had material to work with. He always had an eye to effect, and his effects were deeply calculated. They were produced by no vulgar means, but the motive was as vulgar as the art was great. To surround his interior with a sort of invidious sanctity, to tantalise society with a sense of exclusion, to make people believe his house was different from every other, to impart to the face that he presented to the world a cold originality—this was the ingenious effort of the personage to whom Isabel had attributed a superior morality. 'He works with superior material,' Ralph said to himself; 'it's rich abundance compared with his former resources.' Ralph was a clever man; but Ralph had never—to his own sense—been so clever as when he observed, *in petto*,* that under the guise of caring only for intrinsic values Osmond lived exclusively for the world. Far from being its master as he pretended to be, he was its very humble servant, and the degree of its attention was his only measure of success. He lived with his eye on it from morning till night, and the world was so stupid it never suspected the trick. Everything he did was *pose*—*pose* so subtly considered that if one were not on the lookout one mistook it for impulse. Ralph had never met a man who lived so much in the land of consideration. His tastes, his studies, his accomplishments, his collections, were all for a purpose. His life on his hill-top at Florence had been the conscious attitude of years. His solitude, his ennui, his love for his daughter, his good manners, his bad manners, were so many features of a mental image constantly present to him as a model of impertinence and mystification. His ambition was not to please the world, but to please himself by exciting the world's curiosity and then declining to satisfy it. It had made him feel great, ever, to play the world a trick. The thing he had done in his life most directly to please himself was his marrying Miss Archer; though in this case indeed the gullible world was in a manner embodied in poor Isabel, who had been mystified to the top of her bent. Ralph of course found a fitness in being consistent; he had embraced a creed, and as he had suffered for it he could not in honour forsake it. I give this little sketch of its articles for what they may at the time have been worth. It was certain that he was very skilful in fitting the facts to his theory—even the fact that during the month he spent in Rome at this period the husband of the woman he loved appeared to regard him not in the least as an enemy.

For Gilbert Osmond Ralph had not now that importance. It was not that he had the importance of a friend; it was rather that he had none at all. He was Isabel's cousin and he was rather unpleasantly ill—it was on this basis that Osmond treated with him. He made the proper enquiries, asked about his health, about Mrs Touchett, about his opinion of winter climates, whether he were comfortable at his hotel. He addressed him, on the few occasions of their meeting, not a word that was not necessary; but his manner had always the urbanity proper to conscious success in the presence of conscious failure. For all this, Ralph had had, toward the end, a sharp inward vision of Osmond's making it of small ease to his wife that she should continue to receive Mr Touchett. He was not jealous—he had not that excuse; no one could be jealous of Ralph. But he made Isabel pay for her old-time kindness, of which so much was still left; and as Ralph had no idea of her paying too much, so when his suspicion had become sharp, he had taken himself off. In doing so he had deprived Isabel of a very interesting occupation: she had been constantly wondering what fine principle was keeping him alive. She had decided that it was his love of conversation; his conversation had been better than ever. He had given up walking; he was no longer a humorous stroller. He sat all day in a chair—almost any chair would serve, and was so dependent on what you would do for him that, had not his talk been highly contemplative, you might have thought he was blind. The reader already knows more about him than Isabel was ever to know, and the reader may therefore be given the key to the mystery. What kept Ralph alive was simply the fact that he had not yet seen enough of the person in the world in whom he was most interested: he was not yet satisfied. There was more to come; he couldn't make up his mind to lose that. He wanted to see what she would make of her husband—or what her husband would make of her. This was only the first act of the drama, and he was determined to sit out the performance. His determination had held good; it had kept him going some eighteen months more, till the time of his return to Rome with Lord Warburton. It had given him indeed such an air of intending to live indefinitely that Mrs Touchett, though more accessible to confusions of thought in the matter of this strange, unremunerative—and unremunerated—son of hers than she had ever been before, had, as we have learned, not scrupled to embark for a distant land. If Ralph had been kept alive by suspense it was with a good deal of the same emotion—the excitement of wondering in what state she should find him—that Isabel mounted to his apartment the day after Lord Warburton had notified her of his arrival in Rome.

She spent an hour with him; it was the first of several visits. Gilbert Osmond called on him punctually, and on their sending their carriage for him Ralph came more than once to Palazzo Roccanera. A fortnight elapsed, at the end of which Ralph announced to Lord Warburton that he thought after all he wouldn't go to Sicily. The two men had been dining together after a day spent by the latter in ranging about the Campagna. They had left the table, and Warburton, before the chimney, was lighting a cigar, which he instantly removed from his lips.

'Won't go to Sicily? Where then will you go?'

'Well, I guess I won't go anywhere,' said Ralph, from the sofa, all shamelessly.

'Do you mean you'll return to England?'

'Oh dear no; I'll stay in Rome.'

'Rome won't do for you. Rome's not warm enough.'

'It will have to do. I'll make it do. See how well I've been.'

Lord Warburton looked at him a while, puffing a cigar and as if trying to see it. 'You've been better than you were on the journey, certainly. I wonder how you lived through that. But I don't understand your condition. I recommend you to try Sicily.'

'I can't try,' said poor Ralph. 'I've done trying. I can't move further. I can't face that journey. Fancy me between Scylla and Charybdis!* I don't want to die on the Sicilian plains—to be snatched away, like Proserpine* in the same locality, to the Plutonian shades.'

'What the deuce then did you come for?' his lordship enquired.

'Because the idea took me. I see it won't do. It really doesn't matter where I am now. I've exhausted all remedies, I've swallowed all climates. As I'm here I'll stay. I haven't a single cousin in Sicily—much less a married one.'

'Your cousin's certainly an inducement. But what does the doctor say?'

'I haven't asked him, and I don't care a fig. If I die here Mrs Osmond will bury me. But I shall not die here.'

'I hope not.' Lord Warburton continued to smoke reflectively. 'Well, I must say,' he resumed, 'for myself I'm very glad you don't insist on Sicily. I had a horror of that journey.'

'Ah, but for you it needn't have mattered. I had no idea of dragging you in my train.'

'I certainly didn't mean to let you go alone.'

'My dear Warburton, I never expected you to come further than this,' Ralph cried.

'I should have gone with you and seen you settled,' said Lord Warburton.

'You're a very good Christian. You're a very kind man.'

'Then I should have come back here.'

'And then you'd have gone to England.'

'No, no; I should have stayed.'

'Well,' said Ralph, 'if that's what we are both up to, I don't see where Sicily comes in!'

His companion was silent; he sat staring at the fire. At last, looking up, 'I say, tell me this,' he broke out; 'did you really mean to go to Sicily when we started?'

'Ah, *vous m'en demandez trop!** Let me put a question first. Did you come with me quite—platonically?'

'I don't know what you mean by that. I wanted to come abroad.'

'I suspect we've each been playing our little game.'

'Speak for yourself. I made no secret whatever of my desiring to be here a while.'

'Yes, I remember you said you wished to see the Minister of Foreign Affairs.'

'I've seen him three times. He's very amusing.'

'I think you've forgotten what you came for,' said Ralph.

'Perhaps I have,' his companion answered rather gravely.

These two were gentlemen of a race which is not distinguished by the absence of reserve, and they had travelled together from London to Rome without an allusion to matters that were uppermost in the mind of each. There was an old subject they had once discussed, but it had lost its recognised place in their attention, and even after their arrival in Rome, where many things led back to it, they had kept the same half-diffident, half-confident silence.

'I recommend you to get the doctor's consent, all the same,' Lord Warburton went on, abruptly, after an interval.

'The doctor's consent will spoil it. I never have it when I can help it.'

'What then does Mrs Osmond think?' Ralph's friend demanded.

'I've not told her. She'll probably say that Rome's too cold and even offer to go with me to Catania. She's capable of that.'

'In your place I should like it.'

'Her husband won't like it.'

'Ah well, I can fancy that; though it seems to me you're not bound to mind his likings. They're his affair.'

'I don't want to make any more trouble between them,' said Ralph.

'Is there so much already?'

'There's complete preparation for it. Her going off with me would make the explosion. Osmond isn't fond of his wife's cousin.'

'Then of course he'd make a row. But won't he make a row if you stop here?'

'That's what I want to see. He made one the last time I was in Rome, and then I thought it my duty to disappear. Now I think it's my duty to stop and defend her.'

'My dear Touchett, your defensive powers—!' Lord Warburton began with a smile. But he saw something in his companion's face that checked him. 'Your duty, in these premises, seems to me rather a nice question,' he observed instead.

Ralph for a short time answered nothing. 'It's true that my defensive powers are small,' he returned at last; 'but as my aggressive ones are still smaller Osmond may after all not think me worth his gunpowder. At any rate,' he added, 'there are things I'm curious to see.'

'You're sacrificing your health to your curiosity then?'

'I'm not much interested in my health, and I'm deeply interested in Mrs Osmond.'

'So am I. But not as I once was,' Lord Warburton added quickly. This was one of the allusions he had not hitherto found occasion to make.

'Does she strike you as very happy?' Ralph enquired, emboldened by this confidence.

'Well, I don't know; I've hardly thought. She told me the other night she was happy.'

'Ah, she told *you*, of course,' Ralph exclaimed, smiling.

'I don't know that. It seems to me I was rather the sort of person she might have complained to.'

'Complained? She'll never complain. She has done it—what she *has* done—and she knows it. She'll complain to you least of all. She's very careful.'

'She needn't be. I don't mean to make love to her again.'

'I'm delighted to hear it. There can be no doubt at least of *your* duty.'

'Ah no,' said Lord Warburton gravely; 'none!'

'Permit me to ask,' Ralph went on, 'whether it's to bring out the fact that you don't mean to make love to her that you're so very civil to the little girl?'

Lord Warburton gave a slight start; he got up and stood before the fire, looking at it hard. 'Does that strike you as very ridiculous?'

'Ridiculous? Not in the least, if you really like her.'

'I think her a delightful little person. I don't know when a girl of that age has pleased me more.'

'She's a charming creature. Ah, she at least is genuine.'

'Of course there's the difference in our ages—more than twenty years.'

'My dear Warburton,' said Ralph, 'are you serious?'

'Perfectly serious—as far as I've got.'

'I'm very glad. And, heaven help us,' cried Ralph, 'how cheered-up old Osmond will be!'

His companion frowned. 'I say, don't spoil it. I shouldn't propose for his daughter to please *him*.'

'He'll have the perversity to be pleased all the same.'

'He's not so fond of me as that,' said his lordship.

'As that? My dear Warburton, the drawback of your position is that people needn't be fond of you at all to wish to be connected with you. Now, with me in such a case, I should have the happy confidence that they loved me.'

Lord Warburton seemed scarcely in the mood for doing

justice to general axioms—he was thinking of a special case. 'Do you judge she'll be pleased?'

'The girl herself? Delighted, surely.'

'No, no; I mean Mrs Osmond.'

Ralph looked at him a moment. 'My dear fellow, what has she to do with it?'

'Whatever she chooses. She's very fond of Pansy.'

'Very true—very true.' And Ralph slowly got up. 'It's an interesting question—how far her fondness for Pansy will carry her.' He stood there a moment with his hands in his pockets and rather a clouded brow. 'I hope, you know, that you're very—very sure. The deuce!' he broke off. 'I don't know how to say it.'

'Yes, you do; you know how to say everything.'

'Well, it's awkward. I hope you're sure that among Miss Osmond's merits her being—a—so near her stepmother isn't a leading one?'

'Good heavens, Touchett!' cried Lord Warburton angrily, 'for what do you take me?'

XL

ISABEL had not seen much of Madame Merle since her marriage, this lady having indulged in frequent absences from Rome. At one time she had spent six months in England; at another she had passed a portion of a winter in Paris. She had made numerous visits to distant friends and gave countenance to the idea that for the future she should be a less inveterate Roman than in the past. As she had been inveterate in the past only in the sense of constantly having an apartment in one of the sunniest niches of the Pincian*—an apartment which often stood empty—this suggested a prospect of almost constant absence; a danger which Isabel at one period had been much inclined to deplore. Familiarity had modified in some degree her first impression of Madame Merle, but it had not essentially altered it; there was still much wonder of admiration in it. That personage was armed at all points; it was a pleasure to see a character so completely equipped for the social battle. She carried her flag discreetly, but her weapons were polished steel, and she used them with a skill which struck Isabel as more and more that of a veteran. She was never weary, never overcome with disgust; she never appeared to need rest or consolation. She had her own ideas; she had of old exposed a great many of them to Isabel, who knew also that under an appearance of extreme self-control her highly-cultivated friend concealed a rich sensibility. But her will was mistress of her life; there was something gallant in the way she kept going. It was as if she had learned the secret of it—as if the art of life were some clever trick she had guessed. Isabel, as she herself grew older, became acquainted with revulsions, with disgusts; there were days when the world looked black and she asked herself with some sharpness what it was that she was pretending to live for. Her old habit had been to live by enthusiasm, to fall in love with suddenly-perceived possibilities, with the idea of some new adventure. As a younger person she had been used to proceed from one little exaltation to the other; there were scarcely any dull places between. But Madame Merle had suppressed enthusiasm; she fell in love now-a-days with nothing; she lived entirely by reason and by wisdom. There were hours when Isabel would have given anything for lessons in this art; if her brilliant friend had been near she would have made an appeal to her. She had become aware more than before of the advantage of being like that—of having made one's self a firm surface, a sort of corselet of silver.

But, as I say, it was not till the winter during which we lately renewed acquaintance with our heroine that the personage in question made again a continuous stay in Rome. Isabel now saw more of her than she had done since her marriage; but by this time Isabel's needs and inclinations had considerably changed. It was not at present to Madame Merle that she would have applied for instruction; she had lost the desire to know this lady's clever trick. If she had troubles she must keep them to herself, and if life was difficult it would not make it easier to confess herself beaten. Madame Merle was doubtless of great use to herself and an ornament to any circle; but was she—would she be—of use to others in periods of refined embarrassment? The best way to profit by her friend—this indeed Isabel had always thought—was to imitate her, to be as firm and bright as she. She recognised no embarrassments, and Isabel, considering this fact, determined for the fiftieth time to brush aside her own. It seemed to her too, on the renewal of an intercourse which had virtually been interrupted, that her old ally was different, was almost detached—pushing to the extreme a certain rather artificial fear of being indiscreet. Ralph Touchett, we know, had been of the opinion that she was prone to exaggeration, to forcing the note—was apt, in the vulgar phrase, to overdo it. Isabel had never admitted this charge—had never indeed quite understood it; Madame Merle's conduct, to her perception, always bore the stamp of good taste, was always 'quiet.' But in this matter of not wishing to intrude upon the inner life of the Osmond family it at last occurred to our young woman that she overdid a little. That of course was not the best taste; that was rather violent. She remembered too much that Isabel was married; that she had now other interests; that though she, Madame Merle, had known Gilbert Osmond and his little Pansy very well, better almost than any one, she was not after all of the inner circle. She was on her guard; she never spoke of their affairs till she was asked, even pressed—as when her opinion was wanted; she had a dread of seeming to meddle. Madame Merle was as candid as we know, and one day she candidly expressed this dread to Isabel.

'I *must* be on my guard,' she said; 'I might so easily, without suspecting it, offend you. You would be right to be offended, even if my intention should have been of the purest. I must not forget that I knew your husband long before you did; I must not let that betray me. If you were a silly woman you might be jealous. You're not a silly woman; I know that perfectly. But neither am I; therefore I'm determined not to get into trouble. A little harm's very soon done; a mistake's made before one knows it. Of course if I had wished to make love to your husband I had ten years to do it in, and nothing to prevent; so it isn't likely I shall begin to-day, when I'm so much less attractive than I was. But if I were to annoy you by seeming to take a place that doesn't belong to me, you wouldn't make that reflection; you'd simply say I was forgetting certain differences. I'm determined not to forget them. Certainly a good friend isn't always thinking of that; one doesn't suspect one's friends of injustice. I don't suspect you, my dear, in the least; but I suspect human nature. Don't think I make myself uncomfortable; I'm not always watching myself. I think I sufficiently prove it in talking to you as I do now. All I wish to say is, however, that if you were to be jealous—that's the form it would take—I should be sure to think it was a little my fault. It certainly wouldn't be your husband's.'

Isabel had had three years to think over Mrs Touchett's theory that Madame Merle had made Gilbert Osmond's marriage. We know how she had at first received it. Madame Merle might have made Gilbert Osmond's marriage, but she certainly had not made Isabel Archer's. That was the work of—Isabel scarcely knew what: of nature, providence, fortune, of the eternal mystery of things. It was true her aunt's complaint had been not so much of Madame Merle's activity as of her duplicity: she had brought about the strange event and then she had denied her guilt. Such guilt would not have been great, to Isabel's mind; she couldn't make a crime of Madame Merle's having been the producing cause of the most important friendship she had ever formed. This had occurred to her just before her marriage, after her little discussion with her aunt and at a time when she was still capable of that large inward reference, the tone almost of the philosophic historian, to her scant young annals. If Madame Merle had desired her change of state she could only say it had been a very happy thought. With her, moreover, she had been perfectly straightforward; she had never concealed her high opinion of Gilbert Osmond. After their union Isabel discovered that her husband took a less convenient view of the matter; he seldom consented to finger, in talk, this roundest and smoothest bead of their social rosary.

'Don't you like Madame Merle?' Isabel had once said to him. 'She thinks a great deal of you.'

'I'll tell you once for all,' Osmond had answered. 'I liked her once better than I do to-day. I'm tired of her, and I'm rather ashamed of it. She's so almost unnaturally good! I'm glad she's not in Italy; it makes for relaxation—for a sort of moral *détente*.* Don't talk of her too much; it seems to bring her back. She'll come back in plenty of time.'

Madame Merle, in fact, had come back before it was too late—too late, I mean, to recover whatever advantage she might have lost. But meantime, if, as I have said, she was sensibly different, Isabel's feelings were also not quite the same. Her consciousness of the situation was as acute as of old, but it was much less satisfying. A dissatisfied mind, whatever else it may miss, is rarely in want of reasons; they bloom as thick as buttercups in June. The fact of Madame Merle's having had a hand in Gilbert Osmond's marriage ceased to be one of her titles to consideration; it might have been written, after all, that there was not so much to thank her for. As time went on there was less and less, and Isabel once said to herself that perhaps without her these things would not have been. That reflection indeed was instantly stifled; she knew an immediate horror at having made it. 'Whatever happens to me let me not be unjust,' she said; 'let me bear my burdens myself and not shift them upon others!' This disposition was tested, eventually, by that ingenious apology for her present conduct which Madame Merle saw fit to make and of which I have given a sketch; for there was something irritating—there was almost an air of mockery—in her neat discriminations and clear convictions. In Isabel's mind to-day there was nothing clear; there was a confusion of regrets, a complication of fears. She felt helpless as she turned away from her friend, who had just made the statements I have quoted: Madame Merle knew so little what she was thinking of! She was herself moreover so unable to explain. Jealous of her—jealous of her with Gilbert? The idea just then suggested no near reality. She almost wished jealousy had been possible; it would have made in a manner for refreshment. Wasn't it in a manner one of the symptoms of happiness? Madame Merle, however, was wise, so wise that she might have been pretending to know Isabel better than Isabel knew herself. This young woman had always been fertile in resolutions—many of them of an elevated character; but at no period had they flourished (in the privacy of her heart) more richly than to-day. It is true that they all had a family likeness; they might have been summed up in the determination that if she was to be unhappy it should not be by a fault of her own. Her poor winged spirit had always had a great desire to do its best, and it had not as yet been seriously discouraged. It wished, therefore, to hold fast to justice—not to pay itself by petty revenges. To associate Madame Merle with its disappointment would be a petty revenge—especially as the pleasure to be derived from that would be perfectly insincere. It might feed her sense of bitterness, but it would not loosen her bonds. It was impossible to pretend that she had not acted with her eyes open; if ever a girl was a free agent she had been. A girl in love was doubtless not a free agent; but the sole source of her mistake had been within herself. There had been no plot, no snare; she had looked and considered and chosen. When a woman had made such a mistake, there was only one way to repair it—just immensely (oh, with the highest grandeur!) to accept it. One folly was enough, especially when it was to last for ever; a second one would not much set it off. In this vow of reticence there was a certain nobleness which kept Isabel going; but Madame Merle had been right, for all that, in taking her precautions.

One day about a month after Ralph Touchett's arrival in Rome Isabel came back from a walk with Pansy. It was not only a part of her general determination to be just that she was at present very thankful for Pansy—it was also a part of her tenderness for things that were pure and weak. Pansy was dear to her, and there was nothing else in her life that had the rightness of the young creature's attachment or the sweetness of her own clearness about it. It was like a soft presence—like a small hand in her own; on Pansy's part it was more than an affection—it was a kind of ardent coercive faith. On her own side her sense of the girl's dependence was more than a pleasure; it operated as a definite reason when motives threatened to fail her. She had said to herself that we must take our duty where we find it, and that we must look for it as much as possible. Pansy's sympathy was a direct admonition; it seemed to say that here was an opportunity, not eminent perhaps, but unmistakeable. Yet an opportunity for what Isabel could hardly have said; in general, to be more for the child than the child was able to be for herself. Isabel could have smiled, in these days, to remember that her little companion had once been ambiguous, for she now perceived that Pansy's ambiguities were simply her own grossness of vision. She had been unable to believe any one could care so much—so extraordinarily much—to please. But since then she had seen this delicate faculty in operation, and now she knew what to think of it. It was the whole creature—it was a sort of genius. Pansy had no pride to interfere with it, and though she was constantly extending her conquests she took no credit for them. The two were constantly together; Mrs Osmond was rarely seen without her stepdaughter. Isabel liked her company; it had the effect of one's carrying a nosegay composed all of the same flower. And then not to neglect Pansy, not under any provocation to neglect her—this she had made an article of religion. The young girl had every appearance of being happier in Isabel's society than in that of any one save her father, whom she admired with an intensity justified by the fact that, as paternity was an exquisite pleasure to Gilbert Osmond, he had always been luxuriously mild. Isabel knew how Pansy liked to be with her and how she studied the means of pleasing her. She had decided that the best way of pleasing her was negative, and consisted in not giving her trouble—a conviction which certainly could have had no reference to trouble already existing. She was therefore ingeniously passive and almost imaginatively docile; she was careful even to moderate the eagerness with which she assented to Isabel's propositions and which might have implied that she could have thought otherwise. She never interrupted, never asked social questions, and though she delighted in approbation, to the point of turning pale when it came to her, never held out her hand for it. She only looked toward it wistfully—an attitude which, as she grew older, made her eyes the prettiest in the world. When during the second winter at Palazzo Roccanera she began to go to parties, to dances, she always, at a reasonable hour, lest Mrs Osmond should be tired, was the first to propose departure. Isabel appreciated the sacrifice of the late dances, for she knew her little companion had a passionate pleasure in this exercise, taking her steps to the music like a conscientious fairy. Society, moreover, had no drawbacks for her; she liked even the tiresome parts—the heat of ball-rooms, the dulness of dinners, the crush at the door, the awkward waiting for the carriage. During the day, in this vehicle, beside her stepmother, she sat in a small fixed, appreciative posture, bending forward and faintly smiling, as if she had been taken to drive for the first time.

On the day I speak of they had been driven out of one of the gates of the city and at the end of half an hour had left the carriage to await them by the roadside while they walked away over the short grass of the Campagna, which even in the winter months is sprinkled with delicate flowers. This was almost a daily habit with Isabel, who was fond of a walk and had a swift length of step, though not so swift a one as on her first coming to Europe. It was not the form of exercise that Pansy loved best, but she liked it, because she liked everything; and she moved with a shorter undulation beside her father's wife, who afterwards, on their return to Rome, paid a tribute to her preferences by making the circuit of the Pincian or the Villa Borghese. She had gathered a handful of flowers in a sunny hollow, far from the walls of Rome, and on reaching Palazzo

Roccanera she went straight to her room, to put them into water. Isabel passed into the drawing-room, the one she herself usually occupied, the second in order from the large ante-chamber which was entered from the staircase and in which even Gilbert Osmond's rich devices had not been able to correct a look of rather grand nudity. Just beyond the threshold of the drawing-room she stopped short, the reason for her doing so being that she had received an impression. The impression had, in strictness, nothing unprecedented; but she felt it as something new, and the soundlessness of her step gave her time to take in the scene before she interrupted it. Madame Merle was there in her bonnet, and Gilbert Osmond was talking to her; for a minute they were unaware she had come in. Isabel had often seen that before, certainly; but what she had not seen, or at least had not noticed, was that their colloquy had for the moment converted itself into a sort of familiar silence, from which she instantly perceived that her entrance would startle them. Madame Merle was standing on the rug, a little way from the fire; Osmond was in a deep chair, leaning back and looking at her. Her head was erect, as usual, but her eyes were bent on his. What struck Isabel first was that he was sitting while Madame Merle stood; there was an anomaly in this that arrested her. Then she perceived that they had arrived at a desultory pause in their exchange of ideas and were musing, face to face, with the freedom of old friends who sometimes exchange ideas without uttering them. There was nothing to shock in this; they were old friends in fact. But the thing made an image, lasting only a moment, like a sudden flicker of light. Their relative positions, their absorbed mutual gaze, struck her as something detected. But it was all over by the time she had fairly seen it. Madame Merle had seen her and had welcomed her without moving; her husband, on the other hand, had instantly jumped up. He presently murmured something about wanting a walk and, after having asked their visitor to excuse him, left the room.

'I came to see you, thinking you would have come in; and as you hadn't I waited for you,' Madame Merle said.

'Didn't he ask you to sit down?' Isabel asked with a smile.

Madame Merle looked about her. 'Ah, it's very true; I was going away.'

'You must stay now.'

'Certainly. I came for a reason; I've something on my mind.'

'I've told you that before,' Isabel said—'that it takes something extraordinary to bring you to this house.'

'And you know what I've told *you*; that whether I come or whether I stay away, I've always the same motive—the affection I bear you.'

'Yes, you've told me that.'

'You look just now as if you didn't believe it,' said Madame Merle.

'Ah,' Isabel answered, 'the profundity of your motives, that's the last thing I doubt!'

'You doubt sooner of the sincerity of my words.'

Isabel shook her head gravely. 'I know you've always been kind to me.'

'As often as you would let me. You don't always take it; then one has to let you alone. It's not to do you a kindness, however, that I've come to-day; it's quite another affair. I've come to get rid of a trouble of my own—to make it over to you. I've been talking to your husband about it.'

'I'm surprised at that; he doesn't like troubles.'

'Especially other people's; I know very well. But neither do you, I suppose. At any rate, whether you do or not, you must help me. It's about poor Mr Rosier.'

'Ah,' said Isabel reflectively, 'it's his trouble then, not yours.'

'He has succeeded in saddling me with it. He comes to see me ten times a week, to talk about Pansy.'

'Yes, he wants to marry her. I know all about it.'

Madame Merle hesitated. 'I gathered from your husband that perhaps you didn't.'

'How should he know what I know? He has never spoken to me of the matter.'

'It's probably because he doesn't know how to speak of it.'

'It's nevertheless the sort of question in which he's rarely at fault.'

'Yes, because as a general thing he knows perfectly well what to think. To-day he doesn't.'

'Haven't you been telling him?' Isabel asked.

Madame Merle gave a bright, voluntary smile. 'Do you know you're a little dry?'

'Yes; I can't help it. Mr Rosier has also talked to me.'

'In that there's some reason. You're so near the child.'

'Ah,' said Isabel, 'for all the comfort I've given him! If you think me dry, I wonder what *he* thinks.'

'I believe he thinks you can do more than you have done.'

'I can do nothing.'

'You can do more at least than I. I don't know what mysterious connection he may have discovered between me and Pansy; but he came to me from the first, as if I held his fortune in my hand. Now he keeps coming back, to spur me up, to know what hope there is, to pour out his feelings.'

'He's very much in love,' said Isabel.

'Very much—for him.'

'Very much for Pansy, you might say as well.'

Madame Merle dropped her eyes a moment. 'Don't you think she's attractive?'

'The dearest little person possible—but very limited.'

'She ought to be all the easier for Mr Rosier to love. Mr Rosier's not unlimited.'

'No,' said Isabel, 'he has about the extent of one's pocket-handkerchief—the small ones with lace borders.' Her humour had lately turned a good deal to sarcasm, but in a moment she was ashamed of exercising it on so innocent an object as Pansy's suitor. 'He's very kind, very honest,' she presently added; 'and he's not such a fool as he seems.'

'He assures me that she delights in him,' said Madame Merle.

'I don't know; I've not asked her.'

'You've never sounded her a little?'

'It's not my place; it's her father's.'

'Ah, you're too literal!' said Madame Merle.

'I must judge for myself.'

Madame Merle gave her smile again. 'It isn't easy to help you.'

'To help me?' said Isabel very seriously. 'What do you mean?'

'It's easy to displease you. Don't you see how wise I am to

be careful? I notify you, at any rate, as I notified Osmond, that I wash my hands of the love-affairs of Miss Pansy and Mr Edward Rosier. *Je n'y peux rien, moi!** I can't talk to Pansy about him. Especially,' added Madame Merle, 'as I don't think him a paragon of husbands.'

Isabel reflected a little; after which, with a smile, 'You don't wash your hands then!' she said. After which again she added in another tone: 'You can't—you're too much interested.'

Madame Merle slowly rose; she had given Isabel a look as rapid as the intimation that had gleamed before our heroine a few moments before. Only this time the latter saw nothing. 'Ask him the next time, and you'll see.'

'I can't ask him; he has ceased to come to the house. Gilbert has let him know that he's not welcome.'

'Ah yes,' said Madame Merle, 'I forgot that—though it's the burden of his lamentation. He says Osmond has insulted him. All the same,' she went on, 'Osmond doesn't dislike him so much as he thinks.' She had got up as if to close the conversation, but she lingered, looking about her, and had evidently more to say. Isabel perceived this and even saw the point she had in view; but Isabel also had her own reasons for not opening the way.

'That must have pleased him, if you've told him,' she answered, smiling.

'Certainly I've told him; as far as that goes I've encouraged him. I've preached patience, have said that his case isn't desperate if he'll only hold his tongue and be quiet. Unfortunately he has taken it into his head to be jealous.'

'Jealous?'

'Jealous of Lord Warburton, who, he says, is always here.'

Isabel, who was tired, had remained sitting; but at this she also rose. 'Ah!' she exclaimed simply, moving slowly to the fireplace. Madame Merle observed her as she passed and while she stood a moment before the mantel-glass and pushed into its place a wandering tress of hair.

'Poor Mr Rosier keeps saying there's nothing impossible in Lord Warburton's falling in love with Pansy,' Madame Merle went on.

Isabel was silent a little; she turned away from the glass. 'It's true—there's nothing impossible,' she returned at last, gravely and more gently.

'So I've had to admit to Mr Rosier. So, too, your husband thinks.'

'That I don't know.'

'Ask him and you'll see.'

'I shall not ask him,' said Isabel.

'Pardon me; I forgot you had pointed that out. Of course,' Madame Merle added, 'you've had infinitely more observation of Lord Warburton's behaviour than I.'

'I see no reason why I shouldn't tell you that he likes my stepdaughter very much.'

Madame Merle gave one of her quick looks again. 'Likes her, you mean—as Mr Rosier means?'

'I don't know how Mr Rosier means; but Lord Warburton has let me know that he's charmed with Pansy.'

'And you've never told Osmond?' This observation was immediate, precipitate; it almost burst from Madame Merle's lips.

Isabel's eyes rested on her. 'I suppose he'll know in time; Lord Warburton has a tongue and knows how to express himself.'

Madame Merle instantly became conscious that she had spoken more quickly than usual, and the reflection brought the colour to her cheek. She gave the treacherous impulse time to subside and then said as if she had been thinking it over a little: 'That would be better than marrying poor Mr Rosier.'

'Much better, I think.'

'It would be very delightful; it would be a great marriage. It's really very kind of him.'

'Very kind of him?'

'To drop his eyes on a simple little girl.'

'I don't see that.'

'It's very good of you. But after all, Pansy Osmond—'

'After all, Pansy Osmond's the most attractive person he has ever known!' Isabel exclaimed.

Madame Merle stared, and indeed she was justly bewildered. 'Ah, a moment ago I thought you seemed rather to disparage her.'

'I said she was limited. And so she is. And so's Lord Warburton.'

'So are we all, if you come to that. If it's no more than Pansy deserves, all the better. But if she fixes her affections on Mr Rosier I won't admit that she deserves it. That will be too perverse.'

'Mr Rosier's a nuisance!' Isabel cried abruptly.

'I quite agree with you, and I'm delighted to know that I'm not expected to feed his flame. For the future, when he calls on me, my door shall be closed to him.' And gathering her mantle together Madame Merle prepared to depart. She was checked, however, on her progress to the door, by an inconsequent request from Isabel.

'All the same, you know, be kind to him.'

She lifted her shoulders and eyebrows and stood looking at her friend. 'I don't understand your contradictions! Decidedly I shan't be kind to him, for it will be a false kindness. I want to see her married to Lord Warburton.'

'You had better wait till he asks her.'

'If what you say's true, he'll ask her. Especially,' said Madame Merle in a moment, 'if you make him.'

'If I make him?'

'It's quite in your power. You've great influence with him.'

Isabel frowned a little. 'Where did you learn that?'

'Mrs Touchett told me. Not you—never!' said Madame Merle, smiling.

'I certainly never told you anything of the sort.'

'You *might* have done so—so far as opportunity went—when we were by way of being confidential with each other. But you really told me very little; I've often thought so since.'

Isabel had thought so too, and sometimes with a certain satisfaction. But she didn't admit it now—perhaps because she wished not to appear to exult in it. 'You seem to have had an excellent informant in my aunt,' she simply returned.

'She let me know you had declined an offer of marriage from Lord Warburton, because she was greatly vexed and was full of the subject. Of course I think you've done better in doing as you did. But if you wouldn't marry Lord Warburton yourself, make him the reparation of helping him to marry some one else.'

Isabel listened to this with a face that persisted in not reflecting the bright expressiveness of Madame Merle's. But in a moment she said, reasonably and gently enough: 'I should be very glad indeed if, as regards Pansy, it could be arranged.' Upon which her companion, who seemed to regard this as a speech of good omen, embraced her more tenderly than might have been expected and triumphantly withdrew.

XLI

OSMOND touched on this matter that evening for the first time; coming very late into the drawing-room, where she was sitting alone. They had spent the evening at home, and Pansy had gone to bed; he himself had been sitting since dinner in a small apartment in which he had arranged his books and which he called his study. At ten o'clock Lord Warburton had come in, as he always did when he knew from Isabel that she was to be at home; he was going somewhere else and he sat for half an hour. Isabel, after asking him for news of Ralph, said very little to him, on purpose; she wished him to talk with her stepdaughter. She pretended to read; she even went after a little to the piano; she asked herself if she mightn't leave the room. She had come little by little to think well of the idea of Pansy's becoming the wife of the master of beautiful Lockleigh, though at first it had not presented itself in a manner to excite her enthusiasm. Madame Merle, that afternoon, had applied the match to an accumulation of inflammable material. When Isabel was unhappy she always looked about her—partly from impulse and partly by theory—for some form of positive exertion. She could never rid herself of the sense that unhappiness was a state of disease—of suffering as opposed to doing. To 'do'—it hardly mattered what—would therefore be an escape, perhaps in some degree a remedy. Besides, she wished to convince herself that she had done everything possible to content her husband; she was determined not to be haunted by visions of his wife's limpness under appeal. It would please him greatly to see Pansy married to an English nobleman, and justly please him, since this nobleman was so sound a character. It seemed to Isabel that if she could make it her duty to bring about such an event she should play the part of a good wife. She wanted to be that; she wanted to be able to believe sincerely, and with proof of it, that she had been that. Then such an undertaking had other recommendations. It would occupy her, and she desired occupation. It would even amuse her, and if she could really amuse herself she perhaps might be saved. Lastly, it would be a service to Lord Warburton, who evidently pleased himself greatly with the charming girl. It was a little 'weird' he should—being what he was; but there was no accounting for such impressions. Pansy might captivate any one—any one at least but Lord Warburton. Isabel would have thought her too small, too slight, perhaps even too artificial for that. There was always a little of the doll about her, and that was not what he had been looking for. Still, who could say what men ever were looking for? They looked for what they found; they knew what pleased them only when they saw it. No theory was valid in such matters, and nothing was more unaccountable or more natural than anything else. If he had cared for *her* it might seem odd he should care for Pansy, who was so different; but he had not cared for her so much as he had supposed. Or if he had, he had completely got over it, and it was natural that, as that affair had failed, he should think something of quite another sort might succeed. Enthusiasm, as I say, had not come at first to Isabel, but it came to-day and made her feel almost happy. It was astonishing what happiness she could still find in the idea of procuring a pleasure for her husband. It was a pity, however, that Edward Rosier had crossed their path!

At this reflection the light that had suddenly gleamed upon that path lost something of its brightness. Isabel was unfortunately as sure that Pansy thought Mr Rosier the nicest of all the young men—as sure as if she had held an interview with her on the subject. It was very tiresome she should be so sure, when she had carefully abstained from informing herself; almost as tiresome as that poor Mr Rosier should have taken it into his own head. He was certainly very inferior to Lord Warburton. It was not the difference in fortune so much as the difference in the men; the young American was really so light a weight. He was much more of the type of the useless fine gentleman than the English nobleman. It was true that there was no particular reason why Pansy should marry a statesman; still, if a statesman admired her, that was his affair, and she would make a perfect little pearl of a peeress.

It may seem to the reader that Mrs Osmond had grown of a sudden strangely cynical, for she ended by saying to herself that this difficulty could probably be arranged. An impediment that was embodied in poor Rosier could not anyhow present itself as a dangerous one; there were always means of levelling secondary obstacles. Isabel was perfectly aware that she had not taken the measure of Pansy's tenacity, which might prove to be inconveniently great; but she inclined to see her as rather letting go, under suggestion, than as clutching under deprecation—since she had certainly the faculty of assent developed in a very much higher degree than that of protest. She would cling, yes, she would cling; but it really mattered to her very little what she clung to. Lord Warburton would do as well as Mr Rosier—especially as she seemed quite to like him; she had expressed this sentiment to Isabel without a single reservation; she had said she thought his conversation most interesting—he had told her all about India. His manner to Pansy had been of the rightest and easiest—Isabel noticed that for herself, as she also observed that he talked to her not in the least in a patronising way, reminding himself of her youth and simplicity, but quite as if she understood his subjects with that sufficiency with which she followed those of the fashionable operas. This went far enough for attention to the music and the barytone. He was careful only to be kind—he was as kind as he had been to another fluttered young chit at Gardencourt. A girl might well be touched by that; she remembered how she herself had been touched, and said to herself that if she had been as simple as Pansy the impression would have been deeper still. She had not been simple when she refused him; that operation had been as complicated as, later, her acceptance of Osmond had been. Pansy, however, in spite of *her* simplicity, really did understand, and was glad that Lord Warburton should talk to her, not about her partners and bouquets, but about the state of Italy, the condition of the peasantry, the famous grist-tax, the *pellagra*,* his impressions of Roman society. She looked at him, as she drew her needle through her tapestry, with sweet submissive eyes, and when she lowered them she gave little quiet oblique glances at his person, his hands, his feet, his clothes, as if she were considering him. Even his person, Isabel might have reminded her, was better than Mr Rosier's. But Isabel contented herself at such moments with wondering where this gentleman was; he came no more at all to Palazzo Roccanera. It was surprising, as I say, the hold it had taken of her—the idea of assisting her husband to be pleased.

It was surprising for a variety of reasons which I shall presently touch upon. On the evening I speak of, while Lord Warburton sat there, she had been on the point of taking the great step of going out of the room and leaving her companions alone. I say the great step, because it was in this light that Gilbert Osmond would have regarded it, and Isabel was trying as much as possible to take her husband's view. She succeeded after a fashion, but she fell short of the point I mention. After all she couldn't rise to it; something held her and made this impossible. It was not exactly that it would be base or insidious; for women as a general thing practise such manœuvres with a perfectly good conscience, and Isabel was instinctively much more true than false to the common genius of her sex. There was a vague doubt that interposed—a sense that she was not quite sure. So she remained in the drawing-room, and after a while Lord Warburton went off to his party, of which he promised to give Pansy a full account on the morrow. After he had gone she wondered if she had prevented something which would have happened if she had absented herself for a quarter of an hour; and then she pronounced—always mentally—that when their distinguished visitor should wish her to go away he would easily find means to let her know it. Pansy said nothing whatever about him after he had gone, and Isabel studiously said nothing, as she had taken a vow of reserve until after he should have declared himself. He was a little longer in coming to this than might seem to accord with the description he had given Isabel of his feelings. Pansy went to bed, and Isabel had to admit that she could not now guess what her stepdaughter was thinking of. Her transparent little companion was for the moment not to be seen through.

She remained alone, looking at the fire, until, at the end of half an hour, her husband came in. He moved about a while in silence and then sat down; he looked at the fire like herself. But she now had transferred her eyes from the flickering flame in the chimney to Osmond's face, and she watched him while he kept his silence. Covert observation had become a habit with her; an instinct, of which it is not an exaggeration to say that it was allied to that of self-defence, had made it habitual. She wished as much as possible to know his thoughts, to know what he would say, beforehand, so that she might prepare her answer. Preparing answers had not been her strong point of old; she had rarely in this respect got further than thinking afterwards of clever things she might have said. But she had learned caution—learned it in a measure from her husband's very countenance. It was the same face she had looked into with eyes equally earnest perhaps, but less penetrating, on the terrace of a Florentine villa; except that Osmond had grown slightly stouter since his marriage. He still, however, might strike one as very distinguished.

'Has Lord Warburton been here?' he presently asked.

'Yes, he stayed half an hour.'

'Did he see Pansy?'

'Yes; he sat on the sofa beside her.'

'Did he talk with her much?'

'He talked almost only to her.'

'It seems to me he's attentive. Isn't that what you call it?'

'I don't call it anything,' said Isabel; 'I've waited for you to give it a name.'

'That's a consideration you don't always show,' Osmond answered after a moment.

'I've determined, this time, to try and act as you'd like. I've so often failed of that.'

Osmond turned his head slowly, looking at her. 'Are you trying to quarrel with me?'

'No, I'm trying to live at peace.'

'Nothing's more easy; you know I don't quarrel myself.'

'What do you call it when you try to make me angry?' Isabel asked.

'I don't try; if I've done so it has been the most natural thing in the world. Moreover I'm not in the least trying now.'

Isabel smiled. 'It doesn't matter. I've determined never to be angry again.'

'That's an excellent resolve. Your temper isn't good.'

'No—it's not good.' She pushed away the book she had

been reading and took up the band of tapestry Pansy had left on the table.

'That's partly why I've not spoken to you about this business of my daughter's,' Osmond said, designating Pansy in the manner that was most frequent with him. 'I was afraid I should encounter opposition—that you too would have views on the subject. I've sent little Rosier about his business.'

'You were afraid I'd plead for Mr Rosier? Haven't you noticed that I've never spoken to you of him?'

'I've never given you a chance. We've so little conversation in these days. I know he was an old friend of yours.'

'Yes; he's an old friend of mine.' Isabel cared little more for him than for the tapestry that she held in her hand; but it was true that he was an old friend and that with her husband she felt a desire not to extenuate such ties. He had a way of expressing contempt for them which fortified her loyalty to them, even when, as in the present case, they were in themselves insignificant. She sometimes felt a sort of passion of tenderness for memories which had no other merit than that they belonged to her unmarried life. 'But as regards Pansy,' she added in a moment, 'I've given him no encouragement.'

'That's fortunate,' Osmond observed.

'Fortunate for me, I suppose you mean. For him it matters little.'

'There's no use talking of him,' Osmond said. 'As I tell you, I've turned him out.'

'Yes; but a lover outside's always a lover. He's sometimes even more of one. Mr Rosier still has hope.'

'He's welcome to the comfort of it! My daughter has only to sit perfectly quiet to become Lady Warburton.'

'Should you like that?' Isabel asked with a simplicity which was not so affected as it may appear. She was resolved to assume nothing, for Osmond had a way of unexpectedly turning her assumptions against her. The intensity with which he would like his daughter to become Lady Warburton had been the very basis of her own recent reflections. But that was for herself; she would recognise nothing until Osmond should have put it into words; she would not take for granted with him that he thought Lord Warburton a prize worth an amount of effort that was unusual among the Osmonds. It was Gilbert's constant intimation that for him nothing in life was a prize; that he treated as from equal to equal with the most distinguished people in the world, and that his daughter had only to look about her to pick out a prince. It cost him therefore a lapse from consistency to say explicitly that he yearned for Lord Warburton and that if this nobleman should escape his equivalent might not be found; with which moreover it was another of his customary implications that he was never inconsistent. He would have liked his wife to glide over the point. But strangely enough, now that she was face to face with him and although an hour before she had almost invented a scheme for pleasing him, Isabel was not accommodating, would not glide. And yet she knew exactly the effect on his mind of her question: it would operate as an humiliation. Never mind; he was terribly capable of humiliating *her*—all the more so that he was also capable of waiting for great opportunities and of showing sometimes an almost unaccountable indifference to small ones. Isabel perhaps took a small opportunity because she would not have availed herself of a great one.

Osmond at present acquitted himself very honourably. 'I should like it extremely; it would be a great marriage. And then Lord Warburton has another advantage: he's an old friend of yours. It would be pleasant for him to come into the family. It's very odd Pansy's admirers should all be your old friends.'

'It's natural that they should come to see me. In coming to see me they see Pansy. Seeing her it's natural they should fall in love with her.'

'So I think. But you're not bound to do so.'

'If she should marry Lord Warburton I should be very glad,' Isabel went on frankly. 'He's an excellent man. You say, however, that she has only to sit perfectly still. Perhaps she won't sit perfectly still. If she loses Mr Rosier she may jump up!'

Osmond appeared to give no heed to this; he sat gazing at the fire. 'Pansy would like to be a great lady,' he remarked in a moment with a certain tenderness of tone. 'She wishes above all to please,' he added.

'To please Mr Rosier, perhaps.'

'No, to please me.'

'Me too a little, I think,' said Isabel.

'Yes, she has a great opinion of you. But she'll do what I like.'

'If you're sure of that, it's very well,' she went on.

'Meantime,' said Osmond, 'I should like our distinguished visitor to speak.'

'He has spoken—to me. He has told me it would be a great pleasure to him to believe she could care for him.'

Osmond turned his head quickly, but at first he said nothing. Then, 'Why didn't you tell me that?' he asked sharply.

'There was no opportunity. You know how we live. I've taken the first chance that has offered.'

'Did you speak to him of Rosier?'

'Oh yes, a little.'

'That was hardly necessary.'

'I thought it best he should know, so that, so that—' And Isabel paused.

'So that what?'

'So that he might act accordingly.'

'So that he might back out, do you mean?'

'No, so that he might advance while there's yet time.'

'That's not the effect it seems to have had.'

'You should have patience,' said Isabel. 'You know Englishmen are shy.'

'This one's not. He was not when he made love to *you*.'

She had been afraid Osmond would speak of that; it was disagreeable to her. 'I beg your pardon; he was extremely so,' she returned.

He answered nothing for some time; he took up a book and fingered the pages while she sat silent and occupied herself with Pansy's tapestry. 'You must have a great deal of influence with him,' Osmond went on at last. 'The moment you really wish it you can bring him to the point.'

This was more offensive still; but she felt the great naturalness of his saying it, and it was after all extremely like what she had said to herself. 'Why should I have influence?' she asked. 'What have I ever done to put him under an obligation to me?'

'You refused to marry him,' said Osmond with his eyes on his book.

'I must not presume too much on that,' she replied.

He threw down the book presently and got up, standing before the fire with his hands behind him. 'Well, I hold that it lies in your hands. I shall leave it there. With a little good-will you may manage it. Think that over and remember how much I count on you.' He waited a little, to give her time to answer; but she answered nothing, and he presently strolled out of the room.

XLII

SHE had answered nothing because his words had put the situation before her and she was absorbed in looking at it. There was something in them that suddenly made vibrations deep, so that she had been afraid to trust herself to speak. After he had gone she leaned back in her chair and closed her eyes; and for a long time, far into the night and still further, she sat in the still drawing-room, given up to her meditation. A servant came in to attend to the fire, and she bade him bring fresh candles and then go to bed. Osmond had told her to think of what he had said; and she did so indeed, and of many other things. The suggestion from another that she had a definite influence on Lord Warburton—this had given her the start that accompanies unexpected recognition. Was it true that there was something still between them that might be a handle to make him declare himself to Pansy—a susceptibility, on his part, to approval, a desire to do what would please her? Isabel had hitherto not asked herself the question, because she had not been forced; but now that it was directly presented to her she saw the answer, and the answer frightened her. Yes, there was something—something on Lord Warburton's part. When he had first come to Rome she believed the link that united them to be completely snapped; but little by little she had been reminded that it had yet a palpable existence. It was as thin as a hair, but there were moments when she seemed to hear it vibrate. For herself nothing was changed; what she once thought of him she always thought; it was needless this feeling should change; it seemed to her in fact a better feeling than ever. But he? had he still the idea that she might be more to him than other women? Had he the wish to profit by the memory of the few moments of intimacy through which they had once passed? Isabel knew she had read some of the signs of such a disposition. But what were his hopes, his pretensions, and in what strange way were they mingled with his evidently very sincere appreciation of poor Pansy? Was he in love with Gilbert Osmond's wife, and if so what comfort did he expect to derive from it? If he was in love with Pansy he was not in love with her stepmother, and if he was in love with her stepmother he was not in love with Pansy. Was she to cultivate the advantage she possessed in order to make him commit himself to Pansy, knowing he would do so for her sake and not for the small creature's own—was this the service her husband had asked of her? This at any rate was the duty with which she found herself confronted—from the moment she admitted to herself that her old friend had still an uneradicated predilection for her society. It was not an agreeable task; it was in fact a repulsive one. She asked herself with dismay whether Lord Warburton were pretending to be in love with Pansy in order to cultivate another satisfaction and what might be called other chances. Of this refinement of duplicity she presently acquitted him; she preferred to believe him in perfect good faith. But if his admiration for Pansy were a delusion this was scarcely better than its being an affectation. Isabel wandered among these ugly possibilities until she had completely lost her way; some of them, as she suddenly encountered them, seemed ugly enough. Then she broke out of the labyrinth, rubbing her eyes, and declared that her imagination surely did her little honour and that her husband's did him even less. Lord Warburton was as disinterested as he need be, and she was no more to him than she need wish. She would rest upon this till the contrary should be proved; proved more effectually than by a cynical intimation of Osmond's.

Such a resolution, however, brought her this evening but little peace, for her soul was haunted with terrors which crowded to the foreground of thought as quickly as a place was made for them. What had suddenly set them into livelier motion she hardly knew, unless it were the strange impression she had received in the afternoon of her husband's being in more direct communication with Madame Merle than she suspected. That impression came back to her from time to time, and now she wondered it had never come before. Besides this, her short interview with Osmond half an hour ago was a striking example of his faculty for making everything wither that he touched, spoiling everything for her that he looked at. It was very well to undertake to give him a proof of loyalty; the real fact was that the knowledge of his expecting a thing raised a presumption against it. It was as if he had had the evil eye; as if his presence were a blight and his favour a misfortune. Was the fault in himself, or only in the deep mistrust she had conceived for him? This mistrust was now the clearest result of their short married life; a gulf had opened between them over which they looked at each other with eyes that were on either side a declaration of the deception suffered. It was a strange opposition, of the like of which she had never dreamed—an opposition in which the vital principle of the one was a thing of contempt to the other. It was not her fault—she had practised no deception; she had only admired and believed. She had taken all the first steps in the purest confidence, and then she had suddenly found the infinite vista of a multiplied life to be a dark, narrow alley with a dead wall at the end. Instead of leading to the high places of happiness, from which the world would seem to lie below one, so that one could look down with a sense of exaltation and advantage, and judge and choose and pity, it led rather downward and earthward, into realms of restriction and depression where the sound of other lives, easier and freer, was heard as from above, and where it served to deepen the feeling of failure. It was her deep distrust of her husband—this was what darkened the world. That is a sentiment easily indicated, but not so easily explained, and so composite in its character that much time and still more suffering had been needed to bring it to its actual perfection. Suffering, with Isabel, was an active condition; it was not a chill, a stupor, a despair; it was a passion of thought, of speculation, of response to every pressure. She flattered herself that she had kept her failing faith to herself, however,—that no one suspected it but Osmond. Oh, he knew it, and there were times when she thought he enjoyed it. It had come gradually—it was not till the first year of their life together, so admirably intimate at first, had closed that she had taken the alarm. Then the shadows had begun to gather; it was as if Osmond deliberately, almost malignantly, had put the lights out one by one. The dusk at first was vague and thin, and she could still see her way in it. But it steadily deepened, and if now and again it had occasionally lifted there were certain corners of her prospect that were impenetrably black. These shadows were not an emanation from her own mind: she was very sure of that; she had done her best to be just and temperate, to see only the truth. They were a part, they were a kind of creation and consequence, of her husband's very presence. They were not his misdeeds, his turpitudes; she accused him of nothing—that is but of one thing, which was *not* a crime. She knew of no wrong he had done; he was not violent, he was not cruel: she simply believed he hated her. That was all she accused him of, and the miserable part of it was precisely that it was not a crime, for against a crime she might have found redress. He had discovered that she was so different, that she was not what he had believed she would prove to be. He had thought at first he could change her, and she had done her best to be what he would like. But she was, after all, herself—she couldn't help that; and now there was no use pretending, wearing a mask or a dress, for he knew her and had made up his mind. She was not afraid of him; she had no apprehension he would hurt her; for the ill-will he bore her was not of that sort. He would if possible never give her a pretext, never put himself in the wrong. Isabel, scanning the future with dry, fixed eyes, saw that he would have the better of her there. She would give him many pretexts, she would often put herself in the wrong. There were times when she almost pitied him; for if she had not deceived him in intention she understood how completely she must have done so in fact. She had effaced herself when he first knew her; she had made herself small, pretending there was less of her than there really was. It was because she had been under the extraordinary charm that he, on his side, had taken pains to put forth. He was not changed; he had not disguised himself, during the year of his courtship, any more than she. But she had seen only half his nature then, as one saw the disk of the moon when it was partly masked by the shadow of the earth. She saw the full moon now—she saw the whole man. She had kept still, as it were, so that he should have a free field, and yet in spite of this she had mistaken a part for the whole.

Ah, she had been immensely under the charm! It had not passed away; it was there still: she still knew perfectly what it was that made Osmond delightful when he chose to be. He had wished to be when he made love to her, and as she had wished to be charmed it was not wonderful he had succeeded. He had succeeded because he had been sincere; it never occurred to her now to deny him that. He admired her—he had told her why: because she was the most imaginative woman he had known. It might very well have been true; for during those months she had imagined a world of things that had no substance. She had had a more wondrous vision of him, fed through charmed senses and oh such a stirred fancy!—she had not read him right. A certain combination of features had touched her, and in them she had seen the most striking of figures. That he was poor and lonely and yet that somehow he was noble—that was what had interested her and seemed to give her her opportunity. There had been an indefinable beauty about him—in his situation, in his mind, in his face. She had felt at the same time that he was helpless and ineffectual, but the feeling had taken the form of a tenderness which was the very flower of respect. He was like a sceptical voyager strolling on the beach while he waited for the tide, looking seaward yet not putting to sea. It was in all this she had found her occasion. She would launch his boat for him; she would be his providence; it would be a good thing to love him. And she had loved him, she had so anxiously and yet so ardently given herself—a good deal for what she found in him, but a good deal also for what she brought him and what might enrich the gift. As she looked back at the passion of those full weeks she perceived in it a kind of maternal strain—the happiness of a woman who felt that she was a contributor, that she came with charged hands. But for her money, as she saw to-day, she would never have done it. And then her mind wandered off to poor Mr Touchett, sleeping under English turf, the beneficent author of infinite woe! For this was the fantastic fact. At bottom her money had been a burden, had been on her mind, which was filled with the desire to transfer the weight of it to some other conscience, to some more prepared receptacle. What would lighten her own conscience more effectually than to make it over to the man with the best taste in the world? Unless she should have given it to a hospital there would have been nothing better she could do with it; and there was no charitable institution in which she had been as much interested as in Gilbert Osmond. He would use her fortune in a way that would make her think better of it and rub off a certain grossness attaching to the good luck of an unexpected inheritance. There had been nothing very delicate in inheriting seventy thousand pounds; the delicacy had been all in Mr Touchett's leaving them to her. But to marry Gilbert Osmond and bring him such a portion—in that there would be delicacy for her as well. There would be less for him—that was true; but that was his affair, and if he loved her he wouldn't object to her being rich. Had he not had the courage to say he was glad she was rich?

Isabel's cheek burned when she asked herself if she had really married on a factitious theory, in order to do something finely appreciable with her money. But she was able to answer quickly enough that this was only half the story. It was because a certain ardour took possession of her—a sense of the earnestness of his affection and a delight in his personal qualities. He was better than any one else. This supreme conviction had filled her life for months, and enough of it still remained to prove to her that she could not have done otherwise. The finest—in the sense of being the subtlest—manly organism she had ever known had become her property, and the recognition of her having but to put out her hands and take it had been originally a sort of act of devotion. She had not been mistaken about the beauty of his mind; she knew that organ perfectly now. She had lived with it, she had lived *in* it almost—it appeared to have become her habitation. If she had been captured it had taken a firm hand to seize her; that reflection perhaps had some worth. A mind more ingenious, more plaint, more cultivated, more trained to admirable exercises, she had not encountered; and it was this exquisite instrument she had now to reckon with. She lost herself in infinite dismay when she thought of the magnitude of *his* deception. It was a wonder, perhaps, in view of this, that he didn't hate her more. She remembered perfectly the first sign he had given of it—it had been like the bell that was to ring up the curtain upon the real drama of their life. He said to her one day that she had too many ideas and that she must get rid of them. He had told her that already, before their marriage; but then she had not noticed it: it had come back to her only afterwards. This time she might well have noticed it, because he had really meant it. The words had been nothing superficially; but when in the light of deepening experience she had looked into them they had then appeared portentous. He had really meant it—he would have liked her to have nothing of her own but her pretty appearance. She had known she had too many ideas; she had more even than he had supposed, many more than she had expressed to him when he had asked her to marry him. Yes, she *had* been hypocritical; she had liked him so much. She had too many ideas for herself; but that was just what one married for, to share them with some one else. One couldn't pluck them up by the roots, though of course one might suppress them, be careful not to utter them. It had not been this, however, his objecting to her opinions; this had been nothing. She had no opinions—none that she would not have been eager to sacrifice in the satisfaction of feeling herself loved for it. What he had meant had been the whole thing—her character, the way she felt, the way she judged. This was what she had kept in reserve; this was what he had not known until he had found himself—with the door closed behind, as it were—set down face to face with it. She had a certain way of looking at life which he took as a personal offence. Heaven knew that now at least it was a very humble, accommodating way! The strange thing was that she should not have suspected from the first that his own had been so different. She had thought it so large, so enlightened, so perfectly that of an honest man and a gentleman. Hadn't he assured her that he had no superstitions, no dull limitations, no prejudices that had lost their freshness? Hadn't he all the appearance of a man living in the open air of the world, indifferent to small considerations, caring only for truth and knowledge and believing that two intelligent people ought to look for them together and, whether they found them or not, find at least some happiness in the search? He had told her he loved the conventional; but there was a sense in which this seemed a noble declaration. In that sense, that of the love of harmony and order and decency and of all the stately offices of life, she went with him freely, and his warning had contained nothing ominous. But when, as the months had elapsed, she had followed him further and he had led her into the mansion of his own habitation, then, *then* she had seen where she really was.

She could live it over again, the incredulous terror with which she had taken the measure of her dwelling. Between those four walls she had lived ever since; they were to surround her for the rest of her life. It was the house of darkness, the house of dumbness, the house of suffocation. Osmond's beautiful mind gave it neither light nor air; Osmond's beautiful mind indeed seemed to peep down from a small high window and mock at her. Of course it had not been physical suffering; for physical suffering there might have been a remedy. She could come and go; she had her liberty; her husband was perfectly polite. He took himself so seriously; it was something appalling. Under all his culture, his cleverness, his amenity, under his good-nature, his facility, his knowledge of life, his egotism lay hidden like a serpent in a bank of flowers. She had taken him seriously, but she had not taken him so seriously as that. How could she—especially when she had known him better? She was to think of him as he thought of himself—as the first gentleman in Europe. So it was that she had thought of him at first, and that indeed was the reason she had married him. But when she began to see what it implied she drew back; there was more in the bond than she had meant to put her name to. It implied a sovereign contempt for every one but some three or four very exalted people whom he envied, and for everything in the world but half a dozen ideas of his own. That was very well; she would have gone with him even there a long distance; for he pointed out to her so much of the baseness and shabbiness of life, opened her eyes so wide to the stupidity, the depravity, the ignorance of mankind, that she had been properly impressed with the infinite vulgarity of things and of the virtue of keeping one's self unspotted by it. But this base, ignoble world, it appeared, was after all what one was to live for; one was to keep it for ever in one's eye, in order not to enlighten or convert or redeem it, but to extract from it some recognition of one's own superiority. On the one hand it was despicable, but on the other it afforded a standard.

Osmond had talked to Isabel about his renunciation, his indifference, the ease with which he dispensed with the usual aids to success; and all this had seemed to her admirable. She had thought it a grand indifference, an exquisite independence. But indifference was really the last of his qualities; she had never seen any one who thought so much of others. For herself, avowedly, the world had always interested her and the study of her fellow creatures been her constant passion. She would have been willing, however, to renounce all her curiosities and sympathies for the sake of a personal life, if the person concerned had only been able to make her believe it was a gain! This at least was her present conviction; and the thing certainly would have been easier than to care for society as Osmond cared for it.

He was unable to live without it, and she saw that he had never really done so; he had looked at it out of his window even when he appeared to be most detached from it. He had his ideal, just as she had tried to have hers; only it was strange that people should seek for justice in such different quarters. His ideal was a conception of high prosperity and propriety, of the aristocratic life, which she now saw that he deemed himself always, in essence at least, to have led. He had never lapsed from it for an hour; he would never have recovered from the shame of doing so. That again was very well; here too she would have agreed; but they attached such different ideas, such different associations and desires, to the same formulas. Her notion of the aristocratic life was simply the union of great knowledge with great liberty; the knowledge would give one a sense of duty and the liberty a sense of enjoyment. But for Osmond it was altogether a thing of forms, a conscious, calculated attitude. He was fond of the old, the consecrated, the transmitted; so was she, but she pretended to do what she chose with it. He had an immense esteem for tradition; he had told her once that the best thing in the world was to have it, but that if one was so unfortunate as not to have it one must immediately proceed to make it. She knew that he meant by this that she hadn't it, but that he was better off; though from what source he had derived his traditions she never learned. He had a very large collection of them, however; that was very certain, and after a little she began to see. The great thing was to act in accordance with them; the great thing not only for him but for her. Isabel had an undefined conviction that to serve for another person than their proprietor traditions must be of a thoroughly superior kind; but she nevertheless assented to this intimation that she too must march to the stately music that floated down from unknown periods in her husband's past; she who of old had been so free of step, so desultory, so devious, so much the reverse of processional. There were certain things they must do, a certain posture they must take, certain people they must know and not know. When she saw this rigid system close about her, draped though it was in pictured tapestries, that sense of darkness and suffocation of which I have spoken took possession of her; she seemed shut up with an odour of mould and decay. She had resisted of course; at first very humorously, ironically, tenderly; then, as the situation grew more serious, eagerly, passionately, pleadingly. She had pleaded the cause of freedom, of doing as they chose, of not caring for the aspect and denomination of their life—the cause of other instincts and longings, of quite another ideal.

Then it was that her husband's personality, touched as it never had been, stepped forth and stood erect. The things she had said were answered only by his scorn, and she could see he was ineffably ashamed of her. What did he think of her—that she was base, vulgar, ignoble? He at least knew now that she had no traditions! It had not been in his prevision of things that she should reveal such flatness; her sentiments were worthy of a radical newspaper or a Unitarian preacher. The real offence, as she ultimately perceived, was her having a mind of her own at all. Her mind was to be his—attached to his own like a small garden-plot to a deer-park. He would rake the soil gently and water the flowers; he would weed the beds and gather an occasional nosegay. It would be a pretty piece of property for a proprietor already far-reaching. He didn't wish her to be stupid. On the contrary, it was because she was clever that she had pleased him. But he expected her intelligence to operate altogether in his favour, and so far from desiring her mind to be a blank he had flattered himself that it would be richly receptive. He had expected his wife to feel with him and for him, to enter into his opinions, his ambitions, his preferences; and Isabel was obliged to confess that this was no great insolence on the part of a man so accomplished and a husband originally at least so tender. But there were certain things she could never take in. To begin with, they were hideously unclean. She was not a daughter of the Puritans, but for all that she believed in such a thing as chastity and even as decency. It would appear that Osmond was far from doing anything of the sort; some of his traditions made her push back her skirts. Did all women have lovers? Did they all lie and even the best have their price? Were there only three or four that didn't deceive their husbands? When Isabel heard such things she felt a greater scorn for them than for the gossip of a village parlour—a scorn that kept its freshness in a very tainted air. There was the taint of her sister-in-law: did her husband judge only by the Countess Gemini? This lady very often lied, and she had practised deceptions that were not simply verbal. It was enough to find these facts assumed among Osmond's traditions—it was enough without giving them such a general extension. It was her scorn of his assumptions, it was this that made him draw himself up. He had plenty of contempt, and it was proper his wife should be as well furnished; but that she should turn the hot light of her disdain upon his own conception of things—this was a danger he had not allowed for. He believed he should have regulated her emotions before she came to it; and Isabel could easily imagine how his ears had scorched on his discovering he had been too confident. When one had a wife who gave one that sensation there was nothing left but to hate her.

She was morally certain now that this feeling of hatred, which at first had been a refuge and a refreshment, had become the occupation and comfort of his life. The feeling was deep, because it was sincere; he had had the revelation that she could after all dispense with him. If to herself the idea was startling, if it presented itself at first as a kind of infidelity, a capacity for pollution, what infinite effect might it not be expected to have had upon *him?* It was very simple; he despised her; she had no traditions and the moral horizon of a

Unitarian minister. Poor Isabel, who had never been able to understand Unitarianism! This was the certitude she had been living with now for a time that she had ceased to measure. What was coming—what was before them? That was her constant question. What would he do—what ought *she* to do? When a man hated his wife what did it lead to? She didn't hate him, that she was sure of, for every little while she felt a passionate wish to give him a pleasant surprise. Very often, however, she felt afraid, and it used to come over her, as I have intimated, that she had deceived him at the very first. They were strangely married, at all events, and it was a horrible life. Until that morning he had scarcely spoken to her for a week; his manner was as dry as a burned-out fire. She knew there was a special reason; he was displeased at Ralph Touchett's staying on in Rome. He thought she saw too much of her cousin—he had told her a week before it was indecent she should go to him at his hotel. He would have said more than this if Ralph's invalid state had not appeared to make it brutal to denounce him; but having had to contain himself had only deepened his disgust. Isabel read all this as she would have read the hour on the clock-face; she was as perfectly aware that the sight of her interest in her cousin stirred her husband's rage as if Osmond had locked her into her room—which she was sure was what he wanted to do. It was her honest belief that on the whole she was not defiant, but she certainly couldn't pretend to be indifferent to Ralph. She believed he was dying at last and that she should never see him again, and this gave her a tenderness for him that she had never known before. Nothing was a pleasure to her now; how could anything be a pleasure to a woman who knew that she had thrown away her life? There was an everlasting weight on her heart—there was a livid light on everything. But Ralph's little visit was a lamp in the darkness; for the hour that she sat with him her ache for herself became somehow her ache for *him*. She felt to-day as if he had been her brother. She had never had a brother, but if she had and she were in trouble and he were dying, he would be dear to her as Ralph was. Ah yes, if Gilbert was jealous of her there was perhaps some reason; it didn't make Gilbert look better to sit for half an hour with Ralph. It was not that they talked of him—it was not that she complained. His name was never uttered between them. It was simply that Ralph was generous and that her husband was not. There was something in Ralph's talk, in his smile, in the mere fact of his being in Rome, that made the blasted circle round which she walked more spacious. He made her feel the good of the world; he made her feel what might have been. He was after all as intelligent as Osmond—quite apart from his being better. And thus it seemed to her an act of devotion to conceal her misery from him. She concealed it elaborately; she was perpetually, in their talk, hanging out curtains and arranging screens. It lived before her again—it had never had time to die—that morning in the garden at Florence when he had warned her against Osmond. She had only to close her eyes to see the place, to hear his voice, to feel the warm, sweet air. How could he have known? What a mystery, what a wonder of wisdom! As intelligent as Gilbert? He was much more intelligent—to arrive at such a judgement as that. Gilbert had never been so deep, so just. She had told him then that from her at least he should never know if he was right; and this was what she was taking care of now. It gave her plenty to do; there was passion, exaltation, religion in it. Women find their religion sometimes in strange exercises, and Isabel at present, in playing a part before her cousin, had an idea that she was doing him a kindness. It would have been a kindness perhaps if he had been for a single instant a dupe. As it was, the kindness consisted mainly in trying to make him believe that he had once wounded her greatly and that the event had put him to shame, but that, as she was very generous and he was so ill, she bore him no grudge and even considerately forbore to flaunt her happiness in his face. Ralph smiled to himself, as he lay on his sofa, at this extraordinary form of consideration; but he forgave her for having forgiven him. She didn't wish him to have the pain of knowing she was unhappy: that was the great thing, and it didn't matter that such knowledge would rather have righted him.

For herself, she lingered in the soundless saloon long after the fire had gone out. There was no danger of her feeling the cold; she was in a fever. She heard the small hours strike, and then the great ones, but her vigil took no heed of time. Her mind, assailed by visions, was in a state of extraordinary activity, and her visions might as well come to her there, where she sat up to meet them, as on her pillow, to make a mockery of rest. As I have said, she believed she was not defiant, and what could be a better proof of it than that she should linger there half the night, trying to persuade herself that there was no reason why Pansy shouldn't be married as you would put a letter in the post-office? When the clock struck four she got up; she was going to bed at last, for the lamp had long since gone out and the candles burned down to their sockets. But even then she stopped again in the middle of the room and stood there gazing at a remembered vision—that of her husband and Madame Merle unconsciously and familiarly associated.

XLIII

THREE nights after this she took Pansy to a great party, to which Osmond, who never went to dances, did not accompany them. Pansy was as ready for a dance as ever; she was not of a generalising turn and had not extended to other pleasures the interdict she had seen placed on those of love. If she was biding her time or hoping to circumvent her father she must have had a prevision of success. Isabel thought this unlikely; it was much more likely that Pansy had simply determined to be a good girl. She had never had such a chance, and she had a proper esteem for chances. She carried herself no less attentively than usual and kept no less anxious an eye upon her vaporous skirts; she held her bouquet very tight and counted over the flowers for the twentieth time. She made Isabel feel old; it seemed so long since she had been in a flutter about a ball. Pansy, who was greatly admired, was never in want of partners, and very soon after their arrival she gave Isabel, who was not dancing, her bouquet to hold. Isabel had rendered her this service for some minutes when she became aware of the near presence of Edward Rosier. He stood before her; he had lost his affable smile and wore a look of almost military resolution. The change in his appearance would have made Isabel smile if she had not felt his case to be at bottom a hard one: he had always smelt so much more of heliotrope than of gunpowder. He looked at her a moment somewhat fiercely, as if to notify her he was dangerous, and then dropped his eyes on her bouquet. After he had inspected it his glance softened and he said quickly: 'It's all pansies; it must be hers!'

Isabel smiled kindly. 'Yes, it's hers; she gave it to me to hold.'

'May I hold it a little, Mrs Osmond?' the poor young man asked.

'No, I can't trust you; I'm afraid you wouldn't give it back.'

'I'm not sure that I should; I should leave the house with it instantly. But may I not at least have a single flower?'

Isabel hestitated a moment, and then, smiling still, held out the bouquet. 'Choose one yourself. It's frightful what I'm doing for you.'

'Ah, if you do no more than this, Mrs Osmond!' Rosier exclaimed with his glass in one eye, carefully choosing his flower.

'Don't put it into your button-hole,' she said. 'Don't for the world!'

'I should like her to see it. She has refused to dance with me, but I wish to show her that I believe in her still.'

'It's very well to show it to her, but it's out of place to show it to others. Her father has told her not to dance with you.'

'And is that all *you* can do for me? I expected more from you, Mrs Osmond,' said the young man in a tone of fine general reference. 'You know our acquaintance goes back very far—quite into the days of our innocent childhood.'

'Don't make me out too old,' Isabel patiently answered. 'You come back to that very often, and I've never denied it. But I must tell you that, old friends as we are, if you had done me the honour to ask me to marry you I should have refused you on the spot.'

'Ah, you don't esteem me then. Say at once that you think me a mere Parisian trifler!'

'I esteem you very much, but I'm not in love with you. What I mean by that, of course, is that I'm not in love with you for Pansy.'

'Very good; I see. You pity me—that's all.' And Edward Rosier looked all round, inconsequently, with his single glass. It was a revelation to him that people shouldn't be more pleased; but he was at least too proud to show that the deficiency struck him as general.

Isabel for a moment said nothing. His manner and appearance had not the dignity of the deepest tragedy; his little glass, among other things, was against that. But she suddenly felt touched; her own unhappiness, after all, had something in common with his, and it came over her, more than before, that here, in recognisable, if not in romantic form, was the most affecting thing in the world—young love struggling with adversity. 'Would you really be very kind to her?' she finally asked in a low tone.

He dropped his eyes devoutly and raised the little flower that he held in his fingers to his lips. Then he looked at her. 'You pity me; but don't you pity *her* a little?'

'I don't know; I'm not sure. She'll always enjoy life.'

'It will depend on what you call life!' Mr Rosier effectively said. 'She won't enjoy being tortured.'

'There'll be nothing of that.'

'I'm glad to hear it. She knows what she's about. You'll see.'

'I think she does, and she'll never disobey her father. But she's coming back to me,' Isabel added, 'and I must beg you to go away.'

Rosier lingered a moment till Pansy came in sight on the arm of her cavalier; he stood just long enough to look her in the face. Then he walked away, holding up his head; and the manner in which he achieved this sacrifice to expediency convinced Isabel he was very much in love.

Pansy, who seldom got disarranged in dancing, looking perfectly fresh and cool after this exercise, waited a moment and then took back her bouquet. Isabel watched her and saw she was counting the flowers; whereupon she said to herself that decidedly there were deeper forces at play than she had recognised. Pansy had seen Rosier turn away, but she said nothing to Isabel about him; she talked only of her partner, after he had made his bow and retired; of the music, the floor, the rare misfortune of having already torn her dress. Isabel was sure, however, she had discovered her lover to have abstracted a flower; though this knowledge was not needed to account for the dutiful grace with which she responded to the appeal of her next partner. That perfect amenity under acute constraint was part of a larger system. She was again led forth by a flushed young man, this time carrying her bouquet; and she had not been absent many minutes when Isabel saw Lord Warburton advancing through the crowd. He presently drew near and bade her good-evening; she had not seen him since the day before. He looked about him, and then 'Where's the little maid?' he asked. It was in this manner that he had formed the harmless habit of alluding to Miss Osmond.

'She's dancing,' said Isabel. 'You'll see her somewhere.'

He looked among the dancers and at last caught Pansy's eye.

'She sees me, but she won't notice me,' he then remarked. 'Are you not dancing?'

'As you see, I'm a wall-flower.'

'Won't you dance with me?'

'Thank you; I'd rather you should dance with the little maid.'

'One needn't prevent the other—especially as she's engaged.'

'She's not engaged for everything, and you can reserve yourself. She dances very hard, and you'll be the fresher.'

'She dances beautifully,' said Lord Warburton, following her with his eyes. 'Ah, at last,' he added, 'she has given me a smile.' He stood there with his handsome, easy, important physiognomy; and as Isabel observed him it came over her, as it had done before, that it was strange a man of his mettle should take an interest in a little maid. It struck her as a great incongruity; neither Pansy's small fascinations, nor his own kindness, his good-nature, not even his need for amusement, which was extreme and constant, were sufficient to account for it. 'I should like to dance with you,' he went on in a moment, turning back to Isabel; 'but I think I like even better to talk with you.'

'Yes, it's better, and it's more worthy of your dignity. Great statesmen oughtn't to waltz.'

'Don't be cruel. Why did you recommend me then to dance with Miss Osmond?'

'Ah, that's different. If you danced with her it would look simply like a piece of kindness—as if you were doing it for her amusement. If you dance with me you'll look as if you were doing it for your own.'

'And pray haven't I a right to amuse myself?'

'No, not with the affairs of the British Empire on your hands.'

'The British Empire be hanged! You're always laughing at it.'

'Amuse yourself with talking to me,' said Isabel.

'I'm not sure it's really a recreation. You're too pointed; I've always to be defending myself. And you strike me as more than usually dangerous to-night. Will you absolutely not dance?'

'I can't leave my place. Pansy must find me here.'

He was silent a little. 'You're wonderfully good to her,' he said suddenly.

Isabel stared a little and smiled. 'Can you imagine one's not being?'

'No indeed. I know how one is charmed with her. But you must have done a great deal for her.'

'I've taken her out with me,' said Isabel, smiling still. 'And I've seen that she has proper clothes.'

'Your society must have been a great benefit to her. You've talked to her, advised her, helped her to develop.'

'Ah yes, if she isn't the rose she has lived near it.'

She laughed, and her companion did as much; but there was a certain visible preoccupation in his face which interfered with complete hilarity. 'We all try to live as near it as we can,' he said after a moment's hesitation.

Isabel turned away; Pansy was about to be restored to her, and she welcomed the diversion. We know how much she liked Lord Warburton; she thought him pleasanter even than the sum of his merits warranted; there was something in his friendship that appeared a kind of resource in case of indefinite need; it was like having a large balance at the bank. She felt happier when he was in the room; there was something reassuring in his approach; the sound of his voice reminded her of the beneficence of nature. Yet for all that it didn't suit her that he should be too near her, that he should take too much of her good-will for granted. She was afraid of that; she averted herself from it; she wished he wouldn't. She felt that if he should come too near, as it were, it might be in her to flash out and bid him keep his distance. Pansy came back to Isabel with another rent in her skirt, which was the inevitable consequence of the first and which she displayed to Isabel with serious eyes. There were too many gentlemen in uniform; they wore those dreadful spurs, which were fatal to the dresses of little maids. It hereupon became apparent that the resources of women are innumerable. Isabel devoted herself to Pansy's desecrated drapery; she fumbled for a pin and repaired the injury; she smiled and listened to her account of her adventures. Her attention, her sympathy were immediate and active; and they were in direct proportion to a sentiment with which they were in no way connected—a lively conjecture as to whether Lord Warburton might be trying to make love to her. It was not simply his words just then; it was others as well; it was the reference and the continuity. This was what she thought about while she pinned up Pansy's dress. If it were so, as she feared, he was of course unwitting; he himself had not taken account of his intention. But this made it none the more auspicious, made the situation none less impossible. The sooner he should get back into right relations with things the better. He immediately began to talk to Pansy—on whom it was certainly mystifying to see that he dropped a smile of chastened devotion. Pansy replied, as usual, with a little air of conscientious aspiration; he had to bend toward her a good deal in conversation, and her eyes, as usual, wandered up and down his robust person as if he had offered it to her for exhibition. She always seemed a little frightened; yet her fright was not of the painful character that suggests dislike; on the contrary, she looked as if she knew that he knew she liked him. Isabel left them together a little and wandered toward a friend whom she saw near and with whom she talked till the music of the following dance began, for which she knew Pansy to be also engaged. The girl joined her presently, with a little fluttered flush, and Isabel, who scrupulously took Osmond's view of his daughter's complete dependence, consigned her, as a precious and momentary loan, to her appointed partner. About all this matter she had her own imaginations, her own reserves; there were moments when Pansy's extreme adhesiveness made each of them, to her sense, look foolish. But Osmond had given her a sort of tableau of her position as his daughter's duenna, which consisted of gracious alternations of concession and contraction; and there were directions of his which she liked to think she obeyed to the letter. Perhaps, as regards some of them, it was because her doing so appeared to reduce them to the absurd.

After Pansy had been led away, she found Lord Warburton drawing near her again. She rested her eyes on him steadily; she wished she could sound his thoughts. But he had no appearance of confusion. 'She has promised to dance with me later,' he said.

'I'm glad of that. I suppose you've engaged her for the cotillion.'

At this he looked a little awkward. 'No, I didn't ask her for that. It's a quadrille.'*

'Ah, you're not clever!' said Isabel almost angrily. 'I told her to keep the cotillion in case you should ask for it.'

'Poor little maid, fancy that!' And Lord Warburton laughed frankly. 'Of course I will if you like.'

'If I like? Oh, if you dance with her only because I like it—!'

'I'm afraid I bore her. She seems to have a lot of young fellows on her book.'

Isabel dropped her eyes, reflecting rapidly; Lord Warburton stood there looking at her and she felt his eyes on her face. She felt much inclined to ask him to remove them. She didn't do so, however; she only said to him, after a minute, with her own raised: 'Please let me understand.'

'Understand what?'

'You told me ten days ago that you'd like to marry my stepdaughter. You've not forgotten it!'

'Forgotten it? I wrote to Mr Osmond about it this morning.'

'Ah,' said Isabel, 'he didn't mention to me that he had heard from you.'

Lord Warburton stammered a little. 'I—I didn't send my letter.'

'Perhaps you forgot *that*.'

'No, I wasn't satisfied with it. It's an awkward sort of letter to write, you know. But I shall send it to-night.'

'At three o'clock in the morning?'

'I mean later, in the course of the day.'

'Very good. You still wish then to marry her?'

'Very much indeed.'

'Aren't you afraid that you'll bore her?' And as her companion stared at this enquiry Isabel added: 'If she can't dance with you for half an hour how will she be able to dance with you for life?'

'Ah,' said Lord Warburton readily, 'I'll let her dance with other people! About the cotillion, the fact is I thought that you—that you—'

'That I would do it with you? I told you I'd do nothing.'

'Exactly; so that while it's going on I might find some quiet corner where we may sit down and talk.'

'Oh,' said Isabel gravely, 'you're much too considerate of me.'

When the cotillion came Pansy was found to have engaged herself, thinking, in perfect humility, that Lord Warburton had no intentions. Isabel recommended him to seek another partner, but he assured her that he would dance with no one but herself. As, however, she had, in spite of the remonstrances of her hostess, declined other invitations on the ground that she was not dancing at all, it was not possible for her to make an exception in Lord Warburton's favour.

'After all I don't care to dance,' he said; 'it's a barbarous amusement: I'd much rather talk.' And he intimated that he had discovered exactly the corner he had been looking for—a quiet nook in one of the smaller rooms, where the music would come to them faintly and not interfere with conversation. Isabel had decided to let him carry out his idea; she wished to be satisfied. She wandered away from the ball-room with him, though she knew her husband desired she should not lose sight of his daughter. It was with his daughter's *prétendant*,* however; that would make it right for Osmond. On her way out of the ball-room she came upon Edward Rosier, who was standing in a doorway, with folded arms, looking at the dance in the attitude of a young man without illusions. She stopped a moment and asked him if he were not dancing.

'Certainly not, if I can't dance with *her!*' he answered.

'You had better go away then,' said Isabel with the manner of good counsel.

'I shall not go till she does!' And he let Lord Warburton pass without giving him a look.

This nobleman, however, had noticed the melancholy youth, and he asked Isabel who her dismal friend was, remarking that he had seen him somewhere before.

'It's the young man I've told you about, who's in love with Pansy.'

'Ah yes, I remember. He looks rather bad.'

'He has reason. My husband won't listen to him.'

'What's the matter with him?' Lord Warburton enquired. 'He seems very harmless.'

'He hasn't money enough, and he isn't very clever.'

Lord Warburton listened with interest; he seemed struck with this account of Edward Rosier. 'Dear me; he looked a well-set-up young fellow.'

'So he is, but my husband's very particular.'

'Oh, I see.' And Lord Warburton paused a moment. 'How much money has he got?' he then ventured to ask.

'Some forty thousand francs a year.'

'Sixteen hundred pounds? Ah, but that's very good, you know.'

'So I think. My husband, however, has larger ideas.'

'Yes; I've noticed that your husband has very large ideas. Is he really an idiot, the young man?'

'An idiot? Not in the least; he's charming. When he was twelve years old I myself was in love with him.'

'He doesn't look much more than twelve to-day,' Lord Warburton rejoined vaguely, looking about him. Then with more point, 'Don't you think we might sit here?' he asked.

'Wherever you please.' The room was a sort of boudoir, pervaded by a subdued, rose-coloured light; a lady and gentleman moved out of it as our friends came in. 'It's very kind of you to take such an interest in Mr Rosier,' Isabel said.

'He seems to me rather ill-treated. He had a face a yard long. I wondered what ailed him.'

'You're a just man,' said Isabel. 'You've a kind thought even for a rival.'

Lord Warburton suddenly turned with a stare. 'A rival! Do you call him my rival?'

'Surely—if you both wish to marry the same person.'

'Yes—but since he has no chance!'

'I like you, however that may be, for putting yourself in his place. It shows imagination.'

'You like me for it?' And Lord Warburton looked at her with an uncertain eye. 'I think you mean you're laughing at me for it.'

'Yes, I'm laughing at you a little. But I like you as somebody to laugh at.'

'Ah well, then, let me enter into his situation a little more. What do you suppose one could do for him?'

'Since I have been praising your imagination I'll leave you to imagine that yourself,' Isabel said. 'Pansy too would like you for that.'

'Miss Osmond? Ah, she, I flatter myself, likes me already.'

'Very much, I think.'

He waited a little; he was still questioning her face. 'Well then, I don't understand you. You don't mean that she cares for him?'

'Surely I've told you I thought she did.'

A quick blush sprang to his brow. 'You told me she would have no wish apart from her father's, and as I've gathered that he would favour me—!' He paused a little and then suggested 'Don't you see?' through his blush.

'Yes, I told you she has an immense wish to please her father, and that it would probably take her very far.'

'That seems to me a very proper feeling,' said Lord Warburton.

'Certainly; it's a very proper feeling.' Isabel remained silent for some moments; the room continued empty; the sound of the music reached them with its richness softened by the interposing apartments. Then at last she said: 'But it hardly strikes me as the sort of feeling to which a man would wish to be indebted for a wife.'

'I don't know; if the wife's a good one and he thinks she does well!'

'Yes, of course you must think that.'

'I do; I can't help it. You call that very British, of course.'

'No, I don't. I think Pansy would do wonderfully well to marry you, and I don't know who should know it better than you. But you're not in love.'

'Ah, yes I am, Mrs Osmond!'

Isabel shook her head. 'You like to think you are while you sit here with me. But that's not how you strike me.'

'I'm not like the young man in the doorway. I admit that. But what makes it so unnatural? Could any one in the world be more loveable than Miss Osmond?'

'No one, possibly. But love has nothing to do with good reasons.'

'I don't agree with you. I'm delighted to have good reasons.'

'Of course you are. If you were really in love you wouldn't care a straw for them.'

'Ah, really in love—really in love!' Lord Warburton exclaimed, folding his arms, leaning back his head and stretching himself a little. 'You must remember that I'm forty-two years old. I won't pretend I'm as I once was.'

'Well, if you're sure,' said Isabel, 'it's all right.'

He answered nothing; he sat there, with his head back, looking before him. Abruptly, however, he changed his position; he turned quickly to his friend. 'Why are you so unwilling, so sceptical?'

She met his eyes, and for a moment they looked straight at each other. If she wished to be satisfied she saw something that satisfied her; she saw in his expression the gleam of an idea that she was uneasy on her own account—that she was perhaps even in fear. It showed a suspicion, not a hope, but such as it was it told her what she wanted to know. Not for an instant should he suspect her of detecting in his proposal of marrying her stepdaughter an implication of increased nearness to herself, or of thinking it, on such a betrayal, ominous. In that brief, extremely personal gaze, however, deeper meanings passed between them than they were conscious of at the moment.

'My dear Lord Warburton,' she said, smiling, 'you may do, so far as I'm concerned, whatever comes into your head.'

And with this she got up and wandered into the adjoining room, where, within her companion's view, she was immediately addressed by a pair of gentlemen, high personages in the Roman world, who met her as if they had been looking for her. While she talked with them she found herself regretting she had moved; it looked a little like running away—all the more as Lord Warburton didn't follow her. She was glad of this, however, and at any rate she was satisfied. She was so well satisfied that when, in passing back into the ball-room, she found Edward Rosier still planted in the doorway, she stopped and spoke to him again. 'You did right not to go away. I've some comfort for you.'

'I need it,' the young man softly wailed, 'when I see you so awfully thick with *him!*'

'Don't speak of him; I'll do what I can for you. I'm afraid it won't be much, but what I can I'll do.'

He looked at her with gloomy obliqueness. 'What has suddenly brought you round?'

'The sense that you are an inconvenience in doorways!' she answered, smiling as she passed him. Half an hour later she took leave, with Pansy, and at the foot of the staircase the two ladies, with many other departing guests, waited a while for their carriage. Just as it approached Lord Warburton came out of the house and assisted them to reach their vehicle. He stood a moment at the door, asking Pansy if she had amused herself; and she, having answered him, fell back with a little air of fatigue. Then Isabel, at the window, detaining him by a movement of her finger, murmured gently: 'Don't forget to send your letter to her father!'

XLIV

THE Countess Gemini was often extremely bored—bored, in her own phrase, to extinction. She had not been extinguished, however, and she struggled bravely enough with her destiny, which had been to marry an unaccommodating Florentine who insisted upon living in his native town, where he enjoyed such consideration as might attach to a gentleman whose talent for losing at cards had not the merit of being incidental to an obliging disposition. The Count Gemini was not liked even by those who won from him; and he bore a name which, having a measurable value in Florence, was, like the local coin of the old Italian states, without currency in other parts of the peninsula. In Rome he was simply a very dull Florentine, and it is not remarkable that he should not have cared to pay frequent visits to a place where, to carry it off, his dullness needed more explanation than was convenient. The Countess lived with her eyes upon Rome, and it was the constant grievance of her life that she had not an habitation there. She was ashamed to say how seldom she had been allowed to visit that city; it scarcely made the matter better that there were other members of the Florentine nobility who never had been there at all. She went whenever she could; that was all she could say. Or rather not all, but all she said she could say. In fact she had much more to say about it, and had often set forth the reasons why she hated Florence and wished to end her days in the shadow of Saint Peter's. They are reasons, however, that do not closely concern us, and were usually summed up in the declaration that Rome, in short, was the Eternal City and that Florence was simply a pretty little place like any other. The Countess apparently needed to connect the idea of eternity with her amusements. She was convinced that society was infinitely more interesting in Rome, where you met celebrities all winter at evening parties. At Florence there were no celebrities; none at least that one had heard of. Since her brother's marriage her impatience had greatly increased; she was so sure his wife had a more brilliant life than herself. She was not so intellectual as Isabel, but she was intellectual enough to do justice to Rome—not to the ruins and the catacombs, not even perhaps to the monuments and museums, the church ceremonies and the scenery; but certainly to all the rest. She heard a great deal about her sister-in-law and knew perfectly that Isabel was having a beautiful time. She had indeed seen it for herself on the only occasion on which she had enjoyed the hospitality of Palazzo Roccanera. She had spent a week there during the first winter of her brother's marriage, but she had not been encouraged to renew this satisfaction. Osmond didn't want her—that she was perfectly aware of; but she would have gone all the same, for after all she didn't care two straws about Osmond. It was her husband who wouldn't let her, and the money question was always a trouble. Isabel had been very nice; the Countess, who had liked her sister-in-law from the first, had not been blinded by envy to Isabel's personal merits. She had always observed that she got on better with clever women than with silly ones like herself; the silly ones could never understand her wisdom, whereas the clever ones—the really clever ones—always understood her silliness. It appeared to her that, different as they were in appearance and general style, Isabel and she had somewhere a patch of common ground that they would set their feet upon at last. It was not very large, but it was firm, and they should both know it when once they had really touched it. And then she lived, with Mrs Osmond, under the influence of a pleasant surprise; she was constantly expecting that Isabel would 'look down' on her, and she as constantly saw this operation postponed. She asked herself when it would begin, like fire-works, or Lent, or the opera season; not that she cared much, but she wondered what kept it in abeyance. Her sister-in-law regarded her with none but level glances and expressed for the poor Countess as little contempt as admiration. In reality Isabel would as soon have thought of despising her as of passing a moral judgement on a grasshopper. She was not indifferent to her husband's sister, however; she was rather a little afraid of her. She wondered at her; she thought her very extraordinary. The Countess seemed to her to have no soul; she was like a bright rare shell, with a polished surface and a remarkably pink lip, in which something would rattle when you shook it. This rattle was apparently the Countess's spiritual principle, a little loose nut that tumbled about inside of her. She was too odd for disdain, too anomalous for comparisons. Isabel would have invited her again (there was no question of inviting the Count); but Osmond, after his marriage, had not scrupled to say frankly that Amy was a fool of the worst species—a fool whose folly had the irrepressibility of genius. He said at another time that she had no heart; and he added in a moment that she had given it all away—in small pieces, like a frosted wedding-cake. The fact of not having been asked was of course another obstacle to the Countess's going again to Rome; but at the period with which this history has now to deal she was in receipt of an invitation to spend several weeks at Palazzo Roccanera. The proposal had come from Osmond himself, who wrote to his sister that she must be prepared to be very quiet. Whether or no she found in this phrase all the meaning he had put into it I am unable to say; but she accepted the invitation on any terms. She was curious, moreover; for one of the impressions of her former visit had been that her brother had found his match. Before the marriage she had been sorry for Isabel, so sorry as to have had serious thoughts—if any of the Countess's thoughts were serious—of putting her on her guard. But she had let that pass, and after a little she was reassured. Osmond was as lofty as ever, but his wife would not be an easy victim. The Countess was not very exact at measurements, but it seemed to her that if Isabel should draw herself up she would be the taller spirit of the two. What she wanted to learn now was whether Isabel had drawn herself up; it would give her immense pleasure to see Osmond overtopped.

Several days before she was to start for Rome a servant brought her the card of a visitor—a card with the simple superscription 'Henrietta C. Stackpole.' The Countess pressed her finger-tips to her forehead; she didn't remember to have known any such Henrietta as that. The servant then remarked that the lady had requested him to say that if the Countess should not recognise her name she would know her well enough on seeing her. By the time she appeared before her visitor she had in fact reminded herself that there was once a literary lady at Mrs Touchett's; the only woman of letters she had ever encountered—that is the only modern one, since she was the daughter of a defunct poetess. She recognised Miss Stackpole immediately, the more so that Miss Stackpole seemed perfectly unchanged; and the Countess, who was thoroughly good-natured, thought it rather fine to be called on by a person of that sort of distinction. She wondered if Miss Stackpole had come on account of her mother—whether she had heard of the American Corinne. Her mother was not at all like Isabel's friend; the Countess could see at a glance that this lady was much more contemporary; and she received an impression of the improvements that were taking place—chiefly in distant countries—in the character (the professional character) of literary ladies. Her mother had been used to wear a Roman scarf thrown over a pair of shoulders timorously bared of their tight black velvet (oh the old clothes!) and a gold laurel-wreath set upon a multitude of glossy ringlets. She had spoken softly and vaguely, with the accent of her 'Creole' ancestors,* as she always confessed; she sighed a great deal and was not at all enterprising. But Henrietta, the Countess could see, was always closely buttoned and compactly braided; there was something brisk and business-like in her appearance; her manner was almost conscientiously familiar. It was as impossible to imagine her ever vaguely sighing as to imagine a letter posted without its address. The Countess could not but feel that the correspondent of the *Interviewer* was much more in the movement than the American Corinne. She explained that she had called on the Countess because she was the only person she knew in Florence, and that when she visited a foreign city she liked to see something more than superficial travellers. She knew Mrs Touchett, but Mrs Touchett was in America, and even if she had been in Florence Henrietta would not have put herself out for her, since Mrs Touchett was not one of her admirations.

'Do you mean by that that I am?' the Countess graciously asked.

'Well, I like you better than I do her,' said Miss Stackpole. 'I seem to remember that when I saw you before you were very interesting. I don't know whether it was an accident or whether it's your usual style. At any rate I was a good deal struck with what you said. I made use of it afterwards in print.'

'Dear me!' cried the Countess, staring and half-alarmed; 'I had no idea I ever said anything remarkable! I wish I had known it at the time.'

'It was about the position of woman in this city,' Miss Stackpole remarked. 'You threw a good deal of light upon it.'

'The position of woman's very uncomfortable. Is that what you mean? And you wrote it down and published it?' the Countess went on. 'Ah, do let me see it!'

'I'll write to them to send you the paper if you like,' Henrietta said. 'I didn't mention your name; I only said a lady of high rank. And then I quoted your views.'

The Countess threw herself hastily backward, tossing up her clasped hands. 'Do you know I'm rather sorry you didn't mention my name? I should have rather liked to see my name in the papers. I forget what my views were; I have so many! But I'm not ashamed of them. I'm not at all like my brother—I suppose you know my brother? He thinks it a kind of scandal to be put in the papers; if you were to quote him he'd never forgive you.'

'He needn't be afraid; I shall never refer to him,' said Miss Stackpole with bland dryness. 'That's another reason,' she added, 'why I wanted to come to see you. You know Mr Osmond married my dearest friend.'

'Ah, yes; you were a friend of Isabel's. I was trying to think what I knew about you.'

'I'm quite willing to be known by that,' Henrietta declared. 'But that isn't what your brother likes to know me by. He has tried to break up my relations with Isabel.'

'Don't permit it,' said the Countess.

'That's what I want to talk about. I'm going to Rome.'

'So am I!' the Countess cried. 'We'll go together.'

'With great pleasure. And when I write about my journey I'll mention you by name as my companion.'

The Countess sprang from her chair and came and sat on the sofa beside her visitor. 'Ah, you must send me the paper!

My husband won't like it, but he need never see it. Besides, he doesn't know how to read.'

Henrietta's large eyes became immense. 'Doesn't know how to read? May I put that into my letter?'

'Into your letter?'

'In the *Interviewer*. That's my paper.'

'Oh yes, if you like; with his name. Are you going to stay with Isabel?'

Henrietta held up her head, gazing a little in silence at her hostess. 'She has not asked me. I wrote to her I was coming, and she answered that she would engage a room for me at a *pension*. She gave no reason.'

The Countess listened with extreme interest. 'The reason's Osmond,' she pregnantly remarked.

'Isabel ought to make a stand,' said Miss Stackpole. 'I'm afraid she has changed a great deal. I told her she would.'

'I'm sorry to hear it; I hoped she would have her own way. Why doesn't my brother like you?' the Countess ingenuously added.

'I don't know and I don't care. He's perfectly welcome not to like me; I don't want every one to like me; I should think less of myself if some people did. A journalist can't hope to do much good unless he gets a good deal hated; that's the way he knows how his work goes on. And it's just the same for a lady. But I didn't expect it of Isabel.'

'Do you mean that she hates you?' the Countess enquired.

'I don't know; I want to see. That's what I'm going to Rome for.'

'Dear me, what a tiresome errand!' the Countess exclaimed.

'She doesn't write to me in the same way; it's easy to see there's a difference. If you know anything,' Miss Stackpole went on, 'I should like to hear it beforehand, so as to decide on the line I shall take.'

The Countess thrust out her under lip and gave a gradual shrug. 'I know very little; I see and hear very little of Osmond. He doesn't like me any better than he appears to like you.'

'Yet you're not a lady correspondent,' said Henrietta pensively.

'Oh, he has plenty of reasons. Nevertheless they've invited me—I'm to stay in the house!' And the Countess smiled almost fiercely; her exultation, for the moment, took little account of Miss Stackpole's disappointment.

This lady, however, regarded it very placidly. 'I shouldn't have gone if she *had* asked me. That is I think I shouldn't; and I'm glad I hadn't to make up my mind. It would have been a very difficult question. I shouldn't have liked to turn away from her, and yet I shouldn't have been happy under her roof. A *pension* will suit me very well. But that's not all.'

'Rome's very good just now,' said the Countess; 'there are all sorts of brilliant people. Did you ever hear of Lord Warburton?'

'Hear of him? I know him very well. Do you consider him very brilliant?' Henrietta enquired.

'I don't know him, but I'm told he's extremely *grand seigneur*.* He's making love to Isabel.'

'Making love to her?'

'So I'm told; I don't know the details,' said the Countess lightly. 'But Isabel's pretty safe.'

Henrietta gazed earnestly at her companion; for a moment she said nothing. 'When do you go to Rome?' she enquired abruptly.

'Not for a week, I'm afraid.'

'I shall go to-morrow,' Henrietta said. 'I think I had better not wait.'

'Dear me, I'm sorry; I'm having some dresses made. I'm told Isabel receives immensely. But I shall see you there; I shall call on you at your *pension*.' Henrietta sat still—she was lost in thought; and suddenly the Countess cried: 'Ah, but if you don't go with me you can't describe our journey!'

Miss Stackpole seemed unmoved by this consideration; she was thinking of something else and presently expressed it. 'I'm not sure that I understand you about Lord Warburton.'

'Understand me? I mean he's very nice, that's all.'

'Do you consider it nice to make love to married women?' Henrietta enquired with unprecedented distinctness.

The Countess stared, and then with a little violent laugh: 'It's certain all the nice men do it. Get married and you'll see!' she added.

'That idea would be enough to prevent me,' said Miss Stackpole. 'I should want my own husband; I shouldn't want any one else's. Do you mean that Isabel's guilty—guilty—?' And she paused a little, choosing her expression.

'Do I mean she's guilty? Oh dear no, not yet, I hope. I only mean that Osmond's very tiresome and that Lord Warburton, as I hear, is a great deal at the house. I'm afraid you're scandalised.'

'No, I'm just anxious,' Henrietta said.

'Ah, you're not very complimentary to Isabel! You should have more confidence. I'll tell you,' the Countess added quickly: 'if it will be a comfort to you I engage to draw him off.'

Miss Stackpole answered at first only with the deeper solemnity of her gaze. 'You don't understand me,' she said after a while. 'I haven't the idea you seem to suppose. I'm not afraid for Isabel—in that way. I'm only afraid she's unhappy—that's what I want to get at.'

The Countess gave a dozen turns of the head; she looked impatient and sarcastic. 'That may very well be; for my part I should like to know whether Osmond is.' Miss Stackpole had begun a little to bore her.

'If she's really changed that must be at the bottom of it,' Henrietta went on.

'You'll see; she'll tell you,' said the Countess.

'Ah, she may *not* tell me—that's what I'm afraid of!'

'Well, if Osmond isn't amusing himself—in his own old way—I flatter myself I shall discover it,' the Countess rejoined.

'I don't care for that,' said Henrietta.

'I do immensely! If Isabel's unhappy I'm very sorry for her, but I can't help it. I might tell her something that would make her worse, but I can't tell her anything that would console her. What did she go and marry him for? If she had listened to me she'd have got rid of him. I'll forgive her, however, if I find she has made things hot for him! If she has simply allowed him to trample upon her I don't know that I shall even pity her. But I don't think that's very likely. I count upon finding that if she's miserable she has at least made *him* so.'

Henrietta got up; these seemed to her, naturally, very dreadful expectations. She honestly believed she had no desire to see Mr Osmond unhappy; and indeed he could not be for her the subject of a flight of fancy. She was on the whole rather disappointed in the Countess, whose mind moved in a narrower circle than she had imagined, though with a capacity for coarseness even there. 'It will be better if they love each other,' she said for edification.

'They can't. He can't love any one.'

'I presumed that was the case. But it only aggravates my fear for Isabel. I shall positively start to-morrow.'

'Isabel certainly has devotees,' said the Countess, smiling very vividly. 'I declare I don't pity her.'

'It may be I can't assist her,' Miss Stackpole pursued, as if it were well not to have illusions.

'You can have wanted to, at any rate; that's something. I believe that's what you came from America for,' the Countess suddenly added.

'Yes, I wanted to look after her,' Henrietta said serenely.

Her hostess stood there smiling at her with small bright eyes and an eager-looking nose; with cheeks into each of which a flush had come. 'Ah, that's very pretty—*c'est bien gentil!** Isn't it what they call friendship?'

'I don't know what they call it. I thought I had better come.'

'She's very happy—she's very fortunate,' the Countess went on. 'She has others besides.' And then she broke out passionately. 'She's more fortunate than I! I'm as unhappy as she—I've a very bad husband; he's a great deal worse than Osmond. And I've no friends. I thought I had, but they're gone. No one, man or woman, would do for me what you've done for her.'

Henrietta was touched; there was nature in this bitter effusion. She gazed at her companion a moment, and then: 'Look here, Countess, I'll do anything for you that you like. I'll wait over and travel with you.'

'Never mind,' the Countess answered with a quick change of tone: 'only describe me in the newspaper!'

Henrietta, before leaving her, however, was obliged to make her understand that she could give no fictitious representation of her journey to Rome. Miss Stackpole was a strictly veracious reporter. On quitting her she took the way to the Lung' Arno, the sunny quay beside the yellow river where the bright-faced inns familiar to tourists stand all in a row. She had learned her way before this through the streets of Florence (she was very quick in such matters), and was therefore able to turn with great decision of step out of the little square which forms the approach to the bridge of the Holy Trinity. She proceeded to the left, toward the Ponte Vecchio, and stopped in front of one of the hotels which overlook that delightful structure. Here she drew forth a small pocket-book, took from it a card and a pencil and, after meditating a moment, wrote a few words. It is our privilege to look over her shoulder, and if we exercise it we may read the brief query: 'Could I see you this evening for a few moments on a very important matter?' Henrietta added that she should start on the morrow for Rome. Armed with this little document she approached the porter, who now had taken up his station in the doorway, and asked if Mr Goodwood were at home. The porter replied, as porters always reply, that he had gone out about twenty minutes before; whereupon Henrietta presented her card and begged it might be handed him on his return. She left the inn and pursued her course along the quay to the severe portico of the Uffizi, through which she presently reached the entrance of the famous gallery of paintings. Making her way in, she ascended the high staircase which leads to the upper chambers. The long corridor, glazed on one side and decorated with antique busts, which gives admission to these apartments, presented an empty vista in which the bright winter light twinkled upon the marble floor. The gallery is very cold and during the midwinter weeks but scantily visited. Miss Stackpole may appear more ardent in her quest of artistic beauty than she has hitherto struck us as being, but she had after all her preferences and admirations. One of the latter was the little Correggio of the Tribune—the Virgin kneeling down before the sacred infant, who lies in a litter of straw, and clapping her hands to him while he delightedly laughs and crows. Henrietta had a special devotion to this intimate scene—she thought it the most beautiful picture in the world. On her way, at present, from New York to Rome, she was spending but three days in Florence, and yet reminded herself that they must not elapse without her paying another visit to her favourite work of art. She had a great sense of beauty in all ways, and it involved a good many intellectual obligations. She was about to turn into the Tribune when a gentleman came out of it; whereupon she gave a little exclamation and stood before Caspar Goodwood.

'I've just been at your hotel,' she said. 'I left a card for you.'

'I'm very much honoured,' Caspar Goodwood answered as if he really meant it.

'It was not to honour you I did it; I've called on you before and I know you don't like it. It was to talk to you a little about something.'

He looked for a moment at the buckle in her hat. 'I shall be very glad to hear what you wish to say.'

'You don't like to talk with me,' said Henrietta. 'But I don't care for that; I don't talk for your amusement. I wrote a word to ask you to come and see me; but since I've met you here this will do as well.'

'I was just going away,' Goodwood stated; 'but of course I'll stop.' He was civil, but not enthusiastic.

Henrietta, however, never looked for great professions, and she was so much in earnest that she was thankful he would listen to her on any terms. She asked him first, none the less, if he had seen all the pictures.

'All I want to. I've been here an hour.'

'I wonder if you've seen my Correggio,' said Henrietta. 'I came up on purpose to have a look at it.' She went into the Tribune and he slowly accompanied her.

'I suppose I've seen it, but I didn't know it was yours. I don't remember pictures—especially that sort.' She had pointed out her favourite work, and he asked her if it was about Correggio she wished to talk with him.

'No,' said Henrietta, 'it's about something less harmonious!' They had the small, brilliant room, a splendid cabinet of treasures, to themselves; there was only a custode hovering about the Medicean Venus. 'I want you to do me a favour,' Miss Stackpole went on.

Caspar Goodwood frowned a little, but he expressed no embarrassment at the sense of not looking eager. His face was that of a much older man than our earlier friend. 'I'm sure it's something I shan't like,' he said rather loudly.

'No, I don't think you'll like it. If you did it would be no favour.'

'Well, let's hear it,' he went on in the tone of a man quite conscious of his patience.

'You may say there's no particular reason why you should do me a favour. Indeed I only know of one: the fact that if you'd let me I'd gladly do *you* one.' Her soft, exact tone, in which there was no attempt at effect, had an extreme sincerity; and her companion, though he presented rather a hard surface, couldn't help being touched by it. When he was touched he rarely showed it, however, by the usual signs; he neither blushed, nor looked away, nor looked conscious. He only fixed his attention more directly; he seemed to consider with added firmness. Henrietta continued therefore disinterestedly, without the sense of an advantage. 'I may say now, indeed—it seems a good time—that if I've ever annoyed you (and I think sometimes I have) it's because I knew I was willing to suffer annoyance for you. I've troubled you—doubtless. But I'd *take* trouble for you.'

Goodwood hesitated. 'You're taking trouble now.'

'Yes, I am—some. I want you to consider whether it's better on the whole that you should go to Rome.'

'I thought you were going to say that!' he answered rather artlessly.

'You *have* considered it then?'

'Of course I have, very carefully. I've looked all round it. Otherwise I shouldn't have come so far as this. That's what I stayed in Paris two months for. I was thinking it over.'

'I'm afraid you decided as you liked. You decided it was best because you were so much attracted.'

'Best for whom, do you mean?' Goodwood demanded.

'Well, for yourself first. For Mrs Osmond next.'

'Oh, it won't do *her* any good! I don't flatter myself that.'

'Won't it do her some harm?—that's the question.'

'I don't see what it will matter to her. I'm nothing to Mrs Osmond. But if you want to know, I do want to see her myself.'

'Yes, and that's why you go.'

'Of course it is. Could there be a better reason?'

'How will it help you?—that's what I want to know,' said Miss Stackpole.

'That's just what I can't tell you. It's just what I was thinking about in Paris.'

'It will make you more discontented.'

'Why do you say "more" so?' Goodwood asked rather sternly. 'How do you know I'm discontented?'

'Well,' said Henrietta, hesitating a little, 'you seem never to have cared for another.'

'How do you know what I care for?' he cried with a big blush. 'Just now I care to go to Rome.'

Henrietta looked at him in silence, with a sad yet luminous expression. 'Well,' she observed at last, 'I only wanted to tell you what I think; I had it on my mind. Of course you think it's none of my business. But nothing is any one's business, on that principle.'

'It's very kind of you; I'm greatly obliged to you for your interest,' said Caspar Goodwood. 'I shall go to Rome and I shan't hurt Mrs Osmond.'

'You won't hurt her, perhaps. But will you help her?—that's the real issue.'

'Is she in need of help?' he asked slowly, with a penetrating look.

'Most women always are,' said Henrietta, with conscientious evasiveness and generalising less hopefully than usual. 'If you go to Rome,' she added, 'I hope you'll be a true friend—not a selfish one!' And she turned off and began to look at the pictures.

Caspar Goodwood let her go and stood watching her while she wandered round the room; but after a moment he rejoined her. 'You've heard something about her here,' he then resumed. 'I should like to know what you've heard.'

Henrietta had never prevaricated in her life, and, though on this occasion there might have been a fitness in doing so, she decided, after thinking some minutes, to make no superficial exception. 'Yes, I've heard,' she answered; 'but as I don't want you to go to Rome I won't tell you.'

'Just as you please. I shall see for myself,' he said. Then inconsistently, for him, 'You've heard she's unhappy!' he added.

'Oh, you won't see that!' Henrietta exclaimed.

'I hope not. When do you start?'

'To-morrow, by the evening train. And you?'

Goodwood hung back; he had no desire to make his journey to Rome in Miss Stackpole's company. His indifference to this advantage was not of the same character as Gilbert Osmond's, but it had at this moment an equal distinctness. It was rather a tribute to Miss Stackpole's virtues than a reference to her faults. He thought her very remarkable, very brilliant, and he had, in theory, no objection to the class to which she belonged. Lady correspondents appeared to him a part of the natural scheme of things in a progressive country, and though he never read their letters he supposed that they ministered somehow to social prosperity. But it was this very eminence of their position that made him wish Miss Stackpole didn't take so much for granted. She took for granted that he was always ready for some allusion to Mrs Osmond; she had done so when they met in Paris, six weeks after his arrival in Europe, and she had repeated the assumption with every successive opportunity. He had no wish whatever to allude to Mrs Osmond; he was *not* always thinking of her; he was perfectly sure of that. He was the most reserved, the least colloquial of men, and this enquiring authoress was constantly flashing her lantern into the quiet darkness of his soul. He wished she didn't care so much; he even wished, though it might seem rather brutal of him, that she would leave him alone. In spite of this, however, he just now made other reflections—which show how widely different, in effect, his ill-humour was from Gilbert Osmond's. He desired to go immediately to Rome; he would have liked to go alone, in the night-train. He hated the European railway-carriages, in which one sat for hours in a vise, knee to knee and nose to nose with a foreigner to whom one presently found one's self objecting with all the added vehemence of one's wish to have the window open; and if they were worse at night even than by day, at least at night one could sleep and dream of an American saloon-car. But he couldn't take a night-train when Miss Stackpole was starting in the morning; it struck him that this would be an insult to an unprotected woman. Nor could he wait until after she had gone unless he should wait longer than he had patience for. It wouldn't do to start the next day. She worried him; she oppressed him; the idea of spending the day in a European railway-carriage with her offered a complication of irritations. Still, she was a lady travelling alone; it was his duty to put himself out for her. There could be no two questions about that; it was a perfectly clear necessity. He looked extremely grave for some moments and then said, wholly without the flourish of gallantry but in a tone of extreme distinctness, 'Of course if you're going to-morrow I'll go too, as I may be of assistance to you.'

'Well, Mr Goodwood, I should hope so!' Henrietta returned imperturbably.

XLV

I HAVE already had reason to say that Isabel knew her husband to be displeased by the continuance of Ralph's visit to Rome. That knowledge was very present to her as she went to her cousin's hotel the day after she had invited Lord Warburton to give a tangible proof of his sincerity; and at this moment, as at others, she had a sufficient perception of the sources of Osmond's opposition. He wished her to have no freedom of mind, and he knew perfectly well that Ralph was an apostle of freedom. It was just because he was this, Isabel said to herself, that it was a refreshment to go and see him. It will be perceived that she partook of this refreshment in spite of her husband's aversion to it, that is partook of it, as she flattered herself, discreetly. She had not as yet undertaken to act in direct opposition to his wishes; he was her appointed and inscribed master; she gazed at moments with a sort of incredulous blankness at this fact. It weighed upon her imagination, however; constantly present to her mind were all the traditionary decencies and sanctities of marriage. The idea of violating them filled her with shame as well as with dread, for on giving herself away she had lost sight of this contingency in the perfect belief that her husband's intentions were as generous as her own. She seemed to see, none the less, the rapid approach of the day when she should have to take back something she had solemnly bestown. Such a ceremony would be odious and monstrous; she tried to shut her eyes to it meanwhile. Osmond would do nothing to help it by beginning first; he would put that burden upon her to the end. He had not yet formally forbidden her to call upon Ralph; but she felt sure that unless Ralph should very soon depart this prohibition would come. How could poor Ralph depart? The weather as yet made it impossible. She could perfectly understand her husband's wish for the event; she didn't, to be just, see how he *could* like her to be with her cousin. Ralph never said a word against him, but Osmond's sore, mute protest was none the less founded. If he should positively interpose, if he should put forth his authority, she would have to decide, and that wouldn't be easy. The prospect made her heart beat and her cheeks burn, as I say, in advance; there were moments when, in her wish to avoid an open rupture, she found herself wishing Ralph would start even at a risk. And it was of no use that, when catching herself in this state of mind, she called herself a feeble spirit, a coward. It was not that she loved Ralph less, but that almost anything seemed preferable to repudiating the most serious act—the single sacred act—of her life. That appeared to make the whole future hideous. To break with Osmond once would be to break for ever; any open acknowledgement of irreconcilable needs would be an admission that their whole attempt had proved a failure. For them there could be no condonement, no compromise, no easy forgetfulness, no formal readjustment. They had attempted only one thing, but that one thing was to have been exquisite. Once they missed it nothing else would do; there was no conceivable substitute for that success. For the moment, Isabel went to the Hôtel de Paris as often as she thought well; the measure of propriety was in the canon of taste, and there couldn't have been a better proof that morality was, so to speak, a matter of earnest appreciation. Isabel's application of that measure had been particularly free to-day, for in addition to the general truth that she couldn't leave Ralph to die alone she had something important to ask of him. This indeed was Gilbert's business as well as her own.

She came very soon to what she wished to speak of. 'I want you to answer me a question. It's about Lord Warburton.'

'I think I guess your question,' Ralph answered from his arm-chair, out of which his thin legs protruded at greater length than ever.

'Very possibly you guess it. Please then answer it.'

'Oh, I don't say I can do that.'

'You're intimate with him,' she said; 'you've a great deal of observation of him.'

'Very true. But think how he must dissimulate!'

'Why should he dissimulate? That's not his nature.'

'Ah, you must remember that the circumstances are peculiar,' said Ralph with an air of private amusement.

'To a certain extent—yes. But is he really in love?'

'Very much, I think. I can make that out.'

'Ah!' said Isabel with a certain dryness.

Ralph looked at her as if his mild hilarity had been touched with mystification. 'You say that as if you were disappointed.'

Isabel got up, slowly smoothing her gloves and eyeing them thoughtfully. 'It's after all no business of mine.'

'You're very philosophic,' said her cousin. And then in a moment: 'May I enquire what you're talking about?'

Isabel stared. 'I thought you knew. Lord Warburton tells me he wants, of all things in the world, to marry Pansy. I've told you that before, without eliciting a comment from you. You might risk one this morning, I think. Is it your belief that he really cares for her?'

'Ah, for Pansy, no!' cried Ralph very positively.

'But you said just now he did.'

Ralph waited a moment. 'That he cared for you, Mrs Osmond.'

Isabel shook her head gravely. 'That's nonsense, you know.'

'Of course it is. But the nonsense is Warburton's, not mine.'

'That would be very tiresome.' She spoke, as she flattered herself, with much subtlety.

'I ought to tell you indeed,' Ralph went on, 'that to me he has denied it.'

'It's very good of you to talk about it together! Has he also told you that he's in love with Pansy?'

'He has spoken very well of her—very properly. He has let me know, of course, that he thinks she would do very well at Lockleigh.'

'Does he really think it?'

'Ah, what Warburton really thinks—!' said Ralph.

Isabel fell to smoothing her gloves again; they were long, loose gloves on which she could freely expend herself. Soon, however, she looked up, and then, 'Ah, Ralph, you give me no help!' she cried abruptly and passionately.

It was the first time she had alluded to the need for help, and the words shook her cousin with their violence. He gave a long murmur of relief, of pity, of tenderness; it seemed to him that at last the gulf between them had been bridged. It was this that made him exclaim in a moment: 'How unhappy you must be!'

He had no sooner spoken than she recovered her self-possession, and the first use she made of it was to pretend she had not heard him. 'When I talk of your helping me I talk great nonsense,' she said with a quick smile. 'The idea of my troubling you with my domestic embarrassments! The matter's very simple; Lord Warburton must get on by himself. I can't undertake to see him through.'

'He ought to succeed easily,' said Ralph.

Isabel debated. 'Yes—but he has not always succeeded.'

'Very true. You know, however, how that always surprised me. Is Miss Osmond capable of giving us a surprise?'

'It will come from him, rather. I seem to see that after all he'll let the matter drop.'

'He'll do nothing dishonourable,' said Ralph.

'I'm very sure of that. Nothing can be more honourable than for him to leave the poor child alone. She cares for another person, and it's cruel to attempt to bribe her by magnificent offers to give him up.'

'Cruel to the other person perhaps—the one she cares for. But Warburton isn't obliged to mind that.'

'No, cruel to her,' said Isabel. 'She would be very unhappy if she were to allow herself to be persuaded to desert poor Mr Rosier. That idea seems to amuse you; of course you're not in love with him. He has the merit—for Pansy—of being in love with Pansy. She can see at a glance that Lord Warburton isn't.'

'He'd be very good to her,' said Ralph.

'He has been good to her already. Fortunately, however, he has not said a word to disturb her. He could come and bid her good-bye to-morrow with perfect propriety.'

'How would your husband like that?'

'Not at all; and he may be right in not liking it. Only he must obtain satisfaction himself.'

'Has he commissioned you to obtain it?' Ralph ventured to ask.

'It was natural that as an old friend of Lord Warburton's—an older friend, that is, than Gilbert—I should take an interest in his intentions.'

'Take an interest in his renouncing them, you mean?'

Isabel hesitated, frowning a little. 'Let me understand. Are you pleading his cause?'

'Not in the least. I'm very glad he shouldn't become your stepdaughter's husband. It makes such a very queer relation to you!' said Ralph, smiling. 'But I'm rather nervous lest your husband should think you haven't pushed him enough.'

Isabel found herself able to smile as well as he. 'He knows me well enough not to have expected me to push. He himself has no intention of pushing, I presume. I'm not afraid I shall not be able to justify myself!' she said lightly.

Her mask had dropped for an instant, but she had put it on again, to Ralph's infinite disappointment. He had caught a glimpse of her natural face and he wished immensely to look into it. He had an almost savage desire to hear her complain of her husband—hear her say that she should be held accountable for Lord Warburton's defection. Ralph was certain that this was her situation; he knew by instinct, in advance, the form that in such an event Osmond's displeasure would take. It could only take the meanest and cruellest. He would have liked to warn Isabel of it—to let her see at least how he judged for her and how he knew. It little mattered that Isabel would know much better; it was for his own satisfaction more than for hers that he longed to show her he was not deceived. He tried and tried again to make her betray Osmond; he felt cold-blooded, cruel, dishonourable almost, in doing so. But it scarely mattered, for he only failed. What had she come for then, and why did she seem almost to offer him a chance to violate their tacit convention? Why did she ask him his advice if she gave him no liberty to answer her? How could they talk of her domestic embarrassments, as it pleased her humorously to designate them, if the principal factor was not to be mentioned? These contradictions were themselves but an indication of her trouble, and her cry for help, just before, was the only thing he was bound to consider. 'You'll be decidedly at variance, all the same,' he said in a moment. And as she answered nothing, looking as if she scarce understood, 'You'll find yourselves thinking very differently,' he continued.

'That may easily happen, among the most united couples!' She took up her parasol; he saw she was nervous, afraid of what he might say. 'It's a matter we can hardly quarrel about, however,' she added; 'for almost all the interest is on his side. That's very natural. Pansy's after all his daughter—not mine.' And she put out her hand to wish him good-bye.

Ralph took an inward resolution that she shouldn't leave him without his letting her know that he knew everything: it seemed too great an opportunity to lose. 'Do you know what his interest will make him say?' he asked as he took her hand. She shook her head, rather dryly—not discouragingly—and he went on. 'It will make him say that your want of zeal is owing to jealousy.' He stopped a moment; her face made him afraid.

'To jealousy?'

'To jealousy of his daughter.'

She blushed red and threw back her head. 'You're not kind,' she said in a voice that he had never heard on her lips.

'Be frank with me and you'll see,' he answered.

But she made no reply; she only pulled her hand out of his own, which he tried still to hold, and rapidly withdrew from the room. She made up her mind to speak to Pansy, and she took an occasion on the same day, going to the girl's room before dinner. Pansy was already dressed; she was always in advance of the time: it seemed to illustrate her pretty patience and the graceful stillness with which she could sit and wait. At present she was seated, in her fresh array, before the bed-room fire; she had blown out her candles on the completion of her toilet, in accordance with the economical habits in which she had been brought up and which she was now more careful than ever to observe; so that the room was lighted only by a couple of logs. The rooms in Palazzo Roccanera were as spacious as they were numerous, and Pansy's virginal bower was an immense chamber with a dark, heavily-timbered ceiling. Its diminutive mistress, in the midst of it, appeared but a speck of humanity, and as she got up, with quick deference, to welcome Isabel, the latter was more than ever struck with her shy sincerity. Isabel had a difficult task—the only thing was to perform it as simply as possible. She felt bitter and angry, but she warned herself against betraying this heat. She was afraid even of looking too grave, or at least too stern; she was afraid of causing alarm. But Pansy seemed to have guessed she had come more or less as a confessor; for after she had moved the chair in which she had been sitting a little nearer to the fire and Isabel had taken her place in it, she kneeled down on a cushion in front of her, looking up and resting her clasped hands on her stepmother's knees. What Isabel wished to do was to hear from her own lips that her mind was not occupied with Lord Warburton; but if she desired the assurance she felt herself by no means at liberty to provoke it. The girl's father would have qualified this as rank treachery; and indeed Isabel knew that if Pansy should display the smallest germ of a disposition to encourage Lord Warburton her own duty was to hold her tongue. It was difficult to interrogate without appearing to suggest; Pansy's supreme simplicity, an innocence even more complete than Isabel had yet judged it, gave to the most tentative enquiry something of the effect of an admonition. As she knelt there in the vague firelight, with her pretty dress dimly shining, her hands folded half in appeal and half in submission, her soft eyes, raised and fixed, full of the seriousness of the situation, she looked to Isabel like a childish martyr decked out for sacrifice and scarcely presuming even to hope to avert it. When Isabel said to her that she had never yet spoken to her of what might have been going on in relation to her getting married, but that her silence had not been indifference or ignorance, had only been the desire to leave her at liberty, Pansy bent forward, raised her face nearer and nearer, and with a little murmur which evidently expressed a deep longing, answered that she had greatly wished her to speak and that she begged her to advise her now.

'It's difficult for me to advise you,' Isabel returned. 'I don't know how I can undertake that. That's for your father; you must get his advice and, above all, you must act on it.'

At this Pansy dropped her eyes; for a moment she said nothing. 'I think I should like your advice better than papa's,' she presently remarked.

'That's not as it should be,' said Isabel coldly. 'I love you very much, but your father loves you better.'

'It isn't because you love me—it's because you're a lady,' Pansy answered with the air of saying something very reasonable. 'A lady can advise a young girl better than a man.'

'I advise you then to pay the greatest respect to your father's wishes.'

'Ah yes,' said the child eagerly, 'I must do that.'

'But if I speak to you now about your getting married it's not for your own sake, it's for mine,' Isabel went on. 'If I try to learn from you what you expect, what you desire, it's only that I may act accordingly.'

Pansy stared, and then very quickly, 'Will you do everything I want?' she asked.

'Before I say yes I must know what such things are.'

Pansy presently told her that the only thing she wanted in life was to marry Mr Rosier. He had asked her and she had told him she would do so if her papa would allow it. Now her papa wouldn't allow it.

'Very well then, it's impossible,' Isabel pronounced.

'Yes, it's impossible,' said Pansy without a sigh and with the same extreme attention in her clear little face.

'You must think of something else then,' Isabel went on; but Pansy, sighing at this, told her that she had attempted that feat without the least success.

'You think of those who think of you,' she said with a faint smile. 'I know Mr Rosier thinks of me.'

'He ought not to,' said Isabel loftily. 'Your father has expressly requested he shouldn't.'

'He can't help it, because he knows I think of *him.*'

'You shouldn't think of him. There's some excuse for him, perhaps; but there's none for you.'

'I wish you would try to find one,' the girl exclaimed as if she were praying to the Madonna.

'I should be very sorry to attempt it,' said the Madonna with unusual frigidity. 'If you knew some one else was thinking of you, would you think of him?'

'No one can think of me as Mr Rosier does; no one has the right.'

'Ah, but I don't admit Mr Rosier's right!' Isabel hypocritically cried.

Pansy only gazed at her, evidently much puzzled; and Isabel, taking advantage of it, began to represent to her the wretched consequences of disobeying her father. At this Pansy stopped her with the assurance that she would never disobey him, would never marry without his consent. And she announced, in the serenest, simplest tone, that, though she might never marry Mr Rosier, she would never cease to think of him. She appeared to have accepted the idea of eternal singleness; but Isabel of course was free to reflect that she had no conception of its meaning. She was perfectly sincere; she was prepared to give up her lover. This might seem an important step toward taking another, but for Pansy, evidently, it failed to lead in that direction. She felt no bitterness toward her father; there was no bitterness in her heart; there was only the sweetness of fidelity to Edward Rosier, and a strange, exquisite intimation that she could prove it better by remaining single than even by marrying him.

'Your father would like you to make a better marriage,' said Isabel. 'Mr Rosier's fortune is not at all large.'

'How do you mean better—if that would be good enough? And I have myself so little money; why should I look for a fortune?'

'Your having so little is a reason for looking for more.' With which Isabel was grateful for the dimness of the room; she felt as if her face were hideously insincere. It was what she was doing for Osmond; it was what one had to do for Osmond! Pansy's solemn eyes, fixed on her own, almost embarrassed her; she was ashamed to think she had made so light of the girl's preference.

'What should you like me to do?' her companion softly demanded.

The question was a terrible one, and Isabel took refuge in timorous vagueness. 'To remember all the pleasure it's in your power to give your father.'

'To marry some one else, you mean—if he should ask me?'

For a moment Isabel's answer caused itself to be waited for; then she heard herself utter it in the stillness that Pansy's attention seemed to make. 'Yes—to marry some one else.'

The child's eyes grew more penetrating; Isabel believed she was doubting her sincerity, and the impression took force from her slowly getting up from her cushion. She stood there a moment with her small hands unclasped and then quavered out: 'Well, I hope no one will ask me!'

'There has been a question of that. Some one else would have been ready to ask you.'

'I don't think he can have been ready,' said Pansy.

'It would appear so—if he had been sure he'd succeed.'

'If he had been sure? Then he wasn't ready!'

Isabel thought this rather sharp; she also got up and stood a moment looking into the fire. 'Lord Warburton has shown you great attention,' she resumed; 'of course you know it's of him I speak.' She found herself, against her expectation, almost placed in the position of justifying herself; which led her to introduce this nobleman more crudely than she had intended.

'He has been very kind to me, and I like him very much. But if you mean that he'll propose for me I think you're mistaken.'

'Perhaps I am. But your father would like it extremely.'

Pansy shook her head with a little wise smile. 'Lord Warburton won't propose simply to please papa.'

'Your father would like you to encourage him,' Isabel went on mechanically.

'How can I encourage him?'

'I don't know. Your father must tell you that.'

Pansy said nothing for a moment; she only continued to smile as if she were in possession of a bright assurance. 'There's no danger—no danger!' she declared at last.

There was a conviction in the way she said this, and a felicity in her believing it, which conduced to Isabel's awkwardness. She felt accused of dishonesty, and the idea was disgusting. To repair her self-respect she was on the point of saying that Lord Warburton had let her know that there *was* a danger. But she didn't; she only said—in her embarrassment rather wide of the mark—that he surely had been most kind, most friendly.

'Yes, he has been very kind,' Pansy answered. 'That's what I like him for.'

'Why then is the difficulty so great?'

'I've always felt sure of his knowing that I don't want—what did you say I should do?—to encourage him. He knows I don't want to marry, and he wants me to know that he therefore won't trouble me. That's the meaning of his kindness. It's as if he said to me: "I like you very much, but if it doesn't please you I'll never say it again.' I think that's very kind, very noble,' Pansy went on with deepening positiveness. 'That is all we've said to each other. And he doesn't care for me either. Ah no, there's no danger.'

Isabel was touched with wonder at the depths of perception of which this submissive little person was capable; she felt afraid of Pansy's wisdom—began almost to retreat before it. 'You must tell your father that,' she remarked reservedly.

'I think I'd rather not,' Pansy unreservedly answered.

'You oughtn't to let him have false hopes.'

'Perhaps not; but it will be good for me that he should. So long as he believes that Lord Warburton intends anything of the kind you say, papa won't propose any one else. And that will be an advantage for me,' said the child very lucidly.

There was something brilliant in her lucidity, and it made her companion draw a long breath. It relieved this friend of a heavy responsibility. Pansy had a sufficient illumination of her own, and Isabel felt that she herself just now had no light to spare from her small stock. Nevertheless it still clung to her that she must be loyal to Osmond, that she was on her honour in dealing with his daughter. Under the influence of this sentiment she threw out another suggestion before she retired—a suggestion with which it seemed to her that she should have done her utmost. 'Your father takes for granted at least that you would like to marry a nobleman.'

Pansy stood in the open doorway; she had drawn back the curtain for Isabel to pass. 'I think Mr Rosier looks like one!' she remarked very gravely.

XLVI

LORD WARBURTON was not seen in Mrs Osmond's drawing-room for several days, and Isabel couldn't fail to observe that her husband said nothing to her about having received a letter from him. She couldn't fail to observe, either, that Osmond was in a state of expectancy and that, though it was not agreeable to him to betray it, he thought their distinguished friend kept him waiting quite too long. At the end of four days he alluded to his absence.

'What has become of Warburton? What does he mean by treating one like a tradesman with a bill?'

'I know nothing about him,' Isabel said. 'I saw him last Friday at the German ball. He told me then that he meant to write to you.'

'He has never written to me.'

'So I supposed, from your not having told me.'

'He's an odd fish,' said Osmond comprehensively. And on Isabel's making no rejoinder he went on to enquire whether it took his lordship five days to indite a letter. 'Does he form his words with such difficulty?'

'I don't know,' Isabel was reduced to replying. 'I've never had a letter from him.'

'Never had a letter? I had an idea that you were at one time in intimate correspondence.'

She answered that this had not been the case, and let the conversation drop. On the morrow, however, coming into the drawing-room late in the afternoon, her husband took it up again.

'When Lord Warburton told you of his intention of writing what did you say to him?' he asked.

She just faltered. 'I think I told him not to forget it.'

'Did you believe there was a danger of that?'

'As you say, he's an odd fish.'

'Apparently he has forgotten it,' said Osmond. 'Be so good as to remind him.'

'Should you like me to write to him?' she demanded.

'I've no objection whatever.'

'You expect too much of me.'

'Ah yes, I expect a great deal of you.'

'I'm afraid I shall disappoint you,' said Isabel.

'My expectations have survived a good deal of disappointment.'

'Of course I know that. Think how I must have disappointed myself! If you really wish hands laid on Lord Warburton you must lay them yourself.'

For a couple of minutes Osmond answered nothing; then he said: 'That won't be easy, with you working against me.'

Isabel started; she felt herself beginning to tremble. He had a way of looking at her through half-closed eyelids, as if he were thinking of her but scarcely saw her, which seemed to her to have a wonderfully cruel intention. It appeared to recognize her as a disagreeable necessity of thought, but to ignore her for the time as a presence. That effect had never been so marked as now. 'I think you accuse me of something very base,' she returned.

'I accuse you of not being trustworthy. If he doesn't after all come forward it will be because you've kept him off. I don't know that it's base: it is the kind of thing a woman always thinks she may do. I've no doubt you've the finest ideas about it.'

'I told you I would do what I could,' she went on.

'Yes, that gained you time.'

It came over her, after he had said this, that she had once thought him beautiful. 'How much you must want to make sure of him!' she exclaimed in a moment.

She had no sooner spoken than she perceived the full reach of her words, of which she had not been conscious in uttering them. They made a comparison between Osmond and herself, recalled the fact that she had once held this coveted treasure in her hand and felt herself rich enough to let it fall. A momentary exultation took possession of her—a horrible delight in having wounded him; for his face instantly told her that none of the force of her exclamation was lost. He expressed nothing otherwise, however; he only said quickly: 'Yes, I want it immensely.'

At this moment a servant came in to usher a visitor, and he was followed the next by Lord Warburton, who received a visible check on seeing Osmond. He looked rapidly from the master of the house to the mistress; a movement that seemed to denote a reluctance to interrupt or even a perception of ominous conditions. Then he advanced, with his English address, in which a vague shyness seemed to offer itself as an element of good-breeding; in which the only defect was a difficulty in achieving transitions. Osmond was embarrassed; he found nothing to say; but Isabel remarked, promptly enough, that they had been in the act of talking about their visitor. Upon this her husband added that they hadn't known what was become of him—they had been afraid he had gone away. 'No,' he explained, smiling and looking at Osmond; 'I'm only on the point of going.' And then he mentioned that he found himself suddenly recalled to England: he should start on the morrow or the day after. 'I'm awfully sorry to leave poor Touchett!' he ended by exclaiming.

For a moment neither of his companions spoke; Osmond only leaned back in his chair, listening. Isabel didn't look at him; she could only fancy how he looked. Her eyes were on their visitor's face, where they were the more free to rest that those of his lordship carefully avoided them. Yet Isabel was sure that had she met his glance she would have found it expressive. 'You had better take poor Touchett with you,' she heard her husband say, lightly enough, in a moment.

'He had better wait for warmer weather,' Lord Warburton answered. 'I shouldn't advise him to travel just now.'

He sat there a quarter of an hour, talking as if he might not soon see them again—unless indeed they should come to England, a course he strongly recommended. Why shouldn't they come to England in the autumn?—that struck him as a very happy thought. It would give him such pleasure to do what he could for them—to have them come and spend a month with him. Osmond, by his own admission, had been to England but once; which was an absurd state of things for a man of his leisure and intelligence. It was just the country for him—he would be sure to get on well there. Then Lord Warburton asked Isabel if she remembered what a good time she had had there and if she didn't want to try it again. Didn't she want to see Gardencourt once more? Gardencourt was really very good. Touchett didn't take proper care of it, but it was the sort of place you could hardly spoil by letting it alone. Why didn't they come and pay Touchett a visit? He surely must have asked them. Hadn't asked them? What an ill-mannered wretch!—and Lord Warburton promised to give the master of Gardencourt a piece of his mind. Of course it was a mere accident; he would be delighted to have them. Spending a month with Touchett and a month with himself, and seeing all the rest of the people they must know there, they really wouldn't find it half bad. Lord Warburton added that it would amuse Miss Osmond as well, who had told him that she had never been to England and whom he had assured it was a country she deserved to see. Of course she didn't need to go to England to be admired—that was her fate everywhere; but she would be an immense success there, she certainly would, if that was any inducement. He asked if she were not at home: couldn't he say good-bye? Not that he liked good-byes—he always funked them. When he left England the other day he hadn't said good-bye to a two-legged creature. He had had half a mind to leave Rome without troubling Mrs Osmond for a final interview. What could be more dreary than final interviews? One never said the things one wanted—one remembered them all an hour afterwards. On the other hand one usually said a lot of things one shouldn't, simply from a sense that one had to say something. Such a sense was upsetting; it muddled one's wits. He had it at present, and that was the effect it produced on him. If Mrs Osmond didn't think he spoke as he ought she must set it down to agitation; it was no light thing to part with Mrs Osmond. He was really very sorry to be going. He had thought of writing to her instead of calling—but he would write to her at any rate, to tell her a lot of things that would be sure to occur to him as soon as he had left the house. They must think seriously about coming to Lockleigh.

If there was anything awkward in the conditions of his visit or in the announcement of his departure it failed to come to the surface. Lord Warburton talked about his agitation; but he showed it in no other manner, and Isabel saw that since he had determined on a retreat he was capable of executing it gallantly.

She was very glad for him; she liked him quite well enough to wish him to appear to carry a thing off. He would do that on any occasion—not from impudence but simply from the habit of success; and Isabel felt it out of her husband's power to frustrate this faculty. A complex operation, as she sat there, went on in her mind. On one side she listened to their visitor; said what was proper to him; read, more or less, between the lines of what he said himself; and wondered how he would have spoken if he had found her alone. On the other she had a perfect consciousness of Osmond's emotion. She felt almost sorry for him; he was condemned to the sharp pain of loss without the relief of cursing. He had had a great hope, and now, as he saw it vanish into smoke, he was obliged to sit and smile and twirl his thumbs. Not that he troubled himself to smile very brightly; he treated their friend on the whole to as vacant a countenance as so clever a man could very well wear. It was indeed a part of Osmond's cleverness that he could look consummately uncompromised. His present appearance, however, was not a confession of disappointment; it was simply a part of Osmond's habitual system, which was to be inexpressive exactly in proportion as he was really intent. He had been intent on this prize from the first; but he had never allowed his eagerness to irradiate his refined face. He had treated his possible son-in-law as he treated every one—with an air of being interested in him only for his own advantage, not for any profit to a person already so generally, so perfectly provided as Gilbert Osmond. He would give no sign now of an inward rage which was the result of a vanished prospect of gain—not the faintest nor subtlest. Isabel could be sure of that, if it was any satisfaction to her. Strangely, very strangely, it was a satisfaction; she wished Lord Warburton to triumph before her husband, and at the same time she wished her husband to be very superior before Lord Warburton. Osmond, in his way, was admirable; he had, like their visitor, the advantage of an acquired habit. It was not that of succeeding, but it was something almost as good—that of not attempting. As he leaned back in his place, listening but vaguely to the other's friendly offers and suppressed explanations—as if it were only proper to assume that they were addressed essentially to his wife—he had at least (since so little else was left him) the comfort of thinking how well he personally had kept out of it, and how the air of indifference, which he was now able to wear, had the added beauty of consistency. It was something to be able to look as if the leave-taker's movements had no relation to his own mind. The latter did well, certainly; but Osmond's performance was in its very nature more finished. Lord Warburton's position was after all an easy one; there was no reason in the world why he shouldn't leave Rome. He had had beneficent inclinations, but they had stopped short of fruition; he had never committed himself, and his honour was safe. Osmond appeared to take but a moderate interest in the proposal that they should go and stay with him and in his allusion to the success Pansy might extract from their visit. He murmured a recognition, but left Isabel to say that it was a matter requiring grave consideration. Isabel, even while she made this remark, could see the great vista which had suddenly opened out in her husband's mind, with Pansy's little figure marching up the middle of it.

Lord Warburton had asked leave to bid good-bye to Pansy, but neither Isabel nor Osmond had made any motion to send for her. He had the air of giving out that his visit must be short; he sat on a small chair, as if it were only for a moment, keeping his hat in his hand. But he stayed and stayed; Isabel wondered what he was waiting for. She believed it was not to see Pansy; she had an impression that on the whole he would rather not see Pansy. It was of course to see herself alone—he had something to say to her. Isabel had no great wish to hear it, for she was afraid it would be an explanation, and she could perfectly dispense with explanations. Osmond, however, presently got up, like a man of good taste to whom it had occurred that so inveterate a visitor might wish to say just the last word of all to the ladies. 'I've a letter to write before dinner,' he said; 'you must excuse me. I'll see if my daughter's disengaged, and if she is she shall know you're here. Of course when you come to Rome you'll always look us up. Mrs Osmond will talk to you about the English expedition: she decides all those things.'

The nod with which, instead of a hand-shake, he wound up this little speech was perhaps rather a meagre form of salutation; but on the whole it was all the occasion demanded. Isabel reflected that after he left the room Lord Warburton would have no pretext for saying, 'Your husband's very angry'; which would have been extremely disagreeable to her. Nevertheless, if he had done so, she would have said: 'Oh, don't be anxious. He doesn't hate *you*: it's me that he hates!'

It was only when they had been left alone together that her friend showed a certain vague awkwardness—sitting down in another chair, handling two or three of the objects that were near him. 'I hope he'll make Miss Osmond come,' he presently remarked. 'I want very much to see her.'

'I'm glad it's the last time,' said Isabel.

'So am I. She doesn't care for me.'

'No, she doesn't care for you.'

'I don't wonder at it,' he returned. Then he added with inconsequence: 'You'll come to England, won't you?'

'I think we had better not.'

'Ah, you owe me a visit. Don't you remember that you were to have come to Lockleigh once, and you never did?'

'Everything's changed since then,' said Isabel.

'Not changed for the worse, surely—as far as we're concerned. To see you under my roof'—and he hung fire but an instant—'would be a great satisfaction.'

She had feared an explanation; but that was the only one that occurred. They talked a little of Ralph, and in another moment Pansy came in, already dressed for dinner and with a little red spot in either cheek. She shook hands with Lord Warburton and stood looking up into his face with a fixed smile—a smile that Isabel knew, though his lordship probably never suspected it, to be near akin to a burst of tears.

'I'm going away,' he said. 'I want to bid you good-bye.'

'Good-bye, Lord Warburton.' Her voice perceptibly trembled.

'And I want to tell you how much I wish you may be very happy.'

'Thank you, Lord Warburton,' Pansy answered.

He lingered a moment and gave a glance at Isabel. 'You ought to be very happy—you've got a guardian angel.'

'I'm sure I shall be happy,' said Pansy in the tone of a person whose certainties were always cheerful.

'Such a conviction as that will take you a great way. But if it should ever fail you, remember—remember—' And her interlocutor stammered a little. 'Think of me sometimes, you know!' he said with a vague laugh. Then he shook hands with Isabel in silence, and presently he was gone.

When he had left the room she expected an effusion of tears from her stepdaughter; but Pansy in fact treated her to something very different.

'I think you *are* my guardian angel!' she exclaimed very sweetly.

Isabel shook her head. 'I'm not an angel of any kind. I'm at the most your good friend.'

'You're a very good friend then—to have asked papa to be gentle with me.'

'I've asked your father nothing,' said Isabel, wondering.

'He told me just now to come to the drawing-room, and then he gave me a very kind kiss.'

'Ah,' said Isabel, 'that was quite his own idea!'

She recognized the idea perfectly; it was very characteristic, and she was to see a great deal more of it. Even with Pansy he couldn't put himself the least in the wrong. They were dining out that day, and after their dinner they went to another entertainment; so that it was not till late in the evening that Isabel saw him alone. When Pansy kissed him before going to bed he returned her embrace with even more than his usual munificence, and Isabel wondered if he meant it as a hint that his daughter had been injured by the machinations of her stepmother. It was a partial expression, at any rate, of what he continued to expect of his wife. She was about to follow Pansy, but he remarked that he wished she would remain; he had something to say to her. Then he walked about the drawing-room a little, while she stood waiting in her cloak.

'I don't understand what you wish to do,' he said in a moment. 'I should like to know—so that I may know how to act.'

'Just now I wish to go to bed. I'm very tired.'

'Sit down and rest; I shall not keep you long. Not there—

take a comfortable place.' And he arranged a multitude of cushions that were scattered in picturesque disorder upon a vast divan. This was not, however, where she seated herself; she dropped into the nearest chair. The fire had gone out; the lights in the great room were few. She drew her cloak about her; she felt mortally cold. 'I think you're trying to humiliate me,' Osmond went on. 'It's a most absurd undertaking.'

'I haven't the least idea what you mean,' she returned.

'You've played a very deep game; you've managed it beautifully.'

'What is it that I've managed?'

'You've not quite settled it, however; we shall see him again.' And he stopped in front of her, with his hands in his pockets, looking down at her thoughtfully, in his usual way, which seemed meant to let her know that she was not an object, but only a rather disagreeable incident, of thought.

'If you mean that Lord Warburton's under an obligation to come back you're wrong,' Isabel said. 'He's under none whatever.'

'That's just what I complain of. But when I say he'll come back I don't mean he'll come from a sense of duty.'

'There's nothing else to make him. I think he has quite exhausted Rome.'

'Ah no, that's a shallow judgement. Rome's inexhaustible.' And Osmond began to walk about again. 'However, about that perhaps there's no hurry,' he added. 'It's rather a good idea of his that we should go to England. If it were not for the fear of finding your cousin there I think I should try to persuade you.'

'It may be that you'll not find my cousin,' said Isabel.

'I should like to be sure of it. However, I shall be as sure as possible. At the same time I should like to see his house, that you told me so much about at one time: what do you call it?—Gardencourt. It must be a charming thing. And then, you know, I've a devotion to the memory of your uncle: you made me take a great fancy to him. I should like to see where he lived and died. That indeed is a detail. Your friend was right. Pansy ought to see England.'

'I've no doubt she would enjoy it,' said Isabel.

'But that's a long time hence; next autumn's far off,' Osmond continued; 'and meantime there are things that more nearly interest us. Do you think me so very proud?' he suddenly asked.

'I think you very strange.'

'You don't understand me.'

'No, not even when you insult me.'

'I don't insult you; I'm incapable of it. I merely speak of certain facts, and if the allusion's an injury to you the fault's not mine. It's surely a fact that you have kept all this matter quite in your own hands.'

'Are you going back to Lord Warburton?' Isabel asked. 'I'm very tired of his name.'

'You shall hear it again before we've done with it.'

She had spoken of his insulting her, but it suddenly seemed to her that this ceased to be a pain. He was going down—down; the vision of such a fall made her almost giddy: that was the only pain. He was too strange, too different; he didn't touch her. Still, the working of his morbid passion was extraordinary, and she felt a rising curiosity to know in what light he saw himself justified. 'I might say to you that I judge you've nothing to say to me that's worth hearing,' she returned in a moment. 'But I should perhaps be wrong. There's a thing that would be worth my hearing—to know in the plainest words of what it is you accuse me.'

'Of having prevented Pansy's marriage to Warburton. Are those words plain enough?'

'On the contrary, I took a great interest in it. I told you so; and when you told me that you counted on me—that I think was what you said—I accepted the obligation. I was a fool to do so, but I did it.'

'You pretended to do it, and you even pretended reluctance to make me more willing to trust you. Then you began to use your ingenuity to get him out of the way.'

'I think I see what you mean,' said Isabel.

'Where's the letter you told me he had written me?' her husband demanded.

'I haven't the least idea; I haven't asked him.'

'You stopped it on the way,' said Osmond.

Isabel slowly got up; standing there in her white cloak, which covered her to her feet, she might have represented the angel of disdain, first cousin to that of pity. 'Oh, Gilbert, for a man who was so fine—!' she exclaimed in a long murmur.

'I was never so fine as you. You've done everything you wanted. You've got him out of the way without appearing to do so, and you've placed me in the position in which you wished to see me—that of a man who has tried to marry his daughter to a lord, but has grotesquely failed.'

'Pansy doesn't care for him. She's very glad he's gone,' Isabel said.

'That has nothing to do with the matter.'

'And he doesn't care for Pansy.'

'That won't do; you told me he did. I don't know why you wanted this particular satisfaction,' Osmond continued; 'you might have taken some other. It doesn't seem to me that I've been presumptions—that I have taken too much for granted. I've been very modest about it, very quiet. The idea didn't originate with me. He began to show that he liked her before I ever thought of it. I left it all to you.'

'Yes, you were very glad to leave it to me. After this you must attend to such things yourself.'

He looked at her a moment; then he turned away. 'I thought you were very fond of my daughter.'

'I've never been more so than to-day.'

'Your affection is attended with immense limitations. However, that perhaps is natural.'

'Is this all you wished to say to me?' Isabel asked, taking a candle that stood on one of the tables.

'Are you satisfied? Am I sufficiently disappointed?'

'I don't think that on the whole you're disappointed. You've had another opportunity to try to stupefy me.'

'It's not that. It's proved that Pansy can aim high.'

'Poor little Pansy!' said Isabel as she turned away with her candle.

XLVII

It was from Henrietta Stackpole that she learned how Caspar Goodwood had come to Rome; an event that took place three days after Lord Warburton's departure. This latter fact had been preceded by an incident of some importance to Isabel—the temporary absence, once again, of Madame Merle, who had gone to Naples to stay with a friend, the happy possessor of a villa at Posilippo. Madame Merle had ceased to minister to Isabel's happiness, who found herself wondering whether the most discreet of women might not also by chance be the most dangerous. Sometimes, at night, she had strange visions; she seemed to see her husband and her friend—his friend—in dim, indistinguishable combination. It seemed to her that she had not done with her; this lady had something in reserve. Isabel's imagination applied itself actively to this elusive point, but every now and then it was checked by a nameless dread, so that when the charming woman was away from Rome she had almost a consciousness of respite. She had already learned from Miss Stackpole that Caspar Goodwood was in Europe, Henrietta having written to make it known to her immediately after meeting him in Paris. He himself never wrote to Isabel, and though he was in Europe she thought it very possible he might not desire to see her. Their last interview, before her marriage, had had quite the character of a complete rupture; if she remembered rightly he had said he wished to take his last look at her. Since then he had been the most discordant survival of her earlier time—the only one in fact with which a permanent pain was associated. He had left her that morning with a sense of the most superfluous of shocks: it was like a collision between vessels in broad daylight. There had been no mist, no hidden current to excuse it, and she herself had only wished to steer wide. He had bumped against her prow, however, while her hand was on the tiller, and—to complete the metaphor—had given the lighter vessel a strain which still occasionally betrayed itself in a faint creaking. It had been horrid to see him, because he represented the only serious harm that (to her belief) she had ever done in the world: he was the only person with an unsatisfied claim on her. She had made him unhappy, she couldn't help it; and his unhappiness was a grim reality. She had cried with rage, after he had left her, at—she hardly knew what: she tried to think it had been at his want of consideration. He had come to her with his unhappiness when her own bliss was so perfect; he had done his best to darken the brightness of those pure rays. He had not been violent, and yet there had been a violence in the impression. There had been a violence at any rate in something somewhere; perhaps it was only in her own fit of weeping and in that after-sense of the same which had lasted three or four days.

The effect of his final appeal had in short faded away, and all the first year of her marriage he had dropped out of her books. He was a thankless subject of reference; it was disagreeable to have to think of a person who was sore and sombre about you and whom you could yet do nothing to relieve. It would have been different if she had been able to doubt, even a little, of his unreconciled state, as she doubted of Lord Warburton's; unfortunately it was beyond question, and this aggressive, uncompromising look of it was just what made it unattractive. She could never say to herself that here was a sufferer who had compensations, as she was able to say in the case of her English suitor. She had no faith in Mr Goodwood's compensations and no esteem for them. A cotton-factory was not a compensation for anything—least of all for having failed to marry Isabel Archer. And yet, beyond that, she hardly knew what he had—save of course his intrinsic qualities. Oh, he was intrinsic enough; she never thought of his even looking for artificial aids. If he extended his business—that, to the best of her belief, was the only form exertion could take with him—it would be because it was an enterprising thing, or good for the business; not in the least because he might hope it would overlay the past. This gave his figure a kind of bareness and bleakness which made the accident of meeting it in memory or in apprehension a peculiar concussion; it was deficient in the social drapery commonly muffling, in an overcivilized age, the sharpness of human contacts. His perfect silence, moreover, the fact that she never heard from him and very seldom heard any mention of him, deepened this impression of his loneliness. She asked Lily for news of him, from time to time; but Lily knew nothing of Boston—her imagination was all bounded on the east by Madison Avenue. As time went on Isabel had thought of him oftener, and with fewer restrictions; she had had more than once the idea of writing to him. She had never told her husband about him—never let Osmond know of his visits to her in Florence; a reserve not dictated in the early period by a want of confidence in Osmond, but simply by the consideration that the young man's disappointment was not her secret but his own. It would be wrong of her, she had believed, to convey it to another, and Mr Goodwood's affairs could have, after all, little interest for Gilbert. When it had come to the point she had never written to him; it seemed to her that, considering his grievance, the least she could do was to let him alone. Nevertheless she would have been glad to be in some way nearer to him. It was not that it ever occurred to her that she might have married him; even after the consequences of her actual union had grown vivid to her that particular reflection, though she indulged in so many, had not had the assurance to present itself. But on finding herself in trouble he had become a member of that circle of things with which she wished to set herself right. I have mentioned how passionately she needed to feel that her unhappiness should not have come to her through her own fault. She had no near prospect of dying, and yet she wished to make her peace with the world—to put her spiritual affairs in order. It came back to her from time to time that there was an account still to be settled with Caspar, and she saw herself disposed or able to settle it to-day on terms easier for him than ever before. Still, when she learned he was coming to Rome she felt all afraid; it would be more disagreeable for him than for any one else to make out—since he *would* make it out, as over a falsified balance-sheet or something of that sort—the intimate disarray of her affairs. Deep in her breast she believed that he had invested his all in her happiness, while the others had invested only a part. He was one more person from whom she should have to conceal her stress. She was reassured, however, after he arrived in Rome, for he spent several days without coming to see her.

Henrietta Stackpole, it may well be imagined, was much more punctual, and Isabel was largely favoured with the society of her friend. She threw herself into it, for now that she had made such a point of keeping her conscience clear, that was one way of proving she had not been superficial—the more so as the years, in their flight, had rather enriched than blighted those peculiarities which had been humorously criticized by persons less interested than Isabel, and which were still marked enough to give loyalty a spice of heroism. Henrietta was as keen and quick and fresh as ever, and as neat and bright and fair. Her remarkably open eyes, lighted like great glazed railway-stations, had put up no shutters; her attire had lost none of its crispness, her opinions none of their national reference. She was by no means quite unchanged, however; it struck Isabel she had grown vague. Of old she had never been vague; though undertaking many enquiries at once, she had managed to be entire and pointed about each. She had a reason for everything she did; she fairly bristled with motives. Formerly, when she came to Europe it was because she wished to see it, but now, having already seen it, she had no such excuse. She didn't for a moment pretend that the desire to examine decaying civilizations had anything to do with her present enterprise; her journey was rather an expression of her independence of the old world than of a sense of further obligations to it. 'It's nothing to come to Europe,' she said to Isabel; 'it doesn't seem to me one needs so many reasons for that. It is something to stay at home; this is much more important.' It was not therefore with a sense of doing anything very important that she treated herself to another pilgrimage to Rome; she had seen the place before and carefully inspected it; her present act was simply a sign of familiarity, of her knowing all about it, of her having as good a right as any one else to be there. This was all very well, and Henrietta was restless; she had a perfect right to be restless too, if one came to that. But she had after all a better reason for coming to Rome than that she cared for it so little. Her friend easily recognized it, and with it the worth of the other's fidelity. She had crossed the stormy ocean in midwinter because she had guessed that Isabel was sad. Henrietta guessed a great deal, but she had never guessed so happily as that. Isabel's satisfactions just now were few, but even if they had been more numerous there would still have been something of individual joy in her sense of being justified in having always thought highly of Henrietta. She had made large concessions with regard to her, and had yet insisted that, with all abatements, she was very valuable. It was not her own triumph, however, that she found good; it was simply the relief of confessing to this confidant, the first person to whom she had owned it, that she was not in the least at her ease. Henrietta had herself approached this point with the smallest possible delay, and had accused her to her face of being wretched. She was a woman, she was a sister; she was not Ralph, not Lord Warburton, nor Caspar Goodwood, and Isabel could speak.

'Yes, I'm wretched,' she said very mildy. She hated to hear herself say it; she tried to say it as judicially as possible.

'What does he do to you?' Henrietta asked, frowning as if she were enquiring into the operations of a quack doctor.

'He does nothing. But he doesn't like me.'

'He's very hard to please!' cried Miss Stackpole. 'Why don't you leave him?'

'I can't change that way,' Isabel said.

'Why not, I should like to know? You won't confess that you've made a mistake. You're too proud.'

'I don't know whether I'm too proud. But I can't publish my mistake. I don't think that's decent. I'd much rather die.'

'You won't think so always,' said Henrietta.

'I don't know what great unhappiness might bring me to; but it seems to me I shall always be ashamed. One must accept one's deeds. I married him before all the world; I was perfectly free; it was impossible to do anything more deliberate. One can't change that way,' Isabel repeated.

'You *have* changed, in spite of the impossibility. I hope you don't mean to say you like him.'

Isabel debated. 'No, I don't like him. I can tell you, because I'm weary of my secret. But that's enough; I can't announce it on the housetops.'

Henrietta gave a laugh. 'Don't you think you're rather too considerate?'

'It's not of him that I'm considerate—it's of myself!' Isabel answered.

It was not surprising Gilbert Osmond should not have taken comfort in Miss Stackpole; his instinct had naturally set him in opposition to a young lady capable of advising his wife to withdraw from the conjugal roof. When she arrived in Rome he had said to Isabel that he hoped she would leave her friend the interviewer alone; and Isabel had answered that he at least had nothing to fear from her. She said to Henrietta that as Osmond didn't like her she couldn't invite her to dine, but they could easily see each other in other ways. Isabel received Miss Stackpole freely in her own sitting-room, and took her repeatedly to drive, face to face with Pansy, who, bending a little forward, on the opposite seat of the carriage, gazed at the celebrated authoress with a respectful attention which Henrietta occasionally found irritating. She complained to Isabel that Miss Osmond had a little look as if she should remember everything one said. 'I don't want to be remembered that way,' Miss Stackpole declared; 'I consider that my conversation refers only to the moment, like the morning papers. Your stepdaughter, as she sits there, looks as if she kept all the back numbers and would bring them out some day against me.' She could not teach herself to think favourably of Pansy, whose absence of initiative, of conversation, of personal claims, seemed to her, in a girl of twenty, unnatural and even uncanny. Isabel presently saw that Osmond would have liked her to urge a little the cause of her friend, insist a little upon his receiving her, so that he might appear to suffer for good manners' sake. Her immediate acceptance of his objections put him too much in the wrong—it being in effect one of the disadvantages of expressing contempt that you cannot enjoy at the same time the credit of expressing sympathy. Osmond held to his credit, and yet he held to his objections—all of which were elements difficult to reconcile. The right thing would have been that Miss Stackpole should come to dine at Palazzo Roccanera once or twice, so that (in spite of his superficial civility, always so great) she might judge for herself how little pleasure it gave him. From the moment, however, that both the ladies were so unaccommodating, there was nothing for Osmond but to wish the lady from New York would take herself off. It was surprising how little satisfaction he got from his wife's friends; he took occasion to call Isabel's attention to it.

'You're certainly not fortunate in your intimates; I wish you might make a new collection,' he said to her one morning in reference to nothing visible at the moment, but in a tone of ripe reflection which deprived the remark of all brutal abruptness. 'It's as if you had taken the trouble to pick out the people in the world that I have least in common with. Your cousin I have always thought a conceited ass—besides his being the most ill-favoured animal I know. Then it's insufferably tiresome that one can't tell him so; one must spare him on account of his health. His health seems to me the best part of him; it gives him privileges enjoyed by no one else. If he's so desperately ill there's only one way to prove it; but he seems to have no mind for that. I can't say much more for the great Warburton. When one really thinks of it, the cool insolence of that performance was something rare! He comes and looks at one's daughter as if she were a suite of apartments; he tries the door-handles and looks out of the windows, raps on the walls and almost thinks he'll take the place. Will you be so good as to draw up a lease? Then, on the whole, he decides that the rooms are too small; he doesn't think he could live on a third floor; he must look out for a *piano nobile*. And he goes away after having got a month's lodging in the poor little apartment for nothing. Miss Stackpole, however, is your most wonderful invention. She strikes me as a kind of monster. One hasn't a nerve in one's body that she doesn't set quivering. You know I never have admitted that she's a woman. Do you know what she reminds me of? Of a new steel pen—the most odious thing in nature. She talks as a steel pen writes; aren't her letters, by the way, on ruled paper? She thinks and moves and walks and looks exactly as she talks. You may say that she doesn't hurt me inasmuch as I don't see her. I don't see her, but I hear her; I hear her all day long. Her voice is in my ears; I can't get rid of it. I know exactly what she says, and every inflexion of the tone in which she says it. She says charming things about me, and they give you great comfort. I don't like at all to think she talks about me—I feel as I should feel if I knew the footman were wearing my hat.'

Henrietta talked about Gilbert Osmond, as his wife assured him, rather less than he suspected. She had plenty of other subjects, in two of which the reader may be supposed to be especially interested. She let her friend know that Caspar Goodwood had discovered for himself that she was unhappy, though indeed her ingenuity was unable to suggest what comfort he hoped to give her by coming to Rome and yet not calling on her. They met him twice in the street, but he had no appearance of seeing them; they were driving, and he had a habit of looking straight in front of him, as if he proposed to take in but one object at a time. Isabel could have fancied she had seen him the day before; it must have been with just that face and step that he had walked out of Mrs Touchett's door at the close of their last interview. He was dressed just as he had been dressed on that day, Isabel remembered the colour of his cravat; and yet in spite of this familiar look there was a strangeness in his figure too, something that made her feel it afresh to be rather terrible he should have come to Rome. He looked bigger and more overtopping than of old, and in those days he certainly reached high enough. She noticed that the people whom he passed looked back after him; but he went straight forward, lifting above them a face like a February sky.

Miss Stackpole's other topic was very different; she gave Isabel the latest news about Mr Bantling. He had been out in the United States the year before, and she was happy to say she had been able to show him considerable attention. She didn't know how much he had enjoyed it, but she would undertake to say it had done him good; he wasn't the same man when he left as he had been when he came. It had opened his eyes and shown him that England wasn't everything. He had been very much liked in most places, and thought extremely simple—more simple than the English were commonly supposed to be. There were people who had thought him affected; she didn't know whether they meant that his simplicity was an affectation. Some of his questions were too discouraging; he thought all the chambermaids were farmers' daughters—or all the farmers' daughters were chambermaids—she couldn't exactly remember which. He hadn't seemed able to grasp the great school system; it had been really too much for him. On the whole he had behaved as if there were too much of everything—as if he could only take in a small part. The part he had chosen was the hotel system and the river navigation. He had seemed really fascinated with the hotels; he had a photograph of every one he had visited. But the river steamers were his principal interest; he wanted to do nothing but sail on the big boats. They had travelled together from New York to Milwaukee, stopping at the most interesting cities on the route; and whenever they started afresh he had wanted to know if they could go by the steamer. He seemed to have no idea of geography—had an impression that Baltimore was a Western city and was perpetually expecting to arrive at the Mississippi. He appeared never to have heard of any river in America but the Mississippi and was unprepared to recognise the existence of the Hudson, though obliged to confess at last that it was fully equal to the Rhine. They had spent some pleasant hours in the palace-cars; he was always ordering ice-cream from the coloured man. He could never get used to that idea—that you could get ice-cream in the cars. Of course you couldn't, nor fans, nor candy, nor anything in the English cars! He found the heat quite overwhelming, and she had told him she indeed expected it was the biggest he had ever experienced. He was now in England, hunting—'hunting round' Henrietta called it. These amusements were those of the American red men; we had left that behind long ago, the pleasures of the chase. It seemed to be generally believed in England that we wore tomahawks and feathers; but such a costume was more in keeping with English habits. Mr Bantling would not have time to join her in Italy, but when she should go to Paris again he expected to come over. He wanted very much to see Versailles again; he was very fond of the ancient *régime*. They didn't agree about that, but that was what she liked Versailles for, that you could see the ancient *régime* had been swept away. There were no dukes and marquises there now; she remembered on the contrary one day when there were five American families, walking all round. Mr Bantling was very anxious that she should take up the subject of England again, and he thought she might get on better with it now; England had changed a good deal within two or three years. He was determined that if she went there he should go to see his sister, Lady Pensil, and that this time the invitation should come to her straight. The mystery about that other one had never been explained.

Caspar Goodwood came at last to Palazzo Roccanera; he had written Isabel a note beforehand, to ask leave. This was promptly granted; she would be at home at six o'clock that afternoon. She spent the day wondering what he was coming for—what good he expected to get of it. He had presented himself hitherto as a person destitute of the faculty of compromise, who would take what he had asked for or take nothing. Isabel's hospitality, however, raised no questions, and she found no great difficulty in appearing happy enough to deceive him. It was her conviction at least that she deceived him, made him say to himself that he had been misinformed. But she also saw, so she believed, that he was not disappointed, as some other men, she was sure, would have been; he had not come to Rome to look for an opportunity. She never found out what he had come for; he offered her no explanation; there could be none but the very simple one that he wanted to see her. In other words he had come for his amusement. Isabel followed up this induction with a good deal of eagerness, and was delighted to have found a formula that would lay the ghost of this gentleman's ancient grievance. If he had come to Rome for his amusement this was exactly what she wanted; for if he cared for amusement he had got over his heartache. If he had got over his heartache everything was as it should be and her responsibilities were at an end. It was true that he took his recreation a little stiffly, but he had never been loose and easy and she had every reason to believe he was satisfied with what he saw. Henrietta was not in his confidence, though he was in hers, and Isabel consequently received no side-light upon his state of mind. He was open to little conversation on general topics; it came back to her that she had said of him once, years before, 'Mr Goodwood speaks a good deal, but he doesn't talk.' He spoke a good deal now, but he talked perhaps as little as ever; considering, that is, how much there was in Rome to talk about. His arrival was not calculated to simplify her relations with her husband, for if Mr Osmond didn't like her friends Mr Goodwood had no claim upon his attention save as having been one of the first of them. There was nothing for her to say of him but that he was the very oldest; this rather meagre synthesis exhausted the facts. She had been obliged to introduce him to Gilbert; it was impossible she should not ask him to dinner, to her Thursday evenings, of which she had grown very weary, but to which her husband still held for the sake not so much of inviting people as of not inviting them.

To the Thursdays Mr Goodwood came regularly, solemnly, rather early; he appeared to regard them with a good deal of gravity. Isabel every now and then had a moment of anger; there was something so literal about him; she thought he might know that she didn't know what to do with him. But she couldn't call him stupid; he was not that in the least; he was only extraordinarily honest. To be as honest as that made a man very different from most people; one had to be almost equally honest with *him*. She made this latter reflection at the very time she was flattering herself she had persuaded him that she was the most light-hearted of women. He never threw any doubt on this point, never asked her any personal questions. He got on much better with Osmond than had seemed probable. Osmond had a great dislike to being counted on; in such a case he had an irresistible need of disappointing you. It was in virtue of this principle that he gave himself the entertainment of taking a fancy to a perpendicular Bostonian whom he had been depended upon to treat with coldness. He asked Isabel if Mr Goodwood also had wanted to marry her, and expressed surprise at her not having accepted him. It would have been an excellent thing, like living under some tall belfry which would strike all the hours and make a queer vibration in the upper air. He declared he liked to talk with the great Goodwood; it wasn't easy at first, you had to climb up an interminable steep staircase, up to the top of the tower; but when you got there you had a big view and felt a little fresh breeze. Osmond, as we know, had delightful qualities, and he gave Caspar Goodwood the benefit of them all. Isabel could see that Mr Goodwood thought better of her husband than he had ever wished to; he had given her the impression that morning in Florence of being inaccessible to a good impression. Gilbert asked him repeatedly to dinner, and Mr Goodwood smoked a cigar with him afterwards and even desired to be shown his collections. Gilbert said to Isabel that he was very original; he was as strong and of as good a style as an English portmanteau,—he had plenty of straps and buckles which would never wear out, and a capital patent lock. Caspar Goodwood took to riding on the Campagna and devoted much time to this exercise; it was therefore mainly in the evening that Isabel saw him. She bethought herself of saying to him one day that if he were willing he could render her a service. And then she added smiling:

'I don't know, however, what right I have to ask a service of you.'

'You're the person in the world who has most right,' he answered. 'I've given you assurances that I've never given any one else.'

The service was that he should go and see her cousin Ralph, who was ill at the Hôtel de Paris, alone, and be as kind to him as possible. Mr Goodwood had never seen him, but he would know who the poor fellow was; if she was not mistaken Ralph had once invited him to Gardencourt. Caspar remembered the invitation perfectly, and, though he was not supposed to be a man of imagination, had enough to put himself in the place of a poor gentleman who lay dying at a Roman inn. He called at the Hôtel de Paris and, on being shown into the presence of the master of Gardencourt, found Miss Stackpole sitting beside his sofa. A singular change had in fact occurred in this lady's relations with Ralph Touchett. She had not been asked by Isabel to go and see him, but on hearing that he was too ill to come out had immediately gone of her own motion. After this she had paid him a daily visit—always under the conviction that they were great enemies. 'Oh yes, we're intimate enemies,' Ralph used to say; and he accused her freely—as freely as the humour of it would allow—of coming to worry him to death. In reality they became excellent friends, Henrietta much wondering that she should never have liked him before. Ralph liked her exactly as much as he had always done; he had never doubted for a moment that she was an excellent fellow. They talked about everything and always differed; about everything, that is, but Isabel—a topic as to which Ralph always had a thin forefinger on his lips. Mr Bantling on the other hand proved a great resource; Ralph was capable of discussing Mr Bantling with Henrietta for hours. Discussion was stimulated of course by their inevitable difference of view—Ralph having amused himself with taking the ground that the genial ex-guardsman was a regular Machiavelli. Caspar Goodwood could contribute nothing to such a debate; but after he had been left alone with his host he found there were various other matters they could take up. It must be admitted that the lady who had just gone out was not one of these; Caspar granted all Miss Stackpole's merits in advance, but had no further remark to make about her. Neither, after the first allusions, did the two men expatiate upon Mrs Osmond—a theme in which Goodwood perceived as many dangers as Ralph. He felt very sorry for that unclassable personage; he couldn't bear to see a pleasant man, so pleasant for all his queerness, so beyond anything to be done. There was always something to be done, for Goodwood, and he did it in this case by repeating several times his visit to the Hôtel de Paris. It seemed to Isabel that she had been very clever; she had artfully disposed of the superfluous Caspar. She had given him an occupation; she had converted him into a caretaker of Ralph. She had a plan of making him travel northward with her cousin as soon as the first mild weather should allow it. Lord Warburton had brought Ralph to Rome and Mr Goodwood should take him away. There seemed a happy symmetry in this, and she was now intensely eager that Ralph should depart. She had a constant fear he would die there before her eyes and a horror of the occurrence of this event at an inn, by her door, which he had so rarely entered. Ralph must sink to his last rest in his own dear house, in one of those deep, dim chambers of Gardencourt where the dark ivy would cluster round the edges of the glimmering window.

There seemed to Isabel in these days something sacred in Gardencourt; no chapter of the past was more perfectly irrecoverable. When she thought of the months she had spent there the tears rose to her eyes. She flattered herself, as I say, upon her ingenuity, but she had need of all she could muster; for several events occurred which seemed to confront and defy her. The Countess Gemini arrived from Florence—arrived with her trunks, her dresses, her chatter, her falsehoods, her frivolity, the strange, the unholy legend of the number of her lovers. Edward Rosier, who had been away somewhere,—no one, not even Pansy, knew where,—reappeared in Rome and began to write her long letters, which she never answered. Madame Merle returned from Naples and said to her with a strange smile: 'What on earth did you do with Lord Warburton?' As if it were any business of hers!

XLVIII

ONE day, toward the end of February, Ralph Touchett made up his mind to return to England. He had his own reasons for this decision, which he was not bound to communicate; but Henrietta Stackpole, to whom he mentioned his intention, flattered herself that she guessed them. She forbore to express them, however; she only said, after a moment, as she sat by his sofa: 'I suppose you know you can't go alone?'

'I've no idea of doing that,' Ralph answered. 'I shall have people with me.'

'What do you mean by "people"? Servants whom you pay?'

'Ah,' said Ralph jocosely, 'after all, they're human beings.'

'Are there any women among them?' Miss Stackpole desired to know.

'You speak as if I had a dozen! No, I confess I haven't a soubrette in my employment.'

'Well,' said Henrietta calmly, 'you can't go to England that way. You must have a woman's care.'

'I've had so much of yours for the past fortnight that it will last me a good while.'

'You've not had enough of it yet. I guess I'll go with you,' said Henrietta.

'Go with me?' Ralph slowly raised himself from his sofa.

'Yes, I know you don't like me, but I'll go with you all the same. It would be better for your health to lie down again.'

Ralph looked at her a little; then he slowly relapsed. 'I like you very much,' he said in a moment.

Miss Stackpole gave one of her infrequent laughs. 'You needn't think that by saying that you can buy me off. I'll go with you, and what is more I'll take care of you.'

'You're a very good woman,' said Ralph.

'Wait till I get you safely home before you say that. It won't be easy. But you had better go, all the same.'

Before she left him, Ralph said to her: 'Do you really mean to take care of me?'

'Well, I mean to try.'

'I notify you then that I submit. Oh, I submit!' And it was perhaps a sign of submission that a few minutes after she had left him alone he burst into a loud fit of laughter. It seemed to him so inconsequent, such a conclusive proof of his having abdicated all functions and renounced all exercise, that he should start on a journey across Europe under the supervision of Miss Stackpole. And the great oddity was that the prospect pleased him; he was gratefully, luxuriously passive. He felt even impatient to start; and indeed he had an immense longing to see his own house again. The end of everything was at hand; it seemed to him he could stretch out his arm and touch the goal. But he wanted to die at home; it was the only wish he had left—to extend himself in the large quiet room where he had last seen his father lie, and close his eyes upon the summer dawn.

That same day Caspar Goodwood came to see him, and he informed his visitor that Miss Stackpole had taken him up and was to conduct him back to England. 'Ah then,' said Caspar, 'I'm afraid I shall be a fifth wheel to the coach. Mrs Osmond has made *me* promise to go with you.'

'Good heavens—it's the golden age! You're all too kind.'

'The kindness on my part is to her; it's hardly to you.'

'Granting that, *she's* kind,' smiled Ralph.

'To get people to go with you? Yes, that's a sort of kindness,' Goodwood answered without lending himself to the joke. 'For myself, however,' he added, 'I'll go so far as to say that I would much rather travel with you and Miss Stackpole than with Miss Stackpole alone.'

'And you'd rather stay here than do either,' said Ralph. 'There's really no need of your coming. Henrietta's extraordinarily efficient.'

'I'm sure of that. But I've promised Mrs Osmond.'

'You can easily get her to let you off.'

'She wouldn't let me off for the world. She wants me to look after you, but that isn't the principal thing. The principal thing is that she wants me to leave Rome.'

'Ah, you see too much in it,' Ralph suggested.

'I bore her,' Goodwood went on; 'she has nothing to say to me, so she invented that.'

'Oh then, if it's a convenience to her I certainly will take you with me. Though I don't see why it should be a convenience,' Ralph added in a moment.

'Well,' said Caspar Goodwood simply, 'she thinks I'm watching her.'

'Watching her?'

'Trying to make out if she's happy.'

'That's easy to make out,' said Ralph. 'She's the most visibly happy woman I know.'

'Exactly so; I'm satisfied,' Goodwood answered dryly. For all his dryness, however, he had more to say. 'I've been watching her; I was an old friend and it seemed to me I had the right. She pretends to be happy; that was what she undertook to be; and I thought I should like to see for myself what it amounts to. I've seen,' he continued with a harsh ring in his voice, 'and I don't want to see any more. I'm now quite ready to go.'

'Do you know it strikes me as about time you should?' Ralph rejoined. And this was the only conversation these gentlemen had about Isabel Osmond.

Henrietta made her preparations for departure, and among them she found it proper to say a few words to the Countess Gemini, who returned at Miss Stackpole's *pension* the visit which this lady had paid her in Florence.

'You were very wrong about Lord Warburton,' she remarked to the Countess. 'I think it right you should know that.'

'About his making love to Isabel? My poor lady, he was at her house three times a day. He has left traces of his passage!' the Countess cried.

'He wished to marry your niece; that's why he came to the house.'

The Countess stared, and then with an inconsiderate laugh: 'Is that the story that Isabel tells? It isn't bad, as such things go. If he wishes to marry my niece, pray why doesn't he do it? Perhaps he has gone to buy the wedding-ring and will come back with it next month, after I'm gone.'

'No, he'll not come back. Miss Osmond doesn't wish to marry him.'

'She's very accommodating! I knew she was fond of Isabel, but I didn't know she carried it so far.'

'I don't understand you,' said Henrietta coldly, and reflecting that the Countess was unpleasantly perverse. 'I really must stick to my point—that Isabel never encouraged the attentions of Lord Warburton.'

'My dear friend, what do you and I know about it? All we know is that my brother's capable of everything.'

'I don't know what your brother's capable of,' said Henrietta with dignity.

'It's not her encouraging Warburton that I complain of; it's her sending him away. I want particularly to see him. Do you suppose she thought I would make him faithless?' the Countess continued with audacious insistence. 'However, she's only keeping him, one can feel that. The house is full of him there; he's quite in the air. Oh yes, he has left traces; I'm sure I shall see him yet.'

'Well,' said Henrietta after a little, with one of those inspirations which had made the fortune of her letters to the *Interviewer*, 'perhaps he'll be more successful with you than with Isabel!'

When she told her friend of the offer she had made Ralph Isabel replied that she could have done nothing that would have pleased her more. It had always been her faith that at bottom Ralph and this young woman were made to understand each other. 'I don't care whether he understands me or not,' Henrietta declared. 'The great thing is that he shouldn't die in the cars.'

'He won't do that,' Isabel said, shaking her head with an extension of faith.

'He won't if I can help it. I see you want us all to go. I don't know what you want to do.'

'I want to be alone,' said Isabel.

'You won't be that so long as you've so much company at home.'

'Ah, they're part of the comedy. You others are spectators.'

'Do you call it a comedy, Isabel Archer?' Henrietta rather grimly asked.

'The tragedy then if you like. You're all looking at me; it makes me uncomfortable.'

Henrietta engaged in this act for a while. 'You're like the

stricken deer, seeking the innermost shade. Oh, you do give me such a sense of helplessness!' she broke out.

'I'm not at all helpless. There are many things I mean to do.'

'It's not you I'm speaking of; it's myself. It's too much, having come on purpose, to leave you just as I find you.'

'You don't do that; you leave me much refreshed,' Isabel said.

'Very mild refreshment—sour lemonade! I want you to promise me something.'

'I can't do that. I shall never make another promise. I made such a solemn one four years ago, and I've succeeded so ill in keeping it.'

'You've had no encouragement. In this case I should give you the greatest. Leave your husband before the worst comes; that's what I want you to promise.'

'The worst? What do you call the worst?'

'Before your character gets spoiled.'

'Do you mean my disposition? It won't get spoiled,' Isabel answered, smiling. 'I'm taking very good care of it. I'm extremely struck,' she added, turning away, 'with the off-hand way in which you speak of a woman's leaving her husband. It's easy to see you've never had one!'

'Well,' said Henrietta as if she were beginning an argument, 'nothing is more common in our Western cities, and it's to them, after all, that we must look in the future.' Her argument, however, does not concern this history, which has too many other threads to unwind. She announced to Ralph Touchett that she was ready to leave Rome by any train he might designate, and Ralph immediately pulled himself together for departure. Isabel went to see him at the last, and he made the same remark that Henrietta had made. It struck him that Isabel was uncommonly glad to get rid of them all.

For all answer to this she gently laid her hand on his, and said in a low tone, with a quick smile: 'My dear Ralph—!'

It was answer enough, and he was quite contented. But he went on in the same way, jocosely, ingenuously: 'I've seen less of you than I might, but it's better than nothing. And then I've heard a great deal about you.'

'I don't know from whom, leading the life you've done.'

'From the voices of the air! Oh, from no one else; I never let other people speak of you. They always say you're "charming," and that's so flat.'

'I might have seen more of you certainly,' Isabel said. 'But when one's married one has so much occupation.'

'Fortunately I'm not married. When you come to see me in England I shall be able to entertain you with all the freedom of a bachelor.' He continued to talk as if they should certainly meet again, and succeeded in making the assumption appear almost just. He made no allusion to his term being near, to the probability that he should not outlast the summer. If he preferred it so, Isabel was willing enough; the reality was sufficiently distinct without their erecting finger-posts in conversation. That had been well enough for the earlier time, though about this, as about his other affairs, Ralph had never been egotistic. Isabel spoke of his journey, of the stages into which he should divide it, of the precautions he should take. 'Henrietta's my greatest precaution,' he went on. 'The conscience of that woman's sublime.'

'Certainly she'll be very conscientious.'

'Will be? She has been! It's only because she thinks it's her duty that she goes with me. There's a conception of duty for you.'

'Yes, it's a generous one,' said Isabel, 'and it makes me deeply ashamed. I ought to go with you, you know.'

'Your husband wouldn't like that.'

'No, he wouldn't like it. But I might go, all the same.'

'I'm startled by the boldness of your imagination. Fancy my being a cause of disagreement between a lady and her husband!'

'That's why I don't go,' said Isabel simply—yet not very lucidly.

Ralph understood well enough, however. 'I should think so, with all those occupations you speak of.'

'It isn't that. I'm afraid,' said Isabel. After a pause she repeated, as if to make herself, rather than him, hear the words: 'I'm afraid.'

Ralph could hardly tell what her tone meant; it was so strangely deliberate—apparently so void of emotion. Did she wish to do public penance for a fault of which she had not been convicted? or were her words simply an attempt at enlightened self-analysis? However this might be, Ralph could not resist so easy an opportunity. 'Afraid of your husband?'

'Afraid of myself!' she said, getting up. She stood there a moment and then added: 'If I were afraid of my husband that would be simply my duty. That's what women are expected to be.'

'Ah yes,' laughed Ralph; 'but to make up for it there's always some man awfully afraid of some woman!'

She gave no heed to this pleasantry, but suddenly took a different turn. 'With Henrietta at the head of your little band,' she exclaimed abruptly, 'there will be nothing left for Mr Goodwood!'

'Ah, my dear Isabel,' Ralph answered, 'he's used to that. There *is* nothing left for Mr Goodwood.'

She coloured and then observed, quickly, that she must leave him. They stood together a moment; both her hands were in both of his. 'You've been my best friend,' she said.

'It was for you that I wanted—that I wanted to live. But I'm of no use to you.'

Then it came over her more poignantly that she should not see him again. She could not accept that; she could not part with him that way. 'If you should send for me I'd come,' she said at last.

'Your husband won't consent to that.'

'Oh yes, I can arrange it.'

'I shall keep that for my last pleasure!' said Ralph.

In answer to which she simply kissed him. It was a Thursday, and that evening Caspar Goodwood came to Palazzo Roccanera. He was among the first to arrive, and he spent some time in conversation with Gilbert Osmond, who almost always was present when his wife received. They sat down together, and Osmond, talkative, communicative, expansive, seemed possessed with a kind of intellectual gaiety. He leaned back with his legs crossed, lounging and chatting, while Goodwood, more restless, but not at all lively, shifted his position, played with his hat, made the little sofa creak beneath him. Osmond's face wore a sharp, aggressive smile; he was as a man whose perceptions have been quickened by good news. He remarked to Goodwood that he was sorry they were to lose him; he himself should particularly miss him. He saw so few intelligent men—they were surprisingly scarce in Rome. He must be sure to come back; there was something very refreshing, to an inveterate Italian like himself, in talking with a genuine outsider.

'I'm very fond of Rome, you know,' Osmond said; 'but there's nothing I like better than to meet people who haven't that superstition. The modern world's after all very fine. Now you're thoroughly modern and yet are not at all common. So many of the moderns we see are such very poor stuff. If they're the children of the future we're willing to die young. Of course the ancients too are often very tiresome. My wife and I like everything that's really new—not the mere pretence of it. There's nothing new, unfortunately, in ignorance and stupidity. We see plenty of that in forms that offer themselves as a revelation of progress, of light. A revelation of vulgarity! There's a certain kind of vulgarity which I believe is really new; I don't think there ever was anything like it before. Indeed I don't find vulgarity, at all, before the present century. You see a faint menace of it here and there in the last, but to-day the air has grown so dense that delicate things are literally not recognised. Now, we've *liked you*—!' With which he hesitated a moment, laying his hand gently on Goodwood's knee and smiling with a mixture of assurance and embarrassment. 'I'm going to say something extremely offensive and patronising, but you must let me have the satisfaction of it. We've liked you because—because you've reconciled us a little to the future. If there are to be a certain number of people like you—*à la bonne heure!** I'm talking for my wife as well as for myself, you see. She speaks for me, my wife; why shouldn't I speak for her? We're as united, you know, as the candlestick and the snuffers. Am I assuming too much when I say that I think I've understood from you that your occupations have been—a—commercial? There's a danger in that, you know; but it's the way you have escaped that strikes us. Excuse me if my little compliment seems in execrable taste; fortunately my wife doesn't hear me. What I mean is that you *might have been*—a—what I was mentioning just now. The whole American world was in a conspiracy to make you so. But you resisted, you've something about you that saved you. And yet you're so modern, so modern; the most modern man we know! We shall always be delighted to see you again.'

I have said that Osmond was in good humour, and these remarks will give ample evidence of the fact. They were infinitely more personal than he usually cared to be, and if Caspar Goodwood had attended to them more closely he might have thought that the defence of delicacy was in rather odd hands. We may believe, however, that Osmond knew very well what he was about, and that if he chose to use the tone of patronage with a grossness not in his habits he had an excellent reason for the escapade. Goodwood had only a vague sense that he was laying it on somehow; he scarcely knew where the mixture was applied. Indeed he scarcely knew what Osmond was talking about; he wanted to be alone with Isabel, and that idea spoke louder to him than her husband's perfectly-pitched voice. He watched her talking with other people and wondered when she would be at liberty and whether he might ask her to go into one of the other rooms. His humour was not, like Osmond's, of the best; there was an element of dull rage in his consciousness of things. Up to this time he had not disliked Osmond personally; he had only thought him very well-informed and obliging and more than he had supposed like the person whom Isabel Archer would naturally marry. His host had won in the open field a great advantage over him, and Goodwood had too strong a sense of fair play to have been moved to underrate him on that account. He had not tried positively to think well of him; this was a flight of sentimental benevolence of which, even in the days when he came nearest to reconciling himself to what had happened, Goodwood was quite incapable. He accepted him as rather a brilliant personage of the amateurish kind, afflicted with a redundancy of leisure which it amused him to work off in little refinements of conversation. But he only half trusted him; he could never make out why the deuce Osmond should lavish refinements of any sort upon *him*. It made him suspect that he found some private entertainment in it, and it ministered to a general impression that his triumphant rival had in his composition a streak of perversity. He knew indeed that Osmond could have no reason to wish him evil; he had nothing to fear from him. He had carried off a supreme advantage and could afford to be kind to a man who had lost everything. It was true that Goodwood had at times grimly wished he were dead and would have liked to kill him; but Osmond had no means of knowing this, for practice had made the younger man perfect in the art of appearing inaccessible to-day to any violent emotion. He cultivated this art in order to deceive himself, but it was others that he deceived first. He cultivated it, moreover, with very limited success; of which there could be no better proof than the deep, dumb irritation that reigned in his soul when he heard Osmond speak of his wife's feelings as if he were commissioned to answer for them.

That was all he had had an ear for in what his host said to him this evening; he had been conscious that Osmond made more of a point even than usual of referring to the conjugal harmony prevailing at Palazzo Roccanera. He had been more careful than ever to speak as if he and his wife had all things in sweet community and it were as natural to each of them to say 'we' as to say 'I'. In all this there was an air of intention that had puzzled and angered our poor Bostonian, who could only reflect for his comfort that Mrs Osmond's relations with her husband were none of his business. He had no proof whatever that her husband misrepresented her, and if he judged her by the surface of things was bound to believe that she liked her life. She had never given him the faintest sign of discontent. Miss Stackpole had told him that she had lost her illusions, but writing for the papers had made Miss Stackpole sensational. She was too fond of early news. Moreover, since her arrival in Rome she had been much on her guard; she had pretty well ceased to flash her lantern at him. This indeed, it may be said for her, would have been quite against her conscience. She had now seen the reality of Isabel's situation, and it had inspired her with a just reserve. Whatever could be done to improve it the most useful form of assistance would not be to inflame her former lovers with a sense of her wrongs. Miss Stackpole continued to take a deep interest in the state of Mr Goodwood's feelings, but she showed it at present only by sending him choice extracts, humorous and other, from the American journals, of which she received several by every post and which she always perused with a pair of scissors in her hand. The articles she cut out she placed in an envelope addressed to Mr Goodwood, which she left with her own hand at his hotel. He never asked her a question about Isabel: hadn't he come five thousand miles to see for himself? He was thus not in the least authorised to think Mrs Osmond unhappy; but the very absence of authorisation operated as an irritant, ministered to the harshness with which, in spite of his theory that he had ceased to care, he now recognised that, so far as she was concerned, the future had nothing more for him. He had not even the satisfaction of knowing the truth; apparently he could not even be trusted to respect her if she *were* unhappy. He was hopeless, helpless, useless. To this last character she had called his attention by her ingenious plan for making him leave Rome. He had no objection whatever to doing what he could for her cousin, but it made him grind his teeth to think that of all the services she might have asked of him this was the one she had been eager to select. There had been no danger of her choosing one that would have kept him in Rome.

To-night what he was chiefly thinking of was that he was to leave her to-morrow and that he had gained nothing by coming but the knowledge that he was as little wanted as ever. About herself he had gained no knowledge; she was imperturbable, inscrutable, impenetrable. He felt the old bitterness, which he had tried so hard to swallow, rise again in his throat, and he knew there are disappointments that last as long as life. Osmond went on talking; Goodwood was vaguely aware that he was touching again upon his perfect intimacy with his wife. It seemed to him for a moment that the man had a kind of demonic imagination; it was impossible that without malice he should have selected so unusual a topic. But what did it matter, after all, whether he were demonic or not, and whether she loved him or hated him? She might hate him to the death without one's gaining a straw one's self. 'You travel, by the by, with Ralph Touchett,' Osmond said. 'I suppose that means you'll move slowly?'

'I don't know. I shall do just as he likes.'

'You're very accommodating. We're immensely obliged to you; you must really let me say it. My wife has probably expressed to you what we feel. Touchett has been on our minds all winter; it has looked more than once as if he would never leave Rome. He ought never to have come; it's worse than an imprudence for people in that state to travel; it's a kind of indelicacy. I wouldn't for the world be under such an obligation to Touchett as he has been to—to my wife and me. Other people inevitably have to look after him, and every one isn't so generous as you.'

'I've nothing else to do,' Caspar said dryly.

Osmond looked at him a moment askance. 'You ought to marry, and then you'd have plenty to do! It's true that in that case you wouldn't be quite so available for deeds of mercy.'

'Do you find that as a married man you're so much occupied?' the young man mechanically asked.

'Ah, you see, being married's in itself an occupation. It isn't always active; it's often passive; but that takes even more attention. Then my wife and I do so many things together. We read, we study, we make music, we walk, we drive—we talk even, as when we first knew each other. I delight, to this hour, in my wife's conversation. If you're ever bored take my advice and get married. Your wife indeed may bore you, in that case; but you'll never bore yourself. You'll always have something to say to yourself—always have a subject of reflection.'

'I'm not bored,' said Goodwood. 'I've plenty to think about and to say to myself.'

'More than to say to others!' Osmond exclaimed with a light laugh. 'Where shall you go next? I mean after you've consigned Touchett to his natural caretakers—I believe his mother's at last coming back to look after him. That little lady's superb; she neglects her duties with a finish—! Perhaps you'll spend the summer in England?'

'I don't know. I've no plans.'

'Happy man! That's a little bleak, but it's very free.'

'Oh yes, I'm very free.'

'Free to come back to Rome I hope,' said Osmond as he saw

a group of new visitors enter the room. 'Remember that when you do come we count on you!'

Goodwood had meant to go away early, but the evening elapsed without his having a chance to speak to Isabel otherwise than as one of several associated interlocutors. There was something perverse in the inveteracy with which she avoided him; his unquenchable rancour discovered an intention where there was certainly no appearance of one. There was absolutely no appearance of one. She met his eyes with her clear hospitable smile, which seemed almost to ask that he would come and help her to entertain some of her visitors. To such suggestions, however, he opposed but a stiff impatience. He wandered about and waited; he talked to the few people he knew, who found him for the first time rather self-contradictory. This was indeed rare with Caspar Goodwood, though he often contradicted others. There was often music at Palazzo Roccanera, and it was usually very good. Under cover of the music he managed to contain himself; but toward the end, when he saw the people beginning to go, he drew near to Isabel and asked her in a low tone if he might not speak to her in one of the other rooms, which he had just assured himself was empty. She smiled as if she wished to oblige him but found herself absolutely prevented. 'I'm afraid it's impossible. People are saying good-night, and I must be where they can see me.'

'I shall wait till they are all gone then.'

She hesitated a moment. 'Ah, that will be delightful!' she exclaimed.

And he waited, though it took a long time yet. There were several people, at the end, who seemed tethered to the carpet. The Countess Gemini, who was never herself till midnight, as she said, displayed no consciousness that the entertainment was over; she had still a little circle of gentlemen in front of the fire, who every now and then broke into a united laugh. Osmond had disappeared—he never bade good-bye to people; and as the Countess was extending her range, according to her custom at this period of the evening, Isabel had sent Pansy to bed. Isabel sat a little apart; she too appeared to wish her sister-in-law would sound a lower note and let the last loiterers depart in peace.

'May I not say a word to you now?' Goodwood presently asked her.

She got up immediately, smiling. 'Certainly, we'll go somewhere else if you like.' They went together, leaving the Countess with her little circle, and for a moment after they had crossed the threshold neither of them spoke. Isabel would not sit down; she stood in the middle of the room slowly fanning herself; she had for him the same familiar grace. She seemed to wait for him to speak. Now that he was alone with her all the passion he had never stifled surged into his senses; it hummed in his eyes and made things swim round him. The bright, empty room grew dim and blurred, and through the heaving veil he felt her hover before him with gleaming eyes and parted lips. If he had seen more distinctly he would have perceived her smile was fixed and a trifle forced—that she was frightened at what she saw in his own face. 'I suppose you wish to bid me good-bye?' she said.

'Yes—but I don't like it. I don't want to leave Rome,' he answered with almost plaintive honesty.

'I can well imagine. It's wonderfully good of you. I can't tell you how kind I think you.'

For a moment more he said nothing. 'With a few words like that you make me go.'

'You must come back some day,' she brightly returned.

'Some day? You mean as long a time hence as possible.'

'Oh no; I don't mean all that.'

'What *do* you mean? I don't understand! But I said I'd go, and I'll go,' Goodwood added.

'Come back whenever you like,' said Isabel with attempted lightness.

'I don't care a straw for your cousin!' Caspar broke out.

'Is that what you wished to tell me?'

'No, no; I didn't want to tell you anything; I wanted to ask you—' he paused a moment, and then—'what have you really made of your life?' he said, in a low, quick tone. He paused again, as if for an answer; but she said nothing, and he went on: 'I can't understand, I can't penetrate you! What am I to believe—what do you want me to think?' Still she said nothing; she only stood looking at him, now quite without pretending to ease. 'I'm told you're unhappy, and if you are I should like to know it. That would be something for me. But you yourself say you're happy, and you're somehow so still, so smooth, so hard. You're completely changed. You conceal everything; I haven't really come near you.'

'You come very near,' Isabel said gently, but in a tone of warning.

'And yet I don't touch you! I want to know the truth. Have you done well?'

'You ask a great deal.'

'Yes—I've always asked a great deal. Of course you won't tell me. I shall never know if you can help it. And then it's none of my business.' He had spoken with a visible effort to control himself, to give a considerate form to an inconsiderate state of mind. But the sense that it was his last chance, that he loved her and had lost her, that she would think him a fool whatever he should say, suddenly gave him a lash and added a deep vibration to his low voice. 'You're perfectly inscrutable, and that's what makes me think you've something to hide. I tell you I don't care a straw for your cousin, but I don't mean that I don't like him. I mean that it isn't because I like him that I go away with him. I'd go if he were an idiot and you should have asked me. If you should ask me I'd go to Siberia to-morrow. Why do you want me to leave the place? You must have some reason for that; if you were as contented as you pretend you are you wouldn't care. I'd rather know the truth about you, even if it's damnable, than have come here for nothing. That isn't what I came for. I thought I shouldn't care. I came because I wanted to assure myself that I needn't think of you any more. I haven't thought of anything else, and you're quite right to wish me to go away. But if I must go, there's no harm in my letting myself out for a single moment, is there? If you're really hurt—if *he* hurts you—nothing *I* say will hurt you. When I tell you I love you it's simply what I came for. I thought it was for something else; but it was for that. I shouldn't say it if I didn't believe I should never see you again. It's the last time—let me pluck a single flower! I've no right to say that, I know; and you've no right to listen. But you don't listen; you never listen, you're always thinking of something else. After this I must go, of course; so I shall at least have a reason. Your asking me is no reason, not a real one. I can't judge by your husband,' he went on irrelevantly, almost incoherently; 'I don't understand him; he tells me you adore each other. Why does he tell me that? What business is it of mine? When I say that to you, you look strange. But you always look strange. Yes, you've something to hide. It's none of my business—very true. But I love you,' said Caspar Goodwood.

As he said, she looked strange. She turned her eyes to the door by which they had entered and raised her fan as if in warning. 'You've behaved so well; don't spoil it,' she uttered softly.

'No one hears me. It's wonderful what you tried to put me off with. I love you as I've never loved you.'

'I know it. I knew it as soon as you consented to go.'

'You can't help it—of course not. You would if you could, but you can't, unfortunately. Unfortunately for me, I mean. I ask nothing—nothing, that is, I shouldn't. But I do ask one sole satisfaction:—that you tell me—that you tell me—!'

'That I tell you what?'

'Whether I may pity you.'

'Should you like that?' Isabel asked, trying to smile again.

'To pity you? Most assuredly! That at least would be doing something. I'd give my life to it.'

She raised her fan to her face, which it covered all except her eyes. They rested a moment on his. 'Don't give your life to it; but give a thought to it every now and then.' And with that she went back to the Countess Gemini.

XLIX

MADAME MERLE had not made her appearance at Palazzo Roccanera on the evening of that Thursday of which I have narrated some of the incidents, and Isabel, though she observed her absence, was not surprised by it. Things had passed between them which added no stimulus to sociability, and to appreciate which we must glance a little backward. It has been mentioned that Madame Merle returned from Naples shortly after Lord Warburton had left Rome, and that on her first meeting with Isabel (whom, to do her justice, she came immediately to see) her first utterance had been an enquiry as to the whereabouts of this nobleman, for whom she appeared to hold her dear friend accountable.

'Please don't talk of him,' said Isabel for answer; 'we've heard so much of him of late.'

Madame Merle bent her head on one side a little, protestingly, and smiled at the left corner of her mouth. 'You've heard, yes. But you must remember that I've not, in Naples. I hoped to find him here and to be able to congratulate Pansy.'

'You may congratulate Pansy still; but not on marrying Lord Warburton.'

'How you say that! Don't you know I had set my heart on it?' Madame Merle asked with a great deal of spirit, but still with the intonation of good-humour.

Isabel was discomposed, but she was determined to be good-humoured too. 'You shouldn't have gone to Naples then. You should have stayed here to watch the affair.'

'I had too much confidence in you. But do you think it's too late?'

'You had better ask Pansy,' said Isabel.

'I shall ask her what you've said to her.'

These words seemed to justify the impulse of self-defence aroused on Isabel's part by her perceiving that her visitor's attitude was a critical one. Madame Merle, as we know, had been very discreet hitherto; she had never criticised; she had been markedly afraid of intermeddling. But apparently she had only reserved herself for this occasion, since she now had a dangerous quickness in her eye and an air of irritation which even her admirable ease was not able to transmute. She had suffered a disappointment which excited Isabel's surprise—our heroine having no knowledge of her zealous interest in Pansy's marriage; and she betrayed it in a manner which quickened Mrs Osmond's alarm. More clearly than ever before Isabel heard a cold, mocking voice proceed from she knew not where, in the dim void that surrounded her, and declare that this bright, strong, definite, worldly woman, this incarnation of the practical, the personal, the immediate, was a powerful agent in her destiny. She was nearer to her than Isabel had yet discovered, and her nearness was not the charming accident she had so long supposed. The sense of accident indeed had died within her that day when she happened to be struck with the manner in which the wonderful lady and her own husband sat together in private. No definite suspicion had as yet taken its place; but it was enough to make her view this friend with a different eye, to have been led to reflect that there was more intention in her past behaviour than she had allowed for at the time. Ah yes, there had been intention, there had been intention, Isabel said to herself; and she seemed to wake from a long pernicious dream. What was it that brought home to her that Madame Merle's intention had not been good? Nothing but the mistrust which had lately taken body and which married itself now to the fruitful wonder produced by her visitor's challenge on behalf of poor Pansy. There was something in this challenge which had at the very outset excited an answering defiance; a nameless vitality which she could see to have been absent from her friend's professions of delicacy and caution. Madame Merle had been unwilling to interfere, certainly, but only so long as there was nothing to interfere with. It will perhaps seem to the reader that Isabel went fast in casting doubt, on mere suspicion, on a sincerity proved by several years of good offices. She moved quickly indeed, and with reason, for a strange truth was filtering into her soul. Madame Merle's interest was identical with Osmond's: that was enough. 'I think Pansy will tell you nothing that will make you more angry,' she said in answer to her companion's last remark.

'I'm not in the least angry. I've only a great desire to retrieve the situation. Do you consider that Warburton has left us for ever?'

'I can't tell you; I don't understand you. It's all over; please let it rest. Osmond has talked to me a great deal about it, and I've nothing more to say or to hear. I've no doubt,' Isabel added, 'that he'll be very happy to discuss the subject with you.'

'I know what he thinks; he came to see me last evening.'

'As soon as you had arrived? Then you know all about it and you needn't apply to me for information.'

'It isn't information I want. At bottom it's sympathy. I had set my heart on that marriage; the idea did what so few things do—it satisfied the imagination.'

'Your imagination, yes. But not that of the persons concerned.'

'You mean by that of course that I'm not concerned. Of course not directly. But when one's such an old friend one can't help having something at stake. You forget how long I've known Pansy. You mean, of course,' Madame Merle added, 'that *you* are one of the persons concerned.'

'No; that's the last thing I mean. I'm very weary of it all.'

Madame Merle hesitated a little. 'Ah yes, your work's done.'

'Take care what you say,' said Isabel very gravely.

'Oh, I take care; never perhaps more than when it appears least. Your husband judges you severely.'

Isabel made for a moment no answer to this; she felt choked with bitterness. It was not the insolence of Madame Merle's informing her that Osmond had been taking her into his confidence as against his wife that struck her most; for she was not quick to believe that this was meant for insolence. Madame Merle was very rarely insolent, and only when it was exactly right. It was not right now, or at least it was not right yet. What touched Isabel like a drop of corrosive acid upon an open wound was the knowledge that Osmond dishonoured her in his words as well as in his thoughts. 'Should you like to know how I judge *him*?' she asked at last.

'No, because you'd never tell me. And it would be painful for me to know.'

There was a pause, and for the first time since she had known her Isabel thought Madame Merle disagreeable. She wished she would leave her. 'Remember how attractive Pansy is, and don't despair,' she said abruptly, with a desire that this should close their interview.

But Madame Merle's expansive presence underwent no contraction. She only gathered her mantle about her and, with the movement, scattered upon the air a faint, agreeable fragrance. 'I don't despair; I feel encouraged. And I didn't come to scold you; I came if possible to learn the truth. I know you'll tell it if I ask you. It's an immense blessing with you that one can count upon that. No, you won't believe what a comfort I take in it.'

'What truth do you speak of?' Isabel asked, wondering.

'Just this: whether Lord Warburton changed his mind quite of his own movement or because you recommended it. To please himself I mean, or to please you. Think of the confidence I must still have in you, in spite of having lost a little of it,' Madame Merle continued with a smile, 'to ask such a question as that!' She sat looking at her friend, to judge the effect of her words, and then went on: 'Now don't be heroic, don't be unreasonable, don't take offence. It seems to me I do you an honour in speaking so. I don't know another woman to whom I would do it. I haven't the least idea that any other woman would tell me the truth. And don't you see how well it is that your husband should know it? It's true that he doesn't appear to have had any tact whatever in trying to extract it; he has indulged in gratuitous suppositions. But that doesn't alter the fact that it would make a difference in his view of his daughter's prospects to know distinctly what really occurred. If Lord Warburton simply got tired of the poor child, that's one thing, and it's a pity. If he gave her up to please you it's another. That's a pity too, but in a different way. Then, in the latter case, you'd perhaps resign yourself to not being pleased—to simply seeing your step-daughter married. Let him off—let us have him!'

Madame Merle had proceeded very deliberately, watching her companion and apparently thinking she could proceed safely. As she went on Isabel grew pale; she clasped her hands more tightly in her lap. It was not that her visitor had at last thought it the right time to be insolent; for this was not what was most apparent. It was a worse horror than that. 'Who are you—what are you?' Isabel murmured. 'What have you to do with my husband?' It was strange that for the moment she drew as near to him as if she had loved him.

'Ah then, you take it heroically! I'm very sorry. Don't think, however, that I shall do so.'

'What have you to do with me?' Isabel went on.

Madame Merle slowly got up, stroking her muff, but not removing her eyes from Isabel's face. 'Everything!' she answered.

Isabel sat there looking up at her, without rising; her face was almost a prayer to be enlightened. But the light of this woman's eyes seemed only a darkness. 'Oh misery!' she murmured at last; and she fell back, covering her face with her hands. It had come over her like a high-surging wave that Mrs Touchett was right. Madame Merle had married her. Before she uncovered her face again that lady had left the room.

Isabel took a drive alone that afternoon; she wished to be far away, under the sky, where she could descend from her carriage and tread upon the daisies. She had long before this taken old Rome into her confidence, for in a world of ruins the ruin of her happiness seemed a less unnatural catastrophe. She rested her weariness upon things that had crumbled for centuries and yet still were upright; she dropped her secret sadness into the silence of lonely places, where its very modern quality detached itself and grew objective, so that as she sat in a sun-warmed angle on a winter's day, or stood in a mouldy church to which no one came, she could almost smile at it and think of its smallness. Small it was, in the large Roman record, and her haunting sense of the continuity of the human lot easily carried her from the less to the greater. She had become deeply, tenderly acquainted with Rome; it interfused and moderated her passion. But she had grown to think of it chiefly as the place where people had suffered. This was what came to her in the starved churches, where the marble columns, transferred from pagan ruins, seemed to offer her a companionship in endurance and the musty incense to be a compound of long-unanswered prayers. There was no gentler nor less consistent heretic than Isabel; the firmest of worshippers, gazing at dark altar-pictures or clustered candles, could not have felt more intimately the suggestiveness of these objects nor have been more liable at such moments to a spiritual visitation. Pansy, as we know, was almost always her companion, and of late the Countess Gemini, balancing a pink parasol, had lent brilliancy to their equipage; but she still occasionally found herself alone when it suited her mood and where it suited the place. On such occasions she had several resorts; the most accessible of which perhaps was a seat on the low parapet which edges the wide grassy space before the high, cold front of Saint John Lateran, whence you look across the Campagna at the far-trailing outline of the Alban Mount and at that mighty plain, between, which is still so full of all that has passed from it. After the departure of her cousin and his companions she roamed more than usual; she carried her sombre spirit from one familiar shrine to the other. Even when Pansy and the Countess were with her she felt the touch of a vanished world. The carriage, leaving the walls of Rome behind, rolled through narrow lanes where the wild honeysuckle had begun to tangle itself in the hedges, or waited for her in quiet places where the fields lay near, while she strolled further and further over the flower-freckled turf, or sat on a stone that had once had a use and gazed through the veil of her personal sadness at the splendid sadness of the scene—at the dense, warm light, the far gradations and soft confusions of colour, the motionless shepherds in lonely attitudes, the hills where the cloud-shadows had the lightness of a blush.

On the afternoon I began with speaking of, she had taken a resolution not to think of Madame Merle; but the resolution proved vain, and this lady's image hovered constantly before her. She asked herself, with an almost childlike horror of the supposition, whether to this intimate friend of several years the great historical epithet of *wicked* were to be applied. She knew the idea only by the Bible and other literary works; to the best of her belief she had had no personal acquaintance with wickedness. She had desired a large acquaintance with human life, and in spite of her having flattered herself that she cultivated it with some success this elementary privilege had been denied her. Perhaps it was not wicked—in the historic sense—to be even deeply false; for that was what Madame Merle had been—deeply, deeply, deeply. Isabel's Aunt Lydia had made this discovery long before, and had mentioned it to her niece; but Isabel had flattered herself at this time that she had a much richer view of things, especially of the spontaneity of her own career and the nobleness of her own interpretations, than poor stiffly-reasoning Mrs Touchett. Madame Merle had done what she wanted; she had brought about the union of her two friends; a reflection which could not fail to make it a matter of wonder that she should so much have desired such an event. There were people who had the match-making passion, like the votaries of art for art; but Madame Merle, great artist as she was, was scarcely one of these. She thought too ill of marriage, too ill even of life; she had desired that particular marriage but had not desired others. She had therefore had a conception of gain, and Isabel asked herself where she had found her profit. It took her naturally a long time to discover, and even then her discovery was imperfect. It came back to her that Madame Merle, though she had seemed to like her from their first meeting at Gardencourt, had been doubly affectionate after Mr Touchett's death and after learning that her young friend had been subject to the good old man's charity. She had found her profit not in the gross device of borrowing money, but in the more refined idea of introducing one of her intimates to the young woman's fresh and ingenuous fortune. She had naturally chosen her closest intimate, and it was already vivid enough to Isabel that Gilbert occupied this position. She found herself confronted in this manner with the conviction that the man in the world whom she had supposed to be the least sordid had married her, like a vulgar adventurer, for her money. Strange to say, it had never before occurred to her; if she had thought a good deal of harm of Osmond she had not done him this particular injury. This was the worst she could think of, and she had been saying to herself that the worst was still to come. A man might marry a woman for her money perfectly well; the thing was often done. But at least he should let her know. She wondered whether, since he had wanted her money, her money would now satisfy him. Would he take her money and let her go? Ah, if Mr Touchett's great charity would but help her to-day it would be blessed indeed! It was not slow to occur to her that if Madame Merle had wished to do Gilbert a service his recognition to her of the boon must have lost its warmth. What must be his feelings to-day in regard to his too zealous benefactress, and what expression must they have found on the part of such a master of irony? It is a singular, but a characteristic, fact that before Isabel returned from her silent drive she had broken its silence by the soft exclamation: 'Poor, poor Madame Merle!'

Her compassion would perhaps have been justified if on this same afternoon she had been concealed behind one of the valuable curtains of time-softened damask which dressed the interesting little *salon* of the lady to whom it referred; the carefully-arranged apartment to which we once paid a visit in company with the discreet Mr Rosier. In that apartment, towards six o'clock, Gilbert Osmond was seated, and his hostess stood before him as Isabel had seen her stand on an occasion commemorated in this history with an emphasis appropriate not so much to its apparent as to its real importance.

'I don't believe you're unhappy; I believe you like it,' said Madame Merle.

'Did I say I was unhappy?' Osmond asked with a face grave enough to suggest that he might have been.

'No, but you don't say the contrary, as you ought in common gratitude.'

'Don't talk about gratitude,' he returned dryly. 'And don't aggravate me,' he added in a moment.

Madame Merle slowly seated herself, with her arms folded and her white hands arranged as a support to one of them and an ornament, as it were, to the other. She looked exquisitely calm but impressively sad. 'On your side, don't try to frighten me. I wonder if you guess some of my thoughts.'

'I trouble about them no more than I can help. I've quite enough of my own.'

'That's because they're so delightful.'

Osmond rested his head against the back of his chair and looked at his companion with a cynical directness which seemed also partly an expression of fatigue. 'You do aggravate me,' he remarked in a moment. 'I'm very tired.'

'*Eh moi donc!*'* cried Madame Merle.

'With you it's because you fatigue yourself. With me it's not my own fault.'

'When I fatigue myself it's for you. I've given you an interest. That's a great gift.'

'Do you call it an interest?' Osmond enquired with detachment.

'Certainly, since it helps you to pass your time.'

'The time has never seemed longer to me than this winter.'

'You've never looked better; you've never been so agreeable, so brilliant.'

'Damn my brilliancy!' he thoughtfully murmured. 'How little, after all, you know me!'

'If I don't know you I know nothing,' smiled Madame Merle. 'You've the feeling of complete success.'

'No, I shall not have that till I've made you stop judging me.'

'I did that long ago. I speak from old knowledge. But you express yourself more too.'

Osmond just hung fire. 'I wish you'd express yourself less!'

'You wish to condemn me to silence? Remember that I've never been a chatterbox. At any rate there are three or four things I should like to say to you first. Your wife doesn't know what to do with herself,' she went on with a change of tone.

'Pardon me; she knows perfectly. She has a line sharply drawn. She means to carry out her ideas.'

'Her ideas to-day must be remarkable.'

'Certainly they are. She has more of them than ever.'

'She was unable to show me any this morning,' said Madame Merle. 'She seemed in a very simple, almost in a stupid, state of mind. She was completely bewildered.'

'You had better say at once that she was pathetic.'

'Ah no, I don't want to encourage you too much.'

He still had his head against the cushion behind him; the ankle of one foot rested on the other knee. So he sat for a while. 'I should like to know what's the matter with you,' he said at last.

'The matter—the matter—!' And here Madame Merle stopped. Then she went on with a sudden outbreak of passion, a burst of summer thunder in a clear sky: 'The matter is that I would give my right hand to be able to weep, and that I can't!'

'What good would it do you to weep?'

'It would make me feel as I felt before I knew you.'

'If I've dried your tears, that's something. But I've seen you shed them.'

'Oh, I believe you'll make me cry still. I mean make me howl like a wolf. I've a great hope, I've a great need, of that. I was vile this morning; I was horrid,' she said.

'If Isabel was in the stupid state of mind you mention she probably didn't perceive it,' Osmond answered.

'It was precisely my deviltry that stupefied her. I couldn't help it; I was full of something bad. Perhaps it was something good; I don't know. You've not only dried up my tears; you've dried up my soul.'

'It's not I then that am responsible for my wife's condition,' Osmond said. 'It's pleasant to think that I shall get the benefit of your influence upon her. Don't you know the soul is an immortal principle? How can it suffer alteration?'

'I don't believe at all that it's an immortal principle. I believe it can perfectly be destroyed. That's what has happened to mine, which was a very good one to start with; and it's you I have to thank for it. You're *very* bad,' she added with gravity in her emphasis.

'Is this the way we're to end?' Osmond asked with the same studied coldness.

'I don't know how we're to end. I wish I did! How do bad people end?—especially as to their *common* crimes. You have made me as bad as yourself.'

'I don't understand you. You seem to me quite good enough,' said Osmond, his conscious indifference giving an extreme effect to the words.

Madame Merle's self-possession tended on the contrary to diminish, and she was nearer losing it than on any occasion on which we have had the pleasure of meeting her. The glow of her eye turned sombre; her smile betrayed a painful effort. 'Good enough for anything that I've done with myself? I suppose that's what you mean.'

'Good enough to be always charming!' Osmond exclaimed, smiling too.

'Oh God!' his companion murmured; and, sitting there in her ripe freshness, she had recourse to the same gesture she had provoked on Isabel's part in the morning: she bent her face and covered it with her hands.

'Are you going to weep after all?' Osmond asked; and on her remaining motionless he went on: 'Have I ever complained to you?'

She dropped her hands quickly. 'No, you've taken your revenge otherwise—you have taken it on *her*.'

Osmond threw back his head further; he looked a while at the ceiling and might have been supposed to be appealing, in an informal way, to the heavenly powers. 'Oh, the imagination of women! It's always vulgar, at bottom. You talk of revenge like a third-rate novelist.'

'Of course you haven't complained. You've enjoyed your triumph too much.'

'I'm rather curious to know what you call my triumph.'

'You've made your wife afraid of you.'

Osmond changed his position; he leaned forward, resting his elbows on his knees and looking a while at a beautiful old Persian rug, at his feet. He had an air of refusing to accept any one's valuation of anything, even of time, and of preferring to abide by his own; a peculiarity which made him at moments an irritating person to converse with. 'Isabel's not afraid of me, and it's not what I wish,' he said at last. 'To what do you want to provoke me when you say such things as that?'

'I've thought over all the harm you can do me,' Madame Merle answered. 'Your wife was afraid of me this morning, but in me it was really you she feared.'

'You may have said things that were in very bad taste; I'm not responsible for that. I didn't see the use of your going to see her at all: you're capable of acting without her. I've not made *you* afraid of me that I can see,' he went on; 'how then should I have made her? You're at least as brave. I can't think where you've picked up such rubbish; one might suppose you knew me by this time.' He got up as he spoke and walked to the chimney, where he stood a moment bending his eye, as if he had seen them for the first time, on the delicate specimens of rare porcelain with which it was covered. He took up a small cup and held it in his hand; then, still holding it and leaning his arm on the mantel, he pursued: 'You always see too much in everything; you overdo it; you lose sight of the real. I'm much simpler than you think.'

'I think you're very simple.' And Madame Merle kept her eye on her cup. 'I've come to that with time. I judged you, as I say, of old; but it's only since your marriage that I've understood you. I've seen better what you have been to your wife than I ever saw what you were for me. Please be very careful of that precious object.'

'It already has a wee bit of a tiny crack,' said Osmond dryly as he put it down. 'If you didn't understand me before I married it was cruelly rash of you to put me into such a box. However, I took a fancy to my box myself; I thought it would be a comfortable fit. I asked very little; I only asked that she should like me.'

'That she should like you so much!'

'So much, of course; in such a case one asks the maximum. That she should adore me, if you will. Oh yes, I wanted that.'

'I never adored you,' said Madame Merle.

'Ah, but you pretended to!'

'It's true that you never accused me of being a comfortable fit,' Madame Merle went on.

'My wife has declined—declined to do anything of the sort,' said Osmond. 'If you're determined to make a tragedy of that, the tragedy's hardly for her.'

'The tragedy's for me!' Madame Merle exclaimed, rising with a long low sigh but having a glance at the same time for the contents of her mantel-shelf. 'It appears that I'm to be severely taught the disadvantages of a false position.'

'You express yourself like a sentence in a copy-book. We must look for our comfort where we can find it. If my wife doesn't like me, at least my child does. I shall look for compensations in Pansy. Fortunately I haven't a fault to find with her.'

'Ah,' she said softly, 'if I had a child—!'

Osmond waited, and then, with a little formal air, 'The children of others may be a great interest!' he announced.

'You're more like a copy-book than I. There's something after all that holds us together.'

'Is it the idea of the harm I may do you?' Osmond asked.

'No; it's the idea of the good I may do for you. It's that,' Madame Merle pursued, 'that made me so jealous of Isabel. I want it to be *my* work,' she added, with her face, which had grown hard and bitter, relaxing to its habit of smoothness.

Her friend took up his hat and his umbrella, and after giving the former article two or three strokes with his coat-cuff, 'On the whole, I think,' he said, 'you had better leave it to me.'

After he had left her she went, the first thing, and lifted from the mantel-shelf the attenuated coffee-cup in which he had mentioned the existence of a crack; but she looked at it rather abstractedly. 'Have I been so vile all for nothing?' she vaguely wailed.

L

As the Countess Gemini was not acquainted with the ancient monuments Isabel occasionally offered to introduce her to these interesting relics and to give their afternoon drive an antiquarian aim. The Countess, who professed to think her sister-in-law a prodigy of learning, never made an objection, and gazed at masses of Roman brickwork as patiently as if they had been mounds of modern drapery. She had not the historic sense, though she had in some directions the anecdotic, and as regards herself the apologetic, but she was so delighted to be in Rome that she only desired to float with the current. She would gladly have passed an hour every day in the damp darkness of the Baths of Titus if it had been a condition of her remaining at Palazzo Roccanera. Isabel, however, was not a severe cicerone; she used to visit the ruins chiefly because they offered an excuse for talking about other matters than the love-affairs of the ladies of Florence, as to which her companion was never weary of offering information. It must be added that during these visits the Countess forbade herself every form of active research; her preference was to sit in the carriage and exclaim that everything was most interesting. It was in this manner that she had hitherto examined the Coliseum, to the infinite regret of her niece, who—with all the respect that she owed her—could not see why she should not descend from the vehicle and enter the building. Pansy had so little chance to ramble that her view of the case was not wholly disinterested; it may be divined that she had a secret hope that, once inside, her parents' guest might be induced to climb to the upper tiers. There came a day when the Countess announced her willingness to undertake this feat—a mild afternoon in March when the windy month expressed itself in occasional puffs of spring. The three ladies went into the Coliseum together, but Isabel left her companions to wander over the place. She had often ascended to those desolate ledges from which the Roman crowd used to bellow applause and where now the wild flowers (when they are allowed) bloom in the deep crevices; and to-day she felt weary and disposed to sit in the despoiled arena. It made an intermission too, for the Countess often asked more from one's attention than she gave in return; and Isabel believed that when she was alone with her niece she let the dust gather for a moment on the ancient scandals of the Arnide. She so remained below therefore, while Pansy guided her undiscriminating aunt to the steep brick staircase at the foot of which the custodian unlocks the tall wooden gate. The great enclosure was half in shadow; the western sun brought out the pale red tone of the great blocks of travertine—the latent colour that is the only living element in the immense ruin. Here and there wandered a peasant or a tourist, looking up at the far skyline where, in the clear stillness, a multitude of swallows kept circling and plunging. Isabel presently became aware that one of the other visitors, planted in the middle of the arena, had turned his attention to her own person and was looking at her with a certain little poise of the head which she had some weeks before perceived to be characteristic of baffled but indestructible purpose. Such an attitude, to-day, could belong only to Mr Edward Rosier; and this gentleman proved in fact to have been considering the question of speaking to her. When he had assured himself that she was unaccompanied he drew near, remarking that though she would not answer his letters she would perhaps not wholly close her ears to his spoken eloquence. She replied that her stepdaughter was close at hand and that she could only give him five minutes; whereupon he took out his watch and sat down upon a broken block.

'It's very soon told,' said Edward Rosier. 'I've sold all my bibelots!' Isabel gave instinctively an exclamation of horror; it was as if he had told her he had had all his teeth drawn. 'I've sold them by auction at the Hôtel Drouot,' he went on. 'The sale took place three days ago, and they've telegraphed me the result. It's magnificent.'

'I'm glad to hear it; but I wish you had kept your pretty things.'

'I have the money instead—fifty thousand dollars. Will Mr Osmond think me rich enough now?'

'Is it for that you did it?' Isabel asked gently.

'For what else in the world could it be? That's the only thing

I think of. I went to Paris and made my arrangements. I couldn't stop for the sale; I couldn't have seen them going off; I think it would have killed me. But I put them into good hands, and they brought high prices. I should tell you I have kept my enamels. Now I have the money in my pocket, and he can't say I'm poor!' the young man exclaimed defiantly.

'He'll say now that you're not wise,' said Isabel, as if Gilbert Osmond had never said this before.

Rosier gave her a sharp look. 'Do you mean that without my bibelots I'm nothing? Do you mean they were the best thing about me? That's what they told me in Paris; oh they were very frank about it. But they hadn't seen *her!*'

'My dear friend, you deserve to succeed,' said Isabel very kindly.

'You say that so sadly that it's the same as if you said I shouldn't.' And he questioned her eyes with the clear trepidation of his own. He had the air of a man who knows he has been the talk of Paris for a week and is full half a head taller in consequence, but who also has a painful suspicion that in spite of this increase of stature one or two persons still have the perversity to think him diminutive. 'I know what happened here while I was away,' he went on. 'What does Mr Osmond expect after she has refused Lord Warburton?'

Isabel debated. 'That she'll marry another nobleman.'

'What other nobleman?'

'One that he'll pick out.'

Rosier slowly got up, putting his watch into his waistcoat-pocket. 'You're laughing at some one, but this time I don't think it's at me.'

'I didn't mean to laugh,' said Isabel. 'I laugh very seldom. Now you had better go away.'

'I feel very safe!' Rosier declared without moving. This might be; but it evidently made him feel more so to make the announcement in rather a loud voice, balancing himself a little complacently on his toes and looking all round the Coliseum as if it were filled with an audience. Suddenly Isabel saw him change colour; there was more of an audience than he had suspected. She turned and perceived that her two companions had returned from their excursion. 'You must really go away,' she said quickly.

'Ah, my dear lady, pity me!' Edward Rosier murmured in a voice strangely at variance with the announcement I have just quoted. And then he added eagerly, like a man who in the midst of his misery is seized by a happy thought: 'Is that lady the Countess Gemini? I've a great desire to be presented to her.'

Isabel looked at him a moment. 'She has no influence with her brother.'

'Ah, what a monster you make him out!' And Rosier faced the Countess, who advanced, in front of Pansy, with an animation partly due perhaps to the fact that she perceived her sister-in-law to be engaged in conversation with a very pretty young man.

'I'm glad you've kept your enamels!' Isabel called as she left him. She went straight to Pansy, who, on seeing Edward Rosier, had stopped short, with lowered eyes. 'We'll go back to the carriage,' she said gently.

'Yes, it's getting late,' Pansy returned more gently still. And she went on without a murmur, without faltering or glancing back.

Isabel, however, allowing herself this last liberty, saw that a meeting had immediately taken place between the Countess and Mr Rosier. He had removed his hat and was bowing and smiling; he had evidently introduced himself, while the Countess's expressive back displayed to Isabel's eye a gracious inclination. These facts, none the less, were presently lost to sight, for Isabel and Pansy took their places again in the carriage. Pansy, who faced her stepmother, at first kept her eyes fixed on her lap; then she raised them and rested them on Isabel's. There shone out of each of them a little melancholy ray—a spark of timid passion which touched Isabel to the heart. At the same time a wave of envy passed over her soul, as she compared the tremulous longing, the definite ideal of the child with her own dry despair. 'Poor little Pansy!' she affectionately said.

'Oh never mind!' Pansy answered in the tone of eager apology.

And then there was a silence; the Countess was a long time coming. 'Did you show your aunt everything, and did she enjoy it?' Isabel asked at last.

'Yes, I showed her everything. I think she was very much pleased.'

'And you're not tired, I hope.'

'Oh no, thank you, I'm not tired.'

The Countess still remained behind, so that Isabel requested the footman to go into the Coliseum and tell her they were waiting. He presently returned with the announcement that the Signora Contessa begged them not to wait—she would come home in a cab!

About a week after this lady's quick sympathies had enlisted themselves with Mr Rosier, Isabel, going rather late to dress for dinner, found Pansy sitting in her room. The girl seemed to have been awaiting her; she got up from her low chair. 'Pardon my taking the liberty,' she said in a small voice. 'It will be the last—for some time.'

Her voice was strange, and her eyes, widely opened, had an excited, frightened look. 'You're not going away!' Isabel exclaimed.

'I'm going to the convent.'

'To the convent?'

Pansy drew nearer, till she was near enough to put her arms round Isabel and rest her head on her shoulder. She stood this way a moment, perfectly still; but her companion could feel her tremble. The quiver of her little body expressed everything she was unable to say. Isabel nevertheless pressed her. 'Why are you going to the convent?'

'Because papa thinks it best. He says a young girl's better, every now and then, for making a little retreat. He says the world, always the world, is very bad for a young girl. This is just a chance for a little seclusion—a little reflexion.' Pansy spoke in short detached sentences, as if she could scarce trust herself; and then she added with a triumph of self-control: 'I think papa's right; I've been so much in the world this winter.'

Her annoucement had a strange effect on Isabel; it seemed to carry a larger meaning than the girl herself knew. 'When was this decided?' she asked. 'I've heard nothing of it.'

'Papa told me half an hour ago; he thought it better it shouldn't be too much talked about in advance. Madame Catherine's to come for me at a quarter past seven, and I'm only to take two frocks. It's only for a few weeks; I'm sure it will be very good. I shall find all those ladies who used to be so kind to me, and I shall see the little girls who are being educated. I'm very fond of little girls,' said Pansy with an effect of diminutive grandeur. 'And I'm also very fond of Mother Catherine. I shall be very quiet and think a great deal.'

Isabel listened to her, holding her breath; she was almost awe-struck. 'Think of *me* sometimes.'

'Ah, come and see me soon!' cried Pansy; and the cry was very different from the heroic remarks of which she had just delivered herself.

Isabel could say nothing more; she understood nothing; she only felt how little she yet knew her husband. Her answer to his daughter was a long, tender kiss.

Half an hour later she learned from her maid that Madame Catherine had arrived in a cab and had departed again with the signorina. On going to the drawing-room before dinner she found the Countess Gemini alone, and this lady characterised the incident by exclaiming, with a wonderful toss of the head, '*En voilà, ma chère, une pose!*'* But if it was an affectation she was at a loss to see what her husband affected. She could only dimly perceive that he had more traditions than she supposed. It had become her habit to be so careful as to what she said to him that, strange as it may appear, she hesitated, for several minutes after he had come in, to allude to his daughter's sudden departure: she spoke of it only after they were seated at table. But she had forbidden herself ever to ask Osmond a question. All she could do was to make a declaration, and there was one that came very naturally. 'I shall miss Pansy very much.'

He looked a while, with his head inclined a little, at the basket of flowers in the middle of the table. 'Ah yes,' he said at last, 'I had thought of that. You must go and see her, you know; but not too often. I dare say you wonder why I sent her to the good sisters; but I doubt if I can make you understand. It doesn't matter; don't trouble yourself about it. That's why I had not spoken of it. I didn't believe you would enter into it. But I've always had the idea; I've always thought it a part of the education of one's daughter. One's daughter should be fresh and fair; she should be innocent and gentle. With the manners of the present time she is liable to become so dusty and crumpled. Pansy's a little dusty, a little dishevelled; she has knocked about too much. This bustling, pushing rabble that calls itself society—one should take her out of it occasionally. Convents are very quiet, very convenient, very salutary. I like to think of her there, in the old garden, under the arcade, among those tranquil virtuous women. Many of them are gentlewomen born; several of them are noble. She will have her books and her drawing, she will have her piano. I've made the most liberal arrangements. There is to be nothing ascetic; there's just to be a certain little sense of sequestration. She'll have time to think, and there's something I want her to think about.' Osmond spoke deliberately, reasonably, still with his head on one side, as if he were looking at the basket of flowers. His tone, however, was that of a man not so much offering an explanation as putting a thing into words—almost into pictures—to see, himself, how it would look. He considered a while the picture he had evoked and seemed greatly pleased with it. And then he went on: 'The Catholics are very wise after all. The convent is a great institution; we can't do without it; it corresponds to an essential need in families, in society. It's a school of good manners; it's a school of repose. Oh, I don't want to detach my daughter from the world,' he added; 'I don't want to make her fix her thoughts on any other. This one's very well, as *she* should take it, and she may think of it as much as she likes. Only she must think of it in the right way.'

Isabel gave an extreme attention to this little sketch; she found it indeed intensely interesting. It seemed to show her how far her husband's desire to be effective was capable of going—to the point of playing theoretic tricks on the delicate organism of his daughter. She could not understand his purpose, no—not wholly; but she understood it better than he supposed or desired, inasmuch as she was convinced that the whole proceeding was an elaborate mystification, addressed to herself and destined to act upon her imagination. He had wanted to do something sudden and arbitrary, something unexpected and refined; to mark the difference between his sympathies and her own, and show that if he regarded his daughter as a precious work of art it was natural he should be more and more careful about the finishing touches. If he wished to be effective he had succeeded; the incident struck a chill into Isabel's heart. Pansy had known the convent in her childhood and had found a happy home there; she was fond of the good sisters, who were very fond of her, and there was therefore for the moment no definite hardship in her lot. But all the same the girl had taken fright; the impression her father desired to make would evidently be sharp enough. The old Protestant tradition had never faded from Isabel's imagination, and as her thoughts attached themselves to this striking example of her husband's genius—she sat looking, like him, at the basket of flowers—poor little Pansy became the heroine of a tragedy. Osmond wished it to be known that he shrank from nothing, and his wife found it hard to pretend to eat her dinner. There was a certain relief presently, in hearing the high, strained voice of her sister-in-law. The Countess too, apparently, had been thinking the thing out, but had arrived at a different conclusion from Isabel.

'It's very absurd, my dear Osmond,' she said, 'to invent so many pretty reasons for poor Pansy's banishment. Why don't you say at once that you want to get her out of my way? Haven't you discovered that I think very well of Mr Rosier? I do indeed; he seems to me *simpaticissimo.** He has made me believe in true love; I never did before! Of course you've made up your mind that with those convictions I'm dreadful company for Pansy.'

Osmond took a sip of a glass of wine; he looked perfectly good-humoured. 'My dear Amy,' he answered, smiling as if he were uttering a piece of gallantry, 'I don't know anything about your convictions, but if I suspected that they interfere with mine it would be much simpler to banish *you.*'

LI

THE Countess was not banished, but she felt the insecurity of her tenure of her brother's hospitality. A week after this incident Isabel received a telegram from England, dated from Gardencourt and bearing the stamp of Mrs Touchett's authorship. 'Ralph cannot last many days,' it ran, 'and if convenient would like to see you. Wishes me to say that you must come only if you've not other duties. Say, for myself, that you used to talk a good deal about your duty and to wonder what it was; shall be curious to see whether you've found it out. Ralph is really dying, and there's no other company.' Isabel was prepared for this news, having received from Henrietta Stackpole a detailed account of her journey to England with her appreciative patient. Ralph had arrived more dead than alive, but she had managed to convey him to Gardencourt, where he had taken to his bed, which, as Miss Stackpole wrote, he evidently would never leave again. She added that she had really had two patients on her hands instead of one, inasmuch as Mr Goodwood, who had been of no earthly use, was quite as ailing, in a different way, as Mr Touchett. Afterwards she wrote that she had been obliged to surrender the field to Mrs Touchett, who had just returned from America and had promptly given her to understand that she didn't wish any interviewing at Gardencourt. Isabel had written to her aunt shortly after Ralph came to Rome, letting her know of his critical condition and suggesting that she should lose no time in returning to Europe. Mrs Touchett had telegraphed an acknowledgement of this admonition, and the only further news Isabel received from her was the second telegram I have just quoted.

Isabel stood a moment looking at the latter missive; then, thrusting it into her pocket, she went straight to the door of her husband's study. Here she again paused an instant, after which she opened the door and went in. Osmond was seated at the table near the window with a folio volume before him, propped against a pile of books. This volume was open at a page of small coloured plates, and Isabel presently saw that he had been copying from it the drawing of an antique coin. A box of water-colours and fine brushes lay before him, and he had already transferred to a sheet of immaculate paper the delicate, finely-tinted disk. His back was turned toward the door, but he recognised his wife without looking round.

'Excuse me for disturbing you,' she said.

'When I come to your room I always knock,' he answered, going on with his work.

'I forgot; I had something else to think of. My cousin's dying.'

'Ah, I don't believe that,' said Osmond, looking at his drawing through a magnifying glass. 'He was dying when we married; he'll outlive us all.'

Isabel gave herself no time, no thought, to appreciate the careful cynicism of this declaration; she simply went on quickly, full of her own intention: 'My aunt has telegraphed for me; I must go to Gardencourt.'

'Why must you go to Gardencourt?' Osmond asked in the tone of impartial curiosity.

'To see Ralph before he dies.'

To this, for some time, he made no rejoinder; he continued to give his chief attention to his work, which was of a sort that would brook no negligence. 'I don't see the need of it,' he said at last. 'He came to see you here. I didn't like that; I thought his being in Rome a great mistake. But I tolerated it because it was to be the last time you should see him. Now you tell me it's not to have been the last. Ah, you're not grateful!'

'What am I to be grateful for?'

Gilbert Osmond laid down his little implements, blew a speck of dust from his drawing, slowly got up, and for the first time looked at his wife. 'For my not having interfered while he was here.'

'Oh yes, I am. I remember perfectly how distinctly you let me know you didn't like it. I was very glad when he went away.'

'Leave him alone then. Don't run after him.'

Isabel turned her eyes away from him; they rested upon his little drawing. 'I must go to England,' she said, with a full consciousness that her tone might strike an irritable man of taste as stupidly obstinate.

'I shall not like it if you do,' Osmond remarked.

'Why should I mind that? You won't like it if I don't. You like nothing I do or don't do. You pretend to think I lie.'

Osmond turned slightly pale; he gave a cold smile. 'That's why you must go then? Not to see your cousin, but to take a revenge on me.'

'I know nothing about revenge.'

'I do,' said Osmond. 'Don't give me an occasion.'

'You're only too eager to take one. You wish immensely that I would commit some folly.'

'I should be gratified in that case if you disobeyed me.'

'If I disobeyed you?' said Isabel in a low tone which had the effect of mildness.

'Let it be clear. If you leave Rome to-day it will be a piece of the most deliberate, the most calculated, opposition.'

'How can you call it calculated? I received my aunt's telegram but three minutes ago.'

'You calculate rapidly; it's a great accomplishment. I don't see why we should prolong our discussion; you know my wish.' And he stood there as if he expected to see her withdraw.

But she never moved; she couldn't move, strange as it may seem; she still wished to justify herself; he had the power, in an extraordinary degree, of making her feel this need. There was something in her imagination he could always appeal to against her judgement. 'You've no reason for such a wish,' said Isabel, 'and I've every reason for going. I can't tell you how unjust you seem to me. But I think you know. It's your own opposition that's calculated. It's malignant.'

She had never uttered her worst thought to her husband before, and the sensation of hearing it was evidently new to Osmond. But he showed no surprise, and his coolness was apparently a proof that he had believed his wife would in fact be unable to resist for ever his ingenious endeavour to draw her out. 'It's all the more intense then,' he answered. And he added almost as if he were giving her a friendly counsel: 'This is a very important matter.' She recognised that; she was fully conscious of the weight of the occasion; she knew that between them they had arrived at a crisis. Its gravity made her careful; she said nothing, and he went on. 'You say I've no reason? I have the very best. I dislike, from the bottom of my soul, what you intend to do. It's dishonourable; it's indelicate; it's indecent. Your cousin is nothing whatever to me, and I'm under no obligation to make concessions to him. I've already made the very handsomest. Your relations with him, while he was here, kept me on pins and needles; but I let that pass, because from week to week I expected him to go. I've never liked him and he has never liked me. That's why you like him—because he hates me,' said Osmond with a quick, barely audible tremor in his voice. 'I've an ideal of what my wife should do and should not do. She should not travel across Europe alone, in defiance of my deepest desire, to sit at the bedside of other men. Your cousin's nothing to you; he's nothing to us. You smile most expressively when I talk about *us*, but I assure you that *we, we*, Mrs Osmond, is all I know. I take our marriage seriously; you appear to have found a way of not doing so. I'm not aware that we're divorced or separated; for me we're indissolubly united. You are nearer to me than any human creature, and I'm nearer to you. It may be a disagreeable proximity; it's one, at any rate, of our own deliberate making. You don't like to be reminded of that, I know; but I'm perfectly willing, because—because—' And he paused a moment, looking as if he had something to say which would be very much to the point. 'Because I think we should accept the consequences of our actions, and what I value most in life is the honour of a thing!'

He spoke gravely and almost gently; the accent of sarcasm had dropped out of his tone. It had a gravity which checked his wife's quick emotion; the resolution with which she had entered the room found itself caught in a mesh of fine threads. His last words were not a command, they constituted a kind of appeal; and, though she felt that any expression of respect on his part could only be a refinement of egotism, they represented something transcendent and absolute, like the sign of the cross or the flag of one's country. He spoke in the name of something sacred and precious—the observance of a magnificent form. They were as perfectly apart in feeling as two disillusioned lovers had ever been; but they had never yet separated in act. Isabel had not changed; her old passion for justice still abode within her; and now, in the very thick of her sense of her husband's blasphemous sophistry, it began to throb to a tune which for a moment promised him the victory. It came over her that in his wish to preserve appearances he was after all sincere, and that this, as far as it went, was a merit. Ten minutes before she had felt all the joy of irreflective action—a joy to which she had so long been a stranger; but action had been suddenly changed to slow renunciation, transformed by the blight of Osmond's touch. If she must renounce, however, she would let him know she was a victim rather than a dupe. 'I know you're a master of the art of mockery,' she said. 'How can you speak of an indissoluble union—how can you speak of your being contented? Where's our union when you accuse me of falsity? Where's your contentment when you have nothing but hideous suspicion in your heart?'

'It is in our living decently together, in spite of such drawbacks.'

'We don't live decently together!' cried Isabel.

'Indeed we don't if you go to England.'

'That's very little; that's nothing. I might do much more.'

He raised his eyebrows and even his shoulders a little: he had lived long enough in Italy to catch this trick. 'Ah, if you've come to threaten me I prefer my drawing.' And he walked back to his table, where he took up the sheet of paper on which he had been working and stood studying it.

'I suppose that if I go you'll not expect me to come back,' said Isabel.

He turned quickly round, and she could see this movement at least was not designed. He looked at her a little, and then, 'Are you out of your mind?' he enquired.

'How can it be anything but a rupture?' she went on; 'especially if all you say is true?' She was unable to see how it could be anything but a rupture; she sincerely wished to know what else it might be.

He sat down before his table. 'I really can't argue with you on the hypothesis of your defying me,' he said. And he took up one of his little brushes again.

She lingered but a moment longer; long enough to embrace with her eye his whole deliberately indifferent yet most expressive figure; after which she quickly left the room. Her faculties, her energy, her passion, were all dispersed again; she felt as if a cold, dark mist had suddenly encompassed her. Osmond possessed in a supreme degree the art of eliciting any weakness. On her way back to her room she found the Countess Gemini standing in the open doorway of a little parlour in which a small collection of heterogeneous books had been arranged. The Countess had an open volume in her hand; she appeared to have been glancing down a page which failed to strike her as interesting. At the sound of Isabel's step she raised her head.

'Ah my dear,' she said, 'you, who are so literary, do tell me some amusing book to read! Everything here's of a dreariness—! Do you think this would do me any good?'

Isabel glanced at the title of the volume she held out, but without reading or understanding it. 'I'm afraid I can't advise you. I've had bad news. My cousin, Ralph Touchett, is dying.'

The Countess threw down her book. 'Ah, he was so simpatico. I'm awfully sorry for you.'

'You would be sorrier still if you knew.'

'What is there to know? You look very badly,' the Countess added. 'You must have been with Osmond.'

Half an hour before Isabel would have listened very coldly to an intimation that she should ever feel a desire for the sympathy of her sister-in-law, and there can be no better proof of her present embarrassment than the fact that she almost clutched at this lady's fluttering attention. 'I've been with Osmond,' she said, while the Countess's bright eyes glittered at her.

'I'm sure then he has been odious!' the Countess cried. 'Did he say he was glad poor Mr Touchett's dying?'

'He said it's impossible I should go to England.'

The Countess's mind, when her interests were concerned, was agile; she already foresaw the extinction of any further brightness in her visit to Rome. Ralph Touchett would die,

Isabel would go into mourning, and then there would be no more dinner-parties. Such a prospect produced for a moment in her countenance an expressive grimace; but this rapid, picturesque play of feature was her only tribute to disappointment. After all, she reflected, the game was almost played out; she had already overstayed her invitation. And then she cared enough for Isabel's trouble to forget her own, and she saw that Isabel's trouble was deep. It seemed deeper than the mere death of a cousin, and the Countess had no hesitation in connecting her exasperating brother with the expression of her sister-in-law's eyes. Her heart beat with an almost joyous expectation, for if she had wished to see Osmond overtopped the conditions looked favourable now. Of course if Isabel should go to England she herself would immediately leave Palazzo Roccanera; nothing would induce her to remain there with Osmond. Nevertheless she felt an immense desire to hear that Isabel would go to England. 'Nothing's impossible for you, my dear,' she said caressingly. 'Why else are you rich and clever and good?'

'Why indeed? I feel stupidly weak.'

'Why does Osmond say it's impossible?' the Countess asked in a tone which sufficiently declared that she couldn't imagine.

From the moment she thus began to question her, however, Isabel drew back; she disengaged her hand, which the Countess had affectionately taken. But she answered this enquiry with frank bitterness. 'Because we're so happy together that we can't separate even for a fortnight.'

'Ah,' cried the Countess while Isabel turned away, 'when I want to make a journey my husband simply tells me I can have no money!'

Isabel went to her room, where she walked up and down for an hour. It may appear to some readers that she gave herself much trouble, and it is certain that for a woman of a high spirit she had allowed herself easily to be arrested. It seemed to her that only now she fully measured the great undertaking of matrimony. Marriage meant that in such a case as this, when one had to choose, one chose as a matter of course for one's husband. 'I'm afraid—yes, I'm afraid,' she said to herself more than once, stopping short in her walk. But what she was afraid of was not her husband—his displeasure, his hatred, his revenge; it was not even her own later judgement of her conduct—a consideration which had often held her in check; it was simply the violence there would be in going when Osmond wished her to remain. A gulf of difference had opened between them, but nevertheless it was his desire that she should stay, it was a horror to him that she should go. She knew the nervous fineness with which he could feel an objection. What he thought of her she knew, what he was capable of saying to her she had felt; yet they were married, for all that, and marriage meant that a woman should cleave to the man with whom, uttering tremendous vows, she had stood at the altar. She sank down on her sofa at last and buried her head in a pile of cushions.

When she raised her head again the Countess Gemini hovered before her. She had come in all unperceived; she had a strange smile on her thin lips and her whole face had grown in an hour a shining intimation. She lived assuredly, it might be said, at the window of her spirit, but now she was leaning far out. 'I knocked,' she began, 'but you didn't answer me. So I ventured in. I've been looking at you for the last five minutes. You're very unhappy.'

'Yes; but I don't think you can comfort me.'

'Will you give me leave to try?' And the Countess sat down on the sofa beside her. She continued to smile, and there was something communicative and exultant in her expression. She appeared to have a deal to say, and it occurred to Isabel for the first time that her sister-in-law might say something really human. She made play with her glittering eyes, in which there was an unpleasant fascination. 'After all,' she soon resumed, 'I must tell you, to begin with, that I don't understand your state of mind. You seem to have so many scruples, so many reasons, so many ties. When I discovered, ten years ago, that my husband's dearest wish was to make me miserable—of late he has simply let me alone—ah, it was a wonderful simplification! My poor Isabel, you're not simple enough.'

'No, I'm not simple enough,' said Isabel.

'There's something I want you to know,' the Countess declared—'because I think you ought to know it. Perhaps you do; perhaps you've guessed it. But if you have, all I can say is that I understand still less why you shouldn't do as you like.'

'What do you wish me to know?' Isabel felt a foreboding that made her heart beat faster. The Countess was about to justify herself, and this alone was portentous.

But she was nevertheless disposed to play a little with her subject. 'In your place I should have guessed it ages ago. Have you never really suspected?'

'I've guessed nothing. What should I have suspected? I don't know what you mean.'

'That's because you've such a beastly pure mind. I never saw a woman with such a pure mind!' cried the Countess.

Isabel slowly got up. 'You're going to tell me something horrible.'

'You can call it by whatever name you will!' And the Countess rose also, while her gathered perversity grew vivid and dreadful. She stood a moment in a sort of glare of intention and, as seemed to Isabel even then, of ugliness; after which she said: 'My first sister-in-law had no children.'

Isabel stared back at her; the announcement was an anti-climax. 'Your first sister-in-law?'

'I suppose you know at least, if one may mention it, that Osmond has been married before! I've never spoken to you of his wife; I thought it mightn't be decent or respectful. But others, less particular, must have done so. The poor little woman lived hardly three years and died childless. It wasn't till after her death that Pansy arrived.'

Isabel's brow had contracted to a frown; her lips were parted in pale, vague wonder. She was trying to follow; there seemed so much more to follow than she could see. 'Pansy's not my husband's child then?'

'Your husband's—in perfection! But no one else's husband's. Some one else's wife's. Ah, my good Isabel,' cried the Countess, 'with you one must dot one's i's!'

'I don't understand. Whose wife's?' Isabel asked.

'The wife of a horrid little Swiss who died—how long?—a dozen, more than fifteen, years ago. He never recognised Miss Pansy, nor, knowing what he was about, would have anything to say to her; and there was no reason why he should. Osmond did, and that was better; though he had to fit on afterwards the whole rigmarole of his own wife's having died in childbirth, and of his having, in grief and horror, banished the little girl from his sight for as long as possible before taking her home from nurse. His wife had really died, you know, of quite another matter and in quite another place: in the Piedmontese mountains, where they had gone, one August, because her health appeared to require the air, but where she was suddenly taken worse—fatally ill. The story passed, sufficiently; it was covered by the appearances so long as nobody heeded, as nobody cared to look into it. But of course *I* knew—without researches,' the Countess lucidly proceeded; 'as also, you'll understand, without a word said between us—I mean between Osmond and me. Don't you see him looking at me, in silence, that way, to settle it?—that is to settle *me* if I should say anything. I said nothing, right or left—never a word to a creature, if you can believe that of me: on my honour, my dear, I speak of the thing to you now, after all this time, as I've never, never spoken. It was to be enough for me, from the first, that the child was my niece—from the moment she was my brother's daughter. As for her veritable mother—!' But with this Pansy's wonderful aunt dropped—as, involuntarily, from the impression of her sister-in-law's face, out of which more eyes might have seemed to look at her than she had ever had to meet.

She had spoken no name, yet Isabel could but check, on her own lips, an echo of the unspoken. She sank to her seat again, hanging her head. 'Why have you told me this?' she asked in a voice the Countess hardly recognised.

'Because I've been so bored with your not knowing. I've been bored, frankly, my dear, with not having told you; as if, stupidly, all this time I couldn't have managed! *Ça me dépasse*,* if you don't mind my saying so, the things, all round you, that you've appeared to succeed in not knowing. It's a sort of assistance—aid to innocent ignorance—that I've always been a bad hand at rendering; and in this connexion, that of keeping quiet for my brother, my virtue has at any rate finally found itself exhausted. It's not a black lie, moreover, you know,' the Countess inimitably added. 'The facts are exactly what I tell you.'

'I had no idea,' said Isabel presently; and looked up at her in a manner that doubtless matched the apparent witlessness of this confession.

'So I believed—though it was hard to believe. Had it never occurred to you that he was for six or seven years her lover?'

'I don't know. Things *have* occurred to me, and perhaps that was what they all meant.'

'She has been wonderfully clever, she has been magnificent, about Pansy!' the Countess, before all this view of it, cried.

'Oh, no idea, for me,' Isabel went on, 'ever *definitely* took that form.' She appeared to be making out to herself what had been and what hadn't. 'And as it is—I don't understand.'

She spoke as one troubled and puzzled, yet the poor Countess seemed to have seen her revelation fall below its possibilities of effect. She had expected to kindle some responsive blaze, but had barely extracted a spark. Isabel showed as scarce more impressed than she might have been, as a young woman of approved imagination, with some fine sinister passage of public history. 'Don't you recognise how the child could never pass for *her* husband's?—that is with M. Merle himself,' her companion resumed. 'They had been separated too long for that, and he had gone to some far country—I think to South America. If she had ever had children—which I'm not sure of—she had lost them. The conditions happened to make it workable, under stress (I mean at so awkward a pinch), that Osmond should acknowledge the little girl. His wife was dead—very true; but she had not been dead too long to put a certain accommodation of dates out of the question—from the moment, I mean, that suspicion wasn't started; which was what they had to take care of. What was more natural than that poor Mrs Osmond, at a distance and for a world not troubling about trifles, should have left behind her, *poverina*,* the pledge of her brief happiness that had cost her her life? With the aid of a change of residence—Osmond had been living with her at Naples at the time of their stay in the Alps, and he in due course left it for ever—the whole history was successfully set going. My poor sister-in-law, in her grave, couldn't help herself, and the real mother, to save *her* skin, renounced all visible property in the child.'

'Ah, poor, poor woman!' cried Isabel, who herewith burst into tears. It was a long time since she had shed any; she had suffered a high reaction from weeping. But now they flowed with an abundance in which the Countess Gemini found only another discomfiture.

'It's very kind of you to pity her!' she discordantly laughed. 'Yes indeed, you have a way of your own—!'

'He must have been false to his wife—and so very soon!' said Isabel with a sudden check.

'That's all that's wanting—that you should take up *her* cause!' the Countess went on. 'I quite agree with you, however, that it was much too soon.'

'But to me, to me—?' And Isabel hesitated as if she had not heard; as if her question—though it was sufficiently there in her eyes—were all for herself.

'To you he has been faithful? Well, it depends, my dear, on what you call faithful. When he married you he was no longer the lover of another woman—*such* a lover as he had been, *cara mia*,* between their risks and their precautions, while the thing lasted! That state of affairs had passed away; the lady had repented, or at all events, for reasons of her own, drawn back: she had always had, too, a worship of appearances so intense that even Osmond himself had got bored with it. You may therefore imagine what it was—when he couldn't patch it on conveniently to *any* of those he goes in for! But the whole past was between them.'

'Yes,' Isabel mechanically echoed, 'the whole past is between them.'

'Ah, this later past is nothing. But for six or seven years, as I say, they had kept it up.'

She was silent a little. 'Why then did she want him to marry me?'

'Ah my dear, that's her superiority! Because you had money; and because she believed you would be good to Pansy.'

'Poor woman—and Pansy who doesn't like her!' cried Isabel.

'That's the reason she wanted some one whom Pansy would like. She knows it, she knows everything.'

'Will she know that you've told me this?'

'That will depend upon whether you tell her. She's prepared for it, and do you know what she counts upon for her defence? On your believing that I lie. Perhaps you do; don't make yourself uncomfortable to hide it. Only, as it happens this time, I don't. I've told plenty of little idiotic fibs, but they've never hurt any one but myself.'

Isabel sat staring at her companion's story as at a bale of fantastic wares some strolling gypsy might have unpacked on the carpet at her feet. 'Why did Osmond never marry her?' she finally asked.

'Because she had no money.' The Countess had an answer for everything, and if she lied she lied well. 'No one knows, no one has ever known, what she lives on, or how she has got all those beautiful things. I don't believe Osmond himself knows. Besides, she wouldn't have married him.'

'How can she have loved him then?'

'She doesn't love him in that way. She did at first, and then, I suppose, she would have married him; but at that time her husband was living. By the time M. Merle had rejoined—I won't say his ancestors, because he never had any—her relations with Osmond had changed, and she had grown more ambitious. Besides, she has never had, about him,' the Countess went on, leaving Isabel to wince for it so tragically afterwards—'she *had* never had, what you might call any illusions of *intelligence*. She hoped she might marry a great man; that has always been her idea. She has waited and watched and plotted and prayed; but she has never succeeded. I don't call Madame Merle a success, you know. I don't know what she may accomplish yet, but at present she has very little to show. The only tangible result she has ever achieved—except, of course, getting to know every one and staying with them free of expense—has been her bringing you and Osmond together. Oh, she did that, my dear; you needn't look as if you doubted it. I've watched them for years; I know everything—everything. I'm thought a great scatterbrain, but I've had enough application of mind to follow up those two. She hates me, and her way of showing it is to pretend to be for ever defending me. When people say I've had fifteen lovers she looks horrified and declares that quite half of them were never proved. She has been afraid of me for years, and she has taken great comfort in the vile, false things people have said about me. She has been afraid I'd expose her, and she threatened me one day when Osmond began to pay his court to you. It was at his house in Florence; do you remember that afternoon when she brought you there and we had tea in the garden? She let me know then that if I should tell tales two could play at that game. She pretends there's a good deal more to tell about me than about her. It would be an interesting comparison! I don't care a fig what she may say, simply because I know *you* don't care a fig. You can't trouble your head about me less than you do already. So she may take her revenge as she chooses; I don't think she'll frighten you very much. Her great idea has been to be tremendously irreproachable—a kind of full-blown lily—the incarnation of propriety. She has always worshipped that god. There should be no scandal about Cæsar's wife, you know; and, as I say, she has always hoped to marry Cæsar. That was one reason she wouldn't marry Osmond; the fear that on seeing her with Pansy people would put things together—would even see a resemblance. She has had a terror lest the mother should betray herself. She has been awfully careful; the mother has never done so.'

'Yes, yes, the mother has done so,' said Isabel, who had listened to all this with a face more and more wan. 'She betrayed herself to me the other day, though I didn't recognise her. There appeared to have been a chance of Pansy's making a great marriage, and in her disappointment at its not coming off she almost dropped the mask.'

'Ah, that's where she'd dish herself!' cried the Countess. 'She has failed so dreadfully that she's determined her daughter shall make it up.'

Isabel started at the words 'her daughter,' which her guest threw off so familiarly. 'It seems very wonderful,' she murmured; and in this bewildering impression she had almost lost her sense of being personally touched by the story.

'Now don't go and turn against the poor innocent child!' the Countess went on. 'She's very nice, in spite of her deplorable origin. I myself have liked Pansy; not, naturally, because she was *hers*, but because she had become yours.'

'Yes, she has become mine. And how the poor woman must have suffered at seeing me—!' Isabel exclaimed while she flushed at the thought.

'I don't believe she has suffered; on the contrary, she has enjoyed. Osmond's marriage has given his daughter a great little lift. Before that she lived in a hole. And do you know what the mother thought? That you might take such a fancy to the child that you'd do something for her. Osmond of course could never give her a portion. Osmond was really extremely poor; but of course you know all about that. Ah, my dear,' cried the Countess, 'why did you ever inherit money?' She stopped a moment as if she saw something singular in Isabel's face. 'Don't tell me now that you'll give her a *dot*. You're capable of that, but I would refuse to believe it. Don't try to be too good. Be a little easy and natural and nasty; feel a little wicked, for the comfort of it, once in your life!'

'It's very strange. I suppose I ought to know, but I'm sorry,' Isabel said. 'I'm much obliged to you.'

'Yes, you seem to be!' cried the Countess with a mocking laugh. 'Perhaps you are—perhaps you're not. You don't take it as I should have thought.'

'How should I take it?' Isabel asked.

'Well, I should say as a woman who has been made use of.' Isabel made no answer to this; she only listened, and the Countess went on. 'They've always been bound to each other; they remained so even after she broke off—or *he* did. But he has always been more for her than she has been for him. When their little carnival was over they made a bargain that each should give the other complete liberty, but that each should also do everything possible to help the other on. You may ask me how I know such a thing as that. I know it by the way they've behaved. Now see how much better women are than men! She has found a wife for Osmond, but Osmond has never lifted a little finger for *her*. She has worked for him, plotted for him, suffered for him; she has even more than once found money for him; and the end of it is that he's tired of her. She's an old habit; there are moments when he needs her, but on the whole he wouldn't miss her if she were removed. And, what's more, to-day she knows it. So you needn't be jealous!' the Countess added humorously.

Isabel rose from her sofa again; she felt bruised and scant of breath; her head was humming with new knowledge. 'I'm much obliged to you,' she repeated. And then she added abruptly, in quite a different tone: 'How do you know all this?'

This enquiry appeared to ruffle the Countess more than Isabel's expression of gratitude pleased her. She gave her companion a bold stare, with which, 'Let us assume that I've invented it!' she cried. She too, however, suddenly changed her tone and, laying her hand on Isabel's arm, said with the penetration of her sharp bright smile: 'Now will you give up your journey?'

Isabel started a little; she turned away. But she felt weak and in a moment had to lay her arm upon the mantel-shelf for support. She stood a minute so, and then upon her arm she dropped her dizzy head, with closed eyes and pale lips.

'I've done wrong to speak—I've made you ill!' the Countess cried.

'Ah, I must see Ralph!' Isabel wailed; not in resentment, not in the quick passion her companion had looked for; but in a tone of far-reaching, infinite sadness.

LII

THERE was a train for Turin and Paris that evening; and after the Countess had left her Isabel had a rapid and decisive conference with her maid, who was discreet, devoted and active. After this she thought (except of her journey) only of one thing. She must go and see Pansy; from her she couldn't turn away. She had not seen her yet, as Osmond had given her to understand that it was too soon to begin. She drove at five o'clock to a high door in a narrow street in the quarter of the Piazza Navona, and was admitted by the portress of the convent, a genial and obsequious person. Isabel had been at this institution before; she had come with Pansy to see the sisters. She knew they were good women, and she saw that the large rooms were clean and cheerful and that the well-used garden had sun for winter and shade for spring. But she disliked the place, which affronted and almost frightened her; not for the world would she have spent a night there. It produced to-day more than before the impression of a well-appointed prison; for it was not possible to pretend Pansy was free to leave it. This innocent creature had been presented to her in a new and violent light, but the secondary effect of the revelation was to make her reach out a hand.

The portress left her to wait in the parlour of the convent while she went to make it known that there was a visitor for the dear young lady. The parlour was a vast, cold apartment, with new-looking furniture; a large clean stove of white porcelain, unlighted, a collection of wax flowers under glass, and a series of engravings from religious pictures on the walls. On the other occasion Isabel had thought it less like Rome than like Philadelphia, but to-day she made no reflexions; the apartment only seemed to her very empty and very soundless. The portress returned at the end of some five minutes, ushering in another person. Isabel got up, expecting to see one of the ladies of the sisterhood, but to her extreme surprise found herself confronted with Madame Merle. The effect was strange, for Madame Merle was already so present to her vision that her appearance in the flesh was like suddenly, and rather awfully, seeing a painted picture move. Isabel had been thinking all day of her falsity, her audacity, her ability, her probable suffering; and these dark things seemed to flash with a sudden light as she entered the room. Her being there at all had the character of ugly evidence, of handwritings, of profaned relics, of grim things produced in court. It made Isabel feel faint; if it had been necessary to speak on the spot she would have been quite unable. But no such necessity was distinct to her; it seemed to her indeed that she had absolutely nothing to say to Madame Merle. In one's relations with this lady, however, there were never any absolute necessities; she had a manner which carried off not only her own deficiencies but those of other people. But she was different from usual; she came in slowly, behind the portress, and Isabel instantly perceived that she was not likely to depend upon her habitual resources. For her too the occasion was exceptional, and she had undertaken to treat it by the light of the moment. This gave her a peculiar gravity; she pretended not even to smile, and though Isabel saw that she was more than ever playing a part it seemed to her that on the whole the wonderful woman had never been so natural. She looked at her young friend from head to foot, but not harshly nor defiantly; with a cold gentleness rather, and an absence of any air of allusion to their last meeting. It was as if she had wished to mark a distinction. She had been irritated then, she was reconciled now.

'You can leave us alone,' she said to the portress; 'in five minutes this lady will ring for you.' And then she turned to Isabel, who, after noting what has just been mentioned, had ceased to notice and had let her eyes wander as far as the limits of the room would allow. She wished never to look at Madame Merle again. 'You're surprised to find me here, and I'm afraid you're not pleased,' this lady went on. 'You don't see why I should have come; it's as if I had anticipated you. I confess I've been rather indiscreet—I ought to have asked your permission.' There was none of the oblique movement of irony in this; it was said simply and mildly; but Isabel, far afloat on a sea of wonder and pain, could not have told herself with what intention it was uttered. 'But I've not been sitting long,'

Madame Merle continued; 'that is I've not been long with Pansy. I came to see her because it occurred to me this afternoon that she must be rather lonely and perhaps even a little miserable. It may be good for a small girl; I know so little about small girls; I can't tell. At any rate it's a little dismal. Therefore I came—on the chance. I knew of course that you'd come, and her father as well; still, I had not been told other visitors were forbidden. The good woman—what's her name? Madame Catherine—made no objection whatever. I stayed twenty minutes with Pansy; she has a charming little room, not in the least conventual, with a piano and flowers. She has arranged it delightfully; she has so much taste. Of course it's all none of my business, but I feel happier since I've seen her. She may even have a maid if she likes; but of course she has no occasion to dress. She wears a little black frock; she looks so charming. I went afterwards to see Mother Catherine, who has a very good room too; I assure you I don't find the poor sisters at all monastic. Mother Catherine has a most coquettish little toilet-table, with something that looked uncommonly like a bottle of eau-de-Cologne. She speaks delightfully of Pansy; says it's a great happiness for them to have her. She's a little saint of heaven and a model to the oldest of them. Just as I was leaving Madame Catherine the portress came to say to her that there was a lady for the signorina. Of course I knew it must be you, and I asked her to let me go and receive you in her place. She demurred greatly—I must tell you that—and said it was her duty to notify the Mother Superior; it was of such high importance that you should be treated with respect. I requested her to let the Mother Superior alone and asked her how she supposed I would treat you!'

So Madame Merle went on, with much of the brilliancy of a woman who had long been a mistress of the art of conversation. But there were phases and gradations in her speech, not one of which was lost upon Isabel's ear, though her eyes were absent from her companion's face. She had not proceeded far before Isabel noted a sudden break in her voice, a lapse in her continuity, which was in itself a complete drama. This subtle modulation marked a momentous discovery—the perception of an entirely new attitude on the part of her listener. Madame

Merle had guessed in the space of an instant that everything was at an end between them, and in the space of another instant she had guessed the reason why. The person who stood there was not the same one she had seen hitherto, but was a very different person—a person who knew her secret. This discovery was tremendous, and from the moment she made it the most accomplished of women faltered and lost her courage. But only for that moment. Then the conscious stream of her perfect manner gathered itself again and flowed on as smoothly as might be to the end. But it was only because she had the end in view that she was able to proceed. She had been touched with a point that made her quiver, and she needed all the alertness of her will to repress her agitation. Her only safety was in her not betraying herself. She resisted this, but the startled quality of her voice refused to improve—she couldn't help it—while she heard herself say she hardly knew what. The tide of her confidence ebbed, and she was able only just to glide into port, faintly grazing the bottom.

Isabel saw it all as distinctly as if it had been reflected in a large clear glass. It might have been a great moment for her, for it might have been a moment of triumph. That Madame Merle had lost her pluck and saw before her the phantom of exposure—this in itself was a revenge, this in itself was almost the promise of a brighter day. And for a moment during which she stood apparently looking out of the window, with her back half-turned, Isabel enjoyed that knowledge. On the other side of the window lay the garden of the convent; but this is not what she saw; she saw nothing of the budding plants and the glowing afternoon. She saw, in the crude light of that revelation which had already become a part of experience and to which the very frailty of the vessel in which it had been offered her only gave an intrinsic price, the dry staring fact that she had been an applied handled hung-up tool, as senseless and convenient as mere shaped wood and iron. All the bitterness of this knowledge surged into her soul again; it was as if she felt on her lips the taste of dishonour. There was a moment during which, if she had turned and spoken, she would have said something that would hiss like a lash. But she closed her eyes, and then the hideous vision dropped. What remained was the cleverest woman in the world standing there within a few feet of her and knowing as little what to think as the meanest. Isabel's only revenge was to be silent still—to leave Madame Merle in this unprecedented situation. She left her there for a period that must have seemed long to this lady, who at last seated herself with a movement which was in itself a confession of helplessness. Then Isabel turned slow eyes, looking down at her. Madame Merle was very pale; her own eyes covered Isabel's face. She might see what she would, but her danger was over. Isabel would never accuse her, never reproach her; perhaps because she never would give her the opportunity to defend herself.

'I'm come to bid Pansy good-bye,' our young woman said at last. 'I go to England to-night.'

'Go to England to-night!' Madame Merle repeated sitting there and looking up at her.

'I'm going to Gardencourt. Ralph Touchett's dying.'

'Ah, you'll feel that.' Madame Merle recovered herself; she had a chance to express sympathy. 'Do you go alone?'

'Yes; without my husband.'

Madame Merle gave a low vague murmur; a sort of recognition of the general sadness of things. 'Mr Touchett never liked me, but I'm sorry he's dying. Shall you see his mother?'

'Yes; she has returned from America.'

'She used to be very kind to me; but she has changed. Others too have changed,' said Madame Merle with a quiet noble pathos. She paused a moment, then added: 'And you'll see dear old Gardencourt again!'

'I shall not enjoy it much,' Isabel answered.

'Naturally—in your grief. But it's on the whole, of all the houses I know, and I know many, the one I should have liked best to live in. I don't venture to send a message to the people,' Madame Merle added; 'but I should like to give my love to the place.'

Isabel turned away. 'I had better go to Pansy. I've not much time.'

While she looked about her for the proper egress, the door opened and admitted one of the ladies of the house, who advanced with a discreet smile, gently rubbing, under her long loose sleeves, a pair of plump white hands. Isabel recognized Madame Catherine, whose acquaintance she had already made, and begged that she would immediately let her see Miss Osmond. Madame Catherine looked doubly discreet, but smiled very blandly and said: 'It will be good for her to see you. I'll take you to her myself.' Then she directed her pleased guarded vision to Madame Merle.

'Will you let me remain a little?' this lady asked. 'It's so good to be here.'

'You may remain always if you like!' And the good sister gave a knowing laugh.

She led Isabel out of the room, through several corridors, and up a long staircase. All these departments were solid and bare, light and clean; so, thought Isabel, are the great penal establishments. Madame Catherine gently pushed open the door of Pansy's room and ushered in the visitor; then stood smiling with folded hands while the two others met and embraced.

'She's glad to see you,' she repeated; 'it will do her good.' And she placed the best chair carefully for Isabel. But she made no movement to seat herself; she seemed ready to retire. 'How does this dear child look?' she asked of Isabel, lingering a moment.

'She looks pale,' Isabel answered.

'That's the pleasure of seeing you. She's very happy. *Elle éclaire la maison*,'* said the good sister.

Pansy wore, as Madame Merle had said, a little black dress; it was perhaps this that made her look pale. 'They're very good to me—they think of everything!' she exclaimed with all her customary eagerness to accommodate.

'We think of you always—you're a precious charge,' Madame Catherine remarked in the tone of a woman with whom benevolence was a habit and whose conception of duty was the acceptance of every care. It fell with a leaden weight on Isabel's ears; it seemed to represent the surrender of a personality, the authority of the Church.

When Madame Catherine had left them together Pansy kneeled down and hid her head in her stepmother's lap. So she remained some moments, while Isabel gently stroked her hair.

Then she got up, averting her face and looking about the room. 'Don't you think I've arranged it well? I've everything I have at home.'

'It's very pretty; you're very comfortable.' Isabel scarcely knew what she could say to her. On the one hand she couldn't let her think she had come to pity her, and on the other it would be a dull mockery to pretend to rejoice with her. So she simply added after a moment: 'I've come to bid you good-bye. I'm going to England.'

Pansy's white little face turned red. 'To England! Not to come back?'

'I don't know when I shall come back.'

'Ah, I'm sorry,' Pansy breathed with faintness. She spoke as if she had no right to criticize; but her tone expressed a depth of disappointment.

'My cousin, Mr Touchett, is very ill; he'll probably die. I wish to see him,' Isabel said.

'Ah yes; you told me he would die. Of course you must go. And will papa go?'

'No; I shall go alone.'

For a moment the girl said nothing. Isabel had often wondered what she thought of the apparent relations of her father with his wife; but never by a glance, by an intimation, had she let it be seen that she deemed them deficient in an air of intimacy. She made her reflexions, Isabel was sure; and she must have had a conviction that there were husbands and wives who were more intimate than that. But Pansy was not indiscreet even in thought; she would as little have ventured to judge her gentle stepmother as to criticize her magnificent father. Her heart may have stood almost as still as it would have done had she seen two of the saints in the great picture in the convent-chapel turn their painted heads and shake them at each other. But as in this latter case she would (for very solemnity's sake) never have mentioned the awful phenomenon, so she put away all knowledge of the secrets of larger lives than her own. 'You'll be very far away,' she presently went on.

'Yes; I shall be far away. But it will scarcely matter,' Isabel explained; 'since so long as you're here I can't be called near you.'

'Yes, but you can come and see me; though you've not come very often.'

'I've not come because your father forbade it. To-day I bring nothing with me. I can't amuse you.'

'I'm not to be amused. That's not what papa wishes.'

'Then it hardly matters whether I'm in Rome or in England.'

'You're not happy, Mrs Osmond,' said Pansy.

'Not very. But it doesn't matter.'

'That's what I say to myself. What does it matter? But I should like to come out.'

'I wish indeed you might.'

'Don't leave me here,' Pansy went on gently.

Isabel said nothing for a minute; her heart beat fast. 'Will you come away with me now?' she asked.

Pansy looked at her pleadingly. 'Did papa tell you to bring me?'

'No; it's my own proposal.'

'I think I had better wait then. Did papa send me no message?'

'I don't think he knew I was coming.'

'He thinks I've not had enough,' said Pansy. 'But I have. The ladies are very kind to me and the little girls come to see me. There are some very little ones—such charming children. Then my room—you can see for yourself. All that's very delightful. But I've had enough. Papa wished me to think a little—and I've thought a great deal.'

'What have you thought?'

'Well, that I must never displease papa.'

'You knew that before.'

'Yes; but I know it better. I'll do anything—I'll do anything,' said Pansy. Then, as she heard her own words, a deep, pure blush came into her face. Isabel read the meaning of it; she saw the poor girl had been vanquished. It was well that Mr Edward Rosier had kept his enamels! Isabel looked into her eyes and saw there mainly a prayer to be treated easily. She laid her hand on Pansy's as if to let her know that her look conveyed no diminution of esteem; for the collapse of the girl's momentary resistance (mute and modest though it had been) seemed only her tribute to the truth of things. She didn't presume to judge others, but she had judged herself; she had seen the reality. She had no vocation for struggling with combinations; in the solemnity of sequestration there was something that overwhelmed her. She bowed her pretty head to authority and only asked of authority to be merciful. Yes; it was very well that Edward Rosier had reserved a few articles!

Isabel got up; her time was rapidly shortening. 'Good-bye then. I leave Rome to-night.'

Pansy took hold of her dress; there was a sudden change in the child's face. 'You look strange; you frighten me.'

'Oh, I'm very harmless,' said Isabel.

'Perhaps you won't come back?'

'Perhaps not. I can't tell.'

'Ah, Mrs Osmond, you won't leave me!'

Isabel now saw she had guessed everything. 'My dear child, what can I do for you?' she asked.

'I don't know—but I'm happier when I think of you.'

'You can always think of me.'

'Not when you're so far. I'm a little afraid,' said Pansy.

'What are you afraid of?'

'Of papa—a little. And of Madame Merle. She has just been to see me.'

'You must not say that,' Isabel observed.

'Oh, I'll do everything they want. Only if you're here I shall do it more easily.'

Isabel considered. 'I won't desert you,' she said at last. 'Good-bye, my child.'

Then they held each other a moment in a silent embrace, like two sisters; and afterwards Pansy walked along the corridor with her visitor to the top of the staircase. 'Madame Merle has been here,' she remarked as they went; and as Isabel answered nothing she added abruptly: 'I don't like Madame Merle!'

Isabel hesitated, then stopped. 'You must never say that—that you don't like Madame Merle.'

Pansy looked at her in wonder; but wonder with Pansy had never been a reason for non-compliance. 'I never will again,' she said with exquisite gentleness. At the top of the staircase they had to separate, as it appeared to be part of the mild but very definite discipline under which Pansy lived that she should not go down. Isabel descended, and when she reached the bottom the girl was standing above. 'You'll come back?' she called out in a voice that Isabel remembered afterwards.

'Yes—I'll come back.'

Madame Catherine met Mrs Osmond below and conducted her to the door of the parlour, outside of which the two stood talking a minute. 'I won't go in,' said the good sister. 'Madame Merle's waiting for you.'

At this announcement Isabel stiffened; she was on the point of asking if there were no other egress from the convent. But a moment's reflexion assured her that she would do well not to betray to the worthy nun her desire to avoid Pansy's other friend. Her companion grasped her arm very gently and, fixing her a moment with wise, benevolent eyes, said in French and almost familiarly: '*Eh bien, chère Madame, qu'en pensez-vous?*'*

'About my step-daughter? Oh, it would take long to tell you.'

'We think it's enough,' Madame Catherine distinctly observed. And she pushed open the door of the parlour.

Madame Merle was sitting just as Isabel had left her, like a woman so absorbed in thought that she had not moved a little finger. As Madame Catherine closed the door she got up, and Isabel saw that she had been thinking to some purpose. She had recovered her balance; she was in full possession of her resources. 'I found I wished to wait for you,' she said urbanely. 'But it's not to talk about Pansy.'

Isabel wondered what it could be to talk about, and in spite of Madame Merle's declaration she answered after a moment: 'Madame Catherine says it's enough.'

'Yes; it also seems to me enough. I wanted to ask you another word about poor Mr Touchett,' Madame Merle added. 'Have you reason to believe that he's really at his last?'

'I've no information but a telegram. Unfortunately it only confirms a probability.'

'I'm going to ask you a strange question,' said Madame Merle. 'Are you very fond of your cousin?' And she gave a smile as strange as her utterance.

'Yes, I'm very fond of him. But I don't understand you.'

She just hung fire. 'It's rather hard to explain. Something has occurred to me which may not have occurred to you, and I give you the benefit of my idea. Your cousin did you once a great service. Have you never guessed it?'

'He has done me many services.'

'Yes; but one was much above the rest. He made you a rich woman.'

'*He* made me—?'

Madame Merle appearing to see herself successful, she went on more triumphantly: 'He imparted to you that extra lustre which was required to make you a brilliant match. At bottom it's him you've to thank.' She stopped; there was something in Isabel's eyes.

'I don't understand you. It was my uncle's money.'

'Yes; it was your uncle's money, but it was your cousin's idea. He brought his father over to it. Ah, my dear, the sum was large!'

Isabel stood staring; she seemed to-day to live in a world illumined by lurid flashes. 'I don't know why you say such things. I don't know what you know.'

'I know nothing but what I've guessed. But I've guessed that.'

Isabel went to the door and, when she had opened it, stood a moment with her hand on the latch. Then she said—it was her only revenge: 'I believed it was you I had to thank!'

Madame Merle dropped her eyes; she stood there in a kind of proud penance. 'You're very unhappy, I know. But I'm more so.'

'Yes; I can believe that. I think I should like never to see you again.'

Madame Merle raised her eyes. 'I shall go to America,' she quietly remarked while Isabel passed out.

LIII

It was not with surprise, it was with a feeling which in other circumstances would have had much of the effect of joy, that as Isabel descended from the Paris Mail at Charing Cross she stepped into the arms, as it were—or at any rate into the hands—of Henrietta Stackpole. She had telegraphed to her friend from Turin, and though she had not definitely said to herself that Henrietta would meet her, she had felt her telegram would produce some helpful result. On her long journey from Rome her mind had been given up to vagueness; she was unable to question the future. She performed this journey with sightless eyes and took little pleasure in the countries she traversed, decked out though they were in the richest freshness of spring. Her thoughts followed their course through other countries—strange-looking, dimly-lighted, pathless lands, in which there was no change of seasons, but only, as it seemed, a perpetual dreariness of winter. She had plenty to think about; but it was neither reflexion nor conscious purpose that filled her mind. Disconnected visions passed through it, and sudden dull gleams of memory, of expectation. The past and the future came and went at their will, but she saw them only in fitful images, which rose and fell by a logic of their own. It was extraordinary the things she remembered. Now that she was in the secret, now that she knew something that so much concerned her and the eclipse of which had made life resemble an attempt to play whist with an imperfect pack of cards, the truth of things, their mutual relations, their meaning, and for the most part their horror, rose before her with a kind of architectural vastness. She remembered a thousand trifles; they started to life with the spontaneity of a shiver. She had thought them trifles at the time; now she saw that they had been weighted with lead. Yet even now they were trifles after all, for of what use was it to her to understand them? Nothing seemed of use to her to-day. All purpose, all intention, was suspended; all desire too save the single desire to reach her much-embracing refuge. Gardencourt had been her starting-point, and to those muffled chambers it was at least a temporary solution to return. She had gone forth in her strength; she would come back in her weakness, and if the place had been a rest to her before, it would be a sanctuary now. She envied Ralph his dying, for if one were thinking of rest that was the most perfect of all. To cease utterly, to give it all up and not know anything more—this idea was as sweet as the vision of a cool bath in a marble tank, in a darkened chamber, in a hot land.

She had moments indeed in her journey from Rome which were almost as good as being dead. She sat in her corner, so motionless, so passive, simply with the sense of being carried, so detached from hope and regret, that she recalled to herself one of those Etruscan figures couched upon the receptacle of their ashes. There was nothing to regret now—that was all over. Not only the time of her folly, but the time of her repentance was far. The only thing to regret was that Madame Merle had been so—well, so unimaginable. Just here her intelligence dropped, from literal inability to say what it was that Madame Merle had been. Whatever it was it was for Madame Merle herself to regret it; and doubtless she would do so in America, where she had announced she was going. It concerned Isabel no more; she only had an impression that she should never again see Madame Merle. This impression carried her into the future, of which from time to time she had a mutilated glimpse. She saw herself, in the distant years, still in the attitude of a woman who had her life to live, and these intimations contradicted the spirit of the present hour. It might be desirable to get quite away, really away, further away than little grey-green England, but this privilege was evidently to be denied her. Deep in her soul—deeper than any appetite for renunciation—was the sense that life would be her business for a long time to come. And at moments there was something inspiring, almost enlivening, in the conviction. It was a proof of strength—it was a proof she should some day be happy again. It couldn't be she was to live only to suffer; she was still young, after all, and a great many things might happen to her yet. To live only to suffer—only to feel the injury of life repeated and enlarged—it seemed to her she was too valuable, too capable, for that. Then she wondered if it were vain and stupid to think so well of herself. When had it even been a guarantee to be valuable? Wasn't all history full of the destruction of precious things? Wasn't it much more probable that if one were fine one would suffer? It involved then perhaps an admission that one had a certain grossness; but Isabel recognised, as it passed before her eyes, the quick vague shadow of a long future. She should never escape; she should last to the end. Then the middle years wrapped her about again and the grey curtain of her indifference closed her in.

Henrietta kissed her, as Henrietta usually kissed, as if she were afraid she should be caught doing it; and then Isabel stood there in the crowd, looking about her, looking for her servant. She asked nothing; she wished to wait. She had a sudden perception that she should be helped. She rejoiced Henrietta had come; there was something terrible in an arrival in London. The dusky, smoky, far-arching vault of the station, the strange, livid light, the dense, dark, pushing crowd, filled her with a nervous fear and made her put her arm into her friend's. She remembered she had once liked these things; they seemed part of a mighty spectacle in which there was something that touched her. She remembered how she walked away from Euston, in the winter dusk, in the crowded streets, five years before. She could not have done that to-day, and the incident came before her as the deed of another person.

'It's too beautiful that you should have come,' said Henrietta, looking at her as if she thought Isabel might be prepared to challenge the proposition. 'If you hadn't—if you hadn't; well, I don't know,' remarked Miss Stackpole, hinting ominously at her powers of disapproval.

Isabel looked about without seeing her maid. Her eyes rested on another figure, however, which she felt she had seen before; and in a moment she recognised the genial countenance of Mr Bantling. He stood a little apart, and it was not in the power of the multitude that pressed about him to make him yield an inch of the ground he had taken—that of abstracting himself discreetly while the two ladies performed their embraces.

'There's Mr Bantling,' said Isabel, gently, irrelevantly, scarcely caring much now whether she should find her maid or not.

'Oh yes, he goes everywhere with me. Come here, Mr Bantling!' Henrietta exclaimed. Whereupon the gallant bachelor advanced with a smile—a smile tempered, however, by the gravity of the occasion. 'Isn't it lovely she has come?' Henrietta asked. 'He knows all about it,' she added; 'we had quite a discussion. He said you wouldn't, I said you would.'

'I thought you always agreed,' Isabel smiled in return. She felt she could smile now; she had seen in an instant, in Mr Bantling's brave eyes, that he had good news for her. They seemed to say he wished her to remember he was an old friend of her cousin—that he understood, that it was all right. Isabel gave him her hand; she thought of him, extravagantly, as a beautiful blameless knight.

'Oh, I always agree,' said Mr Bantling. 'But she doesn't, you know.'

'Didn't I tell you that a maid was a nuisance?' Henrietta enquired. 'Your young lady has probably remained at Calais.'

'I don't care,' said Isabel, looking at Mr Bantling, whom she had never found so interesting.

'Stay with her while I go and see,' Henrietta commanded, leaving the two for a moment together.

They stood there at first in silence, and then Mr Bantling asked Isabel how it had been on the Channel.

'Very fine. No, I believe it was very rough,' she said, to her companion's obvious surprise. After which she added: 'You've been to Gardencourt, I know.'

'Now how do you know that?'

'I can't tell you—except that you look like a person who has been to Gardencourt.'

'Do you think I look awfully sad? It's awfully sad there, you know.'

'I don't believe you ever look awfully sad. You look awfully kind,' said Isabel with a breadth that cost her no effort. It seemed to her she should never again feel a superficial embarrassment.

Poor Mr Bantling, however, was still in this inferior stage. He blushed a good deal and laughed, he assured her that he was often very blue, and that when he was blue he was awfully fierce. 'You can ask Miss Stackpole, you know. I was at Gardencourt two days ago.'

'Did you see my cousin?'

'Only for a little. But he had been seeing people; Warburton had been there the day before. Ralph was just the same as usual, except that he was in bed and that he looks tremendously ill and that he can't speak,' Mr Bantling pursued. 'He was awfully jolly and funny all the same. He was just as clever as ever. It's awfully wretched.'

Even in the crowded, noisy station this simple picture was vivid. 'Was that late in the day?'

'Yes; I went on purpose. We thought you'd like to know.'

'I'm greatly obliged to you. Can I go down to-night?'

'Ah, I don't think *she'll* let you go,' said Mr Bantling. 'She wants you to stop with her. I made Touchett's man promise to telegraph me to-day, and I found the telegram an hour ago at my club. "Quiet and easy," that's what it says, and it's dated two o'clock. So you see you can wait till to-morrow. You must be awfully tired.'

'Yes, I'm awfully tired. And I thank you again.'

'Oh,' said Mr Bantling, 'we were certain you would like the last news.' On which Isabel vaguely noted that he and Henrietta seemed after all to agree. Miss Stackpole came back with Isabel's maid, whom she had caught in the act of proving her utility. This excellent person, instead of losing herself in the crowd, had simply attended to her mistress's luggage, so that the latter was now at liberty to leave the station. 'You know you're not to think of going to the country to-night,' Henrietta remarked to her. 'It doesn't matter whether there's a train or not. You're to come straight to me in Wimpole Street. There isn't a corner to be had in London, but I've got you one all the same. It isn't a Roman palace, but it will do for a night.'

'I'll do whatever you wish,' Isabel said.

'You'll come and answer a few questions; that's what I wish.'

'She doesn't say anything about dinner, does she, Mrs Osmond?' Mr Bantling enquired jocosely.

Henrietta fixed him a moment with her speculative gaze. 'I see you're in a great hurry to get your own. You'll be at the Paddington Station to-morrow morning at ten.'

'Don't come for my sake, Mr Bantling,' said Isabel.

'He'll come for mine,' Henrietta declared as she ushered her friend into a cab. And later, in a large dusky parlour in Wimpole Street—to do her justice there had been dinner enough—she asked those questions to which she had alluded at the station. 'Did your husband make you a scene about your coming?' That was Miss Stackpole's first enquiry.

'No; I can't say he made a scene.'

'He didn't object then?'

'Yes, he objected very much. But it was not what you'd call a scene.'

'What was it then?'

'It was a very quiet conversation.'

Henrietta for a moment regarded her guest. 'It must have been hellish,' she then remarked. And Isabel didn't deny that it had been hellish. But she confined herself to answering Henrietta's questions, which was easy, as they were tolerably definite. For the present she offered her no new information. 'Well,' said Miss Stackpole at last, 'I've only one criticism to make. I don't see why you promised little Miss Osmond to go back.'

'I'm not sure I myself see now,' Isabel replied. 'But I did then.'

'If you've forgotten your reason perhaps you won't return.'

Isabel waited a moment. 'Perhaps I shall find another.'

'You'll certainly never find a good one.'

'In default of a better my having promised will do,' Isabel suggested.

'Yes; that's why I hate it.'

'Don't speak of it now. I've a little time. Coming away was a complication, but what will going back be?'

'You must remember, after all, that he won't make you a scene!' said Henrietta with much intention.

'He will, though,' Isabel answered gravely. 'It won't be the scene of a moment; it will be a scene of the rest of my life.'

For some minutes the two women sat and considered this remainder, and then Miss Stackpole, to change the subject, as

Isabel had requested, announced abruptly: 'I've been to stay with Lady Pensil!'

'Ah, the invitation came at last!'

'Yes; it took five years. But this time she wanted to see me.'

'Naturally enough.'

'It was more natural than I think you know,' said Henrietta, who fixed her eyes on a distant point. And then she added, turning suddenly: 'Isabel Archer, I beg your pardon. You don't know why? Because I criticised you, and yet I've gone further than you. Mr Osmond, at least, was born on the other side!'

It was a moment before Isabel grasped her meaning; this sense was so modestly, or at least so ingeniously, veiled. Isabel's mind was not possessed at present with the comicality of things; but she greeted with a quick laugh the image that her companion had raised. She immediately recovered herself, however, and with the right excess of intensity, 'Henrietta Stackpole,' she asked, 'are you going to give up your country?'

'Yes, my poor Isabel, I am. I won't pretend to deny it; I look the fact in the face. I'm going to marry Mr Bantling and locate right here in London.'

'It seems very strange,' said Isabel, smiling now.

'Well yes, I suppose it does. I've come to it little by little. I think I know what I'm doing; but I don't know as I can explain.'

'One can't explain one's marriage,' Isabel answered. 'And yours doesn't need to be explained. Mr Bantling isn't a riddle.'

'No, he isn't a bad pun—or even a high flight of American humour. He has a beautiful nature,' Henrietta went on. 'I've studied him for many years and I see right through him. He's as clear as the style of a good prospectus. He's not intellectual, but he appreciates intellect. On the other hand he doesn't exaggerate its claims. I sometimes think we do in the United States.'

'Ah,' said Isabel, 'you're changed indeed! It's the first time I've ever heard you say anything against your native land.'

'I only say that we're too infatuated with mere brainpower; that, after all, isn't a vulgar fault. But I *am* changed; a woman has to change a good deal to marry.'

'I hope you'll be very happy. You will at last—over here—see something of the inner life.'

Henrietta gave a little significant sigh. 'That's the key to the mystery, I believe. I couldn't endure to be kept off. Now I've as good a right as any one!' she added with artless elation.

Isabel was duly diverted, but there was a certain melancholy in her view. Henrietta, after all, had confessed herself human and feminine, Henrietta whom she had hitherto regarded as a light keen flame, a disembodied voice. It was a disappointment to find she had personal susceptibilities, that she was subject to common passions, and that her intimacy with Mr Bantling had not been completely original. There was a want of originality in her marrying him—there was even a kind of stupidity; and for a moment, to Isabel's sense, the dreariness of the world took on a deeper tinge. A little later indeed she reflected that Mr Bantling himself at least was original. But she didn't see how Henrietta could give up her country. She herself had relaxed her hold of it, but it had never been her country as it had been Henrietta's. She presently asked her if she had enjoyed her visit to Lady Pensil.

'Oh yes,' said Henrietta, 'she didn't know what to make of me.'

'And was that very enjoyable?'

'Very much so, because she's supposed to be a master mind. She thinks she knows everything; but she doesn't understand a woman of my modern type. It would be so much easier for her if I were only a little better or a little worse. She's so puzzled; I believe she thinks it's my duty to go and do something immoral. She thinks it's immoral that I should marry her brother; but, after all, that isn't immoral enough. And she'll never understand my mixture—never!'

'She's not so intelligent as her brother then,' said Isabel. 'He appears to have understood.'

'Oh no, he hasn't!' cried Miss Stackpole with decision. 'I really believe that's what he wants to marry me for—just to find out the mystery and the proportions of it. That's a fixed idea—a kind of fascination.'

'It's very good in you to humour it.'

'Oh well,' said Henrietta, 'I've something to find out too!'

And Isabel saw that she had not renounced an allegiance, but planned an attack. She was at last about to grapple in earnest with England.

Isabel also perceived, however, on the morrow, at the Paddington Station, where she found herself, at ten o'clock, in the company both of Miss Stackpole and Mr Bantling, that the gentleman bore his perplexities lightly. If he had not found out everything he had found out at least the great point—that Miss Stackpole would not be wanting in initiative. It was evident that in the selection of a wife he had been on his guard against this deficiency.

'Henrietta has told me, and I'm very glad,' Isabel said as she gave him her hand.

'I dare say you think it awfully odd,' Mr Bantling replied, resting on his neat umbrella.

'Yes, I think it awfully odd.'

'You can't think it so awfully odd as I do. But I've always rather liked striking out a line,' said Mr Bantling serenely.

LIV

ISABEL'S arrival at Gardencourt on this second occasion was even quieter than it had been on the first. Ralph Touchett kept but a small household, and to the new servants Mrs Osmond was a stranger; so that instead of being conducted to her own apartment she was coldly shown into the drawing-room and left to wait while her name was carried up to her aunt. She waited a long time; Mrs Touchett appeared in no hurry to come to her. She grew impatient at last; she grew nervous and scared—as scared as if the objects about her had begun to show for conscious things, watching her trouble with grotesque grimaces. The day was dark and cold; the dusk was thick in the corners of the wide brown rooms. The house was perfectly still—with a stillness that Isabel remembered; it had filled all the place for days before the death of her uncle She left the drawing-room and wandered about—strolled into the library and along the gallery of pictures, where, in the deep silence, her footstep made an echo. Nothing was changed; she recognised everything she had seen years before; it might have been only yesterday she had stood there. She envied the security of valuable 'pieces' which change by no hair's breadth, only grow in value, while their owners lose inch by inch youth, happiness, beauty; and she became aware that she was walking about as her aunt had done on the day she had come to see her in Albany. She was changed enough since then—that had been the beginning. It suddenly struck her that if her Aunt Lydia had not come that day in just that way and found her alone, everything might have been different. She might have had another life and she might have been a woman more blest. She stopped in the gallery in front of a small picture—a charming and precious Bonington*—upon which her eyes rested a long time. But she was not looking at the picture; she was wondering whether if her aunt had not come that day in Albany she would have married Caspar Goodwood.

Mrs Touchett appeared at last, just after Isabel had returned to the big uninhabited drawing-room. She looked a good deal older, but her eye was as bright as ever and her head as erect; her thin lips seemed a repository of latent meanings. She wore a little grey dress of the most undecorated fashion, and Isabel wondered, as she had wondered the first time, if her remarkable kinswoman resembled more a queen-regent or the matron of a gaol. Her lips felt very thin indeed on Isabel's hot cheek.

'I've kept you waiting because I've been sitting with Ralph,' Mrs Touchett said. 'The nurse had gone to luncheon and I had taken her place. He has a man who's supposed to look after him, but the man's good for nothing; he's always looking out of the window—as if there were anything to see! I didn't wish to move, because Ralph seemed to be sleeping and I was afraid the sound would disturb him. I waited till the nurse came back; I remembered you knew the house.'

'I find I know it better even than I thought; I've been walking everywhere,' Isabel answered. And then she asked if Ralph slept much.

'He lies with his eyes closed; he doesn't move. But I'm not sure that it's always sleep.'

'Will he see me? Can he speak to me?'

Mrs Touchett declined the office of saying. 'You can try him,' was the limit of her extravagance. And then she offered to conduct Isabel to her room. 'I thought they had taken you there; but it's not my house, it's Ralph's; and I don't know what they do. They must at least have taken your luggage; I don't suppose you've brought much. Not that I care, however. I believe they've given you the same room you had before; when Ralph heard you were coming he said you must have that one.'

'Did he say anything else?'

'Ah, my dear, he doesn't chatter as he used!' cried Mrs Touchett as she preceded her niece up the staircase.

It was the same room, and something told Isabel it had not been slept in since she occupied it. Her luggage was there and was not voluminous; Mrs Touchett sat down a moment with her eyes upon it. 'Is there really no hope?' our young woman asked as she stood before her.

'None whatever. There never has been. It has not been a successful life.'

'No—it has only been a beautiful one.' Isabel found herself already contradicting her aunt; she was irritated by her dryness.

'I don't know what you mean by that; there's no beauty without health. That is a very odd dress to travel in.'

Isabel glanced at her garment. 'I left Rome at an hour's notice; I took the first that came.'

'Your sisters, in America, wished to know how you dress. That seemed to be their principal interest. I wasn't able to tell them—but they seemed to have the right idea: that you never wear anything less than black brocade.'

'They think I'm more brilliant than I am; I'm afraid to tell them the truth,' said Isabel. 'Lily wrote me you had dined with her.'

'She invited me four times, and I went once. After the second time she should have let me alone. The dinner was very good; it must have been expensive. Her husband has a very bad manner. Did I enjoy my visit to America? Why should I have enjoyed it? I didn't go for my pleasure.'

These were interesting items, but Mrs Touchett soon left her niece, whom she was to meet in half an hour at the midday meal. For this repast the two ladies faced each other at an abbreviated table in the melancholy dining-room. Here, after a little, Isabel saw her aunt not to be so dry as she appeared, and her old pity for the poor woman's inexpressiveness, her want of regret, of disappointment, came back to her. Unmistakeably she would have found it a blessing to-day to be able to feel a defeat, a mistake, even a shame or two. She wondered if she were not even missing those enrichments of consciousness and privately trying—reaching out for some aftertaste of life, dregs of the banquet; the testimony of pain or the cold recreation of remorse. On the other hand perhaps she was afraid; if she should begin to know remorse at all it might take her too far. Isabel could perceive, however, how it had come over her dimly that she had failed of something, that she saw herself in the future as an old woman without memories. Her little sharp face looked tragical. She told her niece that Ralph had as yet not moved, but that he probably would be able to see her before dinner. And then in a moment she added that he had seen Lord Warburton the day before; an announcement which startled Isabel a little, as it seemed an intimation that this personage was in the neighbourhood and that an accident might bring them together. Such an accident would not be happy; she had not come to England to struggle again with Lord Warburton. She none the less presently said to her aunt that he had been very kind to Ralph; she had seen something of that in Rome.

'He has something else to think of now,' Mrs Touchett returned. And she paused with a gaze like a gimlet.

Isabel saw she meant something, and instantly guessed what she meant. But her reply concealed her guess; her heart beat faster and she wished to gain a moment. 'Ah yes—the House of Lords and all that.'

'He's not thinking of the Lords; he's thinking of the ladies. At least he's thinking of one of them; he told Ralph he's engaged to be married.'

'Ah, to be married!' Isabel mildly exclaimed.

'Unless he breaks it off. He seemed to think Ralph would like to know. Poor Ralph can't go to the wedding, though I believe it's to take place very soon.'

'And who's the young lady?'

'A member of the aristocracy; Lady Flora, Lady Felicia—something of that sort.'

'I'm very glad,' Isabel said. 'It must be a sudden decision.'

'Sudden enough, I believe; a courtship of three weeks. It has only just been made public.'

'I'm very glad,' Isabel repeated with a larger emphasis. She knew her aunt was watching her—looking for the signs of some imputed soreness, and the desire to prevent her companion from seeing anything of this kind enabled her to speak in the tone of quick satisfaction, the tone almost of relief. Mrs Touchett of course followed the tradition that ladies, even married ones, regard the marriage of their old lovers as an offence to themselves. Isabel's first care therefore was to show that however that might be in general she was not offended now. But meanwhile, as I say, her heart beat faster; and if she sat for some moments thoughtful—she presently forgot Mrs Touchett's observation—it was not because she had lost an admirer. Her imagination had traversed half Europe; it halted, panting, and even trembling a little, in the city of Rome. She figured herself announcing to her husband that Lord Warburton was to lead a bride to the altar, and she was of course not aware how extremely wan she must have looked while she made this intellectual effort. But at last she collected herself and said to her aunt: 'He was sure to do it some time or other.'

Mrs Touchett was silent; then she gave a sharp little shake of the head. 'Ah, my dear, you're beyond me!' she cried suddenly. They went on with their luncheon in silence; Isabel felt as if she had heard of Lord Warburton's death. She had known him only as a suitor, and now that was all over. He was dead for poor Pansy; by Pansy he might have lived. A servant had been hovering about; at last Mrs Touchett requested him to leave them alone. She had finished her meal; she sat with her hands folded on the edge of the table. 'I should like to ask you three questions,' she observed when the servant had gone.

'Three are a great many.'

'I can't do with less; I've been thinking. They're all very good ones.'

'That's what I'm afraid of. The best questions are the worst,' Isabel answered. Mrs Touchett had pushed back her chair, and as her niece left the table and walked, rather consciously, to one of the deep windows, she felt herself followed by her eyes.

'Have you ever been sorry you didn't marry Lord Warburton?' Mrs Touchett enquired.

Isabel shook her head slowly, but not heavily. 'No, dear aunt.'

'Good. I ought to tell you that I propose to believe what you say.'

'Your believing me's an immense temptation,' she declared, smiling still.

'A temptation to lie? I don't recommend you to do that, for when I'm misinformed I'm as dangerous as a poisoned rat. I don't mean to crow over you.'

'It's my husband who doesn't get on with me,' said Isabel.

'I could have told him he wouldn't. I don't call that crowing over *you*,' Mrs Touchett added. 'Do you still like Serena Merle?' she went on.

'Not as I once did. But it doesn't matter, for she's going to America.'

'To America? She must have done something very bad.'

'Yes—very bad.'

'May I ask what it is?'

'She made a convenience of me.'

'Ah,' cried Mrs Touchett, 'so she did of me! She does of every one.'

'She'll make a convenience of America,' said Isabel, smiling again and glad that her aunt's questions were over.

It was not till the evening that she was able to see Ralph. He had been dozing all day; at least he had been lying unconscious. The doctor was there, but after a while went away—the local doctor, who had attended his father and whom Ralph liked. He came three or four times a day; he was deeply interested in his patient. Ralph had had Sir Matthew Hope, but he had got tired of this celebrated man, to whom he had asked his mother to send word he was now dead and was therefore without further need of medical advice. Mrs Touchett had simply written to Sir Matthew that her son disliked him. On the day of Isabel's arrival Ralph gave no sign, as I have related, for many hours; but toward evening he raised himself and said he knew that she had come. How he knew was not apparent, inasmuch as for fear of exciting him no one had offered the information. Isabel came in and sat by his bed in the dim light; there was only a shaded candle in a corner of the room. She told the nurse she might go—she herself would sit with him for the rest of the evening. He had opened his eyes and recognised her, and had moved his hand, which lay helpless beside him, so that she might take it. But he was unable to speak; he closed his eyes again and remained perfectly still, only keeping her hand in his own. She sat with him a long time—till the nurse came back; but he gave no further sign. He might have passed away while she looked at him; he was already the figure and pattern of death. She had thought him far gone in Rome, and this was worse; there was but one change possible now. There was a strange tranquillity in his face; it was as still as the lid of a box. With this he was a mere lattice of bones; when he opened his eyes to greet her it was as if she were looking into immeasurable space. It was not till midnight that the nurse came back; but the hours, to Isabel, had not seemed long; it was exactly what she had come for. If she had come simply to wait she found ample occasion, for he lay three days in a kind of grateful silence. He recognised her and at moments seemed to wish to speak; but he found no voice. Then he closed his eyes again, as if he too were waiting for something—for something that certainly would come. He was so absolutely quiet that it seemed to her what was coming had already arrived; and yet she never lost the sense that they were still together. But they were not always together; there were other hours that she passed in wandering through the empty house and listening for a voice that was not poor Ralph's. She had a constant fear; she thought it possible her husband would write to her. But he remained silent, and she only got a letter from Florence and from the Countess Gemini. Ralph, however, spoke at last—on the evening of the third day.

'I feel better to-night,' he murmured, abruptly, in the soundless dimness of her vigil; 'I think I can say something.' She sank upon her knees beside his pillow; took his thin hand in her own; begged him not to make an effort—not to tire himself. His face was of necessity serious—it was incapable of the muscular play of a smile; but its owner apparently had not lost a perception of incongruities. 'What does it matter if I'm tired when I've all eternity to rest? There's no harm in making an effort when it's the very last of all. Don't people always feel better just before the end? I've often heard of that; it's what I was waiting for. Ever since you've been here I thought it would come. I tried two or three times; I was afraid you'd get tired of sitting there.' He spoke slowly, with painful breaks and long pauses; his voice seemed to come from a distance. When he ceased he lay with his face turned to Isabel and his large unwinking eyes open into her own. 'It was very good of you to come,' he went on. 'I thought you would; but I wasn't sure.'

'I was not sure either till I came,' said Isabel.

'You've been like an angel beside my bed. You know they

talk about the angel of death. It's the most beautiful of all. You've been like that; as if you were waiting for me.'

'I was not waiting for your death; I was waiting for—for this. This is not death, dear Ralph.'

'Not for you—no. There's nothing makes us feel so much alive as to see others die. That's the sensation of life—the sense that we remain. I've had it—even I. But now I'm of no use but to give it to others. With me it's all over.' And then he paused. Isabel bowed her head further, till it rested on the two hands that were clasped upon his own. She couldn't see him now; but his far-away voice was close to her ear. 'Isabel,' he went on suddenly, 'I wish it were over for you.' She answered nothing; she had burst into sobs; she remained so, with her buried face. He lay silent, listening to her sobs; at last he gave a long groan. 'Ah, what is it you have done for me?'

'What is it you did for me?' she cried, her now extreme agitation half smothered by her attitude. She had lost all her shame, all wish to hide things. Now he must know; she wished him to know, for it brought them supremely together, and he was beyond the reach of pain. 'You did something once—you know it. O Ralph, you've been everything! What have I done for you—what can I do to-day? I would die if you could live. But I don't wish you to live; I would die myself, not to lose you.' Her voice was as broken as his own and full of tears and anguish.

'You won't lose me—you'll keep me. Keep me in your heart; I shall be nearer to you than I've ever been. Dear Isabel, life is better; for in life there's love. Death is good—but there's no love.'

'I never thanked you—I never spoke—I never was what I should be!' Isabel went on. She felt a passionate need to cry out and accuse herself, to let her sorrow possess her. All her troubles, for the moment, became single and melted together into this present pain. 'What must you have thought of me? Yet how could I know? I never knew, and I only know to-day because there are people less stupid than I.'

'Don't mind people,' said Ralph. 'I think I'm glad to leave people.'

She raised her head and her clasped hands; she seemed for a moment to pray to him. 'Is it true—is it true?' she asked.

'True that you've been stupid? Oh no,' said Ralph with a sensible intention of wit.

'That you made me rich—that all I have is yours?'

He turned away his head, and for some time said nothing. Then at last: 'Ah, don't speak of that—that was not happy.' Slowly he moved his face toward her again, and they once more saw each other. 'But for that—but for that—!' And he paused. 'I believe I ruined you,' he wailed.

She was full of the sense that he was beyond the reach of pain; he seemed already so little of this world. But even if she had not had it she would still have spoken, for nothing mattered now but the only knowledge that was not pure anguish—the knowledge that they were looking at the truth together. 'He married me for the money,' she said. She wished to say everything; she was afraid he might die before she had done so.

He gazed at her a little, and for the first time his fixed eyes lowered their lids. But he raised them in a moment, and then, 'He was greatly in love with you,' he answered.

'Yes, he was in love with me. But he wouldn't have married me if I had been poor. I don't hurt you in saying that. How can I? I only want you to understand. I always tried to keep you from understanding; but that's all over.'

'I always understood,' said Ralph.

'I thought you did, and I didn't like it. But now I like it.'

'You don't hurt me—you make me very happy.' And as Ralph said this there was an extraordinary gladness in his voice. She bent her head again, and pressed her lips to the back of his hand. 'I always understood,' he continued, 'though it was so strange—so pitiful. You wanted to look at life for yourself—but you were not allowed; you were punished for your wish. You were ground in the very mill of the conventional!'

'Oh yes, I've been punished,' Isabel sobbed.

He listened to her a little, and then continued: 'Was he very bad about your coming?'

'He made it very hard for me. But I don't care.'

'It is all over then between you?'

'Oh no; I don't think anything's over.'

'Are you going back to him?' Ralph gasped.

'I don't know—I can't tell. I shall stay here as long as I may. I don't want to think—I needn't think. I don't care for anything but you, and that's enough for the present. It will last a little yet. Here on my knees, with you dying in my arms, I'm happier than I have been for a long time. And I want you to be happy—not to think of anything sad; only to feel that I'm near you and I love you. Why should there be pain? In such hours as this what have we to do with pain? That's not the deepest thing; there's something deeper.'

Ralph evidently found from moment to moment greater difficulty in speaking; he had to wait longer to collect himself. At first he appeared to make no response to these last words; he let a long time elapse. Then he murmured simply: 'You must stay here.'

'I should like to stay—as long as seems right.'

'As seems right—as seems right?' He repeated her words. 'Yes, you think a great deal about that.'

'Of course one must. You're very tired,' said Isabel.

'I'm very tired. You said just now that pain's not the deepest thing. No—no. But it's very deep. If I could stay—'

'For me you'll always be here,' she softly interrupted. It was easy to interrupt him.

But he went on, after a moment: 'It passes, after all; it's passing now. But love remains. I don't know why we should suffer so much. Perhaps I shall find out. There are many things in life. You're very young.'

'I feel very old,' said Isabel.

'You'll grow young again. That's how I see you. I don't believe—I don't believe—' But he stopped again; his strength failed him.

She begged him to be quiet now. 'We needn't speak to understand each other,' she said.

'I don't believe that such a generous mistake as yours can hurt you for more than a little.'

'Oh Ralph, I'm very happy now,' she cried through her tears.

'And remember this,' he continued, 'that if you've been hated you've also been loved. Ah but, Isabel—*adored!*' he just audibly and lingeringly breathed.

'Oh my brother!' she cried with a movement of still deeper prostration.

LV

He had told her, the first evening she ever spent at Gardencourt, that if she should live to suffer enough she might some day see the ghost with which the old house was duly provided. She apparently had fulfilled the necessary condition; for the next morning, in the cold, faint dawn, she knew that a spirit was standing by her bed. She had lain down without undressing, it being her belief that Ralph would not outlast the night. She had no inclination to sleep; she was waiting, and such waiting was wakeful. But she closed her eyes; she believed that as the night wore on she should hear a knock at her door. She heard no knock, but at the time the darkness began vaguely to grow grey she started up from her pillow as abruptly as if she had received a summons. It seemed to her for an instant that he was standing there—a vague, hovering figure in the vagueness of the room. She stared a moment; she saw his white face—his kind eyes; then she saw there was nothing. She was not afraid; she was only sure. She quitted the place and in her certainty passed through dark corridors and down a flight of oaken steps that shone in the vague light of a hall-window. Outside Ralph's door she stopped a moment, listening, but she seemed to hear only the hush that filled it. She opened the door with a hand as gentle as if she were lifting a veil from the face of the dead, and saw Mrs Touchett sitting motionless and upright beside the couch of her son, with one of his hands in her own. The doctor was on the other side, with poor Ralph's further wrist resting in his professional fingers. The two nurses were at the foot between them. Mrs Touchett took no notice of Isabel, but the doctor looked at her very hard; then he gently placed Ralph's hand in a proper position, close beside him. The nurse looked at her very hard too, and no one said a word; but Isabel only looked at what she had come to see. It was fairer than Ralph had ever been in life, and there was a strange resemblance to the face of his father, which, six years before, she had seen lying on the same pillow. She went to her aunt and put her arm around her; and Mrs

Touchett, who as a general thing neither invited nor enjoyed caresses, submitted for a moment to this one, rising, as might be, to take it. But she was stiff and dry-eyed; her acute white face was terrible.

'Dear Aunt Lydia,' Isabel murmured.

'Go and thank God you've no child,' said Mrs Touchett, disengaging herself.

Three days after this a considerable number of people found time, at the height of the London 'season,' to take a morning train down to a quiet station in Berkshire and spend half an hour in a small grey church which stood within an easy walk. It was in the green burial-place of this edifice that Mrs Touchett consigned her son to earth. She stood herself at the edge of the grave, and Isabel stood beside her; the sexton himself had not a more practical interest in the scene than Mrs Touchett. It was a solemn occasion, but neither a harsh nor a heavy one; there was a certain geniality in the appearance of things. The weather had changed to fair; the day, one of the last of the treacherous May-time, was warm and windless, and the air had the brightness of the hawthorn and the blackbird. If it was sad to think of poor Touchett, it was not too sad, since death, for him, had had no violence. He had been dying so long; he was so ready; everything had been so expected and prepared. There were tears in Isabel's eyes, but they were not tears that blinded. She looked through them at the beauty of the day, the splendour of nature, the sweetness of the old English churchyard, the bowed heads of good friends. Lord Warburton was there, and a group of gentlemen all unknown to her, several of whom, as she afterwards learned, were connected with the bank; and there were others whom she knew. Miss Stackpole was among the first, with honest Mr Bantling beside her; and Caspar Goodwood, lifting his head higher than the rest—bowing it rather less. During much of the time Isabel was conscious of Mr Goodwood's gaze; he looked at her somewhat harder than he usually looked in public, while the others had fixed their eyes upon the churchyard turf. But she never let him see that she saw him; she thought of him only to wonder that he was still in England. She found she had taken for granted that after accompanying Ralph to Gardencourt he had gone away; she remembered how little it was a country that pleased him. He was there, however, very distinctly there; and something in his attitude seemed to say that he was there with a complex intention. She wouldn't meet his eyes, though there was doubtless sympathy in them; he made her rather uneasy. With the dispersal of the little group he disappeared, and the only person who came to speak to her—though several spoke to Mrs Touchett—was Henrietta Stackpole. Henrietta had been crying.

Ralph had said to Isabel that he hoped she would remain at Gardencourt, and she made no immediate motion to leave the place. She said to herself that it was but common charity to stay a little with her aunt. It was fortunate she had so good a formula; otherwise she might have been greatly in want of one. Her errand was over; she had done what she had left her husband to do. She had a husband in a foreign city, counting the hours of her absence; in such a case one needed an excellent motive. He was not one of the best husbands, but that didn't alter the case. Certain obligations were involved in the very fact of marriage, and were quite independent of the quantity of enjoyment extracted from it. Isabel thought of her husband as little as might be; but now that she was at a distance, beyond its spell, she thought with a kind of spiritual shudder of Rome. There was a penetrating chill in the image, and she drew back into the deepest shade of Gardencourt. She lived from day to day, postponing, closing her eyes, trying not to think. She knew she must decide, but she decided nothing; her coming itself had not been a decision. On that occasion she had simply started. Osmond gave no sound and now evidently would give none; he would leave it all to her. From Pansy she heard nothing, but that was very simple: her father had told her not to write.

Mrs Touchett accepted Isabel's company, but offered her no assistance; she appeared to be absorbed in considering, without enthusiasm but with perfect lucidity, the new conveniences of her own situation. Mrs Touchett was not an optimist, but even from painful occurrences she managed to extract a certain utility. This consisted in the reflexion that, after all, such things happened to other people and not to herself.

Death was disagreeable, but in this case it was her son's death, not her own; she had never flattered herself that her own would be disagreeable to any one but Mrs Touchett. She was better off than poor Ralph, who had left all the commodities of life behind him, and indeed all the security; since the worst of dying was, to Mrs Touchett's mind, that it exposed one to be taken advantage of. For herself she was on the spot; there was nothing so good as that. She made known to Isabel very punctually—it was the evening her son was buried—several of Ralph's testamentary arrangements. He had told her everything, had consulted her about everything. He left her no money; of course she had no need of money. He left her the furniture of Gardencourt, exclusive of the pictures and books and the use of the place for a year; after which it was to be sold. The money produced by the sale was to constitute an endowment for a hospital for poor persons suffering from the malady of which he died; and of this portion of the will Lord Warburton was appointed executor. The rest of his property, which was to be withdrawn from the bank, was disposed of in various bequests, several of them to those cousins in Vermont to whom his father had already been so bountiful. Then there were a number of small legacies.

'Some of them are extremely peculiar,' said Mrs Touchett; 'he has left considerable sums to persons I never heard of. He gave me a list, and I asked then who some of them were, and he told me they were people who at various times had seemed to like him. Apparently he thought you didn't like him, for he hasn't left you a penny. It was his opinion that you had been handsomely treated by his father, which I'm bound to say I think you were—though I don't mean that I ever heard him complain of it. The pictures are to be dispersed; he has distributed them about, one by one, as little keepsakes. The most valuable of the collection goes to Lord Warburton. And what do you think he has done with his library? It sounds like a practical joke. He has left it to your friend Miss Stackpole—"in recognition of her services to literature." Does he mean her following him up from Rome? Was that a service to literature? It contains a great many rare and valuable books, and as she can't carry it about the world in her trunk he recommends her to sell it at auction. She will sell it of course at Christie's, and with the proceeds she'll set up a newspaper. Will that be a service to literature?'

This question Isabel forbore to answer, as it exceeded the little interrogatory to which she had deemed it necessary to submit on her arrival. Besides, she had never been less interested in literature than to-day, as she found when she occasionally took down from the shelf one of the rare and valuable volumes of which Mrs Touchett had spoken. She was quite unable to read; her attention had never been so little at her command. One afternoon, in the library, about a week after the ceremony in the churchyard, she was trying to fix it for an hour; but her eyes often wandered from the book in her hand to the open window, which looked down the long avenue. It was in this way that she saw a modest vehicle approach the door and perceived Lord Warburton sitting, in rather an uncomfortable attitude, in a corner of it. He had always had a high standard of courtesy, and it was therefore not remarkable, under the circumstances, that he should have taken the trouble to come down from London to call on Mrs Touchett. It was of course Mrs Touchett he had come to see, and not Mrs Osmond; and to prove to herself the validity of this thesis Isabel presently stepped out of the house and wandered away into the park. Since her arrival at Gardencourt she had been but little out of doors, the weather being unfavourable for visiting the grounds. This evening, however, was fine, and at first it struck her as a happy thought to have come out. The theory I have just mentioned was plausible enough, but it brought her little rest, and if you had seen her pacing about you would have said she had a bad conscience. She was not pacified when at the end of a quarter of an hour, finding herself in view of the house, she saw Mrs Touchett emerge from the portico accompanied by her visitor. Her aunt had evidently proposed to Lord Warburton that they should come in search of her. She was in no humour for visitors and, if she had had a chance, would have drawn back behind one of the great trees. But she saw she had been seen and that nothing was left her but to advance. As the lawn at Gardencourt was a vast expanse this took some time; during which she observed that, as he walked beside his hostess, Lord Warburton kept his hands rather stiffly behind him and his eyes upon the ground. Both persons apparently were silent; but Mrs Touchett's thin little glance, as she directed it toward Isabel, had even at a distance an expression. It seemed to say with cutting sharpness: 'Here's the eminently amenable nobleman you might have married!' When Lord Warburton lifted his own eyes, however, that was not what they said. They only said 'This is rather awkward, you know, and I depend upon you to help me.' He was very grave, very proper and, for the first time since Isabel had known him, greeted her without a smile. Even in his days of distress he had always begun with a smile. He looked extremely self-conscious.

'Lord Warburton has been so good as to come out to see me,' said Mrs Touchett. 'He tells me he didn't know you were still here. I know he's an old friend of yours, and as I was told you were not in the house I brought him out to see for himself.'

'Oh, I saw there was a good train at 6.40, that would get me back in time for dinner,' Mrs Touchett's companion rather irrelevantly explained. 'I'm so glad to find you've not gone.'

'I'm not here for long, you know,' Isabel said with a certain eagerness.

'I suppose not; but I hope it's for some weeks. You came to England sooner than—a—than you thought?'

'Yes, I came very suddenly.'

Mrs Touchett turned away as if she were looking at the condition of the grounds, which indeed was not what it should be, while Lord Warburton hesitated a little. Isabel fancied he had been on the point of asking about her husband—rather confusedly—and then had checked himself. He continued immitigably grave, either because he thought it becoming in a place over which death had just passed, or for more personal reasons. If he was conscious of personal reasons it was very fortunate that he had the cover of the former motive; he could make the most of that. Isabel thought of all this. It was not that his face was sad, for that was another matter; but it was strangely inexpressive.

'My sisters would have been so glad to come if they had known you were still here—if they had thought you would see them,' Lord Warburton went on. 'Do kindly let them see you before you leave England.'

'It would give me great pleasure; I have such a friendly recollection of them.'

'I don't know whether you would come to Lockleigh for a day or two? You know there's always that old promise.' And his lordship coloured a little as he made this suggestion, which gave his face a somewhat more familiar air. 'Perhaps I'm not right in saying that just now; of course you're not thinking of visiting. But I meant what would hardly be a visit. My sisters are to be at Lockleigh at Whitsuntide for five days; and if you could come then—as you say you're not to be very long in England—I would see that there should be literally no one else.'

Isabel wondered if not even the young lady he was to marry would be there with her mamma; but she did not express this idea. 'Thank you extremely,' she contented herself with saying; 'I'm afraid I hardly know about Whitsuntide.'

'But I have your promise—haven't I?—for some other time.'

There was an interrogation in this; but Isabel let it pass. She looked at her interlocutor a moment, and the result of her observation was that—as had happened before—she felt sorry for him. 'Take care you don't miss your train,' she said. And then she added: 'I wish you every happiness.'

He blushed again, more than before, and he looked at his watch. 'Ah yes, 6.40; I haven't much time, but I've a fly at the door. Thank you very much.' It was not apparent whether the thanks applied to her having reminded him of his train or to the more sentimental remark. 'Good-bye, Mrs Osmond; good-bye.' He shook hands with her, without meeting her eyes, and then he turned to Mrs Touchett, who had wandered back to them. With her his parting was equally brief; and in a moment the two ladies saw him move with long steps across the lawn.

'Are you very sure he's to be married?' Isabel asked of her aunt.

'I can't be surer than he; but he seems sure. I congratulated him, and he accepted it.'

'Ah,' said Isabel, 'I give it up!'—while her aunt returned to the house and to those avocations which the visitor had interrupted.

She gave it up, but she still thought of it—thought of it while she strolled again under the great oaks whose shadows were long upon the acres of turf. At the end of a few minutes she found herself near a rustic bench, which, a moment after she had looked at it, struck her as an object recognised. It was not simply that she had seen it before, nor even that she had sat upon it; it was that on this spot something important had happened to her—that the place had an air of association. Then she remembered that she had been sitting there, six years before, when a servant brought her from the house the letter in which Caspar Goodwood informed her that he had followed her to Europe; and that when she had read the letter she looked up to hear Lord Warburton announcing that he should like to marry her. It was indeed an historical, an interesting, bench; she stood and looked at it as if it might have something to say to her. She wouldn't sit down on it now—she felt rather afraid of it. She only stood before it, and while she stood the past came back to her in one of those rushing waves of emotion by which persons of sensibility are visited at odd hours. The effect of this agitation was a sudden sense of being very tired, under the influence of which she overcame her scruples and sank into the rustic seat. I have said that she was restless and unable to occupy herself; and whether or no, if you had seen her there, you would have admired the justice of the former epithet, you would at least have allowed that at this moment she was the image of a victim of idleness. Her attitude had a singular absence of purpose; her hands, hanging at her sides, lost themselves in the folds of her black dress; her eyes gazed vaguely before her. There was nothing to recall her to the house; the two ladies, in their seclusion, dined early and had tea at an indefinite hour. How long she had sat in this position she could not have told you; but the twilight had grown thick when she became aware that she was not alone. She quickly straightened herself, glancing about, and then saw what had become of her solitude. She was sharing it with Caspar Goodwood, who stood looking at her, a few yards off, and whose footfall on the unresonant turf, as he came near, she had not heard. It occurred to her in the midst of this that it was just so Lord Warburton had surprised her of old.

She instantly rose, and as soon as Goodwood saw he was seen he started forward. She had had time only to rise when, with a motion that looked like violence, but felt like—she knew not what, he grasped her by the wrist and made her sink again into the seat. She closed her eyes; he had not hurt her; it was only a touch, which she had obeyed. But there was something in his face that she wished not to see. That was the way he had looked at her the other day in the churchyard; only at present it was worse. He said nothing at first; she only felt him close to her—beside her on the bench and pressingly turned to her. It almost seemed to her that no one had ever been so close to her as that. All this, however, took but an instant, at the end of which she had disengaged her wrist, turning her eyes upon her visitant. 'You've frightened me,' she said.

'I didn't mean to,' he answered, 'but if I did a little, no matter. I came from London a while ago by the train, but I couldn't come here directly. There was a man at the station who got ahead of me. He took a fly that was there, and I heard him give the order to drive here. I don't know who he was, but I didn't want to come with him; I wanted to see you alone. So I've been waiting and walking about. I've walked all over, and I was just coming to the house when I saw you here. There was a keeper, or some one, who met me; but that was all right, because I had made his acquaintance when I came here with your cousin. Is that gentleman gone? Are you really alone? I want to speak to you.' Goodwood spoke very fast; he was as excited as when they had parted in Rome. Isabel had hoped that condition would subside; and she shrank into herself as she perceived that, on the contrary, he had only let out sail. She had a new sensation; he had never produced it before; it was a feeling of danger. There was indeed something really formidable in his resolution. She gazed straight before her; he, with a hand on each knee, leaned forward, looking deeply into her face. The twilight seemed to darken round them. 'I want to speak to you,' he repeated; 'I've something particular to say. I don't want to trouble you—as I did the other day in Rome. That was of no use; it only distressed you. I couldn't help it; I knew I was wrong. But I'm not wrong now; please don't think I am,' he went on with his hard, deep voice melting a moment into entreaty. 'I came here to-day for a purpose. It's very different. It was vain for me to speak to you then; but now I can help you.'

She couldn't have told you whether it was because she was afraid, or because such a voice in the darkness seemed of necessity a boon; but she listened to him as she had never listened before; his words dropped deep into her soul. They produced a sort of stillness in all her being; and it was with an effort, in a moment, that she answered him. 'How can you help me?' she asked in a low tone, as if she were taking what he had said seriously enough to make the enquiry in confidence.

'By inducing you to trust me. Now I know—to-day I know. Do you remember what I asked you in Rome? Then I was quite in the dark. But to-day I know on good authority; everything's clear to me to-day. It was a good thing when you made me come away with your cousin. He was a good man, a fine man, one of the best; he told me how the case stands for you. He explained everything; he guessed my sentiments. He was a member of your family and he left you—so long as you should be in England—to my care,' said Goodwood as if he were making a great point. 'Do you know what he said to me the last time I saw him—as he lay there where he died? He said: "Do everything you can for her; do everything she'll let you." '

Isabel suddenly got up. 'You had no business to talk about me!'

'Why not—why not, when we talked in that way?' he demanded, following her fast. 'And he was dying—when a man's dying it's different.' She checked the movement she had made to leave him; she was listening more than ever; it was true that he was not the same as that last time. That had been aimless, fruitless passion, but at present he had an idea, which she scented in all her being. 'But it doesn't matter!' he exclaimed, pressing her still harder, though now without touching a hem of her garment. 'If Touchett had never opened his mouth I should have known all the same. I had only to look at you at your cousin's funeral to see what's the matter with you. You can't deceive me any more; for God's sake be honest with a man who's so honest with you. You're the most unhappy of women, and your husband's the deadliest of fiends.'

She turned on him as if he had struck her. 'Are you mad?' she cried.

'I've never been so sane; I see the whole thing. Don't think it's necessary to defend him. But I won't say another word against him; I'll speak only of you,' Goodwood added quickly. 'How can you pretend you're not heart-broken? You don't know what to do—you don't know where to turn. It's too late to play a part; didn't you leave all that behind you in Rome? Touchett knew all about it, and I knew it too—what it would cost you to come here. It will have cost you your life? Say it will'—and he flared almost into anger: 'give me one word of truth! When I know such a horror as that, how can I keep myself from wishing to save you? What would you think of me if I should stand still and see you go back to your reward? "It's awful, what she'll have to pay for it!"—that's what Touchett said to me. I may tell you that, mayn't I? He was such a near relation!' cried Goodwood, making his queer grim point again. 'I'd sooner have been shot than let another man say those things to me; but he was different; he seemed to me to have the right. It was after he got home—when he saw he was dying, and when I saw it too. I understand all about it: you're afraid to go back. You're perfectly alone; you don't know where to turn. You can't turn anywhere; you know that perfectly. Now it is therefore that I want you to think of *me*.'

'To think of "you"?' Isabel said, standing before him in the dusk. The idea of which she had caught a glimpse a few moments before now loomed large. She threw back her head a little; she stared at it as if it had been a comet in the sky.

'You don't know where to turn. Turn straight to *me*. I want to persuade you to trust me,' Goodwood repeated. And then he paused with his shining eyes. 'Why should you go back—why should you go through that ghastly form?'

'To get away from *you*!' she answered. But this expressed only a little of what she felt. The rest was that she had never been loved before. She had believed it, but this was different;

this was the hot wind of the desert, at the approach of which the others dropped dead, like mere sweet airs of the garden. It wrapped her about; it lifted her off her feet, while the very taste of it, as of something potent, acrid and strange, forced open her set teeth.

At first, in rejoinder to what she had said, it seemed to her that he would break out into greater violence. But after an instant he was perfectly quiet; he wished to prove he was sane, that he had reasoned it all out. 'I want to prevent that, and I think I may, if you'll only for once listen to me. It's too monstrous of you to think of sinking back into that misery, of going to open your mouth to that poisoned air. It's you that are out of your mind. Trust me as if I had the care of you. Why shouldn't we be happy—when it's here before us, when it's so easy? I'm yours for ever—for ever and ever. Here I stand; I'm as firm as a rock. What have you to care about? You've no children; that perhaps would be an obstacle. As it is you've nothing to consider. You must save what you can of your life; you mustn't lose it all simply because you've lost a part. It would be an insult to you to assume that you care for the look of the thing, for what people will say, for the bottomless idiocy of the world. We've nothing to do with all that; we're quite out of it; we look at things as they are. You took the great step in coming away; the next is nothing; it's the natural one. I swear, as I stand here, that a woman deliberately made to suffer is justified in anything in life—in going down into the streets if that will help her! I know how you suffer, and that's why I'm here. We can do absolutely as we please; to whom under the sun do we owe anything? What is it that holds us, what is it that has the smallest right to interfere in such a question as this? Such a question is between ourselves—and to say that is to settle it! Were we born to rot in our misery—were we born to be afraid? I never knew *you* afraid! If you'll only trust me, how little you will be disappointed! The world's all before us—and the world's very big. I know something about that.'

Isabel gave a long murmur, like a creature in pain; it was as if he were pressing something that hurt her. 'The world's very small,' she said at random; she had an immense desire to appear to resist. She said it at random, to hear herself say something; but it was not what she meant. The world, in truth, had never seemed so large; it seemed to open out, all round her, to take the form of a mighty sea, where she floated in fathomless waters. She had wanted help, and here was help; it had come in a rushing torrent. I know not whether she believed everything he said; but she believed just then that to let him take her in his arms would be the next best thing to her dying. This belief, for a moment, was a kind of rapture, in which she felt herself sink and sink. In the movement she seemed to beat with her feet, in order to catch herself, to feel something to rest on.

'Ah, be mine as I'm yours!' she heard her companion cry. He had suddenly given up argument, and his voice seemed to come, harsh and terrible, through a confusion of vaguer sounds.

This however, of course, was but a subjective fact, as the metaphysicians say; the confusion, the noise of waters, all the rest of it, were in her own swimming head. In an instant she became aware of this. 'Do me the greatest kindness of all,' she panted. 'I beseech you to go away!'

'Ah, don't say that. Don't kill me!' he cried.

She clasped her hands; her eyes were streaming with tears. 'As you love me, as you pity me, leave me alone!'

He glared at her a moment through the dusk, and the next instant she felt his arms about her and his lips on her own lips. His kiss was like white lightning, a flash that spread, and spread again, and stayed; and it was extraordinarily as if, while she took it, she felt each thing in his hard manhood that had least pleased her, each aggressive fact of his face, his figure, his presence, justified of its intense identity and made one with this act of possession. So had she heard of those wrecked and under water following a train of images before they sink. But when darkness returned she was free. She never looked about her: she only darted from the spot. There were lights in the windows of the house; they shone far across the lawn. In an extraordinarily short time—for the distance was considerable—she had moved through the darkness (for she saw nothing) and reached the door. Here only she paused. She looked all about her; she listened a little; then she put her hand on the latch. She had not known where to turn; but she knew now. There was a very straight path.

Two days afterwards Caspar Goodwood knocked at the door of the house in Wimpole Street in which Henrietta Stackpole occupied furnished lodgings. He had hardly removed his hand from the knocker when the door was opened and Miss Stackpole herself stood before him. She had on her hat and jacket; she was on the point of going out. 'Oh, good-morning,' he said, 'I was in hopes I should find Mrs Osmond.'

Henrietta kept him waiting a moment for her reply; but there was a good deal of expression about Miss Stackpole even when she was silent. 'Pray what led you to suppose she was here?'

'I went down to Gardencourt this morning, and the servant told me she had come to London. He believed she was to come to you.'

Again Miss Stackpole held him—with an intention of perfect kindness—in suspense. 'She came here yesterday, and spent the night. But this morning she started for Rome.'

Caspar Goodwood was not looking at her; his eyes were fastened on the doorstep. 'Oh, she started—?' he stammered. And without finishing his phrase or looking up he stiffly averted himself. But he couldn't otherwise move.

Henrietta had come out, closing the door behind her, and now she put out her hand and grasped his arm. 'Look here, Mr Goodwood,' she said; 'just you wait!'

On which he looked up at her—but only to guess, from her face, with a revulsion, that she simply meant he was young. She stood shining at him with that cheap comfort, and it added, on the spot, thirty years to his life. She walked him away with her, however, as if she had given him now the key to patience.

EXPLANATORY NOTES

5 *disponibles*: available; to be disposed.

que cela manque souvent d'architecture: that it often lacks structure.

6 *Il en serait bien embarrassé*: he would be hard put to it.

the image en disponibilité: the free-floating image.

15 *ficelle*: string; attachment.

50 *bonne*: maid.

107 *car-conductor*: official in railway train.

108 *charming Constable*: John Constable (1776–1837), the epitome of English landscape painting.

116 *tenue*: bearing.

131 *bêtise*: silliness.

136 *the Civil strife*: the American Civil War (1861–5).

139 *Caliban . . . Ariel*: the earthy and airy creatures who act as servants thanks to Prospero's magic powers in Shakespeare's late romance *The Tempest*.

146 *inns described by Dickens*: perhaps in *The Pickwick Papers*, which involves stage-coach travel.

the Abbey: Westminster Abbey. James names a cluster of standard London tourist spots, ranging from the cultural to the historical.

Doctor Johnson . . . Goldsmith . . . Addison: distinguished figures of eighteenth-century London literary society.

the Duke's Head in Covent Garden: public house in notorious haunt of loose women.

at my club: they were exclusively masculine institutions. James was a guest of seven London clubs before his election to the Reform Club in 1878 and later to honorary membership of the Athenaeum.

159 *Piccadilly*: a 'good' area of central London. James lived at Bolton Street, Piccadilly, 1876–83.

London . . . in the month of September: before the autumn social season.

161 *that brighter palace of art*: Crystal Palace. Constructed largely of

glass in Hyde Park for the Great Exhibition of 1851, it was moved in 1854 to Sydenham.

162 *Lady Jane Grey*: like Isabel, a casualty of others' matrimonial plans, since she was intended as a bride to Henry VIII's delicate son Edward VI. When he died she was put on the throne, but removed after nine days, and later executed.

fête-champêtre: picnic outing.

163 *Byron*: a notorious womanizer as well as an aristocrat and Romantic poet.

164 *Wilmington, Delaware . . . Jermyn Street*: remote or central to British 'civilization': Henrietta ignores such distinctions.

170 *'I should kill the goose that supplies me with the material of my inimitable omelettes'*: Ralph ironically conflates two sayings: 'Don't kill the goose that lays the golden eggs' and 'You can't make an omelette without breaking eggs.'

185 *brown holland*: coarse linen.

193 *du bout des doigts*: with my fingertips.

196 *the Brooklyn navy-yard*: not a birthplace of distinction.

a Juno or a Niobe: ironic parallels. Juno was the jealous wife of Jupiter, ruler of the Roman gods; Niobe, the mythological embodiment of grieving mother-love: when her children were murdered, she turned into a stone, 'weeping' a stream of tears.

214 *she would some day a tale unfold*: echoes the ominous words of the ghost of Hamlet's father (*Hamlet* I. v. 15), also picking up the earlier mention of 'horror'.

217 *carte blanche*: a free hand.

je viens de loin: I go back a long way.

218 *je vous demande un peu*: let me ask you.

carrière: profession.

tout bêtement: quite simply.

220 *Cartes sur table*: to show my hand.

224 *parti*: good catch.

226 *ignis fatuus*: literally 'foolish fire': will o' the wisp.

the new Republic: of France: the Third Republic was established in 1870.

ex-Lancer: former cavalryman.

231 *Cimabue Madonna*: image of the Virgin mother by this Florentine artist (active 1272–1302) in the Byzantine tradition.

233 *Louis Philippe*: King of France 1830–48.

234 *Empire*: of Napoleon III, 1852–70.

235 '*defended*': from the French *défendre*, to forbid: a mistranslation ironically apt to Isabel's current situation.

236 *Almanach de Gotha*: a *Who's Who* of European aristocracy.

237 *sans blague*: seriously.

je ne vous dis que ça: I'll say no more.

Louis Quinze . . . First Empire . . . Queen Anne: styles of furniture ranging from the most precious French to less elaborate English.

salon: drawing-room.

procédure: legal process. The French *Code Napoléon* of Civil Law (1804) saw marriage as a civil contract open to divorce and distinct from the indissoluble religious sacrament.

242 *dame de compagnie*: lady companion.

243 *quarter of the signorino*: young master's rooms.

252 *Ce n'est pas ma partie*: that is not my task.

253 *ces dames*: these ladies.

ma mère: mother.

254 *gentille*: ladylike.

Le couvent n'est pas comme le monde, monsieur: the convent is not like the world, sir.

Le monde y gagnera: the world will gain by it.

255 *là-bas*: there.

Que Dieu vous garde, ma fille: may God bless you, my daughter.

257 *Je vous salue, mesdames*: good-day, ladies.

261 *mignonne*: my sweet.

265 *En écus bien comptés*: in hard cash: a near-quotation from Molière's *L'Avare* (v. i), a play which turns on the question of a dowry.

274 *de confiance*: with confidence.

275 *Aristides the Just*: the Athenian voted to have him exiled because he became so irritated by this constant epithet.

276 *négociant*: businessman.

279 *the Uffizi and the Pitti*: the great art galleries of Florence.

282 *Medici*: ruling family in Florence from the fourteenth century.

Savonarola: Dominican monk who attacked Florentine luxury; he was burned as a heretic in 1498.

282 *Ghirlandaio*: (1449–94), Florentine Renaissance artist.

283 *à fond*: in depth.

Machiavelli: Niccolo Machiavelli (1469–1527), Florentine author of *The Prince*, notorious as a theory of political pragmatism.

Vittoria Colonna: (1492–1547), woman poet.

Metastasio: (1698–1782), spendthrift who turned to libretto writing after exhausting his inheritance.

287 *ciceroni*: guides.

290 *Correggio*: (1494–1524), baroque artist of sentimental voluptuousness.

293 *Longhi*: (1702–65), Venetian master of 'conversation-piece' intimate images of luxurious society.

Goya: (1746–1828), Spanish artist who anticipated the Romantic movement.

toilette: outfit.

303 *jeune fille*: young lady.

305 *Corinne*: heroine of Madame de Staël's novel (1807), a type of the female poet.

308 *malaria*: a seasonal and serious hazard, thought to be caused by a poisonous 'miasma', but actually carried by mosquitoes in the marshes around Rome.

Whyte-Melville: George John Whyte-Melville (1821–78) was himself a product of Eton and the Coldstream Guards, and served in the Crimea as Major in the Turkish irregular cavalry; he wrote many sporting novels.

309 *Niobe of Nations*: from Byron's *Childe Harold*, Canto IV: 'The Niobe of Nations! there she stands, | Childless and crownless, in her voiceless woe.'

311 *Dame*: of course.

312 *Murray*: John Murray and Son's *Handbooks for Travellers* were the standard British guidebooks to Italy.

314 *long journey*: Lord Warburton's route is that of the extended tour, beyond Europe to the Near East. Thomas Cook and Co. instituted a Nile and Palestine tour in 1869.

317 *Clapham Junction*: major railway intersection in London.

326 *the Dying Gladiator*: antique statue of the vanquished combatant.

328 *Antinous and the Faun*: antique image of male beauty and grace.

332 *Ampère*: nineteenth-century French scientific philosopher.

339 *Ah, comme cela se trouve*: what a coincidence.

342 *dot*: dowry.

344 *portone*: double doors.

348 *The world lay before her—she could do whatever she chose*: a version of the closing line of Milton's *Paradise Lost*, as Adam and Eve leave Eden: 'The world was all before them, where to choose | Their place of rest.'

350 *éprouvée*: experienced.

367 *Terpsichore*: muse of dance.

Bernini: seventeenth-century baroque sculptor.

369 '*Willing to wound and yet afraid to strike*': from Alexander Pope's 'Epistle to Dr Arbuthnot' (1735), of the underhand critic.

387 *Louis Quatorze*: distinguished antique French furniture.

388 *belle-mère*: stepmother.

389 *faience*: pottery, not porcelain.

391 *Gardez-vous-en bien*: don't even think of it.

392 *piazzetta*: square.

393 *Caravaggio*: (1573–1610), noted for chiaroscuro of tragic violence.

piano nobile: main floor.

395 *Osmond put out his left hand*: a calculated insult: Osmond's manners consistently act as an index of his morality.

396 *Capo di Monte*: precious decorative porcelain.

398 *Infanta of Velasquez*: Diego Velasquez (1590–1660) became portraitist to the Spanish royal family in 1623.

jeune fille: marriageable young lady.

Sir Walter Scott: the one securely respectable author in a suspect genre.

401 *salottino*: small drawing-room.

402 *majolica*: Italian earthenware.

424 *in petto*: to himself.

426 *Scylla and Charybdis*: mythical monster and whirlpool between which Odysseus had to steer his ship home.

Proserpine: daughter of the Greek goddess of harvest, Demeter, she was carried off by Pluto, god of the underworld, to be queen of Hades: a sorry fate which led to winter on earth.

427 *vous m'en demandez trop*: you are asking too much of me.

431 *Pincian*: hill, a good district of Rome with extensive public gardens.

434 *détente*: easing of diplomatic relations.

441 *Je n'y peux rien, moi*: I can't do anything about it.

447 *pellagra*: disease endemic amongst the peasantry of Lombardy.

474 *cotillion . . . quadrille*: the quadrille is the more formal dance, involving four couples.

475 *prétendant*: suitor.

483 *her 'Creole' ancestors*: this West Indian strain casts an ironical sidelight on her brother Osmond's supposed 'traditions' too.

486 *grand seigneur*: grand; blue-blooded.

488 *c'est bien gentil*: that's very kind.

538 *à la bonne heure*: let it come on.

555 *Eh moi donc*: what about me.

565 *En voilà, ma chère, une pose*: my dear, what affectation.

567 *simpaticissimo*: a darling.

577 *Ça me dépasse*: it's beyond me.

578 *poverina*: poor little thing.

579 *cara mia*: my dear.

589 *Elle éclaire la maison*: she lights up the house.

593 *Eh bien, chère Madame, qu'en pensez-vous?*: Well, Madame, what do you think?

604 *a charming and precious Bonington*: precious partly because Richard Parkes Bonington (1802–28), like Ralph, was cut off by an early death.

THE WORLD'S CLASSICS

A Select List

HANS ANDERSEN: Fairy Tales
Translated by L. W. Kingsland
Introduction by Naomi Lewis
Illustrated by Vilhelm Pedersen and Lorenz Frølich

JANE AUSTEN: Emma
Edited by James Kinsley and David Lodge

Mansfield Park
Edited by James Kinsley and John Lucas

J. M. BARRIE: Peter Pan in Kensington Gardens & Peter and Wendy
Edited by Peter Hollindale

WILLIAM BECKFORD: Vathek
Edited by Roger Lonsdale

CHARLOTTE BRONTË: Jane Eyre
Edited by Margaret Smith

THOMAS CARLYLE: The French Revolution
Edited by K. J. Fielding and David Sorensen

LEWIS CARROLL: Alice's Adventures in Wonderland *and* Through the Looking Glass
Edited by Roger Lancelyn Green
Illustrated by John Tenniel

MIGUEL DE CERVANTES: Don Quixote
Translated by Charles Jarvis
Edited by E. C. Riley

GEOFFREY CHAUCER: The Canterbury Tales
Translated by David Wright

ANTON CHEKHOV: The Russian Master and Other Stories
Translated by Ronald Hingley

JOSEPH CONRAD: Victory
Edited by John Batchelor
Introduction by Tony Tanner

DANTE ALIGHIERI: The Divine Comedy
Translated by C. H. Sisson
Edited by David Higgins

CHARLES DICKENS: Christmas Books
Edited by Ruth Glancy

FEDOR DOSTOEVSKY: Crime and Punishment
Translated by Jessie Coulson
Introduction by John Jones

The Idiot
Translated by Alan Myers
Introduction by W. J. Leatherbarrow

GEORGE ELIOT: Daniel Deronda
Edited by Graham Handley

ELIZABETH GASKELL: Cousin Phillis and Other Tales
Edited by Angus Easson

KENNETH GRAHAME: The Wind in the Willows
Edited by Peter Green

THOMAS HARDY: A Pair of Blue Eyes
Edited by Alan Manford

JAMES HOGG: The Private Memoirs and Confessions of a Justified Sinner
Edited by John Carey

THOMAS HUGHES: Tom Brown's Schooldays
Edited by Andrew Sanders

HENRIK IBSEN: An Enemy of the People, The Wild Duck, Rosmersholm
Edited and Translated by James McFarlane

HENRY JAMES: The Ambassadors
Edited by Christopher Butler

JOCELIN OF BRAKELOND:
Chronicle of the Abbey of Bury St. Edmunds
Translated by Diana Greenway and Jane Sayers

GWYN JONES (Transl.):
Eirik the Red and Other Icelandic Sagas

CHARLOTTE LENNOX: The Female Quixote
Edited by Margaret Dalziel
Introduction by Margaret Anne Doody

JACK LONDON: The Call of the Wild, White Fang, and other Stories
Edited by Earle Labor and Robert C. Leitz III

KATHERINE MANSFIELD: Selected Stories
Edited by D. M. Davin

KARL MARX AND FRIEDRICH ENGELS: The Communist Manifesto
Edited by David McLellan

HERMAN MELVILLE: The Confidence-Man
Edited by Tony Tanner

PROSPER MÉRIMÉE: Carmen and Other Stories
Translated by Nicholas Jotcham

MYTHS FROM MESOPOTAMIA
Translated and Edited by Stephanie Dalley

EDGAR ALLAN POE: Selected Tales
Edited by Julian Symons

PAUL SALZMAN (Ed.):
An Anthology of Elizabethan Prose Fiction

OLIVE SCHREINER: The Story of an African Farm
Edited by Joseph Bristow

TOBIAS SMOLLETT: The Expedition of Humphry Clinker
Edited by Lewis M. Knapp
Revised by Paul-Gabriel Boucé

ROBERT LOUIS STEVENSON: Kidnapped and Catriona
Edited by Emma Letley

The Strange Case of Dr. Jekyll and Mr. Hyde
and Weir of Hermiston
Edited by Emma Letley

BRAM STOKER: Dracula
Edited by A. N. Wilson

WILLIAM MAKEPEACE THACKERAY: Barry Lyndon
Edited by Andrew Sanders

LEO TOLSTOY: Anna Karenina
Translated by Louise and Aylmer Maude
Introduction by John Bayley

ANTHONY TROLLOPE: The American Senator
Edited by John Halperin

VIRGIL: The Aeneid
Translated by C. Day Lewis
Edited by Jasper Griffin

HORACE WALPOLE : The Castle of Otranto
Edited by W. S. Lewis

IZAAK WALTON and CHARLES COTTON:
The Compleat Angler
Edited by John Buxton
Introduction by John Buchan

OSCAR WILDE: Complete Shorter Fiction
Edited by Isobel Murray

The Picture of Dorian Gray
Edited by Isobel Murray

VIRGINIA WOOLF: Orlando
Edited by Rachel Bowlby

ÉMILE ZOLA:
The Attack on the Mill and other stories
Translated by Douglas Parmée

Azure in Action

Azure in Action

CHRIS HAY
BRIAN H. PRINCE

MANNING
Greenwich
(74° w. long.)

For online information and ordering of this and other Manning books, please visit www.manning.com. The publisher offers discounts on this book when ordered in quantity. For more information, please contact:

Special Sales Department
Manning Publications Co.
180 Broad Street
Suite 1323
Stamford, CT 06901
Email: orders@manning.com

Manning Publications Co.
180 Broad Street
Suite 1323
Stamford, CT 06901

Development editor: Lianna Wlasiuk
Copyeditor: Joan Celmer
Proofreader: Katie Tennant
Illustrator: Martin Murtonen
Designer: Marija Tudor

ISBN: 9781935182481

Printed in the United States of America

1 2 3 4 5 6 7 8 9 10 – MAL – 16 15 14 13 12 11 10

brief contents

contents

preface

Both of us have a passion for cloud computing and Windows Azure, and in this book we'd like to share with you what we've learned from working with the technology. We want to show you how to get the most out of Azure and how to best use the cloud.

Writing a book is a far more complex project than either of us expected, involving a lot of people, a lot of collaboration, and plenty of late nights hunched over a keyboard. We did it because we wanted to help you understand what happens inside Azure, how it works, and how you can leverage it as you work with your applications. We wanted to show you not only how to run your complete system in the cloud, but all the other ways you can leverage the cloud, specifically by using hybrid applications and distributed applications.

As we worked with all sorts of developers in our day jobs, we knew they could easily learn how to use the cloud, but they were all scared. We hadn't seen people so afraid of a new technology that could help so much since web services came onto the scene years ago. We knew if developers would take a minute to play with Azure just a little bit, it would become less scary and more approachable. Ultimately, we wanted this book to answer the question, "What can Azure do, and why do I care?" We hope we've succeeded.

We've leveraged a lot of resources to write this book, and you might have been one of them. We worked in forums, we worked with other cloud techs, we crawled through every scrap of public Azure information we could find (even obscure blog posts in the dark corners of the internet), and we had personal conversations with Azure team members and anyone else we could get to take our calls. We leveraged our own experience and insight. Sometimes we guessed at how things work based on how we would have built Azure, and then pushed Microsoft to give us more details to see if we were right. We wrote a lot of code, and tried out ideas that we would get asked about at conferences, in forums, over email, and as responses to our articles.

The rest is history, with about a year of writing, rewriting, reviews, intense discussion, and coding. We faced two big challenges as a writing team. The first was PDC 2009. We knew that would be the coming-out party for Windows Azure with its official 1.0 release, and that a lot of what we had written up to that point would change. This involved rewriting most of our code, retaking all our screen shots, and changing a lot of our text. The second challenge was the time zone differences between us. With up to fourteen time zones separating us at times, our combined travel schedules exacerbated the time zone challenge. Much of this book was written in airports, hotels, at conferences, during late weekend hours, and at every other conceivable time and place.

Windows Azure was released for commercial availability on February 1, 2010, and by all accounts has been a huge success. Microsoft won't publicly state how many applications have been deployed to Azure, but you can infer some trends from the case studies and press releases they make available. It looks like tens of thousands of applications (from small test apps to major internet-scale applications) have been deployed to Azure globally. The Azure teams ship new features about every 2–3 months. As a developer, it's exciting to see so much innovation coming out of Microsoft on a platform you use. It's gratifying to see the features that customers have asked for being deployed.

For book authors, the pace can be a little grueling, with things changing in the technology all the time, but maybe that just sets us up for a second edition. We hope you enjoy the book.

acknowledgments

We would like to thank all the people who helped us during the writing process; their input made this a much better book. First on the list is our amazing editor at Manning, Lianna Wlasiuk. She showed an endless amount of patience and had a seemingly inexhaustible supply of the proverbial red ink. Her feedback and guidance turned these cloud geeks into writers.

Secondly, a big thanks to Mike Stephens. He's a great guy who did an amazing job in shaping this project. We'd also like to thank our publisher Marjan Bace for his insight and vision. Those early conversations with him helped us go in the right direction. And thanks to Christina Rudhoff for kicking off the book in the first place, and to Mary Piergies for her management of the production process. You guys are awesome.

We would also like to thank the other staff at Manning. While any author can ship a book, Manning knows that shipping a great book is a team sport, and they have an excellent team in place. Their constant support and guidance—and the challenge to push the book further—are greatly appreciated.

There's another group of people who were key to making this book successful, the group of reviewers that read the manuscript four or five times over the past year, pointing out weak parts of the story, plot holes, and places where better code samples could be provided. We'd like to thank James Hatheway, Alex Thissen, Scott Turner, Darren Neimke, Christian Siegers, Margriet Bruggeman, Nikander Bruggeman, Eric Nelson, Ray Booysen, Jonas Bandi, Frank Wang, Wade Wegner, Mark Monster, Lester Lobo, Shreekanth Joshi, Berndt Hamboeck, Jason Jung, and Kunal Mittal.

Special thanks to Michael Wood who served as the technical proofreader of the book, reviewing it again shortly before it went to press and testing the code. We couldn't have done it without you.

Our early readers, people who bought the book through the Early Access program, before it was even done, were a big help too. They suffered through drafts, impartial chapters, and early cuts of code. Their feedback in the forums was critical to where we went with the book.

Chris Hay

I don't want this to sound like an Oscar acceptance speech (boo hoo, I want to thank my goldfish, blah blah blah), but it's gonna be a little like that as I really do want to call out a few folks. I guess I lose my right to laugh at those blubbering celebrities in the future.

The biggest thanks of all go to my wonderful wife, who woke up one morning to discover that due to the UK/US time zone difference, I had negotiated a book deal whilst she was sleeping. In spite of this, she gave me her full support, without which this book would never have happened. She is totally awesome and I love her very much. Thank you, Katy, for being so cool and supportive.

I want to apologize to my dogs (Sascha and Tufty) for the impact on their walking time and thank them for distracting me when I got bogged down with too much work. They brought me their bouncy balls and even figured out how to shut down my computer.

Big thanks to my parents and my brother (please don't read anything into the order of thanks; you really don't come after the dogs). Thanks for the great start in life, especially buying me that ZX81 when I was 4 years old.

Thanks to Nathan for being my sounding board; truly appreciated it, dude.

Thanks to Brian and Michael for doing the production work on the book while I was working 18-hour days in India. You guys are awesome, thank you.

Santa Claus, thank you for bringing me presents every year, and Tooth Fairy, thank you for making tooth loss more bearable.

I'd like to thank all the guys at NxtGenUG (especially Rich, Dave, John, and Allister) for their support. P.S. If you have never gone to a .NET User Group then be sure to do so—it's a lot of fun. Big thanks to the UK/US community in general (you guys know who you are, thank you).

Also thanks to Girls Aloud, the Pussycat Dolls, and Alesha Dixon for making cool music and helping me keep my sanity throughout the writing process. And if you are reading this book, then something has gone wrong with the universe which will require The Doctor to fix.

Finally, thanks to you, dear reader, for buying the book. I love you, kiss, kiss, kiss, boo hoo, wah wah ;)

Brian H. Prince

I started learning how to write code when I was ten. My parents were supportive and understanding when they figured out that their middle son wasn't normal, that he was a geek. Back then, geeks hadn't risen to their current social prominence. They picked me up after work from UMF, and they didn't kick me out of the house after I caused a small electrical fire while trying to control the box fan in my room with my CoCo 3. Thanks, Mom and Dad. A few years later, one of my aunts suggested I stick with computers as I grew up. She expected they would be important in the future. That sounds like a trivial prediction today, but back then, it seemed like something out of Nostradamus's writings.

I also want to thank everyone at Microsoft for their encouragement, including my manager, Brian, who supported me in the extra work that writing a book takes.

Above all, I owe a tremendous debt to my family. My kids, Miranda and Elliot, kept me from totally disappearing into my office for 10 months with regular forced breaks. Elliot would come in and declare a 15-minute recess to go and play Xbox with him. Miranda would come in and write cute notes of support on my whiteboard or tell me about that latest book she was reading. Thanks kids, you're the best!

But the one person I owe the most to is my beautiful wife. She kept me motivated; she gave me the time and quiet to write when I needed to write and the push to take a break when I needed to release pressure. I'd heard rumors about how hard it is to live with an author in the house from friends who gave me advice along the way (thanks Bill, Jim, and Jason). Without her I wouldn't have been able to complete this huge project. She spent hours helping me simplify the story, revise the approaches, and dream up segues. Joanne, I would not be without you, and without you I would not be.

about this book

This book will teach you about Windows Azure, Microsoft's cloud computing platform. We'll cover all aspects and components of Windows Azure from a developer's point of view.

The book is written from the perspective of a .NET developer who's using C#. We feel that most developers using Azure will be using .NET. Everything in this book applies to any platform that uses Azure. You'll need to use the appropriate SDK for your development tools and platform of choice.

You should be fairly familiar with .NET, but you don't have to be an expert. We expect a developer with a few years of experience to be able to get the most out of this book. Someone new to development, or perhaps even a manager, can still read the book to get a grasp of the broad concepts of Azure. If that's your situation, skip over the code samples and try to understand what the moving parts are.

Roadmap

This book is broken into six parts, each with its own focus.

Part 1 is titled "Welcome to the cloud" and that's exactly what it is: a welcome to the world of cloud computing. Chapters 1 and 2 explain what cloud computing is, and what the big moving parts of Windows Azure are. You'll build and deploy some simple applications in this part, just to whet your appetite.

Part 2 is called "Understanding the Azure service model." Chapter 3 gives you a peek behind the curtain and shows you how Azure works. Chapters 4 and 5 cover how to run and configure your applications in Azure.

Part 3, "Running your site with web roles," covers running web applications in Azure. This part includes chapter 6, which describes scaling your application, and chapter 7, which covers using native code in Azure.

Part 4 is called "Working with BLOB storage," and covers the first part of Windows Azure storage, BLOBs. Chapter 8 discusses the conceptual basics of BLOBs, chapter 9 covers how to work with them in your code, and chapter 10 tells you when to use BLOBs outside Azure.

Part 5, "Working with structured data," tells you all about Windows Azure tables and SQL Azure. Chapters 11 and 12 focus on tables, chapter 13 dives into SQL Azure, and chapter 14 takes a broader look at how to work with data in the cloud and how to make decisions on what strategies to use.

Part 6, titled "Doing work with messages," covers the last several parts of Azure, including specialized aspects of using worker roles, which is detailed in chapter 15. We discuss working with queues in chapter 16. Connecting your applications together and securing your services are delved into in chapter 17. Finally, chapter 18 describes how to work with diagnostics and how to manage your infrastructure in the cloud.

About the source code

All source code in listings or in text is in a `fixed-width font like this` to separate it from ordinary text. Code annotations accompany many of the listings, highlighting important concepts. In some cases, numbered bullets link to explanations that follow the listing.

Source code for all working examples in this book is available for download from the publisher's website at www.manning.com/AzureinAction.

To work with the sample code in this book, you'll need Windows Vista, Windows 7, or Windows Server 2008. You'll also need either Visual Studio 2008 or 2010. We used VS2010 in this book for samples and screen shots. Additionally, you need to install the Azure SDK and the AppFabric SDK. Both of these can be found at Azure.com.

Author Online

The purchase of *Azure in Action* includes free access to a private forum run by Manning Publications where you can make comments about the book, ask technical questions, and receive help from the author and other users. You can access and subscribe to the forum at www.manning.com/AzureinAction. This page provides information on how to get on the forum once you're registered, what kind of help is available, and the rules of conduct in the forum.

Manning's commitment to our readers is to provide a venue where a meaningful dialogue between individual readers and between readers and authors can take place. It isn't a commitment to any specific amount of participation on the part of the authors, whose contributions to the book's forum remain voluntary (and unpaid). We suggest you try asking the authors some challenging questions, lest their interest stray!

The Author Online forum and the archives of previous discussions will be accessible from the publisher's website as long as the book is in print.

about the authors

Chris Hay is a Microsoft MVP in Client App Dev, an international conference speaker, and cofounder of a .NET usergroup in Cambridge, UK (http://nxtgenug.net/). He has spent part of the past year working and living in India. Brian H. Prince is an Architect Evangelist for Microsoft, cofounder of the nonprofit organization CodeMash (www.codemash.org), and a speaker at various regional and national technology events. He lives in Westerville, Ohio. In their own words, here's what they say about how they came to Azure.

Chris Hay

My day job involves building some of the largest m-commerce systems in the world. When Microsoft announced Windows Azure to the world at the Professional Developers Conference in Los Angeles in 2008, I immediately thought of how I could use the cloud as part of the systems I was actively building.

Of all of the key scenarios for using the cloud, dynamic scaling is one of the most well-known. I was hoping that the promise of massive numbers of servers and a simplified platform would be able to meet my enormous scale needs, while making it easier to build large-scale systems. Azure offered the promise of being able to deploy an application into the cloud and have an automated deployment and provisioning system, with a complete abstraction of the underlying physical infrastructure. This book is focused on exploring those promises, and seeing how they worked out.

Coupling this newfound passion with my long-held desire to someday write a book, I settled down to write the proposal that I would send to Manning, pitching my idea for a book titled *Azure in Action*. And a year later, here it is!

BRIAN H. PRINCE

While working for Microsoft in recent years, I found myself spending more and more of my time focusing on Windows Azure (or Red Dog, as it was called internally at Microsoft at the time) and cloud computing. I was already at work on another *In Action* book when I made a comment in one of my many meetings with Manning that I was surprised they weren't planning a book for each piece of the upcoming Microsoft cloud platform. Thinking that writing my first book ever wasn't enough work, I further commented that I would love to get involved and help with the Azure book.

This simple comment initiated a lot of work for the editors at Manning as they started looking for experienced authors who could write a series of books on Microsoft's cloud platform. They approached me to see if I would pitch in and help write *Azure in Action* with Chris. I agreed, and after a few chats with Chris over Skype, we finalized the draft table of contents and submitted it to Manning. The rest is history and you are now holding that book in your hands.

about the cover illustration

The figure on the cover of *Azure in Action* is captioned "Woman with child from Durdevac." The illustration is taken from a reproduction of an album of Croatian traditional costumes from the mid-nineteenth century by Nikola Arsenovic, published by the Ethnographic Museum in Split, Croatia, in 2003. The illustrations were obtained from a helpful librarian at the Ethnographic Museum in Split, itself situated in the Roman core of the medieval center of the town: the ruins of Emperor Diocletian's retirement palace from around AD 304. The book includes finely colored illustrations of figures from different regions of Croatia, accompanied by descriptions of the costumes and of everyday life.

The village of Durdevac is near the town of Osijek in Slavonia, a geographical and historical region in eastern Croatia. Women in Slavonia were known for their intricate embroidery and sewing skills, and everything they wore was made by hand requiring the weaving of textiles and dyeing of wool. Slavonian women typically wore long white skirts and white linen shirts with a collar, topped with long black and brown vests embroidered along the edges in wool of different colors, with white headscarves and necklaces made of red coral beads. The long aprons that completed the traditional costume were elaborately embroidered with colorful patterns of flowers or geometric designs.

Dress codes and lifestyles have changed over the last 200 years, and the diversity by region, so rich at the time, has faded away. It is now hard to tell apart the inhabitants of different continents, let alone of different hamlets or towns separated by only a few miles. Perhaps we have traded cultural diversity for a more varied personal life—certainly for a more varied and fast-paced technological life.

Manning celebrates the inventiveness and initiative of the computer business with book covers based on the rich diversity of regional life of two centuries ago, brought back to life by illustrations from old books and collections like this one.

Part 1

Welcome to the cloud

Part 1 is all about dipping your toes into the water and getting ready to dive in headfirst.

We cover what Azure is in chapter 1—what the moving parts are, and why people are so excited about cloud computing.

We throw you in the deep end of the pool in chapter 2, building and deploying—step-by-step—your first cloud application. We've all written Hello, World apps; after you've read part 1, you'll begin to see how you can easily scale them to hundreds of servers.

1 Getting to know Windows Azure

This chapter covers

- Overview of Windows Azure
- Building your first Windows Azure web role
- Windows Azure infrastructure
- How Windows Azure implements core cloud concepts
- Flagship Windows Azure platform services

Imagine a world where your applications were no longer constrained by hardware and you could consume whatever computing power you needed, when you needed it. More importantly, imagine a world where you paid only for the computing power that you used.

Now that your imagination is running wild, imagine you don't need to care about managing hardware infrastructure and you can focus on the software that you develop. In this world, you can shift your focus from managing servers to managing applications.

If this is the sort of thing you daydream about, then you should burn your server farm and watch the smoke form into a cloud in the perfect azure sky. Welcome to the cloud, and welcome to Windows Azure. We also suggest that if this is the sort of thing you daydream about, you might want to lie to your non-IT friends.

We'll slowly introduce lots of new concepts to you throughout this book, eventually giving you the complete picture about cloud computing. In this chapter, we'll keep things relatively simple. As you get more comfortable with this new paradigm, and as the book progresses, we'll introduce more of Azure's complexities. To get the ball rolling, we'll start by looking at the big Azure picture: the entire platform.

1.1 What's the Windows Azure platform?

As you might have already gathered, the Windows Azure platform encompasses Microsoft's complete cloud offering. Every service that Microsoft considers to be part of the cloud will be included under this banner. If the whole cloud thing passed you by, there isn't really anything magical about it. The *cloud* refers to a bunch of servers that host and run your applications, or to an offering of services that are consumed (think web service).

The main difference between a cloud offering and a noncloud offering is that the infrastructure is abstracted away—in the cloud, you don't care about the physical hardware that hosts your service. Another difference is that most public cloud solutions are offered as a metered service, meaning you pay for the resources that you use (compute time, disk space, bandwidth, and so on) as and when you use them.

Based on the Azure release announced in November 2009 at the Professional Developers Conference (PDC) held in Los Angeles, the Windows Azure platform splits into the three parts shown in figure 1.1: Windows Azure, SQL Azure, and the Windows Azure platform AppFabric. You can expect the parts included in the platform to

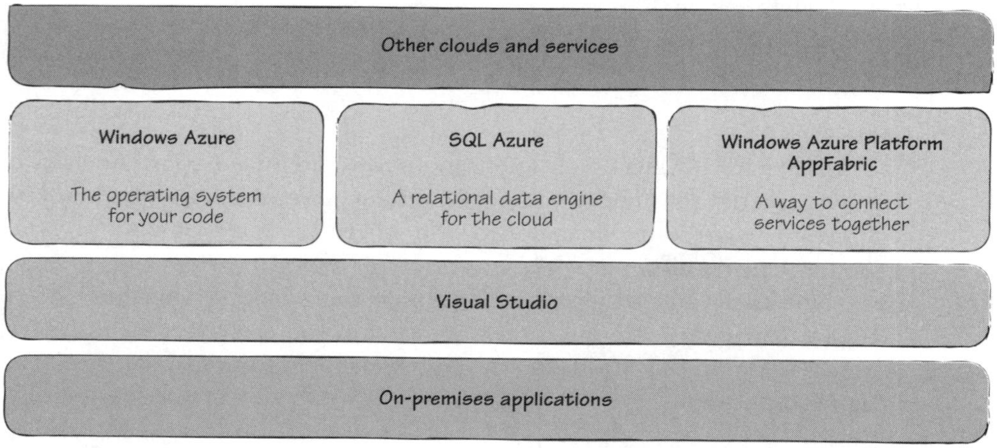

Figure 1.1 The parts that make up the Windows Azure platform include the Windows Azure operating system, SQL Azure, and AppFabric.

increase over time; in fact, we wouldn't be surprised to see Microsoft Flight Simulator in the cloud.

As cool as AppFabric and SQL Azure are, for now we're going to stay focused on the Windows Azure part of the Windows Azure platform and ignore all the other platform-specific stuff until the end of the chapter. Talking about Windows Azure immediately gets a little confusing. Unfortunately, when most folks refer to Windows Azure, it's not clear whether they're referring to the Windows Azure platform, the complete cloud offering, or to Windows Azure, which is a part of the platform.

It's kind of like the ESPN naming convention. The ESPN Network has multiple channels (ESPN, ESPN2, ESPN News, and so on), yet we tend to refer to these channels collectively as ESPN rather than as the ESPN Network. To confuse matters further, we also refer to the individual ESPN channel as ESPN, also. If you ask someone what game is on ESPN tonight, it's not clear if you mean all the channels on ESPN (including ESPN News and ESPN2) or if you mean just the channel named ESPN (not including ESPN2 and the others).To keep things consistent, whenever we talk about the platform as a whole, we'll refer to the *Windows Azure platform* or *the platform*; but if we're talking about the core Windows Azure product, then we'll use the term *Windows Azure*, or just *Azure*.

So, what exactly is Windows Azure? Microsoft calls Azure its core operating system for the cloud. OK, so now you know what Windows Azure is, and we can skip on, right? Not so fast! Let's break it down, strip away all the hype, and find out what Azure is all about.

1.1.1 Windows is in the title, so it must be an operating system

Windows Azure is an operating system that provides the ability to run applications in a highly scalable manner on Microsoft servers, in Microsoft's data centers, in a manageable way. You can host either your web applications, such as a website that sells Hawaiian shirts, or backend processing services, such as an MP3-to-WMA file converter, in Microsoft's data centers.

If you need more computing power (more instances of your website or more instances of your backend service) to run your application, you can allocate more resources to the application, which are then spread across many servers. By increasing the number of resources to your application, you'll ultimately be able to process more data or handle more incoming traffic.

Hmmm...how exactly is that an operating system? To answer that question, we have to define what it means to be a *cloud operating system*.

When Microsoft refers to Windows Azure as an operating system for the cloud, it doesn't literally mean an operating system as you might know it (Windows 7, Windows Vista, Leopard, Snow Leopard, and so on). What Microsoft means is that Windows Azure performs jobs that are similar to those that a traditional operating system might perform. What does an operating system do? Well, it has four tasks in life:

- Host and run applications
- Remove the complexities of hardware from applications

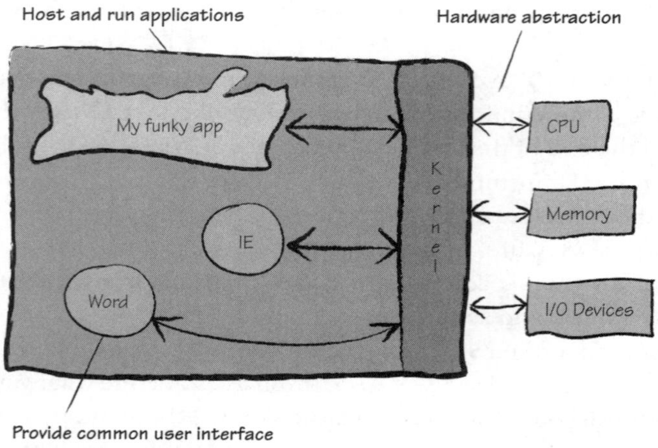

Figure 1.2 A typical representation of an operating system interacting with applications and resources. Notice that applications don't directly interact with CPU, memory, or I/O devices.

- Provide an interface between users and applications
- Provide a mechanism that manages what's running where and enforces permissions in the system

Figure 1.2 shows how a traditional operating system achieves these tasks in a typical PC environment.

The applications shown in figure 1.2 are running within an operating system. The applications don't have direct access to the hardware; all interactions must come through the kernel, the low-level operating system component that performs all the tasks we're discussing: processing, memory management, and device management. We'll look at how some components of Windows Azure fill the role of the kernel in the cloud later in this chapter.

The analogy of Windows Azure being an operating system looks like it could work out after all. Over the next few sections, we'll use this analogy to see how Windows Azure fares as an operating system, which will give you a good overview of how Windows Azure works and what services it provides.

1.1.2 Hosting and running applications the Azure way

Hosting and running applications might be the most important task of an operating system. Without applications, we're just moving a mouse around with no purpose. Let's look at the types of applications that can be run in both traditional operating systems and in Windows Azure.

TYPES OF APPLICATIONS: WHAT'S IN A NAME?

In a traditional operating system, such as Windows 7, we can consider most of the following to be applications:

- Microsoft Word (yep, it's an app)
- Internet Explorer or Firefox (still an app)
- Killer Mutant Donkey Zombie Blaster game (even that's an app)

Remember those applications running in the context of a typical PC operating system in figure 1.1? Instead of hosting client applications (games, Word, Excel, and so on), the types of applications that you host in Windows Azure are server applications, such as web applications (for example, a Hawaiian Shirt Shop website) or background computational applications (for example, an MP3 file converter).

Figure 1.3 shows these server applications running in a traditional operating system.

Turns out (see figures 1.2 and 1.3) that there's no real difference between Microsoft Excel and a Hawaiian Shirt Shop website. As far as a traditional operating system is concerned, they're both applications.

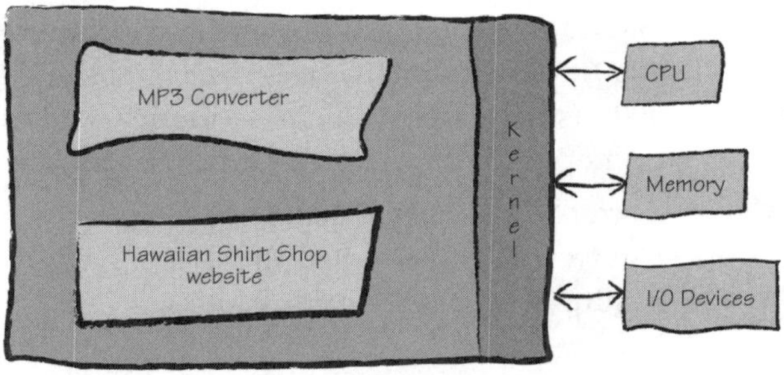

Figure 1.3 Windows Azure–type applications running in a traditional OS. Azure applications function in an OS the same way that traditional applications do.

RUNNING APPLICATIONS ACROSS THOUSANDS OF SERVERS

The traditional operating system is responsible for allocating CPU time and memory space that allows your application to run (as seen in both figures 1.1 and 1.2). Not only is the operating system responsible for allocating these resources, but it's also responsible for managing these resources. For example, if an application fails, then it's the operating system's job to clean up the application's resource usage and restart the application, if necessary. This level of abstraction is perfect for an operating system that manages a single server, but it isn't scalable when it comes to a cloud operating system. With Windows Azure, your application doesn't necessarily run on a single server; it can potentially run in parallel on thousands of servers.

A cloud operating system can't be responsible for allocating CPU time and memory on thousands of physically separate servers. This responsibility has to be abstracted away from the OS. In Windows Azure, that responsibility is given to *virtual machines* (VMs). Figure 1.4 shows how your applications might be distributed among the VMs in a Windows Azure data center.

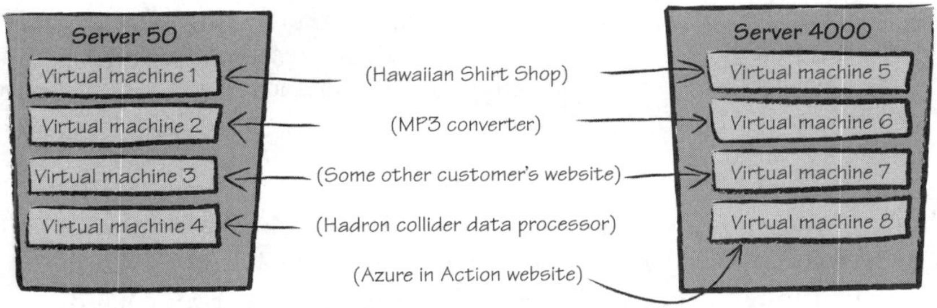

Figure 1.4 Applications split across many VMs in a Windows Azure data center

Your cloud operating system is no longer responsible for assigning your applications' resources by CPU and memory, but is instead responsible for allocating resources using VMs. Windows Azure uses VMs to achieve separation of services across physical servers. Each physical server is divided into multiple VMs. An application from another customer on the same physical hardware as yours won't interfere with your application.

In figure 1.4, the Hawaiian Shirt Shop website is allocated across two VMs (VM1 and VM5), which are hosted on two different physical servers (server 50 and server 4000), whereas the *Azure in Action* website is allocated only a single VM (VM8) on server 4000 (shirt shops make more money, so they get more resources).

Let's drill down and take a closer look at what constitutes a VM.

ANATOMY OF A VIRTUAL MACHINE

Figure 1.5 shows what the VM hosting a web application looks like.

The physical server is split up into one or more VMs. Every instance of your service (web role or worker role) is installed onto its own VM, which is a base installation of Windows Server 2008 (with some extra Azure bits). The VM hosts the web application within Internet Information Services (IIS) 7.0.

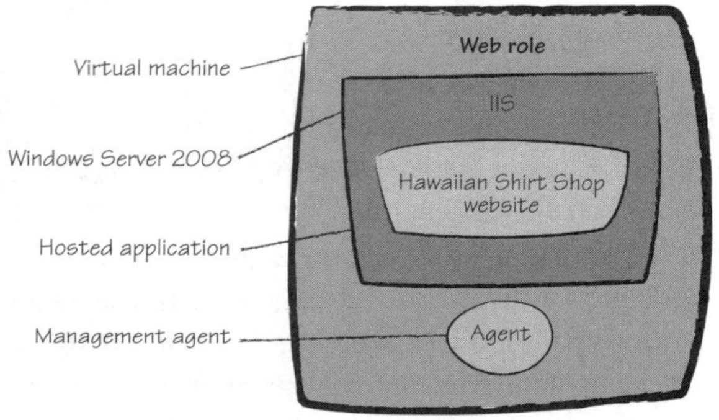

Figure 1.5 A logical representation of the VM that hosts your web application

Although your application runs on a VM, the VM is abstracted away from you, and you only have a view of the role instance, never of the VM. A single instance of your web application is assigned to a single VM, and no other applications will be assigned to that VM. In this way, every instance of your web application is isolated from other applications running on the same physical server. The VM image also runs an agent process. We'll explain what this agent does in chapter 3 when we discuss the Red Dog Agent.

> **Web role and worker role**
>
> A role is another name for your application. The role refers to the base VM image that hosts your application. A web role is a VM that hosts your application within IIS. A worker role is the same as a web role, but without IIS. It's intended for typical backend processing workloads.

To be honest, we're now itching for some code. Let's look at how you can build a simple ASP.NET website that you can run in one of those Windows Azure VMs. Don't worry; we'll continue dissecting Windows Azure after you get your hands dirty with a little code.

1.2 Building your first Windows Azure web application

Although you're going to build an ASP.NET website in this example, the good news is that almost any website that can currently be hosted in IIS on Windows Server 2008 can be hosted in Windows Azure.

The following are examples of the types of web applications Azure supports out of the box:

- ASP.NET 3.5 web applications
- ASP.NET MVC 1.0, 2.0 web applications
- Web services (WCF, ASMX)
- Any FastCGI-based website such as PHP or Python
- Java and Ruby applications

Although Windows Azure supports the ability to host different types of websites, for now you'll create a simple Hello World web application using ASP.NET 3.5 SP1. In chapters 7 and 15, we'll look at how you can create PHP websites, WCF Web Services, and ASP.NET MVC websites.

To get started developing an ASP.NET 3.5 SP1 website, you'll need to download the Windows Azure software development kit (SDK).

1.2.1 Setting up your environment

The SDK contains a whole bunch of things that'll make your life easier when developing for Windows Azure, including the following:

- Windows Azure development fabric (a simulation of the live fabric)
- Visual Studio templates for creating web applications
- Windows Azure storage environment
- Deployment tools
- A glimpse of a bright new world

In chapter 2, we'll take a deeper look at some of the items in the SDK. For now, you'll just install it. If you're an experienced ASP.NET developer, you should be able to install the SDK by clicking the Next button a few times. You can grab the SDK from www.Azure.com.

Before installing the SDK, check your version of Windows and Visual Studio. A local instance of some flavor of SQL Server (either Express, which is installed with Visual Studio, or full-blown SQL Server) is required to use the SDK. We'll explain this in more depth in chapter 9.

SUPPORTED OPERATING SYSTEMS

Before you attempt to install the SDK, make sure that you have a suitable version of Windows. Supported versions of Windows currently include the following:

- Windows 7 (which you should be running because it's lovely)
- Windows Vista
- Windows Server 2008 (and beyond)

NOTE Windows XP isn't supported by Windows Azure. Before you jump up and down about Windows XP, there isn't some conspiracy against it. XP isn't supported because Windows Azure web roles are heavily built on IIS 7.0. Windows XP and Windows 2003 use earlier versions of IIS that won't work with Windows Azure.

SUPPORTED VERSIONS OF VISUAL STUDIO

To develop Windows Azure applications in Visual Studio, you'll need either Visual Studio 2008 or Visual Studio 2010. If you're still running Visual Studio 2005, you now have the excuse you need to upgrade. If for some reason you can't get Visual Studio or your company won't upgrade you, then you can use the Web Express versions of either Visual Studio 2008 or 2010 for free, or you can use Visual Studio 2008. We'll be using Visual Studio 2010 throughout this book. The windows and dialog boxes shown in the figures might differ slightly from those in Visual Studio 2008 or the Express Edition, but, all in all, it works in the same way.

STARTING VISUAL STUDIO

To launch your Windows Azure application in the development fabric from Visual Studio, you need Administrator privileges. Get into the habit (for Azure development) of right-clicking your Visual Studio icon and selecting Run as Administrator.

Now we'll help you create your first Azure web application.

1.2.2 *Creating a new project*

Your first step is to create a new project. Open Visual Studio and select File > New > Project. Select the Cloud Service project type, which gives you the option to select the Cloud Service template, as shown in figure 1.6.

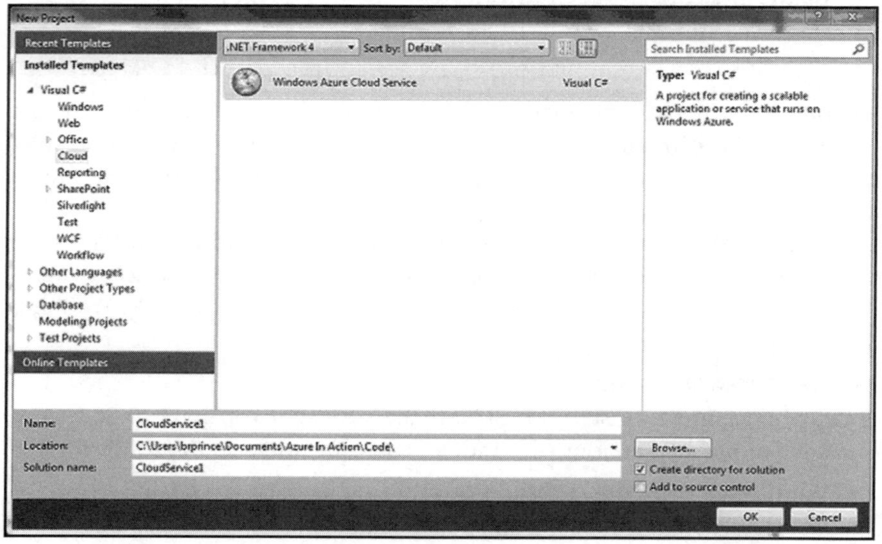

Figure 1.6 The Cloud Service template in the New Project dialog box of Visual Studio 2010

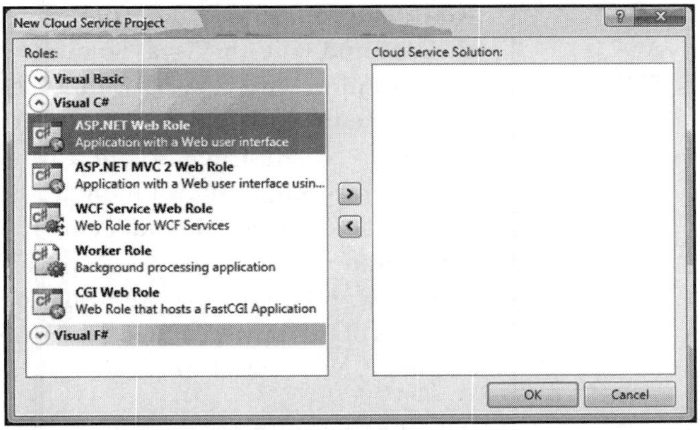

Figure 1.7 New Cloud Service Project dialog box. From here, you can add several Azure projects to your solution.

After you select the Cloud Service template, enter a name for your project and solution, and then click OK. The dialog box shown in figure 1.7 opens, in which you select the type of Windows Azure project that you want to create.

You can create the following types of roles:

- ASP.NET web roles
- ASP.NET MVC 2 web roles
- WCF service web roles
- Worker roles
- CGI-based web roles

You can create your projects in either Visual Basic or C#. In this book, we use C# rather than Visual Basic. This is no disrespect to Visual Basic; we've found over time that although C# developers typically aren't comfortable with Visual Basic, Visual Basic developers are comfortable with both languages (you have to be though, because most samples are in C#).

Select the ASP.NET Web Role project, and then click the right arrow button to add the project to the Cloud Service Solution panel, as shown in figure 1.8.

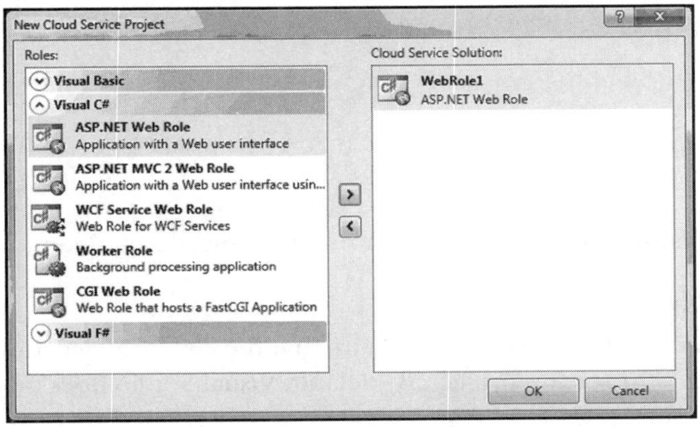

Figure 1.8 Selecting a web role project from the New Cloud Service Project dialog box. Click the default name WebRole1 to change it to something more to your liking.

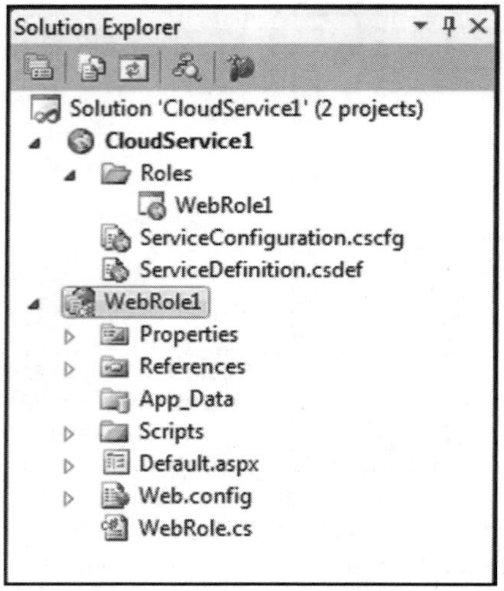

Figure 1.9 Solution Explorer for your newly created web role project. The top project (CloudService1) defines your application to Azure. The bottom one (WebRole1) is a regular ASP.NET project with a starter template.

Now that you've selected your web project, click OK and wait for Visual Studio to generate your solution. After Visual Studio has taken some time to set up your solution and project, it'll have created a new solution for you with two new projects, as shown in figure 1.9.

The first project (CloudService1) contains configuration that's specific to your Windows Azure web role. For now, we won't look at the contents of this project and instead save that for chapter 2. Next, you'll create a simple web page.

1.2.3 *Modifying the web page*

The second project (WebRole1) in figure 1.9 is a regular old ASP.NET web application. You can modify the default.aspx file as you would normally. In this case, modify the file to display Hello World, as shown in the following listing.

Listing 1.1 Modifying the default.aspx file to display Hello World

```
<%@ Page Language="C#" AutoEventWireup="true"
CodeBehind="Default.aspx.cs" Inherits="WebRole1._Default" %>

<!DOCTYPE html PUBLIC "-//W3C//DTD XHTML 1.0 Transitional//EN"
 "http://www.w3.org/TR/xhtml1/DTD/xhtml1-transitional.dtd">

<html xmlns="http://www.w3.org/1999/xhtml" >
<head runat="server">
    <title>Hello World</title>
</head>
<body>
    <form id="form1" runat="server">
    <div>
       Hello World
    </div>
    </form>
</body>
</html>
```

Now that you've created your web page, you can run it in your development fabric.

1.2.4 *Running the web page*

Before you run your new web role, you must ensure that the cloud service, rather than the ASP.NET project, is your startup project. By default, Visual Studio does this for you when you create your new project. If the ASP.NET project is the startup project, Visual Studio will run it with the built-in development web server and not the Azure SDK.

Now for the exciting part: you're about to run your first web application in the Windows Azure development fabric. Press F5 as you would for any other Visual Studio application. Visual Studio fires up the development fabric and launches your web page in your browser just like any other web page. Unlike regular ASP.NET web applications, the development fabric hosts your web page rather than the Visual Studio Web Development Server (Cassini). Figure 1.10 shows your web page running in the development fabric.

Figure 1.10 ASP.NET 3.5 Hello World running in the development fabric

Congratulations! You've developed your first cloud application. In chapter 2, we'll look in more detail at the development SDK, the development fabric, and how to deploy your service to the live production servers.

Let's return now to our big-picture discussion of Azure.

1.3 Putting all the Azure pieces together

Even Hello World web applications often require multiple instances as the result of the levels of traffic they receive. To understand all that's involved in multiple instances, you first need to understand the Windows Azure logical infrastructure and how it makes it so easy to deploy and run applications in the cloud. As you can see in figure 1.11, the web role is just one piece of the overall infrastructure.

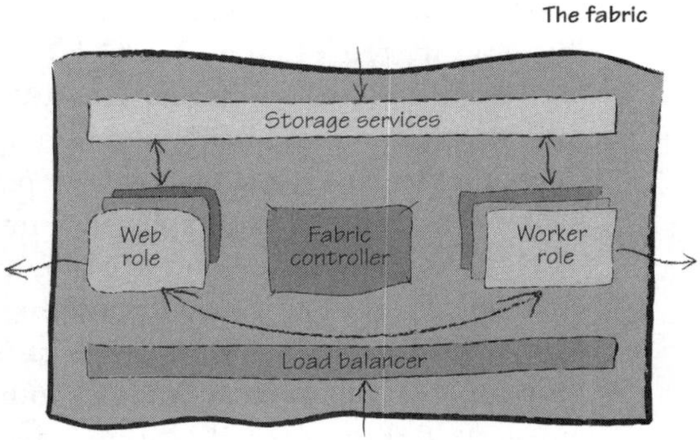

Figure 1.11 The Windows Azure compute infrastructure involves several components. They all work together to run your application.

Over the next couple of sections, we'll look at how the other components—worker roles, the fabric and the Fabric Controller, and the storage services—fit together. First, let's take a closer look at the *load balancer* (the component at the bottom of figure 1.11).

1.3.1 How the load balancer works

Note in figure 1.11 that neither your web roles (web applications) nor your worker roles (background services) have direct incoming traffic from the internet. For both worker and web roles, all incoming traffic must be forwarded via one or more load balancers. The load balancer provides four important functions, as listed in table 1.1.

Table 1.1 Primary load balancer functions

Function	Purpose
Minimize attack surface area	Improves security
Load distribution	Enables incoming requests to be forwarded to multiple instances
Fault tolerance	Routes traffic to another instance during a fault
Maintenance	Routes traffic to another instance during an upgrade

Not only can a role receive incoming traffic, but roles can also initiate communication with services hosted outside the Windows Azure data centers, with roles inside the data center, and with storage services.

Now that you understand the load balancer's job of distributing requests across multiple instances of web roles, we'll take a brief look at Azure's other type of supported role, the worker role.

1.3.2 Creating worker roles

Worker roles are a lot like web roles and will be covered in depth in chapter 15. The biggest difference is that they lack IIS, which means they can't host a web application, at least not in the traditional sense. Worker roles are best suited for hosting backend processing and a wide variety of web services. These types of servers are often referred to as *application servers* in many IT departments.

At this point, we've explored a few tasks an operating system performs (hosting and running applications). What we haven't explained is how the kernel fits into this analogy of Azure as a cloud operating system. You need something that will manage your applications and all your VMs running in the Windows Azure data center. It's one thing to host an application; it's another to manage what's running and enforce permissions and resource allocation. In a normal operating system, the kernel performs these tasks. In Windows Azure, the kernel is the Fabric Controller (it sits right in the center of figure 1.11).

1.3.3 How the fabric and the Fabric Controller work

Azure contains a massive number of servers, and there isn't any way they can possibly be managed on an individual basis. This is where the Azure operating system concept comes into play. By abstracting away all of those individual servers into a swarm or cloud, you only have to manage the cloud as a whole. This swarm of servers is called the *fabric*, and your applications run in the fabric when you deploy them to the cloud.

The fabric is managed by a software overlord known as the *Fabric Controller*. The Fabric Controller plays the role of the kernel and is aware of every hardware and software asset in the fabric. It's responsible for installing your web and worker roles onto the physical or virtual servers living in the fabric (this process is similar to how the kernel assigns memory or CPU to an application in a traditional operating system). The Fabric Controller is responsible for maintaining its inventory by monitoring the health of all its assets. If any of the assets are unhealthy, it's responsible for taking steps to resolve the fault, which might include the following:

- Restarting your role
- Restarting a server
- Reprogramming a load balancer to remove the server from the active pool
- Managing upgrades
- Moving instances of your role in fault situations

Windows Azure follows a cloud computing paradigm known as the fabric, which is another way of describing the data center. Like in the movie *The Matrix*, the fabric is everywhere. Every single piece of hardware (server, router, switch, network cable, and so on) and every VM is connected together to form the fabric. Each resource in the fabric is designed and monitored for fault tolerance. The fabric forms an abstract representation of the physical data center, allowing your applications to run in the fabric without knowledge of the underlying infrastructure.

Figure 1.11 shows how the Fabric Controller monitors and interacts with the servers. It's the central traffic cop, managing the servers and the code that's running on those servers. The Fabric Controller performs the job of the kernel (except across multiple servers at a server level rather than at CPU and memory level) in terms of allocating resources and monitoring resources.

One of the jobs that the Fabric Controller doesn't do (but that a kernel does) is the abstraction of the I/O devices. In Azure, this job is performed by storage services, which we'll discuss next (the storage services component sits near the top of figure 1.11).

1.4 Storing data in the cloud with Azure

Suppose you're developing a new podcasting application for Windows 7. For this application, you want to convert MP3 files to WMA. To convert an MP3 file, you first need to read the file from a hard disk (and eventually write the result). Even though there are thousands of different disk drives, you don't need to concern yourself with the implementation of these drives because the operating system provides you with an abstracted view of the disk drive. To save the converted file to the disk, you can write the file to the filesystem; the operating system manages how it's written to the physical device. The same piece of code that you would use to save your podcast will work, regardless of the physical disk drive.

In the same way that Windows 7 abstracts the complexities of the physical hardware of a desktop PC away from your application, Windows Azure abstracts the physical cloud infrastructure away from your applications using configuration and managed APIs.

Applications can't subsist on code alone; they usually need to store and retrieve data to provide any real value. In the next section, we'll discuss how Azure provides you with shared storage, and then we'll take a quick tour of the BLOB storage service, messaging, and the Table storage service. Each of these is covered in detail in their related sections later in this book.

1.4.1 Understanding Azure's shared storage mechanism

If we consider the MP3 example in the context of Windows Azure, rather than abstracting your application away from a single disk, Windows Azure needs to abstract your application away from the physical server (not just the disk). Your application doesn't have to be directly tied to the storage infrastructure of Azure. You're abstracted away from it so that changes in the infrastructure don't impact your code or application. Also, the data needs to be stored in shared space, which isn't tied to a physical server and can be accessed by multiple physical servers. Figure 1.12 shows this logical abstraction.

You can see how storage is logically represented in figure 1.12, but how does this translate into the world of Windows Azure? Your services won't always be continually running on the same physical machine. Your roles (web or worker) could be shut down and moved to another machine at any time to handle faults or upgrades. In the case of web roles, the load balancer could be distributing requests to a pool of web servers, meaning that an incoming request could be performed on any machine.

To run services in such an environment, all instances of your roles (web and worker) need access to a consistent, durable, and scalable storage service. Windows Azure provides scalable storage service, which can be accessed both inside and outside the Microsoft data centers. When you register for Windows Azure, you'll be able to create your own storage accounts with a set of endpoint URIs that you can use to access access the storage services for your account. The storage services are accessed via a set of REST APIs that's secured by an authentication token. We'll take a more detailed look at these APIs in parts 4 and 5 of this book.

Windows Azure storage services are hosted in the fabric in the same way as your own roles are hosted. Windows Azure is a scalable solution; you never need to worry about running out of capacity.

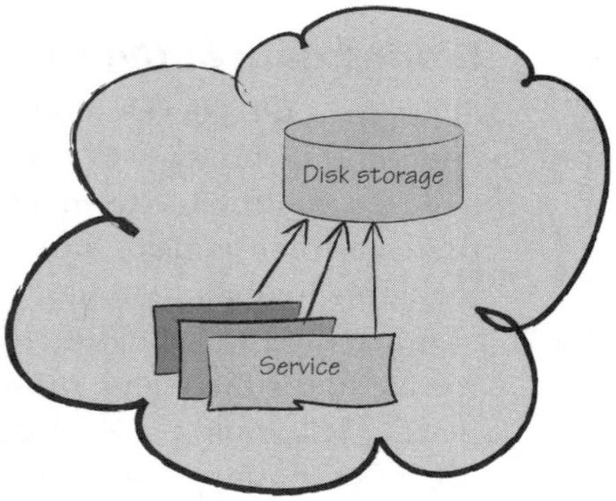

Figure 1.12 Multiple instances of your service (that don't care what physical server they live on) talking to an abstracted logical filesystem, rather than to a physical drive

1.4.2 Storing and accessing BLOB data

Windows Azure provides the ability to store binary files (BLOBs) in a storage area known as *BLOB storage*.

In your storage account, you create a set of containers (similar to folders) that you can store your binary files in. In the initial version of the BLOB storage service, containers can either be restricted to private access (you must use an authentication key to access the files held in this container) or to public access (anyone on the internet can access the file, without using an authentication key).

In figure 1.13, we return to the audio file conversion (MP3 to WMA) scenario. In this example, you're converting a source recording of your podcast (Podcast01.mp3) to Windows Media Audio (Podcast01.wma). The source files are held in BLOB storage in a private container called *Source Files*, and the destination files are held in BLOB storage in a public container called *Converted Files*. Anyone in the world can access the converted files because they're held in a public container, but only you can access the files in the private container because it's secured by your authentication token. Both the private and public containers are held in the storage account called *MyStorage*.

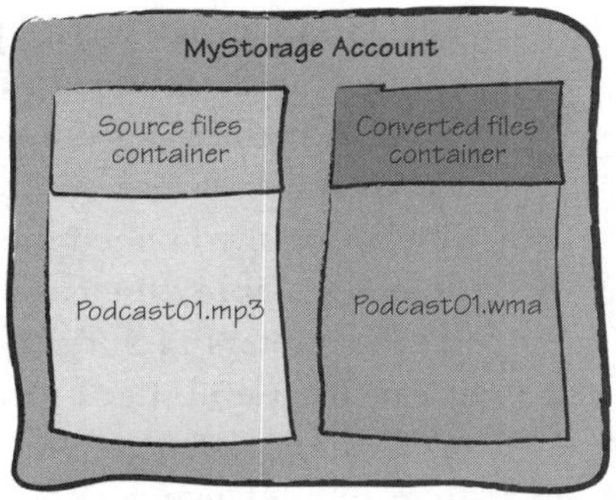

Figure 1.13 Audio files held in BLOB storage

BLOBs can be split up into more manageable chunks known as *blocks* for more efficient uploading of files. This is only the tip of the iceberg in terms of what you can do with BLOB storage in Azure. In part 4, we'll explore BLOB storage and usage in much more detail.

BLOBs play the role of a filesystem in the cloud, but there are other important aspects of the storage subsystem. One of those is the ability to store and forward messages to other services through a message queue.

1.4.3 *Messaging via queues*

Message queues are the primary mechanism for communicating with worker roles. Typically, a web role or an external service places a message in the queue for processing. Instances of the worker role poll the queue for any new messages and then process the retrieved message. After a message is read from the queue, it's not available to any other instances of the worker role. Queues are considered part of the Azure storage system because the messages are stored in a durable manner while they wait to be picked up in the queue.

In the audio file conversion example, after the source podcast BLOB (Podcast01.mp3) is placed in the Source Files container, a web role or external service places a message (containing the location of the BLOB) in the queue. A worker role retrieves the message and performs the conversion. After the worker role converts the file from MP3 to WMA, it places the converted file (Podcast01.wma) in the Converted Files container.

If you're experiencing information overload at this point, don't worry! In part 6, we'll look at message queues in much greater detail and give you some concrete examples to chew on. Windows Azure also provides you with the ability to store data in a highly scalable, simple Table storage service.

1.4.4 Storing data in tables

The Table storage service provides the ability to store serialized entities in a big table; entities can then be partitioned across multiple servers.

Using tables is a simple storage mechanism that's particularly suitable for session management or user authentication. Tables don't provide a relational database in the cloud, and if you need the power of a database (such as when using server-side joins), then SQL Azure, discussed in chapter 13, is a more appropriate technology.

In chapters 11 and 12, you'll learn how to use Table storage and in what scenarios it can be useful. Let's turn now to the question of why you might want to run your applications in the cloud. You'll want to read the next section, if for no other reason than to convince your boss to let you use it. But you should probably have a better argument prepared than "it's real cool, man" or "this book told me to."

1.5 Why run in the cloud?

So far in this chapter, we've said, "Isn't Azure shiny and cool?" We've also said, "Wow, it's so great I can take my existing IT app and put it in the cloud." But what we haven't asked is, "Why would I want to stick it in the cloud? Why would I want to host my applications with Microsoft rather than host them myself? What advantages do I get using this new platform?" The answers to these questions include the following:

- You can save lots of money.
- You won't need to buy any infrastructure to run your application.
- You don't need to manage the infrastructure to run your application.
- Your application runs on the same infrastructure that Microsoft uses to host its services, not some box under a desk.
- You can scale out your application on demand to use whatever resources it needs to meet its demands.
- You pay only for the resources that you use, when you use them.
- You're provided with a framework that allows you to develop scalable software that runs in the Windows Azure platform so your applications can run at internet scale.
- You can focus on what you're good at: developing software.
- You can watch football and drink milkshakes without being disturbed because someone pulled out the server power cable so they could do the vacuuming.
- You can save lots of money.

In case you think we're repeating ourselves by saying "You can save lots of money" twice, well, it's the key point: you can save a lot. We're often involved in large-scale systems for which the infrastructure costs millions (and most of the time, the servers sit idle). That's not including the cost of running these systems. The equivalent systems in Azure are about 10 percent of the cost.

With that in mind, this section will show you a few of the ways the Windows Azure platform can help you out and save lots of money.

1.5.1 Treating computing power as a utility service

In traditional on-premises or managed-hosting solutions, you either rent or own the infrastructure that your service is hosted on. You're paying for future capacity that you're currently not using. The Windows Azure platform, like other cloud platforms, follows a model of utility computing.

Utility computing treats computing power or storage in the same way you treat a utility service (such as gas or electricity). Your usage of the Windows Azure platform is metered, and you pay only for what you consume.

PAY AS YOU GROW

If you have to pay only for the resources you use, you can launch a scalable service without making a huge investment up front in hardware. In the early days of a new venture, a start-up company survives from investment funding and generates very little income. The less money the company spends, the more chance it has of surviving long enough to generate sufficient income to sustain itself. If the service is successful, then the generated income will pay for the use of the resources.

It's not unusual for technology start-ups to purchase large and expensive hardware solutions for new ventures to cope with predicted future demand. If the service is successful, then it'll require the extra capacity; in the meantime, the start-up is paying for resources that it's not using. Utility computing offers the best of both worlds, giving you the ability to use extra capacity as the service grows without making up-front investments in hardware, and to pay only for the resources that that you use.

SCALE ON DEMAND

Some situations involve large, unpredictable growth; you want to handle the load, but not pay for the unused capacity. This situation might appear in the following scenarios:

- Viral marketing campaigns
- Referrals by a popular website
- Concert ticket sales

Let's say you run a Hawaiian Shirt Shop, and you typically have a predictable pattern of usage. If, for example, Ashton Kutcher (who has 2,000,000 Twitter followers) tweets that he buys his shirts from your website, and he posts a link to your site to all his followers, it's likely that your website will experience a surge in traffic.

Look at the graph in figure 1.14. It shows that your website normally receives around 1,000 hits per day. After Ashton Kutcher tweeted about your website, that increased to

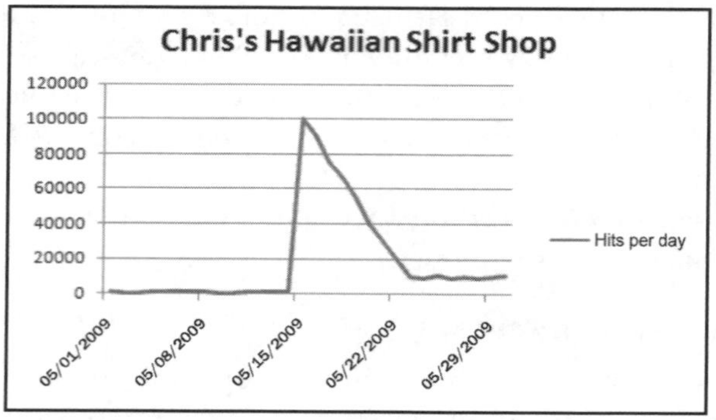

Figure 1.14 Traffic before, during, and after Ashton Kutcher plugged your site

100,000 hits per day. The traffic dropped off after about a week, and then the website had a new baseline of around 10,000 hits per day.

With Windows Azure, you can dynamically scale up to handle the increased traffic load for that week (and get all the extra shirt sales); then, as the traffic decreases, you can scale back down again, paying only for the resources you use. Scaling up and down in Azure is quite simple, and we'll discuss how to do it in detail in chapter 6. You have several options at your disposal. It's important to remember that Azure doesn't scale your service for you. Because it costs money, you have to tell Azure how many servers you want. Azure gives you tools to do this. You can simply log into the portal and make a small change to a configuration file, which is the easy, manual way. You can also use the Service Management API (covered in chapter 18). This API lets you change the resources you have allocated to your application in an automated way.

It's not only possible to scale up and down for predictable (or unpredictable) bursts of growth; you can also dynamically scale your service based on normal, varied usage patterns.

VARIED USAGE PATTERNS

Returning to the Hawaiian Shirt Shop example: after the Ashton Kutcher hype died down a little, your website leveled off at around 10,000 hits per day. Figure 1.15 shows how this traffic varies over the course of a day. Most of the time there's little traffic on the site, apart from during lunch and in the evening. Evidently, most people don't buy Hawaiian shirts when they're at work.

Because it takes only a few minutes to provision a new web server in Windows Azure, you can dynamically scale your website as your usage patterns dictate. For the Hawaiian Shirt Shop, you might decide to run one instance of the website during the day, but in the evening to run three instances to deal with the increased traffic.

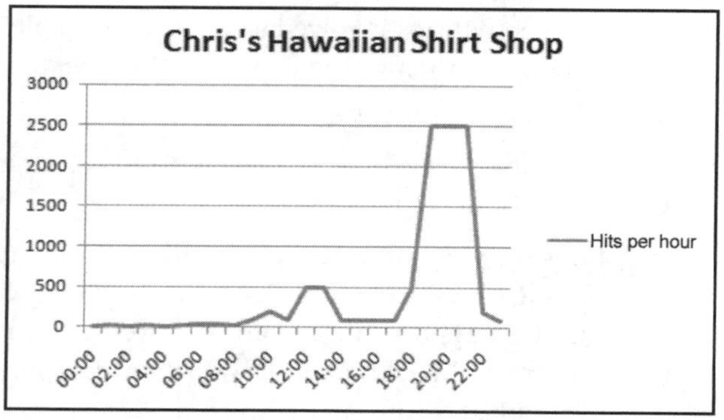

Figure 1.15 Distribution of website traffic over a single day

This sort of scenario is a perfect example of when cloud computing, specifically using Windows Azure, is a perfect fit for your business. If you need to scale beyond a single web server for certain periods of the day when traffic is high, Windows Azure is a cost-effective choice because it allows you to scale back when traffic dies down. Cloud computing solutions are the only offerings that give you this elastic scalability. Other solutions typically require you to over-provision your hardware to cope with the peak periods, but that hardware is underused at off-peak times.

Enough capacity

This example of utility computing can be extended further in regard to available capacity. It's fair to say that most people don't have any idea of the available spare electricity capacity of the network supplying their home, but most of us are confident that if we plug in an extra television, the required electricity will be supplied. The same holds true in Windows Azure. We have no idea how much spare capacity the Microsoft data centers have, but we do know that there's enough. If you require an extra instance of your website, web service, or backend service to be hosted, this will be provisioned for you, within minutes. If the data that your service stores is much larger than you originally anticipated due to the level of growth, more disk space will be allocated to you. You never have to worry about running out of disk space or running out of computing power. You only have to worry about running out of money to pay for the services.

Growth is difficult to model effectively, so knowing there's always enough capacity to grow allows you to concentrate on providing your service rather than worrying about capacity planning, provisioning of new servers, and all their associated tasks.

So far, we've discussed the cost savings you can achieve by scaling your application up and down. Let's now look at how you can save money in maintenance costs.

1.5.2 Simplified data-center management

In this section, we'll look at how the effort involved in operationally maintaining your application is reduced in the Windows Azure environment.

BUILT-IN FAULT TOLERANCE

In Windows Azure, if the physical hardware that your service instance resides on fails, that failed instance is redeployed to another machine. Hardware maintenance resides solely in Microsoft's domain, and you don't have to worry about it.

When you have more than two instances of your application running in Windows Azure, each instance of your web role doesn't live on the same physical server as another instance. This arrangement ensures that if the hardware for one instance dies, the other instance can continue to perform incoming requests. Not only does the second instance live on a different physical server, but it also lives on a different rack (in case the server rack fails). The server rack where the second instance resides is connected to a different network and power grid from the first rack. This level of fault tolerance ensures that if there's a failure on the physical server, the server rack, the network, or in the electricity supply, your service continues to run and is able to service requests.

When you install your application, Windows Azure decides what servers to place your instances on, with the intention of providing the maximum levels of fault tolerance. Because all data-center assets are tracked and mapped, the placement of applications on each physical server is determined by an algorithm designed to match the fault-tolerance criteria. Even with only two instances of an application, these considerations are pretty complex, but Windows Azure maximizes fault tolerance even when there are hundreds of instances.

Although fault tolerance is maintained within a physical data center, Azure doesn't currently run across the data centers, but runs only within a single data center. You still need to perform offsite backups (if you need them). You can replicate your data to a second data center and run your applications in more than one data center if georedundancy is required.

One of the key differences between Windows Azure–hosted applications and regular on-premises solutions or other cloud solutions is that Windows Azure abstracts away everything about the infrastructure, including the underlying operating system, leaving you to focus on your application. Let's see how Azure's ability to maintain the servers your applications run on reduces cost.

SERVER SOFTWARE MAINTENANCE BEGONE!

Whether you're running an entire data center or hosting a website on a dedicated server at a hosting company, maintaining the operating system is usually your responsibility. Maintenance tasks can include managing antivirus protection, installing Windows updates, applying service packs, and providing security. If you're running your own dedicated machine on your own premises rather than it being hosted for you, then you're even responsible for performing backups.

In Windows Azure, because the tasks associated with maintaining the server are the responsibility of Microsoft, you can focus completely on your application. This situation greatly simplifies and reduces the cost of running a service.

A final cost consideration is that if you have a service hosted in Windows Azure, you don't have to worry about the licensing costs for the underlying operating system. You gain all the benefits of running under the latest version of Windows without paying for the costs of maintaining that software. The underlying software is abstracted away from your service, but the base underlying operating system of your service is Windows Server 2008. If you're running multiple servers, the cost of licensing usually runs into thousands of dollars.

Although you don't have to worry about hardware or software maintenance from an operational or cost perspective, you do have to worry about it from a software design perspective.

DESIGNING FOR DISTRIBUTION

Your services won't always be running on the same machine, and they might be failed over to another machine at any time. Failover might be caused by hardware failures, software maintenance cycles, or load distribution. You must design your software so that it can handle these failures. This might mean automatically retrying a failed operation when an exception occurs or reloading any local caches when a service restarts. We'll delve further into these issues in chapter 18.

Let's switch gears now and look at what the Windows Azure *platform* is all about.

1.6 Inside the Windows Azure platform

To reiterate, the major difference between Windows Azure and the Windows Azure platform is the first one is the operating system, and the latter is the broader ecosystem of related services and components. In this section, we'll briefly overview the flagship cloud services provided by the Windows Azure platform (beyond Windows Azure itself): namely, a relational database using SQL Azure, and a set of enterprise services that use the Windows Azure platform AppFabric.

The Windows Azure platform provides many services. In this book, we don't cover every last aspect of every service that's offered across the platform because each component could probably justify its own dedicated book. We'll give you an overview of what's offered, when it's useful, and how you can use the more common scenarios.

Let's get started with the service that you're most likely to use: SQL Azure.

1.6.1 SQL Server capability in the cloud

Although Windows Azure does offer support for storing data in tables, this is a basic storage capability that's suited only for certain core scenarios, which we discuss in chapters 11 and 12.

If you need to create more advanced databases, need to migrate existing SQL databases to Azure, or can't cope with learning another data storage technology, then SQL Azure is the best solution for you. SQL Azure is a relational database (very similar to SQL Server Express Edition) that's hosted within the Windows Azure platform.

A history lesson

When SQL Azure was first announced and made available as a Community Technology Preview (CTP), it was architected differently from the way it currently is. The initial previews of what was known as SQL Server Data Services (SSDS) were of a nonrelational model that was similar to Windows Azure storage services. The feedback given to the product teams made it clear that customers wanted a relational database in the cloud, and SSDS was later retired. Prior to being renamed as SQL Azure, SSDS was renamed SQL Data Services, but there was never a public CTP under this name.

WHAT IS SQL AZURE?

Version 1.0 of SQL Azure, which was released at PDC 2009, provides the core capabilities of SQL Server in the cloud. The first release can be likened to running an instance of SQL Server Express Edition on a shared host, with some changes to security so that you can't mess with other databases on the same server.

Communication with SQL Azure is via the Tabular Data Stream (TDS) protocol, which is the same protocol that's used for the on-premises editions of SQL Server. You can connect SQL Management Studio directly to your database hosted in the cloud, as if it were hosted locally.

NOTE In the first release of SQL Azure, security is limited to SQL Server user accounts. Windows Integrated Security isn't yet supported. Expect some sort of support beyond SQL Security at a later date.

Because you can connect to SQL Azure with a regular connection string, any existing data access layers continue to work normally. Figure 1.16 shows communication between SQL Azure and applications that are hosted both inside and outside Windows Azure.

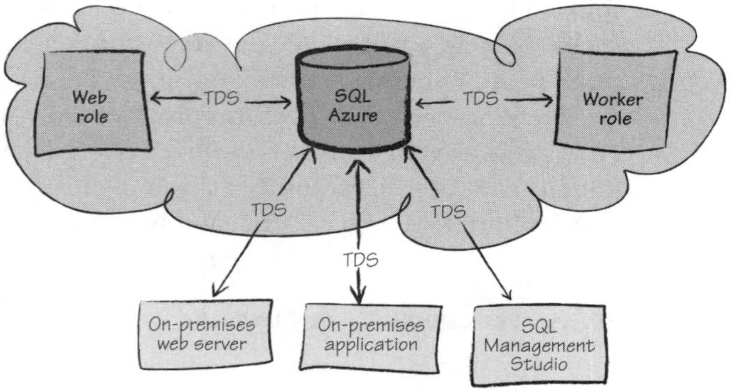

Figure 1.16 On-premises, Azure-hosted applications and SQL Management Studio communicating with SQL Azure via TDS

If your application works today using SQL Server Express Edition and doesn't use some of the more advanced features of SQL Server (see chapter 13), then your application should work in the cloud with little or no modification.

Although on-premises applications can talk to SQL Azure, latency might make this a less attractive option. The closer your application is to the database, the faster it'll go. You can reduce the impact of latency by making your application less chatty.

HOW SCALABLE IS SQL AZURE?

In version 1.0 of SQL Azure, there's no built-in support for data partitioning (the ability to split your data across multiple servers). The initial release is targeted for databases that are sized up to 10 GB; larger databases aren't suitable for SQL Azure in this initial release, but support for larger databases will be available in future service updates. If you need to perform partitioning, you need to implement it in the application layer.

Let's turn now to Azure platform's enterprise services. Known as AppFabric, these services include the Access Control Service (ACS) and the Service Bus.

1.6.2 *Enterprise services in the cloud*

The Windows Azure platform AppFabric (formerly .NET Services) is a set of services that's more oriented toward enterprise applications and is comprised of the following components:

- AppFabric ACS
- AppFabric Service Bus

AppFabric is a large set of technologies that would require its own book to cover in any depth. In this section, we'll give you an overview of the technologies. In chapter 17, we'll show you how to get started using them and discuss a couple of key scenarios in which to use the technology.

> **Velocity and Dublin: where are they now?**
>
> In addition to the Windows Azure platform AppFabric product, there's also an on-premises product known as Windows Server AppFabric. This is a completely different product set, which currently includes AppFabric Caching (formerly Velocity) and AppFabric Service Workflow and Management (formerly Dublin).
>
> Although these services aren't currently part of the Windows Azure platform (PDC 2009), you can expect them to appear at some point. Depending on when you're reading this book, they could be available right now. Alternatively, you could be reading this in the far future (relative to PDC 2009) and there's no need for this technology because we're all plugged in to the Matrix.

ACCESS CONTROL SERVICE

User authentication security and management is a fairly standard requirement for any service used in an enterprise organization. Enterprises require that their employees, customers, and vendors be able to access all services in the organization with a single login; typically, the authentication process occurs using the Windows login. After you're authenticated, you're typically issued a token, which is automatically passed to other services in the enterprise as you access them. The automatic passing and authentication of this token means you don't have to continually log in each time you access a service.

Services in the enterprise don't implement their own individual authentication and user-management systems but hook directly into the organization's identity-management service (such as Active Directory). This single sign-on process provides many benefits to the company (centralized and simplified user management and security) and is a much more integrated and less frustrating user experience.

Traditionally, identity management and access control have been restricted to the enterprise space. With the advent of Web 2.0 social platforms, such as Live Services and Facebook, this level of integration is now creeping into everyday websites. Web users are now more concerned about data privacy and are reluctant to cheaply give away personal information to third-party websites. They don't want a long list of user names and passwords for various sites and want a much richer social experience on the web. For example, it's increasingly common for people to want to be able to tell their friends on Facebook about their latest purchase. Between Facebook, Live Services, OpenID (and its differing implementations), and all the various enterprise identity-management systems, access control has now became a complex task.

AppFabric ACS abstracts away the nuances of the various third-party providers by using a simple rules-based authentication service that manages authentication across multiple providers for users with multiple credentials. We'll look more closely at ACS in chapter 17 and show you how to use it in a couple of key scenarios.

APPFABRIC SERVICE BUS

The Service Bus is a cool piece of technology that allows you to message with applications that aren't necessarily running in the Azure data centers. If you have a custom, proprietary service that you need to continue to host, but you want to use Azure for all other aspects of your service offering, then the Service Bus is a good way to integrate with those services.

The Service Bus is effectively an Enterprise Message Bus that's hosted in the cloud. We'll explore in more detail what this means and look at a couple of key scenarios where you could use this technology in chapter 17.

1.7 Summary

In one chapter, you've learned about cloud computing, Windows Azure, and the Windows Azure platform. Although both Windows and Windows Azure are operating systems, providing all the needed functions, they differ greatly in terms of scale. Windows is an operating system for a single machine, whereas Windows Azure is an operating system for a whole fabric of machines, devices, networks, and other related items.

You learned that you can easily scale applications that run in Windows Azure to support the future needs of your application, but you pay only for your current needs.

We also briefly discussed why you might want to use the cloud. The cloud can give you new capabilities, such as dynamic scaling, disposable resources, and the freedom from manning any of it. But the real reason anyone uses the cloud always boils down to money. The rationale is simple: functionality you can't afford to provide in a normal data center is affordable in the cloud.

You developed your first Windows Azure web application and saw that developing in Windows Azure builds on your existing skills. You can now easily write code that runs locally or runs in the cloud—depending on your needs, not your skills or tools.

Like a desktop operating system, the Windows Azure platform consists of a lot of different parts. The platform includes SQL Azure, which provides a traditional relational database that gives you a familiar setting and makes it easier to migrate applications. Azure can also run your applications and manage storage.

We looked at how the Windows Azure platform AppFabric fits into the equation. AppFabric provides both a Service Bus you use to connect your applications together and a simple, standards-based way to secure your services called Access Control Service (ACS).

In chapter 2, we'll continue our discussion of Azure by showing you how to take your first steps with a web role and how to work with code that goes beyond Hello World.

2 Your first steps with a web role

This chapter covers

- Building a basic website
- Signing up for Azure
- Deploying your first cloud application

With the first chapter out of the way, you should have gotten a feeling for the lay of the land, installed the Windows Azure SDK, and run a Hello World application locally. Let's dive right in to building a website to run on Azure. In this chapter, we'll cover all the steps involved:

- Starting a new Visual Studio project
- Building the XHTML and code for the website
- Running and debugging the site locally
- Deploying the site to the Azure staging environment
- Moving the site to the Azure production environment

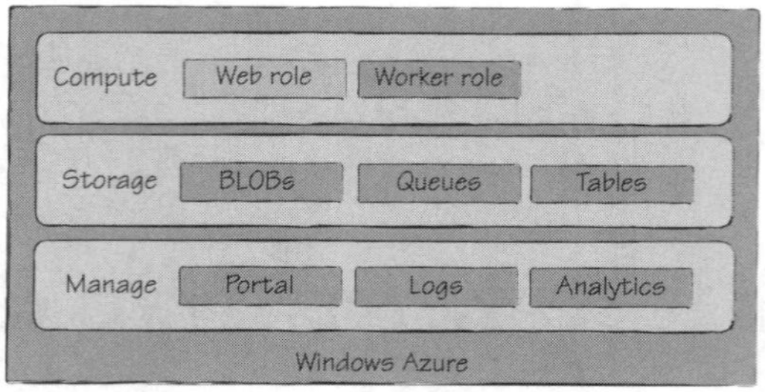

Figure 2.1 The basic components of Windows Azure. In this chapter, we'll focus on how you use the web role in Azure.

Don't let these steps daunt you. If you've ever developed a website with ASP.NET, you're already ahead of the game. You'll have to complete far fewer steps to deploy an application with Azure than you would with a traditional server.

In a large enterprise project one of us worked on, 15 percent of the work hours was spent planning the development, quality assurance, and production environments. Most of this time was used to define hardware requirements, acquire capital expenditure approval, and deal with vendor management. We could've shipped much sooner if we'd been able to focus on the application and not the underlying infrastructure and platform. Many organizations take three to six months just to deploy a server! You won't require this much time to complete the entire process using Windows Azure.

In this chapter, we'll focus on the basic process of deploying a simple website using the web role in Azure, which is highlighted in figure 2.1.

Before we start discussing the web role in detail, let's take a closer look at the Azure SDK.

2.1 Getting around the Azure SDK

After you install the SDK, a folder structure is created on your computer that's filled with tools, goodies, and documentation. The default path is C:\Program Files\Windows

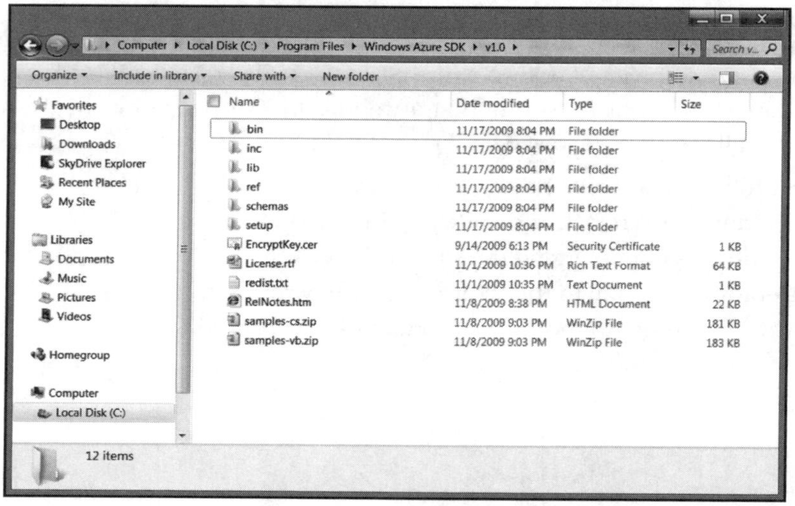

Figure 2.2 The directories that the Azure SDK installs for you. You should examine these because they contain lots of handy tools.

Azure SDK\v1.1. (Pay attention to the path name. It'll vary, depending on the version of the SDK you've installed. In our case, we have version 1.1 installed.) The contents of this directory are shown in figure 2.2.

You should explore these folders briefly, to be familiar with what's available. There are several tools included in the SDK that are quite powerful. Some tools can help you automate build environments and the management of your live Azure applications.

2.1.1 Exploring the SDK folders

Two of the more important SDK folders are bin and inc. The bin folder contains the assemblies and tools that you need to work with Azure packages and to run the development fabric. The inc folder holds a header file that you use if you're working with C++. Table 2.1 lists the tools included in the bin directory.

Table 2.1 The most important tools included in the SDK are found in the bin directory.

Visual Studio tool	Purpose
`CSmonitor`	This tool loads the local development fabric. You'll see the icon appear in your systray.
`CSpack`	Use this tool to manually create deployment packages to upload to the Azure portal when you're ready to run your application in the cloud.
`CSrun`	This tool lets you deploy a package generated by `CSpack` to run on the local development fabric.
`DFUI`	This script starts the management UI for the local development fabric.
`DSinit`	Use this tool to run the initialization needed for the Development storage service on a new SQL instance. If you're using SQL Server Express, the initialization is usually run once, on first startup. You'll need to run this yourself if you're running a local instance of SQL Server. This tool is located in the devstore subdirectory, under the bin folder.

The SDK provides tools you can use when you aren't using Visual Studio or when you're automating some of your processes. For example, if you're using Eclipse to write Java code for Windows Azure, you'll need to run these programs yourself, whereas Visual Studio will run them for you automatically.

2.1.2 Using the Cloud Service project templates

When you installed the SDK, a new project template group called Cloud Service was created in Visual Studio. This group includes several templates for you to start working with. You can use them when you're adding a new project to your solution. Never fear; you can also add an existing project, which is handy when you're migrating an application to the cloud.

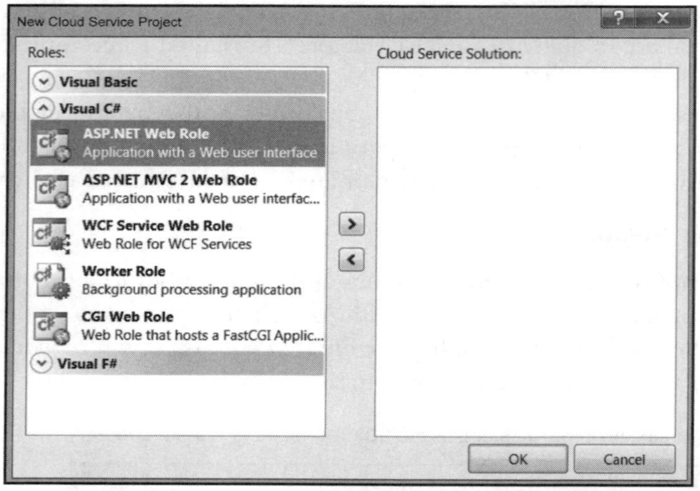

Figure 2.3 You have several options when it comes to adding an Azure project to your solution. These project templates are provided with the SDK.

Let's look at the Cloud Service project options that are available to you. The New Cloud Service Project window is shown in figure 2.3.

The SDK provides the following Visual Basic templates that you can use in your solutions:

- *ASP.NET Web Role*—This template creates an ASP.NET project, preconfigured with an accompanying Azure project.
- *ASP.NET MVC2 Web Role*—This template creates a project similar to the ASP.NET Web Role template, but is prewired to support the MVC2 framework.
- *WCF Service Web Role*—Planning on hosting a Windows Communication Foundation (WCF) service instead of a normal web application? Then this is the project for you. You set this up like a normal WCF project, using sample files for your first service.
- *Worker Role*—This template creates a class library project, preconfigured with a related Azure project. You should use this project if you're building a background processing service.
- *CGI Web Role*—This project template creates the required files needed to host a FastCGI project, which we'll cover in chapter 6.
- *Blank Cloud Service*—This isn't really a template, but if you click OK without adding any projects, you'll have a solution that contains an Azure project without any supporting application projects.

NOTE We're using Visual Studio 2010 in this book. You can use Visual Studio 2008. If you do, your experience will be similar to that depicted in this book, but some screenshots will look different, and the installation process is slightly different.

2.1.3 Running the cloud locally

We talked in chapter 1 about the internal web server that Visual Studio has included for the past few versions, called *Cassini*. This server makes it easy for a web developer to develop locally, without having to install full-blown server software on their desktop. Cassini was also designed to be lightweight and to respond only to local web requests, which enhances performance and security. The Azure SDK includes similar services that help the developer develop cloud websites and services locally.

The SDK installs the development fabric service and the development storage service. Both these services are started automatically by Visual Studio when you run an Azure project. (If you aren't using Visual Studio, or if the services don't start for you, you can start them from the Windows Start menu or from the Azure command prompt using `CSMonitor.exe`.) Although these services are separate processes, they appear as a single icon in the notification area of your task bar, shown in figure 2.4. Each service has several different processes related to it, which handle load balancing, node management, and a few other tasks. These processes allow you to run and debug your cloud services locally, before you deploy them to the cloud. They effectively work together, with a local instance of SQL Server Express, to simulate the real Azure storage and runtime environment. Because the environment is simulated, there are some limitations, which we'll discuss later in this chapter.

Figure 2.4 You can find the local cloud service icons in your notification area. The blue Windows flag tells you that the development fabric and the development storage services are running. Right-click the icon to show the UI you use to manage the services.

When these services start, both services continue to run until you stop them with the taskbar UI. We recommend that you leave them running while you're developing, and then shut them down when you're done for the day.

You can use an existing local instance of SQL Server instead of SQL Server Express to support the storage service. The SDK includes a tool called `DSinit` that you can use to initialize the storage databases. To configure the storage service to use your local SQL instance, use the `/sqlInstance` parameter with the name of the SQL instance you want to initialize. You can use a single period to represent the default instance for the server running, so you don't have to look up the name you gave the instance when you installed SQL Server: `DSinit.exe /sqlInstance.`

The SDK also includes a variety of samples that you can use to get a good idea of how to approach supported scenarios. One of the best ways to learn Azure is to walk through the code in the samples and understand how they work. The samples are provided in a zip file in the root of the SDK folder. Extract them to a folder to work with the code.

2.1.4 How the local and cloud environments differ

Although the SDK tools try to provide a complete simulation of the production cloud environment, there are some limitations developers should be aware of. Most of these limitations exist because the local environment is running on one machine, with limited resources. Others exist because the local storage service is based on a local SQL Server Express instance. We think that over time, the gaps between the local environment and the cloud environment will shrink. Table 2.2 summarizes the differences between the environments. The SDK documentation has a complete and up-to-date list of all the differences.

Table 2.2 Differences between the local and Azure cloud environments

Feature	Local environment	Cloud environment
Storage environment access	Uses a special account key for access.	Storage environment access is different from your cloud key.
HTTPS support	Doesn't support the use of HTTPS.	Cloud storage supports both HTTP and HTTPS.
Storage performance	Local storage is intended only for a few local connections, nothing more.	Expect the performance of the cloud-based storage to be much faster.
URI management	Because the Azure Domain Name System (DNS) is not part of the local environment, storage URIs are different in the local environment.	URIs are based on the Azure DNS system.
Storage management	The local storage subsystem doesn't provide extended error information.	Cloud storage provides extended error information.
BLOB storage	BLOBs in the local store are limited to 2 GB in size.	BLOBs in the cloud can be as big as 1 TB.

One way to minimize the impact of the local storage limitations is to shift to a blended model during your development. Early on in your project, you can configure your application to use local storage. As you start to bump up against the limits, adjust the configuration of the application to use the cloud-based storage. In this blended mode, you continue to run your application locally. Running your code locally with your data in the cloud during development will incur some slight charges for the bandwidth and storage of your data. We believe the cost is worth it because you'll be developing against the real storage infrastructure and not the local simulation provided by the SDK. Eventually, you'll deploy your application to the cloud staging environment, with the application configured to use the cloud storage.

To get a feel for how the SDK and tools work, you're now going to create a simple website.

2.2 Taking Hello World to the next level

You're going to build a second web application now, and it'll be a bit more complicated than the Hello World sample in chapter 1. This new website isn't going to have a lot of functionality, just a bit of XHTML and a cascading style sheet (CSS), with some simple code. You aren't going to be using any databases or advanced topics. Your goal is to make sure that the SDK and tools are installed correctly, and to learn the general workflow of working with a web application in Azure.

The one-page website that you're going to create lists the different shirts available at Chris's Hawaiian Shirt Shop. In addition to walking through the basic workflow, we'll also show you that in many scenarios, running a website in Azure is like running a website on your own server, and that it's as easy, if not easier, to deploy it. We're going to walk you through only the pertinent code; you can review the complete code listing in the sample code provided with this book.

2.2.1 Creating the project

Your first step is to create the project. Open Visual Studio and select File > New > Project. Visual Studio displays a list of available templates; select the Cloud Service template group, and then select Windows Azure Cloud Service in the menu. Give the project a name, such as HawaiianShirtShop, and click OK. A pop-up menu opens in which you pick the project types you want to add to your Azure solution. Because you're building a simple website, without any backend processing, choose the ASP.NET Web Role template. After you add the web role to the project, you can rename it; then click OK. You'll see the New Cloud Service Project window with one solution, as shown in figure 2.5.

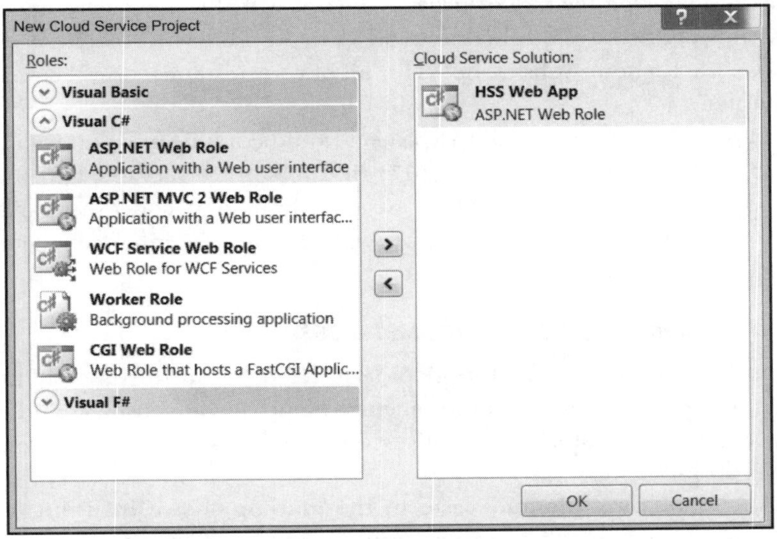

Figure 2.5 Creating a new Azure Application project is easy. Just add the different roles you'll need in your solution.

Visual Studio starts to build a solution file for you that contains a few projects. The first project is given the name that you entered on the New Project window. This new project will be the Azure project, and it doesn't contain a lot. It merely contains the model and configuration Azure needs to run your website. You can think of this information as the metadata for your whole Azure application. The project also contains links to other projects in your solution, and the role type those projects play in your application. These links are stored in the Roles folder. The solution and project structure is shown in figure 2.6.

Figure 2.6 The projects that Visual Studio creates for you. The bolded project is the Azure project, which holds the cloud configuration data for your application. Also shown is the HSS Web App project, which is linked to the Azure project as a web role.

Visual Studio also created an ASP.NET web application project for you, and linked it to the Azure project as a web role. Remember that you can name the subprojects when you select them from the list of roles (figure 2.5) by clicking the pencil icon. This icon shows up when you hover over the projects in the Cloud Service Solution list.

This ASP.NET project is typical in almost every way. Because Visual Studio knew the project was going to be part of an Azure application, it created assembly references to three Azure-related assemblies for you. The three assemblies are part of the `Microsoft.WindowsAzure` namespace. The `Diagnostics` assembly covers logging needs, the `ServiceRuntime` assembly provides methods for interacting with the Azure fabric, and the `StorageClient` assembly makes it easy to work with the Azure storage services. Visual Studio also added a file called webrole.cs or webrole.vb. This file is similar to the global.asax file for your website, but is for all of your instances. We'll cover this file in a later chapter.

You could press F5 right now and the project would compile and run locally. Visual Studio would start the local development Fabric and storage services, and then package and deploy your application. Of course, without any code or markup, you wouldn't see too much, except for an empty web browser. To enhance your app, you need to give it some content.

2.2.2 Laying down some markup with XHTML and a CSS

Now that you have the empty shell in place, you need to put in the content for the website. This new page is going to announce the name of your business and list a few of the shirts you have for sale. When you've completed this task, you'll have a simple web page that looks like figure 2.7.

Open the default.aspx file and paste in the markup shown in listing 2.1. With Azure, you don't usually need any special tags or changes to your website to do what

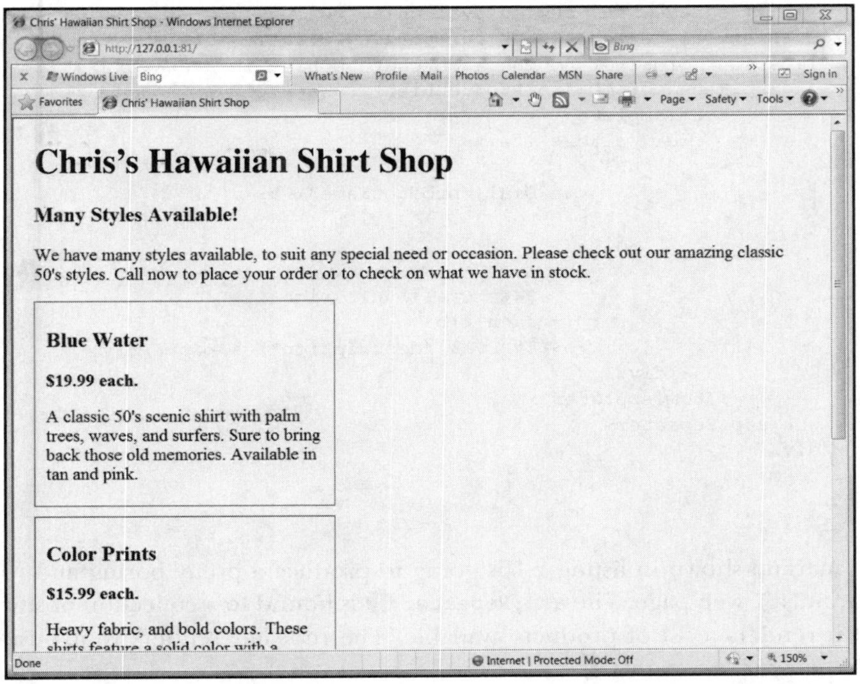

Figure 2.7 After you add some simple XML and a CSS, your web page will look like this.

you've always done. This is one thing that makes it easy for a web developer to learn how to use Azure and quickly move to the cloud.

Listing 2.1 The simple ASP.NET XHTML markup for your web page content

```
<%@ Page Language="C#" AutoEventWireup="true"
 CodeBehind="Default.aspx.cs" Inherits="HSS_Web_App._Default" %>

<!doctype html public "-//w3c//dtd xhtml 1.0 transitional//en"
➥   "http://www.w3.org/tr/xhtml1/dtd/xhtml1-transitional.dtd">
<html xmlns="http://www.w3.org/1999/xhtml">
<head id="Head1" runat="server">
    <title>Chris's Hawaiian Shirt Shop</title>
    <link rel="stylesheet" href="Main.css" type="text/css" />
</head>
<body>
    <form id="form1" runat="server">
    <div id="header">
        <h1>
            Chris's Hawaiian Shirt Shop</h1>
    </div>
    <div id="mainContent">
        <h3>
            Many Styles Available!</h3>
        <p>
```

```
        We have many styles available, to suit any special need or
    occasion. Please check out our amazing classic 50's styles. Call now to
    place your order or to check on what we have in stock.</p>
      <asp:Repeater ID="rptProductList" runat="server">          <-- 1 Lists the shirts
        <ItemTemplate>
          <div class="item">
            <h3>
              <%# Eval("productName") %>
            </h3>
            <div>
              <b>                                                  2 Renders only shirt data
                $<%# Eval("unitPrice")%>
                each.</b>
              <p><%# Eval("description") %></p></div>
          </div>
        </ItemTemplate>
      </asp:Repeater>
    </div>
    </form>
</body>
</html>
```

The markup shown in listing 2.1 is going to produce a pretty boring and run-of-the-mill ASP.NET web page. The `asp:Repeater` 1 is bound to a collection of shirt data so that it renders a list of products available. The repeater renders your business data with the `eval` statements 2.

2.2.3 Binding your data in the code-behind

The next step in your simple sample is to get the product data from a stub that will provide sample data, and then bind it to the repeater control in the markup. Let's call the stub `ProductInfo`. The complete code for the `ProductInfo` class can be found in the sample code provided with this book. A lot of developers would call this class `ProductService`, but we think the *service* word is overloaded as it is and makes things confusing. (You should feel free to roll the way you want; it's your code.) You'll also have a data transfer object (a simple class that has no methods, only properties), called `Product`, to hold your product data. You'll use a generic list collection to hold the multiple product classes as you bind them to the repeater control. You can place these classes in a new C# class file in your project:

```
public class Product
{
     public Product()
     {
     }

    public int sku { get; set; }
    public string productName { get; set; }              1 Accessors for product properties
    public decimal unitPrice { get; set; }
    public string description { get; set; }
}
```

Because we're trying to keep things simple, we're suggesting you use simple property accessors ❶ around the business data. Next, you'll add the `Page_Load` code that'll gather the product data and bind it to the fields on the form, as shown in the following code:

```
   ProductInfo productInfoSource = new ProductInfo();
IList<Product> allProducts = productInfoSource.GetAllProducts();

rptProductList.DataSource = allProducts;
rptProductList.DataBind();
```

❶ **Connects to data source and calls DataBind()**

When the page is loaded, it creates a `ProductInfo` object. The page uses that object to get a collection of `Product` objects, which is then bound ❶ to the `ProductList` repeater on the web form.

When you've entered the code correctly and run the application, Visual Studio starts the local Azure services (you'll see their icon in your task base like in figure 2.3), and launches the website in your browser. When you're running Azure applications locally, you must run Visual Studio as an administrator. If you forget to do this, Visual Studio will kindly remind you when you press F5.

If you look closely at the code, your web project doesn't have or do anything a normal website wouldn't have or do. The only differences are the Azure project, which tells either the local services or the Azure cloud how to run your application, and the webrole.cs file, which acts as a global event handler for your web role instances.

The Azure Fabric Controller knows how to deploy and manage your application, based on the settings included in the Azure project in your solution. There are several parts to this configuration that we need to cover now.

2.2.4 Just another place to run your code

We're going to spend a lot of time in this book discussing the unique capabilities the Azure platform has. You've probably heard a lot about cloud computing, and might be a little confused or intimidated. Don't worry! Until you fully grok the powers of the cloud, the easiest way to wrap your head around it is to think of it as just another place to run your code. If you boil it down to this simple concept, then its most powerful aspect is the simplicity of the deployment and management of applications.

Each cloud project defines a service model for the application. This model defines how the app should be deployed and run in the cloud. With this model, there isn't a 30-page deployment document with obscure and arcane instructions for deploying and upgrading. You can simply deploy your application with a few clicks and a few minutes of time. Azure knows what to do with your code because of the configuration and service model in the Azure project in your solution.

2.2.5 Configuring the Azure service model

The most important aspects of the Azure project are the links, which tell Visual Studio which projects in the solution are parts of the application, and what role they play. These links appear in the portal as elements that can be configured and scaled separately. A class library in your solution should be referenced with a project assembly reference as usual, and not linked to from the Azure project file. Besides these links, the Azure project also includes two configuration files:

- *ServiceDefinition.csdef*—This file defines which services are part of the application, and whether the services have any endpoints or connections that need to be provisioned. The information includes the public port that a website might need in order to receive traffic from the internet. This file mainly concerns itself with the configuration of the infrastructure.
- *ServiceConfiguration.cscfg*—This file determines the configuration of the services and how they should be provisioned by Azure. The configuration includes how many instances of each role should be deployed, and other operational characteristics.

We'll investigate each of these files in more depth in chapter 3.

2.2.6 Running the website in the local development fabric

When you run an Azure application locally, Visual Studio starts the development fabric and storage services, and then launches the application. Part of this process includes removing old temporary files and packaging the project to be deployed to the local services.

After the services are loaded, you can run their UIs to see what's happening in the local environment. Right-click the icon in the system tray and select Show Development Fabric UI. Each time you run your application, a new deployment is created, each with a successive number. Other deployments from your applications might show up in the UI, in addition to the one you're currently running.

The UI lists the deployments in the left panel. Each deployment displays the details of that service, as well as a list of the different roles and their instances that are

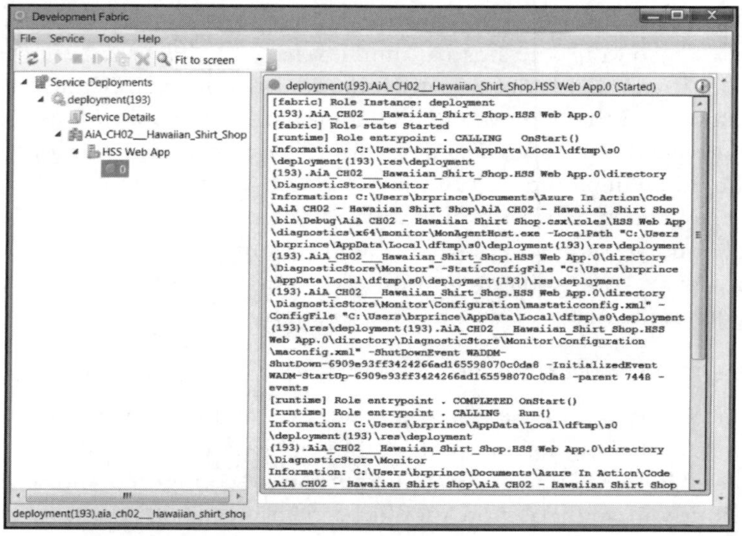

Figure 2.8 The UI of the development fabric. This UI shows that there is one web role running; it also shows the log history for that instance.

running. In figure 2.8, you can see one role, a web role called HSS Web App, which was the ASP.NET project in your solution that was linked to from the Azure project. That role has one instance running. In the UI the instances are numbered, starting with 0, because we're all geeks. In the right panel you see the log history for that instance.

With this UI you can pause or stop the different services, which is helpful during debugging. You can also change the logging levels of each service, which better refines what the log is capturing, and which is also helpful during debugging.

Now that you know how to install and use the Azure SDK and how to run your applications locally using the development fabric and storage services, we're going to show you how to deploy your little website to the cloud, and then become rich selling Hawaiian shirts.

2.3 Deploying with the Azure portal

The Azure portal is one of the three major components you use to manage your Azure applications. The other two components are your system logs (often referred to as diagnostics), and the analytical and billing tools. These components are highlighted in figure 2.9.

Before you can log in to the portal to manage your applications, you need to create an Azure account.

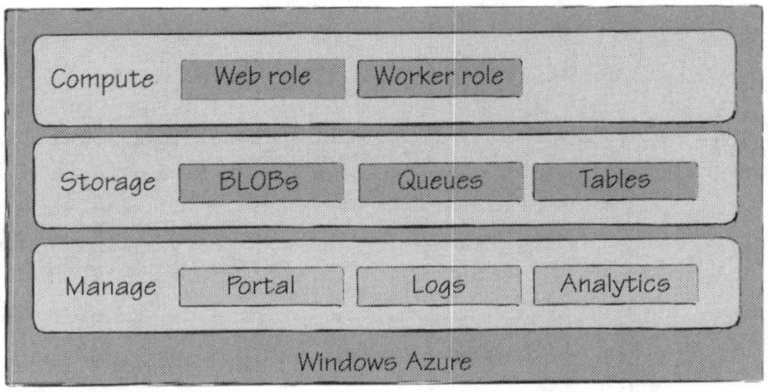

Figure 2.9 The management components of Azure include the portal, system logs, and the analytical tools.

2.3.1 Signing up for Azure

You need to sign up for an account and provide a live ID and billing details. You'll need to visit www.Azure.com to sign up. Go to the account section and click Get Your Account. You should open two accounts and provide two live IDs: one for business purposes such as billing and contract details, and another that's limited to the technical aspects of the system. Having two accounts cleanly separates the management of the business aspects from the management of the technical aspects. The business account manager is prevented from accidentally shutting down the applications or reconfiguring them. The cloud doesn't remove the risk of human mistakes; Azure just tries to automate these mistakes so that they cause trouble faster and more efficiently.

You'll need to give your credit card information so that they know who to bill for the time you use. Even if you have access to free time in the cloud through MSDN or some other channel, you'll still need to provide a credit card number in case you go over your free allocation.

Now that you have your account provisioned, you're ready to create a project on Azure to host your account. To do this, you use the Azure portal.

2.3.2 The Azure portal

The Azure portal is your central management tool for all aspects of running your application in the Azure environment. As shown in figure 2.10, across the top you'll be able to view the technical details (using the Summary tab) or the account details (using the Account tab) of your services. When you click one of these tabs, any services that you've created (websites, services, storage, and so on) are listed in the Windows Azure section on the left.

The following tabs are available on the portal:

- *Summary*—Lists your projects, and gives you access to managing them. From here you can upload new versions, flip staging and production, and manage log files.
- *Account*—Helps you manage your affinity groups, certificates, and any other broad configuration that affects all services under your account.
- *Help and Resources*—Brings together all the help options available to you, including technical support and public forums.

Azure will show you the different types of services available to you on your Azure account. You'll see icons for Storage Account and Hosted Services. You might also see icons for the other services that are part of the greater Azure Services platform, such as the AppFabric and SQL Azure.

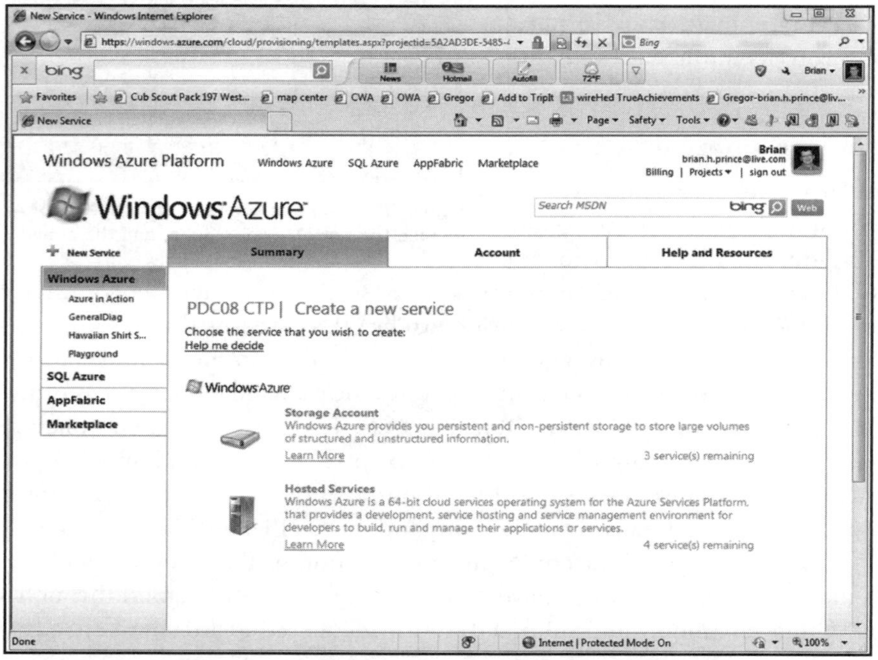

Figure 2.10 The Windows Azure portal. After you've created an application to run in the cloud, choose the Hosted Services project type. This window also shows how many more storage services you can create; the current user is allowed to create three more storage services.

Now that you have your account provisioned, you need to create a project on Azure to host your account.

2.3.3 Setting up your service online

Log in to your Azure portal with the live ID you created your Azure account with. On the home page, click the New Service link at the top right of the window. The process of creating a new service begins; you'll push your code to this new service. The term *service* is used as a general term on the Azure portal to represent some usage of the system, which might be a storage account or one of several websites that you've deployed.

Click the Hosted Services icon shown in figure 2.10 to start the new service wizard. Oh, how we love wizards.

The first step is to provide some basic properties for your project. You need to provide a project name and a description. These are for your own use, but by being careful in how you name and describe your project, you can make it easier to manage your projects over the long haul. After you provide the requested information, click Next to proceed. You're ready for the second step, which is to provide a name for the service and information about affinity groups. You enter this information in the window shown in figure 2.11.

The most important part of this window is the service name. (Remember that pretty much any code running in Azure is called a service, even if it's a simple website like our sample.) This service name will carry over into almost everything you do with the service you're deploying, so choose wisely. Selecting an embarrassing childhood nickname is tempting (such as Doogie Howser or Brainy Smurf), but this should be a name that supports the way you're going to manage your Azure environment.

The name you provide will be the first part of the URL for your service. For example, if your service name is `HawaiianShirtShop`, the Azure DNS server would refer to this site as `HawaiianShirtShop.cloudapp.net`. Because this isn't the name you embroidered on thousands of T-shirts (preferring instead the URL www.HawaiianShirtShop.com), you can use your own DNS tricks to refer people to the correct URL. A simple CNAME record in your DNS server can direct people to your service with any domain name you want to use.

The service name has to be unique across all of Azure. Click the Availability button to find out if the name you want is available. We're going to enter `AzureInAction`, and see if it's available. Because we're doing this, that name won't be available to you; go ahead and check.

The lower half of this window has to do with what Azure calls *affinity groups.* Affinity groups are used to make it easy to deploy services that are related to each other to the same regional data center for performance purposes, or to different data centers for disaster recovery or geo-distribution purposes. As you create more services, instead of having to remember which geographic area to set for your new service, you can select a customer affinity group. Later, when you want to move your services, you just update the affinity group as a whole.

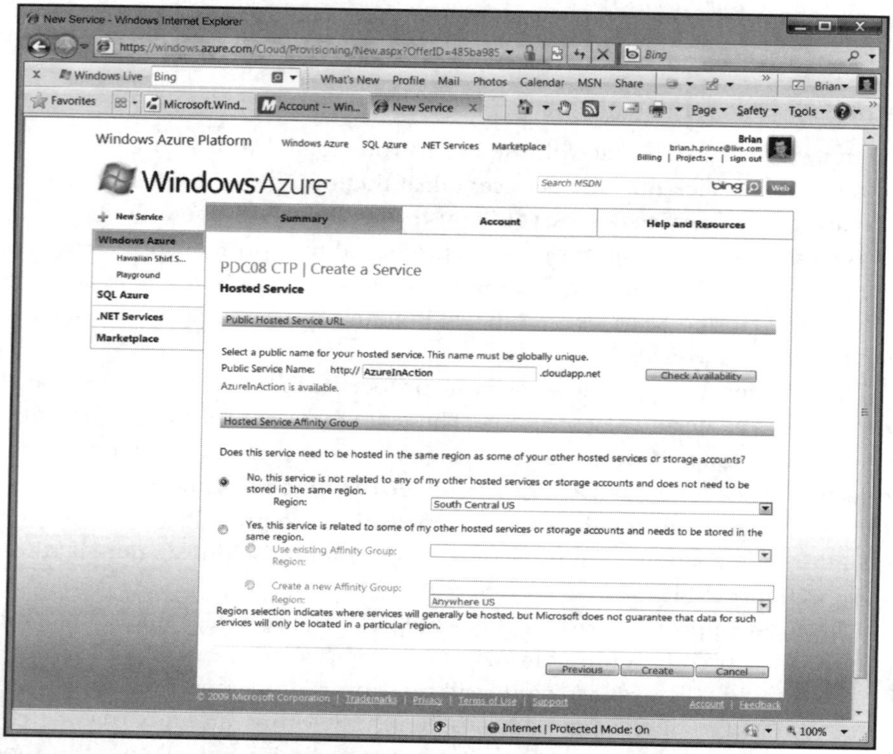

Figure 2.11 In this window you complete the second step in creating an Azure hosted services project. You can provide the name that will be in the URL for your site, as well as the affinity group for geo-distribution. Assign a name carefully; it will permeate everything you do with you service.

Click Create to finish the process. At this point, a project has been provisioned, and is ready for you to deploy an application to. The portal displays the project page for the project you just created.

Each project contains two zones, staging and production. The typical process of deploying your application involves uploading it to the staging environment, testing it, and *flipping* it to the production environment. This flipping is called a *VIP swap*. *VIP* stands for virtual IP.

When you flip your application to a new environment, nothing is actually moved. The Azure Fabric Controller labels the current running instances `production`, and the other instances are labeled `staging`. The Azure Fabric Controller adjusts the assignment of DNS and IP addresses in the Azure data center. The fact that nothing moves makes it fast to do a cutover and reduces the chance of deployment issues. It also makes it easy to flip back to the old setup if the new configuration doesn't work out as planned (not that that has ever happened to us).

Before you set up your storage environment, we should say a few words about logging and the diagnostic agent.

2.3.4 *Putting on your logging boots*

Logging is important in Azure. Like most production environments, you can't attach your debugger to the code running in the cloud. If there's a problem, you need to have good logging in place to help in diagnosing that problem.

Learn to instrument your code with logging commands so that you have the right information at your fingertips when you need it. Every time you fix a bug, you should consider adding some information to the log as well.

Azure runs a diagnostic agent on your virtual server while the server is running. This agent gathers logs and diagnostic information. You can configure it in code, and manage it remotely with the Azure management APIs. The default project templates provided by the SDK include code that'll start the diagnostic agent when your role instance starts.

The diagnostic agent uses the custom error log extensions to gather logs from several standard sources and from any source you can think of. The standard sources include Azure logs, Windows logs, IIS logs, the Windows event log, and performance counters. The data is transferred to an Azure storage account of your choosing. The diagnostic data is collected and then transferred, either on demand or according to a schedule you set. When the data is there, you can do anything you want to with it. Some data sources are copied to an Azure table, while others are copied to an Azure blog account. The type of destination storage depends on the type of the source.

We'll cover logging in greater depth in chapter 18. For now, you need to set up the storage environment you'll need for your basic application.

2.3.5 *Setting up your storage environment*

Open your application in Visual Studio and make one more run locally to make sure that it's running fine. There's one default setting you need to change when you're ready to deploy to the cloud. The default configuration specifies that the diagnostic monitor uses development storage. Before you upload your code, you need to reconfigure it to use the cloud for storage; cloud apps can't reach your development storage on your local desktop.

Return to the portal and create a new service. But instead of choosing Hosted Service, choose Storage Account for the type of service that you create. Figure 2.12 shows that the process is similar to creating a hosted service. As before, you need to provide a service name and a description.

After the storage account is created, you'll be given an account key that you can use to securely access your online data, as shown in figure 2.13. We'll go much deeper into storage accounts in chapter 8, but for now just roll with it.

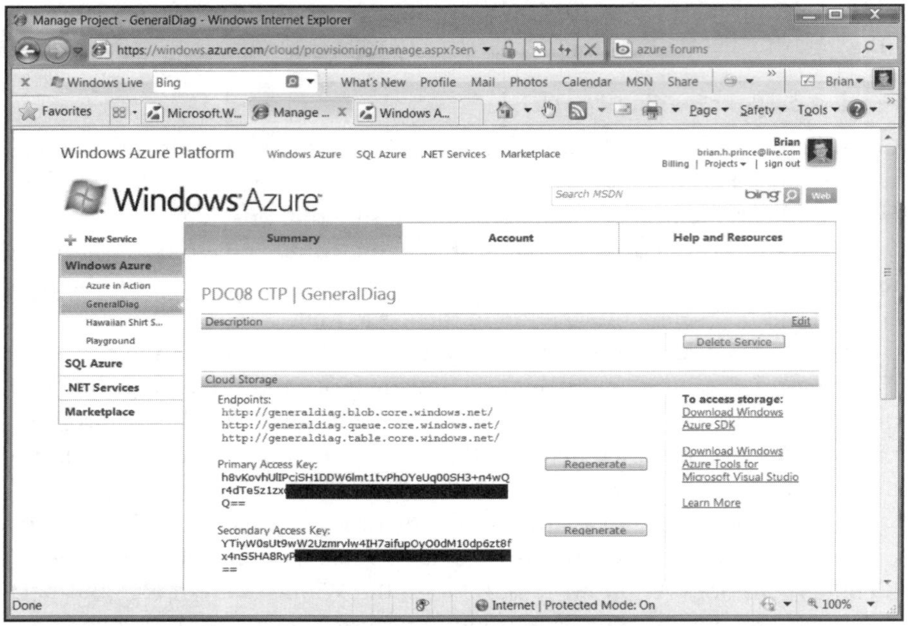

Figure 2.12 You need to create a storage account to store your logs and diagnostic data in. Creating a storage account is similar to creating a hosted service.

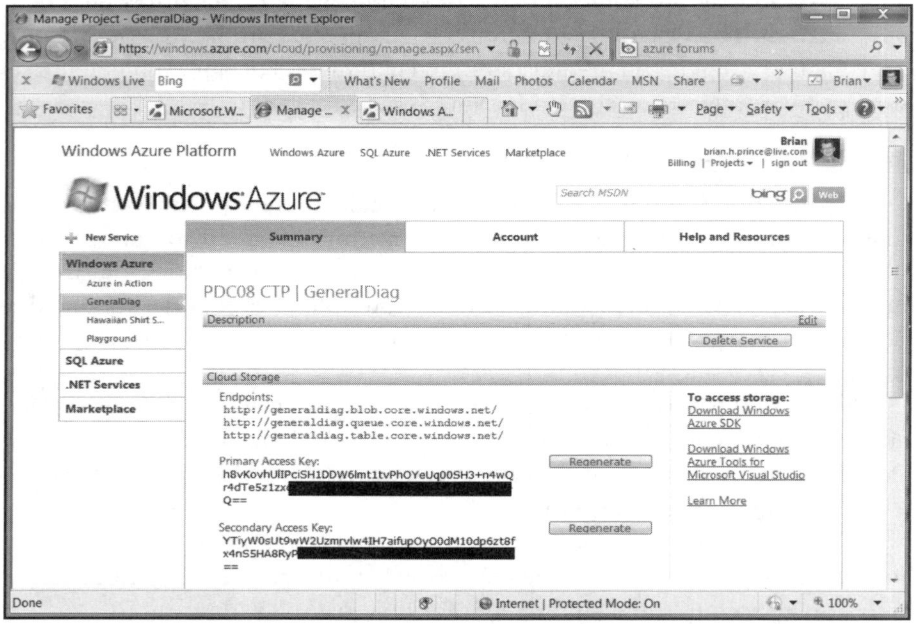

Figure 2.13 You can access your access keys after you've set up the storage account. These keys give anyone access to your data, so keep them safe. They're redacted here for that reason.

Open the ServiceConfiguration.cscfg file and replace the following line to include your storage account settings. This change reconfigures the diagnostic system to store log data into your storage account.

The old setting:

```
<Setting name="DiagnosticsConnectionString"
      value="UseDevelopmentStorage=true" />
```

The new setting:

```
<Setting name="DiagnosticsConnectionString"
     value="DefaultEndpointsProtocol=https;AccountName=YourAccountName;
     AccountKey=YourAccountKey" />
```

The `AccountName` parameter needs to be lowercase and URL friendly; we'll cover why in the chapters about Azure storage. The access key and the account name will be important later on when you want to connect to your storage in the cloud. Your application will still run locally; you've merely pointed the diagnostic system to store its logs in your cloud-based storage system. After you've made this change, you're ready to package your fabulous shirt website and move it to the cloud.

2.3.6 Packaging and deploying your application

You have an Azure account, you've created a hosted services project, and you have some parts for an application sitting on your local disk. Now you're going to take your application, and its configuration, and create a CS package for deployment.

> **What does CS stand for?**
>
> You'll see the acronym CS throughout the SDK and the tools for Azure. VB.NETers don't need to get upset; CS doesn't stand for C#, but for Cloud Service.

One way to create the package is to use the `CSpack` utility in the SDK. Although this is great for scripting, it can be tedious for those who live inside Visual Studio all day. A quicker method is to right-click the Azure project in your solution (named `AiA CH02 - Hawaiian Shirt Shop` in our sample), and choose Publish.

The `publish` command calls `CSpack` for you, which creates the package, opens a file explorer window that points to where the package files are placed, and then opens a browser window to your Azure project portal page. Sign in to your portal, and then select the project you want to deploy to in the Windows Azure section on the left. By default, only the production environment is displayed. Click the small arrow on the right side of the screen to show the staging environment. Click the Deploy button under the gelatinous staging cube, and use the screen to upload the package and the configuration file from the file explorer window that was opened for you. After you select these files, we suggest that you use the text box on the bottom of the form to give the deployment a label for history purposes. We usually use either a build number or version number, but the label can be anything you want. In this example, we're going to enter `version 1, build 14, ch2 sample preview, sp1 spring refresh`.

After you click the Deploy button, the files are uploaded, and you're redirected to the service page on the Azure portal. You can choose to deploy directly to the production environment, but we recommend that you always deploy to the staging environment first. When the files are uploaded, the state of the service is set to Stopped.

Deployment is as easy as uploading a few files and clicking the Run button, at least for you. For Azure, the Fabric Controller kicks in, identifies some unused CPU cores, deploys a virtual server image, copies over your bits, wires up a VLAN for your instances only, reconfigures the load balancers, and then updates the service directories. While all this is happening, which can take from seconds to minutes, depending on what you're deploying, you'll see the status of your environment flip to Initializing; when Azure is finished, the status changes to Started. When things are deployed, the cube turns a nice shade of blue, and the status flips to Staging, as shown in figure 2.14. Note

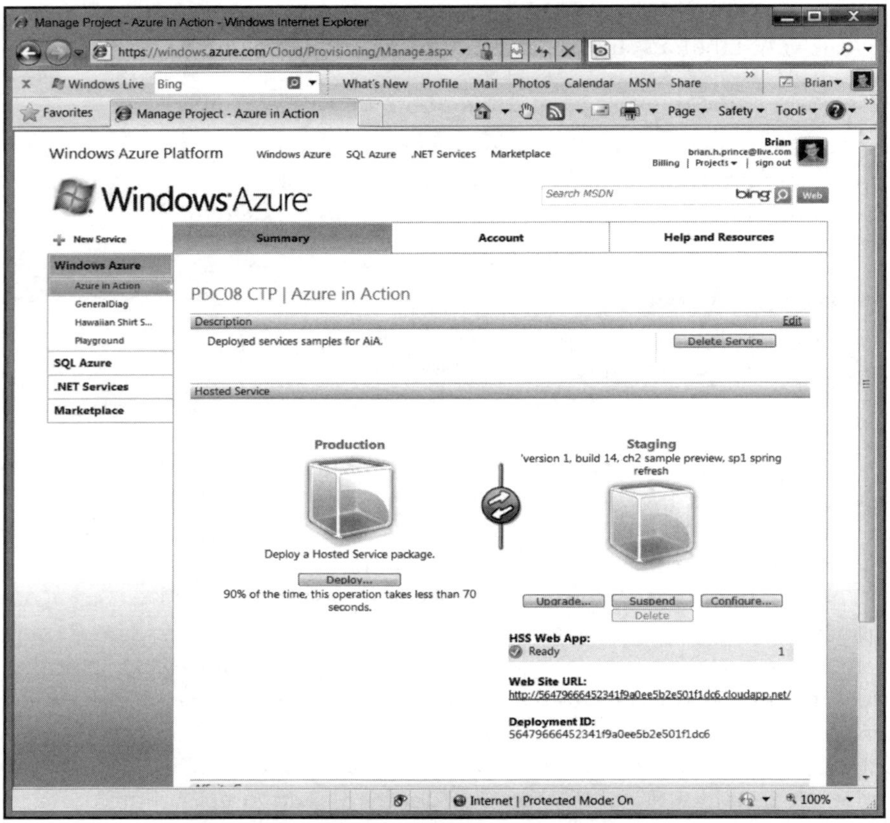

Figure 2.14 Your sample application has been deployed to the staging environment and is fully initialized. It's assigned an easy-to-remember GUID-based host name so that you can test your deployment.

that servers are reserved for you when you do the initial upload of your code with the Deploy button, and before you click Run. At this point, the cube turns blue, and you'll start being charged, even before you click Run. A little saying to remind you when you'll be charged is, "If the cube is grey, you're O.K. If the cube is blue, a bill is due."

While your application is in the staging environment, it has a temporary URL with a GUID as the host name of the service. The friendly name you picked when you created the Azure project won't be used until you migrate your application to production. Before you do that, test your application while it's in staging by using the temporary URL, which is located toward the bottom of the window.

When your application is running, the Run button changes to a Suspend button. If you click this button, you'll take your application offline. Azure is stopping the IIS application in the background when you do this, and even though it's suspended, you're still using a VM; the Azure hours for your billing continue to accrue.

Now that you've tested your application in the staging environment, you can move it to production.

2.3.7 Moving to production

Remember, when you move your application to production, you aren't moving the application or the settings. When you flip the button, Azure reconfigures the fabric to route all new traffic from the outside world to this particular instance. The old production environment becomes the new staging environment. Because nothing actually moves, you can easily roll back to the old version if things go wrong.

To move your application to production, click the circular arrows in the center of the screen. When you click them, you're prompted to make sure that you want to do that, and then the magic happens. Because Azure is making only a small configuration change, the cutover takes only a moment.

Congratulations! In only a few pages you've created a website where you can sell awesome shirts, tested it in a local simulation of the cloud, published it to staging, and promoted it to production. Now that business is rolling in, you'll want to monitor how much your application is costing you. Microsoft provides detailed information about your usage of the Azure platform on a regular basis. You can look at these reports at any time on the Azure portal and see where you are.

2.4 Summary

In this chapter we took you on a broad tour of how to start working with Azure. The SDK is important to be able to build Azure applications, including all of the different tools, APIs, and documentation needed to get started.

In a few pages, if you were following along, you developed and deployed a web application. Before either of us started using Windows Azure, we had never been able to deploy a web application with several load-balanced nodes without weeks or months of meetings, arguments, and planning the deployment and the production configuration.

The one thing you should've noticed is how little difference there is, code-wise, between what you would normally write for a website and what you write for Windows Azure. The web application you built has nothing special about it, and it'll run on a normal on-premises server. Azure is just another place to run your code, much more dynamic than any data center you've ever worked with, but the same. Our sample was simple and didn't delve into the more advanced scenarios, but the point is still valid. The strength of Azure, for a developer, is how *not* different it is from what you do every day.

Deployment is almost a trivial matter. It doesn't take a lot of effort to create a service, upload the package, and promote it to production. The simple staging and production environments make it easy to roll back to the old code in case the new deployment goes horribly wrong.

We'll look into what's under the covers in the next chapter, and see what Microsoft had to do to build such a powerful platform, yet keep it simple.

Part 2

Understanding the Azure service model

With the cloud basics and Windows Azure concepts under your belt, we dial it up a notch. In part 2, we look at all the parts of the service model.

Chapter 3 explains what the service model is, how Azure uses it, and how Azure works behind the scenes. A brilliant chapter if there ever was one.

The quality only gets better as we move into chapter 4, which discusses how to reference the Azure APIs in your code and how to exploit the service runtime.

In chapter 5, we trot out how to configure your service model using the configuration files and the portal. An exciting chapter, especially if you like XML and angle braces.

3 How Windows Azure works

This chapter covers

- How Microsoft built Azure
- What a cloud operating system is
- How your application is provisioned and managed in the cloud

Now that you have a basic understanding of what you can do with Azure, let's drill deeper into the pieces of Azure and how to best work with them. In this chapter, we'll discuss how Windows Azure is architected and how it does the cloud magic that it does. Understanding this background will help you develop better services, be a better person, and get the most out of your Azure infrastructure.

3.1 The big shift

When Azure was first announced at the PDC in 2008, Microsoft wasn't a recognized player in the cloud industry. It was the underdog to the giants Google and Amazon, which had been offering cloud services for years by that time. Building and deploying Azure was a big bet for Microsoft. It was a major change in the company's direction, from where Microsoft had been and where it needed to go in the future. Up until that time, Microsoft had been a product company. It designed and built a product, burnt it to CD, and sold it to customers. Over time, the product was enhanced, but the product was installed and operated in the client's environment. The trick was to build the right product at the right time, for the right market.

With the addition of Ray Ozzie to the Microsoft culture, there was a giant shift toward services. Microsoft wasn't abandoning the selling of products, but it was expanding its expertise and portfolio to offer its products as services. Every product team at Microsoft was asked if what they were doing could be enhanced and extended with services. They wanted to do much more than just put Exchange in a data center and rent it to customers. This became a fundamental shift in how Microsoft developed code, how the code was shipped, and how it was marketed and sold to customers.

This shift toward services wasn't an executive whim, thought up during an exclusive executive retreat at a resort we'll never be able to afford to even drive by. It was based on the trends and patterns the leaders saw in the market, in the needs of their customers, and on the continuing impact of the internet on our world. Those in charge saw that people needed to use their resources in a more flexible way, more flexible than even the advances in virtualization were providing. Companies needed to easily respond to a product's sudden popularity as social networking spread the word. Modern businesses were screaming that six months was too long to wait for an upgrade to their infrastructure; they needed it now.

Customers were also becoming more sensitive to the massive power consumption and heat that was generated by their data centers. Power and cooling bills were often the largest component of their total data-center cost. Coupling this with a concern over global warming, customers were starting to talk about the greening of IT. They wanted to reduce the carbon footprint that these beasts produced. Not only did they want to reduce the power and cooling waste, but also the waste of lead, packing materials, and the massive piles of soda cans produced by the huge number of server administrators that they had to employ.

3.1.1 The data centers of yore

Microsoft is continually improving all the important aspects of its data centers. It closely manages all the costs of a data center, including power, cooling, staff, local laws, risk of disaster, availability of natural resources, and many other factors. While managing all this, it has designed its fourth generation of data centers. Microsoft didn't just show up at this party; it planned it by building on a deep expertise in building and running global data centers over the past few decades.

The first generation of data centers is still the most common in the world. Think of the special room with servers in it. It has racks, cable ladders, raised floors, cooling, uninterruptable power supplies (UPSs), maybe a backup generator, and it's cooled to a temperature that could safely house raw beef. The focus is placed on making sure the servers are running; no thought or concern is given to the operating costs of the data center. These data centers are built to optimize the capital cost of building them, with little thought given to costs accrued beyond the day the center opens. (By the way, the collection of servers under your desk doesn't qualify as a Generation 1 data center. Please be careful not to kick a cord loose while you do your work.)

Generation 2 data centers take all the knowledge learned by running Generation 1 data centers and apply a healthy dose of thinking about what happens on the second day of operation. Ongoing operational costs are reduced by optimizing for sustainability and energy efficiency. To meet these goals, Microsoft powers its Quincy, Washington, data center with clean hydroelectric power. Its data center in San Antonio, Texas, uses recycled civic gray water to cool the data center, reducing the stress on the water sources and infrastructure in the area.

3.1.2 The latest Azure data centers

Even with the advances found in Generation 2 data centers, companies couldn't find the efficiencies and scale needed to combat rising facility costs, let alone meet the demands that the cloud would generate. The density of the data center needed to go up dramatically, and the costs of operations had to plummet. The first Generation 3 data center, located in Chicago, Illinois, went online on June 20, 2009. Microsoft considers it to be a mega data center, which is a class designation that defines how large the data center is. The Chicago data center looks like a large parking deck, with parking spaces and ramps for tractor trailers. Servers are placed into containers, called *CBlox*, which are parked in this structure. A smaller building that looks more like a traditional data center is also part of the complex. This area is for high-maintenance workloads that can't run in Azure.

CBlox are made out of the shipping containers that you see on ocean-going vessels and on eighteen wheelers on the highways. They're sturdily built and follow a standard size and shape that are easy to move around. One CBlox can hold anywhere from 1,800 to 2,500 servers. This is a massive increase in data-center density, 10 times more dense than a traditional data center. The Chicago mega data center holds about 360,000 servers and is the only primary consumer of a dedicated nuclear power plant core run by Chicago Power & Light. How many of your data centers are nuclear powered?

Each parking spot in the data center is anchored by a refrigerator-size device that acts as the primary interconnect to the rest of the data center. Microsoft developed a standard coupler that provides power, cooling, and network access to the container. Using this interconnect and the super-dense containers, massive amounts of capacity can be added in a matter of hours. Compare how long it would take your company to plan, order, deploy, and configure 2,500 servers. It would take at least a year, and a lot of people, not to mention how long it would take to recycle all the cardboard and extra parts you always seem to have after racking a server. Microsoft's goal with this strategy is to make it as cheap and easy as possible to expand capacity as demand increases.

The containers are built to Microsoft's specifications by a vendor and delivered on site, ready for burn-in tests and allocation into the fabric. Each container includes networking gear, cooling infrastructure, servers, and racks, and is sealed against the weather.

Not only are the servers now packaged and deployed in containers, but the necessary generators and cooling machinery are designed to be modular as well. To set up an edge data center, one that's located close to a large-demand population, all that's needed is the power and network connections, and a level paved surface. The trucks with the power and cooling equipment show up first, and the equipment is deployed. Then the trucks with the computing containers back in and drop their trailers, leaving the containers on the wheels that were used to deliver them. The facility is protected by a secure wall and doorway with monitoring equipment. The use of laser fences is pure speculation and just a rumor, as far as we know. The perimeter security is important, because the edge data center doesn't have a roof! Yes, no roof! Not using a roof reduces the construction time and the cooling costs. A roof isn't needed because the containers are completely sealed.

Microsoft opened a second mega data center, the first outside the United States, in Dublin, Ireland, on July 1, 2009. When Azure became commercially available in January 2010, the following locations were known to have an Azure data center: Texas, Chicago, Ireland, Amsterdam, Singapore, and Hong Kong. Although Microsoft won't tell where all its data centers are for security reasons, it purports to have more than 10 and fewer than 100 data centers. Microsoft already has data centers all over the world to support its existing services, such as Virtual Earth, Bing Search, Xbox Live, and others. If we assume there are only 10, and each one is as big as Chicago, then Microsoft needs to manage 3.5 million servers as part of Azure. That's a lot of work.

3.1.3 How many administrators do you need?

Data centers are staffed with IT pros to care and feed the servers. Data centers need a lot of attention, ranging from hardware maintenance to backup, disaster recovery, and monitoring. Think of your company. How many people are allocated to manage your servers? Depending on how optimized your IT center is, the ratio of person-to-servers can be anywhere from 1:10 to 1:100. With that ratio, Microsoft would need 35,000 server managers. Hiring that many server administrators would be hard, considering that Microsoft employs roughly 95,000 people already.

To address this demand, Azure was designed to use as much automation as possible, using a strategy called *lights-out operations*. This strategy seeks to centralize and automate as much of the work as possible by reducing complexity and variability. The result is a person-to-servers ratio closer to 1:30,000 or higher.

Microsoft is achieving this level of automation mostly by using its own off-the-shelf software. Microsoft is literally eating its own dog food. It's using System Center Operations Manager and all the related products to oversee and automate the management of the underlying machines. It's built custom automation scripts and profiles, much like any customer would do.

One key strategy in effectively managing a massive number of servers is to provision them with identical hardware. In traditional data centers where we've worked, each year brought the latest and greatest of server technology, resulting in a wide variety of technology and hardware diversity. We even gave each server a distinct name, such as Protoss, Patty, and Zelda. With this many servers, you can't name them; you have to number them. Not just by server, but by rack, room, and facility. Diversity is usually a great thing, but not when you're managing millions of boxes.

The hardware in each Azure server is optimized for power, cost, density, and management. The optimization process drives exactly which motherboard, chipset, and every other component needs to be in the server; this is truly bang for your buck in action. Then that server recipe is kept for a specific lifecycle, only moving to a new bill of materials when there are significant advantages to doing so.

3.1.4 Data center: the next generation

Microsoft isn't done. It's already spent years planning the fourth generation of data centers. Much like the edge data center we described previously, the whole data center is located outside. The containers make it easy to scale out the computing resources as demand increases; prior generations of data centers had to have the complete data center shell built and provisioned, which meant provisioning the cooling and power systems as if the data center were at maximum capacity from day one. The older systems were too expensive to expand dynamically. The fourth generation data centers are using an extendable spine of infrastructure that the computing containers need, so that both the infrastructure and the computing resources are easily scaled out (see figure 3.1). All of this is outside, in a field of grass, without a roof. They'll be the only data centers in the world that need a grounds crew.

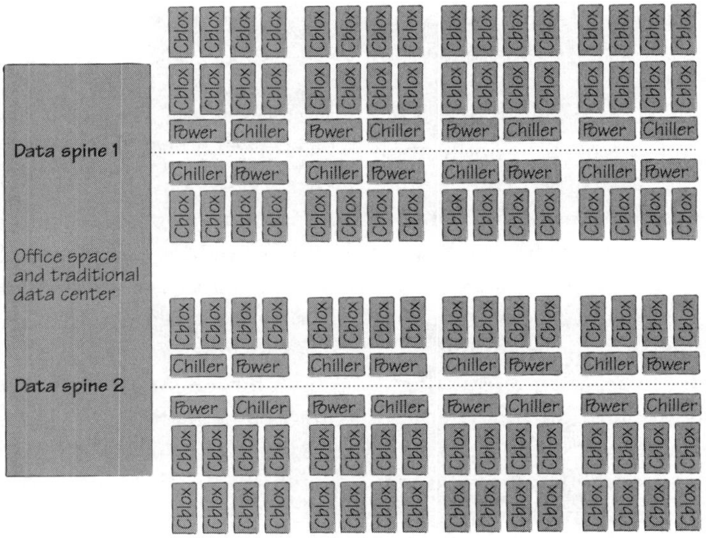

Figure 3.1 Generation 4 data centers are built on extensible spines. This configuration makes it easy to add not only computational capacity, but the required infrastructure as well, including power and cooling.

OK, you're impressed. Microsoft has a lot of servers, some of them are even outside, and all the servers are managed in an effective way. But how does the cloud really work?

3.2 Windows Azure, an operating system for the cloud

Think of the computer on your desk today. When you write code for that computer, you don't have to worry about which sound card it uses, which type of printer it's connected to, or which or how many monitors are used for the display. You don't worry, to a degree, about the CPU, about memory, or even about how storage is provided (solid-state drive [SSD], carrier pigeon, or hard disk drive). The operating system on that computer provides a layer of abstraction away from all of those gritty details, frees you up to focus on the application you need to write, and makes it easy to consume the resources you need. The desktop operating system protects you from the details of the hardware, allocates time on the CPU to the code that's running, makes sure that code is allowed to run, plays traffic cop by controlling shared access to resources, and generally holds everything together.

Now think of that enterprise application you want to deploy. You need a DNS, networking, shared storage, load balancers, plenty of servers to handle load, a way to control access and permissions in the system, and plenty of other moving parts. Modern systems can get complicated. Dealing with all of that complexity by hand is like compiling your own video driver; it doesn't provide any value to the business. Windows Azure does all this work, but on a much grander scale and for distributed applications (see figure 3.2) by using something called the *fabric*. Let's look into this fabric and see how it works.

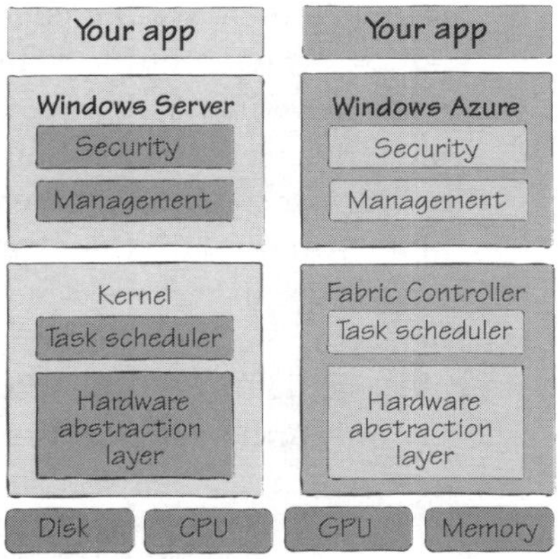

Figure 3.2 The Fabric Controller is like the kernel of your desktop operating system. It's responsible for many of the same tasks, including resource sharing, code security, and management.

Windows Azure takes care of the whole platform so you can focus on your application. The term *fabric* is used because of the similarity of the Azure fabric to a woven blanket. Each thread on its own is weak and can't do a lot. When they're woven together into a fabric, the whole blanket becomes strong and warm. The Azure fabric consists of thousands of servers, woven together and working as a cohesive unit. In Azure, you don't need to worry about which hardware, which node, what underlying operating system, or even how the nodes are load balanced or clustered. Those are just gritty details best left to someone else. You just need to worry about your application and whether it's operating effectively. How much time do you spend wrangling with these details for your on-premises projects? It's probably at least 10–20 percent of the total project cost in meetings alone. There are savings to be gained by abstracting away these issues.

In fact, Azure manages much more than just servers. There are plenty of other assets that are managed. Azure manages routers, switches, IP addresses, DNS servers, load balancers, and dynamic virtual local area networks (VLANs). In a static data center, managing all these assets is a complex undertaking. It's even more complex when you're managing multiple data centers that need to operate as one cohesive pool of resources, in a dynamic and real-time way.

If the fabric is the operating system, then the *Fabric Controller* is the kernel.

3.3 The Fabric Controller

Operating systems have at their core a kernel. This kernel is responsible for being the traffic cop in the system. It manages the sharing of resources, schedules the use of precious assets (CPU time), allocates work streams as appropriate, and keeps an eye on security. The fabric has a kernel called the Fabric Controller (FC). Figure 3.3 shows the relationship between Azure, the fabric, and the FC. Understanding these relationships will help you get the most out of the platform.

The FC handles all of the jobs a normal operating system's kernel would handle. It manages the running servers, deploys code, and makes sure that everyone is happy and has a seat at the table.

The FC is an Azure application in and of itself, running multiple copies of itself for redundancy's sake. It's largely written in managed code. The FC contains the complete state of the fabric internally, which is replicated in real time to all the nodes that are part of the FC. If one of the primary nodes goes offline, the latest state information is available to the remaining nodes, which then elect a new primary node.

The FC manages a state machine for each service deployed, setting a goal state that's based on what the service model for the service requires. Everything the FC does is in an effort to reach this state and then to maintain that state when it's reached. We'll go into the details of what the service model is in the next few pages, but for now, just think of it as a model that defines the needs and expectations that your service has.

The FC is obviously very busy. Let's look at how it manages to seamlessly perform all these tasks.

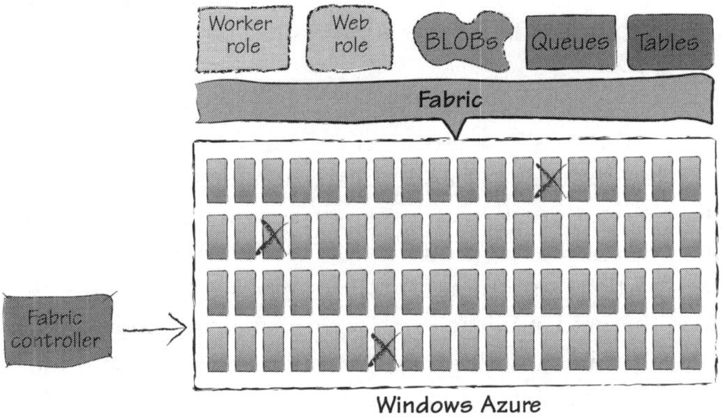

Figure 3.3 The relationship between Azure, the fabric, and the Fabric Controller (FC). The fabric is an abstract model of the massive number of servers in the Azure data center. The FC manages everything. For example, it recovers failed servers and moves your application to a healthy server.

3.3.1 How the FC works: the driver model

The FC follows a driver model, just like a conventional OS. Windows has no idea how to specifically work with your video card. What it does know is how to speak to a video driver, which in turn knows how to work with a specific video card. The FC works with a series of drivers for each type of asset in the fabric. These assets include the machines, as well as the routers, switches, and load balancers.

Although the variability of the environment is low today, over time new types of each asset are likely to be introduced. The goal is to reduce unnecessary diversity, but you'll have business needs that require breadth in the platform. Perhaps you'll get a software load balancer for free, but you'll have to pay a little bit more per month to use a hardware load balancer. A customer might choose a certain option, such as a hardware load balancer, to meet a specific need. The FC would have a different driver for each piece of infrastructure it controls, allowing it to control and communicate with that infrastructure.

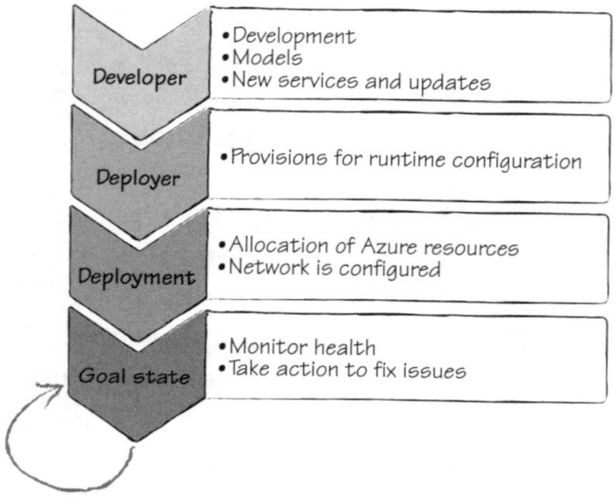

Figure 3.4 How the lifecycle of an Azure service progresses towards a running state. Each role on your team has a different set of responsibilities. From here the FC does what it needs to make sure your servers are always running.

The FC uses these drivers to send commands to each device that help these devices reach the desired running state. The commands might create a new VLAN to a switch or allocate a pool of virtual IP addresses. These commands help the FC move the state of the service towards the goal state. Figure 3.4 shows how a service progresses to the goal state, from the developer writing the code and defining the service model to the FC allocating and managing the resources the service requires.

While the FC is moving all your services toward the running state, it's also allocating resources and managing the health of the nodes in the fabric and of your services.

3.3.2 Resource allocation

One of the key jobs of the FC is to allocate resources to services. It analyzes the service model of the service, including the fault and update domains, and the availability of resources in the fabric. Using a greedy resource allocation algorithm, it finds which nodes can support the needs of each instance in the model. When it has reserved the capacity, the FC updates its data structures in one transaction. After the update, the goal state of each node is changed, and the FC starts moving each node towards its goal state by deploying the proper images and bits, starting up services, and issuing other commands through the driver model to all the resources needed for the change.

3.3.3 Instance management

The FC is also responsible for managing the health of all of the nodes in the fabric, as well as the health of the services that are running. If it detects a fault in a service, it tries to remediate that fault, perhaps by restarting the node or taking it offline and replacing it with a different node in the fabric.

When a new container is added to the data center, the FC performs a series of burn-in tests to ensure that the hardware delivered is working correctly. Part of this process results in the new resource being added into the inventory for the data center, making it available to be allocated by the FC.

If hardware is determined to be faulty, either during installation or during a fault, the hardware is flagged in the inventory as being unusable and is left alone until later. When a container has enough failures, the remaining workloads are moved to different containers and then the whole container is taken offline for repair. After the problems have been fixed, the whole container is retested and returned into service.

3.4 The service model and you

The driving force behind what the FC does is the service model that you define for your service (see figure 3.5). You define the service model indirectly by defining the following things when you're developing a service:

- Some configuration about what the pieces to your service are
- How the pieces communicate
- Expectations you have about the availability of the service

The service model is broken into two pieces of configuration and is deployed with your service. Each piece focuses on a different aspect of the model. In the following sections, you're going to learn about these configuration pieces and how to customize them. We'll also show you how best to manage all the pieces of your configuration.

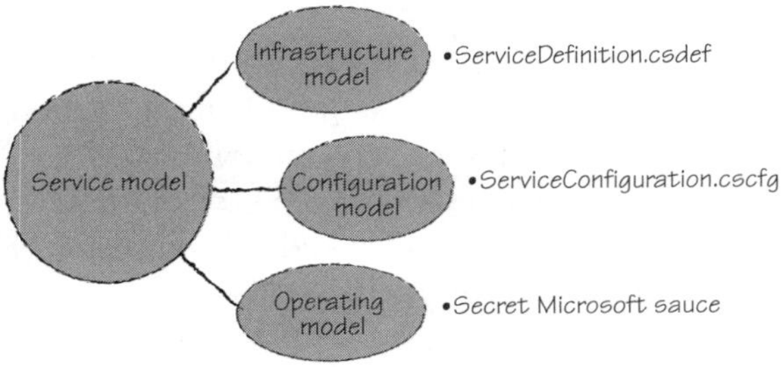

Figure 3.5 The service model consists of several different pieces of information. This model helps Azure run your application correctly.

3.4.1 Defining configuration

Your solution in Visual Studio contains these two pieces of configuration in different files, both of which are found in the Azure Service project in your solution:

- Service definition file (ServiceDefinition.csdef)
- Service configuration file (ServiceConfiguration.cscfg)

The service definition file defines what the roles and their communication endpoints are in your service. This includes public HTTP traffic for a website, or the endpoint details for a web service. You can also configure your service to use local storage (which is different from Azure storage) and any custom configuration elements of the service configuration file. The service definition can't be changed at runtime; any change requires a new deployment of your service. Your service is restricted to using only the network endpoints and resources that are defined in this model. We're going to look at the service definition file in depth in chapter 4; for now you can think of this piece of the configuration as defining what the infrastructure of your service is, and how the parts fit together.

The service configuration file, which we'll discuss in detail in chapter 5, includes the entire configuration needed for the role instances in your service. Each role has its own dedicated part of the configuration. The contents of the configuration file can be changed at runtime, which removes the need to redeploy your application when some part of the role configuration changes. You can also access the configuration in code, similar to how you might read a web.config file in an ASP.NET application.

3.4.2 Adding a custom configuration element

In many applications, you store connection strings, default settings, and secret passwords (please don't!) in the app.config or web.config file. You'll often do the same with an Azure application. First, you need to declare the format of the new configuration setting in the .csdef file by adding a `ConfigurationSettings` node inside the role you want the configuration to belong to:

```
<ConfigurationSettings>
  <Setting name="BannerText"/>
</ConfigurationSettings>
```

Adding this node defines the schema of the .cscfg file for that role, which strongly types the configuration file itself. If there's an error in the configuration file during a build, you'll receive a compiler warning. This is a great feature because there's nothing worse than deploying code when there's a simple little problem in a configuration file.

Now that you've told Azure the new format of your configuration files, namely, that you want a new setting called `BannerText`, you can add that node to the service configuration file. Add the following XML into the appropriate role node in the .cscfg file:

```
<ConfigurationSettings>
  <Setting name="BannerText" value="KlatuBaradaNikto"/>
</ConfigurationSettings>
```

During runtime, you want to read in this configuration data and use it for some purpose. Remember that all configuration settings are stored as strings and must be cast to the appropriate type as needed. In this case, you want a string to assign to your label control text, so that you can use it as is.

```
txtPassword.Text = RoleEnvironment.GetConfigurationSettingValue("BannerText");
```

Having lines of code like this all over your application can get messy and hard to manage. Sometimes developers consolidate their configuration access code into one class. This class's only job is to be a façade into the configuration system.

3.4.3 Centralizing file-reading code

It's a best practice to move your entire configuration file-reading code from wherever it's sprinkled into a `ConfigurationManager` class of your own design. Many people use the term *service* instead of *manager*, but we think that the term *service* is too overloaded and that *manager* is just as clear. Moving your code centralizes all the code that knows how to read the configuration in one place, making it easier to maintain. More importantly, it removes the complexity of reading the configuration from the relying code, which illustrates the principle of *separation of concerns*. Moving the code to a centralized location also makes it easier to mock out the implementation of the `ConfigurationManager` class for easier testing purposes (see figure 3.6). Over time, when the APIs for accessing configuration change or if the location of your configuration changes, you'll have only one place to go to make the changes you need.

Reading configuration data in this manner might look familiar to you. You've probably done this for your current applications, reading in the settings stored in a web.config or an app.config file. When migrating an existing application to Azure, you might be tempted to keep the configuration settings where they are. Although keeping them in place reduces the amount of change to your code as you migrate it to Azure, it does come at a cost. Unfortunately, the configuration files that are part of your roles are frozen and are read-only at runtime; you can't make changes to them after your package is deployed. If you want to change settings at runtime, you'll need to store those settings in the .cscfg file. Then, when you want to make a change, you only have to upload a new .cscfg file or click Configure on the service management page in the portal.

The FC takes these configuration files and builds a sophisticated service model that it uses to manage your service. At this time, there are about three different core model templates that all other service models inherit from. Over time, Azure will expose more of the service model to the developer, so that you can have more fine-grained control over the platform your service is running on.

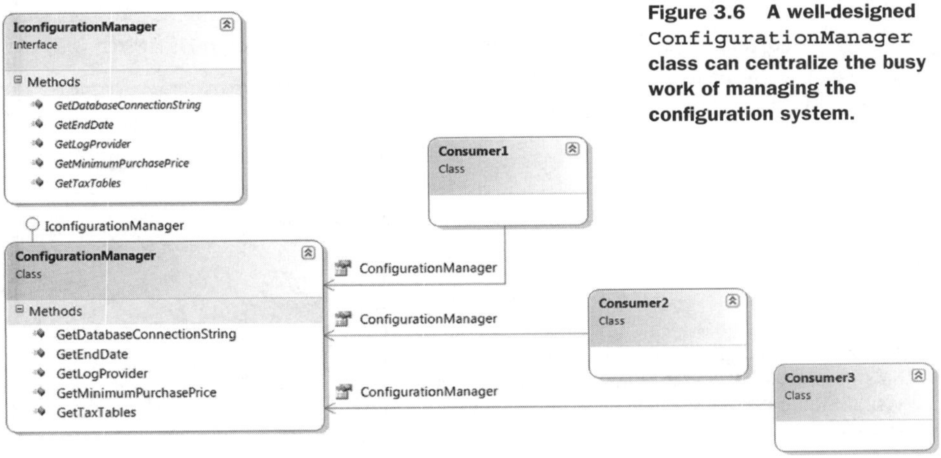

Figure 3.6 A well-designed `ConfigurationManager` class can centralize the busy work of managing the configuration system.

3.4.4 The many sizes of roles

Each role defined in your service model is basically a template for a server you want to be deployed in the fabric. Each role can have a different job and a different configuration. Part of that configuration includes local storage and the number of instances of that role that should be deployed. How these roles connect and work together is part of why the service model exists.

Because each role might have different needs, there are a variety of VM sizes that you can request in your model. Table 3.1 lists each VM size. Each step up in size doubles the resources of the size below it.

Table 3.1 The available sizes of the Azure VMs

VM size	Dedicated CPU cores	Available memory	Local disk space
Small	1	1.7 GB	250 GB
Medium	2	3.5 GB	500 GB
Large	4	7 GB	1,000 GB
Extra large	8	15 GB	2,000 GB

Each size is basically a slice of how big a physical server is, which makes it easy to allocate resources and keeps the numbers round. Because each physical server has eight CPU cores, allocating an extra-large VM to a role is like dedicating a whole physical machine to that instance. You'll have all the CPU, RAM, and disk available on that machine. Which size you want is defined in the ServiceDefinition.csdef file on a role-by-role basis. The default size, if you don't declare one, is small. To change the default size, add the following code, substituting `ExtraLarge` with the size that you want:

```
<WorkerRole name="ImageCompresser" vmsize="ExtraLarge">
```

If you're using Visual Studio 2010, you can define the role configuration by double-clicking the name of your web role in the Roles folder of your Cloud Service project. Choose Properties and click the Configuration tab, as shown in figure 3.7.

The service model is also used to define fault domains and update domains, which we'll look at next.

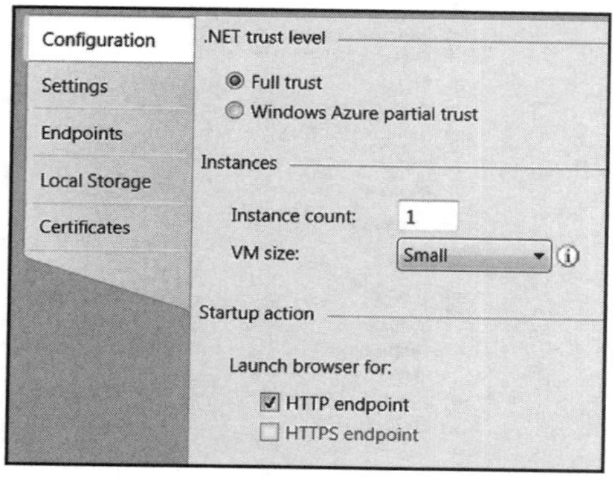

Figure 3.7 Configuring your role doesn't have to be a gruesome XML affair. You can easily do it in Visual Studio 2010 when you view the properties information for the role you want to configure.

3.5 It's not my fault

Fault domains and update domains determine what portions of your service can be offline at the same time, but for different reasons. They're the way that you define your uptime requirements to the FC and how you describe how your service updates will happen when you have new code to deploy.

Let's examine each type of domain in detail. Then we'll present a service model scenario that shows you how fault and update domains help increase fault tolerance in your cloud service.

3.5.1 Fault domains

Fault domains are used to make sure that a set of elements in your service isn't tied to a single point of failure. Fault domains are based more on the physical structure of the data center than on your architecture. Your service should typically have three or more fault domains. If you have only one fault domain, all the parts of your service could potentially be running on one rack, in the same container, connected to the same switch. If there's any failure in that chain, there's a high likelihood of catastrophic failure for your service. If that rack fails, or the switch in use fails, then your service is completely offline. By breaking your service into several fault domains, the FC ensures that those fault domains don't share any dependent infrastructure, which protects your service against single points of failure.

In general, the FC will define three fault domains, meaning that only about a third of them can become unavailable because of a single fault. In a failure scenario, the FC immediately tries to deploy your roles to new nodes in the fabric to make up for the failed nodes. Currently, the Azure SDK and service model don't let you define your own number of fault domains; the default number is thought to be three domains.

3.5.2 Update domains

The second type of domain defined in the service model is the *update domain*. The concept of an update domain is similar to a fault domain. An update domain is the unit of update you've declared for your service. When performing a rolling update, code changes are rolled out across your service one update domain at a time. Cloud services tend to be big and tend to always need to be available. The update domain allows a rolling update to be used to upgrade your service, without having to bring the entire service down. These domains are usually defined to be orthogonal to your fault domains. In this manner, if an update is being pushed out while there's a massive fault, you won't lose all of your resources, just a piece of them.

You can define the number of update domains for your service in your ServiceDefinition.csdef file as part of the `ServiceDefinition` tag at the top of the file.

```
<ServiceDefinition xmlns="http://schemas.microsoft.com/ServiceHosting/
2008/10/ServiceDefinition"
name="HawaiianShirtShop"
upgradeDomainCount="3">
```

If you don't define your own update domain setting, the service model will default to five update domains. Your role instances are assigned to update domains as they're started up, and the FC tries to keep the domains balanced with regard to how many instances are in each domain.

3.5.3 A service model example

If you had a service running on Azure, you might need six role instances to handle the demand on your service, but you should request nine instances instead. You request more than you need because you want a high degree of tolerance in your architecture. As shown in figure 3.8, you would have three fault domains and three update domains defined. If there's a fault, only a third of your nodes are affected. Also, only a third of the nodes will ever be updated at one time, controlling the number of nodes taken out of service for updates, as well as reducing the risk of any update taking down the whole service.

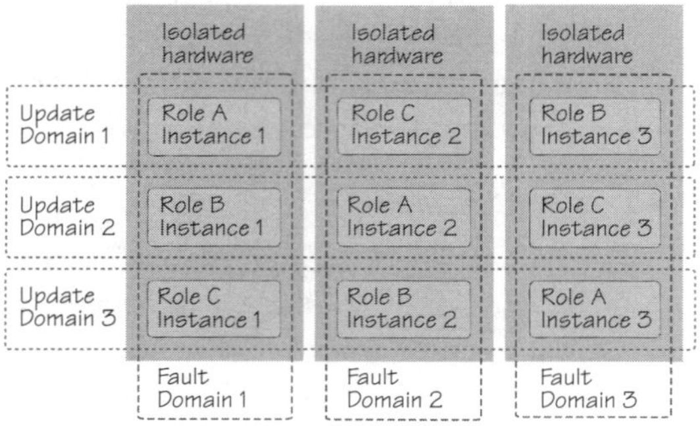

Figure 3.8 Fault and update domains help increase fault tolerance in your cloud service. This figure shows three instances of each of three roles.

In this scenario, a broken switch might take down the first fault domain, but the other two fault domains would not be affected and would keep operating. The FC can manage these fault domains because of the detailed models it has for the Azure data center assets.

The cloud is not about perfect computing, it's about deploying services and managing systems that are fault tolerant. You need to plan for the faults that are inevitable. The magic of cloud computing makes it easy to scale big enough so that a few node failures don't really impact your service.

All this talk about service models and an overlord FC is nice, but at the end of the day, the cloud is built from individual pieces of hardware. There's a lot of hardware, and it all needs to be managed in a hands-off way. There are several approaches to applying updates to a service that's running. You'll see in the next section that you can perform either manual or automated rolling upgrades, or you can perform a full static upgrade (also called a VIP swap).

3.6 Rolling out new code

No matter how great your code is, you'll have to perform an upgrade at some point if for no other reason than to deploy a new feature a user has requested. It's important that you have a plan for updating the application and have a full understanding of the moving parts. There are two major ways to roll out an upgrade: a *static upgrade* or a *rolling upgrade.*

When you perform a static upgrade, you do everything at once and you have to take down your system, at least for a while. You should carefully plan your application architecture to avoid a static upgrade because it impacts the uptime of your service and can be more complicated to roll out. A rolling upgrade keeps your service up and running the whole time. You should always consider performing the upgrade in the staging environment first to make sure the deployment goes well. After a full battery of end-to-end and integration tests are passed, you can proceed with your plans for the production environment.

If the number of endpoints for a role has changed, or if the port numbers have changed, you won't be able to do either a static or a rolling upgrade. You'll be forced to tear down the deployment and redeploy.

3.6.1 Static upgrades

A static upgrade is sometimes referred to as a *forklift upgrade* because you're touching everything all at once. You usually need to do a static upgrade when there's a significant change in the architecture and plumbing of your application. Perhaps there's a whole new architecture of how the services are structured and the database has been completely redesigned. In this case, it can be hard to upgrade just one piece at a time because of interdependencies in the system. This type of upgrade is required if you're changing the service model in any way.

This approach is also called a *VIP swap* because the FC is swapping the virtual IP addresses that are assigned to your resources. When a swap is done, the old staging environment becomes your new production environment and your old production environment becomes your new staging environment (see figure 3.9). This can happen pretty fast, but your service will be down while it's happening and you need to

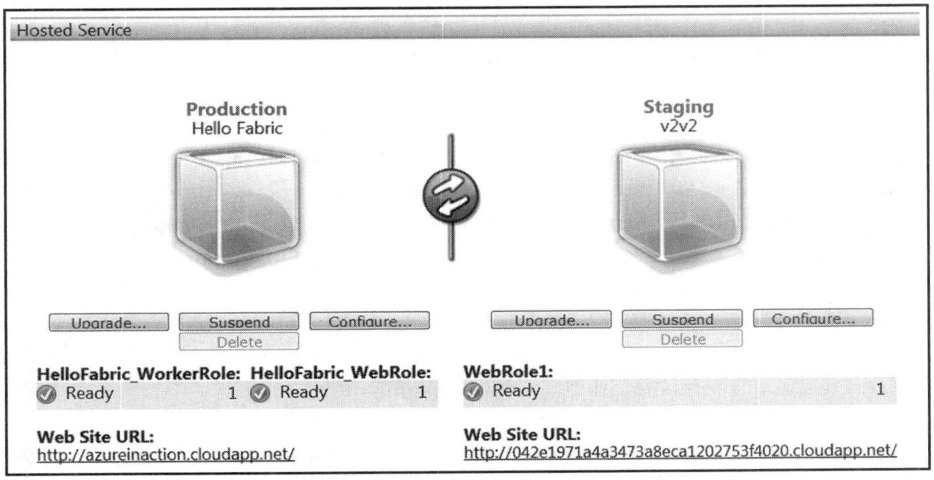

Figure 3.9 Performing a VIP swap, or static upgrade, is as easy as clicking the arrows. If things go horribly awry, you can always swap back to the way things were. It's like rewind for your environment.

plan for that. The one great advantage to this approach is that you can easily swap things back to the way they were if things don't work out.

Your upgrade plan should consider how long the new staging (aka old production) environment should stay around. You might want to keep it for a few days until you know the upgrade has been successful. At that point, you can completely tear down the environment to save resources and money.

To perform a VIP swap, log in to the Azure portal, choose the service that you want to upgrade in the Windows Azure section, and then click the Summary tab. Next, deploy your new application version to the staging environment. After everything is all set up and you're happy with it, click the circular button in the middle. The changeover takes only a few minutes. If the new version isn't working as expected, you can easily click the button again and swap the two environments back where they came from. Voila! The old version is back online.

You can also use the service management API to perform the swap operation. This is one reason why you want to make sure that you've named your deployments clearly, at least more clearly than we did in this example.

VIP swaps are nice, but some customers need more flexibility in the way they perform their rollouts. For them, there's the rolling upgrade.

3.6.2 Rolling upgrades

If your roles are carrying state and you don't want to lose that state as you completely change to a new set of servers, then rolling upgrades are for you. Or maybe you want to upgrade the instances of a specific role instead of all of the roles. For example, you might want to deploy an updated version of the website, without impacting the processing of the shopping carts that's being performed by the backend worker roles. Remember that when doing a rolling upgrade, you can't change the service model of the service that you're upgrading. If you've changed the structure of the service configuration, the number of endpoints, or the number of roles, you'll have to do a VIP swap instead.

There are two types of rolling upgrades: the automatic and the manual. When you perform an automatic rolling upgrade, the FC drains the traffic to the set of instances that's in the first update domain (they're numbered, starting with 0) by removing them from the load balancer's configuration. After the traffic is drained, the instances are stopped, the new code is deployed, and then the instances are restarted. After they're back up and running, they're added back into the load balancer's list of machines to route traffic to. At this point, the FC moves on to the next update domain in the list. It'll proceed in this fashion until all the update domains have been serviced. Each domain should take only a few minutes.

If your situation requires that you control how the progression moves from one domain to the next, you can choose to do a manual rolling upgrade. When you choose this option, the FC stops after updating a domain and waits for your permission to move on to the next one. This gives you a chance to check the status of the machines and the environment before moving forward with the rollout.

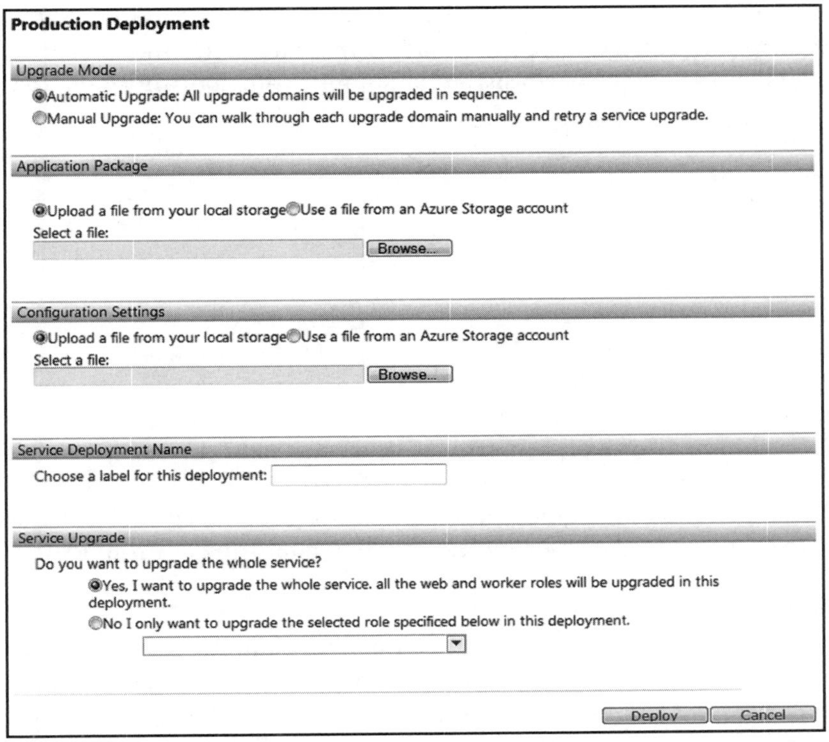

Figure 3.10 Performing a rolling upgrade is easy. Click Upgrade on the Summary page for the service to see this page and choose your options. You can upgrade all of the roles or just one role during an upgrade.

To perform a rolling upgrade, log in to the Azure portal, choose the service that you want to upgrade in the Windows Azure section, and then click the Summary tab. Click the Upgrade button for the deployment you want to upgrade. You're presented with some options, as shown in figure 3.10.

You can choose to perform an automatic or a manual upgrade. You can upgrade all the roles in the package or just one of them. As in a normal deployment, you also need to provide a service package, configuration, and a deployment name.

If you choose to upgrade a single role, then only the instances for that role in each domain are taken offline for upgrading. The other role instances are left untouched.

You can also perform a rolling upgrade by using the service management API. When you use the management API, you have to store the package in BLOB storage before starting the process. As with a VIP swap, you need to post a command to a specific URL (all these commands are covered in detail in chapter 18). Customize the URL to match the settings for the deployment you want to upgrade:

```
https://management.core.windows.net/<subscription-id>/services/
     hostedservices/<service-name>
/deployments/<deployment-name>/?comp=upgrade
```

The body of the command needs to contain the elements shown in the following code. You need to change the code to supply the parameters that match your situation. The following sample performs a fully automatic upgrade on all the roles.

```
<?xml version="1.0" encoding="utf-8"?>
<UpgradeDeployment xmlns="http://schemas.microsoft.com/windowsazure">
  <Mode>auto</Mode>
  <PackageUrl>http://azureinaction.blob.core.windows.net/
deployment_container/new_code.cspkg </PackageUrl>
  <Configuration>***the contents of the config file***</Configuration>
  <Label>v3.2</Label>
</UpgradeDeployment>
```

Performing a manual rolling update with the service management API is a little trickier, and requires several calls to the `WalkUpgradeDomain` method. The upgrades are performed in an asynchronous manner; the first command starts the process. As the upgrade is being performed, you can check on the status by using `Get Operation Status` with the operation ID that was supplied to you when you started the operation.

We've covered how to upgrade running instances and talked about what the fabric is. Now we'll go one level deeper and explore the underlying environment.

3.7 The bare metal

No one outside of the Azure team truly knows the nature of the underlying servers and other hardware, and that's OK because it's all abstracted away by the cloud OS. But you can still look at how your instances are provisioned and how automation is used to do this without hiring the entire population of southern Maine to manage it.

Each instance is really a VM running Windows Server 2008 Enterprise Edition x64 bit, on top of *Hyper-V*. Hyper-V is Microsoft's enterprise virtualization solution, and it's available to anyone. Hyper-V is based on a hypervisor, which manages and controls the virtual servers running on the physical server. One of the virtual servers is chosen to be the host OS. The host OS is a virtual server as well, but it has the additional responsibilities of managing the hypervisor and the underlying hardware.

Hyper-V has two features that help in maximizing the performance of the virtual servers, while reducing the overall cost of running those servers. One of these features is core-and-socket parking; the other is the reduced footprint of Hyper-V itself. Core-and-socket parking needs to be supported by the physical CPU.

Let's drill way down into the workings of Hyper-V, how the virtual servers connect to it, and the processes of booting up these servers and getting your instances up and running.

3.7.1 Free parking

The first feature of Hyper-V is core-and-socket parking. Hyper-V can monitor the use of each core and CPU (which is in a socket on the motherboard) as a whole. Hyper-V moves the processes around on the cores to consolidate the work to as few cores as possible. Any cores not needed at that time are put into a low energy state. They can come back online quickly if needed but consume much less power while they wait.

Hyper-V can do this at the socket level as well. If it notices that each CPU socket is being used at only 10 percent of capacity, for example, it can condense the workload to one socket and park the unused sockets, placing them in a low energy state. This helps data centers use less power and require less cooling. In Azure, you have exclusive access to your assigned CPU core. Hyper-V won't condense your core with someone else's. It will, however, turn off cores that aren't in use.

3.7.2 A special blend of spices

The version of Hyper-V used by Azure is a special version that the team created by removing anything they didn't need. Their goal was to reduce the footprint of Hyper-V as much as possible to make it faster and easier to manage. Because they knew exactly the type of hardware and guest operating systems that will run on it, they could rip out a lot of code. For example, they removed support for 32-bit hosts and guest machines, support needed for other types of operating systems, and support for hardware they weren't supporting at all.

Not stopping there, they further tuned the hypervisor scheduler for better performance while working with cloud data-center workloads. They wanted the scheduler to be more predictable in its use of resources and fairer to the different workloads that were running, because each would be running at the same priority level. They also enhanced Hyper-V to support a heavier I/O load on the VM bus.

3.7.3 Creating instances on the fly

When a new server is ready to be used, it's booted. At this point, it's a naked server with a bare hard drive. You can see the steps involved in starting the server, adding an instance to your service, and adding an additional server in figure 3.11.

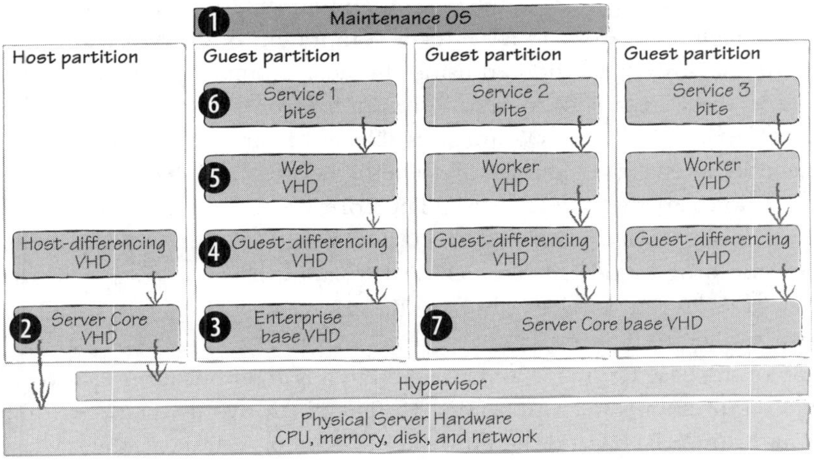

Figure 3.11 The structure of a physical server and virtual instance servers in Azure. This figure illustrates the process involved in starting the server (❶ and ❷). It also shows the process of starting an instance and adding it to your service (❸ through ❻), and adding another virtual server (❼). All these steps are coordinated by the FC and take only a few minutes.

During boot up, the server locates a maintenance OS on the network, using standard Preboot Execution Environment (PXE) protocols. (PXE is a process for booting to an operating system image that can be found on the network.) The server downloads the image and boots to it (❶ in figure 3.11).

The maintenance OS

The maintenance OS is based on Windows Preinstallation Environment (Windows PE). It's a thin OS that's used by many IT organizations for low-level troubleshooting and maintenance. The tools and protocols for Windows PE are available on any Windows server and are used by a lot of companies to easily distribute machine images and automate deployment.

The maintenance OS connects with the FC and acts as an agent for the FC to execute any local commands needed to prepare the disk and machine. The agent prepares the local disk and streams down a Windows Server 2008 Server Core image to the local disk ❷. This image is a virtual hard drive (VHD) and is a common file format used to store the contents of hard drives for VMs. (VHDs are large files representing the complete or partial hard drive for a VM.) The machine is then reconfigured to boot from this core VHD. This image becomes the host OS that manages the machine and interacts with the hypervisor. The host OS is Windows Server 2008 Core because almost all but the most necessary modules have been removed from the operating system. You might be running this in your own data center.

The Azure team worked with the Windows Server team to develop the technology needed to boot a machine natively from a VHD that's stored on the local hard drive. The Windows 7 team liked the feature so much that they added it to their product as well. Being able to boot from a VHD is a key component of the Azure automation.

After the machine has rebooted using the host OS image, the maintenance OS is removed and the FC can start allocating resources from the machine to services that need to be deployed. A base OS image is selected from the prepared image library that'll meet the needs of the service that's being deployed ❸. This image (a VHD file) is streamed down to the physical disk. The core OS VHDs are marked as read-only, allowing multiple service instances to share a single image. A differencing VHD is stacked on top of the read-only base OS VHD to allow for changes specific to that virtual server ❹. Different services can have different base OS images, based on the service model applied to that service.

On top of the base OS image and attached to it is an application VHD that contains additional requirements for your service ❺. The bits for your service are downloaded to the application VHD ❻, and then the stack is booted. As it starts, the stack reports its health to the FC. The FC then enrolls the stack into the service group, configuring the VLAN assigned to your service and updating the load balancer, IP allocation, and DNS configuration. When this process is completed, the new node is ready to service requests to your application.

Much of the image deployment can be completed before the node is needed, cutting down on the time it can take to start a new instance and add it to your service.

Each server can contain several VMs. This allows for the optimal use of computing resources and the flexibility to move instances around as needed. As a second or third virtual server is added, it might use the base OS VHD that has already been downloaded ❼ or it can download a different base OS VHD based on its needs. This second machine then follows the same process of downloading the application VHD, booting up, and enrolling into the cloud.

All these steps are coordinated by the FC and are usually accomplished in a few minutes.

3.7.4 Image is everything

If the key to the automation of Azure is Hyper-V, then the base VM images and their management are the cornerstone. Images are centrally created, also in an automated fashion, and stored in a library, ready to be deployed by the FC as needed.

A variety of images are managed, allowing for the smallest footprint each role might need. If a role doesn't need IIS, then there's an image that doesn't have IIS installed. This is an effort to shrink the size and runtime footprint of the image, but also to reduce any possible attack surfaces or patching opportunities.

All images are deployed using an Xcopy deployment model. This model keeps deployment simple. If the FC relied on complex scripts and tools, then it would never truly know what the state of each server would be and it would take a lot longer to deploy an instance. Again, diversity is the devil in this environment.

This same approach is used when deploying patches. When the OS needs to be patched, Microsoft doesn't download and execute the patch locally as you might on your workstation at home. Doing so would lead to too much risk, having irregular results on some of the machines. Instead, the patch is applied to an image and the new image is stored in the library. The FC then plans a rollout of the upgrade, taking into account the layout of the cloud and the update domains defined by the various service models that are being managed.

The updated image is copied in the background to all of the servers used by the service. After the files have been staged to the local disk, which can take some time, each update domain group is restarted in turn. In this way, the FC knows exactly what's on the server. The new image is merely wired up to the existing service bits that have already been copied locally. The old image is kept locally for a period of time as an escape hatch in case something goes wrong with the new image. If that happens, the server is reconfigured to use the old image and rebooted, according to the update domains in the service model. This process dramatically reduces the service window of the servers, increasing uptime and reducing the cost of maintenance on the cloud.

We've covered how images are used to manage the environment. Now we're going to explain what you can see when you look inside a running role instance.

3.8 The innards of the web role VM

Your first experience with roles in Azure is likely to be with the web role. To help you develop your web applications more effectively, it's worth looking in more detail at the VM that your web role is hosted in. In this section, we'll look at the following items:

- The details of the VM
- The hosting process of your web role (`WaWebHost`)
- The `RDAgent` process

3.8.1 Exploring the VM details

You can use the power of native code execution to see some of the juicy details about the VM that your web role runs on. Figure 3.12 shows an ASP.NET web page that shows some of the internal details, including the machine name, domain name, and the user name that the code is running under.

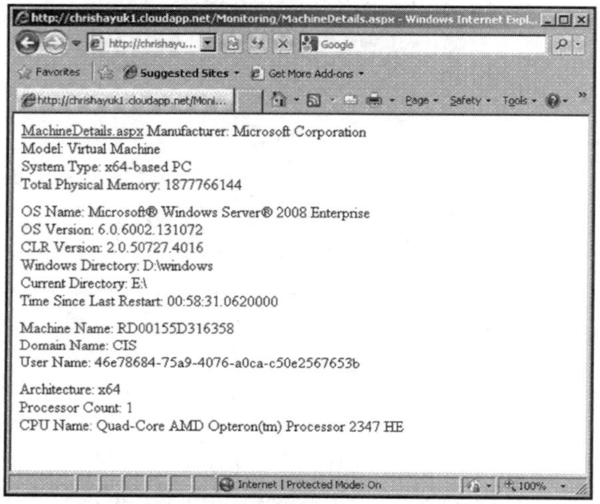

Figure 3.12 Using native code, you can see some of the machine details of a web role in Windows Azure. In this example, Microsoft is using Windows Server 2008 Enterprise x64. Notice that the user name that the process is running as is a GUID.

If you want, you can easily generate the web page shown in figure 3.12 by creating a simple ASPX page with some labels that represent the text, as follows:

```
<div>
   ProcessorCount:
         <asp:Label ID="lblProcessorCount" runat="server" />
</div>
```

Finally, you can display the internal details of the VM using the code-behind in the following listing.

Listing 3.1 Using code behind to display machine details

```
using System.Management;

public partial class _Default : System.Web.UI.Page
    {
        protected void Page_Load(object sender, EventArgs e)
        {

            // Initialize
            var computer = new Microsoft.VisualBasic.Devices.Computer();
            lblMachineName.Text = computer.Name;
```

Class fetches information about server

```
    // OS Details
    lblOSName.Text = computer.Info.OSFullName;
    lblOSVersion.Text = computer.Info.OSVersion;
    lblMachineName.Text = computer.Name;

    // Computer System Details
    lblProcessorCount.Text =
    ➥  System.Environment.ProcessorCount.ToString();
    lblCLRVersion.Text = System.Environment.Version.ToString();
    lblCurrentDirectory.Text = GetCurrentDirectory();
    lblTimeSinceLastRestart.Text = GetTimeSinceLastRestart();
    lblDomainName.Text = System.Environment.UserDomainName;
    lblUserName.Text = System.Environment.UserName;
    lblCPUName.Text = GetCPUName();
    lblArchitecture.Text = GetArchitecture();
}

private string GetCurrentDirectory()
{
    try
    {
        return System.Environment.CurrentDirectory;
    }
    catch
    {
        return "unavailable";
    }
}

private string GetTimeSinceLastRestart()
{
    try
    {
        TimeSpan time = new TimeSpan(0, 0, 0, 0,
        ➥  System.Environment.TickCount);
        return time.ToString();
    }
    catch
    {
        return "unavailable";
    }
}

private string GetCPUName()
{
    try
    {
        using (ManagementObject Mo = new
        ➥  ManagementObject("Win32_Processor.DeviceID='CPU0'"))
        {
            return (string)(Mo["Name"]);
        }
    }
    catch
    {
        return "unavailable";
```

Gets length of time server has been running (GetTimeSinceLastRestart)

Gets domain name server is running on (UserDomainName)

Gets user name service is running as (UserName)

```
                }
            }

            private string GetArchitecture()
            {
                try
                {
                    using (ManagementObject Mo = new
                    ➥ ManagementObject("Win32_Processor.DeviceID='CPU0'"))
                    {
                        ushort result = (ushort)(Mo["Architecture"]);
                        switch (result)
                        {
                            case 0:
                                return "x86";
                            case 9:
                                return "x64";
                            default:
                                return "other";
                        }
                    }
                }
                catch
                {
                    return "unavailable";
                }
            }
        }
```

You can now, of course, deploy your web page to Windows Azure and see the inner details of your web role, which were shown in figure 3.12. These machine details provide you with some interesting facts:

- Web roles run on Windows 2008 Enterprise Edition x64
- They run quad core AMD processors and one core is assigned
- The domain name of the web role is CIS
- This VM has been running for an hour
- The Windows directory lives on the D:\ drive
- The web application lives on the E:\ drive

This is just the beginning; feel free to experiment and discover whatever information you need to satisfy your curiosity about the internals of Windows Azure by using calls similar to those shown in listing 3.1.

3.8.2 *The process list*

Now that we're rummaging around the VM, it might be worth having a look at what processes are actually running on the VM. To do that, you'll build an ASP.NET web page that'll return all the processes in a pretty little grid, as shown in figure 3.13.

To generate the list shown in figure 3.13, create a new web page in your web role with a `GridView` component called `processGridView`:

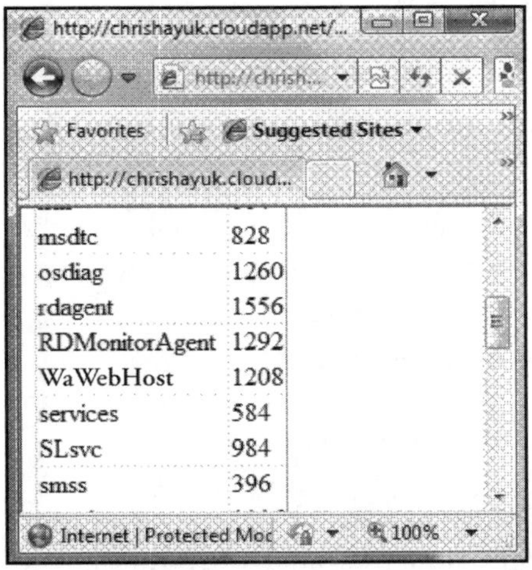

Figure 3.13 The process list of a Windows Azure VM. The RDAgent process is related to Red Dog, which was the code name for Azure while it was being developed.

```
<asp:GridView ID="processGridView" runat="server"/>
```

Next, add a using `System.Diagnostics` statement at the top of the code-behind and then add the following code to the `Page_Load` event:

```
var processes = Process.GetProcesses();              <-- Gets list of running processes

processGridView.DataSource = from process in processes
                             orderby process.ProcessName
                             select new
                             {
                                Name = process.ProcessName,
                                Id = process.Id.ToString() };   <-- Uses LINQ query to streamline data returned
                             }
processGridView.DataBind();                   <-- Binds query result to grid for screen output
```

This code will list all the processes on a server and bind the returned list to a `GridView` on a web page, as displayed in figure 3.13. If you look at the process list displayed in figure 3.13, you'll see the two Windows Azure–specific services that we're interested in: `WaWebHost` and `RDAgent`.

We'll now spend the next couple of subtopics looking at these processes in more detail.

3.8.3 The hosting process of your website (WaWebHost)

If you were to look at the process list for a live web role (shown in figure 3.13), or if you were to fire up your web application in Windows Azure and click the Process tab, you would notice that the typical IIS worker process (w3wp.exe) isn't present when your web server is running.

You would also notice that if you stop your IIS server by issuing `IISReset - stop`, your web server continues to run. You know from installing the Windows Azure SDK that web roles are run under IIS 7.0. So, why can't you see your roles in IIS, or restart the server using `IISReset`?

HOSTABLE WEB CORE

Although Windows Azure uses IIS 7.0, it makes use of a new feature, called *hostable web core*, which allows you to host the IIS runtime in-process. In the case of Windows Azure, the `WaWebHost` process hosts the IIS 7.0 runtime. If you were to look at the process list on the live server or on the development fabric, you would see that as you interact with the web server, the utilization of this process changes.

WHY IS AZURE RUN IN-PROCESS RATHER THAN USING PLAIN OLD IIS?

The implementation of the web role is quite different from that of a normal web server. Rather than using a system administrator to manage the running of the web servers, the data center overlord—the FC—performs that task. The FC needs the ability to interact and report on the web roles in a consistent manner. Instead of attempting to use the Windows Management Instrumentation (WMI) routines of IIS, the Windows Azure team opted for a custom Windows Communication Foundation (WCF) approach.

This custom in-process approach also allows your application instances to interact with the `WaWebHost` processing using a custom API via the `RoleEnvironment` class. You can read more about the `RoleEnvironment` class in chapter 4.

3.8.4 The health of your web role (RDAgent)

The `RDAgent` process collects the health status of the role and the following management information on the VM:

- Server time
- Machine name
- Disk capacity
- OS version
- Memory
- Performance statistics (CPU usage, disk usage)

The role instance and the `RDAgent` process use named pipes to communicate with each other. If the instance needs to notify the FC of its current state of health, notification is communicated from the web role to the `RDAgent` process using the named pipe.

All the information collected by the `RDAgent` process is ultimately made available to the FC; it determines how to best run the data center. The FC uses the `RDAgent` process as a proxy between itself, the VM, and the instance. If the FC decides to shut down an instance, it instructs the `RDAgent` process to perform this task.

3.9 Summary

Hopefully, you've learned a little bit about how Azure is architected and how Microsoft runs the cloud OS. You also know how data centers have changed over the generations of their development. Microsoft has spent billions of dollars and millions of work hours building these data centers and the OS that runs them.

Windows Azure truly is an operating system for the cloud, abstracting away the details of the massive data centers, servers, networks, and other gear so you can simply focus on your application. The FC controls what's happening in the cloud and acts as the kernel in the operating system. With the power of the FC and the massive data centers, you can define the structure of your system and dynamically scale it up or down as needed. The infrastructure makes it easy to do rolling upgrades across your infrastructure, leading to minimal downtime of your service.

The service model that you define consists of the service definition and service configuration files and describes, to the FC, how your application should be deployed and managed. This model is the magic behind the data center automation. New configuration settings are held in the ServiceDefinition.csdef and ServiceConfiguration.cscfg files. Centralizing all your configuration file-reading code into one neat, handy `ConfigurationManager` class is a real time saver.

Fault and update domains describe how the group of servers running your application should be separated to protect against failures and outages. Fault domains ensure that your service is not tied to a single point of failure, which could be catastrophic to your service. An update domain provides the ability to perform a rolling upgrade, keeping you from having to take down your whole service to do an upgrade.

When you need to upgrade your application, you can perform either a static upgrade or a rolling upgrade, which you can do via the Azure portal. All you do is choose a few options and click a button, or you can use the service management API.

The automated nature of Azure is thanks to Hyper-V, Microsoft's enterprise virtualization solution. Hyper-V consolidates work to as few cores as possible by monitoring the use of each core and CPU, all while maintaining a small footprint.

In the next few chapters, we'll work much more closely with the service runtime. We'll look at how you know when you're running in the fabric, and the configuration magic of the service model.

4 It's time to run with the service

This chapter covers

- Interacting with Windows Azure via the `ServiceRuntime` assembly
- Defining your Windows Azure role
- Configuring your Windows Azure role

In the last chapter we got into the guts of the infrastructure and architecture of Windows Azure. During that chapter we introduced the concept of the service model and how it's used by the FC to manage your role.

In this chapter we'll take some time out to look at the parts of the service model that we didn't get to mess around with much (specifically the service definition and service configuration files). But first, let's spend a little time with the Service Management API.

4.1 Using the Windows Azure Service Management API

In both chapter 1 and chapter 2, you created a brand new Windows Azure web role from scratch. As we pointed out then, a web role hosted by Windows Azure is

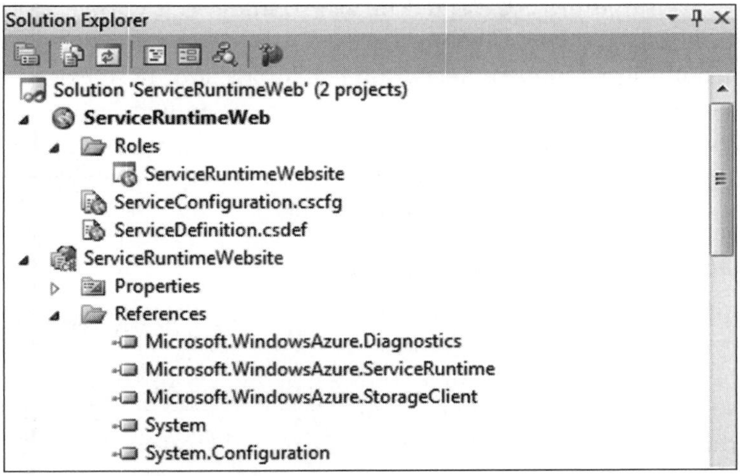

Figure 4.1 Three assemblies to play with in your new web role

a regular old ASP.NET web application with a little bit of extra magic that allows you to interact with Windows Azure. That extra magic is three new assemblies that are automatically added to your new web application when you create a new Windows Azure Cloud Service project in Visual Studio. Figure 4.1 shows these assemblies listed in the Visual Studio 2010 Solution Explorer.

In this chapter we'll focus only on the `Microsoft.WindowsAzure.ServiceRuntime` assembly. We'll look at `Diagnostics` in chapter 18, and the `StorageClient` in chapters 9 through 12 and 16.

The `ServiceRuntime` assembly acts as a bridge between the Windows Azure runtime and your application. Although you don't need to include the `ServiceRuntime` assembly in your web role, you should. Without this assembly, your applications have no way to interact with Windows Azure and make use of the APIs that it exposes to you. This assembly provides the following helper routines that we'll explore throughout this chapter:

- Checking whether your application is running in the cloud
- Retrieving configuration settings
- Getting a reference to a file held in the local cache

This assembly provides some valuable methods that you'll need to fully use the power of Windows Azure. We'll take a look at how you can include this assembly in your projects.

4.1.1 Adding the ServiceRuntime assembly to your application

As you saw earlier, when you create a new ASP.NET web role in Visual Studio, the new assemblies from the SDK are automatically referenced within your project. That's great if you're creating a new role, but what if you're migrating an existing ASP.NET application to the cloud, or if you want to access the API from another assembly?

The ASP.NET web role project created in Visual Studio is a normal ASP.NET web application with three extra assembly references. If you need to migrate your existing application (or use it in another project), you can always add those extra assemblies via the Add Reference dialog box. You can find these assemblies in the c:\Program Files\Windows Azure SDK\v1.1\ref\ directory.

Now that you know how to reference the `ServiceRuntime` assembly, let's take a look at some of the API calls and how you can use them.

4.1.2 Is your application running in Windows Azure?

One of the static properties that the `ServiceRuntime` exposes via the `RoleEnvironment` static class is the ability to check whether your application is running in Windows Azure. You can perform this check using the `RoleEnvironment.IsAvailable` property.

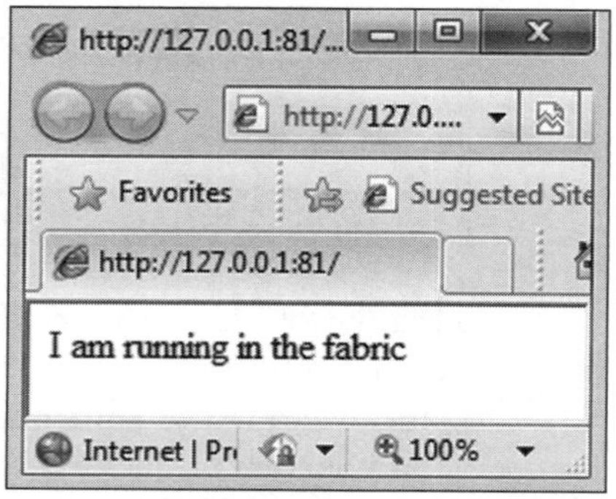

Figure 4.2 A funky little web page that tells you that you're running in the fabric

To see this check in action, you're going to quickly create a web page that displays a label that states whether your application is running in Windows Azure. Figure 4.2 shows that web page running in the development fabric.

To create the web page shown in figure 4.2, create a new cloud service solution called `ServiceRuntimeWeb` with a new ASP.NET web role called `ServiceRuntimeWebsite`. In the web project, modify the Default.aspx page to include the following label:

```
<asp:label id="runningInTheFabricLabel" runat="server"/>
```

After you've added this label to your web page and a `using` statement for the `ServiceRuntime` namespace, you can then display the result of the `RoleEnvironment.IsAvailable` call in the contents of the label by adding the following code to the `Page_Load` event:

```
runningInTheFabricLabel.Text = RoleEnvironment.IsAvailable ?
                "I am running in the fabric" : "Not in the fabric";
```

As you know, web roles are standard ASP.NET web applications; they can still be run on a standard IIS web server (if you like retro computing). If you launched this page in IIS (or the ASP.NET Web Development Server by selecting the ASP.NET project and pressing F5), then it would display the message `Not in the fabric`. If you were to now fire up your web page in the Windows Azure development fabric, it would display `I am running in the fabric` (as shown in figure 4.2).

The `RoleEnvironment.IsAvailable` call is not only useful for announcing to the world that your web application is in heaven (I mean in the cloud), but it's also useful for building applications (or libraries) that will be hosted both inside and outside Windows Azure. Because most of Windows Azure's APIs aren't available outside Windows

Azure, you might want to check that you're running inside Windows Azure before using one of these APIs. Later in this section we'll look at some of these situations and possible solutions that you can use when working with shared code.

We've introduced you to the `ServiceRuntime` assembly. Now let's take a look at some of the other differences between a standard ASP.NET web application and a Windows Azure ASP.NET web role.

4.2 Defining your service

In chapter 3, we spent quite a bit of time discussing the infrastructure and architecture of Windows Azure. In that chapter, we introduced the concept of the service model and how it comprises three elements: the service definition, the service configuration, and the operating model.

In this section, we'll look at the first piece of the service model puzzle, which is the *service definition file* (we'll look at some of the other stuff later on). In chapter 3, we described how the FC uses the service definition file (ServiceDefinition.csdef) to manage your service; in this chapter we'll show you how you can effectively define your service.

The following information is held in the service definition file:

- The number of required upgrade domains (see chapter 3)
- The endpoint of your service (port and protocol)
- Whether the role runs in partial or full trust
- Whether the role has any configuration settings
- The amount of local disk space that the role requires for local file storage
- The required size of the VM

In the following subsections, we'll take a look at how you can define some of that information. Before we do that, let's return to the service definition file itself.

4.2.1 The format of the service definition file

When you created your Cloud Service project in chapter 1, the service definition file was automatically added to your project. The following listing shows the service definition file for the `ServiceRuntimeWeb` project that you created in chapter 1.

Listing 4.1 Service definition file of the `ServiceRuntimeWeb` project

```
<ServiceDefinition name="ServiceRuntimeWeb"
xmlns="http://schemas.microsoft.com/ServiceHosting/2008/10/
  ➥ ServiceDefinition">
  <WebRole name="ServiceRuntimeWebsite">
    <InputEndpoints>
      <InputEndpoint name="HttpIn" protocol="http" port="80" />
    </InputEndpoints>
    <ConfigurationSettings>
      <Setting name="DiagnosticsConnectionString" />
    </ConfigurationSettings>
  </WebRole>
</ServiceDefinition>
```

Name of your cloud project

Name of your web role

HTTP port and protocol your application runs on (1)

Any special configuration elements you want (2)

As shown in listing 4.1, the service definition file adheres to the following format:

- Cloud project (`ServiceDefinition` element)
  - Role definition (web role)
    - Input endpoints ❶
    - Internal endpoints (not shown in listing 4.1)
    - Configuration settings ❷
    - Certificates (not shown in listing 4.1)
    - Local storage (not shown in listing 4.1)

Throughout the course of the next few sections we'll explore the items that define your role in more detail.

Because your Cloud Service project contains only a single web role, you'll see only a single role definition in your service definition file. If your project contained multiple roles, these roles would also be included in the file. The XML in the following listing shows how this would be structured in the service definition file.

Listing 4.2 Configuring multiple roles in the service definition file

```
<?xml version="1.0" encoding="utf-8"?>
<ServiceDefinition name="ServiceRuntimeWeb" xmlns="http://
     schemas.microsoft.com/ServiceHosting/
2008/10/ServiceDefinition">
  <WebRole name="ServiceRuntimeWebsite">

  </WebRole>
  <WorkerRole name="WorkerRole1">

  </WorkerRole>
</ServiceDefinition>
```

In this example, there are two roles in the project: a web role called `ServiceRuntime-Website` and a worker role called `WorkerRole1` (note that the definition of a worker role is exactly the same as the configuration of a web role, except that the definition element is called `WorkerRole` instead of `WebRole`).

You have an idea of the structure of the service definition file, but what sort of information describing your service would you put in that file?

4.2.2 *Configuring the endpoint of your web role*

If you look at the service definition file for your web role in listing 4.1, you'll see that the HTTP port and protocol that your application runs on is defined at ❶.

Windows Azure allows web roles to receive incoming HTTP or HTTPS messages (usually via port 80 and port 443 respectively) via your virtual IP address only (see chapter 3). Any other traffic that's sent to your virtual IP address is either filtered out by the firewalls or is not forwarded to your web role from the load balancer. Figure 4.3 shows the interaction between a client browser, the load balancer, and your web role. Worker roles are not held to this protocol restriction. (We'll cover worker roles in chapter 15.)

By locking down the available protocols, Windows Azure reduces the surface area of attack for your web role. Any incoming requests to your web role (outside of the port and protocol combinations defined in the service definition) are filtered out by the firewalls and load balancers; the request never reaches the servers that your web role is hosted on. This level of protection protects your web role from port attacks, as well as from distributed denial-of-service (DDoS) attacks.

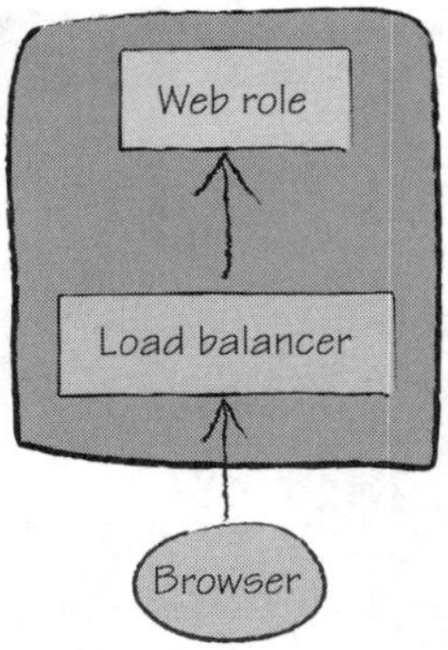

Figure 4.3 The load balancer protects the galaxy (or at least your web role) from the threat of invasion.

By default, Visual Studio correctly configures your web role to use HTTP and port 80 in your service definition file. (This configuration is shown at ❶ in listing 4.1.)

```
<InputEndpoint name="HttpIn" protocol="http" port="80" />
```

If you wanted to expose your service via HTTPS, you would change the `InputEndpoint` in the service definition file to the following:

```
<InputEndpoint name="HttpsIn" protocol="https" port="443" />
```

If you need to run your application in both HTTP and HTTPS, define two `InputEndpoint` tags:

```
<InputEndpoints>
   <InputEndpoint name="HttpIn" protocol="http" port="80"/>
   <InputEndpoint name="HttpsIn" protocol="https" port="443"/>
</InputEndpoints>
```

You can configure other ports for the protocols as well (for example, you can define an endpoint with the port 8080). You would usually configure other ports when there are multiple web roles in the same solution. Such a configuration would allow each web role to be accessed on a different port.

WHERE'S THE GUI?

If you're currently thinking to yourself "I'll never remember all that XML syntax," then good news: the service definition file has an XSD (XML Schema Definition language) associated with it. You get full IntelliSense support when you edit this file in Visual Studio. If you edit in Notepad, you don't get the benefit of this support.

Alternatively, if you feel that we've moved beyond text files and are in a Windows Presentation Foundation (WPF) Minority Report-style GUI interface era, then you'll be pleased to hear that you can edit the service definition file by using a dialog box in Visual Studio 2010. To open the dialog box, double-click the name of your web role in the Roles folder of your Cloud Service project (for example, double-click `ServiceRuntimeWebsite` in the Roles folder in the `ServiceRuntimeWeb` cloud project, as shown in figure 4.1).

To modify the endpoints in the editor, select the Endpoints tab, shown in figure 4.4.

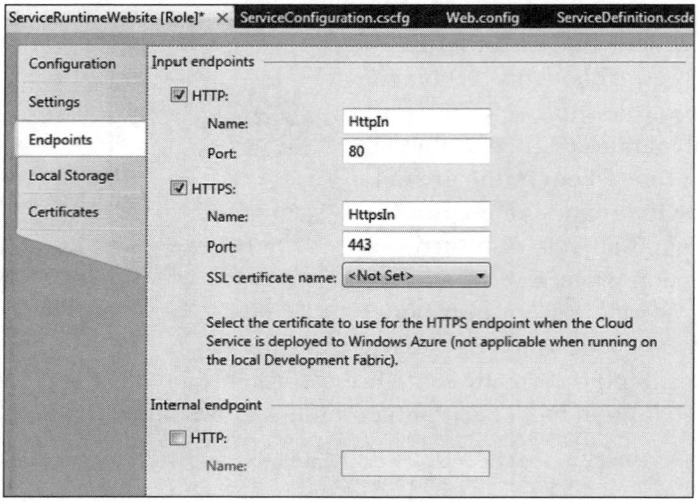

Figure 4.4 If you don't want to use pure XML to configure your endpoints, you can use this GUI by double-clicking the name of your web role in the Roles folder of your Cloud Service project.

There are several reasons why you might want to use a port other than port 80 or 443, but for the most part, these are the traditional ports used with HTTP and HTTPS and are considered best practices.

IGNORING BEST PRACTICES WHEN DEVELOPING

Although security best practices are great for production servers, they can be a real pain to follow during development. We can all thank Ray Ozzie at Microsoft for making this a little easier in the development fabric by allowing us to run our web roles on any port.

Figure 4.4 shows how you can easily set this value via the editor. Because we have an XML fetish, let's look at how it's done in the service definition file. The following bit of configuration shows how you can run your web role on port 87 over HTTP in the development fabric:

```
<InputEndpoint name="HttpIn" protocol="http" port="87" />
```

The development fabric is pretty lenient when it comes to configuring available ports. If a port is already taken (if IIS is hogging port 80), it gives you the next available port. For example, if you asked for port 80, it would fire up your application on port 81 instead.

INTRAROLE COMMUNICATION

You might have noticed in figure 4.4 that there's a little section called Internal Endpoint (go on, look, if you didn't see it already). If you need to host a web role internally (you don't want that web role to be available outside the Windows Azure fabric) but you want to make that web role available to another role, this check box is for you. A typical reason for wanting this functionality is that a web role or worker role is reliant on an internal web service (as is the case with service-oriented-architecture-type applications).

You can configure the internal endpoint of this role by setting the name, port, and protocol of the internal endpoint in this way:

```
<InternalEndpoint name="MyInternalRole" protocol="http"/>
```

Alternatively, you can use the editor, as shown in figure 4.4.

It's worth pointing out that web roles support only HTTP internal endpoints and can't be secured with certificates. You should use the HTTP protocol only for internal endpoints that are legacy web services (old ASP.NET Web Services [ASMX] and the like). If you're considering using this approach for WCF services, you should host your service with a worker role and expose it via TCP instead. TCP generally provides better performance for internal services than does HTTP.

WORKER ROLE ENDPOINTS

Although the service definition file is a common file that's used by both web roles and worker roles, we're going to look at only web roles in this chapter. We'll leave the examples on how to host worker roles that accept incoming requests across various protocols and ports to later in the book.

The configuration of a worker role uses the same `InputEndpoint` tag as the web role. The following XML shows the endpoint for a worker role hosted on TCP port 10000:

```
<InputEndpoint name="MyEndpoint" protocol="tcp" port="10000" />
```

Figure 4.5 shows the GUI for configuring a worker role endpoint.

You can use the editor shown in figure 4.5 to set internal endpoints. Remember, internal endpoints are dynamically assigned ports and you can't manually set the port number. The following XML defines an internal endpoint called `MyEndpoint` that uses TCP (rather than HTTP or HTTPS) as a protocol:

```
<InternalEndpoint name="MyEndpoint" protocol="tcp" />
```

As we said earlier, we intended to give only a brief description about how this configuration applies to worker roles. We'll return to this later on, but now we're going to take a little detour and examine other things you can do in the editor.

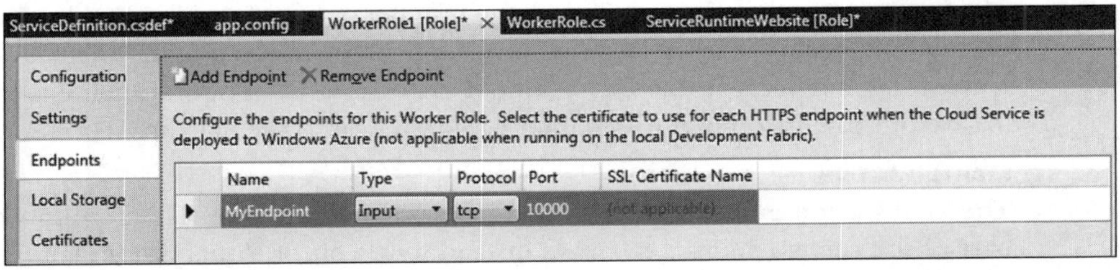

Figure 4.5 Setting a worker role to be hosted via TCP on port 10000 to the external world using the Visual Studio GUI

4.2.3 *Configuring trust level, instances, and startup action*

When you click the Configuration tab, you see the options shown in figure 4.6.

There are three sections on this page: .NET Trust Level, Instances, and Startup Action. We'll be looking at these sections in more detail later in the book, but for the moment let's have a quick introduction to them.

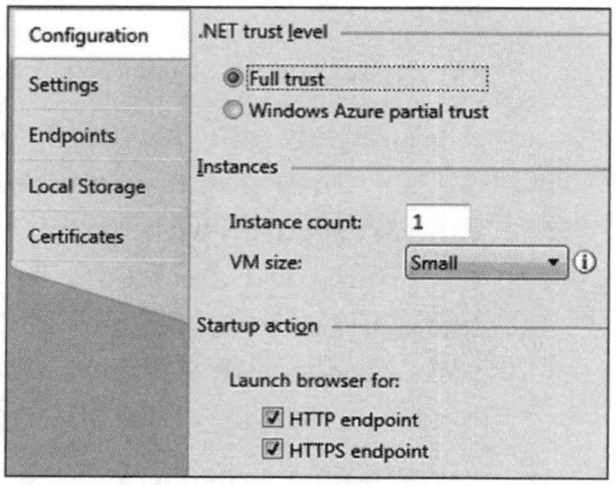

Figure 4.6 The Configuration tab for your role in Visual Studio

.NET TRUST LEVEL

Windows Azure supports two levels of trust: full trust and partial trust. Partial trust is similar to ASP.NET's medium trust level. It restricts the operations that your application can perform to only those that it trusts. Whenever possible, you should run your application in partial-trust mode because it provides a greater level of security (I sleep like a baby at night whenever my application is running under partial trust). If, however, you need to perform big scary actions that would make a security freak's skin crawl (such as C++, Reflection, or P/Invoke) then you'll need to set your application to full trust.

Using the dialog box shown in figure 4.6 is probably the easiest way to set your trust level, but because we all love messing with configuration files, let's modify the service definition file directly.

To configure partial trust, set the `enableNativeExecution` attribute on your role to `false`. For full trust, you can either set the attribute to `true` or not configure it at all (full trust is the default level). The following XML shows how to set your earlier web role to partial trust:

```
<WebRole name="ServiceRuntimeWebsite"
         enableNativeExecution="false">
```

In chapter 6, we'll look in more detail at the supported trust levels. Now let's move on to the Instances section.

INSTANCES

The Instances section allows you to set the number of instances of your role and the size of your VM (small, medium, large, or extra large). The number of instances is an important setting, but because this setting is held in the service configuration file, we're going to save our discussion of it for chapter 6. Now it's on to the Startup Action section.

STARTUP ACTION

The final section on the Configuration page is Startup Action. This section isn't really part of the service definition, but is instead a wee bit of Visual Studio configuration. The following two check boxes are in this section:

- Launch browser for HTTP endpoint
- Launch browser for HTTPS endpoint

These check boxes tell Visual Studio which endpoints you want to launch in the development environment when you press F5.

That's about it for what you can do on the Configuration page in the Visual Studio editor. Let's take a look now at the Local Storage page and find out how to configure your local storage.

4.2.4 Configuring local storage

Local storage is a temporary filesystem storage area that's made available to a role instance to store and retrieve data locally. The local storage area is available only to a single role instance and can't be shared across multiple role instances.

If the VM for your role instance dies and never recovers, you'll lose the data stored in this area forever. Only volatile data should be stored in this storage area; never store any data that you might need to rely on later in a court of law. Any data that you store in local storage should also be stored in a nonvolatile storage area such as a BLOB, Table storage, or SQL Azure.

IF IT'S SO VOLATILE, WHY DO I NEED IT?

Although BLOBs, Table storage, and SQL Azure can be accessed by all instances of a role, the convenience of centralized storage mechanisms comes at a cost: latency. Those other, nonvolatile storage areas are all hosted on separate servers in another part of the data center, whereas local storage is part of your VM. Because the disks are hosted on the same server as your VM, local storage is much faster than the other storage mechanisms.

BLOBs, Table storage, and SQL Azure are suitable for most scenarios, but if you're processing high volumes of data, you might want to use local storage to temporarily cache that data. Let's look at how to set that up.

SETTING UP LOCAL STORAGE

As always, there are two ways to configure local storage. You can either do it manually via the service definition file, or you can use the role editor in Visual Studio 2010 and let it modify the service definition file for you. Figure 4.7 shows the GUI for configuring local storage in Visual Studio.

When you define a local storage resource, you can define the following three items:

- The name of the resource
- The amount of space required, in megabytes
- Whether you want the temporary data deleted when the role is recycled

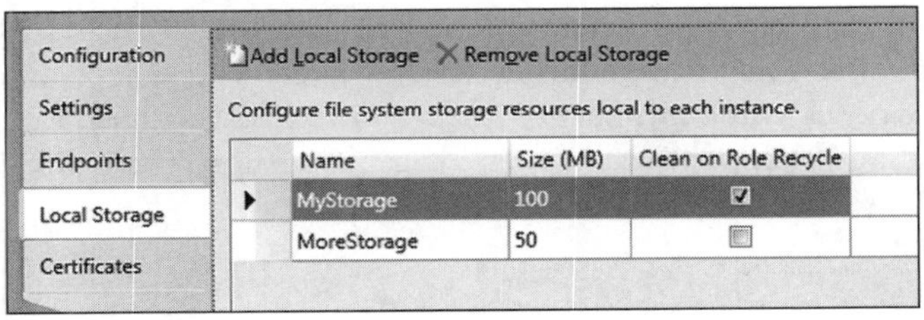

Figure 4.7 Configuring some temporary local storage space in your role using Visual Studio 2010

The maximum amount of local storage that you can use for a single role instance is 20 GB. If you need more than 20 GB of temporary storage space, you might want to rethink the architecture of your application.

The information that you supply in the editor is reflected in the service definition file, as shown in the following listing.

Listing 4.3 Configuring local storage in the service definition file

```
<WebRole name="ServiceRuntimeWebsite">
   <LocalResources>
      <LocalStorage name="MyStorage"
                    cleanOnRoleRecycle="true"
                    sizeInMB="100" />
      <LocalStorage name="MoreStorage"
                    cleanOnRoleRecycle="false"
                    sizeInMB="50" />
   </LocalResources>
</WebRole>
```

In the current version of Windows Azure, you can't dynamically change this setting at runtime, which is why this code lives in the service definition file and not in the service configuration file. If you incorrectly size your temporary storage area and need to request a larger size, you have to redeploy your application. Why is that?

The FC uses the requested size of local storage as part of its algorithm to decide which physical servers will host your VM. If the FC allowed you to modify the local storage dynamically without a redeployment, it might not be able to satisfy your request with the servers that are currently hosting your role instances (there might be too many other roles hosted on that server that have high local storage requirements). By forcing a redeployment of the application, the FC can safely redeploy your role instances to the servers that most appropriately satisfy your request.

Now that you know how to set up local storage, let's take a quick look at how to use it in your application.

USING LOCAL STORAGE

If you need to be able to use local storage in your role (web or worker), then you can make a request to retrieve information about your role using the `RoleEnvironment` class in the `ServiceRuntime`. Use the following call to request information about your local storage resource.

```
LocalResource myStorage =
                    RoleEnvironment.GetLocalResource("myStorage");
```

You need to call `RoleEnvironment.GetLocalResource`, passing in the name of the local storage resource that you defined earlier (`myStorage`). The object returned by `GetLocalResource` exposes three properties (`Name`, `MaximumSizeInMegabytes`, and `RootPath`). The `Name` and `MaximumSizeInMegabytes` properties return the information that you set in the service definition file:

```
string name = myStorage.Name;
int maxSizeInMB = myStorage.MaximumSizeInMegabytes;
```

The RootPath property returns the physical path of the folder where your temporary storage area has been assigned. Using the RootPath property, you can use standard .NET methods to store and retrieve data in this folder. The following code creates a text file called HelloWorld.txt that contains the text "Goodbye World".

```
System.IO.File.WriteAllText(myStorage.RootPath + "HelloWorld.txt",
                            "Goodbye World");
```

It's pretty simple to use local storage. It's built on all the existing system.I/O classes that we all know and love.

Before we leave the subject of local storage, we want to cover one final thing: the Clean on Role Recycle setting.

RECYCLING A ROLE

Use the Clean on Role Recycle setting to indicate whether you want to lose or keep your local storage data if one of the following things occurs:

- An upgrade (you deploy a new version or an OS patch is applied)
- A fault (the server dies)
- You request that the role be recycled

It's pretty hard to test how your application responds to losing your temporary data as part of an upgrade or a fault, but you can manually request that your roles be recycled. All you need to do is call the RequestRecycle method in the RoleEnvironment class:

```
RoleEnvironment.RequestRecycle();
```

This call not only allows you to test that your application handles local storage correctly when your role instance is recycled; it also allows you to test whether the rest of your application behaves gracefully.

If your application needs to know when a role instance is stopping (because it's cleaning up resources, notifying a monitor, or performing some other such task), you can always use the RoleEnvironment.Stopping event:

```
public class WebRole : RoleEntryPoint
{
   public override bool OnStart()
  {
            DiagnosticMonitor.Start("DiagnosticsConnectionString");

            RoleEnvironment.Stopping += new
               EventHandler<RoleEnvironmentStoppingEventArgs>
(RoleEnvironment_Stopping);

            return base.OnStart();
   }

   void RoleEnvironment_Stopping(object sender,
     RoleEnvironmentStoppingEventArgs e)
   {
      Trace.WriteLine("Stopping");
   }
}
```

You can easily stick any cleanup code that you need in the event handler for this event. When this handler is called, your code has only 30 seconds to respond. This time limit protects Windows Azure from sloppy tear-down code or freezes in the cleanup process. This limit is similar to the limit local Windows services face when they're told to stop by the user or the OS.

You now know almost everything you need to know about local storage. We'll revisit this topic in part 4, when we show how you can use this in combination with BLOBs and how local storage can help you when you're building massively scalable worker processes built on MapReduce.

Now let's turn our attention to the tabs in the role editor that we haven't covered yet. So far we've looked at the Configuration, Endpoints, and Local Storage tabs. That leaves the Certificates and Settings tabs. When we looked at configuring endpoints, we discussed HTTPS but we didn't mention how to configure the SSL certificate for your site. Let's return to that subject and look at certificate management in Windows Azure.

4.3 Setting up certificates in Windows Azure

We want to look at how to generate, add, and configure certificates in Azure. Let's look at how to generate one first; then we'll cover how to add and configure them. Certificates are widely used to encrypt, and thereby protect, data as it travels over the network. In this section, when we refer to certificates, we mean the type you'll use for HTTPS/SSL or for your own encryption needs. We're not referring to the management certificates we'll cover in chapter 18.

4.3.1 Generating a certificate

For live production applications you should use a purchased certificate from a trusted authority. If you're just experimenting or testing an application, you can use a test certificate. Because you've already bought this lovely book, we'll save your wallet from more troubles and show you how to generate a test certificate that you can use on the production or development fabric.

To generate a test X.509 certificate, you can use a tool called `makecert`, which is included with both Visual Studio and the .NET Framework. To start using the tool, fire up an instance of the Visual Studio command prompt as an administrator. Using the command prompt, you can generate a test certificate with the following command:

```
makecert -r -pe -a sha1
-n "CN=Windows Azure Authentication Certificate"
-ss My -len 2048
-sp "Microsoft Enhanced RSA and AES Cryptographic Provider"
-sy 24 MyCertificate.cer
```

This command generates a test X.509 certificate called MyCertficate.cer, and stores it in the CurrentUser/Personal store. You'll need to use the certificate management tool in Windows to export it as a PFX-formatted certificate, which is suitable for use in Windows Azure. For more details about the `makecert` tool, you can always visit the following URL: http://msdn.microsoft.com/en-us/library/bfsktky3(VS.80).aspx.

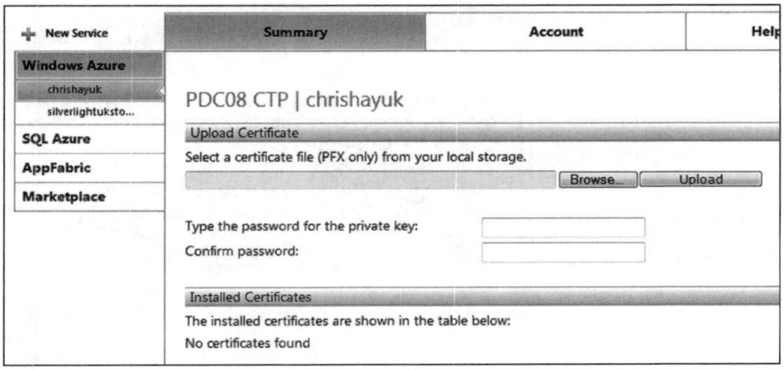

Figure 4.8 To install a certificate using the Windows Azure portal, select the certificate and click Upload. It's that easy.

With your brand new certificate in hand, you can install the certificate in both the production fabric and the development fabric.

4.3.2 Adding certificates

The production fabric and the development fabric both have different methods of managing certificates. Let's look at how to add certificates on the live system first.

ADDING CERTIFICATES TO THE PRODUCTION FABRIC

As you might expect, you manage certificates via the Azure portal. Select your hosted service in the portal, and then click Manage in the Certificates section. You'll see the window shown in figure 4.8.

If you need to install your certificate using your own code, you can use the management APIs. We won't cover how to do this in this book because it's not a typical scenario for most folks. If you're automatically installing lots of websites, then using your own code could be useful; the rest of you should use the portal.

ADDING CERTIFICATES TO THE DEVELOPMENT FABRIC

If you need to test HTTPS in your development fabric, you'll need the appropriate certificate on your development machine. To upload your certificate into the development fabric, click the Certificates tab in the role editor, as shown in figure 4.9.

You can set the name, location (`LocalMachine`, `CurrentUser`), store name (`My`, `Root`, `CA`, `Trust`), and the certificate.

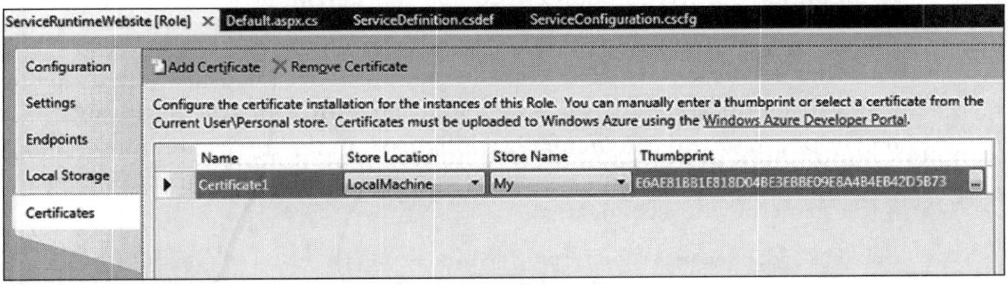

Figure 4.9 Adding certificates to the development fabric

To set the certificate, you can either enter the thumbprint manually or select a certificate from your personal store. If you click the button in the Thumbprint cell, the Select a Certificate dialog box opens (already armed with the test certificate that you generated earlier), as shown in figure 4.10.

Figure 4.10 The Select a Certificate dialog box shows the certificates you've already generated. This example shows the certificate you generated earlier with `makecert`.

Now that you've selected your certificate, you might be wondering how this is reflected in the service definition file. Don't worry. Your XML-obsessed authors are here to help you out. The following listing shows how the certificate is represented.

Listing 4.4 Adding a certificate to the service definition file

```
<WebRole name="ServiceRuntimeWebsite">
    <InputEndpoints>
      <InputEndpoint name="HttpsIn" protocol="https" port="443" />
    </InputEndpoints>
    <Certificates>
      <Certificate name="MyCertificate"
         storeLocation="LocalMachine"
         storeName="My" />
    </Certificates>
</WebRole>
```

Same information shown in figure 4.9

Everything that you set in figure 4.9 is present in the service definition file, except for the thumbprint, which is stored in the service configuration file. The thumbprint is a configurable setting, not a definable attribute of the service; that's why it's in the configuration file. We're going to talk more about the thumbprint in chapter 5; now let's use that new certificate.

4.3.3 Configuring your HTTPS endpoint to use the certificate

The last thing you need to do is to configure your endpoint to use the new certificate. With your certificate installed, you can either use the SSL Certificate drop-down menu shown in figure 4.4 (which is now populated with your test certificate) to configure the endpoint, or you can manually configure it in the service definition file. To configure the endpoint manually, set the certificate attribute of the `InputEndpoint` element to the name of your certificate:

```
<InputEndpoint name="HttpsIn" protocol="https" port="443"
               certificate="MyCertificate"/>
```

If you expose a worker role externally using an `InputEndpoint` element, you can also secure that service with a certificate. You manage and configure certificates for a worker role in the same way as you do a web role.

4.4 Summary

It's probably a good time to stop and review where we've been. In this chapter, you've taken everything that you've learned about how Windows Azure works (from chapter 3) and started to define how you want your application to run in the environment.

We talked about the `ServiceRuntime` assembly and how you can use that to interact with Windows Azure. This assembly provides several APIs that can help you to get the most out of Windows Azure. You can use the `ServiceRuntime` assembly to determine whether your application is up and running in Azure.

Next, we examined the service definition file, which defines your service. The information in this file instructs the FC about how to manage your application. In this file, you configure the endpoint of your web role, the trust level you want to use, your instances, your local storage, and the certificates you'll use. We showed how you can do all this using either the Visual Studio editor or by putting the information directly into the file in XML.

In the next chapter you'll take what you've learned about defining your service and configure it to work in Windows Azure.

Configuring your service

5

This chapter covers

- Understanding the service configuration file
- Handling configuration at runtime
- Handling non-application settings, based on configuration
- Sharing configuration between Azure and non-Azure applications

In the previous chapter, we concentrated on how you define your role using the service definition file. We'll now look at the second part of the service model picture: the service configuration file.

5.1 Working with the service configuration file

In chapter 4, we described how the service definition file (ServiceDefinition.csdef) describes your role and how it's used by the Fabric Controller (FC) to effectively manage your role. You learned that if you need to change any of the settings in your service definition file, you also need to redeploy your role.

You can change some other settings without redeploying your role. You can even change some of your settings dynamically without restarting the role (surely not; because we develop on Microsoft products, we love a good restart). These dynamic settings are typically stored in the *service configuration file* (ServiceConfiguration.cscfg).

In the service configuration file, you can dynamically configure standard Windows Azure runtime settings (the number of role instances and the certificate thumbprint) and your own custom settings. Let's see how you configure this information and how you can dynamically modify these settings at runtime.

5.1.1 The format of the service configuration file

Let's now take a look at the standard service configuration file that Visual Studio creates when you create a web role. The following listing shows the service configuration file that was generated when you created your `ServiceRuntimeWeb` project in chapter 1.

Listing 5.1 Service configuration file of the `ServiceRuntimeWeb` project

```
<?xml version="1.0"?>
<ServiceConfiguration serviceName="ServiceRuntimeWeb"     <-- Same name as
xmlns="http://schemas.microsoft.com/ServiceHosting/            cloud project
➥ 2008/10/ServiceConfiguration">
  <Role name="ServiceRuntimeWebsite">              <-- Same name
    <Instances count="1"/>                             as web role
    <ConfigurationSettings>
      <Setting name="DiagnosticsConnectionString"
      ➥ value="UseDevelopmentStorage=true"/>
    </ConfigurationSettings>
  </Role>
</ServiceConfiguration>
```

Before you start thinking, "Oh no, not another XML file," don't worry; you can configure everything you see in this file in the Visual Studio editor. It's useful to understand the structure of this file, because it'll help you understand which settings are dynamic. You might find yourself editing this file in the Azure portal where there isn't a nice GUI, just a plain old text editor. Also, if things go wrong, you might need to recover the file with Notepad.

As shown in listing 5.1, the service configuration file adheres to the following format:

- Cloud project (`ServiceConfiguration` element)
  - Role definition
    - Instances
    - Configuration settings
    - Certificates

Because your Cloud Service project contains only a single web role, only one role definition appears in your service configuration file. The same was true for the service definition file. If your project contained multiple roles, then these would also appear in the file. The following XML shows how multiple roles would be structured in the service configuration file:

```
<ServiceConfiguration serviceName="ServiceRuntimeWeb" xmlns="http://
     schemas.microsoft.com/ServiceHosting/
     ➥ 2008/10/ServiceConfiguration">
  <Role name="ServiceRuntimeWebsite">
     ...
  </Role>
  <Role name="WorkerRole1">
     ...
  </Role>
</ServiceConfiguration>
```

The XML shows two roles in this project: a web role called `ServiceRuntimeWebsite` and a worker role called `WorkerRole1` (remember, the configuration of a worker role is exactly the same as the configuration of a web role).

You have a pretty good idea of how the service configuration file is structured; let's look at how you can configure some of the standard settings.

5.1.2 Configuring standard settings

As of the PDC 2009 release, there are only two types of standard settings that you can configure in Windows Azure:

- The number of instances of your role
- The certificate thumbprint

All other settings are custom settings (which we'll look at in the next section).

NUMBER OF INSTANCES

We're now going to briefly look at the most important piece of configuration in Windows Azure: the number of instances that your role has. The following XML defines five instances of your role:

```
<Role name="ServiceRuntimeWebsite">
    <Instances count="5"/>
</Role>
```

If you need to increase the number of instances required for your web role, you can modify this value in your service configuration file. During development, you can also modify this value using the Configuration tab in the Visual Studio GUI.

If you're currently wondering why this setting is in the service configuration file and not in the service definition file, the answer is quite simple. This setting doesn't define the service (the service hasn't changed); you just want more instances of it. By storing this setting in the service configuration file, you can scale the number of services up and down dynamically without having to redeploy your application (after all, no code has changed). Later on in this section we'll look at how you can modify the service configuration file at runtime via the Azure portal.

Now let's return to a topic that we had parked earlier: certificates.

CERTIFICATES

We talked about certificates in chapter 4. To recap, in that section, we showed you how to do the following:

- Generate a test certificate
- Install a certificate into the development fabric and production fabric
- Associate a certificate with your HTTPS endpoint

When you installed your certificate in the development fabric, you saw that it stored the following XML in your service definition:

```
<WebRole name="ServiceRuntimeWebsite">
    <InputEndpoints>
      <InputEndpoint name="HttpsIn" protocol="https" port="443" />
    </InputEndpoints>
    <Certificates>
      <Certificate name="MyCertificate"
         storeLocation="LocalMachine"
         storeName="My" />
    </Certificates>
</WebRole>
```

If we return to the Certificates page in Visual Studio (as shown in figure 4.9), the thumbprint shown there isn't present in the service definition file. That's because this value is stored in the service configuration file, as shown below:

```
<?xml version="1.0"?>
<ServiceConfiguration serviceName="ServiceRuntimeWeb" xmlns="http://
     schemas.microsoft.com/ServiceHosting/
     ➥ 2008/10/ServiceConfiguration">
  <Role name="ServiceRuntimeWebsite">
    <Instances count="1"/>
    <Certificates>
      <Certificate name="Certificate1"
     thumbprint="E6AE81BB1E818D04BE3EBBE09E8A4B4EB42D5B73"
     ➥ thumbprintAlgorithm="sha1" />
    </Certificates>
  </Role>
</ServiceConfiguration>
```

Why is certificate information split across two configuration files (service definition and service configuration)? Think about the intention of this functionality. The definition of your role is as follows: the web role `ServiceRunTimeWebsite` is hosted on port 443 using the protocol HTTPS and it requires a certificate called `MyCertificate`, which you've uploaded.

In reality, certificates aren't a fixed entity. You might want to use a test certificate in the staging environment but use your production certificate only in the production environment. Certificates expire, and you might need to change your certificate over time. For these reasons, the certificate associated with your service is dynamic and configurable, which is why the thumbprint lives in the service configuration file. Do you really want to redeploy your application to change certificates when you switch your application from staging to production?

What's the thumbprint used for? The name of the certificate in the service definition file (`MyCertificate`, the one you typed in Visual Studio) is internal to Windows Azure. This name isn't tied back to the name of the certificate that you generated earlier. You need to be able to retrieve the correct certificate from the store, and the thumbprint is that search parameter. Windows Azure uses the `FindByThumbprint` functionality built into Windows to retrieve the actual certificate.

If you have a production certificate from a trusted authority that you can't install in your development environment and you need to configure that in Windows Azure via the portal, then you can always manually configure the certificate in the service configuration file using the thumbprint.

We've covered the standard configuration settings. Let's look at how you configure your own custom settings.

5.1.3 Configuring runtime settings

As with any other application, when you're working with web or worker roles you need to be able to dynamically configure runtime settings without rebuilding the application from its source. In conventional web applications, the following settings (among others) are typically stored in configuration files:

- Database connection strings
- Service endpoints
- Filesystem paths
- Timeout settings

Although these configuration settings are considered dynamic, in most applications they're rarely changed. The main reason for storing these runtime configuration settings in a configuration file is so that you can easily deploy your application between different environments (development, test, staging, and production). Typically, your production environment talks to different web services, a different database, or a different storage account from your development or staging environment. Using configuration files (rather than rebuilding your source code) to modify these endpoints greatly reduces the complexity, increases the maintainability, and simplifies the deployment process of your application.

In this section we'll look at the following aspects of configuring your runtime settings:

- Configuring runtime settings in conventional web apps
- Defining your runtime configuration settings in Windows Azure
- Initially configuring your runtime configuration settings
- Reading your configuration settings
- Modifying your configuration settings dynamically at runtime

Before we look at how to define your runtime configuration settings in Windows Azure, let's look at how you would do this in conventional ASP.NET web applications.

CONFIGURING RUNTIME SETTINGS IN CONVENTIONAL ASP.NET WEB APPLICATIONS

In conventional ASP.NET web applications, you typically store any configurable runtime settings in the web.config file. Windows Azure provides the ability to read application settings from web.config (as we'll now demonstrate), but this isn't the method that you should use to read the configuration settings.

You're going to build a small web page that'll read and display a setting from the `appSettings` section of web.config. Then you're going to modify this page in future sections of this chapter to use the Windows Azure configuration settings functionality. Figure 5.1 shows the output of the web page that you're going to create. The text "Hello Birds Hello Trees" is read from web.config.

Figure 5.1 Displaying configuration settings in a web page. This text is being read from the `appSettings` section of the web.config file. Because you can't modify this text without redeploying your application, a better place to store it is in the ServiceDefinition.csdef file.

In your ASP.NET web project, add a new ASP.NET web page called ConfigurationSettings.aspx that you'll use to develop the page shown in figure 5.1. Next, add the following label to the page:

```
<asp:label id="mySettingLbl" runat="server"/>
```

The text "Hello Birds Hello Trees" that you'll display in the label `mySettingLbl` is stored in the `appSettings` section of web.config. In the web.config file for your web application, replace the `appSettings` tag with the following:

```
<appSettings>
   <add key="mySetting" value="Hello Birds Hello Trees"/>
</appSettings>
```

Add a using `System.Configuration` line to the top of your code. Then, on the `Page_Load` event of the ConfigurationSettings.aspx page, add the following code to display the contents of the `mySetting` application setting:

```
mySettingLbl.Text = ConfigurationManager.AppSettings["mySetting"];
```

If you were to now run this application in the Web Development Server, IIS, the development fabric, or on the live Windows Azure production fabric, the application would run correctly and display the page shown in figure 5.1.

ISSUES WITH USING WEB.CONFIG

Although Windows Azure can read anything stored in the `appSettings` section of your web.config file, it doesn't provide you with the ability to modify these settings at runtime. If you need to modify a value in your web.config file, then Windows Azure requires you to redeploy your entire application.

In conventional web applications, you would need to modify web.config for each instance if you wanted to change runtime settings. Unfortunately, this approach isn't scalable beyond a single server. If you need to modify 100 instances of a web application, dealing with each individual web.config file is likely to be slow and cause synchronization issues. In such a scenario, you'll need to store the configuration settings centrally and then distribute the changes to each instance. It makes sense to remove the configuration settings from web.config (after all, there's more than just application settings in that file) and provide a new mechanism to feed runtime settings. Let's see how this is done.

SETTING CONFIGURATION IN THE SERVICE DEFINITION

Any configuration settings that your application uses must be defined first in the service definition file (ServiceDefinition.csdef). To display the message "Hello Birds Hello Trees" in your web page, you need to define a new setting in the service definition file. Add the name of the new setting (`mySetting`) to the `ConfigurationSettings` section of the file. The following configuration shows how the `ConfigurationSettings` section should look:

```
<ConfigurationSettings>
   <Setting name="mySetting"/>
   <Setting name="DiagnosticsConnectionString"/>
</ConfigurationSettings>
```

Now the service definition file looks like what's shown in the following listing.

Listing 5.2 Adding a new setting to the service definition file for your project

```
<?xml version="1.0" encoding="utf-8"?>
<ServiceDefinition name="ServiceRuntimeWeb"
     xmlns="http://schemas.microsoft.com/ServiceHosting/
     ➥ 2008/10/ServiceDefinition">
  <WebRole name="ServiceRuntimeWebsite">
    <InputEndpoints>
      <InputEndpoint name="HttpIn" protocol="http" port="80" />
    </InputEndpoints>
    <ConfigurationSettings>
      <Setting name="mySetting"/>
         <Setting name="DiagnosticsConnectionString"
                  value="UseDevelopmentStorage=true" />

    </ConfigurationSettings>
  </WebRole>
</ServiceDefinition>
```

Notice that in the service definition file, you specify only the name of the setting; you don't set the configured value at this point.

SETTING YOUR CONFIGURATION VALUE IN THE SERVICE CONFIGURATION FILE

After you define the configuration settings in the service definition file that'll be used by your application, you need to set the actual value of the setting that'll be used by the website. The configuration settings are stored in the ServiceConfiguration.cscfg file in your Cloud Service project.

To set your runtime configuration setting, make a copy of the configuration setting in the service definition file and paste it into the service configuration file. Then add a new attribute called `value` that you can set to your default runtime value. The following code shows how your new setting should look:

```
<Setting name="mySetting" value="Hello Birds Hello Trees"/>
```

Now your ServiceConfiguration.cscfg file should look like what's shown in the following listing.

Listing 5.3 Adding a new setting to the service configuration file for your project

```
<?xml version="1.0"?>
<ServiceConfiguration serviceName="ServiceRuntimeWeb"
➥ xmlns="http://schemas.microsoft.com/ServiceHosting/
➥ 2008/10/ServiceConfiguration">
  <Role name="ServiceRuntimeWebsite">
    <Instances count="1"/>
    <ConfigurationSettings>
      <Setting name="mySetting" value="Hello Birds Hello Trees"/>
         <Setting name="DiagnosticsConnectionString"
                  value="UseDevelopmentStorage=true" />

    </ConfigurationSettings>
  </Role>
</ServiceConfiguration>
```

You've set up your ServiceConfiguration.cscfg file and the `ConfigurationSettings` section in the ServiceDefinition.csd file to contain your runtime configuration settings. Now you need to modify your application to use the Windows Azure Service Runtime to read the configuration data.

READING THE CONFIGURATION SETTING

You can access the runtime values of the configuration setting by using the `RoleEnvironment` static class that you used earlier. To retrieve the value of a configuration setting, you can use the following method:

```
RoleEnvironment.GetConfigurationSettingValue(SettingName);
```

To modify your existing web page to read the configuration setting from the Windows Azure configuration settings file rather than from the web.config file, add a using statement for `Microsoft.WindowsAzure.ServiceRuntime` at the top of your code and change the code-behind of your website to the following:

```
mySettingLbl.Text =
RoleEnvironment.GetConfigurationSettingValue("mySetting");
```

Now you can run the CloudService project to see the value displayed in your web page, as shown in figure 5.1.

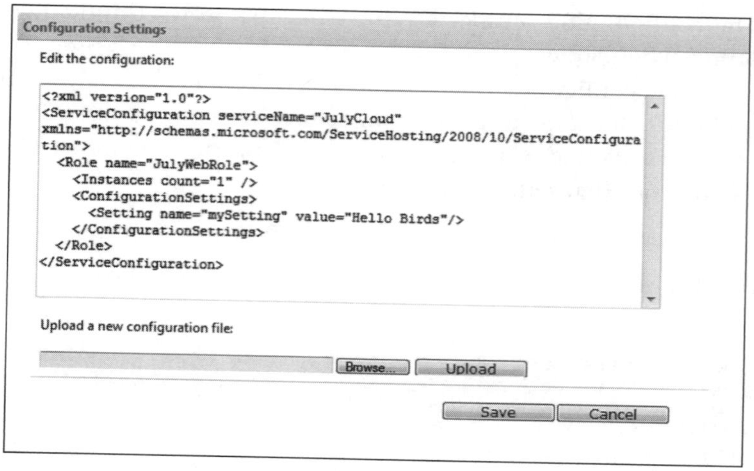

Figure 5.2 Modifying configuration settings in the Azure portal

5.2 Handling configuration at runtime

Congratulations! You understand the service configuration file and how to read those configuration settings. Now let's modify these configuration settings at runtime and find out how to track changes when they occur.

5.2.1 Modifying configuration settings in the Azure portal

You can modify the values that you set in the service configuration file dynamically at runtime by using the Azure portal. First, though, you have to redeploy your application. If you need a little help, skip back to chapter 2 and review that information.

After your application is redeployed and running in the fabric, you can easily modify any of your configuration settings. Select either the production or staging version of the role, and then click Configure. You're redirected to the page shown in figure 5.2, in which you can modify the runtime configuration settings for the role that you selected.

The Azure portal doesn't have any fancy editors; all you see is a big text box with your service configuration file in it. Bet you're glad you paid attention during XML school now.

The Azure portal lets you directly edit the contents of the configuration settings or upload a new version of the service configuration file. After you apply your changes, they're instantly replicated to all instances of your web role; in some cases you don't have to restart any of the roles.

Figure 5.3 shows that you've modified the configuration setting `mySetting` from "Hello Birds Hello Trees" to "Hello Birds".

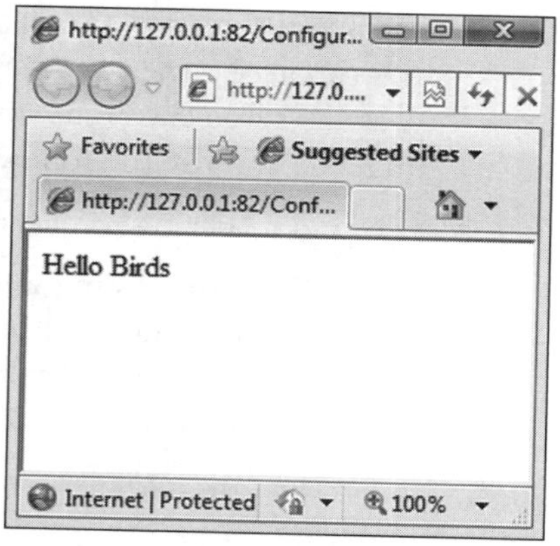

Figure 5.3 Your web page showing a configuration setting that you modified via the Azure portal

Wow, modifying your configuration settings is easily achieved through the Azure portal. What's even cooler is that your role can pick up and run with the changes without needing a restart. The only issue is that you might need to store a local copy of the previous setting whenever that setting changes. Let's see how to do that.

5.2.2 Tracking service configuration changes

When you change a configuration setting, Windows Azure raises two events that your application can handle:

- `RoleEnvironment.Changing`—Fires before the changes to the setting are applied. You can still read the existing setting before the change is applied.
- `RoleEnvironment.Changed`—Fires after the changes to the setting are applied. You might use this event to set up a new shared resource after a cleanup of a shared resource.

To hook up and define one of these events, you can use the code shown in the following listing.

Listing 5.4 Tracking changes to the service configuration

```
public class WebRole : RoleEntryPoint
 {
       public override bool OnStart()
       {
           DiagnosticMonitor.Start("DiagnosticsConnectionString");

           RoleEnvironment.Changing += RoleEnvironmentChanging;

           return base.OnStart();
       }

       private void RoleEnvironmentChanging
       ➥ (object sender, RoleEnvironmentChangingEventArgs e)
       {
           if (e.Changes.Any(change => change is
           ➥ RoleEnvironmentConfigurationSettingChange))
           {
               Trace.WriteLine("Configuration Setting Changed");

               // Set e.Cancel to true to restart this role instance
               e.Cancel = true;
           }
       }
   }
```

So far we've had a good look at how to use the `ConfigurationSettings` functionality in Windows Azure. The problem is that the `ConfigurationSettings` section of the service configuration file is only a replacement for the data that you would normally store in the `appSettings` section of the web.config file. How do you handle other types of configuration data?

5.3 Configuring non-application settings

In this section we'll take a look at when you would use the service configuration file and when you would use regular old application settings to set up configuration data. We're going to look specifically at where you should store the following kinds of information:

- Database connection strings
- Application build configuration
- Tweakable configuration
- Endpoint configuration

5.3.1 Database connection strings

For database connection strings (such as SQL Azure DB), you might have different development, staging, and production connection strings. In standard ASP.NET web applications, you would store the connection string in the `connectionStrings` element of the web.config file. Like `appSettings`, Windows Azure doesn't provide you with the ability to change data stored in the `connectionStrings` element at runtime. You can, however, treat a connection string like an application setting and store it in the service configuration. Using configuration settings allows you to modify the connection string at runtime via the Azure portal.

5.3.2 Application build configuration

Some configuration data can be tweaked on an individual server via web.config but is never different between various deployments. This configuration should remain in web.config and be treated as part of the application build rather than as a runtime setting. Typical examples include the `httpModules` and `httpHandlers` sections of web.config.

5.3.3 Tweakable configuration

It can be useful to tweak some configuration settings when an unexpected issue comes up, without redeploying the application. For example, a user might upload a file that's larger than you originally configured the web server to handle. In this case, you might decide to modify the maximum HTTP request size in web.config to allow larger files to upload. The following configuration shows this web.config setting:

```
<httpRuntime maxRequestLength="1048576"/>
```

In a conventional production environment, you would probably test this change on a staging environment and then roll out the change to the live environment without redeploying the entire application. Typically, this change would be reflected in source control so that all future builds would have the new settings.

The web.config file you're used to editing at runtime to change behavior is read-only in the cloud. Because you can't change the web.config file dynamically in Windows Azure, you would have to redeploy the full application in the Azure portal to deploy a changed web.config file. Instead, you can move these configuration elements to the cloud service definition. Then you can update the settings during runtime through the portal. This might cause a restart of your instances (in a controlled upgrade-style manner), but you aren't deploying new code.

5.3.4 Endpoint configuration

Let's say you have an ASP.NET web page that communicates via WCF to an external WCF service. You might have a different endpoint that you communicate with between the development, production, and staging systems. How can you configure your applications hosted by Windows Azure to use external endpoints, such as WCF services?

The following extract from web.config represents the WCF configuration for a typical WCF client proxy (in this example, we've omitted the binding configuration).

```
<client>
   <endpoint address="http://myservice.com/services/timeservice.svc"
             binding="basicHttpBinding"
             bindingConfiguration="BasicHttpBinding_ITimeService"
             contract="TimeService.ITimeService"
             name="BasicHttpBinding_ITimeService" />
</client>
```

Because you can't modify this information in the Windows Azure portal, you can't change the endpoint between staging and production without redeploying the application. What you can do though is extract the information that can change dynamically (in this case, `http://myservice.com/services/timeservice.svc`) and store it in the service configuration file, leaving all the other configuration as it is (accepting that if that needs to change it will require a redeploy). You can then modify the endpoint in a WCF proxy by modifying the endpoint address on the proxy:

```
var timeServiceProxy = new TimeServiceClient();

Uri timeServiceEndpointAddress =
   new
     Uri(RoleEnvironment.GetConfigurationSettingValue("timeServiceEndpoint"))
     ;

timeServiceProxy.Endpoint.Address =
   new EndpointAddress(timeServiceEndpointAddress);
```

You're doing well so far. You know all about how to configure your own custom runtime settings and how to modify them at runtime. You can configure an ASP.NET web application to work in Windows Azure and you're familiar with the sorts of things you can and can't do in Windows Azure with regard to configuration. Now let's revisit how you can develop an application that'll work in both environments.

5.4 Developing a common code base

Because you've just seen how configuration settings are dramatically different between Windows Azure and standard ASP.NET, let's talk about how to develop a unified system that'll work in both environments. Typically, there are two situations in which you might want to use a common code base for configuration settings:

- You have a common library shared across multiple projects.
- There are two versions of your web application (a cloud version and an on-premises version).

To successfully share configuration settings across Windows Azure applications and applications not running in the cloud, abstract your configuration settings so they can be read either directly from the web.config or app.config file, or via the `RoleEnvironment` class. You can implement this in one of two ways: use the `RoleEnvironment.IsAvailable` property or the configuration settings inversion of control container. Let's examine each of these implementations.

5.4.1 Using the RoleEnvironment.IsAvailable property

Unfortunately, if you attempt to access configuration settings outside the Windows Azure fabric using the `RoleEnvironment.GetConfigurationSettingValue` method, a very large, nasty exception will be thrown. The reason is that the `GetConfigurationSettingValue` method is a Windows Azure–only method that isn't supported in standard .NET applications.

You can get around this issue by performing a check to see whether you're running in Azure using the `RoleEnvironment.IsAvailable` property, as shown in the following code:

```
public static string GetSetting(string settingName)
{
   if (RoleEnvironment.IsAvailable)
   {
      return RoleEnvironment.GetConfigurationSettingValue(settingName);
   }
   else
   {
      return ConfigurationManager.AppSettings[settingName];
   }
}
```

This is probably the simplest method of sharing configuration settings that span across applications that are hosted by Windows Azure and applications that aren't.

In the example code, the `GetSetting` method checks whether the ASP.NET web application is running in the fabric using the `RoleEnvironment.IsAvailable` property. If the application is hosted in Windows Azure (development fabric or live system), then it uses the `RoleEnvironment` class to retrieve the configuration setting; otherwise, it uses the standard method of retrieving a setting from `appSettings`.

Although the previous example is a simple one, using this method will ensure that your non-Windows Azure applications will reference Windows Azure assemblies even though your applications aren't running in the Windows Azure environment. One final thing to remember: your common libraries and any versions of your applications that aren't running in the cloud need to reference the Microsoft.WindowsAzure.ServiceRuntime assembly.

5.4.2 *Pluggable configuration settings using inversion of control*

If you want to keep your application layers clean, consider using the *inversion of control* (IoC) pattern. The IoC pattern is pluggable architecture that allows you to decouple the execution of an operation from its implementation. Call GetSetting in a common layer and let the application figure out the implementation to use (appSettings or RoleEnvironment), as appropriate. In the following four sections we'll use the *Unity Application Block*, or *Unity* (which is part of Microsoft Enterprise Library 4.1) to implement this pattern, but you can use any IoC framework.

DEFINING YOUR CONFIGURATION SETTINGS INTERFACE

To support a pluggable architecture you need an interface that both the RoleEnvironment and appSettings versions of your ConfigurationSettings classes can access, such as the following:

```
public interface IConfigurationSettings
{
   string GetSetting(string settingName);
}
```

This interface exposes a single method that will accept the name of the setting to retrieve and return the value of the setting.

IMPLEMENTING YOUR INTERFACE IN STANDARD WEB APPLICATIONS

Now that you've got your interface, you can implement that interface to return the setting value from the appSettings section of the web.config or app.config file using the following code:

```
public class AppConfigConfiguratonSettings : IConfigurationSettings
{
   public string GetSetting(string settingName)
   {
      return ConfigurationManager.AppSettings[settingName];
   }
}
```

The class above implements IConfigurationSettings and uses System.Configuration.ConfigurationManager to return the setting value. The AppConfigConfigurationSettings class should ideally be located in the same assembly as the interface and both IConfigurationSettings and AppConfigConfigurationSettings should be located in a common assembly that all your applications can access.

IMPLEMENTING YOUR INTERFACE IN WINDOWS AZURE WEB ROLES

Finally, you need to provide an implementation of IConfigurationSettings that can be used to retrieve the configuration settings from the service configuration file via RoleEnvironment:

```
public class RoleEnvironmentConfigurationSettings : IConfigurationSettings
{
```

```
    public string GetSetting(string settingName)
    {
       return RoleEnvironment.GetConfigurationSettingValue(settingName);
    }
}
```

This class can be provided in a separate assembly that's not included with non-Windows Azure instances of your web application and that's not referenced by any of the common layers. As you can see from this implementation, the common layers have no references to any of the Windows Azure SDK assemblies.

CALLING THE CORRECT IMPLEMENTATION

Now that you've defined your pluggable classes, how do you call the correct implementation of the interface? Using the Unity implementation of IoC, reference the Unity assembly (Microsoft.Practices.Unity.dll) from your common assembly and add the following namespaces:

```
using Microsoft.Practices.Unity;
using Microsoft.Practices.Unity.Configuration;
using Microsoft.Practices.Unity.StaticFactory;
```

> **Using Unity**
>
> Download Unity from Microsoft's Patterns and Practices group as part of Enterprise Library 4, Enterprise Library 5, or stand-alone. See http://unity.codeplex.com/ for details.
>
> Unity isn't the only implementation of IoC available; it just happens to be the one used in this example. For more information about Unity or IoC, go to http://msdn.microsoft.com/en-us/library/ff647202(v=pandp.10.aspx.

Then, when you need to retrieve a configuration setting in your application, you call the following code:

```
IUnityContainer myContainer = new UnityContainer();

IConfigurationSettings configurationSettings =
    myContainer.Resolve<IConfigurationSettings>();

configurationSettings.GetSetting("mySetting");
```

When you call the `Resolve` method, that method determines which configuration settings provider is registered, and returns an instance of that class. Then you can retrieve the configuration setting from the registered provider (`appSettings` version or `RoleEnvironment` version) using the interface method `GetSetting`.

Finally, if you want a class to use the `appSettings` version in your applications that aren't hosted by Windows Azure, register it using the following code:

```
IUnityContainer myContainer = new UnityContainer();

myContainer.RegisterType<IConfigurationSettings,
                              AppConfigConfiguratonSettings>();
```

To register the Windows Azure version, you could call the following code instead from your application:

```
IUnityContainer myContainer = new UnityContainer();

myContainer.RegisterType<IConfigurationSettings,
                         RoleEnvironmentConfigurationSettings>();
```

Unity supports both configuration via code, which is what you see above, and via configuration files. You could easily determine which `IConfigurationSettings` to load using the `RoleEnvironment.IsAvailable` method to tell you whether the code was running in the fabric, or you could extract which version to load into a configuration file. Using the configuration file allows you to be a little more flexible by having one configuration file for on-premises and one for the cloud.

Now you know how to share your data across Windows Azure and other applications by using the `RoleEnvironment` class to interact with the Windows Azure runtime. We think it might be interesting to rip away some of the covers and look at how this interaction happens.

5.5 The RoleEnvironment class and callbacks

The `RoleEnvironment` class is hosted by the `Microsoft.WindowsAzure.ServiceRuntime` assembly, which is provided as part of the Windows Azure SDK. On startup of your application, the `WaWebHost` service attempts to call `RoleEnvironment.Initialize` on any hosted web role application. This call populates a singleton instance of the `RoleEnvironment` class (private static variable called at runtime), which is used by static wrapper methods such as `GetConfigurationSettingValue` and `IsAvailable`.

When the `RoleEnvironment` class initializes, a callback is created between the `RoleHost` and the `RoleEnvironment` runtime instance. If any configuration changes are made on the Azure portal and propagated to the VM, the `RoleHost` invokes the callback and notifies the web role that some configuration has changed. This callback mechanism is created across a named pipe. Figure 5.4 shows the communication between your application and the role host.

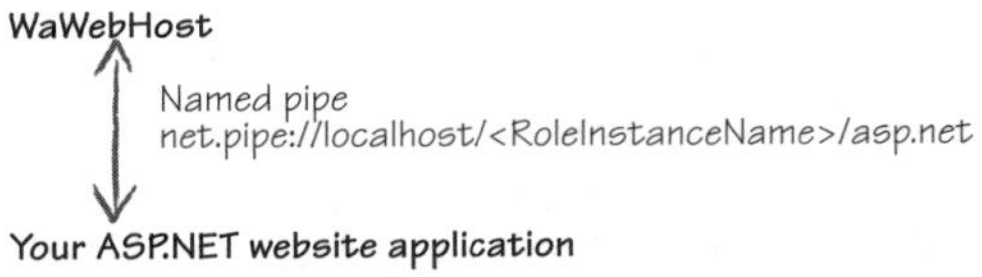

Figure 5.4 Named-pipe communication between the web role host and the service runtime

If the application isn't running in the fabric, then the `Initialize` method is never called; the singleton instance is null. `RoleEnvironment.IsAvailable` checks whether that singleton object is null.

So what happens under the hood when `RoleEnvironment.GetConfigurationSettingValue` is called? The `GetConfigurationSettingValue` static method is calling `GetConfigurationSettings` on an instance of `InteropRoleManager` to retrieve the value. Any changes to the configuration are propagated via a callback over the named pipe. In this way, any configuration settings can be retrieved quickly from an in-memory copy of the configuration settings that were populated as part of the `AcceptConfigurationChanges` callback.

5.6 Summary

In this chapter, we looked at the final piece of the service model puzzle, configuration. You should now fully understand the service model of Windows Azure and be able to effectively define and configure your service inside and outside Windows Azure. With this knowledge, you should understand the effect of the service model and how it applies to your application.

The service configuration file (ServiceConfiguration.cscfg) stores your dynamic configuration settings. You can change the settings in this file without redeploying your role. You configure the most important piece of information in Windows Azure, the number of instances for your role, in this file. We also looked at configuring certificate information and how to dynamically change these settings at runtime.

Comparing conventional ASP.NET applications with Windows Azure applications is a good way to think about how to define, configure, and dynamically modify your runtime configuration settings. Using its `ConfigurationSettings` functionality, Windows Azure can read application settings from the web.config file. A better way to read those settings is to use the `RoleEnvironment` class.

Sharing code between applications running in Windows Azure and other applications not running in the cloud is just a matter of using the `RoleEnvironment.GetConfigurationSettingValue` method to share your configuration settings. Alternatively, you can use the IoC pattern to achieve the same outcome.

We explained the internals of the `RoleEnvironment` class as exposed via the `ServiceRuntime` class. The `RoleEnvironment.IsAvailable` class works in both Azure and non-Azure environments, but you can't use the class `RoleEnvironment.GetConfigurationSettingValue` outside Azure (because there's no named-pipe interface in a non-Azure environment). There's no performance hit involved when you use the `RoleEnvironment` class because all data is cached in memory.

With all your newly gained knowledge, it's time to move on. We're going to enlighten you as to the mysteries and wonders of web roles.

Part 3

Running your site with web roles

By now, you should know that Azure supports two types of server templates, called *roles*. This part dives super deep into web roles.

Chapter 6 discusses how to scale your web roles for performance reasons. Chapter 7 shows you how to run non-.NET code, like PHP, Ruby, Java, and so on. We also uncover all sorts of code dark magic, like spawning processes and threads, and calling native code.

6 Scaling web roles

This chapter covers

- What happens to your web server under extreme load
- Scaling your web role
- The load balancer
- Session management
- Caching

One of the coolest things about Windows Azure is that you can dynamically scale your application. Whenever you need more computing power, you can just ask for it and get it (as long as you can afford it). The downside is that in order to harness such power, you need to design your application correctly. In this chapter, we'll look at what happens when your application is under pressure and how you can use Windows Azure to effectively scale your web application.

6.1 What happens to your web server under extreme load?

Back in chapter 1, we talked about the challenges of handling and predicting growth for typical websites. In this section, we want to show you what happens to a web server when it's under extreme load and how it handles itself. Using the Ashton

Kutcher example from chapter 1, what would happen to your web server if Ashton Kutcher twittered about your little Hawaiian Shirt Shop and you suddenly found thousands of users trying to access your website at the same time?

In an ideal world, if your website (or service) reached its maximum operating capacity, all other requests would be queued and the application could handle the load at a graceful, yet throttled, rate. In the real world, your website is likely to explode into a ball of flames because the web server will continue to attempt to process all requests (regardless of the rate at which they occur). The processing time of the requests will increase, which results in a longer response time to the client. Eventually, the server will become flooded with requests and it won't be able to service those requests anymore. The server is effectively rendered useless until the requests reduce in volume.

In this section, we'll look at how a web server performs both under normal and extreme load by doing the following:

- Building a sample application that can run under extreme load
- Building an application that can simulate extreme load on your web server
- Looking at how your sample application responds when the server is under load
- Increasing the ability to process requests by scaling up or out

To do all this you need to build a small ASP.NET web page sample application that you can use in all these scenarios.

6.1.1 Web server under normal load

The web page that you're about to build will perform an AJAX poll that returns the time a request was made. Under normal operation, the page should return the current server time every 5 seconds. Figure 6.1 shows this AJAX web page adequately handling the load during normal operation.

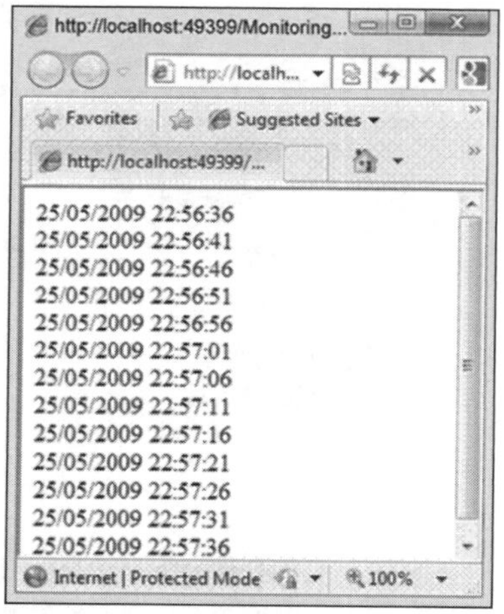

Figure 6.1 An ASP.NET web page making an AJAX request and returning the server time every 5 seconds

Let's take a look at how you can build this web page. The following listing gives the code for the ASP.NET AJAX web poll shown in figure 6.1.

Listing 6.1 AJAX poll web form

```
<asp:ScriptManager ID="ScriptManager1" runat="server" />
<asp:UpdatePanel   ID="RequestsPanel" runat="server"
                   UpdateMode="Always">
   <ContentTemplate>
      <asp:Timer ID="Timer1" runat="server"
                 Interval="5000" OnTick="Timer1_Tick" />
      <asp:Label ID="resultLabel" runat="server" />
   </ContentTemplate>
</asp:UpdatePanel>
```

❶ Normal AJAX panel makes easy screen updates

❷ Timer refreshes the panel

❸ Label contains date output

At ❶ is a standard ASP.NET AJAX update panel that contains a timer ❷, which is set to poll the web server every 5 seconds. When the timer expires, the `resultLabel` ❸ is concatenated with the current date and time using the following code:

```
protected void Timer1_Tick(object sender, EventArgs e)
{
   resultLabel.Text += DateTime.Now.ToString() + " <br/>";
}
```

So far, everything is fine and dandy. Let's now try to simulate what would happen if your server came under extreme load.

6.1.2 Simulating extreme load

To simulate extreme load, you're going to build a web page that will put your server on an extreme diet (you're going to starve it). You'll build an ASP.NET web form that will send the current thread to sleep for 10 seconds. If you then make enough requests to your web server, you should starve the thread pool, making your website behave like a server under extreme load.

THE LONG-RUNNING WEB PAGE

The following code shows the markup for your empty ASP.NET page:

```
<form id="form1" runat="server">
  <div>There is no need for any code in this sample</div>
</form>
```

This code is for a simple web page; you don't need your web page to display anything exciting. You just need the code-behind for your page to simulate a long-running request by sending the current thread to sleep for 10 seconds, as shown below:

```
protected void Page_Load(object sender, EventArgs e)
{
   Thread.Sleep(10000);
}
```

Now that you have a web page that simulates long-running requests, you need to put your web server under extreme load by hammering it with requests.

HAMMERING YOUR LONG-RUNNING WEB PAGE WITH LOTS OF REQUESTS

To simulate lots of users accessing your website, create a new console application that will spawn 100 threads. Each thread will make 30 asynchronous calls to your new web page.

> **NOTE** Your mileage might vary! You might need to increase the number of threads or calls to effectively hammer the web server.

The following listing shows the code for the console application.

Listing 6.2 Console application code for simulating extreme load

```
static void Main(string[] args)
{
```

```
   Console.WriteLine("Creating 100 threads");
   var webAddress =
      new Uri("http://localhost:49399/Monitoring/CPUThrash.aspx");   <-- 1 Defines the URI
for (int i = 0; i < 100; i++)
{
   var t1 = new System.Threading.Thread                              <-- 2 Defines the thread
   ( () =>
     {
        for (int j = 0; j < 30; j++)
        {
          WebClient client = new WebClient();
          client.DownloadStringAsync(webAddress);                    <-- 3 Calls the page
        }
     }
   );

   t1.Start();                                                       <-- 4 Spawns the thread
}

Console.ReadKey();
}
```

In listing 6.2, you define the URI of your long-running web page at ❶. Then you iterate through a loop 100 times, creating a new thread at ❷, which you'll spawn at ❹. You'll spawn 100 threads.

Each thread will execute the code defined at ❷ within the lambda expression. This thread will loop 30 times, making an asynchronous request to the web page at ❸. In the end, you should be making around 300 simultaneous requests to your website. How is the web server going to perform?

6.1.3 How the web server responds under extreme load

In figure 6.1, you saw the response time of a simple AJAX website being polled every 5 seconds under normal load. In that example, there were no real issues and the page was served up with ease.

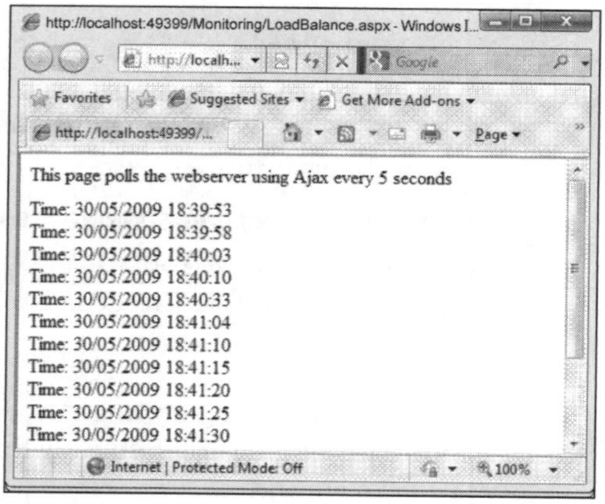

Figure 6.2 AJAX poll under extreme load (running at the same time as your console application)

Figure 6.2 shows that same web application, this time coughing and spluttering as it struggles to cope with the simulated extreme load. The extreme load that this page is suffering from is the result of running your console application (listing 6.2) at the same time as your polling application.

Figure 6.2 shows that your polling web page is no longer consistently taking 5 seconds to return a result. At one point (between 18:40:33 and 18:41:04), it took more than 20 seconds to return the result. This type of response is typical of a web server under extreme load. Because the web server is under extreme load, it attempts to service all requests at once until it's so loaded that it can't effectively service any requests. What you need to do now is scale out your application.

6.1.4 Handling increased requests by scaling up or out

If you're hitting the limits of a single instance, then you should consider hosting your website across multiple instances for those busy periods (you can always scale back down when you're not busy). Let's take a quick look at how you can do that manually in Windows Azure.

SCALING OUT

By default, a Windows Azure web role is configured to run in a single instance. If you want to manually set the number of instances that your web role is configured to run on, set the `instances count` value in your service configuration file in the following way:

```
<WebRole name="MyWebRole"
  <Instances count="1" />
  <ConfigurationSettings />
</WebRole>
```

This configuration shows that your web role is configured to run in a single instance. If you need to increase the number of active web roles to two, you could just modify that value from `1` to `2`:

```
<Instances count="2" />
```

Because the number of instances that a web role should run on is stored in the service configuration file, you can modify the configured value via the Azure Service portal at runtime. For more information about how to modify the service configuration file at runtime, see chapter 5.

Scaling out automatically

If you don't fancy increasing your web role instances manually, but you want to take advantage of the ability to increase and decrease the number of instances depending on the load, you can do this automatically by using Windows Azure APIs.

You can use the diagnostics API to monitor the number of requests, CPU usage, and so on. Then, if you hit a threshold, use the service management APIs to increase the number of instances of your web role.

Alternatively, you could increase or decrease the number of instances, based on the time of day, using a model derived from your web logs. For example, you could run one instance between 3:00 a.m. and 4:00 a.m., but run four instances between 7:00 p.m. and 9:00 p.m. To use this kind of schedule, you create a Windows Scheduler job to call the service management API at those times.

In chapter 15, we'll look at how you can automatically scale worker roles. The techniques used in that chapter also apply to scaling web roles.

You've increased the number of instances that host your web role. Now, if you were to rerun your AJAX polling sample and your console application, you would see your polling application responding every 5 seconds as if it were under normal load (rather than taking 30 seconds or so to respond).

Scaling out your web role is great if you designed your application to use this method, but what if you didn't think that far ahead? Well, then, you can scale it up.

SCALING UP

Uh-oh. You didn't design your application to scale out. Maybe your application has an affinity to a particular instance of a web role (it uses in-process sessions, in-memory caches, or the like); in that case, you might not be able to scale out your web role instance. What you can do is run your web application on a bigger box by modifying the `vmsize` value in the service definition file:

```
<WebRole name="MyWebRole" vmsize="Medium">
```

By default, the web role is hosted on a small VM that has 1 GB of memory and one CPU core. In the example above, you've upgraded your web role to run under a medium VM, which means that your web role has an extra CPU core and more memory. For full details about the available VM sizes, see chapter 3, section 3.4.4.

By increasing the size of the VM, your ASP.NET AJAX web polling application should be able to handle the extreme load being placed on the server (or at least process requests a little quicker).

> **Try to avoid scaling up and scale out instead**
>
> Although scaling up will get you out a hole, it's not an effective long-term strategy. Wherever possible, you should scale out rather than up. At the end of the day, when you scale up, you can only scale up to the largest VM size (and no further). Even that might not be enough for your most extreme needs.
>
> Also, it's not easy to dynamically scale your application up and down, based on load. Scaling out requires only a change to the service configuration file. Scaling up requires you to upgrade your application (because it requires a change to the service definition file).

Now you understand what happens when your server is placed under extreme load and how to effectively handle that situation by scaling your application. What you need to know now is how requests are distributed across multiple web role instances via the load balancer.

6.2 How the load balancer distributes requests

In this section, we'll look at how the load balancer distributes requests across multiple servers and how it reacts under failover conditions. In the end, you'll understand how your application will react and behave when you use multiple instances of your web role.

We're going to look at two load balancers: the development fabric load balancer and the production load balancer. Before we do that, you're going to build a sample application to demonstrate the effects of the load balancer coordinating requests between multiple servers.

6.2.1 Multi-instance sample application

The sample application that you're about to build is a web page that consists of a label that displays the name of the web server that processed the request, and a button that posts back to the server when it's clicked. Every time the page is loaded (either on first load or when the button is clicked), the page writes a message to the diagnostic log. Figure 6.3 shows the web page and its log output in the development fabric.

Now we'll walk you through the steps of creating this simple web role so that you'll be able to be able to see the kind of output shown in figure 6.3.

CREATE THE WEB PAGE

To build the sample application shown in figure 6.3, create a new ASP.NET web role (if you're unsure how to do this, refer to chapter 1). In the web role project that you just created, add a new ASP.NET web page called MultipleInstances.aspx.

Before you can run this web page, you must enable native execution in your service definition file in your Cloud Service project:

```
<WebRole name="MyWebRole"
         enableNativeCodeExecution="true">
```

THE ASPX MARKUP

Now that you've added the page, add the following markup in MultipleInstances.aspx:

```
<div>
   Machine Name: <asp:Label ID="lblMachineName" runat="server" />
</div>
<asp:Button ID="btnClickMe" runat="server" Text="Click Me"/>
```

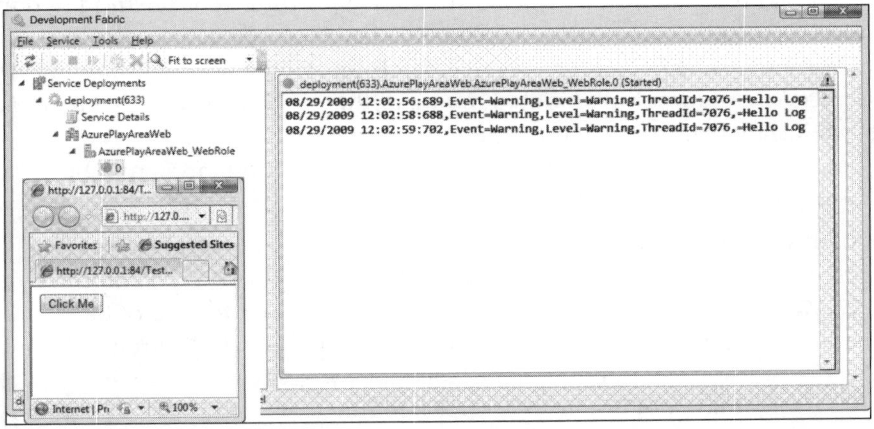

Figure 6.3 A single instance of your web role running in the development fabric, writing out to the diagnostic log

This code represents the page displayed in figure 6.3. There's a label that displays the name of the machine and a button that will post back to the web server when it's clicked.

THE CODE-BEHIND

If you look at figure 6.3, you can see that each time the page is loaded, the name of the web server that processed the request is displayed. To display the web server name that's in the `lblMachineName` label, add the following code to the `Page_Load` event of the ASP.NET page:

```
var computer = new Microsoft.VisualBasic.Devices.Computer();
lblMachineName.Text = Environment.MachineName;
```

Finally, in order to write some data to the log as shown in figure 6.3, you need to write a message to the log on page load. Add the following code to the `Page_Load` event of the ASP.NET page:

```
System.Diagnostics.Trace.WriteLine("Hello Log");
```

Now, fire up the application in the development fabric. You'll see a message written to the log displayed in the development fabric UI every time the page is loaded.

Great! You've got your application working. Now let's go back and take a look at how the load balancers route requests.

6.2.2 *The development fabric load balancer*

In typical ASP.NET web farms, it's not easy to simulate the load balancing of requests. With Windows Azure, a development version of the load balancer is provided so you can simulate the effects of the real load balancer. The development fabric load balancer helps you find and debug any potential issues that you might have in your development environment (yep, there's a debugger, too). So let's take a look at how the development fabric load balancer behaves.

If you were to fire up your web application in the development fabric with two web roles configured, you would notice two instances of your web role displayed in the UI. Similar to the live production system, the development fabric distributes requests between the instances of your web role. Each time someone clicks the button on the web page, the request is distributed to one of the web role instances. Figure 6.4 shows the two instances of the web role in the development fabric UI.

You can see two instances of your web role in the development fabric, but how is this represented on your development machine?

MULTIPLE INSTANCES OF WAWEBHOST.EXE

In chapter 4, you discovered that Windows Azure hosts the IIS 7.0 runtime in-process in the WaWebHost.exe process using the Hostable Web Core feature of IIS 7.0 rather than using the default w3wp.exe process. Because your web application is hosted by the WaWebHost.exe process, multiple instances of WaWebHost.exe are instantiated if you increase the number of instances of your web role that need to be hosted (one process

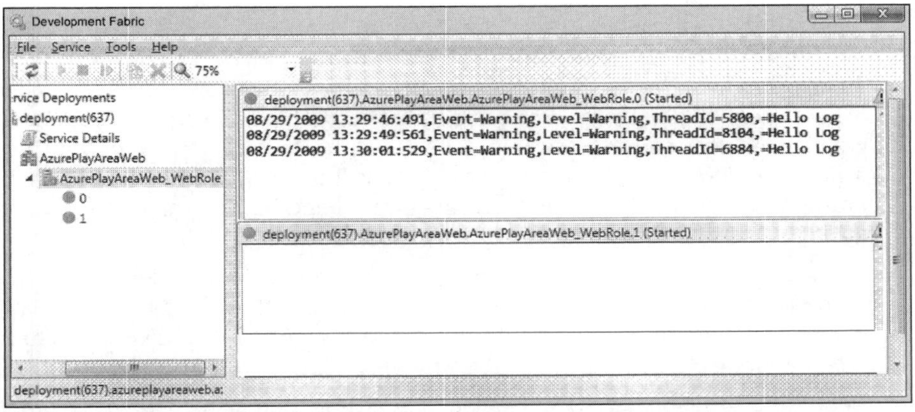

Figure 6.4 Multiple instances of the web role in the development fabric

per instance is instantiated). Figure 6.5 shows the process list of a development machine when it's running multiple instances of the web role.

In figure 6.5 there are two instances of `WaWebHost` in the Processes list, one per web role instance.

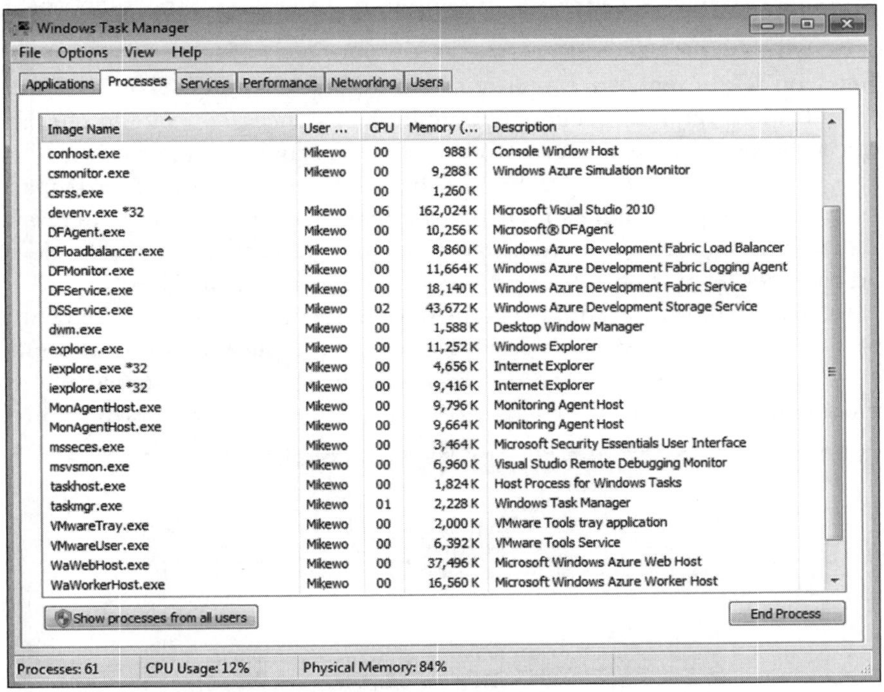

Figure 6.5 Multiple instances of `WaWebHost` shown in the Processes list

> **Development fabric load balancer process**
>
> To help simulate the live production environment, the Windows Azure SDK includes a development load balancer that's used to simulate the hardware load balancers that run in the Windows Azure data centers. Without the development fabric load balancer, it would be difficult to simulate issues that occur across multiple requests (you can't attach a debugger in the live production environment, but you can in the development environment).
>
> The process that simulates the load balancer in the development fabric is called DFLoadBalancer.exe, which is shown in figure 6.5. All HTTP requests that you make in the development fabric are sent to this process first and then distributed to the appropriate `WaWebHost` instance of the web role.
>
> If you were to kill one of the `WaWebHost` instances, then all requests made to the development fabric load balancer would be redistributed to the other instance of `WaWebHost`; the other `WaWebHost` process would be automatically restarted. By performing this test, you can simulate what will happen to your application if there's a hardware or software failure in the live environment.
>
> If you were to kill your DFLoadBalancer.exe process, the entire development fabric on your machine would be shut down and would require restarting.

TESTING WITH MULTIPLE BROWSER INSTANCES

When you're testing your application in the development fabric to see how it responds when requests occur across multiple instances, you should check that your requests haven't just been processed by a single instance of the process.

In the development fabric, the load balancer tends to favor a particular instance (per browser request) unless that role is under load. If you look at figure 6.4, you'll see that although there are two instances of your web role running, the development load balancer seems to be routing all traffic to a single instance.

Because each browser window in the development fabric tends to have affinity with a particular web role instance, you should test your application using multiple browser instances. Figure 6.6 shows the outcome of a test in which both instances of the web role are being used by alternately clicking the button in two different browser instances.

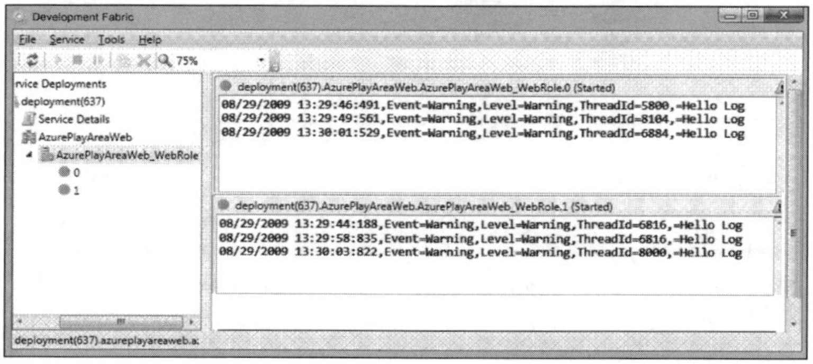

Figure 6.6 Multiple instances of the web role with requests distributed

Now that two different web pages are running, the requests are distributed across both instances of the development fabric.

Although spinning up multiple instances of your web application with multiple browser instances will allow you to test, in your development fabric, that your application will work with multiple roles, it won't test the effects of requests being redistributed to another server. To test that your application behaves as expected in your development fabric when running multiple instances, there are two things that you can do: you can restart one of the `WaWebHost` instances, or you can test your application under load.

RESTARTING THE WAWEBHOST INSTANCE

Although the development fabric load balancer creates affinity between your process and an instance of `WaWebHost`, if you kill that `WaWebHost` instance, the affinity is broken. When the affinity is broken, the request is redistributed to another instance of `WaWebHost`, which creates a new affinity between the web browser and that instance of the web role. Figure 6.7 shows the changing of affinity between a browser and a web role instance when a WaWebHost.exe process is killed.

In the example shown in figure 6.7, two instances of the web role are running (instance 0 and instance 1), and there's a single web browser. Instance 1 didn't process any requests prior to the restarting of the WaWebHost.exe process of instance 0; the browser had affinity with instance 0. When instance 0 was restarted, instance 1 then processed all incoming requests and instance 0 no longer processed any requests from the browser because a new affinity was created.

This test is fairly important for you to perform in the development fabric. Restarting one of your `WaWebHost` instances helps to ensure that your application can truly run against multiple instances of your web role and can recover from a disaster. We'll look at these situations in more detail when we look at session, cache, and local storage later in this chapter.

TESTING UNDER LOAD

The second way to test that your application behaves correctly when it's redistributed to multiple instances is to test your application under load. The best method of testing

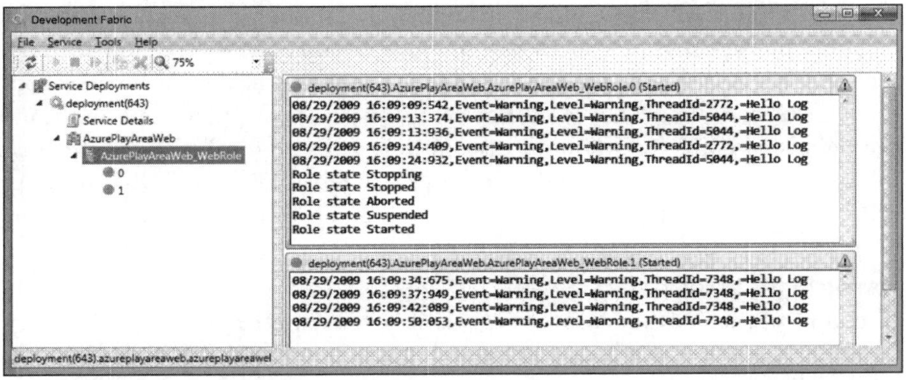

Figure 6.7 Changing of affinity between browser and web role host in the development fabric

this scenario is to use a load testing tool such as Visual Studio Team System Web Load Tester. If you want to ensure that the development fabric load balancer redistributes requests under load, you can simulate this by modifying the sample application that you built earlier. Now, you're going to simulate load by sending the thread to sleep for 10 seconds on page load. You can do this by modifying your `Page_Load` event to include the following code:

```
Thread.Sleep(10000);
```

If you were to now spin up multiple instances of your web page, you would see that as the result of the increase in load, the development fabric load balancer doesn't maintain affinity and starts redistributing the requests more evenly.

Asynchronous AJAX requests

Although the development fabric load balancer keeps affinity between your browser instance and a web role (unless under load), it tends to redistribute requests evenly when performing AJAX requests.

In section 6.1, you created an ASP.NET AJAX web page that asynchronously calls the backend web page every 5 seconds and displays the name of the server that processed the request. If you modify that sample to write to the log, the development fabric load balancer evenly distributes the request, rather than maintaining affinity with a particular web role instance.

Now that you have an understanding of how the development fabric load balancer behaves and how you can effectively test how your application will behave in failover situations, let's look at how things happen in the live environment.

6.2.3 *Load balancing in the live environment*

We've spent quite a bit of time looking at the development fabric load balancer. Hopefully you have a good understanding of how the load balancer works and how it interacts with multiple instances of your web role. Although the development fabric load balancer doesn't behave exactly like the load balancer in the real environment, there are some tricks that you can do to ensure that your application will behave correctly in the live environment. That said, there are some cases in which your application might not behave as expected when it's distributed across physical servers, which isn't something you can easily test for in the development fabric. To ensure that your application will behave correctly prior to making your application live, you'll need to perform some testing in the staging environment.

TESTING IN THE STAGING ENVIRONMENT

In chapter 2, we showed you how to deploy your application to the staging environment and how to move your staging web application to the production environment via the Windows Azure portal. In that chapter, you also learned that when you switch

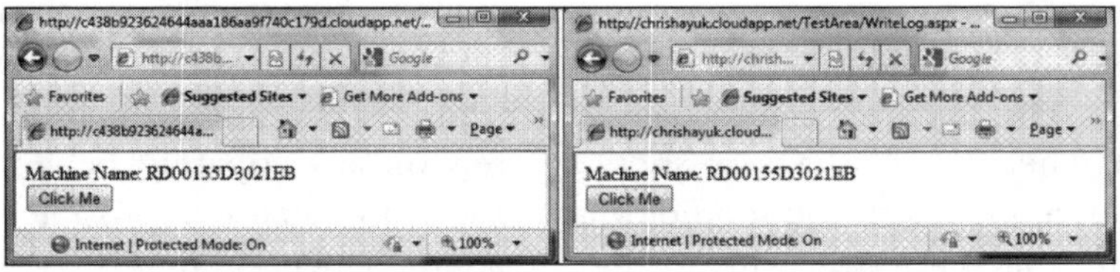

Figure 6.8 Your web application running in the staging environment (left) and in the production environment (right)

your application from staging to production, the application continues to run on the same server as before and the load balancers simply redirect traffic to the correct servers. If you want to, you can prove this by deploying the sample that you built earlier in this chapter to the staging environment (noting the machine name) and then switching over to the production environment (noting the machine name once again). Figure 6.8 shows your application running in the staging environment and in the live environment.

In figure 6.8, the browser on the left is pointed to the staging environment and is running on machine RD00155D3021EB. The browser on the right is your web application running in production after the switchover. Notice that your application is still running on the same server even though you're now running in production (rather than in staging).

Because the staging servers will eventually become the production servers, you should be able to iron out, during your staging testing phase, any errors that might occur when you're running multiple instances of your web role.

Nothing beats production environments

You can't always be sure that an application that works in your development environment will work in your staging environment. On your development machine, `WaWebHost` runs under your user account; anything you can do, it can do. That's not necessarily true with the production servers.

STAGING AND PRODUCTION LOAD BALANCERS

If you modify your ASP.NET web polling application from section 6.1 to display the machine name, and then run it in the staging environment, you get a result that's similar to what's shown in figure 6.9.

The requests are distributed between two different servers, which is great news.

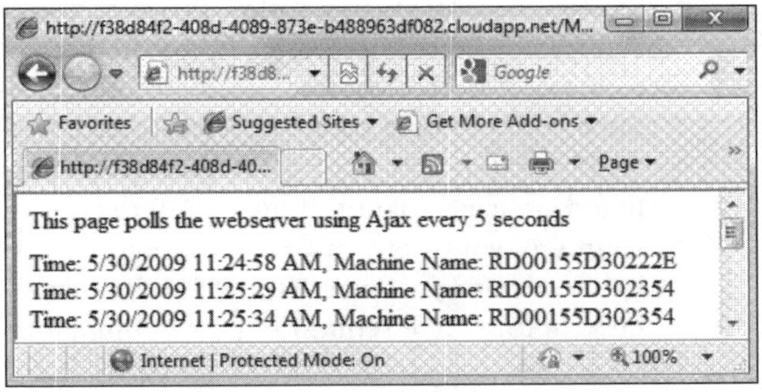

Figure 6.9 Web roles running in the staging environment

You can be sure that the staging environment will host each instance of your web role on a separate physical machine (a test that you can't perform in your development environment). This behavior could change over time, as Windows Azure matures and is expanded. The point is that you shouldn't rely on any apparent behavior when designing your application. You should design it to be as stateless as possible, with the understanding that successive trips to the server won't necessarily always go to the same server.

> **Quirky affinitization**
>
> Both the staging and the production environments can be a little quirky in how they distribute requests between servers. In some instances, requests will be evenly distributed between all servers (for example, AJAX requests are distributed this way), but generally both environments will maintain affinity between a connection and a web role. If you're testing whether your application works with multiple instances of your web role, you should capture the machine name in your request to ensure that your server can handle requests distributed across instances. Then run your sample applications in both the staging and production environments and monitor how the machine name changes.

INDUCING FAILOVER

In the development fabric, you tested how your application handles failover by killing the WaWebHost.exe process and then monitoring the application's behavior. If you need to, you can perform the same test in the staging and production environments. In the live environment, the web role is also hosted in a process called WaWebHost.exe, so you can kill the process on the live environment using the following command (remember that native execution must be enabled for this to work):

```
System.Diagnostics.Process.GetProcessesByName("WaWebHost").First().Kill();
```

Create a new web page with a button that will execute the above command when it's clicked. Then you can run the AJAX polling application in one browser, kill the `WaWebHost` process in another browser, and watch how the load balancer handles the redirection of traffic. Typically, on the live system (at the time of writing), all traffic is redirected to the single node. When the FC is convinced that the failed role is behaving again, the load balancer starts to direct requests to that server.

If you want to test what happens when all roles are killed, you can execute the command on each role until they're all dead. If no web roles are running in the live environment, your web application won't process requests anymore and your end user will be faced with an error. Typically, your service will be automatically restarted and will be able to service requests again within about a minute.

That's how requests are load balanced across multiple web roles. Now let's take a look at those aspects of a website that are generally affected when running with multiple roles, namely:

- Session management
- Caching
- Local storage

Let's start with session management.

6.3 Session management

HTTP is a stateless protocol. Each HTTP request is an independent call that has no knowledge of state from any previous requests. Using sessions is one method of persisting data so that it can be accessed across multiple requests. In ASP.NET, you can use the following methods of persisting data across requests:

- Sessions
- `ViewState`
- Cookies
- Application state
- Profile
- Database

Throughout the course of this chapter (and future chapters), we'll be looking at the methods of persisting data that you'll use that are affected when you scale to multiple web roles. We won't look at `ViewState` or cookies in this book; these methods aren't used differently in a Windows Azure environment.

In this section, we'll look at how running Windows Azure across multiple roles affects your ASP.NET session and the different types of session providers that you can use. Specifically, we're going to talk about how a session works, and you're going to build a sample session application. We'll also discuss in-process sessions and Table storage sessions.

Although the concept of sessions is probably familiar to most of you, we want to recap the purpose of the session and the `Session` object.

6.3.1 How do sessions work?

A session is effectively a temporary store that's created server-side for a limited window of time for a particular browser instance. Your ASP.NET web application can use this temporary store to store and retrieve data throughout the course of that session.

If we go back to the Hawaiian Shirt Shop example, you can store the shopping cart in a session. Using a session as a storage area lets you store items in the cart, but still have access to the cart across multiple requests. When the session is terminated (the

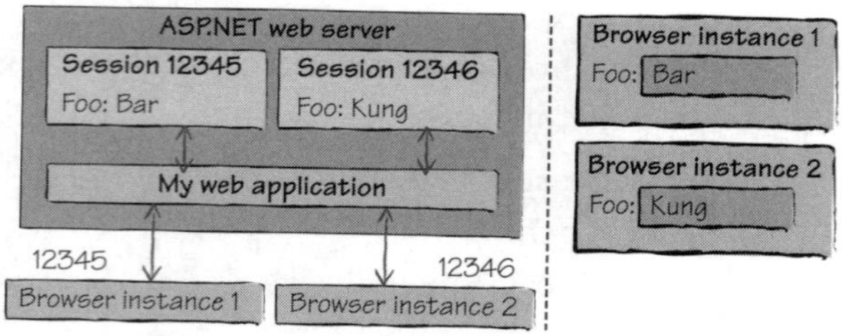

Figure 6.10 Session independence and the temporary store

user closes his browser), the session is destroyed and the data stored in the session is no longer accessible. Similarly, if the user opens a new browser instance, a new independent session is assigned to this new browser instance and it has no access to session data associated with the other browser instances (and vice versa). Figure 6.10 shows how a session is treated with respect to the browser instance and the web server.

In figure 6.10, browser instance 1 is associated with session ID 12345; the session key `Foo` has an associated value of `Bar`; browser instance 2 is associated with session ID 12346; and the session key `Foo` has an associated value of `Kung`. If you were to look at the output of browser instance 1 and browser instance 2, they would display the correct values from their associated temporary store.

When a browser makes a request to an ASP.NET website, it passes a session ID in a cookie as part of the request. This session ID is used to marry the request to a session store. For example, in figure 6.10, browser instance 1 has a session ID of 12345 and browser instance 2 has a session ID of 12346. If no session ID is passed in the request, then a new session is created and that session ID is passed back to the browser in the response, to be used by future requests.

If you need to be able to access data beyond a browser session, then you should consider a more permanent storage mechanism such as Table storage or the SQL Azure Database.

Now that we've reminded you how sessions work in ASP.NET, you're going to build a small sample application that you can use to demonstrate the effects of using sessions on your web applications in Windows Azure.

6.3.2 Sample session application

To get started, you need a web page where you can store a value in the session for later retrieval. Add this new ASP.NET web page, called SessionAdd.aspx, to an ASP.NET web role project. Add the following markup to the page:

```
<asp:TextBox ID="txtSessionText" Text="" runat="server"/>
<asp:Button ID="btnAdd" Text="Add"
            runat="server" onclick="btnAdd_Click"/>
```

The markup shows that the page consists of a text box and a button. Use the following code to set the value of the session key `Foo` to what the text box contains when the button is clicked:

```
protected void btnAdd_Click(object sender, EventArgs e)
{
   Session["Foo"] = txtSessionText.Text;
}
```

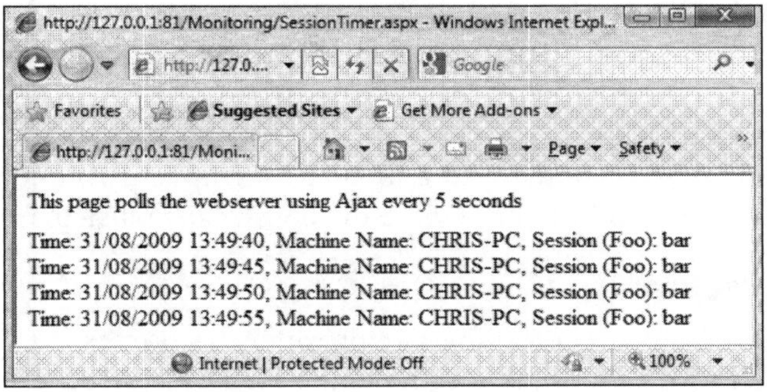

Figure 6.11 Session timer page. Notice that your session is maintained for each request.

Now that you can store some session data in your page, you need a page that you can use to display whatever is stored in `Foo`. For this example, you'll use an ASP.NET AJAX polling timer (similar to the one that you used earlier) that will display whatever is stored in `Foo` every 5 seconds. Figure 6.11 shows how this web page looks (prior to running this page, we used the SessionAdd.aspx page to set the value of `Foo` to `bar`).

To create the page displayed in figure 6.11, add a new ASP.NET page to the project called SessionTimer.aspx that contains the following markup:

```
<div>
   <asp:ScriptManager ID="ScriptManager1" runat="server" />

   <div style="padding-bottom: 10px;">
      This page polls the webserver using Ajax every 5 seconds
   </div>

   <div>
      <asp:UpdatePanel ID="RequestsPanel"
                       runat="server"
                       UpdateMode="Always">
            <ContentTemplate>
               <asp:Label ID="lblResult" runat="server" />
                  <asp:Timer ID="Timer1"
                             runat="server"
                             Interval="5000"
                             OnTick="Timer1_Tick" />
         </ContentTemplate>
      </asp:UpdatePanel>
   </div>
</div>
```

To display the result of `Foo` in the web page, add the following code-behind to the SessionTimer.aspx page:

```
protected void Timer1_Tick(object sender, EventArgs e)
{

   lblResult.Text +=
      string.Format("Time: {0}, Machine Name: {1}, Session (Foo):{2}<br/>",
      ➥ DateTime.Now.ToString(), Environment.MachineName,
      ➥ Session["Foo"] as string);
}
```

Every 5 seconds the SessionTimer.aspx page makes an AJAX request back to the web server where the request is logged. Then, the name of the computer, the time of the request, and the value stored in the session for `Foo` is returned, all of which is then displayed in the SessionAdd.aspx page.

Using this sample, you can see in both the development and live environments which machine processed the request and what the value of `Foo` is at any particular time.

6.3.3 In-process session management

By default, ASP.NET uses an in-process session state provider to store session data. The in-process session state provider stores all session data in memory that's scoped to the web worker process (`w3wp` in standard web servers, or `WaWebHost` in Windows Azure). Let's see how this session provider works.

KILLING YOUR SESSION BY KILLING WAWEBHOST

If the worker process were to be restarted, you would lose any session data because that data is stored in memory. You can simulate this situation in your development environment using your SessionTimer page.

> **TIP** Before you attempt to lose your session, ensure that your ASP.NET web role is running with a single instance.

Go ahead and fire up the SessionAdd.aspx page that you created earlier and set the value of `Foo` to `bar`. After you set this value, open SessionTimer.aspx in the same browser instance. Let the `session` value display a few times and then kill the `WaWebHost` process. As you discovered earlier, if you kill the `WaWebHost` process, the development fabric automatically restarts the process, but all session data is lost. Figure 6.12 shows the result of killing the process.

In figure 6.12, `bar` was displayed up until 13:49:55; just after that point, you killed the `WaWebHost` process. From that point on, the session was lost and no data was returned for all other requests.

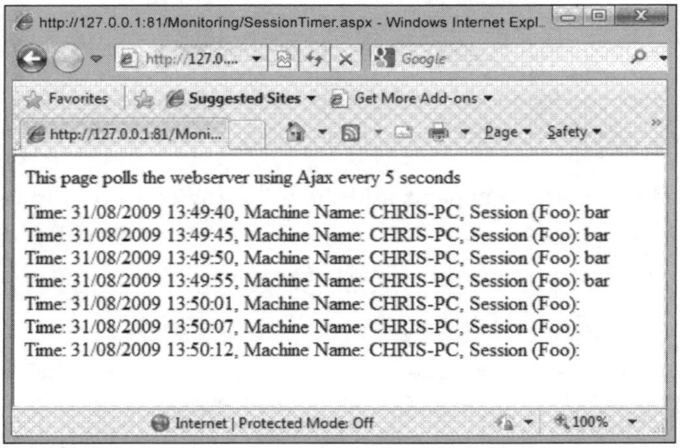

Figure 6.12 Killing the web role that's using in-process sessions

IN-PROCESS SESSION STATE WITH MULTIPLE INSTANCES OF THE WEB ROLE

There are some issues with using the in-process session provider in Windows Azure, but this one is the real killer: if you're using multiple web role instances, Windows Azure doesn't consistently implement sticky sessions in the production environment. Any requests made to a web role might not be routed to the same web role.

As we noted earlier, the production systems generally maintain affinity with a web role but will sometimes evenly distribute requests among roles. In the case of AJAX applications, because requests are likely to be distributed across multiple roles, an in-process session state provider can't be used; the other role won't have access to session data stored in a previous request. Figure 6.13 shows your AJAX polling application running across multiple web roles.

In figure 6.13, you can see that any request made to the first role returns the session data, but any time the request is distributed to another web role, the session data stored in the first web role is no longer accessible. When you're testing your applications in the development environment, you need to keep in mind that sticky sessions aren't always implemented by Windows Azure.

MEMORY CONSUMPTION

If at first you need to run your web role on only a single instance, then you can get better performance by running your application with in-process session management. You should consider this option if you're unconcerned that a user's session might be trashed if the web role is moved to another server (if, for example, the role instance was moved because of a hardware failure). If you need to scale out to multiple servers at a later date, you can always move to a session state provider that'll work cross multiple web roles (such as Table storage) when required.

Before you decide to run with the in-process session state provider, there's one other issue that you should be aware of. If you have a large number of users on your website and they're storing a large amount of session data, you might quickly run into `Out of Memory` exceptions. The web role host doesn't automatically free up any active

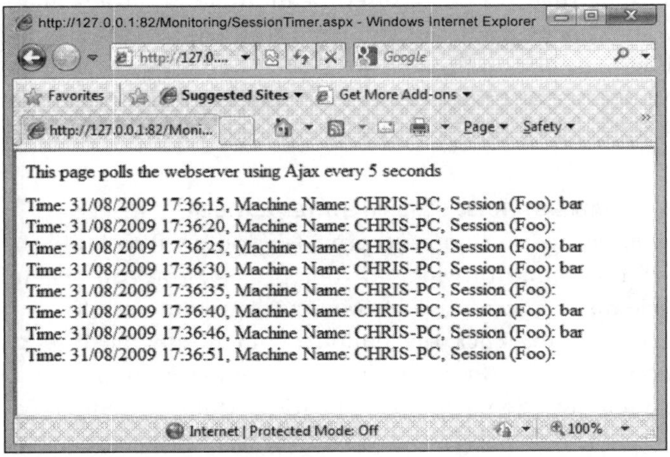

Figure 6.13 Loss of session data across multiple web role instances

session data until sessions start to expire. Remember that your VM only has 2 GB of memory allocated to it if you're running on the smallest (default) size, so you'll run out of memory quite quickly.

If you want to test how your application responds to adding a large amount of session data, you can modify the SessionAdd.aspx page to include a button that will add a large amount of data to the session when clicked. Add the following markup to your SessionAdd.aspx page:

```
<asp:Button ID="btnLarge" Text="Large"
            runat="server" onclick="btnLarge_Click"/>
```

The following code will add a lot of data to the session when the button is clicked:
protected void btnLarge_Click(object sender, EventArgs e)

```
{
   StringBuilder sb = new StringBuilder();

   for (int i = 0; i < 100000; i++)
   {
      sb.Append("Hello World");
   }

   for (int i = 0;  i < 10; i++)
      Session[Guid.NewGuid().ToString()] = sb.ToString();
}
```

By repeatedly clicking this new button on your website, you'll find that the memory usage of your WaWebHost.exe process increases until you start getting `Out of Memory` exceptions.

> **NOTE** In Windows Azure, the state server, or out-of-process session state provider, isn't supported.

6.3.4 *Table-storage session state sample provider*

To maintain a session state that can be accessed by multiple web roles that can have requests evenly distributed between them, you need to use a persistence mechanism that can be accessed by all web roles. In typical ASP.NET web farms, SQL Server is typically used, mainly because ASP.NET has a built-in provider that supports it.

There's a sample online for a Table-storage session state provider that you can use in your ASP.NET web applications.

GETTING STARTED WITH THE TABLE-STORAGE SESSION STATE PROVIDER

To start using the Table-storage session state provider, you need to build the sample provider and then reference that provider in your project. You can get the sample provider at http://code.msdn.microsoft.com/windowsazuresamples.

To build the project, double-click the buildme.cmd file in the directory. After you've built the sample project, add a reference to the assembly in your web role project. Because the Table-storage session state provider is implemented as a custom provider, you'll need to modify your web.config file to include the provider in the system.web settings:

```
<sessionState mode="Custom"
              customProvider="TableStorageSessionStateProvider">
   <providers>
      <clear/>
         <add name="TableStorageSessionStateProvider"
type="Microsoft.Samples.ServiceHosting.AspProviders
➥ .TableStorageSessionStateProvider"
             allowInsecureRemoteEndpoints="false"
             accountName="devstoreaccount1"
             sharedKey="Eby8vdM02xNOcqFlqUwJPLlmEtlCDXJ1
             ➥ OUzFT50uSRZ6IFsuFq2UVErCz4I6tq/K1SZFPTOtr/KBHBeksoGMGw=="
             containerName="sessionstate"
             applicationName="ProviderTest"
             blobServiceBaseUri="http://127.0.0.1:10000/devstoreaccount1"
             tableServiceBaseUri="http://127.0.0.1:10002/devstoreaccount2"
             sessionTableName="Sessions" />

   </providers>
</sessionState>
```

The above configuration is for using the Table-storage and BLOB-storage providers in the development fabric. The creation of the appropriate tables in the Table-storage account is automatically taken care of for you by the provider. On deployment of your application, you'll need to modify web.config to use your live Table-storage account.

If you now run your application in either the development fabric or the live environment, you'll find that you can store and retrieve session data across multiple instances of your web role.

> **Ever-growing tables**
>
> One word of warning about the Table-storage provider: it doesn't clean up after itself with respect to expired sessions. Because Table storage is a paid, metered service, we advise you to have either a worker role, a simulated worker role (discussed later in this chapter), or a background thread that cleans up any expired sessions from the table. If you don't clean up this data, you'll be paying storage costs for data that is no longer used.

PERFORMANCE CONSIDERATIONS

Although Table storage gives you a session state that's accessible across multiple server instances in a load-balanced environment, it does incur a performance hit. To test the performance of the live system, we modified the Table-storage provider to record the time that lapsed between requesting an item from the session and retrieving a response. Because session state is reloaded from the session provider on every page load, this test will allow you to see the impact of the Table-storage session state provider

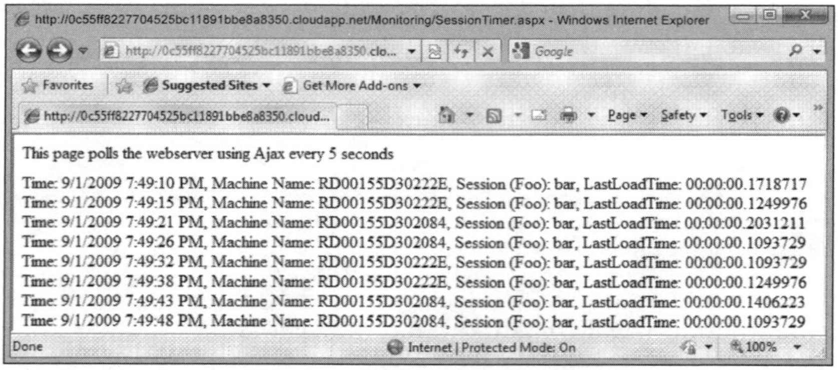

Figure 6.14 Response times of the Table-storage session state provider for a single small item

on your website. Figure 6.14 is a modified version of the SessionTimer.aspx page that you built earlier that also displays the time recorded to load the session during the page load.

You can see in figure 6.14 that although you're storing only one item in the session (`bar` in session key `foo`), it still takes somewhere between 0.1 to 0.2 seconds to retrieve the session state. This load time is probably acceptable for most applications. Table storage is a good solution for the session in Windows Azure until a more performant solution, such as a cache-based session provider, is available.

If you store a large amount of data in the session, you might find the performance of the Table-storage provider a little too slow at the moment. Figure 6.15 shows the SessionTimer.aspx page after we added a large amount of data to the session by clicking the large session button that we built earlier twice.

In figure 6.15, you can see that the performance of the session provider seriously degrades when a large amount of data is stored in the session. In this example, it took 1 to 2 seconds just to load the session. In cases when you need minimal session load times or when you're storing large amounts of data, you should consider another session provider solution (for example, SQL Azure Database or a cache-based session provider).

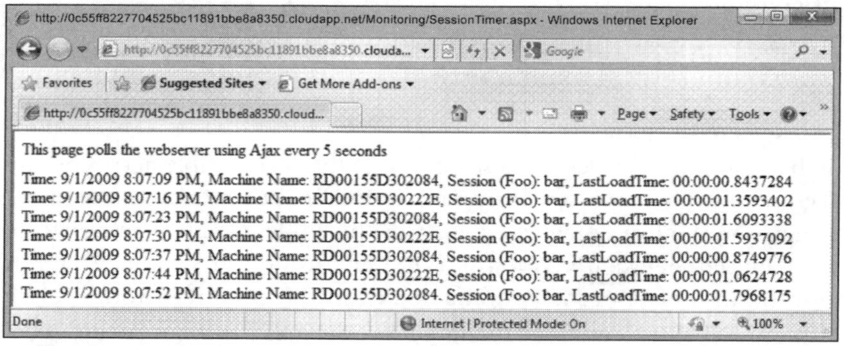

Figure 6.15 Large session state response load times using the Table-storage provider

SQL Azure session state provider

In typical ASP.NET web farms, SQL session state providers are generally used as the session provider. Although this works, it's not the best use of a SQL database; it's not querying across sessions, but rather it's acting as a central storage area.

To date, there isn't a SQL Azure session state provider available (although this could change). Rather than trying to mess with SQL Azure to make it work with sessions, it's probably best to either stick to Table storage, use a cache-based session provider, use an in-process provider, or architect your application so it's not so reliant on sessions.

6.4 Cache management

In any typical website, there's usually some element of static reference data in the system. This static reference data might never change or might change infrequently. Rather than continually querying for the same data from the database, storing the data in a cache can provide great performance benefits.

A *cache* is a temporary, in-memory store that contains duplicated data populated from a persisted backing store, such as a database. Because the cache is an in-memory data store, retrieving data from the cache is fast (compared to database retrieval). Because a cache is an in-memory temporary store, if the host process or underlying hardware dies, the cached data is lost and the cache needs to be rebuilt from its persistent store.

Never rely on data stored in a cache. You should always populate cache data from a persisted storage medium, such as Table storage, which allows you to persist back to that medium if the data isn't present in the cache.

NOTE For small sets of static reference data, a copy of the cached data resides on each server instance. Because the data resides on the actual server, there's no latency with cross-server roundtrips, resulting in the fastest possible response time.

In most systems, there are typically two layers of cache that are used: the in-process cache and the distributed cache. Let's take a look at the first and most simple type of cache you can have in Windows Azure, which is the ASP.NET in-process cache.

6.4.1 In-process caching with the ASP.NET cache

As of the PDC 2009 release, the only caching technology available to Windows Azure web roles is the built-in ASP.NET cache, which is an in-process individual-server cache. Figure 6.16 shows how the cache is related to your web role instances within Windows Azure.

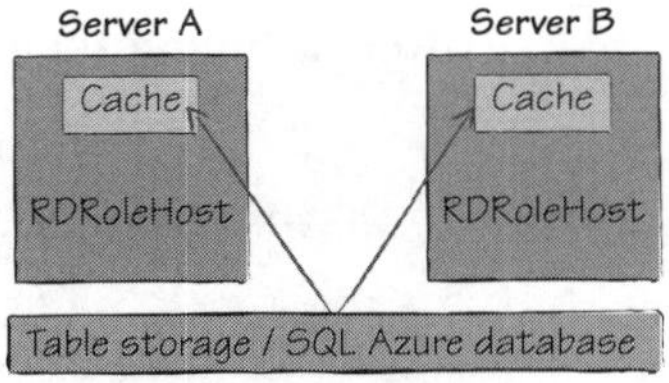

Figure 6.16 The ASP.NET cache; notice that each server maintains its own copy of the cache.

Figure 6.16 shows that both server A and server B maintain their cache of the data that's been retrieved from the data store (either from Table storage or from

SQL Azure database). Although there's some duplication of data, the performance gains make using this cache worthwhile.

In-process memory cache

You should also notice in figure 6.16 that the default ASP.NET cache is an individual-server cache that's tied to the web server worker process (`WaWebHost`). In Windows Azure, any data you cache is held in the `WaWebHost` process memory space. If you were to kill the `WaWebHost` process, the cache would be destroyed and would need to be repopulated as part of the process restart.

Because the VM has a maximum of 1 GB of memory available to the server, you should keep your server cache as lean as possible.

Although in-memory caching is suitable for static data, it's not so useful when you need to cache data across multiple load-balanced web servers. To make that scenario possible, we need to turn to a distributed cache such as Memcached.

6.4.2 Distributed caching with Memcached

Memcached is an open source caching provider that was originally developed for the blogging site *Live Journal*. Essentially it's a big hash table that you can distribute across multiple servers. Figure 6.17 shows three Windows Azure web roles accessing data from a cache hosted in two Windows Azure worker roles.

TIP In figure 6.17, you can see that your web roles can communicate directly with worker roles. In chapter 15, we'll look at how you can do this in Windows Azure.

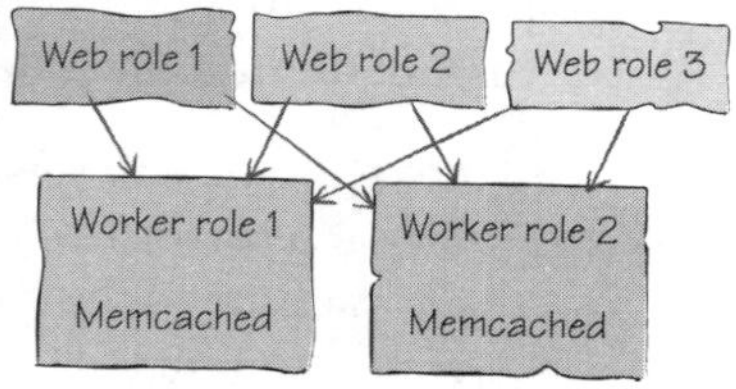

Figure 6.17 Three web roles accessing data stored in two worker role instances of Memcached

Microsoft has developed a solution accelerator that you can use as an example of how to use Memcached in Windows Azure. This accelerator contains a sample website and the worker roles that host Memcached. You can download this accelerator from http://code.msdn.microsoft.com/winazurememcached. Be aware that memcached.exe isn't included in the download. Use version 1.2.1 from http://jehiah.cz/projects/memcached-win32/.

Hosting Memcached

In chapter 7, we'll look at how you can launch executables (such as Memcached) from a Windows Azure role.

Although we're using a worker role to host your cache, you could also host Memcached in your web role (saves a bit of cash).

To get started with the solution accelerator, you just need to download the code and follow the instructions to build the solution. Although we won't go through the downloaded sample, let's take a peek at how you store and retrieve data using the accelerator.

SETTING DATA IN THE CACHE

If you want to store some data in Memcached, you can use the following code:

```
AzureMemcached.Client.Store(Enyim.Caching.
➥ Memcached.StoreMode.Set, "myKey", "Hello World");
```

In this example, the value `"Hello World"` is stored against the key `"myKey"`. Now that you have data stored, let's take a look at how you can get it back (regardless of which web role you're load balanced to).

RETRIEVING DATA FROM THE CACHE

Retrieving data from the cache is pretty simple. The following code will retrieve the contents of the cache using the AzureMemcached library:

```
var myData = AzureMemcached.Client.Get<string>("myKey"));
```

In this example, the value `"Hello World"` that you set earlier for the key `"myKey"` would be returned.

Although our Memcached example is cool, you'll notice that we're not using the ASP.NET `Cache` object to access and store the data. The reason for this is that unlike the `Session` object, the `Cache` object (in .NET Framework 3.5SP1, 3.5, or 2.0) doesn't use the provider factory model; the `Cache` object can be used only in conjunction with the ASP.NET cache provider.

6.4.3 *Cache extensibility in ASP.NET 4.0*

Using ASP.NET 4.0, you'll be able to specify a cache provider other than the standard ASP.NET in-memory cache. Although this feature was introduced to support Microsoft's new distributed cache product, Windows Server AppFabric Caching (which was code-named Velocity), it can be used to support other cache providers, such as Memcached. The configuration of a cache provider is similar to the configuration of a session provider. You could use the following configuration to configure your cache to use AppFabric caching:

```
<system.caching>
   <cache defaultProvider="FrameworkCacheProvider">
      <providers>
       <add name="myVelocityInstances"

     type="System.Data.Caching.VelocityCacheProvider,System.Data.Caching"
                remoteServerName="myServer"
                remoteServerPort="4435"
                namedCache="myCache"
                securityToken="DEC3D34CA29112" />
      </providers>
   </cache>
</system.caching>
```

Although the Windows Azure team will allow you to hook into any cache provider that you like, the real intention is for you to use a Windows Azure-hosted shared-cache role (that's probably based on AppFabric caching).

> **Cache-based session provider**
>
> Now that you can see the benefits of a distributed cache, it's worth revisiting session providers. As stated earlier, most ASP.NET web farms tend to use SQL Server as the session provider. With the increasing popularity of distributed caches, it's now becoming more common for web farms to use a cache-based session provider rather than a SQL Server–based provider.
>
> When a distributed cache is used in a web farm, it makes sense to leverage it whenever possible to maximize its value. Typically, distributed caches perform better than do databases such as SQL Server; you can improve the performance of your web application by using a faster session provider. Because session state is ultimately volatile data (not unlike cached data), a transactional data storage mechanism such as SQL Server is typically overkill for the job required.
>
> If you want to use a Memcached-based session provider (your session data is stored in your Memcached instance), you can download a ready-made provider from http://www.codeplex.com/memcachedproviders.

6.5 Summary

OK, so you've probably learned everything that's relevant about scaling your web applications from this chapter (and even from some of the earlier chapters). You should've come to realize that websites can't cope with being under pressure and the best thing that you can do is design your web application to scale out. If, for whatever reason (and there isn't a good one that we can think of), you can't scale out, you can always host your website on a bigger box until you can.

In this chapter, we also looked at how Windows Azure distributes requests and how you can test them in your own environment using the development fabric load balancer. Although you can't test every scenario, you can get a sense as to how your application will behave when you run under multiple instances. Finally, you learned how to handle sessions and caching across multiple servers (if you want to do that).

Now that we're starting to look at some of the more advanced web scenarios, in the next chapter we're going to take a peek at how you can use Windows Azure support for full-trust applications, how to build non-ASP.NET–based websites, and how to execute non-.NET Framework applications.

7 Running full-trust, native, and other code

This chapter covers
- Running any Common Gateway Interface (CGI) interpreter you want
- Spawning processes and calling local executables
- Calling native libraries with P/Invoke

Microsoft is committed to making Windows the best place to run any type of application. To that end, it's making Azure an open system, where you can run anything you want. Microsoft could have easily made Azure .NET-only. Azure would've been easier for Microsoft to manage, and easier to design the infrastructure for. But Microsoft didn't do that. It opened Azure up, as wide as the on-premises version of Windows is, so that its customers can run almost anything on Azure that can be run on Windows today. Azure can run unmanaged code (C++, for example), any code that needs full trust on the local machine, and code from any other platform that runs on Windows. There's support for PHP, Python, Ruby, and Java. But Microsoft didn't even stop there.

Microsoft worked with a series of open source teams to provide useful and valuable SDKs for each platform, so that they're equal citizens in the cloud. A plug-in for Eclipse was developed in a partnership between Microsoft and an open source team so that Eclipse developers can have an integrated experience.

The openness of Azure is its power. The core of this openness is Azure's support for running in a full-trust environment. After this environment was enabled, you could run anything on Azure, including FastCGI. Because you can run FastCGI, you can run most other web platforms, including PHP. For some, the challenge isn't about just running a different web platform; it's about running legacy code in a better way. Azure also supports spawning processes and calling into native libraries with P/Invoke so that developers can squeeze all the power out of those massive eight-way servers out there.

Enough background information. Let's talk about how you can harness all the power that Azure has to offer.

7.1 Enabling full-trust support

When any code is run in Windows, it's run in a particular trust level. This trust level defines what the code is allowed to do. For example, code in a partial-trust level can't access local hardware and system resources, whereas code running in a full-trust environment has access to just about anything.

Trust is only one piece of the equation. The user account permissions must allow an operation, in addition to the trust level. Trust level is enforced by *code access security* (CAS). CAS is a way to define what an application is allowed to do and is applied at the Common Language Runtime (CLR) level. A CAS policy can determine what methods and libraries you use and what level of local-system access your code has access to. ASP.NET comes with several standard trust policies, expressed in CAS. One of them is the ASP.NET medium-trust policy, which restricts the application to just being able to run itself, without any access to the broader system at play. The Azure team took this policy, tweaked it to fit its needs, and published a modified medium-trust policy.

You should try to run in the lowest trust level possible. Doing so minimizes the damage that can be done if your application is hijacked, or if your code runs amok. This concept is called *least privileged* and refers to always running your code with the least amount of privileges needed to get the job done. If your code doesn't need access to the registry, it shouldn't have access. Running in this way restricts what the bad guys can do if your system is compromised, or the damage you might cause if some code in your application becomes self-aware and starts to run amok. Bad outcomes might include files being placed in the system folders, your desktop wallpaper being changed to lolcats, or naughty things being written to the registry.

You should run your code in full trust only when you absolutely have to. Unfortunately, full trust is required for any unmanaged code you might want to run and for accessing the Azure diagnostics systems.

There are times when your application legitimately needs advanced permissions. It could be because you're referencing a library that requires them, or you're accessing the local system somehow. When you need this kind of permission, you can change the configuration of your cloud service to run in a full-trust model. While you're running in a full-trust model, you have access to do just about anything you want. The identity your application is running under is still that of a limited user on the server, which keeps you from creating Windows user accounts and formatting the hard drive. While your code is able to run any opcode through the CLR that can possibly be run, the local user permissions are limited, such that you can only do things for your application and not system wide.

Full trust is enabled by default. To disable full trust, set the `enableNativeCodeExecution` setting to `false`:

```
<WorkerRole name="VerifyOrder" enableNativeCodeExecution="false">
    <ConfigurationSettings>
      <Setting name="InboundQueue"/>
      <Setting name="OutboundQueue"/>
      <Setting name="AccountName" />
      <Setting name="AccountSharedKey" />
      <Setting name="QueueStorageEndpoint" />
      <Setting name="TableStorageEndpoint" />
    </ConfigurationSettings>
  </WorkerRole>
```

Full trust is the doorway to running just about any code you can think of. Another option that will be released soon is the ability to run your own VMs in the Azure data center. There isn't a lot of information about this yet as it was just announced at the PDC 2009, but it promises to let customers run any machine they have today up in the cloud, including any off-the-shelf applications.

That's all you need to know about full trust for now. If trust level is important to your existing code, understand that you have access to the same tools in Azure. Now we're going to look at some scenarios that you might be doing today on-premises. We're going to show how they work the same way in the cloud.

7.2 FastCGI in Windows Azure

FastCGI is a module in IIS 7 that provides a way to run CGI-based applications. CGI is a standard interface that modules can be written to, to plug in to any web server. The web server then pipes each request through these modules, letting each module work on responding to the request. Sometimes a simple static resource module immediately responds with an image file. Other modules execute a whole application to respond with HTML. Modules responding to web requests is how any web server works, especially ASP.NET and PHP. IIS 7 supports this standard with its FastCGI module that's run in the IIS 7 pipeline (when the pipeline is configured correctly).

To take advantage of FastCGI in Azure, you need to configure the FastCGI support for your development workstation, and then configure your web role to enable the PHP interpreter. After you've completed the configuration, your Azure application will be able to host a PHP application and respond to PHP requests from web clients.

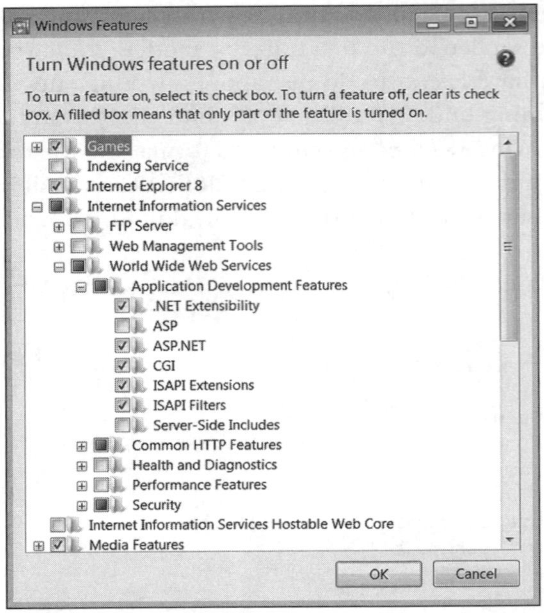

Figure 7.1 If you use Windows 7 for your development workstation, you'll need to enable CGI support for your local instance of IIS. You can do this by using the Windows Features applet in the control panel.

7.2.1 Enabling FastCGI in your local cloud environment

The first step you need to take to run PHP in Azure is a local step. If you want to run and debug PHP running in the local cloud environment, you need to reconfigure the local instance of IIS. The readme for the SDK contains all the gory details for enabling FastCGI. The short steps are to enable the CGI feature of the web server role, if you're running Windows Server 2008. If you're running Vista or Windows 7, you'll need to enable the CGI feature in the Application Development Features group in the Windows Features applet, as shown in figure 7.1.

Easy, right? Now, you've got FastCGI and PHP enabled. Let's configure them.

7.2.2 Configuring Azure for FastCGI and PHP

To run FastCGI in Azure, you need to do more than just tweak one setting in the service definition file, but it isn't too complicated. You need to include a new file in your web role project called web.roleConfig, shown in listing 7.1. The file needs to be in the root of the web project, and needs to be modified from the default contents when you add it. To avoid some of these steps, you can create a CGI web role instead of a normal web role when you create your project. We'll cover that a little later.

Listing 7.1 The web.roleConfig file configures IIS for the use of FastCGI

```
<?xml version="1.0" encoding="utf-8" ?>
<configuration>
  <system.webServer>
    <fastCgi>
```

```
      <application fullPath="%RoleRoot%\approot\myinterpreter.exe"/>
    </fastCgi>
    </system.webServer>
</configuration>
```

After you add the web.roleConfig file, include the CGI interpreter for your platform in the project. If you're upgrading a normal web role project, change the build action of both the interpreter and the web.roleConfig file to `content`. If you're using a CGI Web Role project, this is already done for you. This setting tells Visual Studio to do nothing with the files, but to include them in the output package that is uploaded to Azure. Modify the `fullPath` attribute to point to the interpreter that you include in your project.

Excellent. You've enabled FastCGI, and uploaded and enabled the PHP interpreter that IIS 7 will use to execute your web pages. Now you need to tell IIS 7 what type of requests should be routed to this new interpreter. Should it be every request, or only requests that end in .php? These routing instructions are called *handlers*, and are configured in the plain old web.config file of your web project. The following example shows the handler for PHP:

```
<add name="PHP with FastCGI" path="*.php" verb="*"
➥ modules="FastCgiModule"
➥ scriptProcessor="%RoleRoot%\php\php-cgi.exe"
➥ resourceType="Unspecified" />
```

The handler definition defines a name for the handler and the *path*. The path is what form of requests should be routed to the interpreter that the handler is configuring. In this example, any request to the web server that ends in .php is sent to `FastCgiModule` for processing. `FastCgiModule` then passes the request on to the PHP interpreter for processing.

All file types have a handler in the configuration. Requests for .aspx are executed by ASP.NET with a handler that's configured for you when you install ASP.NET. Requests for static files such as .gif, .jpg, and other simple files are routed to the static file handler. When writing the configuration, keep in mind that you need to use the macro `%RoleRoot%` to point to the root of where your files will be running from. Currently this root is a small drive called E:\ in the Azure server. Don't rely on it to always be E:\; it could change, which is why the `%RoleRoot%` macro is provided.

Add the handler configuration to the `handlers` section of the `system.webServer` part of the web.config file for your web project. Now IIS can set up the handler and start accepting requests.

Let's give IIS some requests to accept by making an application that'll accept and process PHP requests. There are several large applications running on WordPress, on PHP, and on Windows Azure.

7.2.3 Setting up HelloAzureWorld.php

This book isn't about PHP, so our sample is going to focus on simply getting some PHP to work in the cloud. We'll leave what to do with PHP up to you, and perhaps to

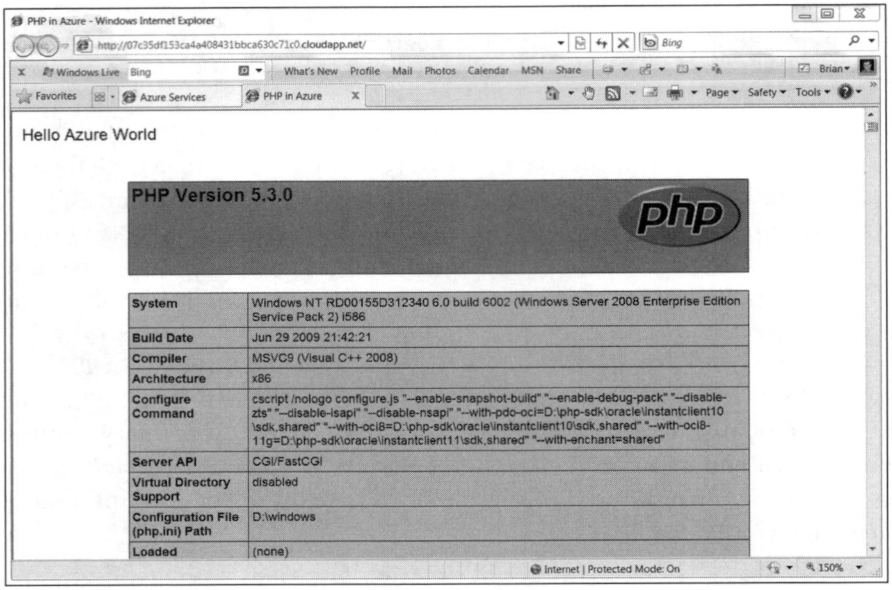

Figure 7.2 Your Hello Azure World PHP web application

another book. For now, you're going to build a simple application that's going to say "Hello Azure World" and display some server information, as shown in figure 7.2.

To build your Hello Azure World PHP application, create a new Cloud Service solution in Visual Studio. Instead of adding a regular web role to the solution, you're going to add a CGI web role. We named ours HelloPHP, as seen in the fabulous figure 7.3. The CGI Web Role template includes the typical changes you'll need to run a CGI-based application in Azure.

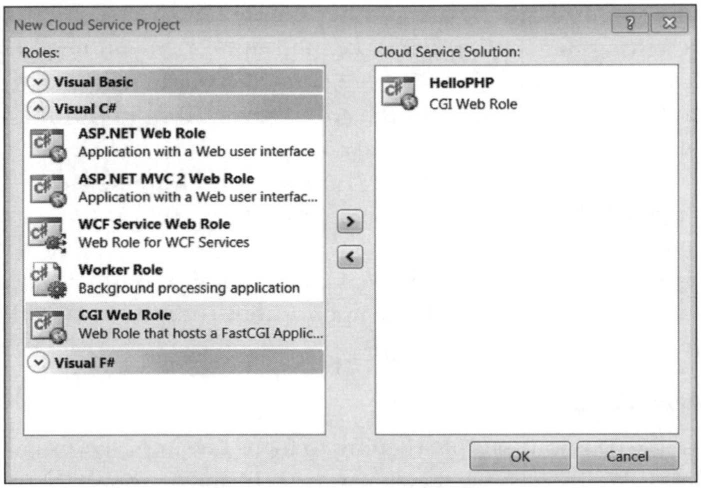

Figure 7.3 Selecting a single web role for your PHP web application. To use FastCGI, choose the CGI Web Role template, which comes prepackaged with the web.roleConfig file you'll need.

The project will already contain a web.roleConfig file, with some notes on how to modify it correctly. The notes remind you to enable native code execution, and to change the path to the interpreter executable (`php-cgi.exe` in this case). You can download the correct version of the PHP interpreter from windows.php.net. (We recommend putting it in a subfolder of the project.) Don't forget to mark any non-.NET files that you add as `content` in the build action for that file. Depending on the version of PHP that you download, you might have to set the time zone in the php.ini file to a valid time zone value, such as `America/New_York`.

The next step is to make some changes to the web.config file. You'll make all these changes in the `system.webServer` section. All lines in this section are used to configure IIS 7, removing the need to use the IIS management tool or to log on to the web server. Not having to use the management tool is great, because now you can put the required web server configuration into the configuration for the web application and it'll travel with your application to whichever web server you deploy it to. You have to configure your application this way in Windows Azure because you can't log in directly to your server.

You need to make two changes to web.config (which are shown in listing 7.2):

- Add a default document section, so that new visitors come to the home page for your web site correctly.
- Add the configuration for the handler, to tell IIS what to do with any web requests that involve PHP.

Listing 7.2 Changing the `web.config` file to run your PHP application

```
<system.webServer>
      <defaultDocument>
        <files>
          <add value="index.php"/>
        </files>
      </defaultDocument>
.
.
.
 <handlers>
.
.
. <add name="FastGGI Handler"
             verb="*"
             path="*.php"
             scriptProcessor="%RoleRoot%\approot\php\php-cgi.exe"
             modules="FastCgiModule"
             resourceType="Unspecified" />
 </handlers>
</sytem.webServer>
```

Your project is set up now, and you can start adding some real PHP code. Add a text file to your web project and name it index.php. Add the following PHP code to index.php:

```
<html>
 <head>
```

```
  <title>PHP in Azure</title>
 </head>
 <body>
  <?php echo '<p>Hello Azure World</p>'; ?> <br />
  <?php phpinfo(); ?>
 </body>
</html>
```

This code does a few basic things. As required by the Union of Demo Code Developers, we have to somehow write to the screen some reference to "Hello World." In this case, you're going to use `echo`, and write out `<p>Hello Azure World</p>`. Lower down in the code, you use the famous `phpinfo()` function. This function writes a bunch of diagnostic information about the version of PHP you're running and information about your web server. You commonly run this function when you first install PHP on a server, to confirm that everything is working correctly. If you deploy your application to the cloud and then browse the results, you'll find some interesting facts about the server running your application: the user name your code is running under is a GUID, and your website files are stored on E:\.

Running PHP in Azure is pretty easy after you set up a few options. That might be why PHP on Azure has proven to be quite popular. Microsoft and WordPress announced at the PDC in 2009 that they're working together, and ICanHazCheeseburger announced that it's been running some of its sites with WordPress running on PHP on Azure.

Now that we have that under our belts, we can start looking at spawning processes in Azure.

7.3 External processes in Windows Azure

Some enterprise applications rely on child processes to be run in an asynchronous way. As a way to show how to work with external processes, you're going to build a small website that converts videos to different video formats. Because we don't want you to write all the video conversion code, you're going to leverage FFmpeg.

FFmpeg is an open source project that provides a cross-platform way to play, convert, and stream media files. You can download it at FFmpeg.org. You'll have to drill around to find the latest build. Also, be aware that it's in a .RAR file, requiring the use of a tool like WinRAR to extract it. For this task, we're using the Windows-compatible binaries. In the package, you'll find an executable called FFmpeg.exe. This is the core executable that you'll be using. Figure 7.4 shows a screen shot of the application you're going to build.

The application will provide a simple way to browse videos in your BLOB account, and to convert one by providing a destination name. The extension of the new filename will tell FFmpeg what format to convert to.

We already have several versions of the Big Buck Bunny trailer uploaded to our BLOB account. Big Buck Bunny is part of the open movie project, and is released under Creative Commons. You can download the whole movie at www.bigbuckbunny.org.

If you enter a destination filename, for example SmallMovie.mpg, the website creates a new background process, executes FFmpeg on the big movie, and then places

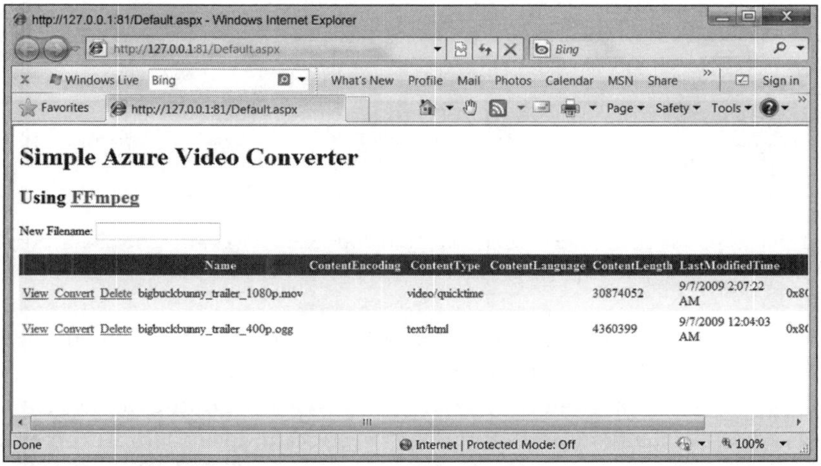

Figure 7.4 A screen shot of the Simple Azure Video Converter, which uses the open source FFmpeg to convert media files. Your web role will call out to the FFmpeg application by launching it as an external process.

the new file (after it's converted into an MPG) back into the BLOB account. Now we're going to tell you how to do that yourself.

7.3.1 *Spawning a sample process*

You can't run this program in the process that's executing your .NET code, so you'll spawn a new process and have it execute the application for you. The SDK has some great sample code for how to spawn this process and how to interact with it. You're going to use the sample as it is, with some tweaks based on what you're doing. You can find the sample as part of the Full Trust demo, which is in the ExecuteProcess.aspx.cs file. The method is called `Run`.

The `Run` method provides ways to capture any output from the process, so that you can use the output in a way that makes sense for you. In the sample application for this section, we've chosen to capture some basic facts about what's happened and pipe that to the Azure log. Use the following shortened `Run` command; for this project, the command is named `ExecuteCommand`.

```
protected int ExecuteCommand(string cmdPath, string arguments)
{
     var process = new Process();
     var startInfo = process.StartInfo;
     startInfo.UseShellExecute = false;
     startInfo.CreateNoWindow = true;
     startInfo.FileName = Server.MapPath(cmdPath);
     startInfo.Arguments = arguments;
     startInfo.WorkingDirectory =
     ➥ Path.GetDirectoryName(startInfo.FileName);
     startInfo.RedirectStandardError = true;
     startInfo.RedirectStandardOutput = true;
```

```
        process.Start();
        process.BeginErrorReadLine();
        process.BeginOutputReadLine();
        process.WaitForExit();
        var elapasedTime = process.ExitTime - process.StartTime;
        RoleManager.WriteToLog("Information", String.Format("Command: {0}
        ➥ {1}", cmdPath, arguments));
        RoleManager.WriteToLog("Information", String.Format("Exit Code: {0}",
        ➥ process.ExitCode));
        RoleManager.WriteToLog("Information", String.Format("Elapsed Time:
        ➥ {0}", elapasedTime));     return process.ExitCode;
}
```

In this method, you're starting a new process on the operating system and telling it to run your executable. The path to the program to run is set to the `FileName` property, and any command-line arguments you want to pass are set to the `Arguments` property. The process isn't actually started until the `Start` method is called. At the end of your method, you're capturing some runtime information and saving that to the Azure log.

When running in the cloud, you can spawn both 32-bit and 64-bit processes. This makes it easy to move legacy code into the cloud. You can spawn 64-bit processes in the local development fabric as well, unless you're running a 32-bit machine. In that case, you'll only be able to spawn 32-bit processes when you're running locally.

You can start multiple processes in your role, but keep in mind that each new process takes up memory and CPU time. Start too many of them and your instance won't be able to get any real work done.

Like most applications you're likely to spawn, FFmpeg works only on files stored on the local filesystem. To accommodate the application, you're going to copy the movie from BLOB storage to the local storage.

7.3.2 Using BLOB storage

The StorageClient library includes some simple methods to make using BLOB storage easy. You call either the `DownloadToFile` or `UploadFile` method on a `Blob` reference. In the sample application, you'll figure out where the BLOB is and where you want to put it. Use the code in the following listing to download the file, run the conversion code, and then upload the new file back to the BLOB container.

Listing 7.3 Copying a BLOB to local storage and back again

```
public void ConvertVideoFromBlob(string _containerName,
➥ string _inputName, string _outputName)
        {
            string inputName = _inputName.ToLower();
            string outputName = _outputName.ToLower();

            CloudBlobContainer videoContainer =
            ➥ blobClient.GetContainerReference(_containerName);
```

```
        videoContainer.CreateIfNotExist();
        videoContainer.GetBlobReference(inputName)
        ➥ .DownloadToFile(inputName);                          ❶ Downloads BLOB to local file

        ConvertVideo(localDisk.RootPath + inputName,
        ➥ localDisk.RootPath + outputName);                     ❷ Converts video using an external process

        videoContainer.GetBlobReference(outputName)
        ➥ .UploadFile(inputName);                              ❸ Uploads new file to BLOB container

        File.Delete(localDisk.RootPath + inputName);
        File.Delete(localDisk.RootPath + outputName);
    }
```

After the movie is copied down to local storage at ❶, you can run the `FFmpeg` command at ❷. To run `FFmpeg` at the command line, use something like the following:

```
FFmpeg.exe -i BigBuckBunny_Trailer_400p.ogg -y SmallerMovie.mpg
```

To execute this command as a process, call the `ExecuteCommand` method with the following code, which spawns the process, executes FFmpeg, passes in the parameters, and waits for the command to finish executing:

```
string VideoArgs = string.Format(@"-i {0} -y {1}",
➥ localInputFilename, localOutputFilename);
ExecuteCommand(@"ffmpeg\ffmpeg.exe", VideoArgs);
```

No matter which way you run `FFmpeg`, the result is a new movie file, of the proper type, in the same local storage folder where the source movie was.

Your next step is to copy the file back into BLOB storage. Copying the file creates a new BLOB in your videos container that has the same name the one that the user asked for in the web application at ❸. First, you get a BLOB reference with the filename that the user wanted. This BLOB doesn't exist yet, it's just a reference. When you call `UploadFile`, the file is uploaded to BLOB storage. When the file is finally uploaded, you clean up after yourself by deleting both local files.

Spawning processes is an important option to have, but you should use it only when you're migrating an application to Azure that relies on an external dependency. You shouldn't intentionally architect a new system to use this feature. For a new system, you should probably use inter-role communication between different role instances, which gives your solution more flexibility when it's time to scale.

Now you're familiar with two ways to use native code in Azure. Let's look at one more way: calling into a native library. Remember, these are important tools to have, but we wouldn't use them unless we absolutely had to.

7.4 Calling native libraries with P/Invoke

We've looked at two ways to leverage native code in Azure: using FastCGI and spawning processes. The third option at your disposal is to call into a native library with P/Invoke. P/Invoke allows you to directly call a native library, such as a Windows dynamic link library (DLL). P/Invoke is shorthand for *platform invoke*. You use P/Invoke when you want to call a platform API directly. If you work mostly in .NET, you're rarely calling the platform API directly; instead, you're using classes out of the .NET Framework or the Base Class library.

The limitation with P/Invoke is that you can call only 64-bit native libraries while running in the cloud. If you happen to be developing on a 32-bit machine, you'll be able to call a 32 bit-library locally, but not in the cloud. You can work around this problem by spawning a 32-bit subprocess, as outlined in section 7.3.1, and calling P/Invoke from there. We think this is too much work though; you should stick with 64-bit libraries.

Calling native libraries is a special skill to begin with, so we aren't going to cover everything you need to know about doing that in .NET. Calling them in the cloud is a lot like when you do it locally.

When working with native libraries, you need to first import the DLL into your namespace, and then provide a façade method into the native libraries method. This will involve a great deal of code that will map native data types to .NET CLR types.

Don't forget to allow native code execution in your cloud service definition file; otherwise, you'll receive a security exception.

The easiest way to implement the signatures you need in your code is to get them from http://www.pinvoke.net, like we do. This website provides the signatures for just about any native call you could possibly want to make.

Now let's get to it and use P/Invoke to call a native library. Although you're free to follow along with how we do this, you might consider skipping to the sample code for the book. It'll be easier to see how it all fits together.

7.4.1 Getting started

You're going to build a simple web application for Azure that will list the files and directories in a given folder. You could easily build this with managed code, without P/Invoke, but we thought it would make for a good example.

The first step is to add the interoperability services namespace to your project:

```
using System.Runtime.InteropServices;
```

Then you import the native methods that you want to call:

```
[DllImport("kernel32", CharSet = CharSet.Unicode)]
public static extern IntPtr FindFirstFile(string lpFileName,
➥ out WIN32_FIND_DATA lpFindFileData);
```

In this example code, you're importing a method called `FindFirstFile` from `kernel32`, which is called by the DLL. This line of code defines a series of parameters you'll need to provide to the method for it to work. The first parameter, `lpFileName`, is the path of the folder you want to look in. The second parameter, `lpFindFileData`, is a variable that the results will be stored in. The `FindFirstFile` method also returns a handle to an object that will be your pointer into the filesystem. You'll use this handle to iterate through the folder you're pointing at by calling another imported method, `FindNextFile`. Always remember to close any handle objects you're using while working with native libraries; otherwise, they'll be left open in memory, causing memory leaks.

It'll often be the case that the method you're importing requires input and output parameters, and return values that use a type that isn't supported in .NET. You'll need to define these types so that they can be used. The following listing shows an example structure that defines the data about the file that the finder just found.

Listing 7.4 Defining a data type to work with a native library

```
[StructLayout(LayoutKind.Sequential, CharSet = CharSet.Unicode)]
        public struct WIN32_FIND_DATA
        {
            public FileAttributes dwFileAttributes;
            public FILETIME ftCreationTime;
            public FILETIME ftLastAccessTime;
            public FILETIME ftLastWriteTime;
            public int nFileSizeHigh;
            public int nFileSizeLow;
            public int dwReserved0;
            public int dwReserved1;
            [MarshalAs(UnmanagedType.ByValTStr, SizeConst = 260)]
            public string cFileName;
            [MarshalAs(UnmanagedType.ByValTStr, SizeConst = 14)]
            public string cAlternate;
        }
```

After you define these types, you'll be able to call into the method just fine.

7.4.2 Calling into the method

In this example, you're going to make the initial `FindFirstFile` call, and then perform a `Do` loop until `FindNextFile` comes back empty. With each iteration of the loop, you'll copy data from the return data structure to a class, `myFileData`, which you also have to define. Then you'll bind a collection of `myFileData` objects to a simple `GridView` on the web form. All this is shown in listing 7.5.

Listing 7.5 Processing each file that's found

```
hFileFinder = FindFirstFile(currentPath, out foundFile);
   do
   {
      fileList.Add(new myFileData()
      { Filename = foundFile.cFileName,
        Filesize = foundFile.nFileSizeLow,
        isDirectory = (foundFile.dwFileAttributes &
        ➥ FileAttributes.Directory) != 0 });
   }
            while (FindNextFile(hFileFinder, out foundFile));

         FindClose(hFileFinder);

         gvFileList.DataSource = fileList;
         gvFileList.DataBind();
```

Working with native libraries and P/Invoke can be complicated. You should look to using this way to use native code only when you can't possibly do what you need to do with a class in the .NET library. Using native libraries can introduce brittleness into your solution by creating external dependencies.

7.5 Summary

Microsoft has provided broad support for running just about anything on Azure. It didn't take the easy way and limit cloud developers to just .NET code because Microsoft wants Azure to be a usable platform with broad adoption. The ability to run FastCGI, spawn processes, and call native libraries makes it easier for you to port existing applications and to support a broader array of applications.

With Azure's support for FastCGI you can leverage any CGI-compatible module in Azure. These modules include PHP, Ruby, and many other web platforms. With just a few simple steps, you can deploy one of these platforms to your web roles in Azure.

Spawning external processes is important when you have an external dependency in a system you might be migrating to the cloud. You can also spawn them to manually parallelize your application.

Some applications that are built with unmanaged code need to access native libraries for system-level access. Using P/Invoke to access these libraries is available in Azure, but it can be complicated. You should leverage this feature only if you truly need it.

Azure isn't just for Web 2.0 web applications with a viral nature; it's also for serious enterprise applications. Those applications often come with a legacy aspect, whether it's calling into a home-grown DLL that can model and calculate the air speed of an unladen swallow, or being able to leverage a forum for your website that happens to run in PHP.

What we've covered in this chapter, especially native calls and process spawning, are great tools with great power. And with great power comes great responsibility. Make sure you use them wisely, or you'll spend a lot of your weekends figuring out why your application isn't working like you want it to.

In our next chapter, we'll start the conversation about how to store files in the cloud using BLOBs. Don't be scared; we know you've probably had a bad experience with BLOBs and traditional databases. BLOBs in Windows Azure aren't nearly as complex.

Part 4

Working with BLOB storage

Part 4 explores BLOB storage, a simple file storage system for the cloud. Many people call file storage *unstructured storage*, and if you saw our desktops, you would know why people call it that. You wouldn't believe how hard it was in these chapters to avoid cheesy, 1950s sci-fi references to BLOB monsters and the like.

Chapter 8 covers BLOB basics: what they are and why you might use them. Chapter 9 shows you how to work with BLOBs inside your applications, and chapter 10 shows you how to use BLOBs from outside Azure.

What? Yes, outside Azure. Hey, by now you should know the cloud isn't all or nothing; the most common use of Azure will likely be of a hybrid nature.

8 The basics of BLOBs

> ***This chapter covers***
> - How files are currently shared in retro systems
> - How Windows Azure allows us to store files (woo hoo, go Azure)
> - How to consume the BLOB storage service

In case you didn't bother reading the blurb at the beginning of part 3, in this chapter (and the next couple of chapters), we'll be looking at how you can store files in Windows Azure's highly scalable, fault tolerant, binary-file storage system (otherwise known as the BLOB storage service).

DEFINITION BLOB stands for *binary large object.* The term has been stolen from the world of relational databases where it used to describe the storage of binary data (such as an image or an MP3 file) in a single entity. We wish they'd used BinLob as the acronym. It more accurately describes what happens when a DBA discovers you stuck a terabyte of data in a single row of his database.

In this chapter, we're going to answer the following questions:

- Why is storing files in a typical scaled-out system so hard?
- How does the BLOB storage service address typical scaling issues?

- How does the BLOB storage service work?
- How can you can get your tools out and start developing against it?
- How do you store BLOBs in the production system?

Before you can appreciate the beauty of the BLOB service, you need to get a little insight into how you might solve the problem of storing files that can be accessed by multiple servers in a scalable fashion.

8.1 Storing files in a scaled-out fashion is a pain in the NAS

Unless you have plenty of cash, you're going to experience some pain if you try to share files across machines. No matter what hat one of us puts on (author, presenter, architect, developer, or computer scientist), we're embarrassed by the following statement: sharing files across machines is incredibly hard. It is; it shouldn't be, but it is. Decoding the genome and making robots climb stairs, that should be hard, but sharing files shouldn't be.

> **BLOB content starts in section 8.1.2**
>
> In this section, we'll be looking at the challenges of storing files in a scalable fashion. If you've had too much coffee and just can't wait to get to some BLOB content, feel free to skip along to section 8.1.2.

To contextualize the problem, let's return to the podcast example that we introduced in chapter 1. In that scenario, we wanted to provide a service where users could upload podcasts that would be converted from MP3 to WMA. To support the predicted demand, we decided to load balance the website across two servers. Because users can upload or download a podcast from any server, a shared storage solution is required.

Figure 8.1 shows a logical representation of two load balanced web servers accessing a podcast from a shared storage mechanism.

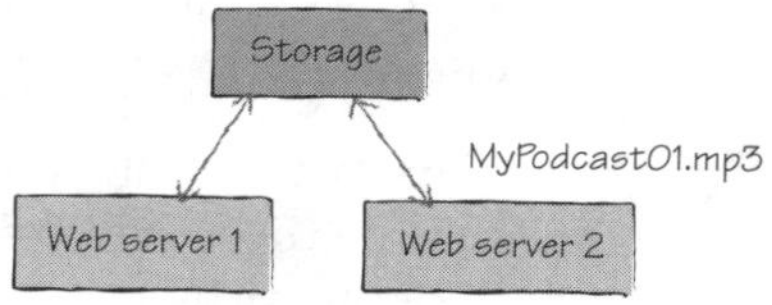

Figure 8.1 Two load balanced servers that require access to a common storage area to serve up MP3 files

To be honest, you don't need to be the greatest architect in the world to draw the solution shown in figure 8.1. It's pretty logical, common sense stuff. Two web servers access a common storage area.

Now you're thinking, "Why did they just say it's common sense, when before they said it was hard? Get me another book that says it's easy." Well, before you start reaching for *Mavis Beacon Teaches Windows Azure*, check out the following questions. As you think about the possible answers, you might begin to see why this is a little harder than it seems to be at first.

- Do you have enough space to store all the files you need?
- How do you add more storage capacity?

- If a disk crashes, where does your data go?
- Is the storage block load balanced?
- What if you lose your connection to the block? Is it redundant?
- At what point do you max out your disk, in terms of reading and writing?
- How do you evenly distribute load across all disks?

The good news is that pretty much all of these problems have been answered and solved already. You can even implement these solutions in your traditional noncloud environments today (well, the lead time is probably longer than a day). The bad news is that the cheap, simple solutions are typically not scalable or fault tolerant. The solutions that are scalable and durable are usually expensive. In the Windows Azure BLOB storage service, all that changes.

Before we look at how easy it is to store and access files (in a scalable, durable fashion) across multiple servers in Windows Azure, let's look at some of the options outside Windows Azure.

8.1.1 Traditional approaches to BLOB management

Over the next few sections we'll look at how you might provide a file storage facility in traditional ASP.NET web server farms, using our podcasting example. We'll specifically look at using the following storage options:

- SQL Server
- Network share
- Distributed File System (DFS)
- Network-attached storage (NAS)
- Direct-attached storage (DAS)
- Storage area network (SAN)

Let's start with one with the typical developer solutions to the problem: the database.

SQL SERVER

Because web servers typically have access to a shared SQL Server database, you could store your podcasts in a table. Although this is a common approach used in many solutions, it's probably not the best use of your expensive database server. It's like racing a truck in a Grand Prix; there are cheaper, simpler, higher performing, and more appropriate solutions for storing files.

Unless you're using a high-availability technology (such as clustering, mirroring, or replication), your database server is likely to be a single point of failure in the system. In figure 8.1, SQL Server would be represented by the Storage block (accessed over a typical network connection).

NETWORK SHARE

Another common approach to providing a shared filesystem across web servers is to use a shared network drive that can be accessed by all instances of the website. This low-cost solution is more lightweight than a database, but it still introduces a single point of failure. This cheapo solution offers no redundancy and provides no ability to scale out. In figure 8.1, an application server with a network share would also be represented by the storage block.

Now that we've looked at some of the lower-end solutions, let's take a look at some of the typical high-scale solutions that are used, starting with Distributed File Systems.

DISTRIBUTED FILE SYSTEM (DFS)

Windows Server 2003/2008 provides a technology known as DFS that allows you to create a peer-to-peer (P2P) filesystem on your network. UNIX/Linux environments have similar tools. If you use DFS to store podcasts, when a new podcast is uploaded, a copy of the file is replicated to all other participating servers. Although this approach requires no new hardware, it's complicated to manage and adds extra performance overhead to all servers involved.

Figure 8.2 shows a DFS solution with a P2P network between two web servers.

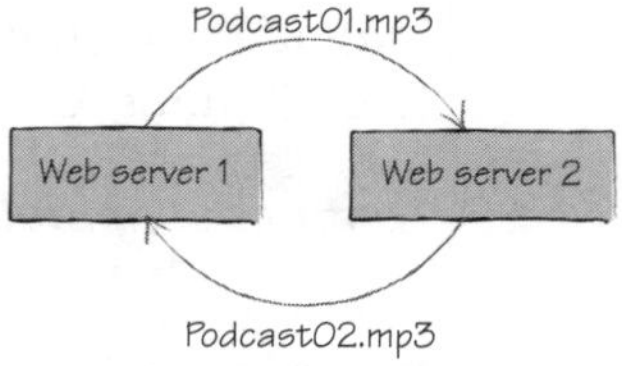

Figure 8.2 Two web servers reading and writing files to a local shared disk. Files are replicated between each server.

Whenever a file is uploaded to a web server, it's automatically replicated to all other servers in the farms. Using replication ensures that there are no single points of failure in this solution and that the data is held on multiple machines. In figure 8.2, Podcast01.mp3 is uploaded to web server 1 and then replicated to web server 2; when Podcast02.mp3 is uploaded to web server 2, it's then replicated to web server 1.

In figure 8.3, the web servers don't hold the files locally, but use a replicated file store held in application servers. In this figure, Podcast01.mp3 was uploaded to app server 1 via web server 1. The file was replicated to app server 2, and then served up to the client from app server 2 via web server 1.

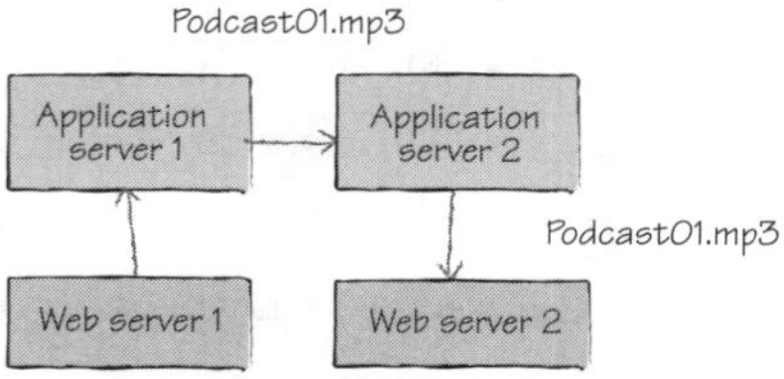

Figure 8.3 Two web servers reading and writing files from a set of replicated file servers

With file replication, any time a file is uploaded to a server there's a small delay between the file being uploaded and it being replicated across all servers. It's therefore possible that the web user could be load balanced onto a server where the file isn't available (because it hasn't been replicated across to that server yet). Although this issue can be alleviated by using sticky sessions, sticky sessions won't help if the original server keels over. Also, using sticky sessions means that incoming requests won't be evenly distributed across all web servers.

Now that we've looked at some of the hook-some-machines-together solutions, we'll look at some of the dedicated disk array–type solutions that are typically used in the market.

> **Sticky sessions**
>
> A sticky session occurs when a load balancer forwards all incoming requests from the same client to the same server for the period of the session.

NETWORK-ATTACHED STORAGE (NAS)

A *network-attached storage* device is a disk array that you can plug into your network and that can be accessed via a network share. NAS devices are responsible for managing the device hardware, the filesystem, and serving files, and can provide varying levels of redundancy, depending on the device and the number of disks in the array.

Although NAS devices reduce load from client operating systems by taking responsibility for file management, they can't scale beyond their own hardware. NAS devices can range from being pretty cheap to very expensive, depending on the levels of scalability, performance, and redundancy that you require from the device. In figure 8.1, the NAS device would be represented by the storage block (connected via the Ethernet).

NAS devices are used to provide capabilities similar to those of a file server, rather than being used as a disk management system in a high-performance application solution.

DIRECT-ATTACHED STORAGE (DAS)

A *direct-attached storage* device is a disk array that you can plug directly into the back of your server and that can be accessed natively by the server. DAS devices are responsible for managing the device hardware and can provide varying levels of redundancy, depending on the device and the number of disks in the array.

Because DAS devices are directly connected to a server, they're treated like a local disk; the server is responsible for the management of the filesystem. DAS devices can support large amounts of data (100 TB or so), can be clustered (there's no single point of failure), and are usually high-performance systems. As such, DAS devices are a common choice for high-performance applications. The cost of the device can range from being pretty cheap to very expensive, depending on the levels of scalability, performance, and redundancy that you require.

Although DAS devices are great, they're limited by the physical hardware. When you reach the physical limits of the hardware (which is quite substantial), you'll be able to scale no further.

In figure 8.1 the DAS device would be represented by the storage block, connected directly to the servers.

STORAGE AREA NETWORK (SAN)

Like DAS devices, SANs are also separate hardware disk arrays; they don't have their own operating system, so file management is performed by the client operating system.

SAN devices are represented on the client operating system as virtual local hard disks that are accessed over a fiber channel. Because you need your web servers to access shared data, the SAN would need to support a shared filesystem. In figure 8.1, the SAN device would be the storage block, attached to the web servers via fiber channels.

SANs are usually quite expensive, require specialized knowledge, and are rarely used outside the enterprise domain. To give you a clue about how expensive they are, Dell doesn't even list the price on its website. As for installing and managing SANs, that's purely in the domain of the long-haired sandal-wearing bearded types. We mere mortals have no chance of making those things work. SAN devices support replication and are highly scalable (they scale much higher than do DAS devices), fault tolerant, high performing, and incredibly expensive. Due to their performance, price, and scalability, this is the solution of choice in the enterprise space. The rest of us can only dream.

Hopefully we've justified our earlier premise that implementing a file storage solution today isn't as easy as it first looks. All the available choices (beyond a certain size) require extensive IT knowledge, skills, and management, not to mention large amounts of cash or a tradeoff between capacity, redundancy, ability to scale, or performance.

This is the state of affairs with regard to the issues with storing files in traditional on-premises solutions. Let's now look at the Windows Azure BLOB storage service and how it tackles these issues.

8.1.2 The BLOB service approach to file management

As we discovered earlier, the BLOB storage service is the Windows Azure solution to providing file storage. Let's take a look at how Azure implements this service.

AN API-BASED SERVICE

Rather than building a native network-share-based solution, Microsoft has provided a set of REST-based APIs that allow you to interact with all the storage services over the HTTP stack, using a standard HTTP request. As mentioned earlier, not only can you use these APIs inside the data center, but you can also use them outside the data center.

> **NOTE** Although you can upload and download files outside the data center, you'll be subject to internet speed; it might take you a few hours to upload or download gigabytes of data. Within the data center, you can copy gigabytes of data between BLOB storage and a worker or web role in seconds. This massive speed difference is the result of the co-location of the storage service and the roles.

SCALABILITY

Using HTTP as the underlying transport layer means that Windows Azure can leverage the web role infrastructure inside Windows Azure to host the storage services. By using the web role infrastructure to host the Windows Azure storage service (with tens of thousands of instances), you can be confident that your application will be able scale to that level. Figure 8.4 shows the abstraction of web instances for the BLOB storage service.

Because BLOB storage is built on the web role infrastructure, web roles can also harness the advantages of utility computing. As the demand for the storage services increases, Microsoft can ramp up the number of instances just like it can for any other web role. You don't need to worry about the scalability of any of the storage services (unless Microsoft runs out of pennies).

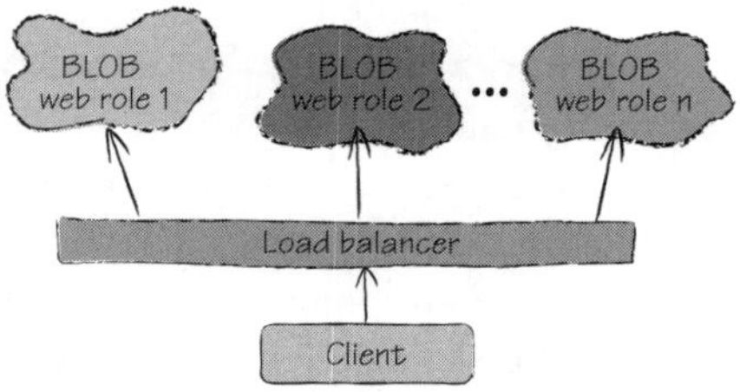

Figure 8.4 Scaling of BLOB storage services in Windows Azure

DISK STORAGE

Just as there are thousands of racks of machines used to host the web and worker roles, there are just as many disk arrays storing your data! Microsoft can grow the storage required in the data center by adding more disks as and when required. This level of enterprise-class storage means that you never need to worry about capacity or scale. Think of the BLOB service as a giant virtual hard disk that will always scale up to meet your demands and never run out of space.

DATA CONSISTENCY WITH REPLICATION

Like the DFS solution, Windows Azure BLOB storage is also a replicated solution (to be honest, you have to be to achieve such massive scale). Although the BLOB service is quite similar to the Amazon Simple Storage System (Amazon S3), replication is one of the areas in which it differs.

With Amazon S3, there's no consistency of data throughout the data center. If you upload a file to Amazon S3 and then request that same file, it's likely that a different server will process that request. As a result of network latency, the file probably won't be available to the new server because the data won't have been replicated from the original server yet. Amazon S3 suffers from the same issues seen with DFS.

This issue of replication latency can never occur in Windows Azure storage services. Windows Azure guarantees a consistent view of your data across all instances that might serve your requests. Internally, inside the Windows Azure storage services, data is replicated throughout the data center as soon as it's written to your storage account. Every piece of data must be replicated at least three times as part of the commit process.

As your data is being replicated across the various disks in Windows Azure, the FC keeps track of which instances can access the latest version of your data. The load balancer will route requests only to an instance that can access the latest version, ensuring that stale data is never served.

Even if a disk failure occurs immediately after the upload, there won't be any data loss; other disks are guaranteed to receive a copy of that data.

So far we've talked about how BLOB storage solves the problems of scalability and fault tolerance, but we haven't talked about performance. Surely performance is going to suffer; it's effectively a REST-based web service, after all.

PERFORMANCE

Sure, the performance of BLOB storage in comparison to SANs or DASs isn't all that great. Ultimately that tradeoff between performance, fault tolerance, and scalability means that performance is lost. However, within the data center, it's generally good enough performance. Because the service is ultimately a load balanced web server, you can expect 50 milliseconds to 100 milliseconds of latency between your role and the storage service. Although the latency is poor, the network connection is fast, so you can expect good enough performance. Sure, you wouldn't allow an application that needs to write to disk very quickly (for example, SQL Server) to write directly to BLOB storage, but not all applications need that kind of speed.

If you do need that level of speed, you can always cache files locally on your role using local storage. This technique will usually give you more acceptable performance for your application. In fact, this is exactly what the Azure Drive (originally called X-Drive) feature uses to ensure performance.

> **What's Azure Drive?**
>
> Although the REST API is flexible and provides great scale, it's no substitute for a good old filesystem. To make life a little easier for those bits of code that are used to talk to directories and files rather than to a web service, Microsoft has provided a new feature called Azure Drive. Azure Drive allows you to mount BLOB storage as a New Technology File System (NTFS) drive, which lets you access BLOB storage just like any other drive. Because this feature is implemented using a special OS driver that was developed specifically for Windows Azure, this feature is only available to your roles; it's not available outside the data center.
>
> As cool as Azure Drive is, it allows only one instance of a role to read and write to the Azure Drive. Multiple role instances can mount the same Azure Drive, but only in a read-only mode, and only against a snapshot of the drive itself.

Now that we've looked at how BLOB storage handles the issues that arise in traditional on-premises solutions, it's worth looking at BLOB storage from a data management perspective.

MANAGEMENT

One of the most compelling arguments for using the Windows Azure storage services is that IT professional management skills aren't required. In traditional systems, a large investment in IT management skills is usually needed to support storage. Management of the storage arrays usually requires expensive specialists who are capable of supporting the data, such as SAN experts, network specialists, technicians, administrators, and DBAs.

To plan such a system, these experts need to be able to design and implement the infrastructure, taking disk management, fault tolerance, networking, lights-out operation, and data distribution into consideration. The day-to-day running of the system includes hardware replacement, managing backups, optimizing infrastructure, health monitoring, and data cleansing, among other endless tasks.

With Windows Azure, you can let Microsoft manage the storage systems and concentrate on using the system via familiar developer APIs. You can focus on your core skill set, which is building software.

8.2 A closer look at the BLOB storage service

You have an idea how the BLOB storage service is hosted in Windows Azure. Let's look at how files are stored in the service. In this section, we'll look at the three layers of BLOB storage:

- The account
- The container
- The BLOB

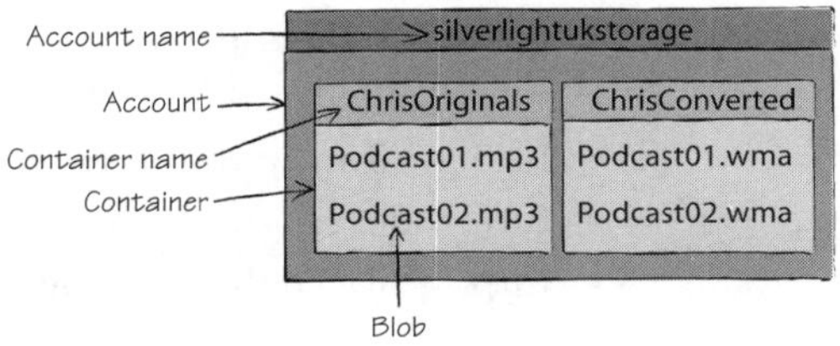

Figure 8.5 Podcast01.mp3 is stored in the ChrisOriginals container in the silverlightukstorage account

To help explain these concepts, we'll use figure 8.5 as a reference. Figure 8.5 shows how an MP3 file might be stored in BLOB storage.

Before we get all technical about accounts, containers, and BLOBs, keep this in mind: an account is simply your account. Dave has an account, Jim has an account, and you have an account. An account is about ownership. A container is somewhere you can store your BLOBs. Containers are about access control (public or private access) and some level of organization.

With that in mind, let's look at some of the specifics.

8.2.1 Accessing the BLOB (file)

In figure 8.5, you can see how files (otherwise known as BLOBs) are stored in BLOB storage. The BLOB Podcast01.wma resides in the container ChrisConverted, which resides in the storage account silverlightukstorage. A BLOB can't directly reside in a storage *account* and must live in a storage *container*. If you do need to make the BLOB available as if it's at the top level of the account (as if it doesn't have a container), you can store the BLOB in the root container; we'll explain this in more detail in chapter 10.

Because storage services use a REST-based architecture, you can retrieve a file from BLOB storage by performing an HTTP GET request to the URI for the BLOB. The following URI would let you retrieve Podcast01.wma from the ChrisConverted container (held in the silverlightukstorage storage account) from the live BLOB storage service: http://silverlightukstorage.blob.core.windows.net/ChrisConverted/Podcast01.wma.

We could formalize the URI for the live storage account as follows: http://<*storageAccount*>.blob.core.windows.net/<*Container*>/<*BlobName*>.

Let's now take a closer look at accounts, containers, and BLOBs to get a clearer understanding of these components.

8.2.2 *Setting up a storage account*

When you sign up for Windows Azure, you can create a storage account in the Azure portal. The storage account is the top level for all storage services (BLOBs, queues, and tables) that reside under it.

When you create your storage account, you'll be assigned a subdomain for each storage service. The following three domains are for the storage services:

- http://<*storageAccountName*>.blob.core.windows.net/
- http://<*storageAccountName*>.queue.core.windows.net/
- http://<*storageAccountName*>.table.core.windows.net/

In our previous example, the name of the storage account was silverlightukstorage, which means that the top-level URI for each service in our account would be as follows:

- http://silverlightukstorage.blob.core.windows.net/
- http://silverlightukstorage.queue.core.windows.net/
- http://silverlightukstorage.table.core.windows.net/

For now we're going to focus on the BLOB service, but in later chapters we'll return to the Table service and the Message Queue service.

> **How do you break up your storage accounts?**
>
> There are a couple of things to consider about your storage account, the major one being this: do you have one large account, or a separate account for each application? Although this is ultimately up to you, a good guide would be access control. If you're a small shop, then one overall account is probably suitable; however, a single account wouldn't work so well in, say, Microsoft or IBM. In these larger organizations, separating by application is probably a more suitable approach.

If you don't like the beautiful subdomain assigned to you for BLOB storage (*xxxxx*.blob.core.windows.net) then you can always assign your own domain name.

8.2.3 *Registering custom domain names*

What we'll do now is step through the process of associating your own domain name with the BLOB storage service. You'll be able to access your WMA file using this URI: http://blobs.chrishayuk.com/ChrisConverted/Podcast01.wma.

To register a custom domain name with a BLOB storage account, you have to do the following:

1. Register a suitable domain with your domain provider.
2. Set up a domain to point at Windows Azure.
3. Validate that you own the domain.
4. Set up the subdomain to point at BLOB storage.

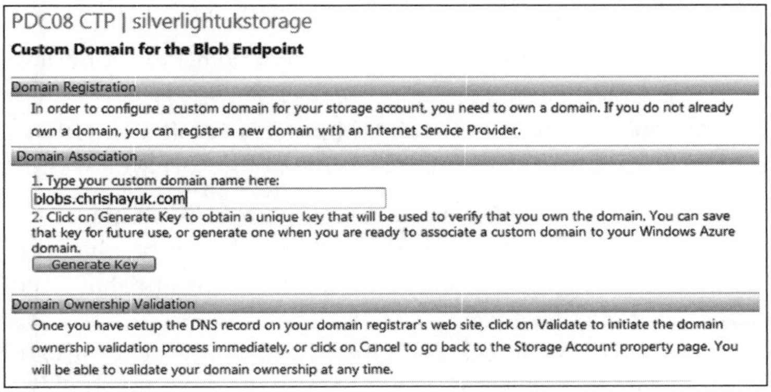

Figure 8.6 Validating in the Azure portal that you're the owner of the domain that you want to point to the BLOB storage account

We're going to skip the registering a suitable domain step. If you don't know how to do that, then I'm sure GoDaddy (or some other provider) will happily provide some instructions so they can extract some lovely dollar bills (or British Pounds, or Euro Euros) from your pocket.

SET UP A SUITABLE DOMAIN

After you've registered your domain (for example, chrishayuk.com), you need to let Windows Azure know that you want to point a suitable subdomain at it. To do that, log in to the Azure portal. Select your storage account (silverlightukstorage), and then click the Manage Domains button. You'll be faced with the page shown in figure 8.6.

After you've entered the name of the domain (including the subdomain) that you want to point to the BLOB storage account, you need to validate the domain.

VALIDATING THAT YOU OWN THE DOMAIN

Validate the domain by clicking the Generate Key button. After you click the button, you'll be presented with the screen shown in figure 8.7.

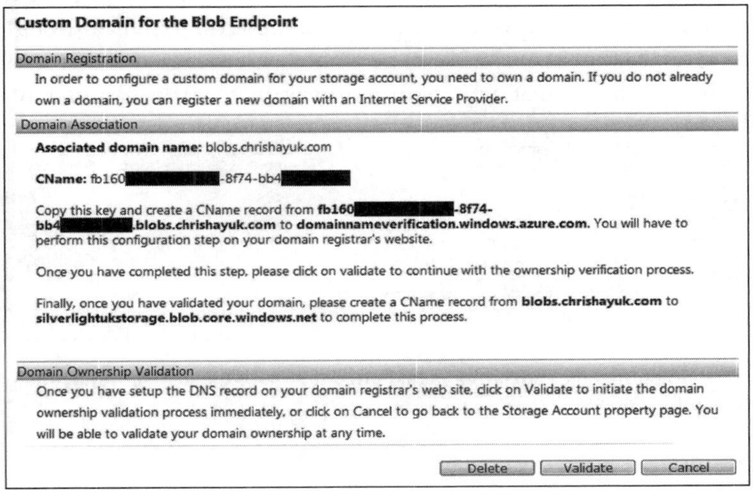

Figure 8.7 Receiving the domain validation CNAME GUID

The window in figure 8.7 indicates that you need to perform two actions:

- Add a new CNAME for the GUID (fb160. . .) that points to verify.windowsazure. com.
- Add a new CNAME for the subdomain (blobs.chrishayuk.com) that points to your BLOB storage account (silverlightukstorage.blob.core.windows.net).

Whichever company you used to register your domain probably manages the DNS for your domain name. Using their web control panel, you should be able to create the subdomain using a CNAME. Figure 8.8 shows the CNAMEs for chrishayuk.com in the GoDaddy Domain Manager.

If you manage your own DNS server, you already know how to set up a CNAME; if not, your system administrator will certainly be able to (although he might not be very pleased that you're looking to replace him with an automated system).

After you've set up your CNAMEs, return to the Windows Azure portal a little later to validate the domain (click the Validate button shown in figure 8.7). As soon as the domain has been validated, you'll be able to use your custom domain name.

Why do you need to come back later? Funnily enough, this is all to do with replication. After you've updated the DNS details on the server that's responsible for maintaining your domain records, this update needs to be replicated to all the other DNS servers in the world. This replication delay is the reason that you'll have to come back later (usually 10 minutes to an hour); it'll take a little time for the Windows Azure DNS servers to receive that update. Perhaps the world's DNS servers should use Windows Azure instead.

OK, you've got your custom domains set up and you understand containers; let's look at how you can use them to store BLOBs.

8.2.4   *Using containers to store BLOBs*

In BLOB storage, you can't store BLOBs directly in a storage account because every BLOB must live in a container. A container is really a top-level folder. Although you can set permissions directly on a BLOB, this can be a pain with a large number of BLOBs. To alleviate that administrative headache, you might want to group similar BLOBs that

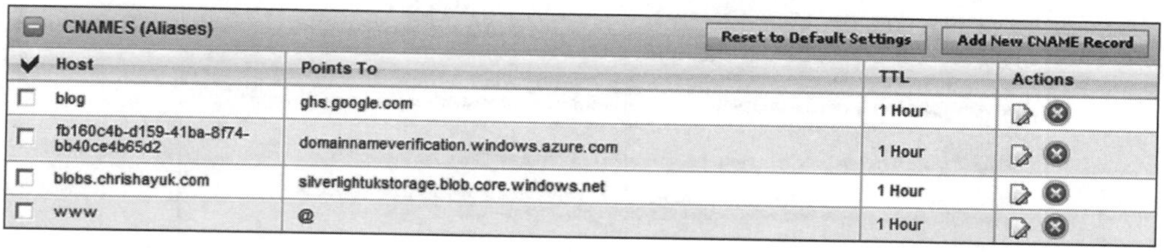

CNAMES (Aliases)		Reset to Default Settings	Add New CNAME Record	
✔ Host	Points To		TTL	Actions
☐ blog	ghs.google.com		1 Hour	📝 ❌
☐ fb160c4b-d159-41ba-8f74-bb40ce4b65d2	domainnameverification.windows.azure.com		1 Hour	📝 ❌
☐ blobs.chrishayuk.com	silverlightukstorage.blob.core.windows.net		1 Hour	📝 ❌
☐ www	@		1 Hour	📝 ❌

Figure 8.8   The CNAME entries for chrishayuk.com; notice that both the domain verification CNAME and the BLOB storage CNAME are listed

have similar access levels in the same container. Then you can set permissions at the container level rather than at the individual BLOB level.

In BLOB storage, there are two levels of access that you can set on a container: private and public.

PRIVATE CONTAINERS

BLOBs in a private container are restricted to the owner of the account. If you need to list the contents or download a BLOB stored in a private container, you need to make a request signed with your shared authentication key (in the next chapter we'll show you how to do this).

In figure 8.5, the container ChrisOriginals is a private container. If you wanted to access the BLOB podcast01.mp3, you would make a GET request to the following URI (this request must be signed with either your account master key or a pregenerated shared key; we'll explain this later): http://silverlightukstorage.blob.core.windows.net/ChrisOriginals/Podcast01.mp3.

FULL PUBLIC READ ACCESS AND PUBLIC READ-ONLY ACCESS FOR BLOBS

If the container is set to full public read access, then you can retrieve any BLOB held in the container over HTTP without providing authentication credentials. Not only that, you can list all the BLOBs in that container and query data about the container.

With public read-only access for BLOBs, anonymous requests will only be able to read a BLOB (you won't be able to read container data or list the BLOBs in the container).

In figure 8.8, the container ChrisConverted is a public container; anyone on the internet would be able to download the file podcast01.wma by making an HTTP `GET` request to http://silverlightukstorage.blob.core.windows.net/ChrisConverted/Podcast01.wma.

If you need to perform any operations beyond the container permission level (for example, if you need to upload or modify a BLOB), you need to provide authentication credentials (account owner or shared access) because these operations are restricted operations.

So far we've talked only about the live BLOB storage service. Now we'll take some time to look at how you can develop against the BLOB storage service by using a development version of the BLOB service that's in the development storage service.

8.3 Getting started with development storage

Development storage hosts all three storage services (BLOB, Queue, and Table storage services) and exposes local endpoints that implement the same APIs as the live service. The production version of the storage services and the development version are two completely different animals. They might expose the same APIs, but the development version is greatly simplified and suitable only for local development.

When you've finished developing your application against your local development storage, you can easily switch to using the live environment by just changing configuration.

SQL Server backing store

Because the development environments and the data centers of Windows Azure are drastically different (we don't have replicated storage arrays on laptops), the SDK can provide only a simulation of the live storage environment. Although development storage and BLOB storage are API–compatible, the underlying implementations are understandably different.

In the development storage version of BLOB storage, SQL Server is used as the backing store.

> **Installation issues**
>
> By default, the development storage database is created in the SQLEXPRESS named instance of SQL Server on your development machine. This instance is normally installed as part of the Visual Studio installation, which is why the SDK assumes that this instance is present. If you need or want to install the database onto a different SQL Server instance, you can use a tool in the SDK called DSInit.exe. You might want to do this if you prefer to run a full-blown version of SQL Server on your machine or if you skipped installing the SQLEXPRESS instance during the Visual Studio installation.

If you want, you can even run queries against the database to ensure that your data is stored as you expected. Figure 8.9 shows all the tables representing the various storage services in the SQL Server implementation.

Figure 8.9 Development storage database in SQL Server

Although the development storage system uses SQL Server (as shown in figure 8.9), the real BLOB storage system uses a higher performing, more scalable, custom solution that makes the best use of the Windows Azure infrastructure. You can be assured that your BLOBs aren't stored in some SQL Server table in the live system.

8.3.2 *Getting around in the development storage UI*

The development storage service is automatically started whenever you run a web or worker role project in Visual Studio. The startup of development storage occurs at the same time as the startup of the development fabric, as described in chapter 2. If you

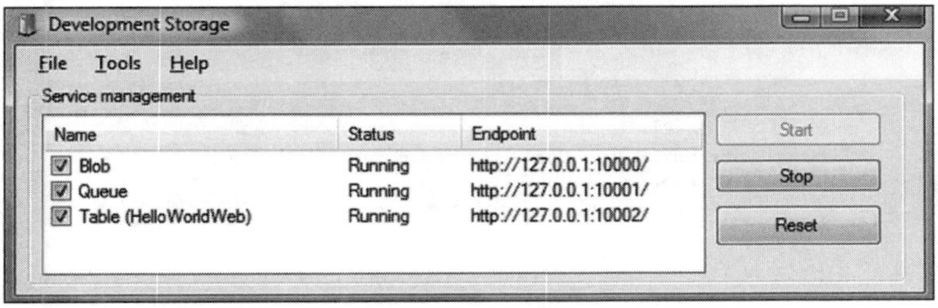

Figure 8.10 Development storage command and control center. You can start, stop, and mess around with all your storage services from here.

right-click the Cloud Services icon in the status bar and select Show Development Storage UI, the Development Storage UI is displayed, as shown in figure 8.10.

The development storage UI shows you the current status of your services and lets you stop and start them if you need to. Although development storage and the development storage UI are automatically launched when you run your application in Visual Studio, you can start them manually using the command line. This can be useful if you're interacting with the storage services from an application that's not hosted in the cloud (a normal WPF application that just uses the BLOB storage service).

> **Starting and shutting down development storage manually**
>
> To start development storage manually, you can use the following command:
>
> ```
> C:\Program Files\Windows Azure SDK\v1.1\bin\devstore\dsservice.exe
> ```
>
> To shut down the service, you can use this command:
>
> ```
> C:\Program Files\Windows Azure SDK\v1.1\bin\devstore\dsservice.exe/shutdown
> ```

With the basics of both BLOB storage and development storage under your belt, get ready! It's time to write your first application that talks to the BLOB service.

8.4 Developing against containers

Before we start writing some code against the containers, we should probably discuss where this type of functionality is useful.

If you just need a shared storage area where you can read BLOBs, you'll probably eventually use the Azure Drive functionality (discussed in chapter 10) rather than interacting with the BLOB storage APIs directly. Even so, it's still useful to understand how the BLOB storage APIs work, because Azure Drive interacts with these APIs too.

If you need a scalable application in which more than one role needs to write to a single shared storage area, then you'll need to use the StorageClient library or the REST APIs directly.

Over the next few sections, we'll be looking at the kinds of operations you can perform against containers. Using containers is particularly interesting when you need to dynamically create storage areas and assign permissions to different parties in a scalable

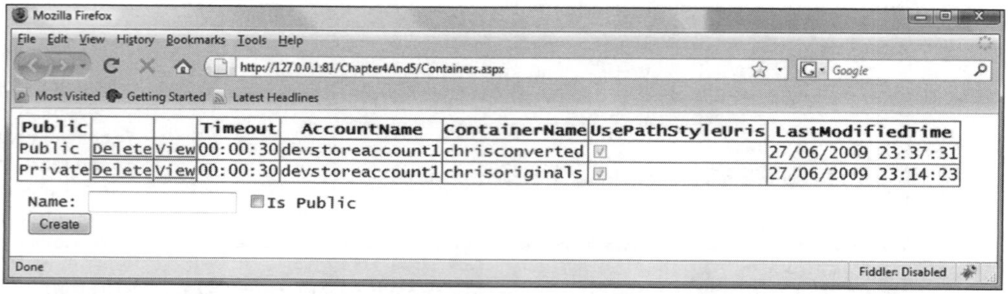

Figure 8.11 When you've finished this section, you'll have an application that can display a list of containers in your storage account using ASP.NET.

fashion. Typical scenarios for using containers are file hosting, enterprise workflows, and data manipulation applications that need to access data. In the next chapter, we'll look at how you can use containers in these kinds of scenarios by generating dynamic keys; we'll also talk about setting permissions on containers.

For now, we'll return to our podcast example. You need a method of creating public and private containers to store your original and converted podcasts in. In this sample application, you'll create an ASP.NET web form page in which to do that. Your final application will look like the screenshot displayed in figure 8.11.

Over the next few sections we'll look at the following topics, which will help you build the web page displayed in figure 8.11:

- Working with the StorageClient library (which is included in the Windows Azure SDK)
- Accessing the development storage account
- Creating a container
- Listing containers
- Deleting a container

By the end of this section, you'll have created the above web page and you'll have a vast knowledge of containers.

Before we get started, you need to create a new web role project in Visual Studio (as described in chapter 1). You should call this web role `PodcastSample`.

8.4.1 Accessing the StorageClient library

There are two ways of interacting with any of the storage services: you can either use the REST API directly or you can use the StorageClient library API. In this book, we're going to look at both methods.

One of the reasons that we'll look at both methods is that the StorageClient library is just a .NET wrapper for the REST API. For new features, Microsoft will often release the REST API call before adding the feature to the StorageClient library. By understanding both methods of interaction, you'll be able to use any new feature immediately (if you need to).

Another reason for looking at the REST API is that the underlying mechanism is heavily abstracted away from you. By understanding the underlying calls, you can make the best decisions architecturally for your application (especially regarding performance).

Now you might be thinking, "If the REST API is so great, why are we using the StorageClient library?" The answer to that is quite simple: as flexible as the REST API is to use, it's one huge pain. Using the REST API directly means we get to write unreadable code; `HttpWebRequest` code with no IntelliSense support. By using the StorageClient library wherever possible, we get to write familiar .NET code (with IntelliSense support), which increases productivity. We can ultimately spend more time doing more important things (like browsing the internet or playing Halo).

Although the StorageClient library (Microsoft.WindowsAzure.StorageClient.dll) is automatically referenced in any new web or worker role projects that you create, you can add the reference manually if you need to. You can find the reference at C:\Program Files\Windows Azure SDK\v1.1\ref\.

You don't need to add this assembly to your project; it's already referenced. But when you're building your own code, you'll probably want to split your code into proper layers. If you do that, you'll need to add the assembly to your own custom assembly.

Now that you know how to reference your assembly, let's look at how you configure the StorageClient library to access your development storage account.

8.4.2 Accessing development storage

To use development storage for storing BLOBs, you need to configure your application to use the development BLOB service in the same way as you would if it were the live system.

There are two ways to tell your code to connect to the local development storage. The first is to use a magic string as your connection string. If you set your connection string to `UseDevelopmentStorage=true`, the development storage fabric will respond to the connections. You can also put in the real development storage fabric connection. The format of the connection string for development storage will look a lot like a production connection string. The following parts are all that's different:

- *Account name*—The only account name that's supported for development storage is the default name, `devstoreaccount1`.
- *Account shared key*—The default name for this value is this:
  ```
  Eby8vdM02xNOcqFlqUwJPLlmEtlCDXJ1OUzFT50u
  ➥ SRZ6IFsuFq2UVErCz4I6tq/K1SZFPTOtr/KBHBeksoGMGw==
  ```
- *Endpoint*—The BLOB storage endpoint for development storage BLOB services is by default 127.0.0.1:10000. To access the BLOB file in the example in section 8.2.1 from the development storage BLOB service, you would use the following URI: http://127.0.0.1:10000/devstoreaccount1/ChrisConverted/Podcast01.wma. This URI can be formalized as http://127.0.0.1:10000/*<StorageAccountName>*/*<Container>*/*<BlobName>*.

You can change the default values for each of these items in the DSService.exe.config file, but it's recommended that you use the default values.

In development storage, there's no ability to create or host multiple storage accounts and there's no Azure portal, so you can't easily generate a new key. The endpoints and URI structure also differ from the live system.

With that knowledge in hand, let's look at how you can use this information to access your account in code.

STORING ACCOUNT DETAILS IN THE SERVICE CONFIGURATION FILE

To make things a little easier, the Windows Azure SDK provides a property that will spin up a `CloudStorageAccount` object with the default development storage settings:

```
CloudStorageAccount = CloudStorageAccount.DevelopmentStorageAccount;
```

Although this is probably the quickest method of getting started, it isn't best practice. Starting this way, you're effectively hardcoding your application to your development account. You'd have to modify and recompile your code before you could deploy your application to the live system, which can complicate your build process and introduce bugs.

The best practice for storing this information is to store the data in the service configuration file, which gives you the option to change this information without redeploying the whole application. For example, if your shared key is compromised, then you would be able to generate a new shared key and modify your application to use the new key by simply changing the service configuration via the Azure portal.

To help you easily use the ServiceConfiguration.cscfg file to store your account details, the StorageClient library provides a method that can extract the account name, shared key, and endpoint from a configuration setting. The following call is used by the library to extract these values:

```
CloudStorageAccount =
   CloudStorageAccount.FromConfigurationSetting("DataConnectionString");
```

In the above example, your account details will be extracted from a configuration setting named `DataConnectionString`.

Although this code is specific to the StorageClient library, you should still store the account details in the service configuration file, even if you're using the REST API directly. Storing the details there will simplify and standardize your code and allow you to easily use both the StorageClient library and the REST API directly within your application (you don't want to have to modify two different settings to access your account).

Now that you know how easy it is to extract an account from your configuration, let's look at how you define that configuration setting.

DEFINING CONFIGURATION SETTINGS

As explained in chapter 4, you'll first need to define your configuration settings in the service definition file before you can configure them. The following setting is the standard method of defining your storage account in your service definition file.

```
<ConfigurationSettings>
   <Setting name="DataConnectionString"/>
</ConfigurationSettings>
```

Notice in this code that `DataConnectionString` is the same name that was passed to the `FromConfigurationSetting` method to extract the account name, shared key, and endpoint values.

COMMUNICATING WITH DEVELOPMENT STORAGE

After you've defined the configuration settings, you can set the runtime values in your service configuration file. The following configuration settings are the defaults used to talk to development storage:

```
<ConfigurationSettings>
  <Setting name="DataConnectionString"
           value="UseDevelopmentStorage=true" />
</ConfigurationSettings>
```

By setting the value of `DataConnectionString` to `UseDevelopmentStorage=true`, you're effectively telling the storage client to extract your settings from the DSService.exe.config file, which gives you the same result as using the `DevelopmentStorageAccount` property.

The advantage of using the `FromConfigurationSetting` method over the `DevelopmentStorageAccount` property is that you can modify the service configuration file to use the live account details (shown later in this chapter) without having to recompile or redeploy your application.

Now that your application is configured to use development storage via the StorageClient library, you can continue on and create your web page.

8.4.3 *Creating a container*

Now you're going to create the web page shown in figure 8.11. In your podcast sample web role project, create a new ASPX page called containers.aspx.

At this stage, you only want to write the code that will create your container; you don't need to see the list of containers. At present, your UI needs to display only the new container name text box and the Create Container button.

The following listing shows the ASPX required for the create-container section of the page.

Listing 8.1 ASPX for creating a container

```
<div>
   <div>
   Name: <asp:TextBox ID="txtContainerName" runat="server" />   <-- Name of the container to create
</div>
<div>
   <asp:Button ID="btnCreate" runat="server"
               Text="Create" OnClick="btnCreate_Click" />   <-- Creates the button
</div>
</div>
```

You've defined your UI. Now you need to create the code that handles the button click. See the following listing, which contains the code-behind for the create button click event.

Listing 8.2 Creating a new container

```
protected void btnCreate_Click(object sender, EventArgs e)
{
   CloudStorageAccount account =
      CloudStorageAccount.FromConfigurationSetting("DataConnectionString");

   CloudBlobClient blobClient =
      account.CreateCloudBlobClient();                    <-- Creates the BLOB client

   CloudBlobContainer container =
      blobClient.GetContainerReference(txtContainerName.Text.ToLower()); <-- Gets reference to container

   container.Create();          <-- Creates container
}
```

Before we explain this code, we want to remind you of its purpose. The user will type in the new container name and then click the button to create the new container. Now let's look at the code.

STORAGE ACCOUNT

The first thing you need to do is retrieve an object that allows you to work with the BLOB storage account. Using the `CloudStorageAccount` object that you used earlier to extract your credentials, you can now instantiate a `CloudBlobClient` object that will allow you to mess with things at an account level by issuing the following call:

```
CloudBlobClient blobClient =
      account.CreateCloudBlobClient();
```

After you've retrieved the `CloudBlobClient` object, you can perform the following operations at an account level on BLOB storage:

- Return a list of all containers in the account (`ListContainers`)
- Get a specific container (`GetContainerReference`)
- List BLOBs (`ListBlobsWithPrefix`)
- Get a specific BLOB (`GetBlobReference`)

As well as performing these operations, you can also set some general policies, including the following ones:

- Block sizes
- Retry policy
- Timeout
- Number of parallel threads

In this example, because you're creating a new container, you need to grab a reference to the container that you want to create. Use the `GetContainerReference` method, passing in the name of your new container:

```
CloudBlobContainer container =
      blobClient.GetContainerReference(txtContainerName.Text.ToLower());
```

In this example, you're setting the container name to whatever the user types in the text box.

> **NOTE** The name of the container is converted to lowercase because the BLOB storage service doesn't allow uppercase characters in the container name.

So far you've just set up the container you want to create; you haven't made any communication with the storage service. The `CloudBlobContainer` object that has been returned by `GetContainerReference` can perform the following operations:

- Create a container (`Create`)
- Delete a container (`Delete`)
- Get and set any custom metadata you want to associate with the container
- Get properties associated with the container (for example, `ETag` and last modified time)
- Get and set container permissions
- List BLOBs (`ListBlobs`)
- Get a specific BLOB

Now make a call to create the container:

```
container.Create();
```

As soon as you call the `Create` method, the storage client generates an HTTP request to the BLOB storage service, requesting that the container be created.

> **Default permissions**
>
> In the `Create` container call, you didn't specify any permissions on the container to be created. By default, a container is created as private access only, meaning that only the account owner can access the container or any of the BLOBs contained within it. In the next chapter, we'll look at how you can set permissions on containers and BLOBs.

You should now be able to run your web role and create some containers in your development storage account. At this point, you won't be able to see the containers that you've created in your web page, but you can check that they're there by running a SQL query against the BlobContainer table in the development storage database.

Now that you can create a container from your web page, you need to modify the page so that you can display all the containers in your storage account.

8.4.4 Listing containers

In the figure 8.11, there's a grid that contains a list of all the containers in the account. To create that grid, you need to update your asp.net page to include an ASP.NET `GridView` component (you're going to eventually bind this grid to a list of containers). You should place the code in the following listing before the code in listing 8.1 in the containers.aspx page.

Listing 8.3 Listing BLOBs with a GridView

```
<asp:GridView ID="gvContainers" runat="server"
              AutoGenerateColumns="true"              <-- Autogenerates columns in grid from bound object
              onrowcommand="gvContainers_RowCommand"
              onrowdeleting="gvContainers_RowDeleting">
   <Columns>
       <asp:TemplateField>                             <-- Deletes container
          <ItemTemplate>
          <asp:LinkButton ID="btnDelete" runat="server"
                          Text="Delete"
                          CommandName="Delete"
  CommandArgument='<%#Eval("Name")%>'/>
          </ItemTemplate>
        </asp:TemplateField>
    <asp:HyperLinkField Text="View"                    Hyperlink for page listing BLOBs
            DataNavigateUrlFields="Name"
            DataNavigateUrlFormatString="Blobs.aspx?Container={0}" />  <--
   </Columns>
</asp:GridView>
```

The code in listing 8.3 is the ASP.NET markup for figure 8.11. Notice that you're allowing the grid to autogenerate all the columns (except the Delete button and the View hyperlink) based on the properties of the object bound to the grid. Listing 8.4 shows the code-behind for your web page that gets a list of containers from the account and binds it to the grid.

Listing 8.4 Binding the grid

```
protected void Page_Load(object sender, EventArgs e)
{
   if (!IsPostBack)
   {
       CloudStorageAccount.SetConfigurationSettingPublisher(
       ➥ (configName, configSetter) =>
          {
            configSetter(RoleEnvironment
            ➥ .GetConfigurationSettingValue(configName));
         });
   BindGrid();
}
}

private void BindGrid()
{
   CloudStorageAccount account =
      CloudStorageAccount.FromConfigurationSetting("DataConnectionString");

   CloudBlobClient blobClient =
      account.CreateCloudBlobClient();
```

```
gvContainers.DataSource =
    blobClient.ListContainers();              <-- Sets grid data source as list
                                                  of containers in account
gvContainers.DataBind();    <-- Binds data grid
                                to its data source
}
```

One interesting thing you'll see in the `Page_Load` method is a call to `SetConfigurationSettingPublisher`. We wouldn't normally put this code here, but it was the easiest place to put it in the book. When you load configuration in ASP.NET, it looks in the web.config file by default. If you're storing your configuration in the .csdef file, ASP.NET will never find it. By including this line of code, you're telling ASP.NET to look in the .cscfg file for the configuration you're trying to load. We would normally put this in the `Role_OnStart` event, or somewhere else where it'll be run once per role instance as it starts up.

Now you have a web page that will display all the containers in your storage account. The page also allows you to create new private containers. To complete your sample, you just need to implement the delete functionality.

8.4.5 Deleting a container

You want to be able to click the Delete button on a particular row in your web page to delete the underlying container. For this to happen, you need to hook in your Delete button. The following listing shows the code-behind for implementing the delete functionality.

Listing 8.5 Deleting the container

```
protected void gvContainers_RowCommand
                        (object sender, GridViewCommandEventArgs e)
{
   if (e.CommandName == "Delete")
   {
       DeleteContainer(e.CommandArgument.ToString());   <-- Calls DeleteContainer
   }                                                        method on receiving
                                                            Delete command
   BindGrid();
}

private void DeleteContainer(string containerName)
{
      CloudStorageAccount account =
         CloudStorageAccount.FromConfigurationSetting
         ➥ ("DataConnectionString");

      CloudBlobClient blobClient =
      account.CreateCloudBlobClient();

      CloudBlobContainer container =
      blobClient.GetContainerReference(containerName);   <-- Gets container from
                                                             BLOB account
   container.Delete();      <-- Deletes container
}
```

```
protected void gvContainers_RowDeleting(object sender,
➥ GridViewDeleteEventArgs e)
{

}
```

Empties RowDeleting handler to avoid exceptions

With the Delete button code hooked in, you should be able to run your application and view all the BLOB containers in development storage, add a container, and then delete it from your web page.

Wow, you've done a great job. You've just completed your first Windows Azure BLOB storage application. All that's left is to make this baby work against the live BLOB storage service.

8.5 Configuring your application to work against the live service

To switch your application from the development storage to the live storage account, you need to create a live storage account and switch your configuration to it. In this section, we won't go through the process of creating a storage account; it's pretty simple and the information you require is available in this chapter. We're going to focus on configuring your application to work against your live storage account.

> **Always set affinity for your storage account**
>
> During the process of creating your storage account, always set affinity, as described in chapter 2 when we discussed the Azure portal. If you don't set affinity, it's possible that your web role might be hosted in Washington State, but your storage account is hosted in Chicago. The latency caused by cross-data-center communication will harm the performance of your application. To gain maximum performance, always set affinity on your web roles, worker roles, and storage accounts to the same data center; this ensures that you achieve the best possible network latency.

8.5.1 Switching to the live storage account

To make your application work against the live system, all you need to do is modify the value of your configuration setting in the service configuration file. That's it, the end, nothing else to do. If you remember earlier, you set your storage account configuration setting to the following:

```
<Setting name="DataConnectionString"
              value="UseDevelopmentStorage=true" />
```

Although this is great for the development storage, it doesn't give you a clue to the structure of the setting for when you want to use the live system. The following setting shows how the string should be structured.

```
<Setting name="DataConnectionString"
              value="DefaultEndpointsProtocol=protocol;
              AccountName=storageaccountname;
              AccountKey=storageaccountkey" />
```

To make this run against the live system, plug in the appropriate values:

```
<Setting name="DataConnectionString"
         value="DefaultEndpointsProtocol=http;
         AccountName=silverlightukstorage;
         AccountKey=Eby8vdM02xNOcqFlqUwJPLlmEtlCDX
         ➥ J1OUzFT50uSRZ6IFsuFq2UVErCz4I6tq/K1SZFPTOtr/KBHBeksoGMGw==
" />
```

Now that you've configured the live settings, you can use the live BLOB storage system either from the development fabric or from the live production fabric. The only thing left to do is to configure the access key.

8.5.2 Configuring the access key

If you're unsure where you get the account key for the storage account, you can always refer to the Azure portal. When a new storage account is created in Windows Azure, a primary and secondary access key is generated for you to secure your API requests. The access key for your live account is used by all storage services and is available from the storage account section of the portal. Figure 8.12 shows the window in which you can retrieve your access key. When you retrieve this key, it replaces the development key held in the service configuration file.

If your access key is compromised at any point, you can generate a new key by clicking the Regenerate button shown in figure 8.12. After a new key has been generated, you'll need to update the key in the service configuration for your application. You also have two keys that are valid at one point in time. Both keys are identical in what they allow the user to do with them. Having two keys is a great way to provide rolling key updates without any downtime in your system.

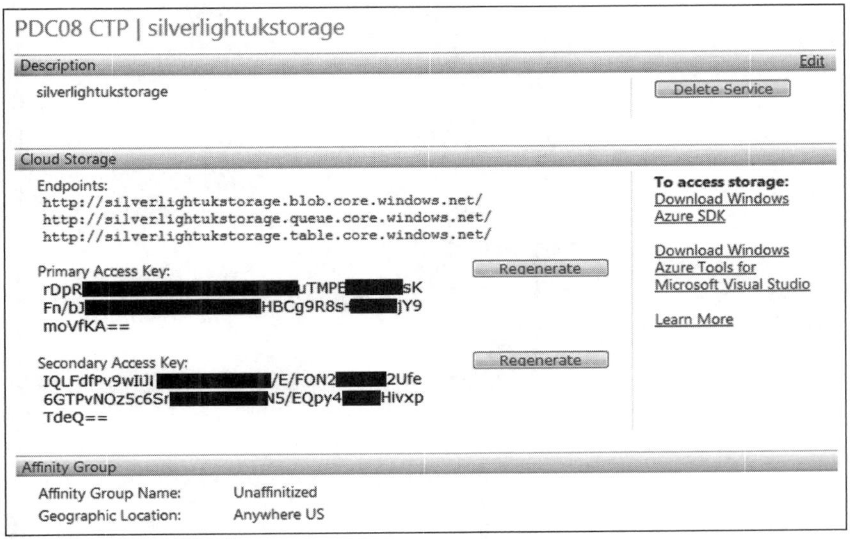

Figure 8.12 Access key in the Azure portal

8.6 Summary

In this chapter, we provided a quick overview of the sorts of problems that you would normally face when trying to provide a shared storage solution in a traditional web farm. Sharing files between multiple servers isn't easy, but Windows Azure provides a neat mechanism that lets you forget about those worries. After a brief introduction to storage services, we showed you how BLOB storage fits into the overall architecture.

Then we jumped right into developing your first application, using the BLOB storage service. First, we used the StorageClient library supplied in the SDK to hit the development environment; then we changed the configuration so it could work against the live production system.

Now you have an appreciation of how easy it is to get started with BLOB storage and containers. Next we're going to look at how to use the APIs that work with BLOB files themselves.

9 Uploading and downloading BLOBs

This chapter covers

- Uploading files
- Downloading files
- Serving files from BLOB storage using an HTTP handler
- Improving performance using local storage
- Using custom metadata
- Blob storage shared access

In the previous chapter, we showed you how to get started with BLOB storage development using the StorageClient library, with a focus on managing accounts and containers. In this chapter, we're going to look at the underlying REST API for the BLOB service and how to manage BLOBs using the StorageClient library.

9.1 Using the REST API

So far we've only used the StorageClient sample library in the SDK and have ignored the REST API. The reason for this is that, as a developer, you're unlikely to be writing code directly against the REST API. In general, you'll prefer to use a more object-oriented structure that uses familiar-looking .NET classes.

The StorageClient library is useful but it's only a wrapper implementation of the REST API (which is the only official API). So although you'll mainly be working against the StorageClient library, there are some instances when you might need to use the REST API directly.

Windows Azure is an evolving platform and the Windows Azure team typically releases new features exposed via the REST API first. At a later date, they might provide an update to the SDK. If there's a new feature that you badly need to use, you might not have the luxury of waiting for the SDK update.

Another reason that you might need to use the REST API directly is that not all features are implemented (or implemented in the way you might expect) in the SDK; you might need to drop down to the REST API to use that feature. Rather than showing you every single feature with the REST API, we'll try to show you the important parts: how to list BLOBs in a public container and how to authenticate private requests using the REST API.

9.1.1 *Listing BLOBs in a public container using REST*

In this example, you're going create a small console application that'll return a list of all the BLOBs in a public container using the REST API. To do that, let's return to the funky little podcasting conversion sample that we were developing in the previous chapter. In that application, let's assume that you've converted a bunch of MP3s to WMA, and now you want to list all the converted podcasts. In the console application that you're going to develop, all the BLOBs stored in the ChrisConverted public container (which holds the WMA files) are going to be returned from the silverlightsukstorage BLOB service account in the live production system. Figure 9.1 shows the information that's returned from the request within your console application. This XML output shows that this container contains a single .wma file called mi2limpbiskit.wma.

file:///C:/AzureBook/Source/PlayArea/AzurePlayArea/WebLoad/bin/Debug/WebLoad.EXE
<EnumerationResults ContainerName="http://silverlightukstorage.blob.core.windows.net/chrisconverted">
<Blobs>
<Blob>
<Name>mi2limpbiskit.wma</Name>
<Url>http://silverlightukstorage.blob.core.windows.net/chrisconverted/mi2limpbiskit.wma</Url>
<LastModified>Sun, 28 Jun 2009 17:21:33 GMT</LastModified>
<Etag>0x8CBC62C04ACF0B0</Etag>
<Size>5128497</Size>
<ContentType>application/octet-stream</ContentType>
<ContentEncoding />
<ContentLanguage />
</Blob>
</Blobs>
<NextMarker />
</EnumerationResults>

Figure 9.1 Console application that returns a list of BLOBs from a public container, using REST

To create the code that returns this output, create a new console application in Visual Studio and replace the existing static main method with the code in the following listing.

Listing 9.1 Listing the BLOBs in a container via REST

```
static void Main(string[] args)
{
   HttpWebRequest hwr =
      CreateHttpRequest(new Uri(@"http://
     silverlightukstorage.blob.core.windows.net/
     ➥ chrisconverted?restype=container&comp=list"),
     ➥ "GET", new TimeSpan(0, 0, 30));                 ❶ Sets up the request with correct destination URI

   using (StreamReader sr =
      new  StreamReader(hwr.GetResponse().GetResponseStream()))   ❷ Gets stream that represents results returned from GET
   {
   XDocument myDocument = XDocument.Parse(sr.ReadToEnd());

   Console.Write(myDocument.ToString());
   }

   Console.ReadKey();
}

private static HttpWebRequest CreateHttpRequest(
➥ Uri uri, string httpMethod, TimeSpan timeout)
{
   HttpWebRequest request = (HttpWebRequest)HttpWebRequest.Create(uri);
request.Timeout = (int)timeout.TotalMilliseconds;
request.ReadWriteTimeout = (int)timeout.TotalMilliseconds;
request.Method = httpMethod;
request.ContentLength = 0;
request.Headers.Add("x-ms-date",
   DateTime.UtcNow.ToString("R", CultureInfo.InvariantCulture));   ❸ Adds correct date header
request.Headers.Add("x-ms-version", "2009-09-19");                 ❹ Adds correct version header
         return request;
}
```

Wow, that's quite a bit of code. All it really does is list the BLOBs in a public container and output the result to the console (as shown in figure 9.1). Unfortunately, whenever you use the REST API directly, your code will get more complex. (I guess you can see why we prefer to use the StorageClient library.)

Remember that the HTTP requests that were generated by the code in listing 9.1 are the same requests that the StorageClient library generates on your behalf.

In listing 9.1, the `GET` request is created at ❶. This verb indicates that you want some data returned from the server rather than have an action performed that'll update the data (such as a create, update, or delete). The request is executed at ❷.

Let's now take a deeper look at the rest of the code in listing 9.1; doing so will give you a better understanding of the communication between your clients and the storage accounts.

THE URI

Look at the URI that you're calling at ❶. There's some interesting information about the request that's being made.

From the domain, you can determine that you're using the live BLOB storage service (`blob.core.windows.net`) and that the request is being made against the storage account silverlightukstorage. Looking at the request, you can also derive that you want a list of whatever is in the container ChrisConverted (`chrisconverted?comp=list`), which we know are BLOBs (in fact, they're the WMA files that were converted from MP3).

Windows Azure follows a standard naming convention for performing requests; as soon as you're familiar with some of the API calls it's easy to infer what other calls might look like. For example, if you required a list of whatever resides in a storage account (containers), you could use the following URI:

```
http://silverlightukstorage.blob.core.windows.net/?comp=list
```

You would need to sign the request with your access key because it isn't a public operation. Listing BLOBs in a public container can be performed without an authorization key because an authorization key is required only for private containers.

THE REQUEST HEADERS

In the code for the standard `CreateHttpRequest` in listing 9.1, two headers are set: `x-ms-version` and `x-ms-date`.

The `x-ms-version` header ❹ is an optional header that should be treated as a required header. The storage service versioning policy is that when a new version of an API is released, any existing APIs will continue to be supported. By providing the correct `x-ms-version` header, you're stating which API you want your request to work against. Using this policy, Microsoft can release new functionality and change existing APIs but allow your existing services to continue to work against the previous API.

> **TIP** You should always check the version of the REST API that you're using to support a particular feature. At ❹ we're using the September 19, 2009 version of the API. If a new feature is released and it isn't working, there's a good chance that you forgot to update the version. The good news is that whenever you download the latest version of the StorageClient library, it'll already be using the correct version.

The `x-ms-date` header is a required header that states the time of the client request. We set this value at ❸ in listing 9.1. The value set in the request header is a representation of the current time in UTC; for example, "Sat, 27 Jun 2009 23:37:31 GMT". This request header serves two purposes:

- It allows the server to generate the same authorization hash as the client
- It prevents replay attacks by denying old requests

> **TIP** If you suddenly start getting errors whenever you call the storage service, it might be worth checking the time on your machine. If the time of the

request is out of synchronization with the server time in the data centers (older than 15 minutes), the request will be rejected with a 403 response code.

We've looked at how to make non-authenticated requests against a public container and how to make requests to the storage accounts via the SDK. We'll now look at how to make authenticated requests via the REST API and give you an understanding of how the REST API calls are authenticated.

9.1.2 Authenticating private requests

In the previous section, you developed a console application to return a list of the files that reside in your public container (ChrisConverted). Now you're going to modify this code to return all the containers in your development storage account. This sample is the direct REST API equivalent of the storage client calls that we performed in the previous chapter.

Because there's only two containers in the development storage account (ChrisOriginals and ChrisConverted), we expect the following XML output from the console application:

```
<EnumerationResults AccountName="http://128.0.0.1:10000/devstoreaccount1/">
  <Containers>
    <Container>
      <Name>chrisconverted</Name>
      <Url>http://128.0.0.1:10000/devstoreaccount1/chrisconverted</Url>
      <LastModified>Sat, 27 Jun 2009 23:37:31 GMT</LastModified>
      <Etag>0x8CBC5975FB7A0D0</Etag>
    </Container>
    <Container>
      <Name>chrisoriginals</Name>
      <Url>http://128.0.0.1:10000/devstoreaccount1/chrisoriginals</Url>
      <LastModified>Sat, 27 Jun 2009 23:14:23 GMT</LastModified>
      <Etag>0x8CBC594247EFB60</Etag>
    </Container>
  </Containers>
  <NextMarker />
</EnumerationResults>
```

Listing 9.2 contains the code that we used to make this request via the REST API. Before you can run this sample, you'll need to reference the storage client because you're going to use some of its library calls to sign the HTTP request with the shared access key. You'll also need the following `using` statement at the top of your class:

```
using Microsoft.WindowsAzure.StorageClient;
```

Listing 9.2 Listing the containers in the development storage account via REST

```
static void Main(string[] args)
{
   HttpWebRequest hwr = CreateHttpRequest(
      new Uri(@"http://127.0.0.1:10000/devstoreaccount1?comp=list"),
      "GET", new TimeSpan(0, 0, 30));
```

Creates HTTP request as before

```
...CloudStorageAccount.SetConfigurationSettingPublisher
➥ ((configName, configSetter) =>
                 { configSetter(ConfigurationManager
                 ➥ .AppSettings[configName]); });

var account =
   CloudStorageAccount.FromConfigurationSetting("DataConnectionString");

account.Credentials.SignRequest(hwr);

using (StreamReader sr =
         new
     StreamReader(hwr.GetResponse().GetResponseStream()))
{
   XDocument myDocument = XDocument.Parse(sr.ReadToEnd());
               Console.Write(myDocument.ToString());
}

   Console.ReadKey();
}
```

Gets account credentials using StorageClient library

Signs request using StorageClient library

Executes request and gets response

The code in listing 9.2 is similar to the code in listing 9.1 except that we're using a different URI (because we're listing containers rather than BLOBs) and signing the request. The URI for listing containers in the development storage account is http://127.0.0.1:10000/devstoreaccount1/?comp=list. This URI will return a list of the contents of the storage account (a list of containers).

Apart from the URI, the only difference between the two listings is that you sign the HTTP web request with your shared-key credentials. The process of signing the request is quite complicated; it's best to use the storage client code as we've done in listing 9.2.

Use the same code that you wrote earlier to extract the configuration setting:

```
var account =
   CloudStorageAccount.FromConfigurationSetting("DataConnectionString");
```

TIP `CloudStorageAccount.FromConfigurationSetting` will work with both Windows Azure `ConfigurationSettings` and regular .NET application settings.

Now sign the request using the request signing functionality built into the StorageClient library:

```
account.Credentials.SignRequest(hwr);
```

Using the `SignRequest` method also adds the `x-ms-date` header information to the request, so you don't have to add it on your own. Be aware that if you add the `x-ms-date` header on your own and you sign the request with `SignRequest`, the header might not be populated correctly.

Even if you do plan to use only the REST API, it's still worth referencing the StorageClient library just to use that bit of code.

SIGNING THE REQUEST

Although the request signing code is already implemented, let's look at the overall process of signing a request.

If you were to look at the HTTP request that you generated in listing 9.2 (you could stick a breakpoint after the request has been signed), you would see that the request contains an Authorization header. The Authorization header for the request in listing 9.2 is

```
SharedKey devstoreaccount1:J5xkbSz7/7Xf8sCNY3RJIzyUEfnj1SJ3ccIBNpDzsq4=
```

The signature in the header (the long string after `devstoreaccount1`) is generated by canonicalizing the request. The canonicalized request is hashed using a SHA-256 algorithm and then encoded as the signature using Base64 encoding.

> **DEFINITION** Canonicalizing is a defined process that converts a request into a predictable request. You can find more information about the canonicalization process at http://msdn.microsoft.com/en-us/library/dd179428.aspx.

PROCESSING THE REQUEST

After the request is received by the server, the server takes the incoming request and performs the same canonicalization and hashing process with the shared key. If the signature that's generated matches the Authorization header, the server can perform the request. Figure 9.2 shows the validation process between the client and the BLOB storage service. Notice that the authorization key generated by the server matches the original client request.

If the signature generated by the server is different from the Authorization header, then the server won't process the request and returns a 400 response code (`Bad Request`). Being able to generate the same authorization key both client-side and server-side means that users who don't have the shared key are prevented from performing unauthorized requests against the account. Because the shared key is never sent between the client and the BLOB storage service, the risk of the key being compromised is substantially reduced.

The authorization key is generated from both the contents of the request and the shared key. Generating the hash with both pieces of information means that the user can't tamper with the request to perform another operation. If, for example, a hacker

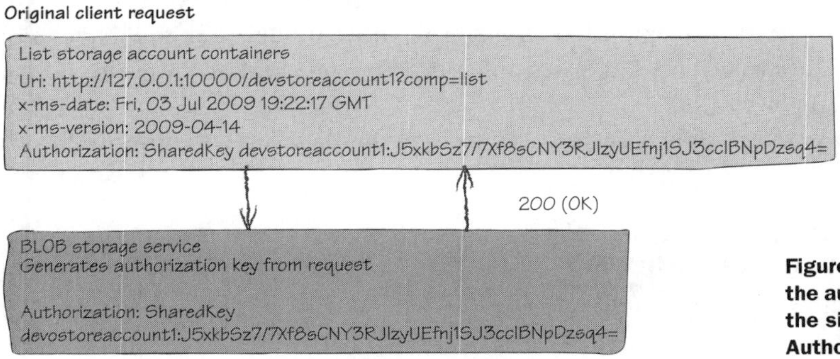

Original client request
List storage account containers
Uri: http://127.0.0.1:10000/devstoreaccount1?comp=list
x-ms-date: Fri, 03 Jul 2009 19:22:17 GMT
x-ms-version: 2009-04-14
Authorization: SharedKey devstoreaccount1:J5xkbSz7/7Xf8sCNY3RJIzyUEfnj1SJ3ccIBNpDzsq4=
200 (OK)
BLOB storage service
Generates authorization key from request
Authorization: SharedKey
devstoreaccount1:J5xkbSz7/7Xf8sCNY3RJIzyUEfnj1SJ3ccIBNpDzsq4=

Figure 9.2 Validation of the authorization key when the signature matches the Authorization header

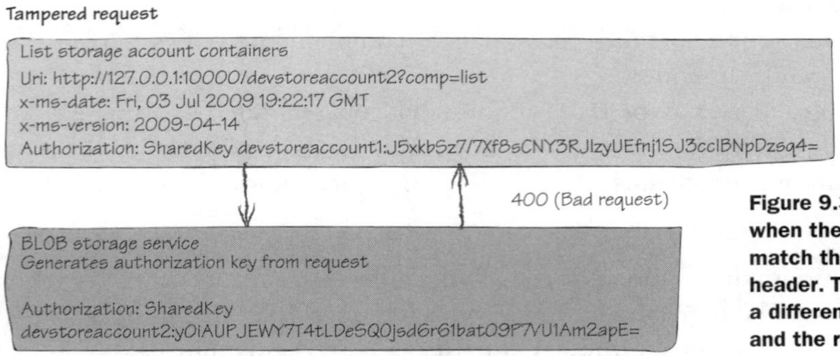
Tampered request
List storage account containers
Uri: http://127.0.0.1:10000/devstoreaccount2?comp=list
x-ms-date: Fri, 03 Jul 2009 19:22:17 GMT
x-ms-version: 2009-04-14
Authorization: SharedKey devstoreaccount1:J5xkbSz7/7Xf8sCNY3RJlzyUEfnj1SJ3cclBNpDzsq4=
400 (Bad request)
BLOB storage service
Generates authorization key from request
Authorization: SharedKey
devstoreaccount2:yOiAUPJEWY7T4tLDeSQ0jsd6r61bat09P7VU1Am2apE=

Figure 9.3 Validation result when the signature doesn't match the Authorization header. The server generates a different authorization key and the request is denied.

were to intercept your previous request, then the generated Authorization header server-side would change and the request would be denied. Figure 9.3 shows the validation process between the client and the BLOB storage service when the original request from figure 9.2 has been tampered with.

In figure 9.3, we've tampered with the original request from figure 9.2 to return any containers from `devstoreaccount2`. Notice that the server generated a different authorization key from the tampered request and therefore the server returns a 400 response code (`Bad Request`).

Now that you understand how the REST API authentication process works, take a break and have a quick beer. Just think, if you had to implement that code yourself rather than Microsoft providing it, you'd probably prefer to have a longer break and drown your sorrows.

9.2 Managing BLOBs using the StorageClient library

Now that you've finished your break and you're rested enough to read this, let's look at how you can use the StorageClient library to list BLOBs in a container, rather than using the REST API directly.

In chapter 8, you developed a sample management application that would allow you to upload podcasts in an MP3 format that were ready to be converted to WMA. You made an ASP.NET page that displayed a grid of all the containers in your storage account. Included in the grid was a hyperlink that would redirect you to another page called blobs.aspx, passing in the name of the selected container in the query string. We're going to extend that example now to develop the page blobs.aspx, shown in figure 9.4. This page is similar to the page that you developed for listing containers in chapter 8.

You can perform the following actions with the page shown in figure 9.4:

- List all BLOBs in the selected container
- Upload a new file
- Delete an existing BLOB
- Download an existing BLOB

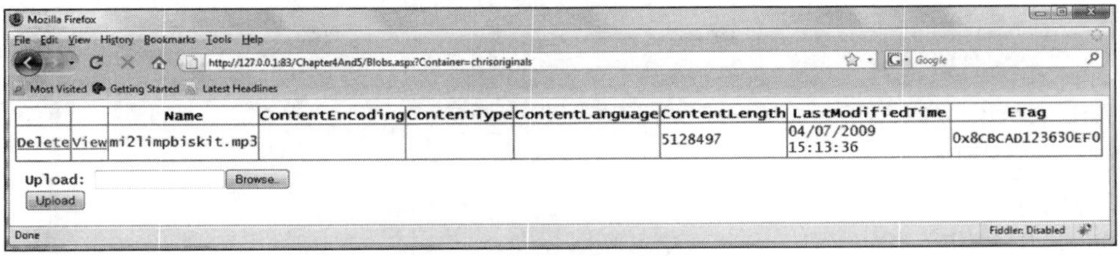

Figure 9.4 An ASP.NET web page that displays all the BLOBs that are in the selected container in a grid control

Let's look at each of these actions in detail.

9.2.1 *Listing BLOBs using the storage client*

In this section, we'll look at how to generate the grid that displays the list of BLOBs. We'll explain how to upload, delete, and view BLOBs later in the chapter. The following listing contains the markup required for the blobs.aspx page shown in figure 9.3.

Listing 9.3 ASPX page that lists the BLOBs in a container

```
<div>
   <asp:GridView ID="gvBlobs" runat="server"
              onrowcommand="gvBlobs_RowCommand"
              onrowdeleting="gvBlobs_RowDeleting">          ❶ Grid of BLOBs
      <Columns>
         <asp:TemplateField>
            <ItemTemplate>
               <asp:LinkButton ID="btnDelete" runat="server"
                               Text="Delete"
                               CommandName="Delete"
                               CommandArgument='<%#Eval("Uri")%>'/>
            </ItemTemplate>
         </asp:TemplateField>
         <asp:TemplateField>
            <ItemTemplate>
               <asp:LinkButton ID="btnView" runat="server"
                             Text="View"
                             CommandName="View"
                             CommandArgument='<%#Eval("Uri")%>'/>   ❷ View BLOB button
             </ItemTemplate>
          </asp:TemplateField>
         <asp:BoundField HeaderText="File" DataField="Uri"/>
       </Columns>
   </asp:GridView>
   <div>
      <div style="padding: 10px;">
         <div>
            Upload: <asp:FileUpload ID="fu" runat="server" />   ❸ File upload control
         </div>
         <div>
```

```
            <asp:Button ID="btnUpload" runat="server"
                        Text="Upload"
                        OnClick="btnUpload_Click" />      <-- 4 Upload button
         </div>
      </div>
   </div>
</div>
```

The ASPX code for displaying the BLOBs is similar to the ASPX we used in chapter 8 to list containers, so this shouldn't be too alien to you.

At ❶ a `GridView` is displayed that lists all the BLOBs in its data source. At ❷ you're defining a hyperlink button that you'll use to download the BLOB, and at ❸ is the standard ASP.NET `FileUpload` control to upload the file.

THE CODE-BEHIND FOR THE WEB PAGE

You've defined how your web page will look. Now you need to bind the grid to the data source on page load. Listing 9.4 shows the code-behind required to display a list of BLOBs for the selected container in your grid.

Listing 9.4 Show the list of BLOBs in the grid

```
protected void Page_Load(object sender, EventArgs e)
{
   if (!IsPostBack)
      BindGrid();
}

private void BindGrid()
{
   CloudStorageAccount account =
      CloudStorageAccount.FromConfigurationSetting("DataConnectionString");

   CloudBlobClient blobClient =
      account.CreateCloudBlobClient();

   CloudBlobContainer container =
      blobClient.GetContainerReference(Request["container"] as string);   <-- 1 Gets container from request query string

   gvBlobs.DataSource = container.ListBlobs();      <-- 2 Lists BLOBs in container
   gvBlobs.DataBind();
```

The code shown in listing 9.4 is again similar to the list containers example in chapter 8. This code is the storage client equivalent to the code you used to display the list of BLOBs with the REST API directly in listing 9.1.

At ❶ you retrieve an instance of the BLOB container by calling the `GetContainer-Reference` method off the BLOB client. Notice that we're passing in the container name from the request query string. Finally, you retrieve a list of the files held in the container by calling the `ListBlobs` method and binding the result to the `GridView` ❷.

Now that you can list and display all of the BLOBs in the selected container, you need to extend the web page so that you can upload new files into the container.

9.2.2 Uploading BLOBs

To upload files from your web page, you're going to use the built-in ASP.NET upload control at ❸ in listing 9.3. On click of the upload button at ❹, you're going to capture the uploaded file and then upload the captured file to BLOB storage. The following listing contains the code-behind for the upload button click event.

Listing 9.5 Posting the uploaded file to BLOB storage

```
protected void btnUpload_Click(object sender, EventArgs e)
{
   CloudStorageAccount account =
      CloudStorageAccount.FromConfigurationSetting("DataConnectionString");

   CloudBlobClient blobClient =
      account.CreateCloudBlobClient();

   CloudBlobContainer container =
      blobClient.GetContainerReference(Request["container"] as string);
          var blob =
        container.GetBlobReference(fu.PostedFile.FileName);    ❶ Gets reference to new BLOB

     blob.UploadByteArray(fu.FileBytes);    ❷ Uploads file contents to BLOB

   BindGrid();
}
```

All the code in listing 9.5 has been discussed in previous examples, except for what's happening at ❶ and ❷. At ❶ you get a reference to the BLOB that you're about to create. We're giving the BLOB the original name of the uploaded file (retrieved from the `UploadFile` control). Then, at ❷ you upload the new file to BLOB storage.

> **TIP** You'll notice that we're extracting the filename and the file contents directly from the ASP.NET file upload control. If you want, you can give the file a name different from the original.

> **Setting the maximum request length**
>
> By default, ASP.NET is configured to allow a maximum upload of 4 MB. If you provide a web role frontend to the BLOB storage as we've done in this sample, you might need to increase the maximum request length.
>
> To increase the default value to a larger value, you need to add the following line under the `system.web` element in the web.config file:
>
> ```
> <httpRuntime executionTimeout="300" maxRequestLength="51200"/>
> ```
>
> The maximum upload size in the above example is 50 MB.

In the previous example, we used the `UploadByteArray` method to upload the BLOB. Three other methods are provided in the StorageClient library that you can use:

UploadFile, UploadText, and UploadFromStream. Depending on your situation, one of these methods might be easier to use than UploadByteArray (for example, UploadFile might be a better choice if you have a local file on disk that you want to store in BLOB storage).

Splitting BLOBs into blocks

The maximum size of a BLOB is 1 TB, but if a file is larger than 64 MB, under the covers the StorageClient library splits the file into smaller blocks of 4 MB each. One of the advantages of the StorageClient library is that you don't need to worry about this. If you're using the REST API, you'll need to implement the splitting of BLOBs into blocks and the committal of blocks and retry logic associated with re-uploading failed blocks (yet another good reason to use the StorageClient library).

If you're a sick and twisted individual who wants to mess around with blocks, then feel free to look in more detail at the online documentation at http://msdn.microsoft.com/en-us/library/ee691964.aspx.

Now that you've spent all that time and effort adding the file to BLOB storage, let's delete it (groan).

9.2.3 Deleting BLOBs

Deleting a BLOB is similar to uploading a file except that you're deleting the BLOB instead of uploading it (cute, huh?). Just like the upload file example in listing 9.5, you get the reference to the BLOB, and then delete the BLOB by calling the following:

```
blob.Delete();
```

The following listing shows the code that will delete the BLOB in your web page.

Listing 9.6 Deleting the BLOB

```
protected void gvBlobs_RowCommand
                        (object sender, GridViewCommandEventArgs e)
{
   if (e.CommandName == "Delete")
   {
       DeleteBlob(e.CommandArgument.ToString());
   }

   BindGrid();
}

private void DeleteBlob(string blobName)
{

   CloudStorageAccount account =
      CloudStorageAccount.FromConfigurationSetting("DataConnectionString");

   CloudBlobClient blobClient =
      account.CreateCloudBlobClient();
```

```
    CloudBlobContainer container =
       blobClient.GetContainerReference(Request["container"] as string);

    var blob =
       container.GetBlobReference(blobName);

    blob.Delete();                                   <-- Deletes the BLOB
}

protected void gvBlobs_RowDeleting(object sender,
➥ GridViewDeleteEventArgs e)
{
}
```

As you can see, deleting a BLOB is pretty simple. Now you can list, upload, and delete BLOBs from your storage account using your ASP.NET management website hosted in your Windows Azure web role. Let's complete the management page example by looking at how you can download BLOBs.

9.3 Downloading BLOBs

In this section we'll look at how to download BLOBs from both a public container and a private container. To take things nice and easy, we'll tell you how to download BLOBs that are stored in a public container first.

9.3.1 Downloading BLOBs from a public container

If your BLOB is hosted in a public container, you can present the URI of the BLOB directly to the user and they'll be able to directly download the file to their browser. In our podcasting sample, the following URI will download podcast01.wma from the ChrisConverted public container in the development storage account: http://127.0.0.1:10000/devstoreaccount1/ChrisConverted/podcast01.wma. Because the BLOB is held in a public container, the user won't need to provide any credentials to access the BLOB.

> **TIP** If you've correctly set the MIME type of your podcast, when the URI is pasted into your browser, the podcast will automatically start playing in Windows Media Player.

In our management web page example, we don't want to expose the podcasts to the world; we want to restrict access to our own credentials. Let's look at how you can do that using your new best friend, the storage client.

9.3.2 Downloading BLOBs from a private container using the storage client

Now we want you to modify your management web page so that if you click the View button for the selected podcast, as shown in figure 9.5, you're prompted to download the file (also shown in figure 9.5).

Although you can store the BLOB in a public container to achieve the same result, in this example you're going to first download the BLOB to your web role and then serve the BLOB from your web role, rather than directly from BLOB storage.

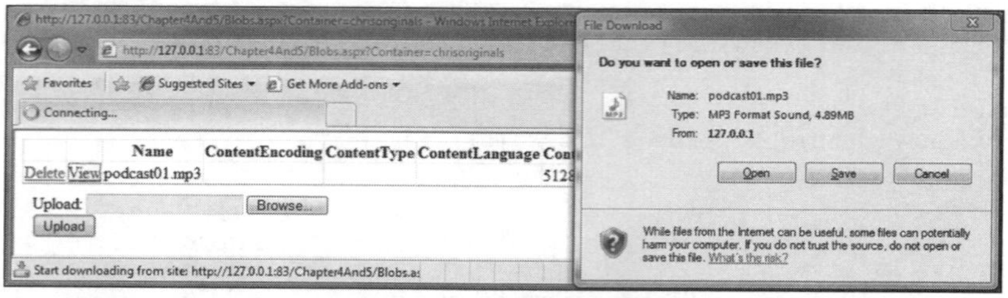

Figure 9.5 Clicking the View button on your BLOBs page opens a Save dialog box

In listing 9.3, we defined the ASPX for your View button; listing 9.7 is where we hook up the code that will download the file when this button is clicked. The code in the following listing will download the selected BLOB and prompt the user with the Save dialog box shown in figure 9.5.

Listing 9.7 Downloading BLOBs from the grid using the storage client

```
protected void gvBlobs_RowCommand(object sender,
➥ GridViewCommandEventArgs e)
{
    if (e.CommandName == "Delete")
    {
        DeleteBlob(e.CommandArgument.ToString());
    }

    if (e.CommandName == "View")
    {
        DownloadBlob(e.CommandArgument.ToString());
    }

    BindGrid();
}

private void DownloadBlob(string blobName)
{
    CloudStorageAccount account =
        CloudStorageAccount.FromConfigurationSetting("DataConnectionString");

    CloudBlobClient blobClient =
        account.CreateCloudBlobClient();

    CloudBlobContainer container =
        blobClient.GetContainerReference(Request["container"] as string);

    var blob =
      container.GetBlobReference(blobName);

    using (var ms = new MemoryStream());
    {
        blob.DownloadToStream(ms);
        Response.ContentType = blob.Properties.ContentType;
        Response.AddHeader("Content-Disposition",
                           "attachment; filename=" blobName);
```

❶ Creates memory stream and downloads BLOB

❷ Sets MIME type

```
        Response.BinaryWrite(ms.ToArray());
    }
}
```

❸ Writes file to response stream

At ❶ you create a new memory stream that writes the contents of the BLOB that's been downloaded from BLOB storage. At ❷ you set the MIME type of the file so that you can allow the browser to perform the correct action based on that type (for example, launch Windows Media Player, Microsoft Word, or some other action), and you add the content-disposition header so that the browser knows to offer a Save file dialog box to the user. Finally, the downloaded BLOB is made available to the client by writing the file to the response stream ❸.

TIP In the previous example, we used the `DownloadToStream` option to download files from BLOB storage but the storage client also offers these methods to download files: `DownloadText`, `DownloadByteArray`, and `DownloadToFile`.

So far we've shown you how to download files that are in public or private containers. What if you want to do something a little more granular, like control access to your BLOBs or containers? For operations like this, you can use a Shared Access Signature. Later on, we'll look at this feature in a little more detail.

Now that you know how to upload and download BLOBs, let's look at how you can integrate BLOB storage with your existing ASP.NET websites.

9.4 Integrating BLOBs with your ASP.NET websites

In typical ASP.NET websites, you usually distribute your assets with your website. Although this strategy works great for small websites, it's pretty much unmanageable when dealing with larger websites. Do you really want to redeploy your entire website just because you have a new Hawaiian shirt in your product range and you need to add an image of it?

There's a better way. In this section, we'll tell you how you can integrate public assets and private assets (such as purchased MP3 files) with your ASP.NET website. Let's return to the Hawaiian Shirt Shop example from chapter 2 to find out how you can integrate your assets.

9.4.1 Integrating ASP.NET websites with table-driven BLOB content

Currently, the shirt shop website displays a list of all the products that you have for sale, but it doesn't display pictures of the shirts. Because the data is currently hard-coded, you could just store the image on the website directly; any changes to the product line would require you to deploy a new version of the website.

In future chapters, you're going to drive the data from an external data source such as Table storage or SQL Azure, so you need a strategy that lets you update static content on the website when the product line is changed, without redeploying the images to the website.

If you stored the pictures of the shirts in BLOB storage, you could store the URI of the BLOB in your external data source. As you add new items to your data source, you

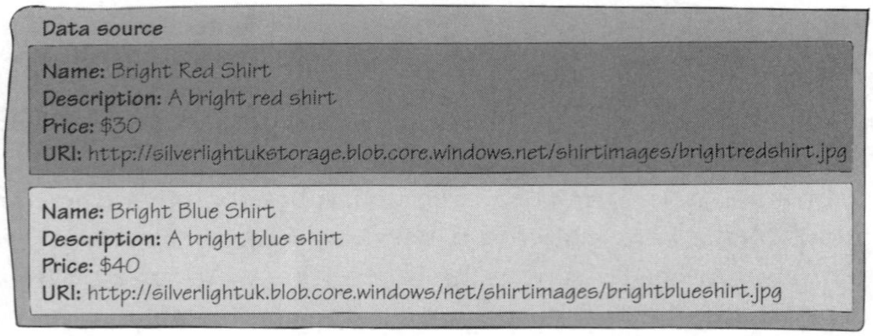

Figure 9.6 Storing URIs in an external data source

can add the associated BLOB at the same time. To expand on the Hawaiian Shirt Shop example, you could store an image of a shirt in BLOB storage as well as add a new shirt to the table. In the table, you would store all the details of the shirt (the name of the shirt, price, description, and so on) and its associated URI. Figure 9.6 shows a representation of this setup.

Because you're happy for the images of your Hawaiian shirts to be in the public domain, you can store the shirt images in a public container and set the URI of your HTML image tag directly to the public URI. The following code shows how this image tag might look:

```
<img src="http://silverlightukstorage.blob.core.windows.net
➥ /shirtimages/greenshirt.jpg" />
```

Using a public container is fine for storing content that you don't mind making available to the world, but it's not an acceptable solution if you want to serve content that you want to keep protected.

> **NOTE** Storing your website assets in BLOB storage is a great way to optimize performance because it takes load away from your web server. In the next chapter, we'll look at how you can take your assets that are stored in BLOB storage and expose them via the Windows Azure Content Delivery Network to make even more performance improvements.

Returning to the podcast example, suppose you decided that you wanted only paid members of your website to be able to download your MP3. In this scenario, you don't want to store the file in a public container; you want to store it in a private container instead.

9.4.2 *Integrating protected, private content*

Earlier in this chapter, in the BLOB management web page, you implemented a download link that allowed you to serve files stored in a private container to your users on a public website. Now we're going to expand that technique to a more integrated, reusable solution by doing the following things:

1. Creating an HTTP handler that serves MP3 files from BLOB storage
2. Registering the HTTP handler
3. Protecting your handler so that only authorized users can use it

HTTP handlers let specified types of HTTP requests be handled by some custom code. In this example, you're going to build a handler that will intercept requests for MP3 files and return the MP3 files from BLOB storage instead of from the local filesystem.

CREATING THE HTTP HANDLER

You're going to build a small sample that will intercept any incoming requests for MP3 files using an HTTP handler. Rather than attempting to serve the MP3 files from your website's filesystem, the handler will retrieve the files from your private BLOB storage container and serve them to the user who requested them. For this task, we're going to build on the techniques that we used in listing 9.7. You can either serve the files directly (useful for images) or initiate a Save dialog box (as shown in figure 9.5). In this example, you'll download a file directly. For example, when the user requests the following URI, they'll be served the file from BLOB storage:

`www.mypodcastwebsite.com/podcast01.mp3`

To implement an HTTP handler, add a new `httphandler` file to your ASP.NET web project. This handler is called `MP3Handler.cs`. Listing 9.8 contains the implementation for `MP3Handler.cs`.

Listing 9.8 An MP3 HTTP handler that serves MP3s from BLOB storage

```
public class MP3Handler : IHttpHandler
{
   public void ProcessRequest(HttpContext context)          ❶ Content is the incoming request
   {
      string blobName = context.Request.Path.Trim('/');     ❷ Parses BLOB name
      var blobData = GetBlob("chrisoriginals", blobName);      and retrieves BLOB

      context.Response.ContentType = "audio/mpeg";          ❸ Sets MIME type as MP3 and
      context.Response.BinaryWrite(blobData);                  writes file to the response
   }

   public bool IsReusable
   {
      get {return false;}
   }

   private byte[] GetBlob(string containerName, string blobName)   ❹ Gets BLOB from BLOB storage
   {
      CloudStorageAccount account =
         CloudStorageAccount
         ➥ .FromConfigurationSetting("DataConnectionString");

      CloudBlobClient blobClient =
         account.CreateCloudBlobClient();

      CloudBlobContainer container =
         blobClient.GetContainerReference(containerName);

      var blob =
        container.GetBlobReference(blobName);
```

```
        blob.DownLoadByteArray();
    }
}
```

The HTTP handler in listing 9.8 will be called whenever an MP3 file request is intercepted at ❶. When the request has been intercepted, the name of the .mp3 file that should be downloaded from BLOB storage from the requested path is extracted ❷. The handler will then download the requested BLOB from the ChrisOriginals private container at ❷ by calling the `GetBlob` method ❹. After the file is retrieved from BLOB storage, you set the MIME type as `MP3` ❸ (we've hardcoded the MIME type but in a more generic sample you could retrieve it from the BLOB properties) and then write the file back to the client.

REGISTERING THE HTTP HANDLER

To register the HTTP handler with your website, add the following line to your web.config file in the `handlers` section under the `system.webServer` element:

```
<add name="MP3Handler" path="*.mp3" verb="GET" type=
➥ "AzurePlayAreaWeb_WebRole.MP3Handler, AzurePlayAreaWeb_WebRole"
➥ resourceType="Unspecified"/>
```

This code will configure your server to route any web requests that end in .mp3 to your new handler. This is a great way to protect assets on your server that would normally be freely accessible. Your handler could check security permissions, route the call to virtual storage, or deny the request.

AUTHORIZATION

If you want to restrict your MP3 files to logged-in users, you can use the built-in ASP.NET authorization and authentication functionality:

```
<authorization>
  <deny users="?"/>
</authorization>
```

Now you have an integrated HTTP handler that can serve protected BLOB files from BLOB storage to authorized users as if it were part of your website. If your website were serving the same file to hundreds of users every day, then continually retrieving the same file from BLOB storage would be inefficient. What you would need to do in that

> **Shared Access Signatures**
>
> Putting BLOBs in local storage to improve performance is useful for showing you how to integrate local storage and BLOB storage together. It's also useful as an option for integrating content. You can use Shared Access Signatures to provide the same result. Using Shared Access Signatures is the preferred approach to protect a BLOB because it's cheaper and takes load off your servers.

case is use BLOB storage and local storage together, to cache requests, so you wouldn't need to continually request the same BLOB from BLOB storage.

9.5 Using local storage with BLOB storage

In the previous section, you used a file handler to intercept MP3 requests from your website and to serve them from BLOB storage rather than from your website. A more efficient approach would be to check whether the file is already on your local filesystem. If the file already exists, then you can just serve the file straight up. If the file doesn't exist, you can retrieve it from BLOB storage, store it on the local filesystem, and then serve the file. All future requests for the file won't need to continually retrieve the file from BLOB storage.

9.5.1 Using a local cache

When you define Windows Azure web roles, you can allocate a portion of the local filesystem for use as a temporary cache. This local storage area allows you to store semi-persistent data that you might use frequently, without having to continually re-request or recalculate the data for every call.

You must be aware that this local storage area isn't shared across multiple instances and the current instance of your web role is the only one that can access that data. Figure 9.7 shows the distribution of BLOBs in local storage across multiple instances.

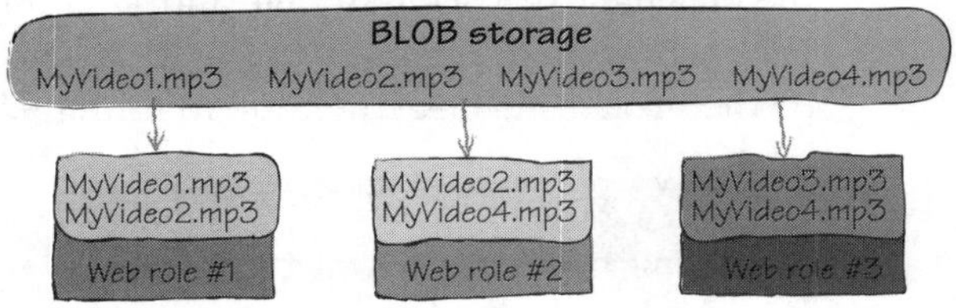

Figure 9.7 Three web role instances, each with different local copies of BLOBs in its local storage

Because the load balancer evenly distributes requests across instances, a user won't always be served by the same web role instance. Any data that you need persisted across multiple requests (such as shopping cart or session data) shouldn't be stored in local storage and must be stored in a data store that all instances can access.

9.5.2 Defining and accessing local storage

As we discussed in chapter 4, you can define how much space you require on your local filesystem in your service definition file. The FC uses this information to assign your web role to a host with enough disk space. The following code is how you would define that you need 100 MB of space to cache MP3 files:

```
<WebRole name="ServiceRuntimeWebsite">
   <LocalResources>
      <LocalStorage name="mp3Cache"
                    cleanOnRoleRecycle="true"
                    sizeInMB="100" />
```

```
  </LocalResources>
</WebRole>
```

To access any of the files held in local storage, you can use the following code to retrieve the location of the file:

```
  LocalResource localCache =
    RoleEnvironment.GetLocalResource("mp3Cache");

 string localCacheRootDirectory = localCache.RootPath;
```

After you've retrieved the root directory of local storage (`RootPath`), you can use standard .NET filesystem calls to modify, create, read, or delete files held in local storage. (For more information about local storage, see chapter 4).

Great! You've configured your local storage area. Now you need to modify your HTTP handler to use your local storage area, where possible.

9.5.3 *Updating your HTTP handler to use local storage*

You're going to modify your HTTP handler to check in local storage to determine whether the requested file exists already. If the file doesn't exist, then you'll retrieve the MP3 file from BLOB storage and store it in local storage. Finally, you'll write the file back to the client from your local filesystem. The following code shows how you modify the `ProcessRequest` method in listing 9.8 to use local storage.

```
public void ProcessRequest(HttpContext context)
{
   string blobName = context.Request.Path.Trim('/');

   var mp3Cache = RoleEnvironment.GetLocalResource("mp3Cache");
   string localFilePath = mp3Cache.RootPath + blobName;

  if (!File.Exists(localFilePath))
  {
     var blobData = GetBlob("chrisoriginals", blobName);
     File.WriteAllBytes(localFilePath, blobData);
  }

  context.Response.ContentType = "audio/mpeg";
  context.Response.WriteFile(localFilePath);
}
```

Using the local storage mechanism in your HTTP handler improves performance by serving the requested file from local storage, rather than always having to retrieve the file from BLOB storage first. Although performance is improved, if the file is changed in BLOB storage, the file that you'll serve will be out of date. Let's look at how you can keep the performance improvement but serve the latest content even if the file has changed in BLOB storage.

TIP Although this sample is focused on web HTTP handlers, this technique can easily be used in worker roles. I currently use this technique with a Windows Azure MapReduce solution that I've built.

file:///C:/AzureBook/Source/PlayArea/AzurePlayArea/WebLoad/bin/Debug/WebLoad.EXE
x-ms-request-id : bc06db6f-90f7-4ec6-97c1-3ca2b55e70ac
Content-Length : 5128497
Date : Sun, 05 Jul 2009 20:20:56 GMT
ETag : 0x8CBCB1016B0929A
Last-Modified : Sat, 04 Jul 2009 22:44:13 GMT
Server : Development Storage Blob Service Version 1.0 Microsoft-HTTPAPI/2.0

Figure 9.8 The output of a `HEAD` request

9.5.4 *Checking properties of a BLOB without downloading it*

If you were to use the HTTP `HEAD` verb instead of the `GET` verb, you could check the properties of the file without downloading the file. Figure 9.8 shows the output of a `HEAD` request.

In figure 9.8, the `Last-Modified` tag shows us the last time the file was updated in BLOB storage. By comparing the header value to the local value in your file properties, you know whether the file has changed.

> **x-ms-request-id**
>
> In figure 9.8, you'll notice that there's a tag called `x-ms-request-id`. Every request made is assigned a unique identifier (GUID) that's returned in the response. Every request and response is logged by Microsoft; if you're experiencing issues, you can always pass this ID with a support request—providing the ID lets Microsoft easily investigate any issues you have.

The listing that follows shows the code for the console application shown in figure 9.8.

Listing 9.9 Showing the output of a HEAD request

```
static void Main(string[] args)
{
      HttpWebRequest hwr = CreateHttpRequest(
         new Uri(@"http://127.0.0.1:10000/devstoreaccount1/chrisoriginals/
         ➥ podcast01.mp3"),
         "HEAD", new TimeSpan(0, 0, 30));                  ❶ HEAD request rather than GET

   var account =
      CloudStorageAccount.FromConfigurationSetting("DataConnectionString");

   account.Credentials.SignRequest(hwr);

   var response = hwr.GetResponse();

   foreach (string header in response.Headers)             ❷ Iterates through returned headers
   {
      Console.WriteLine("{0} : {1}", header, response.Headers[header]);
   }

   Console.ReadKey();
}
```

In the code example shown in listing 9.9, you make the same request that you've made before, but it's a `HEAD` request instead of a `GET` request. You're making a `HEAD` request for the file podcast01.mp3 in the ChrisOriginals container in your development storage account ❶. At ❷ you loop through all the returned headers, outputting the header key and value to the console screen.

USING THE STORAGECLIENT LIBRARY

In listing 9.9, you retrieved the last modified time using the REST API directly, although you could've used the StorageClient library. The following code performs a `HEAD` request that returns the last modified time:

```
blob.FetchAttributes();
var lastModifiedTime = blob.Properties.LastModifiedUtc;
```

`FetchAttributes` is the StorageClient library equivalent of `HEAD`. It returns all the properties and custom metadata of the BLOB, without downloading the actual file. Table 9.1 lists the BLOB properties and their descriptions.

Table 9.1 BLOB properties

Property name	Description
`BlobType`	`PageBlob, BlockBlob`
`CacheControl`	Allows you to instruct the browser on how to cache the BLOB
`ContentEncoding`	Encoding of the header
`ContentLanguage`	Language header of the BLOB
`ContentMD5`	MD5 hash of the content header
`ContentType`	The MIME type of the BLOB
`Etag`	Unique identifier of the request (changes every time a BLOB is modified)
`LastModifiedTimeUtc`	Last time the BLOB was modified
`LeaseStatus`	Used with page blocks: `Locked, Unlocked`; not available in the StorageClient library.
`Length`	Size of the BLOB, in bytes

Now that you're familiar with BLOB properties and how to retrieve them without downloading the file, let's look at how you can use this knowledge to improve the performance of your handler.

9.5.5 *Improving your handler to check the last modified time*

Because you can retrieve the last modified time, you can modify your handler to check whether the file has changed since you last downloaded it. If it has changed, you can download another copy of the file. The following listing shows the modified code for your handler.

Listing 9.10 Checking the last modified date

```
blob.FetchAttributes();
   var lastModifiedTime = blob.Properties.LastModifiedUtc;

   if (!File.Exists(localFilePath) ||
       File.GetLastAccessTimeUtc(localFilePath) < lastModifiedTime)
{
    var blobData = GetBlob("chrisoriginals", blobName);
    File.WriteAllBytes(localFilePath, blobData);
    File.SetLastWriteTimeUtc(localFilePath, lastModifiedTime);
}
```

❶ Gets BLOB properties and metadata

❷ Checks whether BLOB has changed

❸ Sets last write time

At ❶ you get the last modified time of the BLOB. This method is the same code that you used in section 9.5.4; you can either use the StorageClient library or the REST API directly to retrieve this data.

After you've gotten the last modified time of the BLOB, then you check ❷ whether you already have the file locally and whether the local file is older than the server file. The final change that you need to make is that you set the last write time of the local file to the last modified time of the BLOB ❸.

So far, we've only looked at the properties of a BLOB. Now let's look at the other part of the BLOB data that's returned in a `HEAD` request: custom metadata.

9.5.6 *Adding and returning custom metadata*

In listing 9.9, we showed you how to view all the headers associated with a BLOB using a console application. In that example, you returned all the standard headers associated with a BLOB (`last-modified`, `x-ms-request-id`, and so on). If you want to associate some custom metadata with a file, that metadata would also be displayed in the response headers.

DISPLAYING CUSTOM METADATA

Let's modify the BLOB podcast01.mp3 to include the author of the file (me) as custom metadata. Figure 9.9 shows the `HEAD` response in the same console application using the same code that we developed in listing 9.10.

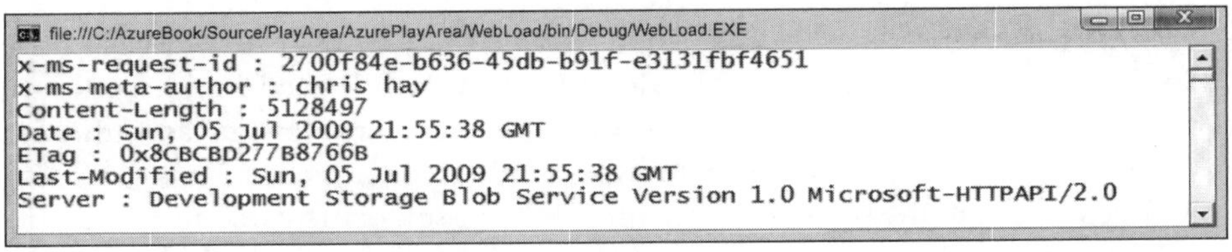
file:///C:/AzureBook/Source/PlayArea/AzurePlayArea/WebLoad/bin/Debug/WebLoad.EXE
x-ms-request-id : 2700f84e-b636-45db-b91f-e3131fbf4651
x-ms-meta-author : chris hay
Content-Length : 5128497
Date : Sun, 05 Jul 2009 21:55:38 GMT
ETag : 0x8CBCBD277B8766B
Last-Modified : Sun, 05 Jul 2009 21:55:38 GMT
Server : Development Storage Blob Service Version 1.0 Microsoft-HTTPAPI/2.0

Figure 9.9 `HEAD` response with custom metadata

Note that with the file podcast01.mp3, there's a new header returned in the response, called `x-ms-meta-author`, with the value `chris hay`. In this example, we returned the metadata from the `HEAD` request, but it's also available in a `GET` request.

SETTING CUSTOM METADATA

If you need to set some custom metadata, you can easily do this with the StorageClient library. The following code sets the metadata for the file podcast01.mp3:

```
blob.Metadata.Add("Author", "Chris Hay");
blob.SetMetadata();
```

This code calls the `UpdateBlobMetadata` method on the container, passing in a `NameValueCollection` of metadata that you want to store against the BLOB.

> **x-ms-meta**
>
> The StorageClient library automatically prefixes all metadata with the tag `x-ms-meta-`. We actually set the key as `author` in the metadata collection, but the response header returned `x-ms-meta-author`. As a matter of fact, the BLOB storage service will only allow you to set metadata with the prefix `x-ms-meta-` and it ignores any attempt to modify any other header associated with a BLOB. Unfortunately, this means you can't modify any standard HTTP header that isn't set by the BLOB storage service.

SCENARIOS FOR USING CUSTOM METADATA

The metadata support for BLOBs allows you to have self-describing BLOBs. If you need to associate extra information with a BLOB (for example, podcast author, recording location, and so on), then this would be a suitable place to store that data; you wouldn't have to resort to an external data source. Any custom attributes associated with a file (such as the author of a Word document) could also be stored in the metadata.

TIP If you need to be able to search for metadata across multiple BLOBs, consider using an external data source (for example, a database or the Table storage service), rather than searching across the BLOBs.

Now that you know how the upload and download operations operate under the covers, let's return to the final part of the uploading and downloading puzzle, namely, copying BLOBs.

9.6 Copying BLOBs

So far in this chapter, you've uploaded files and downloaded files in and out of your account. But you don't always want to transfer files outside your account; sometimes you might want to take a copy of an existing file in the account.

Let's return to the podcasting example for a lesson on why you might want to do this. Let's say that during the conversion of a WMA file to MP3, you decide that you don't want to make the converted file immediately available. In this case, your converted MP3 file would reside in a private container that isn't available to the general public. At a later date, you decide to make the file available to the public by moving it into your public downloads container. To do this, you copy your converted file from one container to another. Figure 9.10 shows a file being copied from one container to another.

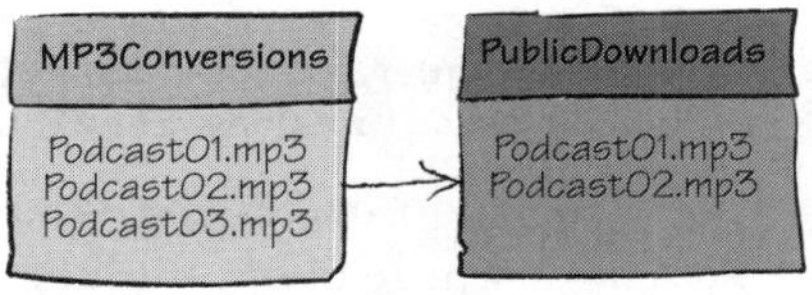

Figure 9.10 Copying podcast03.mp3 in the MP3Conversions container to the PublicDownloads container

In figure 9.10, the BLOB isn't being uploaded or downloaded; the BLOB podcast01.mp3 is just being copied from the MP3Conversions container and the copy is being placed in the PublicDownloads container.

Although you could do this using a download followed by an upload, this would be much slower than just doing an internal copy within the data center. Likewise, performing an upload followed by a download would be incredibly slow and wasteful of network resources if the calling client was based outside the Windows Azure data center.

Listing 9.11 shows the code used to copy a very large filename podcast03.mp3 to the PublicDownloads container from the MP3Conversions container via the REST API.

Listing 9.11 Copying a BLOB between containers

```
    HttpWebRequest hwr = CreateHttpRequest(
       new Uri(@"http://127.0.0.1:10000/devstoreaccount1/publicdownloads/
       ➥ podcast03.mp3"),
       "PUT", new TimeSpan(0, 0, 30));                 <-- ❶ PUT request to destination container

    hwr.Headers.Add("x-ms-copy-source",
       "/silverlightukstorage/mp3conversions/podcast03.mp3"); <-- ❷ Source location of file

var account =
    CloudStorageAccount.FromConfigurationSetting("DataConnectionString");

account.Credentials.SignRequest(hwr);

hwr.GetResponse();
```

As you can see in listing 9.11, the basics of making the HTTP request is pretty much the same as any other REST request you've made. In this case, you're setting the destination container ❶ as the URI for the request, and you're setting the request to be a `PUT` (rather than a `GET`, `HEAD`, or `POST`).

At ❷ you set the location of the source BLOB to be copied. The header `x-ms-copy-source` is where you define the location of the file; notice that we're including the storage account name (`silverlightukstorage`), the container (`mp3conversions`), and the BLOB name (`podcast03.mp3`) in the header value.

9.6.1 *Copying files via the StorageClient library*

Listing 9.11 uses the REST API directly to copy the BLOB, but you could make this call by making the simpler StorageClient library call:

```
var sourceBlob = sourceContainer.GetBlobReference("podcast01.mp3");
var targetBlob = targeCcontainer.GetBlobReference("podcast01.mp3");
targetBlob.CopyFromBlob(sourceBlob);
```

This code makes the same call as in listing 9.11, this time using the StorageClient library instead of using the REST API directly.

NOTE Although you can use the REST API, using the StorageClient library is much easier. Save yourself a lot of heartache and use the REST API only when necessary. Try to stick to using the lovely StorageClient library.

Snapshotting BLOBs

The problem of copying BLOBs is that you have to pay storage costs to the Microsoft bean counters for keeping duplicate copies of the data. If you're only copying the BLOB to maintain some sort of version control, you should consider snapshotting instead. A snapshot pins a version of your BLOB at the date and time you created the snapshot. The snapshot is read only (it can't be modified) and can be used to revert to earlier versions of a BLOB. Only changes made between versions of snapshots are chargeable.

To create a snapshot, you can make the following call:

```
var snapshotBlob = blob.CreateSnapshot();
```

To retrieve a snapshot via the REST API, you can use the following URI:

http://accountname.blob.core.windows.net/containername/blobname?snapshot=<DateTime>

You can also retrieve a snapshot using the StorageClient library:

```
var snapshotBlob = container.GetBlobReference("blobname?snapshot=<DateTime>");
```

For more details about snapshotting, go to http://msdn.microsoft.com/en-us/library/ee691971.aspx.

9.7 *Setting shared access permissions*

Access to a BLOB is controlled by the container that it lives in. If the BLOB lives in a public container, it's available to the world. If the BLOB lives in a private container, you can access it only with your private authentication key.

WARNING Don't distribute your private authentication key. Doing so is a surefire way to have some evildoer trash your data.

These levels of access are a little too extreme; we need a more granular way of controlling access to our BLOBs, namely Shared Access Signatures. Using shared access, you can set a policy on a private container (or BLOB), and anyone who makes a request with the correct signature can perform the appropriate action on the BLOB (say, download the BLOB).

Although you can assign permissions at an individual BLOB level, this is a pain to maintain. It's easier to maintain permissions at a container level (you can always have a container that consists of a single BLOB).

Let's now return to the podcast example and look at how you can control download access to one of your podcasts.

9.7.1 Setting shared access permissions on a container

Let's say your podcasting business has gone well and you've decided to start selling some of your podcasts to the general public. In this scenario, after some rich dude has purchased the podcast, you need to provide a way for them to download the podcast without making it public (you obviously don't want to give them your owner authentication key). To achieve this, you're going to store your podcast (podcast03.mp3) in its own private container (Podcast03), which isn't available to the general public.

After your customer has purchased the podcast, you'll generate a Shared Access Signature that will give that customer permission to read any BLOBs (in this case, podcast03.mp3) in the Podcast03 container, for a period of 24 hours. After the 24-hour period has expired, the customer will no longer be able to download the podcast.

The first thing you need to do is generate a shared access policy that will restrict the download period to the next 24 hours, using the following code:

```
var oneDayDownloadpolicy = new SharedAccessPolicy();
oneDayDownloadpolicy.SharedAccessStartTime = DateTime.Now;
oneDayDownloadpolicy.SharedAccessExpiryTime = DateTime.Now.AddDays(1);
oneDayDownloadpolicy.Permissions = SharedAccessPermissions.Read;
```

As shown in the code, you can specify both a start time and an expiry time for the policy. If you don't specify a start time, the value now is substituted as a default. After you've specified this policy, apply it to the container.

```
var permissions = new BlobContainerPermissions();
permissions.SharedAccessPolicies.Clear();
permissions.SharedAccessPolicies.Add("CustomerA", oneDayDownloadPolicy);
container.SetPermissions(permissions);
```

Finally, you can generate a URI that customers will be able to use to download the BLOB, using the following code:

```
string sharedAccessSignature = container.
➥ GetSharedAccessSignature(oneDayDownloadpolicy);
string uri = blob.Uri.AbsoluteUri + sharedAccessSignature;
```

The generated URI will look something like this:

```
https://chrishayuk.blob.core.windows.net/podcast03/podcast03.mp3?st=
➥ 2010-01-04T12%3A08%3A00Z&se=2010-01-05T12%3A08%3A00Z&sr=
    ➥ b&sp=r&sig=ByfV3a1SXOXT04G4GF%2FNQo%2B9cxx4vrRE45kYxbhFhJk%3D
```

And that's about it; you can now dynamically assign permission to read BLOBs that are in containers.

> **Assigning other types of permissions**
>
> What if you want to be able to assign permissions at a BLOB level (rather than at a container level) or if you want to provide more than just read permissions? You can generate Shared Access Signatures that give users permissions to write to certain BLOBs in your container. This scenario is a little too detailed for what we would like to show in this book, but feel free to visit the online documentation for more details at http://msdn.microsoft.com/en-us/library/ee395415.aspx.

9.8 Summary

And....breathe. It's fairly safe to say we've covered how to manage BLOBs stored in BLOB storage in great depth.

In this chapter, we built upon the knowledge you gained in chapter 8 and looked at how you can upload and download files using the StorageClient library. You know how much the StorageClient library can do for you. We figure that the real take-away from that section is that you shouldn't use the REST API and you should stick to the StorageClient library; otherwise, you have to worry about blocks and retries.

Not only did we look at how to use BLOB storage, but you also learned how you can integrate with your ASP.NET website solutions. BLOB storage is the ideal place to store your ASP.NET website assets. It's perfectly suited to providing controlled access to content you want to protect, such as paid MP3 files.

We used two different methods of serving up content: the HTTP handler and the container-level access policy. Although you should probably use the container-level access policy whenever possible (it's cheaper), the techniques that you learned when you built the HTTP handler are invaluable for synchronizing access between local storage and BLOB storage.

In chapter 8, we focused on managing accounts and containers. In this chapter, we showed you how to work with the actual BLOBs. Not only did we look at how to develop against the BLOB service, but we also showed you how you can use the service with your ASP.NET websites.

In the next chapter, we'll build on your BLOB knowledge and look at how you can use the BLOB storage service without a web role, worker role, or server, and run it as a standalone service. We think you'll agree that it opens up some interesting scenarios.

10 When the BLOB stands alone

This chapter covers

- Hosting static websites in BLOB storage
- Hosting Silverlight applications in BLOB storage
- Hosting website assets in BLOB storage
- Using BLOB storage to progressively download video

Although BLOB storage is generally used as a durable storage area for web and worker roles, it can also be used as a standalone service; you can use the service for your applications without hosting a worker or web role.

So far in this book we've focused on using web roles to host websites. Now we're going to tell you how you can use BLOB storage to host a static HTML website without needing a web role.

10.1 Hosting static HTML websites

You learned in chapter 9 that BLOBs held in a public container are accessible to the outside via a public URI over an HTTP connection. Those files can be accessed with standard web browsers such as Internet Explorer. BLOB storage also lets you configure the MIME types associated with contained files; the web browser can correctly handle the served content. These capabilities make BLOB storage not just a networked hard disk but rather a full-fledged web server farm (as shown in figure 10.1).

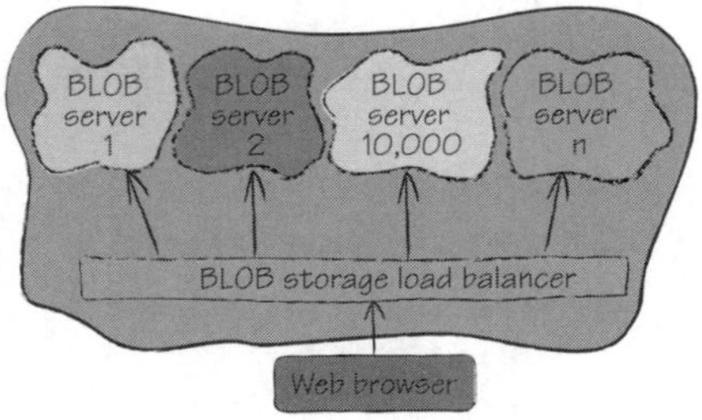

Figure 10.1 BLOB storage acting as a web farm (look, no web roles)

BLOB storage can serve up all modern content types (including standard HTML pages, JavaScript files, CSS files, images, movies, Word documents, PDF documents, Silverlight applications, and Flash applications), making BLOB storage a viable consideration for hosting static websites.

> **Why would I want to use BLOB storage rather than a web role?**
>
> Although web roles are the recommended solution for most scenarios, in some instances it might be more cost effective to use BLOB storage to host your website. If your website is a standard static HTML website that doesn't perform any server-side processing, then it's a suitable candidate for hosting in BLOB storage.
>
> For example, informational sites such as local business websites, static corporate websites, and Silverlight (or Flash) games are good candidates for BLOB-storage hosting. You might conclude that a static website is a fairly uncommon scenario, but it's far more common than you might think. For example, www.sagentia.com is a typical corporate website. Apart from a search facility (which could be implemented using Google and JavaScript), there are no interactive parts to this website. There's no reason why this website couldn't be hosted in BLOB storage rather than using ASP.NET or JSP.
>
> Quite simply, if you want a cheap method of hosting websites in a scalable fashion and you don't need to dynamically generate pages, you can save yourself the cost of web roles and just pay per request.

In this section, we'll show you how BLOB-storage hosting works by showing you how to create and then publish a simple static HTML website. We'll also look at a couple of issues related to using BLOB storage as a host. Now let's get to it and create a static website that you can host in BLOB storage.

10.1.1 Creating a static HTML website

The website that you're about to build is a simple HTML page with a JavaScript calculator, as shown in figure 10.2. When we say calculator, it really just adds two numbers together; abacus++ is probably a more accurate term.

After the user enters two values and clicks the equals button, the result appears (with a gratuitous smiley face graphic), as shown in figure 10.3.

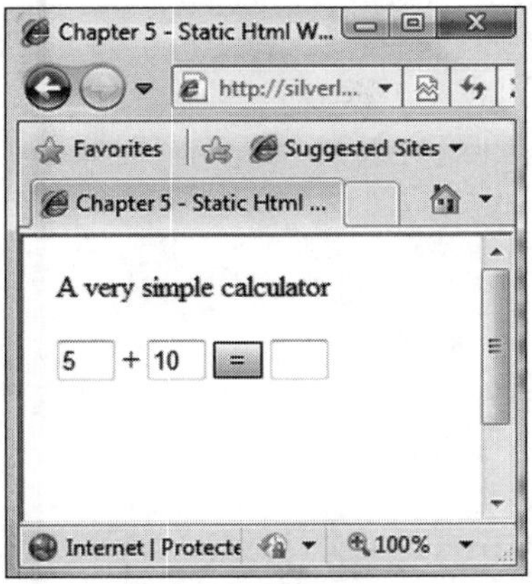

Figure 10.2 A simple static HTML website hosted in BLOB storage

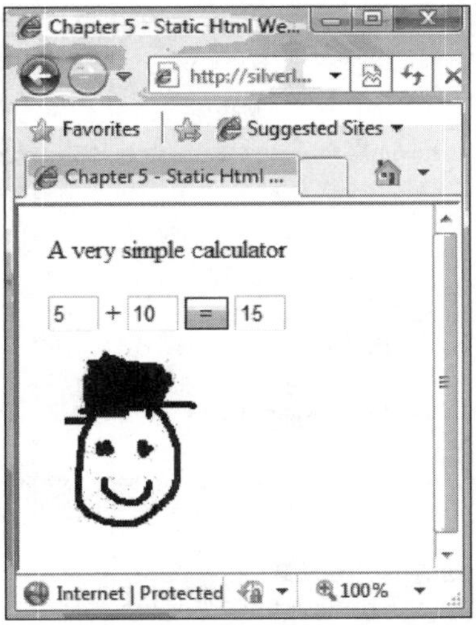

Figure 10.3 On click of the equals button, the result is displayed (along with a badly drawn smiley face)

Although this web page is a simple example, it does consist of all the major parts of a typical website: HTML, CSS, JavaScript, and assets (such as images). Table 10.1 gives a quick overview of the contents of this site.

Table 10.1 A breakdown of all the files in the website shown in figure 10.3

Website file	Purpose
default.htm	HTML page with buttons, text boxes, and stuff.
standard.css	All good web designers use CSS for their markup.
calculator.js	The complicated JavaScript that adds two numbers together.
happy.jpg	The smiley face that appears in figure 10.3.

That's what makes up this website. Now let's take a look at some of the code. The listing that follows contains the HTML for this page.

Listing 10.1 Calculator page website HTML

```
<!DOCTYPE html PUBLIC "-//W3C//DTD XHTML 1.0
➥ Transitional//EN" "http://www.w3.org/TR/xhtml1/DTD/
➥ xhtml1-transitional.dtd">
<html xmlns="http://www.w3.org/1999/xhtml" >
<head>
    <title>Chapter 10 - Static Html Website hosted in Blob Storage</title>
    <link rel="stylesheet" type="text/css" href="standard.css" />
    <script type="text/javascript" src="calculator.js"></script>
    <script type="text/javascript">
        function calculate() {
            document.getElementById('result').value =
                add(
```

Reference to JavaScript file

Reference to CSS file

(1) Calculates the value

```
                    document.getElementById('number1').value,
                    document.getElementById('number2').value
                   );

            document.getElementById('piccy').className = "visible";
        }
    </script>
</head>
<body>
    <div class="standarddiv">
        A very simple calculator
    </div>
    <div class="standarddiv">

        <input id="number1" type="text"
               value="5" class="standardtextbox"/>

        <span>+</span>
        <input id="number2" type="text"
               value="10" class="standardtextbox"/>

        <input type="submit" value="="
               class="standardbutton"
               onclick="calculate();"/>                ❷ Calculate button

        <input id="result" type="text"
               class="standardtextbox"
               readonly="readonly"/>

        <div id="piccy" class="hidden">                ❸ Happy picture
            <img src="happy.jpg"/>
        </div>
    </div></body>
</html>
```

We're not going to explain this code in much detail. It's fairly simple HTML and this is chapter 10; if you've gotten this far, you've probably figured out HTML already. We'll cover the important bits, though. On click of the equals button at ❷ in listing 10.1, the JavaScript function at ❶ is invoked. This function takes the contents of the two text boxes (`number1` and `number2`), calls the add function, and displays the result in the result text box. Finally, when the calculation is complete, the style at ❸ is changed from `hidden` to `visible` and the smiley face graphic as seen in figure 10.3 is displayed.

Now that we've pushed technology to its absolute limit by building a web page that can add numbers together (woo-hoo, go us), you're going to publish your work of art to BLOB storage for hosting.

10.1.2 Publishing your website to BLOB services

In previous examples, you've programmatically added your BLOBs to the storage service. In this example, you'll make use of a tool called Chris Hay's Azure Blob Browser (can you guess from the title who created it?) to upload the files to BLOB storage. Figure 10.4 shows the addition of the calculator.js file to BLOB storage via the tool.

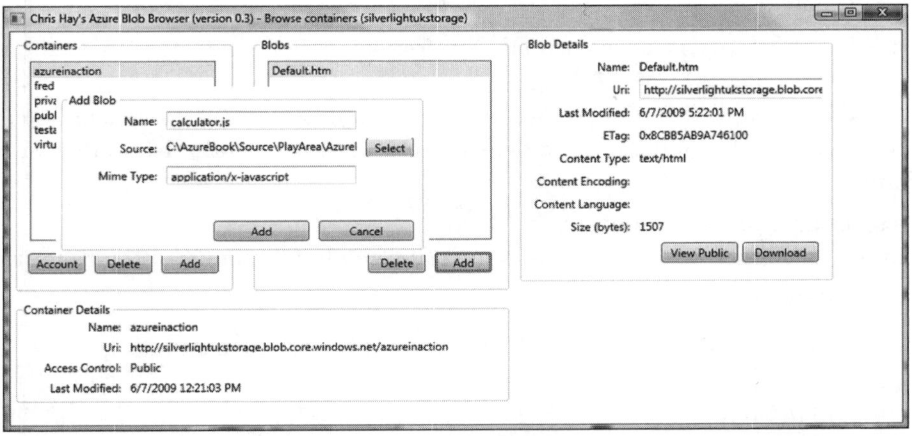

Figure 10.4 Adding calculator.js to BLOB storage via Chris Hay's Azure Blob Browser

Using the BLOB browser, you can add each file of the website (default.htm, calculator.js, standard.css, and happy.jpg) by selecting the file to upload, setting the MIME type (which is automatically predicted for you, but is also editable), and clicking the Add button.

After all the files are uploaded into the appropriate public container, you can access the website with a standard web browser using the following URI structure: http://silverlightukstorage.blob.core.windows.net/azureinaction/default.htm.

Note that you must include the filename (default.htm) because BLOB storage doesn't support default documents.

> **TIP** If you're hosting your website or web application in BLOB storage, you probably don't want your clients to use the BLOB.core.windows.net domain. You need to host your website on your own custom domain, for example, http://www.noddyjavascriptcalculator.com/. For details about how to do this, see chapter 8.

SETTING THE CORRECT MIME TYPE

If the correct MIME type isn't set, the web browser won't be able to render the downloaded file. Some browsers, such as Internet Explorer, will render the content in some situations even if the MIME type is incorrect; other browsers, such as Firefox, require the MIME type to be set explicitly.

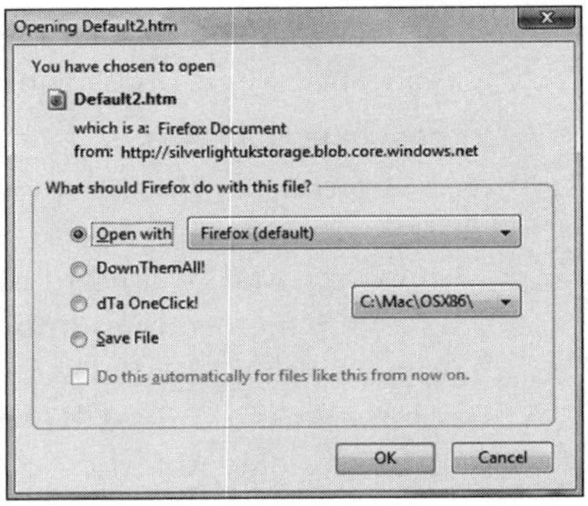

Figure 10.5 Accessing a file that has an incorrect MIME type in Firefox

Figure 10.5 shows how Firefox handles HTML documents that don't have the correct MIME type (text or HTML) but instead use the default Azure BLOB storage services MIME type (application/octet-stream). Figure 10.5

shows that Firefox can't display the page and requires further instructions from the user. If the MIME type is set correctly, Firefox will show the web page that's shown in figure 10.3.

Now that your first static HTML website is running in BLOB storage, let's look at how you can move beyond flat directory structures and store and retrieve files within hierarchies.

HANDLING DIRECTORY STRUCTURE

In our calculator example, we used the following flat directory structure for the files:

- default.htm
- calculator.js
- standard.css
- happy.jpg

Although this kind of structure is useful for small websites, it's limiting for websites with a large hierarchy. BLOB storage technically doesn't support directories within a container, but you can simulate such support by using a slash (/) as a separator in the BLOB name, which creates a hierarchy for the files. The following list shows how you can represent your files in BLOB storage:

- Chapter10/default.htm
- Chapter10/javascript/calculator.js
- Chapter10/css/standard.css
- Chapter10/images/happy.jpg

Using the slash separator in the BLOB name means that the default.htm page would be accessed using the following URI structure: http://silverlightukstorage.blob.core.windows.net/azureinaction/Chapter10/default.htm.

The `CloudBlobDirectory` class in the StorageClient library provides a way around the limitation of containers not having subcontainers (or subfolders) by providing a set of methods that allows you to pretend that there's a real directory structure in a container. It's driven by the slashes you put in your BLOB filename.

Now that you've made this example website, you can tell that using BLOB storage as a web server is pretty cool and simple. There is, however, one drawback.

LOGGING BLOB REQUESTS

As of version 1, BLOB requests aren't logged. This level of logging is vital for analyzing who's visiting your website, where they've come from, and what parts of your site are popular. If you're used to running your own website, you usually have access to your IIS logs, which contain information such as page requested, IP address, referrer, and so on. Because the BLOB storage service doesn't provide such information, if you're going to use it to host HTML websites, you need to use an external analytics service, such as Google Analytics.

In this section, we showed you how to display static HTML websites in BLOB storage services. Next, we'll look at hosting Rich Internet Applications (RIAs), specifically Silverlight applications.

10.2 Hosting Silverlight applications in BLOB storage

Although you'll usually host your Silverlight applications in a standard Windows Azure web role, you can host your Silverlight applications in BLOB storage, if required. Depending on your web application, you can effectively use BLOB storage to achieve massive scale for minimal cost. For example, in our podcasting example from the previous chapters, it might make financial sense to have your website hosted in a web role, but to also have a Silverlight media player hosted in BLOB storage. If you run a foreign currency exchange website, you might want to host the main site (which could offer the option to purchase currency) in a web role, but host an exchange rate calculator in BLOB storage.

> **NOTE** In this chapter, we're focusing on Silverlight because it's familiar to .NET developers. Although we're looking exclusively at Silverlight, the techniques discussed in this section are applicable to other RIA solutions (for example, Flash, Flex, Air, and so on).

In this section, we'll look at how you can enable such scenarios by showing you how you can do the following using BLOB storage:

- Host a standalone Silverlight application that's contained in a static HTML page
- Host a standalone Silverlight application that's contained in an ASP.NET web page
- Get your Silverlight application that's hosted in BLOB storage to communicate with external web services
- Store external Silverlight application access files

And now for the details that will enable you to do all this wonderful stuff with BLOB storage.

10.2.1 Hosting the Silverlight Spectrum emulator

If you've developed a standalone Silverlight application that requires no interaction with any backend services, BLOB storage is a cost-effective candidate for hosting your Silverlight application. These types of applications typically include games, tax calculators, and other widgets.

For our next example, we'll show you how to host a small Silverlight application in BLOB storage. The application that you'll host is a Silverlight ZX Spectrum emulator, which was an 8-bit home computer of the 1980s, very like a Commodore 64 (actually, that's not true; it was much worse, but it had spirit). Figure 10.6 shows the emulator running from BLOB storage.

The ZX Spectrum emulator not only allows you to play games from the 1980s, but as you can see from figure 10.6, you can even write BASIC programs in it. Now, we don't want you to lose focus on this book as soon as you load this thing. As cool as Jet Set Willy is, it won't help you deliver your amazing cloud-based application. You'll have to continue to pay attention to learn how to do that.

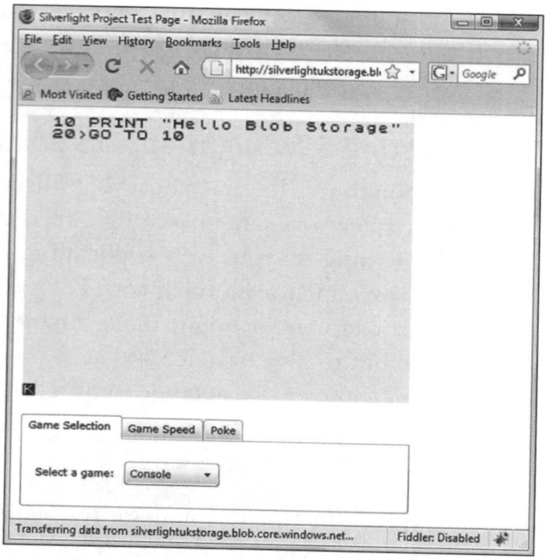

Figure 10.6 Silverlight application running in BLOB storage

To store the application in BLOB storage, upload ZXSilverlight.xap using the same procedure you used in the previous section. (You can download this Silverlight application and its source code from http://www.azureinaction.com.) You must set the BLOB with the correct MIME type; otherwise, the browser won't be able to launch the application. The MIME type for a Silverlight application is `application/x-silverlight-app`.

You're also going to store the HTML page that hosts the Silverlight application in BLOB storage. The following listing shows the HTML that runs the ZX Spectrum emulator Silverlight application (ZXSilverlight.app).

Listing 10.2 HTML for the ZX Spectrum emulator Silverlight application

```
<html xmlns="http://www.w3.org/1999/xhtml" >
<head>
    <title>Silverlight Project Test Page </title>

    <style type="text/css">
        html, body {height: 100%; overflow: auto;}
        #silverlightControlHost {height: 100%;}
    </style>
    <script type="text/javascript" src="Silverlight.js"></script>
</head>
<body>
    <div id="silverlightControlHost">
        <object data="data:application/x-silverlight,"
                type="application/x-silverlight-2"
                width="100%" height="100%">
                <param name="source" value="ZXSilverlight.xap"/>
                <param name="background" value="white" />
        </object>
    </div>
</body>
</html>
```

Specifies Silverlight plug-in

Specifies Silverlight 2 application

Specifies location of Silverlight application

By looking at listing 10.2, you can see that the HTML page doesn't have any logic in it. Its job is to host the Silverlight application. Because this web page is just a host for a Silverlight application, using a full-fledged web server would be a little over the top (and expensive); a static HTML page hosted in BLOB storage will do the job perfectly.

> **TIP** If you have an existing web page that you host outside BLOB storage (you're using a web role or an existing web hosting provider to host it), you can still host your Silverlight application in BLOB storage but keep your site with your existing host. To do so, you need to change the `source` parameter of the Silverlight plug-in (see listing 10.2) to point to your BLOB storage URI.

This standalone Silverlight application doesn't require access to any backend web services, but what if you want to host an application that does? You can still host your application in BLOB services, but you'll need to understand how a cross-domain policy works.

10.2.2 Communicating with third-party sites

Suppose your Silverlight application requires communication with an external website or web service (WCF, ASMX, REST, POX, or HTTP). For example, what if you want to host a Silverlight exchange rate calculator?

Your Silverlight application needs to poll a web service for live data, so you might be thinking that you should host your entire solution as an ASP.NET-hosted website. Although this is a perfectly valid solution, it's still quite expensive for what you require. In this scenario, it might be more cost effective to host your web service in ASP.NET (or use a third-party service if one is available), but host your Silverlight application (and website) in BLOB storage. Figure 10.7 shows a Silverlight application communicating with an external web service.

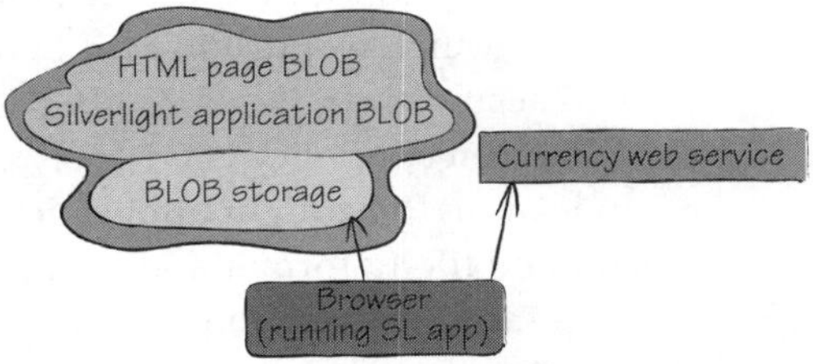

Figure 10.7 Silverlight application communicating with an external web service

For the Silverlight application to communicate with a third-party domain, the external site must host a suitable cross-domain policy.

HOSTING A CROSS-DOMAIN POLICY

The following listing shows a typical cross-domain policy file (ClientAccessPolicy.xml) used to give permissions to a Silverlight application.

Listing 10.3 ClientAccessPolicy.xml file for Silverlight permissions

```
<?xml version="1.0" encoding="utf-8"?>
<access-policy>
  <cross-domain-access>
    <policy>
      <allow-from http-request-headers="*">
```

```
      <domain uri="http://silverlightukstorage.blob.core.windows.net/"/>   ❶ URI of BLOB storage domain
      </allow-from>
      <grant-to>
        <resource path="/" include-subpaths="true"/>
      </grant-to>
    </policy>
  </cross-domain-access>
</access-policy>
```

> **Cross-domain policy**
>
> For security purposes, Silverlight applications (and Flash applications) can, by default, communicate only with the domain that the container web page is hosted on. If your Silverlight application needs to communicate with a third-party domain, the external website needs to host a cross-domain policy file (ClientAccessPolicy.xml or CrossDomain.xml) to give your application permission to communicate with it.

The ClientAccessPolicy.xml file displayed in listing 10.3 states at ❶ that any Silverlight application hosted at http://silverlightukstorage.blob.core.windows.net/ (the BLOB storage account of your Silverlight application) can access the third-party web service. Your application would also be able to access the service if the domain URI at ❶ was set to *, which would indicate that any Silverlight application hosted at any website could access it.

ClientAccessPolicy.xml is a cross-domain policy file that's used solely by Silverlight applications. Silverlight applications can also access web services that host a CrossDomain.xml file (a format that's supported by both Flash and Silverlight). The following listing shows a CrossDomain.xml file that your BLOB storage-hosted application could communicate with.

Listing 10.4 CrossDomain.xml file

```
<?xml version="1.0" ?>
<!DOCTYPE cross-domain-policy  SYSTEM
➥ "http://www.macromedia.com/xml/dtds/cross-domain-policy.dtd">
<cross-domain-policy>
    <allow-access-from domain="*" />          ❶ Allows access to all domains
</cross-domain-policy>
```

The CrossDomain.xml file displayed in listing 10.4 states at ❶ that any website hosting a browser-based application (Silverlight or Flash) can communicate with this service. If the owner of the web service wanted to restrict access to your application only, then it would replace the * at ❶ with `silverlightukstorage.blob.core.windows.net` (your BLOB storage account).

> **$root container**
>
> If you need to allow third-party Silverlight or Flash applications to access assets held in your BLOB storage account, store your CrossDomain.xml or ClientAccessPolicy.xml file in a public container named $root.
>
> This special container allows you to store any file in the root of your URI, for example: http://chrishayuk.blob.core.windows.net/crossdomain.xml.

Now let's build a Silverlight web search application that uses Yahoo's Search API to search the internet.

BUILDING A SILVERLIGHT WEB SEARCH APPLICATION

Figure 10.8 shows the Silverlight application that we're going to show you how to build.

The HTML page for the application that you're going to build (shown in figure 10.8) is no different from the one in listing 10.2 (well, there is one small difference: the `source` parameter value references the new Silverlight application (.XAP file).

To create the application, create a new Silverlight application as you normally would; then rename the default XAML (Extensible Application Markup Language) to YahooSearch.xaml. Replace the default `Grid` provided in the template with the XAML shown in the following listing.

Listing 10.5 XAML for Silverlight web search application

```
<Grid x:Name="LayoutRoot" Background="White">
        <StackPanel>
            <StackPanel Orientation="Horizontal">
```

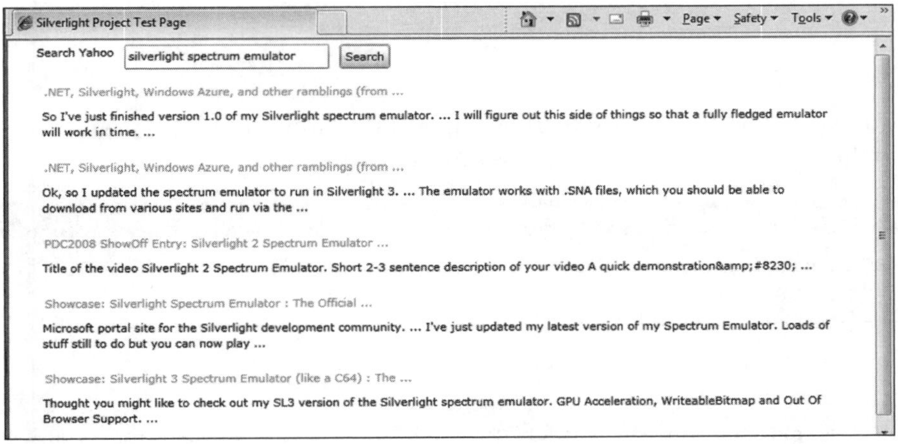

Figure 10.8 A Silverlight search application hosted in BLOB storage that communicates with the Yahoo Search API.

```
            <TextBlock  Text="Search Yahoo"
                        VerticalAlignment="Top"
                        Margin="5"/>
            <TextBox x:Name="txtSearch"                    <-- Enters the
                                VerticalAlignment="Top"        search term
                                Height="25" Width="200"
                                Margin="5"/>
            <Button x:Name="btnSearch"
                    Content="Search"
                    VerticalAlignment="Top"
                    Height="25" Width="50"
                    Margin="5"
                    Click="btnSearch_Click"/>
        </StackPanel>
            <ItemsControl x:Name="itemsResults">           <-- Displays the
                <ItemsControl.ItemTemplate>                    search results
                    <DataTemplate>
                        <Grid Margin="10">
                            <Grid.RowDefinitions>
                                <RowDefinition Height="25"/>
                                <RowDefinition Height="*"/>
                            </Grid.RowDefinitions>
                            <HyperlinkButton
                               Grid.Row="0"
                               Content="{Binding Title}"
                               NavigateUri="{Binding Url}"/>
                            <TextBlock
                               Grid.Row="1"
                               Text="{Binding Summary}"
                               TextWrapping="Wrap">
                            </TextBlock>
                        </Grid>
                    </DataTemplate>
                </ItemsControl.ItemTemplate>
            </ItemsControl>
        </StackPanel>
    </Grid>
```

After you've pasted the XAML in listing 10.5 into your Silverlight page, you can hook up the code-behind for the page, as shown in listing 10.6.

Listing 10.6 Code-behind for Silverlight web search application XAML page

```
public partial class YahooSearch : UserControl
{
        public YahooSearch()
        {
            InitializeComponent();
        }

        private void btnSearch_Click(object sender, RoutedEventArgs e)
        {
            Search mySearch = new Search();
            mySearch.SearchResultsReturned += new
            ➥ Search.SearchResultReturnedDelegate
            ➥ (mySearch_SearchResultsReturned);
```

```
            mySearch.Execute(txtSearch.Text);        ❶ Sends search request
        }                                               to Yahoo API

        void mySearch_SearchResultsReturned(SearchResultSet results)
        {
            itemsResults.ItemsSource = results.Results;   ❷ Binds results of
        }                                                    search to data grid
}
```

In the code-behind for the Silverlight page shown in listing 10.6, you can see that when the Search button is clicked, the `execute` method of your `Search` class is invoked at ❶. The search term is sent to the Yahoo Search API, and then the results are returned asynchronously. When the search results are received, the results are bound to the data grid at ❷.

> **Yahoo Search**
>
> Yahoo was a popular search engine many years ago, at a time before we Googled for everything. Here at *Azure in Action*, we like to support the little guy; come on Yahoo, you can be big again.
>
> Actually, the reason we use Yahoo is that it has a nice, simple, REST-based API that we can easily use from Silverlight.

Listing 10.7 shows the code-behind for the Yahoo `Search` class.

Listing 10.7 Code-behind for the Yahoo `Search` class

```
public class Search
{
    public delegate void SearchResultReturnedDelegate
    ➥ (SearchResultSet results);
    public event SearchResultReturnedDelegate SearchResultsReturned;

    private const string _baseUri =
    ➥ "http://search.yahooapis.com/WebSearchService/
    ➥ V1/webSearch?appid={0}&query={1}&start={2}&results={3}";
    private const string _applicationId =
    ➥ @"Jk.kKH_V34FIj5WGgtm6iimK.37hiKF
    ➥ 0A5EVnJkoltzGoydU.Z0notpjqa0DxTiJULlbg--";

        public void Execute(string keyword)
        {

            Uri searchUri = new Uri(string.Format
            ➥ (_baseUri, _applicationId, keyword,1,5));

            Execute(searchUri);                          Calls the search
        }

        private void Execute(Uri address)
        {
```

```
            WebClient searchClient = new WebClient();

            searchClient.DownloadStringCompleted +=
            ➥ new DownloadStringCompletedEventHandler
            ➥ searchClient_DownloadStringCompleted);

            searchClient.DownloadStringAsync(address);
        }

        void searchClient_DownloadStringCompleted
               (object sender, DownloadStringCompletedEventArgs e)
        {

            if (SearchResultsReturned != null)
            {

                XElement xeResult = XElement.Parse(e.Result);

                                     SearchResultSet resultSet =
                                     ➥ new SearchResultSet(xeResult);

                SearchResultsReturned(resultSet);        <-- Returns the search results
            }
        }
}

public class SearchResultItem
{
    public string Title { get; set; }
    public string Summary { get; set; }
    public Uri Url { get; set; }
}

public class SearchResultSet
{

    public SearchResultSet()
    {

        Results = new List<SearchResultItem>();
    }

    public SearchResultSet(XElement resultsXml)
    {

        Results = new List<SearchResultItem>();


        XNamespace ns = "urn:yahoo:srch";

        var xeResults = from xeResult in
        ➥ resultsXml.Elements(ns + "Result")      <-- LINQ to reform the results
             select new SearchResultItem
             {
```

```
                Title = xeResult
                ➥ .Element(ns + "Title").Value,
                Summary = xeResult
                ➥ .Element(ns + "Summary").Value,
                Url = new Uri(
                ➥ xeResult.Element(ns + "Url").Value)
            };

        Results.AddRange(xeResults);
    }

    public List<SearchResultItem> Results { get; set; }

}
```

We're not going to spend any time explaining the code in listing 10.7, except to say that it makes an HTTP request to the Yahoo Search API and returns a set of results that you can bind to your Silverlight data grid.

Now that you have an idea of how to store static HTML websites and Silverlight applications in BLOB storage, let's look at how you can use BLOB storage as a media server.

10.3 Using BLOB storage as a media server

In this section, we'll return to our podcasting example. Previously, you've used BLOB storage as a place to store your video and audio podcasts; now you're going to use BLOB storage as a mechanism for serving your videos to customers.

Because BLOB storage provides a URI for any files held in public containers, you could just make the link available to your customers to download the files offline, for example, http://storageaccount.blobs.core.windows.net/container/mypodcast.wmv. This probably wouldn't provide the greatest user experience in the world.

An alternative to downloading an entire media file is to use streaming. When media is streamed, the streaming server starts sending a byte stream of the video to the client. The client media player creates a buffer of the downloaded bytes, and starts playing the video when the buffer is sufficiently full. While the user is watching the video from the buffer, the client continues to download the data in the background.

Media streaming lets the user start watching the video within seconds, rather than requiring the user to wait for the entire movie to download. If the user decides to watch only the first few seconds of the movie, the service provider will have served up only some of the movie, which results in cheaper bandwidth bills. Unfortunately, streaming isn't currently available as an option in Windows Azure and the Windows Azure BLOB storage service. If you want to use such a solution, you need to use a third-party streaming service.

An even better solution is to use progressive downloading, in which a file is downloaded in small chunks and is stitched together by the client application. After a few chunks are downloaded, the client application can start playing the movie while the rest of the file chunks are downloaded in the background. Progressive downloading has the same performance advantages as streaming and provides a similar user experience. The main difference between progressive downloading and streaming is that the file being streamed never physically resides on disk and remains only in memory.

10.3.1 Building a Silverlight or WPF video player

By default, Silverlight supports the ability to progressively download files. In this example, we'll tell you how to build a small Silverlight video player that will allow you to play movies on your web page that are hosted by BLOB storage. Figure 10.9 shows a small video player that you'll build. The video player is playing a video served directly from BLOB storage using the public URI.

You can build a WPF or Silverlight media player like that shown in figure 10.9 by creating a WPF or Silverlight application and using the following XAML:

```
<MediaElement x:Name="myVideo"
➥ Source="http://storageaccount.blobs.core.windows.net
➥ /container/videopodcast01.wmv"
/>
```

Wow, is that really it? Yup, that's how easy it is to create a progressive downloading video player that shows videos hosted in BLOB storage.

Although Silverlight does progressively download the video player, the download is performed in a linear fashion, downloading from a single file, from a single website. If you have very large files (they're up to gigabytes), you might want to use a slightly different technique. For large files, you can download video much faster if you split up and chunk your files manually (and eventually split them across multiple servers).

Figure 10.9 WPF video player showing a video that features a giant bunny rabbit (Big Buck Bunny)

10.3.2 A WPF-based adaptive-streaming video player

Now we're going to tell you how to build a WPF-based media player that can adaptively stream your video. Your media player will look exactly like the WPF media player displayed in figure 10.9.

Adaptive streaming is a technique that most content delivery networks (CDNs) use to deliver high-performance video. This technique is also used in IIS adaptive streaming, although BLOB storage won't deliver in multiple bitrates.

> **WARNING** The following code is intended as an example to show you how you can use adaptive streaming. This isn't production-quality code (not by a long shot).

PLAYING THE VIDEO

The following XAML is used to play the video in WPF:

```
<MediaElement x:Name="myVideo" Source="videopodcast01.wmv"
              LoadedBehavior="Manual"/>
```

`MediaElement` is a built-in control that allows you to play movies in WPF applications. In this example, we're downloading the movie (mymovie.wmv) to the same folder that the WPF movie player application resides in. The source attribute states where the `MediaElement` should look for the movie.

By default, the `MediaElement` automatically starts playing the movie on startup. Because the movie hasn't been downloaded yet, you need to prevent the movie from automatically playing by setting the attribute `LoadedBehavior` to `Manual`.

THE CHUNKING METHODOLOGY FOR WPF

You're going to download the movie in chunks of 100 Kb. Only one chunk will be downloaded at a time and each newly downloaded chunk will be appended to the previously downloaded chunk. Listing 10.8 shows that as soon as the movie player is loaded, it starts downloading the chunks. After 10 seconds, the movie starts playing.

Listing 10.8 Chunking movies with the WPF movie player

```
private void Window_Loaded(object sender, RoutedEventArgs e)
{
   movieStream =
      File.Open("videopodcast01.wmv",
         FileMode.Append, FileAccess.Write, FileShare.ReadWrite);   <-- Creates empty movie file

GetNextChunk();                  <-- Starts downloading video from BLOB storage
Thread.Sleep(10000);             <-- Waits 10 seconds
myVideo.Play();                  <-- Starts playing video
}
```

Before we look more carefully at the code used to progressively download the video, let's talk a bit about the `Range` header.

USING THE RANGE HEADER

When a GET request is made using either the storage client or via an HTTP request, the entire file is downloaded by default. The code shown in listing 10.9 will download videopodcast01.wmv from the public container, podcasts.

Listing 10.9 Using the storage client to download a video file

```
CloudStorageAccount account =
   CloudStorageAccount.FromConfigurationSetting("DataConnectionString");

CloudBlobClient blobClient =
   account.CreateCloudBlobClient();

CloudBlobContainer container =
   blobClient.GetContainerReference("podcasts");      <-- Gets podcasts container

container.GetBlobReference("videopodcast01.wmv");     <-- Gets reference to BLOB videopodcast01.wmv
container.DownloadFile("videopodcast01.wmv");         <-- Downloads videopodcast01.wmv BLOB
```

The code in listing 10.9 will download the entire movie; in this example, we want to split the movie up into manageable chunks. Currently, the storage client sample code doesn't provide the ability to download a specified portion of the file, even though the underlying REST API does support this. The code shown in listing 10.10 will download the entire podcast using `HttpWebRequest`.

Listing 10.10 Using `HttpWebRequest` to download a video file

```
string baseUri = @"http://silverlightukstorage.blob.core.windows.net/";
HttpWebRequest hwr =                                   <-- (1) Generates HttpWebRequest
   CreateHttpRequest(new Uri(baseUri +"podcasts/videopodcast01.wmv"),
                     "GET", new TimeSpan(0, 0, 30));
// TODO: Range Header goes here                        <-- (2) Restricts download size using Range header
DownloadFile(hwr," videopodcast01.wmv");               <-- (3) Downloads the file
```

At (1), you generate the `HttpWebRequest` with the standard required headers using the `CreateHttpRequest` method that we used in chapter 8. At (3), you use the `DownloadFile` method to invoke the request and download the file to disk. The implementation of the `DownloadFile` method is available in the online samples.

If you don't want to download the entire video file, you can use the `Range` header to specify the range of bytes that you want to download. The following code would restrict the download to the first 100,000 bytes of the file, and can be used in listing 10.10 at (2):

```
hwr.AddRange(0, 100000);
```

Not only can you restrict the number of bytes using the `Range` header, you can also use it to progressively download the file in chunks.

DOWNLOADING CHUNKS OF DATA

When the WPF movie player was loaded, we made a call to `GetNextChunk()` in listing 10.8. In listing 10.11, we show you how `GetNextChunk` is implemented, and how to use the `Range` header to progressively download the movie.

Listing 10.11 Downloading the data in chunks

```
private int size 100000;
private int nextSize = 0;
private Stream movieStream;

private void GetNextChunk()
{
string baseUri = @"http://silverlightukstorage.blob.core.windows.net/";
HttpWebRequest hwr =
    CreateHttpRequest(new Uri(baseUri +"podcasts/videopodcast01.wmv"),
                              "GET", new TimeSpan(0, 0, 30));

hwr.AddRange(nextRange, nextRange + size);
nextRange += (size + 1);
hwr.BeginGetResponse(new AsyncCallback(webRequest_Callback), hwr);
}

private void webRequest_Callback(IAsyncResult asynchronousResult)
{
   try
   {
      HttpWebRequest request =
         (HttpWebRequest)asynchronousResult.AsyncState;

      HttpWebResponse response =
         (HttpWebResponse)request.EndGetResponse(asynchronousResult);

      SaveChunk(response.GetResponseStream());
      response.Close();

      GetNextChunk();
   }
   catch { }
}

private void SaveChunk(Stream incomingStream)
{
   int READ_CHUNK = 1024 * 1024;
int WRITE_CHUNK = 1000 * 1024;
byte[] buffer = new byte[READ_CHUNK];

Stream stream = incomingStream;

while (true)
{
```

1. Creates web request
2. Adds Range header to restrict download size
3. Makes request, providing callback
4. The callback function
5. Saves downloaded file section

```
        int read = stream.Read(buffer, 0, READ_CHUNK);
        if (read <= 0)
           break;
        int to_write = read;

        while (to_write > 0)
        {
           movieStream.Write(buffer, 0, Math.Min(to_write, WRITE_CHUNK));
           to_write -= Math.Min(to_write, WRITE_CHUNK);
        }
    }
}
```

The GetNextChunk method will download 100 Kb of data from the BLOB storage service asynchronously. This method will be called every time you need to download a new chunk of video; it's called for the first time when the application is loaded in the fourth line in listing 10.8.

In listing 10.11, you create a standard HTTP web request at ❶; this is the same method that you used to create requests earlier. The video (videopodcast01.wmv) that you're downloading resides in a public container called *podcasts* that's held in your storage account. After you've created the request, you add the Range header ❷ to restrict the download to the next 100 Kb chunk.

At ❸ you're making an asynchronous HTTP web request to the BLOB storage service, with a callback to ❹. On the request callback ❹, the downloaded data is retrieved, and you call the SaveChunk method ❺, which will append the downloaded chunk to the videopodcast01.wmv file on the local disk. Finally, you call GetNextChunk again to get the next chunk of data.

Time-based buffering

In our simple example, we used time-based buffering to delay the playback of the movie. Although time-based buffering is suitable for our example, in a production scenario you should start playing the movie after a portion of the movie has been downloaded. We also don't make any provision for variable download speeds; you might want to extend the sample to handle situations in which the playback speed is faster than the download speed.

Now you have a working version of a WPF progressive-downloading media player, which shows that you can use BLOB storage as a storage service for desktop clients. With some tweaks you can build media players that perform similarly to a streaming service.

10.3.3 A Silverlight-based chunking media player

In the previous section, we showed you how to build a desktop progressive-downloading media player for video podcasts. Although the desktop application is great for that richer client experience, we also want to show you how to provide a web-based cross-platform Silverlight experience.

CHUNKING VIDEO IN SILVERLIGHT

Go back to the Silverlight player that you created earlier and modify the XAML to the following:

```
<MediaElement x:Name="myVideo" AutoPlay="False"/>
```

Although the XAML is similar to the WPF version, there are some subtle differences. In the Silverlight version, you use `AutoPlay="False"` to specify that you don't want the video to play automatically; in the WPF version, you set `LoadedBehavior="Manual"`. You're also not going to set a source for the `MediaElement`; you'll do this programmatically in the code-behind.

Listing 10.12 shows the `On_Load` event of the Silverlight media player.

Listing 10.12 `On_Load` event of the Silverlight media player

```
private void UserControl_Loaded(object sender, RoutedEventArgs e)
{
            GetNextChunk();                    ❶ Retrieves first chunk of video
            Thread.Sleep(10000);               ❷ Delays start of video
            using (IsolatedStorageFile isf =   ❸ Starts playing from isolated storage
      IsolatedStorageFile.GetUserStoreForApplication())
                {
                    var iosf = isf.OpenFile("videopodcast01.wmv",
                    ➥ FileMode.Open,
                    ➥ FileAccess.Read,
                    ➥ FileShare.ReadWrite);
                    myVideo.SetSource(iosf);
                    myVideo.Play();
                }
}
```

At ❶ the code calls `GetNextChunk` to start downloading the chunks of data and at ❷ playing the video is delayed for 10 seconds by sending the thread to sleep. At ❸ the video starts playing back from isolated storage.

> **WARNING** Sending the thread to sleep is bad production practice. You should never send the UI thread to sleep. In production, use a background timer that monitors the download progress, and start playing the video back at a suitable threshold.

THE CHUNKING METHODOLOGY FOR SILVERLIGHT

You'll use the same methodology to chunk the data that you used in the WPF example. You're going to split the data into manageable chunks and then stitch the chunks back together client-side.

> **Restricted headers**
>
> The browser plug-in model prevents the use of certain request headers because they're considered reserved and are available only to the browser. The following restricted headers are used by BLOB storage APIs and are unavailable to use in Silverlight: `Authorization` (discussed in the section "Setting shared access permissions" in chapter 9), `Date` (you can use `x-ms-date` as a workaround), and `Range` (you can use `x-ms-range` as a workaround).

Although you could split the files using the `x-ms-range` header (instead of using the `Range` header as you did in the WPF version), it might be kind of interesting to presplit the files into chunks and store the chunks in BLOB storage.

To split the files, use the same code that we used in the WPF example, but instead of stitching the file back together, you're going to save a separate file for each chunk. For example, the file VideoPodcast01.wmv would be split into the following chunks: VideoPodcast01_1.wmv, VideoPodcast01_2.wmv, . . ., VideoPodcast01_12.wmv.

Finally, you need to upload each chunk to BLOB storage using a tool like Chris Hay's Azure Blob Browser.

> **TIP** By presplitting the files, you can potentially distribute the files across a greater number of servers (or even domains). Distributing files in this way would be useful if you decided to use a content delivery network (CDN) (discussed later in this chapter) in combination with BLOB storage. You could also instruct the browser to cache the chunks (see chapters 6 and 9); if the file wasn't fully downloaded, the next download would be much quicker.

To use the presplit version of the chunks, your Silverlight application needs to use the following code to replace the WPF version of the `GetNextChunk` method:

```
private void GetNextChunk()
{
string baseUri = @"http://silverlightukstorage.blob.core.windows.net/";
string videoUri = baseUri+"podcasts/videopodcast01_"+nextRange+".wmv";
nextRange++;
HttpWebRequest hwr =
     CreateHttpRequest(new Uri(videoUri), "GET", new TimeSpan(0, 0, 30));
hwr.BeginGetResponse(new AsyncCallback(webRequest_Callback), hwr);
}
```

This code manually requests the chunk that's stored in your container by continually incrementing the chunk in the URI for each download request.

The major difference between this example and using adaptive streaming is that we don't have multiple encodings of the video at different bitrates. You could easily modify these samples to have videos encoded at different bitrates available and to detect the best bitrate for the client.

SAVING TO ISOLATED STORAGE

Silverlight can directly access the filesystem only via a user-initiated action. Silverlight applications can, however, write data directly to an isolated storage area without user initiation.

> **Saving to the actual filesystem**
>
> If you don't mind user-initiated actions, you can always use the `SaveFileDialog` rather than isolated storage.
>
> You need to be aware that if you're downloading files of any real size, you'll probably need a user-initiated action to increase the isolated storage default limits. In this case, you'd probably do just as well to use the `SaveFileDialog`.

In the Silverlight version of the media player, you're going to use the isolated storage area to save the video locally. Although the video podcast has been presplit into chunks, you still have to combine the chunks into a single file so the media player can play back the video. The method of saving and combining the chunks is similar to that used in the WPF version except that you're using isolated storage. Listing 10.13 shows the Silverlight version of `SaveChunk`.

Listing 10.13 `SaveChunk` for Silverlight

```
private void SaveChunk(Stream incomingStream)
{
int READ_CHUNK = 1024 * 1024;
            int WRITE_CHUNK = 1000 * 1024;
            byte[] buffer = new byte[READ_CHUNK];
            using (IsolatedStorageFile isf =
            ➥ IsolatedStorageFile.GetUserStoreForApplication())
            {
                using (IsolatedStorageFileStream isostream = new
                ➥ IsolatedStorageFileStream("videopodcast01.wmv",
                ➥ FileMode.Append, FileAccess.Write,
                ➥ FileShare.ReadWrite, isf))
                {
                    Stream stream = incomingStream;
                    stream.Position = 0;

                    while (true)
                    {
                        int read = stream.Read(buffer, 0, READ_CHUNK);
                        if (read <= 0)
                            break;
                        int to_write = read;

                        while (to_write > 0)
                        {
                            isostream.Write(buffer,
                            ➥ 0,
                            ➥ Math.Min(to_write, WRITE_CHUNK));
```

Gets isolated storage area for Silverlight application

Appends chunk to video in isolated storage

```
                    to_write -= Math.Min(to_write, WRITE_CHUNK);
                }
            }
            isostream.Close();
        }
    }
}
```

Although you've had to do some slight workarounds, now you've got a working version of the media player in Silverlight.

Congratulations! You've built a WPF video player and a Silverlight video player. Now let's look at how you can improve the performance of the video delivery by using content delivery networks (CDNs).

10.4 Content delivery networks

If your website customers are geographically dispersed, using a CDN can significantly improve the user experience. In this section, we'll discuss CDNs and how you can use them in conjunction with the Windows Azure BLOB storage service.

10.4.1 What's a CDN?

A CDN is a large number of web servers that are distributed across the world. These web servers usually sit close to the internet backbone and can quickly serve up large files. When a user makes a request to the CDN for a file, the CDN figures out which data center in the CDN is closest to the user's location and serves up the content from that data center.

Figure 10.10 shows that if you're based in Edinburgh, your files are served from the Dublin data center, rather than from one in Hong Kong.

In a CDN, a user makes a request via the nearest edge server and the origin server answers the request. Let's look at these servers in more detail.

EDGE SERVERS

Figure 10.10 shows that the CDN network has the following data centers

- Los Angeles
- New York
- Dublin
- London
- Dubai

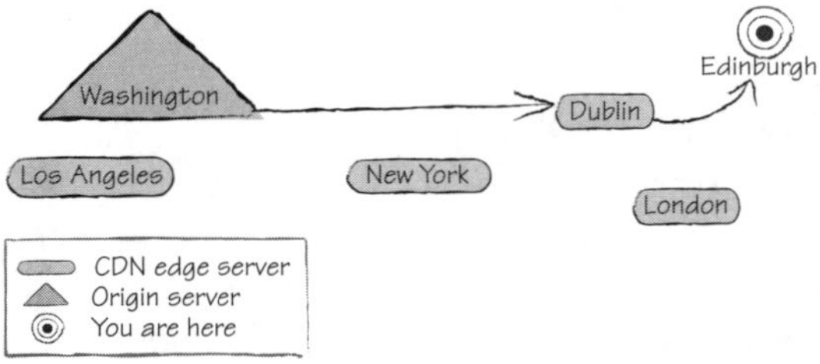

Figure 10.10 A CDN delivers files using the server closest to you.

- Hong Kong
- Tokyo

These data centers, which are represented by circles in figure 10.10, are known as edge servers. An edge server is the name used for one of the geographically dispersed web servers that are responsible for serving your content.

ORIGIN SERVER

The origin server is the web server that contains the original version of the content being distributed. In figure 10.10, the origin server is represented by the triangle and resides in Washington State. For Windows Azure, the origin server could be either your web role or a public container in your BLOB storage account. The content held on your origin server would never be accessed directly by your end user; the origin server only serves content to the edge servers.

When a request is made for a file held in a CDN, the request is redirected to the nearest edge server. If the edge server doesn't have a local copy of that file, it requests the file from the origin server and caches it locally.

> **NOTE** A CDN web server is similar to a BLOB storage web server; it can serve up any static file with the correct MIME type, but it has no backend server processing capabilities. For this reason, a CDN is suitable for serving up static content such as HTML, JavaScript, CSS, Silverlight and Flash applications, PDF documents, audio files, videos, and so on.

10.4.2 CDN performance advantages

Using a CDN network is a simple method of improving performance on your web servers without significantly changing your architecture or code. How so, you ask? Well, read on.

REDUCED LOAD FROM YOUR WEB APPLICATION SERVERS

If your static content is offloaded from your web application servers, your web servers will have more capacity to handle incoming requests. The reduced load will reduce active connections, CPU use, and network traffic on the server.

INCREASED CLIENT-SIDE PERFORMANCE

The largest bottleneck on web applications tends to be the time it takes to download static content from the web server, not the time it takes to serve the HTML page. Figure 10.11 shows the number of requests made to www.manning.com and the length of time it has taken for the content to be served.

If you look carefully at figure 10.11, you'll see that it takes only 1.72 seconds to serve up the HTML page, but an additional 3.5 seconds to serve the static content. This extra time is used because most internet browsers (including Firefox and Internet Explorer) can download only two files simultaneously from the same domain. If more than two files are requested at the same time, all other requests from the same domain are queued. The graph in figure 10.12 shows that the .gif files from manning.com are being downloaded only two files at a time, but the files being served from google-analytics.com can be downloaded at the same time as the manning.com gifs.

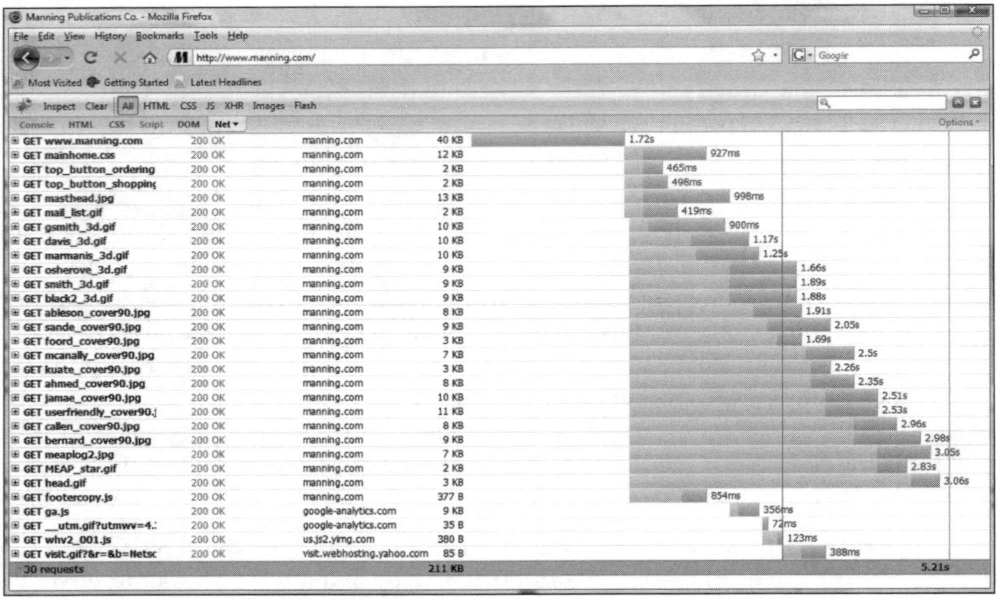

Figure 10.11 Comparison of the number of seconds it takes to serve HTML pages versus the number of seconds it takes to download the static content at www.mannning.com

A CDN moves static content to other subdomains, which allows the browser to simultaneously download more files and reduces the time it takes to render content on the client browser.

With the reduced network latency, faster internet connections, and the increased number of distributed web servers, any static content served from the CDN is delivered more quickly than it would be from a standard web server.

> **Using CDNs means your web server does less work**
>
> Any request that you can push off to the CDN (images, movies, CSS, JavaScript) results in fewer files that the web servers hosting your web application need to serve. Ultimately, this means that to meet the demands of your web traffic, you'll need fewer web role instances, which saves you money. Now, that's a good thing.

OK, you've got the message that you need to use CDNs, so pay close attention while we tell you how to use them with Windows Azure.

10.4.3 Using the Windows Azure CDN

So far, we've looked at CDNs from a generic standpoint; in this section, we'll take a look at what options are available in Windows Azure. In particular, we'll look at how you can use Windows Azure as an origin server and what options you have regarding edge servers.

Although in this section we're showing you how to use the Windows Azure CDN (c'mon, it's a Windows Azure book, after all), you can use other CDN providers, such as Akamai and Amazon Cloud Front. As you're about to discover, using the Windows Azure CDN is probably the easiest option (we have no idea whether it's the cheapest; you'll need to use our JavaScript calculator to work that one out).

USING BLOB STORAGE AS AN ORIGIN SERVER

Although web roles can be used as origin servers with non-Windows Azure CDNs, using them is a more expensive option than using BLOB storage. Because edge servers can serve only static content, there's no need for them to be able to generate dynamic server-side content. An efficient cost-effective solution is to use your storage account as an origin server rather than use a web role.

> **NOTE** With the Windows Azure CDN, you can use only BLOB storage as an origin server; you can't use web roles.

To use our movie player example, the original version of the Big Buck Bunny movie, or even the original presplit chunk files, would be stored in BLOB storage, and BLOB storage would act as the origin server.

ENABLING THE WINDOWS AZURE CDN

To enable the Windows Azure CDN, open the storage account in the Windows Azure Developer portal and click Enable CDN, as shown in figure 10.12.

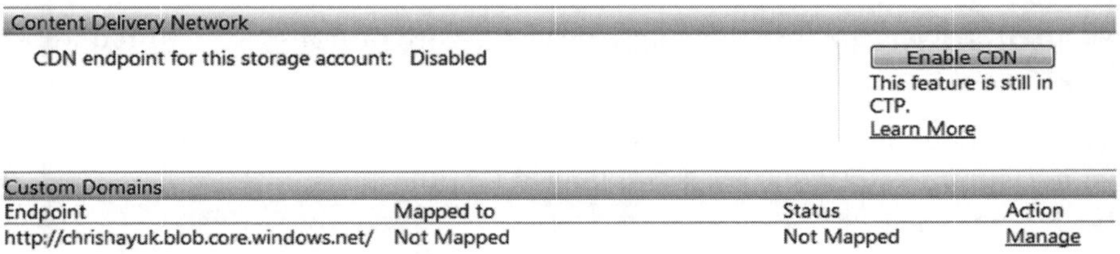

Figure 10.12 Enabling a CDN in the Windows Azure Developer portal

After you click this button, any BLOBs stored in public containers will be available on the CDN after about an hour. Figure 10.13 shows the Developer portal after your CDN account has been enabled.

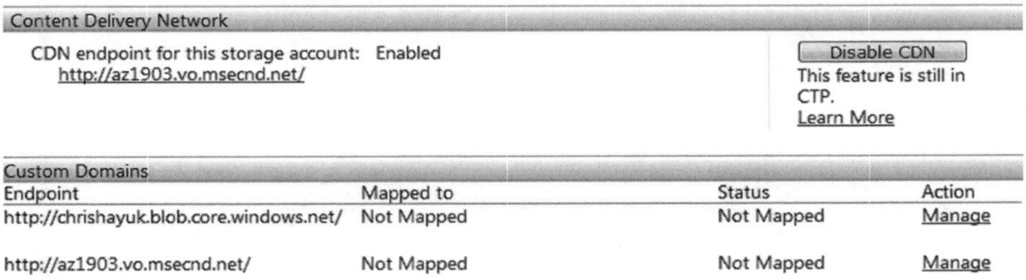

Figure 10.13 An enabled CDN account in the Windows Azure Developer portal

A new custom domain is assigned to your CDN-enabled BLOBs. In figure 10.13, the CDN domain is http://az1903.vo.msecdn.net/. All you need to do now is replace where we used http://chrishayuk.blob.core.windows.net/ with http://az1903.vo.msecdn.net/, and the files will start being fed from the Windows Azure CDN instead of from our BLOB storage account.

If you don't like the assigned subdomain, you can assign your own custom domain to the CDN domain; for details on how to do that, see chapter 8.

> **TIP** If you want to improve the amount of parallel downloads on your site, assign half your assets to the assigned CDN domain, and the other half to a custom domain name.

10.5 Summary

Over the course of part 4 (chapters 8, 9, and 10), we've explored BLOB storage pretty thoroughly and you should now be able to use this storage service effectively in your applications.

In this chapter, you've discovered that BLOB storage can be more than just a hard disk for your web and worker roles. BLOB storage is a powerful storage mechanism that can do the following things for you:

- Host static websites
- Host RIAs, such as Silverlight
- Act as a media server
- Host assets for your existing websites (Azure or non-Azure hosted websites)
- Act as a CDN

We're going to move away now from BLOB storage and build upon the knowledge you gained with this storage service and look at another part of the storage services puzzle, the Table service.

Part 5

Working with structured data

Now that you have working with files under your belts, we can turn our attention to how to work with structured data. There are two options in Azure.

Chapter 11 covers the first option, Azure Table storage. This stuff is really different from your dad's SQL Server and relational data engines. Take off your mental blinders or your mind will be blown!

Don't like to work with high-level APIs? Do you prefer to set the value of AX yourself? Then chapter 12 is for you. Chapter 12 looks at how to work with Azure tables, using the REST interface. Hardcore stuff, but easy for you.

For those who had their minds blown in chapter 11, we'll put them back together again when we cover SQL Azure in chapter 13. Have an app you want to move to the cloud, but you're using an old-fashioned relational data model? You can easily move to the cloud using SQL Azure and all its foreign-key-indexed-relationships-and-transactions supporting goodness.

Finally, we polish off part 5 with chapter 14 and look at how and when you might choose Azure tables and SQL Azure. We try to end the debate in a peaceful way and help you make solid decisions for your data platform.

11 The Table service, a whole different entity

This chapter covers

- Introducing the Table service
- Getting started developing with the Table service
- Using the Table service in a production environment

In typical web applications, you'd normally store your data in a relational database, such as SQL Server. SQL Server is great at representing relational data and is a suitable data store for many situations, but it's very difficult to design scalable SQL Server databases at low cost. To get around the problems of scalability, Windows Azure provides its own table-based storage mechanism called the Table service.

Problems of scale in relational databases

As the web server load increases for a site, you may need to scale up the number of servers to cope with the increase in demand. But what do you do if you need to

(continued)

increase the capacity of your data store? Unfortunately, most databases aren't designed to scale beyond a single server, which means the only way to cope with the increase in demand is either to scale up your hardware or redesign your application.

Although it's possible to design scalable federated databases with SQL Server, the licensing costs, the design complexity, the cost of development, and the operational costs of running such a system make it very difficult to justify for many companies on a budget.

Let's now take a brief look at what the Table service is.

11.1 A brief overview of the Table service

The Table service component of the Windows Azure storage services (which includes the BLOB service, Table service, and Queue service) is a very simple, highly scalable, cost-effective solution that can be used to store data. In many scenarios it can replace traditional SQL Server–based designs.

> **NOTE** Like all other storage services, the Table service is hosted within the Windows Azure data centers, leveraging the web role infrastructure. Access to the service is provided through an HTTP-based REST API. For more details on the infrastructure of the service see chapter 9.

The Table service provides you with the ability to create very simple tables that you can use to store serialized versions of your entities. Figure 11.1 shows how entities are stored in the Table service.

In figure 11.1 you can see that there are two tables (Products and ShoppingCart) in a storage account (silverlightukstorage). The Products table could represent the product list for the Hawaiian Shirt Shop website that we introduced in chapter 2, and each entity stored in the Products table (Red Shirt, Blue Shirt, and Blue Frilly Shirt) would represent different types of shirts.

It's important to point out that although the Table service offers the ability to store data in tables, it's an entity storage mechanism, not a relational database. That means it doesn't offer the sort of functionality that you may be used to:

- It can't create foreign key relationships between tables.
- It can't perform server-side joins between tables.
- It can't create custom indexes on tables.

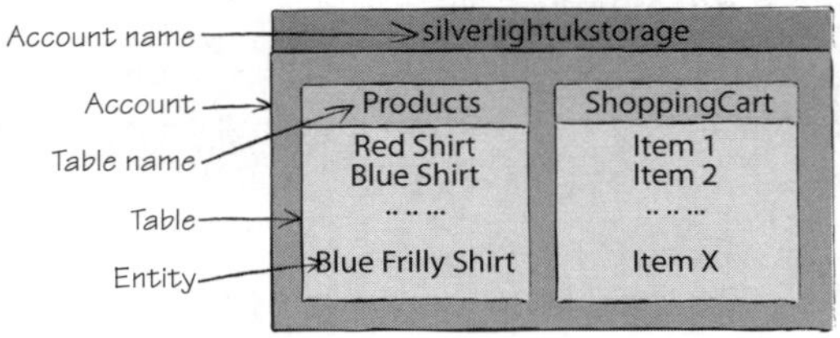

Figure 11.1 The Hawaiian shirts (which are represented as entities) are stored in the Products table. Tables are very similar to BLOB containers (but they hold entities rather than BLOBs). Like BLOB containers, tables are housed within your storage account. Here you can see that the Products and ShoppingCart tables live in the silverlightukstorage account.

If you do require relational database storage, you can look at SQL Azure, which is a Windows Azure platform–hosted SQL Server database.

I always need a relational database, don't I?

We've become a little conditioned to store data in a relational form, even when it's not strictly necessary.

If you can expand your mind and accept that there are other ways of storing data, you can use the Table service to store your data in a highly scalable (and cheaper) fashion.

As you'll see later in this book, many applications (including shopping carts, blogs, content management systems, and so on) could potentially use the simple Table service rather than a relational database.

Now that you know what the Table service is and isn't, it's nearly time to look at how entities are stored in the Table service. But before we do that, let's take a look at how we'd normally represent data in non-Windows Azure environments.

NOTE In the next section, we'll look at how we'd represent an entity in a typical SQL Server solution, and we'll compare this to Table service solutions. If you have no patience or are addicted to caffeine and need to get to Table service code right now, feel free to skip along to section 11.3.

11.2 How we'd normally represent entities outside of Azure

To keep things simple, we'll return to the Hawaiian Shirt Shop website that we introduced in chapter 2. Over the next few sections, we'll look at how we'd typically store shirt data in a noncloud database. We'll focus on the following:

- How would we represent a shirt in C#?
- How would we store shirt data in SQL Server?
- How would we map and transfer data between the two platforms?

By understanding how we'd represent our shirt data in typical solutions, we can then see how this translates to the Table service.

11.2.1 How we'd normally represent an entity in C#

In chapter 2, we defined a Hawaiian shirt using the following data transfer object (DTO) entity.

```
public class Product
{
   public int Id { get; set; }
   public string Name { get; set; }
   public string Description { get; set; }
}
```

The `Product` entity class that we're using to represent Hawaiian shirts contains three properties that we're interested in (`Id`, `Name`, and `Description`).

In chapter 2, we chose to keep the example simple by hardcoding the list of products rather than retrieving it from a data store such as the Table service or SQL Server. The following code is a hardcoded list of the three shirt entities displayed in figure 11.1 (Red Shirt, Blue Shirt, and Blue Frilly Shirt).

```
var products =
   new List<Product>
   {
     new Product
     {
        Id = 1,
        Name = "Red Shirt",
        Description = "Red"
     },
     new Product
     {
        Id = 2,
        Name = "Blue Shirt",
        Description = "A Blue Shirt"
     },
     new Product
     {
        Id = 3,
        Name = "Blue Frilly Shirt",
        Description = "A Frilly Blue Shirt"
     },

};
```

In the preceding code, we simply defined the list of products as a hardcoded list. Obviously this isn't a very scalable pattern—you don't want to redeploy the application every time your shop offers a new product—so let's look at how you can store that data using a non-Windows Azure environment, such as SQL Server.

11.2.2 How we'd normally store an entity in SQL Server

To store an entity in SQL Server, you first need to define a table where you can store the entity data. Figure 11.2 shows how the Products table could be structured in SQL Server.

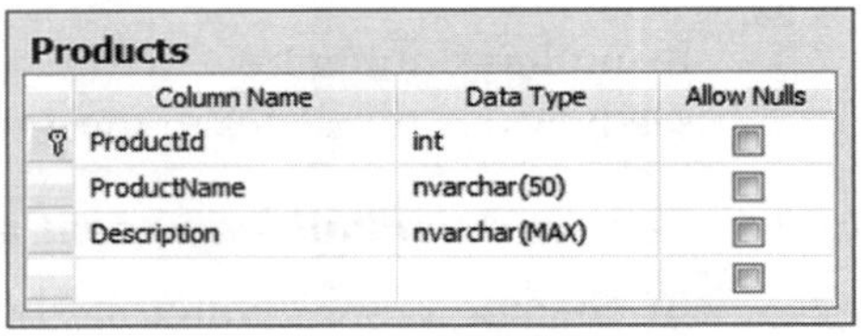

Products
Column Name
Data Type
Allow Nulls
ProductId
int
ProductName
nvarchar(50)
Description
nvarchar(MAX)

Figure 11.2 A representation of how you could store the Hawaiian shirt data in SQL Server

Figure 11.2 shows a table called Products with three columns (ProductId, ProductName, and Description). In this table, ProductId would be the primary key and would uniquely identify shirts in the table. Table 11.1 shows how the shirt data would be represented in SQL Server.

Table 11.1 Logical representation of the Products table in SQL Server

ProductId	ProductName	Description
1	Red Shirt	Red
2	Blue Shirt	A Blue Shirt
3	Blue Frilly Shirt	A Frilly Blue Shirt

In table 11.1 we've enforced a fixed schema in our SQL Server representation of the Hawaiian shirts. If you wanted to store extra information about the product (a thumbnail URI, for example) you'd need to add an extra column to the Products table and a new property to the `Product` entity.

Now that we can represent the Hawaiian shirt product as both an entity and as a table in SQL Server, we'll need to map the entity to the table.

11.2.3 Mapping an entity to a SQL Server database

Although you can manually map entities to SQL Server data, you'd typically use a data-access layer framework that provides mapping capabilities. Typical frameworks include the following:

- ADO.NET Entity Framework
- LINQ's many varieties, like LINQ to SQL and LINQ to DataSet
- NHibernate

The following code maps the Products table returned from SQL Server as a dataset to the `Product` entity class using LINQ to DataSet.

```
var products = ds.Tables["Products"].AsEnumerable().Select
   (
      row => new Product
      {
        Id = row.Field<int>("ProductId"),
        Name = row.Field<string>("ProductName"),
        Description = row.Field<string>("Description")
      }
   );
```

In this example, we convert the dataset to an enumerable list of data rows and then reshape the data to return a list of `Product` entities. For each property in the `Product` entity (`Id`, `Name`, and `Description`) we map the corresponding columns (ProductId, ProductName, and Description) from the returned data row.

We've now seen how we'd normally define entities in C#, how we'd represent entities in SQL Server, and how we could map the entity layer to the database. Let's look at what the differences are when using the Table service.

11.3 Modifying an entity to work with the Table service

Before we look at how we can start coding against the Table service, you need to understand how your data is stored in the Table service and how that differs from the SQL-based solution we looked at in the previous sections. In the next couple of sections, we'll look at the following:

- How can we modify an entity so it can be stored in the Table service?
- How is an entity stored in the Table service?

As these points suggest, before you can store the shirt data with the Table service, you need to do a little bit of jiggery pokery with the entity definition. Let's look at what you need to do.

11.3.1 Modifying an entity definition

To be able to store the C# entity in the Table service, each entity must have the following properties:

- `Timestamp`
- `PartitionKey`
- `RowKey`

Therefore, to store the `Product` entity in the Azure Table service, you'd have to modify the previous definition of the `Product` entity to look something like this:

```
[DataServiceKey("PartitionKey", "RowKey")]
public class Product
{
   public string Timestamp{ get; set; }
   public string PartitionKey { get; set; }
   public string RowKey { get; set; }
   public string Name { get; set; }
   public string Description { get; set; }
}
```

In the preceding code the original `Product` entity is modified to include those properties required for Table storage (`Timestamp`, `PartitionKey`, and `RowKey`). Don't worry if you don't recognize these properties—we'll explain what they mean shortly.

To generate a hardcoded list of shirts using the new version of the `Product` entity, you'd need to change the hardcoded product list (shown earlier in section 11.2.1) to something like this:

```
var products =
   new List<Product>
   {
     new Product
     {
        PartitionKey = "Shirts",
```

```
            RowKey= "1",
            Name = "Red Shirt",
            Description = "Red"
        },
        new Product
        {
            PartitionKey = "Shirts",
            RowKey = "2",
            Name = "Blue Shirt",
            Description = "A Blue Shirt"
        },
        new Product
        {
            PartitionKey = "Shirts",
            RowKey = "3",
            Name = "Frilly Blue Shirt",
            Description = "A Frilly Blue Shirt"
        }

};
```

As you can see from the preceding code, the only difference is that you're now setting a couple of extra properties (`PartitionKey` and `RowKey`).

Look, no `Timestamp`

Notice that the revised object-creation code doesn't set the `Timestamp` property. That's because it's generated on the server side and is only available to us as a read-only property. The `Timestamp` property holds the date and time that the entity was inserted into the table, and if you did set this property, the Table service would just ignore the value.

The `Timestamp` property is typically used to handle concurrency. Prior to updating an entity in the table, you could check that the timestamp for your local version of the entity was the same as the server version. If the timestamps were different, you'd know that another process had modified the data since you last retrieved your local version of the entity.

Now that you've seen how to modify your entities so that you can store them in the Table service, let's take a look at how these entities would be stored in a Table service table.

11.3.2 Table service representation of products

In table 11.1 you saw how we'd normally store our list of Hawaiian shirt product entities in SQL Server, and table 11.2 shows how those same entities would logically be stored in the Windows Azure Table service.

Table 11.2 Logical representation of the Products table in Windows Azure

Timestamp	PartitionKey	RowKey	PropertyBag
2009-07-01T16:20:32	Shirts	1	Name: Red Shirt Description: Red
2009-07-01T16:20:33	Shirts	2	Name: Blue Shirt Description: A Blue Shirt
2009-07-01T16:20:33	Shirts	3	Name: Frilly Blue Shirt Description: A Frilly Blue Shirt

As you can see in table 11.2, entities are represented in the Table service differently from how they'd be stored in SQL Server. In the SQL Server version of the Products table, we maintained a fixed schema where each property of the entity was represented by a column in the table. In table 11.2 the Table service maintains a fairly minimal schema; it doesn't rigidly fix the schema. The only properties that the Table service requires, and that are therefore logically represented by their own columns, are `Timestamp`, `PartitionKey`, and `RowKey`. All other properties are lumped together in a property bag.

EXTENDING AN ENTITY DEFINITION

Because all tables created in the Table service have the same minimal fixed schema (`Timestamp`, `PartitionKey`, `RowKey`, and `PropertyBag`) you don't need to define the entity structure to the Table service in advance.

This flexibility means that you can also change the entity class definition at any time. If you wanted to show a picture of a Hawaiian shirt on the website, you could change the `Product` entity to include a thumbnail URI property as follows:

```
[DataServiceKey("PartitionKey", "RowKey")]
public class Product
{
   public string Timestamp{ get; set; }
   public string PartitionKey { get; set; }
   public string RowKey { get; set; }
   public string Name { get; set; }
   public string Description { get; set; }
   public string ThumbnailUri { get; set; }
}
```

Once you've modified the entity to include a thumbnail URI, you can store that entity directly in the existing Products table without modifying either the table structure or the existing data. Table 11.3 shows a list of shirts that include the new property.

Table 11.3 The modified entity with a new property can happily coexist with older entities that don't have the new property.

Timestamp	PartitionKey	RowKey	PropertyBag
2009-07-01T16:20:32	Shirts	1	Name: Red Shirt Description: Red
2009-07-01T16:20:33	Shirts	2	Name: Blue Shirt Description: A Blue Shirt
2009-07-01T16:20:33	Shirts	3	Name: Frilly Blue Shirt Description: A Frilly Blue Shirt
2009-07-05T10:30:21	Shirts	4	Name: Frilly Pink Shirt Description: A Frilly Pink Shirt ThumbnailUri: frillypinkshirt.png

In the list of shirts in table 11.3, you can see that existing shirts (Red Shirt, Blue Shirt, and Frilly Blue Shirt) have the same data that was stored in table 11.2—they don't contain the new `ThumbnailUri` property. But the data for the new shirt (Frilly Pink Shirt) does have the new `ThumbnailUri` property.

11.3.3 Storing completely different entities

Due to the flexible nature of the Table service, you could even store entities of different types in the same table. For example, you could store the `Product` entity in the same table as a completely different entity, such as this `Customer` entity:

```
[DataServiceKey("PartitionKey", "RowKey")]
public class Customer
{
   public string Timestamp{ get; set; }
   public string PartitionKey { get; set; }
   public string RowKey { get; set; }
   public string Firstname { get; set; }
   public string Surname { get; set; }
}
```

As you can see from the `Customer` entity, although the entity must contain the standard properties (`Timestamp`, `PartitionKey`, and `RowKey`) no other properties are shared between the Customer and Product entities; they even have different class names.

Even though these entities have very different definitions, they could be stored in the table, as shown in table 11.4. The Table service allows for different entities to have different schemas.

Table 11.4 Storing completely different entities in the same table

Timestamp	PartitionKey	RowKey	PropertyBag
2009-07-01T16:20:32	Shirts	1	Name: Red Shirt Description: Red
2009-07-01T16:20:33	Shirts	2	Name: Blue Shirt Description: A Blue Shirt
2009-07-01T16:20:33	Shirts	FredJones	Firstname: Fred Surname: Jones
2009-07-05T10:30:21	Shirts	4	Name: Frilly Pink Shirt Description: A Frilly Pink Shirt ThumbnailUri: frillypinkshirt.png

CHALLENGES OF STORING DIFFERENT ENTITY TYPES

Although the Table service is flexible enough to store entities of different types in the same table, as shown in table 11.4, you should be very careful if you're considering such an approach. If every entity you retrieve has a different schema, you'll need to write some custom code that will serialize the data to the correct object type.

Following this approach will lead to more complex code, which will be difficult to maintain. This code is likely to be more error prone and difficult to debug. We encourage you to only store entities of different types in a single table when absolutely necessary.

CHALLENGES OF EXTENDING ENTITIES

On a similar note, if you need to modify the definition of existing entities, you should take care to ensure that your existing entities don't break your application after the upgrade.

There are a few rules you should keep in mind to prevent you from running into too much trouble:

- Treat entity definitions as data contracts; breaking the contract will have a serious effect on your application, so don't do it lightly.
- Code any new properties as additional rather than required. This strategy means that existing data will be able to serialize to the new data structure. If your code requires existing entities to contain data for the new properties, you should migrate your existing data to the new structure.
- Continue to support existing property names for existing data. If you need to change a property name, you should either support both the old and new names in your new entity or support two versions of your entity (old definition

and new definition). If you only want to support one entity definition, you'll need to migrate any existing data to the new structure.

Now that you've seen how entities are stored within the Table service, let's look at what makes this scalable.

11.4 Partitioning data across lots of servers

In the last couple of sections, we've skipped past a few topics, namely, accounts, partition keys, and row keys. We'll now return to these topics and explain how the Windows Azure Table service is such a scalable storage mechanism.

In this section, we'll look at how the Table service scales using partitioning at the storage account and table levels. To achieve a highly scalable service, the Table service will split your data into more manageable partitions that can then be apportioned out to multiple servers. As developers, we can control how this data is partitioned to maximize the performance of our applications.

Let's look at how this is done at the storage account layer.

11.4.1 Partitioning the storage account

In this section, we'll look at how data is partitioned, but we'll leave performance optimization to a later section.

In figure 11.1, there were two tables within a storage account (ShoppingCart and Products). As the Table service isn't a relational database, there's no way to join these two tables on the server side. Because there's no physical dependency between any two tables in the Table service, Windows Azure can scale the data storage beyond a single server and store tables on separate physical servers.

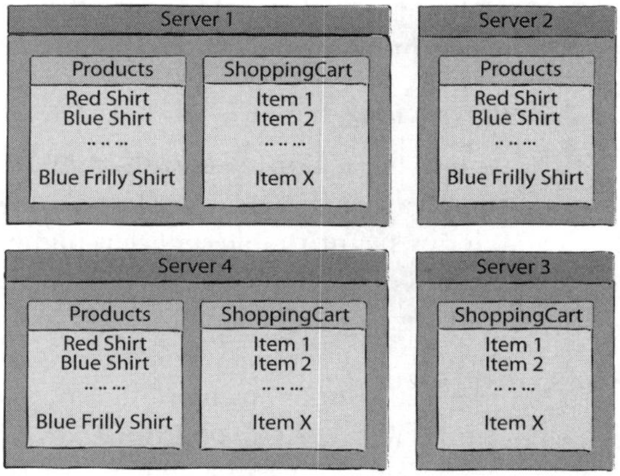

Figure 11.3 Tables within a storage account split across multiple servers

Figure 11.3 shows how these tables could be split across the Windows Azure data center. In this figure, you'll notice that the Products table lives on servers 1, 2, and 4, whereas the ShoppingCart table resides on servers 1, 3, and 4. In the Windows Azure data center, you have no control over where your tables will be stored. The tables could reside on the same server (as in the case of servers 1 and 4) but they could easily live on completely separate servers (servers 2 and 3). In most situations, you can assume that your tables will physically reside on different servers.

Data replication

In order to protect you from data loss, Windows Azure guarantees to replicate your data to at least three different servers as part of the transaction. This data replication guarantee means that if there's a hardware failure after the data has been committed, another server will have a copy of your data.

Once a transaction is committed (and your data has therefore been replicated at least three times), the Table service is guaranteed to serve the new data and will never serve older versions. This means that if you insert a new Hawaiian shirt entity on server 1, you can only be load balanced onto one of the servers that has the latest version of your data. If server 2 was not part of the replication process and contains stale data, you won't be load balanced onto that server. You can safely perform a read of your data straight after a write, knowing that you'll receive the latest copy of the data.

The Amazon SimpleDB database (which has roughly the same architecture as the Windows Azure Table service) doesn't have this replication guarantee by default. Due to replication latency, it isn't uncommon in SimpleDB for newly written data not to exist or to be stale when a read is performed straight after a write. This situation can never occur with the Windows Azure Table service.

Now that you've seen how different tables within a single account will be spread across multiple servers to achieve scalability, it's worth looking at how you can partition data a little more granularly, and split data within a single table across multiple servers.

11.4.2 Partitioning tables

One of the major issues with traditional SQL Server–based databases is that individual tables can grow too large, slowing down all operations against the table. Although the Windows Azure Table service is highly efficient, storing too much data in a single table can still degrade data access performance.

The Table service allows you to specify how your table could be split into smaller partitions by requiring each entity to contain a partition key. The Table service can then scale out by storing different partitions of data on separate physical servers. Any entities with the same partition key must reside together on the same physical server.

In tables 11.2 through to 11.4, all the data was stored in the same partition (Shirts), meaning that all three shirts would always reside together on the same server, as shown in figure 11.3. Table 11.5 shows how you could split your data into multiple partitions.

Table 11.5 Splitting partitions by partition key

Timestamp	PartitionKey	RowKey	PropertyBag
2009-07-01T16:20:32	Red	1	Name: Red Shirt Description: Red

Table 11.5 Splitting partitions by partition key *(continued)*

Timestamp	PartitionKey	RowKey	PropertyBag
2009-07-01T16:20:33	Blue	1	Name: Blue Shirt Description: A Blue Shirt
2009-07-01T16:20:33	Blue	2	Name: Frilly Blue Shirt Description: A Frilly Blue Shirt
2009-07-05T10:30:21	Red	2	Name: Frilly Pink Shirt Description: A Frilly Pink Shirt ThumbnailUri: frillypinkshirt.png

In table 11.5 the Red Shirt and the Frilly Pink Shirt now reside in the Red partition, and the Blue Shirt and the Frilly Blue shirt are now stored in the Blue partition. Figure 11.4 shows the shirt data from table 11.5 split across multiple servers. In this figure, the Red partition data (Red Shirt and Pink Frilly Shirt) lives on server A and the Blue partition data (Blue Shirt and Frilly Blue Shirt) is stored on server B. Although the partitions have been separated out to different physical servers, all entities within the same partition always reside together on the same physical server.

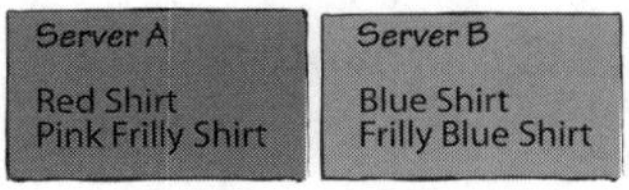

Figure 11.4 Splitting partitions across multiple servers

ROW KEYS

The final property to explain is the row key. The row key uniquely identifies an entity within a partition, meaning that no two entities in the same partition can have the same row key, but any two entities that are stored in different partitions can have the same key. If you look at the data stored in table 11.5, you can see that the row key is unique within each partition but not unique outside of the partition. For example, Red Shirt and Blue Shirt both have the same row key but live in different partitions (Red and Blue).

The partition key and the row key combine to uniquely identify an entity—together they form a composite primary key for the table.

INDEXES

Now that you have a basic understanding of how data is logically stored within the data service, it's worth talking briefly about the indexing of the data.

There are a few rules of thumb regarding data-access speeds:

- Retrieving an entity with a unique partition key is the fastest access method.
- Retrieving an entity using the partition key and row key is very fast (the Table service needs to use only the index to find your data).
- Retrieving an entity using the partition key and no row key is slower (the Table service needs to read all properties for each entity in the partition).

- Retrieving an entity using no partition key and no row key is very slow, relatively speaking (the Table service needs to read all properties for all entities across all partitions, which can span separate physical servers).

We'll explore these points in more detail as we go on.

> **Load balancing of requests**
>
> Because data is partitioned and replicated across multiple servers, all requests via the REST API can be load balanced. This combination of data replication, data partitioning, and a large web server farm provides you with a highly scalable storage solution that can evenly distribute data and requests across the data center. This level of horsepower and data distribution means that you shouldn't need to worry about overloading server resources.

Now that we've covered the theory of table storage, it's time to put it into practice. Let's open Visual Studio and start storing some data.

11.5 Developing with the Table service

Now that you have an understanding of how data is stored in the Table service, it's time to develop a web application that can use it. In the previous section, we defined an entity for storing the Hawaiian shirt product, and we looked at how it would be stored in the Table service. Here you'll build a new application that will manage the product inventory for the Hawaiian Shirt Shop website.

11.5.1 Creating a project

Rather than returning to the solution you built in chapter 2, here you'll develop a new product-management web page in a new web application project. Create a new Cloud Service web role project called `ShirtManagement`. If you need a refresher on how to set up your development environment or how to create a web role project, refer back to chapter 2.

Like the other storage services, communication with the Table service occurs through the REST API (which we'll discuss in detail in the next chapter). Although you can use this API directly, you're likely to be more productive using the StorageClient library provided in the Windows Azure SDK.

Whenever you create a new Cloud Service project, this library will be automatically referenced. But if you're building a brand new class library or migrating an existing project, you can reference the following storage client assembly manually:

- `Microsoft.WindowsAzure.StorageClient`

In addition, you'll need to reference the ADO.NET Data Services assemblies:

- `System.Data.Services`
- `System.Data.Services.Client`

> **ADO.NET Data Services**
>
> The Table service exposes its HTTP REST APIs through its implementation of the ADO.NET Data Services framework. By using this framework, we can utilize the ADO.NET Data Services client assemblies to communicate with the service rather than having to develop or use a custom REST wrapper.
>
> Because ADO.NET Data Services is used by the storage client SDK, you'll need to reference those assemblies too.

Now that you've set up your project, let's look at how you can add the `Product` entity class to the project.

11.5.2 Defining an entity

Before you create your product-management web page, you need to create an entity in the web project. At this stage, we'll just show you how to add the entity directly to the web page, but in the next chapter you'll see how to architecturally separate a class into an entity layer.

To keep this example simple, we'll just store the shirt name and description, as before. Add a new class to your web project named `Product.cs` and define the class as shown in the following listing.

Listing 11.1 `Product` entity

```
public class Product : TableServiceEntity
{
   public string Name { get; set; }
   public string Description { get; set; }
}
```

In listing 11.1, the `Product` class inherits from the `TableServiceEntity` base class (`Microsoft.WindowsAzure.TableService.TableServiceEntity`). This base class contains the three properties required by all table storage entities:

- `Timestamp`
- `PartitionKey`
- `RowKey`

Now that you've set up your project and defined your entity, you need to create a table to store the entity in. The same method can be used in both the development and live environments.

11.5.3 Creating a table

The simplest method of creating a table is to create a PowerShell script or to use one of the many storage clients that are available. In this chapter we'll use Azure Storage Explorer, which you can download from CodePlex: http://azurestorageexplorer.codeplex.com/.

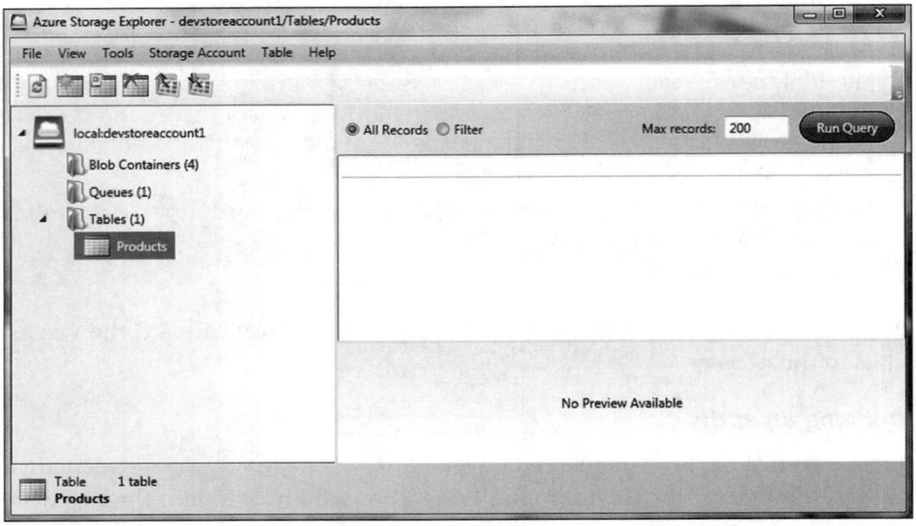

Figure 11.5 The Azure Storage Explorer showing the newly created Products table

In this section, we'll look at how to create a table in two ways: using Azure Storage Explorer and using code.

CREATING A TABLE USING THE AZURE STORAGE EXPLORER

Once you have downloaded and fired up Azure Storage Explorer, it will automatically connect you to your development storage account as long as your local development storage service is running.

To create a new table in your storage account, all you need to is select Table > New Table and enter the name of your table (Products, in this case). Figure 11.5 shows the newly created Products table in Azure Storage Explorer.

Although using a tool such as Azure Storage Explorer is probably the easiest method of creating a new table, you may wish to do this manually in C#.

CREATING A TABLE IN CODE

In this example, you'll manually create a console application that will create a new table in the storage account when it's run. Although we'll have you use a console application in this example, you could easily use a web application, Windows Forms application, or Windows Presentation Foundation application. The deployment application doesn't need to be a cloud application (web or worker role); it can be a standard application that you run locally.

To create the application, perform the following steps:

1. Create a console application targeting .NET 3.5.
2. Add a reference to `System.Data.Services`.
3. Add a reference to `System.Data.Services.Client`.

4 Add a reference to `Microsoft.WindowsAzure.StorageClient`.
5 Add an app.config or web.config entry with your storage account credentials.
6 Add the following code to create the table:

```
CloudStorageAccount.SetConfigurationSettingPublisher((configName,
➥ configSetter) =>
            {
configSetter(RoleEnvironment.GetConfigurationSettingValue(configName));
            });

var storageAccount =

  CloudStorageAccount.FromConfigurationSetting("DataConnectionString");

CloudTableClient tableClient =
   storageAccount.CreateCloudTableClient();

tableClient.CreateTableIfNotExist("Products");
```

The code added in step 6 retrieves storage account information from the app.config and then calls the `CreateTableIfNotExist` method from the `CloudTableClient` object, passing in the name of the table to create (Products).

Deploying to live

The code used to create a new table will work not only on your development storage account, but will also work against the live system. All you need to do to make this code work against the live system is to change the `DataConnectionString` configuration setting to your live account.

Now that you know how to create a table both in the live system and in development storage, it's worth taking a quick peek at how this is implemented in the development storage backing store. Figure 11.6 shows how tables are represented in the development storage SQL Server database.

As you can see in figure 11.6, the SQL Server database that stores the entities is pretty flexible. The TableContainer table keeps a list of all the tables stored in the development storage account. Because you can create tables dynamically, any new table created will contain a new entry in this table.

Each row in the TableRow table in figure 11.6 stores a serialized version of the entity. As you can see from this table definition, the only fixed data that's stored in this table is AccountName, TableName, PartitionKey, RowKey, and TimeStamp. All other properties are stored in the Data column. As you can see, the actual development storage schema relates to the logical representation that you saw in table 11.4.

Now that you've seen how tables are represented in development storage, let's look at how you can start working with your entities.

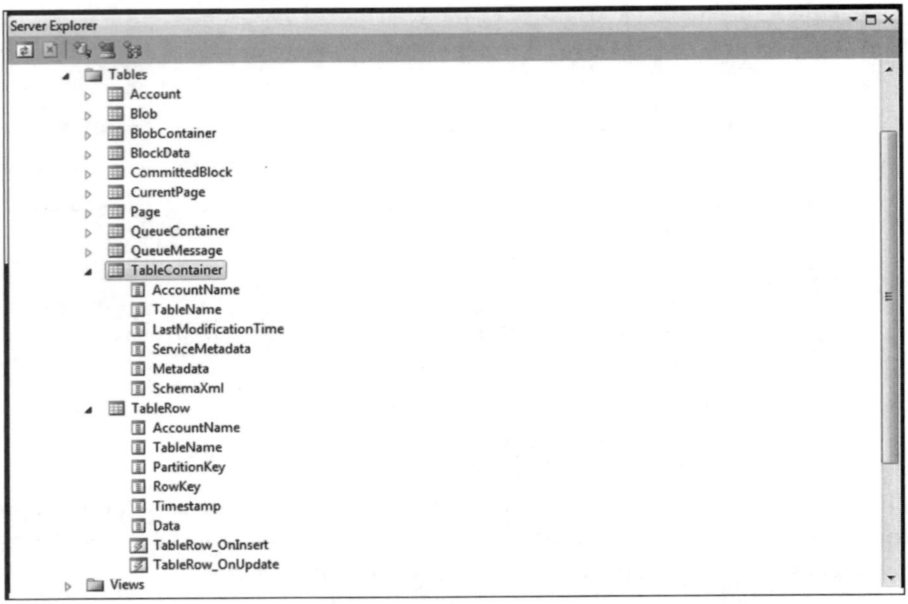

Figure 11.6 How tables are represented in the development storage SQL Server database

11.6 Doing CRUDy stuff with the Table service

In this section, you'll build a new product-management web page to manage the Hawaiian shirt product list stored in the Table service. Through this web page, you'll be able to *create, read, update,* and *delete* (also known as CRUD) data in the table. Figure 11.7 shows what the web page will look like.

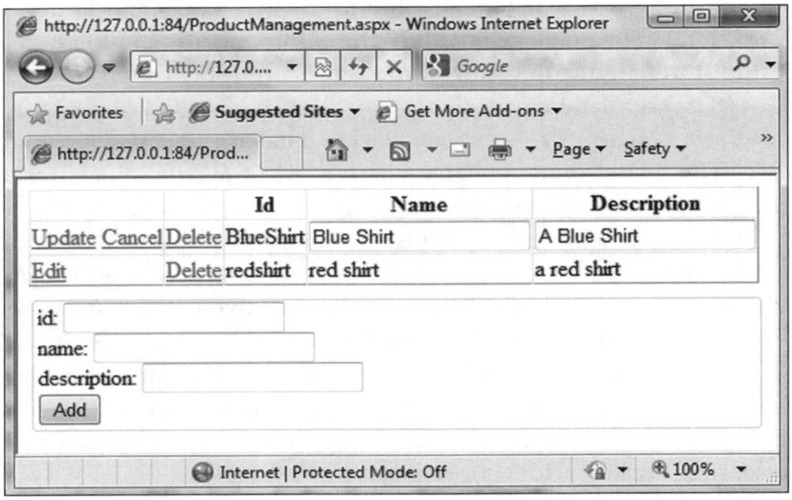

Figure 11.7 Product-management web page

The product-management web page shown in figure 11.7 will allow us to do several things:

- Add new shirts
- List all shirts
- Edit existing shirts
- Delete shirts

You've already set up the entity and registered the entity table in the development storage. It's time to develop the product-management web page shown in figure 11.7. The first step is to set up a context class for your entity.

11.6.1 Creating a context class

In order to work with entities in any way (query, add, insert, delete) using ADO.NET Data Services, you first need to set up a context object.

The context class is really a bridge between an entity and ADO.NET Data Services. It will define the endpoint of the storage account, the name of the table that we'll query, and the entity that will be returned. The following listing shows the context class for the Products table.

Listing 11.2 Product context class

```
public class ProductsContext : TableServiceContext
{
   private static CloudStorageAccount storageAccount =      <- Reads account details from config
      CloudStorageAccount.FromConfigurationSetting("DataConnectionString");

   public ProductsContext()
      : base(storageAccount. TableEndpoint.AbsoluteUri (),
                storageAccount.Credentials)            <- Uses account details to populate context
   {

   }

   public DataServiceQuery<Product> Product           <- Passes LINQ queries through to table
   {
      get
      {
         return CreateQuery<Product>("Products");
      }
   }
}
```

Listing 11.2 shows the context object for the Hawaiian shirt `Product` entity. As you can see, most of the complexity of the context class is abstracted away in the classes that you inherit from. The `TableServiceContext` class inherits from the standard ADO.NET Data Services context class, `DataServicesContext`. The `TableServiceContext` class provides some additional functionality beyond what is provided out of the box with ADO.NET Data Services, including retry policies.

In listing 11.2, the storage account details and credentials are automatically populated from the service configuration. This allows you to simplify your calling classes—you don't need to get the endpoint and credentials every time you wish to use the context class.

Finally, the `Product` property is what you'll use to perform LINQ queries on the Products table.

> **TIP** Code generation is outside the scope of this book, but if you're generating a large number of tables and entities, you may wish to consider using a code generation tool such as T4 to autogenerate code where possible. Typical areas to consider generating code automatically would include table context classes and table-creation scripts.

Let's look at how you can start using this.

11.6.2 Adding entities

Now that you have your context class, you can start creating your product-management web page. To do this, you need to add a new ASP.NET web page called products.aspx.

At this stage, we won't generate the grid listing all the Hawaiian shirts for sale; we'll only write the code required to add shirts to the Products table. Therefore, you only need to add the markup for the bottom section of the products page.

The listing that follows contains the ASPX code that you should add to the products.aspx page.

Listing 11.3 Adding the shirt section of the products.aspx page

```
<fieldset>
   <div>
      <div>id:
<asp:TextBox id="txtId" runat="server" />
</div>                                              <-- Id text box
      <div>name:
<asp:TextBox id="txtName" runat="server" />
</div>
      <div>
          description:
          <asp:TextBox id="txtDescription"
runat="server" />
      </div>
      <asp:button id="btnAdd" text="Add"
                  runat="server"
onclick="btnAdd_Click" />                             <-- Add button
   </div>
</fieldset>
```

When the Add button is clicked in listing 11.3, the shirt entity will be added to the Products table.

Listing 11.4 contains the code for the Add button's click event. This code should be added to the products.aspx code-behind.

Listing 11.4 Add the entity to the Products table

```
protected void btnAdd_Click(object sender, EventArgs e)
{
   var shirtContext = new ProductsContext();          ❶ Creates context to connect with table

   var newShirt = new Product                         ❷ Creates object to store in table
       {
          PartitionKey = "Shirts",
          RowKey = txtId.Text,
          Name = txtName.Text,
          Description = txtDescription.Text
       };

   shirtContext.AddObject("Products", newShirt);      ❸ Adds new object to context

   shirtContext.SaveChanges();                        ❹ Commits changes in context to table

   }
```

To add the new shirt details, which were entered on the web page, to the Products table, you need to extract all the information entered about the product (ID, name, and description) and create a new instance of the `Product` class called `newShirt` ❷. Once you've created an instance of the shirt ❸, you add the shirt entity to a tracking list held in the context object ❶ for the product list.

When you add the entity to the tracking list ❸, you also specify the table that the entity should be added to. The product context object (`shirtContext`) maintains a list of all objects that you have changed as part of this operation. You can create, update, or delete objects from the product list, and you can add all these changes locally to the tracking list.

Eventually, when you wish to perform all the changes on the server side, you can invoke the `SaveChanges` method on the context object ❹, which will apply all the tracked changes on the server side using ADO.NET Data Services via the REST API.

In the next chapter, we'll look at some of the more advanced scenarios for applying changes, such as batching changes, concurrency, retry logic, and transactions.

WAS THE ENTITY ADDED?

You should now be able to run the product-management web page and add new shirts to the product list. We haven't yet implemented the grid to display the list of entities in the product list—we'll do that in the next section. In the meantime you can always check that your entity exists by querying the development storage database using the following statement in SQL Management Studio:

```
SELECT * FROM TableRow
```

11.6.3 Listing entities

It's now time to extend the products.aspx web page to display the list of shirts stored in the Products table. The following listing contains the code required for your grid. This code should be placed above the code in listing 11.3.

Listing 11.5 ASP.NET grid for displaying shirts

```
<asp:GridView ID="GridView1"
              OnRowCommand="GridView1_RowCommand"
              OnRowDeleting="GridView1_RowDeleting"
              OnRowEditing="GridView1_RowEditing"
              OnRowCancelingEdit="GridView1_RowCancelingEdit"
              OnRowUpdating="GridView1_RowUpdating"
              AutoGenerateColumns="false"
              AutoGenerateEditButton="true"
              runat="server">
   <Columns>
      <asp:TemplateField>
         <ItemTemplate>
            <asp:LinkButton ID="btnDelete" runat="server"
                            Text="Delete"
                            CommandName="Delete"
                            CommandArgument=
                            '<%#Eval("RowKey")%>'/>     <-- Passes in product ID (row key)
         </ItemTemplate>
      </asp:TemplateField>
      <asp:BoundField HeaderText="Id"
                      DataField="RowKey"
                      ReadOnly="true"/>     <-- Displays product ID (row key) as read-only field
      <asp:BoundField HeaderText="Name"
                      DataField="Name" />     <-- Displays product name
      <asp:BoundField HeaderText="Description"
                      DataField="Description" />     <-- Displays product description
   </Columns>
</asp:GridView>
```

The grid in listing 11.5 will display the product ID, name, and description for each shirt in the Products table. The name and description columns will both be editable, but the product ID won't be.

At this stage, you've defined the markup required to edit and delete the shirts in the table, but we won't write the code-behind for these events just yet. The following listing contains the code-behind for the products.aspx page, which you'll require to populate the new grid with the list of shirts.

Listing 11.6 Populating the list of shirts

```
protected void Page_Load(object sender, EventArgs e)
{
   if (!IsPostBack)
   {
      BindGrid();
```

```
    }
}

private void BindGrid()
{
    var shirtContext = new ProductContext();          <-- ❶ Creates context to connect to table
    GridView1.DataSource = shirtContext.Product;      <-- ❷ Sets grid's data source to Products table
    GridView1.DataBind();                             <-- ❸ Binds grid
}
```

As you can see, the code to bind the `GridView` to the list of shirts held in the Products table is pretty simple. On the first load of the web page ❶, the `BindGrid` method ❷ is called to populate the grid with the list of shirts retrieved from the Products table.

To retrieve the list of shirts, you instantiate the product context object (`shirtContext`) ❷ and set the data source of the grid to the `Product` property of the context object.

If you look back to the code used to define the product context in listing 11.2, you'll see that the `Product` property returns an `IQueryable` list of products. By returning an `IQueryable` list of products from the context object, you can define a query using LINQ that will be executed on the server side when you enumerate the list of objects, which happens when the grid is data bound ❸.

To keep this example simple, we won't perform any server-side filtering at this stage. We'll simply return a list of all shirts in the Products table as shown at ❷. In the next chapter, we'll look at how to build efficient server-side queries using LINQ.

11.6.4 *Deleting entities*

In listing 11.5 we included some event definitions in the markup to handle deletes. It's now time to implement those event handlers so that when you click the Delete button in the grid, it will delete the corresponding shirt from the Products table in the Table service.

In the listing that follows you'll see the code-behind that relates to the Delete button.

Listing 11.7 Code-behind to delete shirts

```
protected void GridView1_RowCommand (object sender,
                        GridViewCommandEventArgs e)      <-- Called when Delete button is clicked
{
    if (e.CommandName == "Delete")
    {
        DeleteShirt(e.CommandArgument.ToString());       <-- Passes product ID (row key)
        BindGrid();
    }
}

private void DeleteShirt(string rowKey)
{
    var shirtContext = new ProductContext();             <-- ❶ Creates context to connect with table
```

```
    var entity = (from item in shirtContext.Product
                  where item.PartitionKey=="Shirts" &&
                  item.RowKey==rowKey
                  select item).First();                    ❷ Uses query to fetch record from table

    shirtContext.DeleteObject(entity);                    ❸ Deletes object locally

    shirtContext.SaveChanges();

    BindGrid();
}

protected void GridView1_RowDeleting(object sender,
➥ GridViewDeleteEventArgs e){}
```

The code in listing 11.7 shows how you can delete a shirt from the Products table when the Delete button is clicked in the grid. The `DeleteShirt` method is very similar to the code in listing 11.4 that you used to add a shirt. You instantiate the shirt context ❶, add the shirt to be deleted to the context object's tracking list ❸, and submit the changes to the Table service. Finally, you rebind the grid to display the updated list.

FINDING THE ENTITY TO DELETE

There are a couple of differences between adding and deleting a shirt. When adding a shirt to the product list, you can simply create a new `Product` object and add that to the tracking list. If you're deleting an object, you first need to get a local copy of the object that you wish to delete (as you did at ❷ in listing 11.7) and then add that object to the tracking list (as shown at ❸).

For the sake of simplicity, you can pass the object to be deleted by refetching the object from the Table service. In production code, you should never refetch an object for deletion because this performs an unnecessary call to the Table service—in the next chapter, we'll look at how to delete an object in a production web scenario. In this example, however, you can take the `ProductId` (row key) that was passed as the Delete button's command argument, and then perform a LINQ query to retrieve that entity from the Table service.

The following code shows the LINQ query we used to retrieve the individual shirt:

```
from item in shirtContext.Product
where item.PartitionKey=="Shirts" && item.RowKey==rowKey
select item
```

Looking at the LINQ query, you can see that we're using the `IQueryable Product` from the `shirtContext` object as the data source. Because this query is `IQueryable`, you can modify the query before it's sent to the server to restrict the result set to only return those entities that reside in the Shirts partition whose row key matches the passed-in `ProductId`. Because this query is manipulated before it's sent to the server, all the filtering is performed by the Table service rather than by the client application.

You'll now be able to add, list, and delete shirts in the Products table.

11.6.5 Updating entities

Finally, you need to update the code-behind to allow editing the grid and saving any changes back to the Products table. The following listing contains the code you need to edit the grid.

Listing 11.8 Updating entities

```
protected void GridView1_RowCommand(object sender,
                                    GridViewCommandEventArgs e)
{
   if (e.CommandName == "Delete")
   {
      DeleteShirt(e.CommandArgument.ToString());
      BindGrid();
   }
   if (e.CommandName == "Edit")
   {
      BindGrid();
   }
}

protected void GridView1_RowEditing
                 (object sender,GridViewEditEventArgs e)
{
   GridView1.EditIndex = e.NewEditIndex;
   GridView1.DataBind();
}

protected void GridView1_RowCancelingEdit(object sender,
                                     GridViewCancelEditEventArgs e)
{
   GridView1.EditIndex = -1;
   GridView1.DataBind();
}

protected void GridView1_RowUpdating(object sender,
                                     GridViewUpdateEventArgs e)
{
   GridViewRow row = GridView1.Rows[e.RowIndex];
   string id = row.Cells[2].Text;

   var shirtContext = new ProductContext();

   var entity = (from item in shirtContext.Product
                 where item.PartitionKey ==
                     "Shirts" && item.RowKey == id
                 select item).First();

   entity.Name = ((TextBox)
                   (row.Cells[3].Controls[0])).Text;
   entity.Description = ((TextBox)
                          (row.Cells[4].Controls[0])).Text;
```

1. Create a context to the table
2. Retrieve the old entity from the table
3. Update the data in the entity from the table

```
    shirtContext.UpdateObject(entity);
    shirtContext.SaveChanges();

    GridView1.EditIndex = -1;
    BindGrid();
}
```

After editing the grid with your new values, you need to store the modified data back to the Products table. Listing 11.8 will be called whenever there's a change to any data in the grid. The `GridView`'s `RowUpdating` event is where you'll perform that update. The process of updating data is very similar to deleting an entity, as shown earlier.

You retrieve the row that has been edited and extract the product ID displayed in the second cell of the row. As before, you instantiate the product context ❶, and at ❷ you retrieve a copy of the edited entity from the Table service using a LINQ query, passing the partition key and the row key. At ❸ you replace the current name and description of the shirt with the modified data extracted from the text boxes of the row being edited. You then add the modified entity to the `shirtContext`'s tracking list via the `UpdateObject` method, commit the changes back to the Table service using the `SaveChanges` method, take the grid out of edit mode, and rebind the grid to a fresh copy of the data returned from the Table service.

11.7 Summary

In this chapter, we gave you an overview of the Table service, explaining how it provides massively scalable storage and how it differs from traditional relational databases, such as SQL Server.

As you've seen, the Table service is a scalable way of storing and querying entities, and it isn't a relational database. We can sometimes assume we need relational databases when there are other ways of representing data in our solution. Designing systems is all about trade-offs, and the trade-off with relational databases is scalability. By using the Table service, you gain scalability, but the cost is that you have to think and design systems in a different way.

You now have enough knowledge to create and deploy web applications that run in the cloud and can store data in the Table service. In the next chapter, we'll expand upon your new knowledge and drill into some of the inner workings of the service by looking at the REST API and seeing how you can efficiently query and update data.

12 Working with the Table service REST API

This chapter covers

- Introducing the StorageClient library and REST API
- Understanding how to effectively modify data
- Querying the Table service

In the previous chapter, we looked at how to get started with the Table service using the StorageClient library and the WCF Data Services client. In this chapter, we'll look at the underlying REST API to gain a better understanding of the communication between applications and the Table service.

WCF Data Services is an implementation of the OData protocol. OData defines how to work with and exchange data over REST-based services. The Table service implements OData, and the StorageClient library acts as a WCF Data Services client. Even with these layers of abstraction, understanding how to query and update data using the REST API will help you to truly understand what is happening under the covers when using the WCF Data Services–based Table service API.

Let's get started by looking at how you can perform operations directly against the REST API.

12.1 Performing storage account operations using REST

For now, we'll concentrate purely on the operations that you can perform against a storage account using the REST API. Although we've already looked at these operations using the StorageClient library, it's still useful to look at the REST API. Ultimately, the StorageClient library is just a wrapper library for the calls we're about to look at. Over the next few sections, we'll look at the following operations:

- Listing tables
- Deleting tables
- Creating tables

In chapters 8–10 on BLOBs, we described how you could interact with the storage services using various endpoints. We won't go over that subject again in this chapter, but it's worth looking at the endpoint URI of the Table service. The URI of the Table service endpoint uses the following structure:

```
http://<storageaccount>.table.core.windows.net/
```

If your storage account was named silverlightukstorage, your URI would be the following:

```
http://silverlightukstorage.table.core.windows.net/
```

For the development storage Table service, you'd use the following URI:

```
http://127.0.0.1:10002/devstoreaccount1/
```

Now that you know what the URIs will look like, let's try using them.

12.1.1 Listing tables in the development storage account using the REST API

In chapter 9, we looked at a small console application that listed all the containers in a BLOB storage account using the REST API. In this section, you'll create a similar console

```
file:///C:/AzureBook/Source/AiAChapter8/RESTAPIConsole/bin/Debug/RESTAPIConsole.EXE
<feed xml:base="http://127.0.0.1:10002/devstoreaccount1/" xmlns:d="http://schema
s.microsoft.com/ado/2007/08/dataservices" xmlns:m="http://schemas.microsoft.com/
ado/2007/08/dataservices/metadata" xmlns="http://www.w3.org/2005/Atom">
  <title type="text">Tables</title>
  <id>http://127.0.0.1:10002/devstoreaccount1/Tables</id>
  <updated>2009-07-26T13:08:29Z</updated>
  <link rel="self" title="Tables" href="Tables" />
  <entry>
    <id>http://127.0.0.1:10002/devstoreaccount1/Tables('ProductTable')</id>
    <title type="text"></title>
    <updated>2009-07-26T13:08:29Z</updated>
    <author>
      <name />
    </author>
    <link rel="edit" title="Table" href="Tables('ProductTable')" />
    <category term="Microsoft.ServiceHosting.DevelopmentStorage.Table.Table" sch
eme="http://schemas.microsoft.com/ado/2007/08/dataservices/scheme" />
    <content type="application/xml">
      <m:properties>
        <d:TableName>ProductTable</d:TableName>
      </m:properties>
    </content>
  </entry>
</feed>
```

Figure 12.1 A console application that returns a list of tables in a storage account—that's a lot of XML just to return a list containing the name of one table.

application that will list all the tables in a development storage account. Figure 12.1 shows the output of this console application.

If you look at the output in figure 12.1 you can see that the Products table (created in the previous chapter) is returned in the list of storage accounts.

> **Does that funny-looking XML follow some sort of standard?**
>
> As you may have already gathered, normal people don't create APIs that output XML like what you see in figure 12.1. You need a standard to generate that level of verboseness and complexity.
>
> The standard that the Table service uses to expose its data is known as AtomPub. We'll discuss it in more detail later.
>
> If you're interested in being able to identify AtomPub documents in the wild, you can always look at the XML namespace. As you can see in figure 12.1, it's referencing the `Atom` namespace:
>
> `xmlns=http://www.w3.org/2005/Atom`

If you wanted to list all the tables in a storage account using the StorageClient library, you could do the following:

```
var storageAccount =
      CloudStorageAccount.Parse(
         ConfigurationManager.AppSettings["DataConnectionString"]);

CloudTableClient tableClient =
   storageAccount.CreateCloudTableClient();

tableClient.ListTables();
```

Let's now take a look at how this could be done using the REST API directly. You might not usually do this directly with REST, but we want you to appreciate what's really happening behind the scenes.

In order to get a list of all tables that exist in the storage account, all you need to do is write some code that will perform a GET request against the following URIs:

```
http://127.0.0.1:10002/devstoreaccount1/Tables (for dev storage)
http://<storageaccount>.table.core.windows.net/Tables (for live)
```

To create the application that generated the output shown in figure 12.1, you'll need to create a new console application in Visual Studio. To keep the example simple, we'll reuse the StorageClient library's credential-signing method. You'll need to add a reference to this assembly—this is the same assembly that you used in the previous chapter.

The following listing contains the code for the console application.

Listing 12.1 Listing the tables in a storage account

```
static void Main(string[] args)
{
```

```
HttpWebRequest hwr =
      CreateHttpRequest(new
      ➥ Uri(@"http://127.0.0.1:10002/
      ➥ devstoreaccount1/Tables"),
      ➥ "GET", new TimeSpan(0, 0, 30));                    ❶ Creates request

var storageAccount =
        CloudStorageAccount.Parse(ConfigurationManager
        ➥ .AppSettings["DataConnectionString"]);           ❷ Uses storage credentials to sign request

storageAccount.Credentials.SignRequestLite(hwr);

   using (StreamReader sr =
   ➥ new StreamReader(hwr.GetResponse()
   ➥ .GetResponseStream()))                                ❸ Processes response
   {
      XDocument myDocument = XDocument.Parse(sr.ReadToEnd());
      Console.Write(myDocument.ToString());
   }
}

private static HttpWebRequest CreateHttpRequest
➥ (Uri uri, string httpMethod, TimeSpan timeout)
{
   HttpWebRequest request = (HttpWebRequest)HttpWebRequest.Create(uri);
   request.Timeout = (int)timeout.TotalMilliseconds;
   request.ReadWriteTimeout = (int)timeout.TotalMilliseconds;
   request.Method = httpMethod;
   request.ContentLength = 0;
   request.ContentType = "application/atom+xml";
   return request;
}
```

The code displayed in listing 12.1 will make a GET request to the development Table service asking for a list of all the tables in the storage account (http://127.0.0.1:10002/devstoreaccount1/Tables).

At ❶, you generate the HTTP request by calling the CreateHttpRequest method. This method creates the HttpRequest for the given URI (http://127.0.0.1:10002/devstoreaccount1/Tables) and HTTP verb (GET) and returns the request to the calling method.

Sign Request Lite

You've probably noticed that listing 12.1 makes use of the storage account credentials from the StorageClient library ❷, even though it's using the REST API. The major reason for this is that signing the HTTP request manually is hard and horrible. Rather than writing that nasty code, it's easier to use the StorageClient library method. We'll discuss request signing in a little more detail in section 12.2.

Finally, with the request generated and signed, you can make the request to the development service ❸. The Table service will return an XML response listing all of the tables in your account, which is written to the console window, as you saw in figure 12.1.

SWITCHING TO THE LIVE SERVICE

In listing 12.1 you made a request to the development storage Table service. If you wanted to change the application to query a live service (such as a silverlightukstorage storage account) you'd need to change the URI at ❶ to http://silverlightukstorage.table.core.windows.net/Tables.

It's worth pointing out that although the URI in listing 12.1 is hardcoded, you could extract it from the `storageAccount` object:

```
storageAccount.TableEndpoint.AbsoluteUri.ToString();
```

This is just the base URI; you'll still need to append `/tables` to access the Table service.

Now that you know how to list tables, let's take a look at how you can change this code to delete a table (and its underlying data).

12.1.2 Deleting tables using the REST API

To delete a table using the StorageClient library, you need to call the `DeleteTable` method of your `CloudTableClient` object, passing in the name of the table that you wish to delete. The following code would delete the Products table:

```
var storageAccount =
      CloudStorageAccount.Parse(
         ConfigurationManager.AppSettings["DataConnectionString"]);

CloudTableClient tableClient =
   storageAccount.CreateCloudTableClient();

tableClient.DeleteTable("Products");
```

If you wanted to delete the same table using the REST API directly, you could perform an HTTP `DELETE` (rather than a `GET`) request using the following URI:

```
http://silverlightukstorage.table.core.windows.net/Tables('Products')
```

To modify listing 12.1 to delete the Products table, you could replace the code at ❶ with the following:

```
HttpWebRequest hwr =
      CreateHttpRequest(
      ➥ new Uri(@"http://silverlightukstorage
      ➥ .table.core.windows.net/Tables('Products')"),
      ➥ "DELETE", new TimeSpan(0, 0, 30));
```

As you can see, this code replaces the original `GET` request with a `DELETE`, and the URI has been modified. Because you no longer need to process an XML response, you'd also need to change the code at ❸ as follows:

```
hwr.GetResponse();
```

Finally, because the code now uses the live Table service rather than the development storage version, you'd also need to set the correct credentials.

You've now had a chance to interact with the Table service both via the StorageClient library and by using the REST API directly, so let's look at some of the technologies used to implement the Table service REST API.

12.1.3 WCF Data Services and AtomPub

WCF Data Services (formerly known as Astoria) is a data-access framework that allows you to create and consume data via REST-based APIs from your existing data sources (such as SQL Server databases) using HTTP.

Rather than creating a whole new protocol for the Table service API, the Windows Azure team built the REST-based APIs using WCF Data Services. Although not all aspects of the Data Services framework have been implemented, the Table service supports a large subset of the framework.

One of the major advantages of WCF Data Services is that if you're already familiar with the framework, getting started with the Windows Azure Table service is pretty easy. Even if you haven't used the WCF Data Services previously, any knowledge gained from developing against Windows Azure storage will help you with future development that may use the framework.

WCF DATA SERVICES CLIENT LIBRARIES

WCF Data Services provides a set of standard client libraries that abstract away the complexities of the underlying REST APIs and allow you to interact with services in a standard fashion regardless of the underlying service. Whether you're using WCF Data Services with the Windows Azure Table service or SQL Server, your client-side code will be pretty much the same. As seen in the previous chapter, using these libraries to communicate with the Table service allows you to develop simple standard code against the Table service quickly.

ATOMPUB

The Windows Azure Table service uses the WCF Data Services implementation of the Atom Publishing Protocol (AtomPub) to interact with the Table service. AtomPub is an HTTP-based REST-like protocol that allows you to publish and edit resources. AtomPub is often used by blog services and content management systems to allow the editing of resources (articles and blog postings) by third-party clients. Windows Live Writer is a well-known example of a blog client that uses AtomPub to publish articles to various blog platforms (Blogspot, WordPress, Windows Live Spaces, and the like). In the case of Windows Azure storage accounts, tables and entities are all considered as resources.

Although WCF Data Services can support other serialization formats (such as JSON) the Table service implementation of WCF Data Services only supports AtomPub. In this book, we won't look at the AtomPub protocol specifically, but we'll point out its usage.

If you were to look at all the previous examples in this chapter (listing and deleting tables in a storage account) and compare them to the AtomPub protocol, you would see that the REST APIs map directly.

If you're interested in reading more about the AtomPub protocol (RFC 5023) you can read the full specification here: http://bitworking.org/projects/atom/rfc5023.html.

Now that you have a basic awareness of AtomPub, we can look at how the AtomPub protocol and the Atom document format are used to create a table using the Table service REST API.

12.1.4 Creating a table using the REST API

In the previous chapter, you created a table using the following StorageClient library call:

```
var storageAccount =
      CloudStorageAccount.Parse(
         ConfigurationManager.AppSettings["DataConnectionString"]);

CloudTableClient tableClient =
   storageAccount.CreateCloudTableClient();

tableClient.CreateTableIfNotExist("ShoppingCartTable");
```

Ultimately the StorageClient library just wraps the REST API that's exposed by the Table service. Let's take a look at how this is done.

CREATING A TABLE USING ATOMPUB

To create a new table, you must perform a POST request against the URI you used earlier to list and delete tables in the silverlightukstorage storage account.

```
POST http://silverlightukstorage.table.core.windows.net/Tables
```

Because the Table service implements the AtomPub protocol, the body of the POST request needs to be in the Atom document format. The following Atom document instructs the Table service to create a new table called ShoppingCartTable in the storage account:

```
<?xml version="1.0" encoding="utf-8" standalone="yes"?>
   <entry xmlns:d="http://schemas.microsoft.com/ado/2007/08/dataservices"
xmlns:m="http://schemas.microsoft.com/ado/2007/08/dataservices/metadata"
xmlns="http://www.w3.org/2005/Atom">
      <title />
      <updated>2009-03-18T11:48:34.9840639-07:00</updated>
      <author>
         <name/>
      </author>
      <id/>
      <content type="application/xml">
        <m:properties>
          <d:TableName>ShoppingCartTable</d:TableName>   <-- Specifies name
        </m:properties>                                      of table to create
      </content>
   </entry>
```

As you can see from this verbose piece of junk, creating a simple table requires a whole bunch of useless information that's never used.

Our two cents about the REST API method of creation

This is a complete rant, and we do apologize for it, but it has to be said. The REST API method of creating tables is unnecessarily complex and verbose. We know you probably won't care because you'll use the StorageClient library to create tables rather than the REST API. We also know that it's not Microsoft's fault—they're just following the standard. But could we not have a simpler API call?

The method of deleting the ShoppingCartTable is pretty simple; it's the HTTP verb `DELETE` with the appropriate URI, such as this one:

```
http://silverlightukstorage.table.core.windows.net/Tables
➥ ('ShoppingCartTable')
```

It's pretty simple, isn't it? Why does AtomPub have that mad method of creating a table? We can't help thinking that a simpler method of creating tables would be to use the same URI as `DELETE` and change the HTTP verb from `DELETE` to `POST`.

Instead of using AtomPub to create tables with a crazy amount of XML, you can do the same thing with the slightly easier-to-use REST API. We'll eventually get to the easiest way to create a table, which is with the StorageClient library.

CREATING THE TABLE USING THE REST API IN A CONSOLE APPLICATION

It's time for you to create a small console application that will generate the ShoppingCartTable in a storage account using AtomPub and the REST API. The listing that follows contains the code for the console application.

Listing 12.2 Creating tables using the REST API and AtomPub

```
static void Main(string[] args)
{
   HttpWebRequest hwr = CreateHttpRequest(new Uri(
     @"http://silverlightukstorage.table.core.windows.net/Tables"),
     "POST", new TimeSpan(0, 0, 30));

  string xml = string.Format(@"<?xml version=""1.0"" encoding=""utf-8""
  ➥ standalone=""yes""?><entry
  ➥ xmlns:d=""http://schemas.microsoft.com/ado/2007/08/dataservices""
  ➥ xmlns:m=""http://schemas.microsoft.com/ado/2007/08/dataservices/metadata""
  ➥ xmlns=""http://www.w3.org/2005/Atom""><title/><updated>{0:yyyy-MM-
  ➥ ddTHH:mm:ss.fffffffZ}</updated><author><name/></author><id/><content
  ➥ type=""application/xml""><m:properties><d:TableName>{1}</d:TableName>
  ➥ </m:properties></content></entry>"
  ➥ , DateTime.UtcNow, "ShoppingCartTable");

   byte[] bytes = Encoding.UTF8.GetBytes(xml);
   hwr.ContentLength = bytes.Length;

   var storageAccount =
      CloudStorageAccount.Parse(
```

```
        ConfigurationManager
        ➥ .AppSettings["DataConnectionString"]);           Gets
                                                            credentials
                                                                        Signs
    storageAccount.Credentials.SignRequestLite(hwr);                    request

    using (Stream requestStream =                           Writes message
    ➥ hwr.GetRequestStream())                           ❶ to the wire
    {
        requestStream.Write(bytes, 0, bytes.Length);
    }

    using (StreamReader sr =
        new StreamReader(hwr.GetResponse()                  Makes request
        ➥ .GetResponseStream()))                           to Table service
    {
        XDocument myDocument =
            XDocument.Parse(sr.ReadToEnd());

        Console.Write(myDocument.ToString());
    }
}
```

The console application in listing 12.2 is pretty much the same as the one in listing 12.1 that listed tables. But there are a few differences between the two applications. In this case, you use the URI of your table endpoint, and you need to change the HTTP verb from `GET` to `DELETE`. You also need to convert the Atom XML you used earlier from a string to a byte array. Finally, you write the Atom XML `byte[]` to the request body.

Over the past few sections, we've looked at how you can interact with the REST API directly. In each example, you've used the StorageClient library to sign the request, but we haven't spent any time explaining that. Let's take a little time out to do that now.

12.2 Authenticating requests against the Table service

In chapter 9 (section 9.7) we described the Shared Key authentication method for BLOBs. This method of authentication is used by both the BLOB and Queue services. The Table service, however, supports two different authentication mechanisms:

- Shared Key authentication for Table service
- Shared Key Lite authentication for Table service

Let's take a look at Shared Key authentication first.

12.2.1 Shared Key authentication

Shared Key authentication for Table service is the most secure method of authenticating against the Table service using the REST API. The method for generating an authentication key is similar to the method used for BLOBs (with a few subtle differences).

In order to generate a shared key, you need to canonicalize the HTTP request and then hash it using a SHA-56 algorithm, storing the hashed value in the Authorization header. The following value represents the Authorization header for a request, hashed using the Shared Key mechanism:

```
SharedKey devstoreaccount1:J5xkbSz7/7Xf8sCNY3RJIzyUEfnj1SJ3ccIBNpDzsq4=
```

The major difference between the shared key for the BLOB service (as well as the Queue service for that matter) and the Table service is that you don't include canonicalized headers in the signature. The following code shows how you would generate the string prior to SHA-256 hashing:

```
unhashedString =
   VERB + "\n" + Content-MD5 + "\n"
+ Content-Type + "\n" + Date + "\n"
+ canonicalizedRequest;
```

Once you've generated the string, you can hash it and stuff it into the Authorization header.

Although you can use the Shared Key mechanism with the Table service, it can only be used with the REST API directly—the WCF Data Services client doesn't support the Shared Key mechanism. Fortunately, the Table service also supports Shared Key Lite as an authentication mechanism (which is supported by the WCF Data Services client). Let's take a look at that authentication mechanism.

12.2.2 Shared Key Lite authentication

The Shared Key Lite authentication mechanism for signing a request is similar to the Shared Key method. Like the Shared Key mechanism, it will canonicalize and hash the request using a SHA-256 algorithm, storing the result in the Authorization header. The following value represents the Authorization header for a request hashed using the Shared Key Lite mechanism:

```
SharedKeyLite devstoreaccount1:0c4bknVWVmQ+L1r5jCIYFiNDkSXHata8ZYW8mjQhPLo=
```

Although Shared Key Lite follows the same process of hashing a request and uses the same key to hash the request as the Shared Key mechanism, Shared Key Lite is a lighter and less secure mechanism. The Shared Key mechanism includes more data as part of the hash, meaning a hacker would have a better chance of tampering with the request when you're using Shared Key Lite rather than Shared Key.

If you look back to listing 12.2, you can see that the request is signed prior to writing the Atom XML to the request body (at ❶). That means the XML isn't part of the hash and can be tampered with.

If an HTTP request is intercepted within the Shared Access Signature time window, a hacker would be able to modify the request to create a table of a different type (such as a NastyHackerTable). The hacker would not be able to perform any other types of requests, however, because the hash prevents the HTTP verb from being tampered with.

> **Which authentication method should you use?**
>
> If you're using WCF Data Services to communicate with the Table service and your application runs purely within the data center, you can continue to use the Shared Key Lite mechanism. (To be honest, you don't have a choice, as it's the only authentication mechanism supported by the WCF Data Services client.)
>
> If you're using the REST API directly, and you have an application communicating with the Table service API outside of the Windows Azure data center, or you want the highest possible security, you should use the REST API directly with Shared Key authentication.

By now, you should have a good feel for storage accounts, the REST API, AtomPub, and which operations you can perform on a storage account using both the REST API directly and the StorageClient library. Now let's look at how to perform CRUDy stuff (inserts, updates, and deletes—we'll do querying later) in conjunction with the REST API and the StorageClient library.

12.3 Modifying entities with the REST API is CRUD

Over the next few sections, we'll focus on how the REST API can be used to communicate with the Table service in regard to entities. In particular, we'll look at

- Inserting entities
- Deleting entities
- Updating entities

Before you can delete or update an entity, you'll need to insert one first.

12.3.1 Inserting entities

Before we look at how to insert an entity using the REST API, let's look at the code you'd write to store an entity in a table using the StorageClient library:

```
var shirtContext = new ProductContext();

shirtContext.AddObject("Products",
   new Product
   {
      PartitionKey = "Shirts",
      RowKey = "RedShirt",
      Name = "Red Shirt",
      Description = "A Red Shirt"
   });

shirtContext.SaveChanges();
```

The preceding example inserts a new instance of the `Product` entity into the Products table. The new `Product` will be stored in the `Shirts` partition with a `RowKey` value of

RedShirt. For a detailed description of how data is stored in the Table service and how to use a context class to insert data into a table, please refer to chapter 11.

> **The Unit of Work pattern**
>
> WCF Data Services, and therefore the StorageClient library, implement the Unit of Work pattern for saving data back to the database. This means that all changes are tracked locally (when you use the AddObject method) and then all changes are saved back to the Table service when the SaveChanges method is called.
>
> A process that doesn't use the Unit of Work pattern would not track the changes to the entities locally and apply the changes directly to the Table service when the AddObject method is called. This removes any batching or cancellation capabilities easily provided by the Unit of Work pattern.

Now that we've reminded ourselves of how to insert a new entity into a table using the StorageClient library, let's look at how this would be done using the REST API directly.

USING THE REST API

To use the AtomPub-based REST API to insert a new entity into a table, you'd need to perform an HTTP POST request to the following URI:

```
http://<storageaccountname>.table.core.windows.net/<TableName>
```

To insert a new entity into the Products table in the silverlightukstorage storage account, you'd use the following URI:

```
http://silverlightukstorage.table.core.windows.net/Products
```

To insert the entity we created at the beginning of section 12.3.1 with the StorageClient library, you'd need to define the request body with the following Atom XML:

```
<?xml version="1.0" encoding="utf-8" standalone="yes"?>
<entry xmlns:d="http://schemas.microsoft.com/
➥ ado/2007/08/dataservices" xmlns:m="http://schemas.microsoft.com/
➥ ado/2007/08/dataservices/metadata"
➥ xmlns="http://www.w3.org/2005/Atom">
  <title />
  <updated>2009-07-27T14:22:48.8875037Z</updated>
  <author>
    <name />
  </author>
  <id />
  <content type="application/xml">
    <m:properties>
      <d:Description>A Red Shirt</d:Description>
      <d:Name>Red Shirt</d:Name>
      <d:PartitionKey>Shirts</d:PartitionKey>
      <d:RowKey>RedShirt</d:RowKey>
      <d:Timestamp m:type="Edm.DateTime">0001-01-01T00:00:00</d:Timestamp>
    </m:properties>
```

```
  </content>
</entry>
```

If you look at the preceding AtomPub XML, you can see that it follows a similar format to the XML used to create the storage account table in section 12.1.4 (in the "Creating a table using AtomPub" subsection). As you can see from the preceding Atom XML, not only are the values of each property of the entity included in the XML, but so is the name and type of each property (notice that the `Timestamp` property is of type `Edm.DateTime`). Because a Table service table is effectively schemaless, and each row could contain an entity with an entirely different set of properties, it's important that the entities being inserted into the table be self-describing.

If you wanted to modify the console application in listing 12.2 to insert an entity instead of creating a table, you could replace the URI generation with the URI we defined earlier and replace the Atom XML with the preceding document.

Now that you've created your lovely entity, let's nuke it!

12.3.2 Deleting entities

In the product-management web page you built in chapter 11, you could delete shirts from the product list using the following call:

```
var shirtContext = new ProductContext();
shirtContext.DeleteObject(shirtToDelete);
shirtContext.SaveChanges();
```

Deleting an entity is similar to adding an entity when using the StorageClient library. If you wished to delete a shirt from the Products table, you'd need to add the shirt to be deleted to the context object's (`shirtContext`) tracking list using the `DeleteObject` method. All changes are again tracked locally by the context object and are only saved back to the Table service when the `SaveChanges` method is called (following the Unit of Work pattern).

Let's now take a look at using the REST API for deleting entities from a table. To delete an entity you need to make a `DELETE` request to the appropriate URI, passing in the correct table name, partition key, and row key:

```
http://silverlightukstorage.table.core.windows.net
➥ /Products(PartitionKey="Shirts", RowKey="RedShirt")
```

The preceding URI would delete an entity called `RedShirt` from the `Shirts` partition of the Products table from a storage account named silverlightukstorage. See the following listing for the code required to the delete the entity from a console application.

Listing 12.3 Deleting entities using the REST API

```
static void Main(string[] args)
{
      HttpWebRequest hwr = CreateHttpRequest(
      ➥ new Uri(@"http://silverlightukstorage
      ➥ .table.core.windows.net/Products(PartitionKey='Shirts'
      ➥ , RowKey='RedShirt')
      ➥ "), "DELETE", new TimeSpan(0, 0, 30));
```

Deletes entity from table

```
        hwr.Headers.Add("If-Match", "*");

    var storageAccount =
        CloudStorageAccount.Parse(
          ConfigurationManager
          ➥ .AppSettings["DataConnectionString"]);

    storageAccount.Credentials.SignRequestLite(hwr)

    hwr.GetResponse();
}
```

Sets up credentials and executes request

OPTIMIZING DELETE PERFORMANCE IN WEB GRIDS

As explained previously, to delete an entity using the StorageClient library, you first need to add a local copy of the entity to your context object's tracking list. In Windows client applications, this isn't such a big issue, as you'll already have a local copy of the entities. In an ASP.NET application, if you listed the entities in a grid (as in the product-management web page), you'd no longer have a local copy of the entity because each web page call is stateless.

Although you could store a copy of all entities in the ASP.NET page state, this would massively increase the page size and reduce overall performance. Similarly, storing the entities in the session would put unnecessary overhead on the web server, again affecting the performance. Even if the grid were populated from a cache, unnecessary calls to the cache would still have a slight impact on performance. So let's look at some other options.

In the product-management web page in chapter 11, we fetched the entity from the Table service (for the sake of simplicity) and then added that entity to the `shirtContext`'s tracking list. The following code shows how we used a LINQ query to fetch the data from the Table service:

```
var entity = new ProductContext();

shirtToDelete = (from item in shirtContext.Products
        where item.PartitionKey == "Shirts"
        && item.RowKey == rowkey
                 select item).First();

shirtContext.DeleteObject(entity);

shirtContext.SaveChanges();
```

Refetching the entity to be deleted isn't something you should consider in a production environment, as any unnecessary calls to the Table service will impact the performance of your application and add to the overall running cost of your service (calls to the Table service are billable).

As you saw in our discussion of the REST API, you really don't need all the data of the object. In fact, you only need the partition key and row key, so rather than fetching the whole object, you could construct a lightweight version of the object to be deleted.

To do this, you can define a lightweight sister class of the Product class that only contains the `PartitionKey` and `RowKey` values. As long as the object held in the tracking list holds the correct `PartitionKey` and `RowKey` (which uniquely identify an entity), you'll have enough information to perform the delete—there's no need to fetch every property of the entity.

The following code shows how you can delete an entity from the Table service using a lightweight instance:

```
var shirtContext = new ProductContext();
shirtContext.DeleteObject
(
   new ProductKey
   {
      PartitionKey = "Shirts",
      RowKey = e.CommandArgument.ToString()
   }
);
   shirtContext.AttachTo("Product", entity, "*");
shirtContext.SaveChanges(saveOptions);
```

As you can see in the preceding code, there's no need to fetch the entity from the Table service because you already know the `PartitionKey` (`Shirts`), and the `RowKey` can be extracted from the command argument of the Delete button. This optimization saves you that extra fetch.

Now that we've explored both inserting and deleting, it's time to complete the set and look at updates.

12.3.3 Updating entities

When deleting an object using the StorageClient library, you need to keep track of the objects to be deleted in the context object for the Products table. You can use similar logic to update objects in your application.

Here's an example:

```
var shirtContext = new ProductContext();

shirtToUpdate = (from item in shirtContext.Products
                 where item.PartitionKey == "Shirts"
                 && item.RowKey == "RedShirt"
                 select item).First();
shirtToUpdate.Description = "I have been modified";
shirtContext.UpdateObject(shirtToUpdate);
shirtContext.SaveChanges(saveOptions);
```

The preceding code retrieves the `RedShirt` entity from the `Shirts` partition in the Products table. The code then modifies the description of the entity and saves the changes back to the Products table.

MERGING DATA

By default, the `SaveChanges` method will *merge* any changes made to the object back to the entity stored in the Table service, rather than performing a replacement update.

Before we can explain what this means, let's look at an extract of Atom XML that describes the entity held in the Table service:

```
<content type="application/xml">
    <m:properties>
      <d:Description>A Red Shirt</d:Description>
      <d:Name>Red Shirt</d:Name>
      <d:PartitionKey>Shirts</d:PartitionKey>
      <d:RowKey>RedShirt</d:RowKey>
      <d:Timestamp m:type="Edm.DateTime">0001-01-01T00:00:00</d:Timestamp>
    </m:properties>
  </content>
```

By choosing to merge the data, you can efficiently send data back to the Table service by only sending the modified data instead of the full entity. Table 12.1 shows how this would work in three scenarios:

- *Remote*—A remote copy of the entity is stored in the Products table.
- *Local*—A local copy of the entity is used.
- *Merged*—The changes in the local version of the entity are merged with the remote version.

Table 12.1 Merging data with updates

Scenario	Partition key	Row key	Name	Description
Remote	Shirts	RedShirt	RedShirt	A Red Shirt
Local	Shirts	RedShirt	RedShirt	A Pink Shirt
Merged	Shirts	RedShirt	RedShirt	A Pink Shirt

As you can see in table 12.1, the only property that has changed for the entity is the description. This means that the client application doesn't need to send back the name property in the Atom XML describing the entity. The following extract of the Atom XML describes what would be returned to the Table service as part of the merge operation:

```
<content type="application/xml">
    <m:properties>
      <d:Description>A Pink Shirt</d:Description>
    </m:properties>
  </content>
```

If you need to replace the entity stored in the Table service with your local version rather than performing a merge, you can use the following setting in your client code:

```
shirtContext.SaveChangesDefaultOptions =
    SaveChangesOptions.ReplaceOnUpdate;
```

In this case, the Atom XML sent using the REST API would contain the full description of the entity rather than just the changed properties.

USING THE REST API TO MERGE OR UPDATE

When you use the REST API to update or merge data, you're really using a combination of the delete and insert REST API functions.

The URI to update or merge the local entity back to the Table storage is the same URI as for the delete operation:

```
http://silverlightukstorage.table.core.windows.net
➥ /Products(PartitionKey='Shirts', RowKey='RedShirt')
```

As you can see, the URI needs to specify the `PartitionKey` and `RowKey` of the entity being modified. Depending on the operation you're performing, you should set the HTTP verb to either `MERGE` or `PUT`. Finally, the body of the HTTP request should be set to the AtomPub XML document that describes the entity (this is the same as the XML used to create the entity).

If you wish to modify the console application from section 12.1.1 to merge instead of insert, you would need to change the URI and HTTP verbs in the code.

Finally, you would need to add a new `If-Match` header to the request. This header is used to ensure that the data held in the remote version of the entity has not changed since you grabbed the local version. If you wish to ensure that data is only modified if the data is unchanged, you should set the `If-Match` header to the e-tag that was originally returned with the entity.

If you wish to perform an unconditional update, the value of the `If-Match` header should be set to `"*"`.

In this section, you've learned how to perform inserts, updates, and deletes against your entities. But you're unlikely to work with single entities, so it's time to learn about some of the complications of updating data—batching and transactions.

12.4 Batching data

In the previous sections, you used both the StorageClient library and the REST API to insert new entities into the Products table. In this section, we'll look at how you can both improve performance and perform transactional changes by batching up data.

The following code inserts multiple entities into the Products table using the StorageClient library:

```
var shirtContext = new ProductContext();

for (int i = 0; i < 10; i++)
{
   shirtContext.AddObject("Products",
   new Product
   {
      PartitionKey = "Shirts",
      RowKey = i.ToString(),
      Name = "Shirt" + i.ToString(),
      Description = "A Shirt"
   });
}
shirtContext.SaveChanges();
```

12	21.950029	192.168.0.5	65.55.33.205	HTTP	POST /ProductTable HTTP/1.1 (application/atom+xml)
16	22.241154	65.55.33.205	192.168.0.5	HTTP	HTTP/1.1 201 Created (application/atom+xml)
17	22.251847	192.168.0.5	65.55.33.205	HTTP	POST /ProductTable HTTP/1.1 (application/atom+xml)
22	22.633432	65.55.33.205	192.168.0.5	HTTP	HTTP/1.1 201 Created (application/atom+xml)
23	22.641256	192.168.0.5	65.55.33.205	HTTP	POST /ProductTable HTTP/1.1 (application/atom+xml)
27	22.898821	65.55.33.205	192.168.0.5	HTTP	HTTP/1.1 201 Created (application/atom+xml)
28	22.906475	192.168.0.5	65.55.33.205	HTTP	POST /ProductTable HTTP/1.1 (application/atom+xml)
32	23.163614	65.55.33.205	192.168.0.5	HTTP	HTTP/1.1 201 Created (application/atom+xml)
33	23.171723	192.168.0.5	65.55.33.205	HTTP	POST /ProductTable HTTP/1.1 (application/atom+xml)
37	23.429996	65.55.33.205	192.168.0.5	HTTP	HTTP/1.1 201 Created (application/atom+xml)
38	23.438125	192.168.0.5	65.55.33.205	HTTP	POST /ProductTable HTTP/1.1 (application/atom+xml)
42	23.694816	65.55.33.205	192.168.0.5	HTTP	HTTP/1.1 201 Created (application/atom+xml)
43	23.702653	192.168.0.5	65.55.33.205	HTTP	POST /ProductTable HTTP/1.1 (application/atom+xml)
47	23.960189	65.55.33.205	192.168.0.5	HTTP	HTTP/1.1 201 Created (application/atom+xml)
48	23.967479	192.168.0.5	65.55.33.205	HTTP	POST /ProductTable HTTP/1.1 (application/atom+xml)
52	24.226081	65.55.33.205	192.168.0.5	HTTP	HTTP/1.1 201 Created (application/atom+xml)
53	24.233846	192.168.0.5	65.55.33.205	HTTP	POST /ProductTable HTTP/1.1 (application/atom+xml)
57	24.491098	65.55.33.205	192.168.0.5	HTTP	HTTP/1.1 201 Created (application/atom+xml)
58	24.499442	192.168.0.5	65.55.33.205	HTTP	POST /ProductTable HTTP/1.1 (application/atom+xml)
62	24.756697	65.55.33.205	192.168.0.5	HTTP	HTTP/1.1 201 Created (application/atom+xml)

Figure 12.2 By default, the context object will save each entity with an individual request rather than saving them all in a batch.

The preceding code will create 10 new shirts and add each new shirt to a list of objects that are to be tracked; it does this by calling the `AddObject` method on the `shirtContext` object. Following the Unit of Work pattern, the context object won't send any changes to the Table service until the `SaveChanges` method is called. It will then iterate through the list of tracked objects and insert them into the Products table.

By default, the `SaveChanges` call will insert the entities into the table one by one rather than batching the inserts into a single call. Figure 12.2 shows the HTTP traffic for the preceding call, captured by using Wireshark (a packet-sniffing tool).

As you can see from figure 12.2, to insert 10 shirts, the application must perform 10 HTTP `POST` requests to the Table service. This method can cause performance problems if you're inserting a large number of entities and your application is outside of Windows Azure or your web or worker role isn't affinitized to the same data center as your storage account.

> **WARNING** Due to latency, inserting 10 shirts using the preceding code took 4 seconds between our local machine and the live Table service. When running the same code as a web role in the Windows Azure data center, it took milliseconds.

Although minimizing latency will give large performance benefits, you can gain larger performance improvements by batching up inserts into single calls using entity group transactions.

> **NOTE** Due to the flexible nature of the Windows Azure platform, you can host your storage account and your web and worker roles in different data centers. As you can see from the previous example, this flexibility comes at a price: latency. For the best performance, always affinitize your web roles, worker roles, and storage service to the same data center to minimize latency.

12.4.1 Entity group transactions

Entity group transactions are a type of batch insert where the whole batch is treated as a transaction, and the whole thing either succeeds or is rolled back entirely. First, let's look at how batch inserts are done.

Passing `SaveChangesOptions.Batch` as a parameter into the `SaveChanges` method calls will batch up all changes into a single HTTP `POST`:

```
shirtContext.SaveChanges(SaveOptions.Batch);
```

Batching up the data like this reduced our insert of 10 shirts (from the local machine to the live service) from 4 seconds to 1 second.

The `SaveOption` parameter can also be passed in with the call to the `SaveChanges` method to specify what happens if the inserts aren't entirely successful:

- `SaveOptions.None`—By default, when no `SaveOption` is passed, or when `SaveOptions.None` is passed, as part of the `SaveChanges` method, and a tracked entity fails to be inserted, the context object will stop attempting to save any further entities. Any entities that were saved successfully won't be rolled back and will remain in the table.
- `SaveOptions.ContinueOnError`—If this option is passed as part of the `SaveChanges` call, and an entity fails to save, the context object will continue to save all other entities.
- `SaveOptions.Batch`—If this option is passed as part of the `SaveChanges` call, all entities will be processed as a batch in the scope of a single transaction—known as an entity group transaction. If any of the entities being inserted as part of the batch fails to be inserted, the whole batch will be rolled back.

These are the rules for using entity group transactions:

1. A maximum of 100 operations can be performed in a single batch.
2. The batch may not exceed 4 MB in size.
3. All entities in the batch must have the same partition key.
4. You can only perform a single operation against an entity in a batch.

In this book, we won't discuss the REST implementation of entity group transactions due to the complexity of the implementation. But it's worth noting that if you decide to use the REST implementation, the Table service only implements a subset of the available functionality. As of the PDC 2009 release, the Table service only supports single changesets (a changeset being a set of inserts, updates, or deletes) within a batch.

> **NOTE** If you're interested in looking at the REST implementation of batching, you should look up the "Performing Entity Group Transactions" MSDN article: http://msdn.microsoft.com/en-us/library/dd894038.aspx.

Entity group transactions are executed using an isolation method known as *snapshot isolation.* This is a standard method of isolation used in relational databases such as SQL Server or Oracle; it's also known as multiversion concurrency control (MVCC). A snapshot of the data is taken at the beginning of a transaction, and it's used for the duration of the transaction. This means that all operations within the transaction will use the same set of isolated data that can't be interfered with by other concurrent processes. Because the data is isolated from all other processes, there's no need for locking on the table, meaning that operations can't be blocked by other processes. On committing the transaction, if any modified data has been changed by another process since the snapshot began, the whole transaction must be rolled back and retried.

12.4.2 Retries

In order to handle the MVCC model, your code must be able to perform retries. The ability to handle retries is built into the StorageClient library and can be configured using the following code:

```
shirtContext.RetryPolicy =
    RetryPolicies.Retry(5, TimeSpan.FromSeconds(1));
```

The preceding retry policy will reattempt the `SaveChanges` operation up to five times, retrying every second. If you don't wish to set a retry policy, you can always set the policy as `NoRetry`:

```
shirtContext.RetryPolicy = RetryPolicies.NoRetry;
```

If you need more complicated retry polices with randomized back-off timings, or if you wish to define your own policy, this can also be achieved by setting an appropriate retry policy. Unfortunately, if you're using the REST API directly, you'll need to roll your own retry logic.

In order to make use of the standard retry logic, you'll need to use the `SaveChangesWithRetries` method rather than the `SaveChanges` method, as follows:

```
shirtContext.SaveChangesWithRetries();
```

Use retries for queries too

Although retry policies are vital when using entity group transactions, they can also be useful when querying data. Your web and worker roles are based in the cloud and can be shut down and restarted at any time by the Fabric Controller (such as in a case of a hardware failure), so to provide a more professional application, it may be advisable to use retry policies when querying data.

So far we've covered the modification of data in quite a lot of detail. But entity group transactions can also be useful for querying data. With that in mind, it's worth breaking away from data updates and focusing on how to retrieve data via the REST API.

12.5 Querying data

In this section, we'll take a look at how to query data held in the Table service by using both the StorageClient library and the REST API directly. The knowledge that you gain from this section will come in useful when we look at how to store data efficiently. In particular we'll look at how you can

- Retrieve entities using the REST API
- Query using LINQ

- Filter data using the REST API
- Filter data using LINQ
- Select data using LINQ
- Page data

To get started, let's look at how to retrieve data from a table using the REST API.

12.5.1 *Retrieving all entities in a table using the REST API*

In this section we'll look at how to build a small console application that will display all the entities in the Product table. This application is similar to the one that you built earlier to list tables in storage accounts.

The base URI used to query the Products table is the same base URI you used to insert, update, and delete table entities. To return all shirts stored in the Products table in the development storage account, you would make an HTTP `GET` request using the following URI:

```
http://127.0.0.1:10002/devstoreaccount1/Products
```

The code in listing 12.4 will return all entities in the Products table and display the result in the console window.

Listing 12.4 Listing the entities in the Products table using the REST API

```
static void Main(string[] args)
{
   HttpWebRequest hwr =
      CreateHttpRequest(new Uri(@"http://127.0.0.1:10002
      ➥ /devstoreaccount1/Products"), "GET",
      ➥ new TimeSpan(0, 0, 30));                        ❶ Specifies URI for request

   var storageAccount =
      CloudStorageAccount.Parse(
        ConfigurationManager
        ➥ .AppSettings["DataConnectionString"]);        Sets up credentials
                                                          and signs request
   storageAccount.Credentials.SignRequestLite(hwr)

   using (StreamReader sr =
          new StreamReader(
          ➥ hwr.GetResponse()                          Executes request
          ➥ .GetResponseStream()))                      and displays output
   {
      XDocument myDocument = XDocument.Parse(sr.ReadToEnd());
      Console.Write(myDocument.ToString());
   }
}
```

The code in listing 12.4 is pretty much the same code as in listing 12.1 (which listed all the tables in a storage account). The only modification you need to make to that code is to change the URI for the HTTP request at ❶ to the URI of the Products table.

The REST API call that you used to list all product entities adheres to the AtomPub protocol, so the result that's returned to the console window will display the entities from the Products table in Atom XML format, as shown in the following listing.

Listing 12.5 Atom XML output from the console application in listing 12.4

```
<feed xml:base="http://127.0.0.1:10002/devstoreaccount1/" xmlns:d="http://
     schemas
.microsoft.com/ado/2007/08/dataservices" xmlns:m="http://
     schemas.microsoft.com/
ado/2007/08/dataservices/metadata" xmlns="http://www.w3.org/2005/Atom">
  <title type="text">Products</title>
  <id>http://127.0.0.1:10002/devstoreaccount1/Products</id>
  <updated>2009-08-01T11:23:48Z</updated>
  <link rel="self" title="Products" href="Products" />
  <entry m:etag="W/&quot;datetime'2009-07-23T19%3A55%3A38.7'&quot;">
    <id>http://127.0.0.1:10002/devstoreaccount
    ➥ /Products(PartitionKey='Shirts',RowKey='BlueShirt')</id>
    <title type="text"></title>
    <updated>2009-08-01T11:23:48Z</updated>
    <author>
      <name />
    </author>
    <link rel="edit" title="Products" href="Product(PartitionKey=
    ➥ 'Shirts',RowKey='BlueShirt')" />
    <category term="AiAChapter7Web_WebRole.Products"
    ➥  scheme="http://schemas.
microsoft.com/ado/2007/08/dataservices/scheme" />
    <content type="application/xml">
      <m:properties>
        <d:Name>Blue Shirt</d:Name>
        <d:Description>A Blue Shirt</d:Description>
        <d:Timestamp m:type="Edm.DateTime">2009-07-
        ➥ 23T19:55:38.7</d:Timestamp>
        <d:PartitionKey>Shirts</d:PartitionKey>
        <d:RowKey>BlueShirt</d:RowKey>
      </m:properties>
    </content>
  </entry>
  <entry m:etag="W/&quot;datetime'2009-07-23T19%3A13%3A28.09'&quot;">
    <id>http://127.0.0.1:10002/devstoreaccount
    ➥ 1/Products(PartitionKey='Shirts',RowKey='RedShirt')
    </id>
    <title type="text"></title>
    <updated>2009-08-01T11:23:48Z</updated>
    <author>
      <name />
    </author>
    <link rel="edit" title="Products" href=
    ➥ "Product(PartitionKey='Shirts',RowKey='RedShirt')" />
    <category term="AiAChapter7Web_WebRole.Products"
    ➥ scheme="http://schemas.microsoft.com/ado
    ➥ /2007/08/dataservices/scheme" />
    <content type="application/xml">
```

```
    <m:properties>
      <d:Name>red shirt</d:Name>
      <d:Description>a red shirt</d:Description>
      <d:Timestamp m:type="Edm.DateTime">2009-07-
      ➥ 23T19:13:28.09</d:Timestamp>
      <d:PartitionKey>Shirts</d:PartitionKey>
      <d:RowKey>RedShirt</d:RowKey>
    </m:properties>
  </content>
 </entry>
</feed>
```

The Atom XML output in listing 12.5 returns all entities stored in the Products table (`RedShirt` and `BlueShirt`). As you can see, the returned XML is very descriptive (and also verbose), including the name of the property, the value, and the data type.

The verbosity of the returned XML means that the returned datasets are usually pretty large. You should be careful to cache data whenever possible and return the minimum amount of data required.

The verbosity of Atom XML

Hopefully, in the future, the Windows Azure Table service team will support a less verbose serialization format, such as JSON, and will also support local data shaping (explained later on in this section). JSON would be an ideal format to support because WCF Data Services (but not the Table service implementation) already supports this method of serialization.

Using JSON would require few changes to your application code, but you'd gain large benefits in terms of reduced bandwidth. The following code shows how the previously returned Atom XML could be represented in JSON:

```
Products:
 [
     {
        "Name" : "blue shirt"
        "Description" : "a Blue Shirt"
        "Timestamp" : "2009-07-23T19:13:28.09"
        "PartitionKey" : "Shirts"
        "RowKey" : "BlueShirt"}
    },
    {
        "Name" : "red shirt"
        "Description" : "A Blue Shirt"
        "Timestamp" : "2009-07-23T19:13:28.09"
        "PartitionKey" : "Shirts"
        "RowKey" : "RedShirt"}
    },
]
```

As you can see, the JSON representation is much more readable and terse, meaning that the size of the returned documents would be greatly reduced and will therefore improve the speed of your application. Hopefully this will be supported in future versions of the Table service.

12.5.2 Querying with LINQ

Because the Table service is implemented using ADO.NET Data Services, you can use the WCF Data Services client library to perform server-side queries using LINQ rather than querying the REST API directly.

The following code shows how the Products table was exposed in the `ProductContext` class created in listing 11.2 (in chapter 11):

```
public DataServiceQuery<Product> Products
{
   get{return CreateQuery<Product>("Products");}
}
```

Rather than executing and returning a list of products from the Products table stored in the Table service, the `Products` property will generate and return a new query that won't be executed until the collection is enumerated. Because the execution of the `DataServiceQuery` is deferred, you can modify the returned query to include any filters that you may require prior to executing the query.

Because `DataServiceQuery` implements the `IQueryable` interface, you can define the query that should be executed by the Table service in your application by using LINQ. The following code is a LINQ query that will return all the products in the `Shirts` partition of the Products table:

```
var shirts = from shirt in shirtContext.Products
             where shirt.PartitionKey == "Shirts"
             select shirt;

foreach (var shirt in shirts)
{
}
```

In the preceding query, the `Products` property of `shirtContext` is `IQueryable`, so you can make this the data source of a LINQ query. Because the query won't be passed to the Table service for execution until the `for` loop is executed, you can add additional filter criteria to the query (such as restricting the returned data to only those shirts that reside in the `Shirts` partition).

> **NOTE** If you don't include the where criteria in the preceding LINQ statement, the underlying REST API that's executed would be the same as the call made in listing 12.4.

12.5.3 Filtering data with the REST API

In the previous section, we looked at a LINQ query that included a `WHERE` clause, restricting the data returned from the Table service to include only those shirts in the `Shirts` partition. We'll now look at how you can modify your use of the REST API to perform server-side filtering.

RETURNING A SINGLE ENTITY

As stated previously, the combination of the `PartitionKey` and `RowKey` uniquely identifies an entity in a table. If you wish to return a single entity from a table, and you know these two values, you can efficiently return the entity. The following URI would return the `RedShirt` entity from the `Shirts` partition:

```
http://127.0.0.1:10002/devstoreaccount1
➥ /Products(PartitionKey='Shirts',RowKey='RedShirt')
```

To execute this query, you could modify the console application in listing 12.4, replacing the URI with one here. The Atom XML returned from the query would be similar to the data returned in listing 12.5, but it would only contain the `RedShirt` entity.

QUERYING ENTITIES

If you need to return zero or more entities based upon some filter criteria (such as all shirts that cost $10), you could use the following URI to define the REST query:

```
http://127.0.0.1:10002/devstoreaccount1/Products$filter=<query>
```

Just replace the `<query>` in the URI with the filter that you want to run server-side. Again, you can modify the console application in listing 12.4 to use this URI. When the query is executed, all entities that match the query will be returned in Atom XML format, as in listing 12.5.

QUERY EXPRESSIONS

Let's take a quick look at the syntax of the query expression applied in the REST API. (We'll look at using these queries in the more familiar LINQ syntax in the next section.)

As of the PDC 2009 release, the Table service only supports the query expressions listed in table 12.2.

Table 12.2 Query expressions supported by the Table service

Supported query expression	Description (C# equivalent operator)
`eq`	Equals (==)
`gt`	Greater than (>)
`ge`	Greater than or equal to (>=)
`lt`	Less than (<)
`le`	Less than or equal to (<=)
`ne`	Not equal to (!=)
`and`	And (&&)—Boolean properties only
`not`	Not (!)—Boolean properties only
`or`	Or (||)—Boolean properties only

You could apply these queries to a REST API query to return all shirts with the description "A Red Shirt". The URI would look like this:

```
http://127.0.0.1:10002/devstoreaccount1/Products?$filter=
➥ Description%20eq%20'A%20Red%20Shirt'
```

To return all shirts in the `Shirts` partition that have the description "A Red Shirt", you'd use the following URI:

```
http://127.0.0.1:10002/devstoreaccount1/Products?$filter=
➥ PartitionKey%20eq%20'Shirts'%20and%20Description%20eq%20
➥ 'A%20Red%20Shirt'%
```

12.5.4 *Filtering data with LINQ*

In the previous section, we looked at how to filter queries server-side using the REST API. We'll now look at how the REST API maps onto the LINQ queries.

As you may have guessed, LINQ queries eventually get resolved to the REST API URIs like the ones we looked at in the previous section. This means that although LINQ has a large and rich syntax, only those methods that map directly to the REST API can be supported.

While you're debugging a LINQ query in Visual Studio, you can either hover over or put a watch on a context object (such as `shirtContext` in figure 12.3) and you'll be able to see the underlying REST API query. Figure 12.3 shows the REST API query for a LINQ query that returns all products in the `Shirts` partition.

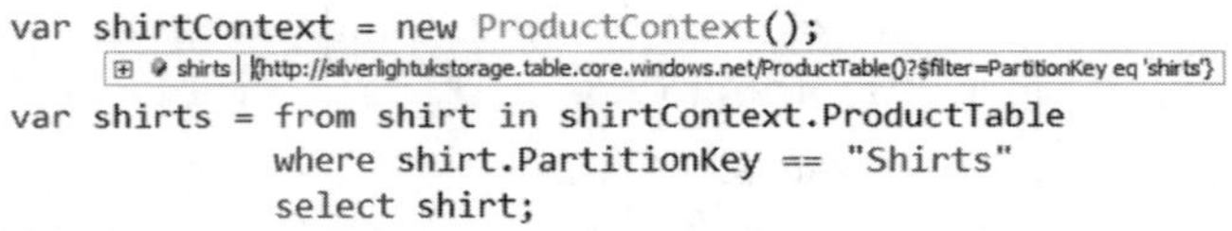

var shirtContext = new ProductContext();
shirts | {http://silverlightukstorage.table.core.windows.net/ProductTable()?$filter=PartitionKey eq 'shirts'}
var shirts = from shirt in shirtContext.ProductTable
where shirt.PartitionKey == "Shirts"
select shirt;

Figure 12.3 Mapping a LINQ query back to the REST API

Let's now look at the typical queries that you'll be able to perform.

EQUALITY COMPARISONS

As you can see from the list in table 12.2, only equality, range comparisons, and Boolean comparisons can be performed using the Table service. The following queries are typical equality comparisons that can be performed:

```
where shirt.RowKey == "Red Shirt"
```

or

```
where shirt.Description != "A Red Shirt"
```

or

```
where shirt.Partition == "Shirts"
  && shirt.Description != "A Red Shirt"
```

RANGE COMPARISONS

The Table service supports the filtering of range data using range queries. For example, the following `WHERE` clause will return those shirts priced at $50 or more, and less than $70:

```
where shirt.Price >= 50 && shirt.Price < 70
```

Because data is stored in the Table service as native types, rather than as string representations, the Table service will perform comparison routines using the native types rather than string comparisons. The following query will return all shirts whose price is greater than or equal to $50.20:

```
where shirt.Price >= 50.20
```

If this query were performed as a string comparison (which you would have to do with Amazon SimpleDB), it would not return shirts priced at $60 (because there are fewer characters in the string than 50.20) unless the price were stored as 60.00.

In Windows Azure Table service, the only time you need to worry about performing equivalent string comparisons is if you store a non-native string type as a partition or row key. Partition and row keys are always represented as strings in the Table service, so if you need to perform range comparisons on these entities, you'll need to ensure that the string lengths of the stored data are correct.

BOOLEAN LOGIC

As stated earlier, the Table service does respect property types. This means you can perform Boolean logic against entity properties that are defined as `bool`. For example, you could perform the following `WHERE` clause against a shirt that's marked as a genuine Hawaiian shirt:

```
where shirt.IsMadeInHawaii && shirt.Price > 50
```

PREFIX QUERIES

Using the range comparison and Boolean logic, you can manipulate your LINQ and REST queries to return all entities that start with a particular string. For example, if you wanted to return all shirts that were present in any of `partition1`, `partition2`, `partition3`, or `partition4`, you could use the following query:

```
where shirt.PartitionKey.CompareTo("Partition1") >= 0 &&
    shirt.PartitionKey.CompareTo("Partition5") < 0
```

LINQ TO OBJECTS QUERIES

Even though only a small subset of the LINQ syntax is available to be executed by the Table service, you can still perform in-memory LINQ queries (LINQ to Objects). In-memory LINQ queries do provide full access to the LINQ syntax, but all queries are executed on the client side, so they require the full dataset to be returned by the Table service first. This approach isn't suitable for situations where you're working with a large set of data.

By now you should have a taste of the types of queries that you can perform against the Table service. Let's now look at how you can shape the data that's returned from your queries.

12.5.5 Selecting data using the LINQ syntax

As you'll have noticed in the supported LINQ syntax list (table 12.2), there was no mention of the `SELECT` statement. You can use the `SELECT` statement to return the entire entity, but you can't use `SELECT` to instruct the Table service to only return a subset of the entity properties.

RETURNING AN ENTIRE ENTITY USING SELECT

To illustrate the limitations of using `SELECT`, let's look again at a LINQ query that returns a product entity in its entirety:

```
var shirts = from shirt in shirtContext.Products
             where shirt.PartitionKey == "Shirts"
             select shirt;
```

This LINQ query was used earlier to return all entities that reside in the Products table. The following code is an Atom XML extract of one of the entities returned by the preceding LINQ query:

```
<content type="application/xml">
   <m:properties>
    <d:PartitionKey>Shirts</d:PartitionKey>
    <d:RowKey>shirts0</d:RowKey>
    <d:Timestamp m:type="Edm.DateTime">
       2009-07-29T21:14:45.022Z
    </d:Timestamp>
    <d:Description>A Shirt</d:Description>
    <d:Name>shirtshirts0</d:Name>
 </m:properties>
</content>
```

As you can see from the XML for the returned entity, every property of the product entity is returned by the Table service (`PartitionKey`, `RowKey`, `Timestamp`, `Description`, and `Name`).

If the Products table was held in SQL Server rather than the Table service, and the LINQ statement was executed against the database using LINQ2SQL or LINQ2Entities, the following SQL statement would be generated and executed on the SQL Server database:

```
SELECT PartitionKey, RowKey, Timestamp, Description, Name
FROM Products
WHERE PartitionKey = 'Shirts'
```

SHAPING THE QUERY

If you're using LINQ2SQL or LINQ2Entities with a SQL Server database, and you don't need to return the entire entity, you might choose to write a more efficient LINQ query that only requests and returns specific columns from the SQL Server Database. The following SQL statement requests just the `Name` and `Description` properties:

```
SELECT Name, Description
FROM Products
WHERE PartitionKey="Shirts"
```

The preceding SQL statement is less intensive to execute on the server (as there is less data being queried) and it will also use less network bandwidth due to the reduced dataset being returned to the application.

When you're using LINQ2SQL or LINQ2Entities, you can modify your less efficient LINQ statements, like this:

```
select entity
```

to generate the more efficient SQL statement:

```
select new
   {
      Name = newShirt.Name,
      Description = newShirt.Description
   };
```

This would modify the previous `select entity` LINQ statement so it looks like this:

```
var shirts = from shirt in shirtContext.Products
             where shirt.PartitionKey == "Shirts"
             select new
             {
                Name = newShirt.Name,
                Description = newShirt.Description
             };
```

Unfortunately, because the Table service doesn't support data shaping using the `SELECT` statement, you'd get a nasty exception if you attempted to run the preceding LINQ query. As a result, whenever you execute queries against the Table service, every property of the entity will always be returned as part of the query.

If you really do need to shape the returned data in your application, and you don't mind that the entire entity will be returned from the server, you can always shape it locally using the following code:

```
var shirts = from newShirt in
             (
                from shirt inshirtContext.Products
                where shirt.PartitionKey == "Shirts"
                select shirt
             ).ToList()
             select new
             {
                Name = newShirt.Name,
                Description = newShirt.Description
             };
```

The preceding code uses the same LINQ query as in section 12.5.2 to filter the data in the Table service, but this time it returns the entire entity. By calling the `ToList` method on the inner LINQ query, you can ensure that the server-side query will return all properties of the entity.

Finally, the result of the `ToList` method is fed into the outer LINQ2Object query, which performs in-memory shaping of the data, returning a new anonymous type containing the two properties that you want.

You should be aware that although this query returns the entities shaped as you specify, it won't improve server-side or bandwidth efficiency. If you have a very large entity with an infrequently used property that you don't need in a particular query, this unused property will still be returned by the Table service.

12.5.6 Paging data

By default, `SELECT` queries will only return 1,000 items in a single result set. Not only is this the default amount of data returned, but it's also the maximum amount of data returned.

If you wish to return a smaller amount of data, you can set this with the `Take` statement in LINQ, as follows:

```
(from shirt inshirtContext.Products
where shirt.PartitionKey == "Shirts"
select shirt).Take(100);
```

The preceding LINQ statement will return the first 100 items in the `Shirts` partition. The LINQ `Take` extension method will be resolved to the following query string parameter in the URI for the REST API call:

```
&top=100
```

If more items could be returned by the query than are present in the result set, continuation tokens will be provided to allow you to retrieve the next set of data in the query. This method of using continuation tokens effectively provides a method of paging.

If you wanted to return all items in the `Shirts` partition of the Products table, but it potentially contains more than 1,000 items, you could run the following REST API query:

```
http://silverlightukstorage.table.core.windows.net/Products?$filter
➥ =PartitionKey%20eq %20'Shirts'
```

Because more than 1,000 items would normally be returned in the query, you'll receive the following continuation tokens in the response:

```
x-ms-continuation-NextPartitionKey: Shirts
x-ms-continuation-NextRowKey: 1001
```

If you wanted to return all the items in the `Shirts` partition that were not returned as part of the original query, you could retrieve the next set of data using the following query:

```
http://silverlightukstorage.table.core.windows.net/Products?$filter
➥ =PartitionKey%20eq %20'Shirts'&NextPartitionKey=Shirts&NextRowKey=1001
```

The preceding query would return all products in the `Shirts` partition from `RowKey` 1001 onwards, or at least the next 1,000 entities.

12.6 Summary

In this chapter, we've taken quite a deep dive into using both the StorageClient library and the Table service REST API.

You've learned how to use the REST API to modify tables in a storage account, and to perform CRUD functions against those tables. We also looked at the AtomPub format and at how this impacts your applications. Finally, we looked at how you can efficiently update and query data.

By gaining an understanding of the REST API, you can maximize the performance of your applications and understand the limits of the service.

Based on the last two chapters, you should now have a pretty good idea of how to use the Table service. Later on in the book, we'll look at how you can apply this knowledge in your applications.

For now, we'll continue with our focus on structured data and look at SQL Azure, the relational database in the cloud.

13 SQL Azure and relational data

This chapter covers

- Leveraging the power of SQL Server for cloud applications
- Easy ways of migrating an on-premises database to the cloud
- Avoiding potholes during migrations

Most applications that work with data today use a relational data model. It's a model we're all familiar with, and we know how to manage and develop with it. SQL Server has been with us for many years, and it's going to be with us as we move into the cloud.

Over the years, SQL Server has matured to meet the different needs of its customers. It started as a spunky departmental server and moved into the desktop space, mobile device space, and the enterprise space. The relational data engine has been the first component to make each of these moves. The rest of the components usually follow shortly after, such as Integration Services (SSIS), Reporting Services (SSRS), and Analysis Services (SSAS). The cloud isn't any different. The SQL

Server team is bringing the data engine to the cloud first, and the rest of the components of the system will follow it quickly.

13.1 The march of SQL Server to the cloud

When Azure was first released as a CTP in November of 2008 at the PDC, SQL Azure wasn't on stage. There was something like SQL involved, but it wasn't a relational engine. It was more like the Azure Table service, but geared for true enterprise needs (beyond the massive scale Tables gives you).

Developers were scared and confused. If they were going to move to the cloud, they surely needed a data platform they were comfortable with—something that made it easy for them to migrate their applications without having to rewrite the data tier. Microsoft heard this feedback, tabled what they had (pun unfortunately intended), and delivered what we now call SQL Azure.

Developers wanted something like SQL in the cloud because they needed a data platform they could easily migrate to from on-premises databases. SQL Azure not only gives you the relational database you're used to, but also supports all of the common tools and APIs you're used to working with, such as ADO.NET and TDS.

You can easily port a traditional database from SQL Server to SQL Azure in a matter of days, if not hours. There are some restrictions, and we'll cover those, but for the most part it's easy and straightforward.

Future versions of SQL Azure are sure to contain the other components of SQL Server. Many customers we speak with want to keep their applications local but move all of their business intelligence applications and their heavy computing needs to the cloud. This is a scenario we have no doubt will be supported at some future date.

13.2 Setting up SQL Azure

The first step in creating a database in SQL Azure is to log into your Azure portal and select the SQL Azure tab on the left.

If you haven't created a SQL Azure server yet, you'll be prompted to create a SQL Azure management account, which is like the SA account for a normal SQL Server installation. You'll need to provide a username and password, and to specify in which data center region you'd like the server to be provisioned. You'll most likely want it in the same region that your Azure applications are running in. The steps are pretty easy, as seen in figure 13.1.

Once your account is created, your server will be provisioned and you'll be given the server name. This screen is where you're able to manage your databases and your SQL Azure firewall settings. In figure 13.2, the server name is mlwwmqca6u. Sometimes you'll need the fully qualified server name, which in this case is mlwwmqca6u.database.windows.net.

Once you have a SQL Azure server provisioned, you'll be able to create a database in that server.

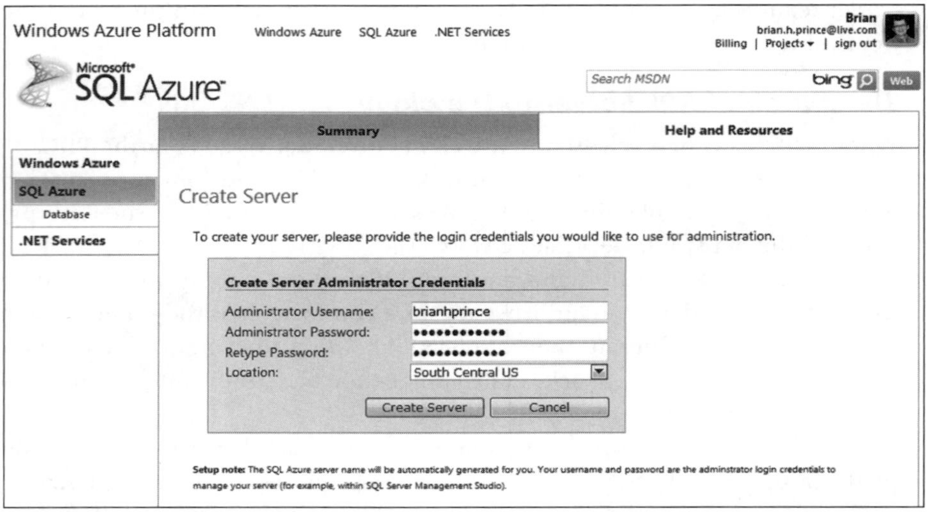

Figure 13.1 Creating a server administrator account for SQL Azure is easy. This is essentially an SA account in the cloud. You can't leave your password blank.

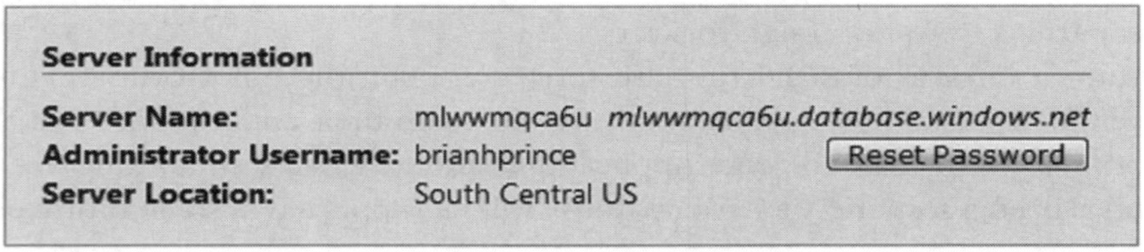

Figure 13.2 Your SQL Azure server name. It's short and easy to remember. I know I can turn this one into a backronym somehow.

An on-premises SQL Server setup has a lot of infrastructure concerns that go along with it: how much RAM it has, what the file group configuration is, what resources are assigned to which instance, what the appropriate resource governing levels should be, and so on. You have none of these concerns with a SQL Azure server, which is just a logical grouping of the databases you've created and doesn't represent a pool of resources at all. The only resource shared by a SQL Azure server is the firewall configuration. Your SQL Server in the cloud isn't really a server, but a collection of settings. It mimics a server when you connect to it, but your databases are actually spread across a farm of commodity hardware running SQL Server.

13.2.1 Creating your database

When you set up a SQL Azure account, you'll be given your own master database, which is listed in the Databases tab shown in figure 13.3. You'll need to use the Create Database button at the bottom of the list to start creating your own databases through the portal.

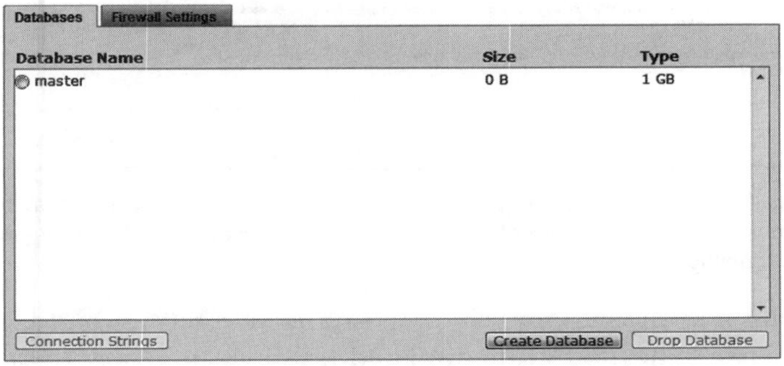

Figure 13.3 Your list of databases and the buttons to manage them. You haven't created any yet, but you were given your own master database. You aren't charged for the master database.

You can also create a database manually by connecting to the master database with the SQLCMD command prompt application and executing a `CREATE DATABASE` command. A sample is shown in figure 13.4. You can provide a `MAXSIZE` parameter to select either the 1 or 10 GB size. If you don't select a size, a 1 GB database will be created. As of the writing of this book, a 50 GB database has been announced, but not yet released.

NOTE You won't be able to connect with SQLCMD, or anything else, until you configure the SQL firewall. We'll cover this in a little bit.

13.2.2 Connecting to your database

Once you click the Create Database button, you'll be prompted to provide a database name and choose the size limit for the database. Your options for a size limit are currently 1 GB and 10 GB. The reasons for these sizes will be discussed later in this chapter.

For this example, we created a database called AzureInAction, with a size of 1 GB. Once you have created your database, you can retrieve the connection string to that

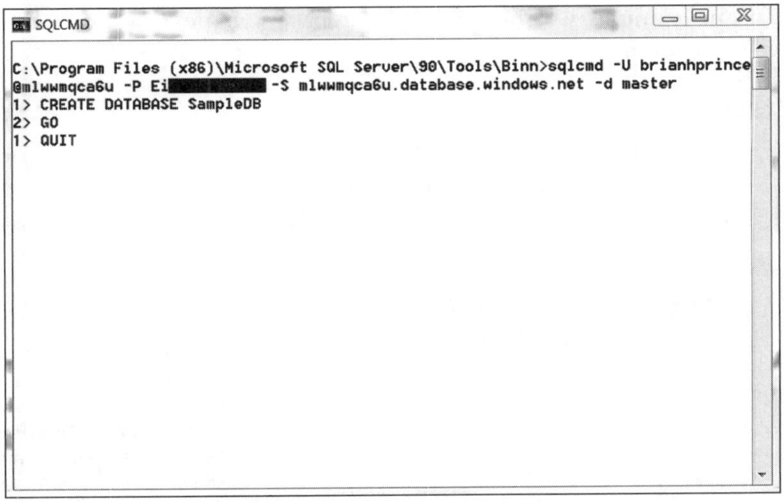

Figure 13.4 Adding a new database to SQL Azure with the SQLCMD tool, just like in the old days. You have to have the firewall configured before you do this.

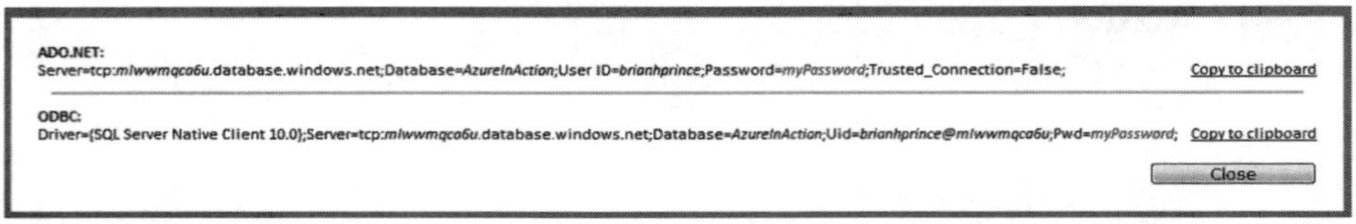

Figure 13.5 SQL Azure connection strings are displayed in the Azure portal, making it easy to know what you need to use in your code. Sometimes changing the connection string is all you need to do to move your application's data to the cloud.

database by selecting it in the list and using the Connection Strings button near the bottom of the list. The connection string displayed (as shown in figure 13.5) will contain the full address of the server, your username, and a place for your password.

You'll eventually create additional SQL user accounts in your database. You should create a special account for each user or application using the database, and not let them use the SA account. The SA account should only be used by you for management purposes.

Notice the brianhprince@mlwwmqca6u username in the ODBC connection string. Some tools will require this form of a username because of how they implement the TDS protocol, which is what underlies all connections to SQL Server.

One last thing you need to do to start using your database is to allow Azure-based applications to connect to the database. This is done on the Firewall Settings tab of the main administration screen. You'll need to check the Allow Microsoft Services Access to This Server check box, as shown in figure 13.6. This will create a default rule allowing Azure-based applications the right to connect to your server. The firewall will be discussed in more detail later in this chapter.

When you've completed these few steps, you'll have created a server, created a database on that server, and retrieved the connection strings you'll need to start using the server. In our example, we chose a 1 GB database; our next step is to discuss why we only have two options.

13.3 Size matters

There are two basic size limits you can choose from in SQL Azure: 1 GB and 10 GB. These are the maximum sizes that databases can be, and these sizes are the basis for how Microsoft will bill you for usage. The 1 GB database (the Web Edition) is charged

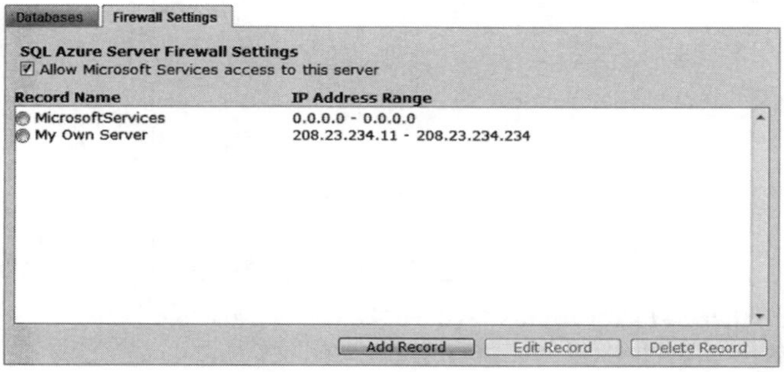

Figure 13.6 Enabling the SQL firewall to allow Azure application traffic to connect to your database. Only IP addresses listed on this screen are allowed to connect to your databases. The check box at the top allows for all Azure services under your account to connect.

at \$9.99 per month, and the 10 GB (called the Business Edition) is charged at \$99.99 per month. The charges are fixed and don't take into account the real size of the database, just the potential maximum size it can have. The size of your master database, logs, and indexes don't count toward the total size of the database when it comes to the size limits and charges.

You'll also be charged for any bandwidth used by your SQL Azure server that crosses a data center boundary. For example, if you have a mobile application accessing the SQL Azure database, bandwidth used by SQL Azure to those clients will be metered and billed for. If your Azure application is using the database, and they both reside in the same data center (aka geographic region), the bandwidth used won't be billed for because you aren't crossing a data center boundary.

The size of a database is fixed when it's created. If a 1 GB database grows too large, it will stop inserting new data. Databases won't automatically upgrade to a larger size. If you need a larger size, you'll need to use an `ALTER DATABASE` command and modify the `MAXSIZE` property.

The biggest reason for this limited size selection is the SLA that Microsoft provides to its customers. SQL Azure runs on a scalable and robust platform, with your data being replicated to different physical servers and disks in real time. The 1 GB and 10 GB sizes are the only sizes they feel they can currently support with the SLA defined as "Monthly Availability" of 99.9 percent. At this time, they couldn't guarantee a high SLA like this with a massive database. How quickly could you restore full function to a 32 TB database after a cataclysmic failure?

You should select the smallest size necessary to run your application. Currently there aren't any differences between the options, except for the size limit. In the future, the higher-end options will include extra features, such as autopartitioning, CLR support, and fanouts.

If your database is larger than 10 GB, you aren't out of luck. You do have a couple of options that are common in the SQL world when a database starts to overwhelm the hardware it's running on: partitioning and sharding. In this case, we'll use these strategies to work around the size limits that SQL Azure presents us.

13.3.1 Partitioning your data

The first option you have in dealing with a database that's too large for SQL Azure is to partition your data.

Imagine a normal application database schema. There are lots of tables, but all tables can be grouped into families. In our fictional DayOldSushiOnline.com website, we might have one set of tables that focus on customer data, a second set focusing on orders and order history, and a third set for product data and pricing, as shown in figure 13.7.

Data partitioning is the strategy of dividing up your database in a vertical manner, breaking your schema along family lines. In our example, this would create three databases with the names DOSO_customers, DOSO_orders, and DOSO_products (see

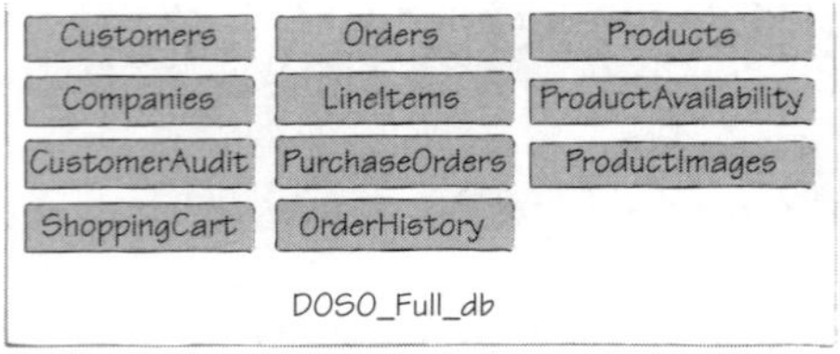

Figure 13.7 A sample application database schema for DayOldSushiOnline.com. The tables naturally fall into three families: customer data, orders and order history, and product data and pricing.

figure 13.8). This does tend to break relationships and queries across these families, requiring a significant amount of rework in your application code related to data handling, as well as in revising the stored procedures and queries in your database.

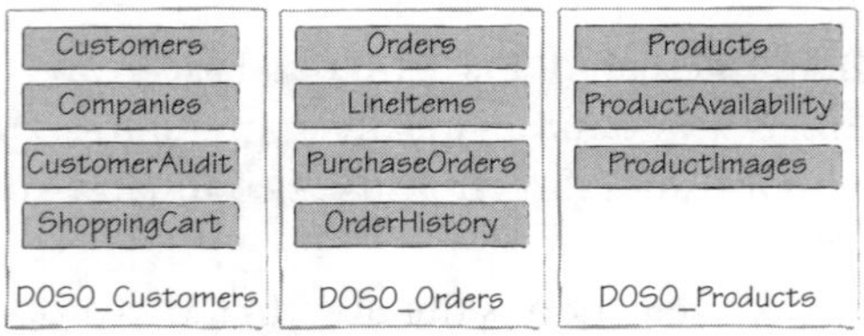

Figure 13.8 Our schema partitioned into families of tables

This strategy will create three smaller databases, each hopefully fitting into the 10 GB limit of SQL Azure. This is commonly done with on-premises databases because it allows the infrastructure team that supports the SQL Servers to tune each database, and its storage system, to the needs of that database. In our example, the products database is going to receive a lot of read traffic, with little write traffic. On the other hand, the orders database is likely to get a mixture of both, with more emphasis on write-related performance. This is a great approach for keeping the load on one part of the database from negatively impacting another part of the database.

This strategy can lead to more complex backup and restore operations, because you'll need to guarantee transactional consistency across the different databases. That isn't much of a challenge when everything is in the same database.

13.3.2 Sharding your data for easier scale

Partitioning your data is fine, but it can become troublesome once your system reaches the true scale only the internet can provide. You might be able to break a family of tables down once more, but you're eventually backed into a corner and have to resort to expensive hardware tricks to continue to scale. This also continues to make your data-access code more and more complex.

Another option is to shard your data. Partitioning involves breaking your schema along vertical lines, whereas sharding is breaking your data along horizontal lines. You can see in figure 13.9 how this might look for the DayOldSushiOnline.com database. Notice we used the word *schema* with the partitioning strategy, and the word *data* with the sharding strategy.

When you shard a database, you create several databases with each new shard having the exact same schema as the original. Then you break the data into chunks, and place each chunk into its own shard. The strategy you use to define the boundaries of your chunks will vary based on the business and growth natures of your system. A simple strategy to start with, but one that will need rebalancing shortly, is to break the

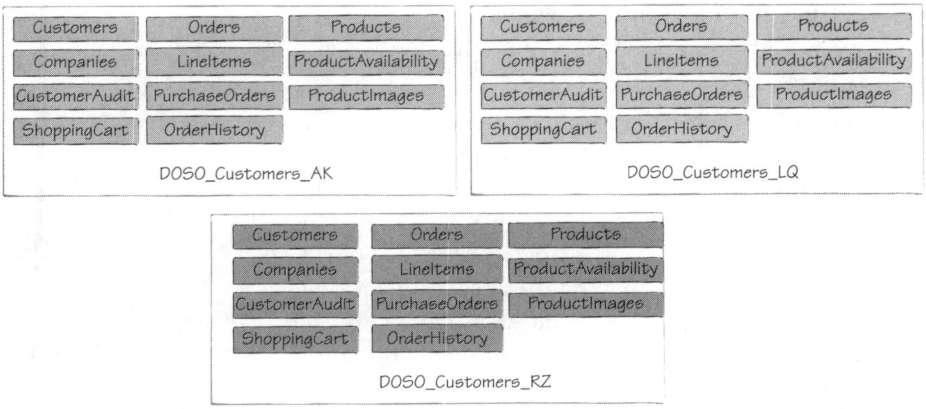

Figure 13.9 What the DayOldSushiOnline.com databases look like after they have been sharded. The result is three identical databases, each with a horizontal slice of the customer data.

chunks on the customer name field, as in figure 13.9. Each shard has its own copy of common or static data—in this case, the product data. This helps performance by providing local replicas of commonly needed data. This data could be partitioned out, but this would result in more complexity in your infrastructure.

In our example, the first shard will have all of the data that's related to any customer with a last name starting with A to K. The other two shards will cover the ranges L to Q, and R to Z. As new customer records are created, they're routed to the appropriate database. This approach can keep your data-layer code fairly straightforward, as all of the code is identical regardless of which database the customer is located in. The only code that needs to be added is some logic to look up which database connection string should be used for that customer. This can easily be isolated in your data-access layer, and the connection strings can be managed through the configuration system.

As we mentioned previously, your shards can become out of balance when you use this simple strategy. Some shards may become significantly larger than others, and this leads to a disproportionate use of the resources on each server. There are better strategies for how you might shard your data. One approach is to mix all of the customers up, and assign each new customer to the latest, smallest database. This, in effect, shards the database based on when the customer account was created, and not by customer name. This makes it easy to create new shards in the future, as the size of each database reaches its effective limit. When the last shard reaches capacity, you dynamically create a new shard, enroll it in the configuration system, and start adding new customers to it.

13.4 How SQL Azure works

Although we say that a SQL Azure database is just SQL Server database in the sky, that's not entirely accurate. Yes, SQL Server and Windows Server are involved, but not like you might think. When you connect to SQL Azure server, and your database, you aren't connecting to a physical SQL Server. You're connecting to a simulation of a server. We'd use the term *virtual*, but it has nothing to do with Hyper-V or application virtualization.

13.4.1 SQL Azure from a logical viewpoint

The endpoint that you connect to with your connection string is a service that's running in the cloud, and it mimics SQL Server, allowing for all of the TDS and other protocols and behavior you would expect to see when connecting to SQL Server.

This "virtual" server then uses intelligence to route your commands and requests to the backend infrastructure that's really running SQL Server. This intermediate virtual layer is how the routing works, and how replication and redundancy are provided, without exposing any of that complexity to the administrator or developer. It's this encapsulation that provides much of the benefit of the Azure platform as a whole, and SQL Azure is no different. The logical architecture of how applications and tools connect with SQL Azure is shown in figure 13.10.

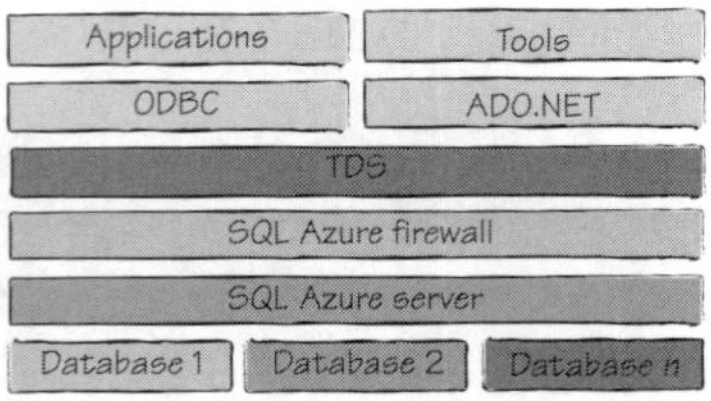

Figure 13.10 The logical shape of SQL Azure, and how your code will see it. The SQL Azure server is really just a service that emulates a real SQL Server. Each of your databases are spread across a farm of SQL Servers.

As a rule of thumb, any command or operation that affects the physical infrastructure isn't allowed. The encapsulation layer removes the concern of the physical infrastructure. When creating a database, you can't set where the files will be, or what they will be called, because you don't know any of those details. The services layer manages these details behind the scenes.

13.4.2 SQL Azure from a physical viewpoint

The data files that represent your database are stored on the infrastructure as a series of replicas. The SQL Azure fabric controls how many replicas are needed, and creates them when there aren't enough available.

There's always one replica that's elected the leader. This is the replica that will receive all of the connections and execute the work. The SQL Azure fabric then makes sure any changes to the data are distributed to the other replicas using a custom replication fabric. If a replica fails for any reason, it's taken out of the pool, a new leader is elected, and a new replica is created on the spot. The physical architecture, relating the different parts of SQL Azure together, is shown in figure 13.11.

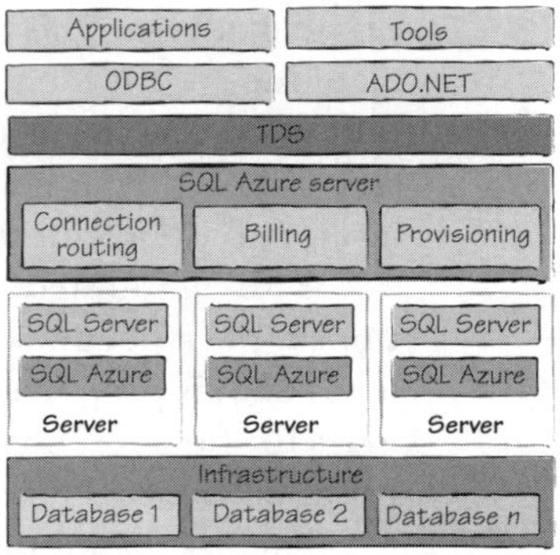

Figure 13.11 How SQL Azure works behind the scenes, encapsulating the physical infrastructure. Your data is replicated three times, and moved around on the SQL Azure fabric as needed to gain performance and reliability.

When a connection is made, the routing engine looks up where the current replica leader is located and routes the request to the correct server. Because all connections come through the router, the lead replica can change and the requests will be rerouted as needed. The fabric can also move a replica from one server to another for performance reasons, keeping the load smooth and even across the farm of servers that run SQL Azure.

What's really happening behind this encapsulation is quite exciting. The infrastructure layer contains the physical disks and networks needed to redundantly and reliably store the bits that are part of your database. This is similar to the common storage area network (SAN) that many database server infrastructures use. The redundancy of the disks and the tight coupling of the networks provide both performance and reliability for your data.

Sitting on top of this infrastructure layer is a series of servers. Each server runs a set of management services, SQL Server itself, and the SQL Azure fabric. The SQL Azure fabric is the component that communicates with the other servers in this layer to help them communicate with one another. The fabric provides the replication, load balancing, and failover features for the platform.

On top of the servers is a series of services that manages the connection routing (including the firewall features), billing, and provisioning. This services layer is the layer that you connect with and the layer that hides all of the magic.

Deep down under all of these covers, SQL Server really is running. Microsoft has added these layers to provide an automated and redundant platform that's easily managed and reliable.

13.5 Managing your database

SQL Azure is heavily automated, and it protects you from the concerns of the physical infrastructure. This frees you up to focus completely on managing your database. There are several aspects to managing a database, and many of them remain the same when the database is in the cloud.

If you ever have a script that needs to know what version of SQL it's running in, you can check the `Edition` and `Engine Edition` values of the server. When running in SQL Azure, you'll receive `SQL Azure` and `5` respectively. This is the query you would execute:

```
SELECT SERVERPROPERTY ('edition'), SERVERPROPERTY ('engineedition')
```

Usually, the first task you have after creating a database is moving your data up into the cloud.

13.5.1 Moving your data

Just because your database is in the cloud and you don't have to manage the disks doesn't mean you don't have to back up your data.

It's true that SQL Azure provides a robust and reliable platform for your data. It stores your data in multiple copies and load balances requests across those copies. In some cases, this might be enough to meet your disaster recovery needs.

But remember that, regardless of the vendor, there isn't any service in the cloud that protects you from stupid, there's no service that makes a bad application work correctly, and there's no platform that can fix bad decisions. What it can do is make them stupider, badder, and break faster, for less money. Don't be lulled into complacency by the scale and redundancy the cloud gives you. You still need to think of the risks to your system, and to your data, and plan for them. The redundancy protects you against the common types of catastrophic loss, related to failing disks and other common issues, but not all loss is catastrophic in nature. For example, this will not protect you if a dinosaur eats Chicago or if you hire that guy Bob. Bob might execute a poorly written update SQL script that renames all of your customers to Terrance. This means you still need to back up your data, to protect your data from yourself and your code.

All of this great redundancy and scale won't protect against the disaster of the data center getting hit by a falling satellite, a radioactive monster, or an oil-eating bacteria. In these cases, having your bits on several servers in the same data center won't help you—you'll need geographic diversity. Only you, and the business you support, can determine what level of disaster recovery you need, and how much you're willing to afford.

Disaster isn't your only risk. What if an upgrade goes awry, and you accidentally delete a customer's data in your system? Or if an automated job takes a left turn and wipes out the order history for the past month? SQL Azure protects you against faults in the platform, but it doesn't protect you against faults in your own code or policies.

Even if you don't need to back up your data, you'll likely need to move data at some point. You'll run into this when you're migrating an existing on-premises database to the cloud, or when you want to move the data from SQL Azure to another location.

Right now there are only three ways to work with SQL Azure data. The first option is to use a developer's API to access the data and save it in some format that you can back up and restore from. There are a lot of options in this case; you could use ADO.NET, ODBC, or WCF Data Services, but this would be tedious and breaks our rule of not writing any plumbing code. We don't want to have to write our own backup tool.

The second option is to use the Bulk Copy Program (BCP), which is used quite often to move large amounts of data into and out of a SQL Server database. It's one of your best bets. When using BCP, it's common for the DBA to disable indexing until the import is completed, to speed up the transfer process. Once the data is loaded, the indexes are enabled and updated based on the new data.

To extract the data from your local SQL Server, you'll need to run BCP from a command prompt. The command is quite simple:

```
bcp databasename.schema.tablename out filename.dat -S servername
➥ -U username -P password -n -q
```

The `bcp` command is straightforward. When exporting data with BCP, you need to use the `out` keyword. Provide the fully qualified table name, the name of the file to write the data to, the server name, and your username and password. The parameters tell BCP to keep the SQL data types native (don't convert them), and to use quoted identities in the connection string. Depending on the size of your table, the copy might take a few minutes. Once it's done, you can open the data file and see what it looks like. When you're done poking around, you can use BCP in the other direction to blast the data into your SQL Azure database. You'll use a similar BCP command to insert the data into your SQL Azure database.

BCP operates at a table level, so you'll need to run it several times, once for each table. A common trick is to write a script that will export all of the tables, one at a time, so you don't have to do it manually. This also helps with automating the procedure, reducing the risk of mistakes, and making it easy to reproduce the process at any time.

Your last option for working with data you have stored, or want to store in SQL Azure, is SQL Server Integration Services (SSIS). SSIS is SQL Server's platform for extracting, transforming, and loading data. It's a common tool used to move data in and out of on-premises SQL servers, and it can connect to almost any data source you need it to. You can also migrate your existing SQL Server 2008 packages to SQL Azure (Azure can't run packages from SQL Server 2005). If you're going to connect with SQL Server Management Studio (SSMS), you'll need to use SSMS 2008 R2 or later; the earlier versions don't support SQL Azure. You can trick them into doing it, but that's material for a shady blog post, and not for a high-profile, self-respecting book.

Regardless of the tool you use to connect to your database, your connection will have to make it past the SQL Azure firewall.

13.5.2 Controlling access to your data with the firewall

Before an incoming connection will be routed to the current leader server for your replicas, the source IP address is checked against a list of allowed sources. If the source address isn't in this list, the connection is denied.

The list of approved sources is a true whitelist, meaning that the IP address must be on the list to be allowed in. There are no other rules supported, just the list of allowed addresses. The list is stored in the master database for your SQL Azure database server.

The most common way to adjust the firewall settings is the one shown earlier in this chapter, namely, by using the SQL Azure portal and making the changes through the admin pages. You can also add entries directly into the master database by using the stored procedures provided. The rules are stored in a table called firewall_rules (shown in figure 13.12), and you can query it like a normal table. Because the table is in the master database, the connection to the database performing the query must be under the system administrator account you set up.

To manage your firewall rules through code, you can create a connection to the master database with your administrator account and use the provided stored procedures: `sp_set_firewall_rule` will create a firewall rule, and `sp_delete_firewall_rule` will remove a rule. When creating a rule, you'll need to provide a unique name, and the two

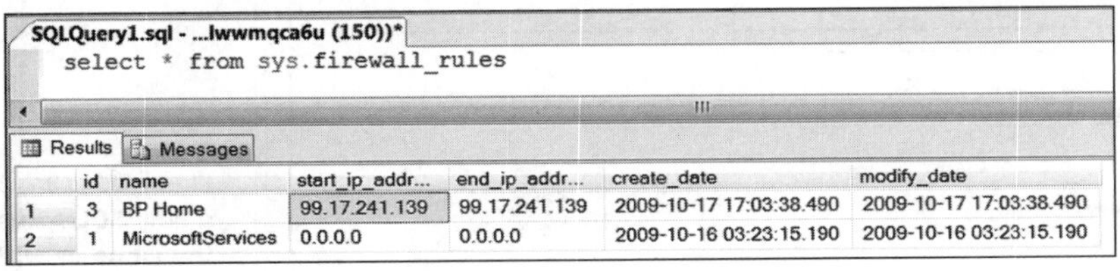

Figure 13.12 You can see what firewall rules are being enforced with `select * from sys.firewall_rules.`

IP addresses that form the range of addresses allowed. These addresses can be the same if you want to grant access to a single IP address. When deleting a rule, you only need to provide the name of the rule to be removed.

Even applications running in Windows Azure can't connect to your server until you grant them permission to connect. Because application servers in Azure use virtual IP addresses, and the roles could shut down and restart anywhere, causing their addresses to change, there's a special rule you can use in the firewall. If you create a rule with 0.0.0.0 as the starting and ending addresses, any Azure application will be able to connect to your server. That connection must still provide a valid username and password.

A common problem is making a change to the firewall and then immediately trying to access the server from that IP address, which then fails. The cache that's used to speed up firewall-rule checks refreshes every 5 minutes. If you make a rule change, it's worth waiting up to 5 minutes before trying to see if the change works.

The second line of defense is the use of SQL credentials to verify that people are allowed to connect to your database.

13.5.3 Creating user accounts

Managing user accounts in SQL Azure works much the same way as in on-premises SQL Servers. A few small differences can be found, mostly with the names of specific roles, but in general it's the same.

Your first step in granting someone access to a database is to create a login for the server itself. You need to connect to the master database in your server using an account with the `loginmanager` role. This would normally be the administrator account you created when you created your server, but any other account with that role will work.

Once connected, you can list the existing logins by executing the `sys.sql_logins` view. To create a login, use the same command you're used to, as shown in figure 13.13:

```
CREATE LOGIN theloginname WITH password='strongpasswordhere';
```

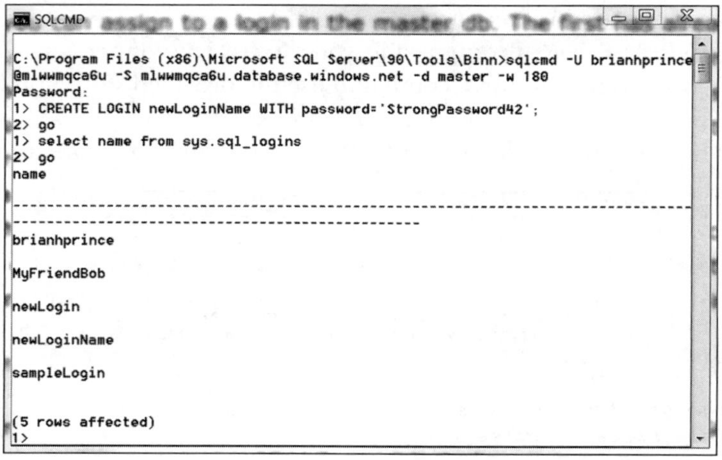

Figure 13.13 Creating a new SQL Azure login the same as with SQL Server on-premises, using the `CREATE LOGIN` command.

There are two roles that you can assign to a login in the master database. The first has already been mentioned, the `loginmanager` role. This role allows the user to manage user accounts and logins on the server. The second is the `dbmanager` role. Granting this role to a user account gives it all the possible permissions it could have, making it equivalent to the administrative account you first created.

Once you've created a server login, you can create a user account in a specific database based on that login. This is the same approach as in on-premises SQL Server installations. Although you can easily do this in SSMS, many DBAs like to do this with SQL commands. You would execute the following command while connected to the database you want to create the user account in:

```
CREATE USER newusername FROM LOGIN theloginname;
```

Once the user is created in the database, you can grant and revoke privileges as you would in a normal SQL database, either with the admin tools, or with the `GRANT` and `REVOKE` commands. SQL Azure only supports SQL users; Windows-based authentication isn't supported by SQL Azure.

Many people ask us when they should use SQL Azure and when they should use the Azure Table service. This is a complex question, and one we've dedicated the whole next section to.

13.6 Migrating an application to SQL Azure

One of the goals Microsoft had in delivering SQL Azure was to make it as easy as possible to migrate an existing application and its database to their Azure platform. Before SQL Azure was released, people were worried they would have to re-architect their systems in order for them to run in the cloud.

There are two basic ways to migrate your on-premises SQL Server data to the cloud. The first is to extract it, and copy it up. This is the same way you might move it from server A to server B in your own data center. The second way is to use an open source tool, SQL Azure Migration Wizard, that was created to help ease the migration process.

13.6.1 Migrating the traditional way

The easiest way to migrate a database to SQL Azure, and one that we have used ourselves, is to find a DBA who already knows how to do it and buy them lunch. Barring that, there are a few steps you can go through, following a traditional approach.

The first step is to make sure that you've created your SQL Azure server and know the administrative username and password. Once that's done, you can create the database that will house your schema and data. Your goal is to script out the existing database, including both schema and data, and then run that script against your cloud server database to recreate it all.

For this example, you'll use SQL Server Management Studio to script out your source database. Navigate to the database in SSMS, and right-click on it. Select Generate Scripts from the Tasks menu, and then walk through the wizard like normal. Make sure that you select the option to script all objects in the database. Then, on the options screen, make your selections according to this list:

- Convert UDDTs to Base Types—True
- Script Extended Properties—False
- Script Logins—False
- Script USE DATABASE—False
- Script Data—True

Finish the wizard. When you're done, the entire script will be loaded in a window.

You now need to remove some parts of the script to make sure it'll work in the cloud:

- Delete any occurrence of `SET ANSI_NULLS ON`.
- Delete any occurrence of `WITH (PAD_INDEX = OFF, STATISTICS_NORECOMPUTE = OFF, IGNORE_DUP_KEY = OFF, ALLOW_ROW_LOCKS = ON, ALLOW_PAGE_LOCKS = ON) ON [PRIMARY]` in a `CREATE TABLE` command.
- Delete any occurrence of `ON [PRIMARY]` in a `CREATE TABLE` command.

Once you've made these changes to the script, you may connect to the destination database and execute the script. You can use SQLCMD for this, or SSMS.

This is a lot of work, and it can be tedious making sure you have modified the script to avoid anything SQL Azure might not support. Thankfully there is an open source tool that can help.

13.6.2 *Migrating with the wizard*

The previous section might have scared you away from ever trying to migrate data to SQL Azure. It wasn't meant to, but there are a lot of little details to be considered. Fortunately, there's an open source project hosted on CodePlex called SQL Azure Migration Wizard that can help you out with this process. The project URL is http://sqlazuremw.codeplex.com.

The wizard can be used in several different scenarios. It can handle moving or analyzing a database from a SQL Server to SQL Azure, from SQL Azure to a SQL Server, or from SQL Azure to SQL Azure. When you run the tool, you can analyze the database for compatibility, generate a compatible script, and migrate the data. You can see the options available to you in figure 13.14.

When you start the tool, you'll need to point it at the source database. You'll be given the options to select the objects in the database you want to analyze and migrate.

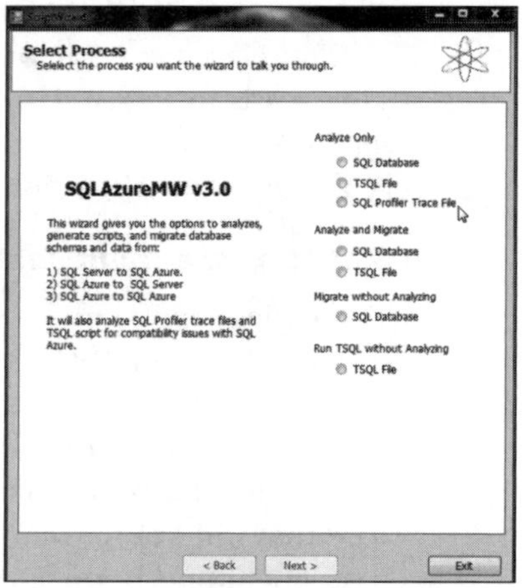

Figure 13.14 The SQL Azure Migration Wizard is a great tool when migrating or planning to migrate data from SQL Server to SQL Azure. It can help in modifying your database so it's compliant, and it also helps move the data.

The wizard is driven by a powerful rules engine with over 1,000 compatibility rules already programmed in. These rules are in an XML file, and it's easy to modify them to meet your needs. The rules detect a condition that isn't supported by SQL Azure, and specify how to fix it. This might be as simple as converting a data type to a type that's supported, or something more intense.

Once the analysis is done, you'll receive a report on the objects that need to be changed to become compatible with SQL Azure. You can stop here and use the report to make decisions, or you can keep going to migrate your data.

You'll need to provide a destination database connection string and credentials if you want the wizard's help in migrating your data. It'll connect to SQL Azure and execute the new script. It'll handle creating the tables and other objects, as well as migrating the data.

Migrating the data tends to be the most difficult part. If you're doing this by hand, even after you sort out the changes you need to make to your script, you still need to worry about timeouts in the connection and batching your data during the upload. You don't want all of your data thrown out because the connection was reset. The migration wizard handles all of this for you, so you don't have to worry about anything.

Because SQL Azure is running in the cloud, there are some limitations. Some of these are related to schemas, and some are related to functional capabilities.

13.7 Limitations of SQL Azure

Although SQL Azure is based on SQL Server, there are some differences and limitations that you'll need to be aware of. We've mentioned some of these in various places in this chapter, but we'll try to cover them all in this section.

The most common reason for any limitation is the services layer that sits on top of the real SQL Servers and simulates SQL Server to the consumer. This abstraction away from the physical implementation, or the routing engine itself, is usually the cause. For example, you can't use the `USE` command in any of your scripts. To get around this limitation, you'll need to make a separate connection for each different database you want to connect with. You should assume that each of your databases are on different servers.

Why you can't use `USE`

You can't use the `USE` command in SQL Azure because the routing layer is stateful, because the underlying TDS protocol is session-based. When you connect to a server, a session is created, which then executes your commands. When you connect in SQL Azure you still have this session, and the fabric routes your commands to the physical SQL Server that's hosting the lead replica for your database. If you call the `USE` command to connect to a different database, that database may not be on the same physical server as the database you're switching from. To avoid this problem, the `USE` command isn't allowed.

Any T-SQL command that refers to the physical infrastructure is also not supported. For example, some of the `CREATE DATABASE` options that can configure which `filegroup` will be used aren't supported, because as a SQL Azure user, you don't know where the files will be stored, or even how they will be named. Some commands are outright not supported, like `BACKUP`.

You can only connect to SQL Azure over port 1433. You can't reconfigure the servers to receive connections over any other port or port range.

You can use transactions with SQL Azure, but you can't use distributed transactions, which are transactions that enroll several different systems into one transaction update. SQL Azure doesn't support the network ports that are required to allow this to happen. Be aware that if you're using a .NET 2.0 TransactionScope, a normal transaction may be elevated to a distributed transaction in some cases. This will cause an error, and you won't know where it's coming from.

Each table in your database schema must have a clustered index. Heap tables (a fancy DBA term for a table without an index) aren't supported. If you import a table without a clustered index, you won't be able to insert records into that table until one has been created.

All commands and queries must execute within 5 to 30 minutes. Currently the system-wide timeout is 30 minutes. Any request taking longer than that will be cancelled, and an error code will be returned. This limit might change in the future, as Microsoft tunes the system to their customers' needs.

There are some limitations that are very niche in nature, and more commands are supported with each new release. Please read the appropriate MSDN documentation to get the most recent list of SQL Azure limitations.

13.8 Common SQL Azure scenarios

People are using SQL Azure in their applications in two general scenarios: *near data* and *far data*. These terms refer to how far away the code that's calling into SQL Server is from the data. If it's creating the connection over what might be a local network (or even closer with named pipes or shared memory), that's a near-data scenario. If the code opening the connection is anywhere else, that's a far-data scenario.

13.8.1 Far-data scenarios

The most common far-data scenario is when you're running your application, perhaps a web application, in an on-premises data center, but you're hosting the data in SQL Azure. You can see this relationship in figure 13.15. This is a good choice if you're slowly migrating to the cloud, or if you want to leverage the amazing high availability and scale SQL Azure has to offer without spending $250,000 yourself.

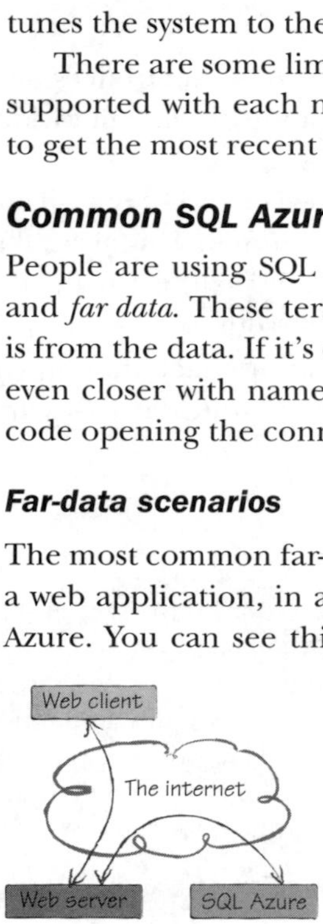

Figure 13.15 A web server using SQL Azure in a far-data scenario. The data is far away from the code that's using it. In this case, the web server is on-premises, and the data is in the cloud with SQL Server.

In a far-data scenario, the client doesn't have to be a web browser over the internet. It might be a desktop WPF application in the same building as the web server, or any other number of scenarios. The one real drawback to far data is the processing time and latency of not being right next to the data. In data-intensive applications this would be a critical flaw, whereas in other contexts it's no big deal.

Far data works well when the data in the far server doesn't need to be accessed in real time. Perhaps you're offloading your data to the cloud as long-term storage, and the real processing happens onsite. Or perhaps you're trying to place the data where it can easily be accessed by many different types of clients, including mobile public devices, web clients, desktop clients, and the like.

13.8.2 Near-data scenarios

A near-data scenario would be doing calculations on the SQL Server directly, or executing a report on the server directly. The code using the data runs close to the data. This is why the SQL team added the ability to run managed code (with CLR support) into the on-premises version of SQL Server. This feature isn't yet available in SQL Azure. Figure 13.16 shows what a near-data scenario looks like.

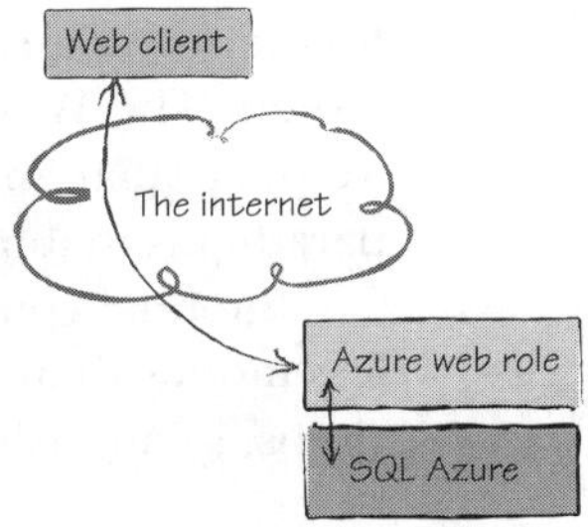

Figure 13.16 Hosting a data service in an Azure web role helps your application be in a near-data scenario. This improves the performance of the application when it comes to working with the data.

One way to convert a far-data application to a near-data one is to move the part of the application accessing the code as close to the data server as possible. With SQL Azure, this means creating a services tier and running that in a role in Azure. Your clients can still be web browsers, mobile devices, and PCs, but they will call into this data service to get the data. This data service will then call into SQL Server. This encapsulates the use of SQL Azure, and helps you provide an extra layer of logic and security in the mix.

13.8.3 SQL Azure versus Azure Tables

SQL Azure and the Azure Table service have some significant differences, which we've tried to cover in this chapter and the chapters on Azure Tables (chapters 11 and 12). These differences help make it a little easier to pick between SQL Azure and Azure Tables, and the deciding factor usually comes down to whether you already have a database to migrate or not.

If you do have a local database, and you want to keep using it, use SQL Azure. If moving it to the cloud would require you to refactor some of the schema to support partitioning or sharding, you might want to consider some options.

If size is the issue, that would be the first sign that you might want to consider Azure Tables. Just make sure the support Tables has for transactions and queries meets your needs. The size limit surely will be sufficient, at 100 TB.

If you're staying with SQL (versus migrating to Azure Tables) and are going to upgrade your database schema to be able to shard or partition, take a moment to think about also upgrading it to support multitenant scenarios. If you have several copies of your database, one for each customer that uses the system, now would be a good time to add the support needed to run those different customers on one database, but still in an isolated manner.

If you're building a new system that doesn't need sophisticated transactions, or a complex authorization model, then using Azure Tables is probably best. People tend to fall into two groups when they think of Tables. They're either from "ye olde country" and think of Tables as a simple data-storage facility that'll only be used for large lookup tables and flat data, or they're able to see the amazing power that a flexible schema model and distributed scale can give them. Looking at Tables without the old blinders on is challenging. We've been beaten over the head with relational databases for decades, and it's hard to consider something that deviates from that expected model. The Windows Azure platform does a good job of providing a platform that we're familiar and comfortable with, while at the same time giving us access to the new paradigms that make the cloud so compelling and powerful.

The final consideration is cost. You can store a lot of data in Azure Tables for a lot less money than you can in SQL Azure. SQL Azure gives you a lot more features to use (joins, relationships, and so on), but it does cost more.

13.9 Summary

SQL Azure is a powerful data platform that's familiar to us. It just happens to be running in the cloud. This makes it easier to move an application to the cloud, or to build something new, using paradigms and tools that we know and love.

We looked at how to create and manage a database in the cloud. The processes and approaches are eerily similar to what you would do when working with a local database, which makes it easy to adopt SQL Azure for your application. There are some limitations because of the "virtual" nature of the SQL Server, and because the database is running in a shared environment.

The sophisticated data engine that is SQL Azure isn't the last stop for SQL in the cloud—it's just the beginning. The tools will be upgraded for full support, and the rest of the SQL family will move into the cloud over time.

Although the firewall and other security features make it easier to trust putting your data in the cloud, you still need to think critically about whether it's the right place for your data, or whether a blended approach is best for your scenario.

Now that you've moved your data to the cloud, it's time to learn more about how best to query and use data in a cloud application. Chapter 14 will look at this from several different angles.

14 Working with different types of data

This chapter covers

- Working with static data
- Working with dynamic data
- Working with infrequently changing data

In previous chapters, we've shown you what you can do with the Table service, SQL Azure, and caching. In this chapter, we'll look at how you can choose when to use these three technologies. Rather than focusing specifically on the technologies, we'll look at the types of data you can store with each of the technologies and at how each technology will help you store different types of data.

We'll look at three types of data in particular: static data, dynamic data, and infrequently changing data. We'll also focus on where you can store the data and how you can efficiently retrieve it.

We'll start with static data.

14.1 Static reference data

Every application typically has some sort of frequently accessed static reference data. This data is usually very small and typically used for data normalization purposes. Let's return to the Hawaiian Shirt Shop website and look at an example.

For each shirt displayed in the Hawaiian Shirt Shop web page, you might wish the customer to be able to specify the following criteria about the shirt they want to buy:

- Shirt personage type (men, ladies, boys, girls)
- Shirt size type (small, medium, large, extra large)
- Shirt material (cotton, silk, wool)

As you can see, the data listed is fairly static, and it's applied across all shirts. All shirts will have a size and a material (admittedly not wool). This data can be considered static, because it's unlikely that it would ever be changed once it's defined. (Hawaiian shirts are unlikely to suddenly start being made in platinum.)

Figure 14.1 shows a page of the website where that data can be selected. The customer can browse shirts that are designed for men or ladies, and for a particular shirt they can choose the size or material (style).

As you can see from figure 14.1, the web page represents the static material (style) and size data with drop-down lists, whereas the personage type is represented as a hyperlink that will perform a search for different shirt types. For now we'll focus on the two drop-down lists (material and size).

The first question you're probably asking is, "Where and how do we represent this data?" Let's take a look at how this could be done using each of these technologies:

- SQL Azure
- Table service
- Cache

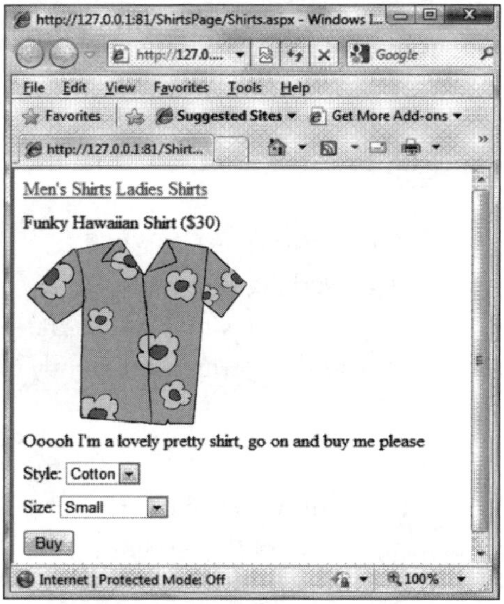

Figure 14.1 Product detail page of the Hawaiian Shirt Shop website

We'll start with SQL Azure, as this is probably the most familiar way of representing data.

14.1.1 Representing simple static data in SQL Azure

As you learned in chapter 13, SQL Azure is a relational database, so you would use a typical relational model to store the data. Figure 14.2 shows a database diagram for the Hawaiian Shirt Shop website in SQL Azure.

In figure 14.2 you can see that the data for each of the drop-down lists (size types and materials) is currently stored in their own tables. As of yet, we haven't defined any

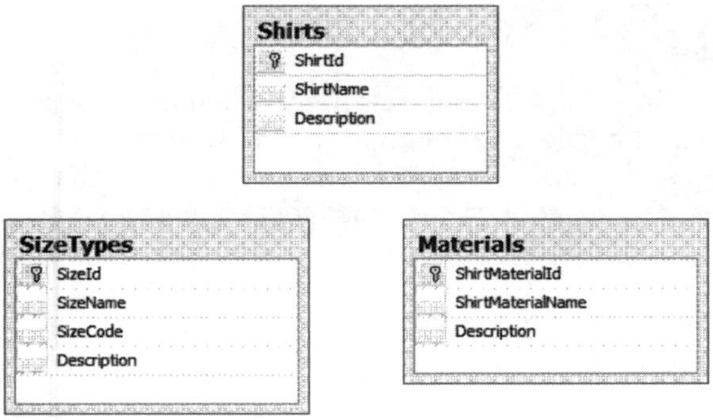

Figure 14.2 A database with Shirts, SizeTypes, and Materials tables in SQL Azure with no relationships defined

relationships between the static tables and the Shirts table (which is the most central table in the relationship).

Now let's take a look at how you would retrieve data from this database and populate the drop-down lists on the web page.

POPULATING DROP-DOWN LISTS

To populate the materials or size types drop-down list directly from a database, you can make a standard ADO.NET call to the database (either using ADO.NET directly or your favorite data-access layer technology, such as Linq2SQL, ADO.NET Entity Framework, or NHibernate).

The following code shows how you could bind the size drop-down list using ADO.NET directly:

```
DataSet ds = new DataSet();
using (SqlConnection conn =
   new SqlConnection(mySqlAzureDBConnectionString))
{
   conn.Open();

   using (SqlDataAdapter da =
      new SqlDataAdapter("SELECT SizeId, SizeName FROM SizeTypes",
          conn))
   {
      da.Fill(ds);
   }
}

sizeDropDown.DataSource = ds.Tables[0];
sizeDropDown.DataTextField= "SizeName";
sizeDropDown.DataValueField = "SizeId";
sizeDropDown.DataBind();
```

The preceding code shows that you can bind your drop-down lists to a table in SQL Azure just as easily as you can with a regular SQL Server database.

> **WARNING** The preceding code obviously isn't up to production standards. You shouldn't mix data-access code with presentation-layer code, but it does illustrate the point.

Cost issues with SQL Azure

SQL Azure uses a fixed-price model, and if your database is tied up servicing static data calls (which always return the same set of data), you may hit the limits of your database quickly and unnecessarily, requiring you to scale out to meet the demand. In this situation, caching the data is probably the most cost-effective approach.

As stated earlier, SQL Azure isn't the only method of storing static data. Let's look at how you could store this data using the Table service.

14.1.2 Representing simple static data in the Table service

Just as easily as each type of static data could be represented in a SQL Azure table, the data could also be represented as entities in a Table service table. The following C# class could represent the `SizeType` entity in the Table service.

```
public class SizeType : TableServiceEntity
{
   public string SizeCode { get; set; }
   public string Description { get; set; }
}
```

In this class, the `PartitionKey` for the `SizeType` entity isn't relevant due to the size of the table, so you could make all entities in the table have the same partition key. You could use the `SizeCode` property to represent the `RowKey`.

NOTE Because the Table service isn't a relational database and you don't need clustered indexes here, you have no need for the `SizeTypeId` surrogate key that's present in the SQL Azure implementation.

The following code represents the data service context class for the SizeTypes table.

```
public class SizeTypeContext : TableServiceContext
{
  private static CloudStorageAccount storageAccount =
  CloudStorageAccount.FromConfigurationSetting("DataConnectionString");

  public SizeTypeContext()
     : base(storageAccount.TableEndpoint.ToString(),
            storageAccount.Credentials)
   {

   }

  public DataServiceQuery<SizeType> SizeTypeTable
  {
     get
     {
        return CreateQuery<SizeType>("SizeTypeTable");
     }
  }
}
```

NOTE For a detailed explanation of the context class, refer to chapter 11.

To store a size in the SizeTypeTable table in the Table service, you could use the following code:

```
var sizeTypeContext = new SizeTypeContext();

var newSizeType = new SizeType
{
          PartitionKey = "SizeTypes",
          RowKey = "Small",
          SizeCode = "S",
          Description = "A shirt for smallish people"
};

sizeTypeContext.AddObject("SizeTypeTable", newSizeType);
sizeTypeContext.SaveChanges();
```

This code will store the “Small” size entity in the SizeTypeTable table. The method used to store the data in the table is explained in more detail in chapter 11, which discusses the Table service.

TIP In this particular example, the SizeTypeTable table will never grow beyond a few rows, so it’s not worth splitting the table across multiple servers. Because all the size data will always be returned together, you can store the data in a single partition called SizeTypes.

Once you have a fully populated SizeTypeTable table, you can bind it to the drop-down list using the following code:

```
var sizeTypeContext = new SizeTypeContext ();
sizeDropDown.DataSource = sizeTypeContext.SizeTypeTable;
sizeDropDown.DataTextField = "RowKey";
sizeDropDown.DataValueField = "SizeCode";
sizeDropDown.DataBind();
```

In this example, the drop-down list is populated directly from the Table service.

Cost issues with the Table service

Because you’re charged for each request that you make to the Table service, reducing the number of requests will reduce your monthly bill. In a website where you receive 1,000 page views of the Product Details page, this would translate to 4,000 Table service requests. Based on these figures, your hosting bill could get very costly very quickly if you follow this model. Caching the data is probably the most efficient thing to do in this situation.

We’ve already talked a little about the performance disadvantages of using SQL Azure or the Table service for accessing static data. Let’s look more closely at why you should avoid chatty applications in Windows Azure.

14.1.3 Performance disadvantages of a chatty interface

In the previous sections, we've discussed how you could store static data, such as shirt sizes and materials, in SQL Azure or the Table service. We'll now look at the call sequences you'd need to make to render the web page (shown previously in figure 14.1) and discuss the pros and cons of each approach.

SYNCHRONOUS CALLS

To retrieve all the data required to display the product details page shown in figure 14.1, you'd need to make at least four calls to the storage provider:

- Retrieve the product details
- Retrieve the list of size types
- Retrieve the list of materials
- Retrieve the list of personage types (men, ladies, and so on)

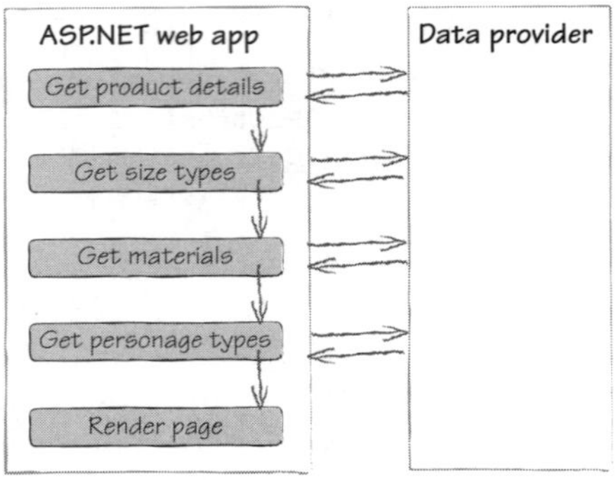

Figure 14.3 Synchronous call sequence; each result must be returned before you can make the next call

When developing an ASP.NET web page, you should consider making asynchronous calls to improve performance, but most developers will typically write synchronous calls to retrieve the data. Figure 14.3 shows the synchronous call sequence for the product details web page.

As you can see, the synchronous nature of the page means you have to wait until you receive data back from the data provider (SQL Azure or the Table service) before you can process the next section of the page. Due to the blocking nature of synchronous calls and the latency involved in cross-server communication, the rendering of this page will be much slower than it needs to be.

ASYNCHRONOUS CALLS

Because size types, materials, and personage types are sets of data that are both independent of each other and independent of the returned product details, you could use asynchronous calls instead. Retrieving the data from the Table service asynchronously means you don't have to wait for one set of data to be returned before retrieving the next set.

Figure 14.4 shows the same call sequence as in figure 14.3, but this time using asynchronous calls.

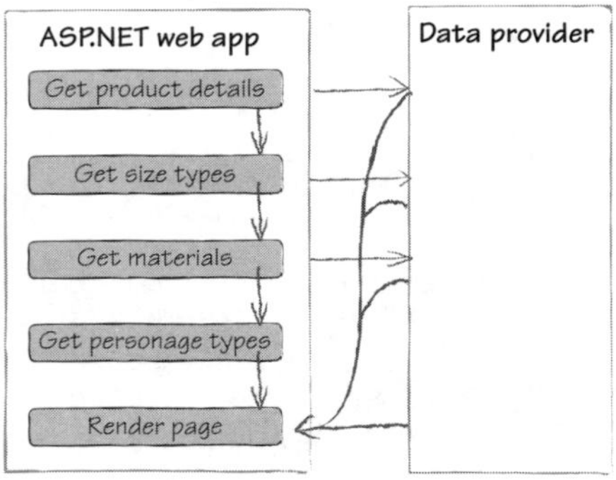

Figure 14.4 Asynchronous call sequence

As you can see in figure 14.4, you no longer have to wait for data to be returned before you process the next statement. Once all the data is returned, you can render the page.

TIP Here we've used static data calls as our example. You can, however, use asynchronous calls whenever you don't have any relationship between sets of data rendered on a page.

Now that you understand how you can store and retrieve static data, let's take a look at how you can improve performance (and reduce the hosting bill) by using cached data instead.

14.1.4 Caching static data

Regardless of your chosen storage platform (SQL Azure or the Table service), you should consider caching static data rather than continually retrieving the same data from a table. This will bring large performance and cost benefits.

Because static reference data hardly ever changes and is usually a pretty small set of data, the in-process memory cache (such as the default ASP.NET cache) is a suitable caching choice. You can always use a cache dependency to keep the cache and the underlying backing store synchronized. For more details on how to set up an in-process cache, refer to chapter 6.

Let's now take a look at how you can use the cache in the Hawaiian Shirt Shop website.

POPULATING THE CACHE

For frequently accessed static data, you should probably populate the web role cache when the application starts up. The following code, placed in the Global.asax file, will do this:

```
protected void Application_Start(object sender, EventArgs e)
{
   var sizeTypeContext = new SizeTypeContext();
   HttpRuntime.Cache["sizeTypes"] = sizeTypeContext.SizeTypeTable;
}
```

In this example we've populated the cache with data from the Table service, but the technique is the same for using SQL Azure. We're using a cache because we're working with static data, and we don't want to hit the data source too often. You might want to consider populating the caching when your role instance starts, instead of when the ASP.NET application starts.

POPULATING THE DROP-DOWN LISTS

Now that you have your data in the cache, let's take a look at how you can populate the drop-down lists with that data:

```
sizeDropDown.DataSource = (IEnumerable<SizeType>)Cache["sizeTypes" ];
sizeDropDown.DataTextField = "RowKey";
sizeDropDown.DataValueField = "SizeCode";
sizeDropDown.DataBind();
```

As you can see from this code, you no longer need to return to the data store to populate the drop-down list—you can use the cache directly.

Because the cache will be scavenged when memory is scarce, you can give static data higher priority than other cache items by using the cache priority mechanism (meaning that other items will be scavenged first):

```
var sizeTypeContext = new SizeTypeContext();
HttpContext.Current.Cache.Insert("sizeTypes",
➥ sizeTypeContext.SizeTypeTable, null, new DateTime(2019, 1, 1),
➥ Cache.NoSlidingExpiration, CacheItemPriority.High, null);
```

In the preceding code, the `SizeTypes` list will be stored in the cache with a `High` priority, and it will have an absolute expiration date of January 1, 2019. If the web role is restarted, the cache will be flushed, but if the process remains running, the data should remain in memory until that date.

If the static data might change in the future, you can set a cache dependency to keep the cache synchronized or manually restart the role when updating the data.

PROTECTING YOUR CODE FROM AN EMPTY CACHE

Because cache data is volatile, you might wish to prevent the cached data from being flushed by checking that the data is cached prior to populating the drop-down list:

```
private IEnumerable<SizeType> GetSizeTypes()
{
   if (Cache["sizeTypes"] == null)
   {
      var sizeTypeContext = new SizeTypeContext();
      Cache["sizeTypes"] = sizeTypeContext.SizeTypeTable;
   }

   return (IEnumberable<SizeType>)Cache["sizeTypes"];
}

sizeDropDown.DataSource = GetSizeTypes();
sizeDropDown.DataTextField = "RowKey";
sizeDropDown.DataValueField = "SizeCode";
sizeDropDown.DataBind();
```

In this code, before the drop-down list is populated, a check is run to make sure that the data is already stored in the cache. If the data isn't held in cache, it repopulates that cache item.

By effectively caching static data, you can both reduce your hosting bill and improve the performance of your application. By using an in-memory cache for static data on the product details page, you now have one data storage call per application start up rather than four.

Using in-memory cache for static data also means that your presentation layer no longer needs to consider where the underlying data is stored.

Please be aware that the examples in this section aren't production-level code and have been simplified to illustrate the concepts. If you're implementing such a solution, you should also take the following guidelines into consideration:

- Abstract your caching code into a separate caching layer
- Don't use magic strings (such as `Cache["sizeTypes"]`)—use constants instead
- Use cache dependencies

- Prioritize your cache properly
- Check that your cache is populated prior to returning data
- Handle exceptions effectively

14.2 Storing static reference data with dynamic data

In the previous section, we looked at how you could represent static data for the purposes of data retrieval. This is only one side of the picture, because typically you'll want to associate the static data with some dynamic data.

For example, people viewing the product details web page shown in figure 14.1 will hopefully purchase the shirt displayed. When they do, how should you store that data so that you can easily retrieve it?

Depending on the implementation of the web page, you can either allow the user to purchase the item directly or add the item to a shopping cart. In either case, the method of storing the data will be the same, so let's look at storing items in a shopping cart.

14.2.1 Representing the shopping cart in SQL Azure

You're probably familiar with relational databases, so we'll first look at how you can store shopping cart data in SQL Azure. (We'll look at using the Table service in section 14.2.3).

THE SHOPPING CART DATA MODEL

The shopping cart can be persisted across sessions, and if the user is a registered logged-in user, you can associate this account with their user ID. Figure 14.5 represents a typical data model for a shopping cart.

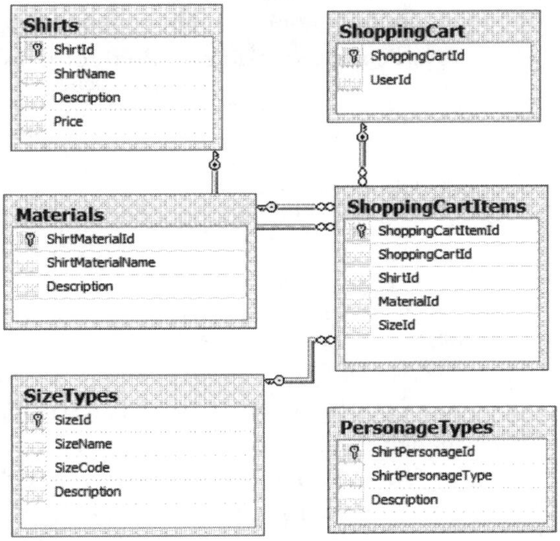

Figure 14.5 Data model for a shopping cart

In figure 14.5, the shopping cart is represented as two tables (ShoppingCart and ShoppingCartItems). The ShoppingCart table represents the shopping cart for each user, and each item in the shopping cart is stored in the ShoppingCartItems table. For each item in the cart, the ShirtId, MaterialId, and SizeId are stored, and the appropriate foreign-key relationships between tables are established.

If the website user is a registered user, the UserId would be stored in the ShoppingCart table; if the user is unregistered, you could use the session ID.

NOTE Although this data model represents a shopping cart, you could model an orders table using the same data structure.

RETRIEVING THE DATA

Because SQL Azure is a relational database, you could query across multiple tables by using JOIN clauses in your SQL statements, if required. For example, to return all items in the shopping cart for UserId 12345, including the shirt name, size, and material, you could issue the following SQL query:

```
SELECT sci.ShoppingCartItemId,
       s.ShirtName,
       s.Description,
       s.Price,
       sz.SizeId,
       sz.SizeName,
       m.MaterialId,
       m.MaterialName
FROM ShoppingCart sc
JOIN ShoppingCartItems sci ON sci.ShoppingCartId = sc.ShoppingCartId
JOIN Shirts s ON s.ShirtId = sci.ShirtId
JOIN SizeTypes sz ON sz.SizeId = sci.SizeId
JOIN Materials m ON m.MaterialId = sci.MaterialId
WHERE sc.UserId = '12345'
```

Because the shopping cart table will never hold a large amount of data, and the static data is held in an in-memory cache, there's no need to return the static data as part of your SQL query. You can, therefore, use the following query instead:

```
SELECT sci.ShoppingCartItemId,
       s.ShirtName,
       s.Description,
       s.Price,
       sci.SizeId,
       sci.MaterialId,
FROM ShoppingCart sc
JOIN ShoppingCartItems sci
   ON sci.ShoppingCartId = sc.ShoppingCartId
JOIN Shirts s ON s.ShirtId = sci.ShirtId
WHERE sc.UserId = '12345'
```

Not returning the static data (SizeTypes and Materials) both improves the performance and reduces the complexity of the query by reducing the number of joins.

Once the data is returned from the database, you can combine it with the in-memory cached data using LINQ to Objects.

> **NOTE** This strategy is perfectly acceptable when dealing with static reference data because the cached data tends to be very small. This would not be an acceptable strategy when dealing with millions of rows of data.

14.2.2 *Partitioning the SQL Azure shopping cart*

The data model in figure 14.5 looks like it's only usable for single-server databases, but this isn't strictly the case. That model will easily scale out, as we'll explain in a second.

One of the issues with using SQL Azure is that currently there's no built-in method of partitioning data across multiple servers. To avoid bottlenecking your application on a single database, you need to partition (or shard) your data across multiple servers in your application layer. In chapter 13, we spent a little time talking about sharding, but here we'll look at how to apply it in relation to the Hawaiian Shirt Shop.

SPLITTING THE DATA MODEL ACROSS MULTIPLE SERVERS

As we said, the data model in figure 14.5 will work across multiple servers—you just have to be a little smart about how you do this. Because the shopping cart tables have no dependencies on any other part of the application, you can separate those tables into their own separate database.

In the application layer, you could therefore separate the shopping cart's data-access layer methods and connection strings into their own layer. By keeping the functionality logically separated, you can split your application across multiple databases if required. In the Hawaiian Shirt Shop example, you could easily maintain separate databases for the shopping cart, orders, customers, products, and static data, if required.

> **All those databases—isn't that expensive?**
>
> The good news about this type of design is that you can still start with a single SQL Azure database when your application has a small number of users. As the traffic increases, you can then split the shopping cart tables into their own separate database when needed. To split out your databases, you could simply create a new SQL Azure database, migrate the shopping cart data across, and then change the connection string for the shopping cart's data layer.

PARTITIONING DATA FURTHER

In your web application, you might get to the point where the shopping cart database is bottlenecking and you need to partition the data further. This isn't as difficult as it sounds.

Because the shopping cart data is only used by a single user and you never query across multiple users, you can easily partition out the data by user. For example, you might have 100,000 registered users who maintain a shopping cart. If you currently have a single database and wish to split it into two or more databases, you could use a partitioning function in your application:

```
If (userId.ToString()[0] < 'N')
{
   // Use Connection String for Database 1
}
else
{
  // Use Connection String for Database 2
}
```

In the preceding example, if the first character of the `userId` begins with `N` or later, they would use the second shopping cart database; otherwise, they'd use the first database. You could break this down into further partitions if required.

As stated earlier, this type of partitioning can only be done in the application layer at present. It's planned that in future releases of SQL Azure there'll be some partitioning built-in on the server side.

Maintaining referential integrity

One of the issues with splitting data across multiple servers is keeping referential integrity.

In the shopping cart example, the data that the shopping cart is referencing is either static (size types, materials, or personage types) or infrequently changing (and administratively controlled), so referential integrity isn't such a big deal. You're ultimately controlling the data, so you can break foreign-key relationships and store the various tables on separate servers.

If you do need to maintain referential integrity, you could keep a copy of the static data on each instance of the database. Although there is data duplication, there's such a small amount of data that you can easily fix the problem by synchronizing the databases. In this case, you'd generally keep one master database allowing one-way synchronization.

In the shopping cart example, because there's no need to query across multiple tables (beyond the cache), you can safely break referential integrity.

Querying across partitions

Unfortunately there is no way of efficiently querying across multiple databases in the current implementation of SQL Azure, which is why you can only partition functionally independent data.

If you need to query across partitions when reporting (such as when reporting on all customer orders in the past week), you can always export data from your SQL Azure real-time database to a large reporting database (outside of Windows Azure) where you can make use of a full-blown version of SQL Server with BI capabilities.

In this example, we've looked at how you can use SQL Azure with Windows Azure when storing dynamic data with static data (and partitioning where necessary). We've purposely not looked at how this works with large sets of infrequently changing data because we'll look at this in section 14.3 of this chapter.

Let's transition over to how we would implement the same concept, but using the Azure Table service instead.

14.2.3 Representing the shopping cart's static data in the Table service

In the previous section, we looked at how you could store the shopping cart in SQL Azure and how you could scale it out horizontally if necessary. Although it's possible to scale out a SQL Azure database, it still requires you to add some manual partitioning code at the application layer. We'll now look at how you could represent the shopping cart table in the Table service, and at how you can use the built-in partitioning model to scale out your tables.

Due to the architecture of the Table service, there's no facility to perform a server-side join between a Shirts table and the ShoppingCart table. This effectively leaves you two options when you have data that resides on two different tables:

- Duplicate the data
- Join the data on the client side

For now, we'll ignore the duplicate data option (we'll cover that in the next section), and we'll focus on client-side data joining. But before we look at joining the data on the client side, let's take a peek at how you could represent the ShoppingCart table in the Table service.

SHOPPINGCART ENTITY

In the SQL Azure implementation of our shopping cart data model, there were two tables (ShoppingCart and ShoppingCartItems). Because the Table service isn't a relational database and doesn't support joining between tables, you can represent the shopping cart as a single table (ShoppingCart). Within the ShoppingCart table you can store the entity as follows:

```
public class ShoppingCartItem : TableServiceEntity
{
   public string Shirt {get;set;}
   public string Material { get; set; }
   public string Size { get; set; }
}
```

Consider the definition of the `ShoppingCartItem` entity. Because both the material and size data are cached in memory, you can simply store a reference to the data (the row key for the material and size) and then perform a client-side join between the shopping cart entity and the cached versions of the Material and SizeType entities. Because the cached data is a small set of static reference data, and it's being joined to a small set of shopping cart data, this technique is appropriate.

> **Partitioning with the Table service**
>
> Unlike SQL Azure, partitioning the Table service implementation of the shopping cart is pretty simple. All you need to do is set a reasonable value for the partition key for the shopping cart table, and the Windows Azure Table service will take care of the rest.
>
> In this case, you'll only be retrieving the shopping cart items for one user at a time, so it would make sense to partition the data by `UserId`. By setting the PartitionKey as the UserId, the data can be physically partitioned to as many servers as necessary, and the data for a single user's shopping cart will always physically reside together.
>
> For more details on how Table service partitioning works, refer back to chapter 11.

To join these two sets of data, you can define a new entity that will represent a strong version of your shopping cart item, as follows:

```
public class StrongShoppingCartItem
{
   public Shirt SelectedShirt { get; set; }
   public SizeType Size { get; set; }
   public Material Material { get; set; }
}
```

As you can see, this code represents the shopping cart item with a reference to each entity rather than the using an ID reference.

Now that you have the stronger version of the entity, you need to populate it, like this:

```
var materials = (IEnumerable<Material>)Cache["materials"];
var sizeTypes = (IEnumerable<SizeType>)Cache["sizeTypes"];

var shoppingCartItemContext = new ShoppingCartItemContext ();
var shoppingCartItems =
   shoppingCartItemContext.ShoppingCartItem.ToList();

var q = from shoppingCartItem in shoppingCartItems
        join sizeType in sizeTypes
           on shoppingCartItem.Size.RowKey equals sizeType.RowKey
        join material in materials
           on shoppingCartItem.Material.RowKey equals material.RowKey
        select new StrongShoppingCartItem
        {
           SelectedShirt = new Shirt(),
           Material = material,
           Size = sizeType
        };
```

The cool thing about the preceding query is that because the size type and materials are cached, you don't need to make any extra table service calls to get the reference data. This is all performed in-memory using LINQ to Objects.

> **WARNING** This technique is super cool for small datasets. Make sure you check your performance on large datasets, such as when you have millions of rows, because it may not meet your needs.

In-memory joins for static data save money

Not only will in-memory joins improve the performance of your application, they'll save you lots of cash. The fewer calls you make to the Table service or SQL Azure, the more money you'll save.

With the Table service, you save money directly by making fewer requests; with SQL Azure, you save money indirectly by requiring fewer SQL databases to service your queries.

The previous example improved performance and saved money by joining static data. Although this works well for static data, it doesn't work so well for nonstatic data—dynamic data or infrequently changing data.

14.3 Joining dynamic and infrequently changing data together

In this section we'll look at the options we have for joining dynamic and infrequently changing data.

In the previous example, we skipped over how you'd represent your shirt in the shopping cart. You have two choices: perform a client-side join (as you did in the previous section with the static data) or duplicate the data. In this section we'll look at how you can duplicate data, and join uncached data.

Let's first look at how we can duplicate data.

14.3.1 Duplicating data instead of joining

Because the shirt data isn't static data but is infrequently changing data, you need to find a different way of associating that data with the dynamic shopping cart item. For this example, you can duplicate the shirt data within the shopping cart item, as shown here:

```
public class ShoppingCartItem : TableServiceEntity
{
   public string ShirtName { get; set; }
   public string ShirtDescription { get; set; }
   public int Price { get; set; }
   public Material Material { get; set; }
   public SizeType Size { get; set; }
}
```

The preceding code stores a complete copy of the selected shirt as part of the shopping cart item's entity.

NOTE This approach will mean that we won't need to perform a join with the Shirts table, but it does mean that our table will be much larger than a traditional relational table, meaning higher storage costs.

Now that you have your shopping cart item, you need to correctly display your `StrongShoppingCartItem` object. The following code shows how you could modify the earlier query (from section 14.2.3) to do this.

```
select new StrongShoppingCartItem
        {
           SelectedShirt = new Shirt {PartitionKey="Shirts",
                             RowKey=shoppingCartItem.ShirtName,
                       Description=shoppingCartItem.ShirtDescription,
                       Price=shoppingCartItem.Price},
           Material = material,
           Size = sizeType
        };
```

As you can see from the preceding code, you can project the duplicate data into the `StrongShoppingCartItem` object by instantiating a new `Shirt` object with the data from the `ShoppingCartItem`.

> **Data synchronization**
>
> Apart from it taking up more space, another issue with duplicating data is data synchronization.
>
> Although the shirt data is infrequently changed, when a change does occur (such as the price), all items that are present in a customer's shopping basket won't be automatically updated with the new price. If your business model allows you to have stale data, this is obviously not a problem. But if your pesky customers want the correct price to be reflected in the shopping basket, you'll need some method of synchronizing the master table to all the duplicates.
>
> A simple method of keeping the data synchronized is to publish a message to a queue, stating that an item has changed. Then you can have a worker role pick up that message and update all items in the table with the correct data.

14.3.2 *Client-side joining of uncached data*

If data synchronization is a big concern and your dynamic data is a very small set of data, you could take the hit of performing a client-side join. To do that, you'd need to modify the `ShoppingCartItem` to support the join:

```
public class ShoppingCartItem : TableServiceEntity
{
   public Shirt Shirt {get;set;}
   public Material Material { get; set; }
   public SizeType Size { get; set; }
}
```

In the preceding code, the duplicate shirt properties have been replaced with a reference to the shirt.

Now that the entity stores a reference, you need to modify your query to join the data together. The following code shows how you could do this:

```
var materials = (IEnumerable<Material>)Cache["materials"];
var sizeTypes = (IEnumerable<SizeType>)Cache["sizeTypes"];

var shoppingCartItemContext = new ShoppingCartItemContext ();
var shoppingCartItems =
   shoppingCartItemContext.ShoppingCartItem.ToList();

var shirtsContext = new ShirtContext();

var q = from shoppingCartItem in shoppingCartItems
        join sizeType in sizeTypes
           on shoppingCartItem.Size.RowKey equals sizeType.RowKey
        join material in materials
           on shoppingCartItem.Material.RowKey equals material.RowKey
```

```
select new ShoppingCartItem
{
   SelectedShirt = (from shirt in shirtsContext.ShirtTable
                    where shirt.PartitionKey=="Shirts" &&
                    shirt.RowKey ==
                    shoppingCartItem
                     .SelectedShirt.RowKey
                    select shirt).First(),
   Material = material,
   Size = sizeType
};
```

The key thing to note about the preceding example is that the shirt query isn't cached, and it will invoke a call to the Table service for each item returned. The following extract shows where this is performed:

```
SelectedShirt = (from shirt in shirtsContext.ShirtTable
                 where shirt.PartitionKey=="Shirts" &&
                 shirt.RowKey == shoppingCartItem.SelectedShirt.RowKey
                 select shirt).First(),
```

Because the data returned from the shopping cart is small, this is a pretty useful technique. If you were dealing with a much larger set of shopping cart data (such as hundreds of items), this would start to perform badly.

> **TIP** If you're working with infrequently changing data (such as the shirt data), you may wish to consider using SQLite to host a local cached version of your data. This would allow you to perform SQL queries on local cached data without calling out to the Table service or SQL Azure.

Not having the ability to join data across tables does present challenges, but not always impossible ones. For the most part, you can use different techniques to get around those limitations. But in some circumstances it's going to be impossible to use the Table service. If you have lots of dynamic data and need to perform live queries across various table joins, you're not going to be able to represent that easily in the Table service. In these instances, SQL Azure is the most appropriate choice. Similarly, if you need to perform transactions across various tables, SQL Azure is again the right choice.

> **Lucene.NET**
>
> If you're storing your data in SQL Azure or the Table service and you need to perform text searches, you can export your data out of these databases and perform searches with Lucene.NET: http://lucene.apache.org/lucene.net/.

14.4 Summary

In this chapter, we've tried to break away from automatically building pure relational database solutions and instead tried to build hybrid solutions that offer the benefits of both platforms.

You've seen that by breaking foreign-key constraints, you can make effective use of the cache to store your static data, allowing you to use either the Table service or SQL Azure as your underlying storage platform.

You've also seen that if you choose to make use of the Table service (which is much more scalable than SQL Azure), you can easily join your dynamic data back to your static reference data without financial or performance penalties.

Although SQL Azure isn't as naturally scalable as the Table service, we looked at how you can shard SQL Azure to build a highly scalable relational database solution.

Finally we saw that when it comes to infrequently changing reference data (such as the shirt data), what you want to do with that data should influence what technologies you choose. In some circumstances, such as live fresh data, transactional data, or data with many joins across dynamic tables, SQL Azure is the only choice. But if you're looking to join dynamic data with infrequently changing data, you can still use the Table service by thinking about your queries and your performance. Take time to work out how your queries should be structured, consider how many round trips will be made, and think about how wasteful some of your "smaller" queries might be. REST is easy to use, but there can be overhead costs because small queries become chatty over the network.

Think about what your application needs to do before you choose a technology. Don't automatically reach for SQL Azure (which is awesome); consider whether the Table service will meet your needs.

Now that you've moved your data to the cloud, it's time to think about how to accomplish the complex backend processing usually associated with relational databases.

Part 6

Doing work with messages

Part 6, the last leg of this journey, covers several advanced topics.

Chapter 15 discusses worker roles. We covered web roles early in the book; most of that also applies to worker roles. This chapter covers some aspects of worker roles, focusing on how they're different from web roles. We also discuss some more advanced topics we saved for the back of the book so you would get to them when you were good and ready.

Chapter 16 covers the last part of Azure storage: queues. We'll look at how you can use queues to decouple your system and peek at some advanced patterns for queues.

Chapter 17 looks at the grandly titled Windows Azure platform AppFabric services. The Access Control Service (ACS) and the Service Bus help you connect to and protect the services you're running in Azure (or, really, that you're running anywhere).

The final chapter, chapter 18 for those keeping count, focuses on how to use the service management API to watch and control your Azure environment. If you want to gather logs and diagnostics, head to this chapter.

That's it, that's the end of the book. You can now put Cloud Surfer on your resume and retire with fame and wealth.

15 Processing with worker roles

This chapter covers

- Scaling the backend
- Processing messages
- Using the service management APIs to control your application

In Azure there are two roles that run your code. The first, the *web role*, has already been discussed. It plays the role of the web server, communicating with the outside world. The second role is the *worker role*. Worker roles act as backend servers—you might use one to run asynchronous or long-running tasks. Worker roles are usually message based and will usually receive these messages by polling a queue or some other shared storage. Like web roles, you can have multiple deployments of code running in different worker roles. Each deployment can have as many instances as you would like running your code (within your Azure subscription limits).

It's important to remember that a worker role is a template for a server in your application. The service model for your application defines how many instances of that role need to be started in the cloud. The role definition is similar to a class definition, and the instances are like objects.

If your system has Windows services or batch jobs, they can easily be ported to a worker role. For example, many systems have a series of regularly scheduled backend tasks. These might process all the new orders each night at 11 p.m. Or perhaps you have a positive pay system for banking, and it needs to connect to your bank each day before 3 p.m., except for banking holidays.

The worker role is intended to be started up and left running to process messages. You'll likely want to dynamically increase and decrease the number of instances of your worker role to meet the demand on your system, as it increases and decreases throughout your business cycle.

When you create worker roles, you'll want to keep in mind that Windows Azure doesn't have a job scheduler facility, so you might need to build your own. You could easily build a scheduling worker role that polls a table representing the schedule of work to do. As jobs need to be executed, it could create the appropriate worker instance, pass it a job's instructions, and then shut down the instance when the work is completed. You could easily do this with the service management APIs, which are discussed in chapter 18.

We're going to start off by building a simple service using a worker role. Once we have done that we'll change it several times, to show you the options you have in communicating with your worker role instances.

15.1 A simple worker role service

When it's all said and done, working with worker roles is quite easy. The core of the code for the worker role is the normal business code that gets the work done. There isn't anything special about this part of a worker role. It's the wrapper or handler around the business code that's interesting. There are also some key concepts you'll want to pay attention to, in order to build a reliable and manageable worker role.

In this section, we'll show you how to build a basic worker role service. You have to have some way to communicate with the worker role, so we'll first send messages to the worker through a queue, showing you how to poll a queue. (We won't go too deep into queues, because they're covered thoroughly in chapter 16.) We'll then upgrade the service so you can use inter-role communication to send messages to your service.

We'll use the term *service* fairly loosely when we're talking about worker roles. We see worker roles as providing a service to the rest of the application, hopefully in a decoupled way. We don't necessarily mean to imply the use of WS-* and Web Service protocols, although that's one way to communicate with the role.

Let's roll up our sleeves and come up with a service that does something a little more than return a string saying "Hello World." In the next few sections, we'll build a new service from scratch.

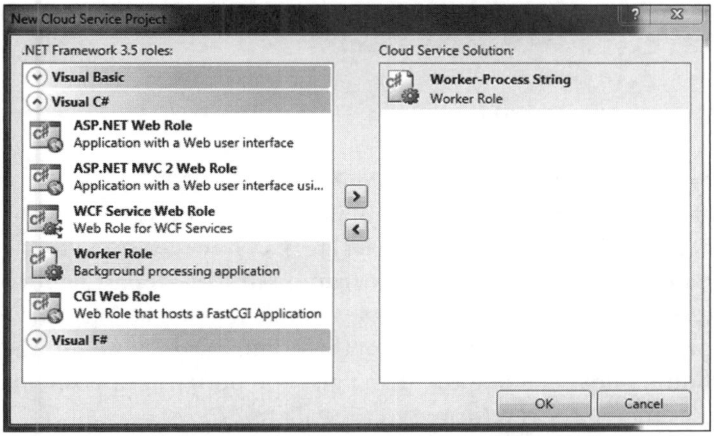

Figure 15.1 To build the service, you'll start with a worker role. It'll do all of the work and make it easy to scale as your business grows, especially during the string-reversal peak season.

15.1.1 No more Hello World

Because Hello World doesn't really cut it as an example this late in any book, we're going to build a service that reverses strings. This is an important service in any business application, and the string-reversal industry is highly competitive.

There will be two parts to this service. The first part will be the code that actually does the work of reversing strings—although it's composed of some unique intellectual property, it isn't very important in our example. This is the business end of the service. The other part of the service gets the messages (requests for work) into the service. This second part can take many shapes, and which design you use comes down to the architectural model you want to support. Some workers never receive messages; they just constantly poll a database, or filesystem, and process what they find.

To build this string-reversal service you need to open up Visual Studio 2010 and start a new cloud project. For this project, add one worker role, and give it the name *Worker-Process String*, as shown in figure 15.1.

At the business end will be our proprietary and award-winning algorithm for reversing strings. We intend to take the string-reversal industry by storm and really upset some industry captains. The core method will be called `ReverseString`, and it will take a string as its only parameter. You can find the secret sauce in the following listing. Careful, don't post it on a blog or anything.

Listing 15.1 The magical string-reversal method

```
private string ReverseString(string originalString)
{
   int lengthOfString = originalString.Length;
   char[]reversedBuffer = new char[lengthOfString];

   for (int i = 0; i < lengthOfString; i++)
```

```
    {
       reversedBuffer [i] = originalString[lengthOfString - 1 - i];
    }

    return new string(reversedBuffer);
}
```

The code in the previous listing is fairly simple—it's normal .NET code that you could write on any platform that supports .NET (mobile, desktop, on-premises servers, and so on), not just for the cloud. The method declares a character array to be a buffer that's the same length as the original string (because our R&D department has discovered that every reversed string is exactly as long as the original string). It then loops over the string, taking characters off the end of the original string and putting them at the front of the buffer, moving along the string and the buffer in opposite directions. Finally, the string in the buffer is returned to the caller.

For this example, we'll put this business logic right in the `WorkerRole.cs` class. Normally this code would be contained in its own class, and would be referenced into the application. You can do that later if you want, but we want to keep the example simple so you can focus on what's important.

We've chosen to put this service in a worker in the cloud so that we can dynamically scale how many servers we have running the service, based on usage and demand. We don't want to distract our fledgling company from writing the next generation of string-reversal software with the details and costs of running servers.

If you ran this project right now, you wouldn't see anything happen. The cloud simulator on your desktop would start up, and the worker role would be instantiated, but nothing would get done. By default, the worker service comes with an infinite polling loop in the `Run` method. This `Run` method is what is called once the role instance is initialized and is ready to run. We like that they called it `Run`, but calling it `DoIt` would have been funnier.

Now that you have your code in the worker role, how do you access it and use it? The next section will focus on the two primary ways you can send messages to a worker role instance in an active way.

15.2 Communicating with a worker role

Worker roles can receive the messages they need to process in either a push or a pull way. Pushing a message to the worker instance is an active approach, where you're directly giving it work to do. The alternative is to have the role instances call out to some shared source to gather work to do, in a sense pulling in the messages they need. When pulling messages in, remember that there will possibly be several instances pulling in work. You'll need a mechanism similar to what the Azure Queue service provides to avoid conflicts between the different worker role instances that are trying to process the same work.

Keep in mind the difference between roles and role instances, which we covered earlier. Although it's sometimes convenient to think of workers as a single entity, they don't run as a role when they're running, but as one or more instances of that role. When you're designing and developing your worker roles, keep this duality in mind. Think of the role as a unit of deployment and management, and the role instance as the unit of work assignment. This will help reduce the number of problems in your architecture.

One advantage that worker roles have over web roles is that they can have as many service endpoints as they like, using almost any transport protocol and port. Web roles are limited to HTTP/S and can have two endpoints at most. We'll use the worker role's flexibility to provide several ways to send it messages.

We'll cover three approaches to sending messages to a worker role instance:

- A pull model, where each worker role instance polls a queue for work to be completed
- A push model, where a producer outside Azure sends messages to the worker role instance
- A push model, where a producer inside the Azure application sends messages to the worker role instance

Let's look first at the pull model.

15.2.1 Consuming messages from a queue

The most common way for a worker role to receive messages is through a queue. This will be covered in depth in chapter 16 (which is on messaging with the queue), but we'll cover it briefly here.

The general model is to have a `while` loop that never quits. This approach is so common that the standard worker role template in Visual Studio provides one for you. The role instance tries to get a new message from the queue it's polling on each iteration of the loop. If it gets a message, it'll process the message. If it doesn't, it'll wait a period of time (perhaps 5 seconds) and then poll the queue again.

The core of the loop calls the business code. Once the loop has a message, it passes the message off to the code that does the work. Once that work is done, the message is deleted from the queue, and the loop polls the queue again.

```
while (true)
{
      CloudQueueMessage msg = queue.GetMessage();
      if (msg != null)
      {
          DoWorkHere(msg);
          queue.DeleteMessage(msg);
      }
      else
      {
           Thread.Sleep(5000);
      }
}
```

You might jump to the conclusion that you could easily poll an Azure Table for work instead of polling a queue. Perhaps you have a property in your table called `Status` that defaults to `new`. The worker role could poll the table, looking for all entities whose `Status` property equals `new`. Once a list is returned, the worker could process each entity and set their `Status` to `complete`. At its base, this sounds like a simple approach.

Unfortunately, this approach is a red herring. It suffers from some severe drawbacks that you might not find until you're in testing or production because they won't show up until you have multiple instances of your role running.

The first problem is of concurrency. If you have multiple instances of your worker role polling a table, they could each retrieve the same entities in their queries. This would result in those entities being processed multiple times, possibly leading to status updates getting entangled. This is the exact concurrency problem the Azure Queue service was designed to avoid.

The other, more important, issue is one of recoverability and durability. You want your system to be able to recover if there's a problem processing a particular entity. Perhaps you have each worker role set the `status` property to the name of the instance to track that the entity is being worked on by a particular instance. When the work is completed, the instance would then set the `status` property to `done`. On the surface, this approach seems to make sense. The flaw is that when an instance fails during processing (which will happen), the entity will never be recovered and processed. It'll remain flagged with the instance name of the worker processing the item, so it'll never be cleared and will never be picked up in the query of the table to be processed. It will, in effect, be "hung." The system administrator would have to go in and manually reset the `status` property back to `new`. There isn't a way for the entity to be recovered from a failure and be reassigned to another instance.

It would take a fair amount of code to overcome the issues of polling a table by multiple consumers, and in the end you'd end up having built the same thing as the Azure Queue service. The Queue service is designed to play this role, and it removes the need to write all of this dirty plumbing code. The Queue service provides a way for work to be distributed among multiple worker instances, and to easily recover that work if the instance fails. A key concept of cloud architecture is to design for failure recoverability in an application. It's to be expected that nodes go down (for one reason or another) and will be restarted and recovered, possibly on a completely different server.

Queues are the easiest way to get messages into a worker role, and they'll be discussed in detail in the next chapter. Now, though, we'll discuss inter-role communication, which lets a worker role receive a message from outside of Azure.

15.2.2 *Exposing a service to the outside world*

Web roles are built to receive traffic from outside of Azure. Their whole point in life is to receive messages from the internet (usually from a browser) and respond with some message (usually HTML). The great thing is that when you have multiple web role instances, they're automatically enrolled in a load balancer. This load balancer automatically distributes the load across the different instances you have running.

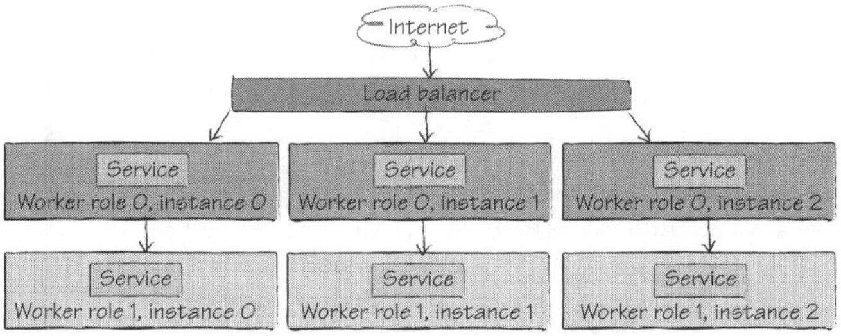

Figure 15.2 Worker roles have two ways of exposing their services. The first is as an input service—these are published to the load balancer and are available externally (role 0). The second is as an internal service, which isn't behind a load balancer and is only visible to your other role instances (role 1).

Worker roles can do much the same thing, but because you aren't running in IIS (which isn't available on a worker role), you have to host the service yourself. The only real option is to build the service as a WCF service.

Our goal is to convert our little string-reversal method into a WCF service, and then expose that externally so that customers can call the service. The first step is to remove the loop that polls the queue and put in some service plumbing. When you host a service in a worker role, regardless of whether it is for external or internal use, you need to declare an endpoint. How you configure this endpoint will determine whether it allows traffic from sources internal or external to the application. The two types of endpoints are shown in figure 15.2. If it's configured to run externally, it will use the Azure load balancers and distribute service calls across all of the role instances running the server, much like how the web role does this. We'll look at internal service endpoints in the next section.

The next step in the process is to define the endpoint. You can do this the macho way in the configuration of the role, or you can do it in the Visual Studio Properties window. If you right-click on the Worker-Process String worker role in the Azure project and choose Properties, you'll see the window in figure 15.3.

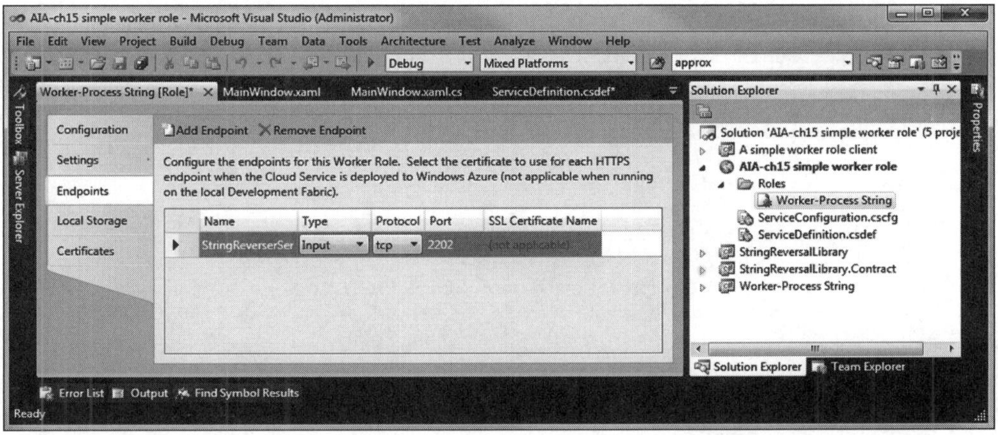

Figure 15.3 Adding an external service endpoint to a worker role. This service endpoint will be managed by Azure and be enrolled in the load balancer. This will make the service available outside of Azure.

Name the service endpoint `StringReverseService` and set it to be an input endpoint, using TCP on port 2202. There's no need to use any certificates or security at this time.

After you save these settings, you'll find the equivalent settings in the ServiceConfiguration.csdef file:

```
<Endpoints>
 <InputEndpoint name="StringReverserService" protocol="tcp" port="2202" />
</Endpoints>
```

You might normally host your service in IIS or WAS, but those aren't available in a worker role. In the future, you might be able to use Windows Server AppFabric, but that isn't available yet, so you'll have to do this the old-fashioned way. You'll have to host the WCF service using `ServiceHost`, which is exactly that, a host that will act as a container to run your service in. It will contain the service, manage the endpoints and configuration, and handle the incoming service requests.

Next you need to add a method called `StartStringReversalService`. This method will wire up the service to the `ServiceHost` and the endpoint you defined. The contents of this method are shown in the following listing.

Listing 15.2 The `StartStringReversalService` method wires up the service

```
private void StartStringReversalService()
{
   this.serviceHost = new ServiceHost(typeof(ReverseStringTools));

   NetTcpBinding binding = new NetTcpBinding(SecurityMode.None);

   RoleInstanceEndpoint externalEndPoint = RoleEnvironment      ❶ Retrieves endpoint
   ➥ .CurrentRoleInstance                                         settings from
   ➥ .InstanceEndpoints["StringReverserService"];                 configuration

serviceHost.AddServiceEndpoint(
        typeof(IReverseString),
        binding,
        String.Format("net.tcp://{0}/StringReverserService",
        ➥ ExternalEndPoint.IPEndpoint));

   try
   {
      this.serviceHost.Open();                  ❷ Starts service host
   }
   catch (Exception ex)
   {
      Trace.TraceError("Could not start string reverser servicehost. {0}",
      ➥ ex.Message);
   }

   while (true)
   {
      Thread.Sleep(500000);                     ❸ Sleeps forever so service host stays open
   }
}
```

Listing 15.2 is an abbreviated version of the real method, shortened so that it fits into the book better. We didn't take out anything that's super important. We took out a series of `trace` commands so we could watch the startup and status of the service. We also abbreviated some of the error handling, something you would definitely want to beef up in a production environment.

Most of this code is normal for setting up a `ServiceHost`. You first have to tell the service host the type of the service that's going to be hosted ❶. In this case, it's the `ReverseStringTools` type.

When you go to add the service endpoint to the service host, you're going to need three things, the ABCs of WCF: address, binding, and contract. The contract is provided by your code, `IReverseString`, and it's a class file that you can reference to share service contract information (or use MEX like a normal web service). The binding is a normal TCP binary binding, with all security turned off. (We would only run with security off for debug and demo purposes!)

Then the address is needed. You can set up the address by referencing the service endpoint from the Azure project. You won't know the real IP address the service will be running under until runtime, so you'll have to build it on the fly by accessing the collection of endpoints from the `RoleEnvironment.CurrentRoleInstance.InstanceEndpoints` collection ❷. The collection is a dictionary, so you can pull out the endpoint you want to reference with the name you used when setting it up—in this case, `StringReverserService`. Once you have a reference to the endpoint, you can access the IP address that you need to set up the service host.

After you have that wired up, you can start the service host. This will plug in all the components, fire them up, and start listening for incoming messages. This is done with the `Open` method ❸.

Once the service is up, you'll want the main execution thread to sleep forever so that the host stays up and running. If you didn't include the sleep loop ❸, the call pointer would fall out of the method, and you'd lose your context, losing the service host. At this point, the worker role instance is sitting there, sleeping, whereas the service host is running, listening for and responding to messages.

We wired up a simple WPF test client, as shown in figure 15.4, to see if our service is working. There are several ways you could write this test harness. If you're using .NET 4,

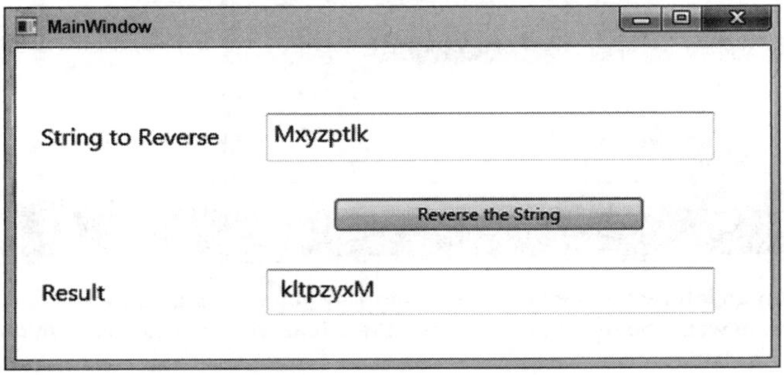

Figure 15.4 A simple client that consumes our super string-reversing service. The service is running in a worker role, running in Azure, behind the load balancers. kltpzyxM! kltpzyxM! kltpzyxM!

it's very common to use unit tests to test your services instead of an interactive WPF client. Your other option would be to use WCFTestClient.exe, which comes with Visual Studio.

Exposing public service endpoints is useful, but there are times when you'll want to expose services for just your use, and you don't want them made public. In this case, you'll want to use inter-role communication, which we'll look at next.

15.2.3 Inter-role communication

Exposing service input endpoints, as we just discussed, can be useful. But many times, you just need a way to communicate between your role instances. Usually you could use a queue, but at times there might be a need for direct communication, either for performance reasons or because the process is synchronous in nature.

You can enable communication directly from one role instance to another, but there are some issues you should be aware of first. The biggest issue is that you'll have direct access to an individual role instance, which means there's no separation that can deal with load balancing. Similarly, if you're communicating with an instance and it goes down, your work is lost. You'll have to write code to handle this possibility on the client side.

To set up inter-role communication, you need to add an internal endpoint in the same way you add an input endpoint, but in this case you'll set the type to `Internal` (instead of `Input`), as shown in figure 15.5. The port will automatically be set to `dynamic` and will be managed for you under the covers by Azure.

Using an internal endpoint is a lot like using an external endpoint, from the point of view of your service. Either way, your service doesn't know about any other instances running the service in parallel. The load balancing is handled outside of your code when you're using an external endpoint, and internal endpoints don't have any available load balancing. This places the choice of which service instance to consume on the shoulders of the service consumer itself.

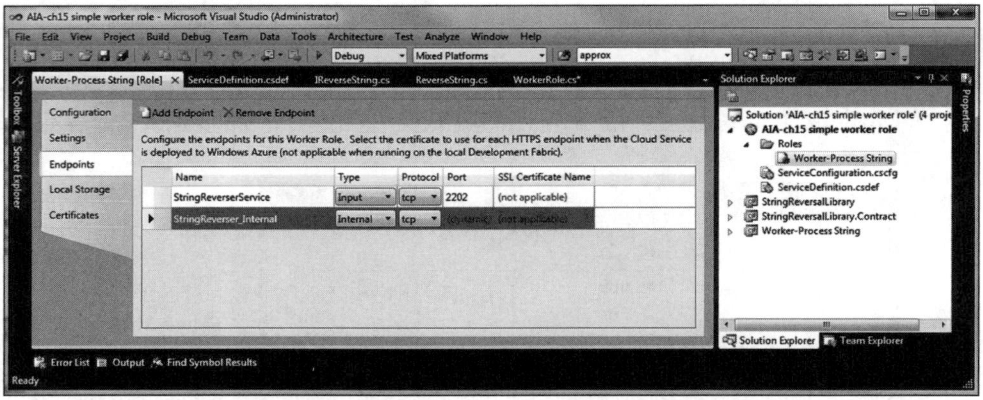

Figure 15.5 You can set up an internal endpoint in the same way you set up an external endpoint. In this case, though, your service won't be load balanced, and the client will have to know which service instance to talk to.

Most of the work involved with internal endpoints is handled on the client side, your service consumer. Because there can be a varying number of instances of your service running at any time, you have to be prepared to decide which instance to talk to, if not all of them. You also have to be wily enough to not call yourself if calling the service from a sibling worker role instance.

You can access the set of instances running, and their exposed internal endpoints, with the `RoleEnvironment` static class:

```
foreach (var instance in
➥ RoleEnvironment.CurrentRoleInstance.Role.Instances)
{
   if (instance != RoleEnvironment.CurrentRoleInstance)
      SendMessage(instance.InstanceEndpoints["MyServiceEndpointName"]);
}
```

The preceding sample code loops through all of the available role instances of the current role. As it loops, it could access a collection of any type of role in the application, including itself. So, for each instance, the code checks to see if that instance is the instance the code is running in. If it isn't, the code will send that instance a message. If it's the same instance, the code won't send it a message, because sending a message to oneself is usually not productive.

All three ways of communicating with a worker role have their advantages and disadvantages, and each has a role to play in your architecture:

- Use a queue for complete separation of your instances from the service consumers.
- Use input endpoints to expose your service publicly and leverage the Azure load balancer.
- Use internal endpoints for direct and synchronous communication with a specific instance of your service.

Now that we've covered how you can communicate with a worker role, we should probably talk about what you're likely to want to do with a worker role.

15.3 Common uses for worker roles

Worker roles are blank slates—you can do almost anything with them. In this section, we're going to explore some common, and some maybe not-so-common, uses for worker roles.

The most common use is to offload work from the frontend. This is a common architecture in many applications, in the cloud or not. We'll also look at how to use multithreading in roles, how to simulate a worker role, and how to break a large process into connected smaller pieces.

15.3.1 Offloading work from the frontend

We're all familiar with the user experience of putting products into a shopping cart and then checking out with an online retailer. You might have even bought this book online. How retailers process your cart and your order is one of the key scenarios for how a worker role might be used in the cloud.

Many large online retailers split the checkout process into two pieces. The first piece is interactive and user-facing. You happily fill your shopping cart with lots of stuff and then check out. At that time, the application gathers your payment details, gives you an order number, and tells you that the order has been processed. Then it emails all of this so you can have it all for your records. This is the notification email shown in figure 15.6.

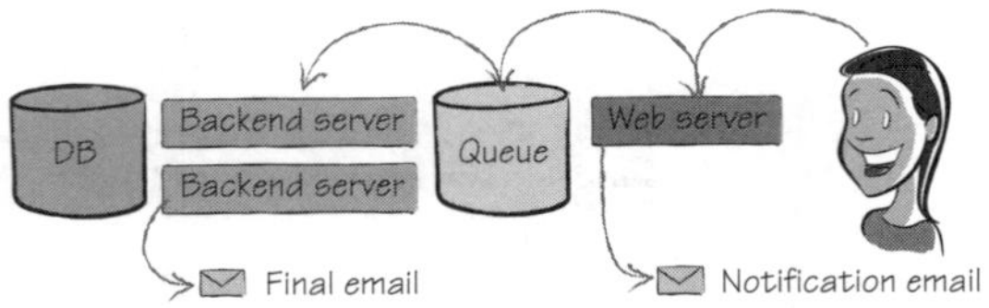

Figure 15.6 The typical online retailer will process a customer's order in two stages. The first saves the cart for processing and immediately sends back a thank you email with an order number. Then the backend servers pick up the order and process it, resulting in a final email with all of the real details.

After the customer-facing work is done, the backend magic kicks in to complete the processing of the order. You see, when the retailer gave you an order number, they were sort of fibbing. All they did was submit the order to the backend processing system via a message queue and give you the order number that can be used to track it. One of the servers that are part of the backend processing group picks up the order and completes the processing. This probably involves charging the credit card, verifying inventory, and determining the ability to ship according to the customer's wishes. Once this backend work is completed, a second email is sent to the customer with an update, usually including the package tracking number and any other final details. This is the final email shown in figure 15.6.

By breaking the system into two pieces, the online retailer gains a few advantages. The biggest is that the user's experience of checking out is much faster, giving them a nice shopping experience. This also takes a lot of load off of the web servers, which should be simple HTML shovels. Because only a fraction of shoppers actually check out (e-tailers call this the conversion rate), it's important to be able to scale the web servers very easily. Having them broken out makes it easy to scale them horizontally (by adding more servers), and makes it possible for each web server to require only simple hardware. The general strategy at the web server tier is to have an army of ants, or many low-end servers.

This two-piece system also makes it easier to plan for failure. You wouldn't want a web server to crash while processing a customer's order and lose the revenue, would you?

This leaves the backend all the time it needs to process the orders. Backend server farms tend to consist of fewer, larger servers, when compared to the web servers. Although you can scale the number of backend servers as well, you won't have to do that as often, because you can just let the flood of orders back up in the queue. As long as your server capacity can process them in a few hours, that's OK.

Azure provides a variety of server sizes for your instances to run on, and sometimes you'll want more horsepower in one box for what you're doing. In that case, you can use threading on the server to tap that entire horsepower.

15.3.2 *Using threads in a worker role*

There may be times when the work assigned to a particular worker role instance needs multithreading, or the ability to process work in parallel by using separate threads of execution. This is especially true when you're migrating an existing application to the Azure platform. Developing and debugging multithreaded applications is very difficult, so deciding to use multithreading isn't a decision you should make lightly.

The worker role does allow for the creation and management of threads for your use, but as with code running on a normal server, you don't want to create too many threads. When the number of threads increases, so does the amount of memory in use. The context-switching cost of the CPU will also hinder efficient use of your resources. You should limit the number of threads you're using to two to four per CPU core.

A common scenario is to spin up an extra thread in the background to process some asynchronous work. Doing this is OK, but if you plan on building a massive computational engine, you're better off using a framework to do the heavy lifting for you. The Parallel Extensions to .NET is a framework Microsoft has developed to help you parallelize your software. The Parallel Extensions to .NET shipped as part of .NET 4.0 in April of 2010.

Although we always want to logically separate our code to make it easier to maintain, sometimes the work involved doesn't need a lot of horsepower, so we may want to deploy both the web and the worker sides of the application to one single web role.

15.3.3 *Simulating worker roles in a web role*

Architecting your application into discrete pieces, some of which are frontend and some of which are backend, is a good thing. But there are times when you need the logical separation, but not the physical separation. This might be for speed reasons, or because you don't want to pay for a whole worker role instance when you just need some lightweight background work done.

MAINTAINING LOGICAL SEPARATION

If you go down this path, you must architect your system so you can easily break it out into a real worker role later on as your needs change. This means making sure that while you're breaking the physical separation, you're at least keeping the logical separation. You should still use the normal methods of passing messages to that worker code. If it would use a queue to process messages in a real worker instance, it should use a queue in the simulated worker instance as well. Take a gander at figure 15.7 to see what we mean. At some point, you'll need to break the code back out to a real worker role, and you won't want to have to rewrite a whole bunch of code.

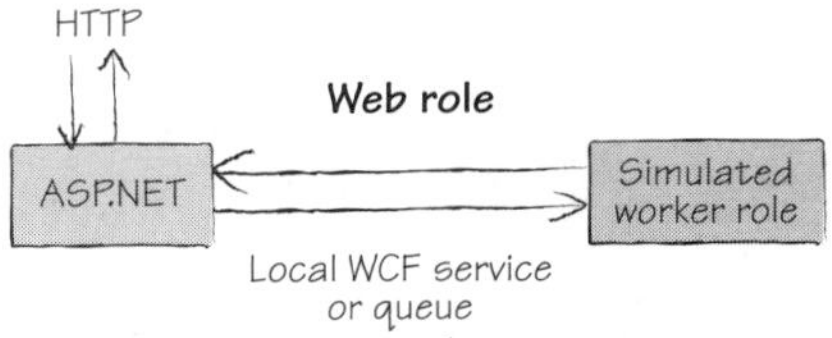

Figure 15.7 You can simulate a worker role in your web role if it's very lightweight.

Be aware that the Fabric Controller will be ignorant of what you're doing, and it won't be able to manage your simulated worker role. If that worker role code goes out of control, it will take down the web instance it's running in, which could cascade to a series of other problems. You've been warned.

If you're going to do this, make sure to put the worker code into a separate library so that primary concerns of the web instance aren't intermingled with the concerns of the faux worker instance. You can then reference that library and execute it in its own thread, passing messages to it however you would like. This will also make it much easier to split it out into its own real worker role later.

UTILIZING BACKGROUND THREADS

The other issue is getting a background thread running so it can execute the faux worker code. An approach we've worked with is to launch the process on a separate thread during the `Session_Start` event of the global.asax. This will fire up the thread once when the web app is starting up, and leave it running.

Our first instinct was to use the `Application_Start` event, but this won't work. The `RoleManager` isn't available in the `Application_Start` event, so it's too early to start the faux worker.

We want to run the following code:

```
Thread t = new Thread(new ThreadStart(FauxWorkerSample.Start));
t.Start();
```

Putting the thread start code in the `Session_Start` event has the effect of trying to start another faux worker every time a new ASP.NET session is started, which is whenever there's a new visitor to the website. To protect against thousands of background faux workers being started, we use the Singleton pattern. This pattern will make sure that only one faux worker is started in that web instance.

When we're about to create the thread, we check a flag in the application state to see if a worker has already been created:

```
object obj = Application["FauxWorkerStarted"];

if (obj == null)
{
     Application["FauxWorkerStarted"] = true;
     Thread t = new Thread(new ThreadStart(FauxWorkerSample.Start));
     t.Start();
}
```

If the worker hasn't been created, the flag won't exist in the application state property bag, so it will equal `null` in that case. If this is the first session, the thread will be created, pointed at the method we give it (`FauxWorkerSample.Start` in this case), and it will start processing in the background.

When you start it in this manner, you'll have access to the `RoleManager` with the ability to write to the log, manage system health, and act like a normal worker instance. You could adapt this strategy to work with the `OnStart` event handler in your webrole.cs file. This might be a cleaner place to put it, but we wanted to show you the dirty work around here.

Our next approach is going to cover how best to handle a large and complex worker role.

15.3.4 State-directed workers

Sometimes the code that a worker role runs is large and complex, and this can lead to a long and risky processing time. In this section, we'll look at a strategy you can use to break this large piece down into manageable pieces, and a way to gain flexibility in your processing.

As we've said time and time again, worker roles tend to be message-centric. The best way to scale them is by having a group of instances take turns consuming messages from a queue. As the load on the queue increases, you can easily add more instances of the worker role. As the queue cools off, you can destroy some instances.

In this section, we'll look at why large worker roles can be problematic, how we can fix this problem, and what the inevitable drawbacks are. Let's start by looking at the pitfalls of using a few, very large workers.

THE PROBLEM

Sometimes the work that's needed on a message is large and complicated, which leads to a heavy, bloated worker. This heaviness also leads to a brittle codebase that's difficult to work with and maintain because of the various code paths and routing logic.

A worker that takes a long time to process a single request is harder to scale and can't process as many messages as a group of smaller workers. A long-running unit of work also exposes your system to more risk. The longer an item takes to be processed, the more likely it is that the work will fail and have to be started over. This is no big deal if the processing takes 3 seconds, but if it takes 20 minutes or 20 hours, you have a significant cost to failure.

This problem can be caused by one message being very complex to process, or by a batch of messages being processed as a group. In either case, the unit of work being performed is large, and this raises risk. This problem is often called the "pig in a python" problem (as shown in figure 15.8), because you end up with one large chunk of work moving through your systems.

We need a way to digest this work a little more gracefully.

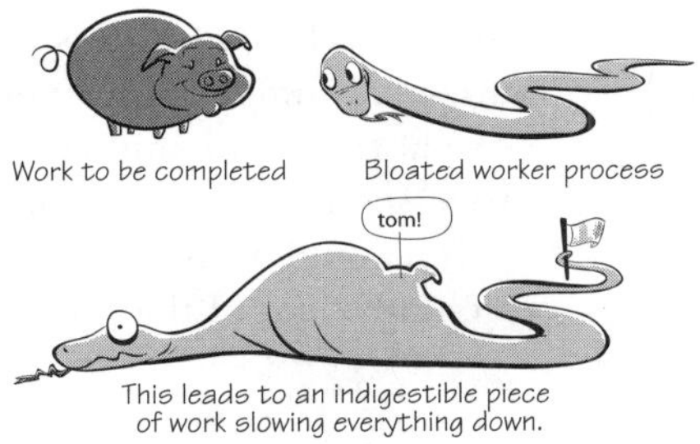
Work to be completed
Bloated worker process
tom!
This leads to an indigestible piece of work slowing everything down.

Figure 15.8 The "pig in a python" problem can often be seen in technology and business. It's when a unit of work takes a long time to complete, like when a python eats a pig. It can take months for the snake to digest the pig, and it can't do much of anything else during that timeframe.

THE SOLUTION

The best way to digest this large pig is to break the large unit of work into a set of smaller processes. This will give you the most flexibility when it comes to scaling and managing your system. But you want to be careful that you don't break the processes down to sizes that are too small. At this level, the latency of communicating with the queue and other storage mechanisms in very chatty ways may introduce more overhead than you were looking for.

When you analyze the stages of processing on the message, you'll likely conceive of several stages to the work. You can figure this out by drawing a flow diagram of the current bloated worker code. For example, when processing an order from an e-commerce site, you might have the following stages:

1. Validate the data in the order.
2. Validate the pricing and discount codes.
3. Enrich the order with all of the relevant customer data.
4. Validate the shipping address.
5. Validate the payment information.
6. Charge the credit card.
7. Verify that the products are in stock and able to be shipped.
8. Enter the shipping orders into the logistics system for the distribution center.
9. Record the transaction in the ERP system.
10. Send a notification email to the customer.
11. Sit back and profit.

You can think of each state the message goes through as a separate worker role, connected together with a queue for each state. Instead of one worker doing all of the work for a single order, it only processes one of the states for each order. The different queues represent the different states the message could have. Figure 15.9 compares a big worker that performs all of the work, to a series of smaller workers that break the work out (validating, shipping, and notifying workers).

There might also be some other processing states you want to plan for. Perhaps one for really bad orders that need to be looked at by a real human, or perhaps you have platinum-level customers who get their orders processed and shipped before normal run-of-the-mill customers. The platinum orders would go into a queue that's processed by a dedicated pool of instances.

You could even have a bad order routed to an Azure table. A customer service representative could then access that data with a CRM application or a simple InfoPath

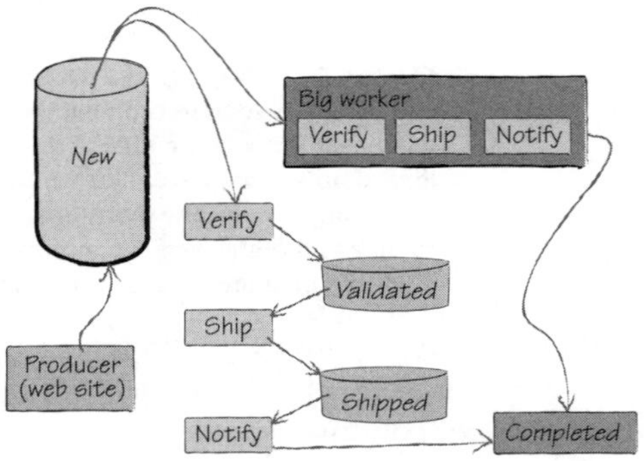

Figure 15.9 A monolithic worker role compared to a state-driven worker role. The big worker completes all the work in one step, leading to the "pig in a python" problem of being harder to maintain and extend as needed. Instead, we can break the process into a series of queues and workers, each dedicated to servicing a specific state or stage of the work to be done.

form, fix the order, and resubmit it back into the proper queue to continue being processed. This process is called *repair and resubmit*, and it's an important element to have in any enterprise processing engine.

You won't be able to put the full order details into the queue message—there won't be enough room. The message should contain a complete work ticket, representing where the order data can be found (perhaps via an order ID), as well as some state information, and any information that would be useful in routing the message through the state machine. This might include the service class of the customer, for example—platinum versus silver.

As the business changes over time, and it will, making changes to how the order is processed is much easier than trying to perform heart surgery on your older, super complicated, and bloated work role code. They don't say spaghetti code for nothing. For example, you might need to add a new step between steps 8 and 9 in our previous list. You could simply create a new queue and a new worker role to process that queue. Then the worker role for the state right before the new one would need to be updated to point to the new queue. Hopefully the changes to the existing parts of the system can be limited to configuration changes.

EVEN COOLER—MAKE THE STATE WORKER ROLE ITS OWN AZURE SERVICE

How you want to manage your application in the cloud should be a primary consideration in how you structure the Visual Studio solution. Each solution becomes a single management point. If you want to manage different pieces without affecting the whole system, those should be split out into separate solutions.

In this scenario, it would make sense to separate each state worker role to its own service in Azure, which would further decouple them from each other. This way, when you need to restart one worker role and its queue, you won't affect the other roles.

In a more dynamic organization, you might need to route a message through these states based on some information that's only available at runtime. The routing information could be stored in a table, with rules for how the flow works, or by simply storing the states and their relationships in the cloud service configuration file. Both of these approaches would let you update how orders were processed at runtime without having to change code. We've done this when orders needed different stages depending on what was in the order, or where it was going. In one case, if a controlled substance was in the order, the processing engine had to execute a series of additional steps to complete the order.

This approach is often called a *poor man's service bus* because it uses a simple way of connecting the states together, and they're fairly firm at runtime. If you require a greater degree of flexibility in the workflow, you would want to look at the Itinerary[1] pattern. This lets the system build up a schedule of processing stops based on the information present at runtime. These systems can get a little more complicated, but they result in a system that's more easily maintained when there's a complex business process.

---

[1] For more information on the Itinerary pattern, see the *Microsoft Application Architecture Guide* from Patterns & Practices at Microsoft. It can be found at http://apparchguide.codeplex.com.

OOPS, IT'S NOT NIRVANA

As you build this out, you'll discover a drawback. You now have many more running worker roles to manage. This can create more costs, and you still have to plan for when you eventually will swallow a pig. If your system is tuned for a slow work day, with one role instance per state, and you suddenly receive a flood of orders, the large amount of orders will move down the state diagram like a pig does when it's eaten by a python. This forces you to scale up the number of worker instances at each state.

Although this flexibility is great, it can get expensive. With this model, you have several pools of instances instead of one general-purpose pool, which results in each pool having to increase and then decrease as the pig (the large flood of work) moves through the pipeline. In the case of a pig coming through, this can lead to a stall in the state machine as each state has to wait for more instances to be added to its pool to handle the pig (flood of work). This can be done easily using the service management APIs, but it takes time to spin up and spin down instances—perhaps 20 minutes.

The next step to take, to avoid the pig in a python problem, is to build your worker roles so that they're generic processors, all able to process any state in the system. You would still keep the separate queues, which makes it easier to know how many messages are in each state.

You could also condense the queues down to one, with each message declaring what state the order is in as part of its data, but we don't like this approach because it leads to favoritism for the most recent orders placed in the processors, and it requires you to restart all of your generic workers when you change the state graph. You can avoid this particular downfall by driving the routing logic with configuration and dependency injection. Then you would only need to update the configuration of the system and deploy a new assembly to change the behavior of the system.

The trick to gaining both flexibility and simplicity in your architecture is to encapsulate the logic for each state in the worker, separating it so it's easily maintainable, while pulling them all together so there's only one pool of workers. The worker, in essence, becomes a router. You can see how this might work in figure 15.10. Each message is routed, based on its state and other runtime data, to the necessary state

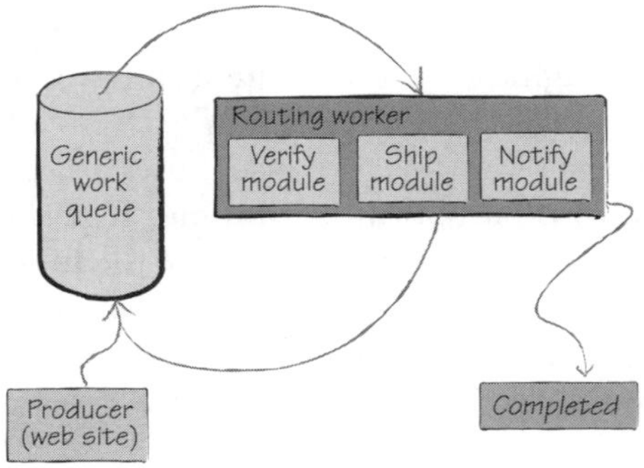

Figure 15.10 By moving to a consolidated state-directed worker, we'll have one queue and one worker. The worker will act as a router, sending each inbound message to the appropriate module based on the message's state and related itinerary. This allows us to have one large pool of workers, but makes it easier to manage and decompose our bulky process.

processor. This functions much like a factory. Each state would have a class that knows how to process that state. Each state class would implement the same interface, perhaps `IorderProcessStage`. This would make it easy for the worker to instantiate the correct class based on the state, and then process it. Most of these classes would then send the message back to the generic queue, with a new state, and the cycle would start again.

There are going to be times when you're working with both web and worker roles and you're either importing legacy code that needs access to a local drive, or what you're doing requires it. That's why we'll discuss local storage next.

15.4 Working with local storage

There are times when the code you're working with will need to read from and write to the local filesystem. Windows Azure allows for you to request and access a piece of the local disk on your role instance.

You can create this space by using the configuration of your role. You won't have control over the path of the directory you're given access to, so you should make sure that the file path your code needs to access is part of your configuration. A hardcoded path will never remain accurate in the cloud environment.

We recommend that you only use local storage when you absolutely have to, because of some limitations we'll cover later in this section. You'll likely need to use local storage the most when you're migrating to the cloud existing frameworks or applications that require local disk access.

15.4.1 Setting up local storage

You can configure the local storage area you need as part of your role by adding a few simple lines of configuration to your role. The tag we're going to work with is the `LocalStorage` tag. It will tell the Fabric Controller to allocate local file storage space on each server the role instance is running on.

In the configuration element, you need to name the storage space. This name will become the name of the folder that's reserved for you. You'll need to define how much filesystem space you'll need. The current limit is 20 GB per role instance, with a minimum of 1 MB.

```
<LocalResources>
      <LocalStorage name="FilesUploaded" cleanOnRoleRecycle="false"
      ➥ sizeInMB="15" />
      <LocalStorage name="VirusScanPending" cleanOnRoleRecycle="true"
      ➥ sizeInMB="5" />
</LocalResources>
```

You can declare multiple local storage resources, as shown in the preceding code snippet. It's important that the local file storage only be used for temporary, unimportant files. The local file store isn't replicated or preserved in any way. If the instance fails and it's moved by the Fabric Controller to a new server, the local file store isn't preserved, which means any files that were present will be lost.

> **TIP** There is one time when the local file storage won't be lost, and that's when the role is recycled, either as part of a service management event on your part, or when the Fabric Controller is responding to a minor issue with your server. In these cases, if you've set the `cleanOnRoleRecyle` parameter to `false`, the current files will still be there when your instance comes back online.

Instances may only access their own local storage. An instance may not access another instance's storage. You should use Azure BLOB storage if you need more than one instance to access the same storage area.

Now that you've defined your local storage, let's look at how you can access it and work with it.

15.4.2 Working with local storage

Working with files in local storage is just like working with normal files. When your role instance is started, the agent creates a folder with the name you defined in the configuration in a special area on the C: drive on your server. Rules are put in place to make sure the folder doesn't exceed its assigned quota for size. To start using it, you simply need to get a handle for it.

To get a handle to your local storage area, you need to use the `GetLocalResource` method. You'll need to provide the name of the local resource you defined in the service definition file. This will return a `LocalResource` object:

```
public static LocalResource uploadFolder =
➥ RoleEnvironment.GetLocalResource("FilesUploaded");
```

After you have this reference to the local folder, you can start using it like a normal directory. To get the physical path, so you can check the directory contents or write files to it, you would use the `uploadFolder` reference from the preceding code.

```
string rootPathName = uploadFolder.RootPath;
```

In the sample code provided with this book, there's a simple web role that uses local storage to store uploaded files. Please remember that this is just a sample, and that you wouldn't normally persist important files to the local store, considering its transient nature. You can view the code we used to do this in listing 15.3. When calling the `RootPath` method in the local development fabric, Brian's storage is located here:

```
C:\Users\brprince\AppData\Local\dftmp\s0\deployment(32)\res\deployment(32)
➥ .AiA_15___Local_Storage_post_pdc.LocalStorage_WebRole.0\directory\File
➥ sUploaded\
```

When we publish this little application to the cloud, it returns the following path:

```
C:\Resources\directory\0c28d4f68a444ea380288bf8160006ae.LocalStorage
➥ _WebRole.FilesUploaded\
```

Listing 15.3 Working with local file storage

```
protected void Page_Load(object sender, EventArgs e)
{
 litName.Text = uploadFolder.Name;
 litMaxSize.Text = uploadFolder.MaximumSizeInMegabytes.ToString();
 litRootPath.Text = uploadFolder.RootPath;
}

protected void cmdUpload1_Click(object sender, EventArgs e)
{
 if (FileUpload1.HasFile)
 {
  FileUpload1.SaveAs
  ➥ (uploadFolder.RootPath + FileUpload1.FileName);
 }

 litUploadedFilePath.Text = uploadFolder.RootPath +
 ➥ FileUpload1.FileName;
 litUploadedFileContents.Text =
 ➥ System.IO.File.OpenText(uploadFolder.RootPath +
 ➥ FileUpload1.FileName).ReadToEnd();
}
```

❶ Path to our local folder

❷ Path to the file uploaded

❸ File contents

Now that we know where the files will be stored, we can start working with them. In the sample application, we have a simple file-upload control ❶. When the web page is loaded, we write out the local file path to the local storage folder that we've been assigned ❷. Once the file is uploaded, we store it in the local storage and write out its filename and path ❸. We then write the file back out to the browser using normal file APIs to do so. Our example code was designed to work only with text files, to keep things simple.

The local storage option is great for volatile local file access, but it isn't durable and may disappear on you. If you need durable storage, look at Azure storage or SQL Azure. If you need shared storage that's super-fast, you should consider the Windows Server AppFabric distributed cache. This is a peer-to-peer caching layer that can run on your roles and provide a shared in-memory cache for your instances to work with.

15.5 Summary

In this chapter, we've looked at how you can process work in the background with the worker role in Azure. The worker role is an important tool for the cloud developer. It lets you do work when there isn't a user present, whether because you've intentionally separated the background process from the user (in the case of a long-running checkout process) or because you've broken your work into a discrete service that will process messages from a queue.

Worker roles scale just like web roles, but they don't have a built-in load balancer like web roles do. You'll usually aggregate worker roles behind a queue, with each instance processing messages from the queue, thereby distributing the work across the group. This gives you the flexibility to increase or decrease the number of worker instances as the need arises.

It's quite possible to have an Azure application consist of only worker roles. You could have some on-premises transaction systems report system activity (such as each time a sale is made) to a queue in the cloud. The worker role would be there to pick up the report and merge the data into the reporting system. This allows you to keep the bulk of your application on-premises, while moving the computing-intensive back-end operations to the cloud. A more robust way of doing this would be to connect the on-premises system with the cloud system using the Windows Azure platform AppFabric Service Bus, which is discussed in chapter 17.

In this chapter we talked a lot about how to work with worker roles, and how to get messages to them. One of the key methods for doing that is to use an Azure queue. We'll work closely with queues in the next chapter.

16 Messaging with the queue

This chapter covers

- Loosely coupling your system
- Distributing work to a group of service providers
- Learning how to use messaging

Queues are the third part of the Azure storage system (after BLOBs and tables). The concept of queues has been around a long time, and it's likely that you've worked with some technology related to queues already.

A common architectural goal during design is to produce a system that's tightly integrated, but also loosely coupled. Any sizable system usually has several components, and whether these components are running in the same memory space, or on different boxes, they need to work closely together. This is what is meant by "tightly integrated." These different components should work as a team to provide the value of the system in an easy and cohesive manner.

If your only goal is tight integration, you'll often end up with a system where the components are tightly coupled as well. Tight coupling leads to a system that's brittle and that responds poorly to changes. This makes it difficult to manage the system and to extend it to meet future needs. In a brittle system, a change in one component can ripple through the whole system, requiring changes in many other components. Such a system is difficult to understand, maintain, and troubleshoot.

The easiest way to create a loosely coupled system is to provide a way for the components to talk with each other through messages, and these messages should follow a "tell, don't ask" approach. You shouldn't ask an object for a bunch of data, do some work with it, and then give the results back to the object for recording. You should just tell the object what you want it to do. This approach should be applied at a component and system level as well—this approach helps to create code that's well abstracted and compartmentalized.

Loose coupling also helps you isolate change from one component to another. For example, an e-commerce website may be communicating with a backend ERP system. When the company chooses to change ERP vendors, the queue will act as a buffer, keeping the change from rippling over the queue boundary. All the producer knows is that it puts messages in a certain format in the queue. The producer has no knowledge of the consuming system, and doesn't care what happens.

The queue also becomes a pivot point for scaling. Later on we'll talk about how you can monitor the length (some use the term *depth*) of a queue to determine whether messages are being consumed quickly enough. If not, you can scale out the number of consumers processing the messages, which reduces the number of waiting messages in the queue.

Be careful, however, that you don't put so much effort into loosely coupling your system that you end up building an overly complex monstrosity that's completely unmanageable. As with many things, balance is the key.

16.1 Decoupling your system with messaging

There are many ways to decouple your system, but they usually center on messaging of some sort. One of the most common ways is to use queues in between the different parts of the system, or between completely different systems that must work together.

Queues have several major components, and we'll walk through each of them in turn. We're first going to look at how queues work in general—how they pass messages around. Then we'll examine what messages are, the shape they have, and how they work. Finally we'll look closely at how an Azure queue works—what its limits are and how to get the most out of it.

16.1.1 How messaging works

Queues have two ends. The producer end, where messages are put into the queue, is usually represented as the bottom. The other end is the consumer end, where a consumer will pull messages off of the top of the queue.

Performance is critical to every part of Azure, and queues are no exception. Each queue, like the rest of the Azure storage services, exists as three instances, each of which is protected by different fault and update domains. This strategy protects your queue from completely failing when a switch goes down or a patch is rolled out.

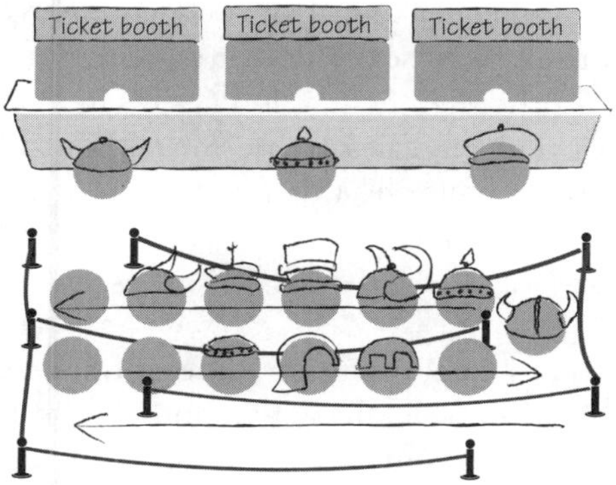

Figure 16.1 A queue forms for tickets on the opening night of a new blockbuster movie. Movie-goers enter (while wearing their fanboy outfits) at the bottom, or end of the line. As the ticket booth (consumer) processes the ticket requests, the movie-goers move forward in the queue until they're at the head of the line.

As the demand for a queue increases, the storage fabric will start serving the requests out of a memory cache. This dramatically increases the performance of the queue and reduces the latency of using the queue.

A queue is a FIFO structure: first in, first out. This contrasts with a stack, which is LIFO: last in, first out. A real-world example of a queue is the line for tickets at a movie theater, as illustrated in figure 16.1. When people arrive, they stand at the end of the line. As the consumer (the ticket booth) completes sales, it works with the next person at the head of the line, and as people buy their tickets, the line moves forward.

At a busy movie theater, there may be many ticket booths consuming customers from the line. Management may open more ticket booths, based on the length of the line or based on how long people have to wait in the line. As the processing capacity of the ticket counter is increased, the theatre is able to sell tickets to more customers each minute. If the line gets short at a particular time, the theater manager might close down ticket booths until only one or two are left open.

Your system can use a similar concept with a queue. As the producer side of your system (the shopping cart checkout process, for example) produces messages, they're placed in the queue. The consumer side of the system (the ERP system that processes the orders and charges credit cards) will pull messages off of the queue. In this way, the two systems are tightly integrated but loosely coupled, because of the queue in between.

Queues are one-way in nature. A message goes in at the bottom, moves towards the top, and is eventually consumed, as you can see in figure 16.2. In order for the consumer message to communicate back to the producer, a separate process must be used. This could be a queue going in the other direction, but it's usually some other mechanism, like a shared storage location.

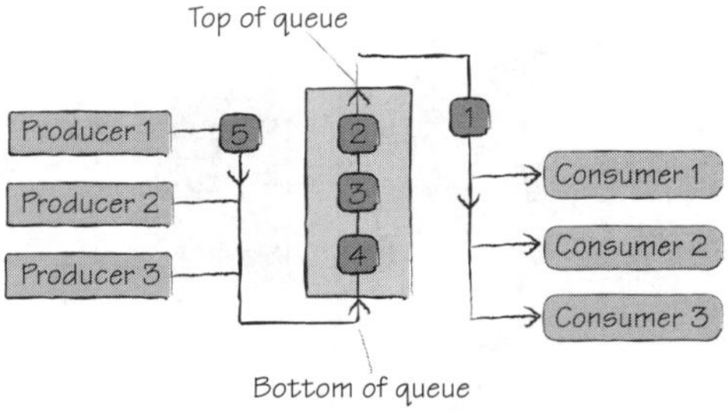

Figure 16.2 Producers place messages into the queue, and consumers get them out. Each queue can have multiple produces and consumers.

There's an inherent order to a queue, but you can't usually rely on queues for strict ordered delivery. In some scenarios, this can be important. A consumer processing checkouts from an e-commerce website won't need the messages in a precise order, but a set of doctor's orders for a patient might. It won't matter which checkout is processed first, as long as it's in a reasonable order, but the order of what tests, drugs, and surgeries are performed on a patient is likely important. We'll explore some ways of handling this situation in Azure later in this chapter.

16.1.2 What is a message?

Your Azure storage account can have many queues; at any time, a queue can have many messages. Messages are the lifeblood of a queue system and should represent the things that a producer is telling a consumer. You can think of a queue as having a name, some properties, and a collection of ordered messages.

In Azure, messages are limited to 8 KB in size. This low limit is designed for performance and scalability reasons. If a message could be up to 1 GB in size, writing to and reading from the queue would take a long time. This would also make it hard for the queue to respond quickly when there were many different consumers reading messages from the top of the queue.

Because of this limit, most Azure queue messages will follow a work ticket pattern. The message will usually not contain the data needed by the consumer itself. Instead, the message will contain a pointer of some sort to the real work that needs to be done.

For example, following along with figure 16.3, a queue that contains messages for video compression won't include the actual video that needs to be compressed. The producer will store the video in a shared storage location ❶, perhaps a BLOB container or a table. Once the video is stored, the producer will then place a message in the queue with the name of the BLOB that needs to be compressed ❷. There'll likely be other jobs in the queue as well.

The consumer will then pick up the work ticket, fetch the proper video from BLOB storage, compress the video ❸, and then store the new video back in BLOB storage ❹. Sometimes the process ends there, with the original producer being smart enough to look in the BLOB storage for the compressed version of the video, or perhaps a flag in a database is flipped to show that the processing has been completed.

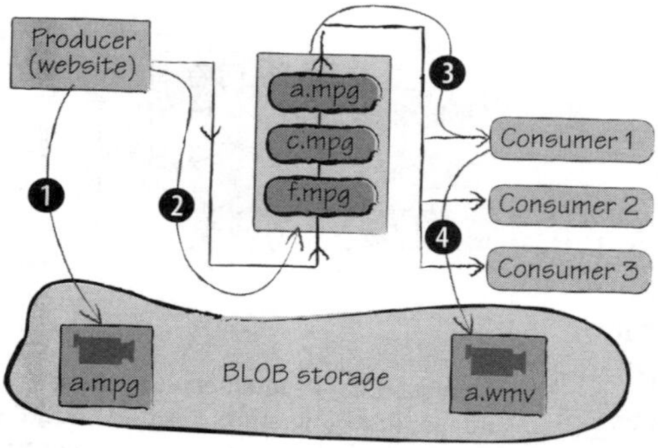

Figure 16.3 Work tickets are used in queues to tell the consumer what work needs to be done. This keeps the messages small, and keeps the queue scalable and performant. The work ticket is usually a pointer to where the real work is.

The content of a queue message is always stored as a string. The string must be in a format that can be included in an XML message and be UTF-8 encoded. This is because a message is returned from the queue in an XML format, with your real message as part of that XML. It's possible to store binary data, but you need to serialize and deserialize the data yourself. Keep in mind that when you're deserializing, the content coming out of the message will be base64 encoded.

The content of the message isn't the only part of the message that you may want to work with. Every message has several important properties, as you can see in the following listing.

Listing 16.1 A message in its native XML format

```
<QueueMessagesList>
 <QueueMessage>
  <MessageId>20be3f61-b70f-47c7-
  ➥ 9f87-abbf4c71182b</MessageId>                    ❶ Unique message ID
  <InsertionTime>Fri, 07 Aug 2009
  ➥ 00:58:41 GMT</InsertionTime>                     ❷ Date and time message was placed on queue
  <ExpirationTime>Fri, 14 Aug 2009 00:58:41 GMT</ExpirationTime>
  <PopReceipt>NzBjM2QwZDYtMzFjMC00MGVhLThiOTEtZ
  ➥ DcxODBlZDczYjA4</PopReceipt>
  <TimeNextVisible>Fri, 07 Aug 2009 00:59:16 GMT</TimeNextVisible>
  <MessageText>PHNhbXBsZT5zYW1wbGUgbWVzc2FnZTwvc2FtcGxlPg==</MessageText>
 </QueueMessage>
</QueueMessagesList>
```

The ID property is assigned by the storage system, and it's unique ❶. This is the only way to uniquely differentiate messages from each other because several messages could contain the same content.

A message also includes the time and date the message was inserted into the queue ❷. It can be handy to see how long the message has been waiting to be processed. For example, you might use this information to determine whether the messages are becoming stale in the queue. This timestamp is also used by the storage service to determine if your message should be garbage collected or not. Any message that's about a week old in any queue will be collected and discarded.

Now that we've discussed what messages are, we're ready to discuss what contains them—the queue itself.

16.1.3 What is a queue?

The queue is the mechanism that holds the messages, in a rough order, until they're consumed. The queue is replicated in triplicate throughout the storage service, like tables and BLOBs, for redundancy and performance reasons.

Queues can be created in a static manner, perhaps as part of deploying your application. They can also be created and destroyed dynamically. This is handy when you need a way to organize and direct messages in different directions based on real-time data or user needs.

Each queue can have an unlimited number of messages. The only real limit is how fast you can process the messages, and whether you can do so before they're garbage collected after one week's time.

Because a queue's name appears in the URI for the REST request, it needs to follow the constraints that DNS names have:

- It must start with a letter or number, and can contain only letters, numbers, and the hyphen (-) character.
- The first and last letters in the queue name must be alphanumeric. The hyphen (-) character may not be the first or last character.
- All letters in a queue name must be lowercase. (This is the requirement that gets me every time.)
- A queue name must be from 3 to 63 characters long.

A queue also has a set of metadata associated with it. This metadata can be up to 8 KB in size and is a simple collection of name/value key pairs. This metadata can help you track and manage your queues. Although the name of a queue can help you understand what the use of the queue is, the metadata can be useful in a more dynamic situation. For example, the name of the queue might be the customer number that the queue is related to, but you could store the customer's service level (tin, silver, molybdenum, and gold) as a piece of metadata. This metadata then lives with the queue and can be accessed by any producer or consumer of the queue.

Queues are both a reliable and persistent way to store and move messages. They're reliable in that you should never lose a message—we'll look at how this works in section 16.4 when we discuss the message lifecycle. Queues are also strict in how they persist your messages. If a server goes down, the messages aren't lost, they remain in the queue. This differs from a purely memory-based system, in which all of the messages would be lost if the server were to have a failure.

16.1.4 StorageClient and the REST API

There are two basic ways to interact with a queue and its messages. The first is the StorageClient library that ships with the Azure SDK. The other mechanism for interacting with queues is to use the REST API directly. You can create and consume REST messages in any way you want. Although this is a little more work, it's worth learning how the REST API works, so that you understand more fully how the storage system works.

The REST entry point will be your key way to access Azure storage when you don't have a handy API lying around, like the StorageClient. Microsoft and several open source teams are working to build SDKs similar to the StorageClient library for every platform, including Python and PHP. All of these libraries use the REST protocols under the hood.

Each call into the REST API has a request header that includes some basic information. The header needs to include which version of the service you're targeting, the date and time of the request, and the authorization header. You can see a sample header in the following listing.

Listing 16.2 A sample REST request header

```
POST /queue21b3c6dfe8626450880b9e16c70e2425e/messages?timeout=30 HTTP/1.1
x-ms-date: Fri, 07 Aug 2009 01:26:38 GMT
Authorization: SharedKey hsslog:Iow8eYFGeodLGqXrgbEcwDuA+aNOR0emEC9uy3Vnggg=
Host: hsslog.queue.core.windows.net
Content-Length: 80
Expect: 100-continue
```

The service version header is useful for preventing an update to the queue service from disrupting your system. You can force your requests to be processed by a specific version of the storage service, allowing you to control when you support and leverage new features in a newer version of the service. If you omit the version header, your request will be routed to the default version of the service.

A queue can't be made public or anonymous. Every operation against a queue must be authenticated with the shared key method. Constructing the authorization header for queue requests is the same as for BLOBs and tables.

Now that you know how to forge the header, or the envelope, for a message, let's look at how to send commands to the queue.

16.2 Working with basic queue operations

To show you how to use the basic queue API operations, we're going to build a queue browser. This little tool (shown in figure 16.4) will help you debug any system you're

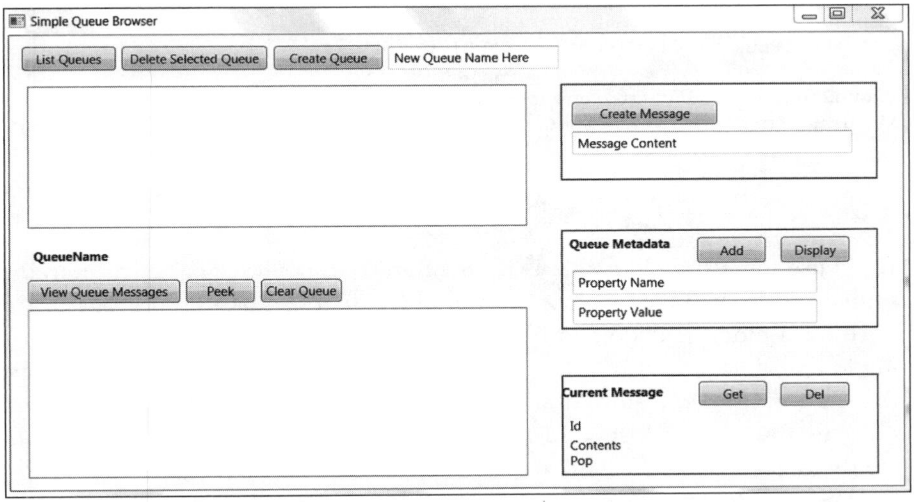

Figure 16.4 A screenshot of the simple queue browser we'll build in this chapter. It's important to note that your authors, while charming, aren't graphic designers or UX specialists. This tool will act as a vehicle for understanding the basics of working with queues.

building, by letting you look at the queues that are being used and see how they're working.

We'll be focusing on creating methods that perform each of the following operations of the browser:

- `ListQueues()`—Lists the queues that exist in your storage account
- `Create()` or `CreateIfNotExist()`—Creates queues in your account
- `SetMetadata()`—Writes metadata
- `Clear()`—Clears a queue of all of its pending messages
- `Delete()`—Deletes a queue or a message from the system

We aren't going to focus on how WPF works, or the best application architecture for this little application. This is meant to be "me-ware"—something that works for you and doesn't have to work for anyone else. You should use it as a harness to play with the different APIs and learn how they work.

16.2.1 Get a list of queues

There are several basic queue operations that you'll need to be able to work with. The first one we're going to look at is a method that will tell you what queues exist in your account. You may not always need this. Usually, you'll know what the queue for your application is and provision it for yourself.

To get a list of the available queues, you need to first connect to the queue service and then call the method. You can see how in the following listing.

Listing 16.3 Connecting to the queue service and getting a list of queues

```
private CloudQueueClient Qsvc;
private IEnumerable<CloudQueue> qList;

CloudStorageAccount storageAccount =
➥ CloudStorageAccount.FromConfigurationSetting("DataConnectionString");

Qsvc = storageAccount.CreateCloudQueueClient();   <-- ❶ Creates queue client to interact with queue

qList = Qsvc.ListQueues();
```

You'll use something like line ❶ quite often. This creates a connection to the service, similar to how you create a connection object to a database. You'll want to create this once for a block of code and hold it in memory so that you aren't always reconnecting to the service. In this little application, we create this object in the constructor for the window itself and store it in a variable at the form level. This makes it available to every method in the form and saves you the trouble of having to continuously recreate the object.

The `CloudStorageAccount` serves as a factory that creates service objects that represent the Azure Queue storage service, called the `CloudQueueClient`. There are several ways to create the `CloudQueueClient`. The most common approach is to create it as in listing 16.3, by using the `FromConfigurationSetting` method. This looks into your configuration and sets up all of the URIs, usernames, account names, and so on. This is better than having to set four or five different parameters when you're newing up the connection.

Once you have a handle to the Queue service, you can call `ListQueues`. This doesn't just return a list of strings, as you might expect, but instead returns a collection of queue objects. Each queue object represents a queue in your account and is fully usable. The equivalent call to get a list of queues in REST would be like the following code. You can see that it's a simple `GET`.

```
GET http://hsslog.queue.core.windows.net/
➥ ?comp=list&maxresults=50&timeout=30
```

If you don't have any queues, you'll get back an empty collection. In this case, your next step would be to create a queue.

16.2.2 Creating a queue

Once you're connected to the queue service you can create a queue with the queue client. You do this by creating a reference to the queue, even if the queue doesn't exist yet. Then you can create the queue using the reference as a control point:

```
CloudQueue q = Qsvc.GetQueueReference("newordersqueue");
q.CreateIfNotExist();
```

In the preceding code, we first create a `CloudQueue` object. This is an empty object, and this line doesn't actually connect to the service. It's merely an empty handle that doesn't point to anything. Then the `CreateIfNotExist` method is called on the queue object. This will check if a queue with that name exists, and if it doesn't, it'll create one. This is very handy.

You can check whether a queue exists before you try to create it by using `q.DoesQueueExist`. This method will return a Boolean value telling you whether the queue exists or not.

Your next step is to attach some metadata to the queue.

16.2.3 Attaching metadata

You can store up to 8 KB of data in the property bag for each queue. You might want to use this to track some core data about the queue, or perhaps some core metrics on how often it should be polled. To work with the metadata, use the following code:

```
CloudQueue q = Qsvc.GetQueueReference("newordersqueue");
q.Metadata.Add("ProjectName", "ElectronReintroductionPhasing");
q.Metadata.Remove("BadKeyNoDoughnut");
q.SetMetadata();
```

The metadata for a queue is attached as a property on the `CloudQueue` object. You work with it like any other name value collection. In this code, we first add a new entry to the metadata called `ProjectName`, with a value of `ElectronReintroductionPhasing`. But this new entry won't be saved back to the queue service until we call `SetMetaData`, which connects to the service and uploads the metadata for the queue in the cloud.

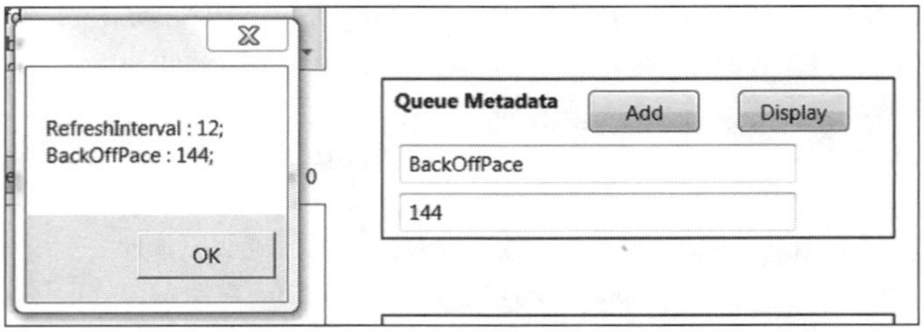

Figure 16.5 Displaying the metadata set on a queue. You can attach up to 8 KB of metadata to a queue. This can help in managing the queue, such as by specifying what the backoff pace rate should be.

You can remove existing properties from the bag if you no longer need them. In this example, the `Remove` method removes `BadKeyNoDoughnut` from use. When you remove an item from the metadata collection, you must follow that with a `SetMetaData` call to persist the changes to the cloud.

In our queue example application, we've set some metadata properties, namely `RefreshInterval` and `BackOffPace`. You can see how we set and fetch these in figure 16.5.

Now that you've created a queue and set its metadata, let's look at how you can delete a queue. On occasion, you'll want to dynamically create and destroy queues.

16.2.4 Deleting a queue

It's good practice to clear a queue before you delete it. This removes all of the messages from the queue. The clear queue method is handy for resetting a system or clearing out poison messages that may have stopped up the flow.

Deleting a queue is as simple as this, when using the client library:

```
CloudQueue q = Qsvc.GetQueueReference("newordersqueue");
q.Clear();
q.Delete();
```

The equivalent REST call would be as follows:

```
DELETE http://hsslog.queue.core.windows.net/newordersqueue?timeout=30
```

Being able to create and destroy queues in a single line of code makes them simple objects to work with. In the past, using a queue in your system would require days, if not weeks, of installing several queue servers (for redundancy purposes). They would also require a lot of care and feeding. Queues in the cloud are much easier to work with and don't require any grooming or maintenance. But the real power of queues is in the messages that flow through them, which we'll delve into in the next section.

16.3 Working with messages

Now that you know how to work with queues, let's look at how you can work with messages. As we mentioned above, a queue is a FIFO structure, similar to a line at the movie theater. The first action we usually take with a queue it to put a message in it, or *enqueue* a message.

16.3.1 Putting a message on the queue

When you put a message on the queue, the new message is placed onto the bottom or end of the queue. When you get a message from the queue, it's from the top or front of the queue. Here we have a few lines of code that show how to add a message to a queue:

```
CloudQueue q = Qsvc.GetQueueReference("newordersqueue");
CloudQueueMessage theNewMessage = new CloudQueueMessage("cart:31415");
q.AddMessage(theNewMessage);
```

To add a message to the queue, you need to get a reference to the queue, as we did in the preceding code. Once you have the queue reference, you can call the `AddMessage` method and pass in a `CloudQueueMessage` object. Creating the message is a simple affair; in this case we're simply passing in text that will be the content of the message. You can also pass in a byte array if you're passing some serialized binary data. Remember that the content of each message is limited to 8 KB in size. When you put a message on a queue, a REST message is generated and sent to the queue. The following listing shows you a sample of what that might look like. This sample is for entertainment purposes only.

Listing 16.4 An example of putting a message onto a queue with REST

```
POST /my-special-queue/messages?timeout=30 HTTP/1.1
x-ms-date: Fri, 07 Aug 2009 01:49:25 GMT
Authorization: SharedKey hsslog:3oJPdtrUK47gMSpHfwrmasdnT5nJpGpszg=
Host: hsslog.queue.core.windows.net
Content-Length: 80
Expect: 100-continue

<QueueMessage><MessageText>cart:31415</MessageText></QueueMessage>
```

In this example, we're adding a message with an order number that can be found in the related Azure table. The consumer will pick up the message, unwrap the content, and process the cart numbered 31415. Their shopping cart is probably filled with pie and pie related accessories.

Before we show you how to get a message, we want to talk about peeking.

16.3.2 Peeking at messages

Peeking is a way to get the content of a message in the queue without taking the message off of the queue. This leaves the message still on the queue, so someone else can grab it. Many people peek at messages to determine if they want to process the message or not, or to determine how they should process the message. You can see how to peek in this snippet of code:

```
CloudQueueMessage m = q.PeekMessage();

private IEnumerable<CloudQueueMessage> mList;
mList = q.PeekMessages(10);
```

Peeking at messages is easy. Calling the PeekMessage method returns a single message—the one at the front of the queue. You can peek at more than one message by calling PeekMessages and providing the number of messages you want returned. In the preceding example, we asked for 10 messages.

Now that you've peeked at the messages, you're ready to get them.

16.3.3 Getting messages

You don't have to peek at a message before getting it, and many times you won't use peek at all. Getting a message off of the queue is simple, as shown here:

```
private CloudQueueMessage currentMsg;
currentMsg = q.GetMessage();
```

If you already have a reference to your queue, getting a message is as simple as calling GetMessage. There's one override that lets you determine the visibility timeout of the get. We'll discuss the lifecycle of a message in section 16.4.

Getting the contents of the message, so that you can work with it, is quite simple, especially if it was string data and not binary data:

```
string s = currentMsg.AsString;
```

Once you have a message, you can use the AsString or AsBytes properties to access the contents of the message. This is the meat of the message, and the part you're most likely interested in.

Once you've processed a message, you'll want to delete it. This takes it off of the queue.

16.3.4 Deleting messages

Deleting a message is as easy as getting it:

```
q.DeleteMessage(currentMsg);
```

To delete a message, you need to pass the message back into the DeleteMessage method of the queue object. You can also do it easily with REST. You can only delete one message at a time. The DELETE command in REST would look like the following example. Notice that all of the pertinent data needed is in the query string.

```
DELETE http://hsslog.queue.core.windows.net/my-special
➥ -queue/messages/f5104ff3-260c-48c8-
➥ 9c35-cd8ffe3d5ace?popreceipt=AgAAAAEAAAAAAAAA1vkQXwEXygE%3d&timeout=30
```

Regardless of how you delete the message, through REST or the API, be prepared to handle any exceptions that might be thrown.

One aspect of messages that we haven't looked at yet is their lifecycle. What happens when a message is retrieved? How does the queue keep the same message from being picked up by several consumers at the same time? Is a message self-aware? These are important questions for a queue service. Never losing a message (known as durability) is critical to a queue.

16.4 Understanding message visibility

A key aspect of a queue is how it manages its messages and their visibility. This is how the queue implements the message durability developers are looking for. The goal is to protect against a consumer getting a message, and then failing to process and delete that message. If that happened, the message would be lost, and this isn't good news for any processing system.

Visibility timeouts and idempotency are the two best tools for making sure your messages are never lost. Understanding how these concepts relate to the queue and understanding the lifecycle of a message are important to the success of your code.

16.4.1 About message visibility and invisibility

Every message has a visibility timeout property. When a message is pulled from the queue, it isn't really deleted; it's just temporarily marked as invisible. The consumer is also given a receipt (called the pop receipt) that's unique to that `GetMessage()` operation. The duration of invisibility can be controlled by the consumer, and it can be as long as 2 hours. If not explicitly set, it will default to 30 seconds. While a message is invisible, it won't be given out in response to new `GetMessage()` operations.

As an example, let's say a producer has placed four messages in a queue, as shown in figure 16.6, and we have two consumers that will be reading messages out of the queue.

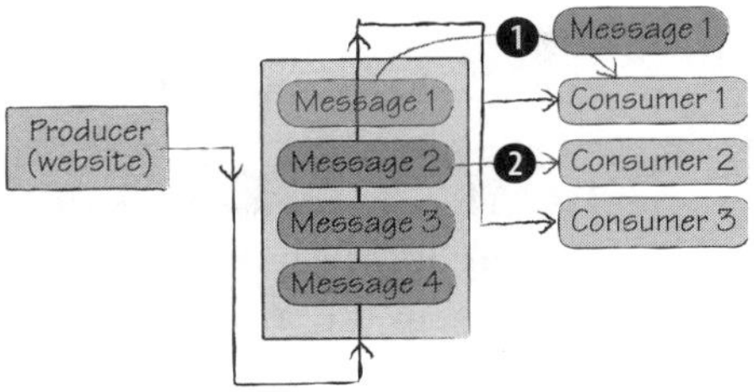

Figure 16.6 Two consumers getting messages from a queue. A message is marked invisible when a `GetMessage()` operation is performed—just like a cloak of invisibility. Note that this effect times out after a while.

Consumer 1 gets a message (msg 1), and that message is marked invisible ❶. Seconds later, consumer 2 performs a get operation as well. Because the first message (msg 1) is invisible, the queue responds with the next message (msg 2) ❷.

Not long thereafter, consumer 1 finishes processing msg 1 and performs a delete operation on the message. As part of the delete operation, the queue checks the pop receipt consumer 1 provides when it passes in the message. This is to make sure consumer 1 is the most recent reader of the message in question. The receipt matches in this case, and the message is deleted.

Consumer 1 then does an immediate read, and gets msg 3. Consumer 1 fails to complete processing within the invisibility time window and fails to delete msg 3 in time. It becomes visible again.

Just at that time, consumer 2 deletes msg 2 and does a get. The queue responds with msg 3, because it's visible again. While consumer 2 is processing msg 3, consumer 1 does finally finish processing msg 3 and tries to delete it. This time, the pop receipt, which consumer 1 has, doesn't match the most recently provided pop receipt, which was given to consumer 2 when msg 3 was handed out for a second time. Because the pop receipt doesn't match, an error is thrown, and the message isn't deleted. You'll likely see a 400 (`Bad Request`) error when this happens. The inner exception details will explain that there aren't any messages with a matching pop receipt available in the queue to be deleted.

16.4.2 Setting visibility timeout

You can set the length of the visibility timeout when you get the message. This lets you determine the proper length of the timeout for each individual message.

When you specify the visibility timeout, you want to balance the expected processing time and how long it will take for the system to recover from an error in processing. If the timeout is too long, it will take a long time for the system to recover a lost message. If the timeout is too short, too many of your messages will be repeatedly reprocessed.

This leads us to an important aspect of queues in general, but specifically the Azure queue system.

16.4.3 Planning on failure

The Queue service guarantee is worded as promising that every message will be processed, *at least once*. You can see this "at least once" business in the previous scenario. Because consumer 1 failed to delete the message in time, the queue handed it out to another consumer. The queue has to assume the original consumer has failed in some way.

This is very useful because it provides a way for your system to take a hit (a server going down) and keep on going. Cloud architecture plans on failure and makes that central to the structure of the system. Queues provide that capability quite nicely.

The downside is that it's possible that a consumer doesn't crash but just takes longer to process the message than intended. In this case, you need to make sure that your processing code is either idempotent, or that it checks before processing each message to make sure it isn't a duplicate copy. Because the message being reprocessed is actually the same message, its ID property will be the same. This makes it easy to check a history table or perhaps the status of a related order before processing starts.

This little bit of complexity might make you think about deleting a message as soon as you receive it—before you process it. Doing so is dangerous and unwise because there will be failure along the way, and when that happens, the message would be lost forever.

16.4.4 Use idempotent processing code

The goal of a messaging system is to make sure you never lose a message. No matter how small or large, you never want to lose an order, or a set of instructions, or anything else you might be processing.

To avoid complexity, it's best to make sure your processing code is *idempotent*. Idempotent means that the process can be executed several times and the system will result in the same state. Suppose you're working with a piece of software that tracks dog food delivery. When the food is delivered to the physical address, the handheld computer sends a message to your queue in the cloud. The software uploads the physical signature of the recipient to BLOB storage and submits an order-delivered message to the queue. The message contains the time of delivery and the order number, which happens to also be the filename of the signature in BLOB storage.

When this message is processed, the consumer copies the signature image to permanent storage, with the proper filename, and marks the order as delivered in the package-tracking database.

If this message were to be processed several times, there would be no detriment to the system. The signature file would be overwritten with the same file. The order status is already set to delivered, so we'd just be setting its status to delivered again. Using the same delivery time doesn't change the overall state of the system.

This is the best way to handle the processing of queue messages, but it isn't always possible. The next section will discuss some common queue-processing patterns, and some of them deal with working around this issue.

16.5 Patterns for message processing

As simple as queues are, they can prove valuable in a lot of complex scenarios. This section will focus on some common approaches developers tend to use with queues.

16.5.1 Shared counters

You might run into a scenario where a piece of work is broken into many small pieces, and you need to make sure all of those small pieces are completed before you move on to the next step in your process. Sometimes these pieces are subsets of the main problem.

This is called *single instruction, multiple data*. The same processing will be performed to each piece of data, but each piece is a subset of the whole. Consider working on an image. If you break the image into 100 pieces and apply the same process to each piece, you need to know for sure that all 100 pieces are completed before you can stitch them back into the larger picture.

If you just break the image into 100 pieces and throw them into the queue, it can be difficult to know for sure when all of the 100 units of work have been completed. This has to do with the visibility timeout and the nondeterministic nature of queues. You might think that you could simply check the estimated length of the queue using `q.ApproximateMessageCount`:

```
q.RetrieveApproximateMessageCount();
if (q.ApproximateMessageCount != null)
   int remainingMsg = q.ApproximateMessageCount;
```

If you do, you must call `RetrieveApproximateMessageCount`, which fetches the information into the `ApproximateMessageCount` property from the queue in the cloud, before you call the property itself. This property returns an approximate count of the items in the queue, not an exact count, for two reasons. The first is that the queue is running in triplicate, and an add operation might have completed on one instance but not the other two, which would lead to an inconsistent result. The second reason is that you might get a zero back from your check, only to have an invisible message turn visible again when its timeout expires. Then you would have a message in the queue you didn't know about.

You need a deterministic way to know for sure that all 100 pieces have been processed. One way to do this is to use a shared counter, perhaps in an Azure table. You can see a visualization of this process in figure 16.7.

When the processing starts, a table is made with a counter set to 0. As items are submitted into the queue by the producer ❷, the counter is incremented ❶. As the work is completed in the consumer and the messages are deleted ❸, the counter is decremented ❹.

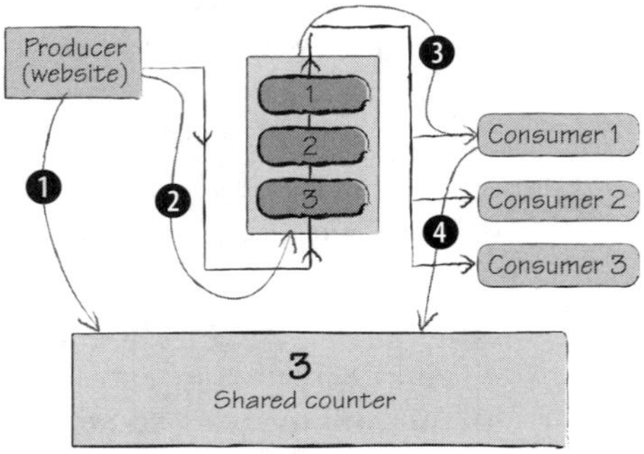

Figure 16.7 Using a shared counter is one way to deterministically track how many messages have been processed. This is a good approach if you have a specific number of messages to process and you need a precise count.

There is one small flaw this approach suffers from, and it's a flaw all shared counters have: it's possible to run into a concurrency problem. If one process reads the counter, adds 1 to it, and then writes it back to the table while another process is doing the same thing, they could end up overwriting each other, resulting in losing track of the count. In order to fix this, you need to use locking on the counter. Another solution, which is used in eventually consistent scenarios, is to read the counter a second time before you write to it, to make sure it wasn't changed by someone else while you weren't looking.

This approach will give you a simple count indicating the progress of the work. What if you want to know which pieces are done and which aren't? No problem. You can do this with a small change to the previous approach.

Instead of writing to a shared counter on each put operation, create a new record in the shared table. This will result in one record per queue message. As they're processed and the queue messages are deleted, the corresponding row should be deleted in the table. Another option would be to mark a property of the row in the table as complete, or store a completed time and date for performance tracking.

In either of these ways—with the shared counter or the shared message tracking table—you can know with a simple query whether all of the work has been completed or not. You should think about wiring up a management portal that monitors the counter or table to show the progress to an administrator.

16.5.2 Work complete receipt

The preceding scenario works when you can control the producer and you have a closed loop. But what if you don't own the producer, or there are too many producers for you to make them also manage a counter? In this case, you can use a return receipt, or a work complete receipt.

In this approach, as work is completed, a message is sent through a separate channel, perhaps another queue, back to the producer. This alerts the producer that the work is done. This is common in scenarios where the process takes a long time to complete, and the producer wants an asynchronous notification when the work is done.

Instead of using a return queue, we've also had the consumer call a small notification web service on the producer side, sending a simple message regarding the status of the work. This makes the consumer an active part of the process, and it removes the need for the producer to monitor a queue and become a consumer itself.

16.5.3 Asymmetric queues versus symmetric queues

Queues are decidedly one-way. They're a way for one or more producers to communicate with one or more consumers, but not the other way around.

Using one queue in this manner is an *asymmetric queue*. Generally, in an asymmetric queue, the producer finds out about the work being completed in a passive way. The new file happens to be in the right place when the user hits Refresh, or the customer receives an email when the order is shipped, or any number of other scenarios.

As was discussed in section 16.5.2 about work complete receipts, sometimes using symmetric queues can be useful. This makes the response from the consumer back to the producer an active one. Using a queue to do this does help decouple the two halves of the system, but it can lead to too much complexity. This also turns the original producer into a consumer in its own right, which can be hard to implement if the original producer was a website. Because websites only respond to outside requests (a person performs a GET or POST with a web browser to view the catalog), they don't have a running process to proactively read the queue and respond to it. How this might work is laid out in figure 16.8.

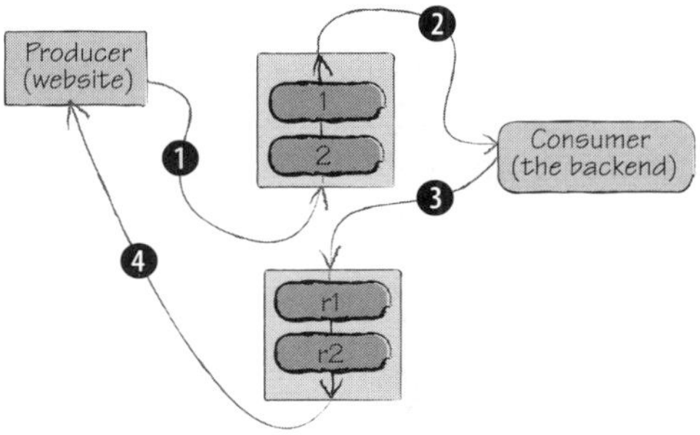

Figure 16.8 A symmetric queue is when two queues are used together to allow for two-way communication between a set of consumers and a set of producers. This keeps both sets of systems loosely coupled. The inbound queue is on the top, and the outbound queue is on the bottom.

In figure 16.8, you can see two queues connecting the consumers and the producers together. The top queue is the inbound queue, sending messages to the consumers. The bottom queue is the outbound queue, bringing messages back to the consumers. A typical message pattern would be for the producer to send a message to the consumer by putting it in the inbound queue ❶. The consumer picks up the message ❷, does some critical business work, like ordering pudding, and submits a confirmation message back to the producer by putting it in the outbound queue ❸. The producer finally receives the confirmation message ❹.

16.5.4 Truncated exponential backoff

It's quite common for a worker role to have an infinite loop that polls the queue, processes the work, and pauses for a period of time if the queue is empty. The following listing shows the typical infinite polling loop.

Listing 16.5 The typical infinite loop to poll a queue

```
while (true)
{
   CloudQueueMessage msg = queue.GetMessage();        ❶ Gets message
   if (msg != null)
   {
      string messageContent = msg.AsString;
      DoWork(messageContent);
      queue.DeleteMessage(msg);        ❷ Does work, deletes message
   }
   else
   {
      System.Threading.Thread.Sleep(1000);        ❸ Sleeps if no messages
   }
}
```

In this listing, a permanent `true` condition starts the loop off, looping until `true` equals `false`, which shouldn't ever happen (and if it does, we're all in for a world of hurt). We grab the first message off of the queue and check to see if it's `null`. If there aren't any messages on the queue, the `GetMessage` ❶ would return a `NULL` message. If there is a message, we process it, not deleting it until the real work is fully completed ❷.

If there wasn't a new message retrieved, the loop sleeps for a period of time ❸, and then tries again.

Sometimes you might find that a queue is polled too often. If this is a concern, you can dynamically change the wait time in the bottom of the loop. A common algorithm used in networking is called *truncated exponential backoff*. You can see an example of how to implement this in listing 16.6. Under this system, each time a queue check doesn't return a message, the loop delay is extended exponentially until a certain ceiling is reached. If the check does return a message, the loop delay is decreased, either back to the lowest setting, or to the next lowest setting in the progression.

Listing 16.6 Adjusting the delay in a polling loop

```
while (true)
{
      CloudQueueMessage msg = q.GetMessage();
      if (msg != null)
      {
```

```
            q.DeleteMessage(msg);

        if (useGradualDecrease)
            if (currentInterval > intervalFloor)
                currentInterval =
                ➥ currentInterval / 2;                  ❶ Decreases sleep interval
            else
                currentInterval = intervalFloor;
        else
            currentInterval = intervalFloor;

    }
    else
    {
        if (currentInterval < intervalCeiling)           ❷ Increases sleep interval
        currentInterval = currentInterval * 2;

        Thread.Sleep(currentInterval * 1000);
    }
}
```

For example, suppose the start value for the delay loop was 2 seconds. After an empty poll, the length would be doubled to 4 seconds. Successive empty checks would result in the time delay increasing to 8, 16, 32, 64, 128, 256, and 512 seconds. You can see the code that produces this progression at ❷. Figure 16.9 shows how the delay is increasing in this example as the queue remains empty.

At 512 seconds, the counter reaches the maximum set for the system, so it doesn't rise above 512 seconds. After some time a message appears. The system processes the message, and then checks the length of the queue. Because there was activity on the queue, the delay setting is set to the next step down the ladder, to 256 seconds at line ❶. The code also supports an immediate drop to the floor interval if you want an aggressive increase in the rate of polling.

Figure 16.9 shows the backoff polling in action. The sample code will randomly put messages in the monitored queue—there's a one-in-three chance of it doing so. The interval started at 2 seconds, and was immediately bumped to 4. Then a message was processed, so it was dialed back down to 2. Then there was a succession of empty calls, leading the code to rapidly increase the polling interval all the way up to 16 seconds between checks.

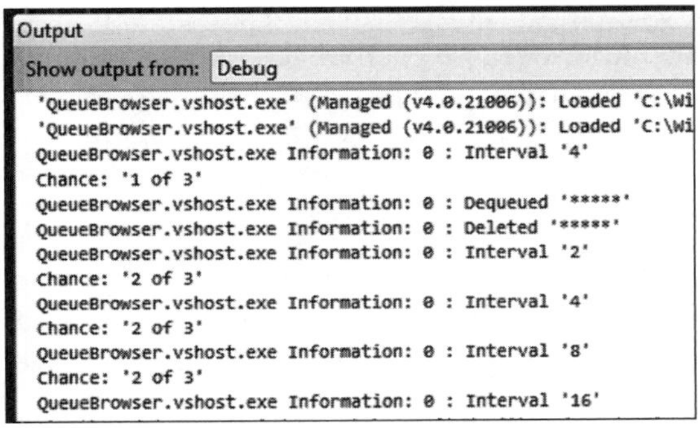

Figure 16.9 The output from running the truncated exponential backoff polling algorithm. You can see the polling interval exponentially increase from 2 to 4 to 8 to 16 as the queue continues to be empty.

16.5.5 Queue creation on startup

One advantage of the Azure storage system is the easy creation and deletion of queues. A common trend is to inspect the storage system on system startup to determine if the needed entities (BLOBs, tables, and queues) exist. If they don't exist, they're created on the spot. This makes it easy to deploy a system, knowing that it will self-provision the storage resources it needs during startup.

A possible drawback to this approach is forgetting to manage the state of these resources carefully. If you're rolling out an upgrade to the system, and the initialization steps clear out the work queues and other storage entities, it's possible that you could lose valuable data or work in progress. Make sure that you test both new deployments and upgrades to your system in a safe environment before relying on the self-provisioning code. The automatic provisioning may also impact performance on system startup, because it will be busy checking the infrastructure and configuring things as needed.

16.5.6 Dynamic queues versus static queues

Most queues in your applications will be static in nature. The design of your system will require whatever queues it needs, and these will be provisioned when the application is deployed and left to run as is.

Alternatively, you can create queues dynamically. For example, you can create a new custom queue for each new order that's being processed by the system. This helps your application dynamically scale, and it also helps you separate different concerns in your system.

Perhaps you're building a system for a value-added network that manages the flow of purchase order messages from vendors and suppliers. All day long you're signing up new vendors and suppliers, and some occasionally stop using your service. A great way to automate the provisioning of the queues that are needed for each customer that signs up is to dynamically create the queues and infrastructure as they sign up and are approved as users of the system.

You want to pay careful attention to the state of each customer, and make sure that any leftover data is cleaned up, and entities are deprovisioned as customers stop using your service. You don't want to have to pay for unneeded infrastructure that's forgotten and left lying around.

Another scenario would be even more short term than the preceding one. Think back to the image-processing scenario. Because each image needs a queue to manage its breakdown and processing, you could dynamically create a queue for each new image job that's submitted. When the processing is complete, the queue could be torn down.

16.5.7 Ordered delivery

Some scenarios require guaranteed ordered delivery, such as some EDI scenarios, but the queue, as it is, doesn't support ordered delivery. There are several approaches for adding this capability on top of the normal queue service.

The simplest approach hinges on the series of messages having a header message that declares the length of the series, or the existence of a trailer message that tells the system when the last message has been received.

The basic approach would be for a process to monitor the normal queue, pull the messages off, and store them in a temporary Azure table. The table should have an integer property that stores the order of that message in the series. Once the defined number of messages are received, or when the trailer message is received, the messages can be properly ordered (usually by some element present in the message themselves) and then sent on to the final system that needed the messages ordered properly.

An optimization would be to have the process that's ordering the messages start trickling them on to the final destination when it knows that it has some of the messages already in order. For example, if messages arrive in the order 1, 2, 3, 5, 6, 4, the message collator could almost immediately send messages 1, 2, and 3. The collator would have to wait for message 4 to arrive before it could forward messages 4, 5, and 6.

16.5.8 Long queues

Most of the queues we've discussed so far have been in the form of an immediately serviced queue, where there are one or more consumers actively processing the messages in the queue.

There are times when it's important to have a long queue in play. This might be a queue that receives messages all day long, without an active consumer. The messages would be processed in a batch later that evening, when the consumer comes online. You might have an application in the field that sends messages into the cloud during the day; then, in the evening, a backend system comes online, processes all of the messages, and goes back offline. This would be a useful scenario when the consuming system isn't always available to process the messages you're holding in the queue.

16.5.9 Dynamically scaling to meet queue demand

The promise of queues is that the processing of messages is decoupled from the production of those messages. By decoupling the backend, you're free to scale the backend to meet the demands of the number of messages in the queue.

In a traditional environment, the number of producers is fairly static. The pool of consumers can be scaled, but it requires all the work of buying an additional server, provisioning it, and deploying it to the pool. This can be time consuming, and you're likely to miss the spike in demand while you're waiting for hardware to be shipped from your vendor.

The promise of cloud computing is the true dynamic allocation of resources to your computing needs. A management tool can be deployed that monitors the length of the queue in question. The tool can then dynamically create additional consumers (by increasing the number of deployed worker role instances using the service management API) based on the length of the queue. The management tool should define a cap on the number of instances that can be created, and also rules as to when instances should be created or destroyed.

For example, you might define the minimum number of instances as zero, with a maximum of five instances. The rule of thumb would be one instance per 20 messages in the queue. The management tool would need to determine the length of the queue on a regular basis, perhaps every 3 minutes. Your rules should always allow for a little reserve buffer capacity. If you run too close to actual demand, the slight delay it takes (a few minutes) to bring on new instances could have a deleterious effect on the performance of your system.

Because Azure is billed based on the number of active instances, and not the actual use of the CPU, this can be a way to not only meet spikes in demand with grace, but also to minimize the costs of the solution.

16.6 Summary

Azure queues are a great way to break your system into pieces that still work together to get the work done, and they're easy to work with. They don't have to connect Azure web and worker roles together. They can be used to help cloud applications, mobile applications, and enterprise applications communicate together. Instead of a mobile application needing to punch through a firewall to submit a new repair ticket, it can submit the ticket into the cloud, where it can be picked up later by the on-premises system.

Queues are often the only on-ramp to a backend system. In this role, they act as the service endpoint for the capability the backend system represents. We showed how simple it is to create and manage queues. They provide a durable way of passing messages, and they're high performance as well.

Although queues are pivotal in leveraging the dynamic power of Azure with their ability to act as load balancers for worker role instances, the real power is in the messages in the system. Messages are the lifeblood of a decoupled system, allowing different components and subsystems to work together without being required to understand dirty implementation details of external parts.

The key to the power and reliability of queues lies in the message lifecycle and how the visibility timeout is managed. This timeout provides a recovery mechanism in case a message is lost in a failed server.

We also explored several patterns that can be used in the design of your application. The two most common manage the polling of the queue with a backoff polling algorithm, and dynamically provision the proper number of consumers based on the depth of the queue.

We'll next explore how to connect all of your on-premises and cloud services together using the Windows Azure Platform AppFabric Service Bus, and how to secure your services with the ACS service. These will allow you to connect to anything anywhere, and to keep it all secure.

17 Connecting in the cloud with AppFabric

This chapter covers

- Securing your services with ACS
- Introducing the Service Bus
- Connecting to your service from anywhere

The Windows Azure platform AppFabric (hereafter referred to as AppFabric) is an important piece of the Windows Azure puzzle. It's part of the larger Azure ecosystem and provides some fundamental features for working with hybrid applications. It performs two major functions: securing REST services and connecting them together.

AppFabric is a big topic—one that deserves its own book. Whenever you start talking about security, you get into long conversations. The same goes for service buses. That's because both of these topics involve a lot of terminology that the average developer is likely not familiar with.

Our goal in this chapter is to give you enough of a look at AppFabric to understand the core scenarios it can be used for, and to understand enough to confidently dive into a detailed book on your own. We'll be visiting the two key services

(Access Control Service and Service Bus) with a simple and straightforward example. You'll need to know a little about Windows Communication Foundation (WCF), but don't worry—WCF isn't scary.

17.1 The road AppFabric has traveled

AppFabric is arguably the most mature part of Windows Azure, at least if you measure by how long it has been publicly available, if not broadly announced. AppFabric started life as BizTalk Services. It was seen as a complementary cloud offering to BizTalk Server. BizTalk is a high-end enterprise-grade messaging and integration platform, and indeed the services fit into that portfolio well. Some joke that it was called BizTalk Services as a clever way to keep it a secret, because BizTalk is one of the most underestimated products Microsoft has. Just ask a BizTalk developer.

When Windows Azure was announced at PDC 2008, the BizTalk Services were renamed to *.NET Services*. Over the following year, there was a push to get developers to work with the services and put the SDK through its paces. Out of that year of real-world testing came a lot of changes.

When Windows Azure went live in early 2010, the services were renamed again to Windows Azure platform AppFabric to tie it more closely to the Windows Azure platform. Some people were confused by the older .NET Services name, thinking it was just the runtime and base class library running in the cloud, which makes no sense whatsoever.

17.1.1 The two AppFabrics

Don't confuse the AppFabric we'll be covering in this chapter with the new Windows Server AppFabric product. They're currently related by name alone. Over time they'll merge to become the same product, but they aren't there quite yet.

Windows Server AppFabric is essentially an extension to Windows Activation Service (WAS) and IIS that makes it easier to host WCF and Windows Workflow Foundation (WF)-based services in your own data center. It supplies tooling and simple infrastructure to provide a base-level messaging infrastructure. It doesn't supply a local instance of the Access Control Service (ACS) or Service Bus service at this time. Likewise, Windows Azure platform AppFabric doesn't provide any of the features that Windows Server AppFabric does, at least today. In early CTPs of Windows Azure platform AppFabric, there was the ability to host WF workflows in the cloud, but this was removed as it moved toward a production release.

The AppFabric we're going to cover in this chapter makes two services available to you: Access Control Service and the Service Bus.

17.1.2 Two key AppFabric services

AppFabric is a library of services that focus on helping you run your services in the cloud and connect them to the rest of the world.

Not everything can run in the cloud, as we've discussed several times already in this book. For example, you could have software running on devices out in the field, a client-side rich application that runs on your customer's computers, or software that works with credit card information and can't be stored off-premises.

The two services in AppFabric are geared to help with these scenarios.

- *Access Control Service (ACS)*—This service provides a way to easily provide claims-based access control for REST services. This means that it abstracts away authentication and the role-based minutia of building an authorization system. Several of Azure's parts use ACS for their access control, including the Service Bus service in AppFabric.
- *Service Bus*—This service provides a bus in the cloud, allowing you to connect your services and clients together so they can be loosely coupled. A bus is simply a way to connect services together and route messages around. An advantage of the Service Bus is that you can connect it to anything, anywhere, without having to figure out the technology and magic that goes into making that possible.

As we look at each of these services, we'll cover some basic examples. All of these examples rely on WCF. The samples will run as normal local applications, not as Azure applications. We did it this way to show you how these services can work outside of the cloud, but also to make the examples easier to use.

Each example has two pieces that need to run: a client and a service. You can run both simultaneously when you press F5 in Visual Studio by changing the startup projects in the solution configuration.

17.2 Controlling access with ACS

Managing identity, authentication, and authorization is hard. It takes a lot of work by developers to get it right. One wrong step and you leave a gaping hole that a bad guy can take advantage of and land your company on the front page of the newspaper. Security is always a high priority on any project, but it's loaded with special terms and more complexity than developers generally want to deal with.

We're going to cover how you can integrate the user's identity inside your company with applications running in the cloud. We'll do this by leveraging claims-based authorization, which allows you to federate your internal identities with applications in the cloud by using standards-based tokens.

17.2.1 Identity in the cloud

When you move all of these concerns out of your own network and into the cloud, these concerns become even bigger issues. The application is no longer sitting right next to the source of authentication; the identity boundaries have been broken. How do you fix this problem?

The short answer is to build yet another identity store (a place to store usernames and passwords) and give every user yet another username and password to remember. They won't remember them—they'll either write it down on a sticky note on their monitor, or they'll call you once a month to remind them what it is. This is a bad experience for the user, and it's dangerous for the owner of the application.

We call this the *identity fishbowl*. Your identity (who you are and what you can do) is fairly easily maintained on your network, but the second you go off-premises you leave your fishbowl. The application in the cloud doesn't have any way to connect to your Active Directory to authenticate you. The way to bridge these worlds is with open standards and the concept of a federated identity.

There are some other challenges, as well. Let's go beyond the previous scenario where you have an internal user trying to access your application in the cloud. What if the user doesn't work for you, but is a customer or vendor of some sort. What if you need to provision 100 user accounts for that new customer, or 10,000 accounts? This is a lot of work for the administrator, it gives your end user yet another identity to remember, and it exposes you to a risk of not deleting an account when it should be. You're on the hook for managing those accounts, not the customer or vendor. If you have user accounts in your identity store that are active and belong to someone who has left the company, you're leaving a wide open hole for them (or an outside evildoer) to compromise that account and access your application when they shouldn't.

What you want is an easy and secure way for your internal users and external users (customers, vendors, and so on) to be able to access your application using the identities they already have. This approach also has to have low impact on the service code. You don't want to have to fix the code every time you enroll a new customer, or find a new protocol to support. You want to write applications, not become enterprise security ninjas. Well, most of us do anyway.

ACS handles all of these concerns for us in a brilliantly elegant way. Before we can really talk about ACS, though, we need a common understanding of some of the core concepts ACS is built on.

17.2.2 Working with actors

The security field is loaded with special vocabulary and concepts that scare most developers. Even knowing the importance of security, many developers just find some sample code and paste it in. They either don't have the understanding needed to work with the code, or they won't change it for fear of making a mistake.

There are several actors in this security play that we need to define. The most important is your service or application—the resource you're trying to protect. It's commonly called the *protected resource* or the *relying party* because it's relying on the security infrastructure.

The next actor is also easily defined: the *client*. This is the application that's trying to access the relying party. Clients are also sometimes called *issuers*. This side can get a little complicated when you have a second client that's being delegated through the first client to the protected resource.

Finally we have the ACS service itself. In security lingo, ACS is called the *authorization server* or *trusted authority*. It provides the security infrastructure the client must use to authenticate and use the protected resource.

In our play, the authorization server is the director, the protected resource is the lead actor, and the client is the supporting actor.

17.2.3 Tokens communicate authorization

Our three actors need some way to communicate, and they do this by passing tokens around. There are many formats for tokens, and there are many ways to pass them around. The messages they pass around usually include a set of claims, which we'll get to in a moment.

You likely use a token every day—your driver's license. You can use it to prove your identity or to prove a claim. A bar might demand you satisfy (prove) your claim that you're over 21. You never have to give them your birth certificate; you just give them your driver's license. You proved who you were, and when you were born, when you applied for your license. The Department of Motor Vehicles validated your credentials and provided you with a token that proves your claim of age on the license. The department is the trusted source, the bar with the beer is the protected resource, and your license is the token. You're the client.

The following figure shows this relationship between you, the bar, and the Department of Motor Vehicles. You first authenticate to the DMV. Once they're satisfied, they give you a secure token that provides data for some claims. You can then use this token to get a frosty beverage at any bar, even if not everybody knows your name. You can see this relationship in figure 17.1.

Some token formats are proprietary and some are an open standard. Microsoft has worked with Google and Yahoo! to develop a new, simple open standard that can be used across the cloud and the web. This standard is called OAuth, short for *open authorization.* There are other open standards that are popular, such as SAML (Security Assertion Markup Language), but they tend to be more complex and geared for SOAP instead of REST. OAuth's goal is to provide a simple token and protocol that makes it easy to secure REST-based services.

NOTE You can read the OAuth specification at http://groups.google.com/group/oauth-wrap-wg.

ACS is based on OAuth, but it knows how to read other types of tokens as well. There are two halves to OAuth. The first is the Web Resource Authorization Protocol (WRAP). This is the protocol used to make authorization requests and to move

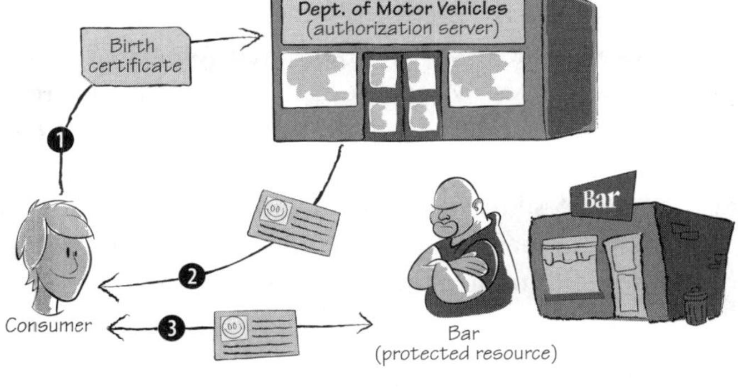

Figure 17.1 A bar doesn't require that you prove your birth date; instead you provide them with a valid and secure token from a trusted authority. You had to prove your birth date to the authority ❶, and they gave you a token ❷. You then use that token to get into the bar ❸.

requests and tokens around on the wire. The other half of OAuth is the Simple Web Token (SWT), which defines the token itself. SWT tokens are simple to read and understand. The goal in designing OAuth and SWT was to build protocols that any platform could leverage to secure REST-based services.

All tokens coming from ACS will be SWT tokens. Here's a sample token:

```
CustomerId%3d31415%26Issuer%3dhttps%253a%252f%252fstringreversalinc.
➥ accesscontrol.windows.net%252f%26Audience%3dhttp%253a%252f%252
➥ flocalhost%252fprocessstring%26ExpiresOn%3d1266231958%26HMACSHA256%
➥ 3dI5g66yaiECux9IQ8y7Ffm2S1p%252bAXF73HWfzSNPyPLOE%253d
```

Notice that this token is URL-encoded. Later on we'll look at code that will let us shred this token and understand the separate parts. If you've ever seen a SAML token, this is far simpler and easier to work with. There isn't even any XML!

The OAuth working group's website includes the specification for these protocols and formats. They're surprisingly easy to read, but they do lack an interesting plot. They're much easier to read than the WS-* and SAML/STS specifications, if that means anything. You can read them all in about 30 minutes.

17.2.4 Making claims about who you are

With all these tokens flying around, we need something to put in them. Although there are other pieces of data stored in tokens, the real reason tokens exist is to deliver what is called "a set of claims."

A *claim set* is a list of claims made about the client or user by the authorization server. What a claim represents is completely open and can be defined by the systems using it. The claim must serialize to plain text—there isn't any fancy XML in OAuth, just a name-value collection of claims. A claim set might include a user's name, their birth date, their customer level, a list of roles or groups they belong to, or anything else your service (the protected resource) needs.

Your service will use these claims to make security and behavior decisions. The first decision is whether the user is allowed to access your service. Then, once you have let them in, you can use the claims to determine what they can do. If their role claim includes *manager*, you might let them apply discounts to existing orders. If the role claim is *staff*, maybe they can only create normal orders. What you ask for in claims and what you do with them once you get them is up to you.

This use of claims moves us away from the traditional role-based access control (RBAC) and toward claims-based access control (CBAC). The concepts are the same; the difference is in how we get the data regarding the user's identity and how we make decisions based on that data.

As you implement ACS, it's possible to add the use of SWT tokens to your system without ripping out the old way of managing identity. This is useful if you're trying to transition to the new platform without breaking what already exists.

17.3 Example: A return to our string-reversing service

In chapter 15, we talked about our amazing string-reversal company, since named String Reversal Inc., and our service that used a new and innovative way to reverse strings. In the time it has taken you to read the intervening chapter, the company has grown and prospered. String-reversal user groups and industry conferences are springing up all over the world.

But our emerging company is running into some trouble. Every time we add a customer, we have to do a lot of work to provision that customer in the system. This overhead is getting in the way of our rapid expansion.

It has also led to a few problems. While you were in the middle of reading the chapter on queues, one of the company's customers, Maine Reversal, was forced to fire an employee, Newton Fernbottom, for insider string-reversing, a horrible, horrible crime. Because that customer didn't notify us that Newton was let go, we never disabled his account. Newton ran home and starting a competing firm, Downeast Reversing, using Maine Reversal's account with our company.

What we need to do now is provide a better way to authorize customers to use our service, and we want to minimize the amount of code we need to change. Because anything can be a client, and anything can be a protected resource with ACS, we're going to move our sample service to a normal local WCF service to make it easier to focus on how ACS works. Everything ACS does can easily be applied to both services and clients running in Azure.

17.3.1 Putting ACS in place

Your first step in upgrading the service is to support a simple scenario where customers will have a shared secret (similar to a username and password) to access the service. Whoever they give that secret to will be able to use the service. They'll be able to change the secret when they need to, just like changing your password every 30 days.

Your first step is to create an AppFabric namespace. This namespace is a lot like a container in BLOB storage—it holds the settings for how you're using the ACS service. You could have several namespaces if you wanted to, perhaps to isolate different services with different configurations.

To create the namespace, you'll use the Azure portal, shown in figure 17.2. Besides creating the namespace, the portal doesn't do much with regards to ACS. There are other tools for that.

To create a namespace, log in to the Azure portal and choose AppFabric on the left side. You'll then see a list of your existing namespaces and a button for creating a new one.

To create a new namespace, you simply need to provide a globally unique name for your namespace. In figure 17.2, you can see that we have selected `StringReversalInc` for our namespace. Once you click the Create button, AppFabric will provision its systems with your namespace.

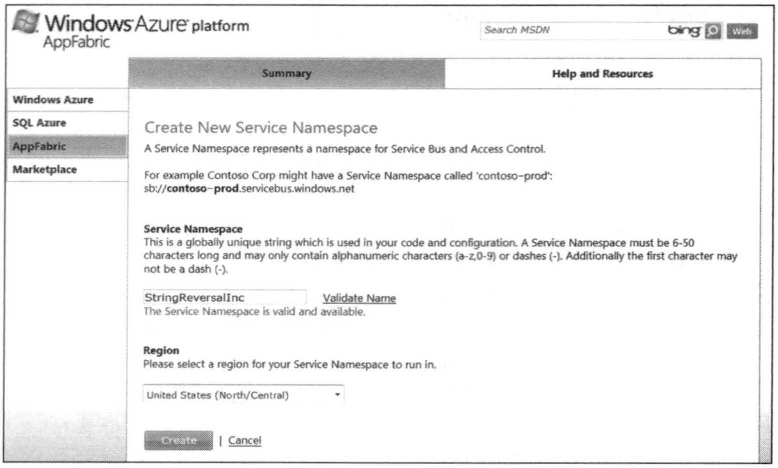

Figure 17.2 To start using AppFabric, you must first create a namespace. This acts like a container for the entire configuration of ACS and the Service Bus. The name of the namespace has to be globally unique.

As you can see in figure 17.3, ACS has configured both a Service Bus and an ACS service for your namespace. The service endpoints for both services will be displayed as shown in the figure. Notice that the namespace is the hostname of the service endpoints.

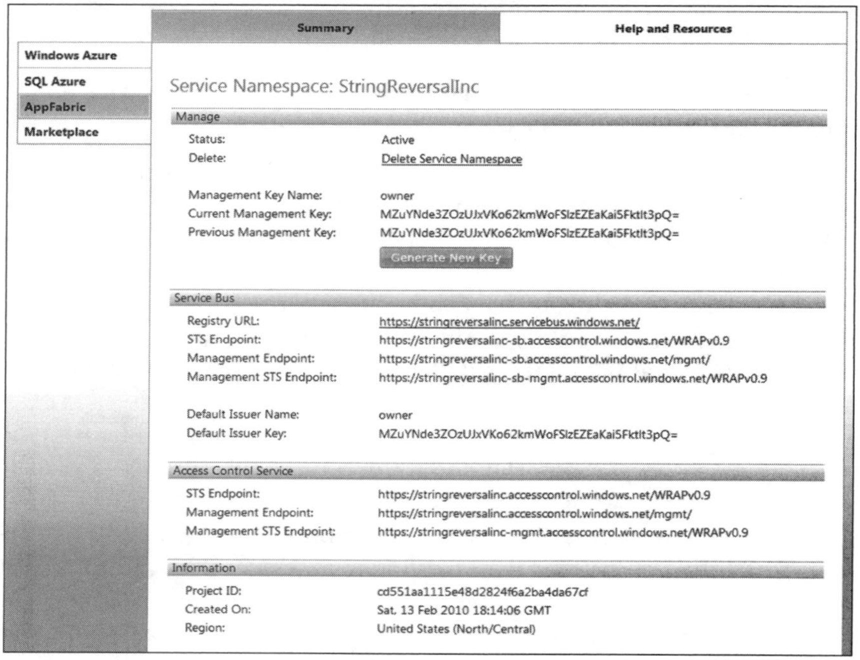

Figure 17.3 Once you create a namespace, AppFabric will provision that namespace with ACS, Service Bus, management endpoints, and security keys.

A management key will be created for you as well. This 32-byte symmetric key is what you'll use when accessing the AppFabric management service to perform operations on your namespace. We won't explore the management service in this chapter, but you should check it out. These keys should not be shared outside your organization, or published in a book where anyone can get ahold of them.

17.3.2 Reviewing the string-reversal service

For this chapter's purposes, we'll use a local REST version of the string-reversal service developed in chapter 15. You can find the complete code for this revised service in the sample code for this chapter. We've removed the entire worker role and Azure-related code to do this. ACS is about securing REST-based services, and our old service used a TCP-based binding. We've changed it to use REST by using the `WebServiceHost` and the `WebHttpBinding` classes.

The following listing shows how we're building our simple little service. This code will start up the service and wait for calls to the service.

Listing 17.1 A simple REST service

```
using System.ServiceModel;
using System.ServiceModel.Web;

public class svcProcessString
{
  public static void Main(string[] args)
  {
    Console.WriteLine("Starting string reversal servicehost...");

    WebServiceHost serviceHost = new
    ➥ WebServiceHost(typeof(ReverseStringTools));        <- Creates host to run service code

    WebHttpBinding binding = new WebHttpBinding(WebHttpSecurityMode.None);

    serviceHost.AddServiceEndpoint(typeof(IReverseString), binding, new
    ➥ Uri("http://localhost/processstring"));

    try
    {
      serviceHost.Open();                                  <- Starts service host with specified configuration
      Console.WriteLine("String reversal servicehost started.");
    }
    catch (Exception ex)
    {
      Console.WriteLine("Could not start string reverser servicehost. {0}",
      ➥ ex.Message);
    }

    Console.ReadLine();
  }
}
```

If you run this sample string-reversal service, you can make all of the requests to the service you want. The sample code includes a simple client that will call the service.

The next few steps are going to center around adding code to the service so that it can read and use SWT tokens. Once that's done, you can upgrade the client so it can fetch a token from ACS and use it during a request to the service.

17.3.3 Accepting tokens from ACS

You'll need to upgrade the service so it can receive and work with ACS tokens. This code is fairly trivial, and much of it is supplied in the AppFabric SDK, which you'll have to install in order to follow these next steps. You can find the SDK on the Azure portal. It also includes several tools that we'll look at in the next section.

Exactly how you get the token and where you process it might change, depending on your business situation and system architecture, but the steps will be generally the same.

The first step is to grab the token from the incoming message. The token will usually be included in the header as an authorization entry. In some situations, it can also be in the URL or in the body of the message, depending on the capabilities of the client.

Exactly how you grab this header will differ based on how you're receiving the message. In WCF it's best to do this in a custom `ServiceAuthorizationManager` class that's added to the WCF pipeline when you set up the channel. Every message will flow through this class, and there you can make a decision about whether to let it through or deny it access.

In a normal WCF service, you need to use the `WebOperationContext` to retrieve the header from the request:

```
string authorizationHeader =
➥ WebOperationContext.Current.IncomingRequest.Headers
➥ [HttpRequestHeader.Authorization];
```

This code will get the raw header. You now need to do a few things to make sure this token is valid, and then you can use it to make decisions.

The SDK has all the sample code you need to build a class called `TokenValidator`. We've included a refactored version of this class in the chapter's sample code that's a little easier to use. The validator will do a series of checks for you, and if they all pass, it'll return `true`. If the validation fails, the validator will deny access.

```
validator = new
➥ ACSTokenValidator("dqSsz5enDOFjUvUnrUe5plozEkplccAfUFyuYpawGW0=",
➥ "StringReversalInc", "http://localhost/stringservice");

if (!validator.ValidateAuthorizationHeader(authorizationHeader))
  DenyAccess();
```

To initialize the validator, you need to pass in three pieces of information:

- The signing key
- The ACS namespace to check against
- The URL of the service the message was sent to

You're passing in the key, the namespace you set up, called `StringReversalInc`, and the URL of the service you're protecting, http://localhost/stringservice.

You then call the `ValidateAuthorizationHeader` on the header you pulled off the message. If this returns `false`, you'll deny access by calling a simple little method, `DenyAccess`, that sets up the deny message:

```
private static void DenyAccess()
{
  WebOperationContext.Current.OutgoingResponse.StatusCode =
  ➥ HttpStatusCode.Unauthorized;
          WebOperationContext.Current.OutgoingRequest.Headers.Add("WWW-
          ➥ Authenticate", "WRAP");
  }
```

That's all you need to receive the header. Most of the work involves making sure it's a valid header and something you can trust. This is the same job the bouncer at the bar does, when he looks at your driver's license to make sure it's a real license and hasn't been tampered with.

17.3.4 Checking the token

We've put all of the token-checking logic into the `ACSTokenValidator` class, and we've just discussed how to new up a validator. The validator includes some custom methods, namely `Validate` and `IsHMACValid`. When you pass in the header, the validator will verify several aspects of it to make sure it's valid. All of these checks test for the negative; if the test passes, you have a bad token and the validator returns `false`.

Table 17.1 summarizes the checks that we do in the code.

Table 17.1 Validation checks performed on a token

Check to be made	Purpose
`string.IsNullOrEmpty(authHeader)`	Makes sure you received a header.
`!authHeader.StartsWith("WRAP ")`	Ensures the header starts with `WRAP`.
`nameValuePair[0] != "access_token"`	Checks that there are two pieces to the header, and that the first is equal to `access_token`.
`!nameValuePair[1].StartsWith("\"") ||` `!nameValuePair[1].EndsWith("\""))`	Checks that the second piece starts and ends with a slash.
`!Validate(GetTokenFromHeader(authHeader))`	Grabs the token part of the header and makes sure it's valid.
`IsHMACValid(token, signingKey)`	Makes sure the token has been signed properly. If this is correct, you know who sent it.
`this.IsExpired(token)`	Checks that the token hasn't expired. Tokens are vulnerable to replay attacks, so this is important.

Table 17.1 Validation checks performed on a token *(continued)*

Check to be made	Purpose
`this.IsIssuerTrusted(token)`	Ensures the sender is recognized as a trusted source. We'll cover this shortly.
`this.IsAudienceTrusted(token)`	Checks that the audience is the intended destination.

If the header passes all of these checks, you know you have a secure token from a trusted source, and that it's meant for you. This is the minimum you'll want to do to allow the message through to the service. You may also want to crack open the claim set in the token to look at what claims have been sent, and make decisions on those claims. In our example, we've mapped in some claims. One is the customer ID number, and the other is the customer's service level. This might be used to determine how long the strings they submit to our service can be. They might have to pay more to reverse longer strings.

That's all you have to do to enable the service and consume and use ACS tokens for authorization. Next we'll look at how you can configure a client to add the authorization header to their requests.

17.3.5 Sending a token as a client

In this section, you're going to build a simple command-line client. This will make it easier to focus on the service aspects of the code. Feel free to make it sexy by using Silverlight or WPF.

For this client, we'll share the contract by sharing a project reference. (Many projects do this, especially when you own both ends of the conversation.) You should either share the contract through a project reference, or through a shared assembly.

In this case, our biggest customer, Maine Reversal, will be building this client. We've set up a trusted relationship with them by swapping keys and configuring them in ACS—we'll look at how to do this in the next section. Maine Reversal won't be sending in any custom claims of their own, just their issuer identity. This process essentially gives them a secure username and password.

We've created a helpful utility class called `ACSTokenValidator` (found in the sample code for this chapter) that encapsulates the process of fetching an ACS header from the AppFabric service. Again, this code is mostly from the SDK samples with some tweaks we wanted to make. (Why write new code when they give us code that works?)

To call the `GetTokenFromACS` method, you'll pass in the service namespace (`StringReversalInc`), the issuer name (the client's name, which is `MaineReversal` in this case), the signing key that Maine Reversal uses, and the URL that represents your protected resource. This doesn't have to be the real URI of the intended destination, but in many cases will be. In security parlance this is referred to as the *audience*. The method call looks like this:

```
string Token = GetTokenFromACS("StringReversalInc",
                "MaineReversal",
                "ltSsoI5l+8DzLSmvsVOhOmflAsKHBYrGeCR8KtCIleE=",
                "http://localhost/processstring");
```

The `GetTokenFromACS` method performs all the work. It uses the `WebClient` class to create the request to ACS. If everything goes well, the ACS service will respond with a token you can put in your authorization header on your request to the string-reversal service.

The following listing shows how you can request a token from the ACS service.

Listing 17.2 How a client gets a token from ACS

```
private static string GetTokenFromACS(string serviceNamespace, string
➥ issuerName, string issuerKey, string scope)
{
  WebClient client = new WebClient();
  client.BaseAddress = string.Format("https://{0}                    ❶ Specifies ACS
  ➥ .accesscontrol.windows.net", serviceNamespace);                    service address

  NameValueCollection values =                      ❷ Sends authorization
  ➥ new NameValueCollection();                        data
  values.Add("wrap_name", issuerName);
  values.Add("wrap_password", issuerKey);
  values.Add("wrap_scope", scope);

  byte[] responseBytes = client.UploadValues("WRAPv0.9", "POST", values);

  string response = Encoding.UTF8.GetString(responseBytes);    ❸ Gives token
                                                                 to caller
  return response
         .Split('&')
         .Single(value => value.StartsWith("wrap_access_token=",
         ➥ StringComparison.OrdinalIgnoreCase))
         .Split('=')[1];
}
```

You have to provide the `GetTokenFromACS` method with the base address for the request ❶. This is a combination of the ACS service address, `accesscontrol.windows.net`, and the namespace for the ACS account, `StringReversalInc`.

To make the call, you need to provide three pieces of data: the issuer name (your name in the ACS configuration), the signing key, and the namespace of the service you're trying to reach ❷.

At this point, ACS will check your credentials. The issuer name is basically your username, and the signing key is your password. If everything checks out, ACS will respond with a valid token that you can attach to your request to the service ❸.

17.3.6 Attaching the token

Attaching the token to the header of the request is fairly simple on most platforms. You can also put the token information in the URL or the message body. Doing either isn't as good as using an authorization header, so only do this if your system doesn't support an authorization header.

To add the token to the authorization header, you can add it to the `OutgoingRequest.Headers` collection:

```
string authorizationHeader =
➥ string.Format("WRAP access_token=\"{0}\"",
➥ httpUtility.UrlDecode(Token));
WebOperationContext.Current.OutgoingRequest.Headers
➥ .Add("authorization", authorizationHeader);
```

To attach the token to the header, you need to use the `UrlDecode` method to decode it, and then wrap it with the WRAP leading text. This tells the destination service that the token is a WRAP token. This text will be stripped off by the server once the token is validated. Then you add the header to the outgoing request using the `WebOperationContext` class.

That's all the client needs to do. Your client should be robust enough to handle any errors in the ACS service call or the ACS token request being denied.

In order for the token validation and generation to work, you have to set up some configuration in the ACS service: a trusted relationship with the issuer, and some rules.

17.3.7 Configuring the ACS namespace

The ACS needs to be configured for your service. You've already learned how to define a namespace, and the namespace is a container for the rest of the ACS configuration. You can also chain namespaces together, which is the key mechanism for providing simple delegation.

Each namespace has four components: issuers, scopes, rules, and token policies. These elements work together to help secure your REST service.

The AppFabric SDK provides two tools for configuring your service, both of which run locally and call into the management service: ACM.exe (used from the command line) and the Azure configuration browser. (You can use the management service as a third option, but that'll require more work on your part.) Beyond the tool that sets up the namespace, there aren't any management tools on the ACS portal.

The ACM.exe tool can be found in the tools folder where you installed the AppFabric SDK. ACM is most useful when you're automating a process or want to script the configuration. But keep in mind that calls to the AppFabric management endpoint aren't free, like the Windows Azure management endpoints are.

The Azure configuration browser is shipped with the SDK, but as a sample in source-code form in a separate download file. You need to load the solution and compile it to use it. This distribution approach is really useful because you can then extend the tool to meet your needs, and the browser is a lot easier to use than the command-line tool.

The configuration browser does have a few limitations. First, it's really ugly, but that's OK. The second is that, at this time, it can't update an existing cloud configuration; it can only deploy a complete configuration. This means that any time you make a change, you have to delete the configuration in the cloud and completely redeploy the new configuration. An advantage of this approach is that you can store your configuration locally in an XML file, which aids in backup and configuration management.

You'll need to provide your service name and your management key with either tool. For the ACM.exe application, you can put your settings in the app.config file, which saves you from having to type them in as part of your commands every single time.

ISSUERS

Issuers are actors in the ACS system and represent consumers of your service. When you create an issuer, you need to provide both a display name and an official issuer name. Once the issuer is created, a signing key will be generated for you. This is the key the issuer must sign their requests with when they ask the ACS service for a token.

To create an issuer from a command line, you would use the following command:

```
acm create issuer
         -name:MaineReversal
         -issuername:MaineReversal
         -autogeneratekey
```

In the configuration browser you'll need to right-click on the Issuers node and choose Create. Figure 17.4 shows how to set up your first client, Maine Reversal.

Setting up an issuer in the system is akin to creating a user. The issuer needs a name (comparable to a username) and a signing key (which is like a password). These are the credentials the issuer will use to request an ACS token.

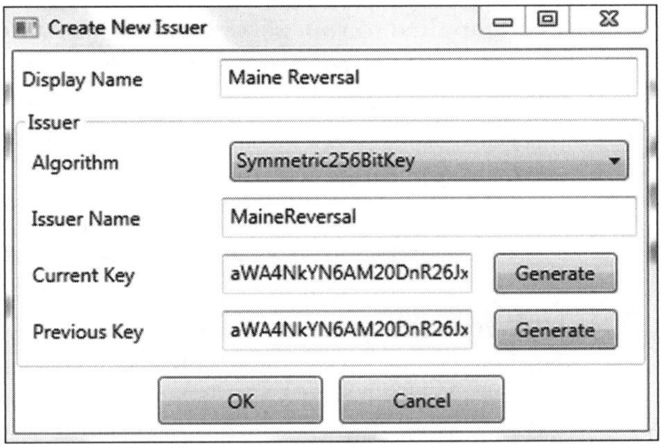

Figure 17.4 Creating an issuer is easy with the ACS configuration browser. You'll need to provide both a display name and an official name for the issuer. You can use the tool to automatically create the signing keys.

TOKEN POLICY

A token policy defines how you want your tokens to be created. Because token-based systems can be vulnerable to token-replay attacks, you'll first want to set a lifetime timeout for the token. This is expressed in seconds. When the token is created, it'll be stamped with the time when the token will expire. Once it's expired, the token will be considered invalid and won't be accepted by a service. You have to check for this expiration explicitly when you validate the token. We check for this in the sample code for the chapter, as seen in the `ACSTokenValidator` class.

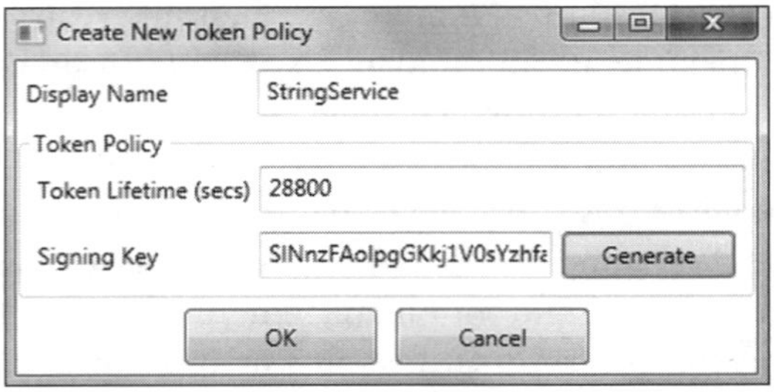

Figure 17.5 You'll need to create a token policy. This will determine the lifetime of your tokens, and the key that will be used to sign your ACS tokens.

The command for creating a token policy at the command line is as follows:

```
acm create tokenpolicy -name:StringReversalInc -autogeneratekey
```

To create a token policy in the configuration browser, right-click on the Token Policy node and select Create. Figure 17.5 shows the Create New Token Policy dialog box, where you can create a policy for your string service.

The second piece of data you'll need for your token policy is the signing key, which can be generated for you. This is the key that will be used to sign the tokens generated for you by the ACS.

SCOPES

A scope is a container that's tied to a service URI. It brings together the rules that you want applied to your service, as well as the token policy you want used for that service.

To create a scope at the command-line level, you'll need the ID of the token policy you want to assign to the scope. You can get the `tokenpolicyid` from the output of the `create tokenpolicy` command discussed in the previous section. This is the command for creating a scope:

```
acm create scope -name:StringServiceScope
           -appliesto:http://localhost/processstring
           -tokenpolicyid:tp_4cb597317c2f42cba0407a91c2553324
```

When you're using the configuration browser, you won't need to provide the token policy ID—you'll be able to choose it from the drop-down list. You can associate a policy to a namespace by creating a scope, as shown in figure 17.6.

There are several advanced uses for scopes that we won't go into in this chapter. These include managing a large number of service endpoints with a few scopes, and chaining namespaces together for delegation.

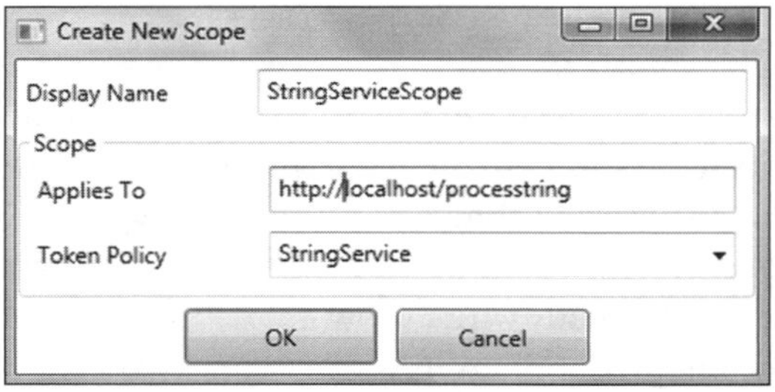

Figure 17.6 It's easy to create a scope. A scope acts as a container for a set of rules for your service. It also associates a token policy with the service. You'll need to define the URI for the service the scope applies to.

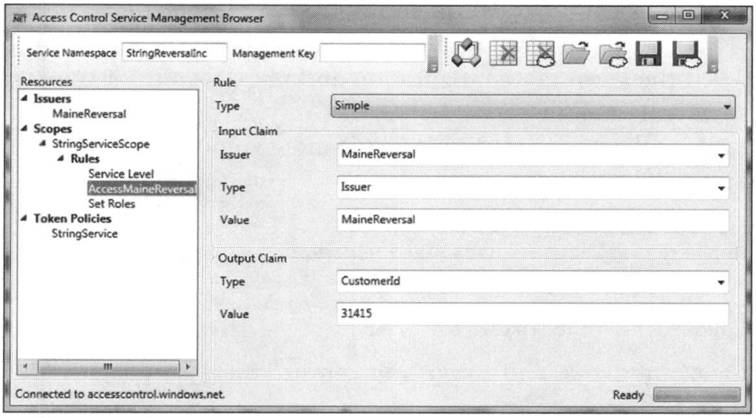

Figure 17.7 Creating a rule to insert a claim that includes the customer's `customerid`. In this case, you're relying on the issuer of the inbound request to know which customer it is.

RULES

Rules are the heart of the ACS system. When a token is created by ACS, the rules for the related scope are executed. This is the process that allows you to transform the consumer's request into something your application can act on. Rules can also be used to create claims out of thin air, and put them in the resulting token.

For example, suppose you wanted to place a claim in the token that represents the consumer's `customerid`, to make it easier for your service to identify the account the request is related to. You could create a rule that says, "If this is for issuer `MaineReversal`, add a claim called `customerid` with a value of `31415`." Figure 17.7 shows how you could create this rule.

Another rule you could use would assign a new role value based on mappings you've worked out with the customer. Perhaps their system tracks their users with a role of ServiceManager—this would be a group the user belongs to at Maine Reversal. Your system doesn't know that role name, and you don't want to add all of your customers' role types to your system—that would get very complex very quickly. The rule in figure 17.8 creates the roles claim with the manager value.

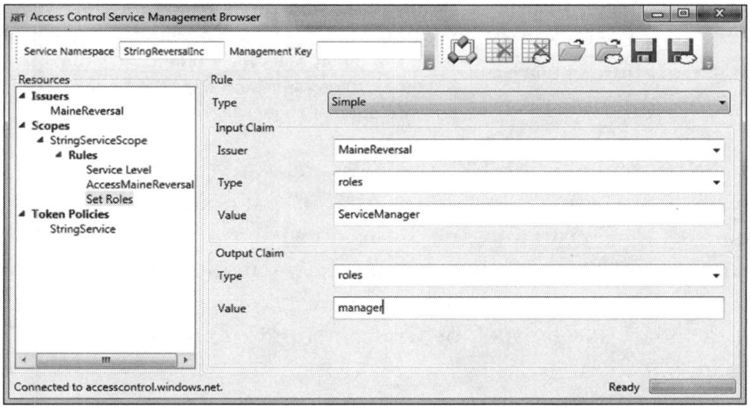

Figure 17.8 Creating a rule that substitutes the inbound roles claim for a new one. Using this rule, you can map the ServiceManager role value that your system doesn't know to one your system does know—manager.

You can then create a rule that finds a claim called `roles` with a value of `Sales-Manager`, and replaces it with a claim called `roles` that has a value of `manager`. In this way you've moved the customer configuration and mapping out of your service and into the authorization service where it belongs.

Creating a rule at the command line is a little more complex than using the configuration browser:

```
acm create rule -name:MaineReversalMap
➥ -scopeid:scp_e7875331c2b880607d5709493eb2751bb7e47044
➥ -inclaimissuerid:iss_6337bf129f06f607dac6a0f6be75a3c287b7c7fa
➥ -inclaimtype:roles -inclaimvalue:ServiceManager
➥ -outclaimtype:roles -outclaimvalue:manager
```

To find the IDs of the scope and issuer, you can use these commands: `acm getall scope` and `acm getall issuer`.

17.3.8 Putting it all together

You've come a long way in stopping illicit use of your service. Now you can control who uses it and how they use it. You've updated your service to consume tokens, you've updated the client to submit tokens with service requests, and you've prepared the ACS service with your configuration.

How does this all work? In this simple scenario, the client requests an access token from ACS, providing its secret key and issuer name. ACS validates this and creates a token, using the scope rules you set up to create claims in the new token. The client then attaches the token to the message in the authorization header.

Figure 17.9 should look familiar; it's much like the DMV example (see figure 17.1), but it shows the technical actors and how they interact.

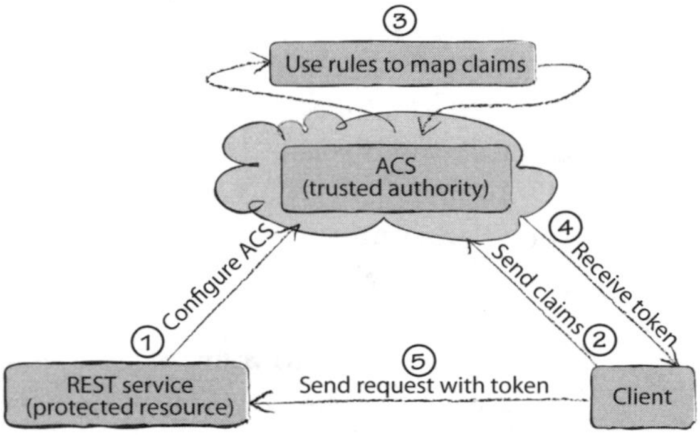

Figure 17.9 How the three actors work together to securely access a REST service. The service configures ACS; the client asks for a token; ACS creates a token, based on rules; and then the client submits this token with its service request.

When your service finally receives the message, you'll grab the token from the header and verify it. You want to make sure that it's valid and hasn't been tampered with. Once you trust it, you can make decisions on what to do.

In our example, you can take the `customerid` value and verify that they're still a paying customer, and if so, respond to their request. You can stop using the token at this point and respond like normal, or you can shred the token and use the claims throughout the application.

If you were protecting an ASP.NET website instead of a REST-based WCF service, you could take those claims, put them in a class that implements `IPrincipal`, and use the class to make role decisions throughout your code.

We've finished a quick lap around ACS. ACS's sibling is the Service Bus, which will let us connect anything to anywhere, with just a little bit of WCF and cloud magic.

17.4 Connecting with the Service Bus

The second major piece of Windows Azure platform AppFabric is the Service Bus. As adoption of service-oriented architecture (SOA) increases, developers are seeking better ways of connecting their services together. At the simplest level, the Service Bus does this for any service out there. It makes it easy for services to connect to each other and for consumers to connect to services.

In this section, we're going to look into what the Service Bus is, why you'd use a bus, and, most importantly, how you can connect your services to it. You'll see how easy it is to use the Service Bus.

17.4.1 What is a Service Bus?

Enterprise service buses (ESBs) have been around for years, and they've grown out of the SOA movement. As services became popular, and as the population of services at companies increased, companies found it harder and harder to maintain the infrastructure. The services and clients became so tightly coupled that the infrastructure became very brittle. This was the exact problem services were created to avoid. ESBs evolved to help fix these problems.

ESBs have several common characteristics, all geared toward building a more dynamic and flexible service environment:

- *ESBs provide a service registry*—Developers and dynamic clients needed ways to find available services, and to retrieve the contract and usage information they needed to consume them.
- *ESBs provide a way to name services*—This involves creating a namespace around services so there isn't a conflict in the service names and the message types defined.
- *ESBs provide some infrastructure for security*—Generally, this includes a way to allow or deny people access to a service, and a way to specify what they're allowed to do on that service.
- *ESBs provide the "bus" part of ESB*—The bus provides a way for the messages to move around from client to service, and back. The important part of the bus is the instrumentation in the endpoints that allows IT to manage the endpoint. IT can track the SLA of the endpoint, performance, and faults on the service.
- *ESBs commonly provide service orchestration*—Orchestration is the concept of composing several services together into a bigger service that performs some business process.

A common model for ESBs is shown in figure 17.10. This is similar to the typical n-tier architecture model, where each tier relies on the abstractions provided by the layer below it.

The orchestration has become not only a way to have lower-level services work together, but it also provides a layer of indirection on top of those services. In the orchestration layer you can route messages based on content, policy, or even service version. This is important as you connect services together, and as they mature.

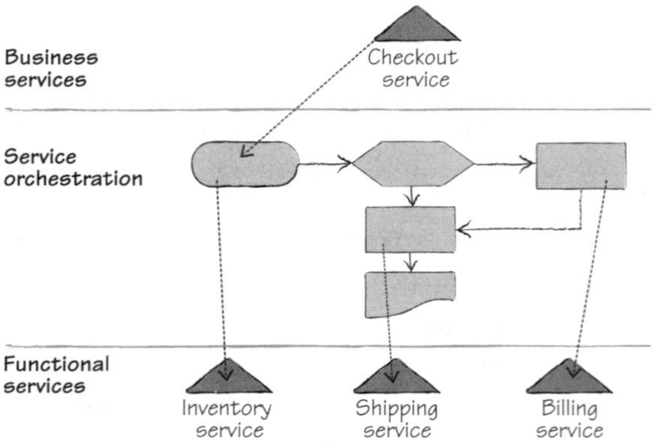

Figure 17.10 Many ESBs support a three-tier concept. The lowest tier consists of functional, discrete services. These services are composed together in the service orchestration layer, and are exposed to provide a comprehensive business service.

17.4.2 Why an ESB is a good idea in the cloud

The problem for ESBs is that they usually only connect internal services and internal clients together. It's hard to publish a service you don't control to your own bus. External dependencies end up getting wrapped in a service you own and published to your ESB as an internal service. Although this avoids the first problem of attaching external services to your ESB, it introduces a new problem, which is yet more code to manage and secure.

If you wanted to expose a service to several vendors, or if you wanted a field application to connect to an internal service, you'd have to resort to all sorts of firewall tricks. You'd have to open ports, provision DNS, and do many other things that give IT managers nightmares. Another challenge is the effort it takes to make sure that an outside application can always connect and use your service.

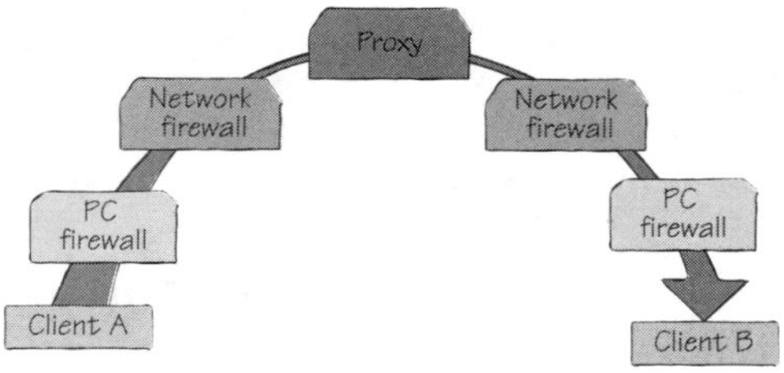

Figure 17.11 Modern networks provide a great number of barriers to easy point-to-point communication. Many computers these days have a local firewall, with one or more firewalls on their network. There are also proxies, NATs, and other devices in the way making it hard to connect in an old-fashioned, direct way.

To go one step farther, it's an even bigger challenge to connect two outside clients together. The problem comes down to the variety of firewalls, NATs, proxies, and other network shenanigans that make point-to-point communication difficult. For example, figure 17.11 might represent the layers between your local software and the services it's calling across the internet.

Take an instant messaging client, for example. When the client starts up, and the user logs in, the client creates an outbound, bidirectional connection to the chat service somewhere. This is always allowed across the network (unless the firewall is configured to explicitly block that type of client), no matter where you are. An outbound connection, especially over port 80 (where HTTP lives) is rarely a problem. Inbound connections, on the other hand, are almost always a problem.

Both clients have these outbound connections, and they're used for signaling and commanding. If client A wants to chat with client B, a message is sent up to the service. The service uses the service registry to figure out where client B's inbound connection is in the server farm, and sends the request to chat down client B's link. If client B accepts the invitation to chat, a new connection is set up between the two clients with a predetermined rendezvous port. In this sense, the two clients are bouncing messages off a satellite in order to always connect, because a direct connection, especially an inbound one, wouldn't be possible. This strategy gets the traffic through a multitude of firewalls—on the PC, on the servers, on the network—on both sides of the conversation.

There is also NATing (network address translation) going on. A network will use private IP addresses internally (usually in the 10.x.x.x range), and will only translate those to an IP address that works on the internet if the traffic needs to go outside the network. It's quite common for all traffic coming from one company or office to have the same source IP address, even if there are hundreds of actual computers. The NAT device keeps a list of which internal addresses are communicating with the outside world. This list uses the TCP session ID (which is buried in each network message) to route inbound traffic back to the individual computer that asked for it.

The "bounce it off a satellite" approach bypasses this problem by having both clients dialing out to the service. Figure 17.12 illustrates how this works.

The Service Bus is here to give you all of that easy messaging goodness without all of the work. Imagine if Skype or Yahoo Messenger could just write a cool application that helped people communicate, instead of spending all of that hard work and time figuring out how to always connect with someone, no matter where they are.

The first step in connecting is knowing who you can connect with, and where they are. To determine this, you need to register your service on the Service Bus.

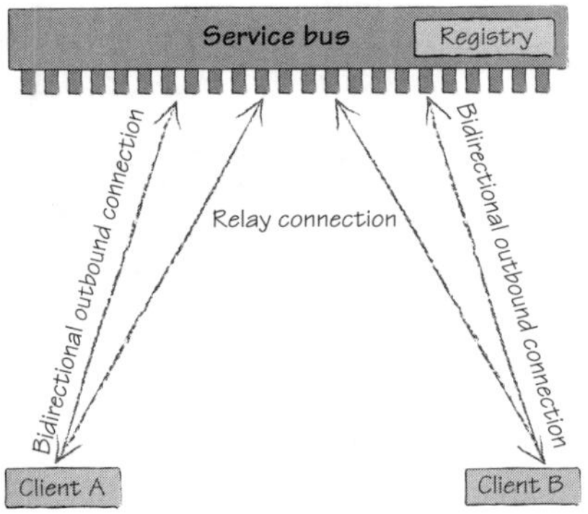

Figure 17.12 Any client can communicate with any other client (which may be a service) from anywhere, on any network, by using the relay bindings with the Service Bus. Each client first registers with the bus so it knows where they're connected. Then when client A wants to connect with client B, they can use the registry to find each other.

17.5 Example: Listening for messages on the bus

Previously in this chapter, as you were configuring ACS, you had to create a namespace. That namespace held configuration for the services you wanted to protect with ACS. Now you'll use that same namespace to register and manage your service on the bus.

Almost all of the magic of the Service Bus is embedded in the new WCF service bindings that are shipped in the AppFabric SDK. All of these bindings start with a protocol identifier of *sb* (you're probably familiar with *http* and others). The binding names also almost always have the word *relay* in them, to indicate that you'll be relaying messages through the Service Bus to their destination.

17.5.1 Connecting the service to the bus

Changing your application to listen for messages from the bus instead of the HTTP endpoint is easy. You need to change the binding and address information to point to the bus.

We've moved the configuration of the service from code to the app.config file to make these changes easier, and you can see these changes in the Service Bus sample code for this chapter. Two things still need to be set up. You need to configure the address and binding information, and you need to configure the service for authentication to the bus.

First, in the configuration, you need to change the address of the endpoint to your namespace on the bus. For this example, you should change it from http://localhost/processstring to sb://stringreversalinc.servicebus.windows.net/processstring. This change tells WCF to use the Service Bus relay bindings, and that the service you're publishing should be registered in the `stringreversalinc` namespace.

```
<endpoint address=
"sb://stringreversalinc.servicebus.windows.net/processstring"
behaviorConfiguration="sharedSecretClientCredentials"
binding="netTcpRelayBinding"
contract="StringReversalLibrary.Contract.IReverseString" />
```

Your service also has to authenticate to the Service Bus when it starts up and registers with the bus. You use ACS to do this. In this example, you can use the simple shared secret we used earlier in this chapter. This will attach the credentials (essentially a username and password) to your request to connect to the Service Bus:

```
<behavior name="sharedSecretClientCredentials">
   <transportClientEndpointBehavior credentialType="SharedSecret">
      <clientCredentials>
         <sharedSecret issuerName="owner"
         ➥ issuerSecret="MZuYNde3ZOzUJxVKo62kmWoFSlzEZEaKai5Fktlt3pQ=" />
      </clientCredentials>
   </transportClientEndpointBehavior>
</behavior>
```

This shared secret behavior that you attach to your service will authenticate to the bus with your issuer name and signing key automatically.

Once you make these changes, you can run the service and it'll start up, authenticate, and start listening for messages coming from the bus. You'll then need to perform similar actions on the client.

17.5.2 Connecting to the service

In the previous section, we looked at what you had to do to connect a service to the Service Bus. You had to change the bindings to point to the bus and update the address. You also had to add some authentication so that the bus knew you were allowed to use your namespace.

You now need to follow the same steps to change the app.config for the client. You need to change the client binding so it's sending messages to the bus. For this example, you can name your endpoint `SBRelayEndpoint`, with the same address the service used.

```
<client>
   <endpoint
      name="SBRelayEndpoint"
      address=
"sb://stringreversalinc.servicebus.windows.net/processstring"
      binding="netTcpRelayBinding"
      contract="StringReversalLibrary.Contract.IReverseString"
      behaviorConfiguration="sharedSecretClientCredentials"
   />
</client>
```

The client is going to have to authenticate to the Service Bus as well—you can configure it to use a shared secret. Use the Maine Reversal issuer from section 17.3.7 of this chapter. Keep in mind that there are two endpoints: one for the ACS service, and one for the Service Bus. They don't share issuers. You can configure the credentials by changing the behavior of the service in the app.config file:

```
<behavior name="sharedSecretClientCredentials">
   <transportClientEndpointBehavior credentialType="SharedSecret">
      <clientCredentials>
         <sharedSecret issuerName=" MaineReversal"
         ➥ issuerSecret=" ltSsoI5l+8DzLSmvsVOhOmflAsKHBYrGeCR8KtCIleE=" />
      </clientCredentials>
   </transportClientEndpointBehavior>
</behavior>
```

Now the client can call your service from anywhere and always be able to connect to it. This makes it easy to provision new customers. In the old, direct method, you had to reconfigure the firewalls to let the new customer through. Now you can point them to the Service Bus address and give them the credentials they'll need.

The binding we used in this example is based on TCP, which is one of the fastest bindings you can use in WCF. It adds the relay capabilities to allow us to message through the bus instead of directly. There are other bindings available that support using the relay.

Now that we've covered what AppFabric can do today, let's consider what its future might hold.

17.6 The future of AppFabric

We normally don't talk about futures in a book because it's entirely possible that priorities will shift and particular features will never ship. The team has been open about what they consider their next steps, but any of this could change, so don't base important strategy on unofficial announcements.

With that said, here are a couple of current goals:

- *Extending OAuth for web identity*—The ACS team wants to extend its use of OAuth and SWT to include common web identity platforms. These are identities on the web that people commonly have, instead of traditional enterprise identities from Active Directory. It will be possible for a user to choose to log into a site not just with an ACS-provisioned issuer ID, or a SAML token, but also with their Google, Yahoo!, and Live ID accounts. This is accomplished by ACS federating with those directories with the updated OAuth protocols. This will also include Facebook and any OpenID provider. This is exciting for people who are building consumer-centric applications.
- *Support for all WS-* protocols*—Right now you can only protect REST services with ACS, and the ACS team wants to extend support for SOAP-based services as well. Once they have support for WS-*, they'll have support for WS-Federation and WS-Trust, which makes it easier to federate enterprise identities. This change will also give them support for CardSpace, which is Windows' identity selector for claims-based authentication systems.

17.7 Summary

This chapter gave you a tour of the Windows Azure platform AppFabric. We looked at how it's a cousin of Windows Server AppFabric, and how maybe over time they'll merge.

The first component of AppFabric we looked at was ACS. ACS's primary concern is securing REST-based services, and it does this with the OAuth and SWT open standards. ACS makes it easy to federate in other token protocols, like SAML, and makes it easy to transform tokens from other parties into a form that your application can consume. You can configure ACS with either the ACM command-line application, or the ACS configuration browser. Both applications use the underlying management REST service, which you can also use directly if you want.

We looked at how a client first authenticates with ACS to prove who they are, and then ACS gives them a token to use to gain access to the service. This removes the concern of authentication from the application, which in turn simplifies the codebase, and makes it easier to adjust to new rules as they evolve.

The second component of AppFabric we looked at was the Service Bus. The Service Bus is a migration of a common enterprise service bus into the cloud. The Service Bus's goal is to make it easy for consumers and services to communicate with each other, no matter where they are or how they're connected.

We adjusted our example to use a `netTCP` binding, but also to relay the messages through the cloud to bypass any firewalls or proxies that might be in the way. You had to make a few adjustments on the service and the client to make this possible. Both sides have to authenticate to ACS before they connect to the bus—this is how you secure your service when it's connected to the bus.

Although this was a simple chapter designed to help you get a feel for AppFabric, we hope that you're comfortable enough with the basics to know when it might make sense to leverage AppFabric. You should be prepared enough to explore on your own and maybe dive deep with a dedicated book on the topic.

The next chapter will zoom out from all of this detail and help you use the diagnostics manager to understand what your applications are doing. The diagnostics manager will help you determine what's happening, and the service management API will help you do something about it.

18 Running a healthy service in the cloud

This chapter covers

- Getting to know the Windows Azure Diagnostics platform
- Using logging to determine what's happening with your service
- Using the service management APIs
- Making your service self-aware with logging and service management

Building an application and deploying it to Azure are just the first steps in a hopefully long application lifecycle. For the rest of its life, the application will be in operation mode, being cared for by loving IT professionals and support developers. The focus shifts from writing quality code to running the application and keeping it healthy. Many tools and techniques are out there to help you manage your infrastructure.

What *healthy* means can be different for every application. It might be a measure of how many simultaneous users there are, or how many transactions per second are processed, or how fast a response can be returned to the service caller. In many cases, it won't be just one metric, but a series of metrics. You have to decide what you're going to measure to determine a healthy state, and what those measurements must be to be considered acceptable. You must make sure these metrics are reasonable and actionable. A metric that demands that the site be as fast as possible isn't really measurable, and it's nearly impossible to test for and fix an issue phrased like that. Better to define the metric as an average response time for a standard request.

To keep your application healthy, you need to instrument and gather diagnostic data. In this chapter, we're going to discuss how you perform diagnostics in the cloud and what tools Azure provides to remediate any issues or under-supply conditions in your system.

18.1 Diagnostics in the cloud

At some point you might need to debug your code, or you'll want to judge how healthy your application is while it's running in the cloud. We don't know about you, but the more experienced we get with writing code, the more we know that our code is less than perfect. We've drastically reduced the amount of debugging we need to do by using test-driven development (TDD), but we still need to fire up the debugger once in a while.

Debugging locally with the SDK is easy, but once you move to the cloud you can't debug at all; instead, you need to log the behavior of the system. For logging, you can use either the infrastructure that Azure provides, or you can use your own logging framework. Logging, like in traditional environments, is going to be your primary mechanism for collecting information about what's happening with your application.

18.1.1 Using Azure Diagnostics to find what's wrong

Logs are handy. They help you find where the problem is, and can act as the flight data recorder for your system. They come in handy when your system has completely burned down, fallen over, and sunk into the swamp. They also come in handy when the worst hasn't happened, and you just want to know a little bit more about the behavior of the system as it's running. You can use logs to analyze how your system is performing, and to understand better how it's behaving. This information can be critical when you're trying to determine when to scale the system, or how to improve the efficiency of your code.

The drawback with logging is that hindsight is 20/20. It's obvious, after the crash, that you should've enabled logging or that you should've logged a particular segment of code. As you write your application, it's important to consider instrumentation as an aspect of your design.

Logging is much more than just remote debugging, 1980s-style. It's about gathering a broad set of data at runtime that you can use for a variety of purposes; debugging is one of those purposes.

18.1.2 Challenges with troubleshooting in the cloud

When you're trying to diagnose a traditional on-premises system, you have easy access to the machine and the log sources on it. You can usually connect to the machine with a remote desktop and get your hands on it. You can parse through log files, both those created by Windows and those created by your application. You can monitor the health of the system by using Performance Monitor, and tap into any source of information on the server. During troubleshooting, it's common to leverage several tools on the server itself to slice and dice the mountain of data to figure out what's gone wrong.

You simply can't do this in the cloud. You can't log in to the server directly, and you have no way of running remote analysis tools. But the bigger challenge in the cloud is the dynamic nature of your infrastructure. On-premises, you have access to a static pool of servers. You know which server was doing what at all times. In the cloud, you don't have this ability. Workloads can be moved around; servers can be created and destroyed at will. And you aren't trying to diagnose the application on one server, but across a multitude of servers, collating and connecting information from all the different sources. The number of servers used in cloud applications can swamp most diagnostic analysis tools. The shear amount of data available can cause bottlenecks in your system.

For example, a typical web user, as they browse your website and decide to check out, can be bounced from instance to instance because of the load balancer. How do you truly find out the load on your system or the cause for the slow response while they were checking out of your site? You need access to all the data that's available on terrestrial servers and you need the data collated for you.

You also need close control over the diagnostic data producers. You need an easy way to dial the level of information from `debug` to `critical`. While you're testing your systems, you need all the data, and you need to know that the additional load it places on the system is acceptable. During production, you want to know only about the most critical issues, and you want to minimize the impact of these issues on system performance.

For all these reasons, the Windows Azure Diagnostics platform sits on top of what is already available in Windows. The diagnostics team at Microsoft has extended and plugged in to the existing platform, making it easy for you to learn, and easy to find the information you need.

18.2 Diagnostics in the cloud is just like normal (almost)

With the challenges of diagnostics at cloud-scale, it's amazing that the solution is so simple and elegant. Microsoft chose to keep everything that you're used to in its place. Every API, tool, log, and data source is the same way it was, which keeps the data sources known and well documented. The diagnostics team provides a small process called MonAgentHost.exe that's started on your instances.

The `MonAgentHost` process is started automatically, and it acts as your agent on the box. It knows how to tap into all the sources, and it knows how to merge the data and move it to the correct locations so you can analyze it. You can configure the process on the fly without having to restart the host it's running on. This is critical. You don't

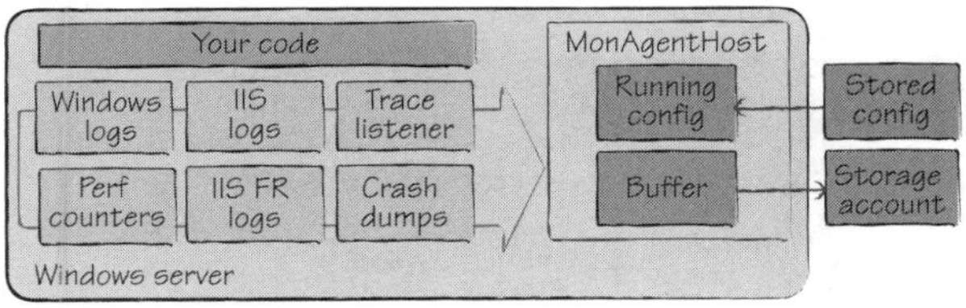

Figure 18.1 The MonAgentHost.exe process gathers, buffers, and transfers many different sources of diagnostic data on your behalf. It's the agent we'll be focusing on in this section.

want to have to take down a web role instance just to dial up the amount of diagnostic information you're collecting. You can control data collection across all your instances with a simple API. All the moving parts of the process are shown in figure 18.1. Your role instance must be running in full-trust mode to be able to run the diagnostic agent. If your role instance is running in partial trust, it won't be able to start.

As the developer, you're always in control of what's being collected and when it's collected. You can communicate with `MonAgentHost` by submitting a configuration change to the process. When you submit the change, the process reloads and starts executing your new commands.

18.2.1 Managing event sources

The local diagnostic agent can find and access any of the normal Windows diagnostic sources; then it moves and collates the data into Windows Azure storage. The agent can even handle full memory dumps in the case of an unhandled exception in one of your processes.

You must configure the agent to have access to a cloud storage account. The agent will place all your data in this account. Depending on the source of the data, it'll either place the information in BLOB storage (if the source is a traditional log file), or it'll put the information in a table.

Some information is stored in a table because of the nature of the data collection activity. Consider when you're collecting data from Performance Monitor. This data is usually stored in a special file with the extension *.blg*. Although this file could be created and stored in BLOB storage, you would have the hurdle of merging several of these files to make any sense of the data (and the information isn't easily viewed in Notepad). You generally want to query that data. For example, you might want to find out what the CPU and memory pressure on the server were for a given time, when a particular request failed to process.

Table 18.1 shows what the most common sources of diagnostic information are, and where the agent stores the data after it's collected. We'll discuss how to configure the sources, logs, and the (tantalizingly named) arbitrary files in later sections.

Table 18.1 Diagnostic data sources

Data source	Default	Destination	Configuration
Arbitrary files	Disabled	BLOB	`DirectoryConfiguration` class
Crash dumps	Disabled	BLOB	`CrashDumps` class

Table 18.1 Diagnostic data sources *(continued)*

Data source	Default	Destination	Configuration
Trace logs	Enabled	Azure table	web.config trace listener
Diagnostic infrastructure logs	Enabled	Azure table	web.config trace listener
IIS failed request logs	Disabled	BLOB	web.config `traceFailedRequests`
IIS logs	Enabled	BLOB	web.config trace listener
Performance counters	Disabled	Azure table	`PerformanceCounterConfiguration` class
Windows event logs	Disabled	Azure table	`WindowsEventLogsBufferConfiguration` class

The agent doesn't just take the files and upload them to storage. The agent can also configure the underlying sources to meet your needs. You can use the agent to start collecting performance data, and then turn the source off when you don't need it anymore. You do all this through configuration.

18.2.2 *It's not just for diagnostics*

We've been focusing pretty heavily on the debugging or diagnostic nature of the Windows Azure Diagnostics platform. Diagnostics is the primary goal of the platform, but you should think of it as a pump of information about what your application is doing. Now that you no longer have to manage infrastructure, you can focus your attention on managing the application much more than you have in the past.

Consider some of the business possibilities you might need to provide for, and as you continue to read this chapter, think about how the diagnostic tools can make some of these scenarios possible.

There are the obvious scenarios of troubleshooting performance and finding out how to tune the system. The common process is that you drive a load on the system and monitor all the characteristics of the system to find out how it responds. This is a good way to find the limits of your code, and to perform A/B tests on your changes. During an A/B test, you test two possible options to see which leads to the better outcome.

Other scenarios aren't technical in nature at all. Perhaps your system is a multitenant system and you need to find out how much work each customer does. In a medical imaging system, you'd want to know how many images are being analyzed and charge a flat fee per image. You could use the diagnostic system to safely log a `new image` event, and then once a day move that to Azure storage to feed into your billing system.

Maybe in this same scenario you need a rock-solid audit that tells you exactly who's accessed each medical record so you can comply with industry and government regulations. The diagnostic system provides a clean way to handle these scenarios.

An even more common scenario might be that you want an analysis of the visitors to your application and their behaviors while they're using your site. Some advanced e-commerce platforms know how their customers shop. With the mountains of data collected over the years, they can predict that 80 percent of customers in a certain scenario will complete the purchase. Armed with this data, they can respond to a user's behavior and provide a way to increase the likelihood that they'll make a purchase. Perhaps this is a timely invitation to a one-on-one chat with a trained customer service person to help them through the process. The diagnostics engine can help your application monitor the key aspects of the user and the checkout process, providing feedback to the e-commerce system to improve business. This is the twenty-first-century version of a salesperson in a store asking if they can help you find anything.

To achieve all of these feats of science with the diagnostic agent, you need to learn how to configure and use it properly.

18.3 Configuring the diagnostic agent

If you're writing your code in Visual Studio, the default Azure project templates include code that automatically starts the diagnostic agent, inserts a listener for the agent in the web.config file, and configures the agent with a default configuration.

You can see this code in the `OnStart()` method in the WebRole.cs file.

```
public override bool OnStart()
{
   DiagnosticMonitor.Start("DiagnosticsConnectionString");    <-- (1) Starts diagnostic agent
   RoleEnvironment.Changing += RoleEnvironmentChanging;
   return base.OnStart();
}
```

The agent starts (1) with the default configuration, all in one line. The line also points to a connection string in the service configuration that provides access to the Azure storage account you want the data to be transferred to. If you're running in the development fabric on your desktop computer, you can configure it with the well-known development storage connection string `UseDevelopmentStorage=true`. This string provides all the data necessary to connect with the local instance of development storage.

You also need to create a trace listener for the diagnostic agent. The trace listener allows you to write to the Azure trace log in your code. Create a trace listener by adding the following lines in your web.config. If you're using a standard template, this code is probably already included.

```
<system.diagnostics>
  <trace>
    <listeners>
      <add type="Microsoft.WindowsAzure.Diagnostics
      ➥ .DiagnosticMonitorTraceListener,
      ➥ Microsoft.WindowsAzure.Diagnostics,
      ➥ Version=1.0.0.0, Culture=neutral,
      ➥ PublicKeyToken=31bf3856ad364e35"
      ➥ name="AzureDiagnostics">
        <filter type="" />
      </add>
```

```
    </listeners>
  </trace>
</system.diagnostics>
```

After you've set up the trace listener, you can use the trace methods to send information to any trace listeners. When you use them, set a category for the log entry. The category will help you filter and find the right data later on. You should differentiate between critical data that you'll always want and verbose logging data that you'll want only when you're debugging an issue. You can use any string for the trace category you want, but be careful and stick to a standard set of categories for your project. If the categories vary too much (for example, you have critical, crit, and important), it'll be too hard to find the data you're looking for. To standardize on log levels, you can use the enumerated type `LogLevel` in `Microsoft.WindowsAzure.Diagnostics`. To write to the trace log, use a line like one of the following:

```
using System.Diagnostics;

System.Diagnostics.Trace.WriteLine(string.Format("Page loaded on {0}",
➥ System.DateTime.Now, "Information");

System.Diagnostics.Trace.WriteLine("Failed to connect to database. ",
➥ "Critical");
```

Only people who have access to your trace information using the diagnostics API will be able to see the log output. That being said, we don't recommend exposing sensitive or personal information in the log. Instead of listing a person's social security number, refer to it in an indirect manner, perhaps by logging the primary key in the customer

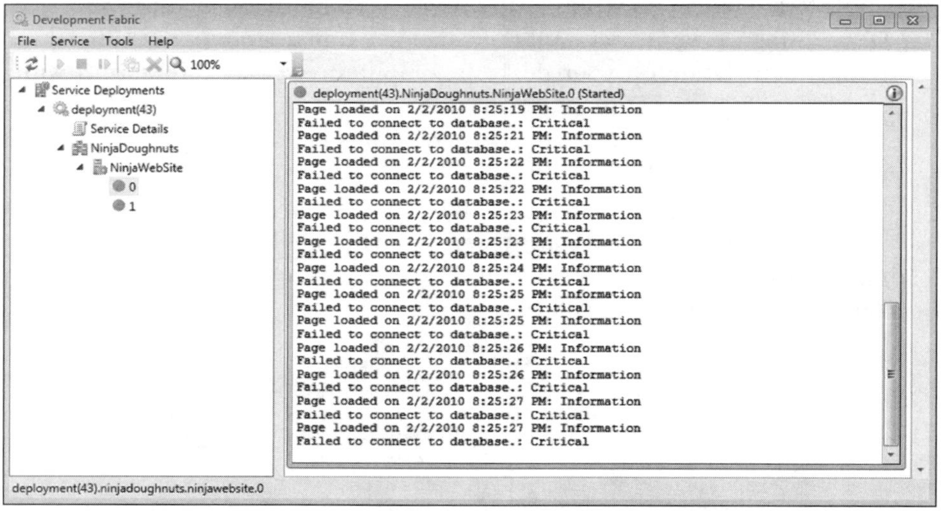

Figure 18.2 When writing to the trace channel, the entries are stored by the Windows Azure diagnostic trace listener to the Azure log, which can then be gathered and stored in your storage account for analysis. The trace output is also displayed in the dev fabric UI during development.

table. That way, if you need the social security number, you can look it up easily, but it won't be left out in plain text for someone to see.

Another benefit of using trace is that the trace output appears in the dev fabric UI, like in figure 18.2.

At a simple level, this is all you need to start the agent and start collecting the most common data. The basic diagnostic setup is almost done for you out of the box because there's so much default configuration that comes with it.

18.3.1 Default configuration

When the diagnostic agent is first started, it has a default configuration. The default configuration collects the Windows Azure trace, diagnostic infrastructure logs, and IIS 7.0 logs automatically. These are the most common sources you're likely to care about in most situations.

When you're configuring the agent, you'll probably follow a common flow. You'll grab the current running configuration (or a default configuration) from the agent, adjust it to your purposes, and then restart the agent. This configuration workflow is shown in figure 18.3.

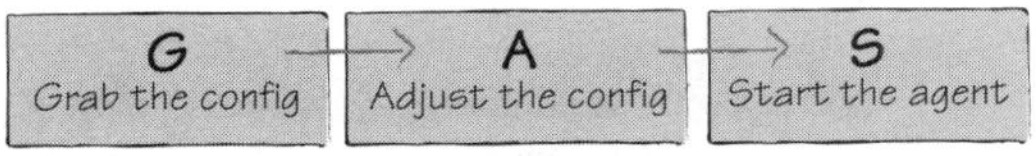

Figure 18.3 Use the GAS process to configure and work with the diagnostic agent. Grab the config, adjust the config, and then start the agent. Sometimes you'll grab the default config and sometimes the running config.

By default, the agent buffers about 4 GB of data locally, and ages out data automatically when the limit is reached. You can change these settings if you want, but most people leave them as is and just transfer the data to storage for long-term keeping.

Although the agent ages out data locally to the role instance, the retention of data after it's moved to Azure storage is up to you. You can keep it there forever, dump it periodically, or download it to a local disk. After it's been transferred to your account, the diagnostic agent doesn't touch your data again. The data will just keep piling up if you let it.

In the next few sections, we'll look at some of the common configuration scenarios, including how to filter the log for the data you're interested in before it's uploaded to storage.

18.3.2 Diagnostic host configuration

You can change the configuration for the agent with code that's running in the role that's collecting data, code that's in another role, or code that's running outside Azure (perhaps a management station in your data center).

CHANGING THE CONFIGURATION IN A ROLE

There will be times when you want to change the configuration of the diagnostic agent from within the role the agent is running in. You'll most likely want to do this during an `OnStart` event, while an instance for your role is starting up. You can change the configuration at any time, but you'll probably want to change it during startup. The following listing shows how to change the configuration during the `OnStart` method for the role instance.

Listing 18.1 Changing the configuration in a role at runtime

```
using Microsoft.WindowsAzure.Diagnostics;

public override bool OnStart()
{
   var config = DiagnosticMonitor.GetDefaultInitialConfiguration();   <-- 1 Grabs the default configuration

   config.PerformanceCounters.DataSources.Add(
    new PerformanceCounterConfiguration()
    {
      CounterSpecifier = @"\Memory\Available MBytes",   <-- 2 Tracks the amount of available memory
      SampleRate = TimeSpan.FromSeconds(5.0)   <-- 3 Sets sample rate of performance counter
    });

config.PerformanceCounters.ScheduledTransferPeriod =
➥ TimeSpan.FromMinutes(1.0);   <-- 4 Sets scheduled transfer time

   DiagnosticMonitor.Start("DiagnosticsConnectionString", config);

   return base.OnStart();
}
```

The first step to change the configuration is to grab the default configuration (1) from the diagnostic agent manager. This is a static method and it gives you a common baseline to start building up the configuration you want running.

In our sample, we're adding a performance counter called `\Memory\Available MBytes` (2). The `CounterSpecifier` property is the path to the performance counter. You can easily find performance counter paths if you use the Performance Monitor, as shown in figure 18.4.

Browse to the counter you want to track to find the specifier (which is like a file path) in the corner. Tell the agent to sample that performance counter every second (3), using the `PerformanceCounterConfiguration` class. Each data source the agent has access to has a configuration class. For each piece of data you want collected, you need to create the right type of configuration object, and add it to the matching configuration collection, which in this case is the `PerformanceCounterConfiguration` collection.

You also want to aggressively upload the performance counter data to Azure storage. Usually this value is set to 20 minutes or longer, but in this case you probably don't want to wait 20 minutes to see whether we're telling you the truth, so set it to once a minute (4). Each data source will have its own data sources collection and its own transfer configuration. You'll be able to transfer different data sources at different intervals. For example, you could transfer the IIS logs once a day, and transfer the performance counters every 5 minutes.

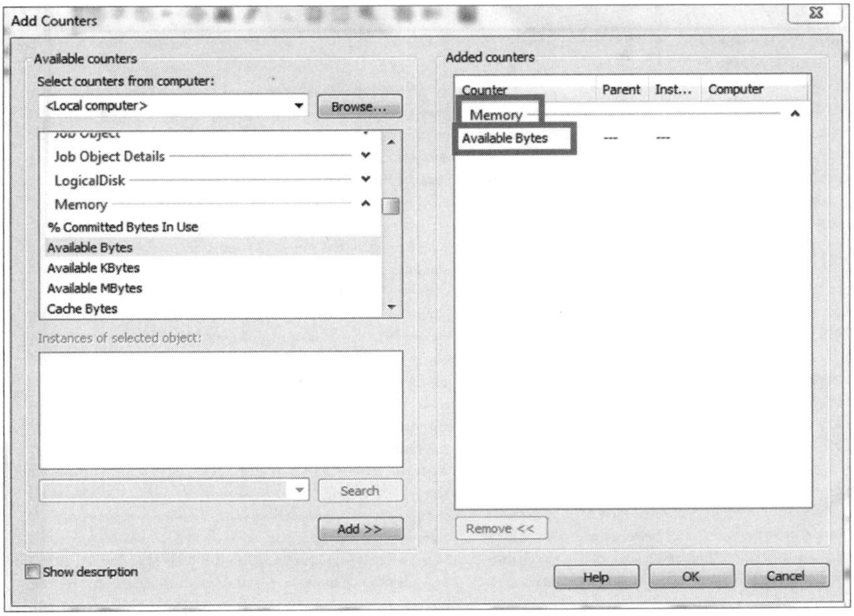

Figure 18.4 Finding the counter specifier using Performance Monitor. Browse to the correct category on the left, choose a counter, and then click Add. You join the category name and counter name with slashes, just like in a folder path. This example is showing `\Memory\Available Bytes`.

Finally, start the diagnostic agent. You need to provide it with the connection string to the storage account that you want the data uploaded to, and the configuration object you just built. The connection string defaults to the value `DiagnosticsConnectionString`, which is an entry in the cloud service configuration file. When you're playing with this on your development machine, you set the value to `UseDevelopmentStorage=true`, but in production you set it to be a connection string to your storage account in the cloud.

The data will be uploaded to different destinations, depending on the data source. In the case of performance counters, the data will be uploaded to an Azure table called WADPerformanceCountersTable, an example of which is shown in figure 18.5.

Figure 18.5 shows the results of the performance counter configuration. The agent tracked the available memory every 5 seconds, and stored that in the table. The entries were uploaded from the role instance to the table every minute, based on the configuration. The high order of the tick count is used as a partition key so that querying by time, which is the most likely dimension to be queried on, is fast and easy.

The RoleInstance column contains the name of the instance, to differentiate entries across the different role instances. In this case, there's only one instance.

Tracking log data can generate a lot of data. To make all this data easier to use, the diagnostic agent supports filters.

Timestamp	EventTickCount	DeploymentId	Role	RoleInstance	CounterName	CounterValue
2010-02-03 03:05:24	634007630871710000	deployment(52)	NinjaWebSite	deployment(52).NinjaDoughnuts.NinjaWebSite.0	\Memory\Available MBytes	3452
2010-02-03 03:05:24	634007630921730000	deployment(52)	NinjaWebSite	deployment(52).NinjaDoughnuts.NinjaWebSite.0	\Memory\Available MBytes	3459
2010-02-03 03:05:24	634007630971710000	deployment(52)	NinjaWebSite	deployment(52).NinjaDoughnuts.NinjaWebSite.0	\Memory\Available MBytes	3459
2010-02-03 03:07:04	634007631021710000	deployment(52)	NinjaWebSite	deployment(52).NinjaDoughnuts.NinjaWebSite.0	\Memory\Available MBytes	3460
2010-02-03 03:07:04	634007631071700000	deployment(52)	NinjaWebSite	deployment(52).NinjaDoughnuts.NinjaWebSite.0	\Memory\Available MBytes	3462
2010-02-03 03:07:04	634007631121720000	deployment(52)	NinjaWebSite	deployment(52).NinjaDoughnuts.NinjaWebSite.0	\Memory\Available MBytes	3462
2010-02-03 03:07:04	634007631171710000	deployment(52)	NinjaWebSite	deployment(52).NinjaDoughnuts.NinjaWebSite.0	\Memory\Available MBytes	3462
2010-02-03 03:07:04	634007631221710000	deployment(52)	NinjaWebSite	deployment(52).NinjaDoughnuts.NinjaWebSite.0	\Memory\Available MBytes	3460
2010-02-03 03:07:04	634007631271710000	deployment(52)	NinjaWebSite	deployment(52).NinjaDoughnuts.NinjaWebSite.0	\Memory\Available MBytes	3432
2010-02-03 03:07:04	634007631321870000	deployment(52)	NinjaWebSite	deployment(52).NinjaDoughnuts.NinjaWebSite.0	\Memory\Available MBytes	3426
2010-02-03 03:07:04	634007631371710000	deployment(52)	NinjaWebSite	deployment(52).NinjaDoughnuts.NinjaWebSite.0	\Memory\Available MBytes	3419
2010-02-03 03:07:04	634007631421710000	deployment(52)	NinjaWebSite	deployment(52).NinjaDoughnuts.NinjaWebSite.0	\Memory\Available MBytes	3422
2010-02-03 03:07:04	634007631471710000	deployment(52)	NinjaWebSite	deployment(52).NinjaDoughnuts.NinjaWebSite.0	\Memory\Available MBytes	3424
2010-02-03 03:07:04	634007631521710000	deployment(52)	NinjaWebSite	deployment(52).NinjaDoughnuts.NinjaWebSite.0	\Memory\Available MBytes	3425
2010-02-03 03:07:04	634007631571700000	deployment(52)	NinjaWebSite	deployment(52).NinjaDoughnuts.NinjaWebSite.0	\Memory\Available MBytes	3426
2010-02-03 03:08:04	634007631621710000	deployment(52)	NinjaWebSite	deployment(52).NinjaDoughnuts.NinjaWebSite.0	\Memory\Available MBytes	3426
2010-02-03 03:08:04	634007631671710000	deployment(52)	NinjaWebSite	deployment(52).NinjaDoughnuts.NinjaWebSite.0	\Memory\Available MBytes	3425
2010-02-03 03:08:04	634007631721720000	deployment(52)	NinjaWebSite	deployment(52).NinjaDoughnuts.NinjaWebSite.0	\Memory\Available MBytes	3427
2010-02-03 03:08:04	634007631771700000	deployment(52)	NinjaWebSite	deployment(52).NinjaDoughnuts.NinjaWebSite.0	\Memory\Available MBytes	3427
2010-02-03 03:08:04	634007631821710000	deployment(52)	NinjaWebSite	deployment(52).NinjaDoughnuts.NinjaWebSite.0	\Memory\Available MBytes	3427
2010-02-03 03:08:04	634007631871710000	deployment(52)	NinjaWebSite	deployment(52).NinjaDoughnuts.NinjaWebSite.0	\Memory\Available MBytes	3421
2010-02-03 03:08:04	634007631921710000	deployment(52)	NinjaWebSite	deployment(52).NinjaDoughnuts.NinjaWebSite.0	\Memory\Available MBytes	3420
2010-02-03 03:08:04	634007631971710000	deployment(52)	NinjaWebSite	deployment(52).NinjaDoughnuts.NinjaWebSite.0	\Memory\Available MBytes	3417
2010-02-03 03:08:04	634007632021700000	deployment(52)	NinjaWebSite	deployment(52).NinjaDoughnuts.NinjaWebSite.0	\Memory\Available MBytes	3430
2010-02-03 03:08:04	634007632071710000	deployment(52)	NinjaWebSite	deployment(52).NinjaDoughnuts.NinjaWebSite.0	\Memory\Available MBytes	3436
2010-02-03 03:08:04	634007632121710000	deployment(52)	NinjaWebSite	deployment(52).NinjaDoughnuts.NinjaWebSite.0	\Memory\Available MBytes	3436
2010-02-03 03:08:04	634007632171710000	deployment(52)	NinjaWebSite	deployment(52).NinjaDoughnuts.NinjaWebSite.0	\Memory\Available MBytes	3432
2010-02-03 03:08:25	634007632221740000	deployment(52)	NinjaWebSite	deployment(52).NinjaDoughnuts.NinjaWebSite.0	\Memory\Available MBytes	3435
2010-02-03 03:08:25	634007632271700000	deployment(52)	NinjaWebSite	deployment(52).NinjaDoughnuts.NinjaWebSite.0	\Memory\Available MBytes	3435
2010-02-03 03:08:25	634007632321710000	deployment(52)	NinjaWebSite	deployment(52).NinjaDoughnuts.NinjaWebSite.0	\Memory\Available MBytes	3434
2010-02-03 03:08:25	634007632371710000	deployment(52)	NinjaWebSite	deployment(52).NinjaDoughnuts.NinjaWebSite.0	\Memory\Available MBytes	3456
2010-02-03 03:08:25	634007632421710000	deployment(52)	NinjaWebSite	deployment(52).NinjaDoughnuts.NinjaWebSite.0	\Memory\Available MBytes	3456
2010-02-03 03:08:25	634007632471710000	deployment(52)	NinjaWebSite	deployment(52).NinjaDoughnuts.NinjaWebSite.0	\Memory\Available MBytes	3452
2010-02-03 03:08:25	634007632521710000	deployment(52)	NinjaWebSite	deployment(52).NinjaDoughnuts.NinjaWebSite.0	\Memory\Available MBytes	3446
2010-02-03 03:08:25	634007632571710000	deployment(52)	NinjaWebSite	deployment(52).NinjaDoughnuts.NinjaWebSite.0	\Memory\Available MBytes	3454
2010-02-03 03:08:25	634007632621710000	deployment(52)	NinjaWebSite	deployment(52).NinjaDoughnuts.NinjaWebSite.0	\Memory\Available MBytes	3454
2010-02-03 03:08:25	634007632671710000	deployment(52)	NinjaWebSite	deployment(52).NinjaDoughnuts.NinjaWebSite.0	\Memory\Available MBytes	3452
2010-02-03 03:08:25	634007632721700000	deployment(52)	NinjaWebSite	deployment(52).NinjaDoughnuts.NinjaWebSite.0	\Memory\Available MBytes	3452
2010-02-03 03:08:25	634007632771720000	deployment(52)	NinjaWebSite	deployment(52).NinjaDoughnuts.NinjaWebSite.0	\Memory\Available MBytes	3447

Figure 18.5 The performance counter data is stored in a table called WADPerformanceCountersTable. In this example, we're tracking the amount of available memory. You can see that the available memory starts at 3,452 MB and slowly drops to 3,436 MB.

FILTERING THE UPLOADED DATA

The amount of data collected by the diagnostic agent can become voluminous. Sometimes you might want to track a great deal of data, but when you're trying to solve a particular problem, you might want only a subset of data to look through. The diagnostic agent configuration provides for filtering of the results.

The agent still collects all the data locally. The filter is applied only when the data is uploaded to Azure storage. Filtering can narrow down the data you need to sift through, make your transfers faster, and reduce your storage cost. You can set the following property to filter based on the log level of the records that you've specified:

```
transferOptions.LogLevelFilter = LogLevel.Error;
```

All the log data remains local to the agent; the agent uploads only the entries that match or exceed the filter level you set.

CHANGING THE CONFIGURATION FROM OUTSIDE THE ROLE

Being able to change the configuration inside the role instance is nice, but you'll probably do this only during the startup of the instance. Dynamic changes to the configuration are more likely to come from outside the role instance. The source of these changes will probably be either an overseer role that's monitoring the first role, or a management application of sorts that's running on your desktop.

The agent's configuration is stored in a file local to the role instance that's running the agent. By default, this file is polled every minute for any configuration changes. You can change the polling interval if you want to by using the `DiagnosticMonitorConfiguration.ConfigurationChangePollInterval` property. You can set this property only from within the role the agent is running in.

To update the configuration remotely, either from another role or from outside Azure, you can use two classes. The `DeploymentDiagnosticManager` class is a factory that returns diagnostic managers for any role you have access to. You can use this manager to change the configuration remotely by using it to create `RoleInstanceDiagnosticManager` objects. Each `RoleInstanceDiagnosticManager` object represents a collection of diagnostic agents for a given role, one for each instance running in that role.

After you've created this object, you can make changes to the configuration like you did in the previous section. The trick is that you have to change the configuration for each instance individually. The following listing shows how to update the configuration for a running role.

Listing 18.2 Remotely changing the configuration of a role's diagnostic agent

```
using Microsoft.WindowsAzure.Diagnostics.Management;
using Microsoft.WindowsAzure.Diagnostics;
using Microsoft.WindowsAzure.ServiceRuntime;

DeploymentDiagnosticManager myDDM = new
➥ DeploymentDiagnosticManager(
➥ RoleEnvironment.GetConfigurationSettingValue
➥ ("DiagnosticsConnectionString"),
➥ txtDeploymentID.Text);

var myRoleInstanceDiagnosticManager =
        myDDM.GetRoleInstanceDiagnostic
        ➥ ManagersForRole("NinjaWebSite");

PerformanceCounterConfiguration CPUTime =        ◁ (1) Creates new configuration
new PerformanceCounterConfiguration()
{
  CounterSpecifier = @"\Processor(_Total)
  ➥ \% Processor Time",
  SampleRate = TimeSpan.FromSeconds(5.0)
};
```

```
foreach (var instanceAgent in myRoleInstanceDiagnosticManager)      <-- Iterates over instance agents (2)
{
DiagnosticMonitorConfiguration
➥ instanceConfiguration =
➥ instanceAgent
      .GetCurrentConfiguration();
   instanceConfiguration
   ➥ .PerformanceCounters.DataSources.Add(CPUTime);     <-- (3) Adds new performance counters

instanceAgent.SetCurrentConfiguration(instanceConfiguration);
}
```

The first thing you do to update the configuration for a running role is get an instance of the `DeploymentDiagnosticManager` for the deployment. One object oversees all the roles in your deployment. Give it a connection string to your storage account for logging. This constructor doesn't take a configuration element like the `DiagnosticsMonitor` class does. You have to pass in a real connection string, or a real connection. The code in listing 18.2 grabs the string out of the role configuration with a call to `GetConfigurationSettingValue`.

From there, you ask for a collection of `RoleInstanceDiagnosticManager` objects for the particular role you want to work with. In this example, we're changing the configuration for the `NinjaWebSite` role. You'll get one `RoleInstanceDiagnosticManager` object for each instance that's running the `NinjaWebSite` role.

Next, you create the new part of the configuration you want to add to the agent ❶. In this example, you'll build another performance counter data source that will track the percentage of CPU in use. Then you'll iterate over your collection ❷ and add the new performance counter `CPUTime` to the current configuration ❸. This process is different from that used when you're changing the configuration in a role. Here you want to add to the configuration, not completely replace it. Finally, you update the configuration for that instance, which updates the configuration file for the diagnostic agent. When the agent polls for a configuration change, it'll pick up the changes and recycle to load them.

Figure 18.6 shows the results of the configuration changes that you've made.

In this sample, we've put this code in the role, but this code would work running from any application that's running outside Azure as well. The only difference would be how you provide the connection string to storage, and how you provide the deployment ID.

We've looked at the standard data sources for Windows Azure diagnostics, but there's one hole remaining. What if you want to manage a diagnostic source that isn't on the official list? This situation is where the escape hatch called *arbitrary diagnostics sources* comes into play.

18.3.3 The other data sources

Up until now, we've discussed how to configure a performance counter data source and how to enable the trace listener in the web.config file. Now let's look briefly at the other data sources that are configured in similar ways.

EventTickCount	DeploymentId	Role	RoleInstance	CounterName	CounterValue
634007737309650000	deployment(54)	NinjaWebSite	deployment(54).NinjaDoughnuts.NinjaWebSite.1	\Memory\Available MBytes	3412
634007737359870000	deployment(54)	NinjaWebSite	deployment(54).NinjaDoughnuts.NinjaWebSite.1	\Processor(_Total)\% Processor Time	26.455785
634007737359870000	deployment(54)	NinjaWebSite	deployment(54).NinjaDoughnuts.NinjaWebSite.1	\Memory\Available MBytes	3410
634007737409610000	deployment(54)	NinjaWebSite	deployment(54).NinjaDoughnuts.NinjaWebSite.1	\Processor(_Total)\% Processor Time	12.953047
634007737409610000	deployment(54)	NinjaWebSite	deployment(54).NinjaDoughnuts.NinjaWebSite.1	\Memory\Available MBytes	3409
634007737459610000	deployment(54)	NinjaWebSite	deployment(54).NinjaDoughnuts.NinjaWebSite.1	\Processor(_Total)\% Processor Time	21.378814
634007737459610000	deployment(54)	NinjaWebSite	deployment(54).NinjaDoughnuts.NinjaWebSite.1	\Memory\Available MBytes	3418
634007737509620000	deployment(54)	NinjaWebSite	deployment(54).NinjaDoughnuts.NinjaWebSite.1	\Processor(_Total)\% Processor Time	10.321144
634007737509620000	deployment(54)	NinjaWebSite	deployment(54).NinjaDoughnuts.NinjaWebSite.1	\Memory\Available MBytes	3418
634007737559600000	deployment(54)	NinjaWebSite	deployment(54).NinjaDoughnuts.NinjaWebSite.1	\Processor(_Total)\% Processor Time	9.487033
634007737559600000	deployment(54)	NinjaWebSite	deployment(54).NinjaDoughnuts.NinjaWebSite.1	\Memory\Available MBytes	3418
634007737609600000	deployment(54)	NinjaWebSite	deployment(54).NinjaDoughnuts.NinjaWebSite.1	\Processor(_Total)\% Processor Time	10.771193
634007737609600000	deployment(54)	NinjaWebSite	deployment(54).NinjaDoughnuts.NinjaWebSite.1	\Memory\Available MBytes	3419
634007737659610000	deployment(54)	NinjaWebSite	deployment(54).NinjaDoughnuts.NinjaWebSite.1	\Processor(_Total)\% Processor Time	9.679234
634007737659610000	deployment(54)	NinjaWebSite	deployment(54).NinjaDoughnuts.NinjaWebSite.1	\Memory\Available MBytes	3419
634007737709630000	deployment(54)	NinjaWebSite	deployment(54).NinjaDoughnuts.NinjaWebSite.1	\Processor(_Total)\% Processor Time	18.414919
634007737709630000	deployment(54)	NinjaWebSite	deployment(54).NinjaDoughnuts.NinjaWebSite.1	\Memory\Available MBytes	3418
634007737759600000	deployment(54)	NinjaWebSite	deployment(54).NinjaDoughnuts.NinjaWebSite.1	\Processor(_Total)\% Processor Time	22.143216
634007737759600000	deployment(54)	NinjaWebSite	deployment(54).NinjaDoughnuts.NinjaWebSite.1	\Memory\Available MBytes	3411
634007737817950000	deployment(54)	NinjaWebSite	deployment(54).NinjaDoughnuts.NinjaWebSite.0	\Processor(_Total)\% Processor Time	23.094753
634007737817950000	deployment(54)	NinjaWebSite	deployment(54).NinjaDoughnuts.NinjaWebSite.0	\Memory\Available MBytes	3404
634007737867950000	deployment(54)	NinjaWebSite	deployment(54).NinjaDoughnuts.NinjaWebSite.0	\Processor(_Total)\% Processor Time	14.653984
634007737867950000	deployment(54)	NinjaWebSite	deployment(54).NinjaDoughnuts.NinjaWebSite.0	\Memory\Available MBytes	3404
634007737917950000	deployment(54)	NinjaWebSite	deployment(54).NinjaDoughnuts.NinjaWebSite.0	\Processor(_Total)\% Processor Time	8.119289
634007737917950000	deployment(54)	NinjaWebSite	deployment(54).NinjaDoughnuts.NinjaWebSite.0	\Memory\Available MBytes	3403
634007737967950000	deployment(54)	NinjaWebSite	deployment(54).NinjaDoughnuts.NinjaWebSite.0	\Processor(_Total)\% Processor Time	15.763015
634007737967950000	deployment(54)	NinjaWebSite	deployment(54).NinjaDoughnuts.NinjaWebSite.0	\Memory\Available MBytes	3395
634007738017950000	deployment(54)	NinjaWebSite	deployment(54).NinjaDoughnuts.NinjaWebSite.0	\Processor(_Total)\% Processor Time	34.482345
634007738017950000	deployment(54)	NinjaWebSite	deployment(54).NinjaDoughnuts.NinjaWebSite.0	\Memory\Available MBytes	3395
634007738068060000	deployment(54)	NinjaWebSite	deployment(54).NinjaDoughnuts.NinjaWebSite.0	\Processor(_Total)\% Processor Time	26.687914
634007738068060000	deployment(54)	NinjaWebSite	deployment(54).NinjaDoughnuts.NinjaWebSite.0	\Memory\Available MBytes	3394

Figure 18.6 You can change the configuration of the Windows Azure diagnostic agent running in each instance quite easily. In this example, we added the % Processor Time performance counter to the agent. You can do this remotely, even from outside Azure.

CRASH DUMPS

Crash dumps are the log file of last resort. They aren't really a log file, but a dump of the status of the computer when a horrible problem has arisen. There are two types of crash dumps. The normal dump includes a copy of all the memory on the machine. The mini dump holds only the most important information, without a complete copy of everything.

If you're running a web application, ASP.NET should handle any errors that aren't handled by your application (in code or in the global.asax). A crash dump usually occurs only during a truly catastrophic error. When your code is running in a worker role, without the soft embrace of ASP.NET, you're likely to see these dumps more often.

Crash dump files are stored in the local data buffer and transferred with the common logs. You can choose which size dump you want by passing in `true` to the `EnableCollection` or `EnableCollectionToDirectory` method for a full dump and passing in `false` for a mini dump.

IIS FAILED REQUEST LOGS

The failed request logs for IIS are a new feature in IIS 7. IIS tracks log data for requests as they come through, but keeps the data only if certain configurable conditions are met. A condition for keeping the log data might be that a response takes too long to complete the request. If the response is completed fast enough, then the log buffer is flushed. You can configure how IIS manages this process in the `tracing` section of the `system.webServer` part of your web.config. After you configure failed request tracing for IIS in this way, the logs are collected with the rest of the data logs.

WINDOWS EVENT LOGS

Windows event logs can provide important clues to serious problems with your applications. Some applications create custom event log sources for their own logging. The diagnostic agent in Azure can collect these logs and transfer them to storage for you.

You need to subscribe to the event data that you want to receive using an XPath expression. Because of the security profile your processes run on, you won't be able to read the security windows event log. If you add this log to your configuration, nothing will be logged, and it won't work correctly until you remove it.

To capture Windows event logs, you can use the following expression:

```
diagConfig.WindowsEventLog.DataSources.Add("System!*");
```

This code grabs everything from the Windows System Event log, which is where you usually want to start your investigations.

18.3.4 Arbitrary diagnostic sources

Windows Azure Diagnostics covers a lot of the diagnostic sources you might use to troubleshoot an issue with your system. It covers IIS logs, performance counters, Windows event logs, and several other things. Over time, you'll probably devise your own diagnostic source; maybe a log you're creating that you need to track. Perhaps this is custom billing data, or a compressed log of the images used in production, or it might just be the output of a third-party logging framework you've chosen to use.

The agent can transfer anything you want. All you need to do is get that data into a file in a designated folder. When you configure the agent, you tell it which custom directories you want it to monitor. You need to configure some local storage and then write your log files to it.

Each data source has a configuration class that you add to the agent's configuration, and custom log locations aren't any different. We'll use the `DirectoryConfiguration` class to tell the agent to monitor a folder. You can set how large that directory is allowed to become, as well as scheduled transfer characteristics, as shown in the following code:

```
DirectoryConfiguration specialLogsDC = new DirectoryConfiguration();

specialLogsDC.Path =
➥ RoleEnvironment.GetLocalResource("specialLogs").RootPath;     <-- Source directory
```

```
specialLogsDC.Container = "speciallogs";            <-- Destination storage container
instanceConfiguration.Directories
➥ .DataSources.Add(specialLogsDC);
```

Windows Azure Diagnostics is a powerful tool you can use to help troubleshoot and diagnose problems. But it isn't just for problems, as we've discussed; you can also use it to help monitor the behavior of the system, or the actions of your users. Although Windows Azure Diagnostics is wonderful, it's only a source of data. You still need to analyze the data to turn it into information, and then take action. Sometimes the action you need to take is to change the configuration of the service model you're running your application in. For example, you might need to add some instances to respond to a spike in traffic. Regardless of the result of your analysis, you'll need to store the data you collect in Azure storage to be able to use it. To do this, you use transfers.

18.4 Transferring diagnostic data

The diagnostic agent does a great job of collecting all the local data and storing it on the machine it's running on. But if the diagnostic information is never moved to Azure storage, it won't be any good to anyone. This is where transfers come into play.

There are two types of transfers, one of which you have already seen in play. We've already talked about the scheduled transfer, which sets up a timer and transfers the related data on a regular basis to your storage account. Each data source category has its own transfer schedule. You can transfer performance counter data at a different rate than you transfer the IIS logs.

The second type of transfer is an on-demand transfer. You usually perform an on-demand transfer when you have a special request of the data.

Let's look at each of these kinds of data transfers in more detail.

18.4.1 Scheduled transfer

In our sample in listing 18.1, a scheduled transfer of the performance counter data is set (4) to occur every minute. As we covered earlier, transferring every minute is quite aggressive, and is probably reasonable only in a testing or debugging environment.

In our next example, we're going to show you how to transfer the IIS logs to storage on a daily basis. The IIS logs are automatically captured by default by the diagnostic agent, so you don't need to add them as a data source. You can set the transfer interval to once a day with this line:

```
instanceConfiguration.Logs.ScheduledTransferPeriod = TimeSpan.FromDays(1.0);
```

Any log files that are captured are sent to a container in BLOB storage, not to a table. Each transfer results in one file in the container. A container hierarchy similar to what you would see on the real server is created for you by the diagnostic agent. Your IIS logs will be in a folder structure similar to what you're used to.

If logs that you don't want to transfer are collected, you can set `ScheduledTransferPeriod` to `0`. This setting disables the transfer of any data for that data source. We typically do this for the Azure diagnostics log themselves, at least until there's a problem with the diagnostic agent itself that requires troubleshooting.

That's how you schedule a transfer. Now let's discuss how you can trigger a transfer on demand.

18.4.2 On-demand transfer

An on-demand transfer lets you configure a onetime transfer of the diagnostics data. This kind of transfer gives you the ability to pick and choose what is transferred and when. A typical scenario is you want an immediate dump of logs because you see that something critical is happening. You can set up an on-demand transfer in much the same way as you would a normal transfer, although there are some differences.

In the following listing, we're initiating an on-demand transfer from within one of the instances, but you can also initiate the transfer from outside the role with an administrative application.

Listing 18.3 Initiating an on-demand transfer

```
DeploymentDiagnosticManager myDDM = new
➥ DeploymentDiagnosticManager(RoleEnvironment
➥ .GetConfigurationSettingValue("DiagnosticsConnectionString"),
➥ txtDeploymentID.Text);

var myRoleInstanceDiagnosticManager =
➥ myDDM.GetRoleInstanceDiagnosticManagersForRole("NinjaWebSite");

DataBufferName datasourceToTransfer =
➥ DataBufferName.PerformanceCounters;                    // ❶ Transfers performance counters
OnDemandTransferOptions transferOptions = new OnDemandTransferOptions();

transferOptions.From = DateTime.UtcNow -
➥ TimeSpan.FromHours(1.0);
transferOptions.To = DateTime.UtcNow;                     // ❷ Selects time filter for data to be sent
transferOptions.NotificationQueueName = "transfernotificationqueue";  // ❸ Provides queue name for notification messages

foreach (var instanceAgent in myRoleInstanceDiagnosticManager)
{
  Guid requestID = instanceAgent
  ➥ .BeginOnDemandTransfer
  ➥ (datasourceToTransfer, transferOptions);              // ❹ Starts transfer for each instance in role
  System.Diagnostics.Trace.WriteLine("on demand started:" +
  ➥ requestID.ToString(), "Information");
}
```

Like in the remote configuration example, you need to get a reference to the `RoleInstanceDiagnosticManagersForRole` class. This reference will let you work with the configuration manager for each instance. In this example, you're going to be transferring the performance counter data over to an Azure table ❶. This transfer will include all counters you might have running from prior configuration changes.

You use the `OnDemandTransferOptions` class to configure how the transfer should happen. This class has several parameters that you'll want to set. Set a time filter at ❷,

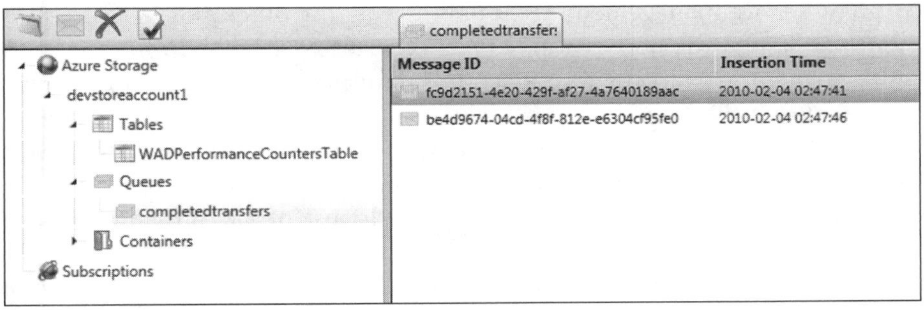

Figure 18.7 You can configure an on-demand transfer to notify you when a transfer is complete by placing a message in a queue you specify. In this example, the role had two instances, so two transfers were completed, one for each instance.

which tells the agent to send over only the performance counter data that's been generated in the last hour. If you're transferring a log, you can also specify a log level filter (informational, critical, and so on).

When you start the transfers, each instance performs its own transfer. The transfer operation is an asynchronous operation; you start it and walk away. In most cases, you'll want to know when the transfers have completed so that you can start analyzing the data. You can have the transfer agent notify you when the transfer for an instance is complete by passing in a queue name ❸. As each transfer is started, you'll be given a unique ID ❹ to track. You can see the completion messages in figure 18.7. Each message contains one of the unique IDs associated with each transfer.

When each transfer is complete, the agent drops a small message onto the queue you designated with that same ID. The message lets you track which transfers have been completed.

A great place to use an on-demand transfer is in the `OnStop` method in your `RoleEntryPoint` override class. Whenever a role is being shut down, either intentionally or otherwise, this method fires. If you do an on-demand transfer in this method, you'll save your log files from being erased during a reboot or a move. These log files can help you troubleshoot instance failures. Because you might not have enough time to transfer gigabytes of log files, make sure that you're transferring only the critical information you need when you do this.

Now that you know how to get data about what's happening with your service, we need to tell you about the APIs that'll help you do something about what you see happening.

18.5 Using the service management API

After your application is up and running in Azure, you'll want to automate some of the management functions. Automation can include scaling your roles, changing configuration, and automating deployments. Almost anything you can do through the Azure portal you can do through the service management API.

The service management API is built like all the other APIs in Azure. It uses REST and XML under the hood, wrapped in a pleasant .NET library. You can use the service management API directly with REST, but most people use either the library or use a tool that calls the APIs.

All the management APIs we're going to discuss can be called from inside or from outside Azure. All management calls are free; they incur no cost to call or execute. The Azure team has said that they monitor the use of the APIs and can throttle back your calls if they're abused.

To start using the service management API, you need to configure your account with certificates for API authentication. After you've done that, you'll be able to send it commands. After we show you how to configure your account, we're going to look at how you can work with your services and containers, how to automate a deployment to the cloud, and how you can use the management API to scale your service up or down.

18.5.1 What the API doesn't do

A little earlier we said that the service management API can do almost as much as the portal. However, you must use the portal to do the following things:

- *Access billing data*—The portal has several tools you can use to monitor your usage and billing in near real time. Monitoring allows you to estimate your charges as they occur. The final numbers are crunched at the end of the month to generate your bill.
- *Create subscriptions and create compute or storage services*—After you've created the subscription and services, you can do everything else from the management API.
- *Deploy management certificates*—You can't use the management service to deploy a management certificate; you have to do this manually.

To make calls with the API, you need to sign them with a certificate, which we'll discuss next.

18.5.2 Setting up the management credentials

The service management API has a lot of power, so all of its calls and responses must be secure. All calls are transferred over HTTPS, using a signed certificate that you associate with your Azure account. Whether you're calling the REST by hand or using the .NET library, you'll need to attach a certificate to your Azure account trusts.

You can use any X.509 v3 certificate that you want to use. Because you have control over which certificates your account trusts, you can use self-signed certificates if you want to. You can also use certificates that you've purchased from a certificate authority like VeriSign.

Your account can hold up to five certificates. You can distribute those certificates to different people or processes, and then eventually revoke them if you need to. All a person needs in order to use the management API on your services is that certificate and your subscription number. We'll look at how to revoke a certificate later in this section.

SETTING UP A CERTIFICATE

To set up your management certificates, you need a certificate to upload. We're going to walk you through the process of creating a certificate locally and then uploading it to your account.

The goal is to create a .cer file that holds the public key for your certificate. You never share the private half of the key. This public key will be uploaded to Azure, and Azure will use it to verify that your private key was used to sign the management API request.

You need to use IIS 7 to create a self-signed certificate. Open the IIS manager and look for the Features view. Listed there is a link for Server Certificates. Click Create Self-Signed Certificate in the Actions pane and follow the steps. You'll give the certificate a name, which will be used whenever you're working with the certificate.

You can also use the Visual Studio command prompt to create a self-signed certificate. Open the command prompt (make sure to run it as an administrator), and then enter the following command:

```
makecert -r -pe
➥ -n "CN=CompanyName"
➥ -a sha1
➥ -len 2048
➥ -ss My "filename.cer"
```

This command creates a certificate that you can use in the local directory.

IMPORTING AND REVOKING A CERTIFICATE

Importing a certificate is as easy as logging into your Azure portal and going to the Account tab. Choose Manage My API Certificates. The window, shown in figure 18.8,

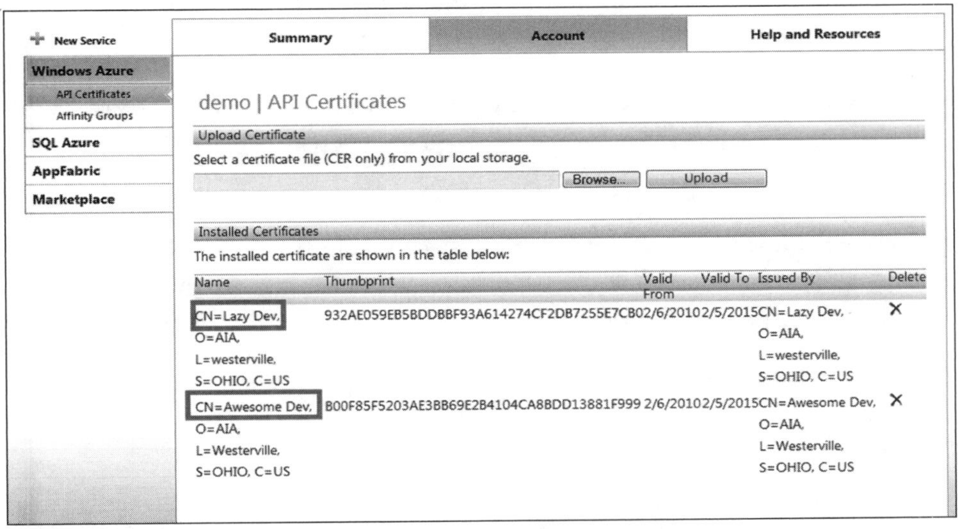

Figure 18.8 This window shows that two X.509 certificates have been imported; one for Lazy Dev and one for Awesome Dev. Certificates are used to authenticate to Azure when you're using the service management API. Guess whose certificate we're going to revoke in the next example?

displays the certificates you've uploaded; you can also upload a new certificate from this window. Your certificate must be in a .cer file. If you have a different format, you can easily convert it by importing it into your Windows certificate store, and then exporting it in the format you want.

You can have up to five certificates in your account at a time; take advantage of them. Each person or system that's using the management API should have their own certificate. If you provide certificates in this way, you'll have an easy way to revoke their access. To revoke a certificate, click the Delete X icon next to the one you want to revoke.

You need to attach your certificate to each request that you send to the API. Attaching your certificate ensures that the message is signed with your private key, which only you should have. When Azure receives your message, it'll check that the message came from you by opening it with the public key you uploaded in the .cer file.

You've got some certificates now and you're ready to learn about some of the things you can use the service management API for.

18.5.3 Listing your services and containers

You can save a lot of time if you learn how to automate your deployments instead of doing them by hand through the portal. We're going to start this section by showing some code you can use to get a list of the service and storage accounts you've created in Azure. This code is fairly primitive and uses the REST API directly. We'll eventually start using a tool that will abstract away the raw REST so that you have something nicer to work with.

You're going to use the `WebRequest` class to work with the REST call you'll be making. You need to pass in the URI of the call you want to make. The following listing shows how to use REST to query for a list of services.

Listing 18.4 Querying for the list of services with REST

```
var request = (HttpWebRequest)WebRequest.Create(
➥ "https://management.core.windows.net/7212af99-206f-dem0-9334-
➥ 380d0f841d0b/services/hostedservices");                    ❶ Required subscription ID

request.Headers.Add("x-ms-version:2009-10-01");
request.ClientCertificates.Add(
➥ X509Certificate2.CreateFromCertFile(@"C:\
➥ \awesomedev.cer"));                                        ❷ Adds certificate to the request

var responseStream = request.GetResponse().GetResponseStream();

var services = XDocument.Parse(new
➥ StreamReader(responseStream).ReadToEnd());
```

In the previous listing, you pass in a string that includes the root of the call, `https://management.core.windows.net/`, and the subscription ID (which can be found on your Accounts tab in the portal) at ❶. You pass this string because you want a list of the services that you've created. Every request into the management service needs this base address. Because for this example we want to include a list of the hosted services you have in your account, add `/services/hostedservices` to the end of your URL.

You also need to attach a version header and your certificate for authentication. The version header tells Azure which version of the management service you intend to call. Right now the latest version to call is the one that was published in October of 2009, so let's use that one. The certificate is easily attached at line ❷. You're attaching it from the file you generated above. You could have used the certificate that's in your secure certificate store.

When you run this code, the result you get in raw XML format is shown in the following listing. All three services that are running in your subscription (`aiademo1`, `aiademo2`, and `aiademo3`) are listed in `HostedService` elements.

Listing 18.5 The raw XML that comes back from our request

```
<HostedServices xmlns="http://schemas.microsoft.com/windowsazure"
➥ xmlns:i="http://www.w3.org/2001/XMLSchema-instance">
  <HostedService>
    <Url>https://management.core.windows.net
    ➥ /7212af99-206f-dem0-9334-80d0f841d0b
    ➥ /services/hostedservices/aiademo1</Url>
    <ServiceName>aiademo1</ServiceName>
  </HostedService>
  <HostedService>
    <Url>https://management.core.windows.net
    ➥ /7212af99-206f-dem0-9334-380d0f841d0b
    ➥ /services/hostedservices/aiademo2</Url>
    <ServiceName>aiademo2</ServiceName>
  </HostedService>
  <HostedService>
    <Url>https://management.core.windows.net
    ➥ /7212af99-206f-dem0-9334-380d0f841d0b
    ➥ /services/hostedservices/aiademo3</Url>
    <ServiceName>aiademo3</ServiceName>
  </HostedService>
</HostedServices>
```

Management URL to the service

Simple name for your service

After you've received the XML, you can use something like Language-Integrated Query (LINQ) to XML to parse through the results. You'll want the URL for each service for later when you're calling back to reference that particular service. You can use the same code to get a list of storage accounts in your Azure account by changing the address of the request from `/hostedservices` to `/storageservices`.

You'll be able to use these endpoints to see the storage and service accounts you have. This part of the API is read-only. To create service or storage accounts, you'll have to use the portal.

Now that you can make simple queries of the management service, let's flip over to csmanage.exe and use it to deploy a simple web application to Azure.

18.5.4 Automating a deployment

Even though you can do everything you need through the naked REST API of the service management service, it's a lot easier to use something that provides a higher level of abstraction. REST is fine, but it's too low-level for us on a daily basis.

There are two popular options to go with. The first is a collection of PowerShell commandlets that have been provided by Microsoft. These are useful when you're integrating cloud management into your existing management scripts. You can find these commandlets at http://code.msdn.microsoft.com/azurecmdlets.

We're going to use csmanage.exe for the rest of this chapter. This small utility is provided by the Azure team and can be found at http://code.msdn.microsoft.com/windowsazuresamples.

We might be using a higher-level tool, but you still need to provide the tool with the subscription ID of your Azure account and the thumbprint for the certificate you'll be using to manage your account. You can enter these into the configuration file for the tool, csmanage.exe.config. The easiest place to find the ID and the thumbprint is on the Azure portal.

The `csmanage` application can work with one of three resources online: hosted services, storage services, or affinity groups. Each command you send will include a reference to the resource you want to work with.

GETTING A LIST OF HOSTED SERVICES

To get a simple list of the hosted services you have in your account, you can execute the following command at a command prompt. This command executes the same query you previously made manually.

```
csmanage.exe /list-hosted-services
```

When you run this command, the application connects to your account in the cloud and returns a list of the services you have. When we executed this command, we had just one hosted service, as shown in figure 18.9.

After you have a list of your services, you next task is to create a deployment of your application.

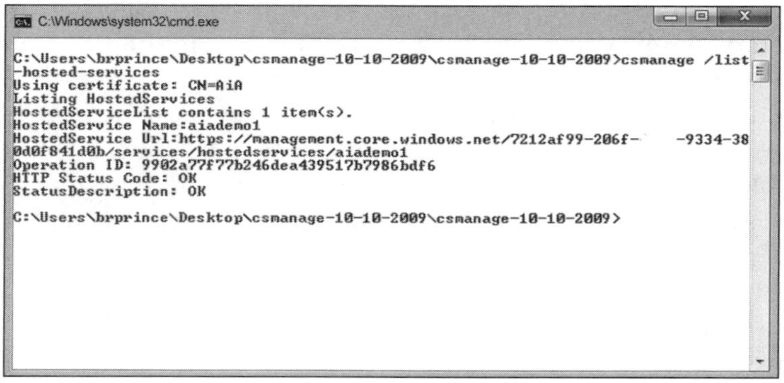

Figure 18.9 You can use the `csmanage` command-line tool to execute management commands against your account in the cloud. In this example, we used a simple command to list the hosted services we have.

CREATING A DEPLOYMENT

First, you need to create the package for your code. You've probably done this a thousand times by now, but right-click the Azure project and choose Publish.

When you're using the management service, a service package has to be in BLOB storage for you to deploy it; you can't upload it as part of the actual `create-deployment` command. What you can do is upload the package through any tool you want to use. In this example, we just want to upload the cspkg file. This BLOB container can be public or private, but it should probably be private. You don't want some jokester on the interweb to download your source package. Because the management call is signed, it'll have access to your private BLOB containers, so you won't have to provide the credentials. The configuration file will be uploaded when you run the `create-deployment` command. The following listing shows the command-line code for deploying a package.

Listing 18.6 Pushing a deployment to the cloud from the command line

```
csmanage.exe
    /create-deployment       /slot:staging
    /hosted-service:aiademo1
    /name:ninjas
    /label:build1234
    /config:ninja.cscfg
    /package:http://aiademostore.blob.core.windows.net/
➥  deployments/NinjaDoughnuts.cspkg
```

Local path of configuration file to upload

URL of package to deploy

That's a lot to type in by hand. The most common use of `csmanage` is in an automated deployment script. You could make the deployment completely hands-off with enough script and PowerShell. When you execute the command in listing 18.6, there'll be a slight pause as the configuration is uploaded and the management service deploys your bits. The output of the command is shown in figure 18.10.

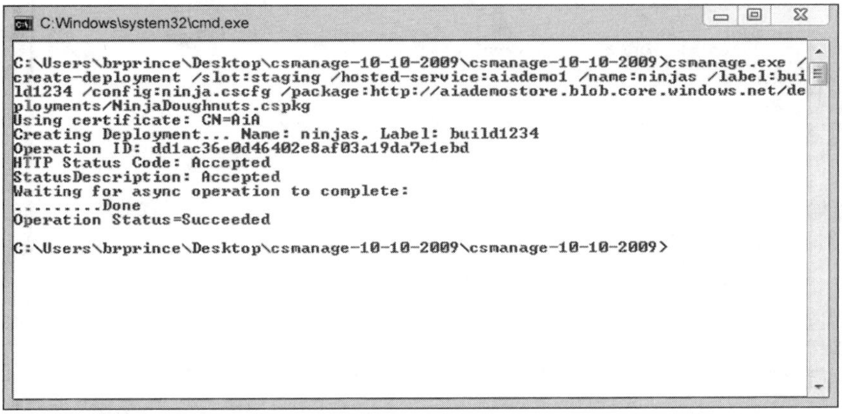
C:\Windows\system32\cmd.exe
C:\Users\brprince\Desktop\csmanage-10-10-2009\csmanage-10-10-2009>csmanage.exe /create-deployment /slot:staging /hosted-service:aiademo1 /name:ninjas /label:build1234 /config:ninja.cscfg /package:http://aiademostore.blob.core.windows.net/deployments/NinjaDoughnuts.cspkg
Using certificate: CN=AiA
Creating Deployment... Name: ninjas, Label: build1234
Operation ID: dd1ac36e0d46402e8af03a19da7e1ebd
HTTP Status Code: Accepted
StatusDescription: Accepted
Waiting for async operation to complete:
.........Done
Operation Status=Succeeded
C:\Users\brprince\Desktop\csmanage-10-10-2009\csmanage-10-10-2009>

Figure 18.10 The output from `csmanage` when you script out a deployment to staging. We're deploying our ninja doughnut application, which has nothing to do with doughnuts or ninjas.

All this is wonderful, but you don't want to just upload and deploy your code; you need to start it.

STARTING THE CODE

You need to start your code so that the FC can start your site. The command to start everything is quite simple:

```
csmanage
➥ /update-deployment
➥ /slot:staging
➥ /hosted-service:aiademo1
➥ /status:running
```

This command tells the management API that you want to update the deployment of your service that's in the staging slot to running. (You can use the same command to set the status to suspended.) After you set the status to running, it can take a few minutes for the FC to get everything up and running. You can check on the status of each instance of your roles by using the `view-deployment` command:

```
csmanage /view-deployment /slot:staging /hosted-service:aiademo1
```

When you execute this command, you'll get a detailed view of each instance. In this example, both of our instances were busy, as shown in figure 18.11. If we just wait a few minutes, they'll flip to ready.

When your instance status reads as ready, you can use a command to perform a VIP swap.

PERFORMING A VIP SWAP

Remember, a VIP swap occurs when you swap the virtual IPs for production and staging, performing a clean cutover from one environment to the other. Using a VIP swap

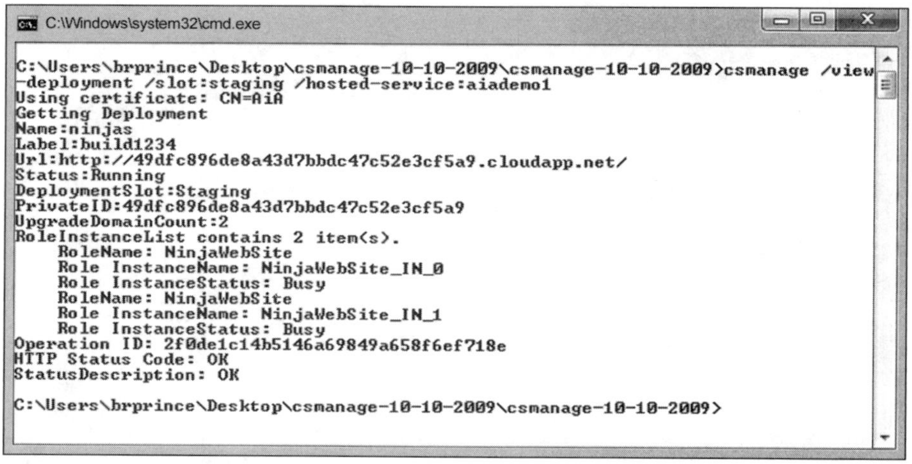

Figure 18.11 You can check the detailed status of each role instance by using the `view-deployment` option. In this example, our instances are busy because we've just deployed the package. In a moment, the status will change to ready.

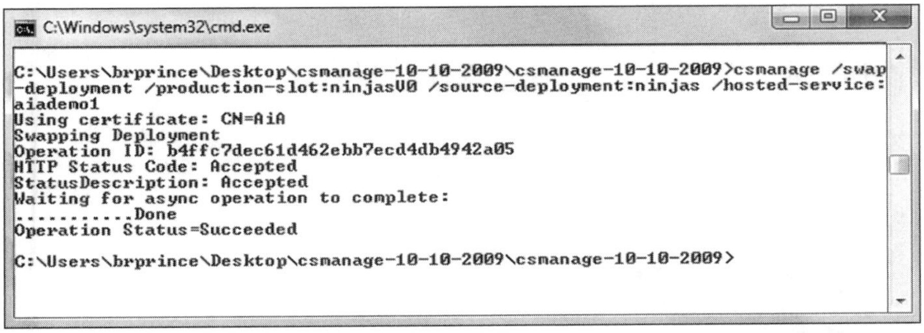
C:\Windows\system32\cmd.exe
C:\Users\brprince\Desktop\csmanage-10-10-2009\csmanage-10-10-2009>csmanage /swap-deployment /production-slot:ninjasV0 /source-deployment:ninjas /hosted-service:aiademo1
Using certificate: CN=AiA
Swapping Deployment
Operation ID: b4ffc7dec61d462ebb7ecd4db4942a05
HTTP Status Code: Accepted
StatusDescription: Accepted
Waiting for async operation to complete:
...........Done
Operation Status=Succeeded
C:\Users\brprince\Desktop\csmanage-10-10-2009\csmanage-10-10-2009>

Figure 18.12 The VIP swap has successfully swapped the staging and production slots. You need to provide the names of the deployments in each slot.

is the simplest way to deploy a new version. You can always do an update domain walk, which is more complicated but provides the capability for a rolling upgrade.

You need a deployment in each slot to perform a VIP swap through the `csmanage` or REST interfaces. If you're deploying for the first time to an empty environment, either deploy your first version into the production slot, or rerun the `swap-deployment` command and adjust the `slot` parameter to `production`.

To perform the VIP swap, execute the following command:

```
csmanage /swap-deployment /production-slot:ninjasV0 /source-deployment:ninjas
     /hosted-service:aiademo1
```

Be careful when you type in this command. The third parameter, `source-deployment`, is different from what you would expect. Because the second parameter is `production-slot`, you would expect the third to be `staging-slot`. The naming isn't terribly consistent. Another mystery is why you need to define the slot names at all. You can have only one slot of each anyway. Go figure.

Figure 18.12 shows the successful completion of the VIP swap.

Now that you've swapped out to production and have fully tested the slot, you can tear down the staging slot.

TEARING DOWN A DEPLOYMENT

Use the following command to suspend the state of the servers, and then delete the deployment:

```
csmanage /update-deployment /slot:staging /hosted-service:aiademo1 /
     status:suspended

csmanage /delete-deployment /slot:staging /hosted-service:aiademo1
```

You need to execute these two commands back-to-back. You can't delete a service while it's running, so you have to wait for the first command to suspend the service to finish.

Figure 18.13 shows the successful completion of these commands.

You've successfully automated the deployment of a cloud service, started it, moved it to production, and then finally stopped and tore down the old version of the service.

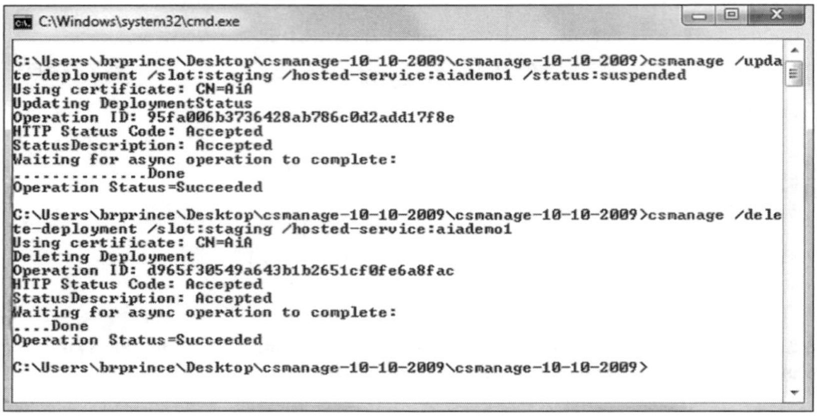
C:\Windows\system32\cmd.exe
C:\Users\brprince\Desktop\csmanage-10-10-2009\csmanage-10-10-2009>csmanage /upda
te-deployment /slot:staging /hosted-service:aiademo1 /status:suspended
Using certificate: CN=AiA
Updating DeploymentStatus
Operation ID: 95fa006b3736428ab786c0d2add17f8e
HTTP Status Code: Accepted
StatusDescription: Accepted
Waiting for async operation to complete:
...............Done
Operation Status=Succeeded
C:\Users\brprince\Desktop\csmanage-10-10-2009\csmanage-10-10-2009>csmanage /dele
te-deployment /slot:staging /hosted-service:aiademo1
Using certificate: CN=AiA
Deleting Deployment
Operation ID: d965f30549a643b1b2651cf0fe6a8fac
HTTP Status Code: Accepted
StatusDescription: Accepted
Waiting for async operation to complete:
....Done
Operation Status=Succeeded
C:\Users\brprince\Desktop\csmanage-10-10-2009\csmanage-10-10-2009>

Figure 18.13 After deploying and swapping your new version to production, you suspend the staging environment and then tear it down to stop the billing. This process involves two steps: first you must suspend the service, and then you delete it.

You've done this without having to use the portal. Even so, you still had to use the portal to upload your management certificates and create the initial service container.

Now to what people really care about in the cloud: dynamically scaling the number of instances that are running your service.

18.5.5 Changing configuration and dynamically scaling your application

One of the golden promises of cloud computing is the dynamic allocation of resources to your service. It's really cool that you can deploy a service from nothing to 20 servers, but you also want to be able to change that from 20 servers to 30 servers if your service experiences a spike of some sort.

CHANGING THE SERVICE CONFIGURATION FILE

As we've discussed in chapters past, your service is based on a service model that's defined in your service configuration file. This file defines how many instances per role your service defines. You can change this file in one of three ways.

The first way to change the file is to edit it online in the portal. This is the simplest way to change it, but it's also the most primitive. You can't wire this up into an automated system or into an enterprise configuration management system.

The second method can use configuration files generated by your enterprise configuration management change system. You can upload a new file (version them with different file names so you can keep track of them) into BLOB storage, and then point to that file when you change the configuration from the portal.

The third option lets you upload a new configuration through the service management REST API. If you don't want to use REST, you can use `csmanage`, like we've been doing in the past few sections.

The FC responds in different ways depending on how you've changed your configuration and how you've coded your `RoleEnvironmentChanging` event. By default, if you've changed anything besides the instance count of a role, the FC tears down and restarts any instances for the affected role. That part of the service comes to a screeching halt while the instances are restarted. The length of the outage isn't very long, but it's there. Be sure to think about which changes should restart your roles and which shouldn't; you can adjust the code in the `RoleEnvironmentChanging` event accordingly.

If you increased the instance count, none of the instances are affected. The FC creates new instances, deploys your bits, configures them, and wires them into the network and load balancer like it does when you've started the role instances from scratch. This process can take several minutes. You won't see an immediate availability, so be patient. Take this slight delay into consideration when you're developing the logic you'll use to detect when you need to add instances.

If you've reduced the number of instances, then the FC uses an undocumented algorithm to decide which instances are shed. They're unwired from the load balancer so that it doesn't receive any new traffic, and then they're torn down.

After you've made changes to the configuration file, you have to deploy it.

DEPLOYING THE NEW CONFIGURATION FILE

You can use `csmanage` to deploy a new configuration file. The command should be fairly easy to understand by now. The .cscfg file that will be uploaded by the following command is in the same folder as `csmanage`. Your file probably isn't in the same folder, so you'll need to provide a path to the configuration file.

```
csmanage /change-deployment-config /config:ninja_daytime.cscfg /
    slot:production /hosted-service:aiademo1
```

When you're using the management API (and `csmanage`), you have to upload a locally stored configuration file. In figure 18.14, you can see that it took quite a while for the

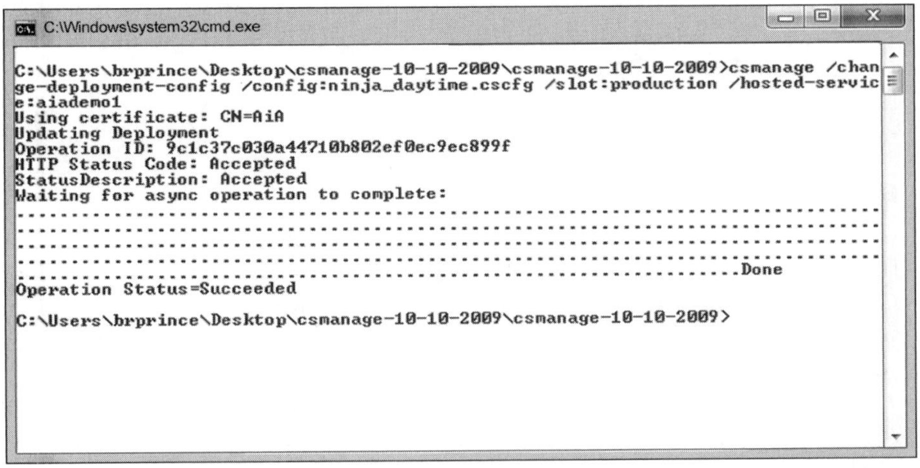
C:\Windows\system32\cmd.exe
C:\Users\brprince\Desktop\csmanage-10-10-2009\csmanage-10-10-2009>csmanage /change-deployment-config /config:ninja_daytime.cscfg /slot:production /hosted-service:aiademo1
Using certificate: CN=AiA
Updating Deployment
Operation ID: 9c1c37c030a44710b802ef0ec9ec899f
HTTP Status Code: Accepted
StatusDescription: Accepted
Waiting for async operation to complete:
Done
Operation Status=Succeeded
C:\Users\brprince\Desktop\csmanage-10-10-2009\csmanage-10-10-2009>

Figure 18.14 We've uploaded a new configuration file for our service. Because we changed only the number of instances for each role, we didn't have any downtime. The FC has spun up new instances to meet our needs.

management service to spin up the new instance. The total time it took in this instance was about 4 minutes.

This might seem like a lot of work. Couldn't Azure do all this for you automatically?

WHY DOESN'T AZURE SCALE AUTOMATICALLY?

Many people wonder why Azure doesn't auto-scale for them. There are a couple of reasons, but they all fall into the "My kid sent 100,000 text messages this month and my cell phone bill is over a million dollars" category.

The first challenge for Azure with auto-scaling your application is that Azure doesn't know what it means for your system to be busy. Is it the depth of the queue? Which queue? Is it the number of hits on the site? Each system defines the status of *busy* different than any other system does. There are too many moving parts for a vendor such as Microsoft to come up with a standard definition that'll make all its customers happy.

Another reason is that Microsoft could be accused of too aggressively scaling up, and not scaling down fast enough, just to increase the charges on your account. We don't think they would do that, but the second someone thinks the algorithm isn't tuned to their liking, Microsoft would get sued for overbilling customers.

Another scenario this approach protects against is a denial of service (DoS) attack. In these attacks, someone tries to flood your server with an unusually high number of requests. These requests overcome the processing power on your servers and the whole system grinds to a halt. If Azure automatically scaled up in this scenario, you would come in on Monday the day after an attack and find 5,000 instances running in production. You would get enough mileage points on your credit card to fly to the moon and back for free, but you probably wouldn't be too happy about it.

Microsoft has given us the tools to manage scaling ourselves. We can adjust the target number of instances at any time in a variety of ways. All we have to add is the logic we want to use to determine what *busy* means for us, and how we want to handle both the busy states and the slow states.

We'll look at some approaches for how to scale your Azure environment in the next section.

18.6 Better together for scaling

Everyone expects that they'll be able to dynamically scale their service in Azure. Dynamic scaling is possible, but it requires some heavy lifting on the developer's part. Over time, vendors will provide this as a service on top of Azure. In the meantime, you'll want to provide some sort of control over the amount of resources allocated to your service.

In this section, we're going to follow the same model that our homes use for heating and cooling. Our homes are driven by a sensor that detects a healthy condition (is the temperature in a pleasant range?), a mechanism to change that temperature, and some simple rules that keep the heater from running for 24 hours straight. We can take this approach and apply it to a cloud service. We'll instrument the cloud service with the diagnostic engine, use the management API to control the infrastructure, and provide some code to control how all that works. You want to respond to events and keep your system healthy so you don't come in on Monday to find that you have 1,500 instances running in the cloud.

In keeping with our heating and cooling metaphor, let's start with the thermostat.

18.6.1 The thermostat

The thermostat in your home is a simple component of a common control system. Other examples include the cruise control in your car, the autopilot in a plane, and many manufacturing systems. Each of these systems has three components.

The first component is the system itself: the car, the plane, the furnace in the house. In Azure, the system is the service you're running. The system needs to have inputs to be able to control important aspects of itself. In the furnace example, you can send it a turn-on signal or a turn-off signal. These signals cause it to generate more heat or to stop generating heat.

The second component is the measurement or input device. This device measures the control aspects of the system. In our house example, it's the thermometer in the thermostat. In Azure, the measurement might be any number of things. A thermostat uses a simple dial to determine what the desired temperature is, as shown in figure 18.15.

The hard part for systems in Azure is deciding what *busy* is for the system. There's not a simple dial, but likely an amalgam of several inputs; perhaps the depth of a messaging queue, the number of pending requests in the IIS queue, and the running average of response time for each web request. Every measurement point you want to monitor to help decide what *busy* means needs to be something you can measure across all your instances.

Busy is sometimes represented as an absolute measure. For example, you could define a concrete amount of time a response is allowed to take under normal conditions. The system is either beneath or above that allotted time. Some definitions for a busy state are relative in nature. Saying that your system is busy whenever there are more than 50 messages in the queue won't work very long. You might instead want to

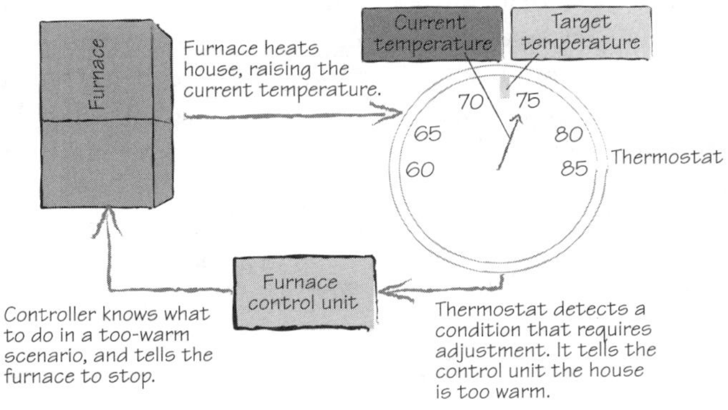

Figure 18.15 A control system you might have in your house. The furnace is the system you want to control. The thermometer measures the temperature of the house and provides feedback on the performance of the system to the controller. The controller is the electronics in your thermostat, which tells the furnace to turn on or off based on the input from the thermostat.

measure 50 messages per instance. Then, if you have five instances, a scenario that has 200 messages in the queue is OK. In this way, you can scale up the definition of *busy* as you scale up the amount of available resources.

The last component is the control logic itself. This is the piece that determines whether anything needs to be done, and how it should be done.

18.6.2 The control system

Your control system has only a few things that it can do with regard to managing performance or scale. In general, the only things the control system can do is add or remove instances of roles. That's about it.

Of course, there are plenty of scale patterns you can implement, and some will help prevent a dramatic scale failure from happening. You'll want to look into shunting, bulkheads, and partitioning. Just look in one of those enterprise patterns books on your bookshelf.

You need to instrument your control system yourself so you know what decisions it's making and how. You want to be able to figure out what went wrong when your service lumbers out of control and eats a village.

The control system can run as a simple role in Azure or as an on-premises application. You might assume an on-premise is a better solution, but remember that you'll need the input of the diagnostic logs; you'll have to download them all the time to make decisions. Having the control for the system running in the cloud puts the code near the data, which makes it both faster and cheaper.

18.6.3 Risks and managing them

A lot of risk is associated with implementing an auto-scaling component for your service; it's not trivial. You'll have to take into consideration a lot of issues and complexities. If things go haywire, they can go haywire badly.

On one hand, you could end up with a large Azure bill if your code goes crazy and spins up 400 instances. On the other hand, if it fails to work properly, you'll end up not responding to a busy state at all, leading to lost orders and unhappy users. Scaling requires a fine balance, and you'll want some protective measures in place.

In your logic, make sure you have an absolute upper boundary in place. No matter what's happening in the feedback system, the scaler won't go above this boundary. If the scaler reaches its ceiling, it should call a human and ask for help (by sending an email or a text message). You should set this boundary to something that's high enough to handle expected spikes (the big spike at the end of month), plus 15 percent for a buffer. In addition to this ceiling, set a floor to the scale value. You might want to make sure you always have two instances for reliability. Of course, some applications are OK with just a single instance, and others are OK to be completely shut down if there isn't any load.

At some point, the spike that caused the controller to create all these instances will pass. After it does, be sure that your controller starts shedding instances to bring the amount of resources deployed back into an acceptable range for the current load.

Pick an algorithm that matches how your load tends to fall off. If it tends to fall very quickly in a steep spike, then you should use an aggressive backoff strategy. In this case, you could use a halving technique in which for each polling cycle that the controller deems is excessive, it cuts the amount of resources by half (going from 32 instances to 16, for example).

In other services, you'll need a slower backoff process, dropping only one instance every time the measure drops by a certain percentage. Do extensive testing on the behavior of your controller to make sure it's working under stressful situations the way you want it to.

Another risk is that the controller might flood the channel with conflicting messages. If the polling cycle is too fast and the traffic too unpredictable, you might end up sending conflicting messages through the channel to the service. If you send a message to add an instance and then immediately follow it with a message to shed an instance, you'll end up thrashing your infrastructure. You also don't want to accidentally send a message to add an instance several times when you want only one net new instance started. To avoid this problem, make sure your controller is stateful, tracking the commands it has sent and whether those commands have been executed yet. You might even want to suspend all polling until the chosen action is completed.

No matter how clever you get with your controlling logic, make sure that you always include wetware somehow. The controller should always have a way to notify a human as to its behavior. If you run into the "we accidentally started up 400 instances last night" problem, you'll likely have a "don't have a job on Monday" problem.

We strongly recommend that you initially build tools that help you watch performance and easily maintain it. Keep the decision to add or remove instances in the control of humans, at least until you have an absolute understanding of how the system responds to stress, and how it responds to increases and decreases in resources.

The cloud does a great job of abstracting away the need to manage the platform, but you still need to manage the application.

18.6.4 Managing service health

Managing service health is critical to your system. Just because the system is running in the cloud doesn't mean there aren't failures and that your system doesn't need to be managed. You still need to manage a system in the cloud, and you need to take into consideration all the aspects that you consider when the system is running on-premises. The cloud doesn't fix problems in a bad system; it makes those problems more obvious.

As you're building your system, think about how you're going to manage disaster recovery, backups, and the ongoing health of the system. The system will be reliable within the Azure data center where the FC can monitor it, but that doesn't protect you against the worst scenario: that data center gets wiped out. In some scenarios, it might be OK to not manage the slight risk of a whole data center disappearing. On the other hand, many companies spend a lot of money running duplicate data centers that aren't near one another, just in case. You need to think about this. If you need to reduce the risk of depending on one data center, then you have a few options. Just to be clear: the FC will manage the state of your system in a data center, but it won't, at this time, manage it across data centers. We think that in the fullness of time, the fabric will be that powerful, but at that time it's likely to be renamed to Microsoft SkyNet.

If the loss to your business isn't likely to be great, and you can deal with a few hours downtime, you can simply plan on redeploying to another data center in the event of a catastrophe. You need to keep a copy of the production bits and service configuration handy. You also need a backup of any data in the cloud. With these in hand, you could completely redeploy to another Azure data center in a matter of minutes to hours (depending on the amount of data that needs to be uploaded).

If you need to minimize downtime, you can run two copies of your service in Azure. Set each copy with a different geographic affinity in the portal. Azure is then forced to run each copy in a different data center. Perhaps the first copy is running in the Chicago data center, and the second is running in the Southwest data center. You could then use a DNS server that is geo-aware, and have it route users to each system, based on their location. In this situation, you'd have to replicate your data across the two systems. One way to do so would be to run them in complete separation, if your business processes can handle that. Then, once a night, you could merge the data sets with a background operation.

In all of these situations, you need to be able to understand the health of your system. One way to do that is to use the management APIs to understand the load on your system, and report the status in a recurring manner.

18.7 Summary

Although this chapter might have seemed like two disparate topics jammed together in one chapter to save space, at this point, you should understand how diagnostics, service management, and good service health instrumentation is important to running a healthy service in the cloud.

We dug deep into the diagnostics API, showing how you collect all sorts of data from many different instances, and merge it all into one place to make it easy to analyze the result. Each data source has its own configuration mechanism and destination. You can tell each data source to transfer its data on a schedule, or you can force an on-demand transfer.

The Azure platform also provides a rich service management API over REST. You can do almost anything over this API that you can do in the portal except for creating hosting and storage services. Although REST is awesome, some people will likely opt to use csmanage.exe, especially when they're automating deployment with a build system.

Finally, we merged diagnostics and the service management API together to discuss how an auto-scaling feature might look, and why Microsoft doesn't provide one out of the box. You now have all of the tools you need to rock out in the cloud, scale your system up and down, and know for sure what's happening with your services. Remember that as you move to the cloud, you want to stop managing servers and start managing services.

index

E

F

G

H

I

N

S

T

X